The Selected Works of
H. G. WELLS

The Seledted Works of
H. G. Wells

The Selected Works of
H. G. WELLS

Wordsworth Editions

For my husband
ANTHONY JOHN RANSON
with love from your wife, the publisher.
Eternally grateful for your unconditional love.

Readers who are interested in other titles from
Wordsworth Editions are invited to visit our website at
www.wordsworth-editions.com

This edition published in 2017 by Wordsworth Editions Limited
8B East Street, Ware, Hertfordshire SG12 9HJ

ISBN 978 1 84022 745 1

Text © Wordsworth Editions Limited 2017

Wordsworth Editions
is the company founded in 1987 by
MICHAEL TRAYLER

Typeset in Great Britain by Antony Gray
Printed and bound by Clays Ltd, St Ives plc

Contents

The Time Machine
An Invention

A novel first published in 1895

The Time Machine was published in Great Britain by William Heinemann in 1895, first in serial form and later that year in a casebound edition; Henry Holt and Company produced an American edition almost simultaneously. Because they differ textually, the two editions are commonly referred to as the 'Heinemann text' and the 'Holt text'.

CHAPTER ONE

THE TIME TRAVELLER (for so it will be convenient to speak of him) was expounding a recondite matter to us. His grey eyes shone and twinkled, and his usually pale face was flushed and animated. The fire burned brightly, and the soft radiance of the incandescent lights in the lilies of silver caught the bubbles that flashed and passed in our glasses. Our chairs, being his patents, embraced and caressed us rather than submitted to be sat upon, and there was that luxurious after-dinner atmosphere when thought roams gracefully free of the trammels of precision. And he put it to us in this way – marking the points with a lean forefinger – as we lazily admired his earnestness over this new paradox (as we thought it) and his fecundity.

'You must follow me carefully. I shall have to controvert one or two ideas that are almost universally accepted. The geometry, for instance, they taught you at school is founded on a misconception.'

'Is not that rather a large thing to expect us to begin upon?' said Filby, an argumentative person with red hair.

'I do not mean to ask you to accept anything without reasonable ground for it. You will soon admit as much as I need from you. You know of course that a mathematical line, a line of thickness *nil*, has no real existence. They taught you that? Neither has a mathematical plane. These things are mere abstractions.'

'That is all right,' said the Psychologist.

'Nor, having only length, breadth, and thickness, can a cube have a real existence.'

'There I object,' said Filby. 'Of course a solid body may exist. All real things – '

'So most people think. But wait a moment. Can an *instantaneous* cube exist?'

'Don't follow you,' said Filby.

'Can a cube that does not last for any time at all, have a real existence?'

Filby became pensive. 'Clearly,' the Time Traveller proceeded, 'any real body must have extension in *four* directions: it must have Length, Breadth, Thickness, and – Duration. But through a natural infirmity of the flesh, which I will explain to you in a moment, we incline to overlook this fact. There are really four dimensions, three which we call the three planes of Space, and a fourth, Time. There is, however, a tendency to draw an unreal distinction between the former three dimensions and the latter, because it

happens that our consciousness moves intermittently in one direction along the latter from the beginning to the end of our lives.'

'That,' said a very young man, making spasmodic efforts to relight his cigar over the lamp; 'that . . . very clear indeed.'

'Now, it is very remarkable that this is so extensively overlooked,' continued the Time Traveller, with a slight accession of cheerfulness. 'Really this is what is meant by the Fourth Dimension, though some people who talk about the Fourth Dimension do not know they mean it. It is only another way of looking at Time. *There is no difference between Time and any of the three dimensions of Space except that our consciousness moves along it.* But some foolish people have got hold of the wrong side of that idea. You have all heard what they have to say about this Fourth Dimension?'

'*I* have not,' said the Provincial Mayor.

'It is simply this. That Space, as our mathematicians have it, is spoken of as having three dimensions, which one may call Length, Breadth, and Thickness, and is always definable by reference to three planes, each at right angles to the others. But some philosophical people have been asking why *three* dimensions particularly – why not another direction at right angles to the other three? – and have even tried to construct a Four-Dimensional geometry. Professor Simon Newcomb was expounding this to the New York Mathematical Society only a month or so ago. You know how on a flat surface, which has only two dimensions, we can represent a figure of a three-dimensional solid, and similarly they think that by models of three dimensions they could represent one of four – if they could master the perspective of the thing. See?'

'I think so,' murmured the Provincial Mayor; and, knitting his brows, he lapsed into an introspective state, his lips moving as one who repeats mystic words. 'Yes, I think I see it now,' he said after some time, brightening in a quite transitory manner.

'Well, I do not mind telling you I have been at work upon this geometry of Four Dimensions for some time. Some of my results are curious. For instance, here is a portrait of a man at eight years old, another at fifteen, another at seventeen, another at twenty-three, and so on. All these are evidently sections, as it were, Three-Dimensional representations of his Four-Dimensioned being, which is a fixed and unalterable thing.'

'Scientific people,' proceeded the Time Traveller, after the pause required for the proper assimilation of this, 'know very well that Time is only a kind of Space. Here is a popular scientific diagram, a weather record. This line I trace with my finger shows the movement of the barometer. Yesterday it was so high, yesterday night it fell, then this morning it rose again, and so gently upward to here. Surely the mercury did not trace this line in any of the dimensions of Space generally recognised? But certainly it traced such a line, and that line, therefore, we must conclude was along the Time-Dimension.'

'But,' said the Medical Man, staring hard at a coal in the fire, 'if Time is

really only a fourth dimension of Space, why is it, and why has it always been, regarded as something different? And why cannot we move in Time as we move about in the other dimensions of Space?'

The Time Traveller smiled. 'Are you sure we can move freely in Space? Right and left we can go, backward and forward freely enough, and men always have done so. I admit we move freely in two dimensions. But how about up and down? Gravitation limits us there.'

'Not exactly,' said the Medical Man. 'There are balloons.'

'But before the balloons, save for spasmodic jumping and the inequalities of the surface, man had no freedom of vertical movement.'

'Still, they could move a little up and down,' said the Medical Man.

'Easier, far easier down than up.'

'And you cannot move at all in Time, you cannot get away from the present moment.'

'My dear sir, that is just where you are wrong. That is just where the whole world has gone wrong. We are always getting away from the present moment. Our mental existences, which are immaterial and have no dimensions, are passing along the Time-Dimension with a uniform velocity from the cradle to the grave. Just as we should travel *down* if we began our existence fifty miles above the earth's surface.'

'But the great difficulty is this,' interrupted the Psychologist. 'You *can* move about in all directions of Space, but you cannot move about in Time.'

'That is the germ of my great discovery. But you are wrong to say that we cannot move about in Time. For instance, if I am recalling an incident very vividly I go back to the instant of its occurrence: I become absent-minded, as you say. I jump back for a moment. Of course we have no means of staying back for any length of Time, any more than a savage or an animal has of staying six feet above the ground. But a civilised man is better off than the savage in this respect. He can go up against gravitation in a balloon, and why should he not hope that ultimately he may be able to stop or accelerate his drift along the Time-Dimension, or even turn about and travel the other way?'

'Oh, *this*,' began Filby, 'is all – '

'Why not?' said the Time Traveller.

'It's against reason,' said Filby.

'What reason?' said the Time Traveller.

'You can show black is white by argument,' said Filby, 'but you will never convince me.'

'Possibly not,' said the Time Traveller. 'But now you begin to see the object of my investigations into the geometry of Four Dimensions. Long ago I had a vague inkling of a machine – '

'To travel through Time!' exclaimed the Very Young Man.

'That shall travel indifferently in any direction of Space and Time, as the driver determines.'

Filby contented himself with laughter.

'But I have experimental verification,' said the Time Traveller.

'It would be remarkably convenient for the historian,' the Psychologist suggested. 'One might travel back and verify the accepted account of the Battle of Hastings, for instance!'

'Don't you think you would attract attention?' said the Medical Man. 'Our ancestors had no great tolerance for anachronisms.'

'One might get one's Greek from the very lips of Homer and Plato,' the Very Young Man thought.

'In which case they would certainly plough you for the Little-go. The German scholars have improved Greek so much.'

'Then there is the future,' said the Very Young Man. 'Just think! One might invest all one's money, leave it to accumulate at interest, and hurry on ahead!'

'To discover a society,' said I, 'erected on a strictly communistic basis.'

'Of all the wild extravagant theories!' began the Psychologist.

'Yes, so it seemed to me, and so I never talked of it until – '

'Experimental verification!' cried I. 'You are going to verify *that*?'

'The experiment!' cried Filby, who was getting brain-weary.

'Let's see your experiment anyhow,' said the Psychologist, 'though it's all humbug, you know.'

The Time Traveller smiled round at us. Then, still smiling faintly, and with his hands deep in his trousers pockets, he walked slowly out of the room, and we heard his slippers shuffling down the long passage to his laboratory.

The Psychologist looked at us. 'I wonder what he's got?'

'Some sleight-of-hand trick or other,' said the Medical Man, and Filby tried to tell us about a conjurer he had seen at Burslem, but before he had finished his preface the Time Traveller came back, and Filby's anecdote collapsed.

The thing the Time Traveller held in his hand was a glittering metallic framework, scarcely larger than a small clock, and very delicately made. There was ivory in it, and some transparent crystalline substance. And now I must be explicit, for this that follows – unless his explanation is to be accepted – is an absolutely unaccountable thing. He took one of the small octagonal tables that were scattered about the room, and set it in front of the fire, with two legs on the hearthrug. On this table he placed the mechanism. Then he drew up a chair, and sat down. The only other object on the table was a small shaded lamp, the bright light of which fell upon the model. There were also perhaps a dozen candles about, two in brass candlesticks upon the mantel and several in sconces, so that the room was brilliantly illuminated. I sat in a low armchair nearest the fire, and I drew this forward so as to be almost between the Time Traveller and the fire-place. Filby sat behind him, looking over his shoulder. The Medical Man

and the Provincial Mayor watched him in profile from the right, the Psychologist from the left. The Very Young Man stood behind the Psychologist. We were all on the alert. It appears incredible to me that any kind of trick, however subtly conceived and however adroitly done, could have been played upon us under these conditions.

The Time Traveller looked at us, and then at the mechanism. 'Well?' said the Psychologist.

'This little affair,' said the Time Traveller, resting his elbows upon the table and pressing his hands together above the apparatus, 'is only a model. It is my plan for a machine to travel through time. You will notice that it looks singularly askew, and that there is an odd twinkling appearance about this bar, as though it was in some way unreal.' He pointed to the part with his finger. 'Also, here is one little white lever, and here is another.'

The Medical Man got up out of his chair and peered into the thing. 'It's beautifully made,' he said.

'It took two years to make,' retorted the Time Traveller. Then, when we had all imitated the action of the Medical Man, he said: 'Now I want you clearly to understand that this lever, being pressed over, sends the machine gliding into the future, and this other reverses the motion. This saddle represents the seat of a time traveller. Presently I am going to press the lever, and off the machine will go. It will vanish, pass into future time, and disappear. Have a good look at the thing. Look at the table too, and satisfy yourselves there is no trickery. I don't want to waste this model and then be told I'm a quack.'

There was a minute's pause perhaps. The Psychologist seemed about to speak to me, but changed his mind. Then the Time Traveller put forth his finger towards the lever. 'No,' he said suddenly. 'Lend me your hand.' And turning to the Psychologist, he took that individual's hand in his own and told him to put out his forefinger. So that it was the Psychologist himself who sent forth the model Time Machine on its interminable voyage. We all saw the lever turn. I am absolutely certain there was no trickery. There was a breath of wind, and the lamp flame jumped. One of the candles on the mantel was blown out, and the little machine suddenly swung round, became indistinct, was seen as a ghost for a second perhaps, as an eddy of faintly glittering brass and ivory; and it was gone – vanished! Save for the lamp the table was bare.

Everyone was silent for a minute. Then Filby said he was damned.

The Psychologist recovered from his stupor, and suddenly looked under the table. At that the Time Traveller laughed cheerfully. 'Well?' he said, with a reminiscence of the Psychologist. Then, getting up, he went to the tobacco jar on the mantel, and with his back to us began to fill his pipe.

We stared at each other. 'Look here,' said the Medical Man, 'are you in earnest about this? Do you seriously believe that that machine has travelled into time?'

'Certainly,' said the Time Traveller, stooping to light a spill at the fire. Then he turned, lighting his pipe, to look at the Psychologist's face. (The Psychologist, to show that he was not unhinged, helped himself to a cigar and tried to light it uncut.) 'What is more, I have a big machine nearly finished in there' – he indicated the laboratory – 'and when that is put together I mean to have a journey on my own account.'

'You mean to say that that machine has travelled into the future?' said Filby.

'Into the future or the past – I don't, for certain, know which.'

After an interval the Psychologist had an inspiration. 'It must have gone into the past if it has gone anywhere,' he said.

'Why?' said the Time Traveller.

'Because I presume that it has not moved in space, and if it travelled into the future it would still be here all this time, since it must have travelled through this time.'

'But,' said I, 'if it travelled into the past it would have been visible when we came first into this room; and last Thursday when we were here; and the Thursday before that; and so forth!'

'Serious objections,' remarked the Provincial Mayor, with an air of impartiality, turning towards the Time Traveller.

'Not a bit,' said the Time Traveller, and to the Psychologist: 'You think. *You* can explain that. It's presentation below the threshold, you know, diluted presentation.'

'Of course,' said the Psychologist, and reassured us. 'That's a simple point of psychology. I should have thought of it. It's plain enough, and helps the paradox delightfully. We cannot see it, nor can we appreciate this machine, any more than we can the spoke of a wheel spinning, or a bullet flying through the air. If it is travelling through time fifty times or a hundred times faster than we are, if it gets through a minute while we get through a second, the impression it creates will of course be only one-fiftieth or one-hundredth of what it would make if it were not travelling in time. That's plain enough.' He passed his hand through the space in which the machine had been. 'You see?' he said, laughing.

We sat and stared at the vacant table for a minute or so. Then the Time Traveller asked us what we thought of it all.

'It sounds plausible enough tonight,' said the Medical Man; 'but wait until tomorrow. Wait for the common sense of the morning.'

'Would you like to see the Time Machine itself?' asked the Time Traveller. And therewith, taking the lamp in his hand, he led the way down the long, draughty corridor to his laboratory. I remember vividly the flickering light, his queer, broad head in silhouette, the dance of the shadows, how we all followed him, puzzled but incredulous, and how there in the laboratory we beheld a larger edition of the little mechanism which we had seen vanish from before our eyes. Parts were of nickel, parts of

ivory, parts had certainly been filed or sawn out of rock crystal. The thing was generally complete, but the twisted crystalline bars lay unfinished upon the bench beside some sheets of drawings, and I took one up for a better look at it. Quartz it seemed to be.

'Look here,' said the Medical Man, 'are you perfectly serious? Or is this a trick – like that ghost you showed us last Christmas?'

'Upon that machine,' said the Time Traveller, holding the lamp aloft, 'I intend to explore time. Is that plain? I was never more serious in my life.'

None of us quite knew how to take it.

I caught Filby's eye over the shoulder of the Medical Man, and he winked at me solemnly.

CHAPTER TWO

I think that at that time none of us quite believed in the Time Machine. The fact is, the Time Traveller was one of those men who are too clever to be believed: you never felt that you saw all round him; you always suspected some subtle reserve, some ingenuity in ambush, behind his lucid frankness. Had Filby shown the model and explained the matter in the Time Traveller's words, we should have shown *him* far less scepticism. For we should have perceived his motives; a pork butcher could understand Filby. But the Time Traveller had more than a touch of whim among his elements, and we distrusted him. Things that would have made the fame of a less clever man seemed tricks in his hands. It is a mistake to do things too easily. The serious people who took him seriously never felt quite sure of his deportment: they were somehow aware that trusting their reputations for judgement with him was like furnishing a nursery with eggshell china. So I don't think any of us said very much about time travelling in the interval between that Thursday and the next, though its odd potentialities ran, no doubt, in most of our minds: its plausibility, that is, its practical incredibleness, the curious possibilities of anachronism and of utter confusion it suggested. For my own part, I was particularly preoccupied with the trick of the model. That I remember discussing with the Medical Man, whom I met on Friday at the Linnaean. He said he had seen a similar thing at Tübingen, and laid considerable stress on the blowing out of the candle. But how the trick was done he could not explain.

The next Thursday I went again to Richmond – I suppose I was one of the Time Traveller's most constant guests – and, arriving late, found four or five men already assembled in his drawing-room. The Medical Man was standing before the fire with a sheet of paper in one hand and his watch in the other. I looked round for the Time Traveller, and – 'It's half-past seven now,' said the Medical Man. 'I suppose we'd better have dinner?'

'Where's — ?' said I, naming our host.

'You've just come? It's rather odd. He's unavoidably detained. He asks me in this note to lead off with dinner at seven if he's not back. Says he'll explain when he comes.'

'It seems a pity to let the dinner spoil,' said the Editor of a well-known daily paper; and thereupon the Doctor rang the bell.

The Psychologist was the only person besides the Doctor and myself who had attended the previous dinner. The other men were Blank, the Editor aforementioned, a certain journalist, and another – a quiet, shy man with a beard – whom I didn't know, and who, as far as my observation went, never opened his mouth all the evening. There was some speculation at the dinner-table about the Time Traveller's absence, and I suggested time travelling, in a half-jocular spirit. The Editor wanted that explained to him, and the Psychologist volunteered a wooden account of the 'ingenious paradox and trick' we had witnessed that day week. He was in the midst of his exposition when the door from the corridor opened slowly and without noise. I was facing the door, and saw it first. 'Hallo!' I said. 'At last!' And the door opened wider, and the Time Traveller stood before us. I gave a cry of surprise. 'Good heavens! man, what's the matter?' cried the Medical Man, who saw him next. And the whole tableful turned towards the door.

He was in an amazing plight. His coat was dusty and dirty, and smeared with green down the sleeves; his hair disordered, and as it seemed to me greyer – either with dust and dirt or because its colour had actually faded. His face was ghastly pale; his chin had a brown cut on it – a cut half healed; his expression was haggard and drawn, as by intense suffering. For a moment he hesitated in the doorway, as if he had been dazzled by the light. Then he came into the room. He walked with just such a limp as I have seen in footsore tramps. We stared at him in silence, expecting him to speak.

He said not a word, but came painfully to the table, and made a motion towards the wine. The Editor filled a glass of champagne, and pushed it towards him. He drained it, and it seemed to do him good: for he looked round the table, and the ghost of his old smile flickered across his face. 'What on earth have you been up to, man?' said the Doctor. The Time Traveller did not seem to hear. 'Don't let me disturb you,' he said, with a certain faltering articulation. 'I'm all right.' He stopped, held out his glass for more, and took it off at a draught. 'That's good,' he said. His eyes grew brighter, and a faint colour came into his cheeks. His glance flickered over our faces with a certain dull approval, and then went round the warm and comfortable room. Then he spoke again, still as it were feeling his way among his words. 'I'm going to wash and dress, and then I'll come down and explain things . . . Save me some of that mutton. I'm starving for a bit of meat.'

He looked across at the Editor, who was a rare visitor, and hoped he was all right. The Editor began a question. 'Tell you presently,' said the Time Traveller. 'I'm – funny! Be all right in a minute.'

He put down his glass, and walked towards the staircase door. Again I remarked his lameness and the soft padding sound of his footfall, and standing up in my place, I saw his feet as he went out. He had nothing on them but a pair of tattered, blood-stained socks. Then the door closed upon him. I had half a mind to follow, till I remembered how he detested any fuss about himself. For a minute, perhaps, my mind was wool-gathering. Then, 'Remarkable Behaviour of an Eminent Scientist,' I heard the Editor say, thinking (after his wont) in headlines. And this brought my attention back to the bright dinner-table.

'What's the game?' said the Journalist. 'Has he been doing the Amateur Cadger? I don't follow.' I met the eye of the Psychologist, and read my own interpretation in his face. I thought of the Time Traveller limping painfully upstairs. I don't think anyone else had noticed his lameness.

The first to recover completely from this surprise was the Medical Man, who rang the bell – the Time Traveller hated to have servants waiting at dinner – for a hot plate. At that the Editor turned to his knife and fork with a grunt, and the Silent Man followed suit. The dinner was resumed. Conversation was exclamatory for a little while, with gaps of wonderment; and then the Editor got fervent in his curiosity. 'Does our friend eke out his modest income with a crossing? or has he his Nebuchadnezzar' phases? he enquired. 'I feel assured it's this business of the Time Machine,' I said, and took up the Psychologist's account of our previous meeting. The new guests were frankly incredulous. The Editor raised objections. 'What *was* this time travelling? A man couldn't cover himself with dust by rolling in a paradox, could he?' And then, as the idea came home to him, he resorted to caricature. Hadn't they any clothes-brushes in the Future? The Journalist, too, would not believe at any price, and joined the Editor in the easy work of heaping ridicule on the whole thing. They were both the new kind of journalist – very joyous, irreverent young men. 'Our Special Correspondent in the Day after Tomorrow reports,' the Journalist was saying – or rather shouting – when the Time Traveller came back. He was dressed in ordinary evening clothes, and nothing save his haggard look remained of the change that had startled me.

'I say,' said the Editor hilariously, 'these chaps here say you have been travelling into the middle of next week! Tell us all about little Rosebery, will you? What will you take for the lot?'

The Time Traveller came to the place reserved for him without a word. He smiled quietly, in his old way. 'Where's my mutton?' he said. 'What a treat it is to stick a fork into meat again!'

'Story!' cried the Editor.

'Story be damned!' said the Time Traveller. 'I want something to eat. I won't say a word until I get some peptone into my arteries. Thanks. And the salt.'

'One word,' said I. 'Have you been time travelling?'

'Yes,' said the Time Traveller, with his mouth full, nodding his head.

'I'd give a shilling a line for a verbatim note,' said the Editor. The Time Traveller pushed his glass towards the Silent Man and rang it with his fingernail; at which the Silent Man, who had been staring at his face, started convulsively, and poured him wine. The rest of the dinner was uncomfortable. For my own part, sudden questions kept on rising to my lips, and I dare say it was the same with the others. The Journalist tried to relieve the tension by telling anecdotes of Hettie Potter. The Time Traveller devoted his attention to his dinner, and displayed the appetite of a tramp. The Medical Man smoked a cigarette, and watched the Time Traveller through his eyelashes. The Silent Man seemed even more clumsy than usual, and drank champagne with regularity and determination out of sheer nervousness. At last the Time Traveller pushed his plate away, and looked round us. 'I suppose I must apologise,' he said. 'I was simply starving. I've had a most amazing time.' He reached out his hand for a cigar, and cut the end. 'But come into the smoking-room. It's too long a story to tell over greasy plates.' And ringing the bell in passing, he led the way into the adjoining room.

'You have told Blank, and Dash, and Chose about the machine?' he said to me, leaning back in his easy-chair and naming the three new guests.

'But the thing's a mere paradox,' said the Editor.

'I can't argue tonight. I don't mind telling you the story, but I can't argue. I will,' he went on, 'tell you the story of what has happened to me, if you like, but you must refrain from interruptions. I want to tell it. Badly. Most of it will sound like lying. So be it! It's true – every word of it, all the same. I was in my laboratory at four o'clock, and since then . . . I've lived eight days . . . such days as no human being ever lived before! I'm nearly worn out, but I shan't sleep till I've told this thing over to you. Then I shall go to bed. But no interruptions! Is it agreed?'

'Agreed,' said the Editor, and the rest of us echoed 'Agreed.' And with that the Time Traveller began his story as I have set it forth. He sat back in his chair at first, and spoke like a weary man. Afterwards he got more animated. In writing it down I feel with only too much keenness the inadequacy of pen and ink – and, above all, my own inadequacy – to express its quality. You read, I will suppose, attentively enough; but you cannot see the speaker's white, sincere face in the bright circle of the little lamp, nor hear the intonation of his voice. You cannot know how his expression followed the turns of his story! Most of us hearers were in shadow, for the candles in the smoking-room had not been lighted, and only the face of the Journalist and the legs of the Silent Man from the knees downward were illuminated. At first we glanced now and again at each other. After a time we ceased to do that, and looked only at the Time Traveller's face.

CHAPTER THREE

'I told some of you last Thursday of the principles of the Time Machine, and showed you the actual thing itself, incomplete in the workshop. There it is now, a little travel-worn, truly; and one of the ivory bars is cracked, and a brass rail bent; but the rest of it's sound enough. I expected to finish it on Friday, but on Friday, when the putting together was nearly done, I found that one of the nickel bars was exactly one inch too short, and this I had to get remade; so that the thing was not complete until this morning. It was at ten o'clock today that the first of all Time Machines began its career. I gave it a last tap, tried all the screws again, put one more drop of oil on the quartz rod, and sat myself in the saddle. I suppose a suicide who holds a pistol to his skull feels much the same wonder at what will come next as I felt then. I took the starting lever in one hand and the stopping one in the other, pressed the first, and almost immediately the second. I seemed to reel; I felt a nightmare sensation of falling; and, looking round, I saw the laboratory exactly as before. Had anything happened? For a moment I suspected that my intellect had tricked me. Then I noted the clock. A moment before, as it seemed, it had stood at a minute or so past ten; now it was nearly half-past three!

'I drew a breath, set my teeth, gripped the starting lever with both hands, and went off with a thud. The laboratory got hazy and went dark. Mrs Watchett came in and walked, apparently without seeing me, towards the garden door. I suppose it took her a minute or so to traverse the place, but to me she seemed to shoot across the room like a rocket. I pressed the lever over to its extreme position. The night came like the turning out of a lamp, and in another moment came tomorrow. The laboratory grew faint and hazy, then fainter and ever fainter. Tomorrow night came black, then day again, night again, day again, faster and faster still. An eddying murmur filled my ears, and a strange, dumb confusedness descended on my mind.

'I am afraid I cannot convey the peculiar sensations of time travelling. They are excessively unpleasant. There is a feeling exactly like that one has upon a switchback – of a helpless headlong motion! I felt the same horrible anticipation, too, of an imminent smash. As I put on pace, night followed day like the flapping of a black wing. The dim suggestion of the laboratory seemed presently to fall away from me, and I saw the sun hopping swiftly across the sky, leaping it every minute, and every minute marking a day. I supposed the laboratory had been destroyed and I had come into the open air. I had a dim impression of scaffolding, but I was already going too fast to be conscious of any moving things. The slowest snail that ever crawled dashed by too fast for me. The twinkling succession of darkness and light was excessively painful to the eye. Then, in the intermittent darknesses, I

saw the moon spinning swiftly through her quarters from new to full, and had a faint glimpse of the circling stars. Presently, as I went on, still gaining velocity, the palpitation of night and day merged into one continuous greyness; the sky took on a wonderful deepness of blue, a splendid luminous colour like that of early twilight; the jerking sun became a streak of fire, a brilliant arch, in space; the moon a fainter fluctuating band; and I could see nothing of the stars, save now and then a brighter circle flickering in the blue.

'The landscape was misty and vague. I was still on the hillside upon which this house now stands, and the shoulder rose above me grey and dim. I saw trees growing and changing like puffs of vapour, now brown, now green: they grew, spread, shivered, and passed away. I saw huge buildings rise up faint and fair, and pass like dreams. The whole surface of the earth seemed changed – melting and flowing under my eyes. The little hands upon the dials that registered my speed raced round faster and faster. Presently I noted that the sun belt swayed up and down, from solstice to solstice, in a minute or less, and that consequently my pace was over a year a minute; and minute by minute the white snow flashed across the world, and vanished, and was followed by the bright, brief green of spring.

'The unpleasant sensations of the start were less poignant now. They merged at last into a kind of hysterical exhilaration. I remarked indeed a clumsy swaying of the machine, for which I was unable to account. But my mind was too confused to attend to it, so with a kind of madness growing upon me, I flung myself into futurity. At first I scarce thought of stopping, scarce thought of anything but these new sensations. But presently a fresh series of impressions grew up in my mind – a certain curiosity and therewith a certain dread – until at last they took complete possession of me. What strange developments of humanity, what wonderful advances upon our rudimentary civilisation, I thought, might not appear when I came to look nearly into the dim elusive world that raced and fluctuated before my eyes! I saw great and splendid architecture rising about me, more massive than any buildings of our own time, and yet, as it seemed, built of glimmer and mist. I saw a richer green flow up the hillside, and remain there, without any wintry intermission. Even through the veil of my confusion the earth seemed very fair. And so my mind came round to the business of stopping.

'The peculiar risk lay in the possibility of my finding some substance in the space which I, or the machine, occupied. So long as I travelled at a high velocity through time, this scarcely mattered; I was, so to speak, attenuated – was slipping like a vapour through the interstices of inter-vening substances! But to come to a stop involved the jamming of myself, molecule by molecule, into whatever lay in my way: meant bringing my atoms into such intimate contact with those of the obstacle that a profound chemical reaction – possibly a far-reaching explosion – would result, and blow myself and my apparatus out of all possible dimensions – into the

Unknown. This possibility had occurred to me again and again while I was making the machine; but then I had cheerfully accepted it as an unavoidable risk – one of the risks a man has got to take! Now the risk was inevitable, I no longer saw it in the same cheerful light. The fact is that, insensibly, the absolute strangeness of everything, the sickly jarring and swaying of the machine, above all, the feeling of prolonged falling, had absolutely upset my nerve. I told myself that I could never stop, and with a gust of petulance I resolved to stop forthwith. Like an impatient fool, I lugged over the lever, and incontinently the thing went reeling over, and I was flung headlong through the air.

'There was the sound of a clap of thunder in my ears. I may have been stunned for a moment. A pitiless hail was hissing round me, and I was sitting on soft turf in front of the overset machine. Everything still seemed grey, but presently I remarked that the confusion in my ears was gone. I looked round me. I was on what seemed to be a little lawn in a garden, surrounded by rhododendron bushes, and I noticed that their mauve and purple blossoms were dropping in a shower under the beating of the hail-stones. The rebounding, dancing hail hung in a cloud over the machine, and drove along the ground like smoke. In a moment I was wet to the skin. "Fine hospitality," said I, "to a man who has travelled innumerable years to see you."

'Presently I thought what a fool I was to get wet. I stood up and looked round me. A colossal figure, carved apparently in some white stone, loomed indistinctly beyond the rhododendrons through the hazy downpour. But all else of the world was invisible.

'My sensations would be hard to describe. As the columns of hail grew thinner, I saw the white figure more distinctly. It was very large, for a silver birch tree touched its shoulder. It was of white marble, in shape something like a winged sphinx, but the wings, instead of being carried vertically at the sides, were spread so that it seemed to hover. The pedestal, it appeared to me, was of bronze, and was thick with verdigris. It chanced that the face was towards me; the sightless eyes seemed to watch me; there was the faint shadow of a smile on the lips. It was greatly weather-worn, and that imparted an unpleasant suggestion of disease. I stood looking at it for a little space – half a minute, perhaps, or half an hour. It seemed to advance and to recede as the hail drove before it denser or thinner. At last I tore my eyes from it for a moment and saw that the hail curtain had worn threadbare, and that the sky was lightening with the promise of the sun.

'I looked up again at the crouching white shape, and the full temerity of my voyage came suddenly upon me. What might appear when that hazy curtain was altogether withdrawn? What might not have happened to men? What if cruelty had grown into a common passion? What if in this interval the race had lost its manliness and had developed into something

inhuman, unsympathetic, and overwhelmingly powerful? I might seem some old-world savage animal, only the more dreadful and disgusting for our common likeness – a foul creature to be incontinently slain.

'Already I saw other vast shapes – huge buildings with intricate parapets and tall columns, with a wooded hillside dimly creeping in upon me through the lessening storm. I was seized with a panic fear. I turned frantically to the Time Machine, and strove hard to readjust it. As I did so the shafts of the sun smote through the thunderstorm. The grey downpour was swept aside and vanished like the trailing garments of a ghost. Above me, in the intense blue of the summer sky, some faint brown shreds of cloud whirled into nothingness. The great buildings about me stood out clear and distinct, shining with the wet of the thunderstorm, and picked out in white by the unmelted hailstones piled along their courses. I felt naked in a strange world. I felt as perhaps a bird may feel in the clear air, knowing the hawk wings above and will swoop. My fear grew to frenzy. I took a breathing space, set my teeth, and again grappled fiercely, wrist and knee, with the machine. It gave under my desperate onset and turned over. It struck my chin violently. One hand on the saddle, the other on the lever, I stood panting heavily in attitude to mount again.

'But with this recovery of a prompt retreat my courage recovered. I looked more curiously and less fearfully at this world of the remote future. In a circular opening, high up in the wall of the nearer house, I saw a group of figures clad in rich soft robes. They had seen me, and their faces were directed towards me.

'Then I heard voices approaching me. Coming through the bushes by the White Sphinx were the heads and shoulders of men running. One of these emerged in a pathway leading straight to the little lawn upon which I stood with my machine. He was a slight creature – perhaps four feet high – clad in a purple tunic, girdled at the waist with a leather belt. Sandals or buskins – I could not clearly distinguish which – were on his feet; his legs were bare to the knees, and his head was bare. Noticing that, I noticed for the first time how warm the air was.

'He struck me as being a very beautiful and graceful creature, but indescribably frail. His flushed face reminded me of the more beautiful kind of consumptive – that hectic beauty of which we used to hear so much. At the sight of him I suddenly regained confidence. I took my hands from the machine.

CHAPTER FOUR

'In another moment we were standing face to face, I and this fragile thing out of futurity. He came straight up to me and laughed into my eyes. The absence from his bearing of any sign of fear struck me at once. Then he

turned to the two others who were following him and spoke to them in a strange and very sweet and liquid tongue.

'There were others coming, and presently a little group of perhaps eight or ten of these exquisite creatures were about me. One of them addressed me. It came into my head, oddly enough, that my voice was too harsh and deep for them. So I shook my head, and, pointing to my ears, shook it again. He came a step forward, hesitated, and then touched my hand. Then I felt other soft little tentacles upon my back and shoulders. They wanted to make sure I was real. There was nothing in this at all alarming. Indeed, there was something in these pretty little people that inspired confidence – a graceful gentleness, a certain childlike ease. And besides, they looked so frail that I could fancy myself flinging the whole dozen of them about like ninepins. But I made a sudden motion to warn them when I saw their little pink hands feeling at the Time Machine. Happily then, when it was not too late, I thought of a danger I had hitherto forgotten, and reaching over the bars of the machine I unscrewed the little levers that would set it in motion, and put these in my pocket. Then I turned again to see what I could do in the way of communication.

'And then, looking more nearly into their features, I saw some further peculiarities in their Dresden-china type of prettiness. Their hair, which was uniformly curly, came to a sharp end at the neck and cheek; there was not the faintest suggestion of it on the face, and their ears were singularly minute. The mouths were small, with bright red, rather thin lips, and the little chins ran to a point. The eyes were large and mild; and – this may seem egotism on my part – I fancied even that there was a certain lack of the interest I might have expected in them.

'As they made no effort to communicate with me, but simply stood round me smiling and speaking in soft cooing notes to each other, I began the conversation. I pointed to the Time Machine and to myself. Then hesitating for a moment how to express time, I pointed to the sun. At once a quaintly pretty little figure in chequered purple and white followed my gesture, and then astonished me by imitating the sound of thunder.

'For a moment I was staggered, though the import of his gesture was plain enough. The question had come into my mind abruptly: were these creatures fools? You may hardly understand how it took me. You see I had always anticipated that the people of the year Eight Hundred and Two Thousand odd would be incredibly in front of us in knowledge, art, everything. Then one of them suddenly asked me a question that showed him to be on the intellectual level of one of our five-year-old children – asked me, in fact, if I had come from the sun in a thunderstorm! It let loose the judgement I had suspended upon their clothes, their frail light limbs, and fragile features. A flow of disappointment rushed across my mind. For a moment I felt that I had built the Time Machine in vain.

'I nodded, pointed to the sun, and gave them such a vivid rendering of a

thunderclap as startled them. They all withdrew a pace or so and bowed. Then came one laughing towards me, carrying a chain of beautiful flowers altogether new to me, and put it about my neck. The idea was received with melodious applause; and presently they were all running to and fro for flowers, and laughingly flinging them upon me until I was almost smothered with blossom. You who have never seen the like can scarcely imagine what delicate and wonderful flowers countless years of culture had created. Then someone suggested that their plaything should be exhibited in the nearest building, and so I was led past the sphinx of white marble, which had seemed to watch me all the while with a smile at my astonishment, towards a vast grey edifice of fretted stone. As I went with them the memory of my confident anticipations of a profoundly grave and intellectual posterity came, with irresistible merriment, to my mind.

'The building had a huge entry, and was altogether of colossal dimensions. I was naturally most occupied with the growing crowd of little people, and with the big open portals that yawned before me shadowy and mysterious. My general impression of the world I saw over their heads was a tangled waste of beautiful bushes and flowers, a long neglected and yet weedless garden. I saw a number of tall spikes of strange white flowers, measuring a foot perhaps across the spread of the waxen petals. They grew scattered, as if wild, among the variegated shrubs, but, as I say, I did not examine them closely at this time. The Time Machine was left deserted on the turf among the rhododendrons.

'The arch of the doorway was richly carved, but naturally I did not observe the carving very narrowly, though I fancied I saw suggestions of old Phoenician decorations as I passed through, and it struck me that they were very badly broken and weather-worn. Several more brightly clad people met me in the doorway, and so we entered, I, dressed in dingy nineteenth-century garments, looking grotesque enough, garlanded with flowers, and surrounded by an eddying mass of bright, soft-coloured robes and shining white limbs, in a melodious whirl of laughter and laughing speech.

'The big doorway opened into a proportionately great hall hung with brown. The roof was in shadow, and the windows, partially glazed with coloured glass and partially unglazed, admitted a tempered light. The floor was made up of huge blocks of some very hard white metal, not plates nor slabs – blocks, and it was so much worn, as I judged by the going to and fro of past generations, as to be deeply channelled along the more frequented ways. Transverse to the length were innumerable tables made of slabs of polished stone, raised perhaps a foot from the floor, and upon these were heaps of fruits. Some I recognised as a kind of hypertrophied raspberry and orange, but for the most part they were strange.

'Between the tables was scattered a great number of cushions. Upon these my conductors seated themselves, signing for me to do likewise. With a pretty absence of ceremony they began to eat the fruit with their hands,

flinging peel and stalks, and so forth, into the round openings in the sides of the tables. I was not loath to follow their example, for I felt thirsty and hungry. As I did so I surveyed the hall at my leisure.

'And perhaps the thing that struck me most was its dilapidated look. The stained-glass windows, which displayed only a geometrical pattern, were broken in many places, and the curtains that hung across the lower end were thick with dust. And it caught my eye that the corner of the marble table near me was fractured. Nevertheless, the general effect was extremely rich and picturesque. There were, perhaps, a couple of hundred people dining in the hall, and most of them, seated as near to me as they could come, were watching me with interest, their little eyes shining over the fruit they were eating. All were clad in the same soft, and yet strong, silky material.

'Fruit, by the by, was all their diet. These people of the remote future were strict vegetarians, and while I was with them, in spite of some carnal cravings, I had to be frugivorous also. Indeed, I found afterwards that horses, cattle, sheep, dogs, had followed the Ichthyosaurus into extinction. But the fruits were very delightful; one, in particular, that seemed to be in season all the time I was there – a floury thing in a three-sided husk – was especially good, and I made it my staple. At first I was puzzled by all these strange fruits, and by the strange flowers I saw, but later I began to perceive their import.

'However, I am telling you of my fruit dinner in the distant future now. So soon as my appetite was a little checked, I determined to make a resolute attempt to learn the speech of these new men of mine. Clearly that was the next thing to do. The fruits seemed a convenient thing to begin upon, and holding one of these up I began a series of interrogative sounds and gestures. I had some considerable difficulty in conveying my meaning. At first my efforts met with a stare of surprise or inextinguishable laughter, but presently a fair-haired little creature seemed to grasp my intention and repeated a name. They had to chatter and explain the business at great length to each other, and my first attempts to make the exquisite little sounds of their language caused an immense amount of amusement. However, I felt like a schoolmaster amidst children, and persisted, and presently I had a score of noun substantives at least at my command; and then I got to demonstrative pronouns, and even the verb "to eat". But it was slow work, and the little people soon tired and wanted to get away from my interrogations, so I determined, rather of necessity, to let them give their lessons in little doses when they felt inclined. And very little doses I found they were before long, for I never met people more indolent or more easily fatigued.

'A queer thing I soon discovered about my little hosts, and that was their lack of interest. They would come to me with eager cries of astonishment, like children, but like children they would soon stop examining me and wander away after some other toy. The dinner and my conversational beginnings ended, I noted for the first time that almost all those who had

surrounded me at first were gone. It is odd, too, how speedily I came to disregard these little people. I went out through the portal into the sunlit world again as soon as my hunger was satisfied. I was continually meeting more of these men of the future, who would follow me a little distance, chatter and laugh about me, and, having smiled and gesticulated in a friendly way, leave me again to my own devices.

'The calm of evening was upon the world as I emerged from the great hall, and the scene was lit by the warm glow of the setting sun. At first things were very confusing. Everything was so entirely different from the world I had known – even the flowers. The big building I had left was situated on the slope of a broad river valley, but the Thames had shifted perhaps a mile from its present position. I resolved to mount to the summit of a crest, perhaps a mile and a half away, from which I could get a wider view of this our planet in the year 802,701 AD. For that, I should explain, was the date the little dials of my machine recorded.

'As I walked I was watching for every impression that could possibly help to explain the condition of ruinous splendour in which I found the world – for ruinous it was. A little way up the hill, for instance, was a great heap of granite, bound together by masses of aluminium, a vast labyrinth of precipitous walls and crumpled heaps, amidst which were thick heaps of very beautiful pagoda-like plants – nettles possibly – but wonderfully tinted with brown about the leaves, and incapable of stinging. It was evidently the derelict remains of some vast structure, to what end built I could not determine. It was here that I was destined, at a later date, to have a very strange experience – the first intimation of a still stranger discovery – but of that I will speak in its proper place.

'Looking round, with a sudden thought, from a terrace on which I rested for a while, I realised that there were no small houses to be seen. Apparently the single house, and possibly even the household, had vanished. Here and there among the greenery were palace-like buildings, but the house and the cottage, which form such characteristic features of our own English landscape, had disappeared.

' "Communism," said I to myself.

'And on the heels of that came another thought. I looked at the half-dozen little figures that were following me. Then, in a flash, I perceived that all had the same form of costume, the same soft hairless visage, and the same girlish rotundity of limb. It may seem strange, perhaps, that I had not noticed this before. But everything was so strange. Now, I saw the fact plainly enough. In costume, and in all the differences of texture and bearing that now mark off the sexes from each other, these people of the future were alike. And the children seemed to my eyes to be but the miniatures of their parents. I judged, then, that the children of that time were extremely precocious, physically at least, and I found afterwards abundant verification of my opinion.

'Seeing the ease and security in which these people were living, I felt that this close resemblance of the sexes was after all what one would expect; for the strength of a man and the softness of a woman, the institution of the family, and the differentiation of occupations are mere militant necessities of an age of physical force. Where population is balanced and abundant, much child-bearing becomes an evil rather than a blessing to the State: where violence comes but rarely and offspring are secure, there is less necessity – indeed there is no necessity – for an efficient family, and the specialisation of the sexes with reference to their children's needs disappears. We see some beginnings of this even in our own time, and in this future age it was complete. This, I must remind you, was my speculation at the time. Later, I was to appreciate how far it fell short of the reality.

'While I was musing upon these things, my attention was attracted by a pretty little structure, like a well under a cupola. I thought in a transitory way of the oddness of wells still existing, and then resumed the thread of my speculations. There were no large buildings towards the top of the hill, and as my walking powers were evidently miraculous, I was presently left alone for the first time. With a strange sense of freedom and adventure I pushed on up to the crest.

'There I found a seat of some yellow metal that I did not recognise, corroded in places with a kind of pinkish rust and half smothered in soft moss, the arm-rests cast and filed into the resemblance of griffins' heads. I sat down on it, and I surveyed the broad view of our old world under the sunset of that long day. It was as sweet and fair a view as I have ever seen. The sun had already gone below the horizon and the west was flaming gold, touched with some horizontal bars of purple and crimson. Below was the valley of the Thames, in which the river lay like a band of burnished steel. I have already spoken of the great palaces dotted about among the variegated greenery, some in ruins and some still occupied. Here and there rose a white or silvery figure in the waste garden of the earth, here and there came the sharp vertical line of some cupola or obelisk. There were no hedges, no signs of proprietary rights, no evidences of agriculture; the whole earth had become a garden.

'So watching, I began to put my interpretation upon the things I had seen, and as it shaped itself to me that evening, my interpretation was something in this way. (Afterwards I found I had got only a half-truth – or only a glimpse of one facet of the truth.)

'It seemed to me that I had happened upon humanity upon the wane. The ruddy sunset set me thinking of the sunset of mankind. For the first time I began to realise an odd consequence of the social effort in which we are at present engaged. And yet, come to think, it is a logical consequence enough. Strength is the outcome of need; security sets a premium on feebleness. The work of ameliorating the conditions of life – the true

civilising process that makes life more and more secure – had gone steadily on to a climax. One triumph of a united humanity over Nature had followed another. Things that are now mere dreams had become projects deliberately put in hand and carried forward. And the harvest was what I saw!

'After all, the sanitation and the agriculture of today are still in the rudimentary stage. The science of our time has attacked but a little department of the field of human disease, but even so, it spreads its operations very steadily and persistently. Our agriculture and horticulture destroy a weed just here and there and cultivate perhaps a score or so of wholesome plants, leaving the greater number to fight out a balance as they can. We improve our favourite plants and animals – and how few they are – gradually by selective breeding; now a new and better peach, now a seedless grape, now a sweeter and larger flower, now a more convenient breed of cattle. We improve them gradually, because our ideals are vague and tentative, and our knowledge is very limited; because Nature, too, is shy and slow in our clumsy hands. Some day all this will be better organised, and still better. That is the drift of the current in spite of the eddies. The whole world will be intelligent, educated, and co-operating; things will move faster and faster towards the subjugation of Nature. In the end, wisely and carefully we shall readjust the balance of animal and vegetable life to suit our human needs.

'This adjustment, I say, must have been done, and done well; done indeed for all time, in the space of time across which my machine had leaped. The air was free from gnats, the earth from weeds or fungi; everywhere were fruits and sweet and delightful flowers; brilliant butterflies flew hither and thither. The ideal of preventive medicine was attained. Diseases had been stamped out. I saw no evidence of any contagious diseases during all my stay. And I shall have to tell you later that even the processes of putrefaction and decay had been profoundly affected by these changes.

'Social triumphs, too, had been effected. I saw mankind housed in splendid shelters, gloriously clothed, and as yet I had found them engaged in no toil. There were no signs of struggle, neither social nor economical struggle. The shop, the advertisement, traffic, all that commerce which constitutes the body of our world, was gone. It was natural on that golden evening that I should jump at the idea of a social paradise. The difficulty of increasing population had been met, I guessed, and population had ceased to increase.

'But with this change in condition comes inevitably adaptations to the change. What, unless biological science is a mass of errors, is the cause of human intelligence and vigour? Hardship and freedom: conditions under which the active, strong, and subtle survive and the weaker go to the wall; conditions that put a premium upon the loyal alliance of capable men, upon self-restraint, patience, and decision. And the institution of the family, and the emotions that arise therein, the fierce jealousy, the tenderness for

offspring, parental self-devotion, all found their justification and support in the imminent dangers of the young. *Now*, where are these imminent dangers? There is a sentiment arising, and it will grow, against connubial jealousy, against fierce maternity, against passion of all sorts; unnecessary things now, and things that make us uncomfortable, savage survivals, discords in a refined and pleasant life.

'I thought of the physical slightness of the people, their lack of intelligence, and those big abundant ruins, and it strengthened my belief in a perfect conquest of Nature. For after the battle comes Quiet. Humanity had been strong, energetic, and intelligent, and had used all its abundant vitality to alter the conditions under which it lived. And now came the reaction of the altered conditions.

'Under the new conditions of perfect comfort and security, that restless energy, that with us is strength, would become weakness. Even in our own time certain tendencies and desires, once necessary to survival, are a constant source of failure. Physical courage and the love of battle, for instance, are no great help – may even be hindrances – to a civilised man. And in a state of physical balance and security, power, intellectual as well as physical, would be out of place. For countless years I judged there had been no danger of war or solitary violence, no danger from wild beasts, no wasting disease to require strength of constitution, no need of toil. For such a life, what we should call the weak are as well equipped as the strong, are indeed no longer weak. Better equipped indeed they are, for the strong would be fretted by an energy for which there was no outlet. No doubt the exquisite beauty of the buildings I saw was the outcome of the last surgings of the now purposeless energy of mankind before it settled down into perfect harmony with the conditions under which it lived – the flourish of that triumph which began the last great peace. This has ever been the fate of energy in security; it takes to art and to eroticism, and then come languor and decay.

'Even this artistic impetus would at last die away – had almost died in the Time I saw. To adorn themselves with flowers, to dance, to sing in the sunlight; so much was left of the artistic spirit, and no more. Even that would fade in the end into a contented inactivity. We are kept keen on the grindstone of pain and necessity, and, it seemed to me, that here was that hateful grindstone broken at last!

'As I stood there in the gathering dark I thought that in this simple explanation I had mastered the problem of the world – mastered the whole secret of these delicious people. Possibly the checks they had devised for the increase of population had succeeded too well, and their numbers had rather diminished than kept stationary. That would account for the abandoned ruins. Very simple was my explanation, and plausible enough – as most wrong theories are!

CHAPTER FIVE

'As I stood there musing over this too perfect triumph of man, the full moon, yellow and gibbous, came up out of an overflow of silver light in the north-east. The bright little figures ceased to move about below, a noiseless owl flitted by, and I shivered with the chill of the night. I determined to descend and find where I could sleep.

'I looked for the building I knew. Then my eye travelled along to the figure of the White Sphinx upon the pedestal of bronze, growing distinct as the light of the rising moon grew brighter. I could see the silver birch against it. There was the tangle of rhododendron bushes, black in the pale light, and there was the little lawn. I looked at the lawn again. A queer doubt chilled my complacency. "No," said I stoutly to myself, "that was not the lawn."

'But it *was* the lawn. For the white leprous face of the sphinx was towards it. Can you imagine what I felt as this conviction came home to me? But you cannot. The Time Machine was gone!

'At once, like a lash across the face, came the possibility of losing my own age, of being left helpless in this strange new world. The bare thought of it was an actual physical sensation. I could feel it grip me at the throat and stop my breathing. In another moment I was in a passion of fear and running with great leaping strides down the slope. Once I fell headlong and cut my face; I lost no time in stanching the blood, but jumped up and ran on, with a warm trickle down my cheek and chin. All the time I ran I was saying to myself: "They have moved it a little, pushed it under the bushes out of the way." Nevertheless, I ran with all my might. All the time, with the certainty that sometimes comes with excessive dread, I knew that such assurance was folly, knew instinctively that the machine was removed out of my reach. My breath came with pain. I suppose I covered the whole distance from the hill crest to the little lawn, two miles perhaps, in ten minutes. And I am not a young man. I cursed aloud, as I ran, at my confident folly in leaving the machine, wasting good breath thereby. I cried aloud, and none answered. Not a creature seemed to be stirring in that moonlit world.

'When I reached the lawn my worst fears were realised. Not a trace of the thing was to be seen. I felt faint and cold when I faced the empty space among the black tangle of bushes. I ran round it furiously, as if the thing might be hidden in a corner, and then stopped abruptly, with my hands clutching my hair. Above me towered the sphinx, upon the bronze pedestal, white, shining, leprous, in the light of the rising moon. It seemed to smile in mockery of my dismay.

'I might have consoled myself by imagining the little people had put the

mechanism in some shelter for me, had I not felt assured of their physical and intellectual inadequacy. That is what dismayed me: the sense of some hitherto unsuspected power, through whose intervention my invention had vanished. Yet, for one thing I felt assured: unless some other age had produced its exact duplicate, the machine could not have moved in time. The attachment of the levers – I will show you the method later – prevented anyone from tampering with it in that way when they were removed. It had moved, and was hid, only in space. But then, where could it be?

'I think I must have had a kind of frenzy. I remember running violently in and out among the moonlit bushes all round the sphinx, and startling some white animal that, in the dim light, I took for a small deer. I remember, too, late that night, beating the bushes with my clenched fist until my knuckles were gashed and bleeding from the broken twigs. Then, sobbing and raving in my anguish of mind, I went down to the great building of stone. The big hall was dark, silent, and deserted. I slipped on the uneven floor, and fell over one of the malachite tables, almost breaking my shin. I lit a match and went on past the dusty curtains, of which I have told you.

'There I found a second great hall covered with cushions, upon which, perhaps, a score or so of the little people were sleeping. I have no doubt they found my second appearance strange enough, coming suddenly out of the quiet darkness with inarticulate noises and the splutter and flare of a match. For they had forgotten about matches. "Where is my Time Machine?" I began, bawling like an angry child, laying hands upon them and shaking them up together. It must have been very queer to them. Some laughed, most of them looked sorely frightened. When I saw them standing round me, it came into my head that I was doing as foolish a thing as it was possible for me to do under the circumstances, in trying to revive the sensation of fear. For, reasoning from their daylight behaviour, I thought that fear must be forgotten.

'Abruptly, I dashed down the match, and, knocking one of the people over in my course, went blundering across the big dining-hall again, out under the moonlight. I heard cries of terror and their little feet running and stumbling this way and that. I do not remember all I did as the moon crept up the sky. I suppose it was the unexpected nature of my loss that maddened me. I felt hopelessly cut off from my own kind – a strange animal in an unknown world. I must have raved to and fro, screaming and crying upon God and Fate. I have a memory of horrible fatigue, as the long night of despair wore away; of looking in this impossible place and that; of groping among moonlit ruins and touching strange creatures in the black shadows; at last, of lying on the ground near the sphinx and weeping with absolute wretchedness. I had nothing left but misery. Then I slept, and when I woke again it was full day, and a couple of sparrows were hopping round me on the turf within reach of my arm.

'I sat up in the freshness of the morning, trying to remember how I had got there, and why I had such a profound sense of desertion and despair. Then things came clear in my mind. With the plain, reasonable daylight, I could look my circumstances fairly in the face. I saw the wild folly of my frenzy overnight, and I could reason with myself. "Suppose the worst?" I said. "Suppose the machine altogether lost – perhaps destroyed? It behoves me to be calm and patient, to learn the way of the people, to get a clear idea of the method of my loss, and the means of getting materials and tools; so that in the end, perhaps, I may make another." That would be my only hope, perhaps, but better than despair. And, after all, it was a beautiful and curious world.

'But probably the machine had only been taken away. Still, I must be calm and patient, find its hiding-place, and recover it by force or cunning. And with that I scrambled to my feet and looked about me, wondering where I could bathe. I felt weary, stiff, and travel-soiled. The freshness of the morning made me desire an equal freshness. I had exhausted my emotion. Indeed, as I went about my business, I found myself wondering at my intense excitement overnight. I made a careful examination of the ground about the little lawn. I wasted some time in futile questionings, conveyed, as well as I was able, to such of the little people as came by. They all failed to understand my gestures; some were simply stolid, some thought it was a jest and laughed at me. I had the hardest task in the world to keep my hands off their pretty laughing faces. It was a foolish impulse, but the devil begotten of fear and blind anger was ill curbed and still eager to take advantage of my perplexity. The turf gave better counsel. I found a groove ripped in it, about midway between the pedestal of the sphinx and the marks of my feet where, on arrival, I had struggled with the overturned machine. There were other signs of removal about, with queer narrow footprints like those I could imagine made by a sloth. This directed my closer attention to the pedestal. It was, as I think I have said, of bronze. It was not a mere block, but highly decorated with deep framed panels on either side. I went and rapped at these. The pedestal was hollow. Examining the panels with care I found them discontinuous with the frames. There were no handles or keyholes, but possibly the panels, if they were doors, as I supposed, opened from within. One thing was clear enough to my mind. It took no very great mental effort to infer that my Time Machine was inside that pedestal. But how it got there was a different problem.

'I saw the heads of two orange-clad people coming through the bushes and under some blossom-covered apple trees towards me. I turned smiling to them and beckoned them to me. They came, and then, pointing to the bronze pedestal, I tried to intimate my wish to open it. But at my first gesture towards this they behaved very oddly. I don't know how to convey their expression to you. Suppose you were to use a grossly improper gesture to a delicate-minded woman – it is how she would look. They went off as if

they had received the last possible insult. I tried a sweet-looking little chap in white next, with exactly the same result. Somehow, his manner made me feel ashamed of myself. But, as you know, I wanted the Time Machine, and I tried him once more. As he turned off, like the others, my temper got the better of me. In three strides I was after him, had him by the loose part of his robe round the neck, and began dragging him towards the sphinx. Then I saw the horror and repugnance of his face, and all of a sudden I let him go.

'But I was not beaten yet. I banged with my fist at the bronze panels. I thought I heard something stir inside – to be explicit, I thought I heard a sound like a chuckle – but I must have been mistaken. Then I got a big pebble from the river, and came and hammered till I had flattened a coil in the decorations, and the verdigris came off in powdery flakes. The delicate little people must have heard me hammering in gusty outbreaks a mile away on either hand, but nothing came of it. I saw a crowd of them upon the slopes, looking furtively at me. At last, hot and tired, I sat down to watch the place. But I was too restless to watch long; I am too Occidental for a long vigil. I could work at a problem for years, but to wait inactive for twenty-four hours – that is another matter.

'I got up after a time, and began walking aimlessly through the bushes towards the hill again. "Patience," said I to myself. "If you want your machine again you must leave that sphinx alone. If they mean to take your machine away, it's little good your wrecking their bronze panels, and if they don't, you will get it back as soon as you can ask for it. To sit among all those unknown things before a puzzle like that is hopeless. That way lies monomania. Face this world. Learn its ways, watch it, be careful of too hasty guesses at its meaning. In the end you will find clues to it all." Then suddenly the humour of the situation came into my mind: the thought of the years I had spent in study and toil to get into the future age, and now my passion of anxiety to get out of it. I had made myself the most complicated and the most hopeless trap that ever a man devised. Although it was at my own expense, I could not help myself. I laughed aloud.

'Going through the big palace, it seemed to me that the little people avoided me. It may have been my fancy, or it may have had something to do with my hammering at the gates of bronze. Yet I felt tolerably sure of the avoidance. I was careful, however, to show no concern and to abstain from any pursuit of them, and in the course of a day or two things got back to the old footing. I made what progress I could in the language, and in addition I pushed my explorations here and there. Either I missed some subtle point or their language was excessively simple – almost exclusively composed of concrete substantives and verbs. There seemed to be few, if any, abstract terms, or little use of figurative language. Their sentences were usually simple and of two words, and I failed to convey or understand any but the simplest propositions. I determined to put the thought of my Time Machine and the mystery of the bronze doors under the sphinx as much as

possible in a corner of memory, until my growing knowledge would lead me back to them in a natural way. Yet a certain feeling, you may understand, tethered me in a circle of a few miles round the point of my arrival.

'So far as I could see, all the world displayed the same exuberant richness as the Thames valley. From every hill I climbed I saw the same abundance of splendid buildings, endlessly varied in material and style, the same clustering thickets of evergreens, the same blossom-laden trees and tree-ferns. Here and there water shone like silver, and beyond, the land rose into blue undulating hills, and so faded into the serenity of the sky. A peculiar feature, which presently attracted my attention, was the presence of certain circular wells, several, as it seemed to me, of a very great depth. One lay by the path up the hill, which I had followed during my first walk. Like the others, it was rimmed with bronze, curiously wrought, and protected by a little cupola from the rain. Sitting by the side of these wells, and peering down into the shafted darkness, I could see no gleam of water, nor could I start any reflection with a lighted match. But in all of them I heard a certain sound: a thud – thud – thud, like the beating of some big engine; and I discovered, from the flaring of my matches, that a steady current of air set down the shafts. Further, I threw a scrap of paper into the throat of one, and, instead of fluttering slowly down, it was at once sucked swiftly out of sight.

'After a time, too, I came to connect these wells with tall towers standing here and there upon the slopes; for above them there was often just such a flicker in the air as one sees on a hot day above a sun-scorched beach. Putting things together, I reached a strong suggestion of an extensive system of subterranean ventilation, whose true import it was difficult to imagine. I was at first inclined to associate it with the sanitary apparatus of these people. It was an obvious conclusion, but it was absolutely wrong.

'And here I must admit that I learned very little of drains and bells and modes of conveyance, and the like conveniences, during my time in this real future. In some of these visions of Utopias and coming times which I have read, there is a vast amount of detail about building, and social arrangements, and so forth. But while such details are easy enough to obtain when the whole world is contained in one's imagination, they are altogether inaccessible to a real traveller amid such realities as I found here. Conceive the tale of London which a negro, fresh from Central Africa, would take back to his tribe! What would he know of railway companies, of social movements, of telephone and telegraph wires, of the Parcels Delivery Company, and postal orders and the like? Yet we, at least, should be willing enough to explain these things to him! And even of what he knew, how much could he make his untravelled friend either apprehend or believe? Then, think how narrow the gap between a negro and a white man of our own times, and how wide the interval between myself and these of the Golden Age! I was sensible of much which was unseen, and

which contributed to my comfort; but save for a general impression of automatic organisation, I fear I can convey very little of the difference to your mind.

'In the matter of sepulture, for instance, I could see no signs of crematoria nor anything suggestive of tombs. But it occurred to me that, possibly, there might be cemeteries (or crematoria) somewhere beyond the range of my explorings. This, again, was a question I deliberately put to myself, and my curiosity was at first entirely defeated upon the point. The thing puzzled me, and I was led to make a further remark, which puzzled me still more: that aged and infirm among this people there were none.

'I must confess that my satisfaction with my first theories of an automatic civilisation and a decadent humanity did not long endure. Yet I could think of no other. Let me put my difficulties. The several big palaces I had explored were mere living places, great dining-halls and sleeping apartments. I could find no machinery, no appliances of any kind. Yet these people were clothed in pleasant fabrics that must at times need renewal, and their sandals, though undecorated, were fairly complex specimens of metalwork. Somehow such things must be made. And the little people displayed no vestige of a creative tendency. There were no shops, no workshops, no sign of import-ations among them. They spent all their time in playing gently, in bathing in the river, in making love in a half-playful fashion, in eating fruit and sleeping. I could not see how things were kept going.

'Then, again, about the Time Machine: something, I knew not what, had taken it into the hollow pedestal of the White Sphinx. *Why?* For the life of me I could not imagine. Those waterless wells, too, those flickering pillars. I felt I lacked a clue. I felt – how shall I put it? Suppose you found an inscription, with sentences here and there in excellent plain English, and interpolated therewith, others made up of words, of letters even, absolutely unknown to you? Well, on the third day of my visit, that was how the world of 802,701 presented itself to me!

'That day, too, I made a friend – of a sort. It happened that, as I was watching some of the little people bathing in a shallow, one of them was seized with cramp and began drifting downstream. The main current ran rather swiftly, but not too strongly for even a moderate swimmer. It will give you an idea, therefore, of the strange deficiency in these creatures, when I tell you that none made the slightest attempt to rescue the weakly crying little thing which was drowning before their eyes. When I realised this, I hurriedly slipped off my clothes, and, wading in at a point lower down, I caught the poor mite and drew her safe to land. A little rubbing of the limbs soon brought her round, and I had the satisfaction of seeing she was all right before I left her. I had got to such a low estimate of her kind that I did not expect any gratitude from her. In that, however, I was wrong.

'This happened in the morning. In the afternoon I met my little woman, as I believe it was, as I was returning towards my centre from an

exploration, and she received me with cries of delight and presented me with a big garland of flowers – evidently made for me and me alone. The thing took my imagination. Very possibly I had been feeling desolate. At any rate I did my best to display my appreciation of the gift. We were soon seated together in a little stone arbour, engaged in conversation, chiefly of smiles. The creature's friendliness affected me exactly as a child's might have done. We passed each other flowers, and she kissed my hands. I did the same to hers. Then I tried talk, and found that her name was Weena, which, though I don't know what it meant, somehow seemed appropriate enough. That was the beginning of a queer friendship which lasted a week, and ended – as I will tell you!

'She was exactly like a child. She wanted to be with me always. She tried to follow me everywhere, and on my next journey out and about it went to my heart to tire her down, and leave her at last, exhausted and calling after me rather plaintively. But the problems of the world had to be mastered. I had not, I said to myself, come into the future to carry on a miniature flirtation. Yet her distress when I left her was very great, her expostulations at the parting were sometimes frantic, and I think, altogether, I had as much trouble as comfort from her devotion. Nevertheless she was, somehow, a very great comfort. I thought it was mere childish affection that made her cling to me. Until it was too late, I did not clearly know what I had inflicted upon her when I left her. Nor until it was too late did I clearly understand what she was to me. For, by merely seeming fond of me, and showing in her weak, futile way that she cared for me, the little doll of a creature presently gave my return to the neighbourhood of the White Sphinx almost the feeling of coming home; and I would watch for her tiny figure of white and gold so soon as I came over the hill.

'It was from her, too, that I learned that fear had not yet left the world. She was fearless enough in the daylight, and she had the oddest confidence in me; for once, in a foolish moment, I made threatening grimaces at her, and she simply laughed at them. But she dreaded the dark, dreaded shadows, dreaded black things. Darkness to her was the one thing dreadful. It was a singularly passionate emotion, and it set me thinking and observing. I discovered then, among other things, that these little people gathered into the great houses after dark, and slept in droves. To enter upon them without a light was to put them into a tumult of apprehension. I never found one out of doors, or one sleeping alone within doors, after dark. Yet I was still such a blockhead that I missed the lesson of that fear, and in spite of Weena's distress I insisted upon sleeping away from these slumbering multitudes.

'It troubled her greatly, but in the end her odd affection for me triumphed, and for five of the nights of our acquaintance, including the last night of all, she slept with her head pillowed on my arm. But my story slips away from me as I speak of her. It must have been the night before her

rescue that I was awakened about dawn. I had been restless, dreaming most disagreeably that I was drowned, and that sea anemones were feeling over my face with their soft palps. I woke with a start, and with an odd fancy that some greyish animal had just rushed out of the chamber. I tried to get to sleep again, but I felt restless and uncomfortable. It was that dim grey hour when things are just creeping out of darkness, when everything is colourless and clear cut, and yet unreal. I got up, and went down into the great hall, and so out upon the flagstones in front of the palace. I thought I would make a virtue of necessity, and see the sunrise.

'The moon was setting, and the dying moonlight and the first pallor of dawn were mingled in a ghastly half-light. The bushes were inky black, the ground a sombre grey, the sky colourless and cheerless. And up the hill I thought I could see ghosts. There several times, as I scanned the slope, I saw white figures. Twice I fancied I saw a solitary white, apelike creature running rather quickly up the hill, and once near the ruins I saw a leash of them carrying some dark body. They moved hastily. I did not see what became of them. It seemed that they vanished among the bushes. The dawn was still indistinct, you must understand. I was feeling that chill, uncertain, early-morning feeling you may have known. I doubted my eyes.

'As the eastern sky grew brighter, and the light of the day came on and its vivid colouring returned upon the world once more, I scanned the view keenly. But I saw no vestige of my white figures. They were mere creatures of the half-light. "They must have been ghosts," I said; "I wonder whence they dated." For a queer notion of Grant Allen's came into my head, and amused me. If each generation die and leave ghosts, he argued, the world at last will get overcrowded with them. On that theory they would have grown innumerable some Eight Hundred Thousand Years hence, and it was no great wonder to see four at once. But the jest was unsatisfying, and I was thinking of these figures all the morning, until Weena's rescue drove them out of my head. I associated them in some indefinite way with the white animal I had startled in my first passionate search for the Time Machine. But Weena was a pleasant substitute. Yet all the same, they were soon destined to take far deadlier possession of my mind.

'I think I have said how much hotter than our own was the weather of this Golden Age. I cannot account for it. It may be that the sun was hotter, or the earth nearer the sun. It is usual to assume that the sun will go on cooling steadily in the future. But people, unfamiliar with such speculations as those of the younger Darwin, forget that the planets must ultimately fall back one by one into the parent body. As these catastrophes occur, the sun will blaze with renewed energy; and it may be that some inner planet had suffered this fate. Whatever the reason, the fact remains that the sun was very much hotter than we know it.

'Well, one very hot morning – my fourth, I think – as I was seeking shelter from the heat and glare in a colossal ruin near the great house where

I slept and fed, there happened this strange thing. Clambering among these heaps of masonry, I found a narrow gallery, whose end and side windows were blocked by fallen masses of stone. By contrast with the brilliancy outside, it seemed at first impenetrably dark to me. I entered it groping, for the change from light to blackness made spots of colour swim before me. Suddenly I halted spellbound. A pair of eyes, luminous by reflection against the daylight without, was watching me out of the darkness.

'The old instinctive dread of wild beasts came upon me. I clenched my hands and steadfastly looked into the glaring eyeballs. I was afraid to turn. Then the thought of the absolute security in which humanity appeared to be living came to my mind. And then I remembered that strange terror of the dark. Overcoming my fear to some extent, I advanced a step and spoke. I will admit that my voice was harsh and ill-controlled. I put out my hand and touched something soft. At once the eyes darted sideways, and something white ran past me. I turned with my heart in my mouth, and saw a queer little apelike figure, its head held down in a peculiar manner, running across the sunlit space behind me. It blundered against a block of granite, staggered aside, and in a moment was hidden in a black shadow beneath another pile of ruined masonry.

'My impression of it is, of course, imperfect; but I know it was a dull white, and had strange large greyish-red eyes; also that there was flaxen hair on its head and down its back. But, as I say, it went too fast for me to see distinctly. I cannot even say whether it ran on all-fours, or only with its forearms held very low. After an instant's pause I followed it into the second heap of ruins. I could not find it at first; but, after a time in the profound obscurity, I came upon one of those round well-like openings of which I have told you, half closed by a fallen pillar. A sudden thought came to me. Could this Thing have vanished down the shaft? I lit a match, and, looking down, I saw a small, white, moving creature, with large bright eyes which regarded me steadfastly as it retreated. It made me shudder. It was so like a human spider! It was clambering down the wall, and now I saw for the first time a number of metal foot and hand rests forming a kind of ladder down the shaft. Then the light burned my fingers and fell out of my hand, going out as it dropped, and when I had lit another the little monster had disappeared.

'I do not know how long I sat peering down that well. It was not for some time that I could succeed in persuading myself that the thing I had seen was human. But, gradually, the truth dawned on me: that Man had not remained one species, but had differentiated into two distinct animals: that my graceful children of the Upper-world were not the sole descendants of our generation, but that this bleached, obscene, nocturnal Thing, which had flashed before me, was also heir to all the ages.

'I thought of the flickering pillars and of my theory of an underground ventilation. I began to suspect their true import. And what, I wondered, was

this Lemur doing in my scheme of a perfectly balanced organisation? How was it related to the indolent serenity of the beautiful Upper-worlders? And what was hidden down there, at the foot of that shaft? I sat upon the edge of the well telling myself that, at any rate, there was nothing to fear, and that there I must descend for the solution of my difficulties. And withal I was absolutely afraid to go! As I hesitated, two of the beautiful Upper-world people came running in their amorous sport across the daylight in the shadow. The male pursued the female, flinging flowers at her as he ran.

'They seemed distressed to find me, my arm against the overturned pillar, peering down the well. Apparently it was considered bad form to remark these apertures; for when I pointed to this one, and tried to frame a question about it in their tongue, they were still more visibly distressed and turned away. But they were interested by my matches, and I struck some to amuse them. I tried them again about the well, and again I failed. So presently I left them, meaning to go back to Weena, and see what I could get from her. But my mind was already in revolution; my guesses and impressions were slipping and sliding to a new adjustment. I had now a clue to the import of these wells, to the ventilating towers, to the mystery of the ghosts; to say nothing of a hint at the meaning of the bronze gates and the fate of the Time Machine! And very vaguely there came a suggestion towards the solution of the economic problem that had puzzled me.

'Here was the new view. Plainly, this second species of Man was sub-terranean. There were three circumstances in particular which made me think that its rare emergence above ground was the outcome of a long-continued underground habit. In the first place, there was the bleached look common in most animals that live largely in the dark – the white fish of the Kentucky caves, for instance. Then, those large eyes, with that capacity for reflecting light, are common features of nocturnal things – witness the owl and the cat. And last of all, that evident confusion in the sunshine, that hasty yet fumbling awkward flight towards dark shadow, and that peculiar carriage of the head while in the light – all reinforced the theory of an extreme sensitiveness of the retina.

'Beneath my feet, then, the earth must be tunnelled enormously, and these tunnellings were the habitat of the new race. The presence of ventilating shafts and wells along the hill slopes – everywhere, in fact, except along the river valley – showed how universal were its ramifications. What so natural, then, as to assume that it was in this artificial Underworld that such work as was necessary to the comfort of the daylight race was done? The notion was so plausible that I at once accepted it, and went on to assume the *how* of this splitting of the human species. I dare say you will anticipate the shape of my theory; though, for myself, I very soon felt that it fell far short of the truth.

'At first, proceeding from the problems of our own age, it seemed clear as daylight to me that the gradual widening of the present merely temporary

and social difference between the Capitalist and the Labourer, was the key to the whole position. No doubt it will seem grotesque enough to you – and wildly incredible! – and yet even now there are existing circumstances to point that way. There is a tendency to utilise underground space for the less ornamental purposes of civilisation; there is the Metropolitan Railway in London, for instance, there are new electric railways, there are subways, there are underground workrooms and restaurants, and they increase and multiply. Evidently, I thought, this tendency had increased till Industry had gradually lost its birthright in the sky. I mean that it had gone deeper and deeper into larger and ever larger underground factories, spending a still-increasing amount of its time therein, till, in the end – ! Even now, does not an East-end worker live in such artificial conditions as practically to be cut off from the natural surface of the earth?

'Again, the exclusive tendency of richer people – due, no doubt, to the increasing refinement of their education, and the widening gulf between them and the rude violence of the poor – is already leading to the closing, in their interest, of considerable portions of the surface of the land. About London, for instance, perhaps half the prettier country is shut in against intrusion. And this same widening gulf – which is due to the length and expense of the higher educational process and the increased facilities for and temptations towards refined habits on the part of the rich – will make that exchange between class and class, that promotion by intermarriage which at present retards the splitting of our species along lines of social stratification, less and less frequent. So, in the end, above ground you must have the Haves, pursuing pleasure and comfort and beauty, and below ground the Have-nots, the Workers getting continually adapted to the conditions of their labour. Once they were there, they would no doubt have to pay rent, and not a little of it, for the ventilation of their caverns; and if they refused, they would starve or be suffocated for arrears. Such of them as were so constituted as to be miserable and rebellious would die; and, in the end, the balance being permanent, the survivors would become as well adapted to the conditions of underground life, and as happy in their way, as the Upper-world people were to theirs. As it seemed to me, the refined beauty and the etiolated pallor followed naturally enough.

'The great triumph of Humanity I had dreamed of took a different shape in my mind. It had been no such triumph of moral education and general co-operation as I had imagined. Instead, I saw a real aristocracy, armed with a perfected science and working to a logical conclusion the industrial system of today. Its triumph had not been simply a triumph over Nature, but a triumph over Nature and the fellow-man. This, I must warn you, was my theory at the time. I had no convenient cicerone in the pattern of the Utopian books. My explanation may be absolutely wrong. I still think it is the most plausible one. But even on this supposition the balanced civilisation that was at last attained must have long since passed its zenith,

and was now far fallen into decay. The too-perfect security of the Upper-worlders had led them to a slow movement of degeneration, to a general dwindling in size, strength, and intelligence. That I could see clearly enough already. What had happened to the Under-grounders I did not yet suspect; but from what I had seen of the Morlocks – that, by the by, was the name by which these creatures were called – I could imagine that the modification of the human type was even far more profound than among the "Eloi", the beautiful race that I already knew.

'Then came troublesome doubts. Why had the Morlocks taken my Time Machine? For I felt sure it was they who had taken it. Why, too, if the Eloi were masters, could they not restore the machine to me? And why were they so terribly afraid of the dark? I proceeded, as I have said, to question Weena about this Underworld, but here again I was disappointed. At first she would not understand my questions, and presently she refused to answer them. She shivered as though the topic was unendurable. And when I pressed her, perhaps a little harshly, she burst into tears. They were the only tears, except my own, I ever saw in that Golden Age. When I saw them I ceased abruptly to trouble about the Morlocks, and was only concerned in banishing these signs of the human inheritance from Weena's eyes. And very soon she was smiling and clapping her hands, while I solemnly burned a match.

CHAPTER SIX

'It may seem odd to you, but it was two days before I could follow up the new-found clue in what was manifestly the proper way. I felt a peculiar shrinking from those pallid bodies. They were just the half-bleached colour of the worms and things one sees preserved in spirit in a zoological museum. And they were filthily cold to the touch. Probably my shrinking was largely due to the sympathetic influence of the Eloi, whose disgust of the Morlocks I now began to appreciate.

'The next night I did not sleep well. Probably my health was a little disordered. I was oppressed with perplexity and doubt. Once or twice I had a feeling of intense fear for which I could perceive no definite reason. I remember creeping noiselessly into the great hall where the little people were sleeping in the moonlight – that night Weena was among them – and feeling reassured by their presence. It occurred to me even then, that in the course of a few days the moon must pass through its last quarter, and the nights grow dark, when the appearances of these unpleasant creatures from below, these whitened Lemurs, this new vermin that had replaced the old, might be more abundant. And on both these days I had the restless feeling of one who shirks an inevitable duty. I felt assured that the Time Machine was only to be recovered by boldly penetrating these underground mysteries. Yet I could not face the mystery. If only I had had a companion it

would have been different. But I was so horribly alone, and even to clamber down into the darkness of the well appalled me. I don't know if you will understand my feeling, but I never felt quite safe at my back.

'It was this restlessness, this insecurity, perhaps, that drove me further and further afield in my exploring expeditions. Going to the south-west-ward towards the rising country that is now called Combe Wood, I observed far off, in the direction of nineteenth-century Banstead, a vast green structure, different in character from any I had hitherto seen. It was larger than the largest of the palaces or ruins I knew, and the façade had an Oriental look: the face of it having the lustre, as well as the pale-green tint, a kind of bluish-green, of a certain type of Chinese porcelain. This difference in aspect suggested a difference in use, and I was minded to push on and explore. But the day was growing late, and I had come upon the sight of the place after a long and tiring circuit; so I resolved to hold over the adventure for the following day, and I returned to the welcome and the caresses of little Weena. But next morning I perceived clearly enough that my curiosity regarding the Palace of Green Porcelain was a piece of self-deception, to enable me to shirk, by another day, an experience I dreaded. I resolved I would make the descent without further waste of time, and started out in the early morning towards a well near the ruins of granite and aluminium.

'Little Weena ran with me. She danced beside me to the well, but when she saw me lean over the mouth and look downward, she seemed strangely disconcerted. "Goodbye, little Weena," I said, kissing her; and then putting her down, I began to feel over the parapet for the climbing hooks. Rather hastily, I may as well confess, for I feared my courage might leak away! At first she watched me in amazement. Then she gave a most piteous cry, and running to me, she began to pull at me with her little hands. I think her opposition nerved me rather to proceed. I shook her off, perhaps a little roughly, and in another moment I was in the throat of the well. I saw her agonised face over the parapet, and smiled to reassure her. Then I had to look down at the unstable hooks to which I clung.

'I had to clamber down a shaft of perhaps two hundred yards. The descent was effected by means of metallic bars projecting from the sides of the well, and these being adapted to the needs of a creature much smaller and lighter than myself, I was speedily cramped and fatigued by the descent. And not simply fatigued! One of the bars bent suddenly under my weight, and almost swung me off into the blackness beneath. For a moment I hung by one hand, and after that experience I did not dare to rest again. Though my arms and back were presently acutely painful, I went on clambering down the sheer descent with as quick a motion as possible. Glancing upward, I saw the aperture, a small blue disk, in which a star was visible, while little Weena's head showed as a round black projection. The thudding sound of a machine below grew louder and

more oppressive. Everything save that little disk above was profoundly dark, and when I looked up again Weena had disappeared.

'I was in an agony of discomfort. I had some thought of trying to go up the shaft again, and leave the Underworld alone. But even while I turned this over in my mind I continued to descend. At last, with intense relief, I saw dimly coming up, a foot to the right of me, a slender loophole in the wall. Swinging myself in, I found it was the aperture of a narrow horizontal tunnel in which I could lie down and rest. It was not too soon. My arms ached, my back was cramped, and I was trembling with the prolonged terror of a fall. Besides this, the unbroken darkness had had a distressing effect upon my eyes. The air was full of the throb and hum of machinery pumping air down the shaft.

'I do not know how long I lay. I was roused by a soft hand touching my face. Starting up in the darkness I snatched at my matches and, hastily striking one, I saw three stooping white creatures similar to the one I had seen above ground in the ruin, hastily retreating before the light. Living, as they did, in what appeared to me impenetrable darkness, their eyes were abnormally large and sensitive, just as are the pupils of the abysmal fishes, and they reflected the light in the same way. I have no doubt they could see me in that rayless obscurity, and they did not seem to have any fear of me apart from the light. But, so soon as I struck a match in order to see them, they fled incontinently, vanishing into dark gutters and tunnels, from which their eyes glared at me in the strangest fashion.

'I tried to call to them, but the language they had was apparently different from that of the Upper-world people; so that I was needs left to my own unaided efforts, and the thought of flight before exploration was even then in my mind. But I said to myself, "You are in for it now," and, feeling my way along the tunnel, I found the noise of machinery grow louder. Presently the walls fell away from me, and I came to a large open space, and striking another match, saw that I had entered a vast arched cavern, which stretched into utter darkness beyond the range of my light. The view I had of it was as much as one could see in the burning of a match.

'Necessarily my memory is vague. Great shapes like big machines rose out of the dimness, and cast grotesque black shadows, in which dim spectral Morlocks sheltered from the glare. The place, by the by, was very stuffy and oppressive, and the faint halitus of freshly shed blood was in the air. Some way down the central vista was a little table of white metal, laid with what seemed a meal. The Morlocks at any rate were carnivorous! Even at the time, I remember wondering what large animal could have survived to furnish the red joint I saw. It was all very indistinct: the heavy smell, the big unmeaning shapes, the obscene figures lurking in the shadows, and only waiting for the darkness to come at me again! Then the match burned down, and stung my fingers, and fell, a wriggling red spot in the blackness.

'I have thought since how particularly ill-equipped I was for such an

experience. When I had started with the Time Machine, I had started with the absurd assumption that the men of the Future would certainly be infinitely ahead of ourselves in all their appliances. I had come without arms, without medicine, without anything to smoke – at times I missed tobacco frightfully – even without enough matches. If only I had thought of a Kodak! I could have flashed that glimpse of the Underworld in a second, and examined it at leisure. But, as it was, I stood there with only the weapons and the powers that Nature had endowed me with – hands, feet, and teeth; these, and four safety-matches that still remained to me.

'I was afraid to push my way in among all this machinery in the dark, and it was only with my last glimpse of light I discovered that my store of matches had run low. It had never occurred to me until that moment that there was any need to economise them, and I had wasted almost half the box in astonishing the Upper-worlders, to whom fire was a novelty. Now, as I say, I had four left, and while I stood in the dark, a hand touched mine, lank fingers came feeling over my face, and I was sensible of a peculiar unpleasant odour. I fancied I heard the breathing of a crowd of those dreadful little beings about me. I felt the box of matches in my hand being gently disengaged, and other hands behind me plucking at my clothing. The sense of these unseen creatures examining me was indescribably unpleasant. The sudden realisation of my ignorance of their ways of thinking and doing came home to me very vividly in the darkness. I shouted at them as loudly as I could. They started away, and then I could feel them approaching me again. They clutched at me more boldly, whispering odd sounds to each other. I shivered violently, and shouted again – rather discordantly. This time they were not so seriously alarmed, and they made a queer laughing noise as they came back at me. I will confess I was horribly frightened. I determined to strike another match and escape under the protection of its glare. I did so, and eking out the flicker with a scrap of paper from my pocket, I made good my retreat to the narrow tunnel. But I had scarce entered this when my light was blown out and in the blackness I could hear the Morlocks rustling like wind among leaves, and pattering like the rain, as they hurried after me.

'In a moment I was clutched by several hands, and there was no mistaking that they were trying to haul me back. I struck another light, and waved it in their dazzled faces. You can scarce imagine how nauseatingly inhuman they looked – those pale, chinless faces and great, lidless, pinkish-grey eyes! – as they stared in their blindness and bewilderment. But I did not stay to look, I promise you: I retreated again, and when my second match had ended, I struck my third. It had almost burned through when I reached the opening into the shaft. I lay down on the edge, for the throb of the great pump below made me giddy. Then I felt sideways for the projecting hooks, and, as I did so, my feet were grasped from behind, and I was violently tugged backwards. I lit my last match . . . and it incontinently

went out. But I had my hand on the climbing bars now, and, kicking violently, I disengaged myself from the clutches of the Morlocks and was speedily clambering up the shaft, while they stayed peering and blinking up at me: all but one little wretch who followed me for some way, and well-nigh secured my boot as a trophy.

'That climb seemed interminable to me. With the last twenty or thirty feet of it a deadly nausea came upon me. I had the greatest difficulty in keeping my hold. The last few yards was a frightful struggle against this faintness. Several times my head swam, and I felt all the sensations of falling. At last, however, I got over the well-mouth somehow, and staggered out of the ruin into the blinding sunlight. I fell upon my face. Even the soil smelt sweet and clean. Then I remember Weena kissing my hands and ears, and the voices of others among the Eloi. Then, for a time, I was insensible.

CHAPTER SEVEN

'Now, indeed, I seemed in a worse case than before. Hitherto, except during my night's anguish at the loss of the Time Machine, I had felt a sustaining hope of ultimate escape, but that hope was staggered by these new discoveries. Hitherto I had merely thought myself impeded by the childish simplicity of the little people, and by some unknown forces which I had only to understand to overcome; but there was an altogether new element in the sickening quality of the Morlocks – a something inhuman and malign. Instinctively I loathed them. Before, I had felt as a man might feel who had fallen into a pit: my concern was with the pit and how to get out of it. Now I felt like a beast in a trap, whose enemy would come upon him soon.

'The enemy I dreaded may surprise you. It was the darkness of the new moon. Weena had put this into my head by some at first incomprehensible remarks about the Dark Nights. It was not now such a very difficult problem to guess what the coming Dark Nights might mean. The moon was on the wane: each night there was a longer interval of darkness. And I now understood to some slight degree at least the reason of the fear of the little Upper-world people for the dark. I wondered vaguely what foul villainy it might be that the Morlocks did under the new moon. I felt pretty sure now that my second hypothesis was all wrong. The Upper-world people might once have been the favoured aristocracy, and the Morlocks their mechanical servants: but that had long since passed away. The two species that had resulted from the evolution of man were sliding down towards, or had already arrived at, an altogether new relationship. The Eloi, like the Carolingian kings, had decayed to a mere beautiful futility. They still possessed the earth on sufferance: since the Morlocks, subterranean _for innumerable generations, had come at last to find the daylit surface

intolerable. And the Morlocks made their garments, I inferred, and main-
tained them in their habitual needs, perhaps through the survival of an old
habit of service. They did it as a standing horse paws with his foot, or as
a man enjoys killing animals in sport: because ancient and departed
necessities had impressed it on the organism. But, clearly, the old order was
already in part reversed. The Nemesis of the delicate ones was creeping on
apace. Ages ago, thousands of generations ago, man had thrust his brother
man out of the ease and the sunshine. And now that brother was coming
back changed! Already the Eloi had begun to learn one old lesson anew.
They were becoming re-acquainted with Fear. And suddenly there came
into my head the memory of the meat I had seen in the Underworld. It
seemed odd how it floated into my mind: not stirred up as it were by the
current of my meditations, but coming in almost like a question from
outside. I tried to recall the form of it. I had a vague sense of something
familiar, but I could not tell what it was at the time.

'Still, however helpless the little people in the presence of their
mysterious Fear, I was differently constituted. I came out of this age of ours,
this ripe prime of the human race, when Fear does not paralyse and mystery
has lost its terrors. I at least would defend myself. Without further delay I
determined to make myself arms and a fastness where I might sleep. With
that refuge as a base, I could face this strange world with some of that
confidence I had lost in realising to what creatures night by night I lay
exposed. I felt I could never sleep again until my bed was secure from them.
I shuddered with horror to think how they must already have examined me.

'I wandered during the afternoon along the valley of the Thames, but
found nothing that commended itself to my mind as inaccessible. All the
buildings and trees seemed easily practicable to such dexterous climbers as
the Morlocks, to judge by their wells, must be. Then the tall pinnacles of
the Palace of Green Porcelain and the polished gleam of its walls came
back to my memory; and in the evening, taking Weena like a child upon my
shoulder, I went up the hills towards the south-west. The distance, I had
reckoned, was seven or eight miles, but it must have been nearer eighteen. I
had first seen the place on a moist afternoon when distances are deceptively
diminished. In addition, the heel of one of my shoes was loose, and a nail was
working through the sole – they were comfortable old shoes I wore about
indoors – so that I was lame. And it was already long past sunset when I came
in sight of the palace, silhouetted black against the pale yellow of the sky.

'Weena had been hugely delighted when I began to carry her, but after a
while she desired me to let her down, and ran along by the side of me,
occasionally darting off on either hand to pick flowers to stick in my
pockets. My pockets had always puzzled Weena, but at the last she had
concluded that they were an eccentric kind of vase for floral decoration. At
least she utilised them for that purpose. And that reminds me! In changing
my jacket I found . . . '

The Time Traveller paused, put his hand into his pocket, and silently placed two withered flowers, not unlike very large white mallows, upon the little table. Then he resumed his narrative.

'As the hush of evening crept over the world and we proceeded over the hill crest towards Wimbledon, Weena grew tired and wanted to return to the house of grey stone. But I pointed out the distant pinnacles of the Palace of Green Porcelain to her, and contrived to make her understand that we were seeking a refuge there from her Fear. You know that great pause that comes upon things before the dusk? Even the breeze stops in the trees. To me there is always an air of expectation about that evening stillness. The sky was clear, remote, and empty save for a few horizontal bars far down in the sunset. Well, that night the expectation took the colour of my fears. In that darkling calm my senses seemed preternaturally sharpened. I fancied I could even feel the hollowness of the ground beneath my feet: could, indeed, almost see through it the Morlocks on their ant-hill going hither and thither and waiting for the dark. In my excitement I fancied that they would receive my invasion of their burrows as a declaration of war. And why had they taken my Time Machine?

'So we went on in the quiet, and the twilight deepened into night. The clear blue of the distance faded, and one star after another came out. The ground grew dim and the trees black. Weena's fears and her fatigue grew upon her. I took her in my arms and talked to her and caressed her. Then, as the darkness grew deeper, she put her arms round my neck, and, closing her eyes, tightly pressed her face against my shoulder. So we went down a long slope into a valley, and there in the dimness I almost walked into a little river. This I waded, and went up the opposite side of the valley, past a number of sleeping houses, and by a statue – a Faun, or some such figure, *minus* the head. Here, too, were acacias. So far I had seen nothing of the Morlocks, but it was yet early in the night, and the darker hours before the old moon rose were still to come.

'From the brow of the next hill I saw a thick wood spreading wide and black before me. I hesitated at this. I could see no end to it, either to the right or the left. Feeling tired – my feet, in particular, were very sore – I carefully lowered Weena from my shoulder as I halted, and sat down upon the turf. I could no longer see the Palace of Green Porcelain, and I was in doubt of my direction. I looked into the thickness of the wood and thought of what it might hide. Under that dense tangle of branches one would be out of sight of the stars. Even were there no other lurking danger – a danger I did not care to let my imagination loose upon – there would still be all the roots to stumble over and the tree-boles to strike against. I was very tired, too, after the excitements of the day; so I decided that I would not face it, but would pass the night upon the open hill.

'Weena, I was glad to find, was fast asleep. I carefully wrapped her in my jacket, and sat down beside her to wait for the moonrise. The hillside was

quiet and deserted, but from the black of the wood there came now and then a stir of living things. Above me shone the stars, for the night was very clear. I felt a certain sense of friendly comfort in their twinkling. All the old constellations had gone from the sky, however: that slow movement which is imperceptible in a hundred human lifetimes, had long since rearranged them in unfamiliar groupings. But the Milky Way, it seemed to me, was still the same tattered streamer of stardust as of yore. Southward (as I judged it) was a very bright red star that was new to me; it was even more splendid than our own green Sirius. And amid all these scintillating points of light one bright planet shone kindly and steadily like the face of an old friend.

'Looking at these stars suddenly dwarfed my own troubles and all the gravities of terrestrial life. I thought of their unfathomable distance, and the slow inevitable drift of their movements out of the unknown past into the unknown future. I thought of the great precessional cycle that the pole of the earth describes. Only forty times had that silent revolution occurred during all the years that I had traversed. And during these few revolutions all the activity, all the traditions, the complex organisations, the nations, languages, literatures, aspirations, even the mere memory of Man as I knew him, had been swept out of existence. Instead were these frail creatures who had forgotten their high ancestry, and the white Things of which I went in terror. Then I thought of the Great Fear that was between the two species, and for the first time, with a sudden shiver, came the clear knowledge of what the meat I had seen might be. Yet it was too horrible! I looked at little Weena sleeping beside me, her face white and starlike under the stars, and forthwith dismissed the thought.

'Through that long night I held my mind off the Morlocks as well as I could, and wiled away the time by trying to fancy I could find signs of the old constellations in the new confusion. The sky kept very clear, except for a hazy cloud or so. No doubt I dozed at times. Then, as my vigil wore on, came a faintness in the eastward sky, like the reflection of some colourless fire, and the old moon rose, thin and peaked and white. And close behind, and overtaking it, and overflowing it, the dawn came, pale at first, and then growing pink and warm. No Morlocks had approached us. Indeed, I had seen none upon the hill that night. And in the confidence of renewed day it almost seemed to me that my fear had been unreasonable. I stood up and found my foot with the loose heel swollen at the ankle and painful under the heel; so I sat down again, took off my shoes, and flung them away.

'I awakened Weena, and we went down into the wood, now green and pleasant instead of black and forbidding. We found some fruit wherewith to break our fast. We soon met others of the dainty ones, laughing and dancing in the sunlight as though there was no such thing in nature as the night. And then I thought once more of the meat that I had seen. I felt assured now of what it was, and from the bottom of my heart I pitied this last feeble rill from the great flood of humanity. Clearly, at some time in the

Long-Ago of human decay the Morlocks' food had run short. Possibly they had lived on rats and suchlike vermin. Even now man is far less discriminating and exclusive in his food than he was – far less than any monkey. His prejudice against human flesh is no deep-seated instinct. And so these inhuman sons of men – ! I tried to look at the thing in a scientific spirit. After all, they were less human and more remote than our cannibal ancestors of three or four thousand years ago. And the intelligence that would have made this state of things a torment had gone. Why should I trouble myself? These Eloi were mere fatted cattle, which the ant-like Morlocks preserved and preyed upon – probably saw to the breeding of. And there was Weena dancing at my side!

'Then I tried to preserve myself from the horror that was coming upon me, by regarding it as a rigorous punishment of human selfishness. Man had been content to live in ease and delight upon the labours of his fellow-man, had taken Necessity as his watchword and excuse, and in the fullness of time Necessity had come home to him. I even tried a Carlyle-like scorn of this wretched aristocracy in decay. But this attitude of mind was impossible. However great their intellectual degradation, the Eloi had kept too much of the human form not to claim my sympathy, and to make me perforce a sharer in their degradation and their Fear.

'I had at that time very vague ideas as to the course I should pursue. My first was to secure some safe place of refuge, and to make myself such arms of metal or stone as I could contrive. That necessity was immediate. In the next place, I hoped to procure some means of fire, so that I should have the weapon of a torch at hand, for nothing, I knew, would be more efficient against these Morlocks. Then I wanted to arrange some contrivance to break open the doors of bronze under the White Sphinx. I had in mind a battering ram. I had a persuasion that if I could enter those doors and carry a blaze of light before me I should discover the Time Machine and escape. I could not imagine the Morlocks were strong enough to move it far away. Weena I had resolved to bring with me to our own time. And turning such schemes over in my mind I pursued our way towards the building which my fancy had chosen as our dwelling.

CHAPTER EIGHT

'I found the Palace of Green Porcelain, when we approached it about noon, deserted and falling into ruin. Only ragged vestiges of glass remained in its windows, and great sheets of the green facing had fallen away from the corroded metallic framework. It lay very high upon a turfy down, and looking north-eastward before I entered it, I was surprised to see a large estuary, or even creek, where I judged Wandsworth and Battersea must once have been. I thought then – though I never followed up the thought –

of what might have happened, or might be happening, to the living things in the sea.

'The material of the Palace proved on examination to be indeed porcelain, and along the face of it I saw an inscription in some unknown character. I thought, rather foolishly, that Weena might help me to interpret this, but I only learned that the bare idea of writing had never entered her head. She always seemed to me, I fancy, more human than she was, perhaps because her affection was so human.

'Within the big valves of the door – which were open and broken – we found, instead of the customary hall, a long gallery lit by many side windows. At the first glance I was reminded of a museum. The tiled floor was thick with dust, and a remarkable array of miscellaneous objects was shrouded in the same grey covering. Then I perceived, standing strange and gaunt in the centre of the hall, what was clearly the lower part of a huge skeleton. I recognised by the oblique feet that it was some extinct creature after the fashion of the Megatherium. The skull and the upper bones lay beside it in the thick dust, and in one place, where rainwater had dropped through a leak in the roof, the thing itself had been worn away. Further in the gallery was the huge skeleton barrel of a Brontosaurus. My museum hypothesis was confirmed. Going towards the side I found what appeared to be sloping shelves, and clearing away the thick dust, I found the old familiar glass cases of our own time. But they must have been airtight to judge from the fair preservation of some of their contents.

'Clearly we stood among the ruins of some latter-day South Kensington! Here, apparently, was the Palaeontological Section, and a very splendid array of fossils it must have been, though the inevitable process of decay that had been staved off for a time, and had, through the extinction of bacteria and fungi, lost ninety-nine hundredths of its force, was nevertheless, with extreme sureness if with extreme slowness at work again upon all its treasures. Here and there I found traces of the little people in the shape of rare fossils broken to pieces or threaded in strings upon reeds. And the cases had in some instances been bodily removed – by the Morlocks as I judged. The place was very silent. The thick dust deadened our footsteps. Weena, who had been rolling a sea urchin down the sloping glass of a case, presently came, as I stared about me, and very quietly took my hand and stood beside me.

'And at first I was so much surprised by this ancient monument of an intellectual age, that I gave no thought to the possibilities it presented. Even my preoccupation about the Time Machine receded a little from my mind.

'To judge from the size of the place, this Palace of Green Porcelain had a great deal more in it than a Gallery of Palaeontology; possibly historical galleries; it might be, even a library! To me, at least in my present circumstances, these would be vastly more interesting than this spectacle of old-time geology in decay. Exploring, I found another short gallery running

transversely to the first. This appeared to be devoted to minerals, and the sight of a block of sulphur set my mind running on gunpowder. But I could find no saltpetre; indeed, no nitrates of any kind. Doubtless they had deliquesced ages ago. Yet the sulphur hung in my mind, and set up a train of thinking. As for the rest of the contents of that gallery, though on the whole they were the best preserved of all I saw, I had little interest. I am no specialist in mineralogy, and I went on down a very ruinous aisle running parallel to the first hall I had entered. Apparently this section had been devoted to natural history, but everything had long since passed out of recognition. A few shrivelled and blackened vestiges of what had once been stuffed animals, desiccated mummies in jars that had once held spirit, a brown dust of departed plants: that was all! I was sorry for that, because I should have been glad to trace the patent readjustments by which the conquest of animated nature had been attained. Then we came to a gallery of simply colossal proportions, but singularly ill-lit, the floor of it running downward at a slight angle from the end at which I entered. At intervals white globes hung from the ceiling – many of them cracked and smashed – which suggested that originally the place had been artificially lit. Here I was more in my element, for rising on either side of me were the huge bulks of big machines, all greatly corroded and many broken down, but some still fairly complete. You know I have a certain weakness for mechanism, and I was inclined to linger among these; the more so as for the most part they had the interest of puzzles, and I could make only the vaguest guesses at what they were for. I fancied that if I could solve their puzzles I should find myself in possession of powers that might be of use against the Morlocks.

'Suddenly Weena came very close to my side. So suddenly that she startled me. Had it not been for her I do not think I should have noticed that the floor of the gallery sloped at all.* The end I had come in at was quite above ground, and was lit by rare slit-like windows. As you went down the length, the ground came up against these windows, until at last there was a pit like the "area" of a London house before each, and only a narrow line of daylight at the top. I went slowly along, puzzling about the machines, and had been too intent upon them to notice the gradual diminution of the light, until Weena's increasing apprehensions drew my attention. Then I saw that the gallery ran down at last into a thick darkness. I hesitated, and then, as I looked round me, I saw that the dust was less abundant and its surface less even. Further away towards the dimness, it appeared to be broken by a number of small narrow footprints. My sense of the immediate presence of the Morlocks revived at that. I felt that I was wasting my time in the academic examination of machinery. I called to mind that it was already far advanced in the afternoon, and that I had still no weapon, no refuge, and no means of making a fire. And then down in the remote blackness of the gallery I heard a peculiar pattering, and the same odd noises I had heard down the well.

'I took Weena's hand. Then, struck with a sudden idea, I left her and turned to a machine from which projected a lever not unlike those in a signal-box. Clambering upon the stand, and grasping this lever in my hands, I put all my weight upon it sideways. Suddenly Weena, deserted in the central aisle, began to whimper. I had judged the strength of the lever pretty correctly, for it snapped after a minute's strain, and I rejoined her with a mace in my hand more than sufficient, I judged, for any Morlock skull I might encounter. And I longed very much to kill a Morlock or so. Very inhuman, you may think, to want to go killing one's own descendants! But it was impossible, somehow, to feel any humanity in the things. Only my disinclination to leave Weena, and a persuasion that if I began to slake my thirst for murder my Time Machine might suffer, restrained me from going straight down the gallery and killing the brutes I heard.

'Well, mace in one hand and Weena in the other, I went out of that gallery and into another and still larger one, which at the first glance reminded me of a military chapel hung with tattered flags. The brown and charred rags that hung from the sides of it, I presently recognised as the decaying vestiges of books. They had long since dropped to pieces, and every semblance of print had left them. But here and there were warped boards and cracked metallic clasps that told the tale well enough. Had I been a literary man I might, perhaps, have moralised upon the futility of all ambition. But as it was, the thing that struck me with keenest force was the enormous waste of labour to which this sombre wilderness of rotting paper testified. At the time I will confess that I thought chiefly of the *Philosophical Transactions* and my own seventeen papers upon physical optics.

'Then, going up a broad staircase, we came to what may once have been a gallery of technical chemistry. And here I had not a little hope of useful discoveries. Except at one end where the roof had collapsed, this gallery was well preserved. I went eagerly to every unbroken case. And at last, in one of the really airtight cases, I found a box of matches. Very eagerly I tried them. They were perfectly good. They were not even damp. I turned to Weena. "Dance," I cried to her in her own tongue. For now I had a weapon indeed against the horrible creatures we feared. And so, in that derelict museum, upon the thick soft carpeting of dust, to Weena's huge delight, I solemnly performed a kind of composite dance, whistling *The Land of the Leal* as cheerfully as I could. In part it was a modest *cancan*, in part a step dance, in part a skirt-dance (so far as my tail coat permitted), and in part original. For I am naturally inventive, as you know.

'Now, I still think that for this box of matches to have escaped the wear of time for immemorial years was a most strange, as for me it was a most fortunate thing. Yet, oddly enough, I found a far unlikelier substance, and that was camphor. I found it in a sealed jar, that by chance, I suppose, had been really hermetically sealed. I fancied at first that it was paraffin wax, and smashed the glass accordingly. But the odour of camphor was unmistakable.

In the universal decay this volatile substance had chanced to survive, perhaps through many thousands of centuries. It reminded me of a sepia painting I had once seen done from the ink of a fossil Belemnite that must have perished and become fossilised millions of years ago. I was about to throw it away, but I remembered that it was inflammable and burned with a good bright flame – was, in fact, an excellent candle – and I put it in my pocket. I found no explosives, however, nor any means of breaking down the bronze doors. As yet my iron crowbar was the most helpful thing I had chanced upon. Nevertheless I left that gallery greatly elated.

'I cannot tell you all the story of that long afternoon. It would require a great effort of memory to recall my explorations in at all the proper order. I remember a long gallery of rusting stands of arms, and how I hesitated between my crowbar and a hatchet or a sword. I could not carry both, however, and my bar of iron promised best against the bronze gates. There were numbers of guns, pistols, and rifles. The most were masses of rust, but many were of some new metal, and still fairly sound. But any cartridges or powder there may once have been had rotted into dust. One corner I saw was charred and shattered; perhaps, I thought, by an explosion among the specimens. In another place was a vast array of idols – Polynesian, Mexican, Grecian, Phoenician, every country on earth I should think. And here, yielding to an irresistible impulse, I wrote my name upon the nose of a steatite monster from South America that particularly took my fancy.

'As the evening drew on, my interest waned. I went through gallery after gallery, dusty, silent, often ruinous, the exhibits sometimes mere heaps of rust and lignite, sometimes fresher. In one place I suddenly found myself near the model of a tin-mine, and then by the merest accident I discovered, in an airtight case, two dynamite cartridges! I shouted "Eureka!" and smashed the case with joy. Then came a doubt. I hesitated. Then, selecting a little side gallery, I made my essay. I never felt such a disappointment as I did in waiting five, ten, fifteen minutes for an explosion that never came. Of course the things were dummies, as I might have guessed from their presence. I really believe that had they not been so, I should have rushed off incontinently and blown Sphinx, bronze doors, and (as it proved) my chances of finding the Time Machine, all together into non-existence.

'It was after that, I think, that we came to a little open court within the palace. It was turfed, and had three fruit trees. So we rested and refreshed ourselves. Towards sunset I began to consider our position. Night was creeping upon us, and my inaccessible hiding-place had still to be found. But that troubled me very little now. I had in my possession a thing that was, perhaps, the best of all defences against the Morlocks – I had matches! I had the camphor in my pocket, too, if a blaze were needed. It seemed to me that the best thing we could do would be to pass the night in the open, protected by a fire. In the morning there was the getting of the Time Machine. Towards that, as yet, I had only my iron mace. But now, with my

growing knowledge, I felt very differently towards those bronze doors. Up to this, I had refrained from forcing them, largely because of the mystery on the other side. They had never impressed me as being very strong, and I hoped to find my bar of iron not altogether inadequate for the work.

CHAPTER NINE

'We emerged from the palace while the sun was still in part above the horizon. I was determined to reach the White Sphinx early the next morning, and ere the dusk I purposed pushing through the woods that had stopped me on the previous journey. My plan was to go as far as possible that night, and then, building a fire, to sleep in the protection of its glare. Accordingly, as we went along I gathered any sticks or dried grass I saw, and presently had my arms full of such litter. Thus loaded, our progress was slower than I had anticipated, and besides Weena was tired. And I began to suffer from sleepiness too; so that it was full night before we reached the wood. Upon the shrubby hill of its edge Weena would have stopped, fearing the darkness before us; but a singular sense of impending calamity, that should indeed have served me as a warning, drove me onward. I had been without sleep for a night and two days, and I was feverish and irritable. I felt sleep coming upon me, and the Morlocks with it.

'While we hesitated, among the black bushes behind us, and dim against their blackness, I saw three crouching figures. There was scrub and long grass all about us, and I did not feel safe from their insidious approach. The forest, I calculated, was rather less than a mile across. If we could get through it to the bare hillside, there, as it seemed to me, was an altogether safer resting-place; I thought that with my matches and my camphor I could contrive to keep my path illuminated through the woods. Yet it was evident that if I was to flourish matches with my hands I should have to abandon my firewood; so, rather reluctantly, I put it down. And then it came into my head that I would amaze our friends behind by lighting it. I was to discover the atrocious folly of this proceeding, but it came to my mind as an ingenious move for covering our retreat.

'I don't know if you have ever thought what a rare thing flame must be in the absence of man and in a temperate climate. The sun's heat is rarely strong enough to burn, even when it is focused by dewdrops, as is sometimes the case in more tropical districts. Lightning may blast and blacken, but it rarely gives rise to widespread fire. Decaying vegetation may occasionally smoulder with the heat of its fermentation, but this rarely results in flame. In this decadence, too, the art of fire-making had been forgotten on the earth. The red tongues that went licking up my heap of wood were an altogether new and strange thing to Weena.

'She wanted to run to it and play with it. I believe she would have cast

herself into it had I not restrained her. But I caught her up, and in spite of her struggles, plunged boldly before me into the wood. For a little way the glare of my fire lit the path. Looking back presently, I could see, through the crowded stems, that from my heap of sticks the blaze had spread to some bushes adjacent, and a curved line of fire was creeping up the grass of the hill. I laughed at that, and turned again to the dark trees before me. It was very black, and Weena clung to me convulsively, but there was still, as my eyes grew accustomed to the darkness, sufficient light for me to avoid the stems. Overhead it was simply black, except where a gap of remote blue sky shone down upon us here and there. I struck none of my matches because I had no hand free. Upon my left arm I carried my little one, in my right hand I had my iron bar.

'For some way I heard nothing but the crackling twigs under my feet, the faint rustle of the breeze above, and my own breathing and the throb of the blood-vessels in my ears. Then I seemed to know of a pattering about me. I pushed on grimly. The pattering grew more distinct, and then I caught the same queer sound and voices I had heard in the Underworld. There were evidently several of the Morlocks, and they were closing in upon me. Indeed, in another minute I felt a tug at my coat, then something at my arm. And Weena shivered violently, and became quite still.

'It was time for a match. But to get one I must put her down. I did so, and, as I fumbled with my pocket, a struggle began in the darkness about my knees, perfectly silent on her part and with the same peculiar cooing sounds from the Morlocks. Soft little hands, too, were creeping over my coat and back, touching even my neck. Then the match scratched and fizzed. I held it flaring, and saw the white backs of the Morlocks in flight amid the trees. I hastily took a lump of camphor from my pocket, and prepared to light it as soon as the match should wane. Then I looked at Weena. She was lying clutching my feet and quite motionless, with her face to the ground. With a sudden fright I stooped to her. She seemed scarcely to breathe. I lit the block of camphor and flung it to the ground, and as it split and flared up and drove back the Morlocks and the shadows, I knelt down and lifted her. The wood behind seemed full of the stir and murmur of a great company!

'She seemed to have fainted. I put her carefully upon my shoulder and rose to push on, and then there came a horrible realisation. In manoeuvring with my matches and Weena, I had turned myself about several times, and now I had not the faintest idea in what direction lay my path. For all I knew, I might be facing back towards the Palace of Green Porcelain. I found myself in a cold sweat. I had to think rapidly what to do. I determined to build a fire and encamp where we were. I put Weena, still motionless, down upon a turfy bole, and very hastily, as my first lump of camphor waned, I began collecting sticks and leaves. Here and there out of the darkness round me the Morlocks' eyes shone like carbuncles.

'The camphor flickered and went out. I lit a match, and as I did so, two white forms that had been approaching Weena dashed hastily away. One was so blinded by the light that he came straight for me, and I felt his bones grind under the blow of my fist. He gave a whoop of dismay, staggered a little way, and fell down. I lit another piece of camphor, and went on gathering my bonfire. Presently I noticed how dry was some of the foliage above me, for since my arrival on the Time Machine, a matter of a week, no rain had fallen. So, instead of casting about among the trees for fallen twigs, I began leaping up and dragging down branches. Very soon I had a choking smoky fire of green wood and dry sticks, and could economise my camphor. Then I turned to where Weena lay beside my iron mace. I tried what I could to revive her, but she lay like one dead. I could not even satisfy myself whether or not she breathed.

'Now, the smoke of the fire beat over towards me, and it must have made me heavy of a sudden. Moreover, the vapour of camphor was in the air. My fire would not need replenishing for an hour or so. I felt very weary after my exertion, and sat down. The wood, too, was full of a slumberous murmur that I did not understand. I seemed just to nod and open my eyes. But all was dark, and the Morlocks had their hands upon me. Flinging off their clinging fingers I hastily felt in my pocket for the matchbox, and – it had gone! Then they gripped and closed with me again. In a moment I knew what had happened. I had slept, and my fire had gone out, and the bitterness of death came over my soul. The forest seemed full of the smell of burning wood. I was caught by the neck, by the hair, by the arms, and pulled down. It was indescribably horrible in the darkness to feel all these soft creatures heaped upon me. I felt as if I was in a monstrous spider's web. I was overpowered, and went down. I felt little teeth nipping at my neck. I rolled over, and as I did so my hand came against my iron lever. It gave me strength. I struggled up, shaking the human rats from me, and, holding the bar short, I thrust where I judged their faces might be. I could feel the succulent giving of flesh and bone under my blows, and for a moment I was free.

'The strange exultation that so often seems to accompany hard fighting came upon me. I knew that both I and Weena were lost, but I determined to make the Morlocks pay for their meat. I stood with my back to a tree, swinging the iron bar before me. The whole wood was full of the stir and cries of them. A minute passed. Their voices seemed to rise to a higher pitch of excitement, and their movements grew faster. Yet none came within reach. I stood glaring at the blackness. Then suddenly came hope. What if the Morlocks were afraid? And close on the heels of that came a strange thing. The darkness seemed to grow luminous. Very dimly I began to see the Morlocks about me – three battered at my feet – and then I recognised, with incredulous surprise, that the others were running, in an incessant stream, as it seemed, from behind me, and away through the wood

in front. And their backs seemed no longer white, but reddish. As I stood agape, I saw a little red spark go drifting across a gap of starlight between the branches, and vanish. And at that I understood the smell of burning wood, the slumbrous murmur that was growing now into a gusty roar, the red glow, and the Morlocks' flight.

'Stepping out from behind my tree and looking back, I saw, through the black pillars of the nearer trees, the flames of the burning forest. It was my first fire coming after me. With that I looked for Weena, but she was gone. The hissing and crackling behind me, the explosive thud as each fresh tree burst into flame, left little time for reflection. My iron bar still gripped, I followed in the Morlocks' path. It was a close race. Once the flames crept forward so swiftly on my right as I ran that I was outflanked and had to strike off to the left. But at last I emerged upon a small open space, and as I did so, a Morlock came blundering towards me, and past me, and went on straight into the fire!

'And now I was to see the most weird and horrible thing, I think, of all that I beheld in that future age. This whole space was as bright as day with the reflection of the fire. In the centre was a hillock or tumulus, surmounted by a scorched hawthorn. Beyond this was another arm of the burning forest, with yellow tongues already writhing from it, completely encircling the space with a fence of fire. Upon the hillside were some thirty or forty Morlocks, dazzled by the light and heat, and blundering hither and thither against each other in their bewilderment. At first I did not realise their blindness, and struck furiously at them with my bar, in a frenzy of fear, as they approached me, killing one and crippling several more. But when I had watched the gestures of one of them groping under the hawthorn against the red sky, and heard their moans, I was assured of their absolute helplessness and misery in the glare, and I struck no more of them.

'Yet every now and then one would come straight towards me, setting loose a quivering horror that made me quick to elude him. At one time the flames died down somewhat, and I feared the foul creatures would presently be able to see me. I was thinking of beginning the fight by killing some of them before this should happen; but the fire burst out again brightly, and I stayed my hand. I walked about the hill among them and avoided them, looking for some trace of Weena. But Weena was gone.

'At last I sat down on the summit of the hillock, and watched this strange incredible company of blind things groping to and fro, and making uncanny noises to each other, as the glare of the fire beat on them. The coiling uprush of smoke streamed across the sky, and through the rare tatters of that red canopy, remote as though they belonged to another universe, shone the little stars. Two or three Morlocks came blundering into me, and I drove them off with blows of my fists, trembling as I did so.

'For the most part of that night I was persuaded it was a nightmare. I bit myself and screamed in a passionate desire to awake. I beat the ground with

my hands, and got up and sat down again, and wandered here and there, and again sat down. Then I would fall to rubbing my eyes and calling upon God to let me awake. Thrice I saw Morlocks put their heads down in a kind of agony and rush into the flames. But, at last, above the subsiding red of the fire, above the streaming masses of black smoke and the whitening and blackening tree stumps, and the diminishing numbers of these dim creatures, came the white light of the day.

'I searched again for traces of Weena, but there were none. It was plain that they had left her poor little body in the forest. I cannot describe how it relieved me to think that it had escaped the awful fate to which it seemed destined. As I thought of that, I was almost moved to begin a massacre of the helpless abominations about me, but I contained myself. The hillock, as I have said, was a kind of island in the forest. From its summit I could now make out through a haze of smoke the Palace of Green Porcelain, and from that I could get my bearings for the White Sphinx. And so, leaving the remnant of these damned souls still going hither and thither and moaning, as the day grew clearer, I tied some grass about my feet and limped on across smoking ashes and among black stems, that still pulsated internally with fire, towards the hiding-place of the Time Machine. I walked slowly, for I was almost exhausted, as well as lame, and I felt the intensest wretchedness for the horrible death of little Weena. It seemed an overwhelming calamity. Now, in this old familiar room, it is more like the sorrow of a dream than an actual loss. But that morning it left me absolutely lonely again – terribly alone. I began to think of this house of mine, of this fireside, of some of you, and with such thoughts came a longing that was pain.

'But as I walked over the smoking ashes under the bright morning sky, I made a discovery. In my trouser pocket were still some loose matches. The box must have leaked before it was lost.

CHAPTER TEN

'About eight or nine in the morning I came to the same seat of yellow metal from which I had viewed the world upon the evening of my arrival. I thought of my hasty conclusions upon that evening and could not refrain from laughing bitterly at my confidence. Here was the same beautiful scene, the same abundant foliage, the same splendid palaces and magnificent ruins, the same silver river running between its fertile banks. The gay robes of the beautiful people moved hither and thither among the trees. Some were bathing in exactly the place where I had saved Weena, and that suddenly gave me a keen stab of pain. And like blots upon the landscape rose the cupolas above the ways to the Underworld. I understood now what all the beauty of the Over-world people covered. Very pleasant was their day, as

pleasant as the day of the cattle in the field. Like the cattle, they knew of no enemies and provided against no needs. And their end was the same.

'I grieved to think how brief the dream of the human intellect had been. It had committed suicide. It had set itself steadfastly towards comfort and ease, a balanced society with security and permanency as its watchword, it had attained its hopes – to come to this at last. Once, life and property must have reached almost absolute safety. The rich had been assured of his wealth and comfort, the toiler assured of his life and work. No doubt in that perfect world there had been no unemployed problem, no social question left unsolved. And a great quiet had followed.

'It is a law of nature we overlook, that intellectual versatility is the compensation for change, danger, and trouble. An animal perfectly in harmony with its environment is a perfect mechanism. Nature never appeals to intelligence until habit and instinct are useless. There is no intelligence where there is no change and no need of change. Only those animals partake of intelligence that have to meet a huge variety of needs and dangers.

'So, as I see it, the Upper-world man had drifted towards his feeble prettiness, and the Underworld to mere mechanical industry. But that perfect state had lacked one thing even for mechanical perfection – absolute permanency. Apparently as time went on, the feeding of the Underworld, however it was effected, had become disjointed. Mother Necessity, who had been staved off for a few thousand years, came back again, and she began below. The Underworld being in contact with machinery, which, however perfect, still needs some little thought outside habit, had probably retained perforce rather more initiative, if less of every other human character, than the Upper. And when other meat failed them, they turned to what old habit had hitherto forbidden. So I say I saw it in my last view of the world of 802,701. It may be as wrong an explanation as mortal wit could invent. It is how the thing shaped itself to me, and as that I give it to you.

'After the fatigues, excitements, and terrors of the past days, and in spite of my grief, this seat and the tranquil view and the warm sunlight were very pleasant. I was very tired and sleepy, and soon my theorising passed into dozing. Catching myself at that, I took my own hint, and spreading myself out upon the turf I had a long and refreshing sleep.

'I awoke a little before sun-setting. I now felt safe against being caught napping by the Morlocks, and, stretching myself, I came on down the hill towards the White Sphinx. I had my crowbar in one hand, and the other hand played with the matches in my pocket.

'And now came a most unexpected thing. As I approached the pedestal of the sphinx I found the bronze valves were open. They had slid down into grooves.

'At that I stopped short before them, hesitating to enter.

'Within was a small apartment, and on a raised place in the corner of this

was the Time Machine. I had the small levers in my pocket. So here, after all my elaborate preparations for the siege of the White Sphinx, was a meek surrender. I threw my iron bar away, almost sorry not to use it.

'A sudden thought came into my head as I stooped towards the portal. For once, at least, I grasped the mental operations of the Morlocks. Suppressing a strong inclination to laugh, I stepped through the bronze frame and up to the Time Machine. I was surprised to find it had been carefully oiled and cleaned. I have suspected since that the Morlocks had even partially taken it to pieces while trying in their dim way to grasp its purpose.

'Now as I stood and examined it, finding a pleasure in the mere touch of the contrivance, the thing I had expected happened. The bronze panels suddenly slid up and struck the frame with a clang. I was in the dark – trapped, So the Morlocks thought. At that I chuckled gleefully.

'I could already hear their murmuring laughter as they came towards me. Very calmly I tried to strike the match. I had only to fix on the levers and depart then like a ghost. But I had overlooked one little thing. The matches were of that abominable kind that light only on the box.

'You may imagine how all my calm vanished. The little brutes were close upon me. One touched me. I made a sweeping blow in the dark at them with the levers, and began to scramble into the saddle of the machine. Then came one hand upon me and then another. Then I had simply to fight against their persistent fingers for my levers, and at the same time feel for the studs over which these fitted. One, indeed, they almost got away from me. As it slipped from my hand, I had to butt in the dark with my head – I could hear the Morlock's skull ring – to recover it. It was a nearer thing than the fight in the forest, I think, this last scramble.

'But at last the lever was fitted and pulled over. The clinging hands slipped from me. The darkness presently fell from my eyes. I found myself in the same grey light and tumult I have already described.

CHAPTER ELEVEN

'I have already told you of the sickness and confusion that comes with time travelling. And this time I was not seated properly in the saddle, but sideways and in an unstable fashion. For an indefinite time I clung to the machine as it swayed and vibrated, quite unheeding how I went, and when I brought myself to look at the dials again I was amazed to find where I had arrived. One dial records days, and another thousands of days, another millions of days, and another thousands of millions. Now, instead of reversing the levers, I had pulled them over so as to go forward with them, and when I came to look at these indicators I found that the thousands hand was sweeping round as fast as the seconds hand of a watch – into futurity.

'As I drove on, a peculiar change crept over the appearance of things. The palpitating greyness grew darker; then – though I was still travelling with prodigious velocity – the blinking succession of day and night, which was usually indicative of a slower pace, returned, and grew more and more marked. This puzzled me very much at first. The alternations of night and day grew slower and slower, and so did the passage of the sun across the sky, until they seemed to stretch through centuries. At last a steady twilight brooded over the earth, a twilight only broken now and then when a comet glared across the darkling sky. The band of light that had indicated the sun had long since disappeared; for the sun had ceased to set – it simply rose and fell in the west, and grew ever broader and more red. All trace of the moon had vanished. The circling of the stars, growing slower and slower, had given place to creeping points of light. At last, some time before I stopped, the sun, red and very large, halted motionless upon the horizon, a vast dome glowing with a dull heat, and now and then suffering a momentary extinction. At one time it had for a little while glowed more brilliantly again, but it speedily reverted to its sullen red heat. I perceived by this slowing down of its rising and setting that the work of the tidal drag was done. The earth had come to rest with one face to the sun, even as in our own time the moon faces the earth. Very cautiously, for I remembered my former headlong fall, I began to reverse my motion. Slower and slower went the circling hands until the thousands one seemed motionless and the daily one was no longer a mere mist upon its scale. Still slower, until the dim outlines of a desolate beach grew visible.

'I stopped very gently and sat upon the Time Machine, looking round. The sky was no longer blue. North-eastward it was inky black, and out of the blackness shone brightly and steadily the pale white stars. Overhead it was a deep Indian red and starless, and south-eastward it grew brighter to a glowing scarlet where, cut by the horizon, lay the huge hull of the sun, red and motionless. The rocks about me were of a harsh reddish colour, and all the trace of life that I could see at first was the intensely green vegetation that covered every projecting point on their south-eastern face. It was the same rich green that one sees on forest moss or on the lichen in caves: plants which like these grow in a perpetual twilight.

'The machine was standing on a sloping beach. The sea stretched away to the south-west, to rise into a sharp bright horizon against the wan sky. There were no breakers and no waves, for not a breath of wind was stirring. Only a slight oily swell rose and fell like a gentle breathing, and showed that the eternal sea was still moving and living. And along the margin where the water sometimes broke was a thick incrustation of salt – pink under the lurid sky. There was a sense of oppression in my head, and I noticed that I was breathing very fast. The sensation reminded me of my only experience of mountaineering, and from that I judged the air to be more rarefied than it is now.

'Far away up the desolate slope I heard a harsh scream, and saw a thing like a huge white butterfly go slanting and fluttering up into the sky and, circling, disappear over some low hillocks beyond. The sound of its voice was so dismal that I shivered and seated myself more firmly upon the machine. Looking round me again, I saw that, quite near, what I had taken to be a reddish mass of rock was moving slowly towards me. Then I saw the thing was really a monstrous crab-like creature. Can you imagine a crab as large as yonder table, with its many legs moving slowly and uncertainly, its big claws swaying, its long antennae, like carters' whips, waving and feeling, and its stalked eyes gleaming at you on either side of its metallic front? Its back was corrugated and ornamented with ungainly bosses, and a greenish incrustation blotched it here and there. I could see the many palps of its complicated mouth flickering and feeling as it moved.

'As I stared at this sinister apparition crawling towards me, I felt a tickling on my cheek as though a fly had lighted there. I tried to brush it away with my hand, but in a moment it returned, and almost immediately came another by my ear. I struck at this, and caught something threadlike. It was drawn swiftly out of my hand. With a frightful qualm, I turned, and I saw that I had grasped the antenna of another monster crab that stood just behind me. Its evil eyes were wriggling on their stalks, its mouth was all alive with appetite, and its vast ungainly claws, smeared with an algal slime, were descending upon me. In a moment my hand was on the lever, and I had placed a month between myself and these monsters. But I was still on the same beach, and I saw them distinctly now as soon as I stopped. Dozens of them seemed to be crawling here and there, in the sombre light, among the foliated sheets of intense green.

'I cannot convey the sense of abominable desolation that hung over the world. The red eastern sky, the northward blackness, the salt Dead Sea, the stony beach crawling with these foul, slow-stirring monsters, the uniform poisonous-looking green of the lichenous plants, the thin air that hurts one's lungs: all contributed to an appalling effect. I moved on a hundred years, and there was the same red sun – a little larger, a little duller – the same dying sea, the same chill air, and the same crowd of earthy crustacea creeping in and out among the green weed and the red rocks. And in the westward sky, I saw a curved pale line like a vast new moon.

'So I travelled, stopping ever and again, in great strides of a thousand years or more, drawn on by the mystery of the earth's fate, watching with a strange fascination the sun grow larger and duller in the westward sky, and the life of the old earth ebb away. At last, more than thirty million years hence, the huge red-hot dome of the sun had come to obscure nearly a tenth part of the darkling heavens. Then I stopped once more, for the crawling multitude of crabs had disappeared, and the red beach, save for its livid green liverworts and lichens, seemed lifeless. And now it was flecked with white. A bitter cold assailed me. Rare white flakes ever and again came

eddying down. To the north-eastward, the glare of snow lay under the starlight of the sable sky and I could see an undulating crest of hillocks pinkish white. There were fringes of ice along the sea margin, with drifting masses further out; but the main expanse of that salt ocean, all bloody under the eternal sunset, was still unfrozen.

'I looked about me to see if any traces of animal life remained. A certain indefinable apprehension still kept me in the saddle of the machine. But I saw nothing moving, in earth or sky or sea. The green slime on the rocks alone testified that life was not extinct. A shallow sandbank had appeared in the sea and the water had receded from the beach. I fancied I saw some black object flopping about upon this bank, but it became motionless as I looked at it, and I judged that my eye had been deceived, and that the black object was merely a rock. The stars in the sky were intensely bright and seemed to me to twinkle very little.

'Suddenly I noticed that the circular westward outline of the sun had changed; that a concavity, a bay, had appeared in the curve. I saw this grow larger. For a minute perhaps I stared aghast at this blackness that was creeping over the day, and then I realised that an eclipse was beginning. Either the moon or the planet Mercury was passing across the sun's disk. Naturally, at first I took it to be the moon, but there is much to incline me to believe that what I really saw was the transit of an inner planet passing very near to the earth.

'The darkness grew apace; a cold wind began to blow in freshening gusts from the east, and the showering white flakes in the air increased in number. From the edge of the sea came a ripple and whisper. Beyond these lifeless sounds the world was silent. Silent? It would be hard to convey the stillness of it. All the sounds of man, the bleating of sheep, the cries of birds, the hum of insects, the stir that makes the background of our lives – all that was over. As the darkness thickened, the eddying flakes grew more abundant, dancing before my eyes; and the cold of the air more intense. At last, one by one, swiftly, one after the other, the white peaks of the distant hills vanished into blackness. The breeze rose to a moaning wind. I saw the black central shadow of the eclipse sweeping towards me. In another moment the pale stars alone were visible. All else was rayless obscurity. The sky was absolutely black.

'A horror of this great darkness came on me. The cold, that smote to my marrow, and the pain I felt in breathing, overcame me. I shivered, and a deadly nausea seized me. Then like a red-hot bow in the sky appeared the edge of the sun. I got off the machine to recover myself. I felt giddy and incapable of facing the return journey. As I stood sick and confused I saw again the moving thing upon the shoal – there was no mistake now that it was a moving thing – against the red water of the sea. It was a round thing, the size of a football perhaps, or, it may be, bigger, and tentacles trailed down from it; it seemed black against the weltering blood-red water, and it

was hopping fitfully about. Then I felt I was fainting. But a terrible dread of lying helpless in that remote and awful twilight sustained me while I clambered upon the saddle.

CHAPTER TWELVE

'So I came back. For a long time I must have been insensible upon the machine. The blinking succession of the days and nights was resumed, the sun got golden again, the sky blue. I breathed with greater freedom. The fluctuating contours of the land ebbed and flowed. The hands spun backward upon the dials. At last I saw again the dim shadows of houses, the evidences of decadent humanity. These, too, changed and passed, and others came. Presently, when the million dial was at zero, I slackened speed. I began to recognise our own pretty and familiar architecture, the thousands hand ran back to the starting-point, the night and day flapped slower and slower. Then the old walls of the laboratory came round me. Very gently, now, I slowed the mechanism down.

'I saw one little thing that seemed odd to me. I think I have told you that when I set out, before my velocity became very high, Mrs Watchett had walked across the room, travelling, as it seemed to me, like a rocket. As I returned, I passed again across that minute when she traversed the laboratory. But now her every motion appeared to be the exact inversion of her previous ones. The door at the lower end opened, and she glided quietly up the laboratory, back foremost, and disappeared behind the door by which she had previously entered. Just before that I seemed to see Hillyer for a moment; but he passed like a flash.

'Then I stopped the machine, and saw about me again the old familiar laboratory, my tools, my appliances just as I had left them. I got off the thing very shakily, and sat down upon my bench. For several minutes I trembled violently. Then I became calmer. Around me was my old workshop again, exactly as it had been. I might have slept there, and the whole thing have been a dream.

'And yet, not exactly! The thing had started from the south-east corner of the laboratory. It had come to rest again in the north-west, against the wall where you saw it. That gives you the exact distance from my little lawn to the pedestal of the White Sphinx, into which the Morlocks had carried my machine.

'For a time my brain went stagnant. Presently I got up and came through the passage here, limping, because my heel was still painful, and feeling sorely begrimed. I saw the *Pall Mall Gazette* on the table by the door. I found the date was indeed today, and looking at the timepiece, saw the hour was almost eight o'clock. I heard your voices and the clatter of plates. I hesitated – I felt so sick and weak. Then I sniffed good wholesome meat,

and opened the door on you. You know the rest. I washed, and dined, and now I am telling you the story.

'I know,' he said, after a pause, 'that all this will be absolutely incredible to you. To me the one incredible thing is that I am here tonight in this old familiar room looking into your friendly faces and telling you these strange adventures.' He looked at the Medical Man. 'No. I cannot expect you to believe it. Take it as a lie – or a prophecy. Say I dreamed it in the workshop. Consider I have been speculating upon the destinies of our race until I have hatched this fiction. Treat my assertion of its truth as a mere stroke of art to enhance its interest. And, taking it as a story, what do you think of it?'

He took up his pipe, and began, in his old accustomed manner, to tap with it nervously upon the bars of the grate. There was a momentary stillness. Then chairs began to creak and shoes to scrape upon the carpet. I took my eyes off the Time Traveller's face, and looked round at his audience. They were in the dark, and little spots of colour swam before them. The Medical Man seemed absorbed in the contemplation of our host. The Editor was looking hard at the end of his cigar – the sixth. The Journalist fumbled for his watch. The others, as far as I remember, were motionless.

The Editor stood up with a sigh. 'What a pity it is you're not a writer of stories!' he said, putting his hand on the Time Traveller's shoulder.

'You don't believe it?'

'Well –'

'I thought not.'

The Time Traveller turned to us. 'Where are the matches?' he said. He lit one and spoke over his pipe, puffing. 'To tell you the truth . . . I hardly believe it myself . . . And yet . . . '

His eye fell with a mute enquiry upon the withered white flowers upon the little table. Then he turned over the hand holding his pipe, and I saw he was looking at some half-healed scars on his knuckles.

The Medical Man rose, came to the lamp, and examined the flowers. 'The gynaeceum's odd,' he said. The Psychologist leant forward to see, holding out his hand for a specimen.

'I'm hanged if it isn't a quarter to one,' said the Journalist. 'How shall we get home?'

'Plenty of cabs at the station,' said the Psychologist.

'It's a curious thing,' said the Medical Man; 'but I certainly don't know the natural order of these flowers. May I have them?'

The Time Traveller hesitated. Then suddenly: 'Certainly not.'

'Where did you really get them?' said the Medical Man.

The Time Traveller put his hand to his head. He spoke like one who was trying to keep hold of an idea that eluded him. 'They were put into my pocket by Weena, when I travelled into Time.' He stared round the room. 'I'm damned if it isn't all going. This room and you and the atmosphere of

every day is too much for my memory. Did I ever make a Time Machine, or a model of a Time Machine? Or is it all only a dream? They say life is a dream, a precious poor dream at times – but I can't stand another that won't fit. It's madness. And where did the dream come from? . . . I must look at that machine. If there *is* one!'

He caught up the lamp swiftly, and carried it, flaring red, through the door into the corridor. We followed him. There in the flickering light of the lamp was the machine sure enough, squat, ugly, and askew; a thing of brass, ebony, ivory, and translucent glimmering quartz. Solid to the touch – for I put out my hand and felt the rail of it – and with brown spots and smears upon the ivory, and bits of grass and moss upon the lower parts, and one rail bent awry.

The Time Traveller put the lamp down on the bench, and ran his hand along the damaged rail. 'It's all right now,' he said. 'The story I told you was true. I'm sorry to have brought you out here in the cold.' He took up the lamp, and, in an absolute silence, we returned to the smoking-room.

He came into the hall with us and helped the Editor on with his coat. The Medical Man looked into his face and, with a certain hesitation, told him he was suffering from over-work, at which he laughed hugely. I remember him standing in the open doorway, bawling good-night.

I shared a cab with the Editor. He thought the tale a 'gaudy lie'. For my own part I was unable to come to a conclusion. The story was so fantastic and incredible, the telling so credible and sober. I lay awake most of the night thinking about it. I determined to go next day and see the Time Traveller again. I was told he was in the laboratory, and being on easy terms in the house, I went up to him. The laboratory, however, was empty. I stared for a minute at the Time Machine and put out my hand and touched the lever. At that the squat substantial-looking mass swayed like a bough shaken by the wind. Its instability startled me extremely, and I had a queer reminiscence of the childish days when I used to be forbidden to meddle. I came back through the corridor. The Time Traveller met me in the smoking-room. He was coming from the house. He had a small camera under one arm and a knapsack under the other. He laughed when he saw me, and gave me an elbow to shake. 'I'm frightfully busy,' said he, 'with that thing in there.'

'But is it not some hoax?' I said. 'Do you really travel through time?'

'Really and truly I do.' And he looked frankly into my eyes. He hesitated. His eye wandered about the room. 'I only want half an hour,' he said. 'I know why you came, and it's awfully good of you. There's some magazines here. If you'll stop to lunch I'll prove you this time travelling up to the hilt, specimens and all. If you'll forgive my leaving you now?'

I consented, hardly comprehending then the full import of his words, and he nodded and went on down the corridor. I heard the door of the laboratory slam, seated myself in a chair, and took up a daily paper. What

was he going to do before lunchtime? Then suddenly I was reminded by an advertisement that I had promised to meet Richardson, the publisher, at two. I looked at my watch, and saw that I could barely save that engagement. I got up and went down the passage to tell the Time Traveller.

As I took hold of the handle of the door I heard an exclamation, oddly truncated at the end, and a click and a thud. A gust of air whirled round me as I opened the door, and from within came the sound of broken glass falling on the floor. The Time Traveller was not there. I seemed to see a ghostly, indistinct figure sitting in a whirling mass of black and brass for a moment – a figure so transparent that the bench behind with its sheets of drawings was absolutely distinct; but this phantasm vanished as I rubbed my eyes. The Time Machine had gone. Save for a subsiding stir of dust, the further end of the laboratory was empty. A pane of the skylight had, apparently, just been blown in.

I felt an unreasonable amazement. I knew that something strange had happened, and for the moment could not distinguish what the strange thing might be. As I stood staring, the door into the garden opened, and the manservant appeared.

We looked at each other. Then ideas began to come. 'Has Mr — gone out that way?' said I.

'No, sir. No one has come out this way. I was expecting to find him here.'

At that I understood. At the risk of disappointing Richardson I stayed on, waiting for the Time Traveller: waiting for the second, perhaps still stranger story, and the specimens and photographs he would bring with him. But I am beginning now to fear that I must wait a lifetime. The Time Traveller vanished three years ago. And, as everybody knows now, he has never returned.

When the Sleeper Wakes

A novel first published in 1899

Contents

When the Sleeper Wakes was originally published in serial form in *The Graphic* in 1899, and was produced in book form later the same year. A reworked version of the novel, entitled *The Sleeper Awakes*, appeared in 1910.

CHAPTER ONE

Insomnia

ONE AFTERNOON, at low water, Mr Isbister, a young artist lodging at Boscastle, walked from that place to the picturesque cove of Pentargen, desiring to examine the caves there. Half-way down the precipitous path to the Pentargen beach he came suddenly upon a man sitting in an attitude of profound distress beneath a projecting mass of rock. The hands of this man hung limply over his knees, his eyes were red and staring before him, and his face was wet with tears.

He glanced round at Isbister's footfall. Both men were disconcerted, Isbister the more so, and, to override the awkwardness of his involuntary pause, he remarked, with an air of mature conviction, that the weather was hot for the time of year.

'Very,' answered the stranger shortly, hesitated a second, and added in a colourless tone, 'I can't sleep.'

Isbister stopped abruptly. 'No?' was all he said, but his bearing conveyed his helpful impulse.

'It may sound incredible,' said the stranger, turning weary eyes to Isbister's face and emphasising his words with a languid hand, 'but I have had no sleep – no sleep at all for six nights.'

'Had advice?'

'Yes. Bad advice for the most part. Drugs. My nervous system . . . They are all very well for the run of people. It's hard to explain. I dare not take . . . sufficiently powerful drugs.'

'That makes it difficult,' said Isbister.

He stood helplessly in the narrow path, perplexed what to do. Clearly the man wanted to talk. An idea natural enough under the circumstances prompted him to keep the conversation going. 'I've never suffered from sleeplessness myself,' he said in a tone of commonplace gossip, 'but in those cases I have known, people have usually found something – '

'I dare make no experiments.'

He spoke wearily. He gave a gesture of rejection, and for a space both men were silent.

'Exercise?' suggested Isbister diffidently, with a glance from his inter-locutor's face of wretchedness to the touring costume he wore.

'That is what I have tried. Unwisely perhaps. I have followed the coast, day after day – from New Quay. It has only added muscular fatigue to the

mental. The cause of this unrest was over-work – trouble. There was something – '

He stopped as if from sheer fatigue. He rubbed his forehead with a lean hand. He resumed speech like one who talks to himself.

'I am a lone wolf, a solitary man, wandering through a world in which I have no part. I am wifeless – childless – who is it speaks of the childless as the dead twigs on the tree of life? I am wifeless, childless – I could find no duty to do. No desire even in my heart. One thing at last I set myself to do.

'I said, I *will* do this, and to do it, to overcome the inertia of this dull body, I resorted to drugs. Great God, I've had enough of drugs! I don't know if *you* feel the heavy inconvenience of the body, its exasperating demand of time from the mind – time – life! Live! We only live in patches. We have to eat, and then comes the dull digestive complacencies – or irritations. We have to take the air or else our thoughts grow sluggish, stupid, run into gulfs and blind alleys. A thousand distractions arise from within and without, and then comes drowsiness and sleep. Men seem to live for sleep. How little of a man's day is his own – even at the best! And then come those false friends, those Thug helpers, the alkaloids that stifle natural fatigue and kill rest – black coffee, cocaine – '

'I see,' said Isbister.

'I did my work,' said the sleepless man with a querulous intonation.

'And this is the price?'

'Yes.'

For a little while the two remained without speaking.

'You cannot imagine the craving for rest that I feel – a hunger and thirst. For six long days, since my work was done, my mind has been a whirlpool, swift, unprogressive and incessant, a torrent of thoughts leading nowhere, spinning round swift and steady – '

He paused. 'Towards the gulf.'

'You must sleep,' said Isbister decisively, and with an air of a remedy discovered. 'Certainly you must sleep.'

'My mind is perfectly lucid. It was never clearer. But I know I am drawing towards the vortex. Presently – '

'Yes?'

'You have seen things go down an eddy? Out of the light of the day, out of this sweet world of sanity – down – '

'But,' expostulated Isbister.

The man threw out a hand towards him, and his eyes were wild, and his voice suddenly high. 'I shall kill myself. If in no other way – at the foot of yonder dark precipice there, where the waves are green, and the white surge lifts and falls, and that little thread of water trembles down. There at any rate is . . . sleep.'

'That's unreasonable,' said Isbister, startled at the man's hysterical gust of emotion. 'Drugs are better than that.'

'There at any rate is sleep,' repeated the stranger, not heeding him.

Isbister looked at him and wondered transitorily if some complex Providence had indeed brought them together that afternoon. 'It's not a cert, you know,' he remarked. 'There's a cliff like that at Lulworth Cove – as high, anyhow – and a little girl fell from top to bottom. And lives today – sound and well.'

'But those rocks there?'

'One might lie on them rather dismally through a cold night, broken bones grating as one shivered, chill water splashing over you. Eh?'

Their eyes met. 'Sorry to upset your ideals,' said Isbister with a sense of devil-may-careish brilliance. 'But a suicide over that cliff (or any cliff for the matter of that), really, as an artist – ' He laughed. 'It's so damned amateurish.'

'But the other thing,' said the sleepless man irritably, 'the other thing. No man can keep sane if night after night – '

'Have you been walking along this coast alone?'

'Yes.'

'Silly sort of thing to do. If you'll excuse my saying so. Alone! As you say; body fag is no cure for brain fag. Who told you to? No wonder; walking! And the sun on your head, heat, fag, solitude, all the day long, and then, I suppose, you go to bed and try very hard – eh?'

Isbister stopped short and looked at the sufferer doubtfully.

'Look at these rocks!' cried the seated man with a sudden force of gesture. 'Look at that sea that has shone and quivered there for ever! See the white spume rush into darkness under that great cliff. And this blue vault, with the blinding sun pouring from the dome of it. It is your world. You accept it, you rejoice in it. It warms and supports and delights you. And for me – '

He turned his head and showed a ghastly face, bloodshot pallid eyes and bloodless lips. He spoke almost in a whisper. 'It is the garment of my misery. The whole world . . . is the garment of my misery.'

Isbister looked at all the wild beauty of the sunlit cliffs about them and back to that face of despair. For a moment he was silent.

He started, and made a gesture of impatient rejection. 'You get a night's sleep,' he said, 'and you won't see much misery out here. Take my word for it.'

He was quite sure now that this was a providential encounter. Only half an hour ago he had been feeling horribly bored. Here was employment the bare thought of which was righteous self-applause. He took possession forthwith. It seemed to him that the first need of this exhausted being was companionship. He flung himself down on the steeply sloping turf beside the motionless seated figure, and deployed forthwith into a skirmishing line of gossip.

His hearer seemed to have lapsed into apathy; he stared dismally seaward,

and spoke only in answer to Isbister's direct questions – and not to all of those. But he made no sign of objection to this benevolent intrusion upon his despair.

In a helpless way he seemed even grateful, and when presently Isbister, feeling that his unsupported talk was losing vigour, suggested that they should reascend the steep and return towards Boscastle, alleging the view into Blackapit, he submitted quietly. Halfway up he began talking to himself, and abruptly turned a ghastly face on his helper. 'What can be happening?' he asked with a gaunt illustrative hand. 'What can be happening? Spin, spin, spin, spin. It goes round and round, round and round for evermore.'

He stood with his hand circling

'It's all right, old chap,' said Isbister with the air of an old friend. 'Don't worry yourself. Trust to me.'

The man dropped his hand and turned again. They went over the brow in single file and to the headland beyond Penally, with the sleepless man gesticulating ever and again, and speaking fragmentary things concerning his whirling brain. At the headland they stood for a space by the seat that looks into the dark mysteries of Blackapit, and then he sat down. Isbister had resumed his talk whenever the path had widened sufficiently for them to walk abreast. He was enlarging upon the complex difficulty of making Boscastle Harbour in bad weather, when suddenly and quite irrelevantly his companion interrupted him again.

'My head is not like what it was,' he said, gesticulating for want of expressive phrases. 'It's not like what it was. There is a sort of oppression, a weight. No – not drowsiness, would God it were! It is like a shadow, a deep shadow falling suddenly and swiftly across something busy. Spin, spin into the darkness. The tumult of thought, the confusion, the eddy and eddy. I can't express it. I can hardly keep my mind on it – steadily enough to tell you.'

He stopped feebly.

'Don't trouble, old chap,' said Isbister. 'I think I can understand. At any rate, it don't matter very much just at present about telling me, you know.'

The sleepless man thrust his knuckles into his eyes and rubbed them. Isbister talked for awhile while this rubbing continued, and then he had a fresh idea. 'Come down to my room,' he said, 'and try a pipe. I can show you some sketches of this Blackapit. If you'd care?'

The other rose obediently and followed him down the steep.

Several times Isbister heard him stumble as they came down, and his movements were slow and hesitating. 'Come in with me,' said Isbister, 'and try some cigarettes and the blessed gift of alcohol. If you take alcohol?'

The stranger hesitated at the garden gate. He seemed no longer clearly aware of his actions. 'I don't drink,' he said slowly, coming up the garden path, and after a moment's interval repeated absently, 'No – I don't drink. It goes round. Spin, it goes – spin – '

He stumbled at the doorstep and entered the room with the bearing of one who sees nothing.

Then he sat down abruptly and heavily in the easy chair, seemed almost to fall into it. He leant forward with his brows on his hands and became motionless.

Presently he made a faint sound in his throat. Isbister moved about the room with the nervousness of an inexperienced host, making little remarks that scarcely required answering. He crossed the room to his portfolio, placed it on the table and noticed the mantel clock.

'I don't know if you'd care to have supper with me,' he said with an unlighted cigarette in his hand – his mind troubled with a design of the furtive administration of chloral. 'Only cold mutton, you know, but passing sweet. Welsh. And a tart, I believe.' He repeated this after momentary silence.

The seated man made no answer. Isbister stopped, match in hand, regarding him.

The stillness lengthened. The match went out, the cigarette was put down unlit. The man was certainly very still. Isbister took up the portfolio, opened it, put it down, hesitated, seemed about to speak. 'Perhaps,' he whispered doubtfully. Presently he glanced at the door and back to the figure. Then he stole on tiptoe out of the room, glancing at his companion after each elaborate pace.

He closed the door noiselessly. The house door was standing open, and he went out beyond the porch, and stood where the monkshood rose at the corner of the garden bed. From this point he could see the stranger through the open window, still and dim, sitting head on hand. He had not moved.

A number of children going along the road stopped and regarded the artist curiously. A boatman exchanged civilities with him. He felt that possibly his circumspect attitude and position seemed peculiar and unaccountable. Smoking, perhaps, might seem more natural. He drew pipe and pouch from his pocket, filled the pipe slowly.

'I wonder,' . . . he said, with a scarcely perceptible loss of complacency. 'At any rate one must give him a chance.' He struck a match in the virile way, and proceeded to light his pipe.

Presently he heard his landlady behind him, coming with his lamp lit from the kitchen. He turned, gesticulating with his pipe, and stopped her at the door of his sitting-room. He had some difficulty in explaining the situation in whispers, for she did not know he had a visitor. She retreated again with the lamp, still a little mystified to judge from her manner, and he resumed his hovering at the corner of the porch, flushed and less at his ease.

Long after he had smoked out his pipe, and when the bats were abroad, his curiosity dominated his complex hesitations, and he stole back into his darkling sitting-room. He paused in the doorway. The stranger was still in the same attitude, dark against the window. Save for the singing of some

sailors aboard one of the little slate-carrying ships in the harbour, the evening was very still. Outside, the spikes of monkshood and delphinium stood erect and motionless against the shadow of the hillside. Something flashed into Isbister's mind; he started, and leaning over the table, listened. An unpleasant suspicion grew stronger; became conviction. Astonishment seized him and became – dread!

No sound of breathing came from the seated figure!

He crept slowly and noiselessly round the table, pausing twice to listen. At last he could lay his hand on the back of the armchair. He bent down until the two heads were ear to ear.

Then he bent still lower to look up at his visitor's face. He started violently and uttered an exclamation. The eyes were void spaces of white.

He looked again and saw that they were open and with the pupils rolled under the lids. He was suddenly afraid. Overcome by the strangeness of the man's condition, he took him by the shoulder and shook him. 'Are you asleep?' he said, with his voice jumping into alto, and again, 'Are you asleep?'

A conviction took possession of his mind that this man was dead. He suddenly became active and noisy, strode across the room, blundering against the table as he did so, and rang the bell.

'Please bring a light at once,' he said in the passage. 'There is something wrong with my friend.'

Then he returned to the motionless seated figure, grasped the shoulder, shook it, and shouted. The room was flooded with yellow glare as his astonished landlady entered with the light. His face was white as he turned blinking towards her. 'I must fetch a doctor at once,' he said. 'It is either death or a fit. Is there a doctor in the village? Where is a doctor to be found?'

CHAPTER TWO

The Trance

The state of cataleptic rigour into which this man had fallen, lasted for an unprecedented length of time, and then he passed slowly to the flaccid state, to a lax attitude suggestive of profound repose. Then it was his eyes could be closed.

He was removed from the hotel to the Boscastle surgery, and from the surgery, after some weeks, to London. But he still resisted every attempt at reanimation. After a time, for reasons that will appear later, these attempts were discontinued. For a great space he lay in that strange condition, inert and still neither dead nor living but, as it were, suspended, hanging midway between nothingness and existence. His was a darkness unbroken by a ray of

thought or sensation, a dreamless inanition, a vast space of peace. The tumult of his mind had swelled and risen to an abrupt climax of silence. Where was the man? Where is any man when insensibility takes hold of him?

'It seems only yesterday,' said Isbister. 'I remember it all as though it happened yesterday – clearer perhaps, than if it had happened yesterday.'

It was the Isbister of the last chapter, but he was no longer a young man. The hair that had been brown and a trifle in excess of the fashionable length, was iron grey and clipped close, and the face that had been pink and white was buff and ruddy. He had a pointed beard shot with grey. He talked to an elderly man who wore a summer suit of drill (the summer of that year was unusually hot). This was Warming, a London solicitor and next of kin to Graham, the man who had fallen into the trance. And the two men stood side by side in a room in a house in London regarding his recumbent figure.

It was a yellow figure lying lax upon a water bed and clad in a flowing shirt, a figure with a shrunken face and a stubby beard, lean limbs and lank nails, and about it was a case of thin glass. This glass seemed to mark off the sleeper from the reality of life about him, he was a thing apart, a strange, isolated abnormality. The two men stood close to the glass, peering in.

'The thing gave me a shock,' said Isbister. 'I feel a queer sort of surprise even now when I think of his white eyes. They were white, you know, rolled up. Coming here again brings it all back to me.'

'Have you never seen him since that time?' asked Warming.

'Often wanted to come,' said Isbister; 'but business nowadays is too serious a thing for much holiday keeping. I've been in America most of the time.'

'If I remember rightly,' said Warming, 'you were an artist?'

'Was. And then I became a married man. I saw it was all up with black and white, very soon – at least for a mediocre man, and I jumped on to process. Those posters on the Cliffs at Dover are by my people.'

'Good posters,' admitted the solicitor, 'though I was sorry to see them there.'

'Last as long as the cliffs, if necessary,' exclaimed Isbister with satisfaction. 'The world changes. When he fell asleep, twenty years ago, I was down at Boscastle with a box of watercolours and a noble, old-fashioned ambition. I didn't expect that some day my pigments would glorify the whole blessed coast of England, from Land's End round again to the Lizard. Luck comes to a man very often when he's not looking.'

Warming seemed to doubt the quality of the luck. 'I just missed seeing you, if I recollect aright.'

'You came back by the trap that took me to Camelford railway station. It was close on the Jubilee, Victoria's Jubilee, because I remember the seats and flags in Westminster, and the row with the cabman at Chelsea.'

'The Diamond Jubilee, it was,' said Warming; 'the second one.'

'Ah, yes! At the proper Jubilee – the Fifty Year affair – I was down at

Wookey – a boy. I missed all that . . . What a fuss we had with him! My landlady wouldn't take him in, wouldn't let him stay – he looked so queer when he was rigid. We had to carry him in a chair up to the hotel. And the Boscastle doctor – it wasn't the present chap, but the GP before him – was at him until nearly two, with me and the landlord holding lights and so forth.'

'It was a cataleptic rigour at first, wasn't it?'

'Stiff! – wherever you bent him he stuck. You might have stood him on his head and he'd have stopped. I never saw such stiffness. Of course this' – he indicated the prostrate figure by a movement of his head – 'is quite different. And, of course, the little doctor – what was his name?'

'Smithers?'

'Smithers it was – was quite wrong in trying to fetch him round too soon, according to all accounts. The things he did. Even now it makes me feel all – ugh! Mustard, snuff, pricking. And one of those beastly little things, not dynamos – '

'Induction coils.'

'Yes. You could see his muscles throb and jump, and he twisted about. There was just two flaring yellow candles, and all the shadows were shivering, and the little doctor nervous and putting on side, and *him* – stark and squirming in the most unnatural ways. Well, it made me dream.'

Pause.

'It's a strange state,' said Warming.

'It's a sort of complete absence,' said Isbister. 'Here's the body, empty. Not dead a bit, and yet not alive. It's like a seat vacant and marked "engaged". No feeling, no digestion, no beating of the heart – not a flutter. *That* doesn't make me feel as if there was a man present. In a sense it's more dead than death, for these doctors tell me that even the hair has stopped growing. Now with the proper dead, the hair will go on growing – '

'I know,' said Warming, with a flash of pain in his expression.

They peered through the glass again. Graham was indeed in a strange state, in the flaccid phase of a trance, but a trance unprecedented in medical history. Trances had lasted for as much as a year before – but at the end of that time it had ever been a waking or a death; sometimes first one and then the other. Isbister noted the marks the physicians had made in injecting nourishment, for that device had been resorted to to postpone collapse; he pointed them out to Warming, who had been trying not to see them.

'And while he has been lying here,' said Isbister, with the zest of a life freely spent, 'I have changed my plans in life; married, raised a family, my eldest lad – I hadn't begun to think of sons then – is an American citizen, and looking forward to leaving Harvard. There's a touch of grey in my hair. And this man, not a day older nor wiser (practically) than I was in my downy days. It's curious to think of.'

Warming turned. 'And I have grown old too. I played cricket with him

when I was still only a lad. And he looks a young man still. Yellow perhaps. But that *is* a young man nevertheless.'

'And there's been the War,' said Isbister.

'From beginning to end.'

'And these Martians.'

'I've understood,' said Isbister after a pause, 'that he had some moderate property of his own?'

'That is so,' said Warming. He coughed primly. 'As it happens – I have charge of it.'

'Ah!' Isbister thought, hesitated and spoke: 'No doubt – his keep here is not expensive – no doubt it will have improved – accumulated?'

'It has. He will wake up very much better off – if he wakes – than when he slept.'

'As a business man,' said Isbister, 'that thought has naturally been in my mind. I have, indeed, sometimes thought that, speaking commercially, of course, this sleep may be a very good thing for him. That he knows what he is about, so to speak, in being insensible so long. If he had lived straight on – '

'I doubt if he would have premeditated as much,' said Warming. 'He was not a far-sighted man. In fact – '

'Yes?'

'We differed on that point. I stood to him somewhat in the relation of a guardian. You have probably seen enough of affairs to recognise that occasionally a certain friction – . But even if that was the case, there is a doubt whether he will ever wake. This sleep exhausts slowly, but it exhausts. Apparently he is sliding slowly, very slowly and tediously, down a long slope, if you can understand me?'

'It will be a pity to lose his surprise. There's been a lot of change these twenty years. It's Rip Van Winkle come real.'

'It's Bellamy,' said Warming. 'There has been a lot of change certainly. And, among other changes, I have changed. I am an old man.'

Isbister hesitated, and then feigned a belated surprise. 'I shouldn't have thought it.'

'I was forty-three when his bankers – you remember you wired to his bankers – sent on to me.'

'I got their address from the cheque book in his pocket,' said Isbister.

'Well, the addition is not difficult,' said Warming.

There was another pause, and then Isbister gave way to an unavoidable curiosity. 'He may go on for years yet,' he said, and had a moment of hesitation. 'We have to consider that. His affairs, you know, may fall some day into the hands of – someone else, you know.'

'That, if you will believe me, Mr Isbister, is one of the problems most constantly before my mind. We happen to be – as a matter of fact, there are no very trustworthy connections of ours. It is a grotesque and unprecedented position.'

'It is,' said Isbister. 'As a matter of fact, it's a case for a public trustee, if only we had such a functionary.'

'It seems to me it's a case for some public body, some practically undying guardian. If he really is going on living – as the doctors, some of them, think. As a matter of fact, I have gone to one or two public men about it. But, so far, nothing has been done.'

'It wouldn't be a bad idea to hand him over to some public body – the British Museum Trustees, or the Royal College of Physicians. Sounds a bit odd, of course, but the whole situation is odd.'

'The difficulty is to induce them to take him.'

'Red tape, I suppose?'

'Partly.'

Pause. 'It's a curious business, certainly,' said Isbister. 'And compound interest has a way of mounting up.'

'It has,' said Warming. 'And now the gold supplies are running short there is a tendency towards . . . appreciation.'

'I've felt that,' said Isbister with a grimace. 'But it makes it better for *him*.'

'*If* he wakes.'

'If he wakes,' echoed Isbister. 'Do you notice the pinched-in look of his nose, and the way in which his eyelids sink?'

Warming looked and thought for a space. 'I doubt if he will wake,' he said at last.

'I never properly understood,' said Isbister, 'what it was brought this on. He told me something about overstudy. I've often been curious.'

'He was a man of considerable gifts, but spasmodic, emotional. He had grave domestic troubles, divorced his wife, in fact, and it was as a relief from that, I think, that he took up politics of the rabid sort. He was a fanatical Radical – a Socialist – or typical Liberal, as they used to call themselves, of the advanced school. Energetic – flighty – undisciplined. Overwork upon a controversy did this for him. I remember the pamphlet he wrote – a curious production. Wild, whirling stuff. There were one or two prophecies. Some of them are already exploded, some of them are established facts. But for the most part to read such a thesis is to realise how full the world is of unanticipated things. He will have much to learn, much to unlearn, when he wakes. If ever a waking comes.'

'I'd give anything to be there,' said Isbister, 'just to hear what he would say to it all.'

'So would I,' said Warming. 'Aye! so would I,' with an old man's sudden turn to self pity. 'But I shall never see him wake.'

He stood looking thoughtfully at the waxen figure. 'He will never wake,' he said at last. He sighed. 'He will never wake again.'

CHAPTER THREE

The Awakening

But Warming was wrong in that. An awakening came.

What a wonderfully complex thing! this simple seeming unity – the self! Who can trace its reintegration as morning after morning we awaken, the flux and confluence of its countless factors interweaving, rebuilding, the dim first stirrings of the soul, the growth and synthesis of the unconscious to the subconscious, the subconscious to dawning consciousness, until at last we recognise ourselves again. And as it happens to most of us after the night's sleep, so it was with Graham at the end of his vast slumber. A dim cloud of sensation taking shape, a cloudy dreariness, and he found himself vaguely somewhere, recumbent, faint, but alive.

The pilgrimage towards a personal being seemed to traverse vast gulfs, to occupy epochs. Gigantic dreams that were terrible realities at the time, left vague perplexing memories, strange creatures, strange scenery, as if from another planet. There was a distinct impression, too, of a momentous conversation, of a name – he could not tell what name – that was subsequently to recur, of some queer long-forgotten sensation of vein and muscle, of a feeling of vast hopeless effort, the effort of a man near drowning in darkness. Then came a panorama of dazzling unstable confluent scenes.

Graham became aware his eyes were open and regarding some unfamiliar thing.

It was something white, the edge of something, a frame of wood. He moved his head slightly, following the contour of this shape. It went up beyond the top of his eyes. He tried to think where he might be. Did it matter, seeing he was so wretched? The colour of his thoughts was a dark depression. He felt the featureless misery of one who wakes towards the hour of dawn. He had an uncertain sense of whispers and footsteps hastily receding.

The movement of his head involved a perception of extreme physical weakness. He supposed he was in bed in the hotel at the place in the valley – but he could not recall that white edge. He must have slept. He remembered now that he had wanted to sleep. He recalled the cliff and waterfall again, and then recollected something about talking to a passer-by . . .

How long had he slept? What was that sound of pattering feet? And that rise and fall, like the murmur of breakers on pebbles? He put out a languid hand to reach his watch from the chair whereon it was his habit to place it, and touched some smooth hard surface like glass. This was so unexpected that it startled him extremely. Quite suddenly he rolled over, stared for a

moment, and struggled into a sitting position. The effort was unexpectedly difficult, and it left him giddy and weak – and amazed.

He rubbed his eyes. The riddle of his surroundings was confusing but his mind was quite clear – evidently his sleep had benefited him. He was not in a bed at all as he understood the word, but lying naked on a very soft and yielding mattress, in a trough of dark glass. The mattress was partly transparent, a fact he observed with a strange sense of insecurity, and below it was a mirror reflecting him greyly. About his arm – and he saw with a shock that his skin was strangely dry and yellow – was bound a curious apparatus of rubber, bound so cunningly that it seemed to pass into his skin above and below. And this strange bed was placed in a case of greenish coloured glass (as it seemed to him), a bar in the white framework of which had first arrested his attention. In the corner of the case was a stand of glittering and delicately made apparatus, for the most part quite strange appliances, though a maximum and minimum thermometer was recognisable.

The slightly greenish tint of the glasslike substance which surrounded him on every hand obscured what lay behind, but he perceived it was a vast apartment of splendid appearance, and with a very large and simple white archway facing him. Close to the walls of the cage were articles of furniture, a table covered with a silvery cloth, silvery like the side of a fish, a couple of graceful chairs, and on the table a number of dishes with substances piled on them, a bottle and two glasses. He realised that he was intensely hungry.

He could see no human being, and after a period of hesitation scrambled off the translucent mattress and tried to stand on the clean white floor of his little apartment. He had miscalculated his strength, however, and staggered and put his hand against the glasslike pane before him to steady himself. For a moment it resisted his hand, bending outward like a distended bladder, then it broke with a slight report and vanished – a pricked bubble. He reeled out into the general space of the hall, greatly astonished. He caught at the table to save himself, knocking one of the glasses to the floor – it rang but did not break – and sat down in one of the armchairs.

When he had a little recovered he filled the remaining glass from the bottle and drank – a colourless liquid it was, but not water, with a pleasing faint aroma and taste and a quality of immediate support and stimulus. He put down the vessel and looked about him.

The apartment lost none of its size and magnificence now that the greenish transparency that had intervened was removed. The archway he saw led to a flight of steps, going downward without the intermediation of a door, to a spacious transverse passage. This passage ran between polished pillars of some white-veined substance of deep ultramarine, and along it came the sound of human movements and voices and a deep undeviating droning note. He sat, now fully awake, listening alertly, forgetting the viands in his attention.

Then with a shock he remembered that he was naked, and casting about him for covering, saw a long black robe thrown on one of the chairs beside him. This he wrapped about him and sat down again, trembling.

His mind was still a surging perplexity. Clearly he had slept, and had been removed in his sleep. But where? And who were those people, the distant crowd beyond the deep blue pillars? Boscastle? He poured out and partially drank another glass of the colourless fluid.

What was this place? – this place that to his senses seemed subtly quivering like a thing alive? He looked about him at the clean and beautiful form of the apartment, unstained by ornament, and saw that the roof was broken in one place by a circular shaft full of light, and, as he looked, a steady, sweeping shadow blotted it out and passed, and came again and passed. 'Beat, beat,' that sweeping shadow had a note of its own in the subdued tumult that filled the air.

He would have called out, but only a little sound came into his throat. Then he stood up, and, with the uncertain steps of a drunkard, made his way towards the archway. He staggered down the steps, tripped on the corner of the black cloak he had wrapped about himself, and saved himself by catching at one of the blue pillars.

The passage ran down a cool vista of blue and purple, and ended remotely in a railed space like a balcony, brightly lit and projecting into a space of haze, a space like the interior of some gigantic building. Beyond and remote were vast and vague architectural forms. The tumult of voices rose now loud and clear, and on the balcony and with their backs to him, gesticulating and apparently in animated conversation, were three figures, richly dressed in loose and easy garments of bright soft colourings. The noise of a great multitude of people poured up over the balcony, and once it seemed the top of a banner passed, and once some brightly coloured object, a pale blue cap or garment thrown up into the air perhaps, flashed athwart the space and fell. The shouts sounded like English, there was a reiteration of 'Wake!' He heard some indistinct shrill cry, and abruptly these three men began laughing.

'Ha, ha, ha!' laughed one – a red-haired man in a short purple robe. 'When the Sleeper wakes – *When!*'

He turned his eyes full of merriment along the passage. His face changed, the whole man changed, became rigid. The other two turned swiftly at his exclamation and stood motionless. Their faces assumed an expression of consternation, an expression that deepened into awe.

Suddenly Graham's knees bent beneath him, his arm against the pillar collapsed limply, he staggered forward and fell upon his face.

CHAPTER FOUR

The Sound of a Tumult

Graham's last impression before he fainted was of a clamorous ringing of bells. He learnt afterwards that he was insensible, hanging between life and death, for the better part of an hour. When he recovered his senses, he was back on his translucent couch, and there was a stirring warmth at heart and throat. The dark apparatus, he perceived, had been removed from his arm, which was bandaged. The white framework was still about him, but the greenish transparent substance that had filled it was altogether gone. A man in a deep violet robe, one of those who had been on the balcony, was looking keenly into his face.

Remote but insistent was a clamour of bells and confused sounds, that suggested to his mind the picture of a great number of people shouting together. Something seemed to fall across this tumult, a door suddenly closed.

Graham moved his head. 'What does this all mean?' he said slowly. 'Where am I?'

He saw the red-haired man who had been first to discover him. A voice seemed to be asking what he had said, and was abruptly stilled.

The man in violet answered in a soft voice, speaking English with a slightly foreign accent, or so at least it seemed to the Sleeper's ears, 'You are quite safe. You were brought hither from where you fell asleep. It is quite safe. You have been here some time – sleeping. In a trance.'

He said something further that Graham could not hear, and a little phial was handed across to him. Graham felt a cooling spray, a fragrant mist played over his forehead for a moment, and his sense of refreshment increased. He closed his eyes in satisfaction.

'Better?' asked the man in violet, as Graham's eyes reopened. He was a pleasant-faced man of thirty, perhaps, with a pointed flaxen beard, and a clasp of gold at the neck of his violet robe.

'Yes,' said Graham.

'You have been asleep some time. In a cataleptic trance. You have heard? Catalepsy? It may seem strange to you at first, but I can assure you everything is well.'

Graham did not answer, but these words served their reassuring purpose. His eyes went from face to face of the three people about him. They were regarding him strangely. He knew he ought to be somewhere in Cornwall, but he could not square these things with that impression.

A matter that had been in his mind during his last waking moments at Boscastle recurred, a thing resolved upon and somehow neglected. He cleared his throat.

'Have you wired my cousin?' he asked. 'E. Warming, 27 Chancery Lane?'

They were all assiduous to hear. But he had to repeat it. 'What an odd *blurr* in his accent!' whispered the red-haired man. 'Wire, sir?' said the young man with the flaxen beard, evidently puzzled.

'He means send an electric telegram,' volunteered the third, a pleasant-faced youth of nineteen or twenty. The flaxen-bearded man gave a cry of comprehension. 'How stupid of me! You may be sure everything shall be done, sir,' he said to Graham. 'I am afraid it would be difficult to – *wire* to your cousin. He is not in London now. But don't trouble about arrangements yet; you have been asleep a very long time and the important thing is to get over that, sir.' (Graham concluded the word was sir, but this man pronounced it '*Sire*.')

'Oh!' said Graham, and became quiet.

It was all very puzzling, but apparently these people in unfamiliar dress knew what they were about. Yet they were odd and the room was odd. It seemed he was in some newly established place. He had a sudden flash of suspicion. Surely this wasn't some hall of public exhibition! If it was he would give Warming a piece of his mind. But it scarcely had that character. And in a place of public exhibition he would not have discovered himself naked.

Then suddenly, quite abruptly, he realised what had happened. There was no perceptible interval of suspicion, no dawn to his knowledge. Abruptly he knew that his trance had lasted for a vast interval; as if by some processes of thought reading he interpreted the awe in the faces that peered into his. He looked at them strangely, full of intense emotion. It seemed they read his eyes. He framed his lips to speak and could not. A queer impulse to hide his knowledge came into his mind almost at the moment of his discovery. He looked at his bare feet, regarding them silently. His impulse to speak passed. He was trembling exceedingly.

They gave him some pink fluid with a greenish fluorescence and a meaty taste, and the assurance of returning strength grew.

'That – that makes me feel better,' he said hoarsely, and there were murmurs of respectful approval. He knew now quite clearly. He made to speak again, and again he could not.

He pressed his throat and tried a third time. 'How long?' he asked in a level voice. 'How long have I been asleep?'

'Some considerable time,' said the flaxen-bearded man, glancing quickly at the others.

'How long?'

'A very long time.'

'Yes – yes,' said Graham, suddenly testy. 'But I want – Is it – it is – some years? Many years? There was something – I forget what. I feel – confused. But you – ' He sobbed. 'You need not fence with me. How long – ?'

He stopped, breathing irregularly. He squeezed his eyes with his knuckles and sat waiting for an answer.

They spoke in undertones.

'Five or six?' he asked faintly. 'More?'

'Very much more than that.'

'More!'

'More.'

He looked at them and it seemed as though imps were twitching the muscles of his face. He looked his question.

'Many years,' said the man with the red beard.

Graham struggled into a sitting position. He wiped a rheumy tear from his face with a lean hand. 'Many years!' he repeated. He shut his eyes tight, opened them, and sat looking about him, from one unfamiliar thing to another.

'How many years?' he asked.

'You must be prepared to be surprised.'

'Well?'

'More than a gross of years.'

He was irritated at the strange word. 'More than a *what?*'

Two of them spoke together. Some quick remarks that were made about 'decimal' he did not catch.

'How long did you say?' asked Graham. 'How long? Don't look like that. Tell me.'

Among the remarks in an undertone, his ear caught six words: 'More than a couple of *centuries.*'

'*What?*' he cried, turning on the youth who he thought had spoken. 'Who says – ? What was that? A couple of centuries!'

'Yes,' said the man with the red beard. 'Two hundred years.'

Graham repeated the words. He had been prepared to hear of a vast repose, and yet these concrete centuries defeated him.

'Two hundred years,' he said again, with the figure of a great gulf opening very slowly in his mind; and then, 'Oh, but – !'

They said nothing.

'You – did you say – ?'

'Two hundred years. Two centuries of years,' said the man with the red beard.

There was a pause. Graham looked at their faces and saw that what he had heard was indeed true.

'But it can't be,' he said querulously. 'I am dreaming. Trances. Trances don't last. That is not right – this is a joke you have played upon me! Tell me – some days ago, perhaps, I was walking along the coast of Cornwall – ?'

His voice failed him.

The man with the flaxen beard hesitated. 'I'm not very strong in history, sir,' he said weakly, and glanced at the others.

'That was it, sir,' said the youngster. 'Boscastle, in the old Duchy of Cornwall – it's in the southwest country beyond the dairy meadows. There is a house there still. I have been there.'

'Boscastle!' Graham turned his eyes to the youngster. 'That was it – Boscastle. Little Boscastle. I fell asleep – somewhere there. I don't exactly remember. I don't exactly remember.'

He pressed his brows and whispered, 'More than *two hundred years!*'

He began to speak quickly with a twitching face, but his heart was cold within him. 'But if it *is* two hundred years, every soul I know, every human being that ever I saw or spoke to before I went to sleep, must be dead.'

They did not answer him.

'The Queen and the Royal Family, her Ministers, of Church and State. High and low, rich and poor, one with another – '

'Is there England still?'

'That's a comfort! Is there London?

'This *is* London, eh? And you are my assistant – custodian; assistant-custodian. And these – ? Eh? Assistant-custodians too!'

He sat with a gaunt stare on his face. 'But why am I here? No! Don't talk. Be quiet. Let me – '

He sat silent, rubbed his eyes, and, uncovering them, found another little glass of pinkish fluid held towards him. He took the dose. It was almost immediately sustaining. Directly he had taken it he began to weep naturally and refreshingly.

Presently he looked at their faces, suddenly laughed through his tears, a little foolishly. 'But – two – hun – dred – years!' he said. He grimaced hysterically and covered up his face again.

After a space he grew calm. He sat up, his hands hanging over his knees in almost precisely the same attitude in which Isbister had found him on the cliff at Pentargen. His attention was attracted by a thick domineering voice, the footsteps of an advancing personage. 'What are you doing? Why was I not warned? Surely you could tell? Someone will suffer for this. The man must be kept quiet. Are the doorways closed? All the doorways? He must be kept perfectly quiet. He must not be told. Has he been told anything?'

The man with the fair beard made some inaudible remark, and Graham looking over his shoulder saw approaching a very short, fat, and thickset beardless man, with aquiline nose and heavy neck and chin. Very thick black and slightly sloping eyebrows that almost met over his nose and overhung deep grey eyes, gave his face an oddly formidable expression. He scowled momentarily at Graham and then his regard returned to the man with the flaxen beard. 'These others,' he said in a voice of extreme irritation. 'You had better go.'

'Go?' said the red-bearded man.

'Certainly – go now. But see the doorways are closed as you go.'

The two men addressed turned obediently, after one reluctant glance at

Graham, and instead of going through the archway as he expected, walked straight to the dead wall of the apartment opposite the archway. And then came a strange thing; a long strip of this apparently solid wall rolled up with a snap, hung over the two retreating men and fell again, and immediately Graham was alone with the new comer and the purple-robed man with the flaxen beard.

For a space the thickset man took not the slightest notice of Graham, but proceeded to interrogate the other – obviously his subordinate – upon the treatment of their charge. He spoke clearly, but in phrases only partially intelligible to Graham. The awakening seemed not only a matter of surprise but of consternation and annoyance to him. He was evidently profoundly excited.

'You must not confuse his mind by telling him things,' he repeated again and again. 'You must not confuse his mind.'

His questions answered, he turned quickly and eyed the awakened sleeper with an ambiguous expression.

'Feel queer?' he asked.

'Very.'

'The world, what you see of it, seems strange to you?'

'I suppose I have to live in it, strange as it seems.'

'I suppose so, now.'

'In the first place, hadn't I better have some clothes?'

'They – ' said the thickset man and stopped, and the flaxen-bearded man met his eye and went away. 'You will very speedily have clothes,' said the thickset man.

'Is it true indeed, that I have been asleep two hundred – ?' asked Graham.

'They have told you that, have they? Two hundred and three, as a matter of fact.'

Graham accepted the indisputable now with raised eyebrows and depressed mouth. He sat silent for a moment, and then asked a question, 'Is there a mill or dynamo near here?' He did not wait for an answer. 'Things have changed tremendously, I suppose?' he said.

'What is that shouting?' he asked abruptly.

'Nothing,' said the thickset man impatiently. 'It's people. You'll understand better later – perhaps. As you say, things have changed.' He spoke shortly, his brows were knit, and he glanced about him like a man trying to decide in an emergency. 'We must get you clothes and so forth, at any rate. Better wait here until some can come. No one will come near you. You want shaving.'

Graham rubbed his chin.

The man with the flaxen beard came back towards them, turned suddenly, listened for a moment, lifted his eyebrows at the older man, and hurried off through the archway towards the balcony. The tumult of shouting grew louder, and the thickset man turned and listened also. He cursed suddenly

under his breath, and turned his eyes upon Graham with an unfriendly expression. It was a surge of many voices, rising and falling, shouting and screaming, and once came a sound like blows and sharp cries, and then a snapping like the crackling of dry sticks. Graham strained his ears to draw some single thread of sound from the woven tumult.

Then he perceived, repeated again and again, a certain formula. For a time he doubted his ears. But surely these were the words: 'Show us the Sleeper! Show us the Sleeper!'

The thickset man rushed suddenly to the archway.

'Wild!' he cried. 'How do they know? Do they know? Or is it guessing?'

There was perhaps an answer.

'I can't come,' said the thickset man; 'I have *him* to see to. But shout from the balcony.'

There was an inaudible reply.

'Say he is not awake. Anything! I leave it to you.'

He came hurrying back to Graham. 'You must have clothes at once,' he said. 'You cannot stop here – and it will be impossible to – '

He rushed away, Graham shouting unanswered questions after him. In a moment he was back.

'I can't tell you what is happening. It is too complex to explain. In a moment you shall have your clothes made. Yes – in a moment. And then I can take you away from here. You will find out our troubles soon enough.'

'But those voices. They were shouting – ?'

'Something about the Sleeper – that's you. They have some twisted idea. I don't know what it is. I know nothing.'

A shrill bell jetted acutely across the indistinct mingling of remote noises, and this brusque person sprang to a little group of appliances in the corner of the room. He listened for a moment, regarding a ball of crystal, nodded, and said a few indistinct words; then he walked to the wall through which the two men had vanished. It rolled up again like a curtain, and he stood waiting.

Graham lifted his arm and was astonished to find what strength the restoratives had given him. He thrust one leg over the side of the couch and then the other. His head no longer swam. He could scarcely credit his rapid recovery. He sat feeling his limbs.

The man with the flaxen beard re-entered from the archway, and as he did so the cage of a lift came sliding down in front of the thickset man, and a lean, grey-bearded man, carrying a roll, and wearing a tightly fitting costume of dark green, appeared therein.

'This is the tailor,' said the thickset man with an introductory gesture. 'It will never do for you to wear that black. I cannot understand how it got here. But I shall. I shall. You will be as rapid as possible?' he said to the tailor.

The man in green bowed, and, advancing, seated himself by Graham on the bed. His manner was calm, but his eyes were full of curiosity. 'You will

find the fashions altered, Sire,' he said. He glanced from under his brows at the thickset man.

He opened the roller with a quick movement, and a confusion of brilliant fabrics poured out over his knees. 'You lived, Sire, in a period essentially cylindrical – the Victorian. With a tendency to the hemisphere in hats. Circular curves always. Now – ' He flicked out a little appliance the size and appearance of a keyless watch, whirled the knob, and behold – a little figure in white appeared kinetoscope fashion on the dial, walking and turning. The tailor caught up a pattern of bluish white satin. 'That is my conception of your immediate treatment,' he said.

The thickset man came and stood by the shoulder of Graham.

'We have very little time,' he said.

'Trust me,' said the tailor. 'My machine follows. What do you think of this?'

'What is that?' asked the man from the nineteenth century.

'In your days they showed you a fashion-plate,' said the tailor, 'but this is our modern development. See here.' The little figure repeated its evolutions, but in a different costume. 'Or this,' and with a click another small figure in a more voluminous type of robe marched on to the dial. The tailor was very quick in his movements, and glanced twice towards the lift as he did these things.

It rumbled again, and a crop-haired anaemic lad with features of the Chinese type, clad in coarse pale blue canvas, appeared together with a complicated machine, which he pushed noiselessly on little castors into the room. Incontinently the little kinetoscope was dropped, Graham was invited to stand in front of the machine and the tailor muttered some instructions to the crop-haired lad, who answered in guttural tones and with words Graham did not recognise. The boy then went to conduct an incomprehensible monologue in the corner, and the tailor pulled out a number of slotted arms terminating in little discs, pulling them out until the discs were flat against the body of Graham, one at each shoulder blade, one at the elbows, one at the neck and so forth, so that at last there were, perhaps, two score of them upon his body and limbs. At the same time, some other person entered the room by the lift, behind Graham. The tailor set moving a mechanism that initiated a faint-sounding rhythmic movement of parts in the machine, and in another moment he was knocking up the levers and Graham was released. The tailor replaced his cloak of black, and the man with the flaxen beard proffered him a little glass of some refreshing fluid. Graham saw over the rim of the glass a pale-faced young man regarding him with a singular fixity.

The thickset man had been pacing the room fretfully, and now turned and went through the archway towards the balcony, from which the noise of a distant crowd still came in gusts and cadences. The crop-headed lad handed the tailor a roll of the bluish satin and the two began fixing this in

the mechanism in a manner reminiscent of a roll of paper in a nineteenth-century printing machine. Then they ran the entire thing on its easy, noiseless bearings across the room to a remote corner where a twisted cable looped rather gracefully from the wall. They made some connection and the machine became energetic and swift.

'What is that doing?' asked Graham, pointing with the empty glass to the busy figures and trying to ignore the scrutiny of the new comer. 'Is that – some sort of force – laid on?'

'Yes,' said the man with the flaxen beard.

'Who is *that*?' He indicated the archway behind him.

The man in purple stroked his little beard, hesitated, and answered in an undertone, 'He is Howard, your chief guardian. You see, Sire, – it's a little difficult to explain. The Council appoints a guardian and assistants. This hall has under certain restrictions been public. In order that people might satisfy themselves. We have barred the doorways for the first time. But I think – if you don't mind, I will leave him to explain.'

'Odd!' said Graham. 'Guardian? Council?' Then turning his back on the new comer, he asked in an undertone, 'Why is this man glaring at me? Is he a mesmerist?'

'Mesmerist! He is a capillotomist.'

'Capillotomist!'

'Yes – one of the chief. His yearly fee is sixdoz lions.'

It sounded sheer nonsense. Graham snatched at the last phrase with an unsteady mind. 'Sixdoz lions?' he said.

'Didn't you have lions? I suppose not. You had the old pounds? They are our monetary units.'

'But what was that you said – sixdoz?'

'Yes. Six dozen, Sire. Of course things, even these little things, have altered. You lived in the days of the decimal system, the Arab system – tens, and little hundreds and thousands. We have eleven numerals now. We have single figures for both ten and eleven, two figures for a dozen, and a dozen dozen makes a gross, a great hundred, you know, a dozen gross a dozand, and a dozand dozand a myriad. Very simple?'

'I suppose so,' said Graham. 'But about this cap – what was it?'

The man with the flaxen beard glanced over his shoulder.

'Here are your clothes!' he said. Graham turned round sharply and saw the tailor standing at his elbow smiling, and holding some palpably new garments over his arm. The crop-headed boy, by means of one finger, was impelling the complicated machine towards the lift by which he had arrived. Graham stared at the completed suit. 'You don't mean to say – !'

'Just made,' said the tailor. He dropped the garments at the feet of Graham, walked to the bed on which Graham had so recently been lying, flung out the translucent mattress, and turned up the looking-glass. As he did so a furious bell summoned the thickset man to the corner. The man

with the flaxen beard rushed across to him and then hurried out by the archway.

The tailor was assisting Graham into a dark purple combination garment, stockings, vest, and pants in one, as the thickset man came back from the corner to meet the man with the flaxen beard returning from the balcony. They began speaking quickly in an undertone, their bearing had an unmistakable quality of anxiety. Over the purple undergarment came a complex but graceful garment of bluish white, and Graham was clothed in the fashion once more and saw himself, sallow-faced, unshaven and shaggy still, but at least naked no longer, and in some indefinable unprecedented way graceful.

'I must shave,' he said regarding himself in the glass.

'In a moment,' said Howard.

The persistent stare ceased. The young man closed his eyes, reopened them, and with a lean hand extended, advanced on Graham. Then he stopped, with his hand slowly gesticulating, and looked about him. 'A seat,' said Howard impatiently, and in a moment the flaxen-bearded man had a chair behind Graham. 'Sit down, please,' said Howard.

Graham hesitated, and in the other hand of the wild-eyed man he saw the glint of steel.

'Don't you understand, Sire?' cried the flaxen-bearded man with hurried politeness. 'He is going to cut your hair.'

'Oh!' cried Graham enlightened. 'But you called him – '

'A capillotomist – precisely! He is one of the finest artists in the world.'

Graham sat down abruptly. The flaxen-bearded man disappeared. The capillotomist came forward with graceful gestures, examined Graham's ears and surveyed him, felt the back of his head, and would have sat down again to regard him but for Howard's audible impatience. Forthwith with rapid movements and a succession of deftly handled implements he shaved Graham's chin, clipped his moustache, and cut and arranged his hair. All this he did without a word, with something of the rapt air of a poet inspired. And as soon as he had finished Graham was handed a pair of shoes.

Suddenly a loud voice shouted – it seemed from a piece of machinery in the corner – 'At once – at once. The people know all over the city. Work is being stopped. Work is being stopped. Wait for nothing, but come.'

This shout appeared to perturb Howard exceedingly. By his gestures it seemed to Graham that he hesitated between two directions. Abruptly he went towards the corner where the apparatus stood about the little crystal ball. As he did so the undertone of tumultuous shouting from the archway that had continued during all these occurrences rose to a mighty sound, roared as if it were sweeping past, and fell again as if receding swiftly. It drew Graham after it with an irresistible attraction. He glanced at the thickset man, and then obeyed his impulse. In two strides he was down the steps and in the passage, and in a score he was out upon the balcony upon which the three men had been standing.

CHAPTER FIVE

The Moving Ways

He went to the railings of the balcony and stared upward. An exclamation of surprise at his appearance, and the movements of a number of people came from the spacious area below.

His first impression was of overwhelming architecture. The place into which he looked was an aisle of Titanic buildings, curving spaciously in either direction. Overhead mighty cantilevers sprang together across the huge width of the place, and a tracery of translucent material shut out the sky. Gigantic globes of cool white light shamed the pale sunbeams that filtered down through the girders and wires. Here and there a gossamer suspension bridge dotted with foot passengers flung across the chasm and the air was webbed with slender cables. A cliff of edifice hung above him, he perceived as he glanced upward, and the opposite façade was grey and dim and broken by great archings, circular perforations, balconies, buttresses, turret projections, myriads of vast windows, and an intricate scheme of architectural relief. Athwart these ran inscriptions horizontally and obliquely in an unfamiliar lettering. Here and there close to the roof cables of a peculiar stoutness were fastened, and drooped in a steep curve to circular openings on the opposite side of the space, and even as Graham noted these a remote and tiny figure of a man clad in pale blue arrested his attention. This little figure was far overhead across the space beside the higher fastening of one of these festoons, hanging forward from a little ledge of masonry and handling some well-nigh invisible strings dependent from the line. Then suddenly, with a swoop that sent Graham's heart into his mouth, this man had rushed down the curve and vanished through a round opening on the hither side of the way. Graham had been looking up as he came out upon the balcony, and the things he saw above and opposed to him had at first seized his attention to the exclusion of anything else. Then suddenly he discovered the roadway! It was not a roadway at all, as Graham understood such things, for in the nineteenth century the only roads and streets were beaten tracks of motionless earth, jostling rivulets of vehicles between narrow footways. But this roadway was three hundred feet across, and it moved; it moved, all save the middle, the lowest part. For a moment, the motion dazzled his mind. Then he understood.

Under the balcony this extraordinary roadway ran swiftly to Graham's right, an endless flow rushing along as fast as a nineteenth-century express train, an endless platform of narrow transverse overlapping slats with little interspaces that permitted it to follow the curvatures of the street. Upon it were seats, and here and there little kiosks, but they swept by too swiftly for

him to see what might be therein. From this nearest and swiftest platform a series of others descended to the centre of the space. Each moved to the right, each perceptibly slower than the one above it, but the difference in pace was small enough to permit anyone to step from any platform to the one adjacent, and so walk uninterruptedly from the swiftest to the motionless middle way. Beyond this middle way was another series of endless platforms rushing with varying pace to Graham's left. And seated in crowds upon the two widest and swiftest platforms, or stepping from one to another down the steps, or swarming over the central space, was an innumerable and wonderfully diversified multitude of people.

'You must not stop here,' shouted Howard suddenly at his side. 'You must come away at once.'

Graham made no answer. He heard without hearing. The platforms ran with a roar and the people were shouting. He perceived women and girls with flowing hair, beautifully robed, with bands crossing between the breasts. These first came out of the confusion. Then he perceived that the dominant note in that kaleidoscope of costume was the pale blue that the tailor's boy had worn. He became aware of cries of 'The Sleeper. What has happened to the Sleeper?' and it seemed as though the rushing platforms before him were suddenly spattered with the pale buff of human faces, and then still more thickly. He saw pointing fingers. He perceived that the motionless central area of this huge arcade just opposite to the balcony was densely crowded with blue-clad people. Some sort of struggle had sprung into life. People seemed to be pushed up the running platforms on either side, and carried away against their will. They would spring off so soon as they were beyond the thick of the confusion, and run back towards the conflict.

'It is the Sleeper. Verily it is the Sleeper,' shouted voices. 'That is never the Sleeper,' shouted others. More and more faces were turned to him. At the intervals along this central area Graham noted openings, pits, apparently the heads of staircases going down with people ascending out of them and descending into them. The struggle it seemed centred about the one of these nearest to him. People were running down the moving platforms to this, leaping dexterously from platform to platform. The clustering people on the higher platforms seemed to divide their interest between this point and the balcony. A number of sturdy little figures clad in a uniform of bright red, and working methodically together, were employed it seemed in preventing access to this descending staircase. About them a crowd was rapidly accumulating. Their brilliant colour contrasted vividly with the whitish-blue of their antagonists, for the struggle was indisputable.

He saw these things with Howard shouting in his ear and shaking his arm. And then suddenly Howard was gone and he stood alone.

He perceived that the cries of 'The Sleeper!' grew in volume, and that the people on the nearer platform were standing up. The nearer swifter

platform he perceived was empty to the right of him, and far across the space the platform running in the opposite direction was coming crowded and passing away bare. With incredible swiftness a vast crowd had gathered in the central space before his eyes; a dense swaying mass of people, and the shouts grew from a fitful crying to a voluminous incessant clamour: 'The Sleeper! The Sleeper!' and yells and cheers, a waving of garments and cries of 'Stop the ways!' They were also crying another name strange to Graham. It sounded like 'Ostrog'. The slower platforms were soon thick with active people, running against the movement so as to keep themselves opposite to him.

'Stop the ways,' they cried. Agile figures ran up swiftly from the centre to the swift road nearest to him, were borne rapidly past him, shouting strange, unintelligible things, and ran back obliquely to the central way. One thing he distinguished: 'It is indeed the Sleeper. It is indeed the Sleeper,' they testified.

For a space Graham stood without a movement. Then he became vividly aware that all this concerned him. He was pleased at his wonderful popularity, he bowed, and, seeking a gesture of longer range, waved his arm. He was astonished at the violence of uproar that this provoked. The tumult about the descending stairway rose to furious violence. He became aware of crowded balconies, of men sliding along ropes, of men in trapeze-like seats hurling athwart the space. He heard voices behind him, a number of people descending the steps through the archway; he suddenly perceived that his guardian Howard was back again and gripping his arm painfully, and shouting inaudibly in his ear.

He turned, and Howard's face was white. 'Come back,' he heard. 'They will stop the ways. The whole city will be in confusion.'

He perceived a number of men hurrying along the passage of blue pillars behind Howard, the red-haired man, the man with the flaxen beard, a tall man in vivid vermilion, a crowd of others in red carrying staves, and all these people had anxious eager faces.

'Get him away,' cried Howard.

'But why?' said Graham. 'I don't see – '

'You must come away!' said the man in red in a resolute voice. His face and eyes were resolute, too. Graham's glances went from face to face, and he was suddenly aware of that most disagreeable flavour in life, compulsion. Someone gripped his arm . . . He was being dragged away. It seemed as though the tumult suddenly became two, as if half the shouts that had come in from this wonderful roadway had sprung into the passages of the great building behind him. Marvelling and confused, feeling an impotent desire to resist, Graham was half led, half thrust, along the passage of blue pillars, and suddenly he found himself alone with Howard in a lift and moving swiftly upward.

CHAPTER SIX

The Hall of the Atlas

From the moment when the tailor had bowed his farewell to the moment when Graham found himself in the lift, was altogether barely five minutes. And as yet the haze of his vast interval of sleep hung about him, as yet the initial strangeness of his being alive at all in this remote age touched everything with wonder, with a sense of the irrational, with something of the quality of a realistic dream. He was still detached, an astonished spectator, still but half involved in life. What he had seen, and especially the last crowded tumult, framed in the setting of the balcony, had a spectacular turn, like a thing witnessed from the box of a theatre. 'I don't understand,' he said. 'What was the trouble? My mind is in a whirl. Why were they shouting? What is the danger?'

'We have our troubles,' said Howard. His eyes avoided Graham's enquiry. 'This is a time of unrest. And, in fact, your appearance, your waking just now, has a sort of connection – '

He spoke jerkily, like a man not quite sure of his breathing. He stopped abruptly.

'I don't understand,' said Graham.

'It will be clearer later,' said Howard.

He glanced uneasily upward, as though he found the progress of the lift slow.

'I shall understand better, no doubt, when I have seen my way about a little,' said Graham puzzled. 'It will be – it is bound to be perplexing. At present it is all so strange. Anything seems possible. Anything. In the details even. Your counting, I understand, is different.'

The lift stopped, and they stepped out into a narrow but very long passage between high walls, along which ran an extraordinary number of tubes and big cables.

'What a huge place this is!' said Graham. 'Is it all one building? What place is it?'

'This is one of the city ways for various public services. Light and so forth.'

'Was it a social trouble – that – in the great roadway place? How are you governed? Have you still a police?'

'Several,' said Howard.

'Several?'

'About fourteen.'

'I don't understand.'

'Very probably not. Our social order will probably seem very complex to

you. To tell you the truth, I don't understand it myself very clearly. Nobody does. You will, perhaps – by and by. We have to go to the Council.'

Graham's attention was divided between the urgent necessity of his enquiries and the people in the passages and halls they were traversing. For a moment his mind would be concentrated upon Howard and the halting answers he made, and then he would lose the thread in response to some vivid unexpected impression. Along the passages, in the halls, half the people seemed to be men in the red uniform. The pale blue canvas that had been so abundant in the aisle of moving ways did not appear. Invariably these men looked at him, and saluted him and Howard as they passed.

He had a clear vision of entering a long corridor, and there were a number of girls sitting on low seats and as though in a class. He saw no teacher, but only a novel apparatus from which he fancied a voice proceeded. The girls regarded him and his conductor, he thought, with curiosity and astonishment. But he was hurried on before he could form a clear idea of the gathering. He judged they knew Howard and not himself, and that they wondered who he was. This Howard, it seemed, was a person of importance. But then he was also merely Graham's guardian. That was odd.

There came a passage in twilight, and into this passage a footway hung so that he could see the feet and ankles of people going to and fro thereon, but no more of them. Then vague impressions of galleries and of casual astonished passers-by turning round to stare after the two of them with their red-clad guard.

The stimulus of the restoratives he had taken was only temporary. He was speedily fatigued by this excessive haste. He asked Howard to slacken his speed. Presently he was in a lift that had a window upon the great street space, but this was glazed and did not open, and they were too high for him to see the moving platforms below. But he saw people going to and fro along cables and along strange, frail-looking bridges.

And thence they passed across the street and at a vast height above it. They crossed by means of a narrow bridge closed in with glass, so clear that it made him giddy even to remember it. The floor of it also was of glass. From his memory of the cliffs between New Quay and Boscastle, so remote in time, and so recent in his experience, it seemed to him that they must be near four hundred feet above the moving ways. He stopped, looked down between his legs upon the swarming blue and red multitudes, minute and foreshortened, struggling and gesticulating still towards the little balcony far below, a little toy balcony, it seemed, where he had so recently been standing. A thin haze and the glare of the mighty globes of light obscured everything. A man seated in a little open-work cradle shot by from some point still higher than the little narrow bridge, rushing down a cable as swiftly almost as if he were falling. Graham stopped involuntarily to watch this strange passenger vanish in a great circular opening below, and then his eyes went back to the tumultuous struggle.

Along one of the swifter ways rushed a thick crowd of red spots. This broke up into individuals as it approached the balcony, and went pouring down the slower ways towards the dense struggling crowd on the central area. These men in red appeared to be armed with sticks or truncheons; they seemed to be striking and thrusting. A great shouting, cries of wrath, screaming, burst out and came up to Graham, faint and thin. 'Go on,' cried Howard, laying hands on him.

Another man rushed down a cable. Graham suddenly glanced up to see whence he came, and beheld through the glassy roof and the network of cables and girders, dim rhythmically passing forms like the vans of windmills, and between them glimpses of a remote and pallid sky. Then Howard had thrust him forward across the bridge, and he was in a little narrow passage decorated with geometrical patterns.

'I want to see more of that,' cried Graham, resisting.

'No, no,' cried Howard, still gripping his arm. 'This way. You must go this way.' And the men in red following them seemed ready to enforce his orders.

Some negroes in a curious wasplike uniform of black and yellow appeared down the passage, and one hastened to throw up a sliding shutter that had seemed a door to Graham, and led the way through it. Graham found himself in a gallery overhanging the end of a great chamber. The attendant in black and yellow crossed this, thrust up a second shutter and stood waiting.

This place had the appearance of an anteroom. He saw a number of people in the central space, and at the opposite end a large and imposing doorway at the top of a flight of steps, heavily curtained but giving a glimpse of some still larger hall beyond. He perceived white men in red and other negroes in black and yellow standing stiffly about those portals.

As they crossed the gallery he heard a whisper from below, 'The Sleeper,' and was aware of a turning of heads, a hum of observation. They entered another little passage in the wall of this antechamber, and then he found himself on an iron-railed gallery of metal that passed round the side of the great hall he had already seen through the curtains. He entered the place at the corner, so that he received the fullest impression of its huge proportions. The black in the wasp uniform stood aside like a well-trained servant, and closed the valve behind him.

Compared with any of the places Graham had see thus far, this second hall appeared to be decorated with extreme richness. On a pedestal at the remote end, and more brilliantly lit than any other object, was a gigantic white figure of Atlas, strong and strenuous, the globe upon his bowed shoulders. It was the first thing to strike his attention, it was so vast, so patiently and painfully real, so white and simple. Save for this figure and for a dais in the centre, the wide floor of the place was a shining vacancy. The dais was remote in the greatness of the area; it would have looked a mere

slab of metal had it not been for the group of seven men who stood about a table on it, and gave an inkling of its proportions. They were all dressed in white robes, they seemed to have arisen that moment from their seats, and they were regarding Graham steadfastly. At the end of the table he perceived the glitter of some mechanical appliances.

Howard led him along the end gallery until they were opposite this mighty labouring figure. Then he stopped. The two men in red who had followed them into the gallery came and stood on either hand of Graham.

'You must remain here,' murmured Howard, 'for a few moments,' and, without waiting for a reply, hurried away along the gallery.

'But, *why* – ?' began Graham.

He moved as if to follow Howard, and found his path obstructed by one of the men in red. 'You have to wait here, Sire,' said the man in red.

'*Why?*'

'Orders, Sire.'

'Whose orders?'

'Our orders, Sire.'

Graham looked his exasperation.

'What place is this?' he said presently. 'Who are those men?'

'They are the lords of the Council, Sire.'

'What Council?'

'*The* Council.'

'Oh!' said Graham, and after an equally ineffectual attempt at the other man, went to the railing and stared at the distant men in white, who stood watching him and whispering together.

The Council? He perceived there were now eight, though how the newcomer had arrived he had not observed. They made no gestures of greeting; they stood regarding him as in the nineteenth century a group of men might have stood in the street regarding a distant balloon that had suddenly floated into view. What council could it be that gathered there, that little body of men beneath the significant white Atlas, secluded from every eavesdropper in this impressive spaciousness? And why should he be brought to them, and be looked at strangely and spoken of inaudibly? Howard appeared beneath, walking quickly across the polished floor towards them. As he drew near he bowed and performed certain peculiar movements, apparently of a ceremonious nature. Then he ascended the steps of the dais, and stood by the apparatus at the end of the table.

Graham watched that visible inaudible conversation. Occasionally, one of the white-robed men would glance towards him. He strained his ears in vain. The gesticulation of two of the speakers became animated. He glanced from them to the passive faces of his attendants . . . When he looked again Howard was extending his hands and moving his head like a man who protests. He was interrupted, it seemed, by one of the white-robed men rapping the table.

The conversation lasted an interminable time to Graham's sense. His eyes rose to the still giant at whose feet the Council sat. Thence they wandered at last to the walls of the hall. It was decorated in long painted panels of a quasi-Japanese type, many of them very beautiful. These panels were grouped in a great and elaborate framing of dark metal, which passed into the metallic caryatidae of the galleries, and the great structural lines of the interior. The facile grace of these panels enhanced the mighty white effort that laboured in the centre of the scheme. Graham's eyes came back to the Council, and Howard was descending the steps. As he drew nearer his features could be distinguished, and Graham saw that he was flushed and blowing out his cheeks. His countenance was still disturbed when presently he reappeared along the gallery.

'This way,' he said concisely, and they went on in silence to a little door that opened at their approach. The two men in red stopped on either side of this door. Howard and Graham passed in, and Graham, glancing back, saw the white-robed Council still standing in a close group and looking at him. Then the door closed behind him with a heavy thud, and for the first time since his awakening he was in silence. The floor, even, was noiseless to his feet.

Howard opened another door, and they were in the first of two contiguous chambers furnished in white and green. 'What Council was that?' began Graham. 'What were they discussing? What have they to do with me?' Howard closed the door carefully, heaved a huge sigh, and said something in an undertone. He walked slantingways across the room and turned, blowing out his cheeks again. 'Ugh!' he grunted, a man relieved.

Graham stood regarding him.

'You must understand,' began Howard abruptly, avoiding Graham's eyes, 'that our social order is very complex. A half explanation, a bare unqualified statement would give you false impressions. As a matter of fact – it is a case of compound interest partly – your small fortune, and the fortune of your cousin Warming which was left to you – and certain other beginnings – have become very considerable. And in other ways that will be hard for you to understand, you have become a person of significance – of very considerable significance – involved in the world's affairs.'

He stopped.

'Yes?' said Graham.

'We have grave social troubles.'

'Yes?'

'Things have come to such a pass that, in fact, it is advisable to seclude you here.'

'Keep me prisoner!' exclaimed Graham.

'Well – to ask you to keep in seclusion.'

Graham turned on him. 'This is strange!' he said.

'No harm will be done you.'

'No harm!'

'But you must be kept here – '

'While I learn my position, I presume.'

'Precisely.'

'Very well then. Begin. Why *harm*?'

'Not now.'

'Why not?'

'It is too long a story, Sire.'

'All the more reason I should begin at once. You say I am a person of importance. What was that shouting I heard? Why is a great multitude shouting and excited because my trance is over, and who are the men in white in that huge council chamber?'

'All in good time, Sire,' said Howard. 'But not crudely, not crudely. This is one of those flimsy times when no man has a settled mind. Your awakening. No one expected your awakening. The Council is consulting.'

'What council?'

'The Council you saw.'

Graham made a petulant movement. 'This is not right,' he said. 'I should be told what is happening.'

'You must wait. Really you must wait.'

Graham sat down abruptly. 'I suppose since I have waited so long to resume life,' he said, 'that I must wait a little longer.'

'That is better,' said Howard. 'Yes, that is much better. And I must leave you alone. For a space. While I attend the discussion in the Council . . . I am sorry.'

He went towards the noiseless door, hesitated and vanished.

Graham walked to the door, tried it, found it securely fastened in some way he never came to understand, turned about, paced the room restlessly, made the circuit of the room, and sat down. He remained sitting for some time with folded arms and knitted brow, biting his fingernails and trying to piece together the kaleidoscopic impressions of this first hour of awakened life; the vast mechanical spaces, the endless series of chambers and passages, the great struggle that roared and splashed through these strange ways, the little group of remote unsympathetic men beneath the colossal Atlas, Howard's mysterious behaviour. There was an inkling of some vast inheritance already in his mind – a vast inheritance perhaps misapplied – of some unprecedented importance and opportunity. What had he to do? And this room's secluded silence was eloquent of imprisonment!

It came into Graham's mind with irresistible conviction that this series of magnificent impressions was a dream. He tried to shut his eyes and succeeded, but that time-honoured device led to no awakening.

Presently he began to touch and examine all the unfamiliar appointments of the two small rooms in which he found himself.

In a long oval panel of mirror he saw himself and stopped astonished. He was clad in a graceful costume of purple and bluish white, with a little grey-shot beard trimmed to a point, and his hair, its blackness streaked now with bands of grey, arranged over his forehead in an unfamiliar but graceful manner. He seemed a man of five-and-forty perhaps. For a moment he did not perceive this was himself.

A flash of laughter came with the recognition. 'To call on old Warming like this!' he exclaimed, 'and make him take me out to lunch!'

Then he thought of meeting first one and then another of the few familiar acquaintances of his early manhood, and in the midst of his amusement realised that every soul with whom he might jest had died many score of years ago. The thought smote him abruptly and keenly; he stopped short, the expression of his face changed to a white consternation.

The tumultuous memory of the moving platforms and the huge façade of that wonderful street reasserted itself. The shouting multitudes came back clear and vivid, and those remote, inaudible, unfriendly councillors in white. He felt himself a little figure, very small and ineffectual, pitifully conspicuous. And all about him, the world was – *strange*.

CHAPTER SEVEN

In the Silent Rooms

Presently Graham resumed his examination of his apartments. Curiosity kept him moving in spite of his fatigue. The inner room, he perceived, was high, and its ceiling dome shaped, with an oblong aperture in the centre, opening into a funnel in which a wheel of broad fans seemed to be rotating, apparently driving the air up the shaft. The faint humming note of its easy motion was the only clear sound in that quiet place. As these vans sprang up one after the other, Graham could get transient glimpses of the sky. He was surprised to see a star.

This drew his attention to the fact that the bright lighting of these rooms was due to a multitude of very faint glow lamps set about the cornices. There were no windows. And he began to recall that along all the vast chambers and passages he had traversed with Howard he had observed no windows at all. Had there been windows? There were windows on the street indeed, but were they for light? Or was the whole city lit day and night for evermore, so that there was no night there?

And another thing dawned upon him. There was no fireplace in either room. Was the season summer, and were these merely summer apartments, or was the whole city uniformly heated or cooled? He became interested in these questions, began examining the smooth texture of the walls, the simply constructed bed, the ingenious arrangements by which the labour

of bedroom service was practically abolished. And over everything was a curious absence of deliberate ornament, a bare grace of form and colour, that he found very pleasing to the eye. There were several very comfortable chairs, a light table on silent runners carrying several bottles of fluids and glasses, and two plates bearing a clear substance like jelly. Then he noticed there were no books, no newspapers, no writing materials. 'The world has changed indeed,' he said.

He observed one entire side of the outer room was set with rows of peculiar double cylinders inscribed with green lettering on white that harmonised with the decorative scheme of the room, and in the centre of this side projected a little apparatus about a yard square and having a white smooth face to the room. A chair faced this. He had a transitory idea that these cylinders might be books, or a modern substitute for books, but at first it did not seem so.

The lettering on the cylinders puzzled him. At first sight it seemed like Russian. Then he noticed a suggestion of mutilated English about certain of the words.

'Thi Man huwdbi Kin' forced itself on him as *The Man who would be King*. 'Phonetic spelling,' he said. He remembered reading a story with that title, then he recalled the story vividly, one of the best stories in the world. But this thing before him was not a book as he understood it. He puzzled out the titles of two adjacent cylinders. *The Heart of Darkness*, he had never heard of before nor *The Madonna of the Future* – no doubt if they were indeed stories, they were by post-Victorian authors.

He puzzled over this peculiar cylinder for some time and replaced it. Then he turned to the square apparatus and examined that. He opened a sort of lid and found one of the double cylinders within, and on the upper edge a little stud like the stud of an electric bell. He pressed this and a rapid clicking began and ceased. He became aware of voices and music, and noticed a play of colour on the smooth front face. He suddenly realised what this might be, and stepped back to regard it.

On the flat surface was now a little picture, very vividly coloured, and in this picture were figures that moved. Not only did they move, but they were conversing in clear small voices. It was exactly like reality viewed through an inverted opera glass and heard through a long tube. His interest was seized at once by the situation, which presented a man pacing up and down and vociferating angry things to a pretty but petulant woman. Both were in the picturesque costume that seemed so strange to Graham. 'I have worked,' said the man, 'but what have you been doing?'

'Ah!' said Graham. He forgot everything else, and sat down in the chair. Within five minutes he heard himself named, heard 'when the Sleeper wakes', used jestingly as a proverb for remote postponement, and passed himself by, a thing remote and incredible. But in a little while he knew those two people like intimate friends.

At last the miniature drama came to an end, and the square face of the apparatus was blank again.

It was a strange world into which he had been permitted to see, unscrupulous, pleasure seeking, energetic, subtle, a world too of dire economic struggle; there were allusions he did not understand, incidents that conveyed strange suggestions of altered moral ideals, flashes of dubious enlightenment. The blue canvas that bulked so largely in his first impression of the city ways appeared again and again as the costume of the common people. He had no doubt the story was contemporary, and its intense realism was undeniable. And the end had been a tragedy that oppressed him. He sat staring at the blankness.

He started and rubbed his eyes. He had been so absorbed in the latterday substitute for a novel, that he awoke to the little green and white room with more than a touch of the surprise of his first awakening.

He stood up, and abruptly he was back in his own wonderland. The clearness of the kinetoscope drama passed, and the struggle in the vast place of streets, the ambiguous Council, the swift phases of his waking hour, came back. These people had spoken of the Council with suggestions of a vague universality of power. And they had spoken of the Sleeper; it had not really struck him vividly at the time that he was the Sleeper. He had to recall precisely what they had said . . .

He walked into the bedroom and peered up through the quick intervals of the revolving fan. As the fan swept round, a dim turmoil like the noise of machinery came in rhythmic eddies. All else was silence. Though the perpetual day still irradiated his apartments, he perceived the little intermittent strip of sky was now deep blue – black almost, with a dust of little stars . . .

He resumed his examination of the rooms. He could find no way of opening the padded door, no bell nor other means of calling for attendance. His feeling of wonder was in abeyance; but he was curious, anxious for information. He wanted to know exactly how he stood to these new things. He tried to compose himself to wait until someone came to him. Presently he became restless and eager for information, for distraction, for fresh sensations.

He went back to the apparatus in the other room, and had soon puzzled out the method of replacing the cylinders by others. As he did so, it came into his mind that it must be these little appliances had fixed the language so that it was still clear and understandable after two hundred years. The haphazard cylinders he substituted displayed a musical fantasia. At first it was beautiful, and then it was sensuous. He presently recognised what appeared to him to be an altered version of the story of Tannhauser. The music was unfamiliar. But the rendering was realistic, and with a contemporary unfamiliarity. Tannhauser did not go to a Venusberg, but to a Pleasure City. What was a Pleasure City? A dream, surely, the fancy of a fantastic, voluptuous writer.

He became interested, curious. The story developed with a flavour of strangely twisted sentimentality. Suddenly he did not like it. He liked it less as it proceeded.

He had a revulsion of feeling. These were no pictures, no idealisations, but photographed realities. He wanted no more of the twenty-second-century Venusberg. He forgot the part played by the model in nineteenth-century art, and gave way to an archaic indignation. He rose, angry and half ashamed at himself for witnessing this thing even in solitude. He pulled forward the apparatus, and with some violence sought for a means of stopping its action. Something snapped. A violet spark stung and convulsed his arm and the thing was still. When he attempted next day to replace these Tannhauser cylinders by another pair, he found the apparatus broken . . .

He struck out a path oblique to the room and paced to and fro, struggling with intolerable vast impressions. The things he had derived from the cylinders and the things he had seen, conflicted, confused him. It seemed to him the most amazing thing of all that in his thirty years of life he had never tried to shape a picture of these coming times. 'We were making the future,' he said, 'and hardly any of us troubled to think what future we were making. And here it is!'

'What have they got to, what has been done? How do I come into the midst of it all?' The vastness of street and house he was prepared for, the multitudes of people. But conflicts in the city ways! And the systematised sensuality of a class of rich men!

He thought of Bellamy, the hero of whose Socialistic Utopia had so oddly anticipated this actual experience. But here was no Utopia, no Socialistic state. He had already seen enough to realise that the ancient antithesis of luxury, waste and sensuality on the one hand and abject poverty on the other, still prevailed. He knew enough of the essential factors of life to understand that correlation. And not only were the buildings of the city gigantic and the crowds in the street gigantic, but the voices he had heard in the ways, the uneasiness of Howard, the very atmosphere spoke of gigantic discontent. What country was he in? Still England it seemed, and yet strangely 'un-English'. His mind glanced at the rest of the world, and saw only an enigmatical veil.

He prowled about his apartment, examining everything as a caged animal might do. He felt very tired, felt that feverish exhaustion that does not admit of rest. He listened for long spaces under the ventilator to catch some distant echo of the tumults he felt must be proceeding in the city.

He began to talk to himself. 'Two hundred and three years!' he said to himself over and over again, laughing stupidly. 'Then I am two hundred and thirty-three years old! The oldest inhabitant. Surely they haven't reversed the tendency of our time and gone back to the rule of the oldest. My claims are indisputable. Mumble, mumble. I remember the Bulgarian

atrocities as though it was yesterday. 'Tis a great age! Ha ha!' He was surprised at first to hear himself laughing, and then laughed again deliberately and louder. Then he realised that he was behaving foolishly. 'Steady,' he said. 'Steady!'

His pacing became more regular. 'This new world,' he said. 'I don't understand it. *Why?* . . . But it is all *why!*'

'I suppose they can fly and do all sorts of things Let me try and remember just how it began.'

He was surprised at first to find how vague the memories of his first thirty years had become. He remembered fragments, for the most part trivial moments, things of no great importance that he had observed. His boyhood seemed the most accessible at first, he recalled school books and certain lessons in mensuration. Then he revived the more salient features of his life, memories of the wife long since dead, her magic influence now gone beyond corruption, of his rivals and friends and betrayers, of the swift decision of this issue and that, and then of his last years of misery, of fluctuating resolves, and at last of his strenuous studies. In a little while he perceived he had it all again; dim perhaps, like metal long laid aside, but in no way defective or injured, capable of re-polishing. And the hue of it was a deepening misery. Was it worth re-polishing? By a miracle he had been lifted out of a life that had become intolerable . . .

He reverted to his present condition. He wrestled with the facts in vain. It became an inextricable tangle. He saw the sky through the ventilator pink with dawn. An old persuasion came out of the dark recesses of his memory. 'I must sleep,' he said. It appeared as a delightful relief from this mental distress and from the growing pain and heaviness of his limbs. He went to the strange little bed, lay down and was presently asleep . . .

He was destined to become very familiar indeed with these apartments before he left them, for he remained imprisoned for three days. During that time no one, except Howard, entered his prison. The marvel of his fate mingled with and in some way minimised the marvel of his survival. He had awakened to mankind it seemed only to be snatched away into this unaccountable solitude. Howard came regularly with subtly sustaining and nutritive fluids, and light and pleasant foods, quite strange to Graham. He always closed the door carefully as he entered. On matters of detail he was increasingly obliging, but the bearing of Graham on the great issues that were evidently being contested so closely beyond the soundproof walls that enclosed him, he would not elucidate. He evaded, as politely as possible, every question on the position of affairs in the outer world.

And in those three days Graham's incessant thoughts went far and wide. All that he had seen, all this elaborate contrivance to prevent him seeing, worked together in his mind. Almost every possible interpretation of his position he debated – even as it chanced, the right interpretation. Things that presently happened to him, came to him at last credible, by

virtue of this seclusion. When at length the moment of his release arrived, it found him prepared . . .

Howard's bearing went far to deepen Graham's impression of his own strange importance; the door between its opening and closing seemed to admit with him a breath of momentous happening. His enquiries became more definite and searching. Howard retreated through protests and difficulties. The awakening was unforeseen, he repeated; it happened to have fallen in with the trend of a social convulsion. 'To explain it I must tell you the history of a gross and a half of years,' protested Howard.

'The thing is this,' said Graham. 'You are afraid of something I shall do. In some way I am arbitrator – I might be arbitrator.'

'It is not that. But you have – I may tell you this much – the automatic increase of your property puts great possibilities of interference in your hands. And in certain other ways you have influence, with your eighteenth-century notions.'

'Nineteenth-century,' corrected Graham.

'With your old-world notions, anyhow, ignorant as you are of every feature of our State.'

'Am I a fool?'

'Certainly not.'

'Do I seem to be the sort of man who would act rashly?'

'You were never expected to act at all. No one counted on your awakening. No one dreamt you would ever awake. The Council had surrounded you with antiseptic conditions. As a matter of fact, we thought that you were dead – a mere arrest of decay. And – but it is too complex. We dare not suddenly – while you are still half awake.'

'It won't do,' said Graham. 'Suppose it is as you say – why am I not being crammed night and day with facts and warnings and all the wisdom of the time to fit me for my responsibilities? Am I any wiser now than two days ago, if it is two days, when I awoke?'

Howard pulled his lip.

'I am beginning to feel – every hour I feel more clearly – a sense of complex concealment of which you are the salient point. Is this Council, or committee, or whatever they are, cooking the accounts of my estate? Is that it?'

'That note of suspicion – ' said Howard.

'Ugh!' said Graham. 'Now, mark my words, it will be ill for those who have put me here. It will be ill. I am alive. Make no doubt of it, I am alive. Every day my pulse is stronger and my mind clearer and more vigorous. No more quiescence. I am a man come back to life. And I want to *live* –'

'*Live!*'

Howard's face lit with an idea. He came towards Graham and spoke in an easy confidential tone.

'The Council secludes you here for your good. You are restless.

Naturally – an energetic man! You find it dull here. But we are anxious that everything you may desire – every desire – every sort of desire . . . There may be something. Is there any sort of company?'

He paused meaningly.

'Yes,' said Graham thoughtfully. 'There is.'

'Ah! *Now!* We have treated you neglectfully.'

'The crowds in yonder streets of yours.'

'That,' said Howard, 'I am afraid – . But – '

Graham began pacing the room. Howard stood near the door watching him. The implication of Howard's suggestion was only half evident to Graham. Company? Suppose he were to accept the proposal, demand some sort of *company?* Would there be any possibilities of gathering from the conversation of this additional person some vague inkling of the struggle that had broken out so vividly at his waking moment? He meditated again, and the suggestion took colour. He turned on Howard abruptly.

'What do you mean by company?'

Howard raised his eyes and shrugged his shoulders. 'Human beings,' he said, with a curious smile on his heavy face.

'Our social ideas,' he said, 'have a certain increased liberality, perhaps, in comparison with your times. If a man wishes to relieve such a tedium as this – by feminine society, for instance. We think it no scandal. We have cleared our minds of formulae. There is in our city a class, a necessary class, no longer despised – discreet – '

Graham stopped dead.

'It would pass the time,' said Howard. 'It is a thing I should perhaps have thought of before, but, as a matter of fact, so much is happening – '.

He indicated the exterior world.

Graham hesitated. For a moment the figure of a possible woman that his imagination suddenly created dominated his mind with an intense attraction. Then he flashed into anger.

'No!' he shouted.

He began striding rapidly up and down the room.

'Everything you say, everything you do, convinces me – of some great issue in which I am concerned. I do not want to pass the time, as you call it. Yes, I know. Desire and indulgence are life in a sense – and Death! Extinction! In my life before I slept I had worked out that pitiful question. I will not begin again. There is a city, a multitude – . And meanwhile I am here like a rabbit in a bag.'

His rage surged high. He choked for a moment and began to wave his clenched fists. He gave way to an anger fit, he swore archaic curses. His gestures had the quality of physical threats.

'I do not know who your party may be. I am in the dark, and you keep me in the dark. But I know this, that I am secluded here for no good purpose.

For no good purpose. I warn you, I warn you of the consequences. Once I come at my power – '

He realised that to threaten thus might be a danger to himself. He stopped. Howard stood regarding him with a curious expression.

'I take it this is a message to the Council,' said Howard.

Graham had a momentary impulse to leap upon the man, fell or stun him. It must have shown upon his face; at any rate Howard's movement was quick. In a second the noiseless door had closed again, and the man from the nineteenth century was alone.

For a moment he stood rigid, with clenched hands half raised. Then he flung them down. 'What a fool I have been!' he said, and gave way to his anger again, stamping about the room and shouting curses. For a long time he kept himself in a sort of frenzy, raging at his position, at his own folly, at the knaves who had imprisoned him. He did this because he did not want to look calmly at his position. He clung to his anger – because he was afraid of Fear.

Presently he found himself reasoning with himself This imprisonment was unaccountable, but no doubt the legal forms – new legal forms – of the time permitted it. It must, of course, be legal. These people were two hundred years further on in the march of civilisation than the Victorian generation. It was not likely they would be less – humane. Yet they had cleared their minds of formulae! Was humanity a formula as well as chastity?

His imagination set to work to suggest things that might be done to him. The attempts of his reason to dispose of these suggestions, though for the most part logically valid, were quite unavailing. 'Why should anything be done to me?'

'If the worst comes to the worst,' he found himself saying at last, 'I can give up what they want. But what do they want? And why don't they ask me for it instead of cooping me up?'

He returned to his former preoccupation with the Council's possible intentions. He began to reconsider the details of Howard's behaviour, sinister glances, inexplicable hesitations. Then, for a time, his mind circled about the idea of escaping from these rooms; but whither could he escape into this vast, crowded world? He would be worse off than a Saxon yeoman suddenly dropped into nineteenth-century London. And besides, how could anyone escape from these rooms?

'How can it benefit anyone if harm should happen to me?'

He thought of the tumult, the great social trouble of which he was so unaccountably the axis. A text, irrelevant enough and yet curiously insistent, came floating up out of the darkness of his memory. This also a Council had said: 'It is expedient for us that one man should die for the people.'

The Roof Spaces

As the fans in the circular aperture of the inner room rotated and permitted glimpses of the night, dim sounds drifted in thereby. And Graham, standing underneath, wrestling darkly with the unknown powers that imprisoned him, and which he had now deliberately challenged, was startled by the sound of a voice.

He peered up and saw in the intervals of the rotation, dark and dim, the face and shoulders of a man regarding him. When a dark hand was extended, the swift fan struck it, swung round and beat on with a little brownish patch on the edge of its thin blade, and something began to fall therefrom upon the floor, dripping silently.

Graham looked down, and there were spots of blood at his feet. He looked up again in a strange excitement. The figure had gone.

He remained motionless – his every sense intent upon the flickering patch of darkness, for outside it was high night. He became aware of some faint, remote, dark specks floating lightly through the outer air. They came down towards him, fitfully, eddyingly, and passed aside out of the uprush from the fan. A gleam of light flickered, the specks flashed white, and then the darkness came again. Warmed and lit as he was, he perceived that it was snowing within a few feet of him.

Graham walked across the room and came back to the ventilator again. He saw the head of a man pass near. There was a sound of whispering. Then a smart blow on some metallic substance, effort, voices, and the vans stopped. A gust of snowflakes whirled into the room, and vanished before they touched the floor. 'Don't be afraid,' said a voice.

Graham stood under the van. 'Who are you?' he whispered.

For a moment there was nothing but a swaying of the fan, and then the head of a man was thrust cautiously into the opening. His face appeared nearly inverted to Graham; his dark hair was wet with dissolving flakes of snow upon it. His arm went up into the darkness holding something unseen. He had a youthful face and bright eyes, and the veins of his forehead were swollen. He seemed to be exerting himself to maintain his position.

For several seconds neither he nor Graham spoke.

'You were the Sleeper?' said the stranger at last.

'Yes,' said Graham. 'What do you want with me?'

'I come from Ostrog, Sire.'

'Ostrog?'

The man in the ventilator twisted his head round so that his profile was

towards Graham. He appeared to be listening. Suddenly there was a hasty exclamation, and the intruder sprang back just in time to escape the sweep of the released fan. And when Graham peered up there was nothing visible but the slowly falling snow.

It was perhaps a quarter of an hour before anything returned to the ventilator. But at last came the same metallic interference again; the fans stopped and the face reappeared. Graham had remained all this time in the same place, alert and tremulously excited.

'Who are you? What do you want?' he said.

'We want to speak to you, Sire,' said the intruder. 'We want – I can't hold the thing. We have been trying to find a way to you – these three days.'

'Is it rescue?' whispered Graham. 'Escape?'

'Yes, Sire. If you will.'

'You are my party – the party of the Sleeper?'

'Yes, Sire.'

'What am I to do?' said Graham.

There was a struggle. The stranger's arm appeared, and his hand was bleeding. His knees came into view over the edge of the funnel. 'Stand away from me,' he said, and he dropped rather heavily on his hands and one shoulder at Graham's feet. The released ventilator whirled noisily. The stranger rolled over, sprang up nimbly and stood panting, hand to a bruised shoulder, and with his bright eyes on Graham.

'You are indeed the Sleeper,' he said. 'I saw you asleep. When it was the law that anyone might see you.'

'I am the man who was in the trance,' said Graham. 'They have imprisoned me here. I have been here since I awoke – at least three days.'

The intruder seemed about to speak, heard something, glanced swiftly at the door, and suddenly left Graham and ran towards it, shouting quick incoherent words. A bright wedge of steel flashed in his hand, and he began tap, tap, a quick succession of blows upon the hinges. 'Mind!' cried a voice. 'Oh!' The voice came from above.

Graham glanced up, saw the soles of two feet, ducked, was struck on the shoulder by one of them, and a heavy weight bore him to the earth. He fell on his knees and forward, and the weight went over his head. He knelt up and saw a second man from above seated before him.

'I did not see you, Sire,' panted the man. He rose and assisted Graham to arise. 'Are you hurt, Sire?' he panted. A succession of heavy blows on the ventilator began, something fell close to Graham's face, and a shivering edge of white metal danced, fell over, and lay flat upon the floor.

'What is this?' cried Graham, confused and looking at the ventilator. 'Who are you? What are you going to do? Remember, I understand nothing.'

'Stand back,' said the stranger, and drew him from under the ventilator as another fragment of metal fell heavily.

'We want you to come, Sire,' panted the newcomer, and Graham glancing at his face again, saw a new cut had changed from white to red on his forehead, and a couple of little trickles of blood starting therefrom. 'Your people call for you.'

'Come where? My people?'

'To the hall about the markets. Your life is in danger here. We have spies. We learned but just in time. The Council has decided – this very day – either to drug or kill you. And everything is ready. The people are drilled, the wind-vane police, the engineers, and half the way-gearers are with us. We have the halls crowded – shouting. The whole city shouts against the Council. We have arms.' He wiped the blood with his hand. 'Your life here is not worth – '

'But why arms?'

'The people have risen to protect you, Sire. What?'

He turned quickly as the man who had first come down made a hissing with his teeth. Graham saw the latter start back, gesticulate to them to conceal themselves, and move as if to hide behind the opening door.

As he did so Howard appeared, a little tray in one hand and his heavy face downcast. He started, looked up, the door slammed behind him, the tray tilted sideways, and the steel wedge struck him behind the ear. He went down like a felled tree, and lay as he fell athwart the floor of the outer room. The man who had struck him bent hastily, studied his face for a moment, rose, and returned to his work at the door.

'Your poison!' said a voice in Graham's ear.

Then abruptly they were in darkness. The innumerable cornice lights had been extinguished. Graham saw the aperture of the ventilator with ghostly snow whirling above it and dark figures moving hastily. Three knelt on the fan. Some dim thing – a ladder – was being lowered through the opening, and a hand appeared holding a fitful yellow light.

He had a moment of hesitation. But the manner of these men, their swift alacrity, their words, marched so completely with his own fears of the Council, with his idea and hope of a rescue, that it lasted not a moment. And his people awaited him!

'I do not understand,' he said, 'I trust. Tell me what to do.'

The man with the cut brow gripped Graham's arm.

'Clamber up the ladder,' he whispered. 'Quick. They will have heard – '

Graham felt for the ladder with extended hands, put his foot on the lower rung, and, turning his head, saw over the shoulder of the nearest man, in the yellow flicker of the light, the first-comer astride over Howard and still working at the door. Graham turned to the ladder again, and was thrust by his conductor and helped up by those above, and then he was standing on something hard and cold and slippery outside the ventilating funnel.

He shivered. He was aware of a great difference in the temperature. Half a dozen men stood about him, and light flakes of snow touched hands and

face and melted. For a moment it was dark, then for a flash a ghastly violet white, and then everything was dark again.

He saw he had come out upon the roof of the vast city structure which had replaced the miscellaneous houses, streets and open spaces of Victorian London. The place upon which he stood was level, with huge serpentine cables lying athwart it in every direction. The circular wheels of a number of windmills loomed indistinct and gigantic through the darkness and snowfall, and roared with a varying loudness as the fitful white light smote up from below, touched the snow eddies with a transient glitter, and made an evanescent spectre in the night; and here and there, low down, some vaguely outlined wind-driven mechanism flickered with livid sparks.

All this he appreciated in a fragmentary manner as his rescuers stood about him. Someone threw a thick soft cloak of fur-like texture about him, and fastened it by buckled straps at waist and shoulders. Things were said briefly, decisively. Someone thrust him forward.

Before his mind was yet clear a dark shape gripped his arm. 'This way,' said this shape, urging him along, and pointed Graham across the flat roof in the direction of a dim semicircular haze of light. Graham obeyed.

'Mind!' said a voice, as Graham stumbled against a cable. 'Between them and not across them,' said the voice. And, 'We must hurry.'

'Where are the people?' said Graham. 'The people you said awaited me?'

The stranger did not answer. He left Graham's arm as the path grew narrower, and led the way with rapid strides. Graham followed blindly. In a minute he found himself running. 'Are the others coming?' he panted, but received no reply. His companion glanced back and ran on. They came to a sort of pathway of open metalwork, transverse to the direction they had come, and they turned aside to follow this. Graham looked back, but the snowstorm had hidden the others.

'Come on!' said his guide. Running now, they drew near a little windmill spinning high in the air. 'Stoop,' said Graham's guide, and they avoided an endless band running roaring up to the shaft of the vane. 'This way!' and they were ankle deep in a gutter full of drifted thawing snow, between two low walls of metal that presently rose waist high. 'I will go first,' said the guide. Graham drew his cloak about him and followed. Then suddenly came a narrow abyss across which the gutter leapt to the snowy darkness of the further side. Graham peeped over the side once and the gulf was black. For a moment he regretted his flight. He dared not look again, and his brain spun as he waded through the half-liquid snow.

Then out of the gutter they clambered and hurried across a wide flat space damp with thawing snow, and for half its extent dimly translucent to lights that went to and fro underneath. He hesitated at this unstable-looking substance, but his guide ran on unheeding, and so they came to and clambered up slippery steps to the rim of a great dome of glass. Round this

they went. Far below a number of people seemed to be dancing, and music filtered through the dome . . . Graham fancied he heard a shouting through the snowstorm, and his guide hurried him on with a new spurt of haste. They clambered panting to a space of huge windmills, one so vast that only the lower edge of its vans came rushing into sight and rushed up again and was lost in the night and the snow. They hurried for a time through the colossal metallic tracery of its supports, and came at last above a place of moving platforms like the place into which Graham had looked from the balcony. They crawled across the sloping transparency that covered this street of platforms, crawling on hands and knees because of the slipperiness of the snowfall.

For the most part the glass was bedewed, and Graham saw only hazy suggestions of the forms below, but near the pitch of the transparent roof the glass was clear, and he found himself looking sheerly down upon it all. For awhile, in spite of the urgency of his guide, he gave way to vertigo and lay spread-eagled on the glass, sick and paralysed. Far below, mere stirring specks and dots, went the people of the unsleeping city in their perpetual daylight, and the moving platforms ran on their incessant journey. Messengers and men on unknown businesses shot along the drooping cables and the frail bridges were crowded with men. It was like peering into a gigantic glass hive, and it lay vertically below him with only a tough glass of unknown thickness to save him from a fall. The street showed warm and lit, and Graham was wet now to the skin with thawing snow, and his feet were numbed with cold. For a space he could not move. 'Come on!' cried his guide, with terror in his voice. 'Come on!'

Graham reached the pitch of the roof by an effort.

Over the ridge, following his guide's example, he turned about and slid backward down the opposite slope very swiftly, amid a little avalanche of snow. While he was sliding he thought of what would happen if some broken gap should come in his way. At the edge he stumbled to his feet ankle deep in slush, thanking heaven for an opaque footing again. His guide was already clambering up a metal screen to a level expanse.

Through the spare snowflakes above this loomed another line of vast windmills, and then suddenly the amorphous tumult of the rotating wheels was pierced with a deafening sound. It was a mechanical shrilling of extraordinary intensity that seemed to come simultaneously from every point of the compass.

'They have missed us already!' cried Graham's guide in an accent of terror, and suddenly, with a blinding flash, the night became day.

Above the driving snow, from the summits of the wind-wheels, appeared vast masts carrying globes of livid light. They receded in illimitable vistas in every direction. As far as his eye could penetrate the snowfall they glared.

'Get on this,' cried Graham's conductor, and thrust him forward to a

long grating of snowless metal that ran like a band between two slightly sloping expanses of snow. It felt warm to Graham's benumbed feet, and a faint eddy of steam rose from it.

'Come on!' shouted his guide ten yards off, and, without waiting, ran swiftly through the incandescent glare towards the iron supports of the next range of wind-wheels. Graham, recovering from his astonishment, followed as fast, convinced of his imminent capture . . .

In a score of seconds they were within a tracery of glare and black shadows shot with moving bars beneath the monstrous wheels. Graham's conductor ran on for some time, and suddenly darted sideways and vanished into a black shadow in the corner of the foot of a huge support. In another moment Graham was beside him.

They cowered panting and stared out.

The scene upon which Graham looked was very wild and strange. The snow had now almost ceased; only a belated flake passed now and again across the picture. But the broad stretch of level before them was a ghastly white, broken only by gigantic masses and moving shapes and lengthy strips of impenetrable darkness, vast ungainly Titans of shadow. All about them, huge metallic structures, iron girders, inhumanly vast as it seemed to him, interlaced, and the edges of wind-wheels, scarcely moving in the lull, passed in great shining curves steeper and steeper up into a luminous haze. Wherever the snow-spangled light struck down, beams and girders, and incessant bands running with a halting, indomitable resolution, passed upward and downward into the black. And with all that mighty activity, with an omnipresent sense of motive and design, this snow-clad desolation of mechanism seemed void of all human presence save themselves, seemed as trackless and deserted and unfrequented by men as some inaccessible Alpine snowfield.

'They will be chasing us,' cried the leader. 'We are scarcely halfway there yet. Cold as it is we must hide here for a space – at least until it snows more thickly again.'

His teeth chattered in his head.

'Where are the markets?' asked Graham staring out. 'Where are all the people?'

The other made no answer.

'*Look!*' whispered Graham, crouched close, and became very still.

The snow had suddenly become thick again, and sliding with the whirling eddies out of the black pit of the sky came something, vague and large and very swift. It came down in a steep curve and swept round, wide wings extended and a trail of white condensing steam behind it, rose with an easy swiftness and went gliding up the air, swept horizontally forward in a wide curve, and vanished again in the steaming specks of snow. And, through the ribs of its body, Graham saw two little men, very minute and active, searching the snowy areas about him, as it seemed to him, with field

glasses. For a second they were clear, then hazy through a thick whirl of snow, then small and distant, and in a minute they were gone.

'*Now!*' cried his companion. 'Come!'

He pulled Graham's sleeve, and incontinently the two were running headlong down the arcade of ironwork beneath the wind-wheels. Graham, running blindly, collided with his leader, who had turned back on him suddenly. He found himself within a dozen yards of a black chasm. It extended as far as he could see right and left. It seemed to cut off their progress in either direction.

'Do as I do,' whispered his guide. He lay down and crawled to the edge, thrust his head over and twisted until one leg hung. He seemed to feel for something with his foot, found it, and went sliding over the edge into the gulf. His head reappeared. 'It is a ledge,' he whispered. 'In the dark all the way along. Do as I did.'

Graham hesitated, went down upon all fours, crawled to the edge, and peered into a velvety blackness. For a sickly moment he had courage neither to go on nor retreat, then he sat and hung his leg down, felt his guide's hands pulling at him, had a horrible sensation of sliding over the edge into the unfathomable, splashed, and felt himself in a slushy gutter, impenetrably dark.

'This way,' whispered the voice, and he began crawling along the gutter through the trickling thaw, pressing himself against the wall. They continued along it for some minutes. He seemed to pass through a hundred stages of misery, to pass minute after minute through a hundred degrees of cold, damp, and exhaustion. In a little while he ceased to feel his hands and feet.

The gutter sloped downwards. He observed that they were now many feet below the edge of the buildings. Rows of spectral white shapes like the ghosts of blind-drawn windows rose above them. They came to the end of a cable fastened above one of these white windows, dimly visible and dropping into impenetrable shadows. Suddenly his hand came against his guide's. '*Still!*' whispered the latter very softly.

He looked up with a start and saw the huge wings of the flying machine gliding slowly and noiselessly overhead athwart the broad band of snow-flecked grey-blue sky. In a moment it was hidden again.

'Keep still; they were just turning.'

For awhile both were motionless, then Graham's companion stood up, and reaching towards the fastenings of the cable fumbled with some indistinct tackle.

'What is that?' asked Graham.

The only answer was a faint cry. The man crouched motionless. Graham peered and saw his face dimly. He was staring down the long ribbon of sky, and Graham, following his eyes, saw the flying machine small and faint and remote. Then he saw that the wings spread on either side, that it headed

towards them, that every moment it grew larger. It was following the edge of the chasm towards them.

The man's movements became convulsive. He thrust two cross bars into Graham's hand. Graham could not see them, he ascertained their form by feeling. They were slung by thin cords to the cable. On the cord were hand grips of some soft elastic substance. 'Put the cross between your legs,' whispered the guide hysterically, 'and grip the holdfasts. Grip tightly, grip!'

Graham did as he was told.

'Jump,' said the voice. 'In heaven's name, jump!'

For one momentous second Graham could not speak. He was glad afterwards that darkness hid his face. He said nothing. He began to tremble violently. He looked sideways at the swift shadow that swallowed up the sky as it rushed upon him.

'Jump! Jump – in God's name! Or they will have us,' cried Graham's guide, and in the violence of his passion thrust him forward.

Graham tottered convulsively, gave a sobbing cry, a cry in spite of himself, and then, as the flying machine swept over them, fell forward into the pit of that darkness, seated on the cross wood and holding the ropes with the clutch of death. Something cracked, something rapped smartly against a wall. He heard the pulley of the cradle hum on its rope. He heard the aeronauts shout. He felt a pair of knees digging into his back . . . He was sweeping headlong through the air, falling through the air. All his strength was in his hands. He would have screamed but he had no breath.

He shot into a blinding light that made him grip the tighter. He recognised the great passage with the running ways, the hanging lights and interlacing girders. They rushed upward and by him. He had a momentary impression of a great circular aperture yawning to swallow him up.

He was in the dark again, falling, falling, gripping with aching hands, and behold! a clap of sound, a burst of light, and he was in a brightly lit hall with a roaring multitude of people beneath his feet. The people! His people! A proscenium, a stage rushed up towards him, and his cable swept down to a circular aperture to the right of this. He felt he was travelling slower, and suddenly very much slower. He distinguished shouts of 'Saved! The Master. He is safe!' The stage rushed up towards him with rapidly diminishing swiftness. Then –

He heard the man clinging behind him shout as if suddenly terrified, and this shout was echoed by a shout from below. He felt that he was no longer gliding along the cable but falling with it. There was a tumult of yells, screams and cries. He felt something soft against his extended hand, and the impact of a broken fall quivering through his arm . . .

He wanted to be still and the people were lifting him. He believed afterwards he was carried to the platform and given some drink, but he was never sure. He did not notice what became of his guide. When his mind was clear again he was on his feet; eager hands were assisting him to stand. He

was in a big alcove, occupying the position that in his previous experience had been devoted to the lower boxes. If this was indeed a theatre.

A mighty tumult was in his ears, a thunderous roar, the shouting of a countless multitude. 'It is the Sleeper! The Sleeper is with us!'

'The Sleeper is with us! The Master – the Owner! The Master is with us. He is safe.'

Graham had a surging vision of a great hall crowded with people. He saw no individuals, he was conscious of a froth of pink faces, of waving arms and garments, he felt the occult influence of a vast crowd pouring over him, buoying him up. There were balconies, galleries, great archways giving remoter perspectives, and everywhere people, a vast arena of people, densely packed and cheering. Across the nearer space lay the collapsed cable like a huge snake. It had been cut by the men of the flying machine at its upper end, and had crumpled down into the hall. Men seemed to be hauling this out of the way. But the whole effect was vague, the very buildings throbbed and leapt with the roar of the voices.

He stood unsteadily and looked at those about him. Someone supported him by one arm. 'Let me go into a little room,' he said, weeping; 'a little room,' and could say no more. A man in black stepped forward, took his disengaged arm. He was aware of officious men opening a door before him. Someone guided him to a seat. He staggered. He sat down heavily and covered his face with his hands; he was trembling violently, his nervous control was at an end. He was relieved of his cloak, he could not remember how; his purple hose he saw were black with wet. People were running about him, things were happening, but for some time he gave no heed to them.

He had escaped. A myriad of cries told him that. He was safe. These were the people who were on his side. For a space he sobbed for breath, and then he sat still with his face covered. The air was full of the shouting of innumerable men.

CHAPTER NINE

The People March

He became aware of someone urging a glass of clear fluid upon his attention, looked up and discovered this was a dark young man in a yellow garment. He took the dose forthwith, and in a moment he was glowing. A tall man in a black robe stood by his shoulder, and pointed to the half-open door into the hall. This man was shouting close to his ear and yet what was said was indistinct because of the tremendous uproar from the great theatre. Behind the man was a girl in a silvery grey robe, whom Graham, even in this confusion, perceived to be beautiful. Her dark eyes, full of wonder and

curiosity, were fixed on him, her lips trembled apart. A partially opened door gave a glimpse of the crowded hall, and admitted a vast uneven tumult, a hammering, clapping and shouting that died away and began again, and rose to a thunderous pitch, and so continued intermittently all the time that Graham remained in the little room. He watched the lips of the man in black and gathered that he was making some clumsy explanation.

He stared stupidly for some moments at these things and then stood up abruptly; he grasped the arm of this shouting person.

'Tell me!' he cried. 'Who am I? Who am I?'

The others came nearer to hear his words. 'Who am I?' His eyes searched their faces.

'They have told him nothing!' cried the girl.

'Tell me, tell me!' cried Graham.

'You are the Master of the Earth. You are owner of half the world.'

He did not believe he heard aright. He resisted the persuasion. He pretended not to understand, not to hear. He lifted his voice again. 'I have been awake three days – a prisoner three days. I judge there is some struggle between a number of people in this city – it is London?'

'Yes,' said the younger man.

'And those who meet in the great hall with the white Atlas? How does it concern me? In some way it has to do with me. Why, I don't know. Drugs? It seems to me that while I have slept the world has gone mad. I have gone mad.

'Who are those Councillors under the Atlas? Why should they try to drug me?'

'To keep you insensible,' said the man in yellow. 'To prevent your interference.'

'But *why*?'

'Because *you* are the Atlas, Sire,' said the man in yellow. 'The world is on your shoulders. They rule it in your name.'

The sounds from the hall had died into a silence threaded by one monotonous voice. Now suddenly, trampling on these last words, came a deafening tumult, a roaring and thundering, cheer crowded on cheer, voices hoarse and shrill, beating, overlapping, and while it lasted the people in the little room could not hear each other shout.

Graham stood, his intelligence clinging helplessly to the thing he had just heard. 'The Council,' he repeated blankly, and then snatched at a name that had struck him. 'But who is Ostrog?' he said.

'He is the organiser – the organiser of the revolt. Our Leader – in your name.'

'In my name? – And you? Why is he not here?'

'He – has deputed us. I am his brother – his half-brother, Lincoln. He wants you to show yourself to these people and then come on to him. That is why he has sent. He is at the wind-vane offices directing. The people are marching.'

'In your name,' shouted the younger man. 'They have ruled, crushed, tyrannised. At last even – '

'In my name! My name! Master?'

The younger man suddenly became audible in a pause of the outer thunder, indignant and vociferous, a high penetrating voice under his red aquiline nose and bushy moustache. 'No one expected you to wake. No one expected you to wake. They were cunning. Damned tyrants! But they were taken by surprise. They did not know whether to drug you, hypnotise you, kill you.'

Again the hall dominated everything.

'Ostrog is at the wind-vane offices ready – . Even now there is a rumour of fighting beginning.'

The man who had called himself Lincoln came close to him. 'Ostrog has it planned. Trust him. We have our organisations ready. We shall seize the flying stages – . Even now he may be doing that. Then – '

'This public theatre,' bawled the man in yellow, 'is only a contingent. We have five myriads of drilled men – '

'We have arms,' cried Lincoln. 'We have plans. A leader. Their police have gone from the streets and are massed in the – ' (inaudible). 'It is now or never. The Council is rocking – They cannot trust even their drilled men – '

'Hear the people calling to you!'

Graham's mind was like a night of moon and swift clouds, now dark and hopeless, now clear and ghastly. He was Master of the Earth, he was a man sodden with thawing snow. Of all his fluctuating impressions the dominant ones presented an antagonism; on the one hand was the White Council, powerful, disciplined, few, the White Council from which he had just escaped; and on the other, monstrous crowds, packed masses of indistinguishable people clamouring his name, hailing him Master. The other side had imprisoned him, debated his death. These shouting thousands beyond the little doorway had rescued him. But why these things should be so he could not understand.

The door opened, Lincoln's voice was swept away and drowned, and a rush of people followed on the heels of the tumult. These intruders came towards him and Lincoln gesticulating. The voices without explained their soundless lips. 'Show us the Sleeper, show us the Sleeper!' was the burden of the uproar. Men were bawling for 'Order! Silence!'

Graham glanced towards the open doorway, and saw a tall, oblong picture of the hall beyond, a waving, incessant confusion of crowded, shouting faces, men and women together, waving pale blue garments, extended hands. Many were standing, one man in rags of dark brown, a gaunt figure, stood on the seat and waved a black cloth. He met the wonder and expectation of the girl's eyes. What did these people expect from him? He was dimly aware that the tumult outside had changed its character, was

in some way beating, marching. His own mind, too, changed. For a space he did not recognise the influence that was transforming him. But a moment that was near to panic passed. He tried to make audible enquiries of what was required of him.

Lincoln was shouting in his ear, but Graham was deafened to that. All the others save the woman gesticulated towards the hall. He perceived what had happened to the uproar. The whole mass of people was chanting together. It was not simply a song, the voices were gathered together and upborne by a torrent of instrumental music, music like the music of an organ, a woven texture of sounds, full of trumpets, full of flaunting banners, full of the march and pageantry of opening war. And the feet of the people were beating time – tramp, tramp.

He was urged towards the door. He obeyed mechanically. The strength of that chant took hold of him, stirred him, emboldened him. The hall opened to him, a vast welter of fluttering colour swaying to the music.

'Wave your arm to them,' said Lincoln. 'Wave your arm to them.'

'This,' said a voice on the other side, 'he must have this.' Arms were about his neck detaining him in the doorway, and a black subtly folding mantle hung from his shoulders. He threw his arm free of this and followed Lincoln. He perceived the girl in grey close to him, her face lit, her gesture onward. For the instant she became to him, flushed and eager as she was, an embodiment of the song. He emerged in the alcove again. Incontinently the mounting waves of the song broke upon his appearing, and flashed up into a foam of shouting. Guided by Lincoln's hand he marched obliquely across the centre of the stage facing the people.

The hall was a vast and intricate space – galleries, balconies, broad spaces of amphitheatral steps, and great archways. Far away, high up, seemed the mouth of a huge passage full of struggling humanity. The whole multitude was swaying in congested masses. Individual figures sprang out of the tumult, impressed him momentarily, and lost definition again. Close to the platform swayed a beautiful fair woman, carried by three men, her hair across her face and brandishing a green staff. Next this group an old careworn man in blue canvas maintained his place in the crush with difficulty, and behind shouted a hairless face, a great cavity of toothless mouth. A voice called that enigmatical word 'Ostrog'. All his impressions were vague save the massive emotion of that trampling song. The multitude were beating time with their feet – marking time, tramp, tramp, tramp, tramp. The green weapons waved, flashed and slanted. Then he saw those nearest to him on a level space before the stage were marching in front of him, passing towards a great archway, shouting 'To the Council!' Tramp, tramp, tramp, tramp. He raised his arm, and the roaring was redoubled. He remembered he had to shout 'March!' His mouth shaped inaudible heroic words. He waved his arm again and pointed to the archway, shouting 'Onward!' They were no longer marking time, they were marching; tramp,

tramp, tramp, tramp. In that host were bearded men, old men, youths, fluttering robed bare-armed women, girls. Men and women of the new age! Rich robes, grey rags fluttered together in the whirl of their movement amidst the dominant blue. A monstrous black banner jerked its way to the right. He perceived a blue-clad negro, a shrivelled woman in yellow, then a group of tall fair-haired, white-faced, blue-clad men pushed theatrically past him. He noted two Chinamen. A tall, sallow, dark-haired, shining-eyed youth, white clad from top to toe, clambered up towards the platform shouting loyally, and sprang down again and receded, looking backward. Heads, shoulders, hands clutching weapons, all were swinging with those marching cadences.

Faces came out of the confusion to him as he stood there, eyes met his and passed and vanished. Men gesticulated to him, shouted inaudible personal things. Most of the faces were flushed, but many were ghastly white. And disease was there, and many a hand that waved to him was gaunt and lean. Men and women of the new age! Strange and incredible meeting! As the broad stream passed before him to the right, tributary gangways from the remote uplands of the hall thrust downward in an incessant replacement of people; tramp, tramp, tramp, tramp. The unison of the song was enriched and complicated by the massive echoes of arches and passages. Men and women mingled in the ranks; tramp, tramp, tramp, tramp. The whole world seemed marching. Tramp, tramp, tramp, tramp; his brain was tramping. The garments waved onward, the faces poured by more abundantly.

Tramp, tramp, tramp, tramp; at Lincoln's pressure he turned towards the archway, walking unconsciously in that rhythm, scarcely noticing his movement for the melody and stir of it. The multitude, the gesture and song, all moved in that direction, the flow of people smote downward until the upturned faces were below the level of his feet. He was aware of a path before him, of a suite about him, of guards and dignities, and Lincoln on his right hand. Attendants intervened, and ever and again blotted out the sight of the multitude to the left. Before him went the backs of the guards in black – three and three and three. He was marched along a little railed way, and crossed above the archway, with the torrent dipping to flow beneath, and shouting up to him. He did not know whither he went; he did not want to know. He glanced back across a flaming spaciousness of hall. Tramp, tramp, tramp, tramp.

CHAPTER TEN

The Battle of the Darkness

He was no longer in the hall. He was marching along a gallery overhanging one of the great streets of the moving platforms that traversed the city. Before him and behind him tramped his guards. The whole concave of the moving ways below was a congested mass of people marching, tramping to the left, shouting, waving hands and arms, pouring along a huge vista, shouting as they came into view, shouting as they passed, shouting as they receded, until the globes of electric light receding in perspective dropped down it seemed and hid the swarming bare heads. Tramp, tramp, tramp, tramp.

The song roared up to Graham now, no longer upborne by music, but coarse and noisy, and the beating of the marching feet, tramp, tramp, tramp, tramp, interwove with a thunderous irregularity of footsteps from the undisciplined rabble that poured along the higher ways.

Abruptly he noted a contrast. The buildings on the opposite side of the way seemed deserted, the cables and bridges that laced across the aisle were empty and shadowy. It came into Graham's mind that these also should have swarmed with people.

He felt a curious emotion – throbbing – very fast! He stopped again. The guards before him marched on; those about him stopped as he did. He saw the direction of their faces. The throbbing had something to do with the lights. He too looked up.

At first it seemed to him a thing that affected the lights simply, an isolated phenomenon, having no bearing on the things below. Each huge globe of blinding whiteness was as it were clutched, compressed in a systole that was followed by a transitory diastole, and again a systole like a tightening grip, darkness, light, darkness, in rapid alternation.

Graham became aware that this strange behaviour of the lights had to do with the people below. The appearance of the houses and ways, the appearance of the packed masses changed, became a confusion of vivid lights and leaping shadows. He saw a multitude of shadows had sprung into aggressive existence, seemed rushing up, broadening, widening, growing with steady swiftness – to leap suddenly back and return reinforced. The song and the tramping had ceased. The unanimous march, he discovered, was arrested, there were eddies, a flow sideways, shouts of 'The lights!' Voices were crying together one thing. 'The lights!' cried these voices. 'The lights!' He looked down. In this dancing death of the lights the area of the street had suddenly become a monstrous struggle. The huge white globes became purple-white, purple with a reddish glow, flickered, flickered

faster and faster, fluttered between light and extinction, ceased to flicker and became mere fading specks of glowing red in a vast obscurity. In ten seconds the extinction was accomplished, and there was only this roaring darkness, a black monstrosity that had suddenly swallowed up those glittering myriads of men.

He felt invisible forms about him; his arms were gripped. Something rapped sharply against his shin. A voice bawled in his ear, 'It is all right – all right.'

Graham shook off the paralysis of his first astonishment. He struck his forehead against Lincoln's and bawled, 'What is this darkness?'

'The Council has cut the currents that light the city. We must wait – stop. The people will go on. They will – '

His voice was drowned. Voices were shouting, 'Save the Sleeper. Take care of the Sleeper.' A guard stumbled against Graham and hurt his hand by an inadvertent blow of his weapon. A wild tumult tossed and whirled about him, growing, as it seemed, louder, denser, more furious each moment. Fragments of recognisable sounds drove towards him, were whirled away from him as his mind reached out to grasp them. Voices seemed to be shouting conflicting orders, other voices answered. There were suddenly a succession of piercing screams close beneath them.

A voice bawled in his ear, 'The red police,' and receded forthwith beyond his questions.

A crackling sound grew to distinctness, and therewith a leaping of faint flashes along the edge of the further ways. By their light Graham saw the heads and bodies of a number of men, armed with weapons like those of his guards, leap into an instant's dim visibility. The whole area began to crackle, to flash with little instantaneous streaks of light, and abruptly the darkness rolled back like a curtain.

A glare of light dazzled his eyes, a vast seething expanse of struggling men confused his mind. A shout, a burst of cheering, came across the ways. He looked up to see the source of the light. A man hung far overhead from the upper part of a cable, holding by a rope the blinding star that had driven the darkness back. He wore a red uniform.

Graham's eyes fell to the ways again. A wedge of red a little way along the vista caught his eye. He saw it was a dense mass of red-clad men jammed on the higher further way, their backs against the pitiless cliff of building, and surrounded by a dense crowd of antagonists. They were fighting. Weapons flashed and rose and fell, heads vanished at the edge of the contest, and other heads replaced them, the little flashes from the green weapons became little jets of smoky grey while the light lasted.

Abruptly the flare was extinguished and the ways were an inky darkness once more, a tumultuous mystery.

He felt something thrusting against him. He was being pushed along the gallery. Someone was shouting – it might be at him. He was too confused to

hear. He was thrust against the wall, and a number of people blundered past him. It seemed to him that his guards were struggling with one another.

Suddenly the cable-hung star-holder appeared again, and the whole scene was white and dazzling. The band of red-coats seemed broader and nearer; its apex was halfway down the ways towards the central aisle. And raising his eyes Graham saw that a number of these men had also appeared now in the darkened lower galleries of the opposite building, and were firing over the heads of their fellows below at the boiling confusion of people on the lower ways. The meaning of these things dawned upon him. The march of the people had come upon an ambush at the very outset. Thrown into confusion by the extinction of the lights they were now being attacked by the red police. Then he became aware that he was standing alone, that his guards and Lincoln were along the gallery in the direction along which he had come before the darkness fell. He saw they were gesticulating to him wildly, running back towards him. A great shouting came from across the ways. Then it seemed as though the whole face of the darkened building opposite was lined and speckled with red-clad men. And they were pointing over to him and shouting. 'The Sleeper! Save the Sleeper!' shouted a multitude of throats.

Something struck the wall above his head. He looked up at the impact and saw a star-shaped splash of silvery metal. He saw Lincoln near him. Felt his arm gripped. Then, pat, pat; he had been missed twice.

For a moment he did not understand this. The street was hidden, everything was hidden, as he looked. The second flare had burned out.

Lincoln had gripped Graham by the arm, was lugging him along the gallery. 'Before the next light!' he cried. His haste was contagious. Graham's instinct of self-preservation overcame the paralysis of his incredulous astonishment. He became for a time the blind creature of the fear of death. He ran, stumbling because of the uncertainty of the darkness, blundered into his guards as they turned to run with him. Haste was his one desire, to escape this perilous gallery upon which he was exposed. A third glare came close on its predecessors. With it came a great shouting across the ways, an answering tumult from the ways. The red-coats below, he saw, had now almost gained the central passage. Their countless faces turned towards him, and they shouted. The white façade opposite was densely stippled with red. All these wonderful things concerned him, turned upon him as a pivot. These were the guards of the Council attempting to recapture him.

Lucky it was for him that these shots were the first fired in anger for a hundred and fifty years. He heard bullets whacking over his head, felt a splash of molten metal sting his ear, and perceived without looking that the whole opposite façade, an unmasked ambuscade of red police, was crowded and bawling and firing at him.

Down went one of his guards before him, and Graham, unable to stop, leapt the writhing body.

In another second he had plunged, unhurt, into a black passage, and incontinently someone, coming, it may be, in a transverse direction, blundered violently into him. He was hurling down a staircase in absolute darkness. He reeled, and was struck again, and came against a wall with his hands. He was crushed by a weight of struggling bodies, whirled round, and thrust to the right. A vast pressure pinned him. He could not breathe, his ribs seemed cracking. He felt a momentary relaxation, and then the whole mass of people moving together, bore him back towards the great theatre from which he had so recently come. There were moments when his feet did not touch the ground. Then he was staggering and shoving. He heard shouts of 'They are coming!' and a muffled cry close to him. His foot blundered against something soft, he heard a hoarse scream under foot. He heard shouts of 'The Sleeper!' but he was too confused to speak. He heard the green weapons crackling. For a space he lost his individual will, became an atom in a panic, blind, unthinking, mechanical. He thrust and pressed back and writhed in the pressure, kicked presently against a step, and found himself ascending a slope. And abruptly the faces all about him leapt out of the black, visible, ghastly-white and astonished, terrified, perspiring, in a livid glare. One face, a young man's, was very near to him, not twenty inches away. At the time it was but a passing incident of no emotional value, but afterwards it came back to him in his dreams. For this young man, wedged upright in the crowd for a time, had been shot and was already dead.

A fourth white star must have been lit by the man on the cable. Its light came glaring in through vast windows and arches and showed Graham that he was now one of a dense mass of flying black figures pressed back across the lower area of the great theatre. This time the picture was livid and fragmentary, slashed and barred with black shadows. He saw that quite near to him the red guards were fighting their way through the people. He could not tell whether they saw him. He looked for Lincoln and his guards. He saw Lincoln near the stage of the theatre surrounded in a crowd of black-badged revolutionaries, lifted up and staring to and fro as if seeking him. Graham perceived that he himself was near the opposite edge of the crowd, that behind him, separated by a barrier, sloped the now vacant seats of the theatre. A sudden idea came to him, and he began fighting his way towards the barrier. As he reached it the glare came to an end.

In a moment he had thrown off the great cloak that not only impeded his movements but made him conspicuous, and had slipped it from his shoulders. He heard someone trip in its folds. In another he was scaling the barrier and had dropped into the blackness on the further side. Then feeling his way he came to the lower end of an ascending gangway. In the darkness the sound of firing ceased and the roar of feet and voices lulled. Then suddenly he came to an unexpected step and tripped and fell. As he did so pools and islands amidst the darkness about him leapt to vivid light

again, the uproar surged louder and the glare of the fifth white star shone through the vast fenestrations of the theatre walls.

He rolled over among some seats, heard a shouting and the whirring rattle of weapons, struggled up and was knocked back again, perceived that a number of black-badged men were all about him firing at the rebels below, leaping from seat to seat, crouching among the seats to reload. Instinctively he crouched amidst the seats, as stray shots ripped the pneumatic cushions and cut bright slashes on their soft metal frames. Instinctively he marked the direction of the gangways, the most plausible way of escape for him so soon as the veil of darkness fell again.

A young man in faded blue garments came vaulting over the seats. 'Hullo!' he said, with his flying feet within six inches of the crouching Sleeper's face.

He stared without any sign of recognition, turned to fire, fired, and, shouting, 'To hell with the Council!' was about to fire again. Then it seemed to Graham that the half of this man's neck had vanished. A drop of moisture fell on Graham's cheek. The green weapon stopped half raised. For a moment the man stood still with his face suddenly expressionless, then he began to slant forward. His knees bent. Man and darkness fell together. At the sound of his fall Graham rose up and ran for his life until a step down to the gangway tripped him. He scrambled to his feet, turned up the gangway and ran on.

When the sixth star glared he was already close to the yawning throat of a passage. He ran on the swifter for the light, entered the passage and turned a corner into absolute night again. He was knocked sideways, rolled over, and recovered his feet. He found himself one of a crowd of invisible fugitives pressing in one direction. His one thought now was their thought also: to escape out of this fighting. He thrust and struck, staggered, ran, was wedged tightly, lost ground and then was clear again.

For some minutes he was running through the darkness along a winding passage, and then he crossed some wide and open space, passed down a long incline, and came at last down a flight of steps to a level place. Many people were shouting, 'They are coming! The guards are coming. They are firing. Get out of the fighting. The guards are firing. It will be safe in Seventh Way. Along here to Seventh Way!' There were women and children in the crowd as well as men. Men called names to him. The crowd converged on an archway, passed through a short throat and emerged on a wider space again, lit dimly. The black figures about him spread out and ran up what seemed in the twilight to be a gigantic series of steps. He followed. The people dispersed to the right and left . . . He perceived that he was no longer in a crowd. He stopped near the highest step. Before him, on that level, were groups of seats and a little kiosk. He went up to this and, stopping in the shadow of its eaves, looked about him panting.

Everything was vague and grey, but he recognised that these great steps

were a series of platforms of the 'ways', now motionless again. The platform slanted up on either side, and the tall buildings rose beyond, vast dim ghosts, their inscriptions and advertisements indistinctly seen, and up through the girders and cables was a faint interrupted ribbon of pallid sky. A number of people hurried by. From their shouts and voices, it seemed they were hurrying to join the fighting. Other less noisy figures flitted timidly among the shadows.

From very far away down the street he could hear the sound of a struggle. But it was evident to him that this was not the street into which the theatre opened. That former fight, it seemed, had suddenly dropped out of sound and hearing. And – grotesque thought! – they were fighting for him!

For a space he was like a man who pauses in the reading of a vivid book, and suddenly doubts what he has been taking unquestioningly. At that time he had little mind for details; the whole effect was a huge astonishment. Oddly enough, while the flight from the Council prison, the great crowd in the hall, and the attack of the red police upon the swarming people were clearly present in his mind, it cost him an effort to piece in his awakening and to revive the meditative interval of the Silent Rooms. At first his memory leapt these things and took him back to the cascade at Pentargen quivering in the wind, and all the sombre splendours of the sunlit Cornish coast. The contrast touched everything with unreality. And then the gap filled, and he began to comprehend his position.

It was no longer absolutely a riddle, as it had been in the Silent Rooms. At least he had the strange, bare outline now. He was in some way the owner of half the world, and great political parties were fighting to possess him. On the one hand was the White Council, with its red police, set resolutely, it seemed, on the usurpation of his property and perhaps his murder; on the other, the revolution that had liberated him, with this unseen 'Ostrog' as its leader. And the whole of this gigantic city was convulsed by their struggle. Frantic development of his world! 'I do not understand,' he cried. 'I do not understand!'

He had slipped out between the contending parties into this liberty of the twilight. What would happen next? What was happening? He figured the red-clad men as busily hunting him, driving the black-badged revolutionists before them.

At any rate chance had given him a breathing space. He could lurk unchallenged by the passers-by, and watch the course of things. His eye followed up the intricate dim immensity of the twilight buildings, and it came to him as a thing infinitely wonderful, that above there the sun was rising, and the world was lit and glowing with the old familiar light of day. In a little while he had recovered his breath. His clothing had already dried upon him from the snow.

He wandered for miles along these twilight ways, speaking to no one,

accosted by no one – a dark figure among dark figures – the coveted man out of the past, the inestimable unintentional owner of half the world. Wherever there were lights or dense crowds, or exceptional excitement he was afraid of recognition, and watched and turned back or went up and down by the middle stairways, into some transverse system of ways at a lower or higher level. And though he came on no more fighting, the whole city stirred with battle. Once he had to run to avoid a marching multitude of men that swept the street. Everyone abroad seemed involved. For the most part they were men, and they carried what he judged were weapons. It seemed as though the struggle was concentrated mainly in the quarter of the city from which he came. Ever and again a distant roaring, the remote suggestion of that conflict, reached his ears. Then his caution and his curiosity struggled together. But his caution prevailed, and he continued wandering away from the fighting – so far as he could judge. He went unmolested, unsuspected through the dark. After a time he ceased to hear even a remote echo of the battle, fewer and fewer people passed him, until at last the Titanic streets became deserted. The frontages of the buildings grew plain and harsh; he seemed to have come to a district of vacant warehouses. Solitude crept upon him – his pace slackened.

He became aware of a growing fatigue. At times he would turn aside and seat himself on one of the numerous seats of the upper ways. But a feverish restlessness, the knowledge of his vital implication in his struggle, would not let him rest in any place for long. Was the struggle on his behalf alone?

And then in a desolate place came the shock of an earthquake – a roaring and thundering – a mighty wind of cold air pouring through the city, the smash of glass, the slip and thud of falling masonry – a series of gigantic concussions. A mass of glass and ironwork fell from the remote roofs into the middle gallery, not a hundred yards away from him, and in the distance were shouts and running. He, too, was startled to an aimless activity, and ran first one way and then as aimlessly back.

A man came running towards him. His self-control returned. 'What have they blown up?' asked the man breathlessly. 'That was an explosion,' and before Graham could speak he had hurried on.

The great buildings rose dimly, veiled by a perplexing twilight, albeit the rivulet of sky above was now bright with day. He noted many strange features, understanding none at the time; he even spelt out many of the inscriptions in Phonetic lettering. But what profits it to decipher a confusion of odd-looking letters resolving itself, after painful strain of eye and mind, into 'Here is Eadhamite', or, 'Labour Bureau – Little Side'? Grotesque thought, that in all probability some or all of these cliff-like houses were his!

The perversity of his experience came to him vividly. In actual fact he had made such a leap in time as romancers have imagined again and again. And that fact realised, he had been prepared, his mind had, as it were, seated itself for a spectacle. And no spectacle, but a great vague danger,

unsympathetic shadows and veils of darkness. Somewhere through the labyrinthine obscurity his death sought him. Would he, after all, be killed before he saw? It might be that even at the next shadowy corner his destruction ambushed. A great desire to see, a great longing to know, arose in him.

He became fearful of corners. It seemed to him that there was safety in concealment. Where could he hide to be inconspicuous when the lights returned? At last he sat down upon a seat in a recess on one of the higher ways, conceiving he was alone there.

He squeezed his knuckles into his weary eyes. Suppose when he looked again he found the dark trough of parallel ways and that intolerable altitude of edifice, gone? Suppose he were to discover the whole story of these last few days, the awakening, the shouting multitudes, the darkness and the fighting, a phantasmagoria, a new and more vivid sort of dream. It must be a dream; it was so inconsecutive, so reasonless. Why were the people fighting for him? Why should this saner world regard him as Owner and Master?

So he thought, sitting blinded, and then he looked again, half hoping in spite of his fears to see some familiar aspect of the life of the nineteenth century, to see, perhaps, the little harbour of Boscastle about him, the cliffs of Pentargen, or the bedroom of his home. But fact takes no heed of human hopes. A squad of men with a black banner tramped athwart the nearer shadows, intent on conflict, and beyond rose that giddy wall of frontage, vast and dark, with the dim incomprehensible lettering showing faintly on its face.

'It is no dream,' he said, 'no dream.' And he bowed his face upon his hands.

CHAPTER ELEVEN

The Old Man Who Knew Everything

He was startled by a cough close at hand.

He turned sharply, and peering, saw a small, hunched-up figure sitting a couple of yards off in the shadow of the enclosure.

'Have ye any news?' asked the high-pitched wheezy voice of a very old man.

Graham hesitated. 'None,' he said.

'I stay here till the lights come again,' said the old man. 'These blue scoundrels are everywhere – everywhere.'

Graham's answer was inarticulate assent. He tried to see the old man but the darkness hid his face. He wanted very much to respond, to talk, but he did not know how to begin.

'Dark and damnable,' said the old man suddenly. 'Dark and damnable. Turned out of my room among all these dangers.'

'That's hard,' ventured Graham. 'That's hard on you.'

'Darkness. An old man lost in the darkness. And all the world gone mad. War and fighting. The police beaten and rogues abroad. Why don't they bring some negroes to protect us? . . . No more dark passages for me. I fell over a dead man.

'You're safer with company,' said the old man, 'if it's company of the right sort,' and peered frankly. He rose suddenly and came towards Graham.

Apparently the scrutiny was satisfactory. The old man sat down as if relieved to be no longer alone. 'Eh!' he said, 'but this is a terrible time! War and fighting, and the dead lying there – men, strong men, dying in the dark. Sons! I have three sons. God knows where they are tonight.'

The voice ceased. Then repeated quavering: 'God knows where they are tonight.'

Graham stood revolving a question that should not betray his ignorance. Again the old man's voice ended the pause.

'This Ostrog will win,' he said. 'He will win. And what the world will be like under him no one can tell. My sons are under the wind-vanes, all three. One of my daughters-in-law was his mistress for a while. His mistress! We're not common people. Though they've sent me to wander tonight and take my chance . . . I knew what was going on. Before most people. But this darkness! And to fall over a dead body suddenly in the dark!'

His wheezy breathing could be heard.

'Ostrog!' said Graham.

'The greatest Boss the world has ever seen,' said the voice.

Graham ransacked his mind. 'The Council has few friends among the people,' he hazarded.

'Few friends. And poor ones at that. They've had their time. Eh! They should have kept to the clever ones. But twice they held election. And Ostrog – . And now it has burst out and nothing can stay it, nothing can stay it. Twice they rejected Ostrog – Ostrog the Boss. I heard of his rages at the time – he was terrible. Heaven save them! For nothing on earth can now, he has raised the Labour Companies upon them. No one else would have dared. All the blue canvas armed and marching! He will go through with it. He will go through.'

He was silent for a little while. 'This Sleeper,' he said, and stopped.

'Yes,' said Graham. 'Well?'

The senile voice sank to a confidential whisper, the dim, pale face came close. 'The real Sleeper – '

'Yes,' said Graham.

'Died years ago.'

'What?' said Graham, sharply.

'Years ago. Died. Years ago.'

'You don't say so!' said Graham.

'I do. I do say so. He died. This Sleeper who's woke up – they changed in the night. A poor, drugged insensible creature. But I mustn't tell all I know. I mustn't tell all I know.'

For a little while he muttered inaudibly. His secret was too much for him. 'I don't know the ones that put him to sleep – that was before my time – but I know the man who injected the stimulants and woke him again. It was ten to one – wake or kill. Wake or kill. Ostrog's way.'

Graham was so astonished at these things that he had to interrupt, to make the old man repeat his words, to re-question vaguely, before he was sure of the meaning and folly of what he heard. And his awakening had not been natural! Was that an old man's senile superstition, too, or had it any truth in it? Feeling in the dark corners of his memory, he presently came on something that might conceivably be an impression of some such stimulating effect. It dawned upon him that he had happened upon a lucky encounter, that at last he might learn something of the new age. The old man wheezed a while and spat, and then the piping, reminiscent voice resumed: 'The first time they rejected him. I've followed it all.'

'Rejected whom?' said Graham. 'The Sleeper?'

'Sleeper? *No.* Ostrog. He was terrible – terrible! And he was promised then, promised certainly the next time. Fools they were – not to be more afraid of him. Now all the city's his millstone, and such as we dust ground upon it. Dust ground upon it. Until he set to work – the workers cut each other's throats, and murdered a Chinaman or a Labour policeman at times, and left the rest of us in peace. Dead bodies! Robbing! Darkness! Such a thing hasn't been this gross of years. Eh! – but 'tis ill on small folks when the great fall out! It's ill.'

'Did you say – there had not been – what? – for a gross of years?'

'Eh?' said the old man.

The old man said something about clipping his words, and made him repeat this a third time. 'Fighting and slaying, and weapons in hand, and fools bawling freedom and the like,' said the old man. 'Not in all my life has there been that. These are like the old days – for sure – when the Paris people broke out – three gross of years ago. That's what I mean hasn't been. But it's the world's way. It had to come back. I know. I know. This five years Ostrog has been working, and there has been trouble and trouble, and hunger and threats and high talk and arms. Blue canvas and murmurs. No one safe. Everything sliding and slipping. And now here we are! Revolt and fighting, and the Council come to its end.'

'You are rather well-informed on these things,' said Graham.

'I know what I hear. It isn't all Babble Machine with me.'

'No,' said Graham, wondering what Babble Machine might be. 'And you are certain this Ostrog – you are certain Ostrog organised this rebellion and

arranged for the waking of the Sleeper? Just to assert himself – because he was not elected to the Council?

'Everyone knows that, I should think,' said the old man. 'Except – just fools. He meant to be master somehow. In the Council or not. Everyone who knows anything knows that. And here we are with dead bodies lying in the dark! Why, where have you been if you haven't heard all about the trouble between Ostrog and the Verneys? And what do you think the troubles are about? The Sleeper? Eh? You think the Sleeper's real and woke of his own accord – eh?'

'I'm a dull man, older than I look, and forgetful,' said Graham. 'Lots of things that have happened – especially of late years – . If I was the Sleeper, to tell you the truth, I couldn't know less about them.'

'Eh!' said the voice. 'Old, are you? You don't sound so very old! But it's not everyone keeps his memory to my time of life – truly. But these notorious things! But you're not so old as me – not nearly so old as me. Well! I ought not to judge other men by myself, perhaps. I'm young – for so old a man. Maybe you're old for so young.'

'That's it,' said Graham. 'And I've a queer history. I know very little. And history! Practically I know no history. The Sleeper and Julius Caesar are all the same to me. It's interesting to hear you talk of these things.'

'I know a few things,' said the old man. 'I know a thing or two. But – . Hark!'

The two men became silent, listening. There was a heavy thud, a concussion that made their seat shiver. The passers-by stopped, shouted to one another. The old man was full of questions; he shouted to a man who passed near. Graham, emboldened by his example, got up and accosted others. None knew what had happened.

He returned to the seat and found the old man muttering vague interrogations in an undertone. For a while they said nothing to one another.

The sense of this gigantic struggle, so near and yet so remote, oppressed Graham's imagination. Was this old man right, was the report of the people right, and were the revolutionaries winning? Or were they all in error, and were the red guards driving all before them? At any time the flood of warfare might pour into this silent quarter of the city and seize upon him again. It behoved him to learn all he could while there was time. He turned suddenly to the old man with a question and left it unsaid. But his motion moved the old man to speech again.

'Eh! but how things work together!' said the old man. 'This Sleeper that all the fools put their trust in! I've the whole history of it – I was always a good one for histories. When I was a boy – I'm that old – I used to read printed books. You'd hardly think it. Likely you've seen none – they rot and dust so – and the Sanitary Company burns them to make ashlarite. But they were convenient in their dirty way. One learnt a lot. These new-fangled Babble Machines – they don't seem new-fangled to you, eh? – they're easy

to hear, easy to forget. But I've traced all the Sleeper business from the first.'

'You will scarcely believe it,' said Graham slowly, 'I'm so ignorant – I've been so preoccupied in my own little affairs, my circumstances have been so odd – I know nothing of this Sleeper's history. Who was he?'

'Eh!' said the old man. 'I know. I know. He was a poor nobody, and set on a playful woman, poor soul! And he fell into a trance. There's the old things they had, those brown things – silver photographs – still showing him as he lay, a gross and a half years ago – a gross and a half of years.'

'Set on a playful woman, poor soul,' said Graham softly to himself, and then aloud, 'Yes – well! go on.'

'You must know he had a cousin named Warming, a solitary man without children, who made a big fortune speculating in roads – the first Eadhamite roads. But surely you've heard? No? Why? He bought all the patent rights and made a big company. In those days there were grosses of grosses of separate businesses and business companies. Grosses of grosses! His roads killed the railroads – the old things – in two dozen years; he bought up and Eadhamited the tracks. And because he didn't want to break up his great property or let in shareholders, he left it all to the Sleeper, and put it under a Board of Trustees that he had picked and trained. He knew then the Sleeper wouldn't wake, that he would go on sleeping, sleeping till he died. He knew that quite well! And plump! a man in the United States, who had lost two sons in a boat accident, followed that up with another great bequest. His trustees found themselves with a dozen myriads of lions'-worth or more of property at the very beginning.'

'What was his name?'

'Graham.'

'No, I mean – that American's.'

'Isbister.'

'Isbister!' cried Graham. 'Why, I don't even know the name.'

'Of course not,' said the old man. 'Of course not. People don't learn much in the schools nowadays. But I know all about him. He was a rich American who went from England, and he left the Sleeper even more than Warming. How he made it? That I don't know. Something about pictures by machinery. But he made it and left it, and so the Council had its start. It was just a council of trustees at first.'

'And how did it grow?'

'Eh! – but you're not up to things. Money attracts money – and twelve brains are better than one. They played it cleverly. They worked politics with money, and kept on adding to the money by working currency and tariffs. They grew – they grew. And for years the twelve trustees hid the growing of the Sleeper's estate, under double names and company titles and all that. The Council spread by title deed, mortgage, share, every political party, every newspaper, they bought. If you listen to the old stories you will

see the Council growing and growing. Billions and billions of lions at last – the Sleeper's estate. And all growing out of a whim – out of this Warming's will, and an accident to Isbister's sons.

'Men are strange,' said the old man. 'The strange thing to me is how the Council worked together so long. As many as twelve. But they worked in cliques from the first. And they've slipped back. In my young days speaking of the Council was like an ignorant man speaking of God. We didn't think they could do wrong. We didn't know of their women and all that! Or else I've got wiser.

'Men are strange,' said the old man. 'Here are you, young and ignorant, and me – sevendy years old, and I might reasonably be forgetting – explaining it all to you short and clear.

'Sevendy,' he said, 'sevendy, and I hear and see – hear better than I see. And reason clearly, and keep myself up to all the happenings of things. Sevendy!

'Life is strange. I was twaindy before Ostrog was a baby. I remember him long before he'd pushed his way to the head of the Wind Vanes Control. I've seen many changes. Eh! I've worn the blue. And at last I've come to see this crush and darkness and tumult and dead men carried by in heaps on the ways. And all his doing! All his doing!'

His voice died away in scarcely articulate praises of Ostrog.

Graham thought. 'Let me see,' he said, 'if I have it right.'

He extended a hand and ticked off points upon his fingers. 'The Sleeper has been asleep – '

'Changed,' said the old man.

'Perhaps. And meanwhile the Sleeper's property grew in the hands of Twelve Trustees, until it swallowed up nearly all the great ownership of the world. The Twelve Trustees – by virtue of this property have become virtually masters of the world. Because they are the paying power – just as the old English Parliament used to be – '

'Eh!' said the old man. 'That's so – that's a good comparison. You're not so – '

'And now this Ostrog – has suddenly revolutionised the world by waking the Sleeper – whom no one but the superstitious, common people had ever dreamt would wake again – raising the Sleeper to claim his property from the Council, after all these years.'

The old man endorsed this statement with a cough. 'It's strange,' he said, 'to meet a man who learns these things for the first time tonight.'

'Aye,' said Graham, 'it's strange.'

'Have you been in a Pleasure City?' said the old man. 'All my life I've longed – ' He laughed. 'Even now,' he said, 'I could enjoy a little fun. Enjoy seeing things, anyhow.' He mumbled a sentence Graham did not understand.

'The Sleeper – when did he awake?' said Graham suddenly.

'Three days ago.'

'Where is he?'

'Ostrog has him. He escaped from the Council not four hours ago. My dear sir, where were you at the time? He was in the hall of the markets – where the fighting has been. All the city was screaming about it. All the Babble Machines! Everywhere it was shouted. Even the fools who speak for the Council were admitting it. Everyone was rushing off to see him – everyone was getting arms. Were you drunk or asleep? And even then! But you're joking! Surely you're pretending. It was to stop the shouting of the Babble Machines and prevent the people gathering that they turned off the electricity – and put this damned darkness upon us. Do you mean to say – ?'

'I had heard the Sleeper was rescued,' said Graham. 'But – to come back a minute. Are you sure Ostrog has him?'

'He won't let him go,' said the old man.

'And the Sleeper. Are you sure he is not genuine? I have never heard – '

'So all the fools think. So they think. As if there wasn't a thousand things that were never heard. I know Ostrog too well for that. Did I tell you? In a way I'm a sort of relation of Ostrog's. A sort of relation. Through my daughter-in-law.'

'I suppose – '

'Well?'

'I suppose there's no chance of this Sleeper asserting himself. I suppose he's certain to be a puppet – in Ostrog's hands or the Council's, as soon as the struggle is over.'

'In Ostrog's hands – certainly. Why shouldn't he be a puppet? Look at his position. Everything done for him, every pleasure possible. Why should he want to assert himself?'

'What are these Pleasure Cities?' said Graham, abruptly.

The old man made him repeat the question. When at last he was assured of Graham's words, he nudged him violently. 'That's too much,' said he. 'You're poking fun at an old man. I've been suspecting you know more than you pretend.'

'Perhaps I do,' said Graham. 'But no! why should I go on acting? No, I do not know what a Pleasure City is.'

The old man laughed in an intimate way.

'What is more, I do not know how to read your letters, I do not know what money you use, I do not know what foreign countries there are. I do not know where I am. I cannot count. I do not know where to get food, nor drink, nor shelter.'

'Come, come,' said the old man, 'if you had a glass of drink, now, would you put it in your ear or your eye?'

'I want you to tell me all these things.'

'He, he! Well, gentlemen who dress in silk must have their fun.' A withered hand caressed Graham's arm for a moment. 'Silk. Well, well! But,

all the same, I wish I was the man who was put up as the Sleeper. He'll have a fine time of it. All the pomp and pleasure. He's a queer-looking face. When they used to let anyone go to see him, I've got tickets and been. The image of the real one, as the photographs show him, this substitute used to be. Yellow. But he'll get fed up. It's a queer world. Think of the luck of it. The luck of it. I expect he'll be sent to Capri. It's the best fun for a greener.'

His cough overtook him again. Then he began mumbling enviously of pleasures and strange delights. 'The luck of it, the luck of it! All my life I've been in London, hoping to get my chance.'

'But you don't know that the Sleeper died,' said Graham, suddenly.

The old man made him repeat his words.

'Men don't live beyond ten dozen. It's not in the order of things,' said the old man. 'I'm not a fool. Fools may believe it, but not me.'

Graham became angry with the old man's assurance. 'Whether you are a fool or not,' he said, 'it happens you are wrong about the Sleeper.'

'Eh?'

'You are wrong about the Sleeper. I haven't told you before, but I will tell you now. You are wrong about the Sleeper.'

'How do you know? I thought you didn't know anything – not even about Pleasure Cities.'

Graham paused.

'You don't know,' said the old man. 'How are you to know? It's very few men – '

'I *am* the Sleeper.'

He had to repeat it.

There was a brief pause. 'There's a silly thing to say, sir, if you'll excuse me. It might get you into trouble in a time like this,' said the old man. Graham, slightly dashed, repeated his assertion.

'I was saying I was the Sleeper. That years and years ago I did, indeed, fall asleep, in a little stone-built village, in the days when there were hedgerows, and villages, and inns, and all the countryside cut up into little pieces, little fields. Have you never heard of those days? And it is I – I who speak to you – who awakened again these four days since.'

'Four days since! – the Sleeper! But they've got the Sleeper. They have him and they won't let him go. Nonsense! You've been talking sensibly enough up to now. I can see it as though I was there. There will be Lincoln like a keeper just behind him; they won't let him go about alone. Trust them. You're a queer fellow. One of these fun pokers. I see now why you have been clipping your words so oddly, but – '

He stopped abruptly, and Graham could see his gesture.

'As if Ostrog would let the Sleeper run about alone! No, you're telling that to the wrong man altogether. Eh! as if I should believe. What's your game? And besides, we've been talking of the Sleeper.'

Graham stood up. 'Listen,' he said. 'I am the Sleeper.'

'You're an odd man,' said the old man, 'to sit here in the dark, talking clipped, and telling a lie of that sort. But – '

Graham's exasperation fell to laughter. 'It is preposterous,' he cried. 'Preposterous. The dream must end. It gets wilder and wilder. Here am I – in this damned twilight – I never knew a dream in twilight before – an anachronism by two hundred years and trying to persuade an old fool that I am myself, and meanwhile – Ugh!'

He moved in gusty irritation and went striding. In a moment the old man was pursuing him. 'Eh! but don't go!' cried the old man. 'I'm an old fool, I know. Don't go. Don't leave me in all this darkness.'

Graham hesitated, stopped. Suddenly the folly of telling his secret flashed into his mind.

'I didn't mean to offend you – disbelieving you,' said the old man coming near. 'It's no manner of harm. Call yourself the Sleeper if it pleases you. 'Tis a foolish trick – '

Graham hesitated, turned abruptly and went on his way.

For a time he heard the old man's hobbling pursuit and his wheezy cries receding. But at last the darkness swallowed him, and Graham saw him no more.

CHAPTER TWELVE

Ostrog

Graham could now take a clearer view of his position. For a long time yet he wandered, but after the talk of the old man his discovery of this Ostrog was clear in his mind as the final inevitable decision. One thing was evident, those who were at the headquarters of the revolt had succeeded very admirably in suppressing the fact of his disappearance. But every moment he expected to hear the report of his death or of his recapture by the Council.

Presently a man stopped before him. 'Have you heard?' he said.

'No!' said Graham starting.

'Near a dozand,' said the man, 'a dozand men!' and hurried on.

A number of men and a girl passed in the darkness, gesticulating and shouting: 'Capitulated! Given up!' 'A dozand of men.' 'Two dozand of men.' 'Ostrog, Hurrah! Ostrog, Hurrah!' These cries receded, became indistinct.

Other shouting men followed. For a time his attention was absorbed in the fragments of speech he heard. He had a doubt whether all were speaking English. Scraps floated to him, scraps like pidgin English, like some sort of dialect, blurred and mangled distortions. He dared accost no one with questions. The impression the people gave him jarred altogether

with his preconceptions of the struggle and confirmed the old man's faith in Ostrog. It was only slowly he could bring himself to believe that all these people were rejoicing at the defeat of the Council, that the Council which had pursued him with such power and vigour was after all the weaker of the two sides in conflict. And if that was so, how did it affect him? Several times he hesitated on the verge of fundamental questions. Once he turned and walked for a long way after a little man of rotund inviting outline, but he was unable to master confidence to address him.

It was only slowly that it came to him that he might ask for the 'wind-vane offices', whatever the 'wind-vane offices' might be. His first enquiry simply resulted in a direction to go on towards Westminster. His second led to the discovery of a short cut in which he was speedily lost. He was told to leave the ways to which he had hitherto confined himself – knowing no other means of transit – and to plunge down one of the middle staircases into the blackness of a crossway. Thereupon came some trivial adventures; chief of these an ambiguous encounter with a gruff-voiced invisible creature speaking in a strange dialect that seemed at first a strange tongue, a thick flow of speech with the drifting corpses of English words therein, the dialect of the latter-day vile. Then another voice drew near, a girl's voice singing, 'tralala tralala'. She spoke to Graham, her English touched with something of the same quality. She professed to have lost her sister, she blundered needlessly into him he thought, caught hold of him and laughed. But a word of vague remonstrance sent her into the unseen again.

The sounds about him increased. Stumbling people passed him, speaking excitedly. 'They have surrendered!' 'The Council! Surely not the Council!' 'They are saying so in the Ways.' The passage seemed wider. Suddenly the wall fell away. He was in a great space and people were stirring remotely. He enquired his way of an indistinct figure. 'Strike straight across,' said a woman's voice. He left his guiding wall, and in a moment had stumbled against a little table on which were utensils of glass. Graham's eyes, now attuned to darkness, made out a long vista with pallid tables on either side. He went down this. At one or two of the tables he heard a clang of glass and a sound of eating. There were people then cool enough to dine, or daring enough to steal a meal in spite of social convulsion and darkness. Far off and high up he presently saw a pallid light of a semicircular shape. As he approached this, a black edge came up and hid it. He stumbled at steps and found himself in a gallery. He heard a sobbing, and found two scared little girls crouched by a railing. These children became silent at the near sound of feet. He tried to console them, but they were very still until he left them. Then as he receded he could hear them sobbing again.

Presently he found himself at the foot of a staircase and near a wide opening. He saw a dim twilight above this and ascended out of the blackness into a street of moving Ways again. Along this a disorderly swarm of people marched shouting. They were singing snatches of the song of the

revolt, most of them out of tune. Here and there torches flared creating brief hysterical shadows. He asked his way and was twice puzzled by that same thick dialect. His third attempt won an answer he could understand. He was two miles from the wind-vane offices in Westminster, but the way was easy to follow.

When at last he did approach the district of the wind-vane offices it seemed to him, from the cheering processions that came marching along the Ways, from the tumult of rejoicing, and finally from the restoration of the lighting of the city, that the overthrow of the Council must already be accomplished. And still no news of his absence came to his ears.

The re-illumination of the city came with startling abruptness. Suddenly he stood blinking, all about him men halted dazzled, and the world was incandescent. The light found him already upon the outskirts of the excited crowds that choked the Ways near the wind-vane offices, and the sense of visibility and exposure that came with it turned his colourless intention of joining Ostrog to a keen anxiety.

For a time he was jostled, obstructed, and endangered by men hoarse and weary with cheering his name, some of them bandaged and bloody in his cause. The frontage of the wind-vane offices was illuminated by some moving picture, but what it was he could not see, because in spite of his strenuous attempts the density of the crowd prevented his approaching it. From the fragments of speech he caught, he judged it conveyed news of the fighting about the Council House. Ignorance and indecision made him slow and ineffective in his movements. For a time he could not conceive how he was to get within the unbroken façade of this place. He made his way slowly into the midst of this mass of people, until he realised that the descending staircase of the central Way led to the interior of the buildings. This gave him a goal, but the crowding in the central path was so dense that it was long before he could reach it. And even then he encountered intricate obstruction, and had an hour of vivid argument first in this guard room and then in that before he could get a note taken to the one man of all men who was most eager to see him. His story was laughed to scorn at one place, and wiser for that, when at last he reached a second stairway he professed simply to have news of extraordinary importance for Ostrog. What it was he would not say. They sent his note reluctantly. For a long time he waited in a little room at the foot of the lift shaft, and thither at last came Lincoln, eager, apologetic, astonished. He stopped in the doorway scrutinising Graham, then rushed forward effusively.

'Yes,' he cried. 'It is you. And you are not dead!'

Graham made a brief explanation.

'My brother is waiting,' explained Lincoln. 'He is alone in the wind-vane offices. We feared you had been killed in the theatre. He doubted – and things are very urgent still in spite of what we are telling them *there* – or he would have come to you.'

They ascended a lift, passed along a narrow passage, crossed a great hall, empty save for two hurrying messengers, and entered a comparatively little room, whose only furniture was a long settee and a large oval disc of cloudy, shifting grey, hung by cables from the wall. There Lincoln left Graham for a space, and he remained alone without understanding the shifting smoky shapes that drove slowly across this disc.

His attention was arrested by a sound that began abruptly. It was cheering, the frantic cheering of a vast but very remote crowd, a roaring exultation. This ended as sharply as it had begun, like a sound heard between the opening and shutting of a door. In the outer room was a noise of hurrying steps and a melodious clinking as if a loose chain was running over the teeth of a wheel.

Then he heard the voice of a woman, the rustle of unseen garments. 'It is Ostrog!' he heard her say. A little bell rang fitfully, and then everything was still again.

Presently came voices, footsteps and movement without. The footsteps of some one person detached itself from the other sounds and drew near, firm, evenly measured steps. The curtain lifted slowly. A tall, white-haired man, clad in garments of cream-coloured silk, appeared, regarding Graham from under his raised arm.

For a moment the white form remained holding the curtain, then dropped it and stood before it. Graham's first impression was of a very broad forehead, very pale blue eyes deep sunken under white brows, an aquiline nose, and a heavily lined resolute mouth. The folds of flesh over the eyes, the drooping of the corners of the mouth contradicted the upright bearing, and said the man was old. Graham rose to his feet instinctively, and for a moment the two men stood in silence, regarding each other.

'You are Ostrog?' said Graham.

'I am Ostrog.'

'The Boss?'

'So I am called.'

Graham felt the inconvenience of the silence. 'I have to thank you chiefly, I understand, for my safety,' he said presently.

'We were afraid you were killed,' said Ostrog. 'Or sent to sleep again – for ever. We have been doing everything to keep our secret – the secret of your disappearance. Where have you been? How did you get here?'

Graham told him briefly.

Ostrog listened in silence.

He smiled faintly. 'Do you know what I was doing when they came to tell me you had come?'

'How can I guess?'

'Preparing your double.'

'My double?'

'A man as like you as we could find. We were going to hypnotise him, to save him the difficulty of acting. It was imperative. The whole of this revolt depends on the idea that you are awake, alive, and with us. Even now a great multitude of people has gathered in the theatre clamouring to see you. They do not trust . . . You know, of course – something of your position?'

'Very little,' said Graham.

'It is like this.' Ostrog walked a pace or two into the room and turned. 'You are absolute owner,' he said, 'of more than half the world. As a result of that you are practically King. Your powers are limited in many intricate ways, but you are the figurehead, the popular symbol of government. This White Council, the Council of Trustees as it is called – '

'I have heard the vague outline of these things.'

'I wondered.'

'I came upon a garrulous old man.'

'I see . . . Our masses – the word comes from your days – you know of course, that we still have masses – regard you as our actual ruler. Just as a great number of people in your days regarded the Crown as the ruler. They are discontented – the masses all over the earth – with the rule of your Trustees. For the most part it is the old discontent, the old quarrel of the common man with his commonness – the misery of work and discipline and unfitness. But your Trustees have ruled ill. In certain matters, in the administration of the Labour Companies, for example, they have been unwise. They have given endless opportunities. Already we of the popular party were agitating for reforms – when your waking came. Came! If it had been contrived it could not have come more opportunely.' He smiled. 'The public mind, making no allowance for your years of quiescence, had already hit on the thought of waking you and appealing to you, and – Flash!'

He indicated the outbreak by a gesture, and Graham moved his head to show that he understood.

'The Council muddled – quarrelled. They always do. They could not decide what to do with you. You know how they imprisoned you?'

'I see. I see. And now – we win?'

'We win. Indeed we win. Tonight, in five swift hours. Suddenly we struck everywhere. The wind-vane people, the Labour Company and its millions, burst the bonds. We got the pull of the aeropiles.'

He paused. 'Yes,' said Graham, guessing that aeropile meant flying machine.

'That was, of course, essential. Or they could have got away. All the city rose, every third man almost was in it! All the blue, all the public services, save only just a few aeronauts and about half the red police. You were rescued, and their own police of the Ways – not half of them could be massed at the Council House – have been broken up, disarmed or killed. All London is ours – now. Only the Council House remains.

'Half of those who remain to them of the red police were lost in that

foolish attempt to recapture you. They lost their heads when they lost you. They flung all they had at the theatre. We cut them off from the Council House there. Truly tonight has been a night of victory. Everywhere your star has blazed. A day ago – the White Council ruled as it has ruled for a gross of years, for a century and a half of years, and then, with only a little whispering, a covert arming here and there, suddenly – So!'

'I am very ignorant,' said Graham. 'I suppose – . I do not clearly understand the conditions of this fighting. If you could explain. Where is the Council? Where is the fight?'

Ostrog stepped across the room, something clicked, and suddenly, save for an oval glow, they were in darkness. For a moment Graham was puzzled.

Then he saw that the cloudy grey disc had taken depth and colour, had assumed the appearance of an oval window looking out upon a strange unfamiliar scene.

At the first glance he was unable to guess what this scene might be. It was a daylight scene, the daylight of a wintry day, grey and clear. Across the picture and halfway as it seemed between him and the remoter view, a stout cable of twisted white wire stretched vertically. Then he perceived that the rows of great wind-wheels he saw, the wide intervals, the occasional gulfs of darkness, were akin to those through which he had fled from the Council House. He distinguished an orderly file of red figures marching across an open space between files of men in black, and realised before Ostrog spoke that he was looking down on the upper surface of latter-day London. The overnight snows had gone. He judged that this mirror was some modern replacement of the camera obscura, but that matter was not explained to him. He saw that though the file of red figures was trotting from left to right, yet they were passing out of the picture to the left. He wondered momentarily, and then saw that the picture was passing slowly, panorama fashion, across the oval.

'In a moment you will see the fighting,' said Ostrog at his elbow. 'Those fellows in red you notice are prisoners. This is the roof space of London – all the houses are practically continuous now. The streets and public squares are covered in. The gaps and chasms of your time have disappeared.'

Something out of focus obliterated half the picture. Its form suggested a man. There was a gleam of metal, a flash, something that swept across the oval, as the eyelid of a bird sweeps across its eye, and the picture was clear again. And now Graham beheld men running down among the wind-wheels, pointing weapons from which jetted out little smoky flashes. They swarmed thicker and thicker to the right, gesticulating – it might be they were shouting, but of that the picture told nothing. They and the wind-wheels passed slowly and steadily across the field of the mirror.

'Now,' said Ostrog, 'comes the Council House,' and slowly a black edge

crept into view and gathered Graham's attention. Soon it was no longer an edge but a cavity, a huge blackened space amidst the clustering edifices, and from it thin spires of smoke rose into the pallid winter sky. Gaunt ruinous masses of the building, mighty truncated piers and girders, rose dismally out of this cavernous darkness. And over these vestiges of some splendid place, countless minute men were clambering, leaping, swarming.

'This is the Council House,' said Ostrog. 'Their last stronghold. And the fools wasted enough ammunition to hold out for a month in blowing up the buildings all about them – to stop our attack. You heard the smash? It shattered half the brittle glass in the city.'

And while he spoke, Graham saw that beyond this sea of ruins, over-hanging it and rising to a great height, was a ragged mass of white building. This mass had been isolated by the ruthless destruction of its surroundings. Black gaps marked the passages the disaster had torn apart; big halls had been slashed open and the decoration of their interiors showed dismally in the wintry dawn, and down the jagged walls hung festoons of divided cables and twisted ends of lines and metallic rods. And amidst all the vast details moved little red specks, the red-clothed defenders of the Council. Every now and then faint flashes illuminated the bleak shadows. At the first sight it seemed to Graham that an attack upon this isolated white building was in progress, but then he perceived that the party of the revolt was not advancing, but sheltered amidst the colossal wreckage that encircled this last ragged stronghold of the red-garbed men, was keeping up a fitful firing.

And not ten hours ago he had stood beneath the ventilating fans in a little chamber within that remote building wondering what was happening in the world!

Looking more attentively as this warlike episode moved silently across the centre of the mirror, Graham saw that the white building was sur-rounded on every side by ruins, and Ostrog proceeded to describe in concise phrases how its defenders had sought by such destruction to isolate themselves from a storm. He spoke of the loss of men that huge downfall had entailed in an indifferent tone. He indicated an improvised mortuary among the wreckage, showed ambulances swarming like cheese-mites along a ruinous groove that had once been a street of moving ways. He was more interested in pointing out the parts of the Council House, the distribution of the besiegers. In a little while the civil contest that had convulsed London was no longer a mystery to Graham. It was no tumultuous revolt had occurred that night, no equal warfare, but a splendidly organised *coup d'état*. Ostrog's grasp of details was astonishing; he seemed to know the business of even the smallest knot of black and red specks that crawled amidst these places.

He stretched a huge black arm across the luminous picture, and showed the room whence Graham had escaped, and across the chasm of ruins the course of his flight. Graham recognised the gulf across which the gutter

ran, and the wind-wheels where he had crouched from the flying machine.
The rest of his path had succumbed to the explosion. He looked again at the
Council House, and it was already half hidden, and on the right a hillside
with a cluster of domes and pinnacles, hazy, dim and distant, was gliding
into view.

'And the Council is really overthrown?' he said.

'Overthrown,' said Ostrog.

'And I – . Is it indeed true that I – ?'

'You are Master of the World.'

'But that white flag – '

'That is the flag of the Council – the flag of the Rule of the World. It will
fall. The fight is over. Their attack on the theatre was their last frantic
struggle. They have only a thousand men or so, and some of these men will
be disloyal. They have little ammunition. And we are reviving the ancient
arts. We are casting guns.'

'But – help. Is this city the world?'

'Practically this is all they have left to them of their empire. Abroad the
cities have either revolted with us or wait the issue. Your awakening has
perplexed them, paralysed them.'

'But haven't the Council flying machines? Why is there no fighting with
them?'

'They had. But the greater part of the aeronauts were in the revolt with
us. They wouldn't take the risk of fighting on our side, but they would not
stir against us. We *had* to get a pull with the aeronauts. Quite half were with
us, and the others knew it. Directly they knew you had got away, those
looking for you dropped. We killed the man who shot at you – an hour ago.
And we occupied the flying stages at the outset in every city we could, and
so stopped and captured the aeroplanes, and as for the little flying machines
that turned out – for some did – we kept up too straight and steady a fire for
them to get near the Council House. If they dropped they couldn't rise
again, because there's no clear space about there for them to get up. Several
we have smashed, several others have dropped and surrendered, the rest
have gone off to the Continent to find a friendly city if they can before their
fuel runs out. Most of these men were only too glad to be taken prisoner
and kept out of harm's way. Upsetting in a flying machine isn't a very
attractive prospect. There's no chance for the Council that way. Its days are
done.'

He laughed and turned to the oval reflection again to show Graham what
he meant by flying stages. Even the four nearer ones were remote and
obscured by a thin morning haze. But Graham could perceive they were
very vast structures, judged even by the standard of the things about them.

And then as these dim shapes passed to the left there came again the sight
of the expanse across which the disarmed men in red had been marching.
And then the black ruins, and then again the beleaguered white fastness of

the Council. It appeared no longer a ghostly pile, but glowing amber in the sunlight, for a cloud shadow had passed. About it the pigmy struggle still hung in suspense, but now the red defenders were no longer firing.

So, in a dusky stillness, the man from the nineteenth century saw the closing scene of the great revolt, the forcible establishment of his rule. With a quality of startling discovery it came to him that this was his world, and not that other he had left behind; that this was no spectacle to culminate and cease; that in this world lay whatever life was still before him, lay all his duties and dangers and responsibilities. He turned with fresh questions. Ostrog began to answer them, and then broke off abruptly. 'But these things I must explain more fully later. At present there are – duties. The people are coming by the moving ways towards this ward from every part of the city – the markets and theatres are densely crowded. You are just in time for them. They are clamouring to see you. And abroad they want to see you. Paris, New York, Chicago, Denver, Capri – thousands of cities are up and in a tumult, undecided, and clamouring to see you. They have clamoured that you should be awakened for years, and now it is done they will scarcely believe – '

'But surely – I can't go . . . '

Ostrog answered from the other side of the room, and the picture on the oval disc paled and vanished as the light jerked back again. 'There are kineto-tele-photographs,' he said. 'As you bow to the people here – all over the world myriads of myriads of people, packed and still in darkened halls, will see you also. In black and white, of course – not like this. And you will hear their shouts reinforcing the shouting in the hall.

'And there is an optical contrivance we shall use,' said Ostrog, 'used by some of the posturers and women dancers. It may be novel to you. You stand in a very bright light, and they see not you but a magnified image of you thrown on a screen – so that even the furtherest man in the remotest gallery can, if he chooses, count your eyelashes.'

Graham clutched desperately at one of the questions in his mind. 'What is the population of London?'

'Eight and twaindy myriads.'

'Eight and what?'

'More than thirty-three millions.'

These figures went beyond Graham's imagination 'You will be expected to say something,' said Ostrog. 'Not what you used to call a Speech, but what our people call a Word – just one sentence, six or seven words. Something formal. If I might suggest – "I have awakened and my heart is with you." That is the sort of thing they want.'

'What was that?' asked Graham.

' "I am awakened and my heart is with you." And bow – bow royally. But first we must get you black robes – for black is your colour. Do you mind? And then they will disperse to their homes.'

Graham hesitated. 'I am in your hands,' he said.

Ostrog was clearly of that opinion. He thought for a moment, turned to the curtain and called brief directions to some unseen attendants. Almost immediately a black robe, the very fellow of the black robe Graham had worn in the theatre, was brought. And as he threw it about his shoulders there came from the room without the shrilling of a high-pitched bell. Ostrog turned in interrogation to the attendant, then suddenly seemed to change his mind, pulled the curtain aside and disappeared.

For a moment Graham stood with the deferential attendant listening to Ostrog's retreating steps. There was a sound of quick question and answer and of men running. The curtain was snatched back and Ostrog reappeared, his massive face glowing with excitement. He crossed the room in a stride, clicked the room into darkness, gripped Graham's arm and pointed to the mirror.

'Even as we turned away,' he said.

Graham saw his index finger, black and colossal, above the mirrored Council House. For a moment he did not understand. And then he perceived that the flagstaff that had carried the white banner was bare.

'Do you mean – ?' he began.

'The Council has surrendered. Its rule is at an end for evermore.

'Look!' and Ostrog pointed to a coil of black that crept in little jerks up the vacant flagstaff, unfolding as it rose.

The oval picture paled as Lincoln pulled the curtain aside and entered.

'They are clamorous,' he said.

Ostrog kept his grip of Graham's arm.

'We have raised the people,' he said. 'We have given them arms. For today at least their wishes must be law.'

Lincoln held the curtain open for Graham and Ostrog to pass through . . .

On his way to the markets Graham had a transitory glance of a long narrow white-walled room in which men in the universal blue canvas were carrying covered things like biers, and about which men in medical purple hurried to and fro. From this room came groans and wailing. He had an impression of an empty blood-stained couch, of men on other couches, bandaged and blood-stained. It was just a glimpse from a railed footway and then a buttress hid the place and they were going on towards the markets . . .

The roar of the multitude was near now: it leapt to thunder. And, arresting his attention, a fluttering of black banners, the waving of blue canvas and brown rags, and the swarming vastness of the theatre near the public markets came into view down a long passage. The picture opened out. He perceived they were entering the great theatre of his first appearance, the great theatre he had last seen as a chequer-work of glare and blackness in his flight from the red police. This time he entered it along a gallery at a level high above the stage. The place was now brilliantly lit

again. He sought the gangway up which he had fled, but he could not tell it from among its dozens of fellows; nor could he see anything of the smashed seats, deflated cushions, and suchlike traces of the fight because of the density of the people. Except the stage the whole place was closely packed. Looking down the effect was a vast area of stippled pink, each dot a still upturned face regarding him. At his appearance with Ostrog the cheering died away, the singing died away, a common interest stilled and unified the disorder. It seemed as though every individual of those myriads was watching him.

CHAPTER THIRTEEN

The End of the Old Order

So far as Graham was able to judge, it was near midday when the white banner of the Council fell. But some hours had to elapse before it was possible to effect the formal capitulation, and so after he had spoken his 'Word' he retired to his new apartments in the wind-vane offices. The continuous excitement of the last twelve hours had left him inordinately fatigued, even his curiosity was exhausted; for a space he sat inert and passive with open eyes, and for a space he slept. He was roused by two medical attendants, come prepared with stimulants to sustain him through the next occasion. After he had taken their drugs and bathed by their advice in cold water, he felt a rapid return of interest and energy, and was presently able and willing to accompany Ostrog through several miles (as it seemed) of passages, lifts, and slides to the closing scene of the White Council's rule.

The way ran deviously through a maze of buildings. They came at last to a passage that curved about, and showed broadening before him an oblong opening, clouds hot with sunset, and the ragged skyline of the ruinous Council House. A tumult of shouts came drifting up to him. In another moment they had come out high up on the brow of the cliff of torn buildings that overhung the wreckage. The vast area opened to Graham's eyes, none the less strange and wonderful for the remote view he had had of it in the oval mirror.

This rudely amphitheatral space seemed now the better part of a mile to its outer edge. It was gold lit on the left hand, catching the sunlight, and below and to the right clear and cold in the shadow. Above the shadowy grey Council House that stood in the midst of it, the great black banner of the surrender still hung in sluggish folds against the blazing sunset. Severed rooms, halls and passages gaped strangely, broken masses of metal projected dismally from the complex wreckage, vast masses of twisted cable dropped like tangled seaweed, and from its base came a tumult of innumerable voices, violent concussions, and the sound of trumpets. All about

this great white pile was a ring of desolation; the smashed and blackened masses, the gaunt foundations and ruinous lumber of the fabric that had been destroyed by the Council's orders, skeletons of girders, Titanic masses of wall, forests of stout pillars. Among the sombre wreckage beneath, running water flashed and glistened, and far away across the space, out of the midst of a vague vast mass of buildings, there thrust the twisted end of a water-main, two hundred feet in the air, thunderously spouting a shining cascade. And everywhere great multitudes of people.

Wherever there was space and foothold, people swarmed, little people, small and minutely clear, except where the sunset touched them to indistinguishable gold. They clambered up the tottering walls, they clung in wreaths and groups about the high-standing pillars. They swarmed along the edges of the circle of ruins. The air was full of their shouting, and they were pressing and swaying towards the central space.

The upper storeys of the Council House seemed deserted, not a human being was visible. Only the drooping banner of the surrender hung heavily against the light. The dead were within the Council House, or hidden by the swarming people, or carried away. Graham could see only a few neglected bodies in gaps and corners of the ruins, and amidst the flowing water.

'Will you let them see you, Sire?' said Ostrog. 'They are very anxious to see you.'

Graham hesitated, and then walked forward to where the broken verge of wall dropped sheer. He stood looking down, a lonely, tall, black figure against the sky.

Very slowly the swarming ruins became aware of him. And as they did so little bands of black-uniformed men appeared remotely, thrusting through the crowds towards the Council House. He saw little black heads become pink, looking at him, saw by that means a wave of recognition sweep across the space. It occurred to him that he should accord them some recognition. He held up his arm, then pointed to the Council House and dropped his hand. The voices below became unanimous, gathered volume, came up to him as multitudinous wavelets of cheering.

The western sky was a pallid bluish green, and Jupiter shone high in the south, before the capitulation was accomplished. Above was a slow insensible change, the advance of night serene and beautiful; below was hurry, excitement, conflicting orders, pauses, spasmodic developments of organisation, a vast ascending clamour and confusion. Before the Council came out, toiling perspiring men, directed by a conflict of shouts, carried forth hundreds of those who had perished in the hand-to-hand conflict within those long passages and chambers . . .

Guards in black lined the way that the Council would come, and as far as the eye could reach into the hazy blue twilight of the ruins, and swarming now at every possible point in the captured Council House and along the

shattered cliff of its circumadjacent buildings, were innumerable people, and their voices even when they were not cheering, were as the soughing of the sea upon a pebble beach. Ostrog had chosen a huge commanding pile of crushed and overthrown masonry, and on this a stage of timbers and metal girders was being hastily constructed. Its essential parts were complete, but humming and clangorous machinery still glared fitfully in the shadows beneath this temporary edifice.

The stage had a small higher portion on which Graham stood with Ostrog and Lincoln close beside him, a little in advance of a group of minor officers. A broader lower stage surrounded this quarter deck, and on this were the black-uniformed guards of the revolt armed with the little green weapons whose very names Graham still did not know. Those standing about him perceived that his eyes wandered perpetually from the swarming people in the twilight ruins about him to the darkling mass of the White Council House, whence the Trustees would presently come, and to the gaunt cliffs of ruin that encircled him, and so back to the people. The voices of the crowd swelled to a deafening tumult.

He saw the Councillors first afar off in the glare of one of the temporary lights that marked their path, a little group of white figures blinking in a black archway. In the Council House they had been in darkness. He watched them approaching, drawing nearer past first this blazing electric star and then that; the minatory roar of the crowd over whom their power had lasted for a hundred and fifty years marched along beside them. As they drew still nearer their faces came out weary, white and anxious. He saw them blinking up through the glare about him and Ostrog. He contrasted their strange cold looks in the Hall of Atlas . . . Presently he could recognise several of them; the man who had rapped the table at Howard, a burly man with a red beard, and one delicate-featured, short, dark man with a peculiarly long skull. He noted that two were whispering together and looking behind him at Ostrog. Next there came a tall, dark and handsome man, walking downcast. Abruptly he glanced up, his eyes touched Graham for a moment, and passed beyond him to Ostrog. The way that had been made for them was so contrived that they had to march past and curve about before they came to the sloping path of planks that ascended to the stage where their surrender was to be made.

'The Master, the Master! God and the Master,' shouted the people. 'To hell with the Council!' Graham looked at their multitudes, receding beyond counting into a shouting haze, and then at Ostrog beside him, white and steadfast and still. His eye went again to the little group of White Councillors. And then he looked up at the familiar quiet stars overhead. The marvellous element in his fate was suddenly vivid. Could that be his indeed, that little life in his memory two hundred years gone by – and this as well?

CHAPTER FOURTEEN

From the Crow's Nest

And so after strange delays and through an avenue of doubt and battle, this man from the nineteenth century came at last to his position at the head of that complex world.

At first when he rose from the long deep sleep that followed his rescue and the surrender of the Council, he did not recognise his surroundings. By an effort he gained a clue in his mind, and all that had happened came back to him, at first with a quality of insincerity like a story heard, like something read out of a book. And even before his memories were clear, the exultation of his escape, the wonder of his prominence were back in his mind. He was owner of half the world; Master of the Earth. This new great age was in the completest sense his. He no longer hoped to discover his experiences a dream; he became anxious now to convince himself that they were real.

An obsequious valet assisted him to dress under the direction of a dignified chief attendant, a little man whose face proclaimed him Japanese, albeit he spoke English like an Englishman. From the latter he learnt something of the state of affairs. Already the revolution was an accepted fact; already business was being resumed throughout the city. Abroad the downfall of the Council had been received for the most part with delight. Nowhere was the Council popular, and the thousand cities of Western America, after two hundred years still jealous of New York, London, and the East, had risen almost unanimously two days before at the news of Graham's imprisonment. Paris was fighting within itself. The rest of the world hung in suspense.

While he was breaking his fast, the sound of a telephone bell jetted from a corner, and his chief attendant called his attention to the voice of Ostrog making polite enquiries. Graham interrupted his refreshment to reply. Very shortly Lincoln arrived, and Graham at once expressed a strong desire to talk to people and to be shown more of the new life that was opening before him. Lincoln informed him that in three hours' time a representative gathering of officials and their wives would be held in the state apartments of the wind-vane Chief. Graham's desire to traverse the ways of the city was, however, at present impossible, because of the enormous excitement of the people. It was, however, quite possible for him to take a bird's eye view of the city from the crow's nest of the wind-vane keeper. To this accordingly Graham was conducted by his attendant. Lincoln, with a graceful compliment to the attendant, apologised for not accompanying them, on account of the present pressure of administrative work.

Higher even than the most gigantic wind-wheels hung this crow's nest, a

clear thousand feet above the roofs, a little disc-shaped speck on a spear of metallic filigree, cable stayed. To its summit Graham was drawn in a little wire-hung cradle. Halfway down the frail-seeming stem was a light gallery about which hung a cluster of tubes – minute they looked from above – rotating slowly on the ring of its outer rail. These were the specula, *en rapport* with the wind-vane keeper's mirrors, in one of which Ostrog had shown him the coming of his rule. His Japanese attendant ascended before him and they spent nearly an hour asking and answering questions.

It was a day full of the promise and quality of spring. The touch of the wind warmed. The sky was an intense blue and the vast expanse of London shone dazzling under the morning sun. The air was clear of smoke and haze, sweet as the air of a mountain glen.

Save for the irregular oval of ruins about the House of the Council and the black flag of the surrender that fluttered there, the mighty city seen from above showed few signs of the swift revolution that had, to his imagination, in one night and one day, changed the destinies of the world. A multitude of people still swarmed over these ruins, and the huge openwork stagings in the distance from which started in times of peace the service of aeroplanes to the various great cities of Europe and America, were also black with the victors. Across a narrow way of planking raised on trestles that crossed the ruins a crowd of workmen were busy restoring the connection between the cables and wires of the Council House and the rest of the city, preparatory to the transfer thither of Ostrog's headquarters from the wind-vane buildings.

For the rest the luminous expanse was undisturbed. So vast was its serenity in comparison with the areas of disturbance, that presently Graham, looking beyond them, could almost forget the thousands of men lying out of sight in the artificial glare within the quasi-subterranean labyrinth, dead or dying of the overnight wounds, forget the improvised wards with the hosts of surgeons, nurses, and bearers feverishly busy, forget, indeed, all the wonder, consternation and novelty under the electric lights. Down there in the hidden ways of the ant-hill he knew that the revolution triumphed, that black everywhere carried the day, black favours, black banners, black festoons across the streets. And out here, under the fresh sunlight, beyond the crater of the fight, as if nothing had happened to the earth, the forest of wind-vanes that had grown from one or two while the Council had ruled, roared peacefully upon their incessant duty.

Far away, spiked, jagged and indented by the wind-vanes, the Surrey Hills rose blue and faint; to the north and nearer, the sharp contours of Highgate and Muswell Hill were similarly jagged. And all over the country-side, he knew, on every crest and hill, where once the hedges had interlaced, and cottages, churches, inns, and farmhouses had nestled among their trees, wind-wheels similar to those he saw and bearing like vast advertisements, gaunt and distinctive symbols of the new age, cast their whirling shadows and stored incessantly the energy that flowed away incessantly through all

the arteries of the city. And underneath these wandered the countless flocks and herds of the British Food Trust with their lonely guards and keepers.

Not a familiar outline anywhere broke the cluster of gigantic shapes below. St Paul's he knew survived, and many of the old buildings in Westminster, embedded out of sight, arched over and covered in among the giant growths of this great age. The Thames, too, made no fall and gleam of silver to break the wilderness of the city; the thirsty water mains drank up every drop of its waters before they reached the walls. Its bed and estuary, scoured and sunken, was now a canal of sea water and a race of grimy bargemen brought the heavy materials of trade from the Pool thereby beneath the very feet of the workers. Faint and dim in the eastward between earth and sky hung the clustering masts of the colossal shipping in the Pool. For all the heavy traffic, for which there was no need of haste, came in gigantic sailing ships from the ends of the earth, and the heavy goods for which there was urgency in mechanical ships of a smaller swifter sort.

And to the south over the hills, came vast aqueducts with sea water for the sewers, and in three separate directions ran pallid lines – the roads, stippled with moving grey specks. On the first occasion that offered he was determined to go out and see these roads. That would come after the flying ship he was presently to try. His attendant officer described them as a pair of gently curving surfaces a hundred yards wide, each one for the traffic going in one direction, and made of a substance called Eadhamite – an artificial substance, so far as he could gather, resembling toughened glass. Along this shot a strange traffic of narrow rubber-shod vehicles, great single wheels, two- and four-wheeled vehicles, sweeping along at velocities of from one to six miles a minute. Railroads had vanished; a few embankments remained as rust-crowned trenches here and there. Some few formed the cores of Eadhamite ways.

Among the first things to strike his attention had been the great fleets of advertisement balloons and kites that receded in irregular vistas northward and southward along the lines of the aeroplane journeys. No aeroplanes were to be seen. Their passages had ceased, and only one little-seeming aeropile circled high in the blue distance above the Surrey Hills, an unimpressive soaring speck.

A thing Graham had already learnt, and which he found very hard to imagine, was that nearly all the towns in the country, and almost all the villages, had disappeared. Here and there only, he understood, some gigantic hotel-like edifice stood amid square miles of some single cultivation and preserved the name of a town – as Bournemouth, Wareham, or Swanage. Yet the officer had speedily convinced him how inevitable such a change had been. The old order had dotted the country with farmhouses, and every two or three miles was the ruling landlord's estate, and the place of the inn and cobbler, the grocer's shop and church – the village. Every eight miles or so was the country town, where lawyer, corn merchant, wool-

stapler, saddler, veterinary surgeon, doctor, draper, milliner and so forth
lived. Every eight miles – simply because that eight-mile marketing journey,
four there and back, was as much as was comfortable for the farmer. But
directly the railways came into play, and after them the light railways, and all
the swift new motor cars that had replaced waggons and horses, and so soon
as the high roads began to be made of wood, and rubber, and Eadhamite,
and all sorts of elastic durable substances – the necessity of having such
frequent market towns disappeared. And the big towns grew. They drew the
worker with the gravitational force of seemingly endless work, the employer
with their suggestions of an infinite ocean of labour.

And as the standard of comfort rose, as the complexity of the mechanism
of living increased, life in the country had become more and more costly,
or narrow and impossible. The disappearance of vicar and squire, the
extinction of the general practitioner by the city specialist, had robbed the
village of its last touch of culture. After telephone, kinematograph and
phonograph had replaced newspaper, book, schoolmaster, and letter, to live
outside the range of the electric cables was to live an isolated savage. In the
country were neither means of being clothed nor fed (according to the
refined conceptions of the time), no efficient doctors for an emergency, no
company and no pursuits.

Moreover, mechanical appliances in agriculture made one engineer the
equivalent of thirty labourers. So, inverting the condition of the city clerk
in the days when London was scarce inhabitable because of the coaly
foulness of its air, the labourers now came hurrying by road or air to the city
and its life and delights at night to leave it again in the morning. The city
had swallowed up humanity; man had entered upon a new stage in his
development. First had come the nomad, the hunter, then had followed the
agriculturist of the agricultural state, whose towns and cities and ports were
but the headquarters and markets of the countryside. And now, logical
consequence of an epoch of invention, was this huge new aggregation
of men. Save London, there were only four other cities in Britain –
Edinburgh, Portsmouth, Manchester and Shrewsbury. Such things as these,
simple statements of fact though they were to contemporary men, strained
Graham's imagination to picture. And when he glanced 'over beyond there'
at the strange things that existed on the Continent, it failed him altogether.

He had a vision of city beyond city, cities on great plains, cities beside
great rivers, vast cities along the sea margin, cities girdled by snowy
mountains. Over a great part of the earth the English tongue was spoken;
taken together with its Spanish American and Hindu and Negro and
'Pidgin' dialects, it was the everyday language of two-thirds of the people
of the earth. On the Continent, save as remote and curious survivals, three
other languages alone held sway – German, which reached to Antioch and
Genoa and jostled Spanish-English at Cadiz, a Gallicised Russian which
met the Indian English in Persia and Kurdistan and the 'Pidgin' English in

Pekin, and French still clear and brilliant, the language of lucidity, which shared the Mediterranean with the Indian English and German and reached through a negro dialect to the Congo.

And everywhere now, through the city-set earth, save in the administered 'black belt' territories of the tropics, the same cosmopolitan social organisation prevailed, and everywhere from Pole to Equator his property and his responsibilities extended. The whole world was civilised; the whole world dwelt in cities; the whole world was property. Over the British Empire and throughout America his ownership was scarcely disguised, Congress and Parliament were usually regarded as antique, curious gatherings. And even in the two Empires of Russia and Germany, the influence of his wealth was conceivably of enormous weight. There, of course, came problems – possibilities, but, uplifted as he was, even Russia and Germany seemed sufficiently remote. And of the quality of the black belt administration, and of what that might mean for him he thought, after the fashion of his former days, not at all. That it should hang like a threat over the spacious vision before him could not enter his nineteenth-century mind. But his mind turned at once from the scenery to the thought of a vanished dread. 'What of the yellow peril?' he asked and Asano made him explain. The Chinese spectre had vanished. Chinaman and European were at peace. The twentieth century had discovered with reluctant certainty that the average Chinaman was as civilised, more moral, and far more intelligent than the average European serf, and had repeated on a gigantic scale the fraternisation of Scot and Englishman that happened in the seventeenth century. As Asano put it, 'They thought it over. They found we were white men after all.' Graham turned again to the view and his thoughts took a new direction.

Out of the dim south-west, glittering and strange, voluptuous, and in some way terrible, shone those Pleasure Cities, of which the kinemato-graph-phonograph and the old man in the street had spoken. Strange places reminiscent of the legendary Sybaris, cities of art and beauty, mercenary art and mercenary beauty, sterile wonderful cities of motion and music, whither repaired all who profited by the fierce, inglorious, economic struggle that went on in the glaring labyrinth below.

Fierce he knew it was. How fierce he could judge from the fact that these latter-day people referred back to the England of the nineteenth century as the figure of an idyllic easy-going life. He turned his eyes to the scene immediately before him again, trying to conceive the big factories of that intricate maze.

Northward he knew were the potters, makers not only of earthenware and china, but of the kindred pastes and compounds a subtler mineralogical chemistry had devised; there were the makers of statuettes and wall ornaments and much intricate furniture; there too were the factories where feverishly competitive authors devised their phonograph discourses and advertisements and arranged the groupings and developments for their

perpetually startling and novel kinematographic dramatic works. Thence, too, flashed the worldwide messages, the worldwide falsehoods of the news-tellers, the chargers of the telephonic machines that had replaced the newspapers of the past.

To the westward beyond the smashed Council House were the voluminous offices of municipal control and government; and to the east-ward, towards the port, the trading quarters, the huge public markets, the theatres, houses of resort, betting palaces, miles of billiard saloons, baseball and football circuses, wild beast rings and the innumerable temples of the Christian and quasi-Christian sects, the Mahomedans, Buddhists, Gnostics, Spook Worshippers, the Incubus Worshippers, the Furniture Worshippers, and so forth; and to the south again a vast manufacture of textiles, pickles, wines and condiments. And from point to point tore the countless multitudes along the roaring mechanical ways. A gigantic hive, of which the winds were tireless servants, and the ceaseless wind-vanes an appropriate crown and symbol.

He thought of the unprecedented population that had been sucked up by this sponge of halls and galleries – the thirty-three million lives that were playing out each its own brief ineffectual drama below him, and the com-placency that the brightness of the day and the space and splendour of the view, and above all the sense of his own importance had begotten, dwindled and perished. Looking down from this height over the city it became at last possible to conceive this overwhelming multitude of thirty-three millions, the reality of the responsibility he would take upon himself, the vastness of the human Maelstrom over which his slender kingship hung.

He tried to figure the individual life. It astonished him to realise how little the common man had changed in spite of the visible change in his conditions. Life and property, indeed, were secure from violence almost all over the world, zymotic diseases, bacterial diseases of all sorts had practically vanished, everyone had a sufficiency of food and clothing, was warmed in the city ways and sheltered from the weather – so much the almost mechanical progress of science and the physical organisation of society had accomplished. But the crowd, he was already beginning to discover, was a crowd still, helpless in the hands of demagogue and organiser, individually cowardly, individually swayed by appetite, collectively incalculable. The memory of countless figures in pale blue canvas came before his mind. Millions of such men and women below him, he knew, had never been out of the city, had never seen beyond the little round of unintelligent grudging participation in the world's business, and un-intelligent dissatisfied sharing in its tawdrier pleasures. He thought of the hopes of his vanished contemporaries, and for a moment the dream of London in Morris's quaint old *News from Nowhere,* and the perfect land of Hudson's beautiful *Crystal Age* – appeared before him in an atmosphere of infinite loss. He thought of his own hopes.

For in the latter days of that passionate life that lay now so far behind him, the conception of a free and equal manhood had become a very real thing to him. He had hoped, as indeed his age had hoped, rashly taking it for granted, that the sacrifice of the many to the few would some day cease, that a day was near when every child born of woman should have a fair and assured chance of happiness. And here, after two hundred years, the same hope, still unfulfilled, cried passionately through the city. After two hundred years, he knew, greater than ever, grown with the city to gigantic proportions, were poverty and helpless labour and all the sorrows of his time.

Already he knew something of the history of the intervening years. He had heard now of the moral decay that had followed the collapse of supernatural religion in the minds of ignoble man, the decline of public honour, the ascendancy of wealth. For men who had lost their belief in God had still kept their faith in property, and wealth ruled a venial world.

His Japanese attendant, Asano, in expounding the political history of the intervening two centuries, drew an apt image from a seed eaten by insect parasites. First there is the original seed, ripening vigorously enough. And then comes some insect and lays an egg under the skin, and behold! in a little while the seed is a hollow shape with an active grub inside that has eaten out its substance. And then comes some secondary parasite, some ichneumon fly, and lays an egg within this grub, and behold! that, too, is a hollow shape, and the new living thing is inside its predecessor's skin which itself is snug within the seed coat. And the seed coat still keeps its shape, most people think it a seed still, and for all one knows it may still think itself a seed, vigorous and alive. 'Your Victorian kingdom,' said Asano, 'was like that – kingship with the heart eaten out. The landowners – the barons and gentry – began ages ago with King John; there were lapses, but they beheaded King Charles, and ended practically with King George, a mere husk of a king . . . the real power in the hands of their parliament. But the Parliament – the organ of the land-holding tenant-ruling gentry – did not keep its power long. The change had already come in the nineteenth century. The franchises had been broadened until it included masses of ignorant men, "urban myriads", who went in their featureless thousands to vote together. And the natural consequence of a swarming constituency is the rule of the party organisation. Power was passing even in the Victorian time to the party machinery, secret, complex, and corrupt. Very speedily power was in the hands of great men of business who financed the machines. A time came when the real power and interest of the Empire rested visibly between the two party councils, ruling by newspapers and electoral organisations – two small groups of rich and able men, working at first in opposition, then presently together.'

There was a reaction of a genteel ineffectual sort. There were numberless books in existence, Asano said, to prove that – the publication of some of them was as early as Graham's sleep – a whole literature of reaction in

fact. The party of the reaction seems to have locked itself into its study and rebelled with unflinching determination – on paper. The urgent necessity of either capturing or depriving the party councils of power is a common suggestion underlying all the thoughtful work of the early twentieth century, both in America and England. In most of these things America was a little earlier than England, though both countries drove the same way.

That counter-revolution never came. It could never organise and keep pure. There was not enough of the old sentimentality, the old faith in righteousness, left among men. Any organisation that became big enough to influence the polls became complex enough to be undermined, broken up, or bought outright by capable rich men. Socialistic and Popular, Reactionary and Purity Parties were all at last mere Stock Exchange counters, selling their principles to pay for their electioneering. And the great concern of the rich was naturally to keep property intact, the board clear for the game of trade. Just as the feudal concern had been to keep the board clear for hunting and war. The whole world was exploited, a battlefield of businesses; and financial convulsions, the scourge of currency manipulation, tariff wars, made more human misery during the twentieth century – because the wretchedness was dreary life instead of speedy death – than had war, pestilence and famine, in the darkest hours of earlier history.

His own part in the development of this time he now knew clearly enough. Through the successive phases in the development of this mechanical civilisation, aiding and presently directing its development, there had grown a new power, the Council, the board of his trustees. At first it had been a mere chance union of the millions of Isbister and Warming, a mere property holding company, the creation of two childless testators' whims, but the collective talent of its first constitution had speedily guided it to a vast influence, until by title deed, loan and share, under a hundred disguises and pseudonyms it had ramified through the fabric of the American and English States.

Wielding an enormous influence and patronage, the Council had early assumed a political aspect; and in its development it had continually used its wealth to tip the beam of political decisions and its political advantages to grasp yet more and more wealth. At last the party organisations of two hemispheres were in its hands; it became an inner council of political control. Its last struggle was with the tacit alliance of the great Jewish families. But these families were linked only by a feeble sentiment, at any time inheritance might fling a huge fragment of their resources to a minor, a woman or a fool, marriages and legacies alienated hundreds of thousands at one blow. The Council had no such breach in its continuity. Steadily, steadfastly it grew.

The original Council was not simply twelve men of exceptional ability; they fused, it was a council of genius. It struck boldly for riches, for political influence, and the two subserved each other. With amazing foresight it

spent great sums of money on the art of flying, holding that invention back against an hour foreseen. It used the patent laws, and a thousand half-legal expedients, to hamper all investigators who refused to work with it. In the old days it never missed a capable man. It paid his price. Its policy in those days was vigorous – unerring, and against it as it grew steadily and incessantly was only the chaotic selfish rule of the casually rich. In a hundred years Graham had become almost exclusive owner of Africa, of South America, of France, of London, of England and all its influence – for all practical purposes, that is – a power in North America – then the dominant power in America. The Council bought and organised China, drilled Asia, crippled the Old World empires, undermined them financially, fought and defeated them.

And this spreading usurpation of the world was so dexterously performed – a proteus – hundreds of banks, companies, syndicates, masked the Council's operations – that it was already far advanced before common men suspected the tyranny that had come. The Council never hesitated, never faltered. Means of communication, land, buildings, governments, municipalities, the territorial companies of the tropics, every human enterprise, it gathered greedily. And it drilled and marshalled its men, its railway police, its roadway police, its house guards, and drain and cable guards, its hosts of land-workers. Their unions it did not fight, but it undermined and betrayed and bought them. It bought the world at last. And, finally, its culminating stroke was the introduction of flying.

When the Council, in conflict with the workers in some of its huge monopolies, did something flagrantly illegal and that without even the ordinary civility of bribery, the old Law, alarmed for the profits of its complaisance, looked about it for weapons. But there were no more armies, no fighting navies; the age of Peace had come. The only possible war ships were the great steam vessels of the Council's Navigation Trust. The police forces they controlled; the police of the railways, of the ships, of their agricultural estates, their timekeepers and order-keepers, outnumbered the neglected little forces of the old country and municipal organisations ten to one. And they produced flying machines. There were men alive still who could remember the last great debate in the London House of Commons – the legal party, the party against the Council was in a minority, but it made a desperate fight – and how the members came crowding out upon the terrace to see these great unfamiliar winged shapes circling quietly overhead. The Council had soared to its power. The last sham of a democracy that had permitted unlimited irresponsible property was at an end.

Within one hundred and fifty years of Graham's falling asleep, his Council had thrown off its disguises and ruled openly, supreme in his name. Elections had become a cheerful formality, a septennial folly, an ancient unmeaning custom; a social Parliament as ineffectual as the convocation of the Established Church in Victorian times assembled now and then; and a

legitimate King of England, disinherited, drunken and witless, played foolishly in a second-rate music-hall. So the magnificent dream of the nineteenth century, the noble project of universal individual liberty and universal happiness, touched by a disease of honour, crippled by a super-stition of absolute property, crippled by the religious feuds that had robbed the common citizens of education, robbed men of standards of conduct, and brought the sanctions of morality to utter contempt, had worked itself out in the face of invention and ignoble enterprise, first to a warring plutocracy, and finally to the rule of a supreme plutocrat. His Council at last had ceased even to trouble to have its decrees endorsed by the constitutional authorities, and he a motionless, sunken, yellow-skinned figure had lain, neither dead nor living, recognisably and immediately Master of the Earth. And awoke at last to find himself – Master of that inheritance! Awoke to stand under the cloudless empty sky and gaze down upon the greatness of his dominion.

To what end had he awakened? Was this city, this hive of hopeless toilers, the final refutation of his ancient hopes? Or was the fire of liberty, the fire that had blazed and waned in the years of his past life, still smouldering below there? He thought of the stir and impulse of the song of the revolution. Was that song merely the trick of a demagogue, to be forgotten when its purpose was served? Was the hope that still stirred within him only the memory of abandoned things, the vestige of a creed outworn? Or had it a wider meaning, an import interwoven with the destiny of man? To what end had he awakened, what was there for him to do? Humanity was spread below him like a map. He thought of the millions and millions of humanity following each other unceasingly for ever out of the darkness of non-existence into the darkness of death. To what end? Aim there must be, but it transcended his power of thought. He saw for the first time clearly his own infinite littleness, saw stark and terrible the tragic contrast of human strength and the craving of the human heart. For that little while he knew himself for the petty accident he was, and knew therewith the greatness of his desire. And suddenly his littleness was intolerable, his aspiration was intolerable, and there came to him an irresistible impulse to pray. And he prayed. He prayed vague, incoherent, contradictory things, his soul strained up through time and space and all the fleeting multitudinous confusion of being, towards something – he scarcely knew what – towards something that could comprehend his striving and endure.

A man and a woman were far below on a roof space to the southward enjoying the freshness of the morning air. The man had brought out a perspective glass to spy upon the Council House and he was showing her how to use it. Presently their curiosity was satisfied, they could see no traces of bloodshed from their position, and after a survey of the empty sky she came round to the crow's nest. And there she saw two little black figures, so

small it was hard to believe they were men, one who watched and one who gesticulated with hands outstretched to the silent emptiness of Heaven.

She handed the glass to the man. He looked and exclaimed: 'I believe it is the Master. Yes. I am sure. It is the Master!'

He lowered the glass and looked at her. 'Waving his hands about almost as if he was praying. I wonder what he is up to. Worshipping the sun? There weren't Parsees in this country in his time, were there?'

He looked again. 'He's stopped it now. It was a chance attitude, I suppose.' He put down the glass and became meditative. 'He won't have anything to do but enjoy himself – just enjoy himself. Ostrog will boss the show of course. Ostrog will have to, because of keeping all these Labourer fools in bounds. Them and their song! And got it all by sleeping, dear eyes – just sleeping. It's a wonderful world.'

CHAPTER FIFTEEN

Prominent People

The state apartments of the Wind Vane Keeper would have seemed astonishingly intricate to Graham had he entered them fresh from his nineteenth-century life, but already he was growing accustomed to the scale of the new time. They can scarcely be described as halls and rooms, seeing that a complicated system of arches, bridges, passages and galleries divided and united every part of the great space. He came out through one of the now familiar sliding panels upon a plateau of landing at the head of a flight of very broad and gentle steps, with men and women far more brilliantly dressed than any he had hitherto seen ascending and descending. From this position he looked down a vista of intricate ornament in lustreless white and mauve and purple, spanned by bridges that seemed wrought of porcelain and filigree, and terminating far off in a cloudy mystery of perforated screens.

Glancing upward, he saw tier above tier of ascending galleries with faces looking down upon him. The air was full of the babble of innumerable voices and of a music that descended from above, a gay and exhilarating music whose source he never discovered.

The central aisle was thick with people, but by no means uncomfortably crowded; altogether that assembly must have numbered many thousands. They were brilliantly, even fantastically dressed, the men as fancifully as the women, for the sobering influence of the Puritan conception of dignity upon masculine dress had long since passed away. The hair of the men, too, though it was rarely worn long, was commonly curled in a manner that suggested the barber, and baldness had vanished from the earth. Frizzy straight-cut masses that would have charmed Rossetti abounded, and one

gentleman, who was pointed out to Graham under the mysterious title of an 'amorist', wore his hair in two becoming plaits *à la* Marguerite. The pigtail was in evidence; it would seem that citizens of Chinese extraction were no longer ashamed of their race. There was little uniformity of fashion apparent in the forms of clothing worn. The more shapely men displayed their symmetry in trunk hose, and here were puffs and slashes, and there a cloak and there a robe. The fashions of the days of Leo the Tenth were perhaps the prevailing influence, but the aesthetic conceptions of the far east were also patent. Masculine embonpoint, which, in Victorian times, would have been subjected to the tightly buttoned perils, the ruthless exaggeration of tight-legged tight-armed evening dress, now formed but the basis of a wealth of dignity and drooping folds. Graceful slenderness abounded also. To Graham, a typically stiff man from a typically stiff period, not only did these men seem altogether too graceful in person, but altogether too expressive in their vividly expressive faces. They gesticulated, they expressed surprise, interest, amusement, above all, they expressed the emotions excited in their minds by the ladies about them with astonishing frankness. Even at the first glance it was evident that women were in a great majority.

The ladies in the company of these gentlemen displayed in dress, bearing and manner alike, less emphasis and more intricacy. Some affected a classical simplicity of robing and subtlety of fold, after the fashion of the First French Empire, and flashed conquering arms and shoulders as Graham passed. Others had closely fitting dresses without seam or belt at the waist, some-times with long folds falling from the shoulders. The delightful confidences of evening dress had not been diminished by the passage of two centuries.

Everyone's movements seemed graceful. Graham remarked to Lincoln that he saw men as Raphael's cartoons walking, and Lincoln told him that the attainment of an appropriate set of gestures was part of every rich person's education. The Master's entry was greeted with a sort of tittering applause, but these people showed their distinguished manners by not crowding upon him nor annoying him by any persistent scrutiny, as he descended the steps towards the floor of the aisle.

He had already learnt from Lincoln that these were the leaders of existing London society; almost every person there that night was either a powerful official or the immediate connection of a powerful official. Many had returned from the European Pleasure Cities expressly to welcome him. The aeronautic authorities, whose defection had played a part in the overthrow of the Council only second to Graham's, were very prominent, and so, too, was the Wind Vane Control. Among others there were several of the more prominent officers of the Food Trust; the controller of the European Piggeries had a particularly melancholy and interesting counten-ance and a daintily cynical manner. A bishop in full canonicals passed athwart Graham's vision, conversing with a gentleman dressed exactly like the traditional Chaucer, including even the laurel wreath.

'Who is that?' he asked almost involuntarily.

'The Bishop of London,' said Lincoln.

'No – the other, I mean.'

'Poet Laureate.'

'You still – ?'

'He doesn't make poetry, of course. He's a cousin of Wotton – one of the Councillors. But he's one of the Red Rose Royalists – a delightful club – and they keep up the tradition of these things.'

'Asano told me there was a King.'

'The King doesn't belong. They had to expel him. It's the Stuart blood, I suppose; but really – '

'Too much?'

'Far too much.'

Graham did not quite follow all this, but it seemed part of the general inversion of the new age. He bowed condescendingly to his first introduction. It was evident that subtle distinctions of class prevailed even in this assembly, that only to a small proportion of the guests, to an inner group, did Lincoln consider it appropriate to introduce him. This first introduction was the Master Aeronaut, a man whose suntanned face contrasted oddly with the delicate complexions about him. Just at present his critical defection from the Council made him a very important person indeed.

His manner contrasted very favourably, according to Graham's ideas, with the general bearing. He made a few commonplace remarks, assurances of loyalty and frank enquiries about the Master's health. His manner was breezy, his accent lacked the easy staccato of latter-day English. He made it admirably clear to Graham that he was a bluff 'aerial dog' – he used that phrase – that there was no nonsense about him, that he was a thoroughly manly fellow and old-fashioned at that, that he didn't profess to know much, and that what he did not know was not worth knowing. He made a manly bow, ostentatiously free from obsequiousness, and passed.

'I am glad to see that type endures,' said Graham

'Phonographs and kinematographs,' said Lincoln, a little spitefully. 'He has studied from the life.' Graham glanced at the burly form again. It was oddly reminiscent.

'As a matter of fact we bought him,' said Lincoln. 'Partly. And partly he was afraid of Ostrog. Everything rested with him.'

He turned sharply to introduce the Surveyor-General of the Public School Trust. This person was a willowy figure in a blue-grey academic gown, he beamed down upon Graham through *pince-nez* of a Victorian pattern, and illustrated his remarks by gestures of a beautifully manicured hand. Graham was immediately interested in this gentleman's functions, and asked him a number of singularly direct questions. The Surveyor-General seemed quietly amused at the Master's fundamental bluntness. He was a little vague as to the monopoly of education his Company possessed; it was done

by contract with the syndicate that ran the numerous London Municipalities, but he waxed enthusiastic over educational progress since the Victorian times. 'We have conquered Cram,' he said, 'completely conquered Cram – there is not an examination left in the world. Aren't you glad?'

'How do you get the work done?' asked Graham.

'We make it attractive – as attractive as possible. And if it does not attract then – we let it go. We cover an immense field.'

He proceeded to details, and they had a lengthy conversation. The Surveyor-General mentioned the names of Pestalozzi and Froebel with profound respect, although he displayed no intimacy with their epoch-making works. Graham learnt that University Extension still existed in a modified form. 'There is a certain type of girl, for example,' said the Surveyor-General, dilating with a sense of his usefulness, 'with a perfect passion for severe studies – when they are not too difficult you know. We cater for them by the thousand. At this moment,' he said with a Napoleonic touch, 'nearly five hundred phonographs are lecturing in different parts of London on the influence exercised by Plato and Swift on the love affairs of Shelley, Hazlitt, and Burns. And afterwards they write essays on the lectures, and the names in order of merit are put in conspicuous places. You see how your little germ has grown? The illiterate middle class of your days has quite passed away.'

'About the public elementary schools,' said Graham. 'Do you control them?'

The Surveyor-General did, 'entirely'. Now, Graham, in his later democratic days, had taken a keen interest in these and his questioning quickened. Certain casual phrases that had fallen from the old man with whom he had talked in the darkness recurred to him. The Surveyor-General, in effect, endorsed the old man's words. 'We have abolished Cram,' he said, a phrase Graham was beginning to interpret as the abolition of all sustained work. The Surveyor-General became sentimental. 'We try and make the elementary schools very pleasant for the little children. They will have to work so soon. Just a few simple principles – obedience – industry.'

'You teach them very little?'

'Why should we? It only leads to trouble and discontent. We amuse them. Even as it is – there are troubles – agitations. Where the labourers get the ideas, one cannot tell. They tell one another. There are socialistic dreams – anarchy even! Agitators will get to work among them. I take it – I have always taken it – that my foremost duty is to fight against popular discontent. Why should people be made unhappy?'

'I wonder,' said Graham thoughtfully. 'But there are a great many things I want to know.'

Lincoln, who had stood watching Graham's face throughout the conversation, intervened. 'There are others,' he said in an undertone.

The Surveyor-General of schools gesticulated himself away. 'Perhaps,'

said Lincoln, intercepting a casual glance, 'you would like to know some of these ladies?'

The daughter of the Manager of the Piggeries of the European Food Trust was a particularly charming little person with red hair and animated blue eyes. Lincoln left him awhile to converse with her, and she displayed herself as quite an enthusiast for the 'dear old times', as she called them, that had seen the beginning of his trance. As she talked she smiled, and her eyes smiled in a manner that demanded reciprocity.

'I have tried,' she said, 'countless times – to imagine those old romantic days. And to you they are memories. How strange and crowded the world must seem to you! I have seen photographs and pictures of the old times, the little isolated houses built of bricks made out of burnt mud and all black with soot from your fires, the railway bridges, the simple advertisements, the solemn savage Puritanical men in strange black coats and those tall hats of theirs, iron railway trains on iron bridges overhead, horses and cattle, and even dogs running half wild about the streets. And suddenly, you have come into this!'

'Into this,' said Graham.

'Out of your life – out of all that was familiar.'

'The old life was not a happy one,' said Graham. 'I do not regret that.'

She looked at him quickly. There was a brief pause. She sighed encouragingly. 'No?'

'No,' said Graham. 'It was a little life – and unmeaning. But this – . We thought the world complex and crowded and civilised enough. Yet I see – although in this world I am barely four days old – looking back on my own time, that it was a queer, barbaric time – the mere beginning of this new order. The mere beginning of this new order. You will find it hard to understand how little I know.'

'You may ask me what you like,' she said, smiling at him.

'Then tell me who these people are. I'm still very much in the dark about them. It's puzzling. Are there any Generals?'

'Men in hats and feathers?'

'Of course not. No. I suppose they are the men who control the great public businesses. Who is that distinguished-looking man?'

'That? He's a most important officer. That is Morden. He is managing director of the Antibilious Pill Company. I have heard that his workers sometimes turn out a myriad myriad pills a day in the twenty-four hours. Fancy a myriad myriad!'

'A myriad myriad. No wonder he looks proud,' said Graham. 'Pills! What a wonderful time it is! That man in purple?'

'He is not quite one of the inner circle, you know. But we like him. He is really clever and very amusing. He is one of the heads of the Medical Faculty of our London University. All medical men, you know, are share-holders in the Medical Faculty Company, and wear that purple. You have to

be – to be qualified. But of course, people who are paid by fees for *doing* something – ' She smiled away the social pretensions of all such people.

'Are any of your great artists or authors here?'

'No authors. They are mostly such queer people – and so preoccupied about themselves. And they quarrel so dreadfully! They will fight, some of them, for precedence on staircases! Dreadful isn't it? But I think Wraysbury, the fashionable capillotomist, is here. From Capri.'

'Capillotomist,' said Graham. 'Ah! I remember. An artist! Why not?'

'We have to cultivate him,' she said apologetically. 'Our heads are in his hands.' She smiled.

Graham hesitated at the invited compliment, but his glance was expressive. 'Have the arts grown with the rest of civilised things?' he said. 'Who are your great painters?'

She looked at him doubtfully. Then laughed. 'For a moment,' she said, 'I thought you meant – ' She laughed again. 'You mean, of course, those good men you used to think so much of because they could cover great spaces of canvas with oil-colours? Great oblongs. And people used to put the things in gilt frames and hang them up in rows in their square rooms. We haven't any. People grew tired of that sort of thing.'

'But what did you think I meant?'

She put a finger significantly on a cheek whose glow was above suspicion, and smiled and looked very arch and pretty and inviting. 'And here,' and she indicated her eyelid.

Graham had an adventurous moment. Then a grotesque memory of a picture he had somewhere seen of Uncle Toby and the Widow flashed across his mind. An archaic shame came upon him. He became acutely aware that he was visible to a great number of interested people. 'I see,' he remarked inadequately. He turned awkwardly away from her fascinating facility. He looked about him to meet a number of eyes that immediately occupied themselves with other things. Possibly he coloured a little. 'Who is that talking with the lady in saffron?' he asked, avoiding her eyes.

The person in question he learnt was one of the great organisers of the American theatres just fresh from a gigantic production at Mexico. His face reminded Graham of a bust of Caligula. Another striking-looking man was the Black Labour Master. The phrase at the time made no deep impression, but afterwards it recurred; – the Black Labour Master? The little lady, in no degree embarrassed, pointed out to him a charming little woman as one of the subsidiary wives of the Anglican Bishop of London. She added encomiums on the episcopal courage – hitherto there had been a rule of clerical monogamy – 'neither a natural nor an expedient condition of things. Why should the natural development of the affections be dwarfed and restricted because a man is a priest?'

'And, by the by,' she added, 'are you an Anglican?' Graham was on the verge of hesitating enquiries about the status of a 'subsidiary wife',

apparently an euphemistic phrase, when Lincoln's return broke off this very suggestive and interesting conversation. They crossed the aisle to where a tall man in crimson, and two charming persons in Burmese costume (as it seemed to him) awaited him diffidently. From their civilities he passed to other presentations.

In a little while his multitudinous impressions began to organise themselves into a general effect. At first the glitter of the gathering had raised all the democrat in Graham; he had felt hostile and satirical. But it is not in human nature to resist an atmosphere of courteous regard. Soon the music, the light, the play of colours, the shining arms and shoulders about him, the touch of hands, the transient interest of smiling faces, the frothing sound of skilfully modulated voices, the atmosphere of compliment, interest and respect, had woven together into a fabric of indisputable pleasure. Graham for a time forgot his spacious resolutions. He gave way insensibly to the intoxication of the position that was conceded him, his manner became less conscious, more convincingly regal, his feet walked assuredly, the black robe fell with a bolder fold and pride ennobled his voice. After all this was a brilliant interesting world.

His glance went approvingly over the shifting colours of the people, it rested here and there in kindly criticism upon a face. Presently it occurred to him that he owed some apology to the charming little person with the red hair and blue eyes. He felt guilty of a clumsy snub. It was not princely to ignore her advances, even if his policy necessitated their rejection. He wondered if he should see her again. And suddenly a little thing touched all the glamour of this brilliant gathering and changed its quality.

He looked up and saw passing across a bridge of porcelain and looking down upon him, a face that was almost immediately hidden, the face of the girl he had seen overnight in the little room beyond the theatre after his escape from the Council. And she was looking with much the same expression of curious expectation, of uncertain intentness, upon his proceedings. For the moment he did not remember when he had seen her, and then with recognition came a vague memory of the stirring emotions of their first encounter. But the dancing web of melody about him kept the air of that great marching song from his memory.

The lady to whom he was talking repeated her remark, and Graham recalled himself to the quasi-regal flirtation upon which he was engaged.

But from that moment a vague restlessness, a feeling that grew to dissatisfaction, came into his mind. He was troubled as if by some half-forgotten duty, by the sense of things important slipping from him amidst this light and brilliance. The attraction that these bright ladies who crowded about him were beginning to exercise ceased. He no longer made vague and clumsy responses to the subtly amorous advances that he was now assured were being made to him, and his eyes wandered for another sight of that face that had appealed so strongly to his sense of beauty. But he

did not see her again until he was awaiting Lincoln's return to leave this assembly. In answer to his request Lincoln had promised that an attempt should be made to fly that afternoon, if the weather permitted. He had gone to make certain necessary arrangements.

Graham was in one of the upper galleries in conversation with a bright-eyed lady on the subject of Eadhamite – the subject was his choice and not hers. He had interrupted her warm assurances of personal devotion with a matter-of-fact enquiry. He found her, as he had already found several other latter-day women that night, less well informed than charming. Suddenly, struggling against the eddying drift of nearer melody, the song of the Revolt, the great song he had heard in the Hall, hoarse and massive, came beating down to him.

He glanced up startled, and perceived above him an *oeil de boeuf* through which this song had come, and beyond, the upper courses of cable, the blue haze, and the pendant fabric of the lights of the public ways. He heard the song break into a tumult of voices and cease. But now he perceived quite clearly the drone and tumult of the moving platforms and a murmur of many people. He had a vague persuasion that he could not account for, a sort of instinctive feeling that outside in the ways a huge crowd must be watching this place in which their Master amused himself. He wondered what they might be thinking.

Though the song had stopped so abruptly, though the special music of this gathering reasserted itself, the *motif* of the marching song, once it had begun, lingered in his mind.

The bright-eyed lady was still struggling with the mysteries of Eadhamite when he perceived the girl he had seen in the theatre again. She was coming now along the gallery towards him; he saw her first before she saw him. She was dressed in a faintly luminous grey, her dark hair about her brows was like a cloud, and as he saw her the cold light from the circular opening into the ways fell upon her downcast face.

The lady in trouble about the Eadhamite saw the change in his expression, and grasped her opportunity to escape. 'Would you care to know that girl, Sire?' she asked boldly. 'She is Helen Wotton – a niece of Ostrog's. She knows a great many serious things. She is one of the most serious persons alive. I am sure you will like her.'

In another moment Graham was talking to the girl, and the bright-eyed lady had fluttered away.

'I remember you quite well,' said Graham. 'You were in that little room. When all the people were singing and beating time with their feet. Before I walked across the Hall.'

Her momentary embarrassment passed. She looked up at him, and her face was steady. 'It was wonderful,' she said, hesitated, and spoke with a sudden effort. 'All those people would have died for you, Sire. Countless people did die for you that night.'

Her face glowed. She glanced swiftly aside to see that no other heard her words.

Lincoln appeared some way off along the gallery, making his way through the press towards them. She saw him and turned to Graham strangely eager, with a swift change to confidence and intimacy. 'Sire,' she said quickly, 'I cannot tell you now and here. But the common people are very unhappy; they are oppressed – they are misgoverned. Do not forget the people, who faced death – death that you might live.'

'I know nothing – ' began Graham.

'I cannot tell you now.'

Lincoln's face appeared close to them. He bowed an apology to the girl.

'You find the new world pleasant, Sire?' asked Lincoln, with smiling deference, and indicating the space and splendour of the gathering by one comprehensive gesture. 'At any rate, you find it changed.'

'Yes,' said Graham, 'changed. And yet, after all, not so greatly changed.'

'Wait till you are in the air,' said Lincoln. 'The wind has fallen; even now an aeropile awaits you.'

The girl's attitude awaited dismissal.

Graham glanced at her face, was on the verge of a question, found a warning in her expression, bowed to her and turned to accompany Lincoln.

CHAPTER SIXTEEN

The Aeropile

For a while, as Graham went through the passages of the Wind Vane Offices with Lincoln, he was preoccupied. But, by an effort, he attended to the things which Lincoln was saying. Soon his preoccupation vanished. Lincoln was talking of flying. Graham had a strong desire to know more of this new human attainment. He began to ply Lincoln with questions. He had followed the crude beginnings of aerial navigation very keenly in his previous life; he was delighted to find the familiar names of Maxim and Pilcher, Langley and Chanute, and, above all, of the aerial proto-martyr Lilienthal, still honoured by men.

Even during his previous life two lines of investigation had pointed clearly to two distinct types of contrivance as possible, and both of these had been realised. On the one hand was the great engine-driven aeroplane, a double row of horizontal floats with a big aerial screw behind, and on the other the nimbler aeropile. The aeroplanes flew safely only in a calm or moderate wind, and sudden storms, occurrences that were now accurately predictable, rendered them for all practical purposes useless. They were built of enormous size – the usual stretch of wing being six hundred feet or more, and the length of the fabric a thousand feet. They were for passenger

traffic alone. The lightly swung car they carried was from a hundred to a hundred and fifty feet in length. It was hung in a peculiar manner in order to minimise the complex vibration that even a moderate wind produced, and for the same reason the little seats within the car – each passenger remained seated during the voyage – were slung with great freedom of movement. The starting of the mechanism was only possible from a gigantic car on the rail of a specially constructed stage. Graham had seen these vast stages, the flying stages, from the crow's nest very well. Six huge blank areas they were, with a giant 'carrier' stage on each.

The choice of descent was equally circumscribed, an accurately plane surface being needed for safe grounding. Apart from the destruction that would have been caused by the descent of this great expanse of sail and metal, and the impossibility of its rising again, the concussion of an irregular surface, a tree-set hillside, for instance, or an embankment, would be sufficient to pierce or damage the framework, to smash the ribs of the body, and perhaps kill those aboard.

At first Graham felt disappointed with these cumbersome contrivances, but he speedily grasped the fact that smaller machines would have been unremunerative, for the simple reason that their carrying power would be disproportionately diminished with diminished size. Moreover, the huge size of these things enabled them – and it was a consideration of primary importance – to traverse the air at enormous speeds, and so run no risks of unanticipated weather. The briefest journey performed, that from London to Paris, took about three-quarters of an hour, but the velocity attained was not high; the leap to New York occupied about two hours, and by timing oneself carefully at the intermediate stations it was possible in quiet weather to go around the world in a day.

The little aeropiles (as for no particular reason they were distinctively called) were of an altogether different type. Several of these were going to and fro in the air. They were designed to carry only one or two persons, and their manufacture and maintenance was so costly as to render them the monopoly of the richer sort of people. Their sails, which were brilliantly coloured, consisted only of two pairs of lateral air floats in the same plane, and of a screw behind. Their small size rendered a descent in any open space neither difficult nor disagreeable, and it was possible to attach pneumatic wheels or even the ordinary motors for terrestrial traffic to them, and so carry them to a convenient starting place. They required a special sort of swift car to throw them into the air, but such a car was efficient in any open place clear of high buildings or trees. Human aeronautics, Graham perceived, were evidently still a long way behind the instinctive gift of the albatross or the flycatcher. One great influence that might have brought the aeropile to a more rapid perfection had been withheld; these inventions had never been used in warfare. The last great international struggle had occurred before the usurpation of the Council.

The Flying Stages of London were collected together in an irregular crescent on the southern side of the river. They formed three groups of two each and retained the names of ancient suburban hills or villages. They were named in order, Roehampton, Wimbledon Park, Streatham, Norwood, Blackheath, and Shooter's Hill. They were uniform structures rising high above the general roof surfaces. Each was about four thousand yards long and a thousand broad, and constructed of the compound of aluminium and iron that had replaced iron in architecture. Their higher tiers formed an openwork of girders through which lifts and staircases ascended. The upper surface was a uniform expanse, with portions – the starting carriers – that could be raised and were then able to run on very slightly inclined rails to the end of the fabric. Save for any aeropiles or aeroplanes that were in port these open surfaces were kept clear for arrivals.

During the adjustment of the aeroplanes it was the custom for passengers to wait in the system of theatres, restaurants, newsrooms, and places of pleasure and indulgence of various sorts that interwove with the prosperous shops below. This portion of London was in consequence commonly the gayest of all its districts, with something of the meretricious gaiety of a seaport or city of hotels. And for those who took a more serious view of aeronautics, the religious quarters had flung out an attractive colony of devotional chapels, while a host of brilliant medical establishments competed to supply physical preparatives for the journey. At various levels through the mass of chambers and passages beneath these, ran, in addition to the main moving ways of the city which laced and gathered here, a complex system of special passages and lifts and slides, for the convenient interchange of people and luggage between stage and stage. And a distinctive feature of the architecture of this section was the ostentatious massiveness of the metal piers and girders that everywhere broke the vistas and spanned the halls and passages, crowding and twining up to meet the weight of the stages and the weighty impact of the aeroplanes overhead.

Graham went to the flying stages by the public ways. He was accompanied by Asano, his Japanese attendant. Lincoln was called away by Ostrog, who was busy with his administrative concerns. A strong guard of the Wind-Vane police awaited the Master outside the Wind-Vane offices, and they cleared a space for him on the upper moving platform. His passage to the flying stages was unexpected, nevertheless a considerable crowd gathered and followed him to his destination. As he went along, he could hear the people shouting his name, and saw numberless men and women and children in blue come swarming up the staircases in the central path, gesticulating and shouting. He could not hear what they shouted. He was struck again by the evident existence of a vulgar dialect among the poor of the city. When at last he descended, his guards were immediately surrounded by a dense excited crowd. Afterwards it occurred to him that some had attempted to reach him with petitions. His guards cleared a passage for him with difficulty.

He found an aeropile in charge of an aeronaut awaiting him on the westward stage. Seen close this mechanism was no longer small. As it lay on its launching carrier upon the wide expanse of the flying stage, its aluminium body skeleton was as big as the hull of a twenty-ton yacht. Its lateral supporting sails braced and stayed with metal nerves almost like the nerves of a bee's wing, and made of some sort of glassy artificial membrane, cast their shadow over many hundreds of square yards. The chairs for the engineer and his passenger hung free to swing by a complex tackle, within the protecting ribs of the frame and well abaft the middle. The passenger's chair was protected by a wind-guard and guarded about with metallic rods carrying air cushions. It could, if desired, be completely closed in, but Graham was anxious for novel experiences, and desired that it should be left open. The aeronaut sat behind a glass that sheltered his face. The passenger could secure himself firmly in his seat, and this was almost unavoidable on landing, or he could move along by means of a little rail and rod to a locker at the stem of the machine, where his personal luggage, his wraps and restoratives were placed, and which also with the seats, served as a make-weight to the parts of the central engine that projected to the propeller at the stern.

The engine was very simple in appearance. Asano, pointing out the parts of this apparatus to him, told him that, like the gas-engine of Victorian days, it was of the explosive type, burning a small drop of a substance called 'fomile' at each stroke. It consisted simply of reservoir and piston about the long fluted crank of the propeller shaft. So much Graham saw of the machine.

The flying stage about him was empty save for Asano and their suite of attendants. Directed by the aeronaut he placed himself in his seat. He then drank a mixture containing ergot – a dose, he learnt, invariably administered to those about to fly, and designed to counteract the possible effect of diminished air pressure upon the system. Having done so, he declared himself ready for the journey. Asano took the empty glass from him, stepped through the bars of the hull, and stood below on the stage waving his hand. Suddenly he seemed to slide along the stage to the right and vanish.

The engine was beating, the propeller spinning, and for a second the stage and the buildings beyond were gliding swiftly and horizontally past Graham's eye; then these things seemed to tilt up abruptly. He gripped the little rods on either side of him instinctively. He felt himself moving upward, heard the air whistle over the top of the windscreen. The propeller screw moved round with powerful rhythmic impulses – one, two, three, pause; one, two, three – which the engineer controlled very delicately. The machine began a quivering vibration that continued throughout the flight, and the roof areas seemed running away to starboard very quickly and growing rapidly smaller. He looked from the face of the engineer through the ribs of the machine. Looking sideways, there was nothing very startling

in what he saw – a rapid funicular railway might have given the same sensations. He recognised the Council House and the Highgate Ridge. And then he looked straight down between his feet.

For a moment physical terror possessed him, a passionate sense of insecurity. He held tight. For a second or so he could not lift his eyes. Some hundred feet or more sheer below him was one of the big wind-vanes of south-west London, and beyond it the southernmost flying stage crowded with little black dots. These things seemed to be falling away from him. For a second he had an impulse to pursue the earth. He set his teeth, he lifted his eyes by a muscular effort, and the moment of panic passed.

He remained for a space with his teeth set hard, his eyes staring into the sky. Throb, throb, throb – beat, went the engine; throb, throb, throb, – beat. He gripped his bars tightly, glanced at the aeronaut, and saw a smile upon his suntanned face. He smiled in return – perhaps a little artificially. 'A little strange at first,' he shouted before he recalled his dignity. But he dared not look down again for some time. He stared over the aeronaut's head to where a rim of vague blue horizon crept up the sky. For a little while he could not banish the thought of possible accidents from his mind. Throb, throb, throb – beat; suppose some trivial screw went wrong in that supporting engine! Suppose – ! He made a grim effort to dismiss all such suppositions. After a while they did at least abandon the foreground of his thoughts. And up he went steadily, higher and higher into the clear air.

Once the mental shock of moving unsupported through the air was over, his sensations ceased to be unpleasant, became very speedily pleasurable. He had been warned of air sickness. But he found the pulsating movement of the aeropile as it drove up the faint south-west breeze was very little in excess of the pitching of a boat head on to broad rollers in a moderate gale, and he was constitutionally a good sailor. And the keenness of the more rarefied air into which they ascended produced a sense of lightness and exhilaration. He looked up and saw the blue sky above fretted with cirrus clouds. His eye came cautiously down through the ribs and bars to a shining flight of white birds that hung in the lower sky. For a space he watched these. Then going lower and less apprehensively, he saw the slender figure of the wind-vane keeper's crow's nest shining golden in the sunlight and growing smaller every moment. As his eye fell with more confidence now, there came a blue line of hills, and then London, already to leeward, an intricate space of roofing. Its near edge came sharp and clear, and banished his last apprehensions in a shock of surprise. For the boundary of London was like a wall, like a cliff, a steep fall of three or four hundred feet, a frontage broken only by terraces here and there, a complex decorative façade.

That gradual passage of town into country through an extensive sponge of suburbs, which was so characteristic a feature of the great cities of the nineteenth century, existed no longer. Nothing remained of it but a waste

of ruins here, variegated and dense with thickets of the heterogeneous growths that had once adorned the gardens of the belt, interspersed among levelled brown patches of sown ground, and verdant stretches of winter greens. The latter even spread among the vestiges of houses. But for the most part the reefs and skerries of ruins, the wreckage of suburban villas, stood among their streets and roads, queer islands amidst the levelled expanses of green and brown, abandoned indeed by the inhabitants years since, but too substantial, it seemed, to be cleared out of the way of the wholesale horticultural mechanisms of the time.

The vegetation of this waste undulated and frothed amidst the countless cells of crumbling house walls, and broke along the foot of the city wall in a surf of bramble and holly and ivy and teazle and tall grasses. Here and there gaudy pleasure palaces towered amidst the puny remains of Victorian times, and cable ways slanted to them from the city. That winter day they seemed deserted. Deserted, too, were the artificial gardens among the ruins. The city limits were indeed as sharply defined as in the ancient days when the gates were shut at nightfall and the robber foreman prowled to the very walls. A huge semicircular throat poured out a vigorous traffic upon the Eadhamite Bath Road. So the first prospect of the world beyond the city flashed on Graham, and dwindled. And when at last he could look vertically downward again, he saw below him the vegetable fields of the Thames valley – innumerable minute oblongs of ruddy brown, intersected by shining threads, the sewage ditches.

His exhilaration increased rapidly, became a sort of intoxication. He found himself drawing deep breaths of air, laughing aloud, desiring to shout. After a time that desire became too strong for him, and he shouted.

The machine had now risen as high as was customary with aeropiles, and they began to curve about towards the south. Steering, Graham perceived, was effected by the opening or closing of one or two thin strips of membrane in one or other of the otherwise rigid wings, and by the movement of the whole engine backward or forward along its supports. The aeronaut set the engine gliding slowly forward along its rail and opened the valve of the leeward wing until the stem of the aeropile was horizontal and pointing southward. And in that direction they drove with a slight list to leeward, and with a slow alternation of movement, first a short, sharp ascent and then a long downward glide that was very swift and pleasing. During these downward glides the propeller was inactive altogether. These ascents gave Graham a glorious sense of successful effort; the descents through the rarefied air were beyond all experience. He wanted never to leave the upper air again.

For a time he was intent upon the minute details of the landscape that ran swiftly northward beneath him. Its minute, clear detail pleased him exceedingly. He was impressed by the ruin of the houses that had once dotted the country, by the vast treeless expanse of country from which all

farms and villages had gone, save for crumbling ruins. He had known the thing was so, but seeing it so was an altogether different matter. He tried to make out places he had known within the hollow basin of the world below, but at first he could distinguish no data now that the Thames valley was left behind. Soon, however, they were driving over a sharp chalk hill that he recognised as the Guildford Hog's Back, because of the familiar outline of the gorge at its eastward end, and because of the ruins of the town that rose steeply on either lip of this gorge. And from that he made out other points, Leith Hill, the sandy wastes of Aldershot, and so forth. The Downs escarpment was set with gigantic slow-moving wind-wheels. Save where the broad Eadhamite Portsmouth Road, thickly dotted with rushing shapes, followed the course of the old railway, the gorge of the Wey was choked with thickets.

The whole expanse of the Downs escarpment, so far as the grey haze permitted him to see, was set with wind-wheels to which the largest of the city was but a younger brother. They stirred with a stately motion before the south-west wind. And here and there were patches dotted with the sheep of the British Food Trust, and here and there a mounted shepherd made a spot of black. Then rushing under the stern of the aeropile came the Wealden Heights, the line of Hindhead, Pitch Hill, and Leith Hill, with a second row of wind-wheels that seemed striving to rob the downland whirlers of their share of breeze. The purple heather was speckled with yellow gorse, and on the further side a drove of black oxen stampeded before a couple of mounted men. Swiftly these swept behind, and dwindled and lost colour, and became scarce moving specks that were swallowed up in haze.

And when these had vanished in the distance Graham heard a peewit wailing close at hand. He perceived he was now above the South Downs, and staring over his shoulder saw the battlements of Portsmouth Landing Stage towering over the ridge of Portsdown Hill. In another moment there came into sight a spread of shipping like floating cities, the little white cliffs of the Needles dwarfed and sunlit, and the grey and glittering waters of the narrow sea. They seemed to leap the Solent in a moment, and in a few seconds the Isle of Wight was running past, and then beneath him spread a wider and wider extent of sea, here purple with the shadow of a cloud, here grey, here a burnished mirror, and here a spread of cloudy greenish blue. The Isle of Wight grew smaller and smaller. In a few more minutes a strip of grey haze detached itself from other strips that were clouds, descended out of the sky and became a coastline – sunlit and pleasant – the coast of northern France. It rose, it took colour, became definite and detailed, and the counterpart of the Downland of England was speeding by below.

In a little time, as it seemed, Paris came above the horizon, and hung there for a space, and sank out of sight again as the aeropile circled about to the north again. But he perceived the Eiffel Tower still standing, and beside it a huge dome surmounted by a pinpoint Colossus. And he perceived, too,

though he did not understand it at the time, a slanting drift of smoke. The aeronaut said something about 'trouble in the underways', that Graham did not heed at the time. But he marked the minarets and towers and slender masses that streamed skyward above the city wind-vanes, and knew that in the matter of grace at least Paris still kept in front of her larger rival. And even as he looked a pale blue shape ascended very swiftly from the city like a dead leaf driving up before a gale. It curved round and soared towards them growing rapidly larger and larger. The aeronaut was saying something. 'What?' said Graham, loath to take his eyes from this. 'Aeroplane, Sire,' bawled the aeronaut pointing.

They rose and curved about northward as it drew nearer. Nearer it came and nearer, larger and larger. The throb, throb, throb – beat, of the aeropile's flight, that had seemed so potent and so swift, suddenly appeared slow by comparison with this tremendous rush. How great the monster seemed, how swift and steady! It passed quite closely beneath them, driving along silently, a vast spread of wire-netted translucent wings, a thing alive. Graham had a momentary glimpse of the rows and rows of wrapped-up passengers, slung in their little cradles behind windscreens, of a white-clothed engineer crawling against the gale along a ladder way, of spouting engines beating together, of the whirling wind screw, and of a wide waste of wing. He exulted in the sight. And in an instant the thing had passed.

It rose slightly and their own little wings swayed in the rush of its flight. It fell and grew smaller. Scarcely had they moved, as it seemed, before it was again only a flat blue thing that dwindled in the sky. This was the aeroplane that went to and fro between London and Paris. In fair weather and in peaceful times it came and went four times a day.

They beat across the Channel, slowly as it seemed now, to Graham's enlarged ideas, and Beachy Head rose greyly to the left of them.

'Land,' called the aeronaut, his voice small against the whistling of the air over the windscreen.

'Not yet,' bawled Graham, laughing. 'Not land yet. I want to learn more of this machine.'

'I meant – ' said the aeronaut.

'I want to learn more of this machine,' repeated Graham. 'I'm coming to you,' he said, and had flung himself free of his chair and taken a step along the guarded rail between them. He stopped for a moment, and his colour changed and his hands tightened. Another step and he was clinging close to the aeronaut. He felt a weight on his shoulder, the pressure of the air. His hat was a whirling speck behind. The wind came in gusts over his windscreen and blew his hair in streamers past his cheek. The aeronaut made some hasty adjustments for the shifting of the centres of gravity and pressure.

'I want to have these things explained,' said Graham. 'What do you do when you move that engine forward?'

The aeronaut hesitated. Then he answered, 'They are complex, Sire.'

'I don't mind,' shouted Graham. 'I don't mind.'

There was a moment's pause. 'Aeronautics is the secret – the privilege – '

'I know. But I'm the Master, and I mean to know.' He laughed, full of this novel realisation of power that was his gift from the upper air.

The aeropile curved about, and the keen fresh wind cut across Graham's face and his garment tugged at his body as the stem pointed round to the west. The two men looked into each other's eyes.

'Sire, there are rules – '

'Not where I am concerned,' said Graham. 'You seem to forget.'

The aeronaut scrutinised his face. 'No,' he said. 'I do not forget, Sire. But in all the earth – no man who is not a sworn aeronaut – has ever a chance. They come as passengers – '

'I have heard something of the sort. But I'm not going to argue these points. Do you know why I have slept two hundred years? To fly!'

'Sire,' said the aeronaut, 'the rules – if I break the rules – '

Graham waved the penalties aside.

'Then if you will watch me – '

'No,' said Graham, swaying and gripping tight as the machine lifted its nose again for an ascent. 'That's not my game. I want to do it myself. Do it myself if I smash for it! No! I will. See. I am going to clamber by this to come and share your seat. Steady! I mean to fly of my own accord if I smash at the end of it. I will have something to pay for my sleep. Of all other things – . In my past it was my dream to fly. Now – keep your balance.'

'A dozen spies are watching me, Sire!'

Graham's temper was at end. Perhaps he chose it should be. He swore. He swung himself round the intervening mass of levers and the aeropile swayed.

'Am I Master of the earth?' he said. 'Or is your Society? Now. Take your hands off those levers, and hold my wrists. Yes – so. And now, how do we turn her nose down to the glide?'

'Sire,' said the aeronaut.

'What is it?'

'You will protect me?'

'Lord! Yes! If I have to burn London. Now!'

And with that promise Graham bought his first lesson in aerial navigation. 'It's clearly to your advantage, this journey,' he said with a loud laugh – for the air was like strong wine – 'to teach me quickly and well. Do I pull this? Ah! So! Hullo!'

'Back, Sire! Back!'

'Back – right. One – two – three – good God! Ah! Up she goes! But this is living!'

And now the machine began to dance the strangest figures in the air. Now it would sweep round a spiral of scarcely a hundred yards diameter, now it would rush up into the air and swoop down again, steeply, swiftly, falling like

a hawk, to recover in a rushing loop that swept it high again. In one of these descents it seemed driving straight at the drifting park of balloons in the south-east, and only curved about and cleared them by a sudden recovery of dexterity. The extraordinary swiftness and smoothness of the motion, the extraordinary effect of the rarefied air upon his constitution, threw Graham into a careless fury.

But at last a queer incident came to sober him, to send him flying down once more to the crowded life below with all its dark insoluble riddles. As he swooped, came a tap and something flying past, and a drop like a drop of rain. Then as he went on down he saw something like a white rag whirling down in his wake. 'What was that?' he asked. 'I did not see.'

The aeronaut glanced, and then clutched at the lever to recover, for they were sweeping down. When the aeropile was rising again he drew a deep breath and replied. 'That,' and he indicated the white thing still fluttering down, 'was a swan.'

'I never saw it,' said Graham.

The aeronaut made no answer, and Graham saw little drops upon his forehead.

They drove horizontally while Graham clambered back to the passenger's place out of the lash of the wind. And then came a swift rush down, with the wind-screw whirling to check their fall, and the flying stage growing broad and dark before them. The sun, sinking over the chalk hills in the west, fell with them, and left the sky a blaze of gold.

Soon men could be seen as little specks. He heard a noise coming up to meet him, a noise like the sound of waves upon a pebbly beach, and saw that the roofs about the flying stage were dark with his people rejoicing over his safe return. A dark mass was crushed together under the stage, a darkness stippled with innumerable faces, and quivering with the minute oscillation of waved white handkerchiefs and waving hands.

CHAPTER SEVENTEEN

Three Days

Lincoln awaited Graham in an apartment beneath the flying stages. He seemed curious to learn all that had happened, pleased to hear of the extraordinary delight and interest which Graham took in flying. Graham was in a mood of enthusiasm. 'I must learn to fly,' he cried. 'I must master that. I pity all poor souls who have died without this opportunity. The sweet swift air! It is the most wonderful experience in the world.'

'You will find our new times full of wonderful experiences,' said Lincoln. 'I do not know what you will care to do now. We have music that may seem novel.'

'For the present,' said Graham, 'flying holds me. Let me learn more of that. Your aeronaut was saying there is some trades union objection to one's learning.'

'There is, I believe,' said Lincoln. 'But for you – ! If you would like to occupy yourself with that, we can make you a sworn aeronaut tomorrow.'

Graham expressed his wishes vividly and talked of his sensations for a while. 'And as for affairs,' he asked abruptly. 'How are things going on?'

Lincoln waved affairs aside. 'Ostrog will tell you that tomorrow,' he said. 'Everything is settling down. The Revolution accomplishes itself all over the world. Friction is inevitable here and there, of course; but your rule is assured. You may rest secure with things in Ostrog's hands.'

'Would it be possible for me to be made a sworn aeronaut, as you call it, forthwith – before I sleep?' said Graham, pacing. 'Then I could be at it the very first thing tomorrow again . . . '

'It would be possible,' said Lincoln thoughtfully. 'Quite possible. Indeed, it shall be done.' He laughed. 'I came prepared to suggest amusements, but you have found one for yourself. I will telephone to the aeronautical offices from here and we will return to your apartments in the Wind-Vane Control. By the time you have dined the aeronauts will be able to come. You don't think that after you have dined, you might prefer – ?' He paused.

'Yes,' said Graham.

'We had prepared a show of dancers – they have been brought from the Capri theatre.'

'I hate ballets,' said Graham, shortly. 'Always did. That other – . That's not what I want to see. We had dancers in the old days. For the matter of that, they had them in ancient Egypt. But flying – '

'True,' said Lincoln. 'Though our dancers – '

'They can afford to wait,' said Graham; 'they can afford to wait. I know. I'm not a Latin. There's questions I want to ask some expert – about your machinery. I'm keen. I want no distractions.'

'You have the world to choose from,' said Lincoln; 'whatever you want is yours.'

Asano appeared, and under the escort of a strong guard they returned through the city streets to Graham's apartments. Far larger crowds had assembled to witness his return than his departure had gathered, and the shouts and cheering of these masses of people sometimes drowned Lincoln's answers to the endless questions Graham's aerial journey had suggested. At first Graham had acknowledged the cheering and cries of the crowd by bows and gestures, but Lincoln warned him that such a recognition would be considered incorrect behaviour. Graham, already a little wearied by rhythmic civilities, ignored his subjects for the remainder of his public progress.

Directly they arrived at his apartments Asano departed in search of kinematographic renderings of machinery in motion, and Lincoln

despatched Graham's commands for models of machines and small machines to illustrate the various mechanical advances of the last two centuries. The little group of appliances for telegraphic communication attracted the Master so strongly that his delightfully prepared dinner, served by a number of charmingly dexterous girls, waited for a space. The habit of smoking had almost ceased from the face of the earth, but when he expressed a wish for that indulgence, enquiries were made and some excellent cigars were discovered in Florida, and sent to him by pneumatic dispatch while the dinner was still in progress. Afterwards came the aeronauts, and a feast of ingenious wonders in the hands of a latter-day engineer. For the time, at any rate, the neat dexterity of counting and numbering machines, building machines, spinning engines, patent doorways, explosive motors, grain and water elevators, slaughterhouse machines and harvesting appliances, was more fascinating to Graham than any bayadère. 'We were savages,' was his refrain, 'we were savages. We were in the stone age – compared with this . . . And what else have you?'

There came also practical psychologists with some very interesting developments in the art of hypnotism. The names of Milne Bramwell, Fechner, Liebault, William James, Myers and Gurney, he found, bore a value now that would have astonished their contemporaries. Several practical applications of psychology were now in general use; it had largely superseded drugs, antiseptics and anaesthetics in medicine; was employed by almost all who had any need of mental concentration. A real enlargement of human faculty seemed to have been effected in this direction. The feats of 'calculating boys', the wonders, as Graham had been wont to regard them, of mesmerisers, were now within the range of anyone who could afford the services of a skilled hypnotist. Long ago the old examination methods in education had been destroyed by these expedients. Instead of years of study, candidates had substituted a few weeks of trances, and during the trances expert coaches had simply to repeat all the points necessary for adequate answering, adding a suggestion of the post-hypnotic recollection of these points. In process mathematics particularly, this aid had been of singular service, and it was now invariably invoked by such players of chess and games of manual dexterity as were still to be found. In fact, all operations conducted under finite rules, of a quasi-mechanical sort that is, were now systematically relieved from the wanderings of imagination and emotion, and brought to an unexampled pitch of accuracy. Little children of the labouring classes, so soon as they were of sufficient age to be hypnotised, were thus converted into beautifully punctual and trustworthy machine minders, and released forthwith from the long, long thoughts of youth. Aeronautical pupils, who gave way to giddiness, could be relieved from their imaginary terrors. In every street were hypnotists ready to print permanent memories upon the mind. If anyone desired to remember a name, a series of numbers, a song or a speech, it could be done by this method, and

conversely memories could be effaced, habits removed, and desires eradicated – a sort of psychic surgery was, in fact, in general use. Indignities, humbling experiences, were thus forgotten, amorous widows would obliterate their previous husbands, angry lovers release themselves from their slavery. To graft desires, however, was still impossible, and the facts of thought transference were yet unsystematised. The psychologists illustrated their expositions with some astounding experiments in mnemonics made through the agency of a troupe of pale-faced children in blue.

Graham, like most of the people of his former time, distrusted the hypnotist, or he might then and there have eased his mind of many painful preoccupations. But in spite of Lincoln's assurances he held to the old theory that to be hypnotised was in some way the surrender of his personality, the abdication of his will. At the banquet of wonderful experiences that was beginning, he wanted very keenly to remain absolutely himself.

The next day, and another day, and yet another day passed in such interests as these. Each day Graham spent many hours in the glorious entertainment of flying. On the third day he soared across middle France, and within sight of the snow-clad Alps. These vigorous exercises gave him restful sleep, and each day saw a great stride in his health from the spiritless anaemia of his first awakening. And whenever he was not in the air, and awake, Lincoln was assiduous in the cause of his amusement; all that was novel and curious in contemporary invention was brought to him, until at last his appetite for novelty was well-nigh glutted. One might fill a dozen inconsecutive volumes with the strange things they exhibited. Each afternoon he held his court for an hour or so. He speedily found his interest in his contemporaries becoming personal and intimate. At first he had been alert chiefly for unfamiliarity and peculiarity; any foppishness in their dress, any discordance with his preconceptions of nobility in their status and manners had jarred upon him, and it was remarkable to him how soon that strangeness and the faint hostility that arose from it, disappeared; how soon he came to appreciate the true perspective of his position, and see the old Victorian days remote and quaint. He found himself particularly amused by the red-haired daughter of the Manager of the European Piggeries. On the second day after dinner he made the acquaintance of a latter-day dancing girl, and found her an astonishing artist. And after that, more hypnotic wonders. On the third day Lincoln was moved to suggest that the Master should repair to a Pleasure City, but this Graham declined, nor would he accept the services of the hypnotists in his aeronautical experiments. The link of locality held him to London; he found a perpetual wonder in topographical identifications that he would have missed abroad. 'Here – or a hundred feet below here,' he could say, 'I used to eat my midday cutlets during my London University days. Underneath here was Waterloo and the perpetual hunt for confusing trains. Often have I stood waiting down there, bag in hand, and stared up into the sky above the forest of signals,

little thinking I should walk some day a hundred yards in the air. And now in that very sky that was once a grey smoke canopy, I circle in an aeropile.'

During those three days Graham was so occupied with such distractions that the vast political movements in progress outside his quarters had but a small share of his attention. Those about him told him little. Daily came Ostrog, the Boss, his Grand Vizier, his mayor of the palace, to report in vague terms the steady establishment of his rule; 'a little trouble' soon to be settled in this city, 'a slight disturbance' in that. The song of the social revolt came to him no more; he never learned that it had been forbidden in the municipal limits; and all the great emotions of the crow's nest slumbered in his mind.

But on the second and third of the three days he found himself, in spite of his interest in the daughter of the Pig Manager, or it may be by reason of the thoughts her conversation suggested, remembering the girl Helen Wotton, who had spoken to him so oddly at the Wind-Vane Keeper's gathering. The impression she had made was a deep one, albeit the incessant surprise of novel circumstances had kept him from brooding upon it for a space. But now her memory was coming to its own. He wondered what she had meant by those broken half-forgotten sentences; the picture of her eyes and the earnest passion of her face became more vivid as his mechanical interests faded. Her beauty came compellingly between him and certain immediate temptations of ignoble passion. But he did not see her again until three full days were past.

CHAPTER EIGHTEEN

Graham Remembers

She came upon him at last in a little gallery that ran from the Wind Vane Offices toward his state apartments. The gallery was long and narrow, with a series of recesses, each with an arched fenestration that looked upon a court of palms. He came upon her suddenly in one of these recesses. She was seated. She turned her head at the sound of his footsteps and started at the sight of him. Every touch of colour vanished from her face. She rose instantly, made a step toward him as if to address him, and hesitated. He stopped and stood still, expectant. Then he perceived that a nervous tumult silenced her, perceived too, that she must have sought speech with him to be waiting for him in this place.

He felt a regal impulse to assist her. 'I have wanted to see you,' he said. 'A few days ago you wanted to tell me something – you wanted to tell me of the people. What was it you had to tell me?'

She looked at him with troubled eyes.

'You said the people were unhappy?'

For a moment she was silent still.

'It must have seemed strange to you,' she said abruptly.

'It did. And yet – '

'It was an impulse.'

'Well?'

'That is all.'

She looked at him with a face of hesitation. She spoke with an effort. 'You forget,' she said, drawing a deep breath.

'What?'

'The people – '

'Do you mean – ?'

'You forget the people.'

He looked interrogative.

'Yes. I know you are surprised. For you do not understand what you are. You do not know the things that are happening.'

'Well?'

'You do not understand.'

'Not clearly, perhaps. But – tell me.'

She turned to him with sudden resolution. 'It is so hard to explain. I have meant to, I have wanted to. And now – I cannot. I am not ready with words. But about you – there is something. It is Wonder. Your sleep – your awakening. These things are miracles. To me at least – and to all the common people. You who lived and suffered and died, you who were a

common citizen, wake again, live again, to find yourself Master almost of the earth.'

'Master of the earth,' he said. 'So they tell me. But try and imagine how little I know of it.'

'Cities – Trusts – the Labour Company – '

'Principalities, powers, dominions – the power and the glory. Yes, I have heard them shout. I know. I am Master. King, if you wish. With Ostrog, the Boss – '

He paused.

She turned upon him and surveyed his face with a curious scrutiny. 'Well?'

He smiled. 'To take the responsibility.'

'That is what we have begun to fear.' For a moment she said no more. 'No,' she said slowly. '*You* will take the responsibility. You will take the responsibility. The people look to you.'

She spoke softly. 'Listen! For at least half the years of your sleep – in every generation – multitudes of people, in every generation greater multitudes of people, have prayed that you might awake – *prayed*.'

Graham moved to speak and did not.

She hesitated, and a faint colour crept back to her cheek. 'Do you know that you have been to myriads – King Arthur, Barbarossa – the King who would come in his own good time and put the world right for them?'

'I suppose the imagination of the people – '

'Have you not heard our proverb, "When the Sleeper wakes"? While you lay insensible and motionless there – thousands came. Thousands. Every first of the month you lay in state with a white robe upon you and the people filed by you. When I was a little girl I saw you like that, with your face white and calm.'

She turned her face from him and looked steadfastly at the painted wall before her. Her voice fell. 'When I was a little girl I used to look at your face . . . it seemed to me fixed and waiting, like the patience of God. That is what we thought of you,' she said. 'That is how you seemed to us.'

She turned shining eyes to him, her voice was clear and strong. 'In the city, in the earth, a myriad myriad men and women are waiting to see what you will do, full of strange incredible expectations.'

'Yes?'

'Ostrog – no one – can take that responsibility.'

Graham looked at her in surprise, at her face lit with emotion. She seemed at first to have spoken with an effort, and to have fired herself by speaking.

'Do you think,' she said, 'that you who have lived that little life so far away in the past, you who have fallen into and risen out of this miracle of sleep – do you think that the wonder and reverence and hope of half the world has gathered about you only that you may live another little life? . . . That you may shift the responsibility to any other man?'

'I know how great this kingship of mine is,' he said haltingly. 'I know how great it seems. But is it real? It is incredible – dreamlike. Is it real, or is it only a great delusion?'

'It is real,' she said; 'if you dare.'

'After all, like all kingship, my kingship is Belief. It is an illusion in the minds of men.'

'If you dare!' she said.

'But – '

'Countless men,' she said, 'and while it is in their minds – they will obey.'

'But I know nothing. That is what I had in mind. I know nothing. And these others – the Councillors, Ostrog. They are wiser, cooler, they know so much, every detail. And, indeed, what are these miseries of which you speak? What am I to know? Do you mean – '

He stopped blankly.

'I am still hardly more than a girl,' she said. 'But to me the world seems full of wretchedness. The world has altered since your day, altered very strangely. I have prayed that I might see you and tell you these things. The world has changed. As if a canker had seized it – and robbed life of – everything worth having.'

She turned a flushed face upon him, moving suddenly. 'Your days were the days of freedom. Yes – I have thought. I have been made to think, for my life – has not been happy. Men are no longer free – no greater, no better than the men of your time. That is not all. This city – is a prison. Every city now is a prison. Mammon grips the key in his hand. Myriads, countless myriads, toil from the cradle to the grave. Is that right? Is that to be – for ever? Yes, far worse than in your time. All about us, beneath us, sorrow and pain. All the shallow delight of such life as you find about you, is separated by just a little from a life of wretchedness beyond any telling. Yes, the poor know it – they know they suffer. These countless multitudes who faced death for you two nights since – ! You owe your life to them.'

'Yes,' said Graham, slowly. 'Yes. I owe my life to them.'

'You come,' she said, 'from the days when this new tyranny of the cities was scarcely beginning. It is a tyranny – a tyranny. In your days the feudal war lords had gone, and the new lordship of wealth had still to come. Half the men in the world still lived out upon the free countryside. The cities had still to devour them. I have heard the stories out of the old books – there was nobility! Common men led lives of love and faithfulness then – they did a thousand things. And you – you come from that time.'

'It was not – . But never mind. How is it now – ?'

'Gain and the Pleasure Cities! Or slavery – unthanked, unhonoured, slavery.'

'Slavery!' he said.

'Slavery.'

'You don't mean to say that human beings are chattels.'

'Worse. That is what I want you to know, what I want you to see. I know you do not know. They will keep things from you, they will take you presently to a Pleasure City. But you have noticed men and women and children in pale blue canvas, with thin yellow faces and dull eyes?'

'Everywhere.'

'Speaking a horrible dialect, coarse and weak.'

'I have heard it.'

'They are the slaves – your slaves. They are the slaves of the Labour Company you own.'

'The Labour Company! In some way – that is familiar. Ah! now I remember. I saw it when I was wandering about the city, after the lights returned, great fronts of buildings coloured pale blue. Do you really mean – ?'

'Yes. How can I explain it to you? Of course the blue uniform struck you. Nearly a third of our people wear it – more assume it now every day. This Labour Company has grown imperceptibly.'

'What is this Labour Company?' asked Graham.

'In the old times, how did you manage with starving people?'

'There was the workhouse – which the parishes maintained.'

'Workhouse! Yes – there was something. In our history lessons. I remember now. The Labour Company ousted the workhouse. It grew – partly – out of something – you, perhaps, may remember it – an emotional religious organisation called the Salvation Army – that became a business company. In the first place it was almost a charity. To save people from workhouse rigours. Now I come to think of it, it was one of the earliest properties your Trustees acquired. They bought the Salvation Army and reconstructed it as this. The idea in the first place was to give work to starving homeless people.'

'Yes.'

'Nowadays there are no workhouses, no refuges and charities, nothing but that Company. Its offices are everywhere. That blue is its colour. And any man, woman or child who comes to be hungry and weary and with neither home nor friend nor resort, must go to the Company in the end – or seek some way of death. The Euthanasy is beyond their means – for the poor there is no easy death. And at any hour in the day or night there is food, shelter and a blue uniform for all comers – that is the first condition of the Company's incorporation – and in return for a day's shelter the Company extracts a day's work, and then returns the visitor's proper clothing and sends him or her out again.'

'Yes?'

'Perhaps that does not seem so terrible to you. In your days men starved in your streets. That was bad. But they died – men. These people in blue – . The proverb runs: "Blue canvas once and ever." The Company trades in their labour, and it has taken care to assure itself of the supply. People come to it starving and helpless – they eat and sleep for a night and day, they work

for a day, and at the end of the day they go out again. If they have worked well they have a penny or so – enough for a theatre or a cheap dancing place, or a kinematograph story, or a dinner or a bet. They wander about after that is spent. Begging is prevented by the police of the ways. Besides, no one gives. They come back again the next day or the day after – brought back by the same incapacity that brought them first. At last their proper clothing wears out, or their rags get so shabby that they are ashamed. Then they must work for months to get fresh. If they want fresh. A great number of children are born under the Company's care. The mother owes them a month thereafter – the children they cherish and educate until they are fourteen, and they pay two years' service. You may be sure these children are educated for the blue canvas. And so it is the Company works.'

'And none are destitute in the city?'

'None. They are either in blue canvas or in prison.'

'If they will not work?'

'Most people will work at that pitch, and the Company has powers. There are stages of unpleasantness in the work – stoppage of food – and a man or woman who has refused to work once is known by a thumb-marking system in the Company's offices all over the world. Besides, who can leave the city poor? To go to Paris costs two lions. And for insubordination there are the prisons – dark and miserable – out of sight below. There are prisons now for many things.'

'And a third of the people wear this blue canvas?'

'More than a third. Toilers, living without pride or delight or hope, with the stories of Pleasure Cities ringing in their ears, mocking their shameful lives, their privations and hardships. Too poor even for the Euthanasy, the rich man's refuge from life. Dumb, crippled millions, countless millions, all the world about, ignorant of anything but limitations and unsatisfied desires. They are born, they are thwarted and they die. That is the state to which we have come.'

For a space Graham sat downcast.

'But there has been a revolution,' he said. 'All these things will be changed. Ostrog – '

'That is our hope. That is the hope of the world. But Ostrog will not do it. He is a politician. To him it seems things must be like this. He does not mind. He takes it for granted. All the rich, all the influential, all who are happy, come at last to take these miseries for granted. They use the people in their politics, they live in ease by their degradation. But you – you who come from a happier age – it is to you the people look. To you.'

He looked at her face. Her eyes were bright with unshed tears. He felt a rush of emotion. For a moment he forgot this city, he forgot the race, and all those vague remote voices, in the immediate humanity of her beauty.

'But what am I to do?' he said with his eyes upon her.

'Rule,' she answered, bending towards him and speaking in a low tone.

'Rule the world as it has never been ruled, for the good and happiness of men. For you might rule it – you could rule it.

'The people are stirring. All over the world the people are stirring. It wants but a word – but a word from you – to bring them all together. Even the middle sort of people are restless – unhappy.

'They are not telling you the things that are happening. The people will not go back to their drudgery – they refuse to be disarmed. Ostrog has awakened something greater than he dreamt of – he has awakened hopes.'

His heart was beating fast. He tried to seem judicial, to weigh considerations.

'They only want their leader,' she said.

'And then?'

'You could do what you would; – the world is yours.'

He sat, no longer regarding her. Presently he spoke. 'The old dreams, and the thing I have dreamt, liberty, happiness. Are they dreams? Could one man – *one man* – ?' His voice sank and ceased.

'Not one man, but all men – give them only a leader to speak the desire of their hearts.'

He shook his head, and for a time there was silence.

He looked up suddenly, and their eyes met. 'I have not your faith,' he said. 'I have not your youth. I am here with power that mocks me. No – let me speak. I want to do – not right – I have not the strength for that – but something rather right than wrong. It will bring no millennium, but I am resolved now that I will rule. What you have said has awakened me . . . You are right. Ostrog must know his place. And I will learn – . . . One thing I promise you. This Labour slavery shall end.'

'And you will rule?'

'Yes. Provided – . There is one thing.'

'Yes?'

'That you will help me.'

'*I!* – a girl!'

'Yes. Does it not occur to you I am absolutely alone?'

She started and for an instant her eyes had pity. 'Need you ask whether I will help you?' she said.

She stood before him, beautiful, worshipful, and her enthusiasm and the greatness of their theme was like a great gulf fixed between them. To touch her, to clasp her hand, was a thing beyond hope. 'Then I will rule indeed,' he said slowly. 'I will rule – ' He paused. 'With you.'

There came a tense silence, and then the beating of a clock striking the hour. She made him no answer. Graham rose.

'Even now,' he said, 'Ostrog will be waiting.' He hesitated, facing her. 'When I have asked him certain questions – . There is much I do not know. It may be, that I will go to see with my own eyes the things of which you have spoken. And when I return – ?'

'I shall know of your going and coming. I will wait for you here again.'

He stood for a moment regarding her.

'I knew,' she said, and stopped.

He waited, but she said no more. They regarded one another steadfastly, questioningly, and then he turned from her towards the Wind Vane Office.

CHAPTER NINETEEN

Ostrog's Point of View

Graham found Ostrog waiting to give a formal account of his day's steward-ship. On previous occasions he had passed over this ceremony as speedily as possible, in order to resume his aerial experiences, but now he began to ask quick short questions. He was very anxious to take up his empire forthwith. Ostrog brought flattering reports of the development of affairs abroad. In Paris and Berlin, Graham perceived that he was saying, there had been trouble, not organised resistance indeed, but insubordinate proceedings. 'After all these years,' said Ostrog, when Graham pressed enquiries, 'the Commune has lifted its head again. That is the real nature of the struggle, to be explicit.' But order had been restored in these cities. Graham, the more deliberately judicial for the stirring emotions he felt, asked if there had been any fighting. 'A little,' said Ostrog. 'In one quarter only. But the Senegalese division of our African agricultural police – the Consolidated African Companies have a very well-drilled police – was ready, and so were the aeroplanes. We expected a little trouble in the continental cities, and in America. But things are very quiet in America. They are satisfied with the overthrow of the Council. For the time.'

'Why should you expect trouble?' asked Graham abruptly.

'There is a lot of discontent – social discontent.'

'The Labour Company?'

'You are learning,' said Ostrog with a touch of surprise. 'Yes. It is chiefly the discontent with the Labour Company. It was that discontent supplied the motive force of this overthrow – that and your awakening.'

'Yes?'

Ostrog smiled. He became explicit. 'We had to stir up their discontent, we had to revive the old ideals of universal happiness – all men equal – all men happy – no luxury that everyone may not share – ideas that have slumbered for two hundred years. You know that? We had to revive these ideals, impossible as they are – in order to overthrow the Council. And now – '

'Well?'

'Our revolution is accomplished, and the Council is overthrown, and people whom we have stirred up remain surging. There was scarcely

enough fighting . . . We made promises, of course. It is extraordinary how violently and rapidly this vague out-of-date humanitarianism has revived and spread. We who sowed the seed even, have been astonished. In Paris, as I say – we have had to call in a little external help.'

'And here?'

'There is trouble. Multitudes will not go back to work. There is a general strike. Half the factories are empty and the people are swarming in the Ways. They are talking of a Commune. Men in silk and satin have been insulted in the streets. The blue canvas is expecting all sorts of things from you . . . Of course there is no need for you to trouble. We are setting the Babble Machines to work with counter suggestions in the cause of law and order. We must keep the grip tight; that is all.'

Graham thought. He perceived a way of asserting himself. But he spoke with restraint.

'Even to the pitch of bringing a negro police,' he said.

'They are useful,' said Ostrog. 'They are fine loyal brutes, with no wash of ideas in their heads – such as our rabble has. The Council should have had them as police of the Ways, and things might have been different. Of course, there is nothing to fear except rioting and wreckage. You can manage your own wings now, and you can soar away to Capri if there is any smoke or fuss. We have the pull of all the great things; the aeronauts are privileged and rich, the closest trades union in the world, and so are the engineers of the wind-vanes. We have the air, and the mastery of the air is the mastery of the earth. No one of any ability is organising against us. They have no leaders – only the sectional leaders of the secret society we organised before your very opportune awakening. Mere busybodies and sentimentalists they are and bitterly jealous of each other. None of them is man enough for a central figure. The only trouble will be a disorganised upheaval. To be frank – that may happen. But it won't interrupt your aeronautics. The days when the People could make revolutions are past.'

'I suppose they are,' said Graham. 'I suppose they are.' He mused. 'This world of yours has been full of surprises to me. In the old days we dreamt of a wonderful democratic life, of a time when all men would be equal and happy.'

Ostrog looked at him steadfastly. 'The day of democracy is past,' he said. 'Past for ever. That day began with the bowmen of Crécy, it ended when marching infantry, when common men in masses ceased to win the battles of the world, when costly cannon, great ironclads, and strategic railways became the means of power. Today is the day of wealth. Wealth now is power as it never was power before – it commands earth and sea and sky. All power is for those who can handle wealth . . . You must accept facts, and these are facts. The world for the Crowd! The Crowd as Ruler! Even in your days that creed had been tried and condemned. Today it has only one believer – a multiplex, silly one – the man in the Crowd.'

Graham did not answer immediately. He stood lost in sombre pre-occupations.

'No,' said Ostrog. 'The day of the common man is past. On the open countryside one man is as good as another, or nearly as good. The earlier aristocracy had a precarious tenure of strength and audacity. They were tempered – tempered. There were insurrections, duels, riots. The first real aristocracy, the first permanent aristocracy, came in with castles and armour, and vanished before the musket and bow. But this is the second aristocracy. The real one. Those days of gunpowder and democracy were only an eddy in the stream. The common man now is a helpless unit. In these days we have this great machine of the city, and an organisation complex beyond his understanding.'

'Yet,' said Graham, 'there is something resists, something you are holding down – something that stirs and presses.'

'You will see,' said Ostrog, with a forced smile that would brush these difficult questions aside. 'I have not roused the force to destroy myself – trust me.'

'I wonder,' said Graham.

Ostrog stared.

'*Must* the world go this way?' said Graham, with his emotions at the speaking point. 'Must it indeed go in this way? Have all our hopes been vain?'

'What do you mean?' said Ostrog. 'Hopes?'

'I came from a democratic age. And I find an aristocratic tyranny!'

'Well, – but you are the chief tyrant.'

Graham shook his head.

'Well,' said Ostrog, 'take the general question. It is the way that change has always travelled. Aristocracy, the prevalence of the best – the suffering and extinction of the unfit, and so to better things.'

'But aristocracy! those people I met – '

'Oh! not *those*!' said Ostrog. 'But for the most part they go to their death. Vice and pleasure! They have no children. That sort of stuff will die out. If the world keeps to one road, that is, if there is no turning back. An easy road to excess, convenient Euthanasia for the pleasure seekers singed in the flame, that is the way to improve the race!'

'Pleasant extinction,' said Graham. 'Yet – .' He thought for an instant. 'There is that other thing – the Crowd, the great mass of poor men. Will that die out? That will not die out. And it suffers, its suffering is a force that even you – '

Ostrog moved impatiently, and when he spoke, he spoke rather less evenly than before.

'Don't you trouble about these things,' he said. 'Everything will be settled in a few days now. The Crowd is a huge foolish beast. What if it does not die out? Even if it does not die, it can still be tamed and driven. I

have no sympathy with servile men. You heard those people shouting and singing two nights ago. They were taught that song. If you had taken any man there in cold blood and asked why he shouted, he could not have told you. They think they are shouting for you, that they are loyal and devoted to you. Just then they were ready to slaughter the Council. Today – they are already murmuring against those who have overthrown the Council.'

'No, no,' said Graham. 'They shouted because their lives were dreary, without joy or pride, and because in me – in me – they hoped.'

'And what was their hope? What is their hope? What right have they to hope? They work ill and they want the reward of those who work well. The hope of mankind – what is it? That some day the Overman may come, that some day the inferior, the weak and the bestial may be subdued or eliminated. Subdued if not eliminated. The world is no place for the bad, the stupid, the enervated. Their duty – it's a fine duty too! – is to die. The death of the failure! That is the path by which the beast rose to manhood, by which man goes on to higher things.'

Ostrog took a pace, seemed to think, and turned on Graham. 'I can imagine how this great world state of ours seems to a Victorian English-man. You regret all the old forms of representative government – their spectres still haunt the world, the voting councils and parliaments and all that eighteenth-century tomfoolery. You feel moved against our Pleasure Cities. I might have thought of that, – had I not been busy. But you will learn better. The people are mad with envy – they would be in sympathy with you. Even in the streets now, they clamour to destroy the Pleasure Cities. But the Pleasure Cities are the excretory organs of the State, attractive places that year after year draw together all that is weak and vicious, all that is lascivious and lazy, all the easy roguery of the world, to a graceful destruction. They go there, they have their time, they die childless, all the pretty silly lascivious women die childless, and mankind is the better. If the people were sane they would not envy the rich their way of death. And you would emancipate the silly brainless workers that we have enslaved, and try to make their lives easy and pleasant again. Just as they have sunk to what they are fit for.' He smiled a smile that irritated Graham oddly. 'You will learn better. I know those ideas; in my boyhood I read your Shelley and dreamt of Liberty. There is no liberty, save wisdom and self-control. Liberty is within – not without. It is each man's own affair. Suppose – which is impossible – that these swarming yelping fools in blue get the upper hand of us, what then? They will only fall to other masters. So long as there are sheep Nature will insist on beasts of prey. It would mean but a few hundred years' delay. The coming of the aristocrat is fatal and assured. The end will be the Overman – for all the mad protests of humanity. Let them revolt, let them win and kill me and my like. Others will arise – other masters. The end will be the same.'

'I wonder,' said Graham doggedly.

For a moment he stood downcast.

'But I must see these things for myself,' he said, suddenly assuming a tone of confident mastery. 'Only by seeing can I understand. I must learn. That is what I want to tell you, Ostrog. I do not want to be King in a Pleasure City; that is not my pleasure. I have spent enough time with aeronautics – and those other things. I must learn how people live now, how the common life has developed. Then I shall understand these things better. I must learn how common people live – the labour people more especially – how they work, marry, bear children, die – '

'You get that from our realistic novelists,' suggested Ostrog, suddenly preoccupied.

'I want reality,' said Graham, 'not realism.'

'There are difficulties,' said Ostrog, and thought. 'On the whole perhaps – 'I did not expect – .

'I had thought – . And yet, perhaps – . You say you want to go through the Ways of the city and see the common people.'

Suddenly he came to some conclusion. 'You would need to go disguised,' he said. 'The city is intensely excited, and the discovery of your presence among them might create a fearful tumult. Still this wish of yours to go into this city – this idea of yours – . Yes, now I think the thing over it seems to me not altogether – . It can be contrived. If you would really find an interest in that! You are, of course, Master. You can go soon if you like. A disguise for this excursion Asano will be able to manage. He would go with you. After all it is not a bad idea of yours.'

'You will not want to consult me in any matter?' asked Graham suddenly, struck by an odd suspicion.

'Oh, dear no! No! I think you may trust affairs to me for a time, at any rate,' said Ostrog, smiling. 'Even if we differ – '

Graham glanced at him sharply.

'There is no fighting likely to happen soon?' he asked abruptly.

'Certainly not.'

'I have been thinking about these negroes. I don't believe the people intend any hostility to me, and, after all, I am the Master. I do not want any negroes brought to London. It is an archaic prejudice perhaps, but I have peculiar feelings about Europeans and the subject races. Even about Paris – '

Ostrog stood watching him from under his drooping brows. 'I am not bringing negroes to London,' he said slowly. 'But if – '

'You are not to bring armed negroes to London, whatever happens,' said Graham. 'In that matter I am quite decided.'

Ostrog, after a pause, decided not to speak, and bowed deferentially.

In the City Ways

And that night, unknown and unsuspected, Graham, dressed in the costume of an inferior wind-vane official keeping holiday, and accompanied by Asano in Labour Company canvas, surveyed the city through which he had wandered when it was veiled in darkness. But now he saw it lit and waking, a whirlpool of life. In spite of the surging and swaying of the forces of revolution, in spite of the unusual discontent, the mutterings of the greater struggle of which the first revolt was but the prelude, the myriad streams of commerce still flowed wide and strong. He knew now something of the dimensions and quality of the new age, but he was not prepared for the infinite surprise of the detailed view, for the torrent of colour and vivid impressions that poured past him.

This was his first real contact with the people of these latter days. He realised that all that had gone before, saving his glimpses of the public theatres and markets, had had its element of seclusion, had been a move-ment within the comparatively narrow political quarter, that all his previous experiences had revolved immediately about the question of his own position. But here was the city at the busiest hours of night, the people to a large extent returned to their own immediate interests, the resumption of the real informal life, the common habits of the new time.

They emerged at first into a street whose opposite ways were crowded with the blue canvas liveries. This swarm Graham saw was a portion of a procession – it was odd to see a procession parading the city *seated*. They carried banners of coarse red stuff with red letters. 'No disarmament,' said the banners, for the most part in crudely daubed letters and with variant spelling, and 'Why should we disarm?' 'No disarming.' 'No disarming.' Banner after banner went by, a stream of banners flowing past, and at last at the end, the song of the revolt and a noisy band of strange instruments. 'They all ought to be at work,' said Asano. 'They have had no food these two days, or they have stolen it.'

Presently Asano made a detour to avoid the congested crowd that gaped upon the occasional passage of dead bodies from hospital to a mortuary, the gleanings after death's harvest of the first revolt.

That night few people were sleeping, everyone was abroad. A vast excite-ment, perpetual crowds perpetually changing, surrounded Graham; his mind was confused and darkened by an incessant tumult, by the cries and enigmatical fragments of the social struggle that was as yet only beginning. Everywhere festoons and banners of black and strange decorations, intensified the quality of his popularity. Everywhere he caught snatches of

that crude thick dialect that served the illiterate class, the class, that is, beyond the reach of phonograph culture, in their commonplace intercourse. Everywhere this trouble of disarmament was in the air, with a quality of immediate stress of which he had no inkling during his seclusion in the Wind-Vane quarter. He perceived that as soon as he returned he must discuss this with Ostrog, this and the greater issues of which it was the expression, in a far more conclusive way than he had so far done. Perpetually that night, even in the earlier hours of their wanderings about the city, the spirit of unrest and revolt swamped his attention, to the exclusion of countless strange things he might otherwise have observed.

This preoccupation made his impressions fragmentary. Yet amidst so much that was strange and vivid, no subject, however personal and insistent, could exert undivided sway. There were spaces when the revolutionary movement passed clean out of his mind, was drawn aside like a curtain from before some startling new aspect of the time. Helen had swayed his mind to this intense earnestness of enquiry, but there came times when she, even, receded beyond his conscious thoughts. At one moment, for example, he found they were traversing the religious quarter, for the easy transit about the city afforded by the moving ways rendered sporadic churches and chapels no longer necessary – and his attention was vividly arrested by the façade of one of the Christian sects.

They were travelling seated on one of the swift upper ways, the place leapt upon them at a bend and advanced rapidly towards them. It was covered with inscriptions from top to base, in vivid white and blue, save where a vast and glaring kinematograph transparency presented a realistic New Testament scene, and where a vast festoon of black to show that the popular religion followed the popular politics, hung across the lettering. Graham had already become familiar with the phonotype writing and these inscriptions arrested him, being to his sense for the most part almost incredible blasphemy. Among the less offensive were 'Salvation on the First Floor and turn to the Right.' 'Put your Money on your Maker.' 'The Sharpest Conversion in London, Expert Operators! Look Slippy!' 'What Christ would say to the Sleeper; – Join the Up-to-date Saints!' 'Be a Christian – without hindrance to your present Occupation.' 'All the Brightest Bishops on the Bench tonight and Prices as Usual.' 'Brisk Blessings for Busy Business Men.'

'But this is appalling!' said Graham, as that deafening scream of mercantile piety towered above them.

'What is appalling?' asked his little officer, apparently seeking vainly for anything unusual in this shrieking enamel.

'This! Surely the essence of religion is reverence.'

'Oh that!' Asano looked at Graham. 'Does it shock you?' he said in the tone of one who makes a discovery. 'I suppose it would, of course. I had forgotten. Nowadays the competition for attention is so keen, and people

simply haven't the leisure to attend to their souls, you know, as they used to do.' He smiled. 'In the old days you had quiet Sabbaths and the countryside. Though somewhere I've read of Sunday afternoons that – '

'But, *that*,' said Graham, glancing back at the receding blue and white. 'That is surely not the only – '

'There are hundreds of different ways. But, of course, if a sect doesn't sell it doesn't pay. Worship has moved with the times. There are high-class sects with quieter ways – costly incense and personal attentions and all that. These people are extremely popular and prosperous. They pay several dozen lions for those apartments to the Council – to you, I should say.'

Graham still felt a difficulty with the coinage, and this mention of a dozen lions brought him abruptly to that matter. In a moment the screaming temples and their swarming touts were forgotten in this new interest. A turn of a phrase suggested, and an answer confirmed the idea that gold and silver were both demonetised, that stamped gold which had begun its reign amidst the merchants of Phoenicia was at last dethroned. The change had been graduated but swift, brought about by an extension of the system of cheques that had even in his previous life already practically superseded gold in all the larger business transactions. The common traffic of the city, the common currency indeed of all the world, was conducted by means of the little brown, green and pink council cheques for small amounts, printed with a blank payee. Asano had several with him, and at the first opportunity he supplied the gaps in his set. They were printed not on tearable paper, but on a semi-transparent fabric of silken flexibility, interwoven with silk. Across them all sprawled a facsimile of Graham's signature, his first encounter with the curves and turns of that familiar autograph for two hundred and three years.

Some intermediary experiences made no impression sufficiently vivid to prevent the matter of the disarmament claiming his thoughts again; a blurred picture of a Theosophist temple that promised MIRACLES in enormous letters of unsteady fire was least submerged perhaps, but then came the view of the dining hall in Northumberland Avenue. That interested him very greatly.

By the energy and thought of Asano he was able to view this place from a little screened gallery reserved for the attendants of the tables. The building was pervaded by a distant muffled hooting, piping and bawling, of which he did not at first understand the import, but which recalled a certain mysterious leathery voice he had heard after the resumption of the lights on the night of his solitary wandering.

He had grown accustomed now to vastness and great numbers of people; nevertheless this spectacle held him for a long time. It was as he watched the table service more immediately beneath, and interspersed with many questions and answers concerning details, that the realisation of the full significance of the feast of several thousand people came to him.

It was his constant surprise to find that points that one might have expected to strike vividly at the very outset never occurred to him until some trivial detail suddenly shaped as a riddle and pointed to the obvious thing he had overlooked. In this matter, for instance, it had not occurred to him that this continuity of the city, this exclusion of weather, these vast halls and ways, involved the disappearance of the household; that the typical Victorian 'home', the little brick cell containing kitchen and scullery, living rooms and bedrooms, had, save for the ruins that diversified the country-side, vanished as surely as the wattle hut. But now he saw what had indeed been manifest from the first, that London, regarded as a living place, was no longer an aggregation of houses but a prodigious hotel, an hotel with a thousand classes of accommodation, thousands of dining halls, chapels, theatres, markets and places of assembly, a synthesis of enterprises, of which he chiefly was the owner. People had their sleeping rooms, with, it might be, antechambers, rooms that were always sanitary at least whatever the degree of comfort and privacy, and for the rest they lived much as many people had lived in the new-made giant hotels of the Victorian days, eating, reading, thinking, playing, conversing, all in places of public resort, going to their work in the industrial quarters of the city or doing business in their offices in the trading section.

He perceived at once how necessarily this state of affairs had developed from the Victorian city. The fundamental reason for the modern city had ever been the economy of co-operation. The chief thing to prevent the merging of the separate households in his own generation was simply the still imperfect civilisation of the people, the strong barbaric pride, passions, and prejudices, the jealousies, rivalries, and violence of the middle and lower classes, which had necessitated the entire separation of contiguous households. But the change, the taming of the people, had been in rapid progress even then. In his brief thirty years of previous life he had seen an enormous extension of the habit of consuming meals from home, the casually patronised horsebox coffee-house had given place to the open and crowded Aërated Bread Shop for instance, women's clubs had had their beginning, and an immense development of reading rooms, lounges and libraries had witnessed to the growth of social confidence. These promises had by this time attained to their complete fulfilment. The locked and barred household had passed away.

These people below him belonged, he learnt, to the lower middle class, the class just above the blue labourers, a class so accustomed in the Victorian period to feed with every precaution of privacy that its members, when occasion confronted them with a public meal, would usually hide their embarrassment under horseplay or a markedly militant demeanour. But these gaily, if lightly dressed people below, albeit vivacious, hurried and uncommunicative, were dexterously mannered and certainly quite at their ease with regard to one another.

He noted a slight significant thing: the table, as far as he could see, was and remained delightfully neat, there was nothing to parallel the confusion, the broadcast crumbs, the splashes of viand and condiment, the overturned drink and displaced ornaments, which would have marked the stormy progress of the Victorian meal. The table furniture was very different. There were no ornaments, no flowers, and the table was without a cloth, being made, he learnt, of a solid substance having the texture and appearance of damask. He discerned that this damask substance was patterned with gracefully designed trade advertisements.

In a sort of recess before each diner was a complete apparatus of porcelain and metal. There was one plate of white porcelain, and by means of taps for hot and cold volatile fluids the diner washed this himself between the courses; he also washed his elegant white metal knife and fork and spoon as occasion required.

Soup and the chemical wine that was the common drink were delivered by similar taps, and the remaining covers travelled automatically in tastefully arranged dishes down the table along silver rails. The diner stopped these and helped himself at his discretion. They appeared at a little door at one end of the table, and vanished at the other. That turn of democratic sentiment in decay, that ugly pride of menial souls, which renders equals loath to wait on one another, was very strong he found among these people. He was so preoccupied with these details that it was only just as he was leaving the place that he remarked the huge advertisement dioramas that marched majestically along the upper walls and proclaimed the most remarkable commodities.

Beyond this place they came into a crowded hall, and he discovered the cause of the noise that had perplexed him. They paused at a turnstile at which a payment was made.

Graham's attention was immediately arrested by a violent, loud hoot, followed by a vast leathery voice. 'The Master is sleeping peacefully,' it vociferated. 'He is in excellent health. He is going to devote the rest of his life to aeronautics. He says women are more beautiful than ever. Galloop! Wow! Our wonderful civilisation astonishes him beyond measure. Beyond all measure. Galloop. He puts great trust in Boss Ostrog, absolute confidence in Boss Ostrog. Ostrog is to be his chief minister; is authorised to remove or reinstate public officers – all patronage will be in his hands. All patronage in the hands of Boss Ostrog! The Councillors have been sent back to their own prison above the Council House.'

Graham stopped at the first sentence, and, looking up, beheld a foolish trumpet face from which this was brayed. This was the General Intelligence Machine. For a space it seemed to be gathering breath, and a regular throbbing from its cylindrical body was audible. Then it trumpeted 'Galloop, Galloop,' and broke out again.

'Paris is now pacified. All resistance is over. Galloop! The black police

hold every position of importance in the city. They fought with great bravery, singing songs written in praise of their ancestors by the poet Kipling. Once or twice they got out of hand, and tortured and mutilated wounded and captured insurgents, men and women. Moral – don't go rebelling. Haha! Galloop, Galloop! They are lively fellows. Lively brave fellows. Let this be a lesson to the disorderly banderlog of this city. Yah! Banderlog! Filth of the earth! Galloop, Galloop!'

The voice ceased. There was a confused murmur of disapproval among the crowd. 'Damned darkies.' A man began to harangue near them. 'Is this the Master's doing, brothers? Is this the Master's doing?'

'Black police!' said Graham. 'What is that? You don't mean – '

Asano touched his arm and gave him a warning look, and forthwith another of these mechanisms screamed deafeningly and gave tongue in a shrill voice. 'Yahaha, Yahah, Yap! Hear a live paper yelp! Live paper. Yaha! Shocking outrage in Paris. Yahahah! The Parisians exasperated by the black police to the pitch of assassination. Dreadful reprisals. Savage times come again. Blood! Blood! Yaha!' The nearer Babble Machine hooted stupendously, 'Galloop, Galloop,' drowned the end of the sentence, and proceeded in a rather flatter note than before with novel comments on the horrors of disorder. 'Law and order must be maintained,' said the nearer Babble Machine.

'But,' began Graham.

'Don't ask questions here,' said Asano, 'or you will be involved in an argument.'

'Then let us go on,' said Graham, 'for I want to know more of this.'

As he and his companion pushed their way through the excited crowd that swarmed beneath these voices, towards the exit, Graham conceived more clearly the proportion and features of this room. Altogether, great and small, there must have been nearly a thousand of these erections, piping, hooting, bawling and gabbling in that great space, each with its crowd of excited listeners, the majority of them men dressed in blue canvas. There were all sizes of machines, from the little gossiping mechanisms that chuckled out mechanical sarcasm in odd corners, through a number of grades to such fifty-foot giants as that which had first hooted over Graham.

This place was unusually crowded, because of the intense public interest in the course of affairs in Paris. Evidently the struggle had been much more savage than Ostrog had represented it. All the mechanisms were discoursing upon that topic, and the repetition of the people made the huge hive buzz with such phrases as 'Lynched policemen,' 'Women burnt alive,' 'Fuzzy Wuzzy.' 'But does the Master allow such things?' asked a man near him. 'Is *this* the beginning of the Master's rule?'

Is *this* the beginning of the Master's rule? For a long time after he had left the place, the hooting, whistling and braying of the machines pursued

him; 'Galloop, Galloop,' 'Yahahah, Yaha, Yap! Yaha!' Is *this* the beginning of the Master's rule?

Directly they were out upon the ways he began to question Asano closely on the nature of the Parisian struggle. 'This disarmament! What was their trouble? What does it all mean?' Asano seemed chiefly anxious to reassure him that it was 'all right'. 'But these outrages!' 'You cannot have an omelette,' said Asano, 'without breaking eggs. It is only the rough people. Only in one part of the city. All the rest is all right. The Parisian labourers are the wildest in the world, except ours.'

'What! the Londoners?'

'No, the Japanese. They have to be kept in order.'

'But burning women alive!'

'A Commune!' said Asano. 'They would rob you of your property. They would do away with property and give the world over to mob rule. You are Master, the world is yours. But there will be no Commune here. There is no need for black police here.

'And every consideration has been shown. It is their own negroes – French-speaking negroes. Senegal regiments, and Niger and Timbuctoo.'

'Regiments?' said Graham, 'I thought there was only one – .'

'No,' said Asano, and glanced at him. 'There is more than one.'

Graham felt unpleasantly helpless.

'I did not think,' he began and stopped abruptly. He went off at a tangent to ask for information about these Babble Machines. For the most part, the crowd present had been shabbily or even raggedly dressed, and Graham learnt that so far as the more prosperous classes were concerned, in all the more comfortable private apartments of the city were fixed Babble Machines that would speak directly a lever was pulled. The tenant of the apartment could connect this with the cables of any of the great News Syndicates that he preferred. When he learnt this presently, he demanded the reason of their absence from his own suite of apartments. Asano stared. 'I never thought,' he said. 'Ostrog must have had them removed.'

Graham stared. 'How was I to know?' he exclaimed.

'Perhaps he thought they would annoy you,' said Asano.

'They must be replaced directly I return,' said Graham after an interval.

He found a difficulty in understanding that this news room and the dining hall were not great central places, that such establishments were repeated almost beyond counting all over the city. But ever and again during the night's expedition his ears, in some new quarter, would pick out from the tumult of the ways the peculiar hooting of the organ of Boss Ostrog, 'Galloop, Galloop!' or the shrill 'Yahaha, Yaha, Yap! – Hear a live paper yelp!' of its chief rival.

Repeated, too, everywhere, were such *crèches* as the one he now entered. It was reached by a lift, and by a glass bridge that flung across the dining hall and traversed the ways at a slight upward angle. To enter the first

section of the place necessitated the use of his solvent signature under Asano's direction. They were immediately attended to by a man in a violet robe and gold clasp, the insignia of practising medical men. He perceived from this man's manner that his identity was known, and proceeded to ask questions on the strange arrangements of the place without reserve.

On either side of the passage, which was silent and padded, as if to deaden the footfall, were narrow little doors, their size and arrangement suggestive of the cells of a Victorian prison. But the upper portion of each door was of the same greenish transparent stuff that had enclosed him at his awakening, and within, dimly seen, lay, in every case, a very young baby in a little nest of wadding. Elaborate apparatus watched the atmosphere and rang a bell far away in the central office at the slightest departure from the optimum of temperature and moisture. A system of such *crèches* had almost entirely replaced the hazardous adventures of the old-world nursing. The attendant presently called Graham's attention to the wet nurses, a vista of mechanical figures, with arms, shoulders and breasts of astonishingly realistic modelling, articulation, and texture, but mere brass tripods below, and having in the place of features a flat disc bearing advertisements likely to be of interest to mothers.

Of all the strange things that Graham came upon that night, none jarred more upon his habits of thought than this place. The spectacle of the little pink creatures, their feeble limbs swaying uncertainly in vague first movements, left alone, without embrace or endearment, was wholly repugnant to him. The attendant doctor was of a different opinion. His statistical evidence showed beyond dispute that in the Victorian times the most dangerous passage of life was the arms of the mother, that there human mortality had ever been most terrible. On the other hand this *crèche* company, the International Crèche Syndicate, lost not one-half per cent of the million babies or so that formed its peculiar care. But Graham's prejudice was too strong even for those figures.

Along one of the many passages of the place they presently came upon a young couple in the usual blue canvas peering through the transparency and laughing hysterically at the bald head of their first-born. Graham's face must have showed his estimate of them, for their merriment ceased and they looked abashed. But this little incident accentuated his sudden realisation of the gulf between his habits of thought and the ways of the new age. He passed on to the crawling rooms and the Kindergarten, perplexed and distressed. He found the endless long playrooms were empty! the latter-day children at least still spent their nights in sleep. As they went through these, the little officer pointed out the nature of the toys, developments of those devised by that inspired sentimentalist Froebel. There were nurses here, but much was done by machines that sang and danced and dandled.

Graham was still not clear upon many points. 'But so many orphans,' he

said perplexed, reverting to a first misconception, and learnt again that they were not orphans.

So soon as they had left the *crèche* he began to speak of the horror the babies in their incubating cases had caused him. 'Is motherhood gone?' he said. 'Was it a cant? Surely it was an instinct. This seems so unnatural – abominable almost.'

'Along here we shall come to the dancing place,' said Asano by way of reply. 'It is sure to be crowded. In spite of all the political unrest it will be crowded. The women take no great interest in politics – except a few here and there. You will see the mothers – most young women in London are mothers. In that class it is considered a creditable thing to have one child – a proof of animation. Few middle-class people have more than one. With the Labour Company it is different. As for motherhood! They still take an immense pride in the children. They come here to look at them quite often.'

'Then do you mean that the population of the world – ?'

'Is falling? Yes. Except among the people under the Labour Company. They are reckless – .'

The air was suddenly dancing with music, and down a way they approached obliquely, set with gorgeous pillars as it seemed of clear amethyst, flowed a concourse of gay people and a tumult of merry cries and laughter. He saw curled heads, wreathed brows, and a happy intricate flutter of gamboge pass triumphant across the picture.

'You will see,' said Asano with a faint smile. 'The world has changed. In a moment you will see the mothers of the new age. Come this way. We shall see those yonder again very soon.'

They ascended a certain height in a swift lift, and changed to a slower one. As they went on the music grew upon them, until it was near and full and splendid, and, moving with its glorious intricacies they could distinguish the beat of innumerable dancing feet. They made a payment at a turnstile, and emerged upon the wide gallery that overlooked the dancing place, and upon the full enchantment of sound and sight.

'Here,' said Asano, 'are the fathers and mothers of the little ones you saw.'

The hall was not so richly decorated as that of the Atlas, but saving that, it was, for its size, the most splendid Graham had seen. The beautiful white limbed figures that supported the galleries reminded him once more of the restored magnificence of sculpture; they seemed to writhe in engaging attitudes, their faces laughed. The source of the music that filled the place was hidden, and the whole vast shining floor was thick with dancing couples. 'Look at them,' said the little officer, 'see how much they show of motherhood.'

The gallery they stood upon ran along the upper edge of a huge screen that cut the dancing hall on one side from a sort of outer hall that showed through broad arches the incessant onward rush of the city ways. In this

outer hall was a great crowd of less brilliantly dressed people, as numerous almost as those who danced within, the great majority wearing the blue uniform of the Labour Company that was now so familiar to Graham. Too poor to pass the turnstiles to the festival, they were yet unable to keep away from the sound of its seductions. Some of them even had cleared spaces, and were dancing also, fluttering their rags in the air. Some shouted as they danced, jests and odd allusions Graham did not understand. Once someone began whistling the refrain of the revolutionary song, but it seemed as though that beginning was promptly suppressed. The corner was dark and Graham could not see. He turned to the hall again. Above the caryatidae were marble busts of men whom that age esteemed great moral emancipators and pioneers; for the most part their names were strange to Graham, though he recognised Grant Allen, Le Gallienne, Nietzsche, Shelley and Goodwin. Great black festoons and eloquent sentiments reinforced the huge inscription that partially defaced the upper end of the dancing place, and asserted that 'The Festival of the Awakening' was in progress.

'Myriads are taking holiday or staying from work because of that, quite apart from the labourers who refuse to go back,' said Asano. 'These people are always ready for holidays.'

Graham walked to the parapet and stood leaning over, looking down at the dancers. Save for two or three remote whispering couples, who had stolen apart, he and his guide had the gallery to themselves. A warm breath of scent and vitality came up to him. Both men and women below were lightly clad, bare-armed, open-necked, as the universal warmth of the city permitted. The hair of the men was often a mass of effeminate curls, their chins were always shaven, and many of them had flushed or coloured cheeks. Many of the women were very pretty, and all were dressed with elaborate coquetry. As they swept by beneath, he saw ecstatic faces with eyes half closed in pleasure.

'What sort of people are these?' he asked abruptly.

'Workers – prosperous workers. What you would have called the middle class. Independent tradesmen with little separate businesses have vanished long ago, but there are store servers, managers, engineers of a hundred sorts. Tonight is a holiday of course, and every dancing place in the city will be crowded, and every place of worship.'

'But – the women?'

'The same. There's a thousand forms of work for women now. But you had the beginning of the independent working-woman in your days. Most women are independent now. Most of these are married more or less – there are a number of methods of contract – and that gives them more money, and enables them to enjoy themselves.'

'I see,' said Graham looking at the flushed faces, the flash and swirl of movement, and still thinking of that nightmare of pink helpless limbs. 'And these are – mothers.'

'Most of them.'

'The more I see of these things the more complex I find your problems. This, for instance, is a surprise. That news from Paris was a surprise.'

In a little while he spoke again: 'These are mothers. Presently, I suppose, I shall get into the modern way of seeing things. I have old habits of mind clinging about me – habits based, I suppose, on needs that are over and done with. Of course, in our time, a woman was supposed not only to bear children, but to cherish them, to devote herself to them, to educate them – all the essentials of moral and mental education a child owed its mother. Or went without. Quite a number, I admit, went without. Nowadays, clearly, there is no more need for such care than if they were butterflies. I see that! Only there was an ideal – that figure of a grave, patient woman, silently and serenely mistress of a home, mother and maker of men – to love her was a sort of worship – '

He stopped and repeated, 'A sort of worship.'

'Ideals change,' said the little man, 'as needs change.'

Graham awoke from an instant reverie and Asano repeated his words. Graham's mind returned to the thing at hand.

'Of course I see the perfect reasonableness of this Restraint, soberness, the matured thought, the unselfish act, they are necessities of the barbarous state, the life of dangers. Dourness is man's tribute to unconquered nature. But man has conquered nature now for all practical purposes – his political affairs are managed by Bosses with a black police – and life is joyous.'

He looked at the dancers again. 'Joyous,' he said.

'There are weary moments,' said the little officer, reflectively.

'They all look young. Down there I should be visibly the oldest man. And in my own time I should have passed as middle-aged.'

'They are young. There are few old people in this class in the work cities.'

'How is that?'

'Old people's lives are not so pleasant as they used to be, unless they are rich to hire lovers and helpers. And we have an institution called Euthanasy.'

'Ah! that Euthanasy!' said Graham. 'The easy death?'

'The easy death. It is the last pleasure. The Euthanasy Company does it well. People will pay the sum – it is a costly thing – long beforehand, go off to some Pleasure City and return impoverished and weary, very weary.'

'There is a lot left for me to understand,' said Graham after a pause. 'Yet I see the logic of it all. Our array of angry virtues and sour restraints was the consequence of danger and insecurity. The Stoic, the Puritan, even in my time, were vanishing types. In the old days man was armed against Pain, now he is eager for Pleasure. There lies the difference. Civilisation has driven pain and danger so far off – for well-to-do people. And only well-to-do people matter now. I have been asleep two hundred years.'

For a minute they leant on the balustrading, following the intricate evolution of the dance. Indeed the scene was very beautiful.

'Before God,' said Graham, suddenly, 'I would rather be a wounded sentinel freezing in the snow than one of these painted fools!'

'In the snow,' said Asano, 'one might think differently.'

'I am uncivilised,' said Graham, not heeding him. 'That is the trouble. I am primitive Palaeolithic. *Their* fountain of rage and fear and anger is sealed and closed, the habits of a lifetime make them cheerful and easy and delightful. You must bear with my nineteenth-century shocks and disgusts. These people, you say, are skilled workers and so forth. And while these dance, men are fighting – men are dying in Paris to keep the world – that they may dance.'

Asano smiled faintly. 'For that matter, men are dying in London,' he said.

There was a moment's silence.

'Where do these sleep?' asked Graham.

'Above and below – an intricate warren.'

'And where do they work? This is – the domestic life.'

'You will see little work tonight. Half the workers are out or under arms. Half these people are keeping holiday. But we will go to the work places if you wish it.'

For a time Graham watched the dancers, then suddenly turned away. 'I want to see the workers. I have seen enough of these,' he said.

Asano led the way along the gallery across the dancing hall. Presently they came to a transverse passage that brought a breath of fresher, colder air.

Asano glanced at this passage as they went past, stopped, went back to it, and turned to Graham with a smile. 'Here, Sire,' he said, 'is something – will be familiar to you at least – and yet – . But I will not tell you. Come!'

He led the way along a closed passage that presently became cold. The reverberation of their feet told that this passage was a bridge. They came into a circular gallery that was glazed in from the outer weather, and so reached a circular chamber which seemed familiar, though Graham could not recall distinctly when he had entered it before. In this was a ladder – the first ladder he had seen since his awakening – up which they went, and came into a high, dark, cold place in which was another almost vertical ladder. This they ascended, Graham still perplexed.

But at the top he understood, and recognised the metallic bars to which he clung. He was in the cage under the ball of St Paul's. The dome rose but a little way above the general contour of the city, into the still twilight, and sloped away, shining greasily under a few distant lights, into a circum-ambient ditch of darkness.

Out between the bars he looked upon the wind-clear northern sky and saw the starry constellations all unchanged. Capella hung in the west, Vega

was rising, and the seven glittering points of the Great Bear swept overhead in their stately circle about the Pole.

He saw these stars in a clear gap of sky. To the east and south the great circular shapes of complaining wind-wheels blotted out the heavens, so that the glare about the Council House was hidden. To the south-west hung Orion, showing like a pallid ghost through a tracery of iron-work and interlacing shapes above a dazzling coruscation of lights. A bellowing and siren screaming that came from the flying stages warned the world that one of the aeroplanes was ready to start. He remained for a space gazing towards the glaring stage. Then his eyes went back to the northward constellations.

For a long time he was silent. 'This,' he said at last, smiling in the shadow, 'seems the strangest thing of all. To stand in the dome of Saint Paul's and look once more upon these familiar, silent stars!'

Thence Graham was taken by Asano along devious ways to the great gambling and business quarters where the bulk of the fortunes in the city were lost and made. It impressed him as a well-nigh interminable series of very high halls, surrounded by tiers upon tiers of galleries into which opened thousands of offices, and traversed by a complicated multitude of bridges, footways, aerial motor rails, and trapeze and cable leaps. And here more than anywhere the note of vehement vitality, of uncontrollable, hasty activity, rose high. Everywhere was violent advertisement, until his brain swam at the tumult of light and colour. And Babble Machines of a peculiarly rancid tone were abundant and filled the air with strenuous squealing and an idiotic slang. 'Skin your eyes and slide,' 'Gewhoop, Bonanza,' 'Gollipers come and hark!'

The place seemed to him to be dense with people either profoundly agitated or swelling with obscure cunning, yet he learnt that the place was comparatively empty, that the great political convulsion of the last few days had reduced transactions to an unprecedented minimum. In one huge place were long avenues of roulette tables, each with an excited, undignified crowd about it; in another a yelping Babel of white-faced women and red-necked leathery-lunged men bought and sold the shares of an absolutely fictitious business undertaking which, every five minutes, paid a dividend of ten per cent and cancelled a certain proportion of its shares by means of a lottery wheel.

These business activities were prosecuted with an energy that readily passed into violence, and Graham approaching a dense crowd found at its centre a couple of prominent merchants in violent controversy with teeth and nails on some delicate point of business etiquette. Something still remained in life to be fought for. Further he had a shock at a vehement announcement in phonetic letters of scarlet flame, each twice the height of a man, that

WE ASSURE THE PROPRAIET'R. WE ASSURE THE PROPRAIET'R.

'Who's the proprietor?' he asked.

'You.'

'But what do they assure me?' he asked. 'What do they assure me?'

'Didn't you have assurance?'

Graham thought. 'Insurance?'

'Yes – Insurance. I remember that was the older word. They are insuring your life. Dozands of people are taking out policies, myriads of lions are being put on you. And further on other people are buying annuities. They do that on everybody who is at all prominent. Look there!'

A crowd of people surged and roared, and Graham saw a vast black screen suddenly illuminated in still larger letters of burning purple.

ANUETES ON THE PROPRAIET'R – x 5 PR. G.

The people began to boo and shout at this, a number of hard-breathing, wild-eyed men came running past, clawing with hooked fingers at the air. There was a furious crush about a little doorway.

Asano did a brief calculation. 'Seventeen per cent per annum is their annuity on you. They would not pay so much per cent if they could see you now, Sire. But they do not know. Your own annuities used to be a very safe investment, but now you are sheer gambling, of course. This is probably a desperate bid. I doubt if people will get their money.'

The crowd of would-be annuitants grew so thick about them that for some time they could move neither forward nor backward. Graham noticed what appeared to him to be a high proportion of women among the speculators, and was reminded again of the economical independence of their sex. They seemed remarkably well able to take care of themselves in the crowd, using their elbows with particular skill, as he learnt to his cost. One curly-headed person caught in the pressure for a space, looked steadfastly at him several times, almost as if she recognised him, and then, edging deliberately towards him, touched his hand with her arm in a scarcely accidental manner, and made it plain by a look as ancient as Chaldea that he had found favour in her eyes. And then a lank, grey-bearded man, perspiring copiously in a noble passion of self-help, blind to all earthly things save that glaring bait, thrust between them in a cataclysmal rush towards that alluring 'x 5 pr. G'.

'I want to get out of this,' said Graham to Asano. 'This is not what I came to see. Show me the workers. I want to see the people in blue. These parasitic lunatics – '

He found himself wedged in a struggling mass of people, and this hopeful sentence went unfinished.

CHAPTER TWENTY-ONE

The Under Side

From the Business Quarter they presently passed by the running ways into a remote quarter of the city, where the bulk of the manufactures was done. On their way the platforms crossed the Thames twice, and passed in a broad viaduct across one of the great roads that entered the city from the North. In both cases his impression was swift and in both very vivid. The river was a broad wrinkled glitter of black sea water, over-arched by buildings, and vanishing either way into a blackness starred with receding lights. A string of black barges passed seaward, manned by blue-clad men. The road was a long and very broad and high tunnel, along which big-wheeled machines drove noiselessly and swiftly. Here, too, the distinctive blue of the Labour Company was in abundance. The smoothness of the double tracks, the largeness and the lightness of the big pneumatic wheels in proportion to the vehicular body, struck Graham most vividly. One lank and very high carriage with longitudinal metallic rods hung with the dripping carcasses of many hundred sheep arrested his attention unduly. Abruptly the edge of the archway cut and blotted out the picture.

Presently they left the way and descended by a lift and traversed a passage that sloped downward, and so came to a descending lift again. The appearance of things changed. Even the pretence of architectural ornament disappeared, the lights diminished in number and size, the architecture became more and more massive in proportion to the spaces as the factory quarters were reached. And in the dusty biscuit-making place of the potters, among the felspar mills in the furnace rooms of the metal workers, among the incandescent lakes of crude Eadhamite, the blue canvas clothing was on man, woman and child.

Many of these great and dusty galleries were silent avenues of machinery, endless raked-out ashen furnaces testified to the revolutionary dislocation, but wherever there was work it was being done by slow-moving workers in blue canvas. The only people not in blue canvas were the over-lookers of the work-places and the orange-clad Labour Police. And fresh from the flushed faces of the dancing halls, the voluntary vigours of the business quarter, Graham could note the pinched faces, the feeble muscles, and weary eyes of many of the latter-day workers. Such as he saw at work were noticeably inferior in physique to the few gaily dressed managers and forewomen who were directing their labours. The burly labourers of the Victorian times had followed the dray horse and all such living force producers, to extinction; the place of his costly muscles was taken by some dexterous machine. The latter-day labourer, male as well as female, was

essentially a machine-minder and feeder, a servant and attendant, or an artist under direction.

The women, in comparison with those Graham remembered, were as a class distinctly plain and flat-chested. Two hundred years of emancipation from the moral restraints of Puritanical religion, two hundred years of city life, had done their work in eliminating the strain of feminine beauty and vigour from the blue canvas myriads. To be brilliant physically or mentally, to be in any way attractive or exceptional, had been and was still a certain way of emancipation to the drudge, a line of escape to the Pleasure City and its splendours and delights, and at last to the Euthanasy and peace. To be steadfast against such inducements was scarcely to be expected of meanly nourished souls. In the young cities of Graham's former life, the newly aggregated labouring mass had been a diverse multitude, still stirred by the tradition of personal honour and a high morality; now it was differentiating into a distinct class, with a moral and physical difference of its own – even with a dialect of its own.

They penetrated downward, ever downward, towards the working places. Presently they passed underneath one of the streets of the moving ways, and saw its platforms running on their rails far overhead, and chinks of white lights between the transverse slits. The factories that were not working were sparsely lighted; to Graham they and their shrouded aisles of giant machines seemed plunged in gloom, and even where work was going on the illumination was far less brilliant than upon the public ways.

Beyond the blazing lakes of Eadhamite he came to the warren of the jewellers, and, with some difficulty and by using his signature, obtained admission to these galleries. They were high and dark, and rather cold. In the first a few men were making ornaments of gold filigree, each man at a little bench by himself, and with a little shaded light. The long vista of light patches, with the nimble fingers brightly lit and moving among the gleaming yellow coils, and the intent face like the face of a ghost, in each shadow' had the oddest effect.

The work was beautifully executed, but without any strength of modelling or drawing, for the most part intricate grotesques or the ringing of the changes on a geometrical motif. These workers wore a peculiar white uniform without pockets or sleeves. They assumed this on coming to work, but at night they were stripped and examined before they left the premises of the Company. In spite of every precaution, the Labour policeman told them in a depressed tone, the Company was not infrequently robbed.

Beyond was a gallery of women busied in cutting and setting slabs of artificial ruby, and next these were men and women busied together upon the slabs of copper net that formed the basis of *cloisonné* tiles. Many of these workers had lips and nostrils a livid white, due to a disease caused by a peculiar purple enamel that chanced to be much in fashion. Asano apologised to Graham for the offence of their faces, but excused himself on

the score of the convenience of this route. 'This is what I wanted to see,' said Graham; 'this is what I wanted to see,' trying to avoid a start at a particularly striking disfigurement that suddenly stared him in the face.

'She might have done better with herself than that,' said Asano.

Graham made some indignant comments.

'But, Sire, we simply could not stand that stuff without the purple,' said Asano. 'In your days people could stand such crudities, they were nearer the barbaric by two hundred years.'

They continued along one of the lower galleries of this *cloisonné* factory, and came to a little bridge that spanned a vault. Looking over the parapet, Graham saw that beneath was a wharf under yet more tremendous archings than any he had seen. Three barges, smothered in floury dust, were being unloaded of their cargoes of powdered felspar by a multitude of coughing men, each guiding a little truck; the dust filled the place with a choking mist, and turned the electric glare yellow. The vague shadows of these workers gesticulated about their feet, and rushed to and fro against a long stretch of white-washed wall. Every now and then one would stop to cough.

A shadowy, huge mass of masonry rising out of the inky water, brought to Graham's mind the thought of the multitude of ways and galleries and lifts, that rose floor above floor overhead between him and the sky. The men worked in silence under the supervision of two of the Labour Police; their feet made a hollow thunder on the planks along which they went to and fro. And as he looked at this scene, some hidden voice in the darkness began to sing.

'Stop that!' shouted one of the policemen, but the order was disobeyed, and first one and then all the white-stained men who were working there had taken up the beating refrain, singing it defiantly, the Song of the Revolt. The feet upon the planks thundered now to the rhythm of the song, tramp, tramp, tramp. The policeman who had shouted glanced at his fellow, and Graham saw him shrug his shoulders. He made no further effort to stop the singing.

And so they went through these factories and places of toil, seeing many painful and grim things. But why should the gentle reader be depressed? Surely to a refined nature our present world is distressing enough without bothering ourselves about these miseries to come. We shall not suffer anyhow. Our children may, but what is that to us? That walk left on Graham's mind a maze of memories, fluctuating pictures of swathed halls, and crowded vaults seen through clouds of dust, of intricate machines, the racing threads of looms, the heavy beat of stamping machinery, the roar and rattle of belt and armature, of ill-lit subterranean aisles of sleeping places, illimitable vistas of pin-point lights. And here the smell of tanning, and here the reek of a brewery and here, unprecedented reeks. And everywhere were pillars and cross archings of such a massiveness as Graham had never before seen, thick Titans of greasy, shining brickwork crushed beneath the vast

weight of that complex city world, even as these anaemic millions were crushed by its complexity. And everywhere were pale features, lean limbs, disfigurement and degradation.

Once and again, and again a third time, Graham heard the song of the revolt during his long, unpleasant research in these places, and once he saw a confused struggle down a passage, and learnt that a number of these serfs had seized their bread before their work was done. Graham was ascending towards the ways again when he saw a number of blue-clad children running down a transverse passage, and presently perceived the reason of their panic in a company of the Labour Police armed with clubs, trotting towards some unknown disturbance. And then came a remote disorder. But for the most part this remnant that worked, worked hopelessly. All the spirit that was left in fallen humanity was above in the streets that night, calling for the Master, and valiantly and noisily keeping its arms.

They emerged from these wanderings and stood blinking in the bright light of the middle passage of the platforms again. They became aware of the remote hooting and yelping of the machines of one of the General Intelligence Offices, and suddenly came men running, and along the platforms and about the ways everywhere was a shouting and crying. Then a woman with a face of mute white terror, and another who gasped and shrieked as she ran.

'What has happened now?' said Graham, puzzled, for he could not understand their thick speech. Then he heard it in English and perceived that the thing that everyone was shouting, that men yelled to one another, that women took up screaming, that was passing like the first breeze of a thunderstorm, chill and sudden through the city, was this: 'Ostrog has ordered the Black Police to London. The Black Police are coming from South Africa . . . The Black Police. The Black Police.'

Asano's face was white and astonished; he hesitated, looked at Graham's face, and told him the thing he already knew. 'But how can they know?' asked Asano.

Graham heard someone shouting. 'Stop all work. Stop all work,' and a swarthy hunchback, ridiculously gay in green and gold, came leaping down the platforms toward him, bawling again and again in good English, 'This is Ostrog's doing, Ostrog, the Knave! The Master is betrayed.' His voice was hoarse and a thin foam dropped from his ugly shouting mouth. He yelled an unspeakable horror that the Black Police had done in Paris, and so passed shrieking, 'Ostrog the Knave!'

For a moment Graham stood still, for it had come upon him again that these things were a dream. He looked up at the great cliff of buildings on either side, vanishing into blue haze at last above the lights, and down to the roaring tiers of platforms, and the shouting, running people who were gesticulating past. 'The Master is betrayed!' they cried. 'The Master is betrayed!'

Suddenly the situation shaped itself in his mind real and urgent. His heart began to beat fast and strong.

'It has come,' he said. 'I might have known. The hour has come.'

He thought swiftly. 'What am I to do?'

'Go back to the Council House,' said Asano.

'Why should I not appeal – ? The people are here.'

'You will lose time. They will doubt if it is you. But they will mass about the Council House. There you will find their leaders. Your strength is there with them.'

'Suppose this is only a rumour?'

'It sounds true,' said Asano.

'Let us have the facts,' said Graham.

Asano shrugged his shoulders. 'We had better get towards the Council House,' he cried. 'That is where they will swarm. Even now the ruins may be impassable.'

Graham regarded him doubtfully and followed him.

They went up the stepped platforms to the swiftest one, and there Asano accosted a labourer. The answers to his questions were in the thick, vulgar speech.

'What did he say?' asked Graham.

'He knows little, but he told me that the Black Police would have arrived here before the people knew – had not someone in the Wind Vane Offices learnt. He said a girl.'

'A girl? Not – ?'

'He said a girl – he did not know who she was. Who came out from the Council House crying aloud, and told the men at work among the ruins.'

And then another thing was shouted, something that turned an aimless tumult into determinate movements, it came like a wind along the street. 'To your Wards, to your Wards. Every man get arms. Every man to his Ward!'

CHAPTER TWENTY-TWO

The Struggle in the Council House

As Asano and Graham hurried along to the ruins about the Council House, they saw everywhere the excitement of the people rising. 'To your Wards! To your Wards!' Everywhere men and women in blue were hurrying from unknown subterranean employments, up the staircases of the middle path – at one place Graham saw an arsenal of the revolutionary committee besieged by a crowd of shouting men, at another a couple of men in the hated yellow uniform of the Labour Police, pursued by a gathering crowd, fled precipitately along the swift way that went in the opposite direction.

The cries of 'To your Wards!' became at last a continuous shouting as they drew near the Government quarter. Many of the shouts were unintelligible. 'Ostrog has betrayed us,' one man bawled in a hoarse voice, again and again, dinning that refrain into Graham's ear until it haunted him. This person stayed close beside Graham and Asano on the swift way, shouting to the people who swarmed on the lower platforms as he rushed past them. His cry about Ostrog alternated with some incomprehensible orders. Presently he went leaping down and disappeared.

Graham's mind was filled with the din. His plans were vague and unformed. He had one picture of some commanding position from which he could address the multitudes, another of meeting Ostrog face to face. He was full of rage, of tense muscular excitement, his hands gripped, his lips were pressed together.

The way to the Council House across the ruins was impassable, but Asano met that difficulty and took Graham into the premises of the central post-office. The post-office was nominally at work, but the blue-clothed porters moved sluggishly or had stopped to stare through the arches of their galleries at the shouting men who were going by outside. 'Every man to his Ward! Every man to his Ward!' Here, by Asano's advice, Graham revealed his identity.

They crossed to the Council House by a cable cradle. Already in the brief interval since the capitulation of the Councillors a great change had been wrought in the appearance of the ruins. The spurting cascades of the ruptured sea water-mains had been captured and tamed, and huge temporary pipes ran overhead along a flimsy-looking fabric of girders. The sky was laced with restored cables and wires that served the Council House, and a mass of new fabric with cranes and other building machines going to and fro upon it, projected to the left of the white pile.

The moving ways that ran across this area had been restored, albeit for once running under the open sky. These were the ways that Graham had seen from the little balcony in the hour of his awakening, not nine days since, and the hall of his Trance had been on the further side, where now shapeless piles of smashed and shattered masonry were heaped together.

It was already high day and the sun was shining brightly. Out of their tall caverns of blue electric light came the swift ways crowded with multitudes of people, who poured off them and gathered ever denser over the wreckage and confusion of the ruins. The air was full of their shouting, and they were pressing and swaying towards the central building. For the most part that shouting mass consisted of shapeless swarms, but here and there Graham could see that a rude discipline struggled to establish itself. And every voice clamoured for order in the chaos. 'To your Wards! Every man to his Ward!'

The cable carried them into a hall which Graham recognised as the antechamber to the Hall of the Atlas, about the gallery of which he had

walked days ago with Howard to show himself to the vanished Council, an hour from his awakening. Now the place was empty except for two cable attendants. These men seemed hugely astonished to recognise the Sleeper in the man who swung down from the cross seat.

'Where is Helen Wotton?' he demanded. 'Where is Helen Wotton?'

They did not know.

'Then where is Ostrog? I must see Ostrog forthwith. He has disobeyed me. I have come back to take things out of his hands.' Without waiting for Asano, he went straight across the place, ascended the steps at the further end, and, pulling the curtain aside, found himself facing the perpetually labouring Titan.

The hall was empty. Its appearance had changed very greatly since his first sight of it. It had suffered serious injury in the violent struggle of the first outbreak. On the right-hand side of the great figure the upper half of the wall had been torn away for nearly two hundred feet of its length, and a sheet of the same glassy film that had enclosed Graham at his awakening had been drawn across the gap. This deadened, but did not altogether exclude the roar of the people outside. 'Wards! Wards! Wards!' they seemed to be saying. Through it there were visible the beams and supports of metal scaffoldings that rose and fell according to the requirements of a great crowd of workmen. An idle building machine, with lank arms of red painted metal that caught the still plastic blocks of mineral paste and swung them neatly into position, stretched gauntly across this green tinted picture. On it were still a number of workmen staring at the crowd below. For a moment he stood regarding these things, and Asano overtook him.

'Ostrog,' said Asano, 'will be in the small offices beyond there.' The little man looked livid now and his eyes searched Graham's face.

They had scarcely advanced ten paces from the curtain before a little panel to the left of the Atlas rolled up, and Ostrog, accompanied by Lincoln and followed by two black-and-yellow-clad negroes, appeared crossing the remote corner of the hall, towards a second panel that was raised and open. 'Ostrog,' shouted Graham, and at the sound of his voice the little party turned astonished.

Ostrog said something to Lincoln and advanced alone.

Graham was the first to speak. His voice was loud and dictatorial. 'What is this I hear?' he asked. 'Are you bringing negroes here – to keep the people down?'

'It is none too soon,' said Ostrog. 'They have been getting out of hand more and more, since the revolt. I underestimated – '

'Do you mean that these infernal negroes are on the way?'

'On the way. As it is, you have seen the people – outside?'

'No wonder! But – after what was said. You have taken too much on yourself, Ostrog.'

Ostrog said nothing, but drew nearer.

'These negroes must not come to London,' said Graham. 'I am Master and they shall not come.'

Ostrog glanced at Lincoln, who at once came towards them with his two attendants close behind him. 'Why not?' asked Ostrog.

'White men must be mastered by white men. Besides – '

'The negroes are only an instrument.'

'But that is not the question. I am the Master. I mean to be the Master. And I tell you these negroes shall not come.'

'The people – '

'I believe in the people.'

'Because you are an anachronism. You are a man out of the Past – an accident. You are Owner perhaps of half the property in the world. But you are not Master. You do not know enough to be Master.'

He glanced at Lincoln again. 'I know now what you think – I can guess something of what you mean to do. Even now it is not too late to warn you. You dream of human equality – of a socialistic order – you have all those worn-out dreams of the nineteenth century fresh and vivid in your mind, and you would rule this age that you do not understand.'

'Listen!' said Graham. 'You can hear it – a sound like the sea. Not voices – but a voice. Do *you* altogether understand?'

'We taught them that,' said Ostrog.

'Perhaps. Can you teach them to forget it? But enough of this! These negroes must not come.'

There was a pause and Ostrog looked him in the eyes.

'They will,' he said.

'I forbid it,' said Graham.

'They have started.'

'I will not have it.'

'No,' said Ostrog. 'Sorry as I am to follow the method of the Council – . For your own good – you must not side with – Disorder. And now that you are here – . It was kind of you to come here.'

Lincoln laid his hand on Graham's shoulder. Abruptly Graham realised the enormity of his blunder in coming to the Council House. He turned towards the curtains that separated the hall from the antechamber. The clutching hand of Asano intervened. In another moment Lincoln had grasped Graham's cloak.

He turned and struck at Lincoln's face, and incontinently a negro had him by collar and arm. He wrenched himself away, his sleeve tore noisily, and he stumbled back, to be tripped by the other attendant. Then he struck the ground heavily and he was staring at the distant ceiling of the hall.

He shouted, rolled over, struggling fiercely, clutched an attendant's leg and threw him headlong, and struggled to his feet.

Lincoln appeared before him, went down heavily again with a blow under the point of the jaw and lay still. Graham made two strides, stumbled.

And then Ostrog's arm was round his neck, he was pulled over backward, fell heavily, and his arms were pinned to the ground. After a few violent efforts he ceased to struggle and lay staring at Ostrog's heaving throat.

'You – are – a prisoner,' panted Ostrog, exulting. 'You – were rather a fool – to come back.'

Graham turned his head about and perceived through the irregular green window in the walls of the hall the men who had been working the building cranes gesticulating excitedly to the people below them. They had seen!

Ostrog followed his eyes and started. He shouted something to Lincoln, but Lincoln did not move. A bullet smashed among the mouldings above the Atlas. The two sheets of transparent matter that had been stretched across this gap were rent, the edges of the torn aperture darkened, curved, ran rapidly towards the framework, and in a moment the Council chamber stood open to the air. A chilly gust blew in by the gap, bringing with it a war of voices from the ruinous spaces without, an elvish babblement, 'Save the Master!' 'What are they doing to the Master?' 'The Master is betrayed!'

And then he realised that Ostrog's attention was distracted, that Ostrog's grip had relaxed, and, wrenching his arms free, he struggled to his knees. In another moment he had thrust Ostrog back, and he was on one foot, his hand gripping Ostrog's throat, and Ostrog's hands clutching the silk about his neck.

But now men were coming towards them from the dais – men whose intentions he misunderstood. He had a glimpse of someone running in the distance towards the curtains of the antechamber, and then Ostrog had slipped from him and these newcomers were upon him. To his infinite astonishment, they seized him. They obeyed the shouts of Ostrog.

He was lugged a dozen yards before he realised that they were not friends – that they were dragging him towards the open panel. When he saw this he pulled back, he tried to fling himself down, he shouted for help with all his strength. And this time there were answering cries.

The grip upon his neck relaxed, and behold! in the lower corner of the rent upon the wall, first one and then a number of little black figures appeared shouting and waving arms. They came leaping down from the gap into the light gallery that had led to the Silent Rooms. They ran along it, so near were they that Graham could see the weapons in their hands. Then Ostrog was shouting in his ear to the men who held him, and once more he was struggling with all his strength against their endeavours to thrust him towards the opening that yawned to receive him. 'They can't come down,' panted Ostrog. 'They daren't fire. It's all right.' 'We'll save him from them yet.'

For long minutes as it seemed to Graham that inglorious struggle continued. His clothes were rent in a dozen places, he was covered in dust, one hand had been trodden upon. He could hear the shouts of his supporters, and once he heard shots. He could feel his strength giving

way, feel his efforts wild and aimless. But no help came, and surely, irresistibly, that black, yawning opening came nearer.

The pressure upon him relaxed and he struggled up. He saw Ostrog's grey head receding and perceived that he was no longer held. He turned about and came full into a man in black. One of the green weapons cracked close to him, a drift of pungent smoke came into his face, and a steel blade flashed. The huge chamber span about him.

He saw a man in pale blue stabbing one of the black and yellow attendants not three yards from his face. Then hands were upon him again.

He was being pulled in two directions now. It seemed as though people were shouting to him. He wanted to understand and could not. Someone was clutching about his thighs, he was being hoisted in spite of his vigorous efforts. He understood suddenly, he ceased to struggle. He was lifted up on men's shoulders and carried away from that devouring panel. Ten thousand throats were cheering.

He saw men in blue and black hurrying after the retreating Ostrogites and firing. Lifted up, he saw now across the whole expanse of the hall beneath the Atlas image, saw that he was being carried towards the raised platform in the centre of the place. The far end of the hall was already full of people running towards him. They were looking at him and cheering. He became aware that a sort of bodyguard surrounded him. Active men about him shouted vague orders. He saw close at hand the black-moustached man in yellow who had been among those who had greeted him in the public theatre, shouting directions. The hall was already densely packed with swaying people, the little metal gallery sagged with a shouting load, the curtains at the end had been torn away, and the antechamber was revealed densely crowded. He could scarcely make the man near him hear for the tumult about them. 'Where has Ostrog gone?' he asked.

The man he questioned pointed over the heads towards the lower panels about the hall on the side opposite the gap. They stood open and armed men, blue clad with black sashes, were running through them and vanishing into the chambers and passages beyond. It seemed to Graham that a sound of firing drifted through the riot. He was carried in a staggering curve across the great hall towards an opening beneath the gap.

He perceived men working with a sort of rude discipline to keep the crowd off him, to make a space clear about him. He passed out of the hall, and saw a crude, new wall rising blankly before him topped by blue sky. He was swung down to his feet; someone gripped his arm and guided him. He found the man in yellow close at hand. They were taking him up a narrow stairway of brick, and close at hand rose the great red-painted masses, the cranes and levers and the still engines of the big building machine.

He was at the top of the steps. He was hurried across a narrow railed footway, and suddenly with a vast shouting the amphitheatre of ruins

opened again before him. 'The Master is with us! The Master! The Master!' The shout swept athwart the lake of faces like a wave, broke against the distant cliff of ruins, and came back in a welter of cries. 'The Master is on our side!'

Graham perceived that he was no longer encompassed by people, that he was standing upon a little temporary platform of white metal, part of a flimsy-seeming scaffolding that laced about the great mass of the Council House. Over all the huge expanse of the ruins, swayed and eddied the shouting people; and here and there the black banners of the revolutionary societies ducked and swayed and formed rare nuclei of organisation in the chaos. Up the steep stairs of wall and scaffolding by which his rescuers had reached the opening in the Atlas Chamber, clung a solid crowd, and little energetic black figures clinging to pillars and projections were strenuous to induce these congested masses to stir. Behind him, at a higher point on the scaffolding, a number of men struggled upwards with the flapping folds of a huge black standard. Through the yawning gap in the walls below him he could look down upon the packed attentive multitudes in the Hall of the Atlas. The distant flying stages to the south came out bright and vivid, brought nearer as it seemed by an unusual translucency of the air. A solitary aeropile beat up from the central stage as if to meet the coming aeroplanes.

'What has become of Ostrog?' asked Graham, and even as he spoke he saw that all eyes were turned from him towards the crest of the Council House building. He looked also in this direction of universal attention. For a moment he saw nothing but the jagged corner of a wall, hard and clear against the sky. Then in the shadow he perceived the interior of a room and recognised with a start the green and white decorations of his former prison. And coming quickly across this opened room and up to the very verge of the cliff of the ruins came a little white clad-figure followed by two other smaller-seeming figures in black and yellow. He heard the man beside him exclaim 'Ostrog,' and turned to ask a question. But he never did, because of the startled exclamation of another of those who were with him and a lank finger suddenly pointing. He looked, and behold the aeropile that had been rising from the flying stage when last he had looked in that direction, was driving towards them. The swift steady flight was still novel enough to hold his attention.

Nearer it came, growing rapidly larger and larger, until it had swept over the further edge of the ruins and into view of the dense multitudes below. It drooped across the space and rose and passed overhead, rising to clear the mass of the Council House, a filmy translucent shape with the solitary aeronaut peering down through its ribs. It vanished beyond the skyline of the ruins.

Graham transferred his attention to Ostrog. He was signalling with his hands, and his attendants were busy breaking down the wall beside him. In

another moment the aeropile came into view again, a little thing far away, coming round in a wide curve and going slower.

Then suddenly the man in yellow shouted: 'What are they doing? What are the people doing? Why is Ostrog left there? Why is he not captured? They will lift him – the aeropile will lift him! Ah!'

The exclamation was echoed by a shout from the ruins. The rattling sound of the green weapons drifted across the intervening gulf to Graham, and, looking down, he saw a number of black and yellow uniforms running along one of the galleries that lay open to the air below the promontory upon which Ostrog stood. They fired as they ran at men unseen, and then emerged a number of pale blue figures in pursuit. These minute fighting figures had the oddest effect; they seemed as they ran like little model soldiers in a toy. This queer appearance of a house cut open gave that struggle amidst furniture and passages a quality of unreality. It was perhaps two hundred yards away from him, and very nearly fifty above the heads in the ruins below. The black and yellow men ran into an open archway, and turned and fired a volley. One of the blue pursuers striding forward close to the edge, flung up his arms, staggered sideways, seemed to Graham's sense to hang over the edge for several seconds, and fell headlong down. Graham saw him strike a projecting corner, fly out, head over heels, head over heels, and vanish behind the red arm of the building machine.

And then a shadow came between Graham and the sun. He looked up and the sky was clear, but he knew the aeropile had passed. Ostrog had vanished. The man in yellow thrust before him, zealous and perspiring, pointing and blatant.

'They are grounding!' cried the man in yellow. 'They are grounding. Tell the people to fire at him. Tell them to fire at him!'

Graham could not understand. He heard loud voices repeating these enigmatical orders.

Suddenly over the edge of the ruins he saw the prow of the aeropile come gliding and stop with a jerk. In a moment Graham understood that the thing had grounded in order that Ostrog might escape by it. He saw a blue haze climbing out of the gulf, perceived that the people below him were now firing up at the projecting stem.

A man beside him cheered hoarsely, and he saw that the blue rebels had gained the archway that had been contested by the men in black and yellow a moment before, and were running in a continual stream along the open passage.

And suddenly the aeropile slipped over the edge of the Council House and fell. It dropped, tilting at an angle of forty-five degrees, and dropping so steeply that it seemed to Graham, it seemed perhaps to most of these below, that it could not possibly rise again.

It fell so closely past him that he could see Ostrog clutching the guides of the seat, with his grey hair streaming; see the white-faced aeronaut

wrenching over the lever that drove the engine along its guides. He heard the apprehensive vague cry of innumerable men below.

Graham clutched the railing before him and gasped. The second seemed an age. The lower fan of the aeropile passed within an ace of touching the people, who yelled and screamed and trampled one another below.

And then it rose.

For a moment it looked as if it could not possibly clear the opposite cliff, and then that it could not possibly clear the wind-wheel that rotated beyond.

And behold! it was clear and soaring, still heeling sideways, upward, upward into the wind-swept sky.

The suspense of the moment gave place to a fury of exasperation as the swarming people realised that Ostrog had escaped them. With belated activity they renewed their fire, until the rattling wove into a roar, until the whole area became dim and blue and the air pungent with the thin smoke of their weapons.

Too late! The aeropile dwindled smaller and smaller, and curved about and swept gracefully downward to the flying stage from which it had so lately risen. Ostrog had escaped.

For a while a confused babblement arose from the ruins, and then the universal attention came back to Graham, perched high among the scaffolding. He saw the faces of the people turned towards him, heard their shouts at his rescue. From the throat of the ways came the song of the revolt spreading like a breeze across that swaying sea of men.

The little group of men about him shouted congratulations on his escape. The man in yellow was close to him, with a set face and shining eyes. And the song was rising, louder and louder; tramp, tramp, tramp, tramp.

Slowly the realisation came of the full meaning of these things to him, the perception of the swift change in his position. Ostrog, who had stood beside him whenever he had faced that shouting multitude before, was beyond there – the antagonist. There was no one to rule for him any longer. Even the people about him, the leaders and organisers of the multitude, looked to see what he would do, looked to him to act, awaited his orders. He was King indeed. His puppet reign was at an end.

He was very intent to do the thing that was expected of him. His nerves and muscles were quivering, his mind was perhaps a little confused, but he felt neither fear nor anger. His hand that had been trodden upon throbbed and was hot. He was a little nervous about his bearing. He knew he was not afraid, but he was anxious not to seem afraid. In his former life he had often been more excited in playing games of skill. He was desirous of immediate action, he knew he must not think too much in detail of the huge complexity of the struggle about him lest he should be paralysed by the sense of its intricacy. Over there those square blue shapes, the flying stages, meant Ostrog; against Ostrog he was fighting for the world.

CHAPTER TWENTY-THREE

While the Aeroplanes were Coming

For a time the Master of the Earth was not even master of his own mind. Even his will seemed a will not his own, his own acts surprised him and were but a part of the confusion of strange experiences that poured across his being. These things were definite, the aeroplanes were coming, Helen Wotton had warned the people of their coming, and he was Master of the Earth. Each of these facts seemed struggling for complete possession of his thoughts. They protruded from a background of swarming halls, elevated passages, rooms jammed with ward leaders in council kinematograph and telephone rooms, and windows looking out on a seething sea of marching men. The man in yellow, and men whom he fancied were called Ward Leaders, were either propelling him forward or following him obediently; it was hard to tell. Perhaps they were doing a little of both. Perhaps some power, unseen and unsuspected, propelled them all. He was aware that he was going to make a proclamation to the People of the Earth, aware of certain grandiose phrases floating in his mind as the thing he meant to say. Many little things happened, and then he found himself with the man in yellow entering a little room where this proclamation of his was to be made.

This room was grotesquely latter-day in its appointments. In the centre was a bright oval lit by shaded electric lights from above. The rest was in shadow, and the double finely fitting doors through which he came from the swarming Hall of the Atlas made the place very still. The dead thud of these as they closed behind him, the sudden cessation of the tumult in which he had been living for hours, the quivering circle of light, the whispers and quick noiseless movements of vaguely visible attendants in the shadows, had a strange effect upon Graham. The huge ears of a phonographic mechanism gaped in a battery for his words, the black eyes of great photographic cameras awaited his beginning, beyond metal rods and coils glittered dimly, and something whirled about with a droning hum. He walked into the centre of the light, and his shadow drew together black and sharp to a little blot at his feet.

The vague shape of the thing he meant to say was already in his mind. But this silence, this isolation, the sudden withdrawal from that contagious crowd, this silent audience of gaping, glaring machines had not been in his anticipation. All his supports seemed withdrawn together; he seemed to have dropped into this suddenly, suddenly to have discovered himself. In a moment he was changed. He found that he now feared to be inadequate, he feared to be theatrical, he feared the quality of his voice, the quality of his wit, astonished, he turned to the man in yellow with a propitiatory gesture.

'For a moment,' he said, 'I must wait. I did not think it would be like this. I must think of the thing I have to say.'

While he was still hesitating there came an agitated messenger with news that the foremost aeroplanes were passing over Arawan.

'Arawan?' he said. 'Where is that? But anyhow, they are coming. They will be here. When?'

'By twilight.'

'Great God! In only a few hours. What news of the flying stages?' he asked.

'The people of the south-west wards are ready.'

'Ready!'

He turned impatiently to the blank circles of the lenses again.

'I suppose it must be a sort of speech. Would to God I knew certainly the thing that should be said! Aeroplanes at Arawan! They must have started before the main fleet. And the people only ready! Surely . . . '

'Oh! what does it matter whether I speak well or ill?' he said, and felt the light grow brighter.

He had framed some vague sentence of democratic sentiment when suddenly doubts overwhelmed him. His belief in his heroic quality and calling he found had altogether lost its assured conviction. The picture of a little strutting futility in a windy waste of incomprehensible destinies replaced it. Abruptly it was perfectly clear to him that this revolt against Ostrog was premature, foredoomed to failure, the impulse of passionate inadequacy against inevitable things. He thought of that swift flight of aeroplanes like the swoop of Fate towards him. He was astonished that he could have seen things in any other light. In that final emergency he debated, thrust debate resolutely aside, determined at all costs to go through with the thing he had undertaken. And he could find no word to begin. Even as he stood, awkward, hesitating, with an indiscreet apology for his inability trembling on his lips, came the noise of many people crying out, the running to and fro of feet. 'Wait,' cried someone, and a door opened. 'She is coming,' said the voices. Graham turned, and the watching lights waned.

Through the open doorway he saw a slight grey figure advancing across a spacious hall. His heart leapt. It was Helen Wotton. Behind and about her marched a riot of applause. The man in yellow came out of the nearer shadows into the circle of light.

'This is the girl who told us what Ostrog had done,' he said.

Her face was aflame, and the heavy coils of her black hair fell about her shoulders. The folds of the soft silk robe she wore streamed from her and floated in the rhythm of her advance. She drew nearer and nearer, and his heart was beating fast. All his doubts were gone. The shadow of the doorway fell athwart her face and she was near him. 'You have not betrayed us?' she cried. 'You are with us?'

'Where have you been?' said Graham.

'At the office of the south-west wards. Until ten minutes since I did not know you had returned. I went to the office of the south-west wards to find the Ward Leaders in order that they might tell the people.'

'I came back so soon as I heard – '

'I knew,' she cried, 'knew you would be with us. And it was I – it was I that told them. They have risen. All the world is rising. The people have awakened. Thank God that I did not act in vain! You are Master still.'

'You told them,' he said slowly, and he saw that in spite of her steady eyes her lips trembled and her throat rose and fell.

'I told them. I knew of the order. I was here. I heard that the negroes were to come to London to guard you and to keep the people down – to keep you a prisoner. And I stopped it. I came out and told the people. And you are Master still.'

Graham glanced at the black lenses of the cameras, the vast listening ears, and back to her face. 'I am Master still,' he said slowly, and the swift rush of a fleet of aeroplanes passed across his thoughts.

'And you did this? You, who are the niece of Ostrog.'

'For you,' she cried. 'For you! That you for whom the world has waited should not be cheated of your power.'

Graham stood for a space, wordless, regarding her. His doubts and questionings had fled before her presence. He remembered the things that he had meant to say. He faced the cameras again and the light about him grew brighter. He turned again towards her.

'You have saved me,' he said; 'you have saved my power. And the battle is beginning. God knows what this night will see – but not dishonour.'

He paused. He addressed himself to the unseen multitudes who stared upon him through those grotesque black eyes. At first he spoke slowly. 'Men and women of the new age,' he said, 'you have arisen to do battle for the race . . . There is no easy victory before us.'

He stopped to gather words. The thoughts that had been in his mind before she came returned, but transfigured, no longer touched with the shadow of a possible irrelevance. 'This night is a beginning,' he cried. 'This battle that is coming, this battle that rushes upon us tonight, is only a beginning. All your lives, it may be, you must fight. Take no thought though I am beaten, though I am utterly overthrown.'

He found the thing in his mind too vague for words. He paused momentarily, and broke into vague exhortations, and then a rush of speech came upon him. Much that he said was but the humanitarian commonplace of a vanished age, but the conviction of his voice touched it to vitality. He stated the case of the old days to the people of the new age, to the woman at his side. 'I come out of the past to you,' he said, 'with the memory of an age that hoped. My age was an age of dreams – of beginnings, an age of noble hopes; throughout the world we had made an end of slavery; throughout

the world we had spread the desire and anticipation that wars might cease, that all men and women might live nobly, in freedom and peace . . . So we hoped in the days that are past. And what of those hopes? How is it with man after two hundred years?

'Great cities, vast powers, a collective greatness beyond our dreams. For that we did not work, and that has come. But how is it with the little lives that make up this greater life? How is it with the common lives? As it has ever been – sorrow and labour, lives cramped and unfulfilled, lives tempted by power, tempted by wealth, and gone to waste and folly. The old faiths have faded and changed, the new faith – . Is there a new faith?'

Things that he had long wished to believe, he found that he believed. He plunged at belief and seized it, and clung for a time at her level. He spoke gustily, in broken incomplete sentences, but with all his heart and strength, of this new faith within him. He spoke of the greatness of self-abnegation, of his belief in an immortal life of Humanity in which we live and move and have our being. His voice rose and fell, and the recording appliances hummed their hurried applause, dim attendants watched him out of the shadow. Through all those doubtful places his sense of that silent spectator beside him sustained his sincerity. For a few glorious moments he was carried away; he felt no doubt of his heroic quality, no doubt of his heroic words, he had it all straight and plain. His eloquence limped no longer. And at last he made an end to speaking. 'Here and now,' he cried, 'I make my will. All that is mine in the world I give to the people of the world. All that is mine in the world I give to the people of the world. I give it to you, and myself I give to you. And as God wills, I will live for you, or I will die.'

He ended with a florid gesture and turned about. He found the light of his present exaltation reflected in the face of the girl. Their eyes met; her eyes were swimming with tears of enthusiasm. They seemed to be urged towards each other. They clasped hands and stood gripped, facing one another, in an eloquent silence. She whispered. 'I knew,' she whispered. 'I knew.' He could not speak, he crushed her hand in his. His mind was the theatre of gigantic passions.

The man in yellow was beside them. Neither had noted his coming. He was saying that the south-west wards were marching. 'I never expected it so soon,' he cried. 'They have done wonders. You must send them a word to help them on their way.'

Graham dropped Helen's hand and stared at him absent-mindedly. Then with a start he returned to his previous preoccupation about the flying stages.

'Yes,' he said. 'That is good, that is good.' He weighed a message. 'Tell them; – well done South West.'

He turned his eyes to Helen Wotton again. His face expressed his struggle between conflicting ideas. 'We must capture the flying stages,' he explained. 'Unless we can do that they will land negroes. At all costs we must prevent that.'

He felt even as he spoke that this was not what had been in his mind before the interruption. He saw a touch of surprise in her eyes. She seemed about to speak and a shrill bell drowned her voice.

It occurred to Graham that she expected him to lead these marching people, that that was the thing he had to do. He made the offer abruptly. He addressed the man in yellow, but he spoke to her. He saw her face respond. 'Here I am doing nothing,' he said.

'It is impossible,' protested the man in yellow. 'It is a fight in a warren. Your place is here.'

He explained elaborately. He motioned towards the room where Graham must wait, he insisted no other course was possible. 'We must know where you are,' he said. 'At any moment a crisis may arise needing your presence and decision.' The room was a luxurious little apartment with news machines and a broken mirror that had once been *en rapport* with the crow's nest specula. It seemed a matter of course to Graham that Helen should stop with him.

A picture had drifted through his mind of such a vast dramatic struggle as the masses in the ruins had suggested. But here was no spectacular battle-field such as he imagined. Instead was seclusion – and suspense. It was only as the afternoon wore on that he pieced together a truer picture of the fight that was raging, inaudibly and invisibly, within four miles of him, beneath the Roehampton stage. A strange and unprecedented contest it was, a battle that was a hundred thousand little battles, a battle in a sponge of ways and channels, fought out of sight of sky or sun under the electric glare, fought out in a vast confusion by multitudes untrained in arms, led chiefly by acclamation, multitudes dulled by mindless labour and enervated by the tradition of two hundred years of servile security against multitudes demoralised by lives of venial privilege and sensual indulgence. They had no artillery, no differentiation into this force or that; the only weapon on either side was the little green metal carbine, whose secret manufacture and sudden distribution in enormous quantities had been one of Ostrog's culminating moves against the Council. Few had had any experience with this weapon, many had never discharged one, many who carried it came unprovided with ammunition; never was wilder firing in the history of warfare. It was a battle of amateurs, a hideous experimental warfare, armed rioters fighting armed rioters, armed rioters swept forward by the words and fury of a song, by the tramping sympathy of their numbers, pouring in countless myriads towards the smaller ways, the disabled lifts, the galleries slippery with blood, the halls and passages choked with smoke, beneath the flying stages, to learn there when retreat was hopeless the ancient mysteries of warfare. And overhead save for a few sharpshooters upon the roof spaces and for a few bands and threads of vapour that multiplied and darkened towards the evening, the day was a clear serenity. Ostrog it seems had no bombs at command and in all the earlier phases of the battle the aeropiles

played no part. Not the smallest cloud was there to break the empty brilliance of the sky. It seemed as though it held itself vacant until the aeroplanes should come.

Ever and again there was news of these, drawing nearer, from this Mediterranean port and then that, and presently from the south of France. But of the new guns that Ostrog had made and which were known to be in the city came no news in spite of Graham's urgency, nor any report of successes from the dense felt of fighting strands about the flying stages. Section after section of the Labour Societies reported itself assembled, reported itself marching, and vanished from knowledge into the labyrinth of that warfare What was happening there? Even the busy Ward Leaders did not know. In spite of the opening and closing of doors, the hasty messengers, the ringing of bells and the perpetual clitter-clack of recording implements, Graham felt isolated, strangely inactive, inoperative.

Their isolation seemed at times the strangest, the most unexpected of all the things that had happened since his awakening. It had something of the quality of that inactivity that comes in dreams. A tumult, the stupendous realisation of a world struggle between Ostrog and himself, and then this confined quiet little room with its mouthpieces and bells and broken mirror!

Now the door would be closed and they were alone together; they seemed sharply marked off then from all the unprecedented world storm that rushed together without, vividly aware of one another, only concerned with one another. Then the door would open again, messengers would enter, or a sharp bell would stab their quiet privacy, and it was like a window in a well-built brightly lit house flung open suddenly to a hurricane. The dark hurry and tumult, the stress and vehemence of the battle rushed in and over-whelmed them. They were no longer persons but mere spectators, mere impressions of a tremendous convulsion. They became unreal even to themselves, miniatures of personality, indescribably small, and the two antagonistic realities, the only realities in being were first the city, that throbbed and roared yonder in a belated frenzy of defence and secondly the aeroplanes hurling inexorably towards them over the round shoulder of the world.

At first their mood had been one of exalted confidence, a great pride had possessed them, a pride in one another for the greatness of the issues they had challenged. At first he had walked the room eloquent with a transitory persuasion of his tremendous destiny. But slowly uneasy intimations of their coming defeat touched his spirit. There came a long period in which they were alone. He changed his theme, became egotistical, spoke of the wonder of his sleep, of the little life of his memories, remote yet minute and clear, like something seen through an inverted opera-glass, and all the brief play of desires and errors that had made his former life. She said little, but the emotion in her face followed the tones in his voice, and it seemed to him

he had at last a perfect understanding. He reverted from pure reminiscence to that sense of greatness she imposed upon him. 'And through it all, this destiny was before me,' he said; 'this vast inheritance of which I did not dream.'

Insensibly their heroic preoccupation with the revolutionary struggle passed to the question of their relationship. He began to question her. She told him of the days before his awakening, spoke with a brief vividness of the girlish dreams that had given a bias to her life, of the incredulous emotions his awakening had aroused. She told him too of a tragic circumstance of her girlhood that had darkened her life, quickened her sense of injustice and opened her heart prematurely to the wider sorrows of the world. For a little time, so far as he was concerned, the great war about them was but the vast ennobling background to these personal things.

In an instant these personal relations were submerged. There came messengers to tell that a great fleet of aeroplanes was rushing between the sky and Avignon. He went to the crystal dial in the corner and assured himself that the thing was so. He went to the chart room and consulted a map to measure the distances of Avignon, New Arawan, and London. He made swift calculations. He went to the room of the Ward Leaders to ask for news of the fight for the stages – and there was no one there. After a time he came back to her.

His face had changed. It had dawned upon him that the struggle was perhaps more than half over, that Ostrog was holding his own, that the arrival of the aeroplanes would mean a panic that might leave him helpless. A chance phrase in the message had given him a glimpse of the reality that came. Each of these soaring giants bore its thousand half-savage negroes to the death grapple of the city. Suddenly his humanitarian enthusiasm showed flimsy. Only two of the Ward Leaders were in their room, when presently he repaired thither, the Hall of the Atlas seemed empty. He fancied a change in the bearing of the attendants in the outer rooms. A sombre disillusionment darkened his mind. She looked at him anxiously when he returned to her.

'No news,' he said with an assumed carelessness in answer to her eyes.

Then he was moved to frankness. 'Or rather – bad news. We are losing. We are gaining no ground and the aeroplanes draw nearer and nearer.'

He walked the length of the room and turned.

'Unless we can capture those flying stages in the next hour – there will be horrible things. We shall be beaten.'

'No!' she said. 'We have justice – we have the people. We have God on our side.'

'Ostrog has discipline – he has plans. Do you know, out there just now I felt – . When I heard that these aeroplanes were a stage nearer. I felt as if I were fighting the machinery of fate.'

She made no answer for a while. 'We have done right,' she said at last.

He looked at her doubtfully. 'We have done what we could. But does this depend upon us? Is it not an older sin, a wider sin?'

'What do you mean?' she asked.

'These blacks are savages, ruled by force, used as force. And they have been under the rule of the whites two hundred years. Is it not a race quarrel? The race sinned – the race pays.'

'But these labourers, these poor people of London – !'

'Vicarious atonement. To stand wrong is to share the guilt.'

She looked keenly at him, astonished at the new aspect he presented.

Without came the shrill ringing of a bell, the sound of feet and the gabble of a phonographic message. The man in yellow appeared. 'Yes?' said Graham.

'They are at Vichy.'

'Where are the attendants who were in the great Hall of the Atlas?' asked Graham abruptly.

Presently the Babble Machine rang again. 'We may win yet,' said the man in yellow, going out to it. 'If only we can find where Ostrog has hidden his guns. Everything hangs on that now. Perhaps this – '

Graham followed him. But the only news was of the aeroplanes. They had reached Orleans.

Graham returned to Helen. 'No news,' he said. 'No news.'

'And we can do nothing?'

'Nothing.'

He paced impatiently. Suddenly the swift anger that was his nature swept upon him. 'Curse this complex world!' he cried, 'and all the inventions of men! That a man must die like a rat in a snare and never see his foe! Oh, for one blow! . . . '

He turned with an abrupt change in his manner. 'That's nonsense,' he said. 'I am a savage.'

He paced and stopped. 'After all London and Paris are only two cities. All the temperate zone has risen. What if London is doomed and Paris destroyed? These are but accidents.' Again came the mockery of news to call him to fresh enquiries. He returned with a graver face and sat down beside her.

'The end must be near,' he said. 'The people it seems have fought and died in tens of thousands, the ways about Roehampton must be like a smoked beehive. And they have died in vain. They are still only at the sub stage. The aeroplanes are near Paris. Even were a gleam of success to come now, there would be nothing to do, there would be no time to do anything before they were upon us. The guns that might have saved us are mislaid. Mislaid! Think of the disorder of things! Think of this foolish tumult, that cannot even find its weapons! Oh, for one aeropile – just one! For the want of that I am beaten. Humanity is beaten and our cause is lost! My kingship, my headlong foolish kingship will not last a night. And I have egged on the people to fight – .'

'They would have fought anyhow.'

'I doubt it. I have come among them – '

'No,' she cried, 'not that. If defeat comes – if you die – . But even that cannot be, it cannot be, after all these years.'

'Ah! We have meant well. But – do you indeed believe – ?'

'If they defeat you,' she cried, 'you have spoken. Your word has gone like a great wind through the world, fanning liberty into a flame. What if the flame sputters a little! Nothing can change the spoken word. Your message will have gone forth . . . '

'To what end? It may be. It may be. You know I said, when you told me of these things – dear God! but that was scarcely a score of hours ago! – I said that I had not your faith. Well – at any rate there is nothing to do now . . . '

'You have not my faith! Do you mean – ? You are *sorry*?'

'No,' he said hurriedly, 'no! Before God – no!' His voice changed. '*But* – . I think – I have been indiscreet. I knew little – I grasped too hastily . . . '

He paused. He was ashamed of this avowal. 'There is one thing that makes up for all. I have known you. Across this gulf of time I have come to you. The rest is done. It is done. With you, too, it has been something more – or something less – '

He paused with his face searching hers, and without clamoured the unheeded message that the aeroplanes were rising into the sky of Amiens.

She put her hand to her throat, and her lips were white. She stared before her as if she saw some horrible possibility. Suddenly her features changed. 'Oh, but I have been honest!' she cried, and then, '*Have* I been honest? I loved the world and freedom, I hated cruelty and oppression. Surely it was that.'

'Yes,' he said, 'yes. And we have done what it lay in us to do. We have given our message, our message! We have started Armageddon! But now – . Now that we have, it may be our last hour, together, now that all these greater things are done . . . '

He stopped. She sat in silence. Her face was a white riddle.

For a moment they heeded nothing of a sudden stir outside, a running to and fro, and cries. Then Helen started to an attitude of tense attention. 'It is – ,' she cried and stood up, speechless, incredulous, triumphant. And Graham, too, heard. Metallic voices were shouting 'Victory!' *yes* it was 'Victory!' He stood up also with the light of a desperate hope in his eyes.

Bursting through the curtains appeared the man in yellow, startled and dishevelled with excitement. 'Victory,' he cried, 'victory! The people are winning. Ostrog's people have collapsed.'

She rose. 'Victory?' And her voice was hoarse and faint.

'What do you mean?' asked Graham. 'Tell me! *What*?'

'We have driven them out of the under galleries at Norwood, Streatham is afire and burning wildly, and Roehampton is ours. Ours! – and we have taken the aeropile that lay thereon.'

For an instant Graham and Helen stood in silence, their hearts were beating fast, they looked at one another. For one last moment there gleamed in Graham his dream of empire, of kingship, with Helen by his side. It gleamed, and passed.

A shrill bell rang. An agitated grey-headed man appeared from the room of the Ward Leaders. 'It is all over,' he cried.

'What matters it now that we have Roehampton? The aeroplanes have been sighted at Boulogne!'

'The Channel!' said the man in yellow. He calculated swiftly. 'Half an hour.'

'They still have three of the flying stages,' said the old man.

'Those guns?' cried Graham.

'We cannot mount them – in half an hour.'

'Do you mean they are found?'

'Too late,' said the old man.

'If we could stop them another hour!' cried the man in yellow.

'Nothing can stop them now,' said the old man, 'they have near a hundred aeroplanes in the first fleet.'

'Another hour?' asked Graham.

'To be so near!' said the Ward Leader. 'Now that we have found those guns. To be so near – . If once we could get them out upon the roof spaces.'

'How long would that take?' asked Graham suddenly.

'An hour – certainly.'

'Too late,' cried the Ward Leader, 'too late.'

'*Is* it too late?' said Graham. 'Even now – . An hour!'

He had suddenly perceived a possibility. He tried to speak calmly, but his face was white. 'There is one chance. You said there was an aeropile – ?'

'On the Roehampton stage, Sire.'

'Smashed?'

'No. It is lying crossways to the carrier. It might be got upon the guides – easily. But there is no aeronaut – .'

Graham glanced at the two men and then at Helen. He spoke after a long pause. 'We have no aeronauts?'

'None.'

'The aeroplanes are clumsy,' he said thoughtfully, 'compared with the aeropiles.'

He turned suddenly to Helen. His decision was made. 'I must do it.'

'Do what?'

'Go to this flying stage – to this aeropile.'

'What do you mean?'

'I am an aeronaut. After all – . Those days for which you reproached me were not altogether wasted.'

He turned to the old man in yellow. 'Put the aeropile upon the guides.'

The man in yellow hesitated.

'What do you mean to do?' cried Helen.

'This aeropile – it is a chance – .'

'You don't mean – ?'

'To fight – yes. To fight in the air. I have thought before – . An aeroplane is a clumsy thing. A resolute man – !'

'But – never since flying began – ' cried the man in yellow.

'There has been no need. But now the time has come. Tell them now – send them my message – to put it upon the guides.'

The old man dumbly interrogated the man in yellow, nodded, and hurried out.

Helen made a step towards Graham. Her face was white. 'But – how can one fight? You will be killed.'

'Perhaps. Yet, not to do it – or to let someone else attempt it – .'

He stopped, he could speak no more, he swept the alternative aside by a gesture, and they stood looking at one another.

'You are right,' she said at last in a low tone. 'You are right. If it can be done . . . You must go.'

He moved a step towards her, and she stepped back, her white face struggled against him and resisted him. 'No,' she gasped. 'I cannot bear – . Go now.'

He extended his hands stupidly. She clenched her fists. 'Go now,' she cried. 'Go now.'

He hesitated and understood. He threw his hands up in a queer half-theatrical gesture. He had no word to say. He turned from her.

The man in yellow moved towards the door with clumsy belated tact. But Graham stepped past him. He went striding through the room where the Ward Leader bawled at a telephone directing that the aeropile should be put upon the guides.

The man in yellow glanced at Helen's still figure, hesitated and hurried after him. Graham did not once look back, he did not speak until the curtain of the antechamber of the great Hall fell behind him. Then he turned his head with curt swift directions upon his bloodless lips.

CHAPTER TWENTY-FOUR

The Coming of the Aeroplanes

Two men in pale blue were lying in the irregular line that stretched along the edge of the captured Roehampton stage from end to end, grasping their carbines and peering into the shadows of the stage called Wimbledon Park. Now and then they spoke to one another. They spoke the mutilated English of their class and period. The fire of the Ostrogites had dwindled and ceased, and few of the enemy had been seen for some time. But the

echoes of the fight that was going on now far below in the lower galleries of that stage, came every now and then between the staccato of shots from the popular side. One of these men was describing to the other how he had seen a man down below there dodge behind a girder, and had aimed at a guess and hit him cleanly as he dodged too far. 'He's down there still,' said the marksman. 'See that little patch. Yes. Between those bars.' A few yards behind them lay a dead stranger, face upward to the sky, with the blue canvas of his jacket smouldering in a circle about the neat bullet hole on his chest. Close beside him a wounded man, with a leg swathed about, sat with an expressionless face and watched the progress of that burning. Gigantic behind them, athwart the carrier lay the captured aeropile.

'I can't see him *now*,' said the second man in a ton of provocation.

The marksman became foul-mouthed and high-voiced in his earnest endeavour to make things plain. And suddenly, interrupting him, came a noisy shouting from the sub-stage.

'What's going on now,' he said, and raised himself on one arm to stare at the stairheads in the central groove of the stage. A number of blue figures were coming up these, and swarming across the stage to the aeropile.

'We don't want all these fools,' said his friend. 'They only crowd up and spoil shots. What are they after?'

'Ssh! – they're shouting something.'

The two men listened. The swarming new-comers had crowded densely about the aeropile. Three Ward Leaders, conspicuous by their black mantles and badges, clambered into the body and appeared above it. The rank and file flung themselves upon the vans, gripping hold of the edges, until the entire outline of the thing was manned, in some places three deep. One of the marksmen knelt up. 'They're putting it on the carrier – that's what they're after.'

He rose to his feet, his friend rose also. 'What's the good?' said his friend. 'We've got no aeronauts.'

'That's what they're doing anyhow.' He looked at his rifle, looked at the struggling crowd, and suddenly turning to the wounded man, 'Mind these, mate,' he said, handing his carbine and cartridge belt; and in a moment he was running towards the aeropile. For a quarter of an hour he was a perspiring Titan, lugging, thrusting, shouting and heeding shouts, and then the thing was done, and he stood with a multitude of others cheering their own achievement. By this time he knew, what indeed everyone in the city knew, that the Master, raw learner though he was, intended to fly this machine himself, was coming even now to take control of it, would let no other man attempt it. 'He who takes the greatest danger, he who bears the heaviest burden, that man is King,' so the Master was reported to have spoken. And even as this man cheered, and while the beads of sweat still chased one another from the disorder of his hair, he heard the thunder of a greater tumult, and in fitful snatches the beat and impulse of the

revolutionary song. He saw through a gap in the people that a thick stream of heads still poured up the stairway. 'The Master is coming,' shouted voices, 'the Master is coming,' and the crowd about him grew denser and denser. He began to thrust himself towards the central groove. 'The Master is coming!' 'The Sleeper, the Master!' 'God and the Master!' roared the voices.

And suddenly quite close to him were the black uniforms of the revolutionary guard, and for the first and last time in his life he saw Graham, saw him quite nearly. A tall, dark man in a flowing black robe, with a white, resolute face and eyes fixed steadfastly before him; a man who for all the little things about him had neither ears nor eyes nor thoughts . . . For all his days that man remembered the passing of Graham's bloodless face. In a moment it had gone and he was fighting in the swaying crowd. A lad weeping with terror thrust against him, pressing towards the stairways, yelling 'Clear for the aeropile!' The bell that clears the flying stage became a loud unmelodious clanging.

With that clanging in his ears Graham drew near the aeropile, marched into the shadow of its tilting wing. He became aware that a number of people about him were offering to accompany him, and waved their offers aside. He wanted to think how one started the engine. The bell clanged faster and faster, and the feet of the retreating people roared faster and louder. The man in yellow was assisting him to mount through the ribs of the body. He clambered into the aeronaut's place, fixing himself very carefully and deliberately. What was it? The man in yellow was pointing to two aeropiles driving upward in the southern sky. No doubt they were looking for the coming aeroplanes. That – presently – the thing to do now was to start. Things were being shouted at him, questions, warnings. They bothered him. He wanted to think about the aeropile, to recall every item of his previous experience. He waved the people from him, saw the man in yellow dropping off through the ribs, saw the crowd cleft down the line of the girders by his gesture.

For a moment he was motionless, staring at the levers, the wheel by which the engine shifted, and all the delicate appliances of which he knew so little. His eye caught a spirit level with the bubble towards him, and he remembered something, spent a dozen seconds in swinging the engine forward until the bubble floated in the centre of the tube. He noted that the people were not shouting, knew they watched his deliberation. A bullet smashed on the bar above his head. Who fired? Was the line clear of people? He stood up to see and sat down again.

In another second the propeller was spinning, and he was rushing down the guides. He gripped the wheel and swung the engine back to lift the stem. Then it was the people shouted. In a moment he was throbbing with the quiver of the engine, and the shouts dwindled swiftly behind, rushed down to silence. The wind whistled over the edges of the screen, and the world sank away from him very swiftly.

Throb, throb, throb – throb, throb, throb; up he drove. He fancied himself free of all excitement, felt cool and deliberate. He lifted the stem still more, opened one valve on his left wing and swept round and up. He looked down with a steady head, and up. One of the Ostrogite aeropiles was driving across his course, so that he drove obliquely towards it and would pass below it at a steep angle. Its little aeronauts were peering down at him. What did they mean to do? His mind became active. One, he saw, held a weapon pointing, seemed prepared to fire. What did they think he meant to do? In a moment he understood their tactics, and his resolution was taken. His momentary lethargy was past. He opened two more valves to his left, swung round, end on to this hostile machine, closed his valves, and shot straight at it, stem and windscreen shielding him from the shot. They tilted a little as if to clear him. He flung up his stem.

Throb, throb, throb – pause – throb, throb – he set his teeth, his face into an involuntary grimace, and crash! He struck it! He struck upward beneath the nearer wing.

Very slowly the wing of his antagonist seemed to broaden as the impetus of his blow turned it up. He saw the full breadth of it and then it slid downward out of his sight.

He felt his stem going down, his hands tightened on the levers, whirled and rammed the engine back. He felt the jerk of a clearance, the nose of the machine jerked upward steeply, and for a moment he seemed to be lying on his back. The machine was reeling and staggering, it seemed to be dancing on its screw. He made a huge effort, hung for a moment on the levers, and slowly the engine came forward again. He was driving upward but no longer so steeply. He gasped for a moment and flung himself at the levers again. The wind whistled about him. One further effort and he was almost level. He could breathe. He turned his head for the first time to see what had become of his antagonists. Turned back to the levers for a moment and looked again. For a moment he could have believed they were annihilated. And then he saw between the two stages to the east was a chasm, and down this something, a slender edge, fell swiftly and vanished, as a sixpence falls down a crack.

At first he did not understand, and then a wild joy possessed him. He shouted at the top of his voice, an inarticulate shout, and drove higher and higher up the sky. Throb, throb, throb, pause, throb, throb, throb. 'Where was the other aeropile?' he thought. 'They too – .' As he looked round the empty heavens he had a momentary fear that this machine had risen above him, and then he saw it alighting on the Norwood stage. They had meant shooting. To risk being rammed headlong two thousand feet in the air was beyond their latter-day courage. The combat was declined.

For a little while he circled, then swooped in a steep descent towards the westward stage. Throb throb throb, throb throb throb. The twilight was creeping on apace, the smoke from the Streatham stage that had been so

dense and dark, was now a pillar of fire, and all the laced curves of the moving ways and the translucent roofs and domes and the chasms between the buildings were glowing softly now, lit by the tempered radiance of the electric light that the glare of the way overpowered. The three efficient stages that the Ostrogites held – for Wimbledon Park was useless because of the fire from Roehampton, and Streatham was a furnace – were glowing with guide lights for the coming aeroplanes. As he swept over the Roehampton stage he saw the dark masses of the people thereon. He heard a clap of frantic cheering, heard a bullet from the Wimbledon Park stage tweet through the air, and went beating up above the Surrey wastes. He felt a breath of wind from the south-west, and lifted his westward wing as he had learnt to do, and so drove upward heeling into the rare swift upper air. Throb throb throb – throb throb throb.

Up he drove and up, to that pulsating rhythm, until the country beneath was blue and indistinct, and London spread like a little map traced in light, like the mere model of a city near the brim of the horizon. The south-west was a sky of sapphire over the shadowy rim of the world, and ever as he drove upward the multitude of stars increased.

And behold! In the southward, low down and glittering swiftly nearer, were two little patches of nebulous light. And then two more, and then a nebulous glow of swiftly driving shapes. Presently he could count them. There were four and twenty. The first fleet of aeroplanes had come! Beyond appeared a yet greater glow.

He swept round in a half circle, staring at this advancing fleet. It flew in a wedgelike shape, a triangular flight of gigantic phosphorescent shapes sweeping nearer through the lower air. He made a swift calculation of their pace, and spun the little wheel that brought the engine forward. He touched a lever and the throbbing effort of the engine ceased. He began to fall, fell swifter and swifter. He aimed at the apex of the wedge. He dropped like a stone through the whistling air. It seemed scarce a second from that soaring moment before he struck the foremost aeroplane.

No man of all that black multitude saw the coming of his fate, no man among them dreamt of the hawk that struck downward upon him out of the sky. Those who were not limp in the agonies of airsickness, were craning their black necks and staring to see the filmy city that was rising out of the haze, the rich and splendid city to which 'Massa Boss' had brought their obedient muscles. Bright teeth gleamed and the glossy faces shone. They had heard of Paris. They knew they were to have lordly times among the 'poor white' trash. And suddenly Graham struck them.

He had aimed at the body of the aeroplane, but at the very last instant a better idea had flashed into his mind. He twisted about and struck near the edge of the starboard wing with all his accumulated weight. He was jerked back as he struck. His prow went gliding across its smooth expanse towards the rim. He felt the forward rush of the huge fabric sweeping him and his

aeropile along with it, and for a moment that seemed an age he could not tell what was happening. He heard a thousand throats yelling, and perceived that his machine was balanced on the edge of the gigantic float, and driving down, down; glanced over his shoulder and saw the backbone of the aeroplane and the opposite float swaying up. He had a vision through the ribs of sliding chairs, staring faces, and hands clutching at the tilting guide bars. The fenestrations in the further float flashed open as the aeronaut tried to right her. Beyond, he saw a second aeroplane leaping steeply to escape the whirl of its heeling fellow. The broad area of swaying wings seemed to jerk upward. He felt his aeropile had dropped clear, that the monstrous fabric, clean overturned, hung like a sloping wall above him.

He did not clearly understand that he had struck the side float of the aeroplane and slipped off, but he perceived that he was flying free on the down glide and rapidly nearing earth. What had he done? His heart throbbed like a noisy engine in his throat and for a perilous instant he could not move his levers because of the paralysis of his hands. He wrenched the levers to throw his engine back, fought for two seconds against the weight of it, felt himself righting, driving horizontally, set the engine beating again.

He looked upward and saw two aeroplanes glide shouting far overhead, looked back, and saw the main body of the fleet opening out and rushing upward and outward; saw the one he had struck fall edgewise on and strike like a gigantic knife-blade along the wind-wheels below it.

He put down his stern and looked again. He drove up heedless of his direction as he watched. He saw the wind-vanes give, saw the huge fabric strike the earth, saw its downward vans crumple with the weight of its descent, and then the whole mass turned over and smashed, upside down, upon the sloping wheels. Throb, throb, throb, pause. Suddenly from the heaving wreckage a thin tongue of white fire licked up towards the zenith. And then he was aware of a huge mass flying through the air towards him, and turned upwards just in time to escape the charge – if it was a charge – of a second aeroplane. It whirled by below, sucked him down a fathom, and nearly turned him over in the gust of its close passage.

He became aware of three others rushing towards him, aware of the urgent necessity of beating above them. Aeroplanes were all about him, circling wildly to avoid him, as it seemed. They drove past him, above, below, eastward and westward. Far away to the westward was the sound of a collision, and two falling flares. Far away to the southward a second squadron was coming. Steadily he beat upward. Presently all the aeroplanes were below him, but for a moment he doubted the height he had of them, and did not swoop again. And then he came down upon a second victim and all its load of soldiers saw him coming. The big machine heeled and swayed as the fear-maddened men scrambled to the stern for their weapons. A score of bullets sung through the air, and there flashed a star in the thick glass

windscreen that protected him. The aeroplane slowed and dropped to foil his stroke, and dropped too low. Just in time he saw the wind-wheels of Bromley Hill rushing up towards him, and spun about and up as the aeroplane he had chased crashed among them. All its voices wove into a felt of yelling. The great fabric seemed to be standing on end for a second among the heeling and splintering vans, and then it flew to pieces. Huge splinters came flying through the air, its engines burst like shells. A hot rush of flame shot overhead into the darkling sky.

'*Two!*' he cried, with a bomb from overhead bursting as it fell, and forthwith he was beating up again. A glorious exhilaration possessed him now, a giant activity. His troubles about humanity, about his inadequacy, were gone for ever. He was a man in battle rejoicing in his power. Aeroplanes seemed radiating from him in every direction, intent only upon avoiding him, the yelling of their packed passengers came in short gusts as they swept by. He chose his third quarry, struck hastily and did but turn it on edge. It escaped him, to smash against the tall cliff of London wall. Flying from that impact he skimmed the darkling ground so nearly he could see a frightened rabbit bolting up a slope. He jerked up steeply, and found himself driving over south London with the air about him vacant. To the right of him a wild riot of signal rockets from the Ostrogites banged tumultuously in the sky. To the south the wreckage of half a dozen air ships flamed, and east and west and north the air ships fled before him. They drove away to the east and north, and went about in the south, for they could not pause in the air. In their present confusion any attempt at evolution would have meant disastrous collisions. He could scarcely realise the thing he had done. In every quarter aeroplanes were receding. They were receding. They dwindled smaller and smaller. They were in flight!

He passed two hundred feet or so above the Roehampton stage. It was black with people and noisy with their frantic shouting. But why was the Wimbledon Park stage black and cheering, too? The smoke and flame of Streatham now hid the three further stages. He curved about and rose to see them and the northern quarters. First came the square masses of Shooter's Hill into sight from behind the smoke, lit and orderly with the aeroplane that had landed and its disembarking negroes. Then came Blackheath, and then under the corner of the reek the Norwood stage. On Blackheath no aeroplane had landed but an aeropile lay upon the guides. Norwood was covered by a swarm of little figures running to and fro in a passionate confusion. Why? Abruptly he understood. The stubborn defence of the flying stages was over, the people were pouring into the under-ways of these last strongholds of Ostrog's usurpation. And then, from far away on the northern border of the city, full of glorious import to him, came a sound, a signal, a note of triumph, the leaden thud of a gun. His lips fell apart, his face was disturbed with emotion.

He drew an immense breath. 'They win,' he shouted to the empty air;

'the people win!' The sound of a second gun came like an answer. And then he saw the aeropile on Blackheath was running down its guides to launch. It lifted clean and rose. It shot up into the air, driving straight southward and away from him.

In an instant it came to him what this meant. It must needs be Ostrog in flight. He shouted and dropped towards it. He had the momentum of his elevation and fell slanting down the air and very swiftly. It rose steeply at his approach. He allowed for its velocity and drove straight upon it.

It suddenly became a mere flat edge, and behold! he was past it, and driving headlong down with all the force of his futile blow.

He was furiously angry. He reeled the engine back along its shaft and went circling up. He saw Ostrog's machine beating up a spiral before him. He rose straight towards it, won above it by virtue of the impetus of his swoop and by the advantage and weight of a man. He dropped headlong – dropped and missed again! As he rushed past he saw the face of Ostrog's aeronaut confident and cool and in Ostrog's attitude a wincing resolution. Ostrog was looking steadfastly away from him – to the south. He realised with a gleam of wrath how bungling his flight must be. Below he saw the Croydon hills. He jerked upward and once more he gained on his enemy.

He glanced over his shoulder and his attention was arrested by a strange thing. The eastward stage, the one on Shooter's Hill, appeared to lift; a flash changing to a tall grey shape, a cowled figure of smoke and dust, jerked into the air. For a moment this cowled figure stood motionless, dropping huge masses of metal from its shoulders, and then it began to uncoil a dense head of smoke. The people had blown it up, aeroplane and all! As suddenly a second flash and grey shape sprang up from the Norwood stage. And even as he stared at this came a dead report, and the air wave of the first explosion struck him. He was flung up and sideways.

For a moment the aeropile fell nearly edgewise with her nose down, and seemed to hesitate whether to overset altogether. He stood on his windshield wrenching the wheel that swayed up over his head. And then the shock of the second explosion took his machine sideways.

He found himself clinging to one of the ribs of his machine, and the air was blowing past him and *upward*. He seemed to be hanging quite still in the air, with the wind blowing up past him. It occurred to him that he was falling. Then he was sure that he was falling. He could not look down.

He found himself recapitulating with incredible swiftness all that had happened since his awakening, the days of doubt, the days of Empire, and at last the tumultuous discovery of Ostrog's calculated treachery. He was beaten but London was saved. London was saved!

The thought had a quality of utter unreality. Who was he? Why was he holding so tightly with his hands? Why could he not leave go? In such a fall as this countless dreams have ended. But in a moment he would wake . . .

His thoughts ran swifter and swifter. He wondered if he should see

Helen again. It seemed so unreasonable that he should not see her again. It *must* be a dream! Yet surely he would meet her. She at least was real. She was real. He would wake and meet her.

Although he could not look at it, he was suddenly aware that the earth was very near.

EPILOGUE

One cannot choose but wonder. Will he ever return? It may be that he swept back into the past, and fell among the blood-drinking, hairy savages of the Age of Unpolished Stone; into the abysses of the Cretaceous Sea; or among the grotesque saurians, the huge reptilian brutes of the Jurassic times. He may even now – if I may use the phrase – be wandering on some plesiosaurus-haunted Oolitic coral reef, or beside the lonely saline lakes of the Triassic Age. Or did he go forward, into one of the nearer ages, in which men are still men, but with the riddles of our own time answered and its wearisome problems solved? Into the manhood of the race: for I, for my own part, cannot think that these latter days of weak experiment, fragmentary theory, and mutual discord are indeed man's culminating time! I say, for my own part. He, I know – for the question had been discussed among us long before the Time Machine was made – thought but cheerlessly of the Advancement of Mankind, and saw in the growing pile of civilisation only a foolish heaping that must inevitably fall back upon and destroy its makers in the end. If that is so, it remains for us to live as though it were not so. But to me the future is still black and blank – is a vast ignorance, lit at a few casual places by the memory of his story. And I have by me, for my comfort, two strange white flowers – shrivelled now, and brown and flat and brittle – to witness that even when mind and strength had gone, gratitude and a mutual tenderness still lived on in the heart of man.

The Island of Doctor Moreau
A Possibility

A novel first published in 1896

Contents

The Island of Doctor Moreau was first published in 1896,
in London by William Heinemann and
in New York by Stone and Kimball.

Foreword

On 1 February 1887, the *Lady Vain* was lost by collision with a derelict when about the latitude 1' S and longitude 107' W.

On 5 January 1888 – that is eleven months and four days after – my uncle, Edward Prendick, a private gentleman, who certainly went aboard the *Lady Vain* at Callao, and who had been considered drowned, was picked up in latitude 5' 3" S and longitude 101' W in a small open boat of which the name was illegible, but which is supposed to have belonged to the missing schooner *Ipecacuanha*. He gave such a strange account of himself that he was supposed demented. Subsequently he alleged that his mind was a blank from the moment of his escape from the *Lady Vain*. His case was discussed among psychologists at the time as a curious instance of the lapse of memory consequent upon physical and mental stress. The following narrative was found among his papers by the undersigned, his nephew and heir, but unaccompanied by any definite request for publication.

The only island known to exist in the region in which my uncle was picked up is Noble's Isle, a small volcanic islet and uninhabited. It was visited in 1891 by HMS *Scorpion*. A party of sailors then landed, but found nothing living thereon except certain curious white moths, some hogs and rabbits, and some rather peculiar rats. No specimen was secured of these – in view of which this narrative is without confirmation in its most essential particular. With that understood, there seems no harm in putting this strange story before the public in accordance, as I believe, with my uncle's intentions. There is at least this much in its behalf: my uncle passed out of human knowledge about latitude 5' S and longitude 105' E, and reappeared in the same part of the ocean after a space of eleven months. In some way he must have lived during the interval. And it seems that a schooner called the *Ipecacuanha* with a drunken captain, John Davies, did start from Africa with a puma and certain other animals aboard in January 1887, that the vessel was well known at several ports in the South Pacific, and that it finally disappeared from those seas (with a considerable amount of copra aboard), sailing to its unknown fate from Bayna in December 1887, a date that tallies entirely with my uncle's story.

CHARLES EDWARD PRENDICK

Edward Prendick's Story

CHAPTER ONE

In the Dinghy of the Lady Vain

I DO NOT PROPOSE to add anything to what has already been written concerning the loss of the *Lady Vain*. As everyone knows, she collided with a derelict when ten days out from Callao. The longboat, with seven of the crew, was picked up eighteen days after by HM gunboat *Myrtle,* and the story of their terrible privations has become quite as well known as the far more horrible *Medusa* case. But I have to add to the published story of the *'Vain* another, possibly as horrible and far stranger. It has hitherto been supposed that the four men who were in the dinghy perished, but this is incorrect. I have the best of evidence for this assertion: I was one of the four men.

But in the first place I must state that there never were four men in the dinghy – the number was three. Constans, who was 'seen by the captain to jump into the gig',* luckily for us and unluckily for himself did not reach us. He came down out of the tangle of ropes under the stays of the smashed bowsprit, some small rope caught his heel as he let go, and he hung for a moment head downward, and then fell and struck a block or spar floating in the water. We pulled towards him, but he never came up.

I say lucky for us he did not reach us, and I might almost say luckily for himself; for we had only a small breaker of water and some soddened ship's biscuits with us, so sudden had been the alarm, so unprepared the ship for any disaster. We thought the people on the launch would be better provisioned (though it seems they were not), and we tried to hail them. They could not have heard us, and the next morning when the drizzle cleared – which was not until past midday – we could see nothing of them. We could not stand up to look about us, because of the pitching of the boat. The two other men who had escaped so far with me were a man named Helmar, a passenger like myself, and a seaman whose name I don't know – a short sturdy man, with a stammer.

We drifted famishing, and, after our water had come to an end, tormented by an intolerable thirst, for eight days altogether. After the second day the sea subsided slowly to a glassy calm. It is quite impossible for the ordinary reader to imagine those eight days. He has not, luckily for himself, anything in his memory to imagine with. After the first day we said little to one another, and lay in our places in the boat and stared at the horizon, or watched, with eyes that grew larger and more haggard every day, the misery and weakness gaining upon our companions. The sun became pitiless. The

water ended on the fourth day, and we were already thinking strange things and saying them with our eyes; but it was, I think, the sixth before Helmar gave voice to the thing we had all been thinking. I remember our voices were dry and thin, so that we bent towards one another and spared our words. I stood out against it with all my might, was rather for scuttling the boat and perishing together among the sharks that followed us; but when Helmar said that if his proposal was accepted we should have drink, the sailor came round to him.

I would not draw lots, however, and in the night the sailor whispered to Helmar again and again, and I sat in the bows with my clasp-knife in my hand, though I doubt if I had the stuff in me to fight; and in the morning I agreed to Helmar's proposal, and we handed halfpence to find the odd man. The lot fell upon the sailor; but he was the strongest of us and would not abide by it, and attacked Helmar with his hands. They grappled together and almost stood up. I crawled along the boat to them, intending to help Helmar by grasping the sailor's leg; but the sailor stumbled with the swaying of the boat, and the two fell upon the gunwale and rolled overboard together. They sank like stones. I remember laughing at that, and wondering why I laughed. The laugh caught me suddenly like a thing from without.

I lay across one of the thwarts for I know not how long, thinking that if I had the strength I would drink sea-water and madden myself to die quickly. And even as I lay there I saw, with no more interest than if it had been a picture, a sail come up towards me over the skyline. My mind must have been wandering, and yet I remember all that happened, quite distinctly. I remember how my head swayed with the seas, and the horizon with the sail above it danced up and down; but I also remember as distinctly that I had a persuasion that I was dead, and that I thought what a jest it was that they should come too late by such a little to catch me in my body.

For an endless period, as it seemed to me, I lay with my head on the thwart watching the schooner (she was a little ship, schooner-rigged fore and aft) come up out of the sea. She kept tacking to and fro in a widening compass, for she was sailing dead into the wind. It never entered my head to attempt to attract attention, and I do not remember anything distinctly after the sight of her side until I found myself in a little cabin aft. There's a dim half-memory of being lifted up to the gangway, and of a big red countenance covered with freckles and surrounded with red hair staring at me over the bulwarks. I also had a disconnected impression of a dark face, with extraordinary eyes, close to mine; but that I thought was a nightmare, until I met it again. I fancy I recollect some stuff being poured in between my teeth; and that is all.

CHAPTER TWO

The Man Who Was Going Nowhere

The cabin in which I found myself was small and rather untidy. A youngish man with flaxen hair, a bristly straw-coloured moustache and a dropping nether lip, was sitting and holding my wrist. For a minute we stared at each other without speaking. He had watery grey eyes, oddly void of expression. Then just overhead came a sound like an iron bedstead being knocked about, and the low angry growling of some large animal. At the same time the man spoke. He repeated his question, 'How do you feel now?'

I think I said I felt all right. I could not recollect how I had got there. He must have seen the question in my face, for my voice was inaccessible to me.

'You were picked up in a boat, starving. The name on the boat was the *Lady Vain*, and there were spots of blood on the gunwale.'

At the same time my eye caught my hand, thin so that it looked like a dirty skin-purse full of loose bones, and all the business of the boat came back to me.

'Have some of this,' said he, and gave me a dose of some scarlet stuff, iced.

It tasted like blood, and made me feel stronger.

'You were in luck,' said he, 'to get picked up by a ship with a medical man aboard.' He spoke with a slobbering articulation, with the ghost of a lisp.

'What ship is this?' I said slowly, hoarse from my long silence.

'It's a little trader from Arica and Callao. I never asked where she came from in the beginning – out of the land of born fools, I guess. I'm a passenger myself, from Arica. The silly ass who owns her – he's captain too, named Davies – he's lost his certificate, or something. You know the kind of man, calls the thing the *Ipecacuanha*, of all silly, infernal names; though when there's much of a sea without any wind, she certainly acts according.'

(Then the noise overhead began again, a snarling growl and the voice of a human being together. Then another voice, telling some 'Heaven-forsaken idiot' to desist.)

'You were nearly dead,' said my interlocutor. 'It was a very near thing, indeed. But I've put some stuff into you now. Notice your arm's sore? Injections. You've been insensible for nearly thirty hours.'

I thought slowly. (I was distracted now by the yelping of a number of dogs.) 'Am I eligible for solid food?' I asked.

'Thanks to me,' he said. 'Even now the mutton is boiling.'

'Yes,' I said with assurance; 'I could eat some mutton.'

'But,' said he with a momentary hesitation, 'you know I'm dying to hear of how you came to be alone in that boat. Damn that howling!' I thought I detected a certain suspicion in his eyes.

He suddenly left the cabin, and I heard him in violent controversy with someone, who seemed to me to talk gibberish in response to him. The matter sounded as though it ended in blows, but in that I thought my ears were mistaken. Then he shouted at the dogs, and returned to the cabin.

'Well?' said he in the doorway. 'You were just beginning to tell me.'

I told him my name, Edward Prendick, and how I had taken to natural history as a relief from the dullness of my comfortable independence.

He seemed interested in this. 'I've done some science myself. I did my biology at University College – getting out the ovary of the earthworm and the radula of the snail, and all that. Lord! It's ten years ago. But go on! go on! tell me about the boat.'

He was evidently satisfied with the frankness of my story, which I told in concise sentences enough, for I felt horribly weak; and when it was finished he reverted at once to the topic of natural history and his own biological studies. He began to question me closely about Tottenham Court Road and Gower Street. 'Is Caplatzi still flourishing? What a shop that was!' He had evidently been a very ordinary medical student, and drifted incontinently to the topic of the music halls. He told me some anecdotes.

'Left it all,' he said, 'ten years ago. How jolly it all used to be! But I made a young ass of myself, played myself out before I was twenty-one. I dare say it's all different now. But I must look up that ass of a cook, and see what he's done to your mutton.'

The growling overhead was renewed, so suddenly and with so much savage anger that it startled me. 'What's that?' I called after him, but the door had closed. He came back again with the boiled mutton, and I was so excited by the appetising smell of it that I forgot the noise of the beast that had troubled me.

After a day of alternate sleep and feeding I was so far recovered as to be able to get from my bunk to the scuttle, and see the green seas trying to keep pace with us. I judged the schooner was running before the wind. Montgomery – that was the name of the flaxen-haired man – came in again as I stood there, and I asked him for some clothes. He lent me some duck things of his own, for those I had worn in the boat had been thrown overboard. They were rather loose for me, for he was large and long in his limbs. He told me casually that the captain was three-parts drunk in his own cabin. As I assumed the clothes, I began asking him some questions about the destination of the ship. He said the ship was bound to Hawaii, but that it had to land him first.

'Where?' said I.

'It's an island, where I live. So far as I know, it hasn't got a name.'

He stared at me with his nether lip dropping, and looked so wilfully stupid of a sudden that it came into my head that he desired to avoid my questions. I had the discretion to ask no more.

CHAPTER THREE

The Strange Face

We left the cabin and found a man at the companion obstructing our way. He was standing on the ladder with his back to us, peering over the combing of the hatchway. He was, I could see, a misshapen man, short, broad and clumsy, with a crooked back, a hairy neck and a head sunk between his shoulders. He was dressed in dark-blue serge, and had peculiarly thick, coarse, black hair. I heard the unseen dogs growl furiously, and forthwith he ducked back, coming into contact with the hand I put out to fend him off from myself. He turned with animal swiftness.

In some indefinable way the black face thus flashed upon me shocked me profoundly. It was a singularly deformed one. The facial part projected, forming something dimly suggestive of a muzzle, and the huge half-open mouth showed as big white teeth as I had ever seen in a human mouth. His eyes were blood-shot at the edges, with scarcely a rim of white round the hazel pupils. There was a curious glow of excitement in his face.

'Confound you!' said Montgomery. 'Why the devil don't you get out of the way?'

The black-faced man started aside without a word. I went on up the companion, staring at him instinctively as I did so. Montgomery stayed at the foot for a moment. 'You have no business here, you know,' he said in a deliberate tone. 'Your place is forward.'

The black-faced man cowered. 'They – won't have me forward.' He spoke slowly, with a queer, hoarse quality in his voice.

'Won't have you forward!' said Montgomery, in a menacing voice. 'But I tell you to go!' He was on the brink of saying something further, then looked up at me suddenly and followed me up the ladder.

I had paused halfway through the hatchway, looking back, still astonished beyond measure at the grotesque ugliness of this black-faced creature. I had never beheld such a repulsive and extraordinary face before, and yet – if the contradiction is credible – I experienced at the same time an odd feeling that in some way I had already encountered exactly the features and gestures that now amazed me. Afterwards it occurred to me that probably I had seen him as I was lifted aboard; and yet that scarcely satisfied my suspicion of a previous acquaintance. Yet how one could have set eyes on so singular a face and yet have forgotten the precise occasion, passed my imagination.

Montgomery's movement to follow me released my attention, and I turned and looked about me at the flush deck of the little schooner. I was already half prepared by the sounds I had heard for what I saw. Certainly I

never beheld a deck so dirty. It was littered with scraps of carrot, shreds of green stuff and indescribable filth. Fastened by chains to the mainmast were a number of grisly staghounds, who now began leaping and barking at me, and by the mizzen a huge puma was cramped in a little iron cage far too small even to give it turning room. Farther under the starboard bulwark were some big hutches containing a number of rabbits, and a solitary llama was squeezed in a mere box of a cage forward. The dogs were muzzled by leather straps. The only human being on deck was a gaunt and silent sailor at the wheel.

The patched and dirty spankers were tense before the wind, and up aloft the little ship seemed carrying every sail she had. The sky was clear, the sun midway down the western sky; long waves, capped by the breeze with froth, were running with us. We went past the steersman to the taffrail, and saw the water come foaming under the stern and the bubbles go dancing and vanishing in her wake. I turned and surveyed the unsavoury length of the ship.

'Is this an ocean menagerie?' said I.

'Looks like it,' said Montgomery.

'What are these beasts for? Merchandise, curios? Does the captain think he is going to sell them somewhere in the South Seas?'

'It looks like it, doesn't it?' said Montgomery, and turned towards the wake again.

Suddenly we heard a yelp and a volley of furious blasphemy from the companion hatchway, and the deformed man with the black face came up hurriedly. He was immediately followed by a heavy red-haired man in a white cap. At the sight of the former the staghounds, who had all tired of barking at me by this time, became furiously excited, howling and leaping against their chains. The black hesitated before them, and this gave the red-haired man time to come up with him and deliver a tremendous blow between the shoulder-blades. The poor devil went down like a felled ox, and rolled in the dirt among the furiously excited dogs. It was lucky for him that they were muzzled. The red-haired man gave a yawp of exultation and stood staggering, and as it seemed to me in serious danger of either going backwards down the companion hatchway or forwards upon his victim.

So soon as the second man had appeared, Montgomery had started forward. 'Steady on there!' he cried, in a tone of remonstrance. A couple of sailors appeared on the forecastle. The black-faced man, howling in a singular voice rolled about under the feet of the dogs. No one attempted to help him. The brutes did their best to worry him, butting their muzzles at him. There was a quick dance of their lithe grey-figured bodies over the clumsy, prostrate figure. The sailors forward shouted, as though it was admirable sport. Montgomery gave an angry exclamation, and went striding down the deck, and I followed him. The black-faced man scrambled up and staggered forward, going and leaning over the bulwark by the main

shrouds, where he remained, panting and glaring over his shoulder at the dogs. The red-haired man laughed a satisfied laugh.

'Look here, captain,' said Montgomery, with his lisp a little accentuated, gripping the elbow of the red-haired man, 'this won't do!'

I stood behind Montgomery. The captain came half round, and regarded him with the dull and solemn eyes of a drunken man. 'Wha' won't do?' he said, and added, after looking sleepily into Montgomery's face for a minute, 'Blasted sawbones!'

With a sudden movement he shook his arm free, and after two in-effectual attempts stuck his freckled fists into his side pockets.

'That man's a passenger,' said Montgomery. 'I'd advise you to keep your hands off him.'

'Go to hell!' said the captain, loudly. He suddenly turned and staggered towards the side. 'Do what I like on my own ship,' he said.

I think Montgomery might have left him then, seeing the brute was drunk; but he only turned a shade paler, and followed the captain to the bulwarks.

'Look you here, captain,' he said; 'that man of mine is not to be ill-treated. He has been hazed ever since he came aboard.'

For a minute, alcoholic fumes kept the captain speechless. 'Blasted saw-bones!' was all he considered necessary.

I could see that Montgomery had one of those slow, pertinacious tempers that will warm day after day to a white heat, and never again cool to forgiveness; and I saw too that this quarrel had been some time growing. 'The man's drunk,' said I, perhaps officiously; 'you'll do no good.'

Montgomery gave an ugly twist to his dropping lip. 'He's always drunk. Do you think that excuses his assaulting his passengers?'

'My ship,' began the captain, waving his hand unsteadily towards the cages, 'was a clean ship. Look at it now!' It was certainly anything but clean. 'Crew,' continued the captain, 'clean, respectable crew.'

'You agreed to take the beasts.'

'I wish I'd never set eyes on your infernal island. What the devil d'you want beasts for on an island like that? Then, that man of yours – understood he was a man. He's a lunatic; and he hadn't no business aft. Do you think the whole damned ship belongs to you?'

'Your sailors began to haze the poor devil as soon as he came aboard.'

'That's just what he is – he's a devil! an ugly devil! My men can't stand him. *I* can't stand him. None of us can't stand him. Nor *you* either!'

Montgomery turned away. '*You* leave that man alone, anyhow,' he said, nodding his head as he spoke.

But the captain meant to quarrel now. He raised his voice. 'If he comes this end of the ship again I'll cut his insides out, I tell you. Cut out his blasted insides! Who are *you*, to tell *me* what *I'm* to do? I tell you I'm captain of this ship – captain and owner. I'm the law here, I tell you – the law and

the prophets. I bargained to take a man and his attendant to and from Arica, and bring back some animals. I never bargained to carry a mad devil and a silly sawbones, a – '

Well, never mind what he called Montgomery. I saw the latter take a step forward, and interposed. 'He's drunk,' said I. The captain began some abuse even fouler than the last. 'Shut up!' I said, turning on him sharply, for I had seen danger in Montgomery's white face. With that I brought the downpour on myself.

However, I was glad to avert what was uncommonly near a scuffle, even at the price of the captain's drunken ill-will. I do not think I have ever heard quite so much vile language come in a continuous stream from any man's lips before, though I have frequented eccentric company enough. I found some of it hard to endure, though I am a mild-tempered man; but, certainly, when I told the captain to 'shut up' I had forgotten that I was merely a bit of human flotsam, cut off from my resources and with my fare unpaid; a mere casual dependant on the bounty, or speculative enterprise, of the ship. He reminded me of it with considerable vigour; but at any rate I prevented a fight.

CHAPTER FOUR

At the Schooner Rail

That night land was sighted after sundown, and the schooner hove to. Montgomery intimated that was his destination. It was too far to see any details; it seemed to me then simply a low-lying patch of dim blue in the uncertain blue-grey sea. An almost vertical streak of smoke went up from it into the sky. The captain was not on deck when it was sighted. After he had vented his wrath on me he had staggered below, and I understand he went to sleep on the floor of his own cabin. The mate practically assumed the command. He was the gaunt, taciturn individual we had seen at the wheel. Apparently he was in an evil temper with Montgomery. He took not the slightest notice of either of us. We dined with him in a sulky silence, after a few ineffectual efforts on my part to talk. It struck me too that the men regarded my companion and his animals in a singularly unfriendly manner. I found Montgomery very reticent about his purpose with these creatures, and about his destination; and though I was sensible of a growing curiosity as to both, I did not press him.

We remained talking on the quarter deck until the sky was thick with stars. Except for an occasional sound in the yellow-lit forecastle and a movement of the animals now and then, the night was very still. The puma lay crouched together, watching us with shining eyes, a black heap in the corner of its cage. Montgomery produced some cigars. He talked to me of

London in a tone of half-painful reminiscence, asking all kinds of questions about changes that had taken place. He spoke like a man who had loved his life there, and had been suddenly and irrevocably cut off from it. I gossiped as well as I could of this and that. All the time the strangeness of him was shaping itself in my mind; and as I talked I peered at his odd, pallid face in the dim light of the binnacle lantern behind me. Then I looked out at the darkling sea, where in the dimness his little island was hidden.

This man, it seemed to me, had come out of Immensity merely to save my life. Tomorrow he would drop over the side, and vanish again out of my existence. Even had it been under commonplace circumstances, it would have made me a trifle thoughtful; but in the first place was the singularity of an educated man living on this unknown little island, and coupled with that the extraordinary nature of his luggage. I found myself repeating the captain's question, What did he want with the beasts? Why, too, had he pretended they were not his when I had remarked about them at first? Then, again, in his personal attendant there was a bizarre quality which had impressed me profoundly. These circumstances threw a haze of mystery round the man. They laid hold of my imagination, and hampered my tongue.

Towards midnight our talk of London died away, and we stood side by side leaning over the bulwarks and staring dreamily over the silent, starlit sea, each pursuing his own thoughts. It was the atmosphere for sentiment, and I began upon my gratitude.

'If I may say it,' said I, after a time, 'you have saved my life.'

'Chance,' he answered. 'Just chance.'

'I prefer to make my thanks to the accessible agent.'

'Thank no one. You had the need, and I had the knowledge; and I injected and fed you much as I might have collected a specimen. I was bored and wanted something to do. If I'd been jaded that day, or hadn't liked your face, well – it's a curious question where you would have been now!'

This damped my mood a little. 'At any rate – ' I began.

'It's chance, I tell you,' he interrupted, 'as everything is in a man's life. Only the asses won't see it! Why am I here now, an outcast from civilisation, instead of being a happy man enjoying all the pleasures of London? Simply because eleven years ago – I lost my head for ten minutes on a foggy night.'

He stopped.

'Yes?' said I.

'That's all.'

We relapsed into silence. Presently he laughed. 'There's something in this starlight that loosens one's tongue. I'm an ass, and yet somehow I would like to tell you.'

'Whatever you tell me, you may rely upon my keeping to myself – if that's it.'

He was on the point of beginning, and then shook his head, doubtfully.

'Don't,' said I. 'It is all the same to me. After all, it is better to keep your secret. There's nothing gained but a little relief if I respect your confidence. If I don't – well?'

He grunted undecidedly. I felt I had him at a disadvantage, had caught him in the mood of indiscretion; and to tell the truth I was not curious to learn what might have driven a young medical student out of London. I have an imagination. I shrugged my shoulders and turned away. Over the taffrail leant a silent black figure, watching the stars. It was Montgomery's strange attendant. It looked over its shoulder quickly with my movement, then looked away again.

It may seem a little thing to you, perhaps, but it came like a sudden blow to me. The only light near us was a lantern at the wheel. The creature's face was turned for one brief instant out of the dimness of the stern towards this illumination, and I saw that the eyes that glanced at me shone with a pale-green light. I did not know then that a reddish luminosity, at least, is not uncommon in human eyes. The thing came to me as stark inhumanity. That black figure with its eyes of fire struck down through all my adult thoughts and feelings, and for a moment the forgotten horrors of childhood came back to my mind. Then the effect passed as it had come. An uncouth black figure of a man, a figure of no particular import, hung over the taffrail against the starlight, and I found Montgomery was speaking to me.

'I'm thinking of turning in, then,' said he, 'if you've had enough of this.'

I answered him incongruously. We went below, and he wished me good-night at the door of my cabin.

That night I had some very unpleasant dreams. The waning moon rose late. Its light struck a ghostly white beam across my cabin, and made an ominous shape on the planking by my bunk. Then the staghounds woke, and began howling and baying; so that I dreamt fitfully, and scarcely slept until the approach of dawn.

CHAPTER FIVE

The Man Who Had Nowhere to Go

In the early morning (it was the second morning after my recovery, and I believe the fourth after I was picked up), I awoke through an avenue of tumultuous dreams – dreams of guns and howling mobs – and became sensible of a hoarse shouting above me. I rubbed my eyes and lay listening to the noise, doubtful for a little while of my whereabouts. Then came a sudden pattering of bare feet, the sound of heavy objects being thrown about, a violent creaking and the rattling of chains. I heard the swish of the water as the ship was suddenly brought round, and a foamy yellow-green

wave flew across the little round window and left it streaming. I jumped into my clothes and went on deck.

As I came up the ladder I saw against the flushed sky – for the sun was just rising – the broad back and red hair of the captain, and over his shoulder the puma spinning from a tackle rigged on to the mizzen spanker-boom.

The poor brute seemed horribly scared, and crouched in the bottom of its little cage.

'Overboard with 'em!' bawled the captain. 'Overboard with 'em! We'll have a clean ship soon of the whole bilin' of 'em.'

He stood in my way, so that I had perforce to tap his shoulder to come on deck. He came round with a start, and staggered back a few paces to stare at me. It needed no expert eye to tell that the man was still drunk.

'Hello!' said he, stupidly; and then with a light coming into his eyes, 'Why, it's Mr – Mr?'

'Prendick,' said I.

'Prendick be damned!' said he. 'Shut-up – that's your name. Mr Shut-up.'

It was no good answering the brute; but I certainly did not expect his next move. He held out his hand to the gangway by which Montgomery stood talking to a massive grey-haired man in dirty-blue flannels, who had apparently just come aboard.

'That way, Mr Blasted Shut-up! that way!' roared the captain.

Montgomery and his companion turned as he spoke.

'What do you mean?' I said.

'That way, Mr Blasted Shut-up, that's what I mean! Overboard, Mr Shut-up – and sharp! We're cleaning the ship out, cleaning the whole blessed ship out; and overboard you go!'

I stared at him dumfounded. Then it occurred to me that it was exactly the thing I wanted. The lost prospect of a journey as sole passenger with this quarrelsome sot was not one to mourn over. I turned towards Montgomery.

'Can't have you,' said Montgomery's companion, concisely.

'You can't have me!' said I, aghast. He had the squarest and most resolute face I ever set eyes upon.

'Look here,' I began, turning to the captain.

'Overboard!' said the captain. 'This ship ain't for beasts and cannibals and worse than beasts, any more. Overboard you go, Mr Shut-up. If they can't have you, you goes overboard. But, anyhow, you go – with your friends. I've done with this blessed island for evermore, amen! I've had enough of it.'

'But, Montgomery,' I appealed.

He distorted his lower lip, and nodded his head hopelessly at the grey-haired man beside him, to indicate his powerlessness to help me.

'I'll see to *you*, presently,' said the captain.

Then began a curious three-cornered altercation. Alternately I appealed

to one and another of the three men, first to the grey-haired man to let me land, and then to the drunken captain to keep me aboard. I even bawled entreaties to the sailors. Montgomery said never a word, only shook his head. 'You're going overboard, I tell you,' was the captain's refrain. 'Law be damned! I'm king here.' At last I must confess my voice suddenly broke in the middle of a vigorous threat. I felt a gust of hysterical petulance, and went aft and stared dismally at nothing.

Meanwhile the sailors progressed rapidly with the task of unshipping the packages and caged animals. A large launch, with two standing lugs, lay under the lea of the schooner; and into this the strange assortment of goods were swung. I did not then see the hands from the island that were receiving the packages, for the hull of the launch was hidden from me by the side of the schooner. Neither Montgomery nor his companion took the slightest notice of me, but busied themselves in assisting and directing the four or five sailors who were unloading the goods. The captain went forward interfering rather than assisting. I was alternately despairful and desperate. Once or twice as I stood waiting there for things to accomplish themselves, I could not resist an impulse to laugh at my miserable quandary. I felt all the wretcheder for the lack of a breakfast. Hunger and a lack of blood-corpuscles take all the manhood from a man. I perceived pretty clearly that I had not the stamina either to resist what the captain chose to do to expel me, or to force myself upon Montgomery and his companion. So I waited passively upon fate; and the work of transferring Montgomery's possessions to the launch went on as if I did not exist.

Presently that work was finished, and then came a struggle. I was hauled, resisting weakly enough, to the gangway. Even then I noticed the oddness of the brown faces of the men who were with Montgomery in the launch; but the launch was now fully laden, and was shoved off hastily. A broadening gap of green water appeared under me, and I pushed back with all my strength to avoid falling headlong. The hands in the launch shouted derisively, and I heard Montgomery curse at them; and then the captain, the mate, and one of the seamen helping him, ran me aft towards the stern.

The dinghy of the *Lady Vain* had been towing behind; it was half full of water, had no oars, and was quite unvictualled. I refused to go aboard her, and flung myself full length on the deck. In the end, they swung me into her by a rope (for they had no stern ladder), and then they cut me adrift. I drifted slowly from the schooner. In a kind of stupor I watched all hands take to the rigging, and slowly but surely she came round to the wind; the sails fluttered, and then bellied out as the wind came into them. I stared at her weather-beaten side heeling steeply towards me; and then she passed out of my range of view.

I did not turn my head to follow her. At first I could scarcely believe what had happened. I crouched in the bottom of the dinghy, stunned, and staring

blankly at the vacant, oily sea. Then I realised that I was in that little hell of mine again, now half swamped; and looking back over the gunwale, I saw the schooner standing away from me, with the red-haired captain mocking at me over the taffrail, and turning towards the island saw the launch growing smaller as she approached the beach.

Abruptly the cruelty of this desertion became clear to me. I had no means of reaching the land unless I should chance to drift there. I was still weak, you must remember, from my exposure in the boat; I was empty and very faint, or I should have had more heart. But as it was I suddenly began to sob and weep, as I had never done since I was a little child. The tears ran down my face. In a passion of despair I struck with my fists at the water in the bottom of the boat, and kicked savagely at the gunwale. I prayed aloud for God to let me die.

CHAPTER SIX

The Evil-Looking Boatman

But the islanders, seeing that I was really adrift, took pity on me. I drifted very slowly to the eastward, approaching the island slantingly; and presently I saw, with hysterical relief, the launch come round and return towards me. She was heavily laden, and I could make out as she drew nearer Montgomery's white-haired, broad-shouldered companion sitting cramped up with the dogs and several packing-cases in the stern sheets. This individual stared fixedly at me without moving or speaking. The black-faced cripple was glaring at me as fixedly in the bows near the puma. There were three other men besides – three strange brutish-looking fellows, at whom the staghounds were snarling savagely. Montgomery, who was steering, brought the boat by me, and rising, caught and fastened my painter to the tiller to tow me, for there was no room aboard.

I had recovered from my hysterical phase by this time and answered his hail, as he approached, bravely enough. I told him the dinghy was nearly swamped, and he reached me a piggin. I was jerked back as the rope tightened between the boats. For some time I was busy baling.

It was not until I had got the water under control (for the water in the dinghy had been shipped; the boat was perfectly sound) that I had leisure to look at the people in the launch again.

The white-haired man I found was still regarding me steadfastly, but with an expression, as I now fancied, of some perplexity. When my eyes met his, he looked down at the staghound that sat between his knees. He was a powerfully-built man, as I have said, with a fine forehead and rather heavy features; but his eyes had that odd drooping of the skin above the lids which often comes with advancing years, and the fall of his heavy mouth at the

corners gave him an expression of pugnacious resolution. He talked to Montgomery in a tone too low for me to hear.

From him my eyes travelled to his three men; and a strange crew they were. I saw only their faces, yet there was something in their faces – I knew not what – that gave me a queer spasm of disgust. I looked steadily at them, and the impression did not pass, though I failed to see what had occasioned it. They seemed to me then to be brown men; but their limbs were oddly swathed in some thin, dirty, white stuff down even to the fingers and feet: I have never seen men so wrapped up before, and women so only in the East. They wore turbans too, and thereunder peered out their elfin faces at me, faces with protruding lower-jaws and bright eyes. They had lank black hair, almost like horsehair, and seemed as they sat to exceed in stature any race of men I have seen. The white-haired man, who I knew was a good six feet in height, sat a head below any one of the three. I found afterwards that really none were taller than myself; but their bodies were abnormally long, and the thigh-part of the leg short and curiously twisted. At any rate, they were an amazingly ugly gang, and over the heads of them under the forward lug peered the black face of the man whose eyes were luminous in the dark. As I stared at them, they met my gaze; and then first one and then another turned away from my direct stare, and looked at me in an odd, furtive manner. It occurred to me that I was perhaps annoying them, and I turned my attention to the island we were approaching.

It was low, and covered with thick vegetation – chiefly a kind of palm, that was new to me. From one point a thin white thread of vapour rose slantingly to an immense height, and then frayed out like a down feather. We were now within the embrace of a broad bay flanked on either hand by a low promontory. The beach was of dull-grey sand, and sloped steeply up to a ridge, perhaps sixty or seventy feet above the sea-level, and irregularly set with trees and undergrowth. Halfway up was a square enclosure of some greyish stone, which I found subsequently was built partly of coral and partly of pumiceous lava. Two thatched roofs peeped from within this enclosure. A man stood awaiting us at the water's edge. I fancied while we were still far off that I saw some other and very grotesque-looking creatures scuttle into the bushes upon the slope; but I saw nothing of these as we drew nearer. This man was of a moderate size, and with a black negroid face. He had a large, almost lipless, mouth, extraordinary lank arms, long thin feet and bow-legs, and stood with his heavy face thrust forward staring at us. He was dressed, like Montgomery and his white-haired companion, in jacket and trousers of blue serge. As we came still nearer, this individual began to run to and fro on the beach, making the most grotesque movements.

At a word of command from Montgomery, the four men in the launch sprang up, and with singularly awkward gestures struck the lugs Montgomery steered us round and into a narrow little dock excavated in the

beach. Then the man on the beach hastened towards us. This dock, as I call it, was really a mere ditch just long enough at this phase of the tide to take the longboat. I heard the bows ground in the sand, staved the dinghy off the rudder of the big boat with my piggin and, freeing the painter, landed. The three muffled men, with the clumsiest movements, scrambled out upon the sand, and forthwith set to landing the cargo, assisted by the man on the beach. I was struck especially by the curious movements of the legs of the three swathed and bandaged boatmen – not stiff they were, but distorted in some odd way, almost as if they were jointed in the wrong place. The dogs were still snarling, and strained at their chains after these men, as the white-haired man landed with them. The three big fellows spoke to one another in odd guttural tones, and the man who had waited for us on the beach began chattering to them excitedly – a foreign language, as I fancied – as they laid hands on some bales piled near the stern. Somewhere I had heard such a voice before, and I could not think where. The white-haired man stood, holding in a tumult of six dogs, and bawling orders over their din. Montgomery, having unshipped the rudder, landed likewise, and all set to work at unloading. I was too faint, what with my long fast and the sun beating down on my bare head, to offer any assistance.

Presently the white-haired man seemed to recollect my presence, and came up to me.

'You look,' said he, 'as though you had scarcely breakfasted.' His little eyes were a brilliant black under his heavy brows. 'I must apologise for that. Now you are our guest, we must make you comfortable, though you are uninvited, you know.' He looked keenly into my face. 'Montgomery says you are an educated man, Mr Prendick; says you know something of science. May I ask what that signifies?'

I told him I had spent some years at the Royal College of Science, and had done some researches in biology under Huxley. He raised his eyebrows slightly at that.

'That alters the case a little, Mr Prendick,' he said, with a trifle more respect in his manner. 'As it happens, we are biologists here. This is a biological station – of a sort.' His eye rested on the men in white who were busily hauling the puma, on rollers, towards the walled yard. 'I and Montgomery, at least,' he added. Then, 'When you will be able to get away, I can't say. We're off the track to anywhere. We see a ship once in a twelve-month or so.'

He left me abruptly, and went up the beach past this group, and I think entered the enclosure. The other two men were with Montgomery, erecting a pile of smaller packages on a low-wheeled truck. The llama was still on the launch with the rabbit hutches; the staghounds were still lashed to the thwarts. The pile of things completed, all three men laid hold of the truck and began shoving the ton-weight or so upon it after the puma. Presently Montgomery left them, and coming back to me held out his hand.

'I'm glad,' said he, 'for my own part. That captain was a silly ass. He'd have made things lively for you.'

'It was you,' said I, 'that saved me again.'

'That depends. You'll find this island an infernally rum place, I promise you. I'd watch my goings carefully, if I were you. *He* – ' He hesitated, and seemed to alter his mind about what was on his lips. 'I wish you'd help me with these rabbits,' he said.

His procedure with the rabbits was singular. I waded in with him, and helped him lug one of the hutches ashore. No sooner was that done than he opened the door of it, and tilting the thing on one end turned its living contents out on the ground. They fell in a struggling heap, one on the top of the other. He clapped his hands, and forthwith they went off with that hopping run of theirs, fifteen or twenty of them I should think, up the beach.

'Increase and multiply, my friends,' said Montgomery. 'Replenish the island. Hitherto we've had a certain lack of meat here.'

As I watched them disappearing, the white-haired man returned with a brandy-flask and some biscuits. 'Something to go on with, Prendick,' said he, in a far more familiar tone than before. I made no ado, but set to work on the biscuits at once, while the white-haired man helped Montgomery to release about a score more of the rabbits. Three big hutches, however, went up to the house with the puma. The brandy I did not touch, for I have been an abstainer from my birth.

CHAPTER SEVEN

The Locked Door

The reader will perhaps understand that at first everything was so strange about me, and my position was the outcome of such unexpected adventures, that I had no discernment of the relative strangeness of this or that thing. I followed the llama up the beach, and was overtaken by Montgomery, who asked me not to enter the stone enclosure. I noticed then that the puma in its cage and the pile of packages had been placed outside the entrance to this quadrangle.

I turned and saw that the launch had now been unloaded, run out again, and was being beached, and the white-haired man was walking towards us. He addressed Montgomery.

'And now comes the problem of this uninvited guest. What are we to do with him?'

'He knows something of science,' said Montgomery.

'I'm itching to get to work again – with this new stuff,' said the white-haired man, nodding towards the enclosure. His eyes grew brighter.

'I dare say you are,' said Montgomery, in anything but a cordial tone.

'We can't send him over there, and we can't spare the time to build him a new shanty; and we certainly can't take him into our confidence just yet.'

'I'm in your hands,' said I. I had no idea of what he meant by 'over there'.

'I've been thinking of the same things,' Montgomery answered. 'There's my room with the outer door – '

'That's it,' said the elder man, promptly, looking at Montgomery; and all three of us went towards the enclosure. 'I'm sorry to make a mystery, Mr Prendick; but you'll remember you're uninvited. Our little establishment here contains a secret or so, is a kind of Blue-Beard's chamber, in fact. Nothing very dreadful, really, to a sane man; but just now, as we don't know you – '

'Decidedly,' said I, 'I should be a fool to take offence at any want of confidence.'

He twisted his heavy mouth into a faint smile – he was one of those saturnine people who smile with the corners of the mouth down – and bowed his acknowledgement of my complaisance. The main entrance to the enclosure we passed; it was a heavy wooden gate, framed in iron and locked, with the cargo of the launch piled outside it; and at the corner we came to a small doorway I had not previously observed. The white-haired man produced a bundle of keys from the pocket of his greasy blue jacket, opened this door, and entered. His keys, and the elaborate locking-up of the place even while it was still under his eye, struck me as peculiar. I followed him, and found myself in a small apartment, plainly but not uncomfortably furnished and with its inner door, which was slightly ajar, opening into a paved courtyard. This inner door Montgomery at once closed. A hammock was slung across the darker corner of the room, and a small unglazed window defended by an iron bar looked out towards the sea.

This the white-haired man told me was to be my apartment; and the inner door, which 'for fear of accidents', he said, he would lock on the other side, was my limit inward. He called my attention to a convenient deckchair before the window, and to an array of old books, chiefly, I found, surgical works and editions of the Latin and Greek classics (languages I cannot read with any comfort), on a shelf near the hammock. He left the room by the outer door, as if to avoid opening the inner one again.

'We usually have our meals in here,' said Montgomery, and then, as if in doubt, went out after the other. 'Moreau!' I heard him call, and for the moment I do not think I noticed. Then as I handled the books on the shelf it came up in consciousness. Where had I heard the name of Moreau before? I sat down before the window, took out the biscuits that still remained to me, and ate them with an excellent appetite. Moreau!

Through the window I saw one of those unaccountable men in white lugging a packing-case along the beach. Presently the window-frame hid him. Then I heard a key inserted and turned in the lock behind me. After a

little while I heard through the locked door the noise of the staghounds that had now been brought up from the beach. They were not barking, but sniffing and growling in a curious fashion. I could hear the rapid patter of their feet, and Montgomery's voice soothing them.

I was very much impressed by the elaborate secrecy of these two men regarding the contents of the place, and for some time I was thinking of that and of the unaccountable familiarity of the name of Moreau; but so odd is the human memory that I could not then recall that well-known name in its proper connection. From that my thoughts went to the indefinable queerness of the deformed man on the beach. I never saw such a gait, such odd motions as he pulled at the box. I recalled that none of these men had spoken to me, though most of them I had found looking at me at one time or another in a peculiarly furtive manner, quite unlike the frank stare of your unsophisticated savage. Indeed, they had all seemed remarkably taciturn, and when they did speak, endowed with very uncanny voices. What was wrong with them? Then I recalled the eyes of Montgomery's ungainly attendant.

Just as I was thinking of him he came in. He was now dressed in white, and carried a little tray with some coffee and boiled vegetables thereon. I could hardly repress a shuddering recoil as he came, bending amiably, and placed the tray before me on the table. Then astonishment paralysed me. Under his stringy black locks I saw his ear; it jumped upon me suddenly close to my face. The man had pointed ears, covered with a fine brown fur!

'Your breakfast, sair,' he said.

I stared at his face without attempting to answer him. He turned and went towards the door, regarding me oddly over his shoulder. I followed him out with my eyes; and as I did so, by some odd trick of unconscious cerebration, there came surging into my head the phrase, 'The Moreau Hollows' – was it? 'The Moreau – ' Ah! It sent my memory back ten years. 'The Moreau Horrors!' The phrase drifted loose in my mind for a moment, and then I saw it in red lettering on a little buff-coloured pamphlet, to read which made one shiver and creep. Then I remembered distinctly all about it. That long-forgotten pamphlet came back with startling vividness to my mind. I had been a mere lad then, and Moreau was, I suppose, about fifty, a prominent and masterful physiologist, well-known in scientific circles for his extraordinary imagination and his brutal directness in discussion.

Was this the same Moreau? He had published some very astonishing facts in connection with the transfusion of blood, and in addition was known to be doing valuable work on morbid growths. Then suddenly his career was closed. He had to leave England. A journalist obtained access to his laboratory in the capacity of laboratory-assistant, with the deliberate intention of making sensational exposures; and by the help of a shocking accident (if it was an accident), his gruesome pamphlet became notorious. On the day of its publication, a wretched dog, flayed and otherwise

mutilated, escaped from Moreau's house. It was in the silly season, and a prominent editor, a cousin of the temporary laboratory-assistant, appealed to the conscience of the nation. It was not the first time that conscience has turned against the methods of research. The doctor was simply howled out of the country. It may be that he deserved to be; but I still think that the tepid support of his fellow-investigators and his desertion by the great body of scientific workers was a shameful thing. Yet some of his experiments, by the journalist's account, were wantonly cruel. He might perhaps have purchased his social peace by abandoning his investigations; but he apparently preferred the latter, as most men would who have once fallen under the overmastering spell of research. He was unmarried, and had indeed nothing but his own interest to consider.

I felt convinced that this must be the same man. Everything pointed to it. It dawned upon me to what end the puma and the other animals – which had now been brought with other luggage into the enclosure behind the house – were destined; and a curious faint odour, the halitus of something familiar, an odour that had been in the background of my consciousness hitherto, suddenly came forward into the forefront of my thoughts. It was the antiseptic odour of the dissecting-room. I heard the puma growling through the wall, and one of the dogs yelped as though it had been struck.

Yet surely, and especially to another scientific man, there was nothing so horrible in vivisection as to account for this secrecy; and by some odd leap in my thoughts the pointed ears and luminous eyes of Montgomery's attendant came back again before me with the sharpest definition. I stared before me out at the green sea, frothing under a freshening breeze, and let these and other strange memories of the last few days chase one another through my mind.

What could it all mean? A locked enclosure on a lonely island, a notorious vivisector, and these crippled and distorted men?

CHAPTER EIGHT

The Crying of the Puma

Montgomery interrupted my tangle of mystification and suspicion about one o'clock, and his grotesque attendant followed him with a tray bearing bread, some herbs and other eatables, a flask of whisky, a jug of water, and three glasses and knives. I glanced askance at this strange creature, and found him watching me with his queer, restless eyes. Montgomery said he would lunch with me, but that Moreau was too preoccupied with some work to come.

'Moreau!' said I. 'I know that name.'

'The devil you do!' said he. 'What an ass I was to mention it to you! I

might have thought. Anyhow, it will give you an inkling of our – mysteries. Whisky?'

'No, thanks; I'm an abstainer.'

'I wish I'd been. But it's no use locking the door after the steed is stolen. It was that infernal stuff which led to my coming here – that, and a foggy night. I thought myself in luck at the time, when Moreau offered to get me off. It's queer – '

'Montgomery,' said I, suddenly, as the outer door closed, 'why has your man pointed ears?'

'Damn!' he said, over his first mouthful of food. He stared at me for a moment, and then repeated, 'Pointed ears?'

'Little points to them,' said I, as calmly as possible, with a catch in my breath; 'and a fine black fur at the edges?'

He helped himself to whisky and water with great deliberation. 'I was under the impression – that his hair covered his ears.'

'I saw them as he stooped by me to put that coffee you sent to me on the table. And his eyes shine in the dark.'

By this time Montgomery had recovered from the surprise of my question. 'I always thought,' he said deliberately, with a certain accentuation of his flavouring of lisp, 'that there *was* something the matter with his ears, from the way he covered them. What were they like?'

I was persuaded from his manner that this ignorance was a pretence. Still, I could hardly tell the man that I thought him a liar. 'Pointed,' I said; 'rather small and furry – distinctly furry. But the whole man is one of the strangest beings I ever set eyes on.'

A sharp, hoarse cry of animal pain came from the enclosure behind us. Its depth and volume testified to the puma. I saw Montgomery wince.

'Yes?' he said.

'Where did you pick up the creature?'

'San Francisco. He's an ugly brute, I admit. Half-witted, you know. Can't remember where he came from. But I'm used to him, you know. We both are. How does he strike you?'

'He's unnatural,' I said. 'There's something about him – don't think me fanciful, but it gives me a nasty little sensation, a tightening of my muscles, when he comes near me. It's a touch – of the diabolical, in fact.'

Montgomery had stopped eating while I told him this. 'Rum!' he said. 'I can't see it.' He resumed his meal. 'I had no idea of it,' he said, and masticated. 'The crew of the schooner must have felt it the same. Made a dead set at the poor devil. You saw the captain?'

Suddenly the puma howled again, this time more painfully. Montgomery swore under his breath. I had half a mind to attack him about the men on the beach. Then the poor brute within gave vent to a series of short, sharp cries.

'Your men on the beach,' said I; 'what race are they?'

'Excellent fellows, aren't they?' said he, absent-mindedly, knitting his brows as the animal yelled out sharply.

I said no more. There was another outcry worse than the former. He looked at me with his dull grey eyes, and then took some more whisky. He tried to draw me into a discussion about alcohol, professing to have saved my life with it. He seemed anxious to lay stress on the fact that I owed my life to him. I answered him distractedly.

Presently our meal came to an end; the misshapen monster with the pointed ears cleared the remains away, and Montgomery left me alone in the room again. All the time he had been in a state of ill-concealed irritation at the noise of the vivisected puma. He had spoken of his odd want of nerve, and left me to the obvious application.

I found myself that the cries were singularly irritating, and they grew in depth and intensity as the afternoon wore on. They were painful at first, but their constant resurgence at last altogether upset my balance. I flung aside a crib of Horace I had been reading, and began to clench my fists, to bite my lips, and to pace the room. Presently I got to stopping my ears with my fingers.

The emotional appeal of those yells grew upon me steadily, grew at last to such an exquisite expression of suffering that I could stand it in that confined room no longer. I stepped out of the door into the slumberous heat of the late afternoon, and walking past the main entrance – locked again, I noticed – turned the corner of the wall

The crying sounded even louder out of doors. It was as if all the pain in the world had found a voice. Yet had I known such pain was in the next room, and had it been dumb, I believe – I have thought since – I could have stood it well enough. It is when suffering finds a voice and sets our nerves quivering that this pity comes troubling us. But in spite of the brilliant sunlight and the green fans of the trees waving in the soothing sea-breeze, the world was a confusion, blurred with drifting black and red phantasms, until I was out of earshot of the house in the chequered wall.

CHAPTER NINE

The Thing in the Forest

I strode through the undergrowth that clothed the ridge behind the house, scarcely heeding whither I went; passed on through the shadow of a thick cluster of straight-stemmed trees beyond it, and so presently found myself some way on the other side of the ridge, and descending towards a streamlet that ran through a narrow valley. I paused and listened. The distance I had come, or the intervening masses of thicket, deadened any sound that might be coming from the enclosure. The air was still. Then with a rustle a rabbit

emerged, and went scampering up the slope before me. I hesitated, and sat down in the edge of the shade.

The place was a pleasant one. The rivulet was hidden by the luxuriant vegetation of the banks save at one point, where I caught a triangular patch of its glittering water. On the farther side I saw through a bluish haze a tangle of trees and creepers, and above these again the luminous blue of the sky. Here and there a splash of white or crimson marked the blooming of some trailing epiphyte. I let my eyes wander over this scene for a while, and then began to turn over in my mind again the strange peculiarities of Montgomery's man. But it was too hot to think elaborately, and presently I fell into a tranquil state midway between dozing and waking.

From this I was aroused, after I know not how long, by a rustling amidst the greenery on the other side of the stream. For a moment I could see nothing but the waving summits of the ferns and reeds. Then suddenly upon the bank of the stream appeared Something – at first I could not distinguish what it was. It bowed its round head to the water, and began to drink. Then I saw it was a man, going on all-fours like a beast. He was clothed in bluish cloth, and was of a copper-coloured hue, with black hair. It seemed that grotesque ugliness was an invariable character of these islanders. I could hear the suck of the water at his lips as he drank.

I leant forward to see him better, and a piece of lava, detached by my hand, went pattering down the slope. He looked up guiltily, and his eyes met mine. Forthwith he scrambled to his feet, and stood wiping his clumsy hand across his mouth and regarding me. His legs were scarcely half the length of his body. So, staring one another out of countenance, we remained for perhaps the space of a minute. Then, stopping to look back once or twice, he slunk off among the bushes to the right of me, and I heard the swish of the fronds grow faint in the distance and die away. Long after he had disappeared, I remained sitting up staring in the direction of his retreat. My drowsy tranquillity had gone.

I was startled by a noise behind me, and turning suddenly saw the flapping white tail of a rabbit vanishing up the slope. I jumped to my feet. The apparition of this grotesque, half-bestial creature had suddenly populated the stillness of the afternoon for me. I looked around me rather nervously, and regretted that I was unarmed. Then I thought that the man I had just seen had been clothed in bluish cloth, had not been naked as a savage would have been; and I tried to persuade myself from that fact that he was after all probably a peaceful character, that the dull ferocity of his countenance belied him.

Yet I was greatly disturbed at the apparition. I walked to the left along the slope, turning my head about and peering this way and that among the straight stems of the trees. Why should a man go on all-fours and drink with his lips? Presently I heard an animal wailing again, and taking it to be the puma, I turned about and walked in a direction diametrically opposite

to the sound. This led me down to the stream, across which I stepped and pushed my way up through the undergrowth beyond.

I was startled by a great patch of vivid scarlet on the ground, and going up to it found it to be a peculiar fungus, branched and corrugated like a foliaceous lichen, but deliquescing into slime at the touch; and then in the shadow of some luxuriant ferns I came upon an unpleasant thing – the dead body of a rabbit covered with shining flies, but still warm and with the head torn off. I stopped aghast at the sight of the scattered blood. Here at least was one visitor to the island disposed of! There were no traces of other violence about it. It looked as though it had been suddenly snatched up and killed; and as I stared at the little furry body came the difficulty of how the thing had been done. The vague dread that had been in my mind since I had seen the inhuman face of the man at the stream grew distincter as I stood there. I began to realise the hardihood of my expedition among these unknown people. The thicket about me became altered to my imagination. Every shadow became something more than a shadow – became an ambush; every rustle became a threat. Invisible things seemed watching me. I resolved to go back to the enclosure on the beach. I suddenly turned away and thrust myself violently, possibly even frantically, through the bushes, anxious to get a clear space about me again.

I stopped just in time to prevent myself emerging upon an open space. It was a kind of glade in the forest, made by a fall; seedlings were already starting up to struggle for the vacant space; and beyond, the dense growth of stems and twining vines and splashes of fungus and flowers closed in again. Before me, squatting together upon the fungoid ruins of a huge fallen tree and still unaware of my approach, were three grotesque human figures. One was evidently a female; the other two were men. They were naked, save for swathings of scarlet cloth about the middle; and their skins were of a dull pinkish-drab colour, such as I had seen in no savages before. They had fat, heavy, chinless faces, retreating foreheads, and a scant bristly hair upon their heads. I never saw such bestial-looking creatures.

They were talking, or at least one of the men was talking to the other two, and all three had been too closely interested to heed the rustling of my approach. They swayed their heads and shoulders from side to side. The speaker's words came thick and sloppy, and though I could hear them distinctly I could not distinguish what he said. He seemed to me to be reciting some complicated gibberish. Presently his articulation became shriller, and spreading his hands he rose to his feet. At that the others began to gibber in unison, also rising to their feet, spreading their hands and swaying their bodies in rhythm with their chant. I noticed then the abnormal shortness of their legs, and their lank, clumsy feet. All three began slowly to circle round, raising and stamping their feet and waving their arms; a kind of tune crept into their rhythmic recitation, and a refrain – 'Aloola,' or 'Balloola,' it sounded like. Their eyes began to sparkle, and

their ugly faces to brighten, with an expression of strange pleasure. Saliva dripped from their lipless mouths.

Suddenly, as I watched their grotesque and unaccountable gestures, I perceived clearly for the first time what it was that had offended me, what had given me the two inconsistent and conflicting impressions of utter strangeness and yet of the strangest familiarity. The three creatures engaged in this mysterious rite were human in shape, and yet human beings with the strangest air about them of some familiar animal. Each of these creatures, despite its human form, its rag of clothing and the rough humanity of its bodily form, had woven into it – into its movements, into the expression of its countenance, into its whole presence – some now irresistible suggestion of a hog, a swinish taint, the unmistakable mark of the beast.

I stood overcome by this amazing realisation and then the most horrible questionings came rushing into my mind. They began leaping in the air, first one and then the other, whooping and grunting. Then one slipped, and for a moment was on all-fours – to recover, indeed, forthwith. But that transitory gleam of the true animalism of these monsters was enough.

I turned as noiselessly as possible, and becoming every now and then rigid with the fear of being discovered, as a branch cracked or a leaf rustled, I pushed back into the bushes. It was long before I grew bolder and dared to move freely. My only idea for the moment was to get away from these foul beings, and I scarcely noticed that I had emerged upon a faint pathway amidst the trees. Then suddenly traversing a little glade, I saw with an unpleasant start two clumsy legs among the trees, walking with noiseless footsteps parallel with my course, and perhaps thirty yards away from me. The head and upper part of the body were hidden by a tangle of creeper. I stopped abruptly, hoping the creature did not see me. The feet stopped as I did. So nervous was I that I controlled an impulse to headlong flight with the utmost difficulty. Then looking hard, I distinguished through the inter-lacing network the head and body of the brute I had seen drinking. He moved his head. There was an emerald flash in his eyes as he glanced at me from the shadow of the trees, a half-luminous colour that vanished as he turned his head again. He was motionless for a moment, and then with a noiseless tread began running through the green confusion. In another moment he had vanished behind some bushes. I could not see him, but I felt that he had stopped and was watching me again.

What on earth was he – man or beast? What did he want with me? I had no weapon, not even a stick. Flight would be madness. At any rate the Thing, whatever it was, lacked the courage to attack me. Setting my teeth hard, I walked straight towards him. I was anxious not to show the fear that seemed chilling my backbone. I pushed through a tangle of tall white-flowered bushes, and saw him twenty paces beyond, looking over his shoulder at me and hesitating. I advanced a step or two, looking steadfastly into his eyes.

'Who are you?' said I.

He tried to meet my gaze. 'No!' he said suddenly, and turning went bounding away from me through the undergrowth. Then he turned and stared at me again. His eyes shone brightly out of the dusk under the trees.

My heart was in my mouth; but I felt my only chance was bluff, and walked steadily towards him. He turned again, and vanished into the dusk. Once more I thought I caught the glint of his eyes, and that was all.

For the first time I realised how the lateness of the hour might affect me. The sun had set some minutes since, the swift dusk of the tropics was already fading out of the eastern sky, and a pioneer moth fluttered silently by my head. Unless I would spend the night among the unknown dangers of the mysterious forest, I must hasten back to the enclosure. The thought of a return to that pain-haunted refuge was extremely disagreeable, but still more so was the idea of being overtaken in the open by darkness and all that darkness might conceal. I gave one more look into the blue shadows that had swallowed up this odd creature, and then retraced my way down the slope towards the stream, going as I judged in the direction from which I had come.

I walked eagerly, my mind confused with many things, and presently found myself in a level place among scattered trees. The colourless clearness that comes after the sunset flush was darkling; the blue sky above grew momentarily deeper, and the little stars one by one pierced the attenuated light; the interspaces of the trees, the gaps in the farther vegetation, that had been hazy blue in the daylight, grew black and mysterious. I pushed on. The colour vanished from the world. The treetops rose against the luminous blue sky in inky silhouette, and all below that outline melted into one formless blackness. Presently the trees grew thinner, and the shrubby undergrowth more abundant. Then there was a desolate space covered with a white sand, and then another expanse of tangled bushes. I did not remember crossing the sand-opening before. I began to be tormented by a faint rustling upon my right hand. I thought at first it was fancy, for whenever I stopped there was silence, save for the evening breeze in the tree-tops. Then when I turned to hurry on again there was an echo to my footsteps.

I turned away from the thickets, keeping to the more open ground, and endeavouring by sudden turns now and then to surprise something in the act of creeping upon me. I saw nothing, and nevertheless my sense of another presence grew steadily. I increased my pace, and after some time came to a slight ridge, crossed it, and turned sharply, regarding it steadfastly from the farther side. It came out black and clear-cut against the darkling sky; and presently a shapeless lump heaved up momentarily against the skyline and vanished again. I felt assured now that my tawny-faced antagonist was stalking me once more; and coupled with that was another unpleasant realisation, that I had lost my way.

For a time I hurried on hopelessly perplexed, and pursued by that stealthy approach. Whatever it was, the Thing either lacked the courage to attack me, or it was waiting to take me at some disadvantage. I kept studiously to the open. At times I would turn and listen; and presently I had half persuaded myself that my pursuer had abandoned the chase, or was a mere creation of my disordered imagination. Then I heard the sound of the sea. I quickened my footsteps almost into a run, and immediately there was a stumble in my rear.

I turned suddenly, and stared at the uncertain trees behind me. One black shadow seemed to leap into another. I listened, rigid, and heard nothing but the creep of the blood in my ears. I thought that my nerves were unstrung, and that my imagination was tricking me, and turned resolutely towards the sound of the sea again.

In a minute or so the trees grew thinner, and I emerged upon a bare, low headland running out into the sombre water. The night was calm and clear, and the reflection of the growing multitude of the stars shivered in the tranquil heaving of the sea. Some way out, the wash upon an irregular band of reef shone with a pallid light of its own. Westward I saw the zodiacal light mingling with the yellow brilliance of the evening star. The coast fell away from me to the east, and westward it was hidden by the shoulder of the cape. Then I recalled the fact that Moreau's beach lay to the west.

A twig snapped behind me, and there was a rustle. I turned, and stood facing the dark trees. I could see nothing – or else I could see too much. Every dark form in the dimness had its ominous quality, its peculiar suggestion of alert watchfulness. So I stood for perhaps a minute, and then, with an eye to the trees still, turned westward to cross the headland; and as I moved, one among the lurking shadows moved to follow me.

My heart beat quickly. Presently the broad sweep of a bay to the westward became visible, and I halted again. The noiseless shadow halted a dozen yards from me. A little point of light shone on the farther bend of the curve, and the grey sweep of the sandy beach lay faint under the starlight. Perhaps two miles away was that little point of light. To get to the beach I should have to go through the trees where the shadows lurked and down a bushy slope.

I could see the Thing rather more distinctly now. It was no animal, for it stood erect. At that I opened my mouth to speak, and found a hoarse phlegm choked my voice. I tried again, and shouted, 'Who is there?' There was no answer. I advanced a step. The Thing did not move, only gathered itself together. My foot struck a stone. That gave me an idea. Without taking my eyes off the black form before me, I stooped and picked up this lump of rock; but at my motion the Thing turned abruptly as a dog might have done, and slunk obliquely into the farther darkness. Then I recalled a schoolboy expedient against big dogs, and twisted the rock into my handkerchief, and gave this a turn round my wrist. I heard a movement farther

off among the shadows, as if the Thing was in retreat. Then suddenly my tense excitement gave way; I broke into a profuse perspiration and fell a-trembling, with my adversary routed and this weapon in my hand.

It was some time before I could summon resolution to go down through the trees and bushes upon the flank of the headland to the beach. At last I did it at a run; and as I emerged from the thicket upon the sand, I heard some other body come crashing after me. At that I completely lost my head with fear, and began running along the sand. Forthwith there came the swift patter of soft feet in pursuit. I gave a wild cry, and redoubled my pace. Some dim, black things about three or four times the size of rabbits went running or hopping up from the beach towards the bushes as I passed.

So long as I live, I shall remember the terror of that chase. I ran near the water's edge, and heard every now and then the splash of the feet that gained upon me. Far away, hopelessly far, was the yellow light. All the night about us was black and still. Splash, splash, came the pursuing feet, nearer and nearer. I felt my breath going, for I was quite out of training; it whooped as I drew it, and I felt a pain like a knife at my side. I perceived the Thing would come up with me long before I reached the enclosure, and, desperate and sobbing for my breath, I wheeled round upon it and struck at it as it came up to me – struck with all my strength. The stone came out of the sling of the handkerchief as I did so. As I turned, the Thing, which had been running on all-fours, rose to its feet, and the missile fell fair on its left temple. The skull rang loud, and the animal-man blundered into me, thrust me back with its hands, and went staggering past me to fall headlong upon the sand with its face in the water; and there it lay still.

I could not bring myself to approach that black heap. I left it there, with the water rippling round it, under the still stars, and giving it a wide berth pursued my way towards the yellow glow of the house; and presently, with a positive effect of relief, came the pitiful moaning of the puma, the sound that had originally driven me out to explore this mysterious island. At that, though I was faint and horribly fatigued, I gathered together all my strength, and began running again towards the light. I thought I heard a voice calling me.

CHAPTER TEN

The Crying of the Man

As I drew near the house I saw that the light shone from the open door of my room; and then I heard coming from out of the darkness at the side of that orange oblong of light, the voice of Montgomery shouting, 'Prendick!' I continued running. Presently I heard him again. I replied by a feeble 'Hello!' and in another moment had staggered up to him.

'Where have you been?' said he, holding me at arm's length, so that the light from the door fell on my face. 'We have both been so busy that we forgot you until about half an hour ago.' He led me into the room and set me down in the deckchair. For awhile I was blinded by the light. 'We did not think you would start to explore this island of ours without telling us,' he said; and then, 'I was afraid – But – what – Hello!'

My last remaining strength slipped from me, and my head fell forward on my chest. I think he found a certain satisfaction in giving me brandy.

'For God's sake,' said I, 'fasten that door.'

'You've been meeting some of our curiosities, eh?' said he.

He locked the door and turned to me again. He asked me no questions, but gave me some more brandy and water and pressed me to eat. I was in a state of collapse. He said something vague about his forgetting to warn me, and asked me briefly when I left the house and what I had seen.

I answered him as briefly, in fragmentary sentences. 'Tell me what it all means,' said I, in a state bordering on hysterics.

'It's nothing so very dreadful,' said he. 'But I think you have had about enough for one day.' The puma suddenly gave a sharp yell of pain. At that he swore under his breath. 'I'm damned,' said he, 'if this place is not as bad as Gower Street, with its cats.'

'Montgomery,' said I, 'what was that thing that came after me? Was it a beast or was it a man?'

'If you don't sleep tonight,' he said, 'you'll be off your head tomorrow.'

I stood up in front of him. 'What was that thing that came after me?' I asked.

He looked me squarely in the eyes, and twisted his mouth askew. His eyes, which had seemed animated a minute before, went dull. 'From your account,' said he, 'I'm thinking it was a bogle.'

I felt a gust of intense irritation, which passed as quickly as it came. I flung myself into the chair again, and pressed my hands on my forehead. The puma began once more.

Montgomery came round behind me and put his hand on my shoulder. 'Look here, Prendick,' he said, 'I had no business to let you drift out into this silly island of ours. But it's not so bad as you feel, man. Your nerves are worked to rags. Let me give you something that will make you sleep. *That* – will keep on for hours yet. You must simply get to sleep, or I won't answer for it.'

I did not reply. I bowed forward, and covered my face with my hands. Presently he returned with a small measure containing a dark liquid. This he gave me. I took it unresistingly, and he helped me into the hammock.

When I awoke, it was broad day. For a little while I lay flat, staring at the roof above me. The rafters, I observed, were made out of the timbers of a ship. Then I turned my head, and saw a meal prepared for me on the table. I perceived that I was hungry, and prepared to clamber out of the hammock,

which, very politely anticipating my intention, twisted round and deposited me upon all-fours on the floor.

I got up and sat down before the food. I had a heavy feeling in my head, and only the vaguest memory at first of the things that had happened over night. The morning breeze blew very pleasantly through the unglazed window, and that and the food contributed to the sense of animal comfort which I experienced. Presently the door behind me – the door inward towards the yard of the enclosure – opened. I turned and saw Montgomery's face.

'All right?' said he. 'I'm frightfully busy.' And he shut the door.

Afterwards I discovered that he forgot to re-lock it. Then I recalled the expression of his face the previous night, and with that the memory of all I had experienced reconstructed itself before me. Even as that fear came back to me, there came a cry from within; but this time it was not the cry of a puma. I put down the mouthful that hesitated upon my lips, and listened. Silence, save for the whisper of the morning breeze. I began to think my ears had deceived me.

After a long pause I resumed my meal, but with my ears still vigilant. Presently I heard something else, very faint and low. I sat as if frozen in my attitude. Though it was faint and low, it moved me more profoundly than all that I had hitherto heard of the abominations behind the wall. There was no mistake this time in the quality of the dim, broken sounds; no doubt at all of their source. For it was groaning, broken by sobs and gasps of anguish. It was no brute this time; it was a human being in torment!

As I realised this I rose, and in three steps had crossed the room, seized the handle of the door into the yard, and flung it open before me.

'Prendick, man! Stop!' cried Montgomery, intervening.

A startled deerhound yelped and snarled. There was blood, I saw, in the sink – brown, and some scarlet – and I smelt the peculiar smell of carbolic acid. Then through an open doorway beyond, in the dim light of the shadow, I saw something bound painfully upon a framework, scarred, red and bandaged; and then blotting this out appeared the face of old Moreau, white and terrible. In a moment he had gripped me by the shoulder with a hand that was smeared red, had twisted me off my feet, and flung me headlong back into my own room. He lifted me as though I was a little child. I fell at full length upon the floor, and the door slammed and shut out the passionate intensity of his face. Then I heard the key turn in the lock, and Montgomery's voice in expostulation.

'Ruin the work of a lifetime,' I heard Moreau say.

'He does not understand,' said Montgomery, with other things that were inaudible.

'I can't spare the time yet,' said Moreau.

The rest I did not hear. I picked myself up and stood trembling, my mind a chaos of the most horrible misgivings. Could it be possible, I thought, that

such a thing as the vivisection of men was carried on here? The question shot like lightning across a tumultuous sky; and suddenly the clouded horror of my mind condensed into a vivid realisation of my own danger.

CHAPTER ELEVEN

The Hunting of the Man

It came before my mind with an unreasonable hope of escape that the outer door of my room was still open to me. I was convinced now, absolutely assured, that Moreau had been vivisecting a human being. All the time since I had heard his name, I had been trying to link in my mind in some way the grotesque animalism of the islanders with his abominations; and now I thought I saw it all. The memory of his work on the transfusion of blood recurred to me. These creatures I had seen were the victims of some hideous experiment. These sickening scoundrels had merely intended to keep me back, to fool me with their display of confidence, and presently to fall upon me with a fate more horrible than death – with torture; and after torture the most hideous degradation it is possible to conceive – to send me off a lost soul, a beast, to the rest of their Comus rout.

I looked round for some weapon. Nothing. Then with an inspiration I turned over the deckchair, put my foot on the side of it, and tore away the side rail. It happened that a nail came away with the wood, and projecting, gave a touch of danger to an otherwise petty weapon. I heard a step outside, and incontinently flung open the door and found Montgomery within a yard of it. He meant to lock the outer door! I raised this nailed stick of mine and cut at his face; but he sprang back. I hesitated a moment, then turned and fled, round the corner of the house. 'Prendick, man!' I heard his astonished cry, 'don't be a silly ass, man!'

Another minute, thought I, and he would have had me locked in, and as ready as a hospital rabbit for my fate. He emerged behind the corner, for I heard him shout, 'Prendick!' Then he began to run after me, shouting things as he ran. This time running blindly, I went north-eastward in a direction at right angles to my previous expedition. Once, as I went running headlong up the beach, I glanced over my shoulder and saw his attendant with him. I ran furiously up the slope, over it, then turning eastward along a rocky valley fringed on either side with jungle I ran for perhaps a mile altogether, my chest straining, my heart beating in my ears; and then hearing nothing of Montgomery or his man, and feeling upon the verge of exhaustion, I doubled sharply back towards the beach as I judged, and lay down in the shelter of a canebrake. There I remained for a long time, too fearful to move, and indeed too fearful even to plan a course of action. The wild scene about me lay sleeping silently under the sun, and the only sound

near me was the thin hum of some small gnats that had discovered me. Presently I became aware of a drowsy breathing sound, the soughing of the sea upon the beach.

After about an hour I heard Montgomery shouting my name, far away to the north. That set me thinking of my plan of action. As I interpreted it then, this island was inhabited only by these two vivisectors and their animalised victims. Some of these no doubt they could press into their service against me if need arose. I knew both Moreau and Montgomery carried revolvers; and, save for a feeble bar of deal spiked with a small nail, the merest mockery of a mace, I was unarmed.

So I lay still there, until I began to think of food and drink; and at that thought the real hopelessness of my position came home to me. I knew no way of getting anything to eat. I was too ignorant of botany to discover any resort of root or fruit that might lie about me; I had no means of trapping the few rabbits upon the island. It grew blanker the more I turned the prospect over. At last, in the desperation of my position, my mind turned to the animal men I had encountered. I tried to find some hope in what I remembered of them. In turn I recalled each one I had seen, and tried to draw some augury of assistance from my memory.

Then suddenly I heard a staghound bay, and at that realised a new danger. I took little time to think, or they would have caught me then, but snatching up my nailed stick, rushed headlong from my hiding-place towards the sound of the sea. I remember a growth of thorny plants, with spines that stabbed like penknives. I emerged bleeding and with torn clothes upon the lip of a long creek opening northward. I went straight into the water without a minute's hesitation, wading up the creek, and presently finding myself knee deep in a little stream. I scrambled out at last on the westward bank, and with my heart beating loudly in my ears, crept into a tangle of ferns to await the issue. I heard the dog (there was only one) draw nearer, and yelp when it came to the thorns. Then I heard no more, and presently began to think I had escaped.

The minutes passed; the silence lengthened out, and at last after an hour of security my courage began to return to me. By this time I was no longer very much terrified or very miserable. I had, as it were, passed the limit of terror and despair. I felt now that my life was practically lost, and that persuasion made me capable of daring anything. I had even a certain wish to encounter Moreau face to face; and as I had waded into the water, I remembered that if I were too hard pressed at least one path of escape from torment still lay open to me – they could not very well prevent my drowning myself. I had half a mind to drown myself then; but an odd wish to see the whole adventure out, a queer, impersonal, spectacular interest in myself, restrained me. I stretched my limbs, sore and painful from the pricks of the spiny plants, and stared around me at the trees; and, so suddenly that it seemed to jump out of the green tracery about it, my eyes

lit upon a black face watching me. I saw that it was the simian creature who had met the launch upon the beach. He was clinging to the oblique stem of a palm tree. I gripped my stick, and stood up facing him. He began chattering. 'You, you, you,' was all I could distinguish at first. Suddenly he dropped from the tree, and in another moment was holding the fronds apart and staring curiously at me.

I did not feel the same repugnance towards this creature which I had experienced in my encounters with the other Beast Men. 'You,' he said, 'in the boat.' He was a man, then – at least as much of a man as Montgomery's attendant – for he could talk.

'Yes,' I said, 'I came in the boat. From the ship.'

'Oh!' he said, and his bright, restless eyes travelled over me, to my hands, to the stick I carried, to my feet, to the tattered places in my coat, and the cuts and scratches I had received from the thorns. He seemed puzzled at something. His eyes came back to my hands. He held his own hand out and counted his digits slowly, 'One, two, three, four, five – eight?'

I did not grasp his meaning then; afterwards I was to find that a great proportion of these Beast People had malformed hands, lacking sometimes even three digits. But guessing this was in some way a greeting, I did the same thing by way of reply. He grinned with immense satisfaction. Then his swift roving glance went round again; he made a swift movement – and vanished. The fern fronds he had stood between came swishing together,

I pushed out of the brake after him, and was astonished to find him swinging cheerfully by one lank arm from a rope of creeper that looped down from the foliage overhead. His back was to me.

'Hello!' said I.

He came down with a twisting jump, and stood facing me.

'I say,' said I, 'where can I get something to eat?'

'Eat!' he said. 'Eat Man's food, now.' And his eye went back to the swing of ropes. 'At the huts.'

'But where are the huts?'

'Oh!'

'I'm new, you know.'

At that he swung round, and set off at a quick walk. All his motions were curiously rapid. 'Come along,' said he.

I went with him to see the adventure out. I guessed the huts were some rough shelter where he and some more of these Beast People lived. I might perhaps find them friendly, find some handle in their minds to take hold of. I did not know how far they had forgotten their human heritage.

My apelike companion trotted along by my side, with his hands hanging down and his jaw thrust forward. I wondered what memory he might have in him. 'How long have you been on this island?' said I.

'How long?' he asked; and after having the question repeated, he held up three fingers.

The creature was little better than an idiot. I tried to make out what he meant by that, and it seems I bored him. After another question or two he suddenly left my side and went leaping at some fruit that hung from a tree. He pulled down a handful of prickly husks and went on, eating the contents. I noted this with satisfaction, for here at least was a hint for feeding. I tried him with some other questions, but his chattering, prompt responses were as often as not quite at cross purposes with my question. Some few were appropriate, others quite parrot-like.

I was so intent upon these peculiarities that I scarcely noticed the path we followed. Presently we came to trees, all charred and brown, and so to a bare place covered with a yellow-white encrustation, across which a drifting smoke, pungent in whiffs to nose and eyes, went drifting. On our right, over a shoulder of bare rock, I saw the level blue of the sea. The path coiled down abruptly into a narrow ravine between two tumbled and knotty masses of blackish scoriae. Into this we plunged.

It was extremely dark, this passage, after the blinding sunlight reflected from the sulphurous ground. Its walls grew steep, and approached each other. Blotches of green and crimson drifted across my eyes. My conductor stopped suddenly. 'Home!' said he, and I stood on the floor of a chasm that was at first absolutely dark to me. I heard some strange noises, and thrust the knuckles of my left hand into my eyes. I became aware of a disagreeable odour, like that of a monkey's cage ill-cleaned. Beyond, the rock opened again upon a gradual slope of sunlit greenery, and on either hand the light smote down through narrow ways into the central gloom.

CHAPTER TWELVE

The Sayers of the Law

Then something cold touched my hand. I started violently, and saw close to me a dim pinkish thing, looking more like a flayed child than anything else in the world. The creature had exactly the mild but repulsive features of a sloth, the same low forehead and slow gestures.

As the first shock of the change of light passed, I saw about me more distinctly. The little sloth-like creature was standing and staring at me. My conductor had vanished. The place was a narrow passage between high walls of lava, a crack in the knotted rock, and on either side interwoven heaps of sea-mat, palm-fans and reeds leaning against the rock formed rough and impenetrably dark dens. The winding way up the ravine between these was scarcely three yards wide, and was disfigured by lumps of decaying fruit-pulp and other refuse, which accounted for the disagreeable stench of the place.

The little pink sloth-creature was still blinking at me when my Ape-man

reappeared at the aperture of the nearest of these dens, and beckoned me in. As he did so a slouching monster wriggled out of one of the places, farther up this strange street, and stood up in featureless silhouette against the bright green beyond, staring at me. I hesitated, having half a mind to bolt the way I had come; and then, determined to go through with the adventure, I gripped my nailed stick about the middle and crawled into the little evil-smelling lean-to after my conductor.

It was a semicircular space, shaped like the half of a beehive; and against the rocky wall that formed the inner side of it was a pile of variegated fruits, coconuts among others. Some rough vessels of lava and wood stood about the floor, and one on a rough stool. There was no fire. In the darkest corner of the hut sat a shapeless mass of darkness that grunted 'Hey!' as I came in, and my Ape-man stood in the dim light of the doorway and held out a split coconut to me as I crawled into the other corner and squatted down. I took it, and began gnawing it, as serenely as possible, in spite of a certain trepidation and the nearly intolerable closeness of the den. The little pink sloth-creature stood in the aperture of the hut, and something else with a drab face and bright eyes came staring over its shoulder.

'Hey!' came out of the lump of mystery opposite. 'It is a man.'

'It is a man,' gabbled my conductor, 'a man, a man, a five-man, like me.'

'Shut up!' said the voice from the dark, and grunted. I gnawed my coconut amid an impressive stillness.

I peered hard into the blackness, but could distinguish nothing.

'It is a man,' the voice repeated. 'He comes to live with us?'

It was a thick voice, with something in it – a kind of whistling overtone – that struck me as peculiar; but the English accent was strangely good.

The Ape-man looked at me as though he expected something. I perceived the pause was interrogative. 'He comes to live with you,' I said.

'It is a man. He must learn the Law.'

I began to distinguish now a deeper blackness in the black, a vague outline of a hunched-up figure. Then I noticed the opening of the place was darkened by two more black heads. My hand tightened on my stick.

The thing in the dark repeated in a louder tone, 'Say the words.' I had missed its last remark. 'Not to go on all-fours; that is the Law,' it repeated in a kind of sing-song.

I was puzzled.

'Say the words,' said the Ape-man, repeating, and the figures in the doorway echoed this, with a threat in the tone of their voices.

I realised that I had to repeat this idiotic formula; and then began the insanest ceremony. The voice in the dark began intoning a mad litany, line by line, and I and the rest to repeat it. As they did so, they swayed from side to side in the oddest way, and beat their hands upon their knees; and I followed their example. I could have imagined I was already dead and in another world. That dark hut, these grotesque dim figures, just flecked here

and there by a glimmer of light, and all of them swaying in unison and chanting,

'Not to go on All-Fours; *that* is the Law. Are we not Men?
Not to suck up Drink; *that* is the Law. Are we not Men?
Not to eat Fish or Flesh; *that* is the Law. Are we not Men?
Not to claw the Bark of Trees; *that* is the Law. Are we not Men?
Not to chase other Men; *that* is the Law. Are we not Men?'

And so from the prohibition of these acts of folly, on to the prohibition of what I thought then were the maddest, most impossible, and most indecent things one could well imagine. A kind of rhythmic fervour fell on all of us; we gabbled and swayed faster and faster, repeating this amazing Law. Superficially the contagion of these brutes was upon me, but deep down within me the laughter and disgust struggled together. We ran through a long list of prohibitions, and then the chant swung round to a new formula.

'*His* is the House of Pain.
His is the Hand that makes.
His is the Hand that wounds.
His is the Hand that heals.'

And so on for another long series, mostly quite incomprehensible gibberish to me about *Him*, whoever he might be. I could have fancied it was a dream, but never before have I heard chanting in a dream.

'*His* is the lightning flash,' we sang. '*His* is the deep, salt sea.'

A horrible fancy came into my head that Moreau, after animalising these men, had infected their dwarfed brains with a kind of deification of himself. However, I was too keenly aware of white teeth and strong claws about me to stop my chanting on that account.

'*His* are the stars in the sky.'

At last that song ended. I saw the Ape-man's face shining with perspiration; and my eyes being now accustomed to the darkness, I saw more distinctly the figure in the corner from which the voice came. It was the size of a man, but it seemed covered with a dull grey hair almost like a Skye terrier. What was it? What were they all? Imagine yourself surrounded by all the most horrible cripples and maniacs it is possible to conceive, and you may understand a little of my feelings with these grotesque caricatures of humanity about me.

'He is a five-man, a five-man, a five-man – like me,' said the Ape-man.

I held out my hands. The grey creature in the corner leant forward.

'Not to run on All-Fours; that is the Law. Are we not Men?' he said.

He put out a strangely distorted talon and gripped my fingers. The thing was almost like the hoof of a deer produced into claws. I could have yelled with surprise and pain. His face came forward and peered at my

nails, came forward into the light of the opening of the hut and I saw with a quivering disgust that it was like the face of neither man nor beast, but a mere shock of grey hair, with three shadowy over-archings to mark the eyes and mouth.

'He has little nails,' said this grisly creature in his hairy beard. 'It is well.'

He threw my hand down, and instinctively I gripped my stick.

'Eat roots and herbs; it is His will,' said the Ape-man.

'I am the Sayer of the Law,' said the grey figure. 'Here come all that be new to learn the Law. I sit in the darkness and say the Law.'

'It is even so,' said one of the beasts in the doorway.

'Evil are the punishments for those who break the Law. None escape.'

'None escape,' said the Beast Folk, glancing furtively at one another.

'None, none,' said the Ape-man, 'none escape. See! I did a little thing, a wrong thing, once. I jabbered, jabbered, stopped talking. None could understand. I am burnt, branded in the hand. He is great. He is good!'

'None escape,' said the grey creature in the corner.

'None escape,' said the Beast People, looking askance at one another.

'For everyone the want is bad,' said the grey Sayer of the Law. 'What you will want we do not know; we shall know. Some want to follow things that move, to watch and slink and wait and spring; to kill and bite, bite deep and rich, sucking the blood. It is bad. "Not to chase other Men; that is the Law. *Are we not Men?* Not to eat Flesh or Fish; that is the Law. *Are we not Men?*" '

'None escape,' said a dappled brute standing in the doorway.

'For everyone the want is bad,' said the grey Sayer of the Law. 'Some want to go tearing with teeth and hands into the roots of things, snuffing into the earth. It is bad.'

'None escape,' said the men in the door.

'Some go clawing trees; some go scratching at the graves of the dead; some go fighting with foreheads or feet or claws; some bite suddenly, none giving occasion; some love uncleanness.'

'None escape,' said the Ape-man, scratching his calf.

'None escape,' said the little pink sloth-creature.

'Punishment is sharp and sure. Therefore learn the Law. Say the words.'

And incontinently he began again the strange litany of the Law, and again I and all these creatures began singing and swaying. My head reeled with this jabbering and the close stench of the place; but I kept on, trusting to find presently some chance of a new development.

'Not to go on All-Fours; that is the Law. *Are we not Men?*'

We were making such a noise that I noticed nothing of a tumult outside, until someone, who I think was one of the two Swine Men I had seen, thrust his head over the little pink sloth-creature and shouted something excitedly, something that I did not catch. Incontinently those at the opening of the hut vanished; my Ape-man rushed out; the thing that had sat in the dark followed him (I only observed that it was big and clumsy, and covered with

silvery hair), and I was left alone. Then before I reached the aperture I heard the yelp of a staghound.

In another moment I was standing outside the hovel, my chair-rail in my hand, every muscle of me quivering. Before me were the clumsy backs of perhaps a score of these Beast People, their misshapen heads half hidden by their shoulder-blades. They were gesticulating excitedly. Other half-animal faces glared interrogation out of the hovels. Looking in the direction in which they faced, I saw coming through the haze under the trees beyond the end of the passage of dens the dark figure and awful white face of Moreau. He was holding the leaping staghound back, and close behind him came Montgomery revolver in hand.

For a moment I stood horror-struck. I turned and saw the passage behind me blocked by another heavy brute, with a huge grey face and twinkling little eyes, advancing towards me. I looked round and saw to the right of me and a half-dozen yards in front of me a narrow gap in the wall of rock through which a ray of light slanted into the shadows.

'Stop!' cried Moreau as I strode towards this, and then, 'Hold him!'

At that, first one face turned towards me and then others. Their bestial minds were happily slow. I dashed my shoulder into a clumsy monster who was turning to see what Moreau meant, and flung him forward into another. I felt his hands fly round, clutching at me and missing me. The little pink sloth-creature dashed at me, and I gashed down its ugly face with the nail in my stick and in another minute was scrambling up a steep side pathway, a kind of sloping chimney, out of the ravine. I heard a howl behind me, and cries of, 'Catch him!' 'Hold him!' and the grey-faced creature appeared behind me and jammed his huge bulk into the cleft. 'Go on! go on!' they howled. I clambered up the narrow cleft in the rock and came out upon the sulphur on the westward side of the village of the Beast Men.

That gap was altogether fortunate for me, for the narrow chimney, slanting obliquely upward, must have impeded the nearer pursuers. I ran over the white space and down a steep slope, through a scattered growth of trees, and came to a low-lying stretch of tall reeds, through which I pushed into a dark, thick undergrowth that was black and succulent underfoot. As I plunged into the reeds, my foremost pursuers emerged from the gap. I broke my way through this undergrowth for some minutes. The air behind me and about me was soon full of threatening cries. I heard the tumult of my pursuers in the gap up the slope, then the crashing of the reeds, and every now and then the crackling crash of a branch. Some of the creatures roared like excited beasts of prey. The staghound yelped to the left. I heard Moreau and Montgomery shouting in the same direction. I turned sharply to the right. It seemed to me even then that I heard Montgomery shouting for me to run for my life.

Presently the ground gave rich and oozy under my feet; but I was

desperate and went headlong into it, struggled through knee deep, and so came to a winding path among tall canes. The noise of my pursuers passed away to my left. In one place three strange, pink, hopping animals, about the size of cats, bolted before my footsteps. This pathway ran uphill, across another open space covered with white encrustation, and plunged into a cane-brake again. Then suddenly it turned parallel with the edge of a steep-walled gap, which came without warning, like the ha-ha of an English park – turned with an unexpected abruptness. I was still running with all my might, and I never saw this drop until I was flying headlong through the air.

I fell on my forearms and head, among thorns, and rose with a torn ear and bleeding face. I had fallen into a precipitous ravine, rocky and thorny, full of a hazy mist which drifted about me in wisps, and with a narrow streamlet, from which this mist came meandering, down the centre. I was astonished at this thin fog in the full blaze of daylight; but I had no time to stand wondering then. I turned to my right, downstream, hoping to come to the sea in that direction, and so have my way open to drown myself. It was only later I found that I had dropped my nailed stick in my fall.

Presently the ravine grew narrower for a space, and carelessly I stepped into the stream. I jumped out again pretty quickly, for the water was almost boiling. I noticed too there was a thin sulphurous scum drifting upon its coiling water. Almost immediately came a turn in the ravine, and the indistinct blue horizon. The nearer sea was flashing the sun from myriad facets. I saw my death before me; but I was hot and panting, with the warm blood oozing out on my face and running pleasantly through my veins. I felt more than a touch of exultation too, at having distanced my pursuers. It was not in me then to go out and drown myself yet. I stared back the way I had come.

I listened. Save for the hum of the gnats and the chirp of some small insects that hopped among the thorns, the air was absolutely still. Then came the yelp of a dog, very faint, and a chattering and gibbering, the snap of a whip, and voices. They grew louder, then fainter again. The noise receded up the stream and faded away. For a while the chase was over; but I knew now how much hope of help for me lay in the Beast People.

CHAPTER THIRTEEN

A Parley

I turned again and went on down towards the sea. I found the hot stream broadened out to a shallow, weedy sand, in which an abundance of crabs and long-bodied, many-legged creatures started from my footfall. I walked to the very edge of the salt water, and then I felt I was safe. I turned and

stared, arms akimbo, at the thick green behind me, into which the steamy ravine cut like a smoking gash. But, as I say, I was too full of excitement and (a true saying, though those who have never known danger may doubt it) too desperate to die.

Then it came into my head that there was one chance before me yet. While Moreau and Montgomery and their bestial rabble chased me through the island, might I not go round the beach until I came to their enclosure – make a flank march upon them, in fact, and then with a rock lugged out of their loosely-built wall, perhaps, smash in the lock of the smaller door and see what I could find (knife, pistol or what not) to fight them with when they returned? It was at any rate something to try.

So I turned to the westward and walked along by the water's edge. The setting sun flashed his blinding heat into my eyes. The slight Pacific tide was running in with a gentle ripple. Presently the shore fell away southward, and the sun came round upon my right hand. Then suddenly, far in front of me, I saw first one and then several figures emerging from the bushes – Moreau, with his grey staghound, then Montgomery and two others. At that I stopped.

They saw me, and began gesticulating and advancing. I stood watching them approach. The two Beast Men came running forward to cut me off from the undergrowth, inland. Montgomery came, running also, but straight towards me. Moreau followed more slowly with the dog.

At last I roused myself from my inaction, and turning seaward walked straight into the water. The water was very shallow at first. I was thirty yards out before the waves reached to my waist. Dimly I could see the intertidal creatures darting away from my feet.

'What are you doing, man?' cried Montgomery.

I turned, standing waist deep, and stared at them. Montgomery stood panting at the margin of the water. His face was bright-red with exertion, his long flaxen hair blown about his head, and his dropping nether lip showed his irregular teeth. Moreau was just coming up, his face pale and firm, and the dog at his hand barked at me. Both men had heavy whips. Farther up the beach stared the Beast Men.

'What am I doing? I am going to drown myself,' said I.

Montgomery and Moreau looked at each other. 'Why?' asked Moreau.

'Because that is better than being tortured by you.'

'I told you so,' said Montgomery, and Moreau said something in a low tone.

'What makes you think I shall torture you?' asked Moreau.

'What I saw,' I said. 'And those – yonder.'

'Hush!' said Moreau, and held up his hand.

'I will not,' said I. 'They were men: what are they now? I at least will not be like them.'

I looked past my interlocutors. Up the beach were M'ling, Mont-

gomery's attendant, and one of the white-swathed brutes from the boat. Farther up, in the shadow of the trees, I saw my little Ape-man, and behind him some other dim figures.

'Who are these creatures?' said I, pointing to them and raising my voice more and more that it might reach them. 'They were men, men like yourselves, whom you have infected with some bestial taint – men whom you have enslaved, and whom you still fear. 'You who listen,' I cried, pointing now to Moreau and shouting past him to the Beast Men, 'You who listen! Do you not see these men still fear you, go in dread of you? Why, then, do you fear them? You are many – '

'For God's sake,' cried Montgomery, 'stop that, Prendick!'

'Prendick!' cried Moreau.

They both shouted together, as if to drown my voice; and behind them lowered the staring faces of the Beast Men, wondering, their deformed hands hanging down, their shoulders hunched up. They seemed, as I fancied, to be trying to understand me, to remember, I thought, something of their human past.

I went on shouting, I scarcely remember what – that Moreau and Montgomery could be killed, that they were not to be feared: that was the burden of what I put into the heads of the Beast People. I saw the green-eyed man in the dark rags, who had met me on the evening of my arrival, come out from among the trees, and others followed him, to hear me better. At last, for want of breath, I paused.

'Listen to me for a moment,' said the steady voice of Moreau; 'and then say what you will.'

'Well?' said I.

He coughed, thought, then shouted: 'Latin, Prendick! bad Latin, schoolboy Latin; but try and understand. *Hi non sunt homines; sunt animalia qui nos habemus* – vivisected. A humanising process. I will explain. Come ashore.'

I laughed. 'A pretty story,' said I. 'They talk, build houses. They *were* men. It's likely I'll come ashore!'

'The water just beyond where you stand is deep – and full of sharks.'

'That's my way,' said I. 'Short and sharp. Presently.'

'Wait a minute.' He took something out of his pocket that flashed back the sun, and dropped the object at his feet. 'That's a loaded revolver,' said he. 'Montgomery here will do the same. Now we are going up the beach until you are satisfied the distance is safe. Then come and take the revolvers.'

'Not I! You have a third between you.'

'I want you to think over things, Prendick. In the first place, I never asked you to come upon this island. If we vivisected men, we should import men, not beasts. In the next, we had you drugged last night, had we wanted to work you any mischief; and in the next, now your first panic is over and you can think a little, is Montgomery here quite up to the character you give him? We have chased you for your good. Because this island is full of

inimical phenomena. Besides, why should we want to shoot you when you have just offered to drown yourself?'

'Why did you set – your people on to me when I was in the hut?'

'We felt sure of catching you, and bringing you out of danger. Afterwards we drew away from the scent, for your good.'

I mused. It seemed just possible. Then I remembered something again. 'But I saw,' said I, 'in the enclosure – '

'That was the puma.'

'Look here, Prendick,' said Montgomery, 'you're a silly ass! Come out of the water and take these revolvers, and talk. We can't do anything more than we could do now.'

I will confess that then, and indeed always, I distrusted and dreaded Moreau; but Montgomery was a man I felt I understood.

'Go up the beach,' said I, after thinking, and added, 'holding your hands up.'

'Can't do that,' said Montgomery, with an explanatory nod over his shoulder. 'Undignified.'

'Go up to the trees, then,' said I, 'as you please.'

'It's a damned silly ceremony,' said Montgomery.

Both turned and faced the six or seven grotesque creatures, who stood there in the sunlight, solid, casting shadows, moving, and yet so incredibly unreal. Montgomery cracked his whip at them, and forthwith they all turned and fled helter-skelter into the trees; and when Montgomery and Moreau were at a distance I judged sufficient, I waded ashore, and picked up and examined the revolvers. To satisfy myself against the subtlest trickery, I discharged one at a round lump of lava, and had the satisfaction of seeing the stone pulverised and the beach splashed with lead. Still I hesitated for a moment.

'I'll take the risk,' said I, at last; and with a revolver in each hand I walked up the beach towards them.

'That's better,' said Moreau, without affectation. 'As it is, you have wasted the best part of my day with your confounded imagination.' And with a touch of contempt which humiliated me, he and Montgomery turned and went on in silence before me.

The knot of Beast Men, still wondering, stood back among the trees. I passed them as serenely as possible. One started to follow me, but retreated again when Montgomery cracked his whip. The rest stood silent – watching. They may once have been animals; but I never before saw an animal trying to think.

CHAPTER FOURTEEN

Doctor Moreau Explains

'And now, Prendick, I will explain,' said Dr Moreau, so soon as we had eaten and drunk. 'I must confess that you are the most dictatorial guest I ever entertained. I warn you that this is the last I shall do to oblige you. The next thing you threaten to commit suicide about, I shan't do – even at some personal inconvenience.'

He sat in my deckchair, a cigar half consumed in his white, dexterous-looking fingers. The light of the swinging lamp fell on his white hair; he stared through the little window out at the starlight. I sat as far away from him as possible, the table between us and the revolvers to hand. Montgomery was not present. I did not care to be with the two of them in such a little room.

'You admit that the vivisected human being, as you called it, is, after all, only the puma?' said Moreau. He had made me visit that horror in the inner room, to assure myself of its inhumanity.

'It is the puma,' I said, 'still alive, but so cut and mutilated as I pray I may never see living flesh again. Of all vile – '

'Never mind that,' said Moreau; 'at least, spare me those youthful horrors. Montgomery used to be just the same. You admit that it is the puma. Now be quiet, while I reel off my physiological lecture to you.'

And forthwith, beginning in the tone of a man supremely bored, but presently warming a little, he explained his work to me. He was very simple and convincing. Now and then there was a touch of sarcasm in his voice. Presently I found myself hot with shame at our mutual positions.

The creatures I had seen were not men, had never been men. They were animals, humanised animals – triumphs of vivisection.

'You forget all that a skilled vivisector can do with living things,' said Moreau. 'For my own part, I'm puzzled why the things I have done here have not been done before. Small efforts, of course, have been made – amputation, tongue-cutting, excisions. Of course you know a squint may be induced or cured by surgery? Then in the case of excisions you have all kinds of secondary changes, pigmentary disturbances, modifications of the passions, alterations in the secretion of fatty tissue. I have no doubt you have heard of these things?'

'Of course,' said I. 'But these foul creatures of yours – '

'All in good time,' said he, waving his hand at me; 'I am only beginning. Those are trivial cases of alteration. Surgery can do better things than that. There is building up as well as breaking down and changing. You have heard, perhaps, of a common surgical operation resorted to in cases where

the nose has been destroyed: a flap of skin is cut from the forehead, turned down on the nose, and heals in the new position. This is a kind of grafting in a new position of part of an animal upon itself. Grafting of freshly obtained material from another animal is also possible – the case of teeth, for example. The grafting of skin and bone is done to facilitate healing: the surgeon places in the middle of the wound pieces of skin snipped from another animal, or fragments of bone from a victim freshly killed. Hunter's cock-spur – possibly you have heard of that – flourished on the bull's neck; and the rhinoceros rats of the Algerian zouaves are also to be thought of – monsters manufactured by transferring a slip from the tail of an ordinary rat to its snout, and allowing it to heal in that position.'

'Monsters manufactured!' said I. 'Then you mean to tell me – '

'Yes. These creatures you have seen are animals carven and wrought into new shapes. To that, to the study of the plasticity of living forms, my life has been devoted. I have studied for years, gaining in knowledge as I go. I see you look horrified, and yet I am telling you nothing new. It all lay in the surface of practical anatomy years ago, but no one had the temerity to touch it. It is not simply the outward form of an animal which I can change. The physiology, the chemical rhythm of the creature, may also be made to undergo an enduring modification – of which vaccination and other methods of inoculation with living or dead matter are examples that will, no doubt, be familiar to you. A similar operation is the transfusion of blood – with which subject, indeed, I began. These are all familiar cases. Less so, and probably far more extensive, were the operations of those mediaeval practitioners who made dwarfs and beggar-cripples, show-monsters – some vestiges of whose art still remain in the preliminary manipulation of the young mountebank or contortionist. Victor Hugo gives an account of them in *L'Homme qui Rit* . . . But perhaps my meaning grows plain now. You begin to see that it is a possible thing to transplant tissue from one part of an animal to another, or from one animal to another; to alter its chemical reactions and methods of growth; to modify the articulations of its limbs; and, indeed, to change it in its most intimate structure.

'And yet this extraordinary branch of knowledge has never been sought as an end, and systematically, by modern investigators until I took it up! Some of such things have been hit upon in the last resort of surgery; most of the kindred evidence that will recur to your mind has been demonstrated as it were by accident – by tyrants, by criminals, by the breeders of horses and dogs, by all kinds of untrained clumsy-handed men working for their own immediate ends. I was the first man to take up this question armed with antiseptic surgery, and with a really scientific knowledge of the laws of growth. Yet one would imagine it must have been practised in secret before. Such creatures as the Siamese Twins . . . And in the vaults of the Inquisition. No doubt their chief aim was artistic torture, but some at least of the inquisitors must have had a touch of scientific curiosity.'

'But,' said I, 'these things – these animals *talk*!'

He said that was so, and proceeded to point out that the possibility of vivisection does not stop at a mere physical metamorphosis. A pig may be educated. The mental structure is even less determinate than the bodily. In our growing science of hypnotism we find the promise of a possibility of superseding old inherent instincts by new suggestions, grafting upon or replacing the inherited fixed ideas. Very much indeed of what we call moral education, he said, is such an artificial modification and perversion of instinct; pugnacity is trained into courageous self-sacrifice, and suppressed sexuality into religious emotion. And the great difference between man and monkey is in the larynx, he continued, – in the incapacity to frame delicately different sound-symbols by which thought could be sustained. In this I failed to agree with him, but with a certain incivility he declined to notice my objection. He repeated that the thing was so, and continued his account of his work.

I asked him why he had taken the human form as a model. There seemed to me then, and there still seems to me now, a strange wickedness in that choice.

He confessed that he had chosen that form by chance. 'I might just as well have worked to form sheep into llamas and llamas into sheep. I suppose there is something in the human form that appeals to the artistic turn of mind more powerfully than any animal shape can. But I've not confined myself to man-making. Once or twice – ' He was silent, for a minute perhaps. 'These years! How they have slipped by! And here I have wasted a day saving your life, and am now wasting an hour explaining myself!'

'But,' said I, 'I still do not understand. Where is your justification for inflicting all this pain? The only thing that could excuse vivisection to me would be some application – '

'Precisely,' said he. 'But, you see, I am differently constituted. We are on different platforms. You are a materialist.'

'I am *not* a materialist,' I began hotly.

'In my view – in my view. For it is just this question of pain that parts us. So long as visible or audible pain turns you sick, so long as your own pains drive you, so long as pain underlies your propositions about sin, so long, I tell you, you are an animal, thinking a little less obscurely what an animal feels. This pain – '

I gave an impatient shrug at such sophistry.

'Oh, but it is such a little thing! A mind truly opened to what science has to teach must see that it is a little thing. It may be that save in this little planet, this speck of cosmic dust, invisible long before the nearest star could be attained – it may be, I say, that nowhere else does this thing called *pain* occur. But the laws we feel our way towards . . . Why, even on this earth, even among living things, what pain is there?'

As he spoke he drew a little penknife from his pocket, opened the smaller

blade, and moved his chair so that I could see his thigh. Then, choosing the place deliberately, he drove the blade into his leg and withdrew it.

'No doubt,' he said, 'you have seen that before. It does not hurt a pinprick. But what does it show? The capacity for pain is not needed in the muscle, and it is not placed there; it is but little needed in the skin, and only here and there over the thigh is a spot capable of feeling pain. Pain is simply our intrinsic medical adviser to warn us and stimulate us. Not all living flesh is painful; nor is all nerve, not even all sensory nerve. There's no taint of pain, real pain, in the sensations of the optic nerve. If you wound the optic nerve, you merely see flashes of light, just as disease of the auditory nerve merely means a humming in our ears. Plants do not feel pain, nor the lower animals; it's possible that such animals as the starfish and crayfish do not feel pain at all. Then with men, the more intelligent they become, the more intelligently they will see after their own welfare, and the less they will need the goad to keep them out of danger. I never yet heard of a useless thing that was not ground out of existence by evolution sooner or later. Did you? And pain gets needless.

'Then I am a religious man, Prendick, as every sane man must be. It may be, I fancy, that I have seen more of the ways of this world's Maker than you – for I have sought his laws, in *my* way, all my life, while you, I understand, have been collecting butterflies. And I tell you, pleasure and pain have nothing to do with heaven or hell. Pleasure and pain – bah! What is your theologian's ecstasy but Mahomet's houri in the dark? This store which men and women set on pleasure and pain, Prendick, is the mark of the beast upon them, the mark of the beast from which they came! Pain, pain and pleasure, they are for us only so long as we wriggle in the dust.

'You see, I went on with this research just the way it led me. That is the only way I ever heard of true research going. I asked a question, devised some method of obtaining an answer, and got a fresh question. Was this possible or that possible? You cannot imagine what this means to an investigator, what an intellectual passion grows upon him! You cannot imagine the strange, colourless delight of these intellectual desires! The thing before you is no longer an animal, a fellow-creature, but a problem! Sympathetic pain – all I know of it I remember as a thing I used to suffer from years ago. I wanted – it was the one thing I wanted – to find out the extreme limit of plasticity in a living shape.'

'But,' said I, 'the thing is an abomination –'

'To this day I have never troubled about the ethics of the matter,' he continued. 'The study of Nature makes a man at last as remorseless as Nature. I have gone on, not heeding anything but the question I was pursuing; and the material has – dripped into the huts yonder . . . It is nearly eleven years since we came here, I and Montgomery and six Kanakas. I remember the green stillness of the island and the empty ocean about us as though it was yesterday. The place seemed waiting for me.

'The stores were landed and the house was built. The Kanakas founded some huts near the ravine. I went to work here upon what I had brought with me. There were some disagreeable things happened at first. I began with a sheep, and killed it after a day and a half by a slip of the scalpel. I took another sheep, and made a thing of pain and fear and left it bound up to heal. It looked quite human to me when I had finished it; but when I went to it I was discontented with it. It remembered me, and was terrified beyond imagination; and it had no more than the wits of a sheep. The more I looked at it the clumsier it seemed, until at last I put the monster out of its misery. These animals without courage, these fear-haunted, pain-driven things, without a spark of pugnacious energy to face torment – they are no good for man-making.

'Then I took a gorilla I had; and upon that, working with infinite care and mastering difficulty after difficulty, I made my first man. All the week, night and day, I moulded him. With him it was chiefly the brain that needed moulding; much had to be added, much changed. I thought him a fair specimen of the negroid type when I had finished him, and he lay bandaged, bound, and motionless before me. It was only when his life was assured that I left him and came into this room again, and found Montgomery much as you are. He had heard some of the cries as the thing grew human – cries like those that disturbed *you* so. I didn't take him completely into my confidence at first. And the Kanakas, too, had realised something of it. They were scared out of their wits by the sight of me. I got Montgomery over to me – in a way; but I and he had the hardest job to prevent the Kanakas deserting. Finally they did; and so we lost the yacht. I spent many days educating the brute – altogether I had him for three or four months. I taught him the rudiments of English; gave him ideas of counting; even made the thing read the alphabet. But at that he was slow, though I've met with idiots slower. He began with a clean sheet, mentally; had no memories left in his mind of what he had been. When his scars were quite healed, and he was no longer anything but painful and stiff, and able to converse a little, I took him yonder and introduced him to the Kanakas as an interesting stowaway.

'They were horribly afraid of him at first, somehow – which offended me rather, for I was conceited about him; but his ways seemed so mild, and he was so abject, that after a time they received him and took his education in hand. He was quick to learn, very imitative and adaptive, and built himself a hovel rather better, it seemed to me, than their own shanties. There was one among the boys a bit of a missionary, and he taught the thing to read, or at least to pick out letters, and gave him some rudimentary ideas of morality; but it seems the beast's habits were not all that is desirable.

'I rested from work for some days after this, and was in a mind to write an account of the whole affair to wake up English physiology. Then I came upon the creature squatting up in a tree and gibbering at two of the Kanakas

who had been teasing him. I threatened him, told him the inhumanity of such a proceeding, aroused his sense of shame, and came home resolved to do better before I took my work back to England. I have been doing better. But somehow the things drift back again: the stubborn beast-flesh grows day by day back again. But I mean to do better things still. I mean to conquer that. This puma. . .

'But that's the story. All the Kanaka boys are dead now; one fell overboard from the launch, and one died of a wounded heel that he poisoned in some way with plant-juice. Three went away in the yacht, and I suppose and hope were drowned. The other one – was killed. Well, I have replaced them. Montgomery went on much as you are disposed to do at first, and then – '

'What became of the other one?' said I, sharply, 'the other Kanaka who was killed?'

'The fact is, after I had made a number of human creatures I made a thing – ' He hesitated.

'Yes,' said I.

'It was killed.'

'I don't understand,' said I; 'do you mean to say – '

'It killed the Kanaka – yes. It killed several other things that it caught. We chased it for a couple of days. It only got loose by accident. I never meant it to get away. It wasn't finished. It was purely an experiment. It was a limbless thing with a horrible face that writhed along the ground in a serpentine fashion. It was immensely strong, and in infuriating pain. It lurked in the woods for some days, until we hunted it; and then it wriggled into the northern part of the island, and we divided the party to close in upon it. Montgomery insisted upon coming with me. The man had a rifle; and when his body was found, one of the barrels was curved into the shape of an S and very nearly bitten through. Montgomery shot the thing. After that I stuck to the ideal of humanity – except for little things.'

He became silent. I sat in silence watching his face.

'So for twenty years altogether – counting nine years in England – I have been going on; and there is still something in everything I do that defeats me, makes me dissatisfied, challenges me to further effort. Sometimes I rise above my level, sometimes I fall below it; but always I fall short of the things I dream. The human shape I can get now, almost with ease, so that it is lithe and graceful, or thick and strong; but often there is trouble with the hands and the claws – painful things, that I dare not shape too freely. But it is in the subtle grafting and reshaping one must needs do to the brain that my trouble lies. The intelligence is often oddly low, with unaccountable blank ends, unexpected gaps. And least satisfactory of all is something that I cannot touch, somewhere – I cannot determine where – in the seat of the emotions. Cravings, instincts, desires that harm humanity, a strange hidden reservoir liable to burst forth suddenly and inundate the whole being of the

creature with anger, hate or fear. These creatures of mine seemed strange and uncanny to you as soon as you began to observe them; but to me, just after I make them, they seem to be indisputably human beings. It's afterwards, as I observe them, that the persuasion fades. First one animal trait, then another, creeps to the surface and stares out at me. But I will conquer yet! Each time I dip a living creature into the bath of burning pain, I say, "This time I will burn out all the animal; this time I will make a rational creature of my own!" After all, what is ten years? Men have been a hundred thousand in the making.'

He thought darkly. 'But I am drawing near the fastness. This puma of mine – '

After a silence, 'And they revert. As soon as my hand is taken from them the beast begins to creep back, begins to assert itself again.'

Another long silence.

'Then you take the things you make into those dens?' said I.

'They go. I turn them out when I begin to feel the beast in them, and presently they wander there. They all dread this house and me. There is a kind of travesty of humanity over there. Montgomery knows about it, for he interferes in their affairs. He has trained one or two of them to our service. He's ashamed of it, but I believe he half likes some of those beasts. It's his business, not mine. They only sicken me with a sense of failure. I take no interest in them. I fancy they follow in the lines the Kanaka missionary marked out, and have a kind of mockery of a rational life, poor beasts! There's something they call the Law. Sing hymns about "all thine". They build themselves their dens, gather fruit, and pull herbs – marry even. But I can see through it all, see into their very souls, and see there nothing but the souls of beasts, beasts that perish – anger and the lust to live and gratify themselves . . . Yet they're odd; complex, like everything else alive. There is a kind of upward striving in them, part vanity, part waste sexual emotion, part waste curiosity. It only mocks me. I have some hope of this puma. I have worked hard at her head and brain.

'And now,' said he, standing up after a long gap of silence, during which we had each pursued our own thoughts, 'what do you think? Are you in fear of me still?'

I looked at him, and saw but a white-faced, white-haired man, with calm eyes. Save for his serenity, the touch almost of beauty that resulted from his set tranquillity and his magnificent build, he might have passed muster among a hundred other comfortable old gentlemen. Then I shivered. By way of answer to his second question, I handed him a revolver with either hand.

'Keep them,' he said, and snatched at a yawn. He stood up, stared at me for a moment, and smiled. 'You have had two eventful days,' said he. 'I should advise some sleep. I'm glad it's all clear. Good-night.'

He thought me over for a moment, then went out by the inner door.

I immediately turned the key in the outer one. I sat down again; sat for a time in a kind of stagnant mood, so weary, emotionally, mentally and physically, that I could not think beyond the point at which he had left me. The black window stared at me like an eye. At last with an effort I put out the light and got into the hammock. Very soon I was asleep.

CHAPTER FIFTEEN

Concerning the Beast Folk

I woke early. Moreau's explanation stood before my mind, clear and definite, from the moment of my awakening. I got out of the hammock and went to the door to assure myself that the key was turned. Then I tried the window-bar, and found it firmly fixed. That these manlike creatures were in truth only bestial monsters, mere grotesque travesties of men, filled me with a vague uncertainty of their possibilities which was far worse than any definite fear.

A tapping came at the door, and I heard the glutinous accents of M'ling speaking. I pocketed one of the revolvers (keeping one hand upon it), and opened to him.

'Good-morning, sair,' he said, bringing in, in addition to the customary herb-breakfast, an ill-cooked rabbit. Montgomery followed him. His roving eye caught the position of my arm and he smiled askew.

The puma was resting to heal that day; but Moreau, who was singularly solitary in his habits, did not join us. I talked with Montgomery to clear my ideas of the way in which the Beast Folk lived. In particular, I was urgent to know how these inhuman monsters were kept from falling upon Moreau and Montgomery and from rending one another. He explained to me that the comparative safety of Moreau and himself was due to the limited mental scope of these monsters. In spite of their increased intelligence and the tendency of their animal instincts to reawaken, they had certain fixed ideas implanted by Moreau in their minds, which absolutely bounded their imaginations. They were really hypnotised; had been told that certain things were impossible, and that certain things were not to be done, and these prohibitions were woven into the texture of their minds beyond any possibility of disobedience or dispute.

Certain matters, however, in which old instinct was at war with Moreau's convenience, were in a less stable condition. A series of propositions called the Law (I had already heard them recited) battled in their minds with the deep-seated, ever-rebellious cravings of their animal natures. This Law they were ever repeating, I found, and ever breaking. Both Montgomery and Moreau displayed particular solicitude to keep them ignorant of the taste of blood; they feared the inevitable suggestions of that flavour. Montgomery

told me that the Law, especially among the feline Beast People, became oddly weakened about nightfall; that then the animal was at its strongest; that a spirit of adventure sprang up in them at the dusk, when they would dare things they never seemed to dream about by day. To that I owed my stalking by the Leopard-man, on the night of my arrival. But during these earlier days of my stay they broke the Law only furtively and after dark; in the daylight there was a general atmosphere of respect for its multifarious prohibitions.

And here perhaps I may give a few general facts about the island and the Beast People. The island, which was of irregular outline and lay low upon the wide sea, had a total area, I suppose, of seven or eight square miles.* It was volcanic in origin, and was now fringed on three sides by coral reefs; some fumaroles to the northward, and a hot spring, were the only vestiges of the forces that had long since originated it. Now and then a faint quiver of earthquake would be sensible, and sometimes the ascent of the spire of smoke would be rendered tumultuous by gusts of steam; but that was all. The population of the island, Montgomery informed me, now numbered rather more than sixty of these strange creations of Moreau's art, not counting the smaller monstrosities which lived in the undergrowth and were without human form. Altogether he had made nearly a hundred and twenty; but many had died, and others – like the writhing Footless Thing of which he had told me – had come by violent ends. In answer to my question, Montgomery said that they actually bore offspring, but that these generally died. When they lived, Moreau took them and stamped the human form upon them. There was no evidence of the inheritance of their acquired human characteristics. The females were less numerous than the males, and liable to much furtive persecution in spite of the monogamy the Law enjoined.

It would be impossible for me to describe these Beast People in detail; my eye has had no training in details, and unhappily I cannot sketch. Most striking, perhaps, in their general appearance was the disproportion between the legs of these creatures and the length of their bodies; and yet – so relative is our idea of grace – my eye became habituated to their forms, and at last I even fell in with their persuasion that my own long thighs were ungainly. Another point was the forward carriage of the head and the clumsy and inhuman curvature of the spine. Even the Ape-man lacked that inward sinuous curve of the back which makes the human figure so graceful. Most had their shoulders hunched clumsily, and their short forearms hung weakly at their sides. Few of them were conspicuously hairy, at least until the end of my time upon the island.

The next most obvious deformity was in their faces, almost all of which were prognathous, malformed about the ears, with large and protuberant noses, very furry or very bristly hair, and often strangely-coloured or strangely-placed eyes. None could laugh, though the Ape-man had a

chattering titter. Beyond these general characters their heads had little in common; each preserved the quality of its particular species: the human mark distorted but did not hide the leopard, the ox, or the sow, or other animal or animals, from which the creature had been moulded. The voices, too, varied exceedingly. The hands were always malformed; and though some surprised me by their unexpected human appearance, almost all were deficient in the number of the digits, clumsy about the fingernails and lacking any tactile sensibility.

The two most formidable animal men were my Leopard-man and a creature made of hyena and swine. Larger than these were the three bull-creatures who pulled in the boat. Then came the silvery-hairy man, who was also the Sayer of the Law, M'ling, and a satyr-like creature of ape and goat. There were three Swine-men and a Swine-woman, a mare-rhinoceros creature, and several other females whose sources I did not ascertain. There were several wolf-creatures, a bear-bull, and a St-Bernard-man. I have already described the Ape-man, and there was a particularly hateful (and evil-smelling) old woman made of vixen and bear, whom I hated from the beginning. She was said to be a passionate votary of the Law. Smaller creatures were certain dappled youths and my little sloth-creature. But enough of this catalogue.

At first I had a shivering horror of the brutes, felt all too keenly that they were still brutes; but insensibly I became a little habituated to the idea of them, and moreover I was affected by Montgomery's attitude towards them. He had been with them so long that he had come to regard them as almost normal human beings. His London days seemed a glorious, impossible past to him. Only once in a year or so did he go to Arica to deal with Moreau's agent, a trader in animals there. He hardly met the finest type of mankind in that seafaring village of Spanish mongrels. The men aboard-ship, he told me, seemed at first just as strange to him as the Beast Men seemed to me – unnaturally long in the leg, flat in the face, prominent in the forehead, suspicious, dangerous and cold-hearted. In fact, he did not like men: his heart had warmed to me, he thought, because he had saved my life. I fancied even then that he had a sneaking kindness for some of these metamorphosed brutes, a vicious sympathy with some of their ways, but that he attempted to veil it from me at first.

M'ling, the black-faced man, Montgomery's attendant, the first of the Beast Folk I had encountered, did not live with the others across the island, but in a small kennel at the back of the enclosure. The creature was scarcely so intelligent as the Ape-man, but far more docile, and the most human-looking of all the Beast Folk; and Montgomery had trained it to prepare food, and indeed to discharge all the trivial domestic offices that were required. It was a complex trophy of Moreau's horrible skill – a bear, tainted with dog and ox, and one of the most elaborately made of all his creatures. It treated Montgomery with a strange tenderness and devotion.

Sometimes he would notice it, pat it, call it half-mocking, half-jocular names, and so make it caper with extraordinary delight; sometimes he would ill-treat it, especially after he had been at the whisky, kicking it, beating it, pelting it with stones or lighted fuses. But whether he treated it well or ill, it loved nothing so much as to be near him.

I say I became habituated to the Beast People, that a thousand things which had seemed unnatural and repulsive speedily became natural and ordinary to me. I suppose everything in existence takes its colour from the average hue of our surroundings. Montgomery and Moreau were too peculiar and individual to keep my general impressions of humanity well defined. I would see one of the clumsy bovine-creatures who worked the launch treading heavily through the undergrowth, and find myself asking, trying hard to recall, how he differed from some really human yokel trudging home from his mechanical labours; or I would meet the Fox-bear-woman's vulpine, shifty face, strangely human in its speculative cunning, and even imagine I had met it before in some city byway.

Yet every now and then the beast would flash out upon me beyond doubt or denial. An ugly-looking man, a hunch-backed human savage to all appearance, squatting in the aperture of one of the dens, would stretch his arms and yawn, showing with startling suddenness scissor-edged incisors and sabre-like canines, keen and brilliant as knives. Or in some narrow pathway, glancing with a transitory daring into the eyes of some lithe, white-swathed female figure, I would suddenly see (with a spasmodic revulsion) that she had slit-like pupils, or glancing down note the curving nail with which she held her shapeless wrap about her. It is a curious thing, by the by, for which I am quite unable to account, that these weird creatures – the females, I mean – had in the earlier days of my stay an instinctive sense of their own repulsive clumsiness, and displayed in consequence a more than human regard for the decency and decorum of extensive costume.

CHAPTER SIXTEEN

How the Beast Folk Taste Blood

My inexperience as a writer betrays me, and I wander from the thread of my story.

After I had breakfasted with Montgomery, he took me across the island to see the fumarole and the source of the hot spring into whose scalding waters I had blundered on the previous day. Both of us carried whips and loaded revolvers. While going through a leafy jungle on our road thither, we heard a rabbit squealing. We stopped and listened, but we heard no more; and presently we went on our way, and the incident dropped out of

our minds. Montgomery called my attention to certain little pink animals with long hind-legs, that went leaping through the undergrowth. He told me they were creatures made of the offspring of the Beast People, that Moreau had invented. He had fancied they might serve for meat, but a rabbit-like habit of devouring their young had defeated this intention. I had already encountered some of these creatures – once during my moonlight flight from the Leopard-man and once during my pursuit by Moreau on the previous day. By chance, one hopping to avoid us leapt into the hole caused by the uprooting of a wind-blown tree; before it could extricate itself we managed to catch it. It spat like a cat, scratched and kicked vigorously with its hind-legs, and made an attempt to bite; but its teeth were too feeble to inflict more than a painless pinch. It seemed to me rather a pretty little creature; and as Montgomery stated that it never destroyed the turf by burrowing, and was very cleanly in its habits, I should imagine it might prove a convenient substitute for the common rabbit in gentlemen's parks.

We also saw on our way the trunk of a tree barked in long strips and splintered deeply. Montgomery called my attention to this. ' "Not to claw Bark of Trees, *that* is the Law," ' he said. 'Much some of them care for it!' It was after this, I think, that we met the Satyr and the Ape-man. The Satyr was a gleam of classical memory on the part of Moreau, his face ovine in expression, like the coarser Hebrew type, his voice a harsh bleat, his nether extremities satyric. He was gnawing the husk of a pod-like fruit as he passed us. Both of them saluted Montgomery.

'Hail,' said they, 'to the Other with the Whip!'

'There's a Third with a Whip now,' said Montgomery. 'So you'd better mind!'

'Was he not made?' said the Ape-man. 'He said – he said he was made.'

The Satyr-man looked curiously at me. 'The Third with the Whip, he that walks weeping into the sea, has a thin white face.'

'He has a thin long whip,' said Montgomery.

'Yesterday he bled and wept,' said the Satyr. 'You never bleed nor weep. The Master does not bleed or weep.'

'Ollendorffian beggar!' said Montgomery, 'you'll bleed and weep if you don't look out!'

'He has five fingers, he is a five-man like me,' said the Ape-man.

'Come along, Prendick,' said Montgomery, taking my arm; and I went on with him.

The Satyr and the Ape-man stood watching us and making other remarks to each other.

'He says nothing,' said the Satyr. 'Men have voices.'

'Yesterday he asked me of things to eat,' said the Ape-man. 'He did not know.'

Then they spoke inaudible things, and I heard the Satyr laughing.

It was on our way back that we came upon the dead rabbit. The red body of the wretched little beast was rent to pieces, many of the ribs stripped white, and the backbone indisputably gnawed.

At that Montgomery stopped. 'Good God!' said he, stooping down, and picking up some of the crushed vertebrae to examine them more closely. 'Good God!' he repeated, 'what can this mean?'

'Some carnivore of yours has remembered its old habits,' I said, after a pause. 'This backbone has been bitten through.'

He stood staring, with his face white and his lip pulled askew. 'I don't like this,' he said slowly.

'I saw something of the same kind,' said I, 'the first day I came here.'

'The devil you did! What was it?'

'A rabbit with its head twisted off.'

'The day you came here?'

'The day I came here. In the undergrowth at the back of the enclosure, when I went out in the evening. The head was completely wrung off.'

He gave a long, low whistle.

'And what is more, I have an idea which of your brutes did the thing. It's only a suspicion, you know. Before I came on the rabbit I saw one of your monsters drinking in the stream.'

'Sucking his drink?'

'Yes.'

' "Not to suck your Drink; *that* is the Law." Much the brutes care for the Law, eh? when Moreau's not about!'

'It was the brute who chased me.'

'Of course,' said Montgomery; 'it's just the way with carnivores. After a kill, they drink. It's the taste of blood, you know . . . What was the brute like?' he continued. 'Would you know him again?' He glanced about us, standing astride over the mess of dead rabbit, his eyes roving among the shadows and screens of greenery, the lurking-places and ambuscades of the forest that bounded us in. 'The taste of blood,' he said again.

He took out his revolver, examined the cartridges in it and replaced it. Then he began to pull at his dropping lip.

'I think I should know the brute again,' I said. 'I stunned him. He ought to have a handsome bruise on the forehead of him.'

'But then we have to *prove* that he killed the rabbit,' said Montgomery. 'I wish I'd never brought the things here.'

I should have gone on, but he stayed there thinking over the mangled rabbit in a puzzle-headed way. As it was, I went to such a distance that the rabbit's remains were hidden.

'Come on!' I said.

Presently he woke up and came towards me. 'You see,' he said, almost in a whisper, 'they are all supposed to have a fixed idea against eating anything that runs on land. If some brute has by any accident tasted blood . . . '

He went on some way in silence. 'I wonder what can have happened,' he said to himself. Then, after a pause again: 'I did a foolish thing the other day. That servant of mine – I showed him how to skin and cook a rabbit. It's odd . . . I saw him licking his hands . . . It never occurred to me – '

Then: 'We must put a stop to this. I must tell Moreau.'

He could think of nothing else on our homeward journey.

Moreau took the matter even more seriously than Montgomery, and I need scarcely say that I was affected by their evident consternation.

'We must make an example,' said Moreau. 'I've no doubt in my own mind that the Leopard-man was the sinner. But how can we prove it? I wish, Montgomery, you had kept your taste for meat in hand, and gone without these exciting novelties. We may find ourselves in a mess yet, through it.'

'I was a silly ass,' said Montgomery. 'But the thing's done now; and you said I might have them, you know.'

'We must see to the thing at once,' said Moreau. 'I suppose if anything should turn up, M'ling can take care of himself?'

'I'm not so sure of M'ling,' said Montgomery. 'I think I ought to know him.'

In the afternoon, Moreau, Montgomery, myself and M'ling went across the island to the huts in the ravine. We three were armed; M'ling carried the little hatchet he used in chopping firewood, and some coils of wire. Moreau had a huge cowherd's horn slung over his shoulder.

'You will see a gathering of the Beast People,' said Montgomery. 'It is a pretty sight!'

Moreau said not a word on the way, but the expression of his heavy, white-fringed face was grimly set.

We crossed the ravine down which smoked the stream of hot water, and followed the winding pathway through the cane-brakes until we reached a wide area covered over with a thick, powdery yellow substance which I believe was sulphur. Above the shoulder of a weedy bank the sea glittered. We came to a kind of shallow natural amphitheatre, and here the four of us halted. Then Moreau sounded the horn, and broke the sleeping stillness of the tropical afternoon. He must have had strong lungs. The hooting note rose and rose amidst its echoes to at last an ear-penetrating intensity.

'Ah!' said Moreau, letting the curved instrument fall to his side again.

Immediately there was a crashing through the yellow canes, and a sound of voices from the dense green jungle that marked the morass through which I had run on the previous day. Then at three or four points on the edge of the sulphurous area appeared the grotesque forms of the Beast People hurrying towards us. I could not help a creeping horror, as I perceived first one and then another trot out from the trees or reeds and come shambling along over the hot dust. But Moreau and Montgomery stood calmly enough; and, perforce, I stuck beside them.

First to arrive was the Satyr, strangely unreal for all that he cast a shadow

and tossed the dust with his hoofs. After him from the brake came a monstrous lout, a thing of horse and rhinoceros, chewing a straw as it came; then appeared the Swine-woman and two Wolf-women; then the Fox-bear witch, with her red eyes in her peaked red face, and then others – all hurrying eagerly. As they came forward they began to cringe towards Moreau and chant, quite regardless of one another, fragments of the latter half of the litany of the Law: 'His is the Hand that wounds; His is the Hand that heals,' and so forth. As soon as they had approached within a distance of perhaps thirty yards they halted, and bowing on knees and elbows began flinging the white dust upon their heads.

Imagine the scene if you can! We three blue-clad men, with our mis-shapen black-faced attendant, standing in a wide expanse of sunlit yellow dust under the blazing blue sky, and surrounded by this circle of crouching and gesticulating monstrosities, some almost human save in their subtle expression and gestures, some like cripples, some so strangely distorted as to resemble nothing but the denizens of our wildest dreams; and, beyond, the reedy lines of a cane-brake in one direction, a dense tangle of palm trees in the other, separating us from the ravine with the huts, and to the north the hazy horizon of the Pacific Ocean.

'Sixty-two, sixty-three,' counted Moreau. 'There are four more.'

'I do not see the Leopard-man,' said I.

Presently Moreau sounded the great horn again, and at the sound of it all the Beast People writhed and grovelled in the dust. Then, slinking out of the cane-brake, stooping near the ground and trying to join the dust-throwing circle behind Moreau's back, came the Leopard-man. The last of the Beast People to arrive was the little Ape-man. The earlier animals, hot and weary with their grovelling, shot vicious glances at him.

'Cease!' said Moreau, in his firm, loud voice; and the Beast People sat back upon their hams and rested from their worshipping.

'Where is the Sayer of the Law?' said Moreau, and the hairy-grey monster bowed his face in the dust.

'Say the words!' said Moreau.

Forthwith all in the kneeling assembly, swaying from side to side and dashing up the sulphur with their hands, – first the right hand and a puff of dust, and then the left, – began once more to chant their strange litany. When they reached, 'Not to eat Fish or Flesh, that is the Law,' Moreau held up his lank white hand.

'Stop!' he cried, and there fell absolute silence upon them all.

I think they all knew and dreaded what was coming. I looked round at their strange faces. When I saw their wincing attitudes and the furtive dread in their bright eyes, I wondered that I had ever believed them to be men.

'That Law has been broken!' said Moreau.

'None escape,' from the faceless creature with the silvery hair. 'None escape,' repeated the kneeling circle of Beast People.

'Who is he?' cried Moreau, and looked round at their faces, cracking his whip. I fancied the Hyena-swine looked dejected, so too did the Leopard-man. Moreau stopped, facing this creature, who cringed towards him with the memory and dread of infinite torment.

'Who is he?' repeated Moreau, in a voice of thunder.

'Evil is he who breaks the Law,' chanted the Sayer of the Law.

Moreau looked into the eyes of the Leopard-man, and seemed to be dragging the very soul out of the creature.

'Who breaks the Law – ' said Moreau, taking his eyes off his victim, and turning towards us. It seemed to me there was a touch of exultation in his voice.

'Goes back to the House of Pain,' they all clamoured; 'goes back to the House of Pain, O Master!'

'Back to the House of Pain, back to the House of Pain,' gabbled the Ape-man, as though the idea was sweet to him.

'Do you hear?' said Moreau, turning back to the criminal, 'my friend . . . Hello!'

For the Leopard-man, released from Moreau's eye, had risen straight from his knees, and now, with eyes aflame and his huge feline tusks flashing out from under his curling lips, leapt towards his tormentor. I am convinced that only the madness of unendurable fear could have prompted this attack. The whole circle of threescore monsters seemed to rise about us. I drew my revolver. The two figures collided. I saw Moreau reeling back from the Leopard-man's blow. There was a furious yelling and howling all about us. Everyone was moving rapidly. For a moment I thought it was a general revolt. The furious face of the Leopard-man flashed by mine, with M'ling close in pursuit. I saw the yellow eyes of the Hyena-swine blazing with excitement, his attitude as if he were half resolved to attack me. The Satyr, too, glared at me over the Hyena-swine's hunched shoulders. I heard the crack of Moreau's pistol, and saw the pink flash dart across the tumult. The whole crowd seemed to swing round in the direction of the glint of fire, and I too was swung round by the magnetism of the movement. In another second I was running, one of a tumultuous shouting crowd, in pursuit of the escaping Leopard-man.

That is all I can tell definitely. I saw the Leopard-man strike Moreau, and then everything spun about me until I was running headlong. M'ling was ahead, close in pursuit of the fugitive. Behind, their tongues already lolling out, ran the Wolf-women in great leaping strides. The Swine folk followed, squealing with excitement, and the two Bull-men in their swathings of white. Then came Moreau in a cluster of the Beast People, his wide-brimmed straw hat blown off, his revolver in hand, and his lank white hair streaming out. The Hyena-swine ran beside me, keeping pace with me and glancing furtively at me out of his feline eyes, and the others came pattering and shouting behind us.

The Leopard-man went bursting his way through the long canes, which sprang back as he passed, and rattled in M'ling's face. We others in the rear found a trampled path for us when we reached the brake. The chase lay through the brake for perhaps a quarter of a mile, and then plunged into a dense thicket, which retarded our movements exceedingly, though we went through it in a crowd together – fronds flicking into our faces, ropy creepers catching us under the chin or gripping our ankles, thorny plants hooking into and tearing cloth and flesh together.

'He has gone on all-fours through this,' panted Moreau, now just ahead of me.

'None escape,' said the Wolf-bear, laughing into my face with the exultation of hunting. We burst out again among rocks, and saw the quarry ahead running lightly on all-fours and snarling at us over his shoulder. At that the Wolf Folk howled with delight. The Thing was still clothed, and at a distance its face still seemed human; but the carriage of its four limbs was feline, and the furtive droop of its shoulder was distinctly that of a hunted animal. It leapt over some thorny yellow-flowering bushes and was hidden. M'ling was halfway across the space.

Most of us now had lost the first speed of the chase, and had fallen into a longer and steadier stride. I saw as we traversed the open that the pursuit was now spreading from a column into a line. The Hyena-swine still ran close to me, watching me as it ran, every now and then puckering its muzzle with a snarling laugh.

At the edge of the rocks the Leopard-man, realising that he was making for the projecting cape upon which he had stalked me on the night of my arrival, had doubled in the undergrowth; but Montgomery had seen the manoeuvre, and turned him again. So, panting, tumbling against rocks, torn by brambles, impeded by ferns and reeds, I helped to pursue the Leopard-man who had broken the Law, and the Hyena-swine ran, laughing savagely, by my side. I staggered on, my head reeling and my heart beating against my ribs, tired almost to death, and yet not daring to lose sight of the chase lest I should be left alone with this horrible companion. I staggered on in spite of infinite fatigue and the dense heat of the tropical afternoon.

At last the fury of the hunt slackened. We had pinned the wretched brute into a corner of the island. Moreau, whip in hand, marshalled us all into an irregular line, and we advanced now slowly, shouting to one another as we advanced and tightening the cordon about our victim. He lurked, noiseless and invisible, in the bushes through which I had run from him during that midnight pursuit.

'Steady!' cried Moreau, 'steady!' as the ends of the line crept round the tangle of undergrowth and hemmed the brute in.

' 'Ware a rush!' came the voice of Montgomery from beyond the thicket. I was on the slope above the bushes; Montgomery and Moreau beat

along the beach beneath. Slowly we pushed in among the fretted network of branches and leaves. The quarry was silent.

'Back to the House of Pain, the House of Pain, the House of Pain!' yelped the voice of the Ape-man, some twenty yards to the right.

When I heard that, I forgave the poor wretch all the fear he had inspired in me. I heard the twigs snap and the boughs swish aside before the heavy tread of the Horse-rhinoceros upon my right. Then suddenly, through a polygon of green, in the half darkness under the luxuriant growth, I saw the creature we were hunting. I halted. He was crouched together into the smallest possible compass, his luminous green eyes turned over his shoulder regarding me.

It may seem a strange contradiction in me – I cannot explain the fact – but now, seeing the creature there in a perfectly animal attitude, with the light gleaming in its eyes and its imperfectly human face distorted with terror, I realised again the fact of its humanity. In another moment other of its pursuers would see it, and it would be overpowered and captured, to experience once more the horrible tortures of the enclosure. Abruptly I slipped out my revolver, aimed between its terror-struck eyes, and fired. As I did so, the Hyena-swine saw the thing, and flung itself upon it with an eager cry, thrusting thirsty teeth into its neck. All about me the green masses of the thicket were swaying and cracking as the Beast People came rushing together. One face and then another appeared.

'Don't kill it, Prendick!' cried Moreau. 'Don't kill it!' and I saw him stooping as he pushed through the under fronds of the big ferns.

In another moment he had beaten off the Hyena-swine with the handle of his whip, and he and Montgomery were keeping away the excited carnivorous Beast People, and particularly M'ling, from the still quivering body. The hairy-grey thing came sniffing at the corpse under my arm. The other animals, in their animal ardour, jostled me to get a nearer view.

'Confound you, Prendick!' said Moreau. 'I wanted him.'

'I'm sorry,' said I, though I was not. 'It was the impulse of the moment.' I felt sick with exertion and excitement. Turning, I pushed my way out of the crowding Beast People and went on alone up the slope towards the higher part of the headland. Under the shouted directions of Moreau, I heard the three white-swathed Bull-men begin dragging the victim down towards the water.

It was easy now for me to be alone. The Beast People manifested a quite human curiosity about the dead body, and followed it in a thick knot, sniffing and growling at it as the Bull-men dragged it down the beach. I went to the headland and watched the Bull-men, black against the evening sky, as they carried the weighted dead body out to sea; and like a wave across my mind came the realisation of the unspeakable aimlessness of things upon the island. Upon the beach among the rocks beneath me were the Ape-man, the Hyena-swine and several other of the Beast People

standing about Montgomery and Moreau. They were all still intensely excited, and all overflowing with noisy expressions of their loyalty to the Law; yet I felt an absolute assurance in my own mind that the Hyena-swine was implicated in the rabbit-killing. A strange persuasion came upon me, that, save for the grossness of the line, the grotesqueness of the forms, I had here before me the whole balance of human life in miniature, the whole interplay of instinct, reason and fate in its simplest form. The Leopard-man had happened to go under: that was all the difference. Poor brute!

Poor brutes! I began to see the viler aspect of Moreau's cruelty. I had not thought before of the pain and trouble that came to these poor victims after they had passed from Moreau's hands. I had shivered only at the days of actual torment in the enclosure. But now that seemed to me the lesser part. Before, they had been beasts, their instincts fitly adapted to their surroundings, and happy as living things may be. Now they stumbled in the shackles of humanity, lived in a fear that never died, fretted by a law they could not understand; their mock-human existence, begun in an agony, was one long internal struggle, one long dread of Moreau – and for what? It was the wantonness of it that stirred me.

Had Moreau had any intelligible object, I could have sympathised at least a little with him. I am not so squeamish about pain as that. I could have forgiven him a little even had his motive been only hate. But he was so irresponsible, so utterly careless! His curiosity, his mad, aimless investigations, drove him on; and the Things were thrown out to live a year or so, to struggle and blunder and suffer, and at last to die painfully. They were wretched in themselves; the old animal hate moved them to trouble one another; the Law held them back from a brief hot struggle and a decisive end to their natural animosities.

In those days my fear of the Beast People went the way of my personal fear of Moreau. I fell indeed into a morbid state, deep and enduring, and alien to fear, which has left permanent scars upon my mind. I must confess that I lost faith in the sanity of the world when I saw it suffering the painful disorder of this island. A blind fate, a vast pitiless mechanism, seemed to cut and shape the fabric of existence, and I, Moreau (by his passion for research), Montgomery (by his passion for drink) and the Beast People with their instincts and mental restrictions were torn and crushed, ruthlessly, inevitably, amid the infinite complexity of its incessant wheels. But this condition did not come all at once: I think indeed that I anticipate a little in speaking of it now.

CHAPTER SEVENTEEN

A Catastrophe

Scarcely six weeks passed before I had lost every feeling but dislike and abhorrence for this infamous experiment of Moreau's. My one idea was to get away from these horrible caricatures of my Maker's image, back to the sweet and wholesome intercourse of men. My fellow-creatures, from whom I was thus separated, began to assume idyllic virtue and beauty in my memory. My first friendship with Montgomery did not increase. His long separation from humanity, his secret vice of drunkenness, his evident sympathy with the Beast People, tainted him for me. Several times I let him go alone among them. I avoided intercourse with them in every possible way. I spent an increasing proportion of my time upon the beach, looking for some liberating sail that never appeared – until one day there fell upon us an appalling disaster, which put an altogether different aspect upon my strange surroundings.

It was about seven or eight weeks after my landing – rather more, I think, though I had not troubled to keep account of the time – when this catastrophe occurred. It happened in the early morning – I should think about six. I had risen and breakfasted early, having been aroused by the noise of three Beast Men carrying wood into the enclosure.

After breakfast I went to the open gateway of the enclosure, and stood there smoking a cigarette and enjoying the freshness of the early morning. Moreau presently came round the corner of the enclosure and greeted me. He passed by me, and I heard him behind me unlock and enter his laboratory. So indurated was I at that time to the abomination of the place, that I heard without a touch of emotion the puma victim begin another day of torture. It met its persecutor with a shriek, almost exactly like that of an angry virago.

Then suddenly something happened. I do not know what it was to this day. I heard a short, sharp cry behind me, a fall, and turning saw an awful face rushing upon me – not human, not animal, but hellish, brown, seamed with red branching scars, red drops starting out upon it, and the lidless eyes ablaze. I threw up my arm to defend myself from the blow that flung me headlong with a broken forearm; and the great monster, swathed in lint and with red-stained bandages fluttering about it, leapt over me and passed. I rolled over and over down the beach, tried to sit up, and collapsed upon my broken arm. Then Moreau appeared, his massive white face all the more terrible for the blood that trickled from his forehead. He carried a revolver in one hand. He scarcely glanced at me, but rushed off at once in pursuit of the puma.

I tried the other arm and sat up. The muffled figure in front ran in great striding leaps along the beach, and Moreau followed her. She turned her head and saw him, then doubling abruptly made for the bushes. She gained upon him at every stride. I saw her plunge into them, and Moreau, running slantingly to intercept her, fired and missed as she disappeared. Then he too vanished in the green confusion. I stared after them, and then the pain in my arm flamed up, and with a groan I staggered to my feet. Montgomery appeared in the doorway, dressed, and with his revolver in his hand.

'Great God, Prendick!' he said, not noticing that I was hurt, 'that brute's loose! Tore the fetter out of the wall! Have you seen them?' Then sharply, seeing I gripped my arm, 'What's the matter?'

'I was standing in the doorway,' said I.

He came forward and took my arm. 'Blood on the sleeve,' said he, and rolled back the flannel. He pocketed his weapon, felt my arm about painfully, and led me inside. 'Your arm is broken,' he said, and then, 'Tell me exactly how it happened – what happened?'

I told him what I had seen; told him in broken sentences, with gasps of pain between them, and very dexterously and swiftly he bound my arm meanwhile. He slung it from my shoulder, stood back and looked at me.

'You'll do,' he said. 'And now?'

He thought. Then he went out and locked the gates of the enclosure. He was absent some time.

I was chiefly concerned about my arm. The incident seemed merely one more of many horrible things. I sat down in the deckchair, and I must admit swore heartily at the island. The first dull feeling of injury in my arm had already given way to a burning pain when Montgomery reappeared. His face was rather pale, and he showed more of his lower gums than ever.

'I can neither see nor hear anything of him,' he said. 'I've been thinking he may want my help.' He stared at me with his expressionless eyes. 'That was a strong brute,' he said. 'It simply wrenched its fetter out of the wall.' He went to the window, then to the door, and there turned to me. 'I shall go after him,' he said. 'There's another revolver I can leave with you. To tell you the truth, I feel anxious somehow.'

He obtained the weapon, and put it ready to my hand on the table; then went out, leaving a restless contagion in the air. I did not sit long after he left, but took the revolver in hand and went to the doorway.

The morning was as still as death. Not a whisper of wind was stirring; the sea was like polished glass, the sky empty, the beach desolate. In my half-excited, half-feverish state, this stillness of things oppressed me. I tried to whistle, and the tune died away. I swore again – the second time that morning. Then I went to the corner of the enclosure and stared inland at the green bush that had swallowed up Moreau and Montgomery. When would they return, and how? Then far away up the beach a little grey Beast Man appeared, ran down to the water's edge and began splashing about. I

strolled back to the doorway, then to the corner again, and so began pacing to and fro like a sentinel upon duty. Once I was arrested by the distant voice of Montgomery bawling, 'Coo-ee – Moreau!' My arm became less painful, but very hot. I got feverish and thirsty. My shadow grew shorter. I watched the distant figure until it went away again. Would Moreau and Montgomery never return? Three sea-birds began fighting for some stranded treasure.

Then from far away behind the enclosure I heard a pistol-shot. A long silence, and then came another. Then a yelling cry nearer, and another dismal gap of silence. My unfortunate imagination set to work to torment me. Then suddenly a shot close by. I went to the corner, startled, and saw Montgomery, his face scarlet, his hair disordered and the knee of his trousers torn. His face expressed profound consternation. Behind him slouched the Beast Man, M'ling, and round M'ling's jaws were some queer dark stains.

'Has he come?' said Montgomery.

'Moreau?' said I. 'No.'

'My God!' The man was panting, almost sobbing. 'Go back in,' he said, taking my arm. 'They're mad. They're all rushing about mad. What can have happened? I don't know. I'll tell you, when my breath comes. Where's some brandy?'

Montgomery limped before me into the room and sat down in the deckchair. M'ling flung himself down just outside the doorway and began panting like a dog. I got Montgomery some brandy-and-water. He sat staring in front of him at nothing, recovering his breath. After some minutes he began to tell me what had happened.

He had followed their track for some way. It was plain enough at first on account of the crushed and broken bushes, white rags torn from the puma's bandages, and occasional smears of blood on the leaves of the shrubs and undergrowth. He lost the track, however, on the stony ground beyond the stream where I had seen the Beast Man drinking, and went wandering aimlessly westward shouting Moreau's name. Then M'ling had come to him carrying a light hatchet. M'ling had seen nothing of the puma affair; had been felling wood and heard him calling. They went on shouting together. Two Beast Men came crouching and peering at them through the undergrowth, with gestures and a furtive carriage that alarmed Montgomery by their strangeness. He hailed them, and they fled guiltily. He stopped shouting after that, and after wandering some time farther in an undecided way, determined to visit the huts.

He found the ravine deserted.

Growing more alarmed every minute, he began to retrace his steps. Then it was he encountered the two Swine-men I had seen dancing on the night of my arrival; blood-stained they were about the mouth, and intensely excited. They came crashing through the ferns, and stopped with fierce

faces when they saw him. He cracked his whip in some trepidation, and forthwith they rushed at him. Never before had a Beast Man dared to do that. One he shot through the head; M'ling flung himself upon the other, and the two rolled grappling. M'ling got his brute under, with his teeth in its throat, and Montgomery shot that too as it struggled in M'ling's grip. He had some difficulty in inducing M'ling to come on with him.

Thence they had hurried back to me. On the way, M'ling had suddenly rushed into a thicket and driven out an undersized Ocelot-man, also blood-stained, and lame through a wound in the foot. This brute had run a little way and then turned savagely at bay, and Montgomery – with a certain wantonness, I thought – had shot him.

'What does it all mean?' said I.

He shook his head, and turned once more to the brandy.

CHAPTER EIGHTEEN

The Finding of Moreau

When I saw Montgomery swallow a third dose of brandy, I took it upon myself to interfere. He was already more than half fuddled. I told him that some serious thing must have happened to Moreau by this time, or he would have returned before this, and that it behoved us to ascertain what that catastrophe was. Montgomery raised some feeble objections, but at last agreed. We had some food, and then all three of us started.

It is possibly due to the tension of my mind at the time, but even now that start into the hot stillness of the tropical afternoon is a singularly vivid impression. M'ling went first, his shoulder hunched, his strange black head moving with quick starts as he peered first on this side of the way and then on that. He was unarmed; his axe he had dropped when he encountered the Swine-man. Teeth were *his* weapons, when it came to fighting. Montgomery followed with stumbling footsteps, his hands in his pockets, his face downcast; he was in a state of muddled sullenness with me on account of the brandy. My left arm was in a sling (it was lucky it was my left), and I carried my revolver in my right. Soon we traced a narrow path through the wild luxuriance of the island, going north-westward; and presently M'ling stopped, and became rigid with watchfulness. Montgomery almost staggered into him, and then stopped too. Then, listening intently, we heard coming through the trees the sound of voices and footsteps approaching us.

'He is dead,' said a deep, vibrating voice.

'He is not dead; he is not dead,' jabbered another.

'We saw, we saw,' said several voices.

'*Hel*-lo!' suddenly shouted Montgomery. 'Hello, there!'

'Confound you!' said I, and gripped my pistol.

There was a silence, then a crashing among the interlacing vegetation, first here, then there, and then half a dozen faces appeared, strange faces, lit by a strange light. M'ling made a growling noise in his throat. I recognised the Ape-man – I had indeed already identified his voice – and two of the white-swathed brown-featured creatures I had seen in Montgomery's boat. With these were the two dappled brutes and that grey, horribly crooked creature who said the Law, with grey hair streaming down its cheeks, heavy grey eyebrows, and grey locks pouring off from a central parting upon its sloping forehead – a heavy, faceless thing, with strange red eyes, looking at us curiously from amid the green.

For a space no one spoke. Then Montgomery hiccoughed, 'Who – said he was dead?'

The Monkey-man looked guiltily at the Hairy Grey Thing. 'He is dead,' said this monster. 'They saw.'

There was nothing threatening about this detachment, at any rate. They seemed awe-stricken and puzzled.

'Where is he?' said Montgomery.

'Beyond,' and the grey creature pointed.

'Is there a Law now?' asked the Monkey-man. 'Is it still to be this and that? Is he dead indeed?'

'Is there a Law?' repeated the man in white. 'Is there a Law, thou Other with the Whip?'

'He is dead,' said the Hairy Grey Thing. And they all stood watching us.

'Prendick,' said Montgomery, turning his dull eyes to me. 'He's dead, evidently.'

I had been standing behind him during this colloquy. I began to see how things lay with them. I suddenly stepped in front of Montgomery and lifted up my voice: – 'Children of the Law,' I said, 'he is *not* dead!' M'ling turned his sharp eyes on me. 'He has changed his shape; he has changed his body,' I went on. 'For a time you will not see him. He is – there,' I pointed upward, 'where he can watch you. You cannot see him, but he can see you. Fear the Law!'

I looked at them squarely. They flinched.

'He is great, he is good,' said the Ape-man, peering fearfully upward among the dense trees.

'And the other Thing?' I demanded.

'The Thing that bled, and ran screaming and sobbing – that is dead too,' said the Grey Thing, still regarding me.

'That's well,' grunted Montgomery.

'The Other with the Whip – ' began the Grey Thing.

'Well?' said I.

'Said he was dead.'

But Montgomery was still sober enough to understand my motive in

denying Moreau's death. 'He is not dead,' he said slowly, 'not dead at all. No more dead than I am.'

'Some,' said I, 'have broken the Law: they will die. Some have died. Show us now where his old body lies – the body he cast away because he had no more need of it.'

'It is this way, Man who walked in the Sea,' said the Grey Thing.

And with these six creatures guiding us, we went through the tumult of ferns and creepers and tree-stems towards the north-west. Then came a yelling, a crashing among the branches, and a little pink homunculus rushed by us shrieking. Immediately after appeared a feral monster in headlong pursuit, blood-bedabbled, who was among us almost before he could stop his career. The Grey Thing leapt aside. M'ling, with a snarl, flew at it, and was struck aside. Montgomery fired and missed, bowed his head, threw up his arm, and turned to run. I fired, and the Thing still came on; fired again, point-blank, into its ugly face. I saw its features vanish in a flash: its face was driven in. Yet it passed me, gripped Montgomery, and holding him, fell headlong beside him and pulled him sprawling upon itself in its death-agony.

I found myself alone with M'ling, the dead brute and the prostrate man. Montgomery raised himself slowly and stared in a muddled way at the shattered Beast Man beside him. It more than half sobered him. He scrambled to his feet. Then I saw the Grey Thing returning cautiously through the trees.

'See,' said I, pointing to the dead brute, 'is the Law not alive? This came of breaking the Law.'

He peered at the body. 'He sends the Fire that kills,' said he, in his deep voice, repeating part of the Ritual. The others gathered round and stared for a space.

At last we drew near the westward extremity of the island. We came upon the gnawed and mutilated body of the puma, its shoulder-bone smashed by a bullet, and perhaps twenty yards farther found at last what we sought. Moreau lay face downward in a trampled space in a cane-brake. One hand was almost severed at the wrist and his silvery hair was dabbled in blood. His head had been battered in by the fetters of the puma. The broken canes beneath him were smeared with blood. His revolver we could not find. Montgomery turned him over. Resting at intervals, and with the help of the seven Beast People (for he was a heavy man), we carried Moreau back to the enclosure. The night was darkling. Twice we heard unseen creatures howling and shrieking past our little band, and once the little pink sloth-creature appeared and stared at us, and vanished again. But we were not attacked again. At the gates of the enclosure our company of Beast People left us, M'ling going with the rest. We locked ourselves in, and then took Moreau's mangled body into the yard and laid it upon a pile of brushwood. Then we went into the laboratory and put an end to all we found living there.

CHAPTER NINETEEN

Montgomery's 'Bank Holiday'

When this was accomplished, and we had washed and eaten, Montgomery and I went into my little room and seriously discussed our position for the first time. It was then near midnight. He was almost sober, but greatly disturbed in his mind. He had been strangely under the influence of Moreau's personality: I do not think it had ever occurred to him that Moreau could die. This disaster was the sudden collapse of the habits that had become part of his nature in the ten or more monotonous years he had spent on the island. He talked vaguely, answered my questions crookedly, wandered into general questions.

'This silly ass of a world,' he said; 'what a muddle it all is! I haven't had any life. I wonder when it's going to begin. Sixteen years being bullied by nurses and schoolmasters at their own sweet will; five in London grinding hard at medicine, bad food, shabby lodgings, shabby clothes, shabby vice, a blunder – I didn't know any better – and hustled off to this beastly island. Ten years here! What's it all for, Prendick? Are we bubbles blown by a baby?'

It was hard to deal with such ravings. 'The thing we have to think of now,' said I, 'is how to get away from this island.'

'What's the good of getting away? I'm an outcast. Where am *I* to join on? It's all very well for *you*, Prendick. Poor old Moreau! We can't leave him here to have his bones picked. As it is . . . And besides, what will become of the decent part of the Beast Folk?'

'Well,' said I, 'that will do tomorrow. I've been thinking we might make that brushwood into a pyre and burn his body – and those other things. But what will happen with the Beast Folk?'

'*I* don't know. I suppose those that were made of beasts of prey will make silly asses of themselves sooner or later. We can't massacre the lot – can we? I suppose that's what *your* humanity would suggest? But they'll change. They are sure to change.'

He talked thus inconclusively until at last I felt my temper going.

'Damnation!' he exclaimed at some petulance of mine; 'can't you see I'm in a worse hole than you are?' And he got up, and went for the brandy. 'Drink!' he said returning. 'You logic-chopping, chalky-faced saint of an atheist, drink!'

'Not I,' said I, and sat grimly watching his face under the yellow paraffin flare as he drank himself into a garrulous misery.

I have a memory of infinite tedium. He wandered into a maudlin defence of the Beast People and of M'ling. M'ling, he said, was the only thing that had ever really cared for him. And suddenly an idea came to him.

'I'm damned!' said he, staggering to his feet and clutching the brandy bottle.

By some flash of intuition I knew what it was he intended. 'You don't give drink to that beast!' I said, rising and facing him.

'Beast!' said he. 'You're the beast. He takes his liquor like a Christian. Come out of the way, Prendick!'

'For God's sake,' said I.

'*Get* – out of the way!' he roared, and suddenly whipped out his revolver.

'Very well,' said I, and stood aside, half-minded to fall upon him as he put his hand upon the latch, but deterred by the thought of my useless arm. 'You've made a beast of yourself – to the beasts you may go.'

He flung the doorway open, and stood half facing me between the yellow lamplight and the pallid glare of the moon; his eye-sockets were blotches of black under his stubbly eyebrows.

'You're a solemn prig, Prendick, a silly ass! You're always fearing and fancying. We're on the edge of things. I'm bound to cut my throat tomorrow. I'm going to have a damned Bank Holiday tonight.' He turned and went out into the moonlight. 'M'ling!' he cried; 'M'ling, old friend!'

Three dim creatures in the silvery light came along the edge of the wan beach, one a white-wrapped creature, the other two blotches of blackness following it. They halted, staring. Then I saw M'ling's hunched shoulders as he came round the corner of the house.

'Drink!' cried Montgomery, 'drink, you brutes! Drink and be men! Damme, I'm the cleverest. Moreau forgot this; this is the last touch. Drink, I tell you!' And waving the bottle in his hand he started off at a kind of quick trot to the westward, M'ling ranging himself between him and the three dim creatures who followed.

I went to the doorway. They were already indistinct in the mist of the moonlight before Montgomery halted. I saw him administer a dose of the raw brandy to M'ling, and saw the five figures melt into one vague patch.

'Sing!' I heard Montgomery shout, 'sing all together, "Confound old Prendick!" ' That's right; now again, "Confound old Prendick!" '

The black group broke up into five separate figures, and wound slowly away from me along the band of shining beach. Each went howling at his own sweet will, yelping insults at me, or giving whatever other vent this new inspiration of brandy demanded. Presently I heard Montgomery's voice shouting, 'Right turn!' and they passed with their shouts and howls into the blackness of the landward trees. Slowly, very slowly, they receded into silence.

The peaceful splendour of the night healed again. The moon was now past the meridian and travelling down the west. It was at its full, and very bright riding through the empty blue sky. The shadow of the wall lay, a yard wide and of inky blackness, at my feet. The eastward sea was a feature-less grey, dark and mysterious; and between the sea and the shadow the grey

sands (of volcanic glass and crystals) flashed and shone like a beach of diamonds. Behind me the paraffin lamp flared hot and ruddy.

Then I shut the door, locked it, and went into the enclosure where Moreau lay beside his latest victims – the staghounds and the llama and some other wretched brutes – with his massive face calm even after his terrible death, and with the hard eyes open, staring at the dead white moon above. I sat down upon the edge of the sink, and with my eyes upon that ghastly pile of silvery light and ominous shadows began to turn over my plans. In the morning I would gather some provisions in the dinghy, and after setting fire to the pyre before me, push out into the desolation of the high sea once more. I felt that for Montgomery there was no help; that he was, in truth, half akin to these Beast Folk, unfitted for human kindred.

I do not know how long I sat there scheming. It must have been an hour or so. Then my planning was interrupted by the return of Montgomery to my neighbourhood. I heard a yelling from many throats, a tumult of exultant cries passing down towards the beach, whooping and howling and excited shrieks that seemed to come to a stop near the water's edge. The riot rose and fell; I heard heavy blows and the splintering smash of wood, but it did not trouble me then. A discordant chanting began.

My thoughts went back to my means of escape. I got up, brought the lamp, and went into a shed to look at some kegs I had seen there. Then I became interested in the contents of some biscuit-tins, and opened one. I saw something out of the tail of my eye – a red flicker – and turned sharply.

Behind me lay the yard, vividly black and white in the moonlight, and the pile of wood and faggots on which Moreau and his mutilated victims lay, one over another. They seemed to be gripping one another in one last revengeful grapple. His wounds gaped, black as night, and the blood that had dripped lay in black patches upon the sand. Then I saw, without understanding, the cause of my phantom, a ruddy glow that came and danced and went upon the wall opposite. I misinterpreted this, fancied it was a reflection of my flickering lamp, and turned again to the stores in the shed. I went on rummaging among them, as well as a one-armed man could, finding this convenient thing and that, and putting them aside for tomorrow's launch. My movements were slow, and the time passed quickly. Insensibly the daylight crept upon me.

The chanting died down, giving place to a clamour; then it began again, and suddenly broke into a tumult. I heard cries of, 'More! more!' a sound like quarrelling, and a sudden wild shriek. The quality of the sounds changed so greatly that it arrested my attention. I went out into the yard and listened. Then cutting like a knife across the confusion came the crack of a revolver.

I rushed at once through my room to the little doorway. As I did so I heard some of the packing-cases behind me go sliding down and smash

together with a clatter of glass on the floor of the shed. But I did not heed these. I flung the door open and looked out.

Up the beach by the boathouse a bonfire was burning, raining up sparks into the indistinctness of the dawn. Around this struggled a mass of black figures. I heard Montgomery call my name. I began to run at once towards this fire, revolver in hand. I saw the pink tongue of Montgomery's pistol lick out once, close to the ground. He was down. I shouted with all my strength and fired into the air. I heard someone cry, 'The Master!' The knotted black struggle broke into scattering units, the fire leapt and sank down. The crowd of Beast People fled in sudden panic before me, up the beach. In my excitement I fired at their retreating backs as they disappeared among the bushes. Then I turned to the black heaps upon the ground.

Montgomery lay on his back, with the Hairy Grey Thing sprawling across his body. The brute was dead, but still gripping Montgomery's throat with its curving claws. Near by lay M'ling on his face and quite still, his neck bitten open and the upper part of the smashed brandy-bottle in his hand. Two other figures lay near the fire – the one motionless, the other groaning fitfully, every now and then raising its head slowly, then dropping it again.

I caught hold of the Grey Thing and pulled it off Montgomery's body; its claws drew down the torn coat reluctantly as I dragged it away. Montgomery was dark in the face and scarcely breathing. I splashed sea-water on his face and pillowed his head on my rolled-up coat. M'ling was dead. The wounded creature by the fire – it was a Wolf-brute with a bearded grey face – lay, I found, with the fore part of its body upon the still glowing timber. The wretched thing was injured so dreadfully that in mercy I blew its brains out at once. The other brute was one of the Bull-men swathed in white. He too was dead. The rest of the Beast People had vanished from the beach.

I went to Montgomery again and knelt beside him, cursing my ignorance of medicine. The fire beside me had sunk down, and only charred beams of timber glowing at the central ends and mixed with a grey ash of brushwood remained. I wondered casually where Montgomery had got his wood. Then I saw that the dawn was upon us. The sky had grown brighter, the setting moon was becoming pale and opaque in the luminous blue of the day. The sky to the eastward was rimmed with red.

Suddenly I heard a thud and a hissing behind me, and, looking round, sprang to my feet with a cry of horror. Against the warm dawn great tumultuous masses of black smoke were boiling up out of the enclosure, and through their stormy darkness shot flickering threads of blood-red flame. Then the thatched roof caught. I saw the curving charge of the flames across the sloping straw. A spurt of fire jetted from the window of my room.

I knew at once what had happened. I remembered the crash I had heard. When I had rushed out to Montgomery's assistance, I had overturned the lamp.

The hopelessness of saving any of the contents of the enclosure stared me in the face. My mind came back to my plan of flight, and turning swiftly I looked to see where the two boats lay upon the beach. They were gone! Two axes lay upon the sands beside me; chips and splinters were scattered broadcast, and the ashes of the bonfire were blackening and smoking under the dawn. Montgomery had burnt the boats to revenge himself upon me and prevent our return to mankind!

A sudden convulsion of rage shook me. I was almost moved to batter his foolish head in as he lay there helpless at my feet. Then suddenly his hand moved, so feebly, so pitifully, that my wrath vanished. He groaned, and opened his eyes for a minute. I knelt down beside him and raised his head. He opened his eyes again, staring silently at the dawn, and then they met mine. The lids fell.

'Sorry,' he said presently, with an effort. He seemed trying to think. 'The last,' he murmured, 'the last of this silly universe. What a mess – '

I listened. His head fell helplessly to one side. I thought some drink might revive him; but there was neither drink nor vessel in which to bring drink at hand. He seemed suddenly heavier. My heart went cold. I bent down to his face, put my hand through the rent in his blouse. He was dead; and even as he died a line of white heat, the limb of the sun, rose eastward beyond the projection of the bay, splashing its radiance across the sky and turning the dark sea into a weltering tumult of dazzling light. It fell like a glory upon his death-shrunken face.

I let his head fall gently upon the rough pillow I had made for him, and stood up. Before me was the glittering desolation of the sea, the awful solitude upon which I had already suffered so much; behind me the island, hushed under the dawn, its Beast People silent and unseen. The enclosure, with all its provisions and ammunition, burnt noisily, with sudden gusts of flame, a fitful crackling, and now and then a crash. The heavy smoke drove up the beach away from me, rolling low over the distant tree-tops towards the huts in the ravine. Beside me were the charred vestiges of the boats and these four dead bodies.

Then out of the bushes came three Beast People, with hunched shoulders, protruding heads, misshapen hands awkwardly held, and inquisitive, un-friendly eyes, and advanced towards me with hesitating gestures.

CHAPTER TWENTY

Alone with the Beast Folk

I faced these people, facing my fate in them, single-handed now – literally single-handed, for I had a broken arm. In my pocket was a revolver with two empty chambers. Among the chips scattered about the beach lay the two axes that had been used to chop up the boats. The tide was creeping in behind me. There was nothing for it but courage. I looked squarely into the faces of the advancing monsters. They avoided my eyes, and their quivering nostrils investigated the bodies that lay beyond me on the beach. I took half a dozen steps, picked up the blood-stained whip that lay beneath the body of the Wolf-man, and cracked it. They stopped and stared at me.

'Salute!' said I. 'Bow down!'

They hesitated. One bent his knees. I repeated my command, with my heart in my mouth, and advanced upon them. One knelt, then the other two.

I turned and walked towards the dead bodies, keeping my face towards the three kneeling Beast Men, very much as an actor passing up the stage faces the audience.

'They broke the Law,' said I, putting my foot on the Sayer of the Law. 'They have been slain – even the Sayer of the Law; even the Other with the Whip. Great is the Law! Come and see.'

'None escape,' said one of them, advancing and peering.

'None escape,' said I. 'Therefore hear and do as I command.' They stood up, looking questioningly at one another.

'Stand there,' said I.

I picked up the hatchets and swung them by their heads from the sling of my arm; I turned Montgomery over, picked up his revolver still loaded in two chambers, and bending down to rummage, found half a dozen cartridges in his pocket.

'Take him,' said I, standing up again and pointing with the whip; 'take him, and carry him out and cast him into the sea.'

They came forward, evidently still afraid of Montgomery, but still more afraid of my cracking red whiplash; and after some fumbling and hesitation, some whip-cracking and shouting, they lifted him gingerly, carried him down to the beach, and went splashing into the dazzling welter of the sea.

'On!' said I, 'on! Carry him far.'

They went in up to their armpits and stood regarding me.

'Let go,' said I; and the body of Montgomery vanished with a splash. Something seemed to tighten across my chest.

'Good!' said I, with a break in my voice; and they came back, hurrying

and fearful, to the margin of the water, leaving long wakes of black in the silver. At the water's edge they stopped, turning and glaring into the sea as though they presently expected Montgomery to arise therefrom and exact vengeance.

'Now these,' said I, pointing to the other bodies.

They took care not to approach the place where they had thrown Montgomery into the water, but instead, carried the four dead Beast People slantingly along the beach for perhaps a hundred yards before they waded out and cast them away.

As I watched them disposing of the mangled remains of M'ling, I heard a light footfall behind me, and turning quickly saw the big Hyena-swine perhaps a dozen yards away. His head was bent down, his bright eyes were fixed upon me, his stumpy hands clenched and held close by his sides. He stopped in this crouching attitude when I turned, his eyes a little averted.

For a moment we stood eye to eye. I dropped the whip and snatched at the pistol in my pocket; for I meant to kill this brute, the most formidable of any left now upon the island, at the first excuse. It may seem treacherous, but so I was resolved. I was far more afraid of him than of any other two of the Beast Folk. His continued life was I knew a threat against mine.

I was perhaps a dozen seconds collecting myself. Then cried I, 'Salute! Bow down!'

His teeth flashed upon me in a snarl. 'Who are *you* that I should – '

Perhaps a little too spasmodically I drew my revolver, aimed quickly and fired. I heard him yelp, saw him run sideways and turn, knew I had missed, and clicked back the cock with my thumb for the next shot. But he was already running headlong, jumping from side to side, and I dared not risk another miss. Every now and then he looked back at me over his shoulder. He went slanting along the beach, and vanished beneath the driving masses of dense smoke that were still pouring out from the burning enclosure. For some time I stood staring after him. I turned to my three obedient Beast Folk again and signalled them to drop the body they still carried. Then I went back to the place by the fire where the bodies had fallen and kicked the sand until all the brown bloodstains were absorbed and hidden.

I dismissed my three serfs with a wave of the hand, and went up the beach into the thickets. I carried my pistol in my hand, my whip thrust with the hatchets in the sling of my arm. I was anxious to be alone, to think out the position in which I was now placed. A dreadful thing that I was only beginning to realise was that over all this island there was now no safe place where I could be alone and secure to rest or sleep. I had recovered strength amazingly since my landing, but I was still inclined to be nervous and to break down under any great stress. I felt that I ought to cross the island and establish myself with the Beast People, and make myself secure in their confidence. But my heart failed me. I went back to the beach, and turning eastward past the burning enclosure, made for a point where a shallow spit

of coral sand ran out towards the reef. Here I could sit down and think, my back to the sea and my face against any surprise. And there I sat, chin on knees, the sun beating down upon my head and unspeakable dread in my mind, plotting how I could live on against the hour of my rescue (if ever rescue came). I tried to review the whole situation as calmly as I could, but it was difficult to clear the thing of emotion.

I began turning over in my mind the reason of Montgomery's despair. 'They will change,' he said; 'they are sure to change.' And Moreau, what was it that Moreau had said? 'The stubborn beast-flesh grows day by day back again.' Then I came round to the Hyena-swine. I felt sure that if I did not kill that brute, he would kill me. The Sayer of the Law was dead: worse luck. They knew now that we of the Whips could be killed even as they themselves were killed. Were they peering at me already out of the green masses of ferns and palms over yonder, watching until I came within their spring? Were they plotting against me? What was the Hyena-swine telling them? My imagination was running away with me into a morass of insubstantial fears.

My thoughts were disturbed by a crying of sea-birds hurrying towards some black object that had been stranded by the waves on the beach near the enclosure. I knew what that object was, but I had not the heart to go back and drive them off. I began walking along the beach in the opposite direction, designing to come round the eastward corner of the island and so approach the ravine of the huts, without traversing the possible ambuscades of the thickets.

Perhaps half a mile along the beach I became aware of one of my three Beast Folk advancing out of the landward bushes towards me. I was now so nervous with my own imaginings that I immediately drew my revolver. Even the propitiatory gestures of the creature failed to disarm me. He hesitated as he approached.

'Go away!' cried I.

There was something very suggestive of a dog in the cringing attitude of the creature. It retreated a little way, very like a dog being sent home, and stopped, looking at me imploringly with canine brown eyes.

'Go away,' said I. 'Do not come near me.'

'May I not come near you?' it said.

'No; go away,' I insisted, and snapped my whip. Then putting my whip in my teeth, I stooped for a stone, and with that threat drove the creature away.

So in solitude I came round by the ravine of the Beast People, and hiding among the weeds and reeds that separated this crevice from the sea I watched such of them as appeared, trying to judge from their gestures and appearance how the death of Moreau and Montgomery and the destruction of the House of Pain had affected them. I know now the folly of my cowardice. Had I kept my courage up to the level of the dawn, had I not

allowed it to ebb away in solitary thought, I might have grasped the vacant sceptre of Moreau and ruled over the Beast People. As it was I lost the opportunity, and sank to the position of a mere leader among my fellows.

Towards noon certain of them came and squatted basking in the hot sand. The imperious voices of hunger and thirst prevailed over my dread. I came out of the bushes, and, revolver in hand, walked down towards these seated figures. One, a Wolf-woman, turned her head and stared at me, and then the others did the same. None attempted to rise or salute me. I felt too faint and weary to insist, and I let the moment pass.

'I want food,' said I, almost apologetically, and drawing near.

'There is food in the huts,' said an Ox-boar-man, drowsily, and looking away from me.

I passed them, and went down into the shadow and odours of the almost deserted ravine. In an empty hut I feasted on some specked and half-decayed fruit; and then after I had propped some branches and sticks about the opening, and placed myself with my face towards it and my hand upon my revolver, the exhaustion of the last thirty hours claimed its own, and I let myself fall into a light slumber, trusting that the flimsy barricade I had erected would cause sufficient noise in its removal to save me from surprise.

CHAPTER TWENTY-ONE

The Reversion of the Beast Folk

In this way I became one among the Beast People on the Island of Doctor Moreau. When I awoke, it was dark about me. My arm ached in its bandages. I sat up, wondering at first where I might be. I heard coarse voices talking outside. Then I saw that my barricade had gone, and that the opening of the hut stood clear. My revolver was still in my hand.

I heard something breathing, saw something crouched together close beside me. I held my breath, trying to see what it was. It began to move slowly, interminably. Then something soft and warm and moist passed across my hand. All my muscles contracted. I snatched my hand away. A cry of alarm began and was stifled in my throat. Then I just realised what had happened sufficiently to stay my fingers on the revolver.

'Who is that?' I said in a hoarse whisper, the revolver still pointed.

'I – Master.'

'Who are you?'

'They say there is no Master now. But I know, I know. I carried the bodies into the sea, O Walker in the Sea! the bodies of those you slew. I am your slave, Master.'

'Are you the one I met on the beach?' I asked.

'The same, Master.'

The Thing was evidently faithful enough, for it might have fallen upon me as I slept. 'It is well,' I said, extending my hand for another licking kiss. I began to realise what its presence meant, and the tide of my courage flowed. 'Where are the others?' I asked.

'They are mad; they are fools,' said the Dog-man. 'Even now they talk together beyond there. They say, "The Master is dead. The Other with the Whip is dead. That Other who walked in the Sea is as we are. We have no Master, no Whips, no House of Pain, any more. There is an end. We love the Law, and will keep it; but there is no Pain, no Master, no Whips for ever again." So they say. But I know, Master, I know.'

I felt in the darkness, and patted the Dog-man's head. 'It is well,' I said again.

'Presently you will slay them all,' said the Dog-man.

'Presently,' I answered, 'I will slay them all – after certain days and certain things have come to pass. Every one of them save those you spare, every one of them shall be slain.'

'What the Master wishes to kill, the Master kills,' said the Dog-man with a certain satisfaction in his voice.

'And that their sins may grow,' I said, 'let them live in their folly until their time is ripe. Let them not know that I am the Master.'

'The Master's will is sweet,' said the Dog-man, with the ready tact of his canine blood.

'But one has sinned,' said I. 'Him I will kill, whenever I may meet him. When I say to you, "*That is he*," see that you fall upon him. And now I will go to the men and women who are assembled together.'

For a moment the opening of the hut was blackened by the exit of the Dog-man. Then I followed and stood up almost in the exact spot where I had been when I had heard Moreau and his staghound pursuing me. But now it was night, and all the miasmatic ravine about me was black; and beyond, instead of a green, sunlit slope, I saw a red fire, before which hunched, grotesque figures moved to and fro. Farther were the thick trees, a bank of darkness, fringed above with the black lace of the upper branches. The moon was just riding up on the edge of the ravine, and like a bar across its face drove the spire of vapour that was forever streaming from the fumaroles of the island.

'Walk by me,' said I, nerving myself; and side by side we walked down the narrow way, taking little heed of the dim Things that peered at us out of the huts.

None about the fire attempted to salute me. Most of them disregarded me – ostentatiously. I looked round for the Hyena-swine, but he was not there. Altogether, perhaps twenty of the Beast Folk squatted, staring into the fire or talking to one another.

'He is dead, he is dead! the Master is dead!' said the voice of the Ape-man to the right of me. 'The House of Pain – there is no House of Pain!'

'He is not dead,' said I, in a loud voice. 'Even now he watches us!'

This startled them. Twenty pairs of eyes regarded me.

'The House of Pain is gone,' said I. 'It will come again. The Master you cannot see; yet even now he listens among you.'

'True, true!' said the Dog-man.

They were staggered at my assurance. An animal may be ferocious and cunning enough, but it takes a real man to tell a lie.

'The Man with the Bandaged Arm speaks a strange thing,' said one of the Beast Folk.

'I tell you it is so,' I said. 'The Master and the House of Pain will come again. Woe be to him who breaks the Law!'

They looked curiously at one another. With an affectation of indifference I began to chop idly at the ground in front of me with my hatchet. They looked, I noticed, at the deep cuts I made in the turf.

Then the Satyr raised a doubt. I answered him. Then one of the dappled things objected, and an animated discussion sprang up round the fire. Every moment I began to feel more convinced of my present security. I talked now without the catching in my breath, due to the intensity of my excitement, that had troubled me at first. In the course of about an hour I had really convinced several of the Beast Folk of the truth of my assertions, and talked most of the others into a dubious state. I kept a sharp eye for my enemy the Hyena-swine, but he never appeared. Every now and then a suspicious movement would startle me, but my confidence grew rapidly. Then, as the moon crept down from the zenith, one by one the listeners began to yawn (showing the oddest teeth in the light of the sinking fire), and first one and then another retired towards the dens in the ravine; and I, dreading the silence and darkness, went with them, knowing I was safer with several of them than with one alone.

In this manner began the longer part of my sojourn upon this Island of Doctor Moreau. But from that night until the end came, there was but one thing happened to tell save a series of innumerable small unpleasant details and the fretting of an incessant uneasiness. So that I prefer to make no chronicle for that gap of time, to tell only one cardinal incident of the ten months I spent as an intimate of these half-humanised brutes. There is much that sticks in my memory that I could write, things that I would cheerfully give my right hand to forget; but they do not help the telling of the story.

In the retrospect it is strange to remember how soon I fell in with these monsters' ways, and gained my confidence again. I had my quarrels with them of course, and could show some of their teethmarks still; but they soon gained a wholesome respect for my trick of throwing stones and for the bite of my hatchet. And my St-Bernard-man's loyalty was of infinite service to me. I found their simple scale of honour was based mainly on the capacity for inflicting trenchant wounds. Indeed, I may say – without

vanity, I hope – that I held something like pre-eminence among them. One or two, whom in a rare access of high spirits I had scarred rather badly, bore me a grudge; but it vented itself chiefly behind my back, and at a safe distance from my missiles, in grimaces.

The Hyena-swine avoided me, and I was always on the alert for him. My inseparable Dog-man hated and dreaded him intensely. I really believe that was at the root of the brute's attachment to me. It was soon evident to me that the former monster had tasted blood, and gone the way of the Leopard-man. He formed a lair somewhere in the forest, and became solitary. Once I tried to induce the Beast Folk to hunt him, but I lacked the authority to make them co-operate for one end. Again and again I tried to approach his den and come upon him unawares; but always he was too acute for me, and saw or winded me and got away. He too made every forest pathway dangerous to me and my ally with his lurking ambuscades. The Dog-man scarcely dared to leave my side.

In the first month or so the Beast Folk, compared with their latter condition, were human enough, and for one or two besides my canine friend I even conceived a friendly tolerance. The little pink sloth-creature displayed an odd affection for me, and took to following me about. The Monkey-man bored me, however; he assumed, on the strength of his five digits, that he was my equal, and was forever jabbering at me – jabbering the most arrant nonsense. One thing about him entertained me a little: he had a fantastic trick of coining new words. He had an idea, I believe, that to gabble about names that meant nothing was the proper use of speech. He called it 'Big Thinks' to distinguish it from 'Little Thinks', the sane everyday interests of life. If ever I made a remark he did not understand, he would praise it very much, ask me to say it again, learn it by heart, and go off repeating it, with a word wrong here or there, to all the milder of the Beast People. He thought nothing of what was plain and comprehensible. I invented some very curious 'Big Thinks' for his especial use. I think now that he was the silliest creature I ever met; he had developed in the most wonderful way the distinctive silliness of man without losing one jot of the natural folly of a monkey.

This, I say, was in the earlier weeks of my solitude among these brutes. During that time they respected the usage established by the Law, and behaved with general decorum. Once I found another rabbit torn to pieces – by the Hyena-swine, I am assured – but that was all. It was about May when I first distinctly perceived a growing difference in their speech and carriage, a growing coarseness of articulation, a growing disinclination to talk. My Monkey-man's jabber multiplied in volume but grew less and less comprehensible, more and more simian. Some of the others seemed altogether slipping their hold upon speech, though they still understood what I said to them at that time. (Can you imagine language, once clear-cut and exact, softening and guttering, losing shape and import, becoming

mere limps of sound again?) And they walked erect with an increasing difficulty. Though they evidently felt ashamed of themselves, every now and then I would come upon one or another running on toes and fingertips, and quite unable to recover the vertical attitude. They held things more clumsily; drinking by suction, feeding by gnawing, grew commoner every day. I realised more keenly than ever what Moreau had told me about the 'stubborn beast-flesh'. They were reverting, and reverting very rapidly.

Some of them – the pioneers in this, I noticed with some surprise, were all females – began to disregard the injunction of decency, deliberately for the most part. Others even attempted public outrages upon the institution of monogamy. The tradition of the Law was clearly losing its force. I cannot pursue this disagreeable subject.

My Dog-man imperceptibly slipped back to the dog again; day by day he became dumb, quadrupedal, hairy. I scarcely noticed the transition from the companion on my right hand to the lurching dog at my side.

As the carelessness and disorganisation increased from day to day, the lane of dwelling places, at no time very sweet, became so loathsome that I left it, and going across the island made myself a hovel of boughs amid the black ruins of Moreau's enclosure. Some memory of pain, I found, still made that place the safest from the Beast Folk.

It would be impossible to detail every step of the lapsing of these monsters – to tell how, day by day, the human semblance left them; how they gave up bandagings and wrappings, abandoned at last every stitch of clothing; how the hair began to spread over the exposed limbs; how their foreheads fell away and their faces projected; how the quasi-human intimacy I had permitted myself with some of them in the first month of my loneliness became a shuddering horror to recall.

The change was slow and inevitable. For them and for me it came without any definite shock. I still went among them in safety, because no jolt in the downward glide had released the increasing charge of explosive animalism that ousted the human day by day. But I began to fear that soon now that shock must come. My St-Bernard-brute followed me to the enclosure every night, and his vigilance enabled me to sleep at times in something like peace. The little pink sloth-thing became shy and left me, to crawl back to its natural life once more among the tree-branches. We were in just the state of equilibrium that would remain in one of those 'Happy Family' cages which animal-tamers exhibit, if the tamer were to leave it for ever.

Of course these creatures did not decline into such beasts as the reader has seen in zoological gardens – into ordinary bears, wolves, tigers, oxen, swine and apes. There was still something strange about each; in each Moreau had blended this animal with that. One perhaps was ursine chiefly, another feline chiefly, another bovine chiefly; but each was tainted with other creatures – a kind of generalised animalism appearing through the

specific dispositions. And the dwindling shreds of the humanity still startled me every now and then – a momentary recrudescence of speech perhaps, an unexpected dexterity of the forefeet, a pitiful attempt to walk erect.

I too must have undergone strange changes. My clothes hung about me as yellow rags, through whose rents showed the tanned skin. My hair grew long, and became matted together. I am told that even now my eyes have a strange brightness, a swift alertness of movement.

At first I spent the daylight hours on the southward beach watching for a ship, hoping and praying for a ship. I counted on the *Ipecacuanha* returning as the year wore on; but she never came. Five times I saw sails, and thrice smoke; but nothing ever touched the island. I always had a bonfire ready, but no doubt the volcanic reputation of the island was taken to account for that.

It was only about September or October that I began to think of making a raft. By that time my arm had healed, and both my hands were at my service again. At first, I found my helplessness appalling. I had never done any carpentry or suchlike work in my life, and I spent day after day in experimental chopping and binding among the trees. I had no ropes, and could hit on nothing wherewith to make ropes; none of the abundant creepers seemed limber or strong enough, and with all my litter of scientific education I could not devise any way of making them so. I spent more than a fortnight grubbing among the black ruins of the enclosure and on the beach where the boats had been burnt, looking for nails and other stray pieces of metal that might prove of service. Now and then some Beast-creature would watch me, and go leaping off when I called to it. There came a season of thunderstorms and heavy rain, which greatly retarded my work; but at last the raft was completed.

I was delighted with it. But with a certain lack of practical sense which has always been my bane, I had made it a mile or more from the sea; and before I had dragged it down to the beach the thing had fallen to pieces. Perhaps it is as well that I was saved from launching it; but at the time my misery at my failure was so acute that for some days I simply moped on the beach, and stared at the water and thought of death.

I did not, however, mean to die, and an incident occurred that warned me unmistakably of the folly of letting the days pass so – for each fresh day was fraught with increasing danger from the Beast People.

I was lying in the shade of the enclosure wall, staring out to sea, when I was startled by something cold touching the skin of my heel, and starting round found the little pink sloth-creature blinking into my face. He had long since lost speech and active movement, and the lank hair of the little brute grew thicker every day and his stumpy claws more askew. He made a moaning noise when he saw he had attracted my attention, went a little way towards the bushes and looked back at me.

At first I did not understand, but presently it occurred to me that he

wished me to follow him; and this I did at last – slowly, for the day was hot. When we reached the trees he clambered into them, for he could travel better among their swinging creepers than on the ground. And suddenly in a trampled space I came upon a ghastly group. My St-Bernard-creature lay on the ground, dead; and near his body crouched the Hyena-swine, gripping the quivering flesh with its misshapen claws, gnawing at it, and snarling with delight. As I approached, the monster lifted its glaring eyes to mine, its lips went trembling back from its red-stained teeth, and it growled menacingly. It was not afraid and not ashamed; the last vestige of the human taint had vanished. I advanced a step farther, stopped, and pulled out my revolver. At last I had him face to face.

The brute made no sign of retreat; but its ears went back, its hair bristled, and its body crouched together. I aimed between the eyes and fired. As I did so, the Thing rose straight at me in a leap, and I was knocked over like a ninepin. It clutched at me with its crippled hand, and struck me in the face. Its spring carried it over me. I fell under the hind part of its body; but luckily I had hit as I meant, and it had died even as it leapt. I crawled out from under its unclean weight and stood up trembling, staring at its quivering body. That danger at least was over; but this, I knew, was only the first of the series of relapses that must come.

I burnt both of the bodies on a pyre of brushwood; but after that I saw that unless I left the island my death was only a question of time. The Beast People by that time had, with one or two exceptions, left the ravine and made themselves lairs according to their taste among the thickets of the island. Few prowled by day, most of them slept, and the island might have seemed deserted to a newcomer; but at night the air was hideous with their calls and howling. I had half a mind to make a massacre of them; to build traps, or fight them with my knife. Had I possessed sufficient cartridges, I should not have hesitated to begin the killing. There could now be scarcely a score left of the dangerous carnivores; the braver of these were already dead. After the death of this poor dog of mine, my last friend, I too adopted to some extent the practice of slumbering in the daytime in order to be on my guard at night. I rebuilt my den in the walls of the enclosure, with such a narrow opening that anything attempting to enter must necessarily make a considerable noise. The creatures had lost the art of fire, too, and recovered their fear of it. I turned once more, almost passionately now, to hammering together stakes and branches to form a raft for my escape.

I found a thousand difficulties. I am an extremely unhandy man (my schooling was over before the days of Slöjd); but most of the requirements of a raft I met at last in some clumsy circuitous way or other, and this time I took care of the strength. The only insurmountable obstacle was that I had no vessel to contain the water I should need if I floated forth upon these untravelled seas. I would have even tried pottery, but the island contained no clay. I used to go moping about the island trying with all my might to

solve this one last difficulty. Sometimes I would give way to wild outbursts of rage, and hack and splinter some unlucky tree in my intolerable vexation. But I could think of nothing.

And then came a day, a wonderful day, which I spent in ecstasy. I saw a sail to the southwest, a small sail like that of a little schooner; and forthwith I lit a great pile of brushwood, and stood by it in the heat of it, and the heat of the midday sun, watching. All day I watched that sail, eating or drinking nothing, so that my head reeled; and the Beasts came and glared at me, and seemed to wonder, and went away. It was still distant when night came and swallowed it up; and all night I toiled to keep my blaze bright and high, and the eyes of the Beasts shone out of the darkness, marvelling. In the dawn the sail was nearer, and I saw it was the dirty lug-sail of a small boat. But it sailed strangely. My eyes were weary with watching, and I peered and could not believe them. Two men were in the boat, sitting low down – one by the bows, the other at the rudder. The head was not kept to the wind; it yawed and fell away.

As the day grew brighter, I began waving the last rag of my jacket to them; but they did not notice me, and sat still, facing each other. I went to the lowest point of the low headland and gesticulated and shouted. There was no response, and the boat kept on her aimless course, making slowly, very slowly, for the bay. Suddenly a great white bird flew up out of the boat, and neither of the men stirred nor noticed it; it circled round, and then came sweeping overhead with its strong wings outspread.

Then I stopped shouting, and sat down on the headland and rested my chin on my hands and stared. Slowly, slowly, the boat drove past towards the west. I would have swum out to it, but something – a cold, vague fear – kept me back. In the afternoon the tide stranded the boat, and left it a hundred yards or so to the westward of the ruins of the enclosure. The men in it were dead, had been dead so long that they fell to pieces when I tilted the boat on its side and dragged them out. One had a shock of red hair, like the captain of the *Ipecacuanha*, and a dirty white cap lay in the bottom of the boat.

As I stood beside the boat, three of the Beasts came slinking out of the bushes and sniffing towards me. One of my spasms of disgust came upon me. I thrust the little boat down the beach and clambered on board her. Two of the brutes were Wolf-beasts, and came forward with quivering nostrils and glittering eyes; the third was the horrible nondescript of bear and bull. When I saw them approaching those wretched remains, heard them snarling at one another and caught the gleam of their teeth, a frantic horror succeeded my repulsion. I turned my back upon them, struck the lug and began paddling out to sea. I could not bring myself to look behind me.

I lay, however, between the reef and the island that night, and the next morning went round to the stream and filled the empty keg aboard with water. Then, with such patience as I could command, I collected a quantity

of fruit, and waylaid and killed two rabbits with my last three cartridges. While I was doing this I left the boat moored to an inward projection of the reef, for fear of the Beast People.

CHAPTER TWENTY-TWO

The Man Alone

In the evening I started, and drove out to sea before a gentle wind from the southwest, slowly, steadily; and the island grew smaller and smaller, and the lank spire of smoke dwindled to a finer and finer line against the hot sunset. The ocean rose up around me, hiding that low, dark patch from my eyes. The daylight, the trailing glory of the sun, went streaming out of the sky, was drawn aside like some luminous curtain, and at last I looked into the blue gulf of immensity which the sunshine hides, and saw the floating hosts of the stars. The sea was silent, the sky was silent. I was alone with the night and silence.

So I drifted for three days, eating and drinking sparingly, and meditating upon all that had happened to me, not desiring very greatly then to see men again. One unclean rag was about me, my hair a black tangle: no doubt my discoverers thought me a madman.

It is strange, but I felt no desire to return to mankind. I was only glad to be quit of the foulness of the Beast People. And on the third day I was picked up by a brig from Apia to San Francisco. Neither the captain nor the mate would believe my story, judging that solitude and danger had made me mad; and fearing their opinion might be that of others, I refrained from telling my adventure further, and professed to recall nothing that had happened to me between the loss of the *Lady Vain* and the time when I was picked up again – the space of a year.

I had to act with the utmost circumspection to save myself from the suspicion of insanity. My memory of the Law, of the two dead sailors, of the ambuscades of the darkness, of the body in the cane-brake, haunted me; and, unnatural as it seems, with my return to mankind came, instead of that confidence and sympathy I had expected, a strange enhancement of the uncertainty and dread I had experienced during my stay upon the island. No one would believe me; I was almost as queer to men as I had been to the Beast People. I may have caught something of the natural wildness of my companions. They say that terror is a disease, and anyhow I can witness that for several years now a restless fear has dwelt in my mind – such a restless fear as a half-tamed lion cub may feel.

My trouble took the strangest form. I could not persuade myself that the men and women I met were not also another, still passably human, Beast People, animals half wrought into the outward image of human souls, and

that they would presently begin to revert – to show first this bestial mark and then that. But I have confided my case to a strangely able man – a man who had known Moreau, and seemed half to credit my story; a mental specialist – and he has helped me mightily, though I do not expect that the terror of that island will ever altogether leave me. At most times it lies far in the back of my mind, a mere distant cloud, a memory and a faint distrust; but there are times when the little cloud spreads until it obscures the whole sky. Then I look about me at my fellow men; and I go in fear. I see faces keen and bright; others dull or dangerous; others unsteady, insincere – none that have the calm authority of a reasonable soul. I feel as though the animal was surging up through them; that presently the degradation of the Islanders will be played over again on a larger scale. I know this is an illusion; that these seeming men and women about me are indeed men and women, men and women for ever, perfectly reasonable creatures, full of human desires and tender solicitude, emancipated from instinct and the slaves of no fantastic Law – beings altogether different from the Beast Folk. Yet I shrink from them, from their curious glances, their enquiries and assistance, and long to be away from them and alone. For that reason I live near the broad free downland, and can escape thither when this shadow is over my soul; and very sweet is the empty downland then, under the windswept sky.

When I lived in London the horror was well-nigh insupportable. I could not get away from men: their voices came through windows; locked doors were flimsy safeguards. I would go out into the streets to fight with my delusion, and prowling women would mew after me; furtive, craving men glance jealously at me; weary, pale workers go coughing by me with tired eyes and eager paces, like wounded deer dripping blood; old people, bent and dull, pass murmuring to themselves; and, all unheeding, a ragged tail of gibing children. Then I would turn aside into some chapel – and even there, such was my disturbance, it seemed that the preacher gibbered 'Big Thinks', even as the Ape-man had done; or into some library, and there the intent faces over the books seemed but patient creatures waiting for prey. Particularly nauseous were the blank, expressionless faces of people in trains and omnibuses; they seemed no more my fellow-creatures than dead bodies would be, so that I did not dare to travel unless I was assured of being alone. And even it seemed that I too was not a reasonable creature, but only an animal tormented with some strange disorder in its brain which sent it to wander alone, like a sheep stricken with gid.

This is a mood, however, that comes to me now, I thank God, more rarely. I have withdrawn myself from the confusion of cities and multitudes, and spend my days surrounded by wise book – bright windows in this life of ours, lit by the shining souls of men. I see few strangers, and have but a small household. My days I devote to reading and to experiments in chemistry, and I spend many of the clear nights in the study of astronomy.

There is – though I do not know how there is or why there is – a sense of infinite peace and protection in the glittering hosts of heaven. There it must be, I think, in the vast and eternal laws of matter, and not in the daily cares and sins and troubles of men, that whatever is more than animal within us must find its solace and its hope. I hope, or I could not live.

And so, in hope and solitude, my story ends.

<div align="right">EDWARD PRENDICK</div>

NOTE The substance of the chapter entitled 'Doctor Moreau Explains', which contains the essential idea of the story, appeared as a middle article in the *Saturday Review* in January 1895. This is the only portion of this story that has been previously published, and it has been entirely recast to adapt it to the narrative form.

The Invisible Man
A Grotesque Romance

A novel first published in 1897

Contents

The Invisible Man was published in Great Britain in 1897, first as a serial in *Pearson's Weekly* and later in the same year in book form by Arthur Pearson Limited, London, and in the United States by Harper Brothers, New York.

CHAPTER ONE

The Strange Man's Arrival

THE STRANGER CAME EARLY in February, one wintry day, through a biting wind and a driving snow, the last snowfall of the year, over the down, walking from Bramblehurst railway station, and carrying a little black portmanteau in his thickly gloved hand. He was wrapped up from head to foot, and the brim of his soft felt hat hid every inch of his face but the shiny tip of his nose; the snow had piled itself against his shoulders and chest, and added a white crest to the burden he carried. He staggered into the Coach and Horses more dead than alive, and flung his portmanteau down. 'A fire,' he cried, 'in the name of human charity! A room and a fire!' He stamped and shook the snow from off himself in the bar, and followed Mrs Hall into her guest parlour to strike his bargain. And with that much introduction, that and a couple of sovereigns flung upon the table, he took up his quarters in the inn.

Mrs Hall lit the fire and left him there while she went to prepare him a meal with her own hands. A guest to stop at Iping in the wintertime was an unheard-of piece of luck, let alone a guest who was no 'haggler', and she was resolved to show herself worthy of her good fortune. As soon as the bacon was well under way, and Millie, her lymphatic maid, had been brisked up a bit by a few deftly chosen expressions of contempt, she carried the cloth, plates and glasses into the parlour and began to lay them with the utmost *éclat*. Although the fire was burning up briskly, she was surprised to see that her visitor still wore his hat and coat, standing with his back to her and staring out of the window at the falling snow in the yard. His gloved hands were clasped behind him, and he seemed to be lost in thought. She noticed that the melting snow that still sprinkled his shoulders dripped upon her carpet. 'Can I take your hat and coat, sir?' she said, 'and give them a good dry in the kitchen?'

'No,' he said without turning.

She was not sure she had heard him, and was about to repeat her question.

He turned his head and looked at her over his shoulder. 'I prefer to keep them on,' he said with emphasis, and she noticed that he wore big blue spectacles with side-lights, and had bushy side-whiskers over his coat-collar that completely hid his cheeks and face.

'Very well, sir,' she said. '*As* you like. In a bit the room will be warmer.'

He made no answer, and had turned his face away from her again, and

Mrs Hall, feeling that her conversational advances were ill-timed, laid the rest of the table things in a quick staccato and whisked out of the room. When she returned he was still standing there, like a man of stone, his back hunched, his collar turned up, his dripping hat-brim turned down, hiding his face and ears completely. She put down the eggs and bacon with considerable emphasis, and called rather than said to him, 'Your lunch is served, sir.'

'Thank you,' he said at the same time, and did not stir until she was closing the door. Then he swung round and approached the table with a certain eager quickness.

As she went behind the bar to the kitchen she heard a sound repeated at regular intervals. Chirk, chirk, chirk, it went, the sound of a spoon being rapidly whisked round a basin. 'That girl!' she said. 'There! I clean forgot it. It's her being so long!' And while she herself finished mixing the mustard, she gave Millie a few verbal stabs for her excessive slowness. She had cooked the ham and eggs, laid the table, and done everything, while Millie (help indeed!) had only succeeded in delaying the mustard. And him a new guest and wanting to stay! Then she filled the mustard pot, and, putting it with a certain stateliness upon a gold and black tea-tray, carried it into the parlour.

She rapped and entered promptly. As she did so her visitor moved quickly, so that she got but a glimpse of a white object disappearing behind the table. It would seem he was picking something from the floor. She rapped down the mustard pot on the table, and then she noticed the overcoat and hat had been taken off and put over a chair in front of the fire, and a pair of wet boots threatened rust to her steel fender. She went to these things resolutely. 'I suppose I may have them to dry now,' she said in a voice that brooked no denial.

'Leave the hat,' said her visitor, in a muffled voice, and turning she saw he had raised his head and was sitting and looking at her.

For a moment she stood gaping at him, too surprised to speak.

He held a white cloth – it was a serviette he had brought with him – over the lower part of his face, so that his mouth and jaws were completely hidden, and that was the reason of his muffled voice. But it was not that which startled Mrs Hall. It was the fact that all his forehead above his blue glasses was covered by a white bandage, and that another covered his ears, leaving not a scrap of his face exposed excepting only his pink, peaked nose. It was bright, pink, and shiny just as it had been at first. He wore a dark-brown velvet jacket with a high, black, linen-lined collar turned up about his neck. The thick black hair, escaping as it could below and between the cross bandages, projected in curious tails and horns, giving him the strangest appearance conceivable. This muffled and bandaged head was so unlike what she had anticipated, that for a moment she was rigid.

He did not remove the serviette, but remained holding it, as she saw

now, with a brown-gloved hand, and regarding her with his inscrutable blue glasses. 'Leave the hat,' he said, speaking very distinctly through the white cloth.

Her nerves began to recover from the shock they had received. She placed the hat on the chair again by the fire. 'I didn't know, sir,' she began, 'that – ' and she stopped embarrassed.

'Thank you,' he said drily, glancing from her to the door and then at her again.

'I'll have them nicely dried, sir, at once,' she said, and carried his clothes out of the room. She glanced at his white-swathed head and blue goggles again as she was going out of the door; but his napkin was still in front of his face. She shivered a little as she closed the door behind her, and her face was eloquent of her surprise and perplexity. 'I *never*,' she whispered. 'There!' She went quite softly to the kitchen, and was too preoccupied to ask Millie what she was messing about with *now*, when she got there.

The visitor sat and listened to her retreating feet. He glanced en-quiringly at the window before he removed his serviette and resumed his meal. He took a mouthful, glanced suspiciously at the window, took another mouthful, then rose and, taking the serviette in his hand, walked across the room and pulled the blind down to the top of the white muslin that obscured the lower panes. This left the room in a twilight. This done, he returned with an easier air to the table and his meal.

'The poor soul's had an accident or an op'ration or somethin',' said Mrs Hall. 'What a turn them bandages did give me, to be sure!'

She put on some more coal, unfolded the clothes-horse, and extended the traveller's coat upon this. 'And they goggles! Why, he looked more like somethin' in a divin' helmet than a human man!' She hung his muffler on a corner of the horse. 'And holdin' that handkerchief over his mouth all the time. Talkin' through it! . . . Perhaps his mouth was hurt too – maybe.' She turned round, as one who suddenly remembers. 'Bless my soul alive!' she said, going off at a tangent; 'ain't you done them taters *yet*, Millie?'

When Mrs Hall went to clear away the stranger's lunch, her idea that his mouth must also have been cut or disfigured, in the accident she supposed him to have suffered, was confirmed, for he was smoking a pipe, and all the time that she was in the room he never loosened the silk muffler he had wrapped round the lower part of his face to put the mouthpiece to his lips. Yet it was not forgetfulness, for she saw he glanced at it as it smouldered out. He sat in the corner with his back to the window-blind and spoke now, having eaten and drunk and being comfortably warmed through, with less aggressive brevity than before. The reflection of the fire lent a kind of red animation to his big spectacles they had lacked hitherto.

'I have some luggage,' he said, 'at Bramblehurst station,' and he asked her how he could have it sent. He bowed his bandaged head quite politely in acknowledgement of her explanation. 'Tomorrow?' he said. 'There is no

speedier delivery?' and seemed quite disappointed when she answered, 'No.' Was she quite sure? No man with a trap who would go over?

Mrs Hall, nothing loath, answered his questions and developed a conversation. 'It's a steep road by the down, sir,' she said in answer to the question about a trap; and then, snatching at an opening, said, 'It was there a carriage was upsettled, a year ago and more. A gentleman killed, besides his coachman. Accidents, sir, happen in a moment, don't they?'

But the visitor was not to be drawn so easily. 'They do,' he said through his muffler, eyeing her quietly through his impenetrable glasses.

'But they take long enough to get well, don't they? . . . There was my sister's son, Tom, jest cut his arm with a scythe, tumbled on it in the 'ayfield, and, bless me! he was three months tied up sir. You'd hardly believe it. It's regular given me a dread of a scythe, sir.'

'I can quite understand that,' said the visitor.

'He was afraid, one time, that he'd have to have an op'ration – he was that bad, sir.'

The visitor laughed abruptly, a bark of a laugh that he seemed to bite and kill in his mouth. '*Was* he?' he said.

'He was, sir. And no laughing matter to them as had the doing for him, as I had – my sister being took up with her little ones so much. There was bandages to do, sir, and bandages to undo. So that if I may make so bold as to say it, sir – '

'Will you get me some matches?' said the visitor, quite abruptly. 'My pipe is out.'

Mrs Hall was pulled up suddenly. It was certainly rude of him, after telling him all she had done. She gasped at him for a moment, and then remembered the two sovereigns. She went for the matches.

'Thanks,' he said concisely, as she put them down, and turned his shoulder upon her and stared out of the window again. It was altogether too discouraging. Evidently he was sensitive on the topic of operations and bandages. She did not 'make so bold as to say', however, after all. But his snubbing way had irritated her, and Millie had a hot time of it that afternoon.

The visitor remained in the parlour until four o'clock, without giving the ghost of an excuse for an intrusion. For the most part he was quite still during that time; it would seem he sat in the growing darkness smoking in the firelight – perhaps dozing.

Once or twice a curious listener might have heard him at the coals, and for the space of five minutes he was audible pacing the room. He seemed to be talking to himself. Then the armchair creaked as he sat down again.

CHAPTER TWO

Mr Teddy Henfrey's First Impression

At four o'clock, when it was fairly dark and Mrs Hall was screwing up her courage to go in and ask her visitor if he would take some tea, Teddy Henfrey, the clock-jobber, came into the bar. 'My sakes! Mrs Hall,' said he, 'but this is terrible weather for thin boots!' The snow outside was falling faster.

Mrs Hall agreed, and then noticed he had his bag with him. 'Now you're here, Mr Teddy,' said she, 'I'd be glad if you'd give th' old clock in the parlour a bit of a look. 'Tis going, and it strikes well and hearty; but the hour-hand won't do nuthin' but point at six.'

And leading the way, she went across to the parlour door and rapped and entered.

Her visitor, she saw as she opened the door, was seated in the armchair before the fire, dozing it would seem, with his bandaged head drooping on one side. The only light in the room was the red glow from the fire – which lit his eyes like adverse railway signals, but left his downcast face in darkness – and the scanty vestiges of the day that came in through the open door. Everything was ruddy, shadowy and indistinct to her, the more so since she had just been lighting the bar lamp, and her eyes were dazzled. But for a second it seemed to her that the man she looked at had an enormous mouth wide open – a vast and incredible mouth that swallowed the whole of the lower portion of his face. It was the sensation of a moment: the white-bound head, the monstrous goggle eyes and this huge yawn below it. Then he stirred, started up in his chair, put up his hand. She opened the door wide, so that the room was lighter, and she saw him more clearly, with the muffler held up to his face just as she had seen him hold the serviette before. The shadows, she fancied, had tricked her.

'Would you mind, sir, this man a-coming to look at the clock, sir?' she said, recovering from the momentary shock.

'Look at the clock?' he said, staring round in a drowsy manner, and speaking over his hand, and then, getting more fully awake, 'certainly.'

Mrs Hall went away to get a lamp, and he rose and stretched himself. Then came the light, and Mr Teddy Henfrey, entering, was confronted by this bandaged person. He was, he says, 'taken aback'.

'Good-afternoon,' said the stranger, regarding him – as Mr Henfrey says, with a vivid sense of the dark spectacles – 'like a lobster.'

'I hope,' said Mr Henfrey, 'that it's no intrusion.'

'None whatever,' said the stranger. 'Though, I understand,' he said turning to Mrs Hall, 'that this room is really to be mine for my own private use.'

'I thought, sir,' said Mrs Hall, 'you'd prefer the clock – ' She was going to say 'mended'.

'Certainly,' said the stranger, 'certainly – but, as a rule, I like to be alone and undisturbed. But I'm really glad to have the clock seen to,' he said, seeing a certain hesitation in Mr Henfrey's manner. 'Very glad.'

Mr Henfrey had intended to apologise and withdraw, but this anticipation reassured him. The stranger turned round with his back to the fireplace and put his hands behind his back. 'And presently,' he said, 'when the clock-mending is over, I think I should like to have some tea. But not till the clock-mending is over.'

Mrs Hall was about to leave the room – she made no conversational advances this time, because she did not want to be snubbed in front of Mr Henfrey – when her visitor asked her if she had made any arrangements about his boxes at Bramblehurst. She told him she had mentioned the matter to the postman, and that the carrier could bring them over on the morrow. 'You are certain that is the earliest?' he said.

She was certain, with a marked coldness.

'I should explain,' he added, 'what I was really too cold and fatigued to do before, that I am an experimental investigator.'

'Indeed, sir,' said Mrs Hall, much impressed.

'And my baggage contains apparatus and appliances.'

'Very useful things indeed they are, sir,' said Mrs Hall.

'And I'm very naturally anxious to get on with my enquiries.'

'Of course, sir.'

'My reason for coming to Iping,' he proceeded, with a certain deliberation of manner, 'was . . . a desire for solitude. I do not wish to be disturbed in my work. In addition to my work, an accident – '

'I thought as much,' said Mrs Hall to herself.

' – necessitates a certain retirement. My eyes – are sometimes so weak and painful that I have to shut myself up in the dark for hours together. Lock myself up. Sometimes – now and then. Not at present, certainly. At such times the slightest disturbance, the entry of a stranger into the room, is a source of excruciating annoyance to me – it is well these things should be understood.'

'Certainly, sir,' said Mrs Hall. 'And if I might make so bold as to ask – '

'That I think, is all,' said the stranger, with that quietly irresistible air of finality he could assume at will. Mrs Hall reserved her question and sympathy for a better occasion.

After Mrs Hall had left the room, he remained standing in front of the fire, glaring, so Mr Henfrey puts it, at the clock-mending. Mr Henfrey not only took off the hands of the clock, and the face, but extracted the works; and he tried to work in as slow and quiet and unassuming a manner as possible. He worked with the lamp close to him, and the green shade threw a brilliant light upon his hands, and upon the frame and wheels, and left

the rest of the room shadowy. When he looked up, coloured patches swam in his eyes. Being constitutionally of a curious nature, he had removed the works – a quite unnecessary proceeding – with the idea of delaying his departure and perhaps falling into conversation with the stranger. But the stranger stood there, perfectly silent and still. So still, it got on Henfrey's nerves. He felt alone in the room and looked up, and there, grey and dim, was the bandaged head and huge blue lenses staring fixedly, with a mist of green spots drifting in front of them. It was so uncanny to Henfrey that for a minute they remained staring blankly at one another. Then Henfrey looked down again. Very uncomfortable position! One would like to say something. Should he remark that the weather was very cold for the time of year?

He looked up as if to take aim with that introductory shot. 'The weather – ' he began.

'Why don't you finish and go?' said the rigid figure, evidently in a state of painfully suppressed rage. 'All you've got to do is to fix the hour-hand on its axle. You're simply humbugging – '

'Certainly, sir – one minute more. I overlooked – ' and Mr Henfrey finished and went.

But he went feeling excessively annoyed. 'Damn it!' said Mr Henfrey to himself, trudging down the village through the thawing snow; 'a man must do a clock at times, sure-lie.'

And again, 'Can't a man look at you? – Ugly!'

And yet again, 'Seemingly not. If the police was wanting you, you couldn't be more wropped and bandaged.'

At Gleeson's corner he saw Hall, who had recently married the stranger's hostess at the Coach and Horses, and who now drove the Iping conveyance, when occasional people required it, to Sidderbridge Junction, coming towards him on his return from that place. Hall had evidently been 'stopping a bit' at Sidderbridge, to judge by his driving.

' 'Ow do, Teddy?' he said, passing.

'You got a rum un up home!' said Teddy.

Hall very sociably pulled up. 'What's that?' he asked.

'Rum-looking customer stopping at the Coach and Horses,' said Teddy. 'My sakes!'

And he proceeded to give Hall a vivid description of his grotesque guest. 'Looks a bit like a disguise, don't it? I'd like to see a man's face if I had him stopping in *my* place,' said Henfrey. 'But women are that trustful – where strangers are concerned. He's took your rooms and he ain't even given a name, Hall.'

'You don't say so!' said Hall, who was a man of sluggish apprehension.

'Yes,' said Teddy. 'By the week. Whatever he is, you can't get rid of him under the week. And he's got a lot of luggage coming tomorrow, so he says. Let's hope it won't be stones in boxes, Hall.'

He told Hall how his aunt at Hastings had been swindled by a stranger with empty portmanteaux. Altogether he left Hall vaguely suspicious. 'Get up, old girl,' said Hall. 'I s'pose I must see 'bout this.'

Teddy trudged on his way with his mind considerably relieved.

Instead of 'seeing 'bout it', however, Hall on his return was severely rated by his wife on the length of time he had spent in Sidderbridge, and his mild enquiries were answered snappishly and in a manner not to the point. But the seed of suspicion Teddy had sown germinated in the mind of Mr Hall in spite of these discouragements. 'You wim' don't know everything,' said Mr Hall, resolved to ascertain more about the personality of his guest at the earliest possible opportunity. And after the stranger had gone to bed, which he did about half-past nine, Mr Hall went very aggressively into the parlour and looked very hard at his wife's furniture, just to show that the stranger wasn't master there, and scrutinised closely and a little contemptuously a sheet of mathematical computations the stranger had left. When retiring for the night he instructed Mrs Hall to look very closely at the stranger's luggage when it came next day.

'You mind your own business, Hall,' said Mrs Hall, 'and I'll mind mine.'

She was all the more inclined to snap at Hall because the stranger was undoubtedly an unusually strange sort of stranger, and she was by no means assured about him in her own mind. In the middle of the night she woke up dreaming of huge white heads like turnips, that came trailing after her, at the end of interminable necks, and with vast black eyes. But being a sensible woman, she subdued her terrors and turned over and went to sleep again.

CHAPTER THREE

The Thousand and One Bottles

So it was that on the twenty-ninth day of February, at the beginning of the thaw, this singular person fell out of infinity into Iping village. Next day his luggage arrived through the slush – and very remarkable luggage it was. There were a couple of trunks indeed, such as a rational man might need, but in addition there were a box of books – big, fat books, of which some were just in an incomprehensible handwriting – and a dozen or more crates, boxes and cases, containing objects packed in straw, as it seemed to Hall, tugging with a casual curiosity at the straw – glass bottles. The stranger, muffled in hat, coat, gloves and wrapper, came out impatiently to meet Fearenside's cart, while Hall was having a word or so of gossip preparatory to helping bring them in. Out he came, not noticing Fearenside's dog, who was sniffing in a dilettante spirit at Hall's legs. 'Come along with those boxes,' he said. 'I've been waiting long enough.'

And he came down the steps towards the tail of the cart as if to lay hands

on the smaller crate. No sooner had Fearenside's dog caught sight of him, however, than it began to bristle and growl savagely, and when he rushed down the steps it gave an undecided hop and then sprang straight at his hand. 'Whup!' cried Hall, jumping back, for he was no hero with dogs, and Fearenside howled, 'Lie down!' and snatched his whip.

They saw the dog's teeth had slipped the hand, heard a kick, saw the dog execute a flanking jump and get home on the stranger's leg, and heard the rip of his trousering. Then the finer end of Fearenside's whip reached his property, and the dog, yelping with dismay, retreated under the wheels of the waggon. It was all the business of a swift half-minute. No one spoke, everyone shouted. The stranger glanced swiftly at his torn glove and at his leg, made as if he would stoop to the latter, then turned and rushed swiftly up the steps into the inn. They heard him go headlong across the passage and up the uncarpeted stairs to his bedroom.

'You brute, you!' said Fearenside, climbing off the waggon with his whip in his hand, while the dog watched him through the wheel. 'Come here,' said Fearenside – 'You'd better.'

Hall had stood gaping. 'He wuz bit,' said Hall. 'I'd better go and see to en,' and he trotted after the stranger. He met Mrs Hall in the passage. 'Carrier's darg,' he said 'bit en.'

He went straight upstairs, and the stranger's door being ajar, he pushed it open and was entering without any ceremony, being of a naturally sympathetic turn of mind.

The blind was down and the room dim. He caught a glimpse of a most singular thing, what seemed a handless arm waving towards him, and a face of three huge indeterminate spots on white, very like the face of a pale pansy. Then he was struck violently in the chest, hurled back, and the door slammed in his face and locked. It was so rapid that it gave him no time to observe. A waving of indecipherable shapes, a blow and a concussion. There he stood on the dark little landing, wondering what it might be that he had seen.

A couple of minutes after, he rejoined the little group that had formed outside the Coach and Horses. There was Fearenside telling about it all over again for the second time; there was Mrs Hall saying his dog didn't have no business to bite her guests; there was Huxter, the general dealer from over the road, interrogative; and Sandy Wadgers from the forge, judicial; besides women and children, all of them saying fatuities: 'Wouldn't let en bite *me*, I knows'; ' 'Tasn't right *have* such dargs'; 'Whad '*e* bite 'n for, then?' and so forth.

Mr Hall, staring at them from the steps and listening, found it incredible that he had seen anything so very remarkable happen upstairs. Besides, his vocabulary was altogether too limited to express his impressions.

'He don't want no help, he says,' he said in answer to his wife's enquiry. 'We'd better be a-takin' of his luggage in.'

'He ought to have it cauterised at once,' said Mr Huxter; 'especially if it's at all inflamed.'

'I'd shoot en, that's what I'd do,' said a lady in the group.

Suddenly the dog began growling again.

'Come along,' cried an angry voice in the doorway, and there stood the muffled stranger with his collar turned up, and his hat-brim bent down. 'The sooner you get those things in the better I'll be pleased.' It is stated by an anonymous bystander that his trousers and gloves had been changed.

'Was you hurt, sir?' said Fearenside. 'I'm rare sorry the darg – '

'Not a bit,' said the stranger. 'Never broke the skin. Hurry up with those things.'

He then swore to himself, so Mr Hall asserts.

Directly the first crate was, in accordance with his directions, carried into the parlour, the stranger flung himself upon it with extraordinary eagerness, and began to unpack it, scattering the straw with an utter disregard of Mrs Hall's carpet. And from it he began to produce bottles – little fat bottles containing powders, small and slender bottles containing coloured and white fluids, fluted blue bottles labelled 'Poison', bottles with round bodies and slender necks, large green-glass bottles, large white-glass bottles, bottles with glass stoppers and frosted labels, bottles with fine corks, bottles with bungs, bottles with wooden caps, wine bottles, salad-oil bottles – putting them in rows on the chiffonnier, on the mantel, on the table under the window, round the floor, on the bookshelf – everywhere. The chemist's shop in Bramblehurst could not boast half so many. Quite a sight it was. Crate after crate yielded bottles, until all six were empty and the table high with straw; the only things that came out of these crates besides the bottles were a number of test-tubes and a carefully packed balance.

And directly the crates were unpacked, the stranger went to the window and set to work, not troubling in the least about the litter of straw, the fire which had gone out, the box of books outside, nor for the trunks and other luggage that had gone upstairs.

When Mrs Hall took his dinner in to him, he was already so absorbed in his work, pouring little drops out of the bottles into test-tubes, that he did not hear her until she had swept away the bulk of the straw and put the tray on the table, with some little emphasis perhaps, seeing the state that the floor was in. Then he half turned his head and immediately turned it away again. But she saw he had removed his glasses; they were beside him on the table, and it seemed to her that his eye sockets were extraordinarily hollow. He put on his spectacles again, and then turned and faced her. She was about to complain of the straw on the floor when he anticipated her.

'I wish you wouldn't come in without knocking,' he said in the tone of abnormal exasperation that seemed so characteristic of him.

'I knocked, but seemingly – '

'Perhaps you did. But in my investigations – my really very urgent and

necessary investigations – the slightest disturbance, the jar of a door – I must ask you – '

'Certainly, sir. You can turn the lock if you're like that, you know. Any time.'

'A very good idea,' said the stranger.

'This stror, sir, if I might make so bold as to remark – '

'Don't. If the straw makes trouble put it down in the bill.' And he mumbled at her – words suspiciously like curses.

He was so odd, standing there, so aggressive and explosive, bottle in one hand and test-tube in the other, that Mrs Hall was quite alarmed. But she was a resolute woman. 'In which case, I should like to know, sir, what you consider – '

'A shilling – put down a shilling. Surely a shilling's enough?'

'So be it,' said Mrs Hall, taking up the tablecloth and beginning to spread it over the table. 'If you're satisfied, of course – '

He turned and sat down, with his coat-collar towards her.

All the afternoon he worked with the door locked and, as Mrs Hall testifies, for the most part in silence. But once there was a concussion and a sound of bottles ringing together as though the table had been hit, and the smash of a bottle flung violently down, and then a rapid pacing athwart the room. Fearing 'something was the matter', she went to the door and listened, not caring to knock.

'I can't go on,' he was raving. 'I *can't* go on. Three hundred thousand, four hundred thousand! The huge multitude! Cheated! All my life it may take me! . . . Patience! Patience indeed! . . . Fool and liar!'

There was a noise of hobnails on the bricks in the bar, and Mrs Hall had very reluctantly to leave the rest of his soliloquy. When she returned the room was silent again, save for the faint crepitation of his chair and the occasional clink of a bottle. It was all over; the stranger had resumed work.

When she took in his tea she saw broken glass in the corner of the room under the concave mirror, and a golden stain that had been carelessly wiped. She called attention to it.

'Put it down in the bill,' snapped her visitor. 'For God's sake don't worry me. If there's damage done, put it down in the bill,' and he went on ticking a list in the exercise book before him.

'I'll tell you something,' said Fearenside, mysteriously. It was late in the afternoon, and they were in the little beer-shop of Iping Hanger.

'Well?' said Teddy Henfrey.

'This chap you're speaking of, what my dog bit. Well – he's black. Leastways, his legs are. I seed through the tear of his trousers and the tear of his glove. You'd have expected a sort of pinky to show, wouldn't you? Well – there wasn't none. Just blackness. I tell you, he's as black as my hat.'

'My sakes!' said Henfrey. 'It's a rummy case altogether. Why, his nose is as pink as paint!'

'That's true,' said Fearenside. 'I knows that. And I tell 'ee what I'm thinking. That marn's a piebald, Teddy. Black here and white there – in patches. And he's ashamed of it. He's a kind of half-breed, and the colour's come off patchy instead of mixing. I've heard of such things before. And it's the common way with horses, as anyone can see.'

CHAPTER FOUR

Mr Cuss Interviews the Stranger

I have told the circumstances of the stranger's arrival in Iping with a certain fullness of detail, in order that the curious impression he created may be understood by the reader. But excepting two odd incidents, the circumstances of his stay until the extraordinary day of the club festival may be passed over very cursorily. There were a number of skirmishes with Mrs Hall on matters of domestic discipline, but in every case until late April, when the first signs of penury began, he over-rode her by the easy expedient of an extra payment. Hall did not like him, and whenever he dared he talked of the advisability of getting rid of him; but he showed his dislike chiefly by concealing it ostentatiously, and avoiding his visitor as much as possible. 'Wait till the summer,' said Mrs Hall sagely, 'when the artisks are beginning to come. Then we'll see. He may be a bit overbearing, but bills settled punctual is bills settled punctual, whatever you'd like to say.'

The stranger did not go to church, and indeed made no difference between Sunday and the irreligious days, even in costume. He worked, as Mrs Hall thought, very fitfully. Some days he would come down early and be continuously busy. On others he would rise late, pace his room, fretting audibly for hours together, smoke, sleep in the armchair by the fire. Communication with the world beyond the village he had none. His temper continued very uncertain; for the most part his manner was that of a man suffering under almost unendurable provocation, and once or twice things were snapped, torn, crushed or broken in spasmodic gusts of violence. He seemed under a chronic irritation of the greatest intensity. His habit of talking to himself in a low voice grew steadily upon him, but though Mrs Hall listened conscientiously she could make neither head nor tail of what she heard.

He rarely went abroad by daylight, but at twilight he would go out muffled up invisibly, whether the weather were cold or not, and he chose the loneliest paths and those most overshadowed by trees and banks. His goggling spectacles and ghastly bandaged face, under the penthouse of his hat, came with a disagreeable suddenness out of the darkness upon one or two home-going labourers, and Teddy Henfrey, tumbling out of the Scarlet Coat one night, at half-past nine, was scared shamefully by the

stranger's skull-like head (he was walking hat in hand) lit by the sudden light of the opened inn door. Such children as saw him at nightfall dreamt of bogies, and it seemed doubtful whether he disliked boys more than they disliked him, or the reverse; but there was certainly a vivid enough dislike on either side.

It was inevitable that a person of so remarkable an appearance and bearing should form a frequent topic in such a village as Iping. Opinion was greatly divided about his occupation. Mrs Hall was sensitive on the point. When questioned, she explained very carefully that he was an 'experimental investigator', going gingerly over the syllables as one who dreads pitfalls. When asked what an experimental investigator was, she would say with a touch of superiority that most educated people knew such things as that, and would thus explain that he 'discovered things'. Her visitor had had an accident, she said, which temporarily discoloured his face and hands, and being of a sensitive disposition, he was averse to any public notice of the fact.

Out of her hearing there was a view largely entertained that he was a criminal trying to escape from justice by wrapping himself up so as to conceal himself altogether from the eye of the police. This idea sprang from the brain of Mr Teddy Henfrey. No crime of any magnitude dating from the middle or end of February was known to have occurred. Elaborated in the imagination of Mr Gould, the probationary assistant in the National School, this theory took the form that the stranger was an Anarchist in disguise, preparing explosives, and he resolved to undertake such detective operations as his time permitted. These consisted for the most part in looking very hard at the stranger whenever they met, or in asking people who had never seen the stranger leading questions about him. But he detected nothing.

Another school of opinion followed Mr Fearenside, and either accepted the piebald view or some modification of it; as, for instance, Silas Durgan, who was heard to assert that 'if he chooses to show enself at fairs he'd make his fortune in no time', and being a bit of a theologian, compared the stranger to the man with the one talent. Yet another view explained the entire matter by regarding the stranger as a harmless lunatic. That had the advantage of accounting for everything straight away.

Between these main groups there were waverers and compromisers. Sussex folk have few superstitions, and it was only after the events of early April that the thought of the supernatural was first whispered in the village. Even then it was only credited among the womenfolk.

But whatever they thought of him, people in Iping, on the whole, agreed in disliking him. His irritability, though it might have been comprehensible to an urban brain-worker, was an amazing thing to these quiet Sussex villagers. The frantic gesticulations they surprised now and then, the head-long pace after nightfall that swept him upon them round quiet corners, the inhuman bludgeoning of all tentative advances of curiosity, the taste for

twilight that led to the closing of doors, the pulling down of blinds, the extinction of candles and lamps – who could agree with such goings on? They drew aside as he passed down the village, and when he had gone by, young humourists would up with coat-collars and down with hat-brims, and go pacing nervously after him in imitation of his occult bearing. There was a song popular at that time called 'The Bogey Man'. Miss Statchell sang it at the schoolroom concert (in aid of the church lamps), and thereafter whenever one or two of the villagers were gathered together and the stranger appeared, a bar or so of this tune, more or less sharp or flat, was whistled in the midst of them. Also belated little children would call 'Bogey Man!' after him, and make off tremulously elated.

Cuss, the general practitioner, was devoured by curiosity. The bandages excited his professional interest, the report of the thousand and one bottles aroused his jealous regard. All through April and May he coveted an opportunity of talking to the stranger, and at last, towards Whitsuntide, he could stand it no longer, but hit upon the subscription-list for a village nurse as an excuse. He was surprised to find that Mr Hall did not know his guest's name. 'He give a name,' said Mrs Hall – an assertion which was quite unfounded – 'but I didn't rightly hear it.' She thought it seemed so silly not to know the man's name.

Cuss rapped at the parlour door and entered. There was a fairly audible imprecation from within. 'Pardon my intrusion,' said Cuss, and then the door closed and cut Mrs Hall off from the rest of the conversation.

She could hear the murmur of voices for the next ten minutes, then a cry of surprise, a stirring of feet, a chair flung aside, a bark of laughter, quick steps to the door, and Cuss appeared, his face white, his eyes staring over his shoulder. He left the door open behind him, and without looking at her strode across the hall and went down the steps, and she heard his feet hurrying along the road. He carried his hat in his hand. She stood behind the door, looking at the open door of the parlour. Then she heard the stranger laughing quietly, and then his footsteps came across the room. She could not see his face where she stood. The parlour door slammed, and the place was silent again.

Cuss went straight up the village to Bunting the vicar. 'Am I mad?' Cuss began abruptly, as he entered the shabby little study. 'Do I look like an insane person?'

'What's happened?' said the vicar, putting the ammonite on the loose sheets of his forthcoming sermon.

'That chap at the inn – '

'Well?'

'Give me something to drink,' said Cuss, and he sat down.

When his nerves had been steadied by a glass of cheap sherry – the only drink the good vicar had available – he told him of the interview he had just had. 'Went in,' he gasped, 'and began to demand a subscription for that

Nurse Fund. He'd stuck his hands in his pockets as I came in, and he sat down lumpily in his chair. Sniffed. I told him I'd heard he took an interest in scientific things. He said yes. Sniffed again. Kept on sniffing all the time; evidently recently caught an infernal cold. No wonder, wrapped up like that! I developed the nurse idea, and all the while kept my eyes open. Bottles – chemicals – everywhere. Balance, test-tubes in stands, and a smell of – evening primrose. Would he subscribe? Said he'd consider it. Asked him, point-blank, was he researching. Said he was. A long research? Got quite cross. "A damnable long research," said he, blowing the cork out, so to speak. "Oh," said I. And out came the grievance. The man was just on the boil, and my question boiled him over. He had been given a prescription, most valuable prescription – what for he wouldn't say. Was it medical? "Damn you! What are you fishing after?" I apologised. Dignified sniff and cough. He resumed. He'd read it. Five ingredients. Put it down; turned his head. Draught of air from window lifted the paper. Swish, rustle. He was working in a room with an open fireplace, he said. Saw a flicker, and there was the prescription burning and lifting chimneyward. Rushed towards it just as it whisked up the chimney. So! Just at that point, to illustrate his story, out came his arm.'

'Well?'

'No hand – just an empty sleeve. Lord! I thought, *that's* a deformity! Got a cork arm, I suppose, and has taken it off. Then, I thought, there's something odd in that. What the devil keeps that sleeve up and open, if there's nothing in it? There was nothing in it, I tell you. Nothing down it, right down to the joint. I could see right down it to the elbow, and there was a glimmer of light shining through a tear of the cloth. "Good God!" I said. Then he stopped. Stared at me with those black goggles of his, and then at his sleeve.'

'Well?'

'That's all. He never said a word; just glared, and put his sleeve back in his pocket quickly. "I was saying," said he, "that there was the prescription burning, wasn't I?" Interrogative cough. "How the devil," said I, "can you move an empty sleeve like that?" "Empty sleeve?" "Yes," said I, "an empty sleeve."

' "It's an empty sleeve, is it? You saw it was an empty sleeve?" He stood up right away. I stood up too. He came towards me in three very slow steps, and stood quite close. Sniffed venomously. I didn't flinch, though I'm hanged if that bandaged knob of his, and those blinkers, aren't enough to unnerve anyone, coming quietly up to you.

' "You said it was an empty sleeve?" he said.

' "Certainly," I said.

Then very quietly he pulled his sleeve out of his pocket again, and raised his arm towards me as though he would show it to me again. He did it very, very slowly. I looked at it. Seemed an age. "Well?" said I, clearing my throat, "there's nothing in it."

'Had to say something. I was beginning to feel frightened. I could see right down it. He extended it straight towards me, slowly, slowly – just like that – until the cuff was six inches from my face. Queer thing to see an empty sleeve come at you like that! And then – '

'Well?'

'Something – exactly like a finger and thumb it felt – nipped my nose.'

Bunting began to laugh.

'There wasn't anything *there*!' said Cuss, his voice running up into a shriek at the 'there'. 'It's all very well for you to laugh, but I tell you I was so startled, I hit his cuff hard, and turned around, and cut out of the room. I left him – '

Cuss stopped. There was no mistaking the sincerity of his panic. He turned round in a helpless way and took a second glass of the excellent vicar's very inferior sherry. 'When I hit his cuff,' said Cuss, 'I tell you, it felt exactly like hitting an arm. And there wasn't an arm! There wasn't the ghost of an arm!'

Mr Bunting thought it over. He looked suspiciously at Cuss. 'It's a most remarkable story,' he said. He looked very wise and grave indeed. 'It's really,' said Mr Bunting with judicial emphasis, 'a most remarkable story.'

CHAPTER FIVE

The Burglary at the Vicarage

The facts of the burglary at the vicarage came to us chiefly through the medium of the vicar and his wife. It occurred in the small hours of Whit Monday, the day devoted in Iping to the Club festivities. Mrs Bunting, it seems, woke up suddenly in the stillness that comes before the dawn, with the strong impression that the door of their bedroom had opened and closed. She did not arouse her husband at first, but sat up in bed listening. She then distinctly heard the pad, pad, pad of bare feet coming out of the adjoining dressing-room and walking along the passage towards the staircase. As soon as she felt assured of this, she aroused the Rev. Mr Bunting as quietly as possible. He did not strike a light, but putting on his spectacles, her dressing-gown and his bath slippers, he went out on the landing to listen. He heard quite distinctly a fumbling going on at his study desk downstairs, and then a violent sneeze.

At that he returned to his bedroom, armed himself with the most obvious weapon, the poker, and descended the staircase as noiselessly as possible. Mrs Bunting came out on the landing.

The hour was about four, and the ultimate darkness of the night was past. There was a faint shimmer of light in the hall, but the study doorway yawned impenetrably black. Everything was still except for the faint creaking of the

stairs under Mr Bunting's tread and the slight movements in the study. Then something snapped, the drawer was opened, and there was a rustle of papers. Then came an imprecation, and a match was struck and the study was flooded with yellow light. Mr Bunting was now in the hall, and through the crack of the door he could see the desk and the open drawer and a candle burning on the desk. But the robber he could not see. He stood there in the hall undecided what to do, and Mrs Bunting, her face white and intent, crept slowly downstairs after him. One thing kept up Mr Bunting's courage; the persuasion that this burglar was a resident in the village.

They heard the chink of money, and realised that the robber had found the housekeeping reserve of gold – two pounds ten in half-sovereigns altogether. At that sound Mr Bunting was nerved to abrupt action. Gripping the poker firmly, he rushed into the room, closely followed by Mrs Bunting. 'Surrender!' cried Mr Bunting, fiercely, and then stopped amazed. Apparently the room was perfectly empty.

Yet their conviction that they had, that very moment, heard somebody moving in the room had amounted to a certainty. For half a minute, perhaps, they stood gaping, then Mrs Bunting went across the room and looked behind the screen, while Mr Bunting, by a kindred impulse, peered under the desk. Then Mrs Bunting turned back the window-curtains, and Mr Bunting looked up the chimney and probed it with the poker. Then Mrs Bunting scrutinised the wastepaper basket and Mr Bunting opened the lid of the coal-scuttle. Then they came to a stop and stood with eyes interrogating each other.

'I could have sworn – ' said Mr Bunting.

'The candle!' said Mr Bunting. 'Who lit the candle?'

'The drawer!' said Mrs Bunting. 'And the money's gone!'

She went hastily to the doorway.

'Of all the strange occurrences – '

There was a violent sneeze in the passage. They rushed out, and as they did so the kitchen door slammed. 'Bring the candle,' said Mr Bunting, and led the way. They both heard a sound of bolts being hastily shot back.

As he opened the kitchen door he saw through the scullery that the back door was just opening, and the faint light of early dawn displayed the dark masses of the garden beyond. He is certain that nothing went out of the door. It opened, stood open for a moment, and then closed with a slam. As it did so, the candle Mrs Bunting was carrying from the study flickered and flared. It was a minute or more before they entered the kitchen.

The place was empty. They refastened the back door, examined the kitchen, pantry and scullery thoroughly, and at last went down into the cellar. There was not a soul to be found in the house, search as they would.

Daylight found the vicar and his wife, a quaintly-costumed little couple, still marvelling about on their own ground floor by the unnecessary light of a guttering candle.

CHAPTER SIX

The Furniture that Went Mad

Now it happened that in the early hours of Whit Monday, before Millie was hunted out for the day, Mr Hall and Mrs Hall both rose and went noiselessly down into the cellar. Their business there was of a private nature, and had something to do with the specific gravity of their beer. They had hardly entered the cellar when Mrs Hall found she had forgotten to bring down a bottle of sarsaparilla from their joint-room. As she was the expert and principal operator in this affair, Hall very properly went upstairs for it.

On the landing he was surprised to see that the stranger's door was ajar. He went on into his own room and found the bottle as he had been directed.

But returning with the bottle, he noticed that the bolts of the front door had been shot back, that the door was in fact simply on the latch. And with a flash of inspiration he connected this with the stranger's room upstairs and the suggestions of Mr Teddy Henfrey. He distinctly remembered holding the candle while Mrs Hall shot these bolts overnight. At the sight he stopped, gaping, then with the bottle still in his hand went upstairs again. He rapped at the stranger's door. There was no answer. He rapped again; then pushed the door wide open and entered. It was as he expected. The bed, the room also, was empty. And what was stranger, even to his heavy intelligence, on the bedroom chair and along the rail of the bed were scattered the garments, the only garments so far as he knew, and the bandages of their guest. His big slouch hat even was cocked jauntily over the bedpost.

As Hall stood there he heard his wife's voice coming out of the depth of the cellar, with that rapid telescoping of the syllables and interrogative cocking up of the final words to a high note, by which the West Sussex villager is wont to indicate a brisk impatience. 'George! You gart whad a wand?'

At that he turned and hurried down to her. 'Janny,' he said, over the rail of the cellar steps, ' 'tas the truth what Henfrey sez. 'E's not in uz room, 'e en't. And the front door's onbolted.'

At first Mrs Hall did not understand, and as soon as she did she resolved to see the empty room for herself. Hall, still holding the bottle, went first. 'If 'e en't there,' he said, ' 'is close are. And what's 'e doin' 'ithout 'is close, then? 'Tas a most curious business.'

As they came up the cellar steps they both, it was afterwards ascertained, fancied they heard the front door open and shut, but seeing it closed and nothing there, neither said a word to the other about it at the time. Mrs

Hall passed her husband in the passage and ran on first upstairs. Someone sneezed on the staircase. Hall, following six steps behind, thought that he heard her sneeze. She, going on first, was under the impression that Hall was sneezing. She flung open the door and stood regarding the room. 'Of all the curious!' she said.

She heard a sniff close behind her head as it seemed, and turning, was surprised to see Hall a dozen feet off on the topmost stair. But in another moment he was beside her. She bent forward and put her hand on the pillow and then under the clothes.

'Cold,' she said. 'He's been up this hour or more.'

As she did so, a most extraordinary thing happened. The bedclothes gathered themselves together, leapt up suddenly into a sort of peak, and then jumped headlong over the bottom rail. It was exactly as if a hand had clutched them in the centre and flung them aside. Immediately after, the stranger's hat hopped off the bedpost, described a whirling flight in the air through the better part of a circle, and then dashed straight at Mrs Hall's face. Then as swiftly came the sponge from the washstand; and then the chair, flinging the stranger's coat and trousers carelessly aside, and laughing drily in a voice singularly like the stranger's, turned itself up with its four legs at Mrs Hall, seemed to take aim at her for a moment, and charged at her. She screamed and turned, and then the chair legs came gently but firmly against her back and impelled her and Hall out of the room. The door slammed violently and was locked. The chair and bed seemed to be executing a dance of triumph for a moment, and then abruptly everything was still.

Mrs Hall was left almost in a fainting condition in Mr Hall's arms on the landing. It was with the greatest difficulty that Mr Hall and Millie, who had been roused by her scream of alarm, succeeded in getting her downstairs, and applying the restoratives customary in such cases.

' 'Tas sperits,' said Mrs Hall. 'I know 'tas sperits. I've read in papers of en. Tables and chairs leaping and dancing . . . '

'Take a drop more, Janny,' said Hall. ' 'Twill steady ye.'

'Lock him out,' said Mrs Hall. 'Don't let him come in again. I half guessed – I might ha' known. With them goggling eyes and bandaged head, and never going to church of a Sunday. And all they bottles – more'n it's right for anyone to have. He's put the sperits into the furniture . . . My good old furniture! 'Twas in that very chair my poor dear mother used to sit when I was a little girl. To think it should rise up against me now!'

'Just a drop more, Janny,' said Hall. 'Your nerves is all upset.'

They sent Millie across the street through the golden five o'clock sunshine to rouse up Mr Sandy Wadgers, the blacksmith. Mr Hall's compliments and the furniture upstairs was behaving most extraordinary. Would Mr Wadgers come round? He was a knowing man, was Mr Wadgers, and very resourceful. He took quite a grave view of the case.

'Arm darmed if thet ent witchcraft,' was the view of Mr Sandy Wadgers. 'You warnt horseshoes for such gentry as he.'

He came round greatly concerned. They wanted him to lead the way upstairs to the room, but he didn't seem to be in any hurry. He preferred to talk in the passage. Over the way Huxter's apprentice came out and began taking down the shutters of the tobacco window. He was called over to join the discussion. Mr Huxter naturally followed over in the course of a few minutes. The Anglo-Saxon genius for parliamentary government asserted itself; there was a great deal of talk and no decisive action. 'Let's have the facts first,' insisted Mr Sandy Wadgers. 'Let's be sure we'd be acting perfectly right in bustin' that there door open. A door onbust is always open to bustin', but ye can't onbust a door once you've busted en.'

And suddenly and most wonderfully the door of the room upstairs opened of its own accord, and as they looked up in amazement, they saw descending the stairs the muffled figure of the stranger staring more blackly and blankly than ever with those unreasonably large blue glass eyes of his. He came down stiffly and slowly, staring all the time; he walked across the passage staring, then stopped.

'Look there!' he said, and their eyes followed the direction of his gloved finger and saw a bottle of sarsaparilla hard by the cellar door. Then he entered the parlour, and suddenly, swiftly, viciously, slammed the door in their faces.

Not a word was spoken until the last echoes of the slam had died away. They stared at one another. 'Well, if that don't lick everything!' said Mr Wadgers, and left the alternative unsaid.

'I'd go in and ask'n 'bout it,' said Wadgers, to Mr Hall. 'I'd d'mand an explanation.'

It took some time to bring the landlady's husband up to that pitch. At last he rapped, opened the door, and got as far as, 'Excuse me – '

'Go to the devil!' said the stranger in a tremendous voice, and, 'Shut that door after you.' So that brief interview terminated.

CHAPTER SEVEN

The Unveiling of the Stranger

The stranger went into the little parlour of the Coach and Horses about half-past five in the morning, and there he remained until near midday, the blinds down, the door shut, and none, after Hall's repulse, venturing near him.

All that time he must have fasted. Thrice he rang his bell, the third time furiously and continuously, but no one answered him. 'Him and his "go to the devil" indeed!' said Mrs Hall. Presently came an imperfect rumour of

the burglary at the vicarage, and two and two were put together. Hall, assisted by Wadgers, went off to find Mr Shuckleforth, the magistrate, and take his advice. No one ventured upstairs. How the stranger occupied himself is unknown. Now and then he would stride violently up and down, and twice came an outburst of curses, a tearing of paper and a violent smashing of bottles.

The little group of scared but curious people increased. Mrs Huxter came over; some gay young fellows resplendent in black ready-made jackets and *piqué* paper ties – for it was Whit Monday – joined the group with confused interrogations. Young Archie Harker distinguished himself by going up the yard and trying to peep under the window-blinds. He could see nothing, but gave reason for supposing that he did, and others of the Iping youth presently joined him.

It was the finest of all possible Whit Mondays, and down the village street stood a row of nearly a dozen booths, a shooting gallery, and on the grass by the forge were three yellow and chocolate waggons and some picturesque strangers of both sexes putting up a coconut shy. The gentlemen wore blue jerseys, the ladies white aprons and quite fashionable hats with heavy plumes. Wodger, of the Purple Fawn, and Mr Jaggers, the cobbler, who also sold second-hand ordinary bicycles, were stretching a string of union-jacks and royal ensigns (which had originally celebrated the first Victorian jubilee) across the road.

And inside, in the artificial darkness of the parlour, into which only one thin jet of sunlight penetrated, the stranger, hungry, we must suppose, and fearful, hidden in his uncomfortable hot wrappings, pored through his dark glasses upon his paper or chinked his dirty little bottles, and occasionally swore savagely at the boys, audible if invisible, outside the windows. In the corner by the fireplace lay the fragments of half a dozen smashed bottles, and a pungent twang of chlorine tainted the air. So much we know from what was heard at the time and from what was subsequently seen in the room.

About noon he suddenly opened his parlour door and stood glaring fixedly at the three or four people in the bar. 'Mrs Hall,' he said. Somebody went sheepishly and called for Mrs Hall.

Mrs Hall appeared after an interval, a little short of breath, but all the fiercer for that. Hall was still out. She had deliberated over this scene, and she came holding a little tray with an unsettled bill upon it. 'Is it your bill you're wanting, sir?' she said.

'Why wasn't my breakfast laid? Why haven't you prepared my meals and answered my bell? Do you think I live without eating?'

'Why isn't my bill paid?' said Mrs Hall. 'That's what I want to know.'

'I told you three days ago I was awaiting a remittance – '

'I told you two days ago I wasn't going to await no remittances. You can't grumble if your breakfast waits a bit, if my bill's been waiting these five days, can you?'

The stranger swore briefly but vividly.

'Nar, nar!' from the bar.

'And I'd thank you kindly, sir, if you'd keep your swearing to yourself, sir,' said Mrs Hall.

The stranger stood looking more like an angry diving-helmet than ever. It was universally felt in the bar that Mrs Hall had the better of him. His next words showed as much.

'Look here, my good woman – ' he began.

'Don't "good woman" *me*,' said Mrs Hall.

'I've told you my remittance hasn't come.'

'Remittance indeed!' said Mrs Hall.

'Still, I dare say in my pocket – '

'You told me three days ago that you hadn't anything but a sovereign's worth of silver upon you.'

'Well, I've found some more – '

' 'Ul–*lo*!' from the bar.

'I wonder where you found it,' said Mrs Hall.

That seemed to annoy the stranger very much. He stamped his foot. 'What do you mean?' he said.

'That I wonder where you found it,' said Mrs Hall. 'And before I take any bills or get any breakfasts, or do any such things whatsoever, you got to tell me one or two things I don't understand, and what nobody don't understand, and what everybody is very anxious to understand. I want to know what you been doing t'my chair upstairs, and I want to know how 'tis your room was empty, and how you got in again. Them as stops in this house comes in by the doors – that's the rule of the house, and that you *didn't* do, and what I want to know is how you *did* come in. And I want to know – '

Suddenly the stranger raised his gloved hands clenched, stamped his foot, and said, 'Stop!' with such extraordinary violence that he silenced her instantly.

'You don't understand,' he said, 'who I am or what I am. I'll show you. By heaven! I'll show you.' Then he put his open palm over his face and withdrew it. The centre of his face became a black cavity. 'Here,' he said. He stepped forward and handed Mrs Hall something which she, staring at his metamorphosed face, accepted automatically. Then, when she saw what it was, she screamed loudly, dropped it, and staggered back. The nose – it was the stranger's nose! pink and shining – rolled on to the floor.

Then he removed his spectacles, and everyone in the bar gasped. He took off his hat, and with a violent gesture tore at his whiskers and bandages. For a moment they resisted him. A flash of horrible anticipation passed through the bar. 'Oh, my Gard!' said someone. Then off they came.

It was worse than anything. Mrs Hall, standing open-mouthed and horror-struck, shrieked at what she saw, and made for the door of the house.

Everyone began to move. They were prepared for scars, disfigurements, tangible horrors, but *nothing*! The bandages and false hair flew across the passage into the bar, making a hobbledehoy jump to avoid them. Everyone tumbled on everyone else down the steps. For the man who stood there, shouting some incoherent explanation, was a solid gesticulating figure up to the coat-collar of him, and then – nothingness, no visible thing at all!

People down the village heard shouts and shrieks, and looking up the street saw the Coach and Horses violently firing out its humanity. They saw Mrs Hall fall down and Mr Teddy Henfrey jump to avoid tumbling over her, and then they heard the frightful screams of Millie, who, emerging suddenly from the kitchen at the noise of the tumult, had come upon the headless stranger from behind.

Forthwith everyone all down the street, the sweetstuff seller, coconut-shy proprietor and his assistant, the swing man, little boys and girls, rustic dandies, smart wenches, smocked elders and aproned gypsies – began running towards the inn, and in a miraculously short space of time a crowd of perhaps forty people, and rapidly increasing, swayed and hooted and enquired and exclaimed and suggested, in front of Mrs Hall's establishment. Everyone seemed eager to talk at once, and the result was Babel. A small group supported Mrs Hall, who was picked up in a state of collapse. There was a conference, and the incredible evidence of a vociferous eye-witness. 'O Bogey!' 'What's he been doin', then?' 'Ain't hurt the girl, 'as 'e?' 'Run at en with a knife, I believe.' 'No 'ed, I tell ye. I don't mean no manner of speaking. I mean *marn 'ithout a 'ed*!' 'Narnsense! 'tis some conjuring trick.' 'Fetched off 'is wrapping, 'e did – '

In its struggles to see in through the open door, the crowd formed itself into a straggling wedge, with the more adventurous apex nearest the inn. 'He stood for a moment, I heerd the gal scream, and he turned. I saw her skirts whisk, and he went after her. Didn't take ten seconds. Back he comes with a knife in uz hand and a loaf; stood just as if he was staring. Not a moment ago. Went in that there door. I tell 'e, 'e ain't gart no 'ed at all. You just missed en – '

There was a disturbance behind, and the speaker stopped to step aside for a little procession that was marching very resolutely towards the house: first Mr Hall, very red and determined, then Mr Bobby Jaffers, the village constable, and then the wary Mr Wadgers. They had come now armed with a warrant.

People shouted conflicting information of the recent circumstances. ' 'Ed or no 'ed,' said Jaffers, 'I got to 'rest en, and 'rest en I *will*.'

Mr Hall marched up the steps, marched straight to the door of the parlour and flung it open. 'Constable,' he said, 'do your duty.'

Jaffers marched in. Hall next, Wadgers last. They saw in the dim light the headless figure facing them, with a gnawed crust of bread in one gloved hand and a chunk of cheese in the other.

'That's him!' said Hall.

'What the devil's this?' came in a tone of angry expostulation from above the collar of the figure.

'You're a damned rum customer, mister,' said Mr Jaffers. 'But 'ed or no 'ed, the warrant says "body", and duty's duty – '

'Keep off!' said the figure, starting back.

Abruptly he whipped down the bread and cheese, and Mr Hall just grasped the knife on the table in time to save it. Off came the stranger's left glove and was slapped in Jaffers's face. In another moment Jaffers, cutting short some statement concerning a warrant, had gripped him by the handless wrist and caught his invisible throat. He got a sounding kick on the shin that made him shout, but he kept his grip. Hall sent the knife sliding along the table to Wadgers, who acted as goalkeeper for the offensive, so to speak, and then stepped forward as Jaffers and the stranger swayed and staggered towards him, clutching and hitting in. A chair stood in the way, and went aside with a crash as they came down together.

'Get the feet,' said Jaffers between his teeth.

Mr Hall, endeavouring to act on instructions, received a sounding kick in the ribs that disposed of him for a moment, and Mr Wadgers, seeing the decapitated stranger had rolled over and got the upper side of Jaffers, retreated towards the door, knife in hand, and so collided with Mr Huxter and the Sidderbridge carter coming to the rescue of law and order. At the same moment down came three or four bottles from the chiffonnier and shot a web of pungency into the air of the room.

'I'll surrender,' cried the stranger, though he had Jaffers down, and in another moment he stood up panting, a strange figure, headless and handless – for he had pulled off his right glove now as well as his left. 'It's no good,' he said, as if sobbing for breath.

It was the strangest thing in the world to hear that voice coming as if out of empty space, but the Sussex peasants are perhaps the most matter-of-fact people under the sun. Jaffers got up also and produced a pair of handcuffs. Then he stared.

'I say!' said Jaffers, brought up short by a dim realisation of the incongruity of the whole business, 'Darn it! Can't use 'em as I can see.'

The stranger ran his arm down his waistcoat, and as if by a miracle the buttons to which his empty sleeve pointed became undone. Then he said something about his shin, and stooped down. He seemed to be fumbling with his shoes and socks.

'Why!' said Huxter, suddenly, 'that's not a man at all. It's just empty clothes. Look! You can see down his collar and the linings of his clothes. I could put my arm – '

He extended his hand; it seemed to meet something in midair, and he drew it back with a sharp exclamation. 'I wish you'd keep your fingers out of my eye,' said the aerial voice, in a tone of savage expostulation. 'The fact is,

I'm all here – head, hands, legs, and all the rest of it, but it happens I'm invisible. It's a confounded nuisance, but I am. That's no reason why I should be poked to pieces by every stupid bumpkin in Iping, is it?'

The suit of clothes, now all unbuttoned and hanging loosely upon its unseen supports, stood up, arms akimbo.

Several other of the men folks had now entered the room, so that it was closely crowded. 'Invisible, eh?' said Huxter, ignoring the stranger's abuse. 'Who ever heard the likes of that?'

'It's strange, perhaps, but it's not a crime. Why am I assaulted by a policeman in this fashion?'

'Ah! that's a different matter,' said Jaffers. 'No doubt you are a bit difficult to see in this light, but I got a warrant and it's all correct. What I'm after ain't no invisibility – it's burglary. There's a house been broke into and money took.'

'Well?'

'And circumstances certainly point – '

'Stuff and nonsense!' said the Invisible Man.

'I hope so, sir; but I've got my instructions.'

'Well,' said the stranger, 'I'll come. I'll *come*. But no handcuffs.'

'It's the regular thing,' said Jaffers.

'No handcuffs,' stipulated the stranger.

'Pardon me,' said Jaffers.

Abruptly the figure sat down, and before anyone could realise was was being done, the slippers, socks and trousers had been kicked off under the table. Then he sprang up again and flung off his coat.

'Here, stop that,' said Jaffers, suddenly realising what was happening. He gripped at the waistcoat; it struggled, and the shirt slipped out of it and left it limp and empty in his hand. 'Hold him!' said Jaffers, loudly. 'Once he gets the things off – '

'Hold him!' cried everyone, and there was a rush at the fluttering white shirt which was now all that was visible of the stranger.

The shirt-sleeve planted a shrewd blow in Hall's face that stopped his open-armed advance, and sent him backwards into old Toothsome the sexton, and in another moment the garment was lifted up and became convulsed and vacantly flapping about the arms, even as a shirt that is being thrust over a man's head. Jaffers clutched at it, and only helped to pull it off; he was struck in the mouth out of the air, and incontinently threw his truncheon and smote Teddy Henfrey savagely upon the crown of his head.

'Look out!' said everybody, fencing at random and hitting at nothing. 'Hold him! Shut the door! Don't let him loose! I got something! Here he is!' A perfect Babel of noises they made. Everybody, it seemed, was being hit all at once, and Sandy Wadgers, knowing as ever and his wits sharpened by a frightful blow in the nose, reopened the door and led the rout. The others, following incontinently, were jammed for a moment in the corner

by the doorway. The hitting continued. Phipps, the Unitarian, had a front tooth broken, and Henfrey was injured in the cartilage of his ear. Jaffers was struck under the jaw, and, turning, caught at something that intervened between him and Huxter in the mêlée, and prevented their coming together. He felt a muscular chest, and in another moment the whole mass of struggling, excited men shot out into the crowded hall.

'I got him!' shouted Jaffers, choking and reeling through them all, and wrestling with purple face and swelling veins against his unseen enemy.

Men staggered right and left as the extraordinary conflict swayed swiftly towards the house door, and went spinning down the half-dozen steps of the inn. Jaffers cried in a strangled voice – holding tight, nevertheless, and making play with his knee – spun around, and fell heavily undermost with his head on the gravel. Only then did his fingers relax.

There were excited cries of 'Hold him!' 'Invisible!' and so forth, and a young fellow, a stranger in the place whose name did not come to light, rushed in at once, caught something, missed his hold, and fell over the constable's prostrate body. Halfway across the road a woman screamed as something pushed by her; a dog, kicked apparently, yelped and ran howling into Huxter's yard, and with that the transit of the Invisible Man was accomplished. For a space people stood amazed and gesticulating, and then came Panic, and scattered them abroad through the village as a gust scatters dead leaves.

But Jaffers lay quite still, face upward and knees bent, at the foot of the steps of the inn.

CHAPTER EIGHT

In Transit

The eighth chapter is exceedingly brief, and relates that Gibbons, the amateur naturalist of the district, while lying out on the spacious open downs without a soul within a couple of miles of him, as he thought, and almost dozing, heard close to him the sound as of a man coughing, sneezing, and then swearing savagely to himself; and looking, beheld nothing. Yet the voice was indisputable. It continued to swear with that breadth and variety that distinguishes the swearing of a cultivated man. It grew to a climax, diminished again, and died away in the distance, going as it seemed to him in the direction of Adderdean. It lifted to a spasmodic sneeze and ended. Gibbons had heard nothing of the morning's occurrences, but the phenomenon was so striking and disturbing that his philosophical tranquillity vanished; he got up hastily, and hurried down the steepness of the hill towards the village, as fast as he could go.

CHAPTER NINE

Mr Thomas Marvel

You must picture Mr Thomas Marvel as a person of copious, flexible visage, a nose of cylindrical protrusion, a liquorish, ample, fluctuating mouth, and a beard of bristling eccentricity. His figure inclined to embonpoint; his short limbs accentuated this inclination. He wore a furry silk hat, and the frequent substitution of twine and shoelaces for buttons, apparent at critical points of his costume, marked a man essentially bachelor.

Mr Thomas Marvel was sitting with his feet in a ditch by the roadside over the down towards Adderdean, about a mile and a half out of Iping. His feet, save for socks of irregular open-work, were bare, his big toes were broad, and pricked like the ears of a watchful dog. In a leisurely manner – he did everything in a leisurely manner – he was contemplating trying on a pair of boots. They were the soundest boots he had come across for a long time, but too large for him; whereas the ones he had were, in dry weather, a very comfortable fit, but too thin-soled for damp. Mr Thomas Marvel hated roomy shoes, but then he hated damp. He had never properly thought out which he hated most, and it was a pleasant day, and there was nothing better to do. So he put the four shoes in a graceful group on the turf and looked at them. And seeing them there among the grass and springing agrimony, it suddenly occurred to him that both pairs were exceedingly ugly to see. He was not at all startled by a voice behind him.

'They're boots, anyhow,' said the Voice.

'They are – charity boots,' said Mr Thomas Marvel, with his head on one side regarding them distastefully; 'and which is the ugliest pair in the whole blessed universe, I'm darned if I know!'

'H'm,' said the Voice.

'I've worn worse – in fact, I've worn none. But none so owdacious ugly – if you'll allow the expression. I've been cadging boots – in particular – for days. Because I was sick of *them*. They're sound enough, of course. But a gentleman on tramp sees such a thundering lot of his boots. And if you'll believe me, I've raised nothing in the whole blessed country, try as I would, but *them*. Look at 'em! And a good country for boots, too, in a general way. But it's just my promiscuous luck. I've got my boots in this country ten years or more. And then they treat you like this.'

'It's a beast of a country,' said the Voice. 'And pigs for people.'

'Ain't it?' said Mr Thomas Marvel. 'Lord! But them boots! It beats it.'

He turned his head over his shoulder to the right, to look at the boots of his interlocutor with a view to comparisons, and lo! where the boots of his interlocutor should have been were neither legs nor boots. He was

irradiated by the dawn of a great amazement. 'Where *are* yer?' said Mr Thomas Marvel over his shoulder and coming on all fours. He saw a stretch of empty downs with the wind swaying the remote green-pointed furze bushes.

'Am I drunk?' said Mr Marvel. 'Have I had visions? Was I talking to myself? What the – '

'Don't be alarmed,' said the Voice.

'None of your ventriloquising *me*,' said Mr Thomas Marvel, rising sharply to his feet. 'Where *are* yer? Alarmed, indeed!'

'Don't be alarmed,' repeated the Voice.

'*You'll* be alarmed in a minute, you silly fool,' said Mr Thomas Marvel. 'Where *are* yer? Lemme get my mark on yer . . .

'Are yer *buried*?' said Mr Thomas Marvel, after an interval.

There was no answer. Mr Thomas Marvel stood bootless and amazed, his jacket nearly thrown off.

'Peewit,' said a peewit, very remote.

'Peewit, indeed!' said Mr Thomas Marvel. 'This ain't no time for foolery.' The down was desolate, east and west, north and south; the road with its shallow ditches and white bordering stakes, ran smooth and empty north and south, and, save for that peewit, the blue sky was empty too. 'So help me,' said Mr Thomas Marvel, shuffling his coat on to his shoulders again. 'It's the drink! I might ha' known.'

'It's not the drink,' said the Voice. 'You keep your nerves steady.'

'Ow!' said Mr Marvel, and his face grew white amidst its patches. 'It's the drink!' his lips repeated noiselessly. He remained staring about him, rotating slowly backwards. 'I could have *swore* I heard a voice,' he whispered.

'Of course you did.'

'It's there again,' said Mr Marvel, closing his eyes and clasping his hand on his brow with a tragic gesture. He was suddenly taken by the collar and shaken violently, and left more dazed than ever. 'Don't be a fool,' said the Voice.

'I'm – off – my – blooming – chump,' said Mr Marvel. 'It's no good. It's fretting about them blarsted boots. I'm off my blessed blooming chump. Or it's spirits.'

'Neither one thing nor the other,' said the Voice. 'Listen!'

'Chump,' said Mr Marvel.

'One minute,' said the Voice, penetratingly, tremulous with self-control.

'Well?' said Mr Thomas Marvel, with a strange feeling of having been dug in the chest by a finger.

'You think I'm just imagination? Just imagination?'

'What else *can* you be?' said Mr Thomas Marvel, rubbing the back of his neck.

'Very well,' said the Voice, in a tone of relief. 'Then I'm going to throw flints at you till you think differently.'

'But where *are* yer?'

The Voice made no answer. Whizz came a flint, apparently out of the air, and missed Mr Marvel's shoulder by a hair's breadth. Mr Marvel, turning, saw a flint jerk up into the air, trace a complicated path, hang for a moment, and then fling at his feet with almost invisible rapidity. He was too amazed to dodge. Whizz it came, and ricocheted from a bare toe into the ditch. Mr Thomas Marvel jumped a foot and howled aloud. Then he started to run, tripped over an unseen obstacle, and came head over heels into a sitting position.

'*Now*,' said the Voice, as a third stone curved upward and hung in the air above the tramp. 'Am I imagination?'

Mr Marvel by way of reply struggled to his feet, and was immediately rolled over again. He lay quiet for a moment. 'If you struggle any more,' said the Voice, 'I shall throw the flint at your head.'

'It's a fair do,' said Mr Thomas Marvel, sitting up, taking his wounded toe in hand and fixing his eye on the third missile. 'I don't understand it. Stones flinging themselves. Stones talking. Put yourself down. Rot away. I'm done.'

The third flint fell.

'It's very simple,' said the Voice. 'I'm an invisible man.'

'Tell us something I don't know,' said Mr Marvel, gasping with pain. 'Where you've hid – how you do it – I *don't* know. I'm beat.'

'That's all,' said the Voice. 'I'm invisible. That's what I want you to understand.'

'Anyone could see that. There is no need for you to be so confounded impatient, mister. *Now* then. Give us a notion. How are you hid?'

'I'm invisible. That's the great point. And what I want you to understand is this – '

'But whereabouts?' interrupted Mr Marvel.

'Here! Six yards in front of you.'

'Oh, *come*! I ain't blind. You'll be telling me next you're just thin air. I'm not one of your ignorant tramps – '

'Yes, I am – thin air. You're looking through me.'

'What! Ain't there any stuff to you. *Vox et* – what is it? – jabber. Is it that?'

'I am just a human being – solid, needing food and drink, needing covering too – But I'm invisible. You see? Invisible. Simple idea. Invisible.'

'What, real like?'

'Yes, real.'

'Let's have a hand of you,' said Marvel, 'if you *are* real. It won't be so darn out-of-the-way like, then – *Lord!*' he said, 'how you made me jump! – gripping me like that!'

He felt the hand that had closed round his wrist with his disengaged fingers, and his fingers went timorously up the arm, patted a muscular chest, and explored a bearded face. Marvel's face was astonishment.

'I'm dashed!' he said. 'If this don't beat cockfighting! Most remarkable! – And there I can see a rabbit clean through you, 'arf a mile away! Not a bit of you visible – except – '

He scrutinised the apparently empty space keenly. 'You 'aven't been eatin' bread and cheese?' he asked, holding the invisible arm.

'You're quite right, and it's not quite assimilated into the system.'

'Ah!' said Mr Marvel. 'Sort of ghostly, though.'

'Of course, all this isn't half so wonderful as you think.'

'It's quite wonderful enough for *my* modest wants,' said Mr Thomas Marvel. 'Howjer manage it! How the dooce is it done?'

'It's too long a story. And besides – '

'I tell you, the whole business fairly beats me,' said Mr Marvel.

'What I want to say at present is this: I need help. I have come to that – I came upon you suddenly. I was wandering, mad with rage, naked, impotent. I could have murdered. And I saw you – '

'*Lord!*' said Mr Marvel.

'I came up behind you – hesitated – went on – '

Mr Marvel's expression was eloquent.

' – then stopped. "Here," I said, "is an outcast like myself. This is the man for me." So I turned back and came to you – you. And – '

'*Lord!*' said Mr Marvel. 'But I'm all in a tizzy. May I ask – How is it? And what you may be requiring in the way of help? – Invisible!'

'I want you to help me get clothes – and shelter – and then, with other things. I've left them long enough. If you won't – well! But you *will – must.*'

'Look here,' said Mr Marvel. 'I'm too flabbergasted. Don't knock me about any more. And leave me go. I must get steady a bit. And you've pretty near broken my toe. It's all so unreasonable. Empty downs, empty sky. Nothing visible for miles except the bosom of nature. And then comes a voice. A voice out of heaven! And stones! And a fist – Lord!'

'Pull yourself together,' said the Voice, 'for you have to do the job I've chosen for you.'

Mr Marvel blew out his cheeks, and his eyes were round.

'I've chosen you,' said the Voice. 'You are the only man, except for some of those fools down there, who knows there is such a thing as an invisible man. You have to be my helper. Help me – and I will do great things for you. An invisible man is a man of power.' He stopped for a moment to sneeze violently.

'But if you betray me,' he said, 'if you fail to do as I direct you – ' He paused and tapped Mr Marvel's shoulder smartly.

Mr Marvel gave a yelp of terror at the touch. '*I* don't want to betray you,' said Mr Marvel, edging away from the direction of the fingers. 'Don't you go a-thinking that, whatever you do. All I want to do is to help you – just tell me what I got to do. (Lord!) Whatever you want done, that I'm most willing to do.'

CHAPTER TEN

Mr Marvel's Visit to Iping

After the first gusty panic had spent itself Iping became argumentative. Scepticism suddenly reared its head – rather nervous scepticism, not at all assured of its back, but scepticism nevertheless. It is so much easier not to believe in an invisible man; and those who had actually seen him dissolve into air, or felt the strength of his arm, could be counted on the fingers of two hands. And of these witnesses Mr Wadgers was presently missing, having retired impregnably behind the bolts and bars of his own house, and Jaffers was lying stunned in the parlour of the Coach and Horses. Great and strange ideas transcending experience often have less effect upon men and women than smaller, more tangible considerations. Iping was gay with bunting, and everybody was in gala dress. Whit Monday had been looked forward to for a month or more. By the afternoon even those who believed in the Unseen were beginning to resume their little amusements in a tentative fashion, on the supposition that he had quite gone away, and with the sceptics he was already a jest. But people, sceptics and believers alike, were remarkably sociable all that day.

Haysman's meadow was gay with a tent, in which Mrs Bunting and other ladies were preparing tea, while, without, the Sunday-school children ran races and played games under the noisy guidance of the curate and the Misses Cuss and Sackbut. No doubt there was a slight uneasiness in the air, but people for the most part had the sense to conceal whatever imaginative qualms they experienced. On the village green an inclined strong rope, down which, clinging the while to a pulley-swung handle, one could be hurled violently against a sack at the other end, came in for considerable favour among the adolescents, as also did the swings and the coconut shies. There was also promenading, and the steam organ attached to a small roundabout filled the air with a pungent flavour of oil and with equally pungent music. Members of the club, who had attended church in the morning, were splendid in badges of pink and green, and some of the gayer-minded had also adorned their bowler hats with brilliant-coloured favours of ribbon. Old Fletcher, whose conceptions of holiday-making were severe, was visible through the jasmine about his window or through the open door (whichever way you chose to look), poised delicately on a plank supported on two chairs, and whitewashing the ceiling of his front room.

About four o'clock a stranger entered the village from the direction of the downs. He was a short, stout person in an extraordinarily shabby top hat, and he appeared to be very much out of breath. His cheeks were alternately limp and tightly puffed. His mottled face was apprehensive, and

he moved with a sort of reluctant alacrity. He turned the corner of the church, and directed his way to the Coach and Horses. Among others old Fletcher remembers seeing him, and indeed the old gentleman was so struck by his peculiar agitation that he inadvertently allowed a quantity of whitewash to run down the brush into the sleeve of his coat while regarding him.

This stranger, to the perceptions of the proprietor of the coconut shy, appeared to be talking to himself, and Mr Huxter remarked the same thing. He stopped at the foot of the Coach and Horses steps, and, according to Mr Huxter, appeared to undergo a severe internal struggle before he could induce himself to enter the house. Finally he marched up the steps, and was seen by Mr Huxter to turn to the left and open the door of the parlour. Mr Huxter heard voices from within the room and from the bar apprising the man of his error. 'That room's private!' said Hall, and the stranger shut the door clumsily and went into the bar.

In the course of a few minutes he reappeared, wiping his lips with the back of his hand with an air of quiet satisfaction that somehow impressed Mr Huxter as assumed. He stood looking about him for some moments, and then Mr Huxter saw him walk in an oddly furtive manner towards the gates of the yard, upon which the parlour window opened. The stranger, after some hesitation, leant against one of the gateposts, produced a short clay pipe, and prepared to fill it. His fingers trembled while doing so. He lit it clumsily, and folding his arms began to smoke in a languid attitude, an attitude which his occasional glances up the yard altogether belied.

All this Mr Huxter saw over the canisters of the tobacco window, and the singularity of the man's behaviour prompted him to maintain his observation.

Presently the stranger stood up abruptly and put his pipe in his pocket. Then he vanished into the yard. Forthwith Mr Huxter, conceiving he was witness of some petty larceny, leapt round his counter and ran out into the road to intercept the thief. As he did so, Mr Marvel reappeared, his hat askew, a big bundle in a blue tablecloth in one hand, and three books tied together – as it proved afterwards with the vicar's braces – in the other. Directly he saw Huxter he gave a sort of gasp, and turning sharply to the left, began to run. 'Stop, thief!' cried Huxter, and set off after him. Mr Huxter's sensations were vivid but brief. He saw the man just before him and spurting briskly for the church corner and the hill road. He saw the village flags and festivities beyond, and a face or so turned towards him. He bawled, 'Stop!' again. He had hardly gone ten strides before his shin was caught in some mysterious fashion, and he was no longer running but flying with inconceivable rapidity through the air. He saw the ground suddenly close to his face. The world seemed to splash into a million whirling specks of light and subsequent proceedings interested him no more.

CHAPTER ELEVEN

In the Coach and Horses

Now, in order clearly to understand what had happened in the inn, it is necessary to go back to the moment when Mr Marvel first came into view of Mr Huxter's window.

At that precise moment Mr Cuss and Mr Bunting were in the parlour. They were seriously investigating the strange occurrences of the morning, and were, with Mr Hall's permission, making a thorough examination of the Invisible Man's belongings. Jaffers had partially recovered from his fall and had gone home in the charge of his sympathetic friends. The stranger's scattered garments had been removed by Mrs Hall and the room tidied up. And on the table under the window where the stranger had been wont to work, Cuss had hit almost at once on three big books in manuscript labelled 'Diary'.

'Diary!' said Cuss, putting the three books on the table. 'Now, at any rate, we shall learn something.' The vicar stood with his hands on the table.

'Diary,' repeated Cuss, sitting down, putting two volumes to support the third, and opening it. 'H'm – no name on the flyleaf. Bother! – cypher. And figures.'

The vicar came round to look over his shoulder.

Cuss turned the pages over with a face suddenly disappointed. 'I'm – dear me! It's all cypher, Bunting.'

'There are no diagrams?' asked Mr Bunting. 'No illustrations throwing light – '

'See for yourself,' said Mr Cuss. 'Some of it's mathematical and some of it's Russian or some such language (to judge by the letters), and some of it's Greek. Now the Greek I thought *you* – '

'Of course,' said Mr Bunting, taking out and wiping his spectacles and feeling suddenly very uncomfortable – for he had no Greek left in his mind worth talking about; 'yes – the Greek, of course, may furnish a clue.'

'I'll find you a place.'

'I'd rather glance through the volumes first,' said Mr Bunting, still wiping. 'A general impression first, Cuss, and *then*, you know, we can go looking for clues.'

He coughed, put on his glasses, arranged them fastidiously, coughed again, and wished something would happen to avert the seemingly inevitable exposure. Then he took the volume Cuss handed him in a leisurely manner. And then something did happen.

The door opened suddenly.

Both gentlemen started violently, looked round, and were relieved to see

a sporadically rosy face beneath a furry silk hat. 'Tap?' asked the face, and stood staring.

'No,' said both gentlemen at once.

'Over the other side, my man,' said Mr Bunting. And, 'Please shut that door,' said Mr Cuss, irritably.

'All right,' said the intruder, as it seemed in a low voice curiously different from the huskiness of its first enquiry. 'Right you are,' said the intruder in the former voice. 'Stand clear!' and he vanished and closed the door.

'A sailor, I should judge,' said Mr Bunting. 'Amusing fellows, they are. Stand clear! indeed. A nautical term, referring to his getting back out of the room, I suppose.'

'I dare say so,' said Cuss. 'My nerves are all loose today. It quite made me jump – the door opening like that.'

Mr Bunting smiled as if he had not jumped. 'And now,' he said with a sigh, 'these books.'

Someone sniffed as he did so.

'One thing is indisputable,' said Bunting, drawing up a chair next to that of Cuss. 'There certainly have been very strange things happen in Iping during the last few days – very strange. I cannot of course believe in this absurd invisibility story – '

'It's incredible,' said Cuss – 'incredible. But the fact remains that I saw – I certainly saw right down his sleeve – '

'But did you – are you sure? Suppose a mirror, for instance – hallucinations are so easily produced. I don't know if you have ever seen a really good conjuror – '

'I won't argue again,' said Cuss. 'We've thrashed that out, Bunting. And just now there's these books – Ah! here's some of what I take to be Greek! Greek letters certainly.'

He pointed to the middle of the page. Mr Bunting flushed slightly and brought his face nearer, apparently finding some difficulty with his glasses. Suddenly he became aware of a strange feeling at the nape of his neck. He tried to raise his head, and encountered an immovable resistance. The feeling was a curious pressure, the grip of a heavy, firm hand, and it bore his chin irresistibly to the table. *'Don't move, little men,'* whispered a voice, *'or I'll brain you both!'* He looked into the face of Cuss, close to his own, and each saw a horrified reflection of his own sickly astonishment.

'I'm sorry to handle you so roughly,' said the Voice, 'but it's unavoidable.

'Since when did you learn to pry into an investigator's private memoranda,' said the Voice; and two chins struck the table simultaneously, and two sets of teeth rattled.

'Since when did you learn to invade the private rooms of a man in misfortune?' and the concussion was repeated.

'Where have they put my clothes?

'Listen,' said the Voice. 'The windows are fastened and I've taken the key

out of the door. I am a fairly strong man, and I have the poker handy – besides being invisible. There's not the slightest doubt that I could kill you both and get away quite easily if I wanted to – do you understand? Very well. If I let you go will you promise not to try any nonsense and do what I tell you?'

The vicar and the doctor looked at one another, and the doctor pulled a face. 'Yes,' said Mr Bunting, and the doctor repeated it. Then the pressure on the necks relaxed, and the doctor and the vicar sat up, both very red in the face and wriggling their heads.

'Please keep sitting where you are,' said the Invisible Man. 'Here's the poker, you see.

'When I came into this room,' continued the Invisible Man, after presenting the poker to the tip of the nose of each of his visitors, 'I did not expect to find it occupied, and I expected to find, in addition to my books of memoranda, an outfit of clothing. Where is it? No – don't rise. I can see it's gone. Now, just at present, though the days are quite warm enough for an invisible man to run about stark, the evenings are quite chilly. I want clothing – and other accommodation; and I must also have those three books.'

CHAPTER TWELVE

The Invisible Man Loses his Temper

It is unavoidable that at this point the narrative should break off again, for a certain very painful reason that will presently be apparent. While these things were going on in the parlour, and while Mr Huxter was watching Mr Marvel smoking his pipe against the gate, not a dozen yards away were Mr Hall and Teddy Henfrey discussing in a state of cloudy puzzlement the one Iping topic.

Suddenly there came a violent thud against the door of the parlour, a sharp cry, and then – silence.

'*Hel*–lo!' said Teddy Henfrey.

'Hel–*lo*!' from the Tap.

Mr Hall took things in slowly but surely. 'That ain't right,' he said, and came round from behind the bar towards the parlour door.

He and Teddy approached the door together, with intent faces. Their eyes considered. 'Summat wrong,' said Hall, and Henfrey nodded agreement. Whiffs of an unpleasant chemical odour met them, and there was a muffled sound of conversation, very rapid and subdued.

'You all right thur?' asked Hall, rapping.

The muttered conversation ceased abruptly, for a moment silence, then the conversation was resumed, in hissing whispers, then a sharp cry of, 'No! no, you don't!' There came a sudden motion and the oversetting of a chair, a brief struggle. Silence again.

'What the dooce?' exclaimed Henfrey, *sotto voce.*

'You – all – right thur?' asked Mr Hall, sharply, again.

The vicar's voice answered with a curious jerking intonation: 'Quite ri-right. Please don't – interrupt.'

'Odd!' said Mr Henfrey.

'Odd!' said Mr Hall.

'Says, "Don't interrupt," ' said Henfrey.

'I heerd'n,' said Hall.

'And a sniff,' said Henfrey.

They remained listening. The conversation was rapid and subdued. 'I *can't*,' said Mr Bunting, his voice rising; 'I tell you, sir, I *will* not.'

'What was that?' asked Henfrey.

'Says he wi' nart,' said Hall. 'Warn't speaking to us, wuz he?'

'Disgraceful!' said Mr Bunting, within.

' "Disgraceful," ' said Mr Henfrey. 'I heard it – distinct.'

'Who's that speaking now?' asked Henfrey.

'Mr Cuss, I s'pose,' said Hall. 'Can you hear – anything?'

Silence. The sounds within indistinct and perplexing.

'Sounds like throwing the tablecloth about,' said Hall.

Mrs Hall appeared behind the bar. Hall made gestures of silence and invitation. This aroused Mrs Hall's wifely opposition. 'What yer listenin' there for, Hall?' she asked. 'Ain't you nothin' better to do – busy day like this?'

Hall tried to convey everything by grimaces and dumb show, but Mrs Hall was obdurate. She raised her voice. So Hall and Henfrey, rather crestfallen, tiptoed back to the bar, gesticulating to explain to her.

At first she refused to see anything in what they had heard at all. Then she insisted on Hall keeping silence, while Henfrey told her his story. She was inclined to think the whole business nonsense – perhaps they were just moving the furniture about.

'I heerd'n say "disgraceful"; *that* I did,' said Hall.

'*I* heerd that, Mrs Hall,' said Henfrey.

'Like as not – ' began Mrs Hall.

'Hsh!' said Mr Teddy Henfrey. 'Didn't I hear the window?'

'What window?' asked Mrs Hall.

'Parlour window,' said Henfrey.

Everyone stood listening intently. Mrs Hall's eyes, directed straight before her, saw without seeing the brilliant oblong of the inn door, the road white and vivid, and Huxter's shop-front blistering in the June sun. Abruptly Huxter's door opened and Huxter appeared, eyes staring with excitement, arms gesticulating. '*Yap!*' cried Huxter. 'Stop thief!' and he ran obliquely across the oblong towards the yard gates, and vanished.

Simultaneously came a tumult from the parlour, and a sound of windows being closed.

Hall, Henfrey, and the human contents of the tap rushed out at once pell-mell into the street. They saw someone whisk round the corner towards the road, and Mr Huxter executing a complicated leap in the air that ended on his face and shoulder. Down the street people were standing astonished or running towards them.

Mr Huxter was stunned. Henfrey stopped to discover this, but Hall and the two labourers from the tap rushed at once to the corner, shouting incoherent things, and saw Mr Marvel vanishing by the corner of the church wall. They appear to have jumped to the impossible conclusion that this was the Invisible Man suddenly become visible, and set off at once along the lane in pursuit. But Hall had hardly run a dozen yards before he gave a loud shout of astonishment and went flying headlong sideways, clutching one of the labourers and bringing him to the ground. He had been charged just as one charges a man at football. The second labourer came round in a circle, stared, and conceiving that Hall had tumbled over of his own accord, turned to resume the pursuit, only to be tripped by the ankle just as Huxter had been. Then, as the first labourer struggled to his feet, he was kicked sideways by a blow that might have felled an ox.

As he went down, the rush from the direction of the village green came round the corner. The first to appear was the proprietor of the coconut shy, a burly man in a blue jersey. He was astonished to see the lane empty save for three men sprawling absurdly on the ground. And then something happened to his rearmost foot, and he went headlong and rolled sideways just in time to graze the feet of his brother and partner, following headlong. The two were then kicked, knelt on, fallen over and cursed by quite a number of over-hasty people.

Now when Hall and Henfrey and the labourers ran out of the house, Mrs Hall, who had been disciplined by years of experience, remained in the bar next the till. And suddenly the parlour door was opened, and Mr Cuss appeared, and without glancing at her rushed at once down the steps towards the corner. 'Hold him!' he cried. 'Don't let him drop that parcel.'

He knew nothing of the existence of Marvel. For the Invisible Man had handed over the books and bundle in the yard. The face of Mr Cuss was angry and resolute, but his costume was defective, a sort of limp white kilt that could only have passed muster in Greece. 'Hold him!' he bawled. 'He's got my trousers! And every stitch of the vicar's clothes!'

' 'Tend to him in a minute!' he cried to Henfrey as he passed the prostrate Huxter, and, coming round the corner to join the tumult, was promptly knocked off his feet into an indecorous sprawl. Somebody in full flight trod heavily on his finger. He yelled, struggled to regain his feet, was knocked against and thrown on all fours again, and became aware that he was involved not in a capture, but a rout. Everyone was running back to the village. He rose again and was hit severely behind the ear. He staggered and

set off back to the Coach and Horses forthwith, leaping over the deserted Huxter, who was now sitting up, on his way.

Behind him as he was halfway up the inn steps he heard a sudden yell of rage, rising sharply out of the confusion of cries, and a sounding smack in someone's face. He recognised the voice as that of the Invisible Man, and the note was that of a man suddenly infuriated by a painful blow.

In another moment Mr Cuss was back in the parlour. 'He's coming back, Bunting!' he said, rushing in. 'Save yourself!'

Mr Bunting was standing in the window engaged in an attempt to clothe himself in the hearthrug and a *West Surrey Gazette*. 'Who's coming?' he said, so startled that his costume narrowly escaped disintegration.

'Invisible Man,' said Cuss, and rushed on to the window. 'We'd better clear out from here! He's fighting mad! Mad!'

In another moment he was out in the yard.

'Good heavens!' said Mr Bunting, hesitating between two horrible alternatives. He heard a frightful struggle in the passage of the inn, and his decision was made. He clambered out of the window, adjusted his costume hastily, and fled up the village as fast as his fat little legs would carry him.

From the moment when the Invisible Man screamed with rage and Mr Bunting made his memorable flight up the village, it became impossible to give a consecutive account of affairs in Iping. Possibly the Invisible Man's original intention was simply to cover Marvel's retreat with the clothes and books. But his temper, at no time very good, seems to have gone completely at some chance blow, and forthwith he set to smiting and overthrowing, for the mere satisfaction of hurting.

You must figure the street full of running figures, of doors slamming and fights for hiding-places. You must figure the tumult suddenly striking on the unstable equilibrium of old Fletcher's planks and two chairs – with cataclysmic results. You must figure an appalled couple caught dismally in a swing. And then the whole tumultuous rush has passed and the Iping street with its gauds and flags is deserted save for the still raging unseen, and littered with coconuts, overthrown canvas screens, and the scattered stock in trade of a sweetstuff stall. Everywhere there is a sound of closing shutters and shoving bolts, and the only visible humanity is an occasional flitting eye under a raised eyebrow in the corner of a window pane.

The Invisible Man amused himself for a little while by breaking all the windows in the Coach and Horses, and then he thrust a street lamp through the parlour window of Mrs Gribble. He it must have been who cut the telegraph wire to Adderdean just beyond Higgins's cottage on the Adderdean road. And after that, as his peculiar qualities allowed, he passed out of human perceptions altogether, and he was neither heard, seen, nor felt in Iping any more. He vanished absolutely.

But it was the best part of two hours before any human being ventured out again into the desolation of Iping Street.

CHAPTER THIRTEEN

Mr Marvel Discusses his Resignation

When the dusk was gathering and Iping was just beginning to peep timorously forth again upon the shattered wreckage of its Bank Holiday, a short, thickset man in a shabby silk hat was marching painfully through the twilight behind the beechwoods on the road to Bramblehurst. He carried three books bound together by some sort of ornamental elastic ligature, and a bundle wrapped in a blue tablecloth. His rubicund face expressed consternation and fatigue; he appeared to be in a spasmodic sort of hurry. He was accompanied by a voice other than his own, and ever and again he winced under the touch of unseen hands.

'If you give me the slip again,' said the Voice, 'if you attempt to give me the slip again – '

'Lord!' said Mr Marvel. 'That shoulder's a mass of bruises as it is.'

'On my honour,' said the Voice, 'I will kill you.'

'I didn't try to give you the slip,' said Marvel, in a voice that was not far remote from tears. 'I swear I didn't. I didn't know the blessed turning, that was all! How the devil was I to know the blessed turning? As it is, I've been knocked about – '

'You'll get knocked about a great deal more if you don't mind,' said the Voice, and Mr Marvel abruptly became silent. He blew out his cheeks, and his eyes were eloquent of despair.

'It's bad enough to let these floundering yokels explode my little secret, without *your* cutting off with my books. It's lucky for some of them they cut and ran when they did! Here am I . . . No one knew I was invisible! And now what am I to do?'

'What am *I* to do?' asked Marvel, *sotto voce*.

'It's all about. It will be in the papers! Everybody will be looking for me; everyone on their guard – ' The Voice broke off into vivid curses and ceased.

The despair of Mr Marvel's face deepened, and his pace slackened.

'Go on!' said the Voice.

Mr Marvel's face assumed a greyish tint between the ruddier patches.

'Don't drop those books, stupid,' said the Voice, sharply – overtaking him.

'The fact is,' said the Voice, 'I shall have to make use of you . . . You're a poor tool, but I must.'

'I'm a *miserable* tool,' said Marvel.

'You are,' said the Voice.

'I'm the worst possible tool you could have,' said Marvel. 'I'm not

strong,' he said after a discouraging silence. 'I'm not over strong,' he repeated.

'No?'

'And my heart's weak. That little business – I pulled it through, of course – but bless you! I could have dropped.'

'Well?'

'I haven't the nerve and strength for the sort of thing you want.'

'*I'll* stimulate you.'

'I wish you wouldn't. I wouldn't like to mess up your plans, you know. But I might – out of sheer funk and misery.'

'You'd better not,' said the Voice, with quiet emphasis.

'I wish I was dead,' said Marvel. 'It ain't justice,' he said; 'you must admit . . . It seems to me I've a perfect right – '

'*Get* on!' said the Voice.

Mr Marvel mended his pace, and for a time they went in silence again.

'It's devilish hard,' said Mr Marvel.

This was quite ineffectual. He tried another tack.

'What do I make by it?' he began again in a tone of unendurable wrong.

'Oh! *shut up!*' said the Voice, with sudden amazing vigour. 'I'll see to you all right. You do what you're told. You'll do it all right. You're a fool and all that, but you'll do – '

'I tell you, sir, I'm not the man for it. Respectfully – but it *is* so – '

'If you don't shut up I shall twist your wrist again,' said the Invisible Man. 'I want to think.'

Presently two oblongs of yellow light appeared through the trees, and the square tower of a church loomed through the gloaming. 'I shall keep my hand on your shoulder,' said the Voice, 'all through the village. Go straight through and try no foolery. It will be the worse for you if you do.'

'I know that,' sighed Mr Marvel. 'I know all that.'

The unhappy-looking figure in the obsolete silk hat passed up the street of the little village with his burdens, and vanished into the gathering darkness beyond the lights of the windows.

CHAPTER FOURTEEN

At Port Stowe

Ten o'clock the next morning found Mr Marvel, unshaven, dirty and travel-stained, sitting with the books beside him and his hands deep in his pockets, looking very weary, nervous and uncomfortable, and inflating his cheeks at infrequent intervals, on the bench outside a little inn on the outskirts of Port Stowe. Beside him were the books, but now they were tied with string. The bundle had been abandoned in the pinewoods beyond Bramblehurst,

in accordance with a change in the plans of the Invisible Man. Mr Marvel sat on the bench, and although no one took the slightest notice of him, his agitation remained at fever heat. His hands would go ever and again to his various pockets with a curious nervous fumbling.

When he had been sitting for the best part of an hour, however, an elderly mariner, carrying a newspaper, came out of the inn and sat down beside him. 'Pleasant day,' said the mariner.

Mr Marvel glanced about him with something very like terror. 'Very,' he said.

'Just seasonable weather for the time of year,' said the mariner, taking no denial.

'Quite,' said Mr Marvel.

The mariner produced a toothpick, and (saving his regard) was engrossed thereby for some minutes. His eyes meanwhile were at liberty to examine Mr Marvel's dusty figure, and the books beside him. As he had approached Mr Marvel he had heard a sound like the dropping of coins into a pocket. He was struck by the contrast of Mr Marvel's appearance with this suggestion of opulence. Thence his mind wandered back again to a topic that had taken a curiously firm hold of his imagination.

'Books?' he said suddenly, noisily finishing with the toothpick.

Mr Marvel started and looked at them. 'Oh, yes,' he said. 'Yes, they're books.'

'There's some extra-ordinary things in books,' said the mariner.

'I believe you,' said Mr Marvel.

'And some extra-ordinary things out of 'em,' said the mariner.

'True likewise,' said Mr Marvel. He eyed his interlocutor, and then glanced about him.

'There's some extra-ordinary things in newspapers, for example,' said the mariner.

'There are.'

'In *this* newspaper,' said the mariner.

'Ah!' said Mr Marvel.

'There's a story,' said the mariner, fixing Mr Marvel with an eye that was firm and deliberate; 'there's a story about an Invisible Man, for instance.'

Mr Marvel pulled his mouth askew and scratched his cheek and felt his ears glowing.

'What will they be writing next?' he asked faintly. 'Ostria, or America?'

'Neither,' said the mariner. '*Here!*'

'Lord!' said Mr Marvel, starting.

'When I say *here*,' said the mariner, to Mr Marvel's intense relief, 'I don't of course mean here in this place, I mean hereabouts.'

'An Invisible Man!' said Mr Marvel. 'And what's *he* been up to?'

'Everything,' said the mariner, controlling Marvel with his eye, and then amplifying, 'every – blessed – thing.'

'I ain't seen a paper these four days,' said Marvel.

'Iping's the place he started at,' said the mariner.

'In-*deed*!' said Mr Marvel.

'He started there. And where he came from, nobody don't seem to know. Here it is: "Pe-culiar Story from Iping". And it says in this paper that the evidence is extra-ordinary strong – extra-ordinary.'

'Lord!' said Mr Marvel.

'But then, it's an extra-ordinary story. There is a clergyman and a medical gent witnesses – saw 'im all right and proper – or leastways didn't see 'im. He was staying, it says, at the Coach an' Horses, and no one don't seem to have been aware of his misfortune, it says, aware of his misfortune, until in an Altercation in the inn, it says, his bandages on his head was torn off. It was then ob-served that his head was invisible. Attempts were At Once made to secure him, but casting off his garments, it says, he succeeded in escaping, but not until after a desperate struggle, in which he had inflicted serious injuries, it says, on our worthy and able constable, Mr J. A. Jaffers. Pretty straight story, eh? Names and everything.'

'Lord!' said Mr Marvel, looking nervously about him, trying to count the money in his pockets by his unaided sense of touch, and full of a strange and novel idea. 'It sounds most astonishing.'

'Don't it? Extra-ordinary, *I* call it. Never heard tell of Invisible Men before, I haven't, but nowadays one hears such a lot of extra-ordinary things – that – '

'That all he did?' asked Marvel, trying to seem at his ease.

'It's enough, ain't it?' said the mariner.

'Didn't go back by any chance?' asked Marvel. 'Just escaped and that's all, eh?'

'All!' said the mariner. 'Why! – ain't it enough?'

'Quite enough,' said Marvel.

'I should think it was enough,' said the mariner. 'I should think it was enough.'

'He didn't have any pals – it don't say he had any pals, does it?' asked Mr Marvel, anxious.

'Ain't one of a sort enough for you?' asked the mariner. 'No, thank heaven, as one might say, he didn't.'

He nodded his head slowly. 'It makes me regular uncomfortable, the bare thought of that chap running about the country! He is at present At Large, and from certain evidence it is supposed that he has taken – *took*, I suppose they mean – the road to Port Stowe. You see we're right *in* it! None of your American wonders, this time. And just think of the things he might do! Where'd you be, if he took a drop over and above, and had a fancy to go for you? Suppose he wants to rob – who can prevent him? He can trespass, he can burgle, he could walk through a cordon of policemen as easy as me or you could give the slip to a blind man! Easier! For these

here blind chaps hear uncommon sharp, I'm told. And wherever there was liquor he fancied – '

'He's got a tremenjous advantage, certainly,' said Mr Marvel. 'And – well . . . '

'You're right,' said the mariner. 'He *has*.'

All this time Mr Marvel had been glancing about him intently, listening for faint footfalls, trying to detect imperceptible movements. He seemed on the point of some great resolution. He coughed behind his hand.

He looked about him again, listened, bent towards the mariner, and lowered his voice: 'The fact of it is – I happen – to know just a thing or two about this Invisible Man. From private sources.'

'Oh!' said the mariner, interested. '*You?*'

'Yes,' said Mr Marvel. 'Me.'

'Indeed!' said the mariner. 'And may I ask – '

'You'll be astonished,' said Mr Marvel behind his hand. 'It's tremenjous.'

'Indeed!' said the mariner.

'The fact is,' began Mr Marvel eagerly in a confidential undertone. Suddenly his expression changed marvellously. 'Ow!' he said. He rose stiffly in his seat. His face was eloquent of physical suffering. 'Wow!' he said.

'What's up?' said the mariner, concerned.

'Toothache,' said Mr Marvel, and put his hand to his ear. He caught hold of his books. 'I must be getting on, I think,' he said. He edged in a curious way along the seat away from his interlocutor.

'But you was just a-going to tell me about this here Invisible Man!' protested the mariner.

Mr Marvel seemed to consult with himself. 'Hoax,' said a Voice. 'It's a hoax,' said Mr Marvel.

'But it's in the paper,' said the mariner.

'Hoax all the same,' said Marvel. 'I know the chap that started the lie. There ain't no Invisible Man whatsoever – Blimey.'

'But how 'bout this paper? D'you mean to say – ?'

'Not a word of it,' said Marvel, stoutly.

The mariner stared, paper in hand. Mr Marvel jerkily faced about. 'Wait a bit,' said the mariner, rising and speaking slowly, 'D'you mean to say – ?'

'I do,' said Mr Marvel.

'Then why did you let me go on and tell you all this blarsted stuff, then? What d'yer mean by letting a man make a fool of himself like that for? Eh?'

Mr Marvel blew out his cheeks.

The mariner was suddenly very red indeed; he clenched his hands. 'I been talking here this ten minutes,' he said; 'and you, you little pot-bellied, leathery-faced son of an old boot, couldn't have the elementary manners – '

'Don't you come bandying words with *me*,' said Mr Marvel.

'Bandying words! I'm a jolly good mind – '

'Come up,' said a Voice, and Mr Marvel was suddenly whirled about and started marching off in a curious spasmodic manner.

'You'd better move on,' said the mariner.

'*Who's* moving on?' said Mr Marvel. He was receding obliquely with a curious hurrying gait, with occasional violent jerks forward. Some way along the road he began a muttered monologue, protests and recriminations.

'Silly devil!' said the mariner, legs wide apart, elbows akimbo, watching the receding figure. 'I'll show you, you silly ass – hoaxing *me*! It's here – in the paper!'

Mr Marvel retorted incoherently and, receding, was hidden by a bend in the road, but the mariner still stood magnificent in the midst of the way, until the approach of a butcher's cart dislodged him. Then he turned himself towards Port Stowe. 'Full of extra-ordinary asses,' he said softly to himself. 'Just to take me down a bit – that was his silly game It's in the paper!'

And there was another extraordinary thing he was presently to hear, that had happened quite close to him. And that was a vision of a 'fist full of money' (no less) travelling without visible agency, along by the wall at the corner of St Michael's Lane. A brother mariner had seen this wonderful sight that very morning. He had snatched at the money forthwith and had been knocked headlong, and when he had got to his feet the butterfly money had vanished. Our mariner was in the mood to believe anything, he declared, but that was a bit *too* stiff. Afterwards, however, he began to think things over.

The story of the flying money was true. And all about that neighbourhood, even from the august London and Country Banking Company, from the tills of shops and inns – doors standing that sunny weather entirely open – money had been quietly and dexterously making off that day in handfuls and rouleaux, floating quietly along by walls and shady places, dodging quickly from the approaching eyes of men. And it had, though no man had traced it, invariably ended its mysterious flight in the pocket of that agitated gentleman in the obsolete silk hat, sitting outside the little inn on the outskirts of Port Stowe.

It was ten days after – and indeed only when the Burdock story was already old – that the mariner collated these facts and began to understand how near he had been to the wonderful Invisible Man.

CHAPTER FIFTEEN

The Man Who was Running

In the early evening time, Dr Kemp was sitting in his study in the belvedere on the hill overlooking Burdock. It was a pleasant little room, with three windows – north, west and south – and bookshelves covered with books and scientific publications, and a broad writing-table, and, under the north window, a microscope, glass slips, minute instruments, some cultures and scattered bottles of reagents. Dr Kemp's solar lamp was lit, albeit the sky was still bright with the sunset light, and his blinds were up because there was no offence of peering outsiders to require them pulled down. Dr Kemp was a tall and slender young man, with flaxen hair and a moustache almost white, and the work he was upon would earn him, he hoped, the fellowship of the Royal Society, so highly did he think of it.

And his eye, presently wandering from his work, caught the sunset blazing at the back of the hill that is over against his own. For a minute perhaps he sat, pen in mouth, admiring the rich golden colour above the crest, and then his attention was attracted by the little figure of a man, inky black, running over the hill-brow towards him. He was a shortish little man, and he wore a high hat, and he was running so fast that his legs verily twinkled.

'Another of those fools,' said Dr Kemp. 'Like that ass who ran into me this morning round a corner, with the " 'Visible Man a-coming, sir!" I can't imagine what possesses people. One might think we were in the thirteenth century.'

He got up, went to the window, and stared at the dusky hillside, and the dark little figure tearing down it. 'He seems in a confounded hurry,' said Dr Kemp, 'but he doesn't seem to be getting on. If his pockets were full of lead, he couldn't run heavier.

'Spurted, sir,' said Dr Kemp.

In another moment the higher of the villas that had clambered up the hill from Burdock had occulted the running figure. He was visible again for a moment, and again, and then again, three times between the three detached houses that came next, and then the terrace hid him.

'Asses!' said Dr Kemp, swinging round on his heel and walking back to his writing-table.

But those who saw the fugitive nearer, and perceived the abject terror on his perspiring face, being themselves in the open roadway, did not share in the doctor's contempt. By the man pounded, and as he ran he chinked like a well-filled purse that is tossed to and fro. He looked neither to the right nor the left, but his dilated eyes stared straight downhill to where the lamps

were being lit, and the people were crowded in the street. And his ill-shaped mouth fell apart, and a glairy foam lay on his lips, and his breath came hoarse and noisy. All he passed stopped and began staring up the road and down, and interrogating one another with an inkling of discomfort for the reason of his haste.

And then presently, far up the hill, a dog playing in the road yelped and ran under a gate, and as they still wondered, something – a wind – a pad, pad, pad – a sound like a panting breathing, rushed by.

People screamed. People sprang off the pavement. It passed in shouts, it passed by instinct down the hill. They were shouting in the street before Marvel was halfway there. They were bolting into houses and slamming the doors behind them, with the news. He heard it and made one last desperate spurt. Fear came striding by, rushed ahead of him, and in a moment had seized the town.

'The Invisible Man is coming! *The Invisible Man!*'

CHAPTER SIXTEEN

In the Jolly Cricketers

The Jolly Cricketers is just at the bottom of the hill, where the tram-lines begin. The barman leant his fat red arms on the counter and talked of horses with an anaemic cabman, while a black-bearded man in grey snapped up biscuit and cheese, drank Burton, and conversed in American with a policeman off duty.

'What's the shouting about!' said the cabman, going off at a tangent, trying to see up the hill over the dirty yellow blind in the low window of the inn. Somebody ran by outside. 'Fire, perhaps,' said the barman.

Footsteps approached, running heavily, the door was pushed open violently, and Marvel, weeping and dishevelled, his hat gone, the neck of his coat torn open, rushed in, made a convulsive turn, and attempted to shut the door. It was held half open by a strap.

'Coming!' he bawled, his voice shrieking with terror. 'He's coming. The 'Visible Man! After me! For Gawd's sake! 'Elp! 'Elp! 'Elp!'

'Shut the doors,' said the policeman. 'Who's coming? What's the row?' He went to the door, released the strap, and it slammed. The American closed the other door.

'Lemme go inside,' said Marvel, staggering and weeping, but still clutching the books. 'Lemme go inside. Lock me in – somewhere. I tell you he's after me. I give him the slip. He said he'd kill me and he will.'

'*You're* safe,' said the man with the black beard. 'The door's shut. What's it all about?'

'Lemme go inside,' said Marvel, and shrieked aloud as a blow suddenly

made the fastened door shiver and was followed by a hurried rapping and a shouting outside. 'Hello,' cried the policeman, 'who's there?' Mr Marvel began to make frantic dives at panels that looked like doors. 'He'll kill me – he's got a knife or something. For Gawd's sake – !'

'Here you are,' said the barman. 'Come in here.' And he held up the flap of the bar.

Mr Marvel rushed behind the bar as the summons outside was repeated. 'Don't open the door,' he screamed. '*Please* don't open the door. *Where* shall I hide?'

'This, this Invisible Man, then?' asked the man with the black beard, with one hand behind him. 'I guess it's about time we saw him.'

The window of the inn was suddenly smashed in, and there was a screaming and running to and fro in the street. The policeman had been standing on the settee staring out, craning to see who was at the door. He got down with raised eyebrows. 'It's that,' he said. The barman stood in front of the bar-parlour door which was now locked on Mr Marvel, stared at the smashed window, and came round to the two other men.

Everything was suddenly quiet. 'I wish I had my truncheon,' said the policeman, going irresolutely to the door. 'Once we open, in he comes. There's no stopping him.'

'Don't you be in too much hurry about that door,' said the anaemic cabman, anxiously.

'Draw the bolts,' said the man with the black beard, 'and if he comes – ' He showed a revolver in his hand.

'That won't do,' said the policeman; 'that's murder.'

'I know what country I'm in,' said the man with the beard. 'I'm going to let off at his legs. Draw the bolts.'

'Not with that blinking thing going off behind me,' said the barman, craning over the blind.

'Very well,' said the man with the black beard, and stooping down, revolver ready, drew them himself. Barman, cabman and policeman faced about.

'Come in,' said the bearded man in an undertone, standing back and facing the unbolted door with his pistol behind him. No one came in, the door remained closed. Five minutes afterwards when a second cabman pushed his head in cautiously, they were still waiting, and an anxious face peered out of the bar-parlour and supplied information. 'Are all the doors of the house shut?' asked Marvel. 'He's going round – prowling round. He's as artful as the devil.'

'Good Lord!' said the burly barman. 'There's the back! Just watch them doors! I say – !' He looked about him helplessly. The bar-parlour door slammed and they heard the key turn. 'There's the yard door and the private door. The yard door – '

He rushed out of the bar.

In a minute he reappeared with a carving-knife in his hand. 'The yard door was open!' he said, and his fat underlip dropped.

'He may be in the house now!' said the first cabman.

'He's not in the kitchen,' said the barman. 'There's two women there, and I've stabbed every inch of it with this little beef slicer. And they don't think he's come in. They haven't noticed – '

'Have you fastened it?' asked the first cabman.

'I'm out of frocks,' said the barman.

The man with the beard replaced his revolver. And even as he did so the flap of the bar was shut down and the bolt clicked, and then with a tremendous thud the catch of the door snapped and the bar-parlour door burst open. They heard Marvel squeal like a caught leveret, and forthwith they were clambering over the bar to his rescue. The bearded man's revolver cracked and the looking-glass at the back of the parlour starred and came smashing and tinkling down.

As the barman entered the room he saw Marvel, curiously crumpled up and struggling against the door that led to the yard and kitchen. The door flew open while the barman hesitated, and Marvel was dragged into the kitchen. There was a scream and a clatter of pans. Marvel, head down, and lugging back obstinately, was forced to the kitchen door, and the bolts were drawn.

Then the policeman, who had been trying to pass the barman, rushed in, followed by one of the cabmen, gripped the wrist of the invisible hand that collared Marvel, was hit in the face and went reeling back. The door opened, and Marvel made a frantic effort to obtain a lodgment behind it. Then the cabman collared something. 'I got him,' said the cabman. The barman's red hands came clawing at the unseen. 'Here he is!' said the barman.

Mr Marvel, released, suddenly dropped to the ground and made an attempt to crawl behind the legs of the fighting men. The struggle blundered round the edge of the door. The voice of the Invisible Man was heard for the first time, yelling out sharply as the policeman trod on his foot. Then he cried out passionately and his fists flew round like flails. The cabman suddenly whooped and doubled up, kicked under the diaphragm. The door into the bar-parlour from the kitchen slammed and covered Mr Marvel's retreat. The men in the kitchen found themselves clutching at and struggling with empty air.

'Where's he gone?' cried the man with the beard. 'Out?'

'This way,' said the policeman, stepping into the yard and stopping.

A piece of tile whizzed by his head and smashed among the crockery on the kitchen table.

'I'll show him,' shouted the man with the black beard, and suddenly a steel barrel shone over the policeman's shoulder, and five bullets had followed one another into the twilight whence the missile had come. As he

fired, the man with the beard moved his hand in a horizontal curve, so that his shots radiated out into the narrow yard like spokes from a wheel.

A silence followed. 'Five cartridges,' said the man with the black beard. 'That's the best of all. Four aces and a joker. Get a lantern, someone, and come and feel about for his body.'

CHAPTER SEVENTEEN

Dr Kemp's Visitor

Dr Kemp had continued writing in his study until the shots aroused him. Crack, crack, crack, they came one after the other.

'Hello!' said Dr Kemp, putting his pen into his mouth again and listening. 'Who's letting off revolvers in Burdock? What are the asses at now?'

He went to the south window, threw it up, and leaning out stared down on the network of windows, beaded gas-lamps and shops, with its black interstices of roof and yard that made up the town at night. 'Looks like a crowd down the hill,' he said, 'by the Cricketers,' and remained watching. Thence his eyes wandered over the town to far away where the ships' lights shone, and the pier glowed – a little illuminated, faceted pavilion like a gem of yellow light. The moon in its first quarter hung over the westward hill, and the stars were clear and almost tropically bright.

After five minutes, during which his mind had travelled into a remote speculation on social conditions of the future and lost itself at last over the time dimension, Dr Kemp roused himself with a sigh, pulled down the window again, and returned to his writing desk.

It must have been about an hour after this that the front-door bell rang. He had been writing slackly, and with intervals of abstraction, since the shots. He sat listening. He heard the servant answer the door, and waited for her feet on the staircase, but she did not come. 'Wonder what that was,' said Dr Kemp.

He tried to resume his work, failed, got up, went downstairs from his study to the landing, rang, and called over the balustrade to the housemaid as she appeared in the hall below. 'Was that a letter?' he asked.

'Only a runaway ring, sir,' she answered.

'I'm restless tonight,' he said to himself. He went back to his study, and this time attacked his work resolutely. In a little while he was hard at work again, and the only sounds in the room were the ticking of the clock and the subdued shrillness of his quill, hurrying in the very centre of the circle of light his lampshade threw on his table.

It was two o'clock before Dr Kemp had finished his work for the night. He rose, yawned, and went downstairs to bed. He had already removed his

coat and waistcoat, when he noticed that he was thirsty. He took a candle and went down to the dining-room in search of a syphon and whisky.

Dr Kemp's scientific pursuits had made him a very observant man, and as he recrossed the hall, he noticed a dark spot on the linoleum near the mat at the foot of the stairs. He went on upstairs, and then it suddenly occurred to him to ask himself what the spot on the linoleum might be. Apparently some subconscious element was at work. At any rate, he turned with his burden, went back to the hall, put down the syphon and whisky, and bending down, touched the spot. Without any great surprise he found it had the stickiness and colour of drying blood.

He took up his burden again, and returned upstairs, looking about him and trying to account for the blood-spot. On the landing he saw something and stopped astonished. The door-handle of his own room was blood-stained.

He looked at his own hand. It was quite clean, and then he remembered that the door of his room had been open when he came down from his study, and that consequently he had not touched the handle at all. He went straight into his room, his face quite calm – perhaps a trifle more resolute than usual. His glance, wandering inquisitively, fell on the bed. On the counterpane was a mess of blood, and the sheet had been torn. He had not noticed this before because he had walked straight to the dressing-table. On the farther side the bedclothes were depressed as if someone had been recently sitting there.

Then he had an odd impression that he had heard a low voice say, 'Good heavens! – Kemp!' But Dr Kemp was no believer in voices.

He stood staring at the tumbled sheets. Was that really a voice? He looked about again, but noticed nothing further than the disordered and blood-stained bed. Then he distinctly heard a movement across the room, near the wash-hand stand. All men, however highly educated, retain some superstitious inklings. The feeling that is called 'eerie' came upon him. He closed the door of the room, came forward to the dressing-table and put down his burdens. Suddenly, with a start, he perceived a coiled and blood-stained bandage of linen rag hanging in mid-air, between him and the wash-hand stand.

He stared at this in amazement. It was an empty bandage, a bandage properly tied but quite empty. He would have advanced to grasp it, but a touch arrested him, and a voice speaking quite close to him.

'Kemp!' said the Voice.

'Eh?' said Kemp, with his mouth open.

'Keep your nerve,' said the Voice. 'I'm an Invisible Man.'

Kemp made no answer for a space, simply stared at the bandage. 'Invisible Man,' he said.

'I am an Invisible Man,' repeated the Voice.

The story he had been active to ridicule only that morning rushed

through Kemp's brain. He does not appear to have been either very much frightened or very greatly surprised at the moment. Realisation came later.

'I thought it was all a lie,' he said. The thought uppermost in his mind was the reiterated arguments of the morning. 'Have you a bandage on?' he asked.

'Yes,' said the Invisible Man.

'Oh!' said Kemp, and then roused himself. 'I say!' he said. 'But this is nonsense. It's some trick.' He stepped forward suddenly, and his hand, extended towards the bandage, met invisible fingers.

He recoiled at the touch and his colour changed.

'Keep steady, Kemp, for God's sake! I want help badly. Stop!'

The hand gripped his arm. He struck at it.

'Kemp!' cried the Voice. 'Kemp! Keep steady!' and the grip tightened.

A frantic desire to free himself took possession of Kemp. The hand of the bandaged arm gripped his shoulder, and he was suddenly tripped and flung backwards upon the bed. He opened his mouth to shout, and the corner of the sheet was thrust between his teeth. The Invisible Man had him down grimly, but his arms were free and he struck and tried to kick savagely.

'Listen to reason, will you?' said the Invisible Man, sticking to him in spite of a pounding in the ribs. 'By heaven! you'll madden me in a minute! Lie still, you fool!' he bawled in Kemp's ear.

Kemp struggled for another moment and then lay still.

'If you shout, I'll smash your face,' said the Invisible Man, relieving his mouth. 'I'm an Invisible Man. It's no foolishness, and no magic. I really am an Invisible Man. And I want your help. I don't want to hurt you, but if you behave like a frantic rustic, I must. Don't you remember me, Kemp? Griffin, of University College?'

'Let me get up,' said Kemp. 'I'll stop where I am. And let me sit quiet for a minute.'

He sat up and felt his neck.

'I am Griffin, of University College, and I have made myself invisible. I am just an ordinary man – a man you have known – made invisible.'

'Griffin?' said Kemp.

'Griffin,' answered the Voice. A younger student than you were, almost an albino, six feet high, and broad, with a pink and white face and red eyes, who won the medal for chemistry.'

'I am confused,' said Kemp. 'My brain is rioting. What has this to do with Griffin?'

'I *am* Griffin.'

Kemp thought. 'It's horrible,' he said. 'But what devilry must happen to make a man invisible?'

'It's no devilry. It's a process, sane and intelligible enough – '

'It's horrible!' said Kemp. 'How on earth – ?'

'It's horrible enough. But I'm wounded and in pain, and tired . . . Great

God! Kemp, you are a man. Take it steady. Give me some food and drink, and let me sit down here.'

Kemp stared at the bandage as it moved across the room, then saw a basket chair dragged across the floor and come to rest near the bed. It creaked, and the seat was depressed a quarter of an inch or so. He rubbed his eyes and felt his neck again. 'This beats ghosts,' he said, and laughed stupidly.

'That's better. Thank heaven, you're getting sensible!'

'Or silly,' said Kemp, and knuckled his eyes.

'Give me some whisky. I'm near dead.'

'It didn't feel so. Where are you? If I get up shall I run into you? *There!* All right. Whisky? Here. Where shall I give it to you?'

The chair creaked and Kemp felt the glass drawn away from him. He let go by an effort; his instinct was all against it. It came to rest poised twenty inches above the front edge of the seat of the chair. He stared at it in infinite perplexity. 'This is – this *must* be – hypnotism. You have suggested you are invisible.'

'Nonsense,' said the Voice.

'It's frantic.'

'Listen to me.'

'I demonstrated conclusively this morning,' began Kemp, 'that invisibility – '

'Never mind what you've demonstrated! – I'm starving,' said the Voice, 'and the night is chilly to a man without clothes.'

'Food?' said Kemp.

The tumbler of whisky tilted itself. 'Yes,' said the Invisible Man rapping it down. 'Have you a dressing-gown?'

Kemp made some exclamation in an undertone. He walked to a wardrobe and produced a robe of dingy scarlet. 'This do?' he asked. It was taken from him. It hung limp for a moment in midair, fluttered weirdly, stood full and decorous buttoning itself, and sat down in his chair. 'Drawers, socks, slippers would be a comfort,' said the Unseen, curtly. 'And food.'

'Anything. But this is the insanest thing I ever was in, in my life!'

He turned out his drawers for the articles, and then went downstairs to ransack his larder. He came back with some cold cutlets and bread, pulled up a light table, and placed them before his guest. 'Never mind knives,' said his visitor, and a cutlet hung in mid-air, with a sound of gnawing.

'Invisible!' said Kemp, and sat down on a bedroom chair.

'I always like to get something about me before I eat,' said the Invisible Man, with a full mouth, eating greedily. 'Queer fancy!'

'I suppose that wrist is all right,' said Kemp.

'Trust me,' said the Invisible Man.

'Of *all* the strange and wonderful – '

'Exactly. But it's odd I should blunder into *your* house to get my

bandaging. My first stroke of luck! Anyhow I meant to sleep in this house tonight. You must stand that! It's a filthy nuisance, my blood showing, isn't it? Quite a clot over there. Gets visible as it coagulates, I see. It's only the living tissue I've changed, and only for as long as I'm alive . . . I've been in the house three hours.'

'But how's it done?' began Kemp, in a tone of exasperation. 'Confound it! The whole business – it's unreasonable from beginning to end.'

'Quite reasonable,' said the Invisible Man. 'Perfectly reasonable.' He reached over and secured the whisky bottle.

Kemp stared at the devouring dressing-gown. A ray of candlelight, penetrating a torn patch in the right shoulder, made a triangle of light under the left ribs. 'What were the shots?' he asked. 'How did the shooting begin?'

'There was a real fool of a man – a sort of confederate of mine – curse him! – who tried to steal my money. *Has* done so.'

'Is *he* invisible too?'

'No.'

'Well?'

'Can't I have some more to eat before I tell you all that? I'm hungry – in pain. And you want me to tell stories!'

Kemp got up. '*You* didn't do any shooting?' he asked.

'Not me,' said his visitor. 'Some fool I'd never seen fired at random. A lot of them got scared. They all got scared at me. Curse them! – I say – I want more to eat than this, Kemp.'

'I'll see what more there is to eat downstairs,' said Kemp. 'Not much, I'm afraid.'

After he had done eating, and he made a heavy meal, the Invisible Man demanded a cigar. He bit the end savagely before Kemp could find a knife, and cursed when the outer leaf loosened. It was strange to see him smoking; his mouth and throat, pharynx and nares, became visible as a sort of whirling smoke cast.

'This blessed gift of smoking!' he said, and puffed vigorously. 'I'm lucky to have fallen upon you, Kemp. You must help me. Fancy tumbling on you just now! I'm in a devilish scrape – I've been mad, I think. The things I have been through! But we will do things yet. Let me tell you – '

He helped himself to more whisky and soda. Kemp got up, looked about him, and fetched a glass from his spare room. 'It's wild – but I suppose I may drink.'

'You haven't changed much, Kemp, these dozen years. You fair men don't. Cool and methodical – after the first collapse. I must tell you. We will work together!'

'But how was it all done?' said Kemp, 'and how did you get like this?'

'For God's sake, let me smoke in peace for a little while! And then I will begin to tell you.'

But the story was not told that night. The Invisible Man's wrist was growing painful; he was feverish, exhausted, and his mind came round to brood upon his chase down the hill and the struggle about the inn. He spoke in fragments of Marvel, he smoked faster, his voice grew angry. Kemp tried to gather what he could.

'He was afraid of me, I could see that he was afraid of me,' said the Invisible Man many times over. 'He meant to give me the slip – he was always casting about! What a fool I was!

'The cur!

'I should have killed him!'

'Where did you get the money?' asked Kemp, abruptly.

The Invisible Man was silent for a space. 'I can't tell you tonight,' he said.

He groaned suddenly and leant forward, supporting his invisible head on invisible hands. 'Kemp,' he said, 'I've had no sleep for near three days, except a couple of dozes of an hour or so. I must sleep soon.'

'Well, have my room – have this room.'

'But how can I sleep? If I sleep – he will get away. Ugh! What does it matter?'

'What's the shot wound?' asked Kemp, abruptly.

'Nothing – scratch and blood. Oh, God! How I want sleep!'

'Why not?'

The Invisible Man appeared to be regarding Kemp. 'Because I've a particular objection to being caught by my fellow men,' he said slowly.

Kemp started.

'Fool that I am!' said the Invisible Man, striking the table smartly. 'I've put the idea into your head.'

CHAPTER EIGHTEEN

The Invisible Man Sleeps

Exhausted and wounded as the Invisible Man was, he refused to accept Kemp's word that his freedom should be respected. He examined the two windows of the bedroom, drew up the blinds and opened the sashes, to confirm Kemp's statement that a retreat by them would be possible. Outside the night was very quiet and still, and the new moon was setting over the down. Then he examined the keys of the bedroom and the two dressing-room doors, to satisfy himself that these also could be made an assurance of freedom. Finally he expressed himself satisfied. He stood on the hearth rug and Kemp heard the sound of a yawn.

'I'm sorry,' said the Invisible Man, 'if I cannot tell you all that I have done tonight. But I am worn out. It's grotesque, no doubt. It's horrible! But

believe me, Kemp, in spite of your arguments of this morning, it is quite a possible thing. I have made a discovery. I meant to keep it to myself. I can't. I must have a partner. And you . . . We can do such things . . . But tomorrow. Now, Kemp, I feel as though I must sleep or perish.'

Kemp stood in the middle of the room staring at the headless garment. 'I suppose I must leave you,' he said. 'It's – incredible. Three things happening like this, overturning all my preconceptions – would make me insane. But it's real! Is there anything more that I can get you?'

'Only bid me good-night,' said Griffin.

'Good-night,' said Kemp, and shook an invisible hand. He walked sideways to the door. Suddenly the dressing-gown walked quickly towards him. 'Understand me!' said the dressing-gown. 'No attempts to hamper me, or capture me! Or – '

Kemp's face changed a little. 'I thought I gave you my word,' he said.

Kemp closed the door softly behind him, and the key was turned upon him forthwith. Then, as he stood with an expression of passive amazement on his face, the rapid feet came to the door of the dressing-room and that too was locked. Kemp slapped his brow with his hand. 'Am I dreaming? Has the world gone mad – or have I?'

He laughed, and put his hand to the locked door. 'Barred out of my own bedroom, by a flagrant absurdity!' he said.

He walked to the head of the staircase, turned, and stared at the locked doors. 'It's fact,' he said. He put his fingers to his slightly bruised neck. 'Undeniable fact!

'But – '

He shook his head hopelessly, turned, and went downstairs.

He lit the dining-room lamp, got out a cigar, and began pacing the room, ejaculating. Now and then he would argue with himself.

'Invisible!' he said.

'Is there such a thing as an invisible animal? . . . In the sea, yes. Thousands – millions. All the larvae, all the little nauplii and tornarias, all the microscopic things, the jellyfish. In the sea there are more things invisible than visible! I never thought of that before. And in the ponds too! All those little pond-life things – specks of colourless translucent jelly! But in air? No!

'It can't be.

'But after all – why not?

'If a man was made of glass he would still be visible.'

His meditation became profound. The bulk of three cigars had passed into the invisible or diffused as a white ash over the carpet before he spoke again. Then it was merely an exclamation. He turned aside, walked out of the room, and went into his little consulting-room and lit the gas there. It was a little room, because Dr Kemp did not live by practice, and in it were the day's newspapers. The morning's paper lay carelessly opened and

thrown aside. He caught it up, turned it over, and read the account of a 'Strange Story from Iping' that the mariner at Port Stowe had spelt over so painfully to Mr Marvel. Kemp read it swiftly.

'Wrapped up!' said Kemp. 'Disguised! Hiding it! "No one seems to have been aware of his misfortune." What the devil *is* his game?'

He dropped the paper, and his eye went seeking. 'Ah!' he said, and caught up the *St James's Gazette*, lying folded up as it arrived. 'Now we shall get at the truth,' said Dr Kemp. He rent the paper open; a couple of columns confronted him. 'An Entire Village in Sussex goes Mad' was the heading.

'Good heavens!' said Kemp, reading eagerly an incredulous account of the events in Iping of the previous afternoon that have already been described. Over the leaf the report in the morning paper had been reprinted.

He re-read it. 'Ran through the streets striking right and left. Jaffers insensible. Mr Huxter in great pain – still unable to describe what he saw. Painful humiliation – vicar. Woman ill with terror! Windows smashed. This extraordinary story probably a fabrication. Too good not to print – *cum grano*!'

He dropped the paper and stared blankly in front of him. 'Probably a fabrication!'

He caught up the paper again, and re-read the whole business. 'But when does the tramp come in? Why the deuce was he chasing a tramp?'

He sat down abruptly on the surgical bench. 'He's not only invisible,' he said, 'but he's mad! Homicidal!'

When dawn came to mingle its pallor with the lamplight and cigar smoke of the dining-room, Kemp was still pacing up and down, trying to grasp the incredible.

He was altogether too excited to sleep. His servants, descending sleepily, discovered him, and were inclined to think that over-study had worked this ill on him. He gave them extraordinary but quite explicit instructions to lay breakfast for two in the belvedere study – and then to confine themselves to the basement and ground-floor. Then he continued to pace the dining-room until the morning's paper came. That had much to say and little to tell, beyond the confirmation of the evening before, and a very badly written account of another remarkable tale from Port Burdock. This gave Kemp the essence of the happenings at the Jolly Cricketers, and the name of Marvel. 'He has made me keep with him twenty-four hours,' Marvel testified. Certain minor facts were added to the Iping story, notably the cutting of the village telegraph-wire. But there was nothing to throw light on the connection between the Invisible Man and the tramp; for Mr Marvel had supplied no information about the three books, or the money with which he was lined. The incredulous tone had vanished and a shoal of reporters and enquirers were already at work elaborating the matter.

Kemp read every scrap of the report and sent his housemaid out to get every one of the morning papers she could. These also he devoured.

'He is invisible!' he said. 'And it reads like rage growing to mania! The things he may do! The things he may do! And he's upstairs free as the air. What on earth ought I to do?

'For instance, would it be a breach of faith if – ? No.'

He went to a little untidy desk in the corner, and began a note. He tore this up half written, and wrote another. He read it over and considered it. Then he took an envelope and addressed it to 'Colonel Adye, Port Burdock'.

The Invisible Man awoke even as Kemp was doing this. He awoke in an evil temper, and Kemp, alert for every sound, heard his pattering feet rush suddenly across the bedroom overhead. Then a chair was flung over and the wash-hand-stand tumbler smashed. Kemp hurried upstairs and rapped eagerly.

CHAPTER NINETEEN

Certain First Principles

'What's the matter?' asked Kemp, when the Invisible Man admitted him.

'Nothing,' was the answer.

'But, confound it! The smash?'

'Fit of temper,' said the Invisible Man. 'Forgot this arm; and it's sore.'

'You're rather liable to that sort of thing.'

'I am.'

Kemp walked across the room and picked up the fragments of broken glass. 'All the facts are out about you,' said Kemp, standing up with the glass in his hand; 'all that happened in Iping, and down the hill. The world has become aware of its invisible citizen. But no one knows you are here.'

The Invisible Man swore.

'The secret's out. I gather it was a secret. I don't know what your plans are, but of course I'm anxious to help you.'

The Invisible Man sat down on the bed.

'There's breakfast upstairs,' said Kemp, speaking as easily as possible, and he was delighted to find his strange guest rose willingly. Kemp led the way up the narrow staircase to the belvedere.

'Before we can do anything else,' said Kemp, 'I must understand a little more about this invisibility of yours.' He had sat down, after one nervous glance out of the window, with the air of a man who has talking to do. His doubts of the sanity of the entire business flashed and vanished again as he looked across to where Griffin sat at the breakfast-table – a headless, handless dressing-gown, wiping unseen lips on a miraculously held serviette.

'It's simple enough – and credible enough,' said Griffin, putting the serviette aside and leaning the invisible head on an invisible hand.

'No doubt, to you, but – ' Kemp laughed.

'Well, yes; to me it seemed wonderful at first, no doubt. But now, great God! . . . But we will do great things yet! I came on the stuff first at Chesilstowe.'

'Chesilstowe?'

'I went there after I left London. You know I dropped medicine and took up physics? No; well, I did. *Light* fascinated me.'

'Ah!'

'Optical density! The whole subject is a network of riddles – a network with solutions glimmering elusively through. And being but two-and-twenty and full of enthusiasm, I said, "I will devote my life to this. This is worth while." You know what fools we are at two-and-twenty?'

'Fools then or fools now,' said Kemp.

'As though knowing could be any satisfaction to a man!

'But I went to work – like a slave. And I had hardly worked and thought about the matter six months before light came through one of the meshes suddenly – blindingly! I found a general principle of pigments and refraction – a formula, a geometrical expression involving four dimensions. Fools, common men, even common mathematicians, do not know anything of what some general expression may mean to the student of molecular physics. In the books – the books that tramp has hidden – there are marvels, miracles! But this was not a method, it was an idea, that might lead to a method by which it would be possible, without changing any other property of matter – except, in some instances colours – to lower the refractive index of a substance, solid or liquid, to that of air – so far as all practical purposes are concerned.'

'Phew!' said Kemp. 'That's odd! But still I don't see quite . . . I can understand that thereby you could spoil a valuable stone, but personal invisibility is a far cry.'

'Precisely,' said Griffin. 'But consider, visibility depends on the action of the visible bodies on light. Either a body absorbs light, or it reflects or refracts it, or does all these things. If it neither reflects nor refracts nor absorbs light, it cannot of itself be visible. You see an opaque red box, for instance, because the colour absorbs some of the light and reflects the rest, all the red part of the light, to you. If it did not absorb any particular part of the light, but reflected it all, then it would be a shining white box. Silver! A diamond box would neither absorb much of the light nor reflect much from the general surface, but just here and there where the surfaces were favourable the light would be reflected and refracted, so that you would get a brilliant appearance of flashing reflections and translucencies – a sort of skeleton of light. A glass box would not be so brilliant, nor so clearly visible, as a diamond box, because there would be less refraction and reflection. See

that? From certain points of view you would see quite clearly through it. Some kinds of glass would be more visible than others, a box of flint glass would be brighter than a box of ordinary window glass. A box of very thin common glass would be hard to see in a bad light, because it would absorb hardly any light and refract and reflect very little. And if you put a sheet of common white glass in water, still more if you put it in some denser liquid than water, it would vanish almost altogether, because light passing from water to glass is only slightly refracted or reflected or indeed affected in any way. It is almost as invisible as a jet of coal gas or hydrogen is in air. And for precisely the same reason!'

'Yes,' said Kemp, 'that is pretty plain sailing.'

'And here is another fact you will know to be true. If a sheet of glass is smashed, Kemp, and beaten into a powder, it becomes much more visible while it is in the air; it becomes at last an opaque white powder. This is because the powdering multiplies the surfaces of the glass at which refraction and reflection occur. In the sheet of glass there are only two surfaces; in the powder the light is reflected or refracted by each grain it passes through, and very little gets right through the powder. But if the white powdered glass is put into water, it forthwith vanishes. The powdered glass and water have much the same refractive index; that is, the light undergoes very little refraction or reflection in passing from one to the other.

'You make the glass invisible by putting it into a liquid of nearly the same refractive index; a transparent thing becomes invisible if it is put in any medium of almost the same refractive index. And if you will consider only a second, you will see also that the powder of glass might be made to vanish in air, if its refractive index could be made the same as that of air; for then there would be no refraction or reflection as the light passed from glass to air.'

'Yes, yes,' said Kemp. 'But a man's not powdered glass!'

'No,' said Griffin. 'He's more transparent!'

'Nonsense!'

'That from a doctor! How one forgets! Have you already forgotten your physics, in ten years? Just think of all the things that are transparent and seem not to be so. Paper, for instance, is made up of transparent fibres, and it is white and opaque only for the same reason that a powder of glass is white and opaque. Oil white paper, fill up the interstices between the particles with oil so that there is no longer refraction or reflection except at the surfaces, and it becomes as transparent as glass. And not only paper, but cotton fibre, linen fibre, wool fibre, woody fibre, and *bone*, Kemp, *flesh*, Kemp, *hair*, Kemp, *nails* and *nerves*, Kemp, in fact the whole fabric of a man except the red of his blood and the black pigment of hair, are all made up of transparent, colourless tissue. So little suffices to make us visible one to the other. For the most part the fibres of a living creature are no more opaque than water.'

'Great heavens!' cried Kemp. 'Of course, of course! I was thinking only last night of the sea larvae and all jellyfish!'

'*Now* you have me! And all that I knew and had in mind a year after I left London – six years ago. But I kept it to myself. I had to do my work under frightful disadvantages. Oliver, my professor, was a scientific bounder, a journalist by instinct, a thief of ideas – he was always prying! And you know the knavish system of the scientific world. I simply would not publish and let him share my credit. I went on working; I got nearer and nearer making my formula into an experiment, a reality. I told no living soul, because I meant to flash my work upon the world with crushing effect and become famous at a blow. I took up the question of pigments to fill up certain gaps. And suddenly, not by design but by accident, I made a discovery in physiology.'

'Yes?'

'You know the red colouring matter of blood; it can be made white – colourless – and remain with all the functions it has now!'

Kemp gave a cry of incredulous amazement.

The Invisible Man rose and began pacing the little study. 'You may well exclaim. I remember that night. It was late at night – in the daytime one was bothered with the gaping, silly students – and I worked then sometimes till dawn. It came suddenly, splendid and complete into my mind. I was alone; the laboratory was still, with the tall lights burning brightly and silently. In all my great moments I have been alone. "One could make an animal – a tissue – transparent! One could make it invisible! All except the pigments. I could be invisible!" I said, suddenly realising what it meant to be an albino with such knowledge. It was overwhelming. I left the filtering I was doing, and went and stared out of the great window at the stars. "I could be invisible!" I repeated.

'To do such a thing would be to transcend magic. And I beheld, unclouded by doubt, a magnificent vision of all that invisibility might mean to a man – the mystery, the power, the freedom. Drawbacks I saw none. You have only to think! And I, a shabby, poverty-struck, hemmed-in demonstrator, teaching fools in a provincial college, might suddenly become – this. I ask you, Kemp, if *you* . . . Anyone, I tell you, would have flung himself upon that research. And I worked three years, and every mountain of difficulty I toiled over showed another from its summit. The infinite details! And the exasperation! A professor, a provincial professor, always prying. "When are you going to publish this work of yours?" was his everlasting question. And the students, the cramped means! Three years I had of it –

'And after three years of secrecy and exasperation, I found that to complete it was impossible – impossible.'

'How?' asked Kemp.

'Money,' said the Invisible Man, and went again to stare out of the window.

He turned around abruptly. 'I robbed the old man – robbed my father.

'The money was not his, and he shot himself.'

CHAPTER TWENTY

At the House in Great Portland Street

For a moment Kemp sat in silence, staring at the back of the headless figure at the window. Then he started, struck by a thought, rose, took the Invisible Man's arm, and turned him away from the outlook.

'You are tired,' he said, 'and while I sit, you walk about. Have my chair.'

He placed himself between Griffin and the nearest window.

For a space Griffin sat silent, and then he resumed abruptly: 'I had left the Chesilstowe cottage already,' he said, 'when that happened. It was last December. I had taken a room in London, a large unfurnished room in a big ill-managed lodging-house in a slum near Great Portland Street. The room was soon full of the appliances I had bought with his money; the work was going on steadily, successfully, drawing near an end. I was like a man emerging from a thicket, and suddenly coming on some unmeaning tragedy. I went to bury him. My mind was still on this research, and I did not lift a finger to save his character. I remember the funeral, the cheap hearse, the scant ceremony, the windy frost-bitten hillside, and the old college friend of his who read the service over him – a shabby, black, bent old man with a snivelling cold.

'I remember walking back to the empty house, through the place that had once been a village and was now patched and tinkered by the jerry builders into the ugly likeness of a town. Every way the roads ran out at last into the desecrated fields and ended in rubble heaps and rank wet weeds. I remember myself as a gaunt black figure, going along the slippery, shiny pavement, and the strange sense of detachment I felt from the squalid respectability, the sordid commercialism of the place.

'I did not feel a bit sorry for my father. He seemed to me to be the victim of his own foolish sentimentality. The current cant required my attendance at his funeral, but it was really not my affair.

'But going along the High Street, my old life came back to me for a space, for I met the girl I had known ten years since. Our eyes met.

'Something moved me to turn back and talk to her. She was a very ordinary person.

'It was all like a dream, that visit to the old places. I did not feel then that I was lonely, that I had come out from the world into a desolate place. I appreciated my loss of sympathy, but I put it down to the general inanity of things. Re-entering my room seemed like the recovery of reality. There were the things I knew and loved. There stood the apparatus, the experiments arranged and waiting. And now there was scarcely a difficulty left, beyond the planning of details.

'I will tell you, Kemp, sooner or later, all the complicated processes. We need not go into that now. For the most part, saving certain gaps I chose to remember, they are written in cypher in those books that tramp has hidden. We must hunt him down. We must get those books again. But the essential phase was to place the transparent object whose refractive index was to be lowered between two radiating centres of a sort of ethereal vibration, of which I will tell you more fully later. No, not those Roentgën vibrations – I don't know that these others of mine have been described. Yet they are obvious enough. I needed two little dynamos, and these I worked with a cheap gas engine. My first experiment was with a bit of white wool fabric. It was the strangest thing in the world to see it in the flicker of the flashes soft and white, and then to watch it fade like a wreath of smoke and vanish.

'I could scarcely believe I had done it. I put my hand into the emptiness, and there was the thing as solid as ever. I felt it awkwardly, and threw it on the floor. I had a little trouble finding it again.

'And then came a curious experience. I heard a miaow behind me, and turning, saw a lean white cat, very dirty, on the cistern cover outside the window. A thought came into my head. "Everything ready for you," I said, and went to the window, opened it, and called softly. She came in, purring – the poor beast was starving, and I gave her some milk. All my food was in a cupboard in the corner of the room. After that she went smelling round the room, evidently with the idea of making herself at home. The invisible rag upset her a bit; you should have seen her spit at it! But I made her comfortable on the pillow of my truckle-bed. And I gave her butter to get her to wash.'

'And you processed her?'

'I processed her. But giving drugs to a cat is no joke, Kemp! And the process failed.'

'Failed!'

'In two particulars. These were the claws and the pigment stuff, what is it? – at the back of the eye in a cat. You know?'

'*Tapetum.*'

'Yes, the *tapetum*. It didn't go. After I'd given the stuff to bleach the blood and done certain other things to her, I gave the beast opium, and put her and the pillow she was sleeping on, on the apparatus. And after all the rest had faded and vanished, there remained two little ghosts of her eyes.'

'Odd!'

'I can't explain it. She was bandaged and clamped, of course – so I had her safe; but she woke while she was still misty, and miaowed dismally, and someone came knocking. It was an old woman from downstairs, who suspected me of vivisecting – a drink-sodden old creature, with only a white cat to care for in all the world. I whipped out some chloroform, applied it, and answered the door. "Did I hear a cat?" she asked. "My cat?" "Not here," said I, very politely. She was a little doubtful and tried to peer past

me into the room; strange enough to her no doubt – bare walls, uncurtained windows, truckle-bed, with the gas engine vibrating, and the seethe of the radiant points, and that faint ghastly stinging of chloroform in the air. She had to be satisfied at last and went away again.'

'How long did it take?' asked Kemp.

'Three or four hours – the cat. The bones and sinews and the fat were the last to go, and the tips of the coloured hairs. And, as I say, the back part of the eye, tough, iridescent stuff it is, wouldn't go at all.

'It was night outside long before the business was over, and nothing was to be seen but the dim eyes and the claws. I stopped the gas engine, felt for and stroked the beast, which was still insensible, and then, being tired, left it sleeping on the invisible pillow and went to bed. I found it hard to sleep. I lay awake thinking weak aimless stuff, going over the experiment over and over again, or dreaming feverishly of things growing misty and vanishing about me, until everything, the ground I stood on, vanished, and so I came to that sickly falling nightmare one gets. About two, the cat began miaowing about the room. I tried to hush it by talking to it, and then I decided to turn it out. I remember the shock I had when striking a light – there were just the round eyes shining green – and nothing round them. I would have given it milk, but I hadn't any. It wouldn't be quiet, it just sat down and miaowed at the door. I tried to catch it, with an idea of putting it out of the window, but it wouldn't be caught, it vanished. Then it began miaowing in different parts of the room. At last I opened the window and made a bustle. I suppose it went out at last. I never saw any more of it.

'Then – heaven knows why – I fell to thinking of my father's funeral again, and the dismal windy hillside, until the day had come. I found sleeping was hopeless, and, locking my door after me, wandered out into the morning streets.'

'You don't mean to say there's an invisible cat at large!' said Kemp.

'If it hasn't been killed,' said the Invisible Man. 'Why not?'

'Why not?' said Kemp. 'I didn't mean to interrupt.'

'It's very probably been killed,' said the Invisible Man. 'It was alive four days after, I know, and down a grating in Great Titchfield Street; because I saw a crowd round the place, trying to see whence the miaowing came.'

He was silent for the best part of a minute. Then he resumed abruptly: 'I remember that morning before the change very vividly. I must have gone up Great Portland Street. I remember the barracks in Albany Street, and the horse soldiers coming out, and at last I found the summit of Primrose Hill. It was a sunny day in January – one of those sunny, frosty days that came before the snow this year. My weary brain tried to formulate the position, to plot out a plan of action.

'I was surprised to find, now that my prize was within my grasp, how inconclusive its attainment seemed. As a matter of fact I was worked out; the intense stress of nearly four years' continuous work left me incapable of

any strength of feeling. I was apathetic, and I tried in vain to recover the enthusiasm of my first enquiries, the passion of discovery that had enabled me to compass even the downfall of my father's grey hairs. Nothing seemed to matter. I saw pretty clearly this was a transient mood, due to overwork and want of sleep, and that either by drugs or rest it would be possible to recover my energies.

'All I could think clearly was that the thing had to be carried through; the fixed idea still ruled me. And soon, for the money I had was almost exhausted. I looked about me at the hillside, with children playing and girls watching them, and tried to think of all the fantastic advantages an invisible man would have in the world. After a time I crawled home, took some food and a strong dose of strychnine, and went to sleep in my clothes on my unmade bed. Strychnine is a grand tonic, Kemp, to take the flabbiness out of a man.'

'It's the devil,' said Kemp. 'It's the palaeolithic in a bottle.'

'I awoke vastly invigorated and rather irritable. You know?'

'I know the stuff.'

'And there was someone rapping at the door. It was my landlord with threats and enquiries, an old Polish Jew in a long grey coat and greasy slippers. I had been tormenting a cat in the night, he was sure – the old woman's tongue had been busy. He insisted on knowing all about it. The laws in this country against vivisection were very severe – he might be liable. I denied the cat. Then the vibration of the little gas engine could be felt all over the house, he said. That was true, certainly. He edged round me into the room, peering about over his German-silver spectacles, and a sudden dread came into my mind that he might carry away something of my secret. I tried to keep between him and the concentrating apparatus I had arranged, and that only made him more curious. What was I doing? Why was I always alone and secretive? Was it legal? Was it dangerous? I paid nothing but the usual rent. His had always been a most respectable house – in a disreputable neighbourhood. Suddenly my temper gave way. I told him to get out. He began to protest, to jabber of his right of entry. In a moment I had him by the collar; something ripped and he went spinning out into his own passage. I slammed and locked the door and sat down quivering.

'He made a fuss outside, which I disregarded, and after a time he went away.

'But this brought matters to a crisis. I did not know what he would do, nor even what he had the power to do. To move to fresh apartments would have meant delay; altogether I had barely twenty pounds left in the world, for the most part in a bank – and I could not afford that. Vanish! It was irresistible. Then there would be an inquiry, the sacking of my room.

'At the thought of the possibility of my work being exposed or interrupted at its very climax, I became very angry and active. I hurried out with my three books of notes, my chequebook – the tramp has them now – and

directed them from the nearest Post Office to a house of call for letters and parcels in Great Portland Street. I tried to go out noiselessly. Coming in, I found my landlord going quietly upstairs; he had heard the door close, I suppose. You would have laughed to see him jump aside on the landing as I came tearing after him. He glared at me as I went by him, and I made the house quiver with the slamming of my door. I heard him come shuffling up to my floor, hesitate, and go down. I set to work upon my preparations forthwith.

'It was all done that evening and night. While I was still sitting under the sickly, drowsy influence of the drugs that decolourise blood, there came a repeated knocking at the door. It ceased, footsteps went away and returned, and the knocking was resumed. There was an attempt to push something under the door – a blue paper. Then in a fit of irritation I rose and went and flung the door wide open. "Now then?" said I.

'It was my landlord, with a notice of ejectment or something. He held it out to me, saw something odd about my hands, I expect, and lifted his eyes to my face.

'For a moment he gaped. Then he gave a sort of inarticulate cry, dropped candle and writ together, and went blundering down the dark passage to the stairs. I shut the door, locked it, and went to the looking-glass. Then I understood his terror . . . My face was white – like white stone.

'But it was all horrible. I had not expected the suffering. A night of racking anguish, sickness and fainting. I set my teeth, though my skin was presently afire, all my body afire; but I lay there like grim death. I under-stood now how it was the cat had howled until I chloroformed it. Lucky it was I lived alone and untended in my room. There were times when I sobbed and groaned and talked. But I stuck to it . . . I became insensible and woke languid in the darkness.

'The pain had passed. I thought I was killing myself and I did not care. I shall never forget that dawn, and the strange horror of seeing that my hands had become as clouded glass, and watching them grow clearer and thinner as the day went by, until at last I could see the sickly disorder of my room through them, though I closed my transparent eyelids. My limbs became glassy, the bones and arteries faded, vanished, and the little white nerves went last. I gritted my teeth and stayed there to the end. At last only the dead tips of the fingernails remained, pallid and white, and the brown stain of some acid upon my fingers.

'I struggled up. At first I was as incapable as a swathed infant – stepping with limbs I could not see. I was weak and very hungry. I went and stared at nothing in my shaving-glass, at nothing save where an attenuated pigment still remained behind the retina of my eyes, fainter than mist. I had to hang on to the table and press my forehead against the glass.

'It was only by a frantic effort of will that I dragged myself back to the apparatus and completed the process.

'I slept during the forenoon, pulling the sheet over my eyes to shut out the light, and about midday I was awakened again by a knocking. My strength had returned. I sat up and listened and heard a whispering. I sprang to my feet and as noiselessly as possible began to detach the connections of my apparatus, and to distribute it about the room, so as to destroy the suggestions of its arrangement. Presently the knocking was renewed and voices called, first my landlord's, and then two others. To gain time I answered them. The invisible rag and pillow came to hand and I opened the window and pitched them out on to the cistern cover. As the window opened, a heavy crash came at the door. Someone had charged it with the idea of smashing the lock. But the stout bolts I had screwed up some days before stopped him. That startled me, made me angry. I began to tremble and do things hurriedly.

'I tossed together some loose paper, straw, packing paper and so forth, in the middle of the room, and turned on the gas. Heavy blows began to rain upon the door. I could not find the matches. I beat my hands on the wall with rage. I turned down the gas again, stepped out of the window on to the cistern cover, very softly lowered the sash, and sat down, secure and invisible, but quivering with anger, to watch events. They split a panel, I saw, and in another moment they had broken away the staples of the bolts and stood in the open doorway. It was the landlord and his two stepsons, sturdy young men of three or four and twenty. Behind them fluttered the old hag of a woman from downstairs.

'You may imagine their astonishment to find the room empty. One of the younger men rushed to the window at once, flung it up and stared out. His staring eyes and thick-lipped bearded face came a foot from my face. I was half minded to hit his silly countenance, but I arrested my doubled fist. He stared right through me. So did the others as they joined him. The old man went and peered under the bed, and then they all made a rush for the cupboard. They had to argue about it at length in Yiddish and cockney English. They concluded I had not answered them, that their imagination had deceived them. A feeling of extraordinary elation took the place of my anger as I sat outside the window and watched these four people – for the old lady came in, glancing suspiciously about her like a cat, trying to understand the riddle of my behaviour.

'The old man, so far as I could understand his *patois*, agreed with the old lady that I was a vivisectionist. The sons protested in garbled English that I was an electrician, and appealed to the dynamos and radiators. They were all nervous about my arrival, although I found subsequently that they had bolted the front door. The old lady peered into the cupboard and under the bed, and one of the young men pushed up the register and stared up the chimney. One of my fellow lodgers, a costermonger who shared the opposite room with a butcher, appeared on the landing, and he was called in and told incoherent things.

'It occurred to me that the radiators, if they fell into the hands of some acute well-educated person, would give me away too much, and watching my opportunity, I came into the room and tilted one of the little dynamos off its fellow on which it was standing, and smashed both apparatus. Then, while they were trying to explain the smash, I dodged out of the room and went softly downstairs.

'I went into one of the sitting-rooms and waited until they came down, still speculating and argumentative, all a little disappointed at finding no "horrors", and all a little puzzled how they stood legally towards me. Then I slipped up again with a box of matches, fired my heap of paper and rubbish, put the chairs and bedding thereby, led the gas to the affair, by means of an india-rubber tube, and waving a farewell to the room left it for the last time.'

'You fired the house!' exclaimed Kemp.

'Fired the house. It was the only way to cover my trail – and no doubt it was insured. I slipped the bolts of the front door quietly and went out into the street. I was invisible, and I was only just beginning to realise the extraordinary advantage my invisibility gave me. My head was already teeming with plans of all the wild and wonderful things I had now impunity to do.'

CHAPTER TWENTY-ONE

In Oxford Street

'In going downstairs the first time I found an unexpected difficulty because I could not see my feet; indeed I stumbled twice, and there was an unaccustomed clumsiness in gripping the bolt. By not looking down, however, I managed to walk on the level passably well.

'My mood, I say, was one of exaltation. I felt as a seeing man might do, with padded feet and noiseless clothes, in a city of the blind. I experienced a wild impulse to jest, to startle people, to clap men on the back, fling people's hats astray, and generally revel in my extraordinary advantage.

'But hardly had I emerged upon Great Portland Street, however (my lodging was close to the big draper's shop there), when I heard a clashing concussion and was hit violently behind, and turning saw a man carrying a basket of soda-water syphons, and looking in amazement at his burden. Although the blow had really hurt me, I found something so irresistible in his astonishment that I laughed aloud. "The devil's in the basket," I said, and suddenly twisted it out of his hand. He let go incontinently, and I swung the whole weight into the air.

'But a fool of a cabman, standing outside a public house, made a sudden rush for this, and his extending fingers took me with excruciating violence

under the ear. I let the whole down with a smash on the cabman, and then, with shouts and the clatter of feet about me, people coming out of shops, vehicles pulling up, I realised what I had done for myself, and cursing my folly, backed against a shop window and prepared to dodge out of the confusion. In a moment I should be wedged into a crowd and inevitably discovered. I pushed by a butcher boy, who luckily did not turn to see the nothingness that shoved him aside, and dodged behind the cabman's four-wheeler. I do not know how they settled the business. I hurried straight across the road, which was happily clear, and hardly heeding which way I went, in the fright of detection the incident had given me, plunged into the afternoon throng of Oxford Street.

'I tried to get into the stream of people, but they were too thick for me, and in a moment my heels were being trodden upon. I took to the gutter, the roughness of which I found painful to my feet, and forthwith the shaft of a crawling hansom dug me forcibly under the shoulder blade, reminding me that I was already bruised severely. I staggered out of the way of the cab, avoided a perambulator by a convulsive movement, and found myself behind the hansom. A happy thought saved me, and as this drove slowly along I followed in its immediate wake, trembling and astonished at the turn of my adventure. And not only trembling, but shivering. It was a bright day in January and I was stark naked and the thin slime of mud that covered the road was freezing. Foolish as it seems to me now, I had not reckoned that, transparent or not, I was still amenable to the weather and all its consequences.

'Then suddenly a bright idea came into my head. I ran round and got into the cab. And so, shivering, scared, and sniffing with the first intimations of a cold, and with the bruises in the small of my back growing upon my attention, I drove slowly along Oxford Street and past Tottenham Court Road. My mood was as different from that in which I had sallied forth ten minutes ago as it is possible to imagine. This invisibility indeed! The one thought that possessed me was – how was I to get out of the scrape I was in.

'We crawled past Mudie's, and there a tall woman with five or six yellow-labelled books hailed my cab, and I sprang out just in time to escape her, shaving a railway van narrowly in my flight. I made off up the roadway to Bloomsbury Square, intending to strike north past the Museum and so get into the quiet district. I was now cruelly chilled, and the strangeness of my situation so unnerved me that I whimpered as I ran. At the northward corner of the square a little white dog ran out of the Pharmaceutical Society's offices, and incontinently made for me, nose down.

'I had never realised it before, but the nose is to the mind of a dog what the eye is to the mind of a seeing man. Dogs perceive the scent of a man moving as men perceive his vision. This brute began barking and leaping, showing, as it seemed to me, only too plainly that he was aware of me. I

crossed Great Russell Street, glancing over my shoulder as I did so, and went some way along Montague Street before I realised what I was running towards.

'Then I became aware of a blare of music, and looking along the street saw a number of people advancing out of Russell Square, red shirts, and the banner of the Salvation Army to the fore. Such a crowd, chanting in the roadway and scoffing on the pavement, I could not hope to penetrate, and dreading to go back and farther from home again, and deciding on the spur of the moment, I ran up the white steps of a house facing the museum railings, and stood there until the crowd should have passed. Happily the dog stopped at the noise of the band too, hesitated, and turned tail, running back to Bloomsbury Square again.

'On came the band, bawling with unconscious irony some hymn about "When shall we see His face?" and it seemed an interminable time to me before the tide of the crowd had washed along the pavement by me. Thud, thud, thud, came the drum with a vibrating resonance, and for the moment I did not notice two urchins stopping at the railings by me. "See 'em," said one. "See what?" said the other. "Why – them footmarks – *bare*. Like what you makes in mud."

'I looked down and saw the youngsters had stopped and were gaping at the muddy footmarks I had left behind me up the newly whitened steps. The passing people elbowed and jostled them, but their confounded intelligence was arrested. "Thud, thud, thud, When, thud, shall we see, thud, His face, thud, thud." "There's a barefoot man gone up them steps, or I don't know nothing," said one. "And he ain't never come down again. And his foot was a-bleeding."

'The thick of the crowd had already passed. "Looky there, Ted," quoth the younger of the detectives, with the sharpness of surprise in his voice, and pointed straight to my feet. I looked down and saw at once the dim suggestion of their outline sketched in splashes of mud. For a moment I was paralysed.

' "Why, that's rum," said the elder. "Dashed rum! It's just like the ghost of a foot, ain't it?" He hesitated and advanced with outstretched hand. A man pulled up short to see what he was catching, and then a girl. In another moment he would have touched me. Then I saw what to do. I made a step, the boy started back with an exclamation, and with a rapid movement I swung myself over into the portico of the next house. But the smaller boy was sharp-eyed enough to follow the movement, and before I was well down the steps and upon the pavement, he had recovered from his momentary astonishment and was shouting out that the feet had gone over the wall.

'They rushed round and saw my new footmarks flash into being on the lower step and upon the pavement. "What's up?" asked someone. "Feet! Look! Feet running!"

'Everybody in the road, except my three pursuers, was pouring along after the Salvation Army, and this blow not only impeded me but them. There was an eddy of surprise and interrogation. At the cost of bowling over one young fellow I got through, and in another moment I was rushing headlong round the circuit of Russell Square, with six or seven astonished people following my footmarks. There was no time for explanation, or else the whole host would have been after me.

'Twice I doubled round corners, thrice I crossed the road and came back upon my tracks, and then, as my feet grew hot and dry, the damp impressions began to fade. At last I had a breathing space and rubbed my feet clean with my hands, and so got away altogether. The last I saw of the chase was a little group of a dozen people perhaps, studying with infinite perplexity a slowly drying footprint that had resulted from a puddle in Tavistock Square, a footprint as isolated and incomprehensible to them as Crusoe's solitary discovery.

'This running warmed me to a certain extent, and I went on with a better courage through the maze of less frequented roads that runs hereabouts. My back had now become very stiff and sore, my tonsils were painful from the cabman's fingers, and the skin of my neck had been scratched by his nails; my feet hurt exceedingly and I was lame from a little cut on one foot. I saw in time a blind man approaching me, and fled limping, for I feared his subtle intuitions. Once or twice accidental collisions occurred and I left people amazed, with unaccountable curses ringing in their ears. Then came something silent and quiet against my face, and across the square fell a thin veil of slowly falling flakes of snow. I had caught a cold, and do as I would I could not avoid an occasional sneeze. And every dog that came in sight, with its pointing nose and curious sniffing, was a terror to me.

'Then came men and boys running, first one and then others, and shouting as they ran. It was a fire. They ran in the direction of my lodging, and looking back down a street I saw a mass of black smoke streaming up above the roofs and telephone wires. It was my lodging burning; my clothes, my apparatus, all my resources indeed, except my chequebook and the three volumes of memoranda that awaited me in Great Portland Street, were there. Burning! I had burnt my boats – if ever a man did! The place was blazing.'

The Invisible Man paused and thought. Kemp glanced nervously out of the window. 'Yes?' he said. 'Go on.'

CHAPTER TWENTY-TWO

In the Emporium

'So last January, with the beginning of a snowstorm in the air about me – and if it settled on me it would betray me! – weary, cold, painful, inexpressibly wretched, and still but half convinced of my invisible quality, I began this new life to which I am committed. I had no refuge, no appliances, no human being in the world in whom I could confide. To have told my secret would have given me away – made a mere show and rarity of me. Nevertheless, I was half-minded to accost some passer-by and throw myself upon his mercy. But I knew too clearly the terror and brutal cruelty my advances would evoke. I made no plans in the street. My sole object was to get shelter from the snow, to get myself covered and warm; then I might hope to plan. But even to me, an Invisible Man, the rows of London houses stood latched, barred, and bolted impregnably.

'Only one thing could I see clearly before me – the cold exposure and misery of the snowstorm and the night.

'And then I had a brilliant idea. I turned down one of the roads leading from Gower Street to Tottenham Court Road, and found myself outside Omniums, the big establishment where everything is to be bought – you know the place: meat, grocery, linen, furniture, clothing, oil paintings even – a huge meandering collection of shops rather than a shop. I had thought I should find the doors open, but they were closed; and as I stood in the wide entrance a carriage stopped outside, and a man in uniform – you know the kind of personage with OMNIUM on his cap – flung open the door. I contrived to enter, and walking down the shop – it was a department where they were selling ribbons and gloves and stockings and that kind of thing – came to a more spacious region devoted to picnic baskets and wicker furniture.

'I did not feel safe there, however; people were going to and fro, and I prowled restlessly about until I came upon a huge section in an upper floor containing multitudes of bedsteads, and over these I clambered, and found a resting-place at last among a huge pile of folded flock mattresses. The place was already lit up and agreeably warm, and I decided to remain where I was, keeping a cautious eye on the two or three sets of shopmen and customers who were meandering through the place, until closing time came. Then I should be able, I thought, to rob the place for food and clothing, and disguised, prowl through it and examine its resources, perhaps sleep on some of the bedding. That seemed an acceptable plan. My idea was to procure clothing to make myself a muffled but acceptable figure, to get money, and then to recover my books and parcels where they awaited me,

take a lodging somewhere and elaborate plans for the complete realisation of the advantages my invisibility gave me (as I still imagined) over my fellow men.

'Closing time arrived quickly enough. It could not have been more than an hour after I took up my position on the mattresses before I noticed the blinds of the windows being drawn, and customers being marched doorwards. And then a number of brisk young men began with remarkable alacrity to tidy up the goods that remained disturbed. I left my lair as the crowds diminished, and prowled cautiously out into the less desolate parts of the shop. I was really surprised to observe how rapidly the young men and women whipped away the goods displayed for sale during the day. All the boxes of goods, the hanging fabrics, the festoons of lace, the boxes of sweets in the grocery section, the displays of this and that, were being whipped down, folded up, slapped into tidy receptacles, and everything that could not be taken down and put away had sheets of some coarse stuff like sacking flung over them. Finally all the chairs were turned up on to the counters, leaving the floor clear. Directly each of these young people had done, he or she made promptly for the door with such an expression of animation as I have rarely observed in a shop assistant before. Then came a lot of youngsters scattering sawdust and carrying pails and brooms. I had to dodge to get out of the way, and as it was, my ankle got stung with the sawdust. For some time, wandering through the swathed and darkened departments, I could hear the brooms at work. And at last a good hour or more after the shop had been closed, came a noise of locking doors. Silence came upon the place, and I found myself wandering through the vast and intricate shops, galleries, showrooms of the place, alone. It was very still; in one place I remember passing near one of the Tottenham Court Road entrances and listening to the tapping of the boot-heels of the passers-by.

'My first visit was to the place where I had seen stockings and gloves for sale. It was dark, and I had the devil of a hunt after matches, which I found at last in the drawer of the little cash desk. Then I had to get a candle. I had to tear down wrappings and ransack a number of boxes and drawers, but at last I managed to turn out what I sought; the box label called them lambs-wool pants, and lambswool vests. Then socks, a thick comforter, and then I went to the clothing place and got trousers, a lounge jacket, an overcoat and a slouch hat – a clerical sort of hat with the brim turned down. I began to feel a human being again, and my next thought was food.

'Upstairs was a refreshment department, and there I got cold meat. There was coffee still in the urn, and I lit the gas and warmed it up again, and altogether I did not do badly. Afterwards, prowling through the place in search of blankets – I had to put up at last with a heap of down quilts – I came upon a grocery section with a lot of chocolate and candied fruits, more than was good for me indeed – and some white burgundy. And near that was a toy department, and I had a brilliant idea. I found some artificial

noses – dummy noses, you know, and I thought of dark spectacles. But Omniums had no optical department. My nose had been a difficulty indeed – I had thought of paint. But the discovery set my mind running on wigs and masks and the like. Finally I went to sleep in a heap of down quilts, very warm and comfortable.

'My last thoughts before sleeping were the most agreeable I had had since the change. I was in a state of physical serenity, and that was reflected in my mind. I thought that I should be able to slip out unobserved in the morning with my clothes upon me, muffling my face with a white wrapper I had taken, purchase, with the money I had taken, spectacles and so forth, and so complete my disguise. I lapsed into disorderly dreams of all the fantastic things that had happened during the last few days. I saw the ugly little Jew of a landlord vociferating in his rooms; I saw his two sons marvelling, and the wrinkled old woman's gnarled face as she asked for her cat. I experienced again the strange sensation of seeing the cloth disappear, and so I came round to the windy hillside and the sniffing old clergyman mumbling, "Earth to earth, ashes to ashes, dust to dust," at my father's open grave.

' "You also," said a voice, and suddenly I was being forced towards the grave. I struggled, shouted, appealed to the mourners, but they continued stonily following the service; the old clergyman, too, never faltered, droning and sniffing through the ritual. I realised I was invisible and inaudible, that overwhelming forces had their grip on me. I struggled in vain, I was forced over the brink, the coffin rang hollow as I fell upon it, and the gravel came flying after me in spadefuls. Nobody heeded me, nobody was aware of me. I made convulsive struggles and awoke.

'The pale London dawn had come, the place was full of a chilly grey light that filtered round the edges of the window blinds. I sat up, and for a time I could not think where this ample apartment, with its counters, its piles of rolled stuff, its heap of quilts and cushions, its iron pillars, might be. Then, as recollection came back to me, I heard voices in conversation.

'Then far down the place, in the brighter light of some department which had already raised its blinds, I saw two men approaching. I scrambled to my feet, looking about me for some way of escape, and even as I did so the sound of my movement made them aware of me. I suppose they saw merely a figure moving quietly and quickly away. "Who's that?" cried one, and "Stop there!" shouted the other. I dashed around a corner and came full tilt – a faceless figure, mind you! – on a lanky lad of fifteen. He yelled and I bowled him over, rushed past him, turned another corner, and by a happy inspiration threw myself behind a counter. In another moment feet went running past and I heard voices shouting, "All hands to the doors!" asking what was "up", and giving one another advice how to catch me.

'Lying on the ground, I felt scared out of my wits. But – odd as it may seem – it did not occur to me at the moment to take off my clothes as I

should have done. I had made up my mind, I suppose, to get away in them, and that ruled me. And then down the vista of the counters came a bawling of, "Here he is!"

'I sprang to my feet, whipped a chair off the counter, and sent it whirling at the fool who had shouted, turned, came into another round a corner, sent him spinning, and rushed up the stairs. He kept his footing, gave a view halloo! and came up the staircase hot after me. Up the staircase were piled a multitude of those bright-coloured pot things – what are they?'

'Art pots,' suggested Kemp.

'That's it! Art pots. Well, I turned at the top step and swung round, plucked one out of a pile and smashed it on his silly head as he came at me. The whole pile of pots went headlong, and I heard shouting and footsteps running from all parts. I made a mad rush for the refreshment place, and there was a man in white like a man cook, who took up the chase. I made one last desperate turn and found myself among lamps and ironmongery. I went behind the counter of this, and waited for my cook, and as he bolted in at the head of the chase, I doubled him up with a lamp. Down he went, and I crouched down behind the counter and began whipping off my clothes as fast as I could. Coat, jacket, trousers, shoes were all right, but a lambswool vest fits a man like a skin. I heard more men coming, my cook was lying quiet on the other side of the counter, stunned or scared speechless, and I had to make another dash for it, like a rabbit hunted out of a woodpile.

' "This way, policeman!" I heard someone shouting. I found myself in my bedstead storeroom again, and at the end of a wilderness of wardrobes. I rushed among them, went flat, got rid of my vest after infinite wriggling, and stood a free man again, panting and scared, as the policeman and three of the shopmen came round the corner. They made a rush for the vest and pants, and collared the trousers. "He's dropping his plunder," said one of the young men. "He *must* be somewhere here."

'But they did not find me all the same.

'I stood watching them hunt for me for a time, and cursing my ill-luck in losing the clothes. Then I went into the refreshment-room, drank a little milk I found there, and sat down by the fire to consider my position.

'In a little while two assistants came in and began to talk over the business very excitedly and like the fools they were. I heard a magnified account of my depredations, and other speculations as to my whereabouts. Then I fell to scheming again. The insurmountable difficulty of the place, especially now it was alarmed, was to get any plunder out of it. I went down into the warehouse to see if there was any chance of packing and addressing a parcel, but I could not understand the system of checking. About eleven o'clock, the snow having thawed as it fell, and the day being finer and a little warmer than the previous one, I decided that the Emporium was hopeless, and went out again, exasperated at my want of success, with only the vaguest plans of action in my mind.'

CHAPTER TWENTY-THREE

In Drury Lane

'But you begin now to realise,' said the Invisible Man, 'the full disadvantage of my condition. I had no shelter – no covering – to get clothing was to forgo all my advantage, to make myself a strange and terrible thing. I was fasting; for to eat, to fill myself with unassimilated matter, would be to become grotesquely visible again.'

'I never thought of that,' said Kemp.

'Nor had I. And the snow had warned me of other dangers. I could not go abroad in snow – it would settle on me and expose me. Rain, too, would make me a watery outline, a glistening surface of a man – a bubble. And fog – I should be like a fainter bubble in a fog, a surface, a greasy glimmer of humanity. Moreover, as I went abroad – in the London air – I gathered dirt about my ankles, floating smuts and dust upon my skin. I did not know how long it would be before I should become visible from that cause also. But I saw clearly it could not be for long.

'Not in London at any rate.

'I went into the slums towards Great Portland Street, and found myself at the end of the street in which I had lodged. I did not go that way, because of the crowd halfway down it opposite to the still smoking ruins of the house I had fired. My most immediate problem was to get clothing. What to do with my face puzzled me. Then I saw in one of those little miscellaneous shops – news, sweets, toys, stationery, belated Christmas tomfoolery, and so forth – an array of masks and noses. I realised that problem was solved. In a flash I saw my course. I turned about, no longer aimless, and went – circuitously in order to avoid the busy ways, towards the back streets north of the Strand; for I remembered, though not very distinctly where, that some theatrical costumiers had shops in that district.

'The day was cold, with a nipping wind down the northward running streets. I walked fast to avoid being overtaken. Every crossing was a danger, every passenger a thing to watch alertly. One man as I was about to pass him at the top of Bedford Street, turned upon me abruptly and came into me, sending me into the road and almost under the wheel of a passing hansom. The verdict of the cab-rank was that he had had some sort of stroke. I was so unnerved by this encounter that I went into Covent Garden Market and sat down for some time in a quiet corner by a stall of violets, panting and trembling. I found I had caught a fresh cold, and had to turn out after a time lest my sneezes should attract attention.

'At last I reached the object of my quest, a dirty, flyblown little shop in a byway near Drury Lane, with a window full of tinsel robes, sham jewels,

wigs, slippers, dominoes and theatrical photographs. The shop was old-fashioned and low and dark, and the house rose above it for four storeys, dark and dismal. I peered through the window and, seeing no one within, entered. The opening of the door set a clanking bell ringing. I left it open, and walked round a bare costume stand, into a corner behind a cheval glass. For a minute or so no one came. Then I heard heavy feet striding across a room, and a man appeared down the shop.

'My plans were now perfectly definite. I proposed to make my way into the house, secrete myself upstairs, watch my opportunity, and when everything was quiet, rummage out a wig, mask, spectacles, and costume, and go into the world, perhaps a grotesque but still a credible figure. And incidentally of course I could rob the house of any available money.

'The man who had just entered the shop was a short, slight, hunched, beetle-browed man, with long arms and very short bandy legs. Apparently I had interrupted a meal. He stared about the shop with an expression of expectation. This gave way to surprise, and then to anger, as he saw the shop empty. "Damn the boys!" he said. He went to stare up and down the street. He came in again in a minute, kicked the door to with his foot spitefully, and went muttering back to the house door.

'I came forward to follow him, and at the noise of my movement he stopped dead. I did so too, startled by his quickness of ear. He slammed the house door in my face.

'I stood hesitating. Suddenly I heard his quick footsteps returning, and the door reopened. He stood looking about the shop like one who was still not satisfied. Then, murmuring to himself, he examined the back of the counter and peered behind some fixtures. Then he stood doubtful. He had left the house door open and I slipped into the inner room.

'It was a queer little room, poorly furnished and with a number of big masks in the corner. On the table was his belated breakfast, and it was a confoundedly exasperating thing for me, Kemp, to have to sniff his coffee and stand watching while he came in and resumed his meal. And his table manners were irritating. Three doors opened into the little room, one going upstairs and one down, but they were all shut. I could not get out of the room while he was there; I could scarcely move because of his alertness, and there was a draught down my back. Twice I strangled a sneeze just in time.

'The spectacular quality of my sensations was curious and novel, but for all that I was heartily tired and angry long before he had done his eating. But at last he made an end and putting his beggarly crockery on the black tin tray upon which he had had his teapot, and gathering all the crumbs up on the mustard-stained cloth, he took the whole lot of things after him. His burden prevented his shutting the door behind him – as he would have done; I never saw such a man for shutting doors – and I followed him into a very dirty underground kitchen and scullery. I had the pleasure of seeing

him begin to wash up, and then, finding no good in keeping down there, and the brick floor being cold on my feet, I returned upstairs and sat in his chair by the fire. It was burning low, and scarcely thinking, I put on a little coal. The noise of this brought him up at once, and he stood aglare. He peered about the room and was within an ace of touching me. Even after that examination, he scarcely seemed satisfied. He stopped in the doorway and took a final inspection before he went down.

'I waited in the little parlour for an age, and at last he came up and opened the upstairs door. I just managed to get by him.

'On the staircase he stopped suddenly, so that I very nearly blundered into him. He stood looking back right into my face and listening. "I could have sworn," he said. His long hairy hand pulled at his lower lip. His eye went up and down the staircase. Then he grunted and went on up again.

'His hand was on the handle of a door, and then he stopped again with the same puzzled anger on his face. He was becoming aware of the faint sounds of my movements about him. The man must have had diabolically acute hearing. He suddenly flashed into rage. "If there's anyone in this house – " he cried with an oath, and left the threat unfinished. He put his hand in his pocket, failed to find what he wanted, and rushing past me went blundering noisily and pugnaciously downstairs. But I did not follow him. I sat on the head of the staircase until his return.

'Presently he came up again, still muttering. He opened the door of the room, and before I could enter, slammed it in my face.

'I resolved to explore the house, and spent some time in doing so as noiselessly as possible. The house was very old and tumbledown, damp so that the paper in the attics was peeling from the walls, and rat infested. Some of the door handles were stiff and I was afraid to turn them. Several rooms I did inspect were unfurnished, and others were littered with theatrical lumber, bought second-hand, I judged, from its appearance. In one room next to his I found a lot of old clothes. I began routing among these, and in my eagerness forgot again the evident sharpness of his ears. I heard a stealthy footstep and, looking up just in time, saw him peering in at the tumbled heap and holding an old-fashioned revolver in his hand. I stood perfectly still while he stared about open-mouthed and suspicious. "It must have been her," he said slowly. "Damn her!"

'He shut the door quietly, and immediately I heard the key turn in the lock. Then his footsteps retreated. I realised abruptly that I was locked in. For a minute I did not know what to do. I walked from door to window and back, and stood perplexed. A gust of anger came upon me. But I decided to inspect the clothes before I did anything further, and my first attempt brought down a pile from an upper shelf. This brought him back, more sinister than ever. That time he actually touched me, jumped back with amazement and stood astonished in the middle of the room.

'Presently he calmed a little. "Rats," he said in an undertone, fingers on

lips. He was evidently a little scared. I edged quietly out of the room, but a plank creaked. Then the infernal little brute started going all over the house, revolver in hand and locking door after door and pocketing the keys. When I realised what he was up to I had a fit of rage – I could hardly control myself sufficiently to watch my opportunity. By this time I knew he was alone in the house, and so I made no more ado, but knocked him on the head.'

'Knocked him on the head?' exclaimed Kemp.

'Yes – stunned him – as he was going downstairs. Hit him from behind with a stool that stood on the landing. He went downstairs like a bag of old boots.'

'But – I say! The common conventions of humanity – '

'Are all very well for common people. But the point was, Kemp, that I had to get out of that house in a disguise without his seeing me. I couldn't think of any other way of doing it. And then I gagged him with a Louis Quatorze vest and tied him up in a sheet.'

'Tied him up in a sheet!'

'Made a sort of bag of it. It was rather a good idea to keep the idiot scared and quiet, and a devilish hard thing to get out of – head away from the string. My dear Kemp, it's no good your sitting glaring as though I was a murderer. It had to be done. He had his revolver. If once he saw me he would be able to describe me – '

'But still,' said Kemp, 'in England – today. And the man was in his own house, and you were – well, robbing.'

'Robbing! Confound it! You'll call me a thief next! Surely, Kemp, you're not fool enough to dance on the old strings. Can't you see my position?'

'And his too,' said Kemp.

The Invisible Man stood up sharply. 'What do you mean to say?'

Kemp's face grew a trifle hard. He was about to speak and checked himself. 'I suppose, after all,' he said with a sudden change of manner, 'the thing had to be done. You were in a fix. But still – '

'Of course I was in a fix – an infernal fix. And he made me wild too – hunting me about the house, fooling about with his revolver, locking and unlocking doors. He was simply exasperating. You don't blame me, do you? You don't blame me?'

'I never blame anyone,' said Kemp. 'It's quite out of fashion. What did you do next?'

'I was hungry. Downstairs I found a loaf and some rank cheese – more than sufficient to satisfy my hunger. I took some brandy and water, and then went up past my impromptu bag – he was lying quite still – to the room containing the old clothes. This looked out upon the street, two lace curtains brown with dirt guarding the window. I went and peered out through their interstices. Outside the day was bright – by contrast with the brown shadows of the dismal house in which I found myself, dazzlingly

bright. A brisk traffic was going by, fruit carts, a hansom, a four-wheeler with a pile of boxes, a fishmonger's cart. I turned with spots of colour swimming before my eyes to the shadowy fixtures behind me. My excitement was giving place to a clear apprehension of my position again. The room was full of a faint scent of benzoline, used, I suppose, in cleaning the garments.

'I began a systematic search of the place. I should judge the hunchback had been alone in the house for some time. He was a curious person. Everything that could possibly be of service to me I collected in the clothes storeroom, and then I made a deliberate selection. I found a handbag I thought a suitable possession, and some powder, rouge and sticking-plaster.

'I had thought of painting and powdering my face and all that there was to show of me, in order to render myself visible, but the disadvantage of this lay in the fact that I should require turpentine and other appliances and a considerable amount of time before I could vanish again. Finally I chose a mask of the better type, slightly grotesque but not more so than many human beings, dark glasses, greyish whiskers and a wig. I could find no underclothing, but that I could buy subsequently, and for the time I swathed myself in calico dominoes and some white cashmere scarfs. I could find no socks, but the hunchback's boots were rather a loose fit and sufficed. In a desk in the shop were three sovereigns and about thirty shillings' worth of silver, and in a locked cupboard I burst in the inner room were eight pounds in gold. I could go forth into the world again, equipped.

'Then came a curious hesitation. Was my appearance really credible? I tried myself with a little bedroom looking-glass, inspecting myself from every point of view to discover any forgotten chink, but it all seemed sound. I was grotesque to the theatrical pitch, a stage miser, but I was certainly not a physical impossibility. Gathering confidence, I took my looking-glass down into the shop, pulled down the shop blinds, and surveyed myself from every point of view with the help of the cheval glass in the corner.

'I spent some minutes screwing up my courage and then unlocked the shop door and marched out into the street, leaving the little man to get out of his sheet again when he liked. In five minutes a dozen turnings intervened between me and the costumier's shop. No one appeared to notice me very pointedly. My last difficulty seemed overcome.'

He stopped again.

'And you troubled no more about the hunchback?' said Kemp.

'No,' said the Invisible Man. 'Nor have I heard what became of him. I suppose he untied himself or kicked himself out. The knots were pretty tight.'

He became silent and went to the window and stared out.

'What happened when you went out into the Strand?'

'Oh! – disillusionment again. I thought my troubles were over. Practically I thought I had impunity to do whatever I chose, everything – save to give

away my secret. So I thought. Whatever I did, whatever the consequences might be, was nothing to me. I had merely to fling aside my garments and vanish. No person could hold me. I could take my money where I found it. I decided to treat myself to a sumptuous feast, and then put up at a good hotel, and accumulate a new outfit of property. I felt amazingly confident; it's not particularly pleasant recalling that I was an ass. I went into a place and was already ordering lunch, when it occurred to me that I could not eat unless I exposed my invisible face. I finished ordering the lunch, told the man I should be back in ten minutes, and went out exasperated. I don't know if you have ever been disappointed in your appetite.'

'Not quite so badly,' said Kemp, 'but I can imagine it.'

'I could have smashed the silly devils. At last, faint with the desire for tasteful food, I went into another place and demanded a private room. "I am disfigured," I said. "Badly." They looked at me curiously, but of course it was not their affair – and so at last I got my lunch. It was not particularly well served, but it sufficed; and when I had had it, I sat over a cigar, trying to plan my line of action. And outside a snowstorm was beginning.

'The more I thought it over, Kemp, the more I realised what a helpless absurdity an Invisible Man was – in a cold and dirty climate and a crowded civilised city. Before I made this mad experiment I had dreamt of a thousand advantages. That afternoon it seemed all disappointment. I went over the heads of the things a man reckons desirable. No doubt invisibility made it possible to get them, but it made it impossible to enjoy them when they are got. Ambition – what is the good of pride of place when you cannot appear there? What is the good of the love of a woman when her name must needs be Delilah? I have no taste for politics, for the blackguardisms of fame, for philanthropy, for sport. What was I to do? And for this I had become a wrapped-up mystery, a swathed and bandaged caricature of a man!'

He paused, and his attitude suggested a roving glance at the window.

'But how did you get to Iping?' said Kemp, anxious to keep his guest busy talking.

'I went there to work. I had one hope. It was a half idea! I have it still. It is a full-blown idea now. A way of getting back! Of restoring what I have done. When I choose. When I have done all I mean to do invisibly. And that is what I chiefly want to talk to you about now.'

'You went straight to Iping?'

'Yes. I had simply to get my three volumes of memoranda and my chequebook, my luggage and underclothing, order a quantity of chemicals to work out this idea of mine – I will show you the calculations as soon as I get my books – and then I started. Jove! I remember the snowstorm now, and the accursed bother it was to keep the snow from damping my pasteboard nose.'

'At the end,' said Kemp, 'the day before yesterday, when they found you out, you rather – to judge by the papers – '

'I did. Rather. Did I kill that fool of a constable?'

'No,' said Kemp. 'He's expected to recover.'

'That's his luck, then. I clean lost my temper, the fools! Why couldn't they leave me alone? And that grocer lout?'

'There are no deaths expected,' said Kemp.

'I don't know about that tramp of mine,' said the Invisible Man, with an unpleasant laugh. 'By heaven, Kemp, you don't know what rage is! . . . To have worked for years, to have planned and plotted, and then to get some fumbling purblind idiot messing across your course! . . . Every conceivable sort of silly creature that has ever been created has been sent to cross me.

'If I have much more of it, I shall go wild – I shall start mowing 'em. As it is, they've made things a thousand times more difficult.'

'No doubt it's exasperating,' said Kemp, drily.

CHAPTER TWENTY-FOUR

The Plan that Failed

'But now,' said Kemp, with a side glance out of the window, 'what are we to do?'

He moved nearer his guest as he spoke in such a manner as to prevent the possibility of a sudden glimpse of the three men who were advancing up the hill road – with an intolerable slowness, as it seemed to Kemp.

'What were you planning to do when you were heading for Port Burdock? *Had* you any plan?'

'I was going to clear out of the country. But I have altered that plan rather since seeing you. I thought it would be wise, now the weather is hot and invisibility possible, to make for the south. Especially as my secret was known, and everyone would be on the lookout for a masked and muffled man. You have a line of steamers from here to France. My idea was to get aboard one and run the risks of the passage. Thence I could go by train into Spain, or else get to Algiers. It would not be difficult. There a man might always be invisible – and yet live. And do things. I was using that tramp as a money box and luggage carrier, until I decided how to get my books and things sent over to meet me.'

'That's clear.'

'And then the filthy brute must needs try and rob me! He *has* hidden my books, Kemp. Hidden my books! If I can lay my hands on him!'

'Best plan to get the books out of him first.'

'But where is he? Do you know?'

'He's in the town police station, locked up, by his own request, in the strongest cell in the place.'

'Cur!' said the Invisible Man.

'But that hangs up your plans a little.'

'We must get those books; those books are vital.'

'Certainly,' said Kemp, a little nervously, wondering if he heard footsteps outside. 'Certainly we must get those books. But that won't be difficult, if he doesn't know they're for you.'

'No,' said the Invisible Man, and thought.

Kemp tried to think of something to keep the talk going, but the Invisible Man resumed of his own accord.

'Blundering into your house, Kemp,' he said, 'changes all my plans. For you are a man that can understand. In spite of all that has happened, in spite of this publicity, of the loss of my books, of what I have suffered, there still remain great possibilities, huge possibilities –

'You have told no one I am here?' he asked abruptly.

Kemp hesitated. 'That was implied,' he said.

'No one?' insisted Griffin.

'Not a soul.'

'Ah! Now – ' The Invisible Man stood up, and sticking his arms akimbo began to pace the study.

'I made a mistake, Kemp, a huge mistake, in carrying this thing through alone. I have wasted strength, time, opportunities. Alone – it is wonderful how little a man can do alone! To rob a little, to hurt a little, and there is the end.

'What I want, Kemp, is a goalkeeper, a helper and a hiding-place, an arrangement whereby I can sleep and eat and rest in peace, and un-suspected. I must have a confederate. With a confederate, with food and rest – a thousand things are possible.

'Hitherto I have gone on vague lines. We have to consider all that invisibility means, all that it does not mean. It means little advantage for eavesdropping and so forth – one makes sounds. It's of little help – a little help perhaps – in housebreaking and so forth. Once you've caught me you could easily imprison me. But on the other hand I am hard to catch. This invisibility, in fact, is only good in two cases. It's useful in getting away, it's useful in approaching. It's particularly useful, therefore, in killing. I can walk round a man, whatever weapon he has, choose my point, strike as I like. Dodge as I like. Escape as I like.'

Kemp's hand went to his moustache. Was that a movement downstairs?

'And it is killing we must do, Kemp.'

'It is killing we must do,' repeated Kemp. 'I'm listening to your plan, Griffin, but I'm not agreeing, mind. *Why* killing?'

'Not wanton killing, but a judicious slaying. The point is, they know there is an Invisible Man – as well as we know there is an Invisible Man. And that Invisible Man, Kemp, must now establish a Reign of Terror. Yes; no doubt it's startling. But I mean it. A Reign of Terror. He must take some town like your Burdock and terrify and dominate it. He must issue his

orders. He can do that in a thousand ways – scraps of paper thrust under doors would suffice. And all who disobey his orders he must kill, and kill all who would defend them.'

'Humph!' said Kemp, no longer listening to Griffin but to the sound of his front door opening and closing.

'It seems to me, Griffin,' he said, to cover his wandering attention, 'that your confederate would be in a difficult position.'

'No one would know he was a confederate,' said the Invisible Man, eagerly. And then suddenly, '*Hush!* What's that downstairs?'

'Nothing,' said Kemp, and suddenly began to speak loud and fast. 'I don't agree to this, Griffin,' he said. 'Understand me, I don't agree to this. Why dream of playing a game against the race? How can you hope to gain happiness? Don't be a lone wolf. Publish your results; take the world – take the nation at least – into your confidence. Think what you might do with a million helpers – '

The Invisible Man interrupted – arm extended. 'There are footsteps coming upstairs,' he said in a low voice.

'Nonsense,' said Kemp.

'Let me see,' said the Invisible Man, and advanced, arm extended, to the door.

And then things happened very swiftly. Kemp hesitated for a second and then moved to intercept him. The Invisible Man started and stood still. 'Traitor!' cried the Voice, and suddenly the dressing-gown opened, and sitting down the Unseen began to disrobe. Kemp made three swift steps to the door, and forthwith the Invisible Man – his legs had vanished – sprang to his feet with a shout. Kemp flung the door open.

As it opened, there came a sound of hurrying feet downstairs and voices.

With a quick movement Kemp thrust the Invisible Man back, sprang aside, and slammed the door. The key was outside and ready. In another moment Griffin would have been alone in the belvedere study, a prisoner. Save for one little thing. The key had been slipped in hastily that morning. As Kemp slammed the door it fell noisily upon the carpet.

Kemp's face became white. He tried to grip the door handle with both hands. For a moment he stood lugging. Then the door gave six inches. But he got it closed again. The second time it was jerked a foot wide, and the dressing-gown came wedging itself into the opening. His throat was gripped by invisible fingers, and he left his hold on the handle to defend himself. He was forced back, tripped and pitched heavily into the corner of the landing. The empty dressing-gown was flung on top of him.

Halfway up the staircase was Colonel Adye, the recipient of Kemp's letter, the chief of the Burdock police. He was staring aghast at the sudden appearance of Kemp, followed by the extraordinary sight of clothing tossing empty in the air. He saw Kemp felled, and struggling to his feet. He saw him rush forward, and go down again, felled like an ox.

Then suddenly he was struck violently. By nothing! A vast weight, it seemed, leapt upon him, and he was hurled headlong down the staircase, with a grip on his throat and a knee in his groin. An invisible foot trod on his back, a ghostly patter passed downstairs, he heard the two police officers in the hall shout and run, and the front door of the house slammed violently.

He rolled over and sat up staring. He saw, staggering down the staircase, Kemp, dusty and dishevelled, one side of his face white from a blow, his lip bleeding, and a pink dressing-gown and some underclothing held in his arms.

'My God!' cried Kemp, 'the game's up! He's gone!'

CHAPTER TWENTY-FIVE

The Hunting of the Invisible Man

For a space Kemp was too inarticulate to make Adye understand the swift things that had just happened. They stood on the landing, Kemp speaking swiftly, the grotesque swathings of Griffin still on his arm. But presently Adye began to grasp something of the situation.

'He is mad,' said Kemp; 'inhuman. He is pure selfishness. He thinks of nothing but his own advantage, his own safety. I have listened to such a story this morning of brutal self-seeking . . . He has wounded men. He will kill them unless we can prevent him. He will create a panic. Nothing can stop him. He is going out now – furious!'

'He must be caught,' said Adye. 'That is certain.'

'But how?' cried Kemp, and suddenly became full of ideas. 'You must begin at once. You must set every available man to work; you must prevent his leaving this district. Once he gets away, he may go through the country-side as he wills, killing and maiming. He dreams of a reign of terror! A reign of terror, I tell you. You must set a watch on trains and roads and shipping. The garrison must help. You must wire for help. The only thing that may keep him here is the thought of recovering some books of notes he counts of value. I will tell you of that! There is a man in your police station – Marvel.'

'I know,' said Adye, 'I know. Those books – yes. But the tramp – '

'Says he hasn't them. But he *thinks* the tramp has. And you must prevent him from eating or sleeping; day and night the country must be astir for him. Food must be locked up and secured, all food, so that he will have to break his way to it. The houses everywhere must be barred against him. Heaven send us cold nights and rain! The whole countryside must begin hunting and keep hunting. I tell you, Adye, he is a danger, a disaster; unless he is pinned and secured, it is frightful to think of the things that may happen.'

'What else can we do?' said Adye. 'I must go down at once and begin organising. But why not come? Yes – you come too! Come, and we must hold a sort of council of war – get Hopps to help – and the railway managers. By Jove! it's urgent. Come along – tell me as we go. What else is there we can do? Put that stuff down.'

In another moment Adye was leading the way downstairs. They found the front door open and the policemen standing outside staring at empty air. 'He's got away, sir,' said one.

'We must go to the central station at once,' said Adye. 'One of you go on down and get a cab to come up and meet us – quickly. And now, Kemp, what else?'

'Dogs,' said Kemp. 'Get dogs. They don't see him, but they wind him. Get dogs.'

'Good,' said Adye. 'It's not generally known, but the prison officials over at Halstead know a man with bloodhounds. Dogs. What else?'

'Bear in mind,' said Kemp, 'his food shows. After eating, his food shows until it is assimilated. So that he has to hide after eating. You must keep on beating. Every thicket, every quiet corner. And put all weapons – all implements that might be weapons, away. He can't carry such things for long. And what he can snatch up and strike men with must be hidden away.'

'Good again,' said Adye. 'We shall have him yet!'

'And on the roads – ' said Kemp, and hesitated.

'Yes?' said Adye.

'Powdered glass,' said Kemp. 'It's cruel, I know. But think of what he may do!'

Adye drew the air in sharply between his teeth. 'It's unsportsman–like. I don't know. But I'll have powdered glass got ready. If he goes too far . . .'

'The man's become inhuman, I tell you,' said Kemp. 'I am as sure he will establish a reign of terror – so soon as he has got over the emotions of this escape – as I am sure I am talking to you. Our only chance is to be ahead. He has cut himself off from his kind. His blood be upon his own head.'

CHAPTER TWENTY-SIX

The Wicksteed Murder

The Invisible Man seems to have rushed out of Kemp's house in a state of blind fury. A little child playing near Kemp's gateway was violently caught up and thrown aside, so that its ankle was broken, and thereafter for some hours the Invisible Man passed out of human perceptions. No one knows where he went nor what he did. But one can imagine him hurrying through the hot June forenoon, up the hill and on to the open downland behind Port Burdock, raging and despairing at his intolerable fate, and sheltering at last,

heated and weary, amid the thickets of Hintondean, to piece together again his shattered schemes against his species. That seems the most probable refuge for him, for there it was he reasserted himself in a grimly tragical manner about two in the afternoon.

One wonders what his state of mind may have been during that time, and what plans he devised. No doubt he was almost ecstatically exasperated by Kemp's treachery, and though we may be able to understand the motives that led to that deceit, we may still imagine and even sympathise a little with the fury the attempted surprise must have occasioned. Perhaps something of the stunned astonishment of his Oxford Street experiences may have returned to him, for he had evidently counted on Kemp's co-operation in his brutal dream of a terrorised world. At any rate he vanished from human ken about midday, and no living witness can tell what he did until about half-past two. It was a fortunate thing, perhaps, for humanity, but for him it was a fatal inaction.

During that time a growing multitude of men scattered over the country-side was busy. In the morning he had still been simply a legend, a terror; in the afternoon, by virtue chiefly of Kemp's drily worded proclamation, he was presented as a tangible antagonist, to be wounded, captured or overcome, and the countryside began organising itself with inconceivable rapidity. By two o'clock even he might still have removed himself out of the district by getting aboard a train, but after two that became impossible. Every passenger train along the lines on a great parallelogram between Southampton, Manchester, Brighton and Horsham, travelled with locked doors, and the goods traffic was almost entirely suspended. And in a great circle of twenty miles round Port Burdock, men armed with guns and bludgeons were presently setting out in groups of three and four, with dogs, to beat the roads and fields.

Mounted policemen rode along the country lanes, stopping at every cottage and warning the people to lock up their houses, and keep indoors unless they were armed, and all the elementary schools had broken up by three o'clock, and the children, scared and keeping together in groups, were hurrying home. Kemp's proclamation – signed indeed by Adye – was posted over almost the whole district by four or five o'clock in the afternoon. It gave briefly but clearly all the conditions of the struggle, the necessity of keeping the Invisible Man from food and sleep, the necessity for incessant watchfulness and for a prompt attention to any evidence of his movements. And so swift and decided was the action of the authorities, so prompt and universal was the belief in this strange being, that before nightfall an area of several hundred square miles was in a stringent state of siege. And before nightfall, too, a thrill of horror went through the whole watching nervous countryside. Going from whispering mouth to mouth, swift and certain over the length and breadth of the country, passed the story of the murder of Mr Wicksteed.

If our supposition that the Invisible Man's refuge was the Hintondean thickets, then we must suppose that in the early afternoon he sallied out again bent upon some project that involved the use of a weapon. We cannot know what the project was, but the evidence that he had the iron rod in hand before he met Wicksteed is to me at least overwhelming.

Of course we can know nothing of the details of that encounter. It occurred on the edge of a gravel pit, not two hundred yards from Lord Burdock's lodge gate. Everything points to a desperate struggle – the trampled ground, the numerous wounds Mr Wicksteed received, his splintered walking-stick; but why the attack was made, save in a murderous frenzy, it is impossible to imagine. Indeed the theory of madness is almost unavoidable. Mr Wicksteed was a man of forty-five or forty-six, steward to Lord Burdock, of inoffensive habits and appearance, the very last person in the world to provoke such a terrible antagonist. Against him it would seem the Invisible Man used an iron rod dragged from a broken piece of fence. He stopped this quiet man, going quietly home to his midday meal, attacked him, beat down his feeble defences, broke his arm, felled him and smashed his head to a jelly.

Of course, he must have dragged this rod out of the fencing before he met his victim – he must have been carrying it ready in his hand. Only two details beyond what has already been stated seem to bear on the matter. One is the circumstance that the gravel pit was not in Mr Wicksteed's direct path home, but nearly a couple of hundred yards out of his way. The other is the assertion of a little girl to the effect that, going to her afternoon school, she saw the murdered man '*trotting*' in a peculiar manner across a field towards the gravel pit. Her pantomime of his action suggests a man pursuing something on the ground before him and striking at it ever and again with his walking-stick. She was the last person to see him alive. He passed out of her sight to his death, the struggle being hidden from her only by a clump of beech trees and a slight depression in the ground.

Now this, to the present writer's mind at least, lifts the murder out of the realm of the absolutely wanton. We may imagine that Griffin had taken the rod as a weapon indeed, but without any deliberate intention of using it in murder. Wicksteed may then have come by and noticed this rod inexplicably moving through the air. Without any thought of the Invisible Man – for Port Burdock is miles away – he may have pursued it. It is quite conceivable that he may not even have heard of the Invisible Man. One can then imagine the Invisible Man making off – quietly in order to avoid discovering his presence in the neighbourhood, and Wicksteed, excited and curious, pursuing this unaccountably locomotive object – finally striking at it.

No doubt the Invisible Man could easily have out-distanced his middle-aged pursuer under ordinary circumstances, but the position in which Wicksteed's body was found suggests that he had the ill luck to drive his quarry into a corner between a drift of stinging nettles and the gravel pit.

To those who appreciate the extraordinary irascibility of the Invisible Man, the rest of the encounter will be easy to imagine.

But this is pure hypothesis. The only undeniable facts – for stories of children are often unreliable – are the discovery of Wicksteed's body, done to death, and of the blood-stained iron rod flung among the nettles. The abandonment of the rod by Griffin suggests that in the emotional excitement of the affair the purpose for which he took it – if he had a purpose – was abandoned. He was certainly an intensely egotistical and unfeeling man, but the sight of his victim, his first victim, bloody and pitiful at his feet, may have released some long pent fountain of remorse which for a time may have flooded whatever scheme of action he had contrived.

After the murder of Mr Wicksteed, he would seem to have struck across the country towards the downland. There is a story of a voice heard about sunset by a couple of men in a field near Fern Bottom. It was wailing and laughing, sobbing and groaning, and ever and again it shouted. It must have been queer hearing. It drove up across the middle of a clover field and died away towards the hills.

That afternoon the Invisible Man must have learnt something of the rapid use Kemp had made of his confidences. He must have found houses locked and secured; he may have loitered about railway stations and prowled about inns, and no doubt he read the proclamations and realised something of the nature of the campaign against him. And as the evening advanced, the fields became dotted here and there with groups of three or four men and noisy with the yelping of dogs. These men-hunters had particular instructions in the case of an encounter as to the way they should support one another. But he avoided them all. We may understand something of his exasperation, and it could have been none the less because he himself had supplied the information that was being used so remorselessly against him. For that day at least he lost heart; for nearly twenty-four hours, save when he turned on Wicksteed, he was a hunted man. In the night, he must have eaten and slept, for in the morning he was himself again, active, powerful, angry and malignant, prepared for his last great struggle against the world.

CHAPTER TWENTY-SEVEN

The Siege at Kemp's House

Kemp read a strange missive, written in pencil on a greasy sheet of paper.

You have been amazingly energetic and clever [this letter ran], though what you stand to gain by it I cannot imagine. You are against me. For a whole day you have chased me; you have tried to rob me of a night's rest. But I have had

food in spite of you, I have slept in spite of you, and the game is only beginning. The game is only beginning. There is nothing for it, but to start the Terror. This announces the first day of the Terror. Port Burdock is no longer under the Queen, tell your colonel of police, and the rest of them; it is under me – the Terror! This is day one of year one of the new epoch – the Epoch of the Invisible Man. I am Invisible Man the First. To begin with the rule will be easy. The first day there will be one execution for the sake of example – a man named Kemp. Death starts for him today. He may lock himself away, hide himself away, get guards about him, put on armour if he likes – Death, the unseen Death, is coming. Let him take precautions; it will impress my people. Death starts from the pillar box by midday. The letter will fall in as the postman comes along, then off! The game begins. Death starts. Help him not, my people, lest Death fall upon you also. Today Kemp is to die.

Kemp read this letter twice. 'It's no hoax,' he said. 'That's his voice! And he means it.'

He turned the folded sheet over and saw on the addressed side of it the postmark Hintondean, and the prosaic detail '2*d*. to pay'.

He got up slowly, leaving his lunch unfinished – the letter had come by the one o'clock post – and went into his study. He rang for his housekeeper, and told her to go round the house at once, examine all the fastenings of the windows, and close all the shutters. He closed the shutters of his study himself. From a locked drawer in his bedroom he took a little revolver, examined it carefully, and put it into the pocket of his lounge jacket. He wrote a number of brief notes, one to Colonel Adye, and gave them to his servant to take, with explicit instructions as to her way of leaving the house. 'There is no danger,' he said, and added a mental reservation, 'to you'. He remained meditative for a space after doing this, and then returned to his cooling lunch.

He ate with gaps of thought. Finally he struck the table sharply. 'We will have him!' he said; 'and I am the bait. He will come too far.'

He went up to the belvedere, carefully shutting every door after him. 'It's a game,' he said, 'an odd game – but the chances are all for me, Mr Griffin, in spite of your invisibility. Griffin *contra mundum* . . . with a vengeance.'

He stood at the window staring at the hot hillside. 'He must get food every day – and I don't envy him. Did he really sleep last night? Out in the open somewhere – secure from collisions. I wish we could get some good cold wet weather instead of the heat.

'He may be watching me now.'

He went close to the window. Something rapped smartly against the brickwork over the frame, and made him start violently back.

'I'm getting nervous,' said Kemp. But it was five minutes before he went to the window again. 'It must have been a sparrow,' he said.

Presently he heard the front-door bell ringing, and hurried downstairs. He unbolted and unlocked the door, examined the chain, put it up, and opened cautiously without showing himself. A familiar voice hailed him. It was Adye.

'Your servant's been assaulted, Kemp,' he said round the door.

'What!' exclaimed Kemp.

'Had that note of yours taken away from her. He's close about here. Let me in.'

Kemp released the chain, and Adye entered through as narrow an opening as possible. He stood in the hall, looking with infinite relief at Kemp refastening the door. 'Note was snatched out of her hand. Scared her horribly. She's down at the station. Hysterics. He's close here. What was it about?'

Kemp swore.

'What a fool I was,' said Kemp. 'I might have known. It's not an hour's walk from Hintondean. Already?'

'What's up?' said Adye.

'Look here!' said Kemp, and led the way into his study. He handed Adye the Invisible Man's letter. Adye read it and whistled softly. 'And you – ?' said Adye.

'Proposed a trap – like a fool,' said Kemp, 'and sent my proposal out by a maidservant. To him.'

Adye followed Kemp's profanity.

'He'll clear out,' said Adye.

'Not he,' said Kemp.

A resounding smash of glass came from upstairs. Adye had a silvery glimpse of a little revolver half out of Kemp's pocket. 'It's a window, upstairs!' said Kemp, and led the way up. There came a second smash while they were still on the staircase. When they reached the study they found two of the three windows smashed, half the room littered with splintered glass, and one big flint lying on the writing table. The two men stopped in the doorway, contemplating the wreckage. Kemp swore again, and as he did so the third window went with a snap like a pistol, hung starred for a moment, and collapsed in jagged, shivering triangles into the room.

'What's this for?' said Adye.

'It's a beginning,' said Kemp.

'There's no way of climbing up here?'

'Not for a cat,' said Kemp.

'No shutters?'

'Not here. All the downstairs rooms – Hello!'

Smash, and then the whack of boards hit hard came from downstairs. 'Confound him!' said Kemp. 'That must be – yes – it's one of the bedrooms. He's going to do all the house. But he's a fool. The shutters are up, and the glass will fall outside. He'll cut his feet.'

Another window proclaimed its destruction. The two men stood on the landing perplexed. 'I have it!' said Adye. 'Let me have a stick or something, and I'll go down to the station and get the bloodhounds put on. That ought to settle him! They're hard by – not ten minutes – '

Another window went the way of its fellows.

'You haven't a revolver?' asked Adye.

Kemp's hand went to his pocket. Then he hesitated. 'I haven't one – at least to spare.'

'I'll bring it back,' said Adye, 'you'll be safe here.'

Kemp, ashamed of his momentary lapse from truthfulness, handed him the weapon.

'Now for the door,' said Adye.

As they stood hesitating in the hall, they heard one of the first-floor bedroom windows crack and crash. Kemp went to the door and began to slip the bolts as silently as possible. His face was a little paler than usual. 'You must step straight out,' said Kemp. In another moment Adye was on the doorstep and the bolts were dropping back into the staples. He hesitated for a moment, feeling more comfortable with his back against the door. Then he marched, upright and square, down the steps. He crossed the lawn and approached the gate. A little breeze seemed to ripple over the grass. Something moved near him. 'Stop a bit,' said a Voice, and Adye stopped dead and his hand tightened on the revolver.

'Well?' said Adye, white and grim, and every nerve tense.

'Oblige me by going back to the house,' said the Voice, as tense and grim as Adye.

'Sorry,' said Adye a little hoarsely, and moistened his lips with his tongue. The Voice was on his left front, he thought. Suppose he were to take his luck with a shot?

'What are you going for?' said the Voice, and there was a quick movement of the two, and a flash of sunlight from the open lip of Adye's pocket.

Adye desisted and thought. 'Where I go,' he said slowly, 'is my own business.' The words were still on his lips, when an arm came round his neck, his back felt a knee, and he was sprawling backward. He drew clumsily and fired absurdly, and in another moment he was struck in the mouth and the revolver wrested from his grip. He made a vain clutch at a slippery limb, tried to struggle up and fell back. 'Damn!' said Adye. The Voice laughed. 'I'd kill you now if it wasn't the waste of a bullet,' it said. He saw the revolver in midair, six feet off, covering him.

'Well?' said Adye, sitting up.

'Get up,' said the Voice.

Adye stood up.

'Attention!' said the Voice, and then fiercely, 'Don't try any games. Remember I can see your face if you can't see mine. You've got to go back to the house.'

'He won't let me in,' said Adye.

'That's a pity,' said the Invisible Man. 'I've got no quarrel with you.'

Adye moistened his lips again. He glanced away from the barrel of the revolver and saw the sea far off very blue and dark under the midday sun, the smooth green down, the white cliff of the Head, and the multitudinous town, and suddenly he knew that life was very sweet. His eyes came back to this little metal thing hanging between heaven and earth, six yards away. 'What am I to do?' he said sullenly.

'What am *I* to do?' asked the Invisible Man. 'You will get help. The only thing is for you to go back.'

'I will try. If he lets me in will you promise not to rush the door?'

'I've got no quarrel with you,' said the Voice.

Kemp had hurried upstairs after letting Adye out, and now, crouching among the broken glass and peering cautiously over the edge of the study window sill, he saw Adye stand parleying with the Unseen. 'Why doesn't he fire?' whispered Kemp to himself. Then the revolver moved a little and the glint of the sunlight flashed in Kemp's eyes. He shaded his eyes and tried to see the source of the blinding beam.

'Surely,' he said, 'Adye hasn't given up the revolver?'

'Promise not to rush the door,' Adye was saying. 'Don't push a winning game too far. Give a man a chance.'

'You go back to the house. I tell you flatly I will not promise anything.'

Adye's decision seemed suddenly made. He turned towards the house, walking slowly with his hands behind him. Kemp watched him – puzzled. The revolver vanished, flashed again into sight, vanished again, and became evident on a closer scrutiny as a little dark object following Adye. Then things happened very quickly. Adye leapt backwards, swung around, clutched at this little object, missed it, threw up his hands and fell forward on his face, leaving a little puff of blue in the air. Kemp did not hear the sound of the shot. Adye writhed, raised himself on one arm, fell forward and lay still.

For a space Kemp remained staring at the quiet carelessness of Adye's attitude. The afternoon was very hot and still, nothing seemed stirring in all the world save a couple of yellow butterflies chasing each other through the shrubbery between the house and the road gate. Adye lay on the lawn near the gate. The blinds of all the villas down the hill-road were drawn, but in one little green summerhouse was a white figure, apparently an old man asleep. Kemp scrutinised the surroundings of the house for a glimpse of the revolver, but it had vanished. His eyes came back to Adye. The game was opening well.

Then came a ringing and knocking at the front door that grew at last tumultuous, but pursuant to Kemp's instructions the servants had locked themselves into their rooms. This was followed by a silence. Kemp sat listening and then began peering cautiously out of the three windows, one

after another. He went to the staircase head and stood listening uneasily. He armed himself with his bedroom poker, and went to examine the interior fastenings of the ground-floor windows again. Everything was safe and quiet. He returned to the belvedere. Adye lay motionless over the edge of the gravel just as he had fallen. Coming along the road by the villas were the housemaid and two policemen.

Everything was deadly still. The three people seemed very slow in approaching. He wondered what his antagonist was doing.

He started. There was a smash from below. He hesitated and went downstairs again. Suddenly the house resounded with heavy blows and the splintering of wood. He heard a smash and the destructive clang of the iron fastenings of the shutters. He turned the key and opened the kitchen door. As he did so, the shutters, split and splintering, came flying inward. He stood aghast. The window frame, save for one crossbar, was still intact, but only little teeth of glass remained in the frame. The shutters had been driven in with an axe, and now the axe was descending in sweeping blows upon the window frame and the iron bars defending it. Then suddenly it leapt aside and vanished. He saw the revolver lying on the path outside, and then the little weapon sprang into the air. He dodged back. The revolver cracked just too late, and a splinter from the edge of the closing door flashed over his head. He slammed and locked the door, and as he stood outside he heard Griffin shouting and laughing. Then the blows of the axe with its splitting and smashing consequences, were resumed.

Kemp stood in the passage trying to think. In a moment the Invisible Man would be in the kitchen. This door would not keep him a moment, and then –

A ringing came at the front door again. It would be the policemen. He ran into the hall, put up the chain and drew the bolts. He made the girl speak before he dropped the chain, and the three people blundered into the house in a heap, and Kemp slammed the door again.

'The Invisible Man!' said Kemp. 'He has a revolver, with two shots – left. He's killed Adye. Shot him anyhow. Didn't you see him on the lawn? He's lying there.'

'Who?' said one of the policemen.

'Adye,' said Kemp.

'We came in the back way,' said the girl.

'What's that smashing?' asked one of the policemen.

'He's in the kitchen – or will be. He has found an axe – '

Suddenly the house was full of the Invisible Man's resounding blows on the kitchen door. The girl stared towards the kitchen, shuddered, and retreated into the dining-room. Kemp tried to explain in broken sentences. They heard the kitchen door give.

'This way,' said Kemp, starting into activity, and bundled the policemen into the dining-room doorway.

'Poker,' said Kemp, and rushed to the fender. He handed the poker he had carried to the policeman and the dining-room one to the other. He suddenly flung himself backwards.

'Whup!' said one policeman, ducked, and caught the axe on his poker. The pistol snapped its penultimate shot and ripped a valuable Sidney Cooper. The second policeman brought his poker down on the little weapon, as one might knock down a wasp, and sent it rattling to the floor.

At the first clash the girl screamed, stood screaming for a moment by the fireplace, and then ran to open the shutters – possibly with an idea of escaping by the shattered window.

The axe receded into the passage, and fell to a position about two feet from the ground. They could hear the Invisible Man breathing. 'Stand away, you two,' he said. 'I want that man Kemp.'

'We want you,' said the first policeman, making a quick step forward and swiping with his poker at the Voice. The Invisible Man must have started back, and he blundered into the umbrella stand.

Then, as the policeman staggered with the swing of the blow he had aimed, the Invisible Man countered with the axe, the helmet crumpled like paper, and the blow sent the man spinning to the floor at the head of the kitchen stairs. But the second policeman, aiming behind the axe with his poker, hit something soft that snapped. There was a sharp exclamation of pain and then the axe fell to the ground. The policeman swiped again at vacancy and hit nothing; he put his foot on the axe, and struck again. Then he stood, poker clubbed, listening intently for the slightest movement.

He heard the dining-room window open, and a quick rush of feet within. His companion rolled over and sat up, with the blood running down between his eye and ear. 'Where is he?' asked the man on the floor.

'Don't know. I've hit him. He's standing somewhere in the hall. Unless he's slipped past you. Dr Kemp – sir.'

Pause.

'Dr Kemp,' cried the policeman again.

The second policeman began struggling to his feet. He stood up. Suddenly the faint pad of bare feet on the kitchen stairs could be heard. 'Yap!' cried the first policeman, and incontinently flung his poker. It smashed a little gas bracket.

He made as if he would pursue the Invisible Man downstairs. Then he thought better of it and stepped into the dining-room.

'Dr Kemp – ' he began, and stopped short.

'Dr Kemp isn't here,' he said, as his companion looked over his shoulder. The dining-room window was wide open, and neither housemaid nor Kemp was to be seen.

The second policeman's opinion of Kemp was terse and vivid.

CHAPTER TWENTY-EIGHT

The Hunter Hunted

Mr Heelas, Mr Kemp's nearest neighbour among the villa holders, was asleep in his summer house when the siege of Kemp's house began. Mr Heelas was one of the sturdy minority who refused to believe 'in all this nonsense' about an Invisible Man. His wife, however, as he was subsequently to be reminded, did. He insisted upon walking about his garden just as if nothing was the matter, and he went to sleep in the afternoon in accordance with the custom of years. He slept through the smashing of the windows, and then woke up suddenly with a curious persuasion of something wrong. He looked across at Kemp's house, rubbed his eyes and looked again. Then he put his feet to the ground, and sat listening. He said he was damned, but still the strange thing was visible. The house looked as though it had been deserted for weeks – after a violent riot. Every window was broken, and every window, save those of the belvedere study, was blinded by the internal shutters.

'I could have sworn it was all right' – he looked at his watch – 'twenty minutes ago.'

He became aware of a measured concussion and the clash of glass, far away in the distance. And then, as he sat open-mouthed, came a still more wonderful thing. The shutters of the drawing-room window were flung open violently, and the housemaid in her outdoor hat and garments, appeared struggling in a frantic manner to throw up the sash. Suddenly a man appeared beside her, helping her – Dr Kemp! In another moment the window was open, and the housemaid was struggling out; she pitched forward and vanished among the shrubs. Mr Heelas stood up, exclaiming vaguely and vehemently at all these wonderful things. He saw Kemp stand on the sill, spring from the window, and reappear almost instantaneously running along a path in the shrubbery and stooping as he ran, like a man who evades observation. He vanished behind a laburnum, and appeared again clambering over a fence that abutted on the open down. In a second he had tumbled over and was running at a tremendous pace down the slope towards Mr Heelas.

'Lord!' cried Mr Heelas, struck with an idea; 'it's that Invisible Man brute! It's right, after all!'

With Mr Heelas to think things like that was to act, and his cook watching him from the top window was amazed to see him come pelting towards the house at a good nine miles an hour. There was a slamming of doors, a ringing of bells, and the voice of Mr Heelas bellowing like a bull. 'Shut the doors, shut the windows, shut everything! – the Invisible Man is

coming!' Instantly the house was full of screams and directions, and scurrying feet. He ran himself to shut the French windows that opened on the verandah; as he did so Kemp's head and shoulders and knee appeared over the edge of the garden fence. In another moment Kemp had ploughed through the asparagus, and was running across the tennis lawn to the house.

'You can't come in,' said Mr Heelas, shutting the bolts. 'I'm very sorry if he's after you, but you can't come in!'

Kemp appeared with a face of terror close to the glass, rapping and then shaking frantically at the French windows. Then, seeing his efforts were useless, he ran along the verandah, vaulted the end, and went to hammer at the side door. Then he ran round by the side gate to the front of the house, and so into the hill-road. And Mr Heelas staring from his window – a face of horror – had scarcely witnessed Kemp vanish, ere the asparagus was being trampled this way and that by feet unseen. At that Mr Heelas fled precipitately upstairs, and the rest of the chase was beyond his purview. But as he passed the staircase window, he heard the side gate slam.

Emerging into the hill-road, Kemp naturally took the downward direction, and so it was he came to run in his own person the very race he had watched with such a critical eye from the belvedere study only four days ago. He ran it well, for a man out of training, and though his face was white and wet, his wits were cool to the last. He ran with wide strides, and wherever a patch of rough ground intervened, wherever there came a patch of raw flints, or a bit of broken glass shone dazzling, he crossed it and left the bare invisible feet that followed to take what line they would.

For the first time in his life Kemp discovered that the hill-road was indescribably vast and desolate, and that the beginnings of the town far below at the hill foot were strangely remote. Never had there been a slower or more painful method of progression than running. All the gaunt villas, sleeping in the afternoon sun, looked locked and barred; no doubt they were locked and barred – by his own orders. But at any rate they might have kept a lookout for an eventuality like this! The town was rising up now, the sea had dropped out of sight behind it, and people down below were stirring. A tram was just arriving at the hill foot. Beyond that was the police station. Was that footsteps he heard behind him? Spurt.

The people below were staring at him, one or two were running, and his breath was beginning to saw in his throat. The tram was quite near now, and the Jolly Cricketers was noisily barring its doors. Beyond the tram were posts and heaps of gravel – the drainage works. He had a transitory idea of jumping into the tram and slamming the doors, and then he resolved to go for the police station. In another moment he had passed the door of the Jolly Cricketers, and was in the blistering fag end of the street, with human beings about him. The tram driver and his helper – arrested by the sight of his furious haste – stood staring with the tram horses unhitched. Farther on the astonished features of navvies appeared above the mounds of gravel.

His pace broke a little, and then he heard the swift pad of his pursuer, and leapt forward again. 'The Invisible Man!' he cried to the navvies, with a vague indicative gesture, and by an inspiration leapt the excavation and placed a burly group between him and the chase. Then, abandoning the idea of the police station, he turned into a little side street, rushed by a greengrocer's cart, hesitated for the tenth of a second at the door of a sweetstuff shop, and then made for the mouth of an alley that ran back into the main Hill Street again. Two or three little children were playing here, and shrieked and scattered at his apparition, and forthwith doors and windows opened and excited mothers revealed their hearts. Out he shot into Hill Street again, three hundred yards from the tramline end, and immediately he became aware of a tumultuous vociferation and running people.

He glanced up the street towards the hill. Hardly a dozen yards off ran a huge navvy, cursing in fragments and slashing viciously with a spade, and hard behind him came the tram conductor with his fists clenched. Up the street others followed these two, striking and shouting. Down towards the town, men and women were running, and he noticed clearly one man coming out of a shop-door with a stick in his hand. 'Spread out! Spread out!' cried someone. Kemp suddenly grasped the altered condition of the chase. He stopped, and looked round, panting. 'He's close here!' he cried. 'Form a line across – '

He was hit hard under the ear, and went reeling, trying to face round towards his unseen antagonist. He just managed to keep his feet, and he struck a vain counter swipe in the air. Then he was hit again under the jaw, and sprawled headlong on the ground. In another moment a knee compressed his diaphragm, and a couple of eager hands gripped his throat, but the grip of one was weaker than the other; he grasped the wrists, heard a cry of pain from his assailant, and then the spade of the navvy came whirling through the air above him, and struck something with a dull thud. He felt a drop of moisture on his face. The grip at his throat suddenly relaxed, and with a convulsive effort, Kemp loosed himself, grasped a limp shoulder and rolled uppermost. He gripped the unseen elbows near the ground. 'I've got him!' screamed Kemp. 'Help! Help – hold! He's down! Hold his feet!'

In another second there was a simultaneous rush upon the struggle, and a stranger coming into the road suddenly might have thought an exceptionally savage game of Rugby football was in progress. And there was no shouting after Kemp's cry – only a sound of blows and feet and heavy breathing.

Then came a mighty effort, and the Invisible Man threw off a couple of his antagonists and rose to his knees. Kemp clung to him in front like a hound to a stag, and a dozen hands gripped, clutched and tore at the Unseen. The tram conductor suddenly got the neck and shoulders and lugged him back.

Down went the heap of struggling men again and rolled over. There was,

I am afraid, some savage kicking. Then suddenly a wild scream of, 'Mercy! Mercy!' that died down swiftly to a sound like choking.

'Get back, you fools!' cried the muffled voice of Kemp, and there was a vigorous shoving back of stalwart forms. 'He's hurt, I tell you. Stand back!'

There was a brief struggle to clear a space, and then the circle of eager faces saw the doctor kneeling, as it seemed, fifteen inches in the air, and holding invisible arms to the ground. Behind him a constable gripped invisible ankles.

'Don't you leave go of en,' cried the big navvy, holding a blood-stained spade; 'he's shamming.'

'He's not shamming,' said the doctor, cautiously raising his knee; 'and I'll hold him.' His face was bruised and already going red; he spoke thickly because of a bleeding lip. He released one hand and seemed to be feeling at the face. 'The mouth's all wet,' he said. And then, 'Good God!'

He stood up abruptly and then knelt down on the ground by the side of the thing unseen. There was a pushing and shuffling, a sound of heavy feet as fresh people turned up to increase the pressure of the crowd. People now were coming out of the houses. The doors of the Jolly Cricketers stood suddenly wide open. Very little was said.

Kemp felt about, his hand seeming to pass through empty air. 'He's not breathing,' he said, and then, 'I can't feel his heart. His side – ugh!'

Suddenly an old woman, peering under the arm of the big navvy, screamed sharply. 'Looky there!' she said, and thrust out a wrinkled finger.

And looking where she pointed, everyone saw, faint and transparent as though it was made of glass, so that veins and arteries and bones and nerves could be distinguished, the outline of a hand, a hand limp and prone. It grew clouded and opaque even as they stared.

'Hello!' cried the constable. 'Here's his feet a-showing!'

And so, slowly, beginning at his hands and feet and creeping along his limbs to the vital centres of his body, that strange change continued. It was like the slow spreading of a poison. First came the little white nerves, a hazy grey sketch of a limb, then the glassy bones and intricate arteries, then the flesh and skin, first a faint fogginess, and then growing rapidly dense and opaque. Presently they could see his crushed chest and his shoulders, and the dim outline of his drawn and battered features.

When at last the crowd made way for Kemp to stand erect, there lay, naked and pitiful on the ground, the bruised and broken body of a young man about thirty. His hair and brow were white – not grey with age, but white with the whiteness of albinism – and his eyes were like garnets. His hands were clenched, his eyes wide open, and his expression was one of anger and dismay.

'Cover his face!' said a man. 'For Gawd's sake, cover that face!' and three little children, pushing forward through the crowd, were suddenly twisted round and sent packing off again.

Someone brought a sheet from the Jolly Cricketers, and having covered him, they carried him into that house. And there it was, on a shabby bed in a tawdry, ill-lighted bedroom, surrounded by a crowd of ignorant and excited people, broken and wounded, betrayed and unpitied, that Griffin, the first of all men to make himself invisible, Griffin, the most gifted physicist the world has ever seen, ended in infinite disaster his strange and terrible career.

The Epilogue

So ends the story of the strange and evil experiments of the Invisible Man. And if you would learn more of him you must go to a little inn near Port Stowe and talk to the landlord. The sign of the inn is an empty board save for a hat and boots, and the name is the title of this story. The landlord is a short and corpulent little man with a nose of cylindrical proportions, wiry hair and a sporadic rosiness of visage. Drink generously, and he will tell you generously of all the things that happened to him after that time, and of how the lawyers tried to do him out of the treasure found upon him.

'When they found they couldn't prove whose money was which, I'm blessed,' he says, 'if they didn't try to make me out a blooming treasure trove! Do I *look* like a Treasure Trove? And then a gentleman gave me a guinea a night to tell the story at the Empire Music 'All – just to tell 'em in my own words – barring one.'

And if you want to cut off the flow of his reminiscences abruptly, you can always do so by asking if there weren't three manuscript books in the story. He admits there were and proceeds to explain, with asseverations that everybody thinks *he* has 'em! But bless you! he hasn't. 'The Invisible Man it was took 'em off to hide 'em when I cut and ran for Port Stowe. It's that Mr Kemp put people on with the idea of *my* having 'em.'

And then he subsides into a pensive state, watches you furtively, bustles nervously with glasses, and presently leaves the bar.

He is a bachelor man – his tastes were ever bachelor, and there are no women folk in the house. Outwardly he buttons – it is expected of him – but in his more vital privacies, in the matter of braces for example, he still turns to string. He conducts his house without enterprise, but with eminent decorum. His movements are slow, and he is a great thinker. But he has a reputation for wisdom and for a respectable parsimony in the village, and his knowledge of the roads of the South of England would beat Cobbett.

And on Sunday mornings, every Sunday morning, all the year round, while he is closed to the outer world, and every night after ten, he goes into his bar parlour, bearing a glass of gin faintly tinged with water, and having placed this down, he locks the door and examines the blinds, and even looks under the table. And then, being satisfied of his solitude, he unlocks the

cupboard and a box in the cupboard and a drawer in that box, and produces three volumes bound in brown leather, and places them solemnly in the middle of the table. The covers are weather-worn and tinged with an algal green – for once they sojourned in a ditch and some of the pages have been washed blank by dirty water. The landlord sits down in an armchair, fills a long clay pipe slowly – gloating over the books the while. Then he pulls one towards him and opens it, and begins to study it – turning over the leaves backwards and forwards.

His brows are knit and his lips move painfully. 'Hex, little two up in the air, cross and a fiddle-de-dee. Lord! what a one he was for intellect!'

Presently he relaxes and leans back, and blinks through his smoke across the room at things invisible to other eyes. 'Full of secrets,' he says. 'Wonderful secrets!

'Once I get the haul of them – *Lord!* I wouldn't do what *he* did, I'd just – well!'

He pulls at his pipe.

So he lapses into a dream, the undying wonderful dream of his life. And though Kemp has fished unceasingly, no human being save the landlord knows those books are there, with the subtle secret of invisibility and a dozen other strange secrets written therein. And none other will know of them until he dies.

The Food of the Gods
And How it Came to Earth

A novel first published in 1904

Contents

BOOK ONE

The Dawn of the Food

The Food of the Gods was first published in 1903
by *Pearson's* magazine in London and
by *Cosmopolitan* magazine in New York.
In 1904 it was published in book form
by Macmillan & Co. in London

CHAPTER ONE

The Discovery of the Food

IN THE MIDDLE YEARS of the nineteenth century there first became abundant in this strange world of ours a class of men, men tending for the most part to become elderly, who are called, and who are very properly called, but who dislike extremely to be called – 'Scientists'. They dislike that word so much that from the columns of *Nature*, which was from the first their distinctive and characteristic paper, it is as carefully excluded as if it were – that other word which is the basis of all really bad language in this country. But the Great Public and its Press know better, and 'Scientists' they are, and when they emerge to any sort of publicity, 'distinguished scientists' and 'eminent scientists' and 'well-known scientists' is the very least we call them.

Certainly both Mr Bensington and Professor Redwood quite merited any of these terms long before they came upon the marvellous discovery of which this story tells. Mr Bensington was a Fellow of the Royal Society and a former president of the Chemical Society, and Professor Redwood was Professor of Physiology in the Bond Street College of the London University, and he had been grossly libelled by the anti-vivisectionists time after time. And they had led lives of academic distinction from their very earliest youth.

They were of course quite undistinguished-looking men, as indeed all true scientists are. There is more personal distinction about the mildest-mannered actor alive than there is about the entire Royal Society. Mr Bensington was short and very, very bald, and he stooped slightly; he wore gold-rimmed spectacles and cloth boots that were abundantly cut open because of his numerous corns, and Professor Redwood was entirely ordinary in his appearance. Until they happened upon the Food of the Gods (as I must insist upon calling it) they led lives of such eminent and studious obscurity that it is hard to find anything whatever to tell the reader about them.

Mr Bensington won his spurs (if one may use such an expression of a gentleman in boots of slashed cloth) by his splendid researches upon the More Toxic Alkaloids, and Professor Redwood rose to eminence – I do not clearly remember how he rose to eminence! I know he was very eminent, and that's all. Things of this sort grow. I fancy it was a voluminous work on Reaction Times with numerous plates of sphygmograph tracings (I write subject to correction) and an admirable new terminology that did the thing for him.

The general public saw little or nothing of either of these gentlemen. Sometimes at places like the Royal Institution and the Society of Arts it did in a sort of way see Mr Bensington, or at least his blushing baldness and something of his collar and coat, and hear fragments of a lecture or paper that he imagined himself to be reading audibly; and once I remember – one midday in the vanished past – when the British Association was at Dover, coming on Section C or D, or some such letter, which had taken up its quarters in a public-house, and following two, serious-looking ladies with paper parcels, out of mere curiosity, through a door labelled 'Billiards' and 'Pool' into a scandalous darkness, broken only by a magic-lantern circle of Redwood's tracings.

I watched the lantern slides come and go, and listened to a voice (I forget what it was saying) which I believe was the voice of Professor Redwood, and there was a sizzling from the lantern and another sound that kept me there, still out of curiosity, until the lights were unexpectedly turned up. And then I perceived that this sound was the sound of the munching of buns and sandwiches and things that the assembled British Associates had come there to eat under cover of the magic-lantern darkness.

And Redwood I remember went on talking all the time the lights were up and dabbing at the place where his diagram ought to have been visible on the screen – and so it was again so soon as the darkness was restored. I remember him then as a most ordinary, slightly nervous-looking dark man, with an air of being preoccupied with something else, and doing what he was doing just then under an unaccountable sense of duty.

I heard Bensington also once – in the old days – at an educational conference in Bloomsbury. Like most eminent chemists and botanists, Mr Bensington was very authoritative upon teaching – though I am certain he would have been scared out of his wits by an average Board School class in half an hour – and so far as I can remember now, he was propounding an improvement of Professor Armstrong's Heuristic method, whereby at the cost of three or four hundred pounds' worth of apparatus, a total neglect of all other studies and the undivided attention of a teacher of exceptional gifts, an average child might with a peculiar sort of thumby thoroughness learn in the course of ten or twelve years almost as much chemistry as one could get in one of those objectionable shilling textbooks that were then so common . . .

Quite ordinary persons you perceive, both of them, outside their science. Or, if anything, on the unpractical side of ordinary. And that you will find is the case with 'scientists' as a class all the world over. What there is great of them is an annoyance to their fellow scientists and a mystery to the general public, and what is not is evident.

There is no doubt about what is not great, no race of men have such obvious littlenesses. They live in a narrow world so far as their human intercourse goes; their researches involve infinite attention and an almost

monastic seclusion; and what is left over is not very much. To witness some queer, shy, misshapen, grey-headed, self-important, little discoverer of great discoveries, ridiculously adorned with the wide ribbon of some order of chivalry and holding a reception of his fellow men, or to read the anguish of *Nature* at the 'neglect of science' when the angel of the birthday honours passes the Royal Society by, or to listen to one indefatigable lichenologist commenting on the work of another indefatigable lichenologist, such things force one to realise the unfaltering littleness of men.

And withal the reef of science that these little 'scientists' built and are yet building is so wonderful, so portentous, so full of mysterious half-shapen promises for the mighty future of man! They do not seem to realise the things that they are doing! No doubt long ago even Mr Bensington, when he chose this calling, when he consecrated his life to the alkaloids and their kindred compounds, had some inkling of the vision – more than an inkling. Without some such inspiration, for such glories and positions only as a 'scientist' may expect, what young man would have given his life to such work, as young men do? No, they *must* have seen the glory, they must have had the vision, but so near that it has blinded them. The splendour has blinded them, mercifully, so that for the rest of their lives they can hold the lights of knowledge in comfort – that we may see!

And perhaps it accounts for Redwood's touch of preoccupation, that – there can be no doubt of it now – he among his fellows was different, he was different inasmuch as something of the vision still lingered in his eyes.

2

The Food of the Gods I call it, this substance that Mr Bensington and Professor Redwood made between them; and having regard now to what it has already done and all that it is certainly going to do, there is surely no exaggeration in the name. So I shall continue to call it therefore throughout my story. But Mr Bensington would no more have called it that in cold blood than he would have gone out from his flat in Sloane Street clad in regal scarlet and a wreath of laurel. The phrase was a mere first cry of astonishment from him. He called it the Food of the Gods in his enthusiasm and for an hour or so at the most altogether. After that he decided he was being absurd. When he first thought of the thing he saw, as it were, a vista of enormous possibilities – literally enormous possibilities; but upon this dazzling vista, after one stare of amazement, he resolutely shut his eyes, even as a conscientious 'scientist' should. After that, the Food of the Gods sounded blatant to the pitch of indecency. He was surprised he had used the expression. Yet for all that something of that clear-eyed moment hung about him and broke out ever and again . . .

'Really, you know,' he said, rubbing his hands together and laughing nervously, 'it has more than a theoretical interest.'

'For example,' he confided, bringing his face close to the professor's and dropping to an undertone, 'it would perhaps, if suitably handled, *sell* . . .

'Precisely,' he said, walking away – 'as a food. Or at least a food ingredient.

'Assuming of course that it is palatable. A thing we cannot know till we have prepared it.'

He turned upon the hearthrug, and studied the carefully designed slits upon his cloth shoes.

'Name?' he said, looking up in response to an enquiry. 'For my part I incline to the good old classical allusion. It – it makes Science res – Gives it a touch of old-fashioned dignity. I have been thinking . . , I don't know if you will think it absurd of me . . . A little fancy is surely occasionally permissible . . . Herakleophorbia. Eh? The nutrition of a possible Hercules? You know it *might* . . .

'Of course if you think *not* – '

Redwood reflected with his eyes on the fire and made no objection.

'You think it would do?'

Redwood moved his head gravely.

'It might be Titanophorbia, you know. Food of Titans . . . You prefer the former?

'You're quite sure you don't think it a little *too* – '

'No.'

'Ah! I'm glad.'

And so they called it Herakleophorbia throughout their investigations, and in their report – the report that was never published, because of the unexpected developments that upset all their arrangements – it is invariably written in that way. There were three kindred substances prepared before they hit on the one their speculations had foretold and these they spoke of as Herakleophorbia I, Herakleophorbia II, and Herakleophorbia III. It is Herakleophorbia IV which I – insisting upon Bensington's original name – call here the Food of the Gods.

3

The idea was Mr Bensington's. But as it was suggested to him by one of Professor Redwood's contributions to the *Philosophical Transactions*, he very properly consulted that gentleman before he carried it further. Besides which it was, as a research, a physiological quite as much as a chemical inquiry.

Professor Redwood was one of those scientific men who are addicted to tracings and curves. You are familiar – if you are at all the sort of reader I

like – with the sort of scientific paper I mean. It is a paper you cannot make head nor tail of, and at the end come five or six long folded diagrams that open out and show peculiar zigzag tracings, flashes of lightning overdone or sinuous inexplicable things called 'smoothed curves' set up on ordinates and rooting in abscissae – and things like that. You puzzle over the thing for a long time and end with the suspicion that not only do you not understand it but that the author does not understand it either. But really you know many of these scientific people understand the meaning of their own papers quite well, it is simply a defect of expression that raises the obstacle between us.

I am inclined to think that Redwood thought in tracings and curves. And after his monumental work upon Reaction Times (the unscientific reader is exhorted to stick to it for a little bit longer and everything will be as clear as daylight) Redwood began to turn out smoothed curves and sphygmo-grapheries upon Growth, and it was one of his papers upon Growth that really gave Mr Bensington his idea.

Redwood, you know, had been measuring growing things of all sorts, kittens, puppies, sunflowers, mushrooms, bean plants and (until his wife put a stop to it) his baby, and he showed that growth went out not at a regular pace, or, as he put it, so,

but with bursts and intermissions of this sort,

and that apparently nothing grew regularly and steadily, and so far as he could make out nothing could grow regularly and steadily; it was as if every living thing had just to accumulate force to grow, grew with vigour only for a time, and then had to wait for a space before it could go on growing again. And in the muffled and highly technical language of the really careful 'scientist', Redwood suggested that the process of growth probably demanded the presence of a considerable quantity of some necessary sub-stance in the blood that was only formed very slowly, and that when this substance was used up by growth, it was only very slowly replaced, and that meanwhile the organism had to mark time. He compared his unknown substance to oil in machinery. A growing animal was rather like an engine, he suggested, that can move a certain distance and must then be oiled before it can run again. ('But why shouldn't one oil the engine from without?' said Mr Bensington, when he read the paper.) And all this, said Redwood, with the delightful nervous inconsecutiveness of his class, might

very probably be found to throw a light upon the mystery of certain of the ductless glands. As though they had anything to do with it at all!

In a subsequent communication Redwood went further. He gave a perfect Brock's benefit of diagrams – exactly like rocket trajectories they were; and the gist of it – so far as it had any gist – was that the blood of puppies and kittens and the sap of sunflowers and the juice of mushrooms in what he called the 'growing phase' differed in the proportion of certain elements from their blood and sap on the days when they were not particularly growing.

And when Mr Bensington, after holding the diagrams sideways and upside down, began to see what this difference was, a great amazement came upon him. Because, you see, the difference might probably be due to the presence of just the very substance he had recently been trying to isolate in his researches upon such alkaloids as are most stimulating to the nervous system. He put down Redwood's paper on the patent reading-desk that swung inconveniently from his armchair, took off his gold-rimmed spectacles, breathed on them and wiped them very carefully.

'By Jove!' said Mr Bensington.

Then replacing his spectacles again he turned to the patent reading-desk, which immediately, as his elbow came against its arm, gave a coquettish squeak and deposited the paper, with all its diagrams in a dispersed and crumpled state, on the floor. 'By Jove!' said Mr Bensington, straining his stomach over the armchair with a patient disregard of the habits of this convenience, and then, finding the pamphlet still out of reach, he went down on all fours in pursuit. It was on the floor that the idea of calling it the Food of the Gods came to him . . .

For you see, if he was right and Redwood was right, then by injecting or administering this new substance of his in food, he would do away with the 'resting phase', and instead of growth going on in this fashion

it would (if you follow me) go thus:

4

The night after his conversation with Redwood Mr Bensington could scarcely sleep a wink. He did seem once to get into a sort of doze, but it was only for a moment, and then he dreamt he had dug a deep hole into the

earth and poured in tons and tons of the Food of the Gods, and the earth was swelling and swelling, and all the boundaries of the countries were bursting, and the Royal Geographical Society was at work like one great guild of tailors letting out the equator . . .

That of course was a ridiculous dream, but it shows the state of mental excitement into which Mr Bensington got and the real value he attached to his idea much better than any of the things he said or did when he was awake and on his guard. Or I should not have mentioned it, because as a general rule I do not think it is at all interesting for people to tell each other about their dreams.

By a singular coincidence Redwood also had a dream that night, and his dream was this:

It was a diagram done in fire upon a long scroll of the abyss. And he (Redwood) was standing on a planet before a sort of black platform lecturing about the new sort of growth that was now possible, to the More than Royal Institution of Primordial Forces – forces which had always previously, even in the growth of races, empires, planetary systems and worlds, gone so:

And even in some cases so:

And he was explaining to them quite lucidly and convincingly that these slow, these even retrogressive methods would be very speedily quite put out of fashion by his discovery.

Ridiculous of course! But that too shows –

That either dream is to be regarded as in any way significant or prophetic beyond what I have categorically said, I do not for one moment suggest.

CHAPTER TWO

The Experimental Farm

Mr Bensington proposed originally to try this stuff, so soon as he was really able to prepare it, upon tadpoles. One always does try this sort of thing upon tadpoles to begin with; this being what tadpoles are for. And it was

agreed that he should conduct the experiments and not Redwood, because Redwood's laboratory was occupied with the ballistic apparatus and animals necessary for an investigation into the Diurnal Variation in the Butting Frequency of the Young Bull Calf, an investigation that was yielding curves of an abnormal and very perplexing sort, and the presence of glass globes of tadpoles was extremely undesirable while this particular research was in progress.

But when Mr Bensington conveyed to his cousin Jane something of what he had in mind, she put a prompt veto upon the importation of any considerable number of tadpoles, or any such experimental creatures, into their flat. She had no objection whatever to his use of one of the rooms of the flat for the purposes of a non-explosive chemistry that, so far as she was concerned, came to nothing; she let him have a gas furnace and a sink and a dust-tight cupboard of refuge from the weekly storm of cleaning she would not forgo. And having known people addicted to drink, she regarded his solicitude for distinction in learned societies as an excellent substitute for the coarser form of depravity. But any sort of living things in quantity, 'wriggly' as they were bound to be alive and 'smelly' dead, she could not and would not abide. She said these things were certain to be unhealthy, and Bensington was notoriously a delicate man – it was nonsense to say he wasn't. And when Bensington tried to make the enormous importance of this possible discovery clear, she said that it was all very well, but if she consented to his making everything nasty and unwholesome in the place (and that was what it all came to) then she was certain he would be the first to complain.

And Mr Bensington went up and down the room, regardless of his corns, and spoke to her quite firmly and angrily without the slightest effect. He said that nothing ought to stand in the way of the Advancement of Science, and she said that the Advancement of Science was one thing and having a lot of tadpoles in a flat was another; he said that in Germany it was an ascertained fact that a man with an idea like his would at once have twenty thousand properly-fitted cubic feet of laboratory placed at his disposal, and she said she was glad and always had been glad that she was not a German; he said that it would make him famous for ever, and she said it was much more likely to make him ill to have a lot of tadpoles in a flat like theirs; he said he was master in his own house, and she said that rather than wait on a lot of tadpoles she'd go as matron to a school; and then he asked her to be reasonable, and she asked *him* to be reasonable then and give up all this about tadpoles; and he said she might respect his ideas, and she said not if they were smelly she wouldn't, and then he gave way completely and said – in spite of the classical remarks of Huxley upon the subject – a bad word. Not a very bad word it was, but bad enough.

And after that she was greatly offended and had to be apologised to, and the prospect of ever trying the Food of the Gods upon tadpoles in their flat at any rate vanished completely in the apology.

So Bensington had to consider some other way of carrying out these experiments in feeding that would be necessary to demonstrate his discovery, so soon as he had his substance isolated and prepared. For some days he meditated upon the possibility of boarding out his tadpoles with some trustworthy person, and then the chance sight of the phrase in a newspaper turned his thoughts to an Experimental Farm.

And chicks. Directly he thought of it, he thought of it as a poultry farm. He was suddenly taken with a vision of wildly growing chicks. He conceived a picture of coops and runs, outsize and still more outsize coops, and runs progressively larger. Chicks are so accessible, so easily fed and observed, so much drier to handle and measure, that for his purpose tadpoles seemed to him now, in comparison with them, quite wild and uncontrollable beasts. He was quite puzzled to understand why he had not thought of chicks instead of tadpoles from the beginning. Among other things it would have saved all this trouble with his cousin Jane. And when he suggested this to Redwood, Redwood quite agreed with him.

Redwood said that in working so much upon needlessly small animals he was convinced experimental physiologists made a great mistake. It is exactly like making experiments in chemistry with an insufficient quantity of material; errors of observation and manipulation become disproportionately large. It was of extreme importance just at present that scientific men should assert their right to have their material *big*. That was why he was doing his present series of experiments at the Bond Street College upon bull calves, in spite of a certain amount of inconvenience to the students and professors of other subjects caused by their incidental levity in the corridors. But the curves he was getting were quite exceptionally interesting, and would, when published, amply justify his choice. For his own part, were it not for the inadequate endowment of science in this country, he would never, if he could avoid it, work on anything smaller than a whale. But a Public Vivarium on a sufficient scale to render this possible was, he feared, at present, in this country at any rate, a Utopian demand. In Germany – etc.

As Redwood's bull calves needed his daily attention, the selection and equipment of the Experimental Farm fell largely on Bensington. The entire cost also, was, it was understood, to be defrayed by Bensington, at least until a grant could be obtained. Accordingly he alternated his work in the laboratory of his flat with farm hunting up and down the lines that run southward out of London, and his peering spectacles, his simple baldness and his lacerated cloth shoes filled the owners of numerous undesirable properties with vain hopes. And he advertised in several daily papers and *Nature* for a responsible couple (married), punctual, active and used to poultry, to take entire charge of an Experimental Farm of three acres.

He found the place he seemed in need of at Hickleybrow, near Urshot, in Kent. It was a queer little isolated place, in a dell surrounded by old pinewoods that were black and forbidding at night. A humped shoulder of

down cut it off from the sunset, and a gaunt well with a shattered penthouse dwarfed the dwelling. The little house was creeperless, several windows were broken, and the cart shed had a black shadow at midday. It was a mile and a half from the end house of the village, and its loneliness was very doubtfully relieved by an ambiguous family of echoes.

The place impressed Bensington as being eminently adapted to the requirements of scientific research. He walked over the premises sketching out coops and runs with a sweeping arm, and he found the kitchen capable of accommodating a series of incubators and foster mothers with the very minimum of alteration. He took the place there and then; on his way back to London he stopped at Dunton Green and closed with an eligible couple that had answered his advertisements, and that same evening he succeeded in isolating a sufficient quantity of Herakleophorbia I to more than justify these engagements.

The eligible couple who were destined under Mr Bensington to be the first almoners on earth of the Food of the Gods were not only very perceptibly aged but also extremely dirty. This latter point Mr Bensington did not observe, because nothing destroys the powers of general observation quite so much as a life of experimental science. They were named Skinner, Mr and Mrs Skinner, and Mr Bensington interviewed them in a small room with hermetically sealed windows, a spotted overmantel looking-glass, and some ailing calceolarias.

Mrs Skinner was a very little old woman, capless, with dirty white hair drawn back very very tightly from a face that had begun by being chiefly, and was now, through the loss of teeth and chin, and the wrinkling up of everything else, ending by being almost exclusively – nose. She was dressed in slate colour (so far as her dress had any colour) slashed in one place with red flannel. She let him in and talked to him guardedly and peered at him round and over her nose, while Mr Skinner she alleged made some alteration in his toilette. She had one tooth that got into her articulations and she held her two long wrinkled hands nervously together. She told Mr Bensington that she had managed fowls for years and knew all about incubators; in fact, they themselves had run a poultry farm at one time, and it had only failed at last through the want of pupils. 'It's the pupils as pay,' said Mrs Skinner.

Mr Skinner, when he appeared, was a large-faced man, with a lisp and a squint that made him look over the top of your head, slashed slippers that appealed to Mr Bensington's sympathies, and a manifest shortness of buttons. He held his coat and shirt together with one hand and traced patterns on the black-and-gold tablecloth with the index finger of the other, while his disengaged eye watched Mr Bensington's sword of Damocles, so to speak, with an expression of sad detachment. 'You don't want to run thith farm for profit. No, thir. Ith all the thame, thir. Ekthperimenth! Prethithely.'

He said they could go to the farm at once. He was doing nothing at Dunton Green except a little tailoring. 'It ithn't the thmart plathe I thought it wath, and what I get ithent thkarthely worth having,' he said, 'tho that if it ith any convenienth to you for uth to come . . .'

And in a week Mr and Mrs Skinner were installed in the farm, and the jobbing carpenter from Hickleybrow was diversifying the task of erecting runs and henhouses with a systematic discussion of Mr Bensington.

'I haven't theen much of 'im yet,' said Mr Skinner. 'But as far as I can make 'im out 'e theems to be a thtewpid o' fool.'

'*I* thought 'e seemed a bit dotty,' said the carpenter from Hickleybrow.

' 'E fanthieth 'imself about poultry,' said Mr Skinner. 'Oh my goodneth! You'd think nobody knew nothin' about poultry thept 'im.'

' 'E *looks* like a 'en,' said the carpenter from Hickleybrow; 'what with them spectacles of 'is.'

Mr Skinner came closer to the carpenter from Hickleybrow, and spoke in a confidential manner, and one sad eye regarded the distant village and one was bright and wicked. 'Got to be meathured every blethed day – every blethed 'en, 'e thays. Tho as to thee they grow properly. What oh . . . eh? Every blethed 'en – every blethed day.'

And Mr Skinner put up his hand to laugh behind it in a refined and contagious manner, and humped his shoulders very much – and only the other eye of him failed to participate in his laughter. Then doubting if the carpenter had quite got the point of it, he repeated in a penetrating whisper: '*Meathured!*'

' 'E's worse than our old guvnor; I'm dratted if 'e ain't,' said the carpenter from Hickleybrow.

2

Experimental work is the most tedious thing in the world (unless it be the reports of it in the *Philosophical Transactions*), and it seemed a long time to Mr Bensington before his first dream of enormous possibilities was replaced by a crumb of realisation. He had taken the Experimental Farm in October, and it was May before the first inklings of success began. Herakleophorbia I and II and III had to be tried, and failed; there was trouble with the rats of the Experimental Farm, and there was trouble with the Skinners. The only way to get Skinner to do anything he was told to do was to dismiss him. Then he would rub his unshaven chin – he was always unshaven most miraculously and yet never bearded – with a flattened hand, and look at Mr Bensington with one eye, and over him with the other, and say, 'Oo, of courthe, thir – if you're *theriouth!*'

But at last success dawned. And its herald was a letter in the long slender handwriting of Mr Skinner.

The new Brood are out [wrote Mr Skinner] and don't quite like the look of them. Growing very rank – quite unlike what the similar lot was before your last directions was given. The last, before the cat got them, was a very nice, stocky chick, but these are Growing like thistles. I never saw. They peck so hard, striking above boot top, that am unable to give exact Measures as requested. They are regular Giants, and eating as such. We shall want more corn very soon, for you never saw such chicks to eat. Bigger than Bantams. Going on at this rate, they ought to be a bird for show, rank as they are. Plymouth Rocks won't be in it. Had a scare last night thinking that cat was at them, and when I looked out at the window could have sworn I see her getting in under the wire. The chicks was all awake and pecking about hungry when I went out, but could not see anything of the cat. So gave them a peck of corn, and fastened up safe. Shall be glad to know if the Feeding to be continued as directed. Food you mixed is pretty near all gone, and do not like to mix any more myself on account of the accident with the pudding. With best wishes from us both, and soliciting continuance of esteemed favours,

 Respectfully yours,

<div align="right">ALFRED NEWTON SKINNER</div>

The allusion towards the end referred to a milk pudding with which some Herakleophorbia II had got itself mixed with painful and very nearly fatal results to the Skinners.

But Mr Bensington, reading between the lines, saw in this rankness of growth the attainment of his long sought goal. The next morning he alighted at Urshot station, and in the bag in his hand he carried, sealed in three tins, a supply of the Food of the Gods sufficient for all the chicks in Kent.

It was a bright and beautiful morning late in May, and his corns were so much better that he resolved to walk through Hickleybrow to his farm. It was three miles and a half altogether, through the park and villages and then along the green glades of the Hickleybrow preserves. The trees were all dusted with the green spangles of high spring, the hedges were full of stitchwort and campion and the woods of blue hyacinths and purple orchid; and everywhere there was a great noise of birds – thrushes, blackbirds, robins, finches, and many more – and in one warm corner of the park some bracken was unrolling, and there was a leaping and rushing of fallow deer.

These things brought back to Mr Bensington his early and forgotten delight in life; before him the promise of his discovery grew bright and joyful, and it seemed to him that indeed he must have come upon the happiest day in his life. And when in the sunlit run by the sandy bank under the shadow of the pine trees he saw the chicks that had eaten the food he had mixed for them, gigantic and gawky, bigger already than many a hen that is married and settled, and still growing, still in their first soft yellow plumage (just faintly marked with brown along the back), he knew indeed that his happiest day had come.

At Mr Skinner's urgency he went into the runs but after he had been pecked through the cracks in his shoes once or twice he got out again, and watched these monsters through the wire netting. He peered close to the netting, and followed their movements as though he had never seen a chick before in his life.

'Whath they'll be when they're grown up ith impothible to think,' said Mr Skinner.

'Big as a horse,' said Mr Bensington.

'Pretty near,' said Mr Skinner.

'Several people could dine off a wing!' said Mr Bensington. 'They'd cut up into joints like butcher's meat.'

'They won't go on growing at thith pathe though,' said Mr Skinner.

'No?' said Mr Bensington.

'No,' said Mr Skinner. 'I know thith thort. They begin rank, but they don't go on, bleth you! No.'

There was a pause.

'It'th management,' said Mr Skinner modestly.

Mr Bensington turned his glasses on him suddenly.

'We got 'em almoth ath big at the other plathe,' said Mr Skinner, with his better eye piously uplifted and letting himself go a little; 'me and the mithith.'

Mr Bensington made his usual general inspection of the premises, but he speedily returned to the new run. It was, you know, in truth ever so much more than he had dared to expect. The course of science is so tortuous and so slow; after the clear promises and before the practical realisation arrives there comes almost always year after year of intricate contrivance, and here – here was the Food of the Gods arriving after less than a year of testing! It seemed too good – too good. That Hope Deferred which is the daily food of the scientific imagination was to be his no more! So at least it seemed to him then. He came back and stared at these stupendous chicks of his, time after time.

'Let me see,' he said. 'They're ten days old. And by the side of an ordinary chick I should fancy – about six or seven times as big . . . '

'Itth about time we artht for a rithe in thkrew,' said Mr Skinner to his wife. 'He'th ath pleathed ath Punth about the way we got thothe chickth on in the further run – pleathed ath Punth he ith.'

He bent confidentially towards her. 'Thinkth it'th that old food of hith,' he said behind his hands and made a noise of suppressed laughter in his pharyngeal cavity . . .

Mr Bensington was indeed a happy man that day. He was in no mood to find fault with details of management. The bright day certainly brought out the accumulating slovenliness of the Skinner couple more vividly than he had ever seen it before. But his comments were of the gentlest. The fencing of many of the runs was out of order, but he seemed to consider it quite

satisfactory when Mr Skinner explained that it was a 'fokth or a dog or thomething' did it. He pointed out that the incubator had not been cleaned.

'That it *asn't*, sir,' said Mrs Skinner with her arms folded, smiling coyly behind her nose. 'We don't seem to have had time to clean it not since we been 'ere . . . '

He went upstairs to see some rat-holes that Skinner said would justify a trap – they certainly were enormous – and discovered that the room in which the Food of the Gods was mixed with meal and bran was in a quite disgraceful order. The Skinners were the sort of people who find a use for cracked saucers and old cans and pickle jars and mustard boxes, and the place was littered with these. In one corner a great pile of apples that Skinner had saved was decaying, and from a nail in the sloping part of the ceiling hung several rabbit skins, upon which he proposed to test his gift as a furrier. ('There ithn't mutth about furth and thingth that *I* don't know,' said Skinner.)

Mr Bensington certainly sniffed critically at this disorder, but he made no unnecessary fuss, and even when he found a wasp regaling itself in a gallipot half full of Herakleophorbia IV, he simply remarked mildly that his substance was better sealed from the damp than exposed to the air in that manner.

And he turned from these things at once to remark – what had been for some time in his mind – 'I *think*, Skinner – you know, I shall kill one of these chicks – as a specimen. I think we will kill it this afternoon, and I will take it back with me to London.'

He pretended to peer into another gallipot and then took off his spectacles to wipe them.

'I should like,' he said, 'I should like very much, to have some relic – some memento – of this particular brood at this particular day.'

'By the by,' he said, 'you don't give those little chicks meat?'

'Oh! *no*, thir,' said Skinner, 'I can athure you, thir, we know far too much about the management of fowlth of all dethcriptionth to do anything of that thort.'

'Quite sure you don't throw your dinner refuse – I thought I noticed the bones of a rabbit scattered about the far corner of the run – '

But when they came to look at them they found they were the larger bones of a cat picked very clean and dry.

'*That's* no chick,' said Mr Bensington's cousin Jane.

'Well, I should *think* I knew a chick when I saw it,' said Mr Bensington's cousin Jane hotly.

'It's too big for a chick, for one thing, and besides you can *see* perfectly well it isn't a chick.

'It's more like a bustard than a chick.'

'For my part,' said Redwood, reluctantly allowing Bensington to drag him into the argument, 'I must confess that, considering all the evidence – '

'Oh! if you do *that*,' said Mr Bensington's cousin Jane, 'instead of using your eyes like a sensible person – '

'Well, but really, Miss Bensington – !'

'Oh! Go *on*!' said Cousin Jane. 'You men are all alike.'

'Considering all the evidence, this certainly falls within the definition – no doubt it's abnormal and hypertrophied, but still – especially since it was hatched from the egg of a normal hen – Yes, I think, Miss Bensington, I must admit – this, so far as one can call it anything, is a sort of chick.'

'You mean it's a chick?' said Cousin Jane.

'I *think* it's a chick,' said Redwood.

'What *nonsense*!' said Mr Bensington's cousin Jane, and 'Oh!' directed at Redwood's head, 'I haven't patience with you,' and then suddenly she turned about and went out of the room with a slam.

'And it's a very great relief for me to see it too, Bensington,' said Redwood, when the reverberation of the slam had died away. 'In spite of its being so big.'

Without any urgency from Mr Bensington he sat down in the low armchair by the fire and confessed to proceedings that even in an un-scientific man would have been indiscreet. 'You will think it very rash of me, Bensington, I know,' he said, 'but the fact is I put a little – not very much of it – but some – into Baby's bottle, very nearly a week ago!'

'But suppose – !' cried Mr Bensington.

'I know,' said Redwood, and glanced at the giant chick upon the plate on the table. 'It's turned out all right, thank goodness,' and he felt in his pocket for his cigarettes.

He gave fragmentary details. 'Poor little chap wasn't putting on weight . . . desperately anxious. Winkles, a frightful duffer . . . former pupil of mine . . . no good . . . Mrs Redwood – unmitigated confidence in Winkles . . . *You* know, man with a manner like a cliff – towering . . . No confidence in *me*, of course . . . Taught Winkles . . . Scarcely allowed in the nursery . . . Something had to be done . . . Slipped in while the nurse was at breakfast . . . got at the bottle.'

'But he'll grow,' said Mr Bensington.

'He's growing. Twenty-seven ounces last week . . . You should hear Winkles. It's management, he said.'

'Dear me! That's what Skinner says!'

Redwood looked at the chick again. 'The bother is to keep it up,' he said. 'They won't trust me in the nursery alone, because I tried to get a growth curve out of Georgina Phyllis – you know – and how I'm to give him a second dose – '

'Need you?'

'He's been crying two days – can't get on with his ordinary food again, anyhow. He wants some more now.'

'Tell Winkles.'

'Hang Winkles!' said Redwood.

'You might get at Winkles and give him powders to give the child '

'That's about what I shall have to do,' said Redwood, resting his chin on his fist and staring into the fire.

Bensington stood for a space smoothing the down on the breast of the giant chick. 'They will be monstrous fowls,' he said.

'They will,' said Redwood, still with his eyes on the glow.

'Big as horses,' said Bensington.

'Bigger,' said Redwood. 'That's just it!'

Bensington turned away from the specimen. 'Redwood,' he said, 'these fowls are going to create a sensation.'

Redwood nodded his head at the fire.

'And by Jove!' said Bensington, coming round suddenly with a flash in his spectacles, 'so will your little boy!'

'That's just what I'm thinking of,' said Redwood.

He sat back, sighed, threw his unconsumed cigarette into the fire and thrust his hands deep into his trouser pockets. 'That's precisely what I'm thinking of. This Herakleophorbia is going to be queer stuff to handle. The pace that chick must have grown at – !'

'A little boy growing at that pace,' said Mr Bensington slowly, and stared at the chick as he spoke.

'I *say*!' said Bensington, 'he'll be Big.'

'I shall give him diminishing doses,' said Redwood. 'Or at any rate Winkles will.'

'It's rather too much of an experiment.'

'Much.'

'Yet still, you know, I must confess – . . . Some baby will sooner or later have to try it.'

'Oh, we'll try it on *some* baby – certainly.'

'Exactly so,' said Bensington, and came and stood on the hearthrug and took off his spectacles to wipe them.

'Until I saw these chicks, Redwood, I don't think I *began* to realise –

anything – of the possibilities of what we were making. It's only beginning to dawn upon me . . . the possible consequences . . . '

And even then, you know, Mr Bensington was far from any conception of the mine that little train would fire.

4

That happened early in June. For some weeks Bensington was kept from revisiting the Experimental Farm by a severe imaginary catarrh, and one necessary flying visit was made by Redwood. He returned an even more anxious-looking parent than he had gone. Altogether there were seven weeks of steady, uninterrupted growth . . .

And then the wasps began their career.

It was late in July and nearly a week before the hens escaped from Hickleybrow that the first of the big wasps was killed. The report of it appeared in several papers, but I do not know whether the news reached Mr Bensington, much less whether he connected it with the general laxity of method that prevailed at the Experimental Farm.

There can be but little doubt now, that while Mr Skinner was plying Mr Bensington's chicks with Herakleophorbia IV, a number of wasps were just as industriously – perhaps more industriously – carrying quantities of the same paste to their early summer broods in the sandbanks beyond the adjacent pinewoods. And there can be no dispute whatever that these early broods found just as much growth and benefit in the substance as Mr Bensington's hens. It is in the nature of the wasp to attain to effective maturity before the domestic fowl – and in fact of all the creatures that were – through the generous carelessness of the Skinners – partaking of the benefits Mr Bensington heaped upon his hens, the wasps were the first to make any sort of figure in the world.

It was a keeper named Godfrey, on the estate of Lieutenant-Colonel Rupert Hick, near Maidstone, who encountered and had the luck to kill the first of these monsters of whom history has any record. He was walking knee high in bracken across an open space in the beechwoods that diversify Lieutenant-Colonel Hick's park, and he was carrying his gun – very fortunately for him a double-barrelled gun – over his shoulder, when he first caught sight of the thing. It was, he says, coming down against the light, so that he could not see it very distinctly, and as it came it made a drone 'like a motor car'. He admits he was frightened. It was evidently as big or bigger than a barn owl, and, to his practised eye, its flight and particularly the misty whirl of its wings must have seemed weirdly unbirdlike. The instinct of self-defence, I fancy, mingled with long habit, when, as he says, he 'let fly, right away'.

The queerness of the experience probably affected his aim; at any rate

most of his shot missed, and the thing merely dropped for a moment with an angry 'Wuzzzz' that revealed the wasp at once, and then rose again, with all its stripes shining against the light. He says it turned on him. At any rate, he fired his second barrel at less than twenty yards and threw down his gun, ran a pace or so, and ducked to avoid it.

It flew, he is convinced, within a yard of him, struck the ground, rose again, came down again perhaps thirty yards away, and rolled over with its body wriggling and its sting stabbing out and back in its last agony. He emptied both barrels into it again before he ventured to go near.

When he came to measure the thing, he found it was twenty-seven and a half inches across its open wings, and its sting was three inches long. The abdomen was blown clean off from its body, but he estimated the length of the creature from head to sting as eighteen inches – which is very nearly correct. Its compound eyes were the size of penny pieces.

That is the first authenticated appearance of these giant wasps. The day after, a cyclist riding, feet up, down the hill between Sevenoaks and Tonbridge, very narrowly missed running over a second of these giants that was crawling across the roadway. His passage seemed to alarm it, and it rose with a noise like a sawmill. His bicycle jumped the footpath in the drama of the moment, and when he could look back, the wasp was soaring away above the woods towards Westerham.

After riding unsteadily for a little time, he put on his brake, dismounted – he was trembling so violently that he fell over his machine in doing so – and sat down by the roadside to recover. He had intended to ride to Ashford, but he did not get beyond Tonbridge that day . . .

After that, curiously enough, there is no record of any big wasps being seen for three days. I find on consulting the meteorological record of those days that they were overcast and chilly with local showers, which may perhaps account for this intermission. Then on the fourth day came blue sky and brilliant sunshine and such an outburst of wasps as the world had surely never seen before.

How many big wasps came out that day it is impossible to guess. There are at least fifty accounts of their apparition. There was one victim, a grocer, who discovered one of these monsters in a sugar-cask and very rashly attacked it with a spade as it rose. He struck it to the ground for a moment, and it stung him through the boot as he struck at it again and cut its body in half. He was first dead of the two . . .

The most dramatic of the fifty appearances was certainly that of the wasp that visited the British Museum about midday, dropping out of the blue serene upon one of the innumerable pigeons that feed in the courtyard of that building, and flying up to the cornice to devour its victim at leisure. After that it crawled for a time over the museum roof, entered the dome of the reading-room by a skylight, buzzed about inside it for some little time – there was a stampede among the readers – and at last

found another window and vanished again with a sudden silence from human observation.

Most of the other reports were of mere passings or descents. A picnic party was dispersed at Aldington Knoll and all its sweets and jam consumed, and a puppy was killed and torn to pieces near Whitstable under the very eyes of its mistress . . .

The streets that evening resounded with the cry, the newspaper placards gave themselves up exclusively in the biggest of letters to the 'Gigantic Wasps in Kent'. Agitated editors and assistant editors ran up and down tortuous staircases bawling things about 'wasps'. And Professor Redwood, emerging from his college in Bond Street at five, flushed from a heated discussion with his committee about the price of bull calves, bought an evening paper, opened it, changed colour, forgot about bull calves and his committee forthwith, and took a hansom headlong for Bensington's flat.

5

The flat was occupied, it seemed to him – to the exclusion of all other sensible objects – by Mr Skinner and his voice, if indeed you can call either him or it a sensible object!

The voice was up very high slopping about among the notes of anguish. 'It'th impothible for uth to thtop, thir. We've thtopped on hoping thingth would get better and they've only got worth, thir. It ithn't on'y the waptheth, thir – there'th big earwigth, thir – big ath that, thir.' (He indicated all his hand and about three inches of fat dirty wrist.) 'They pretty near give Mithith Thkinner fitth, thir. And the thtinging nettleth by the runth, thir, *they're* growing, thir, and the canary creeper, thir, what we thowed near the think, thir– it put it'th tendril through the window in the night, thir, and very nearly caught Mithith Thkinner by the legth, thir. It'th that food of yourth, thir. Wherever we thplathed it about, thir, a bit, it'th thet everything growing ranker, thir, than I ever thought anything could grow. It'th impothible to thtop a month, thir. It'th more than our liveth are worth, thir. Even if the waptheth don't thting uth, we thall be thuffocated by the creeper, thir. You can't imagine, thir– unleth you come down to thee, thir– '

He turned his superior eye to the cornice above Redwood's head. ' 'Ow do we know the ratth 'aven't got it, thir! That 'th what I think of motht, thir. I 'aven't theen any big ratth, thir, but 'ow do I know, thir. We been frightened for dayth becauth of the earwigth we've theen – like lobthters they wath – two of 'em, thir– and the frightful way the canary creeper wath growing, and directly I heard the waptheth – directly I 'eard 'em, thir, I underthtood. I didn't wait for nothing exthept to thow on a button I'd lortht, and then I came on up. Even now, thir, I'm arf wild with angthiety, thir.

'Ow do *I* know watth happenin' to Mithith Thkinner, thir! There'th the creeper growing all over the plathe like a thnake, thir – thwelp me but you 'ave to watch it, thir, and jump out of itth way! – and the earwigth gettin' bigger and bigger, and the waptheth – She 'athen't even got a Blue Bag, thir– if anything thould happen, thir!'

'But the hens,' said Mr Bensington; 'how are the hens?'

'We fed 'em up to yethterday, thwelp me,' said Mr Skinner, 'but thith morning we didn't *dare*, thir. The noithe of the waptheth wath – thomet-hing awful, thir. They wath coming ont – dothenth. Ath big ath 'enth. I thayth, to 'er, I thayth you juth thow me on a button or two, I thayth, for I can't go to London like thith, I thayth, and I'll go up to Mithter Benthington, I thayth, and ekthplain thingth to 'im. And you thtop in thith room till I come back to you, I thayth, and keep the windowth thut juth ath tight ath ever you can, I thayth.'

'If you hadn't been so confoundedly untidy – ' began Redwood.

'Oh! don't thay *that*, thir,' said Skinner. 'Not now, thir. Not with me tho diththrethed, thir, about Mithith Thkinner, thir! Oh, *don't*, thir! I 'aven't the 'eart to argue with you. Thwelp me, thir, I 'aven't! It'th the ratth I keep a thinking of – 'Ow do I know they 'aven't got at Mithith Thkinner while I been up 'ere?'

'And you haven't got a solitary measurement of all these beautiful growth curves!' said Redwood.

'I been too upthet, thir,' said Mr Skinner. 'If you knew what we been through – me and the mithith! All thith latht month. We 'aven't known what to make of it, thir. What with the henth gettin' tho rank, and the earwigth, and the canary creeper. I dunno if I told you, thir – the canary creeper . . .'

'You've told us all that,' said Redwood. 'The thing is, Bensington, what are we to do?'

'What are *we* to do?' said Mr Skinner.

'You'll have to go back to Mrs Skinner,' said Redwood. 'You can't leave her there alone all night.'

'Not alone, thir, I won't. Not if there wath a dothen Mithith Thkinnerth. It'th Mithter Benthington – '

'Nonsense,' said Redwood. 'The wasps will be all right at night. And the earwigs will get out of your way – '

'But about the ratth?'

'There aren't any rats,' said Redwood.

Mr Skinner might have forgone his chief anxiety. Mrs Skinner did not stop out her day.

About eleven the canary creeper, which had been quietly active all the morning, began to clamber over the window and darken it very greatly, and the darker it got the more and more clearly Mrs Skinner perceived that her position would speedily become untenable. And also that she had lived many ages since Skinner went. She peered out of the darkling window, through the stirring tendrils, for some time, and then went very cautiously and opened the bedroom door and listened . . .

Everything seemed quiet, and so, tucking her skirts high about her, Mrs Skinner made a bolt for the bedroom, and having first looked under the bed and locked herself in, proceeded with the methodical rapidity of an experienced woman to pack for departure. The bed had not been made, and the room was littered with pieces of the creeper that Skinner had hacked off in order to close the window overnight, but these disorders she did not heed. She packed in a decent sheet. She packed all her own wardrobe and a velveteen jacket that Skinner wore in his finer moments, and she packed a jar of pickles that had not been opened, and so far she was justified in her packing. But she also packed two of the hermetically closed tins containing Herakleophorbia IV that Mr Bensington had brought on his last visit. (She was honest, good woman – but she was a grandmother, and her heart had burned within her to see such good growth lavished on a lot of dratted chicks.)

And having packed all these things, she put on her bonnet, took off her apron, tied a new bootlace round her umbrella, and after listening for a long time at door and window, opened the door and sallied out into a perilous world. The umbrella was under her arm and she clutched the bundle with two gnarled and resolute hands. It was her best Sunday bonnet, and the two poppies that reared their heads amidst its splendours of band and bead seemed instinct with the same tremulous courage that possessed her.

The features about the roots of her nose wrinkled with determination. She had had enough of it! All alone there! Skinner might come back there if he liked.

She went out by the front door, going that way not because she wanted to go to Hickleybrow (her goal was Cheasing Eyebright, where her married daughter resided), but because the back door was impassable on account of the canary creeper that had been growing so furiously ever since she upset the can of food near its roots. She listened for a space and closed the front door very carefully behind her.

At the corner of the house she paused and reconnoitred . . .

An extensive sandy scar upon the hillside beyond the pinewoods marked the nest of the giant wasps, and this she studied very earnestly. The coming and going of the morning was over, not a wasp chanced to be in sight then, and except for a sound scarcely more perceptible than a steam wood-saw at work amidst the pines would have been, everything was still. As for earwigs, she could see not one. Down among the cabbage indeed something was stirring, but it might just as probably be a cat stalking birds. She watched this for a time.

She went a few paces past the corner, came in sight of the run containing the giant chicks and stopped again. 'Ah!' she said, and shook her head slowly at the sight of them. They were at that time about the height of emus, but of course much thicker in the body – a larger thing altogether. They were all hens and five all told, now that the two cockerels had killed each other. She hesitated at their drooping attitudes. 'Poor dears!' she said, and put down her bundle; 'they've got no water. And they've 'ad no food these twenty-four hours! And such appetites, too, as they 'ave!' She put a lean finger to her lips and communed with herself.

Then this dirty old woman did what seems to me a quite heroic deed of mercy. She left her bundle and umbrella in the middle of the brick path and went to the well and drew no fewer than three pailfuls of water for the chickens' empty trough, and then while they were all crowding about that, she undid the door of the run very softly. After which she became extremely active, resumed her package, got over the hedge at the bottom of the garden, crossed the rank meadows (in order to avoid the wasps' nest) and toiled up the winding path towards Cheasing Eyebright.

She panted up the hill, and as she went she paused ever and again to rest her bundle and get her breath and stare back at the little cottage beside the pinewood below. And when at last, when she was near the crest of the hill, she saw afar off three several wasps dropping heavily westward, it helped her greatly on her way.

She soon got out of the open and into the high-banked lane beyond (which seemed a safer place to her), and so up by Hicklebrow Coombe to the downs. There at the foot of the downs where a big tree gave an air of shelter she rested for a space on a stile.

Then on again very resolutely . . .

You figure her, I hope, with her white bundle, a sort of erect black ant, hurrying along the little white path-thread athwart the downland slopes under the hot sun of the summer afternoon. On she struggled after her resolute indefatigable nose, and the poppies in her bonnet quivered perpetually and her spring-sided boots grew whiter and whiter with the downland dust. Flip-flap, flip-flap went her footfalls through the still heat of the day, and persistently, incurably, her umbrella sought to slip from under the elbow that retained it. The mouth wrinkle under her nose was pursed to an extreme resolution, and ever and again she told her umbrella to come up or

gave her tightly clutched bundle a vindictive jerk. And at times her lips mumbled with fragments of some foreseen argument between herself and Skinner.

And far away, miles and miles away, a steeple and a hanger grew insensibly out of the vague blue to mark more and more distinctly the quiet corner where Cheasing Eyebright sheltered from the tumult of the world, recking little or nothing of the Herakleophorbia concealed in that white bundle that struggled so persistently towards its orderly retirement.

7

So far as I can gather, the pullets came into Hickleybrow about three o'clock in the afternoon. Their coming must have been a brisk affair, though nobody was out in the street to see it. The violent bellowing of little Skelmersdale seems to have been the first announcement of anything out of the way. Miss Durgan of the Post Office was at the window as usual, and saw the hen that had caught the unhappy child in violent flight up the street with its victim, closely pursued by two others. You know that swinging stride of the emancipated athletic latter-day pullet! You know the keen insistence of the hungry hen! There was Plymouth Rock in these birds, I am told, and even without Herakleophorbia that is a gaunt and striding strain.

Probably Miss Durgan was not altogether taken by surprise. In spite of Mr Bensington's insistence upon secrecy, rumours of the great chickens Mr Skinner was producing had been about the village for some weeks. 'Lor!' she cried, 'it's what I expected.'

She seems to have behaved with great presence of mind. She snatched up the sealed bag of letters that was waiting to go on to Urshot, and rushed out of the door at once. Almost simultaneously Mr Skelmersdale himself appeared down the village, gripping a watering-pot by the spout and very white in the face. And, of course, in a moment or so everyone in the village was rushing to the door or window. The spectacle of Miss Durgan all across the road, with the entire day's correspondence of Hickleybrow in her hand, gave pause to the pullet in possession of Master Skelmersdale. She halted through one instant's indecision and then turned for the open gates of Fulcher's yard. That instant was fatal. The second pullet ran in neatly, got possession of the child by a well-directed peck, and went over the wall into the vicarage garden.

'Charawk, chawk, chawk, chawk, chawk, chawk!' shrieked the hindmost hen, hit smartly by the watering-can Mr Skelmersdale had thrown, and fluttered wildly over Mrs Glue's cottage and so into the doctor's field, while the rest of those gargantuan birds pursued the pullet in possession of the child across the vicarage lawn.

'Good heavens!' cried the curate, or (as some say) something much more

manly, and ran, whirling his croquet mallet and shouting, to head off the chase.

'Stop, you wretch!' cried the curate, as though giant hens were the commonest facts in life.

And then, finding he could not possibly intercept her, he hurled his mallet with all his might and main, and out it shot in a gracious curve within a foot or so of Master Skelmersdale's head and through the glass lantern of the conservatory. Smash! The new conservatory! The vicar's wife's beautiful new conservatory!

It frightened the hen. It might have frightened anyone. She dropped her victim into a Portugal laurel (from which he was presently extracted, disordered but, save for his less delicate garments, uninjured), made a flapping leap for the roof of Fulcher's stables, put her foot through a weak place in the tiles, and descended, so to speak, out of the infinite into the contemplative quiet of Mr Bumps the paralytic – who, it is now proved beyond all cavil, did, on this one occasion in his life, get down the entire length of his garden and indoors without any assistance whatever, bolt the door after him, and immediately relapse again into Christian resignation and helpless dependence upon his wife . . .

The rest of the pullets were headed off by the other croquet players, and went through the vicar's kitchen garden into the doctor's field, to which rendezvous the fifth also came at last, clucking disconsolately after an unsuccessful attempt to walk on the cucumber frames in Mr Witherspoon's place.

They seem to have stood about in a hen-like manner for a time, and scratched a little and chirrawked meditatively, and then one pecked at and pecked over a hive of the doctor's bees, and after that they set off in a gawky, jerky, feathery, fitful sort of way across the fields towards Urshot, and Hickleybrow Street saw them no more. Near Urshot they really came upon commensurate food in a field of swedes; and pecked for a space with gusto, until their fame overtook them.

The chief immediate reaction of this astonishing irruption of gigantic poultry upon the human mind was to arouse an extraordinary passion to whoop and run and throw things, and in quite a little time almost all the available manhood of Hickleybrow, and several ladies, were out with a remarkable assortment of flappish and whangable articles in hand – to commence the scooting of the giant hens. They drove them into Urshot, where there was a rural fête, and Urshot took them as the crowning glory of a happy day. They began to be shot at near Findon Beeches, but at first only with a rook rifle. Of course birds of that size could absorb an unlimited quantity of small shot without inconvenience. They scattered somewhere near Sevenoaks, and near Tonbridge one of them fled clucking for a time in excessive agitation, somewhat ahead of and parallel with the afternoon boat express – to the great astonishment of everyone therein.

And about half-past five two of them were caught very cleverly by a circus proprietor at Tunbridge Wells, who lured them into a cage, rendered vacant through the death of a widowed dromedary, by scattering cakes and bread . . .

8

When the unfortunate Skinner got out of the South-Eastern train at Urshot that evening it was already nearly dusk. The train was late, but not inordinately late – and Mr Skinner remarked as much to the station-master. Perhaps he saw a certain pregnancy in the station-master's eye. After the briefest hesitation and with a confidential movement of his hand to the side of his mouth he asked if 'anything' had happened that day.

'How d'yer *mean*?' said the station-master, a man with a hard, emphatic voice.

'Thethe 'ere waptheth and thingth.'

'We 'aven't 'ad much time to think of *waptheth*,' said the station- master agreeably. 'We've been too busy with your brasted 'ens,' and he broke the news of the pullets to Mr Skinner as one might break the window of an adverse politician.

'You ain't 'eard anything of Mithith Thkinner?' asked Skinner, amidst that missile shower of pithy information and comment.

'No fear!' said the station-master – as though even he drew the line somewhere in the matter of knowledge.

'I mutht make enquireth bout thith,' said Mr Skinner, edging out of reach of the station-master's concluding generalisations about the responsibility attaching to the excessive nurture of hens . . .

Going through Urshot Mr Skinner was hailed by a lime-burner from the pits over by Hankey and asked if he was looking for his hens.

'You ain't 'eard anything of Mithith Thkinner?' he asked.

The lime-burner – his exact phrases need not concern us – expressed his superior interest in hens . . .

It was already dark – as dark at least as a clear night in the English June can be – when Skinner – or his head at any rate – came into the bar of the Jolly Drovers and said: ' 'Ello! You 'aven't 'eard anything of thith 'ere thtory bout my 'enth, 'ave you?'

'Oh, *'aven't* we!' said Mr Fulcher. 'Why, part of the story's been and bust into my stable roof and one chapter smashed a 'ole in Missis Vicar's green 'ouse – I beg 'er pardon – conservarratory.'

Skinner came in. 'I'd like thomething a little comforting,' he said, ' 'ot gin and water'th about my figure,' and everybody began to tell him things about the pullets.

'*Grathuth* me!' said Skinner.

'You 'aven't 'eard anything about Mithith Thkinner, 'ave you?' he asked in a pause.

'That we 'aven't!' said Mr Witherspoon. 'We 'aven't thought of 'er. We ain't thought nothing of either of you.'

'Ain't you been 'ome today?' asked Fulcher over a tankard.

'If one of those brasted birds 'ave pecked 'er,' began Mr Witherspoon, and left the full horror to their unaided imaginations . . .

It appeared to the meeting at the time that it would be an interesting end to an eventful day to go on with Skinner and see if anything *had* happened to Mrs Skinner. One never knows what luck one may have when accidents are at large. But Skinner, standing at the bar and drinking his hot gin and water, with one eye roving over the things at the back of the bar and the other fixed on the Absolute, missed the psychological moment.

'I thuppothe there 'athen't been any trouble with any of thethe big waptheth today anywhere?' he asked, with an elaborate detachment of manner.

'Been too busy with your 'ens,' said Fulcher.

'I thuppothe they've all gone in now anyhow,' said Skinner.

'What – the 'ens?'

'I wath thinking of the waptheth more particularly,' said Skinner.

And then, with an air of circumspection that would have awakened suspicion in a week-old baby, and laying the accent heavily on most of the words he chose, he asked, 'I *thuppothe nobody* 'athn't 'eard of any other *big* thingth about, 'ave they? Big *dogth* or *catth* or anything of *that* thort? Theemth to me if there'th big henth and big waptheth comin' on – '

He laughed with a fine pretence of talking idly.

But a brooding expression came upon the faces of the Hickleybrow men. Fulcher was the first to give their condensing thought the concrete shape of words.

'A cat to match them 'ens – ' said Fulcher.

'Ay!' said Witherspoon, 'a cat to match they 'ens.'

' 'Twould be a tiger,' said Fulcher.

'More'n a tiger,' said Witherspoon . . .

When at last Skinner followed the lonely footpath over the swelling field that separated Hickleybrow from the sombre pine-shaded hollow in whose black shadows the gigantic canary-creeper grappled silently with the Experimental Farm, he followed it alone.

He was distinctly seen to rise against the skyline, against the warm clear immensity of the northern sky – for so far public interest followed him – and to descend again into the night, into an obscurity from which it would seem he will nevermore emerge. He passed – into a mystery. No one knows to this day what happened to him after he crossed the brow. When later on the two Fulchers and Witherspoon, moved by their own imaginations, came up the hill and stared after him, the flight had swallowed him up altogether.

The three men stood close. There was not a sound out of the wooded blackness that hid the farm from their eyes.

'It's all right,' said young Fulcher, ending a silence.

'Don't see any lights,' said Witherspoon.

'You wouldn't from here.'

'It's misty,' said the elder Fulcher.

They meditated for a space.

' 'E'd 'ave come back if anything was wrong,' said young Fulcher, and this seemed so obvious and conclusive that presently old Fulcher said, 'Well,' and the three went home to bed – thoughtfully I will admit . . .

A shepherd out by Huckster's Farm heard a squealing in the night that he thought was foxes, and in the morning one of his lambs had been killed, dragged halfway towards Hickleybrow and partially devoured . . .

The inexplicable part of it all is the absence of any indisputable remains of Skinner!

Many weeks after, amidst the charred ruins of the Experimental Farm, there was found something which may or may not have been a human shoulder-blade and in another part of the ruins a long bone greatly gnawed and equally doubtful. Near the stile going up towards Eyebright there was found a glass eye, and many people discovered thereupon that Skinner owed much of his personal charm to such a possession. It stared out upon the world with that same inevitable effect of detachment, that same severe melancholy that had been the redemption of his else worldly countenance.

And about the ruins industrious research discovered the metal rings and charred coverings of two linen buttons, three shanked buttons entire, and one of that metallic sort which is used in the less conspicuous sutures of the human Oeconomy. These remains have been accepted by persons in authority as conclusive of a destroyed and scattered Skinner, but for my own entire conviction, and in view of his distinctive idiosyncrasy, I must confess I should prefer fewer buttons and more bones.

The glass eye of course has an air of extreme conviction, but if it really *is* Skinner's – and even Mrs Skinner did not certainly know if that immobile eye of his was glass – something has changed it from a liquid brown to a serene and confident blue. That shoulder-blade is an extremely doubtful document, and I would like to put it side by side with the gnawed scapulae of a few of the commoner domestic animals before I admitted its humanity.

And where were Skinner's boots, for example? Perverted and strange as a rat's appetite must be, is it conceivable that the same creatures that could leave a lamb only half eaten, would finish up Skinner – hair, bones, teeth and boots?

I have closely questioned as many as I could of those who knew Skinner at all intimately, and they one and all agree that they cannot imagine *anything* eating him. He was the sort of man, as a retired seafaring person

living in one of Mr W. W. Jacobs's cottages at Dunton Green told me, with a guarded significance of manner not uncommon in those parts, who would 'get washed up anyhow', and as regards *the* devouring element was 'fit to put a fire out'. He considered that Skinner would be as safe on a raft as anywhere. The retired seafaring man added that he wished to say nothing whatever against Skinner; facts were facts. And rather than have his clothes made by Skinner, the retired seafaring man remarked he would take his chance of being locked up. These observations certainly do not present Skinner in the light of an appetising object.

To be perfectly frank with the reader, I do not believe he ever went back to the Experimental Farm. I believe he hovered through long hesitations about the fields of the Hickleybrow glebe, and finally, when that squealing began, took the line of least resistance out of his perplexities into the Incognito.

And in the Incognito, whether of this or of some other world unknown to us, he obstinately and quite indisputably has remained to this day . . .

CHAPTER THREE

The Giant Rats

It was two nights after the disappearance of Mr Skinner that the Podbourne doctor was out late near Hankey, driving in his buggy. He had been up all night assisting another undistinguished citizen into this curious world of ours, and his task accomplished, he was driving homeward in a drowsy mood enough. It was about two o'clock in the morning, and the waning moon was rising. The summer night had gone cold, and there was a low-lying whitish mist that made things indistinct. He was quite alone – for his coachman was ill in bed – and there was nothing to be seen on either hand but a drifting mystery of hedge running athwart the yellow glare of his lamps, and nothing to hear but the clitter-clatter of his horse and the echo of his wheels. His horse was as trustworthy as himself, and one does not wonder that he dozed . . .

You know that intermittent drowsing as one sits, the drooping of the head, the nodding to the rhythm of the wheels then chin upon the breast, and at once the sudden start up again.

Pitter, litter, patter.

'What was that?'

It seemed to the doctor he had heard a thin shrill squeal close at hand. In a moment he was quite awake. He said a word or two of undeserved rebuke to his horse, and looked about him. He tried to persuade himself that he had heard the distant squeal of a fox – or perhaps a young rabbit gripped by a ferret.

Swish, swish, swish, pitter, patter, swish . . .

What was that?

He felt he was getting fanciful. He shook his shoulders and told his horse to get on. He listened, and heard nothing.

Or was it nothing?

He had the queerest impression that something had just peeped over the hedge at him, a queer big head. With round ears! He peered hard, but he could see nothing.

'Nonsense,' said he.

He sat up with an idea that he had dropped into a nightmare, gave his horse the slightest touch of the whip, spoke to it and peered again over the hedge. The glare of his lamp, however, together with the mist, rendered things indistinct, and he could distinguish nothing. It came into his head, he says, that there could be nothing there, because if there was his horse would have shied at it. Yet for all that his senses remained nervously awake.

Then he heard quite distinctly a soft pattering of feet in pursuit along the road.

He would not believe his ears about that. He could not look round, for the road had a sinuous curve just there. He whipped up his horse and glanced sideways again. And then he saw quite distinctly where a ray from his lamp leapt a low stretch of hedge, the curved back of – some big animal, he couldn't tell what, going along in quick convulsive leaps.

He says he thought of the old tales of witchcraft – the thing was so utterly unlike any animal he knew, and he tightened his hold on the reins for fear of the fear of his horse. Educated man as he was, he admits he asked himself if this could be something that his horse could not see.

Ahead, and drawing near in silhouette against the rising moon, was the outline of the little hamlet of Hankey, comforting, though it showed never a light, and he cracked his whip and spoke again, and then in a flash the rats were at him!

He had passed a gate, and as he did so, the foremost rat came leaping over into the road. The thing sprang upon him out of vagueness into the utmost clearness, the sharp, eager, round-eared face, the long body exaggerated by its movement; and what particularly struck him, the pink, webbed forefeet of the beast. What must have made it more horrible to him at the time was that he had no idea the thing was any created beast he knew. He did not recognise it as a rat, because of the size. His horse gave a bound as the thing dropped into the road beside it. The little lane woke into tumult at the report of the whip and the doctor's shout. The whole thing suddenly went fast.

Rattle-clatter, clash, clatter.

The doctor, one gathers, stood up, shouted to his horse, and slashed with all his strength. The rat winced and swerved most reassuringly at his blow – in the glare of his lamp he could see the fur furrow under the lash – and he

slashed again and again, heedless and unaware of the second pursuer that gained upon his offside.

He let the reins go, and glanced back to discover the third rat in pursuit behind . . .

His horse bounded forward. The buggy leapt high at a rut. For a frantic minute perhaps everything seemed to be going in leaps and bounds . . .

It was sheer good luck the horse came down in Hankey, and not either before or after the houses had been passed.

No one knows how the horse came down, whether it stumbled or whether the rat on the offside really got home with one of those slashing down strokes of the teeth (given with the full weight of the body); and the doctor never discovered that he himself was bitten until he was inside the brickmaker's house, much less did he discover when the bite occurred, though bitten he was and badly – a long slash like the slash of a double tomahawk that had cut two parallel ribbons of flesh from his left shoulder.

He was standing up in his buggy at one moment, and in the next he had leapt to the ground, with his ankle, though he did not know it, badly sprained, and he was cutting furiously at a third rat that was flying directly at him. He scarcely remembers the leap he must have made over the top of the wheel as the buggy came over, so obliteratingly hot and swift did his impressions rush upon him. I think myself the horse reared up with the rat biting again at its throat, and fell sideways, and carried the whole affair over; and that the doctor sprang, as it were, instinctively. As the buggy came down, the receiver of the lamp smashed, and suddenly poured a flare of blazing oil, a thud of white flame, into the struggle.

That was the first thing the brickmaker saw.

He had heard the clatter of the doctor's approach and – though the doctor's memory has nothing of this – wild shouting. He had got out of bed hastily, and as he did so came the terrific smash, and up shot the glare outside the rising blind. 'It was brighter than day,' he says. He stood, blind cord in hand, and stared out of the window at a nightmare transformation of the familiar road before him. The black figure of the doctor with its whirling whip danced out against the flame. The horse kicked indistinctly, half hidden by the blaze, with a rat at its throat. In the obscurity against the churchyard wall, the eyes of a second monster shone wickedly. Another – a mere dreadful blackness with red-lit eyes and flesh-coloured hands – clutched unsteadily on the wall coping to which it had leapt at the flash of the exploding lamp.

You know the keen face of a rat, those two sharp teeth, those pitiless eyes. Seen magnified to near six times its linear dimensions, and still more magnified by darkness and amazement and the leaping fancies of a fitful blaze, it must have been an ill sight for the brickmaker – still more than half asleep.

Then the doctor had grasped the opportunity, that momentary respite

the flare afforded, and was out of the brickmaker's sight below battering the door with the butt of his whip . . .

The brickmaker would not let him in until he had got a light.

There are those who have blamed the man for that, but until I know my own courage better, I hesitate to join their number.

The doctor yelled and hammered . . .

The brickmaker says he was weeping with terror when at last the door was opened.

'Bolt,' said the doctor, 'bolt' – he could not say 'bolt the door'. He tried to help, and was of no service. The brickmaker fastened the door, and the doctor had to sit on the chair beside the clock for a space before he could go upstairs . . .

'I don't know what they *are*!' he repeated several times. 'I don't know what they *are*' – with a high note on the 'are'.

The brickmaker would have got him whisky, but the doctor would not be left alone with nothing but a flickering light just then.

It was long before the brickmaker could get him to go upstairs . . .

And when the fire was out the giant rats came back, took the dead horse, dragged it across the churchyard into the brickfield and ate at it until it was dawn, none even then daring to disturb them . . .

2

Redwood went round to Bensington about eleven the next morning with the second editions of three evening papers in his hand.

Bensington looked up from a despondent meditation over the forgotten pages of the most distracting novel the Brompton Road librarian had been able to find him. 'Anything fresh?' he asked.

'Two men stung near Chartham.'

'They ought to let us smoke out that nest. They really did. It's their own fault.'

'It's their own fault, certainly,' said Redwood.

'Have you heard anything – about buying the farm?'

'The House Agent,' said Redwood, 'is a thing with a big mouth and made of dense wood. It pretends someone else is after the house – it always does, you know – and won't understand there's a hurry. "This is a matter of life and death," I said, "don't you understand?" It drooped its eyes half shut and said, "Then why don't you go the other two hundred pounds?" I'd rather live in a world of solid wasps than give in to the stonewalling stupidity of that offensive creature. I – '

He paused, feeling that a sentence like that might very easily be spoiled by its context.

'It's too much to hope,' said Bensington, 'that one of the wasps – '

'The wasp has no more idea of public utility than a – than a house agent,' said Redwood.

He talked for a little while about house agents and solicitors and people of that sort, in the unjust, unreasonable way that so many people do somehow get to talk of these business calculi ('Of all the cranky things in this cranky world, the most cranky of all to my mind is that while we expect honour, courage, efficiency from a doctor or a soldier as a matter of course, a solicitor or a house agent is not only permitted but expected to display nothing but a sort of greedy, greasy, obstructive, over-reaching imbecility – ' etc.) and then, greatly relieved, he went to the window and stared out at the Sloane Street traffic.

Bensington had put the most exciting novel conceivable on the little table that carried his electric standard. He joined the fingers of his opposed hands very carefully and regarded them 'Redwood,' he said. 'Do they say much about *Us?*'

'Not so much as I should expect.'

'They don't denounce us at all?'

'Not a bit. But, on the other hand, they don't back up what I point out must be done. I've written to *The Times*, you know, explaining the whole thing – '

'We take the *Daily Chronicle*,' said Bensington.

'And *The Times* has a long leader on the subject – a very high-class, well-written leader, with three pieces of *Times* Latin – *status quo* is one – and it reads like the voice of Somebody Impersonal of the Greatest Importance suffering from Influenza Headache and talking through sheets and sheets of felt without getting any relief from it whatever. Reading between the lines, you know, it's pretty clear that *The Times* considers that it is useless to mince matters and that something (indefinite, of course) has to be done at once. Otherwise still more undesirable consequences – *Times* English, you know, for more wasps and stings. Thoroughly statesmanlike article!'

'And meanwhile this Bigness is spreading in all sorts of ugly ways.'

'Precisely.'

'I wonder if Skinner was right about those big rats – '

'Oh no! That would be too much,' said Redwood.

He came and stood by Bensington's chair.

'By the by,' he said, with a slightly lowered voice, 'how does *she* – ?'

He indicated the closed door.

'Cousin Jane? She simply knows nothing about it. Doesn't connect us with it and won't read the articles. "Gigantic wasps!" she says, "I haven't patience to read the papers." '

'That's very fortunate,' said Redwood.

'I suppose – Mrs Redwood – ?'

'No,' said Redwood, 'just at present it happens – she's terribly worried about the child. You know, he keeps on.'

'Growing?'

'Yes. Put on forty-one ounces in ten days. Weighs nearly four stone. And only six months old! Naturally rather alarming.'

'Healthy?'

'Vigorous. His nurse is leaving because he kicks so forcibly. And everything, of course, shockingly outgrown. Everything, you know, has had to be made fresh, clothes and everything. Perambulator – light affair – broke one wheel, and the youngster had to be brought home on the milkman's hand-truck. Yes. Quite a crowd . . . And we've put Georgina Phyllis back into his cot and put him into the bed of Georgina Phyllis. His mother – naturally alarmed. Proud at first and inclined to praise Winkles. Not now. Feels the thing *can't* be wholesome. *You* know.'

'I imagined you were going to put him on diminishing doses.'

'I tried it.'

'Didn't it work?'

'Howls. In the ordinary way the cry of a child is loud and distressing; it is for the good of the species that this should be so – but since he has been on the Herakleophorbia treatment – '

'Mm,' said Bensington, regarding his fingers with more resignation than he had hitherto displayed.

'Practically the thing *must* come out. People will hear of this child, connect it up with our hens and things, and the whole thing will come round to my wife . . . How she will take it I haven't the remotest idea.'

'It *is* difficult,' said Mr Bensington, 'to form any plan – certainly.'

He removed his glasses and wiped them carefully.

'It is another instance,' he generalised, 'of the thing that is continually happening. We – if indeed I may presume to the adjective – *scientific* men – we work of course always for a theoretical result – a purely theoretical result. But, incidentally, we do set forces in operation – *new* forces. We mustn't control them – and nobody else *can*. Practically, Redwood, the thing is out of our hands. *We* supply the material – '

'And they,' said Redwood, turning to the window, 'get the experience.'

'So far as this trouble down in Kent goes I am not disposed to worry further.'

'Unless they worry us.'

'Exactly. And if they like to muddle about with solicitors and petti-foggers and legal obstructions and weighty considerations of the tomfool order, until they have got a number of new gigantic species of vermin well established . . . Things always *have* been in a muddle, Redwood.'

Redwood traced a twisted, tangled line in the air.

'And our real interest lies at present with your boy.'

Redwood turned about and came and stared at his collaborator.

'What do you think of him, Bensington? You can look at this business with a greater detachment than I can. What am I to do about him?'

'Go on feeding him.'

'On Herakleophorbia?'

'On Herakleophorbia.'

'And then he'll grow.'

'He'll grow, as far as I can calculate from the hens and the wasps, to the height of about five-and-thirty feet – with everything in proportion – '

'And then what'll he do?'

'That,' said Mr Bensington, 'is just what makes the whole thing so interesting.'

'Confound it, man! Think of his clothes.'

'And when he's grown up,' said Redwood, 'he'll only be one solitary Gulliver in a pigmy world.'

Mr Bensington's eye over his gold rim was pregnant.

'Why solitary?' he said, and repeated still more darkly, '*Why solitary?*'

'But you don't propose – ?'

'I said,' said Mr Bensington, with the self-complacency of a man who has produced a good significant saying, 'Why solitary?'

'Meaning that one might bring up other children – ?'

'Meaning nothing beyond my enquiry.'

Redwood began to walk about the room. 'Of course,' he said, 'one might – But still! What are we coming to?'

Bensington evidently enjoyed his line of high intellectual detachment. 'The thing that interests me most, Redwood, of all this, is to think that his brain at the top of him will also, so far as my reasoning goes, be five-and-thirty feet or so above our level . . . What's the matter?'

Redwood stood at the window and stared at a news placard on a paper-cart that rattled up the street.

'What's the matter?' repeated Bensington, rising.

Redwood exclaimed violently.

'What is it?' said Bensington.

'Get a paper,' said Redwood, moving doorwards.

'Why?'

'Get a paper. Something – I didn't quite catch – Gigantic rats – !'

'Rats?'

'Yes, rats. Skinner was right after all!'

'What do you mean?'

'How the deuce am *I* to know till I see a paper? Great rats! Good Lord! I wonder if he's been eaten!'

He glanced for his hat, and decided to go hatless.

As he rushed downstairs two steps at a time, he could hear along the street the mighty howlings to and fro of the hooligan paper-sellers making a Boom.

' 'Orrible affair in Kent – 'orrible affair in Kent. Doctor . . . eaten by rats. 'Orrible affair – 'orrible affair – rats – eaten by Stchewpendous rats. Full perticulars – 'orrible affair.'

Cossar, the well-known civil engineer, found them in the great doorway of the flat mansions, Redwood holding out the damp pink paper, and Bensington on tiptoe reading over his arm. Cossar was a large-bodied man with gaunt inelegant limbs casually placed at convenient corners of his body, and a face like a carving abandoned at an early stage as altogether too unpromising for completion. His nose had been left square, and his lower jaw projected beyond his upper. He breathed audibly. Few people considered him handsome. His hair was entirely tangential, and his voice, which he used sparingly, was pitched high, and had commonly a quality of bitter protest. He wore a grey-cloth jacket suit and a silk hat on all occasions. He plumbed an abysmal trouser pocket with a vast red hand, paid his cabman, and came panting resolutely up the steps, a copy of the pink paper clutched about the middle, like Jove's thunderbolt, in his hand.

'Skinner?' Bensington was saying, regardless of his approach.

'Nothing about him,' said Redwood. 'Bound to be eaten. Both of them. It's too terrible . . . Hello! Cossar!'

'This your stuff?' asked Cossar, waving the paper.

'*Yes!* Well, why don't you stop it?' he demanded.

' *Can't* be jiggered!' said Cossar.

'*Buy the place?*' he cried. 'What nonsense! Burn it! I knew you chaps would fumble this.

'*What are you to do?* Why – what I tell you.

'*You? Do?* Why! Go up the street to the gunsmith's, of course.

'*Why?* For guns. Yes – there's only one shop. Get eight guns! Rifles. Not elephant guns – no! Too big. Not army rifles – too small. Say it's to kill – kill a bull. Say it's to shoot buffalo! See? Eh? Rats? No! How the deuce are they to understand that? Because we *want* eight. Get a lot of ammunition. Don't get guns without ammunition – No! Take the lot in a cab to – where's the place? *Urshot?* Charing Cross, then. There's a train – Well, the first train that starts after two. Think you can do it? All right. Licence? Get eight at a post-office, of course. Gun licences, you know. Not game. Why? It's rats, man.

'You – Bensington. Got a telephone? Yes. I'll ring up five of my chaps from Ealing. *Why* five? Because it's the right number!

'Where you going, Redwood? Get a hat! *Nonsense*. Have mine. You want guns, man – not hats. Got money? Enough? All right. So long.

'Where's the telephone, Bensington?'

Bensington wheeled about obediently and led the way.

Cossar used and replaced the instrument. 'Then there's the wasps,' he said. 'Sulphur and nitre'll do that. Obviously. Plaster of Paris. You're a

chemist. Where can I get sulphur by the ton in portable sacks? *What for?* Why, Lord *bless* my heart and soul! – to smoke out the nest, of course! I suppose it must be sulphur, eh? You're a chemist. Sulphur best, eh?'

'Yes, I should *think* sulphur.'

'Nothing better? Right. That's your job. That's all right. Get as much sulphur as you can – saltpetre to make it burn. Sent? Charing Cross. Right away. See they do it. Follow it up. Anything?'

He thought a moment.

'Plaster of Paris – any sort of plaster – bung up nest – holes – you know. That *I'd* better get.'

'How much?'

'How much what?'

'Sulphur.'

'Ton. See?'

Bensington tightened his glasses with a hand tremulous with determination. 'Right,' he said, very curtly.

'Money in your pocket?' asked Cossar. 'Hang cheques. They may not know you. Pay cash. Obviously. Where's your bank? All right. Stop on the way and get forty pounds – notes and gold.'

Another meditation. 'If we leave this job for public officials we shall have all Kent in tatters,' said Cossar. 'Now is there – anything? *No! Hi!*'

He stretched a vast hand towards a cab that became convulsively eager to serve him ('Cab, sir?' said the cabman. 'Obviously,' said Cossar); and Bensington, still hatless, paddled down the steps and prepared to mount.

'I *think*,' he said, with his hand on the cab apron, and a sudden glance up at the windows of his flat, 'I *ought* to tell my cousin Jane – '

'More time to tell her when you come back,' said Cossar, thrusting him in with a vast hand expanded over his back . . .

'Clever chaps,' remarked Cossar, 'but no initiative whatever. Cousin Jane indeed! I know her. Rot, these Cousin Janes! Country infested with 'em. I suppose I shall have to spend the whole blessed night seeing they do what they know perfectly well they ought to have done all along. I wonder if it's Research makes 'em like that or Cousin Jane or what?'

He dismissed this obscure problem, meditated for a space upon his watch, and decided there would be just time to drop into a restaurant and get some lunch before he hunted up the plaster of Paris and took it to Charing Cross.

The train started at five minutes past three, and he arrived at Charing Cross at a quarter to three, to find Bensington in heated argument between two policemen and his van-driver outside, and Redwood in the luggage office involved in some technical obscurity about this ammunition. Everybody was pretending not to know anything or to have any authority, in the way dear to South-Eastern officials when they catch you in a hurry.

'Pity they can't shoot all these officials and get a new lot,' remarked

Cossar with a sigh. But the time was too limited for anything fundamental, and so he swept through these minor controversies, disinterred what may or may not have been the station-master from some obscure hiding-place, walked about the premises holding him and giving orders in his name, and was out of the station with everybody and everything aboard before that official was fully awake to the breaches in the most sacred routines and regulations that were being committed.

'Who *was* he?' said the high official, caressing the arm Cossar had gripped, and smiling with knit brows.

' 'E was a gentleman, sir,' said a porter, 'anyhow. 'Im and all 'is party travelled first class.'

'Well, we got him and his stuff off pretty sharp – whoever he was,' said the high official, rubbing his arm with something approaching satisfaction.

And as he walked slowly back, blinking in the unaccustomed daylight, towards that dignified retirement in which the higher officials at Charing Cross shelter from the importunity of the vulgar, he smiled still at his unaccustomed energy. It was a very gratifying revelation of his own possibilities, in spite of the stiffness of his arm. He wished some of those confounded armchair critics of railway management could have seen it.

4

By five o'clock that evening this amazing Cossar, with no appearance of hurry at all, had got all the stuff for his fight with insurgent Bigness out of Urshot and on the road to Hickleybrow. Two barrels of paraffin and a load of dry brushwood he had bought in Urshot; plentiful sacks of sulphur, eight big-game guns and ammunition, three light breechloaders, with small-shot ammunition for the wasps, a hatchet, two billhooks, a pick and three spades, two coils of rope, some bottled beer, soda and whisky, one gross of packets of rat poison, and cold provisions for three days, had come down from London. All these things he had sent on in a coal trolley and a hay waggon in the most businesslike way, except the guns and ammunition, which were stuck under the seat of the Red Lion waggonette appointed to bring on Redwood and the five picked men who had come up from Ealing at Cossar's summons.

Cossar conducted all these transactions with an invincible air of commonplace, in spite of the fact that Urshot was in a panic about the rats, and all the drivers had to be specially paid. All the shops were shut in the place, and scarcely a soul abroad in the street, and when he banged at a door a window was apt to open. He seemed to consider that the conduct of business from open windows was an entirely legitimate and obvious method. Finally he and Bensington got the Red Lion dogcart and set off with the waggonette to overtake the baggage. They did this a little beyond the crossroads, and so reached Hickleybrow first.

Bensington, with a gun between his knees, sitting beside Cossar in the dogcart, developed a long germinated amazement. All they were doing was, no doubt, as Cossar insisted, quite the obvious thing to do, only – ! In England one so rarely does the obvious thing. He glanced from his neighbour's feet to the boldly sketched hands upon the reins. Cossar had apparently never driven before, and he was keeping the line of least resistance down the middle of the road by some no doubt quite obvious but certainly unusual light of his own.

'Why don't we all do the obvious?' thought Bensington. 'How the world would travel if one did! I wonder for instance why I don't do such a lot of things I know would be all right to do – things I *want* to do. Is everybody like that, or is it peculiar to me!' He plunged into obscure speculation about the Will. He thought of the complex organised futilities of the daily life, and in contrast with them the plain and manifest things to do, the sweet and splendid things to do, that some incredible influences will never permit us to do. Cousin Jane? Cousin Jane he perceived was important in the question, in some subtle and difficult way. Why should we after all eat, drink and sleep, remain unmarried, go here, abstain from going there, all out of deference to Cousin Jane? She became symbolical without ceasing to be incomprehensible!

A stile and a path across the fields caught his eye and reminded him of that other bright day, so recent in time, so remote in its emotions, when he had walked from Urshot to the Experimental Farm to see the giant chicks.

Fate plays with us.

'Tcheck, tcheck,' said Cossar. 'Get up.'

It was a hot midday afternoon, not a breath of wind, and the dust was thick on the roads. Few people were about, but the deer beyond the park palings browsed in profound tranquillity. They saw a couple of big wasps stripping a gooseberry bush just outside Hickleybrow, and another was crawling up and down the front of the little grocer's shop in the village street trying to find an entry. The grocer was dimly visible within, with an ancient fowling-piece in hand, watching its endeavours. The driver of the waggonette pulled up outside the Jolly Drovers and informed Redwood that his part of the bargain was done. In this contention he was presently joined by the drivers of the waggon and the trolley. Not only did they maintain this, but they refused to let the horses be taken farther.

'Them big rats is nuts on 'orses,' the trolley driver kept on repeating.

Cossar surveyed the controversy for a moment.

'Get the things out of that waggonette,' he said, and one of his men, a tall, fair, dirty engineer, obeyed.

'Gimme that shotgun,' said Cossar.

He placed himself between the drivers. 'We don't want *you* to drive,' he said. 'You can say what you like,' he conceded, 'but we want these horses.'

They began to argue, but he continued speaking.

'If you try and assault us I shall, in self-defence, let fly at your legs. The horses are going on.'

He treated the incident as closed. 'Get up on that waggon, Flack,' he said to a thickset, wiry little man. 'Boon, take the trolley.'

The two drivers blustered to Redwood.

'You've done your duty to your employers,' said Redwood. 'You stop in this village until we come back. No one will blame you, seeing we've got guns. We've no wish to do anything unjust or violent, but this occasion is pressing. I'll pay if anything happens to the horses, never fear.'

'*That's* all right,' said Cossar, who rarely promised.

They left the waggonette behind, and the men who were not driving went afoot. Over each shoulder sloped a gun. It was the oddest little expedition for an English country road, more like a Yankee party, trekking west in the good old Indian days.

They went up the road, until at the crest by the stile they came into sight of the Experimental Farm. They found a little group of men there with a gun or so – the two Fulchers were among them – and one man, a stranger from Maidstone, stood out before the others and watched the place through an opera-glass.

These men turned about and stared at Redwood's party.

'Anything fresh?' said Cossar.

'The waspses keeps a comin' and a goin',' said old Fulcher. 'Can't see as they bring anything.'

'The canary creeper's got in among the pine trees now,' said the man with the lorgnette. 'It wasn't there this morning. You can see it grow while you watch it.'

He took out a handkerchief and wiped his object-glasses with careful deliberation.

'I reckon you're going down there,' ventured Skelmersdale.

'Will you come?' said Cossar.

Skelmersdale seemed to hesitate.

'It's an all-night job.'

Skelmersdale decided that he wouldn't.

'Rats about?' asked Cossar.

'One was up in the pines this morning – rabbiting, we reckon.'

Cossar slouched on to overtake his party.

Bensington, regarding the Experimental Farm under his hand, was able to gauge now the vigour of the Food. His first impression was that the house was smaller than he had thought – very much smaller; his second was to perceive that all the vegetation between the house and the pinewood had become extremely large. The roof over the well peeped amidst tussocks of grass a good eight feet high, and the canary creeper wrapped about the chimney stack and gesticulated with stiff tendrils towards the heavens. Its flowers were vivid yellow splashes, distinctly visible as separate specks this

mile away. A great green cable had writhed across the big wire enclosures of the giant hens' run, and flung twining leaf stems about two outstanding pines. Fully half as tall as these was the grove of nettles running round behind the cart-shed. The whole prospect, as they drew nearer, became more and more suggestive of a raid of pigmies upon a dolls' house that has been left in a neglected corner of some great garden.

There was a busy coming and going from the wasps' nest, they saw. A swarm of black shapes interlaced in the air above the rusty hill-front beyond the pine cluster, and ever and again one of these would dart up into the sky with incredible swiftness and soar off upon some distant quest. Their humming became audible at more than half a mile's distance from the Experimental Farm. Once a yellow-striped monster dropped towards them and hung for a space watching them with its great compound eyes, but at an ineffectual shot from Cossar it darted off again. Down in a corner of the field, away to the right, several were crawling about over some ragged bones that were probably the remains of the lamb the rats had brought from Huxter's Farm. The horses became very restless as they drew near these creatures. None of the party was an expert driver, and they had to put a man to lead each horse and encourage it with the voice.

They could see nothing of the rats as they came up to the house, and everything seemed perfectly still except for the rising and falling 'whoozzzzzzZZZ, whoooo-zoo-oo' of the wasps' nest.

They led the horses into the yard, and one of Cossar's men, seeing the door open – the whole of the middle portion of the door had been gnawed out – walked into the house. Nobody missed him for the time, the rest being occupied with the barrels of paraffin, and the first intimation they had of his separation from them was the report of his gun and the whizz of his bullet. 'Bang, bang,' both barrels, and his first bullet it seems went through the cask of sulphur, smashed out a stave from the farther side, and filled the air with yellow dust. Redwood had kept his gun in hand and let fly at something grey that leapt past him. He had a vision of the broad hind-quarters, the long scaly tail and long soles of the hind-feet of a rat, and fired his second barrel. He saw Bensington drop as the beast vanished round the corner.

Then for a time everybody was busy with a gun. For three minutes lives were cheap at the Experimental Farm, and the banging of guns filled the air. Redwood, careless of Bensington in his excitement, rushed in pursuit, and was knocked headlong by a mass of brick fragments, mortar, plaster and rotten lath splinters that came flying out at him as a bullet whacked through the wall.

He found himself sitting on the ground with blood on his hands and lips, and a great stillness brooded over all about him.

Then a flattish voice from within the house remarked: 'Gee-whizz!'

'Hello!' said Redwood.

'Hello there!' answered the voice.

And then: 'Did you chaps get 'im?'

A sense of the duties of friendship returned to Redwood. 'Is Mr Bensington hurt?' he said.

The man inside heard imperfectly. 'No one ain't to blame if I ain't,' said the voice inside.

It became clearer to Redwood that he must have shot Bensington. He forgot the cuts upon his face, arose and came back to find Bensington seated on the ground and rubbing his shoulder. Bensington looked over his glasses. 'We peppered him, Redwood,' he said, and then: 'He tried to jump over me, and knocked me down. But I let him have it with both barrels, and my! how it has hurt my shoulder, to be sure.'

A man appeared in the doorway. 'I got him once in the chest and once in the side,' he said.

'Where's the waggons?' said Cossar, appearing amidst a thicket of gigantic canary-creeper leaves.

It became evident, to Redwood's amazement, first, that no one had been shot, and, secondly, that the trolley and waggon had shifted fifty yards, and were now standing with interlocked wheels amidst the tangled distortions of Skinner's kitchen garden. The horses had stopped their plunging. Half-way towards them, the burst barrel of sulphur lay in the path with a cloud of sulphur dust above it. He indicated this to Cossar and walked towards it. 'Has anyone seen that rat?' shouted Cossar, following. 'I got him in between the ribs once, and once in the face as he turned on me.'

They were joined by two men, as they worried at the locked wheels.

'I killed that rat,' said one of the men.

'Have they got him?' asked Cossar.

'Jim Bates has found him, beyond the hedge. I got him jest as he came round the corner . . . Whack behind the shoulder . . . '

When things were a little shipshape again Redwood went and stared at the huge misshapen corpse. The brute lay on its side, with its body slightly bent. Its rodent teeth overhanging its receding lower jaw gave its face a look of colossal feebleness, of weak avidity. It seemed not in the least ferocious or terrible. Its forepaws reminded him of lank emaciated hands. Except for one neat round hole with a scorched rim on either side of its neck, the creature was absolutely intact. He meditated over this fact for some time. 'There must have been two rats,' he said at last, turning away.

'Yes. And the one that everybody hit – got away.'

'I am certain that my own shot –'

A canary-creeper-leaf tendril, engaged in that mysterious search for a holdfast which constitutes a tendril's career, bent itself engagingly towards his neck and made him step aside hastily.

'Whoo–z–z z–z–z–z–Z–Z–Z,' from the distant wasps' nest, 'whoo-oo zoo-oo.'

This incident left the party alert but not unstrung.

They got their stores into the house, which had evidently been ransacked by the rats after the flight of Mrs Skinner, and four of the men took the two horses back to Hickleybrow. They dragged the dead rat through the hedge and into a position commanded by the windows of the house, and incidentally came upon a cluster of giant earwigs in the ditch. These creatures dispersed hastily, but Cossar reached out incalculable limbs and managed to kill several with his boots and gun-butt. Then two of the men hacked through several of the main stems of the canary creeper – huge cylinders they were, a couple of feet in diameter, that came out by the sink at the back; and while Cossar set the house in order for the night, Bensington, Redwood and one of the assistant electricians went cautiously round by the fowl runs in search of the rat-holes.

They skirted the giant nettles widely, for these huge weeds threatened them with poison-thorns a good inch long. Then round beyond the gnawed, dismantled stile they came abruptly on the huge cavernous throat of the most westerly of the giant rat-holes, an evil-smelling profundity that drew them up into a line together.

'I *hope* they'll come out,' said Redwood, with a glance at the pent-house of the well.

'If they don't – ' reflected Bensington.

'They will,' said Redwood.

They meditated.

'We shall have to rig up some sort of flare if we *do* go in,' said Redwood.

They went up a little path of white sand through the pinewood and halted presently within sight of the wasp-holes.

The sun was setting now, and the wasps were coming home for good; their wings in the golden light made twirling haloes about them. The three men peered out from under the trees – they did not care to go right to the edge of the wood – and watched these tremendous insects drop and crawl for a little and enter and disappear. 'They will be still in a couple of hours from now,' said Redwood . . . 'This is like being a boy again.'

'We can't miss those holes,' said Bensington, 'even if the night is dark. By the by – about the light – '

'Full moon,' said the electrician. 'I looked it up.'

They went back and consulted with Cossar.

He said that 'obviously' they must get the sulphur, nitre and plaster of Paris through the wood before twilight, and for that they broke bulk and carried the sacks. After the necessary shouting of the preliminary directions, never a word was spoken, and as the buzzing of the wasps' nest died away

there was scarcely a sound in the world but the noise of footsteps, the heavy breathing of burthened men and the thud of the sacks. They all took turns at that labour except Mr Bensington, who was manifestly unfit. He took post in the Skinners' bedroom with a rifle, to watch the carcass of the dead rat; and of the others, they took turns to rest from sack-carrying and to keep watch two at a time upon the rat-holes behind the nettle grove. The pollen sacs of the nettles were ripe, and every now and then the vigil would be enlivened by the dehiscence of these, the bursting of the sacs sounding exactly like the crack of a pistol, and the pollen grains as big as buckshot pattered all about them.

Mr Bensington sat at his window on a hard horse-hair-stuffed armchair, covered by a grubby antimacassar that had given a touch of social distinction to the Skinners' sitting-room for many years. His unaccustomed rifle rested on the sill, and his spectacles anon watched the dark bulk of the dead rat in the thickening twilight, anon wandered about him in curious meditation. There was a faint smell of paraffin without, for one of the casks leaked, and it mingled with a less unpleasant odour arising from the hacked and crushed creeper.

Within, when he turned his head, a blend of faint domestic scents, beer, cheese, rotten apples and old boots as the leading *motifs*, was full of reminiscences of the vanished Skinners. He regarded the dim room for a space. The furniture had been greatly disordered – perhaps by some inquisitive rat – but a coat upon a clothes-peg on the door, a razor and some dirty scraps of paper, and a piece of soap that had hardened through years of disuse into a horny cube, were redolent of Skinner's distinctive personality. It came to Bensington's mind with a complete novelty of realisation that in all probability the man had been killed and eaten, at least in part, by the monster that now lay dead there in the darkling.

To think of all that a harmless-looking discovery in chemistry may lead to!

Here he was in homely England and yet in infinite danger, sitting out alone with a gun in a twilit, ruined house, remote from every comfort, his shoulder dreadfully bruised from a gun-kick, and – by Jove!

He grasped now how profoundly the order of the universe had changed for him. He had come right away to this amazing experience, *without even saying a word to his cousin Jane*!

What must she be thinking of him?

He tried to imagine it and he could not. He had an extraordinary feeling that she and he were parted for ever and would never meet again. He felt he had taken a step and come into a world of new immensities. What other monsters might not those deepening shadows hide? The tips of the giant nettles came out sharp and black against the pale green and amber of the western sky. Everything was very still – very still indeed. He wondered why he could not hear the others away there round the corner of the house. The shadow in the cart-shed was now an abysmal black.

Bang . . . Bang . . . Bang.

A sequence of echoes and a shout.

A long silence.

Bang and a *diminuendo* of echoes.

Stillness.

Then, thank goodness! Redwood and Cossar were coming out of the inaudible darkness, and Redwood was calling, 'Bensington! Bensington! We've bagged another of the rats! Cossar's bagged another of the rats!'

6

When the Expedition had finished refreshment, the night had fully come. The stars were at their brightest, and a growing pallor towards Hankey heralded the moon. The watch on the rat-holes had been maintained, but the watchers had shifted to the hill slope above the holes, feeling this a safer firing-point. They squatted there in a rather abundant dew, fighting the damp with whisky. The others rested in the house, and the three leaders discussed the night's work with the men. The moon rose towards midnight, and as soon as it was clear of the downs, everyone except the rat-hole sentinels started off in single file, led by Cossar, towards the wasps' nest.

So far as the wasps' nest went, they found their task exceptionally easy – astonishingly easy. Except that it was a longer labour, it was no graver affair than any common wasps' nest might have been. Danger there was, no doubt, danger to life, but it never so much as thrust its head out of that portentous hillside. They stuffed in the sulphur and nitre, they bunged the holes soundly and fired their trains. Then with a common impulse all the party but Cossar turned and ran athwart the long shadows of the pines, and, finding Cossar had stayed behind, came to a halt together in a knot, a hundred yards away, convenient to a ditch that offered cover. Just for a minute or two the moonlit night, all black and white, was heavy with a suffocated buzz that rose and mingled to a roar, a deep abundant note, and culminated and died, and then almost incredibly the night was still.

'By Jove!' said Bensington, almost in a whisper, '*it's done!*'

All stood intent. The hillside above the black point-lace of the pine shadows seemed as bright as day and as colourless as snow. The setting plaster in the holes positively shone. Cossar's loose framework moved towards them.

'So far – ' said Cossar.

Crack – *bang!*

A shot from near the house and then – stillness.

'What's *that*?' said Bensington.

'One of the rats put its head out,' suggested one of the men.

'By the by, we left our guns up there,' said Redwood. 'By the sacks.'

Everyone began to walk towards the hill again.

'That must be the rats,' said Bensington.

'Obviously,' said Cossar, gnawing his fingernails.

Bang!

'Hello?' said one of the men.

Then abruptly came a shout, two shots, a loud shout that was almost a scream, three shots in rapid succession and a splintering of wood. All these sounds were very clear and very small in the immense stillness of the night. Then for some moments nothing but a minute muffled confusion from the direction of the rat-holes, and then again a wild yell . . . Each man found himself running hard for the guns.

Two shots.

Bensington found himself, gun in hand, going hard through the pine trees after a number of receding backs. It is curious that the thought uppermost in his mind at that moment was the wish that his cousin Jane could see him. His bulbous slashed boots flew out in wild strides, and his face was distorted into a permanent grin, because that wrinkled his nose and kept his glasses in place. Also he held the muzzle of his gun projecting straight before him as he flew through the chequered moonlight. The man who had run away met them full tilt – he had dropped his gun.

'Hello,' said Cossar, and caught him in his arms. 'What's this?'

'They came out together,' said the man.

'The rats?'

'Yes, six of them.'

'Where's Flack?'

'Down.'

'What's he say?' panted Bensington, coming up, unheeded. 'Flack's down?'

'He fell down.'

'They came out one after the other.'

'What?'

'Made a rush. I fired both barrels first.'

'You left Flack?'

'They were on to us.'

'Come on,' said Cossar. 'You come with us. Where's Flack? Show us.'

The whole party moved forward. Further details of the engagement dropped from the man who had run away. The others clustered about him, except Cossar, who led.

'Where are they?'

'Back in their holes, perhaps. I cleared. They made a rush for their holes.'

'What do you mean? Did you get behind them?'

'We got down by their holes. Saw 'em come out, you know, and tried to cut 'em off. They lolloped out – like rabbits. We ran down and let fly. They ran about wild after our first shot and suddenly came at us. *Went* for us.'

'How many?'

'Six or seven.'

Cossar led the way to the edge of the pinewood and halted.

'D'yer mean they *got* Flack?' asked someone.

'One of 'em was on to him.'

'Didn't you shoot?'

'How *could* I?'

'Everyone loaded?' said Cossar over his shoulder.

There was a confirmatory movement.

'But Flack – ' said one.

'D'yer mean – Flack? – ' said another.

'There's no time to lose,' said Cossar, and shouted, 'Flack!' as he led the way. The whole force advanced towards the rat-holes, the man who had run away a little to the rear. They went forward through the rank exaggerated weeds and skirted the body of the second dead rat. They were extended in a bunchy line, each man with his gun pointing forward, and they peered about them in the clear moonlight for some crumpled, ominous shape, some crouching form. They found the gun of the man who had run away very speedily.

'Flack!' cried Cossar. 'Flack!'

'He ran past the nettles and fell down,' volunteered the man who ran away.

'Where?'

'Round about there.'

'Where did he fall?'

He hesitated and led them athwart the long black shadows for a space and turned judicially. 'About here, I think.'

'Well, he's not here now.'

'But his gun – ?'

'Confound it!' swore Cossar, 'where's everything got to?' He strode a step towards the black shadows on the hillside that masked the holes and stood staring. Then he swore again. 'If they *have* dragged him in! – '

So they hung for a space tossing each other the fragments of thoughts. Bensington's glasses flashed like diamonds as he looked from one to the other. The men's faces changed from cold clearness to mysterious obscurity as they turned them to or from the moon. Everyone spoke, no one completed a sentence. Then abruptly Cossar chose his line. He flapped limbs this way and that and expelled orders in pellets. It was obvious he wanted lamps. Everyone except Cossar was moving towards the house.

'You're going into the holes?' asked Redwood.

'Obviously,' said Cossar.

He made it clear once more that the lamps of the cart and trolley were to be got and brought to him.

Bensington, grasping this, started off along the path by the well. He

glanced over his shoulder, and saw Cossar's gigantic figure standing out as if he were regarding the holes pensively. At the sight Bensington halted for a moment and half turned. They were all leaving Cossar – !

Cossar was able to take care of himself, of course!

Suddenly Bensington saw something that made him shout a windless 'HI!' In a second three rats had projected themselves from the dark tangle of the creeper towards Cossar. For three seconds Cossar stood unaware of them, and then he had become the most active thing in the world. He didn't fire his gun. Apparently he had no time to aim, or to think of aiming; he ducked a leaping rat, Bensington saw, and then smashed at the back of its head with the butt of his gun. The monster gave one leap and fell over itself.

Cossar's form went right down out of sight among the reedy grass, and then he rose again, running towards another of the rats and whirling his gun overhead. A faint shout came to Bensington's ears, and then he perceived the remaining two rats bolting divergently, and Cossar in pursuit towards the holes.

The whole thing was an affair of misty shadows; all three fighting monsters were exaggerated and made unreal by the delusive clearness of the light. At moments Cossar was colossal, at moments invisible. The rats flashed athwart the eye in sudden unexpected leaps, or ran with a movement of the feet so swift, they seemed to run on wheels. It was all over in half a minute. No one saw it but Bensington. He could hear the others behind him still receding towards the house. He shouted something inarticulate and then ran back towards Cossar, while the rats vanished. He came up to him outside the holes. In the moonlight the distribution of shadows that constituted Cossar's visage intimated calm. 'Hello,' said Cossar, 'back already? Where's the lamps? They're all back now in their holes. One I broke the neck of as it ran past me . . . See? There!' And he pointed a gaunt finger.

Bensington was too astonished for conversation.

The lamps seemed an interminable time in coming. At last they appeared, first one unwinking luminous eye, preceded by a swaying yellow glare, and then, winking now and then and then shining out again, two others. About them came little figures with little voices, and then enormous shadows. This group made as it were a spot of inflammation upon the gigantic dreamland of moonshine.

'Flack,' said the voices. 'Flack.'

An illuminating sentence floated up. 'Locked himself in the attic.'

Cossar was continually more wonderful. He produced great handfuls of cotton wool and stuffed them in his ears – Bensington wondered why. Then he loaded his gun with a quarter charge of powder. Who else could have thought of that? Wonderland culminated with the disappearance of Cossar's twin realms of boot sole up the central hole.

Cossar was on all fours with two guns, one trailing on each side from a

string under his chin; and his most trusted assistant, a little dark man with a grave face, was to go in stooping behind him, holding a lantern over his head. Everything had been made as sane and obvious and proper as a lunatic's dream. The wool, it seems, was on account of the concussion of the rifle; the man had some too. Obviously! So long as the rats turned tail on Cossar no harm could come to him, and directly they headed for him he would see their eyes and fire between them. Since they would have to come down the cylinder of the hole, Cossar could hardly fail to hit them. It was, Cossar insisted, the obvious method, a little tedious perhaps, but absolutely certain. As the assistant stooped to enter, Bensington saw that the end of a ball of twine had been tied to the tail of his coat. By this he was to draw in the rope if it should be needed to drag out the bodies of the rats.

Bensington perceived that the object he held in his hand was Cossar's silk hat.

How had it got there?

It would be something to remember him by, anyhow.

At each of the adjacent holes stood a little group with a lantern on the ground shining up the hole, and with one man kneeling and aiming at the round void before him, waiting for anything that might emerge.

There was an interminable suspense.

Then they heard Cossar's first shot, like an explosion in a mine.

Everyone's nerves and muscles tightened at that, and bang! bang! bang! the rats had tried a bolt, and two more were dead. Then the man who held the ball of twine reported a twitching. 'He's killed one in there,' said Bensington, 'and he wants the rope.'

He watched the rope creep into the hole, and it seemed as though it had become animated by a serpentine intelligence – for the darkness made the twine invisible. At last it stopped crawling, and there was a long pause. Then what seemed to Bensington the queerest monster of all crept slowly from the hole, and resolved itself into the little engineer emerging backwards. After him, and ploughing deep furrows, Cossar's boots thrust out, and then came his lantern-illuminated back . . .

Only one rat was left alive now, and this poor, doomed wretch cowered in the inmost recesses until Cossar and the lantern went in again and slew it; and finally Cossar, that human ferret, went through all the runs to make sure.

'We got 'em,' he said to his nearly awestricken company at last. 'And if I hadn't been a mud-headed mucker I should have stripped to the waist. Obviously. Feel my sleeves, Bensington! I'm wet through with perspiration. Jolly hard to think of everything. Only a halfway-up of whisky can save me from a cold.'

There were moments during that wonderful night when it seemed to Bensington that he was planned by nature for a life of fantastic adventure. This was particularly the case for an hour or so after he had taken a stiff whisky. 'Shan't go back to Sloane Street,' he confided to the tall, fair, dirty engineer.

'You won't, eh?'

'No fear,' said Bensington, nodding darkly.

The exertion of dragging the seven dead rats to the funeral pyre by the nettle grove left him bathed in perspiration, and Cossar pointed out the obvious physical reaction of whisky to save him from the otherwise inevitable chill. There was a sort of brigands' supper in the old bricked kitchen, with the row of dead rats lying in the moonlight against the hen-runs outside, and after thirty minutes or so of rest, Cossar roused them all to the labours that were still to do. 'Obviously,' as he said, they had to 'wipe the place out. No litter – no scandal. See?' He stirred them up to the idea of making destruction complete. They smashed and splintered every fragment of wood in the house; they built trails of chopped wood wherever big vegetation was springing; they made a pyre for the rat bodies and soaked them in paraffin.

Bensington worked like a conscientious navvy. He had a sort of climax of exhilaration and energy towards two o'clock. When in the work of destruction he wielded an axe the bravest fled his neighbourhood. Afterwards he was a little sobered by the temporary loss of his spectacles, which were found for him at last in his side coat-pocket.

Men went to and fro about him – grimy, energetic men. Cossar moved among them like a god.

Bensington drank that delight of human fellowship that comes to happy armies, to sturdy expeditions – never to those who live the life of the sober citizen in cities. After Cossar had taken his axe away and set him to carry wood he went to and fro, saying they were all 'good fellows'. He kept on – long after he was aware of fatigue.

At last all was ready, and the broaching of the paraffin began. The moon, robbed now of all its meagre night retinue of stars, shone high above the dawn.

'Burn everything,' said Cossar, going to and fro – 'burn the ground and make a clean sweep of it. See?'

Bensington became aware of him, looking now very gaunt and horrible in the pale beginnings of the daylight, hurrying past with his lower jaw projected and a flaring torch of touchwood in his hand.

'Come away!' said someone, pulling Bensington's arm.

The still dawn – no birds were singing there – was suddenly full of a tumultuous crackling; a little dull red flame ran about the base of the pyre, changed to blue upon the ground, and set out to clamber, leaf by leaf, up the stem of a giant nettle. A singing sound mingled with the crackling.

They snatched their guns from the corner of the Skinners' living-room, and then everyone was running. Cossar came after them with heavy strides . . .

Then they were standing looking back at the Experimental Farm. It was boiling up; the smoke and flames poured out like a crowd in a panic, from doors and windows and from a thousand cracks and crevices in the roof. Trust Cossar to build a fire! A great column of smoke, shot with blood-red tongues and darting flashes, rushed up into the sky. It was like some huge giant suddenly standing up, straining upward and abruptly spreading his great arms out across the sky. It cast the night back upon them, utterly hiding and obliterating the incandescence of the sun that rose behind it. All Hickleybrow was soon aware of that stupendous pillar of smoke, and came out upon the crest, in various deshabille, to watch them coming.

Behind, like some fantastic fungus, this smoke pillar swayed and fluctuated, up, up, into the sky – making the downs seem low and all other objects petty, and in the foreground, led by Cossar, the makers of this mischief followed the path, eight little black figures coming wearily, guns shouldered, across the meadow.

As Bensington looked back there came into his jaded brain, and echoed there, a familiar formula. What was it? 'You have lit today – ? You have lit today – ?' Then he remembered Latimer's words: 'We have lit this day such a candle in England as no man may ever put out again – '

What a man Cossar was, to be sure! He admired his back view for a space, and was proud to have held that hat. Proud! Although he was an eminent investigator and Cossar only engaged in applied science.

Suddenly he fell to shivering and yawning enormously and wishing he was warmly tucked away in bed in his little flat that looked out upon Sloane Street. (It didn't do even to think of Cousin Jane.) His legs became cotton strands, his feet lead. He wondered if anyone would get them coffee in Hickleybrow. He had never been up all night for three-and-thirty years.

8

And while these eight adventurers fought with rats about the Experimental Farm, nine miles away, in the village of Cheasing Eyebright, an old lady with an excessive nose struggled with great difficulties by the light of a flickering candle. She gripped a sardine-tin opener in one gnarled hand, and in the other she held a tin of Herakleophorbia, which she had resolved to open or die. She struggled indefatigably, grunting at each fresh effort,

while through the flimsy partition the voice of the Caddles infant wailed.

'Bless 'is poor 'art,' said Mrs Skinner; and then, with her solitary tooth biting her lip in an ecstasy of determination, 'Come *up!*'

And presently, '*Jab!*' a fresh supply of the Food of the Gods was let loose to wreak its powers of giantry upon the world.

<div align="center">

CHAPTER FOUR

The Giant Children

</div>

For a time at least the spreading circle of residual consequences about the Experimental Farm must pass out of the focus of our narrative – how for a long time a power of bigness, in fungus and toadstool, in grass and weed, radiated from that charred but not absolutely obliterated centre. Nor can we tell here at any length how those mournful spinsters, the two surviving hens, made a wonder of and a show, spent their remaining years in eggless celebrity. The reader who is hungry for fuller details in these matters is referred to the newspapers of the period – to the voluminous, in-discriminate files of the modern Recording Angel. Our business lies with Mr Bensington at the focus of the disturbance.

He had come back to London to find himself a quite terribly famous man. In a night the whole world had changed with respect to him. Every-body understood. Cousin Jane, it seemed, knew all about it; the people in the streets knew all about it; the newspapers all and more. To meet Cousin Jane was terrible, of course, but when it was over not so terrible after all. The good woman had limits even to her power over facts; it was clear that she had communed with herself and accepted the Food as something in the nature of things.

She took the line of huffy dutifulness. She disapproved highly, it was evident, but she did not prohibit. The flight of Bensington, as she must have considered it, may have shaken her, and her worst was to treat him with bitter persistence for a cold he had not caught and fatigue he had long since forgotten, and to buy him a new sort of hygienic all-wool combination underwear that was apt to get involved and turned partially inside out and partially not and was as difficult to get into for an absent-minded man as – Society. And so for a space, and as far as this convenience left him leisure, he still continued to participate in the development of this new element in human history, the Food of the Gods.

The public mind, following its own mysterious laws of selection, had chosen him as the one and only responsible Inventor and Promoter of this new wonder; it would hear nothing of Redwood, and without a protest it allowed Cossar to follow his natural impulse into a terribly prolific obscurity. Before he was aware of the drift of these things, Mr Bensington

was, so to speak, stark and dissected upon the hoardings. His baldness, his curious general pinkness and his golden spectacles had become a national possession. Resolute young men with large expensive-looking cameras and a general air of complete authorisation took possession of the flat for brief but fruitful periods, let off flashlights in it that filled it for days with dense, intolerable vapour, and retired to fill the pages of the syndicated magazines with their admirable photographs of Mr Bensington complete and at home in his second-best jacket and his slashed shoes. Other resolute-mannered persons of various ages and sexes dropped in and told him things about Boomfood – it was *Punch* first called the stuff 'Boomfood' – and afterwards reproduced what they had said as his own original contribution to the interview. The thing became quite an obsession with Broadbeam, the Popular Humourist. He scented another confounded thing he could not understand, and he fretted dreadfully in his efforts to 'laugh the thing down'. One saw him in clubs, a great clumsy presence with the evidences of his midnight-oil burning manifest upon his large unwholesome face, explaining to everyone he could buttonhole: 'These Scientific chaps, you know, haven't a Sense of Humour, you know. That's what it is. This Science – kills it.' His jests at Bensington became malignant libels.

An enterprising press-cutting agency sent Bensington a long article about himself from a sixpenny weekly, entitled 'A New Terror', and offered to supply one hundred such disturbances for a guinea, and two extremely charming young ladies, totally unknown to him, called, and, to the speechless indignation of Cousin Jane, had tea with him and afterwards sent him their birthday books for his signature. He was speedily quite hardened to seeing his name associated with the most incongruous ideas in the public press, and to discover in the reviews articles written about Boomfood and himself in a tone of the utmost intimacy by people he had never heard of. And whatever delusions he may have cherished in the days of his obscurity about the pleasantness of Fame were dispelled utterly and for ever.

At first – except for Broadbeam – the tone of the public mind was quite free from any touch of hostility. It did not seem to occur to the public mind as anything but a mere playful supposition that any more Herakleophorbia was going to escape again. And it did not seem to occur to the public mind that the growing little band of babies now being fed on the food would presently be growing more 'up' than most of us ever grow. The sort of thing that pleased the public mind was caricatures of eminent politicians after a course of Boomfeeding, uses of the idea on hoardings, and such edifying exhibitions as the dead wasps that had escaped the fire and the remaining hens.

Beyond that the public did not care to look, until very strenuous efforts were made to turn its eyes to the remoter consequences, and even then for a while its enthusiasm for action was partial. 'There's always somethin' New,'

said the public – a public so glutted with novelty that it would hear of the earth being split as one splits an apple without surprise, and, 'I wonder what they'll do next.'

But there were one or two people outside the public, as it were, who did already take that further glance, and some it seems were frightened by what they saw there. There was young Caterham, for example, cousin of the Earl of Pewterstone, and one of the most promising of English politicians, who, taking the risk of being thought a faddist, wrote a long article in *The Nineteenth Century and After* to suggest its total suppression. And – in certain of his moods there was Bensington.

'They don't seem to realise – ' he said to Cossar.

'No, they don't.'

'And do we? Sometimes, when I think of what it means – This poor child of Redwood's – And, of course, your three . . . Forty feet high, perhaps! After all, *ought* we to go on with it?'

'Go on with it!' cried Cossar, convulsed with inelegant astonishment and pitching his note higher than ever. 'Of *course* you'll go on with it! What d'you think you were made for? Just to loaf about between meal-times?

'Serious consequences,' he screamed, 'of course! Enormous. Obviously. Ob-viously. Why, man, it's the only chance you'll ever get of a serious consequence! And you want to shirk it!' For a moment his indignation was speechless, 'It's downright Wicked!' he said at last, and repeated explosively, 'Wicked!'

But Bensington worked in his laboratory now with more emotion than zest. He couldn't tell whether he wanted serious consequences to his life or not; he was a man of quiet tastes. It was a marvellous discovery, of course, quite marvellous – but – He had already become the proprietor of several acres of scorched, discredited property near Hickleybrow, at a price of nearly £90 an acre, and at times he was disposed to think this as serious a consequence of speculative chemistry as any unambitious man could wish. Of course he was Famous – terribly Famous. More than satisfying, altogether more than satisfying, was the Fame he had attained.

But the habit of Research was strong in him . . .

And at moments, rare moments in the laboratory chiefly, he would find something else than habit and Cossar's arguments to urge him to his work. This little spectacled man, poised perhaps with his slashed shoes wrapped about the legs of his high stool and his hand upon the tweezer of his balance weights, would have again a flash of that adolescent vision, would have a momentary perception of the eternal unfolding of the seed that had been sown in his brain, would see as it were in the sky, behind the grotesque shapes and accidents of the present, the coming world of giants and all the mighty things the future has in store – vague and splendid, like some glittering palace seen suddenly in the passing of a sunbeam far away . . . And presently it would be with him as though that distant splendour had never

shone upon his brain, and he would perceive nothing ahead but sinister shadows, vast declivities and darknesses, inhospitable immensities, cold, wild and terrible things.

2

Amidst the complex and confused happenings, the impacts from the great outer world that constituted Mr Bensington's fame, a shining and active figure presently became conspicuous – became almost, as it were, a leader and marshal of these externalities in Mr Bensington's eyes. This was Dr Winkles, that convincing young practitioner who has already appeared in this story as the means whereby Redwood was able to convey the Food to his son. Even before the great outbreak, it was evident that the mysterious powders Redwood had given him had awakened this gentleman's interest immensely, and so soon as the first wasps came he was putting two and two together.

He was the sort of doctor that is in manners, in morals, in methods and appearance, most succinctly and finally expressed by the word 'rising'. He was large and fair, with a hard, alert, superficial, aluminium-coloured eye and hair like chalk mud, even-featured and muscular about the clean-shaven mouth, erect in figure and energetic in movement, quick and spinning on the heel, and he wore long frock coats, black silk ties and plain gold studs and chains and his silk hats had a special shape and brim that made him look wiser and better than anybody. He looked as young or old as anybody grown up. And after that first wonderful outbreak he took to Bensington and Redwood and the Food of the Gods with such a convincing air of proprietorship, that at times, in spite of the testimony of the press to the contrary, Bensington was disposed to regard him as the original inventor of the whole affair.

'These accidents,' said Winkles, when Bensington hinted at the dangers of further escapes, 'are nothing. Nothing. The discovery is everything. Properly developed, suitably handled, sanely controlled, we have – we have something very portentous indeed in this food of ours . . . We must keep our eye on it . . . We mustn't let it out of control again, and – we mustn't let it rest.'

He certainly did not mean to do that. He was at Bensington's now almost every day. Bensington, glancing from the window, would see the faultless equipage come spanking up Sloane Street and after an incredibly brief interval Winkles would enter the room with a light, strong motion, and pervade it, and protrude some newspaper and supply information and make remarks.

'Well,' he would say, rubbing his hands, 'how are we getting on?' and so pass to the current discussion about it.

'Do you see,' he would say, for example, 'that Caterham has been talking about our stuff at the Church Association?'

'Dear me!' said Bensington, 'that's a cousin of the Prime Minister, isn't it?'

'Yes,' said Winkles, 'a very able young man – very able. Quite wrong-headed, you know, violently reactionary – but thoroughly able. And he's evidently disposed to make capital out of this stuff of ours. Takes a very emphatic line. Talks of our proposal to use it in the elementary schools – '

'Our proposal to use it in the elementary schools!'

'I said something about that the other day – quite in passing – little affair at a Polytechnic. Trying to make it clear the stuff was really highly beneficial. Not in the slightest degree dangerous, in spite of those first little accidents. Which cannot possibly occur again . . . You know it *would* be rather good stuff – But he's taken it up.'

'What did you say?'

'Mere obvious nothings. But as you see – ! Takes it up with perfect gravity. Treats the thing as an attack. Says there is already a sufficient waste of public money in elementary schools without this. Tells the old stories about piano lessons again – *you* know. No one, he says, wishes to prevent the children of the lower classes obtaining an education suited to their condition, but to give them a food of this sort will be to destroy their sense of proportion utterly. Expands the topic. What Good will it do, he asks, to make poor people six-and-thirty feet high? He really believes, you know, that they *will* be thirty-six feet high.'

'So they would be,' said Bensington, 'if you gave them our food at all regularly. But nobody said anything – '

'I said something.'

'But, my dear Winkles – !'

'They'll be bigger, of course,' interrupted Winkles, with an air of knowing all about it, and discouraging the crude ideas of Bensington. 'Bigger indisputably. But listen to what he says! Will it make them happier? That's his point. Curious, isn't it? Will it make them better? Will they be more respectful to properly constituted authority? Is it fair to the children themselves? Curious how anxious his sort are for justice – so far as any future arrangements go. Even nowadays, he says, the cost of feeding and clothing children is more than many of their parents can contrive, and if this sort of thing is to be permitted – ! Eh?

'You see he makes my mere passing suggestion into a positive proposal. And then he calculates how much a pair of breeches for a growing lad of twenty feet high or so will cost. Just as though he really believed . . . Ten pounds, he reckons, for the merest decency. Curious this Caterham! So concrete! The honest and struggling ratepayer will have to contribute to that, he says. He says we have to consider the Rights of the Parent. It's all here. Two columns. Every parent has a right to have his children brought up in his own size . . .

'Then comes the question of school accommodation, cost of enlarged desks and forms for our already too greatly burthened National Schools. And to get what? – a proletariat of hungry giants. Winds up with a very serious passage, says even if this wild suggestion – mere passing fancy of mine, you know, and misinterpreted at that – this wild suggestion about the schools comes to nothing, that doesn't end the matter. This is a strange food, so strange as to seem to him almost wicked. It has been scattered recklessly – so he says – and it may be scattered again. Once you've taken it, it's poison unless you go on with it. ['So it is,' said Bensington.] And in short he proposes the formation of a National Society for the Preservation of the Proper Proportions of Things. Odd? Eh? People are hanging on to the idea like anything.'

'But what do they propose to do?'

Winkles shrugged his shoulders and threw out his hands. 'Form a Society,' he said, 'and fuss. They want to make it illegal to manufacture this Herakleophorbia – or at any rate to circulate the knowledge of it. I've written about a bit to show that Caterham's idea of the stuff is very much exaggerated – very much exaggerated indeed, but that doesn't seem to check it. Curious how people are turning against it. And the National Temperance Association, by the by, has founded a branch for Temperance in Growth.'

'Mm,' said Bensington and stroked his nose.

'After all that has happened there's bound to be this uproar. On the face of it the thing's – *startling*.'

Winkles walked about the room for a time, hesitated, and departed.

It became evident there was something at the back of his mind, some aspect of crucial importance to him, that he waited to display. One day, when Redwood and Bensington were at the flat together, he gave them a glimpse of this something in reserve.

'How's it all going?' he said; rubbing his hands together.

'We're getting together a sort of report.'

'For the Royal Society?'

'Yes.'

'Hm,' said Winkles, very profoundly, and walked to the hearthrug. 'Hm. But – Here's the point. *Ought* you?'

'Ought we – what?'

'Ought you to publish?'

'We're not in the Middle Ages,' said Redwood.

'I know.'

'As Cossar says, swapping wisdom – that's the true scientific method.'

'In most cases, certainly. But – this is exceptional.'

'We shall put the whole thing before the Royal Society in the proper way,' said Redwood.

Winkles returned to that on a later occasion.

'It's in many ways an Exceptional Discovery.'

'That doesn't matter,' said Redwood.

'It's the sort of knowledge that could easily be subject to grave abuse – grave dangers, as Caterham puts it.'

Redwood said nothing.

'Even carelessness, you know – '

'If we were to form a committee of trustworthy people to control the manufacture of Boomfood – Herakleophorbia, I *should* say – we might – '

He paused, and Redwood, with a certain private discomfort, pretended that he did not see any sort of interrogation . . .

Outside the apartments of Redwood and Bensington, Winkles, in spite of the incompleteness of his instructions, became a leading authority upon Boomfood. He wrote letters defending its use; he made notes and articles explaining its possibilities, he jumped up irrelevantly at the meetings of the scientific and medical associations to talk about it; he identified himself with it. He published a pamphlet called 'The Truth about Boomfood', in which he minimised the whole of the Hickleybrow affair almost to nothing. He said that it was absurd to say Boomfood would make people thirty-seven feet high. That was 'obviously exaggerated'. It would make them bigger, of course, but that was all . . .

Within that intimate circle of two it was chiefly evident that Winkles was extremely anxious to help in the making of Herakleophorbia, help in correcting any proofs there might be of any paper there might be in preparation upon the subject – do anything indeed that might lead up to his participation in the details of the making of Herakleophorbia. He was continually telling them both that he felt it was a Big Thing, that it had big possibilities. If only they were – 'safeguarded in some way'. And at last one day he asked outright to be told just how it was made.

'I've been thinking over what you said,' said Redwood.

'Well?' said Winkles brightly.

'It's the sort of knowledge that could easily be subject to grave abuse,' said Redwood.

'But I don't see how that applies,' said Winkles.

'It does,' said Redwood.

Winkles thought it over for a day or so. Then he came to Redwood and said that he doubted if he ought to give powders about which he knew nothing to Redwood's little boy; it seemed to him it was uncommonly like taking responsibility in the dark. That made Redwood thoughtful.

'You've seen that the Society for the Total Suppression of Boomfood claims to have several thousand members,' said Winkles, changing the subject. 'They've drafted a Bill,' said Winkles. 'They've got young Caterham to take it up – readily enough. They're in earnest. They're forming local committees to influence candidates. They want to make it penal to prepare and store Herakleophorbia without special licence, and a

felony – matter of imprisonment without option – to administer Boomfood
– that's what they call it, you know – to any person under one-and-twenty.
But there's collateral societies, you know. All sorts of people. The Society
for the Preservation of Ancient Statures is going to have Mr Frederic
Harrison on the council, they say. You know he's written an essay about
it; says it is vulgar, and entirely inharmonious with that Revelation of
Humanity that is found in the teachings of Comte. It is the sort of thing the
Eighteenth Century *couldn't* have produced even in its worst moments. The
idea of the Food never entered the head of Comte – which shows how
wicked it really is. No one, he says, who really understood Comte . . . '

'But you don't mean to say – ' said Redwood, alarmed out of his disdain
for Winkles.

'They'll not do all that,' said Winkles. 'But public opinion is public
opinion, and votes are votes. Everybody can see you are up to a disturbing
thing. And the human instinct is all against disturbance, you know.
Nobody seems to believe Caterham's idea of people thirty-seven feet high,
who won't be able to get inside a church, or a meeting-house, or any social
or human institution. But for all that they're not so easy in their minds
about it. They see there's something – something more than a common
discovery – '

'There is,' said Redwood, 'in every discovery.'

'Anyhow, they're getting – restive. Caterham keeps harping on what may
happen if it gets loose again. I say over and over again, it won't, and it can't.
But – there it is!'

And he bounced about the room for a little while as if he meant to reopen
the topic of the secret, and then thought better of it and went.

The two scientific men looked at one another. For a space only their eyes
spoke.

'If the worst comes to the worst,' said Redwood at last, in a strenuously
calm voice, 'I shall give the Food to my little Teddy with my own hands.'

3

It was only a few days after this that Redwood opened his paper to find that
the Prime Minister had promised a Royal Commission on Boomfood. This
sent him, newspaper in hand, round to Bensington's flat.

'Winkles, I believe, is making mischief for the stuff. He plays into the
hands of Caterham. He keeps on talking about it, and what it is going to
do, and alarming people. If he goes on, I really believe he'll hamper our
enquiries. Even as it is – with this trouble about my little boy – '

Bensington wished Winkles wouldn't.

'Do you notice how he has dropped into the way of calling it Boomfood?'

'I don't like that name,' said Bensington, with a glance over his glasses.

'It is just so exactly what it is – to Winkles.'

'Why does he keep on about it? It isn't his!'

'It's something called Booming,' said Redwood. '*I* don't understand. If it isn't his, everybody is getting to think it is. Not that *that* matters.'

'In the event of this ignorant, this ridiculous agitation becoming – serious – ' began Bensington.

'My little boy can't get on without the stuff,' said Redwood. 'I don't see how I can help myself now. If the worst comes to the worst – '

A slight bouncing noise proclaimed the presence of Winkles. He became visible in the middle of the room rubbing his hands together.

'I wish you'd knock,' said Bensington, looking vicious over the gold rims.

Winkles was apologetic. Then he turned to Redwood. 'I'm glad to find you here,' he began; 'the fact is – '

'Have you seen about this Royal Commission?' interrupted Redwood.

'Yes,' said Winkles, thrown out. 'Yes.'

'What do you think of it?'

'Excellent thing,' said Winkles. 'Bound to stop most of this clamour. Ventilate the whole affair. Shut up Caterham. But that's not what I came round for, Redwood. The fact is – '

'I don't like this Royal Commission,' said Bensington.

'I can assure you it will be all right. I may say – I don't think it's a breach of confidence – that very possibly *I* may have a place on the Commission – '

'Oom,' said Redwood, looking into the fire.

'I can put the whole thing right. I can make it perfectly clear, first, that the stuff is controllable, and, secondly, that nothing short of a miracle is needed before anything like that catastrophe at Hickleybrow can possibly happen again. That is just what is wanted, an authoritative assurance. Of course, I could speak with more confidence if I knew – But that's quite by the way. And just at present there's something else, another little matter, upon which I'm wanting to consult you. Ahem. The fact is – Well – I happen to be in a slight difficulty, and you can help me out.'

Redwood raised his eyebrows, and was secretly glad.

'The matter is – highly confidential.'

'Go on,' said Redwood. 'Don't worry about that.'

'I have recently been entrusted with a child – the child of – of an Exalted Personage.'

Winkles coughed.

'You're getting on,' said Redwood.

'I must confess it's largely your powders – and the reputation of my success with your little boy – There is, I cannot disguise, a strong feeling against its use. And yet I find that among the more intelligent – One must go quietly in these things, you know – little by little. Still, in the case of Her Serene High – I mean this new little patient of mine . . . As a matter of fact – the suggestion came from the parent. Or I should never – '

He struck Redwood as being embarrassed.

'I thought you had a doubt of the advisability of using these powders,' said Redwood.

'Merely a passing doubt.'

'You don't propose to discontinue – '

'In the case of your little boy? Certainly not!'

'So far as I can see, it would be murder.'

'I wouldn't do it for the world.'

'You shall have the powders,' said Redwood.

'I suppose you couldn't – '

'No fear,' said Redwood. 'There isn't a recipe. It's no good, Winkles, if you'll pardon my frankness. I'll make you the powders myself.'

'Just as well, perhaps,' said Winkles, after a momentary hard stare at Redwood – 'just as well.' And then: 'I can assure you I really don't mind in the least.'

4

When Winkles had gone Bensington came and stood on the hearthrug and looked down at Redwood.

'Her Serene Highness!' he remarked.

'Her Serene Highness!' said Redwood.

'It's the Princess of Weser Dreiburg!'

'No further than a third cousin.'

'Redwood,' said Bensington; 'it's a curious thing to say, I know, but – do you think Winkles understands?'

'What?'

'Just what it is we have made.'

'Does he really understand,' said Bensington, dropping his voice and keeping his eye doorwards, 'that in the Family – the Family of his new patient – '

'Go on,' said Redwood.

'Who have always been if anything a little *under* – '

'The Average?'

'Yes. And so *very* tactfully undistinguished in *any* way, he is going to produce a royal personage – an outsize royal personage – of *that* size. You know, Redwood, I'm not sure whether there is not something almost – *treasonable* . . .'

He transferred his eyes from the door to Redwood.

Redwood flung a momentary gesture – index finger erect – at the fire. 'By Jove!' he said, 'he *doesn't* know!'

'That man,' said Redwood, 'doesn't know anything. That was his most exasperating quality as a student. Nothing. He passed all his examinations,

he had all his facts – and he had just as much knowledge – as a rotating bookshelf containing *The Times Encyclopedia*. And he doesn't know anything *now*. He's Winkles, and incapable of really assimilating anything not immediately and directly related to his superficial self. He is utterly void of imagination and, as a consequence, incapable of knowledge. No one could possibly pass so many examinations and be so well dressed, so well done, and so successful as a doctor without that precise incapacity. That's it. And in spite of all he's seen and heard and been told, there he is – he has no idea whatever of what he has set going. He has got a Boom on, he's working it well on Boomfood, and someone has let him in to this new Royal Baby – and that's Boomier than ever! And the fact that Weser Dreiburg will presently have to face the gigantic problem of a thirty-odd-foot princess not only hasn't entered his head, but couldn't – it couldn't!'

'There'll be a fearful row,' said Bensington.

'In a year or so.'

'So soon as they really see she is going on growing.'

'Unless after their fashion – they hush it up.'

'It's a lot to hush up.'

'Rather!'

'I wonder what they'll do?'

'They never do anything – Royal tact.'

'They're bound to do something.'

'Perhaps *she* will.'

'Oh Lord! Yes.'

'They'll suppress her. Such things have been known.'

Redwood burst into desperate laughter. 'The redundant royalty – the bouncing babe in the Iron Mask!' he said. 'They'll have to put her in the tallest tower of the old Weser Dreiburg castle and make holes in the ceilings as she grows from floor to floor! Well, I'm in the very same pickle. And Cossar and his three boys. And – Well, well.'

'There'll be a fearful row,' Bensington repeated, not joining in the laughter. 'A *fearful* row.'

'I suppose,' he argued, 'you've really thought it out thoroughly, Redwood. You're quite sure it wouldn't be wiser to warn Winkles, wean your little boy gradually, and – and rely upon the Theoretical Triumph?'

'I wish to goodness you'd spend half an hour in my nursery when the Food's a little late,' said Redwood, with a note of exasperation in his voice; 'then you wouldn't talk like that, Bensington. Besides – Fancy warning Winkles . . . No! The tide of this thing has caught us unawares, and whether we're frightened or whether we're not – *we've got to swim!*'

'I suppose we have,' said Bensington, staring at his toes. 'Yes. We've got to swim. And your boy will have to swim, and Cossar's boys – he's given it to all three of them. Nothing partial about Cossar – all or nothing! And Her Serene Highness. And everything. We are going on making the Food.

Cossar also. We're only just in the dawn of the beginning, Redwood. It's evident all sorts of things are to follow. Monstrous great things. But I can't imagine them, Redwood. Except – '

He scanned his fingernails. He looked up at Redwood with eyes bland through his glasses.

'I've half a mind,' he adventured, 'that Caterham is right. At times. It's going to destroy the Proportion of Things. It's going to dislocate – What isn't it going to dislocate?'

'Whatever it dislocates,' said Redwood, 'my little boy must have the Food.'

They heard someone falling rapidly upstairs. Then Cossar put his head into the fiat. 'Hello!' he said at their expressions, and entering, 'Well?'

They told him about the princess.

'*Difficult question!*' he remarked. 'Not a bit of it. *She'll* grow. Your boy'll grow. All the others you give it to'll grow. Everything. Like anything. What's difficult about that? That's all right. A child could tell you that. Where's the bother?'

They tried to make it clear to him.

'*Not go on with it!*' he shrieked. 'But – ! You can't help yourselves now. It's what you're for. It's what Winkles is for. It's all right. Often wondered what Winkles was for. *Now* it's obvious. What's the trouble?'

'*Disturbance?* Obviously. *Upset things?* Upset everything. Finally – upset every human concern. Plain as a pikestaff. They're going to try and stop it, but they're too late. It's their way to be too late. You go on and start as much of it as you can. Thank God He has a use for you!'

'But the conflict!' said Bensington, 'the stress! I don't know if you have imagined – '

'You ought to have been some sort of little vegetable, Bensington,' said Cossar – 'that's what you ought to have been. Something growing over a rockery. Here you are, fearfully and wonderfully made, and all you think you're made for is just to sit about and take your vittles. D'you think this world was made for old women to mope about in? Well, anyhow, you can't help yourselves now – you've *got* to go on.'

'I suppose we must,' said Redwood. 'Slowly – '

'No!' said Cossar, in a huge shout. 'No! Make as much as you can and as soon as you can. Spread it about!'

He was inspired to a stroke of wit. He parodied one of Redwood's curves with a vast upward sweep of his arm.

'Redwood!' he said, to point the allusion, 'make it SO!'

There is, it seems, an upward limit to the pride of maternity, and this in the case of Mrs Redwood was reached when her offspring completed his sixth month of terrestrial existence, broke down his high-class bassinet-perambulator and was brought home, bawling, in the milk-truck. Young Redwood at that time weighed fifty-nine and a half pounds, measured forty-eight inches in height, and gripped about sixty pounds. He was carried upstairs to the nursery by the cook and housemaid. After that, discovery was only a question of days. One afternoon Redwood came home from his laboratory to find his unfortunate wife deep in the fascinating pages of *The Mighty Atom*, and at the sight of him she put the book aside and ran violently forward and burst into tears on his shoulder.

'Tell me what you have *done* to him,' she wailed. 'Tell me what you have done.' Redwood took her hand and led her to the sofa, while he tried to think of a satisfactory line of defence.

'It's all right, my dear,' he said; 'it's all right. You're only a little over-wrought. It's that cheap perambulator. I've arranged for a bath-chair man to come round with something stouter tomorrow – '

Mrs Redwood looked at him tearfully over the top of her handkerchief.

'A baby in a bath-chair?' she sobbed.

'Well, why not?'

'It's like a cripple.'

'It's like a young giant, my dear, and you've no cause to be ashamed of him.'

'You've done something to him, Dandy,' she said. 'I can see it in your face.'

'Well, it hasn't stopped his growth, anyhow,' said Redwood heartlessly.

'I *knew*,' said Mrs Redwood, and clenched her pocket-handkerchief ball fashion in one hand. She looked at him with a sudden change to severity. 'What have you done to our child, Dandy?'

'What's wrong with him?'

'He's so big. He's a monster.'

'Nonsense. He's as straight and clean a baby as ever a woman had. What's wrong with him?'

'Look at his size.'

'That's all right. Look at the puny little brutes about us! He's the finest baby – '

'He's *too* fine,' said Mrs Redwood.

'It won't go on,' said Redwood reassuringly; 'it's just a start he's taken.'

But he knew perfectly well it would go on. And it did. By the time this baby was twelve months old he tottered just one inch under five feet high and scaled eight stone three; he was as big in fact as a St Peter's *in Vaticano*

cherub, and his affectionate clutch at the hair and features of visitors became the talk of West Kensington. They had an invalid's chair to carry him up and down to his nursery, and his special nurse, a muscular young person just out of training, used to take him for his airings in a Panhard 8 h.p. hill-climbing perambulator specially made to meet his requirements. It was lucky in every way that Redwood had his expert-witness connection in addition to his professorship.

When one got over the shock of little Redwood's enormous size, he was, I am told by people who used to see him almost daily *teufteufing* slowly about Hyde Park, a singularly bright and pretty baby. He rarely cried or needed a dummy. Commonly he clutched a big rattle, and sometimes he went along hailing the bus-drivers and policemen along the road outside the railings as 'Dadda!' and 'Babba!' in a sociable, democratic way.

'There goes that there great Boomfood baby,' the bus-driver used to say.

'Looks 'ealthy,' the forward passenger would remark.

'Bottle fed,' the bus-driver would explain. 'They say it 'olds a gallon and 'ad to be specially made for 'im.'

'Very 'ealthy child any'ow,' the forward passenger would conclude.

When Mrs Redwood realised that his growth was indeed going on indefinitely and logically – and this she really did for the first time when the motor-perambulator arrived – she gave way to a passion of grief. She declared she never wished to enter her nursery again, wished she was dead, wished the child was dead, wished everybody was dead, wished she had never married Redwood, wished no one ever married anybody, Ajaxed a little, and retired to her own room, where she lived almost exclusively on chicken broth for three days. When Redwood came to remonstrate with her, she banged pillows about and wept and tangled her hair.

'*He's* all right,' said Redwood. 'He's all the better for being big. You wouldn't like him smaller than other people's children.'

'I want him to be *like* other children, neither smaller nor bigger. I wanted him to be a nice little boy, just as Georgina Phyllis is a nice little girl, and I wanted to bring him up nicely in a nice way, and here he is' – and the unfortunate woman's voice broke – 'wearing number four grown-up shoes and being wheeled about by – boohoo! – petroleum!

'I can never love him,' she wailed, 'never! He's too much for me! I can never be a mother to him, such as I meant to be!'

But at last they contrived to get her into the nursery, and there was Edward Monson Redwood ('Pantagruel' was only a later nickname) swinging in a specially strengthened rocking-chair and smiling and talking 'goo' and 'wow'. And the heart of Mrs Redwood warmed again to her child, and she went and held him in her arms and wept.

'They've done something to you,' she sobbed, 'and you'll grow and grow, dear; but whatever I can do to bring you up nice I'll do for you, whatever your father may say.'

And Redwood, who had helped to bring her to the door, went down the passage much relieved.

(Eh! but it's a base job this being a man – with women as they are!)

6

Before the year was out there were, in addition to Redwood's pioneer vehicle, quite a number of motor-perambulators to be seen in the west of London. I am told there were as many as eleven; but the most careful enquiries yield trustworthy evidence of only six within the Metropolitan area at that time. It would seem the stuff acted differently upon different types of constitution. At first Herakleophorbia was not adapted to injection, and there can be no doubt that quite a considerable proportion of human beings are incapable of absorbing this substance in the normal course of digestion. It was given, for example, to Winkles's youngest boy; but he seems to have been as incapable of growth as, if Redwood was right, his father was incapable of knowledge. Others again, according to the Society for the Total Suppression of Boomfood, became in some inexplicable way corrupted by it, and perished at the onset of infantile disorders. The Cossar boys took to it with amazing avidity.

Of course a thing of this kind never comes with absolute simplicity of application into the life of man; growth in particular is a complex thing, and all generalisations must needs be a little inaccurate. But the general law of the Food would seem to be this, that when it could be taken into the system in any way it stimulated it in very nearly the same degree in all cases. It increased the amount of growth from six to seven times, and it did not go beyond that, whatever amount of the Food in excess was taken. Excess of Herakleophorbia indeed beyond the necessary minimum led, it was found, to morbid disturbances of nutrition, to cancer and tumours, ossifications and the like. And once growth upon the large scale had begun, it was soon evident that it could only continue upon that scale, and that the continuous administration of Herakleophorbia in small but sufficient doses was imperative.

If it was discontinued while growth was still going on, there was first a vague restlessness and distress, then a period of voracity – as in the case of the young rats at Hankey – and then the growing creature had a sort of exaggerated anaemia and sickened and died. Plants suffered in a similar way. This, however, applied only to the growth period. So soon as adolescence was attained – in plants this was represented by the formation of the first flower-buds – the need and appetite for Herakleophorbia diminished, and so soon as the plant or animal was fully adult, it became altogether independent of any further supply of the food. It was, as it were, completely established on the new scale. It was so completely established on the new scale that, as

the thistles about Hickleybrow and the grass of the down side already demonstrated, its seed produced giant offspring after its kind.

And presently little Redwood, pioneer of the new race, first child of all who ate the food, was crawling about his nursery, smashing furniture, biting like a horse, pinching like a vice and bawling gigantic babytalk at his 'Nanny' and 'Mammy' – and the rather scared and awestricken 'Daddy' who had set this mischief going.

The child was born with good intentions. 'Padda be good, be good,' he used to say as the breakables flew before him. 'Padda' was his rendering of Pantagruel, the nickname Redwood imposed on him. And Cossar, disregarding certain Ancient Lights that presently led to trouble, did, after a conflict with the local building regulations, get building on a vacant piece of ground adjacent to Redwood's home a comfortable well-lit playroom, schoolroom and nursery for their four boys – sixty feet square about this room was, and forty feet high.

Redwood fell in love with that great nursery as he and Cossar built it, and his interest in curves faded, as he had never dreamt it could fade, before the pressing needs of his son. 'There is much,' he said, 'in fitting a nursery. Much.

'The walls, the things in it, they will all speak to this new mind of ours, a little more, a little less eloquently, and teach it or fail to teach it a thousand things.'

'Obviously,' said Cossar, reaching hastily for his hat.

They worked together harmoniously, but Redwood supplied most of the educational theory required.

They had the walls and woodwork painted with a cheerful vigour; for the most part a slightly warmed white prevailed, but there were bands of bright clean colour to enforce the simple lines of construction. 'Clean colours we *must* have,' said Redwood, and in one place had a neat horizontal band of squares, in which crimson and purple, orange and lemon, blues and greens, in many hues and many shades, did themselves honour. These squares the giant children should arrange and rearrange to their pleasure. 'Decorations must follow,' said Redwood; 'let them first get the range of all the tints, and then this may go away. There is no reason why one should bias them in favour of any particular colour or design.'

Then, 'The place must be full of interest,' said Redwood. 'Interest is food for a child, and blankness torture and starvation. He must have pictures galore.' There were no pictures hung about the room for any permanent service, however, but blank frames were provided into which new pictures would come and pass thence into a portfolio so soon as their fresh interest had passed. There was one window that looked down the length of a street, and in addition, for an added interest, Redwood had contrived above the roof of the nursery a camera obscura that watched the Kensington High Street and not a little of the Gardens.

In one corner that most worthy implement, an abacus, four feet square, a specially strengthened piece of ironmongery with rounded corners, awaited the young giants' incipient computations. There were few woolly lambs and suchlike idols, but instead Cossar, without explanation, had brought one day in three four-wheelers a great number of toys (all just too big for the coming children to swallow) that could be piled up, arranged in rows, rolled about, bitten, made to flap and rattle, smacked together, felt over, pulled out, opened, closed, and mauled and experimented with to an interminable extent. There were many bricks of wood in diverse colours, oblong and cuboid, bricks of polished china, bricks of transparent glass and bricks of india-rubber; there were slabs and slates; there were cones, truncated cones, and cylinders; there were oblate and prolate spheroids, balls of varied substances, solid and hollow, many boxes of diverse size and shape, with hinged lids and screw lids and fitting lids, and one or two to catch and lock; there were bands of elastic and leather, and a number of rough and sturdy little objects of a size together that could stand up steadily and suggest the shape of a man. 'Give 'em these,' said Cossar. 'One at a time.'

These things Redwood arranged in a locker in one corner. Along one side of the room, at a convenient height for a six- or eight-foot child, there was a blackboard, on which the youngsters might flourish in white and coloured chalk, and near by a sort of drawing block, from which sheet after sheet might be torn, and on which they could draw in charcoal; and a little desk there was, furnished with great carpenter's pencils of varying hardness and a copious supply of paper on which the boys might first scribble and then draw more neatly. And moreover Redwood gave orders, so far ahead did his imagination go, for specially large tubes of liquid paint and boxes of pastels against the time when they should be needed. He laid in a cask or so of plasticine and modelling clay. 'At first he and his tutor shall model together,' he said, 'and when he is more skilful he shall copy casts and perhaps animals. And that reminds me, I must also have made for him a box of tools!

'Then books. I shall have to look out a lot of books to put in his way, and they'll have to be big type. Now what sort of books will he need? There is his imagination to be fed. That, after all, is the crown of every education. The crown – as sound habits of mind and conduct are the throne. No imagination at all is brutality; a base imagination is lust and cowardice; but a noble imagination is God walking the earth again. He must dream too of a dainty fairyland and of all the quaint little things of life, in due time. But he must feed chiefly on the splendid real; he shall have stories of travel through all the world, travels and adventures and how the world was won; he shall have stories of beasts, great books splendidly and clearly done of animals and birds and plants and creeping things, great books about the deeps of the sky and the mystery of the sea; he shall have histories and maps of all the empires the world has seen, pictures and stories of all the tribes and habits

and customs of men. And he must have books and pictures to quicken his sense of beauty, subtle Japanese pictures to make him love the subtler beauties of bird and tendril and falling flower, and Western pictures too, pictures of gracious men and women, sweet groupings and broad views of land and sea. He shall have books on the building of houses and palaces; he shall plan rooms and invent cities –

'I think I must give him a little theatre.

'Then there is music!'

Redwood thought that over and decided that his son might best begin with a very pure-sounding harmonicon of one octave, to which afterwards there could be an extension. 'He shall play with this first, sing to it and give names to the notes,' said Redwood, 'and afterwards? – '

He stared up at the window-sill overhead and measured the size of the room with his eye.

'They'll have to build his piano in here,' he said. 'Bring it in in pieces.'

He hovered about amidst his preparations, a pensive, dark, little figure. If you could have seen him there he would have looked to you like a ten-inch man amidst common nursery things. A great rug – indeed it was a Turkey carpet – four hundred square feet of it, upon which young Redwood was soon to crawl – stretched to the grill-guarded electric radiator that was to warm the whole place. A man from Cossar's hung amidst scaffolding over-head, fixing the great frame that was to hold the transitory pictures. A blotting-paper book for plant specimens as big as a house door leant against the wall, and from it projected a gigantic stalk, a leaf edge or so and one flower of chickweed, all of that gigantic size that was soon to make Urshot famous throughout the botanical world.

A sort of incredulity came to Redwood as he stood among these things.

'If it really *is* going on – ' said Redwood, staring up at the remote ceiling.

From far away came a sound like the bellowing of a Mafficking bull, almost as if in answer.

'It's going on all right,' said Redwood. 'Evidently.'

There followed resounding blows upon a table, followed by a vast crowing shout, 'Gooloo! Boozoo! Bzz . . .'

'The best thing I can do,' said Redwood, following out some divergent line of thought, 'is to teach him myself.'

That beating became more insistent. For a moment it seemed to Red-wood that it caught the rhythm of an engine's throbbing – the engine he could have imagined of some great train of events that bore down upon him. Then a descendant flight of sharper beats broke up that effect, and were repeated.

'Come in,' he cried, perceiving that someone rapped, and the door that was big enough for a cathedral opened slowly a little way. The new winch ceased to creak, and Bensington appeared in the crack, gleaming benevolently under his protruded baldness and over his glasses.

'I've ventured round to *see*,' he whispered in a confidentially furtive manner.

'Come in,' said Redwood, and he did, shutting the door behind him.

He walked forward, hands behind his back, advanced a few steps, and peered up with a birdlike movement at the dimensions about him. He rubbed his chin thoughtfully.

'Every time I come in,' he said, with a subdued note in his voice, 'it strikes me as – *Big*.'

'Yes,' said Redwood, surveying it all again also, as if in an endeavour to keep hold of the visible impression. 'Yes. They're going to be big, too, you know.'

'I know,' said Bensington, with a note that was nearly awe. '*Very* big.'

They looked at one another, almost, as it were, apprehensively.

'Very big indeed,' said Bensington, stroking the bridge of his nose, and with one eye that watched Redwood doubtfully for a confirmatory expression. 'All of them, you know – fearfully big. I don't seem able to imagine – even with this – just how big they're all going to be.'

CHAPTER FIVE

The Minimificence of Mr Bensington

It was while the Royal Commission on Boomfood was preparing its report that Herakleophorbia really began to demonstrate its capacity for leakage. And the earliness of this second outbreak was the more unfortunate, from the point of view of Cossar at any rate, since the draft report still in existence shows that the commission had, under the tutelage of that most able member, Dr Stephen Winkles (FRS, MD, FRCP, DSC, JP, DL, etc.), already quite made up its mind that accidental leakages were impossible, and was prepared to recommend that to entrust the preparation of Boom-food to a qualified committee (Winkles chiefly), with an entire control over its sale, was quite enough to satisfy all reasonable objections to its free diffusion. This committee was to have an absolute monopoly. And it is, no doubt, to be considered as a part of the irony of life that the first and most alarming of this second series of leakages occurred within fifty yards of a little cottage at Keston occupied during the summer months by Dr Winkles.

There can be little doubt now that Redwood's refusal to acquaint Winkles with the composition of Herakleophorbia IV had aroused in that gentleman a novel and intense desire towards analytical chemistry. He was not a very expert manipulator, and for that reason probably he saw fit to do his work not in the excellently equipped laboratories that were at his disposal in London, but, without consulting anyone, and almost with an

air of secrecy, in a rough little garden laboratory at the Keston establishment. He does not seem to have shown either very great energy or very great ability in this quest; indeed one gathers he dropped the inquiry after working at it intermittently for about a month.

This garden laboratory, in which the work was done, was very roughly equipped, supplied by a standpipe tap with water and draining into a pipe that ran down into a swampy rush-bordered pool under an alder tree in a secluded corner of the common just outside the garden hedge. The pipe was cracked, and the residuum of the Food of the Gods escaped through the crack into a little puddle amidst clumps of rushes, just in time for the spring awakening.

Everything was astir with life in that scummy little corner. There was frog spawn adrift, tremulous with tadpoles just bursting their gelatinous envelopes; there were little pond snails creeping out into life; and under the green skin of the rush stems the larvae of a big water beetle were struggling out of their egg cases. I doubt if the reader knows the larva of the beetle called (I know not why) Dytiscus. It is a jointed, queer-looking thing, very muscular and sudden in its movements, and given to swimming head downward with its tail out of water; the length of a man's top thumb joint it is, and more – two inches, that is for those who have not eaten the Food – and it has two sharp jaws that meet in front of its head – tubular jaws with sharp points – through which its habit is to suck its victim's blood.

The first things to get at the drifting grains of the Food were the little tadpoles and the little water snails; the little wriggling tadpoles in particular, once they had the taste of it, took to it with zest. But scarcely did one of them begin to grow into a conspicuous position in that little tadpole world and try a smaller brother or so as an aid to a vegetarian dietary, when nip! one of the beetle larva had its curved bloodsucking prongs gripping into his heart, and with that red stream went Herakleophorbia IV, in a state of solution, into the being of a new client. The only thing that had a chance with these monsters to get any share of the Food were the rushes and slimy green scum in the water and the seedling weeds in the mud at the bottom. A clean up of the study presently washed a fresh spate of the Food into the puddle, and overflowed it, and carried all this sinister expansion of the struggle for life into the adjacent pool under the roots of the alder . . .

The first person to discover what was going on was a Mr Lukey Carrington, a special science teacher under the London Education Board, and, in his leisure, a specialist in freshwater algae, and he is certainly not to be envied his discovery. He had come down to Keston Common for the day to fill a number of specimen tubes for subsequent examination, and he came, with a dozen or so corked tubes clanking faintly in his pocket, over the sandy crest and down towards the pool, spiked walking stick in hand. A garden lad standing on the top of the kitchen steps clipping Dr Winkles's hedge saw him in this unfrequented corner, and found him and his

occupation sufficiently inexplicable and interesting to watch him pretty closely.

He saw Mr Carrington stoop down by the side of the pool, with his hand against the old alder stem, and peer into the water, but of course he could not appreciate the surprise and pleasure with which Mr Carrington beheld the big unfamiliar-looking blobs and threads of the algal scum at the bottom. There were no tadpoles visible – they had all been killed by that time – and it would seem Mr Carrington saw nothing at all unusual except the excessive vegetation. He bared his arm to the elbow, leant forward, and dipped deep in pursuit of a specimen. His seeking hand went down. Instantly there flashed out of the cool shadow under the tree roots something –

Flash! It had buried its fangs deep into his arm – a bizarre shape it was, a foot long and more, brown and jointed like a scorpion.

Its ugly apparition and the sharp amazing painfulness of its bite were too much for Mr Carrington's equilibrium. He felt himself going, and yelled aloud. Over he toppled, face foremost, splash! into the pool.

The boy saw him vanish, and heard the splashing of his struggle in the water. The unfortunate man emerged again into the boy's field of vision, hatless and streaming with water, and screaming!

Never before had the boy heard screams from a man.

This astonishing stranger appeared to be tearing at something on the side of his face. There appeared streaks of blood there. He flung out his arms as if in despair, leapt in the air like a frantic creature, ran violently ten or twelve yards, and then fell and rolled on the ground and over and out of sight of the boy. The lad was down the steps and through the hedge in a trice – happily with the garden shears still in hand. As he came crashing through the gorse bushes, he says he was half minded to turn back, fearing he had to deal with a lunatic, but the possession of the shears reassured him. 'I could 'ave jabbed his eyes,' he explained, 'anyhow.' Directly Mr Carrington caught sight of him, his demeanour became at once that of a sane but desperate man. He struggled to his feet, stumbled, stood up, and came to meet the boy.

'Look!' he cried, 'I can't get 'em off!'

And with a qualm of horror the boy saw that, attached to Mr Carrington's cheek, to his bare arm and to his thigh, and lashing furiously with their lithe brown muscular bodies, were three of these horrible larvae, their great jaws buried deep in his flesh and sucking for dear life. They had the grip of bulldogs, and Mr Carrington's efforts to detach the monsters from his face had only served to lacerate the flesh to which it had attached itself, and streak face and neck and coat with living scarlet.

'I'll cut 'em,' cried the boy; ' 'old on, sir.'

And with the zest of his age in such proceedings, he severed one by one the heads from the bodies of Mr Carrington's assailants. 'Yup,' said the boy

with a wincing face as each one fell before him. Even then, so tough and determined was their grip that the severed heads remained for a space, still fiercely biting home and still sucking, with the blood streaming out of their necks behind. But the boy stopped that with a few more slashes of his scissors – in one of which Mr Carrington was implicated.

'I couldn't get 'em off!' repeated Carrington, and stood for a space, swaying and bleeding profusely. He dabbed feeble hands at his injuries and examined the result upon his palms. Then he gave way at the knees and fell headlong in a dead faint at the boy's feet, between the still leaping bodies of his defeated foes. Very luckily it didn't occur to the boy to splash water on his face – for there were still more of these horrors under the alder roots – and instead he passed back by the pond and went into the garden with the intention of calling assistance. And there he met the gardener-coachman and told him of the whole affair.

When they got back to Mr Carrington he was sitting up, dazed and weak, but able to warn them against the danger in the pool.

2

Such were the circumstances by which the world had its first notification that the Food was loose again. In another week Keston Common was in full operation as what naturalists call a centre of distribution. This time there were no wasps or rats, no earwigs and no nettles, but there were at least three water-spiders, several dragonfly larvae which presently became dragonflies, dazzling all Kent with their hovering sapphire bodies, and a nasty gelatinous, scummy growth that swelled over the pond margin, and sent its slimy green masses surging halfway up the garden path to Dr Winkles's house. And there began a growth of rushes and equisetum and potamogeton that ended only with the drying of the pond.

It speedily became evident to the public mind that this time there was not simply one centre of distribution, but quite a number of centres. There was one at Ealing – there can be no doubt now – and from that came the plague of flies and red spiders; there was one at Sunbury, productive of ferocious great eels that could come ashore and kill sheep; and there was one in Bloomsbury that gave the world a new strain of cockroaches of a quite terrible sort – an old house it was in Bloomsbury, and much inhabited by undesirable things. Abruptly the world found itself confronted with the Hickleybrow experiences all over again, with all sorts of queer exaggerations of familiar monsters in the place of the giant hens and rats and wasps. Each centre burst out with its own characteristic local fauna and flora.

We know now that every one of these centres corresponded to one of the patients of Dr Winkles, but that was by no means apparent at the time.

Dr Winkles was the last person to incur any odium in the matter. There was a panic quite naturally, a passionate indignation, but it was indignation not against Dr Winkles but against the Food, and not so much against the Food as against the unfortunate Bensington, whom from the very first the popular imagination had insisted upon regarding as the sole and only person responsible for this new thing.

The attempt to lynch him that followed is just one of those explosive events that bulk largely in history and are in reality the least significant of occurrences.

The history of the outbreak is a mystery. The nucleus of the crowd certainly came from an Anti-Boomfood meeting in Hyde Park organised by extremists of the Caterham party, but there seems no one in the world who actually first proposed, no one who ever first hinted a suggestion of the outrage at which so many people assisted. It is a problem for M. Gustave le Bon – a mystery in the psychology of crowds. The fact emerges that about three o'clock on Sunday afternoon a remarkably big and ugly London crowd, entirely out of hand, came rolling down Thursday Street intent on Bensington's exemplary death as a warning to all scientific investigators, and that it came nearer accomplishing its object than any London crowd has ever come since the Hyde Park railings came down in remote middle-Victorian times. This crowd came so close to its object indeed, that for the space of an hour or more a word would have settled the unfortunate gentleman's fate.

The first intimation he had of the thing was the noise of the people outside. He went to the window and peered, realising nothing of what impended. For a minute perhaps he watched them seething about the entrance, disposing of an ineffectual dozen of policemen who barred their way, before he fully realised his own importance in the affair. It came upon him in a flash – that that roaring, swaying multitude was after him. He was all alone in the flat – fortunately perhaps – his cousin Jane having gone down to Ealing to have tea with a relation on her mother's side, and he had no more idea of how to behave under such circumstances than he had of the etiquette of the Day of Judgement. He was still dashing about the flat asking his furniture what he should do, turning keys in locks and then unlocking them again, making darts at door and window and bedroom – when the porter for his floor came to him.

'There isn't a moment, sir,' he said. 'They've got your number from the board in the hall! They're coming straight up!'

He ran Mr Bensington out into the passage, already echoing with the approaching tumult from the great staircase, locked the door behind them, and led the way into the opposite flat by means of his duplicate key.

'It's our only chance now,' he said.

He flung up a window which opened on a ventilating shaft, and showed that the wall was set with iron staples that made the rudest and most

perilous of wall ladders to serve as a fire escape from the upper flats. He shoved Mr Bensington out of the window, showed him how to cling on, and pursued him up the ladder, goading and jabbing his legs with a bunch of keys whenever he desisted from climbing. It seemed to Bensington at times that he must climb that vertical ladder for evermore. Above, the parapet was inaccessibly remote, a mile perhaps; below – He did not care to think of things below.

'Steady on!' cried the porter, and gripped his ankle. It was quite horrible having his ankle gripped like that, and Mr Bensington tightened his hold on the iron staple above to a drowning clutch, and gave a faint squeal of terror.

It became evident the porter had broken a window, and then it seemed he had leapt a vast distance sideways, and there came the noise of a window-frame sliding in its sash. He was bawling things.

Mr Bensington moved his head round cautiously until he could see the porter. 'Come down six steps,' the porter commanded.

All this moving about seemed very foolish, but very, very cautiously Mr Bensington lowered a foot.

'Don't pull me!' he cried, as the porter made to help him from the open window.

It seemed to him that to reach the window from the ladder would be a very respectable feat for a flying fox, and it was rather with the idea of a decent suicide than in any hope of accomplishing it that he made the step at last, and quite ruthlessly the porter pulled him in. 'You'll have to stop here,' said the porter; 'my keys are no good here. It's an American lock. I'll get out and slam the door behind me and see if I can find the man of this floor. You'll be locked in. Don't go to the window, that's all. It's the ugliest crowd I've ever seen. If only they think you're out they'll probably content themselves by breaking up your stuff – '

'The indicator said In,' said Bensington.

'The devil it did! Well, anyhow, I'd better not be found – '

He vanished with a slam of the door.

Bensington was left to his own initiative again.

It took him under the bed.

There presently he was found by Cossar.

Bensington was almost comatose with terror when he was found, for Cossar had burst the door in with his shoulder by jumping at it across the breadth of the passage.

'Come out of it, Bensington,' he said. 'It's all right. It's me. We've got to get out of this. They're setting the place on fire. The porters are all clearing out. The servants are gone. It's lucky I caught the man who knew.

'Look here!'

Bensington, peering from under the bed, became aware of some un-accountable garments on Cossar's arm, and, of all things, a black bonnet in his hand!

'They're having a clear out,' said Cossar. 'If they don't set the place on fire they'll come here. Troops may not be here for an hour yet. Fifty per cent hooligans in the crowd, and the more furnished flats they go into the better they'll like it. Obviously . . . They mean a clear out. You put this skirt and bonnet on, Bensington, and clear out with me.'

'D'you *mean* – ?' began Bensington, protruding a head, tortoise fashion.

'I mean, put 'em on and come! Obviously,' And with a sudden vehemence he dragged Bensington from under the bed and began to dress him for his new impersonation of an elderly woman of the people.

He rolled up his trousers and made him kick off his slippers, took off his collar and tie and coat and waistcoat, slipped a black skirt over his head, and put on a red-flannel bodice and over it a blouse. He made him take off his all-too-characteristic spectacles and clapped the bonnet on his head. 'You might have been born an old woman,' he said as he tied the strings. Then came the spring-sided boots – a terrible wrench for corns – and the shawl, and the disguise was complete. 'Up and down,' said Cossar, and Bensington obeyed.

'You'll do,' said Cossar.

And in this guise it was, stumbling awkwardly over his unaccustomed skirts, shouting womanly imprecations upon his own head in a weird falsetto to sustain his part, assailed by the roaring note of a crowd bent upon lynching him, that the original discoverer of Herakleophorbia IV proceeded down the corridor of Chesterfield Mansions, mingled with that inflamed disorderly multitude and passed out altogether from the thread of events that constitutes our story.

Never once after that escape did he meddle again with the stupendous development of the Food of the Gods he of all men had done most to begin.

3

This little man who started the whole thing passes out of the story, and after a time he passed altogether out of the world of things, visible and tellable. But because he started the whole thing it is seemly to give his exit an intercalary page of attention. One may picture him in his later days as Tunbridge Wells came to know him. For it was at Tunbridge Wells he reappeared after a temporary obscurity, so soon as he fully realised how transitory, how quite exceptional and unmeaning that fury of rioting was. He reappeared under the wing of Cousin Jane, treating himself for nervous shock to the exclusion of all other interests, and totally indifferent, as it seemed, to the battles that were raging then about those new centres of distribution, and about the baby Children of the Food.

He took up his quarters at the Mount Glory Hydrotherapeutic Hotel, where there are quite extraordinary facilities for baths: Carbonated Baths,

Creosote Baths, Galvanic and Faradic Treatment, Massage, Pine Baths, Starch and Hemlock Baths, Radium Baths, Light Baths, Heat Baths, Bran and Needle Baths, Tar and Birdsdown Baths – all sorts of baths; and he devoted his mind to the development of that system of curative treatment that was still imperfect when he died. And sometimes he would go out in a hired vehicle and a sealskin-trimmed coat, and sometimes, when his feet permitted, he would walk to the Pantiles, and there he would sip chalybeate water under the eye of his cousin Jane.

His stooping shoulders, his pink appearance, his beaming glasses, became a 'feature' of Tunbridge Wells. No one was the least bit unkind to him, and indeed the place and the hotel seemed very glad to have the distinction of his presence. Nothing could rob him of that distinction now. And though he preferred not to follow the development of his great invention in the daily papers, yet when he crossed the lounge of the hotel or walked down the Pantiles and heard the whisper, 'There he is! That's him!' it was not dissatisfaction that softened his mouth and gleamed for a moment in his eye.

This little figure, this minute little figure, launched the Food of the Gods upon the world! One does not know which is the most amazing, the greatness or the littleness of these scientific and philosophical men. You figure him there on the Pantiles, in the overcoat trimmed with fur. He stands under that chinaware window where the spring spouts, and holds and sips the glass of chalybeate water in his hand. One bright eye over the gilt rim is fixed, with an expression of inscrutable severity, on Cousin Jane, 'Mm,' he says, and sips.

So we make our souvenir, so we focus and photograph this discoverer of ours for the last time, and leave him, a mere dot in our foreground, and pass to the greater picture that has developed about him, to the story of his Food, how the scattered Giant Children grew up day by day into a world that was all too small for them, and how the net of Boomfood Laws and Boomfood Conventions, which the Boomfood Commission was weaving even then, drew closer and closer upon them with every year of their growth. Until –

BOOK TWO

The Food in the Village

CHAPTER ONE

The Coming of the Food

Our theme, which began so compactly in Mr Bensington's study, has already spread and branched, until it points this way and that, and henceforth our whole story is one of dissemination. To follow the Food of the Gods farther is to trace the ramifications of a perpetually branching tree; in a little while, in the quarter of a lifetime, the Food had trickled and increased from its first spring in the little farm near Hickleybrow until it had spread – it and the report and shadow of its power – throughout the world. It spread beyond England very speedily. Soon in America, all over the continent of Europe, in Japan, in Australia, at last all over the world, the thing was working towards its appointed end. Always it worked slowly, by indirect courses and against resistance. It was bigness insurgent. In spite of prejudice, in spite of law and regulation, in spite of all that obstinate conservatism that lies at the base of the formal order of mankind, the Food of the Gods, once it had been set going, pursued its subtle and invincible progress.

The Children of the Food grew steadily through all these years; that was the cardinal fact of the time. But it is the leakages make history. The children who had eaten grew, and soon there were other children growing; and all the best intentions in the world could not stop further leakages and still further leakages. The Food insisted on escaping with the pertinacity of a thing alive. Flour treated with the stuff crumbled in dry weather almost as if by intention into an impalpable powder, and would lift and travel before the lightest breeze. Now it would be some fresh insect won its way to a temporary fatal new development, now some fresh outbreak from the sewers of rats and suchlike vermin. For some days the village of Pangbourne in Berkshire fought with giant ants. Three men were bitten and died. There would be a panic, there would be a struggle, and the salient evil would be fought down again, leaving always something behind, in the obscurer things of life, changed for ever. Then again another acute and startling outbreak, a swift upgrowth of monstrous weedy thickets, a drifting dissemination about the world of inhumanly growing thistles, of cockroaches men fought with shotguns, or a plague of mighty flies.

There were some strange and desperate struggles in obscure places. The Food begot heroes in the cause of littleness . . .

And men took such happenings into their lives, and met them by the expedients of the moment, and told one another there was 'no change in the

essential order of things'. After the first great panic, Caterham, in spite of his power of eloquence, became a secondary figure in the political world, remained in men's minds as the exponent of an extreme view.

Only slowly did he win a way towards a central position in affairs. 'There was no change in the essential order of things' – that eminent leader of modern thought, Dr Winkles, was very clear upon this – and the exponents of what was called in those days Progressive Liberalism grew quite sentimental upon the essential insincerity of their progress. Their dreams, it would appear, ran wholly on little nations, little languages, little households, each self-supported on its little farm. A fashion for the small and neat set in. To be big was to be 'vulgar', and dainty, neat, mignon, miniature, 'minutely perfect', became the key-words of critical approval . . .

Meanwhile, quietly, taking their time as children must, the Children of the Food, growing into a world that changed to receive them, gathered strength and stature and knowledge, became individual and purposeful, rose slowly towards the dimensions of their destiny. Presently they seemed a natural part of the world; all these stirrings of bigness seemed a natural part of the world, and men wondered how things had been before their time. There came to men's ears stories of things the giant boys could do, and they said, 'Wonderful!' – without a spark of wonder. The popular papers would tell of the three sons of Cossar, and how these amazing children would lift great cannons, hurl masses of iron for hundreds of yards and leap two hundred feet. They were said to be digging a well, deeper than any well or mine that man had ever made, seeking, it was said, for treasures hidden in the earth since ever the earth began.

These Children, said the popular magazines, will level mountains, bridge seas, tunnel your earth to a honeycomb. 'Wonderful!' said the little folks, 'isn't it? What a lot of conveniences we shall have!' and went about their business as though there was no such thing as the Food of the Gods on earth. And indeed these things were no more than the first hints and promises of the powers of the Children of the Food. It was still no more than child's play with them, no more than the first use of a strength in which no purpose had arisen. They did not know themselves for what they were. They were children – slow-growing children of a new race. The giant strength grew day by day – the giant will had still to grow into purpose and an aim.

Looking at it in a shortened perspective of time, those years of transition have the quality of a single consecutive occurrence; but indeed no one saw the coming of Bigness in the world, as no one in all the world till centuries had passed saw, as one happening, the Decline and Fall of Rome. They who lived in those days were too much among these developments to see them together as a single thing. It seemed even to wise men that the Food was giving the world nothing but a crop of unmanageable, disconnected irrelevancies, that might shake and trouble indeed, but could do no more to the established order and fabric of mankind.

To one observer at least the most wonderful thing throughout that period of accumulating stress is the invincible inertia of the great mass of people, their quiet persistence in all that ignored the enormous presences, the promise of still more enormous things, that grew among them. Just as many a stream will be at its smoothest, will look most tranquil, running deep and strong, at the very verge of a cataract, so all that is most conservative in man seemed settling quietly into a serene ascendency during these latter days. Reaction became popular: there was talk of the bankruptcy of science, of the dying of Progress, of the advent of the Mandarins – talk of such things amidst the echoing footsteps of the Children of the Food. The fussy pointless revolutions of the old time, a vast crowd of silly little people chasing some silly little monarch and the like, had indeed died out and passed away; but Change had not died out. It was only Change that had changed. The New was coming in its own fashion and beyond the common understanding of the world.

To tell fully of its coming would be to write a great history, but everywhere there was a parallel chain of happenings. To tell therefore of the manner of its coming in one place is to tell something of the whole. It chanced one stray seed of Immensity fell into the pretty, petty village of Cheasing Eyebright in Kent, and from the story of its queer germination there and of the tragic futility that ensued one may attempt – following one thread, as it were – to show the direction in which the whole great interwoven fabric of the thing rolled off the loom of Time.

2

Cheasing Eyebright had of course a vicar. There are vicars and vicars, and of all sorts I love an innovating vicar, a piebald progressive professional reactionary, the least. But the vicar of Cheasing Eyebright was one of the least innovating of vicars, a most worthy, plump, ripe and conservative-minded little man. It is becoming to go back a little in our story to tell of him. He matched his village, and one may figure them best together as they used to be, on the sunset evening when Mrs Skinner – you will remember her flight! – brought the Food with her all unsuspected into these rustic serenities.

The village was looking its very best just then, under that western light. It lay down along the valley beneath the beechwoods of the hanger, a beading of thatched and red-tiled cottages – cottages with trellised porches and pyracanthus-lined faces, that clustered closer and closer as the road dropped from the yew trees by the church towards the bridge. The vicarage peeped not too ostentatiously between the trees beyond the inn, an early Georgian front ripened by time, and the spire of the church rose happily in the depression made by the valley in the outline of the hills. A winding

stream, a thin intermittency of sky blue and foam, glittered amidst a thick margin of reeds and loosestrife and overhanging willows, along the centre of a sinuous pennant of meadow. The whole prospect had that curiously English quality of ripened cultivation – that look of still completeness – that apes perfection, under the sunset warmth.

And the vicar too looked mellow. He looked habitually and essentially mellow, as though he had been a mellow baby born into a mellow class, a ripe and juicy little boy. One could see, even before he mentioned it, that he had gone to an ivy-clad public school in its anecdotage, with magnificent traditions, aristocratic associations, and no chemical laboratories, and proceeded thence to a venerable college in the very ripest Gothic. Few books he had younger than a thousand years; of these, Yarrow and Ellis and good pre-Methodist sermons made the bulk. He was a man of moderate height, a little shortened in appearance by his equatorial dimensions, and a face that had been mellow from the first was now climacterically ripe. The beard of a David hid his redundancy of chin; he wore no watch-chain out of refinement, and his modest clerical garments were made by a West End tailor . . . And he sat with a hand on either shin, blinking at his village in beatific approval. He waved a plump palm towards it. His burthen sang out again. What more could anyone desire?

'We are fortunately situated,' he said, putting the thing tamely.

'We are in a fastness of the hills,' he expanded.

He explained himself at length. 'We are out of it all.'

For they had been talking, he and his friend, of the Horrors of the Age, of Democracy, and Secular Education, and Sky Scrapers, and Motor Cars, and the American Invasion, the Scrappy Reading of the Public, and the disappearance of any Taste at all.

'We are out of it all,' he repeated, and even as he spoke the footsteps of someone coming smote upon his ear, and he rolled over and regarded her.

You figure the old woman's steadfastly tremulous advance, the bundle clutched in her gnarled lank hand, her nose (which was her countenance) wrinkled with breathless resolution. You see the poppies nodding fatefully on her bonnet, and the dust-white spring-sided boots beneath her skimpy skirts, pointing with an irrevocable slow alternation east and west. Beneath her arm, a restive captive, waggled and slipped a scarcely valuable umbrella. What was there to tell the vicar that this grotesque old figure was – so far as his village was concerned at any rate – no less than Fruitful Chance and the Unforeseen, the Hag weak men call Fate. But for us, you understand, no more than Mrs Skinner.

As she was too much encumbered for a curtsey, she pretended not to see him and his friend at all, and so passed, flip-flop, within three yards of them, onward down towards the village. The vicar watched her slow transit in silence, and ripened a remark the while . . .

The incident seemed to him of no importance whatever. Old woman-

kind, *aere perennius*, has carried bundles since the world began. What difference has it made?

'We are out of it all,' said the vicar. 'We live in an atmosphere of simple and permanent things, Birth and Toil, simple seed-time and simple harvest. The Uproar passes us by.' He was always very great upon what he called the permanent things. 'Things change,' he would say, 'but Humanity – *aere perennius*.'

Thus the vicar. He loved a classical quotation subtly misapplied. Below, Mrs Skinner, inelegant but resolute, had involved herself curiously with Wilmerding's stile.

3

No one knows what the vicar made of the giant puff-balls.

No doubt he was among the first to discover them. They were scattered at intervals up and down the path between the near down and the village end – a path he frequented daily in his constitutional round. Altogether, of these abnormal fungi there were, from first to last, quite thirty. The vicar seems to have stared at each severally, and to have prodded most of them with his stick once or twice. One he attempted to measure with his arms, but it burst at his Ixion embrace.

He spoke to several people about them, and said they were 'marvellous!', and he related to at least seven different persons the well-known story of the flagstone that was lifted from the cellar floor by a growth of fungi beneath. He looked up his Sowerby to see if it was *Lycoperdon coelatum* or *giganteum* – like all his kind since Gilbert White became famous, he Gilbert-Whited. He cherished a theory that *giganteum* is unfairly named.

One does not know if he observed that those white spheres lay in the very track that old woman of yesterday had followed, or if he noted that the last of the series swelled not a score of yards from the gate of the Caddleses' cottage. If he observed these things, he made no attempt to place his observation on record. His observation in matters botanical was what the inferior sort of scientific people call a 'trained observation' – you look for certain definite things and neglect everything else. And he did nothing to link this phenomenon with the remarkable expansion of the Caddleses' baby that had been going on now for some weeks, indeed ever since Caddles walked over one Sunday afternoon a month or more ago to see his mother-in-law and hear Mr Skinner (since defunct) brag about his management of hens.

The growth of the puff-balls following on the expansion of the Caddleses' baby really ought to have opened the vicar's eyes. The latter fact had already come right into his arms at the christening – almost over-poweringly . . .

The youngster bawled with deafening violence when the cold water that sealed its divine inheritance and its right to the name of 'Albert Edward Caddles' fell upon its brow. It was already beyond maternal porterage, and Caddles, staggering indeed, but grinning triumphantly at quantitatively inferior parents, bore it back to the free-sitting occupied by his party.

'I never saw such a child!' said the vicar. This was the first public intimation that the Caddleses' baby, which had begun its earthly career a little under seven pounds, did after all intend to be a credit to its parents. Very soon it was clear it meant to be not only a credit but a glory. And within a month their glory shone so brightly as to be, in connection with people in the Caddleses' position, improper.

The butcher weighed the infant eleven times. He was a man of few words, and he soon got through with them. The first time he said, ' 'E's a good un'; the next time he said, 'My word!'; the third time he said, '*Well*, mum,' and after that he simply blew enormously each time, scratched his head, and looked at his scales with an unprecedented mistrust. Everyone came to see the Big Baby – so it was called by universal consent – and most of them said, ' 'E's a Bouncer,' and almost all remarked to him, '*Did* they?' Miss Fletcher came and said she 'never *did*', which was perfectly true.

Lady Wondershoot, the village tyrant, arrived the day after the third weighing, and inspected the phenomenon narrowly through glasses that filled it with howling terror. 'It's an unusually Big child,' she told its mother, in a loud instructive voice. 'You ought to take unusual care of it, Caddles. Of course it won't go on like this, being bottle fed, but we must do what we can for it. I'll send you down some more flannel.'

The doctor came and measured the child with a tape, and put the figures in a notebook, and old Mr Drifthassock, who farmed by Up Marden, brought a manure traveller two miles out of their way to look at it. The traveller asked the child's age three times over, and said finally that he was blowed. He left it to be inferred how and why he was blowed; apparently it was the child's size blowed him. He also said it ought to be put into a baby show. And all day long, out of school hours, little children kept coming and saying, 'Please, Mrs Caddles, mum, may we have a look at your baby, please, mum?' until Mrs Caddles had to put a stop to it. And amidst all these scenes of amazement came Mrs Skinner, and stood and smiled, standing somewhat in the background, with each sharp elbow in a lank gnarled hand,

and smiling, smiling under and about her nose, with a smile of infinite profundity.

'It makes even that old wretch of a grandmother look quite pleasant,' said Lady Wondershoot. 'Though I'm sorry she's come back to the village.'

Of course, as with almost all cottagers' babies, the eleemosynary element had already come in, but the child soon made it clear by colossal bawling that so far as the filling of its bottle went, it hadn't come in yet nearly enough.

The baby was entitled to a nine days' wonder, and everyone wondered happily over its amazing growth for twice that time and more. And then you know, instead of its dropping into the background and giving place to other marvels, it went on growing more than ever!

Lady Wondershoot heard Mrs Greenfield, her housekeeper, with infinite amazement

'Caddles downstairs again? No food for the child! My dear Greenfield, it's impossible. The creature eats like a hippopotamus! I'm sure it can't be true.'

'I'm sure I hope you're not being imposed upon, my lady,' said Mrs Greenfield.

'It's so difficult to tell with these people,' said Lady Wondershoot. 'Now I do wish, my good Greenfield, that you'd just go down there yourself this afternoon and *see* – see it have its bottle. Big as it is, I cannot imagine that it needs more than six pints a day.'

'It hasn't no business to, my lady,' said Mrs Greenfield.

The hand of Lady Wondershoot quivered, with that code-of-silence sort of emotion, that suspicious rage that stirs in all true aristocrats at the thought that possibly the meaner classes are after all as mean as their betters, and – where the sting lies – scoring points in the game.

But Mrs Greenfield could observe no evidence of peculation, and the order for an increasing daily supply to the Caddleses' nursery was issued. Scarcely had the first instalment gone, when Caddles was back again at the great house in a state abjectly apologetic.

'We took the greates' care of 'em, Mrs Greenfield, I do assure you, mum, but he's regular bust 'em! They flew with such vilence, mum, that one button broke a pane of the window, mum, and one hit me a regular stinger jest 'ere, mum.'

Lady Wondershoot, when she heard that this amazing child had positively burst out of its beautiful charity clothes, decided that she must speak to Caddles herself. He appeared in her presence with his hair hastily wetted and smoothed by hand, breathless, and clinging to his hat brim as though it was a life-belt, and he stumbled at the carpet edge out of sheer distress of mind.

Lady Wondershoot liked bullying Caddles. Caddles was her ideal lower-class person, dishonest, faithful, abject, industrious and inconceivably incapable of responsibility. She told him it was a serious matter, the way his

child was going on. 'It's 'is appetite, my ladyship,' said Caddles, with a rising note.

'Check 'im, my ladyship, you can't,' said Caddles. 'There 'e lies, my ladyship, and kicks out 'e does, and 'owls – it's that distressin'. We 'aven't the 'eart, my ladyship. If we 'ad – the neighbours would interfere . . . '

Lady Wondershoot consulted the parish doctor.

'What I want to know,' said Lady Wondershoot, 'is it *right* this child should have such an extraordinary quantity of milk?'

'The proper allowance for a child of that age,' said the parish doctor, 'is a pint and a half to two pints in the twenty-four hours. I don't see that you are called upon to provide more. If you do, it is your own generosity. Of course we might try the legitimate quantity for a few days. But the child, I must admit, seems for some reason to be physiologically different. Possibly what is called a Sport. A case of General Hypertrophy.'

'It isn't fair to the other parish children,' said Lady Wondershoot. 'I am certain we shall have complaints if this goes on.'

'I don't see that anyone can be expected to give more than the recognised allowance. We might insist on its doing with that, or if it wouldn't, send it as a case into the Infirmary.'

'I suppose,' said Lady Wondershoot, reflecting, 'that apart from the size and the appetite, you don't find anything else abnormal – nothing monstrous?'

'No. No, I don't. But no doubt if this growth goes on, we shall find grave moral and intellectual deficiencies. One might almost prophesy that from Max Nordau's law. A most gifted and celebrated philosopher, Lady Wondershoot. He discovered that the abnormal is – abnormal, a most valuable discovery, and well worth bearing in mind. I find it of the utmost help in practice. When I come upon anything abnormal, I say at once, "This is abnormal." ' His eyes became profound, his voice dropped, his manner verged upon the intimately confidential. He raised one hand stiffly. 'And I treat it in that spirit,' he said.

<div align="center">

5

</div>

'Tut, tut!' said the vicar to his breakfast things – the day after the coming of Mrs Skinner. 'Tut, tut! what's this?' and poised his glasses at his paper with a general air of remonstrance. 'Giant wasps! What's the world coming to? American journalists, I suppose! Hang these Novelties! Giant gooseberries are good enough for me.

'Nonsense!' said the vicar, and drank off his coffee at a gulp, eyes steadfast on the paper, and smacked his lips incredulously.

'Bosh!' said the vicar, rejecting the hint altogether.

But the next day there was more of it, and the light came.

Not all at once, however. When he went for his constitutional that day he was still chuckling at the absurd story his paper would have had him believe. Wasps indeed – killing a dog! Incidentally as he passed by the site of that first crop of puff-balls he remarked that the grass was growing very rank there, but he did not connect that in any way with the matter of his amusement. 'We should certainly have heard something of it,' he said; 'Whitstable can't be twenty miles from here.'

Beyond he found another puff-ball, one of the second crop, rising like a roc's egg out of the abnormally coarsened turf.

The thing came upon him in a flash.

He did not take his usual round that morning. Instead he turned aside by the second stile and came round to the Caddleses' cottage. 'Where's that baby?' he demanded, and at the sight of it, 'Goodness me!'

He went up the village blessing his heart, and met the doctor full tilt coming down. He grasped his arm. 'What does this *mean*?' he said. 'Have you seen the paper these last few days?'

The doctor said he had.

'Well, what's the matter with that child? What's the matter with everything – wasps, puff-balls, babies, eh? What's making them grow so big? This is most unexpected. In Kent too! If it was America now – '

'It's a little difficult to say just what it is,' said the doctor. 'So far as I can grasp the symptoms – '

'Yes?'

'It's Hypertrophy – General Hypertrophy.'

'Hypertrophy?'

'Yes. General – affecting all the bodily structures – all the organism. I may say that in my own mind, between ourselves, I'm very nearly convinced it's that . . . But one has to be careful.'

'Ah,' said the vicar, a good deal relieved to find the doctor equal to the situation. 'But how is it it's breaking out in this fashion, all over the place?'

'That again,' said the doctor, 'is difficult to say.'

'Urshot. Here. It's a pretty clear case of spreading.'

'Yes,' said the doctor. 'Yes. I think so. It has a strong resemblance at any rate to some sort of epidemic. Probably Epidemic Hypertrophy will meet the case.'

'Epidemic!' said the vicar. 'You don't mean it's contagious?'

The doctor smiled gently and rubbed one hand against the other. 'That I couldn't say,' he said.

'But – !' cried the vicar, round-eyed. 'If it's *catching* – it – it affects *us*!'

He made a stride up the road and turned about.

'I've just been there,' he cried. 'Hadn't I better – ? I'll go home at once and have a bath and fumigate my clothes.'

The doctor regarded his retreating back for a moment, and then turned about and went towards his own house . . .

But on the way he reflected that one case had been in the village a month without anyone catching the disease, and after a pause of hesitation decided to be as brave as a doctor should be and take the risks like a man.

And indeed he was well advised by his second thoughts. Growth was the last thing that could ever happen to him again. He could have eaten – and the vicar could have eaten – Herakleophorbia by the truckful. For growth had done with them. Growth had done with these two gentlemen for evermore.

6

It was a day or so after this conversation – a day or so, that is, after the burning of the Experimental Farm – that Winkles came to Redwood and showed him an insulting letter. It was an anonymous letter, and an author should respect his character's secrets. 'You are only taking credit for a natural phenomenon,' said the letter, 'and trying to advertise yourself by your letter to *The Times*. You and your Boomfood! Let me tell you, this absurdly named food of yours has only the most accidental connection with those big wasps and rats. The plain fact is there is an epidemic of Hypertrophy – Contagious Hypertrophy – which you have about as much claim to control as you have to control the solar system. The thing is as old as the hills. There was Hypertrophy in the family of Anak. Quite outside your range, at Cheasing Eyebright, at the present time there is a baby – '

'Shaky up-and-down writing. Old gentleman apparently,' said Redwood. 'But it's odd a baby – '

He read a few lines further, and had an inspiration.

'By Jove!' said he. 'That's my missing Mrs Skinner!'

He descended upon her suddenly in the afternoon of the following day.

She was engaged in pulling onions in the little garden before her daughter's cottage when she saw him coming through the garden gate. She stood for a moment 'consternated', as the country folks say, and then folded her arms, and with the little bunch of onions held defensively under her left elbow, awaited his approach. Her mouth opened and shut several times; she mumbled her remaining tooth, and once quite suddenly she curtsied, like the blink of an arc-light.

'I thought I should find you,' said Redwood.

'I thought you might, sir,' she said, without joy.

'Where's Skinner?'

' 'E ain't never written to me, sir, not once, nor come nigh of me since I came here, sir.'

'Don't you know what's become of him?'

'Him not having written, no, sir,' and she edged a step towards the left with an imperfect idea of cutting off Redwood from the barn door.

'No one knows what has become of him,' said Redwood.

'I dessay 'e knows,' said Mrs Skinner.

'He doesn't tell.'

'He was always a great one for looking after 'imself and leaving them that was near and dear to 'im in trouble, was Skinner. Though clever as could be,' said Mrs Skinner.

'Where's this child?' asked Redwood abruptly.

She begged his pardon.

'This child I hear about, the child you've been giving our stuff to – the child that weighs two stone.'

Mrs Skinner's hands worked, and she dropped the onions. 'Reely, sir,' she protested, 'I don't hardly know, sir, what you mean. My daughter, sir, Mrs Caddles, 'as a baby, sir.' And she made an agitated curtsey and tried to look innocently enquiring by tilting her nose to one side.

'You'd better let me see that baby, Mrs Skinner,' said Redwood.

Mrs Skinner unmasked an eye at him as she led the way towards the barn. 'Of course, sir, there may 'ave been a *little*, in a little can of Nicey I give his father to bring over from the farm, or a little perhaps what I happened to bring about with me, so to speak. Me packing in a hurry and all . . .'

'Um!' said Redwood, after he had cluckered to the infant for a space. 'Oom!'

He told Mrs Caddles the baby was a very fine child indeed, a thing that was getting well home to her intelligence – and he ignored her altogether after that. Presently she left the barn – through sheer insignificance.

'Now you've started him, you'll have to keep on with him, you know,' he said to Mrs Skinner.

He turned on her abruptly. 'Don't splash it about *this* time,' he said.

'Splash it about, sir?'

'Oh! *you* know.'

She indicated knowledge by convulsive gestures.

'You haven't told these people here? The parents, the squire and so on at the big house, the doctor, no one?'

Mrs Skinner shook her head.

'I wouldn't,' said Redwood.

He went to the door of the barn and surveyed the world about him. The door of the barn looked between the end of the cottage and some disused piggeries through a five-barred gate upon the high road. Beyond was a high, red brick-wall rich with ivy and wallflower and pennywort, and set along the top with broken glass. Beyond the corner of the wall, a sunlit noticeboard amidst green and yellow branches reared itself above the rich tones of the first fallen leaves and announced that 'Trespassers in these Woods will be Prosecuted.' The dark shadow of a gap in the hedge threw a stretch of barbed wire into relief.

'Um,' said Redwood, then in a deeper note, 'Oom!'

There came a clatter of horses and the sound of wheels, and Lady Wondershoot's greys came into view. He marked the faces of coachman and footman as the equipage approached. The coachman was a very fine specimen, full and fruity, and he drove with a sort of sacramental dignity. Others might doubt their calling and position in the world, he at any rate was sure – he drove her ladyship. The footman sat beside him with folded arms and a face of inflexible certainties. Then the great lady herself became visible, in a hat and mantle disdainfully inelegant, peering through her glasses. Two young ladies protruded necks and peered also.

The vicar passing on the other side swept off the hat from his David's brow unheeded . . .

Redwood remained standing in the doorway for a long time after the carriage had passed, his hands folded behind him. His eyes went to the green-grey upland of down, and into the cloud curdled sky, and came back to the glass-set wall. He turned upon the cool shadows within, and amidst spots and blurs of colour regarded the giant child amidst that Rembrandtesque gloom, naked except for a swathing of flannel, seated upon a huge truss of straw and playing with its toes.

'I begin to see what we have done,' he said.

He mused, and young Caddles and his own child and Cossar's brood mingled in his musing. He laughed abruptly. 'Good Lord!' he said at some passing thought.

He roused himself presently and addressed Mrs Skinner. 'Anyhow he mustn't be tortured by a break in his food. That at least we can prevent. I shall send you a can every six months. That ought to do for him all right.'

Mrs Skinner mumbled something about 'if you think so, sir,' and 'probably got packed by mistake . . . Thought no harm in giving him a little,' and so by the aid of various aspen gestures indicated that she understood.

So the child went on growing.

And growing.

'Practically,' said Lady Wondershoot, 'he's eaten up every calf in the place. If I have any more of this sort of thing from that man Caddles – '

7

But even so secluded a place as Cheasing Eyebright could not rest for long in the theory of Hypertrophy – Contagious or not – in view of the growing hubbub about the Food. In a little while there were painful explanations for Mrs Skinner – explanations that reduced her to speechless mumblings of her remaining tooth – explanations that probed her and ransacked her and exposed her – until at last she was driven to take refuge from a universal convergence of blame in the dignity of inconsolable widowhood.

She turned her eye – which she constrained to be watery – upon the angry Lady of the Manor, and wiped suds from her hands.

'You forget, my lady, what I'm bearing up under.'

And she followed up this warning note with a slightly defiant: 'It's 'IM I think of, my lady, night *and* day.'

She compressed her lips, and her voice flattened and faltered: 'Bein' et, my lady.'

And having established herself on these grounds, she repeated the affirmation her ladyship had refused before. 'I 'ad no more idea what I was giving the child, my lady, than anyone *could* 'ave . . . '

Her ladyship turned her mind in more hopeful directions, wigging Caddles of course tremendously by the way. Emissaries, full of diplomatic threatenings, entered the whirling lives of Bensington and Redwood. They presented themselves as parish councillors, stolid and clinging phonographically to prearranged statements. 'We hold you responsible, Mr Bensington, for the injury inflicted upon our parish, sir. We hold you responsible.'

A firm of solicitors, with a snake of a style – Banghurst, Brown, Flapp, Codlin, Brown, Tedder and Snoxton, they called themselves, and appeared invariably in the form of a small rufous cunning-looking gentleman with a pointed nose – said vague things about damages, and there was a polished personage, her ladyship's agent, who came in suddenly upon Redwood one day and asked, 'Well, sir, and what do you propose to do?'

To which Redwood answered that he proposed to discontinue supplying the food for the child if he or Bensington were bothered any further about the matter. 'I give it for nothing as it is,' he said, 'and the child will yell your village to ruins before it dies if you don't let it have the stuff. The child's on your hands, and you have to keep it. Lady Wondershoot can't always be Lady Bountiful and Earthly Providence of her parish without sometimes meeting a responsibility, you know.'

'The mischief's done,' Lady Wondershoot decided when they told her – with expurgations – what Redwood had said.

'The mischief's done,' echoed the vicar.

Though indeed as a matter of fact the mischief was only beginning.

CHAPTER TWO

The Brat Gigantic

The giant child was ugly – the vicar would insist. 'He always had been ugly – as all excessive things must be.' The vicar's views had carried him out of sight of just judgement in this matter. The child was much subjected to snapshots even in that rustic retirement, and their net testimony is against

the vicar, testifying that the young monster was at first almost pretty, with a copious curl of hair reaching to his brow and a great readiness to smile. Usually Caddles, who was slightly built, stands smiling behind the baby, perspective emphasising his relative smallness.

After the second year the good looks of the child became more subtle and more contestable. He began to grow, as his unfortunate grandfather would no doubt have put it, 'rank'. He lost colour and developed an increasing effect of being somehow, albeit colossal, yet slight. He was vastly delicate. His eyes and something about his face grew finer – grew, as people say, 'interesting'. His hair, after one cutting, began to tangle into a mat. 'It's the degenerate strain coming out in him,' said the parish doctor, marking these things, but just how far he was right in that, and just how far the youngster's lapse from ideal healthfulness was the result of living entirely in a white-washed barn upon Lady Wondershoot's sense of charity tempered by justice, is open to question.

The photographs of him that present him from three to six show him developing into a round-eyed, flaxen-haired youngster with a truncated nose and a friendly stare. There lurks about his lips that never very remote promise of a smile that all the photographs of the early giant children display. In summer he wears loose garments of ticking tacked together with string; there is usually one of those straw baskets upon his head that workmen use for their tools, and he is barefooted. In one picture he grins broadly and holds a bitten melon in his hand.

The winter pictures are less numerous and satisfactory. He wears huge sabots – no doubt of beechwood, and (as fragments of the inscription 'John Stickells, Iping', show) sacks for socks, and his trousers and jacket are unmistakably cut from the remains of a gaily patterned carpet. Underneath that there were rude swathings of flannel; five or six yards of flannel are tied comforter-fashion about his neck. The thing on his head is probably another sack. He stares, sometimes smiling, sometimes a little ruefully, at the camera. Even when he was only five years old, one sees that half-whimsical wrinkling over his soft brown eyes that characterised his face.

He was from the first, the vicar always declared, a terrible nuisance about the village. He seems to have had a proportionate impulse to play, much curiosity and sociability, and in addition there was a certain craving within him – I grieve to say – for more to eat. In spite of what Mrs Greenfield called an '*excessively* generous' allowance of food from Lady Wondershoot, he displayed what the doctor perceived at once was the 'Criminal Appetite'. It carries out only too completely Lady Wondershoot's worst experiences of the lower classes that, in spite of an allowance of nourishment in-ordinately beyond what is known to be the maximum necessity even of an adult human being, the creature was found to steal. And what he stole he ate with an inelegant voracity. His great hand would come over garden walls; he would covet the very bread in the bakers' carts. Cheeses went from

Marlow's store loft, and never a pig trough was safe from him. Some farmer walking over his field of swedes would find the great spoor of his feet and the evidence of his nibbling hunger – a root picked here, a root picked there, and the holes, with childish cunning, heavily erased. He ate a swede as one devours a radish. He would stand and eat apples from a tree, if no one was about, as normal children eat blackberries from a bush. In one way at any rate this shortness of provisions was good for the peace of Cheasing Eyebright – for many years he ate up every grain very nearly of the Food of the Gods that was given him.

Indisputably the child was troublesome and out of place. 'He was always about,' the vicar used to say. He could not go to school; he could not go to church by virtue of the obvious limitations of its cubical content. There was some attempt to satisfy the spirit of that 'most foolish and destructive law' – I quote the vicar – the Elementary Education Act of 1870, by getting him to sit outside the open window while instruction was going on within. But his presence there destroyed the discipline of the other children. They were always popping up and peering at him, and every time he spoke they laughed together. His voice was so odd! So they let him stay away.

Nor did they persist in pressing him to come to church, for his vast proportions were of little help to devotion. Yet there they might have had an easier task; there are good reasons for guessing there were the germs of religious feeling somewhere in that big carcass. The music perhaps drew him. He was often in the churchyard on a Sunday morning, picking his way softly among the graves after the congregation had gone in, and he would sit the whole service out beside the porch, listening as one listens outside a hive of bees.

At first he showed a certain want of tact; the people inside would hear his great feet crunch restlessly round their place of worship, or become aware of his dim face peering in through the stained glass, half curious, half envious, and at times some simple hymn would catch him unawares, and he would howl lugubriously in a gigantic attempt at unison. Whereupon little Sloppet, who was organ-blower and verger and beadle and sexton and bell-ringer on Sundays, besides being postman and chimney-sweep all the week, would go out very briskly and valiantly and send him mournfully away. Sloppet, I am glad to say, felt it – in his more thoughtful moments at any rate. It was like sending a dog home when you start out for a walk, he told me.

But the intellectual and moral training of young Caddles, though fragmentary, was explicit. From the first, vicar, mother, and all the world, combined to make it clear to him that his giant strength was not for use. It was a misfortune that he had to make the best of. He had to mind what was told him, do what was set him, be careful never to break anything nor hurt anything. Particularly he must not go treading on things or jostling against things or jumping about. He had to salute the gentlefolks respectful and be

grateful for the food and clothing they spared him out of their riches. And he learnt all these things submissively, being by nature and habit a teachable creature and only by food and accident gigantic.

For Lady Wondershoot, in these early days, he displayed the profoundest awe. She found she could talk to him best when she was in short skirts and had her dog-whip, and she gesticulated with that and was always a little contemptuous and shrill. But sometimes the vicar played master – a minute, middle-aged, rather breathless David pelting a childish Goliath with reproof and reproach and dictatorial command. The monster was now so big that it seems it was impossible for anyone to remember he was after all only a child of seven, with all a child's desire for notice and amusement and fresh experience, with all a child's craving for response, attention and affection, and all a child's capacity for dependence and unrestricted dullness and misery.

The vicar, walking down the village road some sunlit morning, would encounter an ungainly eighteen feet of the Inexplicable, as fantastic and unpleasant to him as some new form of Dissent, as it padded fitfully along with craning neck, seeking, always seeking the two primary needs of childhood – something to eat and something with which to play.

There would come a look of furtive respect into the creature's eyes and an attempt to touch the matted forelock.

In a limited way the vicar had an imagination – at any rate, the remains of one – and with young Caddles it took the line of developing the huge possibilities of personal injury such vast muscles must possess. Suppose a sudden madness – ! Suppose a mere lapse into disrespect – ! However, the truly brave man is not the man who does not feel fear but the man who overcomes it. Every time and always the vicar got his imagination under. And he used always to address young Caddles stoutly in a good clear service tenor.

'Being a good boy, Albert Edward?'

And the young giant, edging closer to the wall and blushing deeply, would answer, 'Yessir – trying.'

'Mind you do,' said the vicar, and would go past him with at most a slight acceleration of his breathing. And out of respect for his manhood he made it a rule, whatever he might fancy, never to look back at the danger when once it was passed.

In a fitful manner the vicar would give young Caddles private tuition. He never taught the monster to read – it was not needed; but he taught him the more important points of the Catechism – his duty to his neighbour for example, and of that Deity who would punish Caddles with extreme vindictiveness if ever he ventured to disobey the vicar and Lady Wondershoot. The lessons would go on in the vicar's yard, and passers-by would hear that great cranky childish voice droning out the essential teachings of the Established Church.

'To onner 'n 'bey the King and allooer put 'nthority under 'im. To s'bmit meself t'all my gov'ners, teachers, spir'shall pastors an' masters. To order myself lowly 'n rev'rently t'all my betters – '

Presently it became evident that the effect of the growing giant on unaccustomed horses was like that of a camel, and he was told to keep off the high road, not only near the shrubbery (where the oafish smile over the wall had exasperated her ladyship extremely), but altogether. That law he never completely obeyed, because of the vast interest the high road had for him. But it turned what had been his constant resort into a stolen pleasure. He was limited at last almost entirely to old pasture and the downs.

I do not know what he would have done if it had not been for the downs. There there were spaces where he might wander for miles, and over these spaces he wandered. He would pick branches from trees and make insane vast nosegays there until he was forbidden, take up sheep and put them in neat rows, from which they immediately wandered (at this he invariably laughed very heartily), until he was forbidden, dig away the turf, great wanton holes, until he was forbidden . . .

He would wander over the downs as far as the hill above Wreckstone, but not farther, because there he came upon cultivated land, and the people, by reason of his depredations upon their root-crops, and inspired moreover by the sort of hostile timidity his big unkempt appearance frequently evoked, always came out against him with yapping dogs to drive him away. They would threaten him and lash at him with cart whips. I have heard that they would sometimes fire at him with shotguns. And in the other direction he ranged within sight of Hickleybrow. From above Thursley Hanger he could get a glimpse of the London, Chatham and Dover railway, but ploughed fields and a suspicious hamlet prevented his nearer access.

And after a time there came boards – great boards with red letters that barred him in every direction. He could not read what the letters said – 'Out of Bounds' – but in a little while he understood. He was often to be seen in those days, by the railway passengers, sitting, chin on knees, perched up on the down hard by the Thursley chalk pits, where afterwards he was set working. The train seemed to inspire a dim emotion of friendliness in him, and sometimes he would wave an enormous hand at it, and sometimes give it a rustic incoherent hail.

'Big,' the peering passenger would say. 'One of these Boom children. They say, sir, quite unable to do anything for itself – little better than an idiot in fact, and a great burden on the locality.'

'Parents quite poor, I'm told.'

'Lives on the charity of the local gentry.'

Every one would stare intelligently at that distant squatting monstrous figure for a space.

'Good thing that was put a stop to,' some spacious thinking mind would suggest. 'Nice to 'ave a few thousand of *them* on the rates, eh?'

And usually there was someone wise enough to tell this philosopher: 'You're about Right there, sir,' in hearty tones.

2

He had his bad days.

There was, for example, that trouble with the river.

He made little boats out of whole newspapers, an art he learnt by watching the Spender boy, and he set them sailing down the stream – great paper cocked-hats. When they vanished under the bridge which marks the boundary of the strictly private grounds about Eyebright House, he would give a great shout and run round and across Tormat's new field – Lord! how Tormat's pigs did scamper, to be sure, and turn their good fat into lean muscle! – and so meet his boats by the ford. Right across the nearer lawns these paper boats of his used to go, right in front of Eyebright House, right under Lady Wondershoot's eyes! Disorganising folded newspapers! A pretty thing!

Gathering enterprise from impunity, he began babyish hydraulic engineering. He delved a huge port for his paper fleets with an old shed door that served him as a spade, and, no one chancing to observe his operations just then, he devised an ingenious canal that incidentally flooded Lady Wondershoot's ice-house, and finally he dammed the river. He dammed it right across with a few vigorous doorfuls of earth – he must have worked like an avalanche – and down came a most amazing spate through the shrubbery and washed away Miss Spinks and her easel and the most promising watercolour sketch she had ever begun, or, at any rate, it washed away her easel and left her wet to the knees and dismally tucked up in flight to the house, and thence the waters rushed through the kitchen garden, and so by the green door into the lane and down into the river-bed again by Short's ditch.

Meanwhile, the vicar, interrupted in conversation with the blacksmith, was amazed to see distressful stranded fish leaping out of a few residual pools, and heaped green weed in the bed of the stream where ten minutes before there had been eight feet and more of clear cool water.

After that, horrified at his own consequences, young Caddles fled his home for two days and nights. He returned only at the insistent call of hunger, to bear with stoical calm an amount of violent scolding that was more in proportion to his size than anything else that had ever before fallen to his lot in the Happy Village.

Immediately after that affair Lady Wondershoot, casting about for exemplary additions to the abuse and fastings she had inflicted, issued a ukase. She issued it first to her butler, and very suddenly, so that she made him jump. He was clearing away the breakfast things, and she was staring out of the tall window on the terrace where the fawns would come to be fed. 'Jobbet,' she said, in her most imperial voice – 'Jobbet, this Thing must work for its living.'

And she made it quite clear not only to Jobbet (which was easy), but to everyone else in the village, including young Caddles, that in this matter, as in all things, she meant what she said.

'Keep him employed,' said Lady Wondershoot. 'That's the tip for Master Caddles.'

'It's the Tip, I fancy, for all Humanity,' said the vicar. 'The simple duties, the modest round, seedtime and harvest – '

'Exactly,' said Lady Wondershoot. 'What *I* always say. Satan finds some mischief still for idle hands to do. At any rate among the labouring classes. We bring up our under-housemaids on that principle, always. What shall we set him to do?'

That was a little difficult. They thought of many things, and meanwhile they broke him in to labour a bit by using him instead of a horse messenger to carry telegrams and notes when extra speed was needed, and he also carried luggage and packing-cases and things of that sort very conveniently in a big net they found for him. He seemed to like employment, regarding it as a sort of game, and Kinkle, Lady Wondershoot's agent, seeing him shift a rockery for her one day, was struck by the brilliant idea of putting him into her chalk quarry at Thursley Hanger, hard by Hickleybrow. This idea was carried out, and it seemed they had settled his problem.

He worked in the chalk pit, at first with the zest of a playing child, and afterwards with an effect of habit – delving, loading, doing all the haulage of the trucks, running the full ones down the lines towards the siding, and hauling the empty ones up by the wire of a great windlass – working the entire quarry at last single-handed.

I am told that Kinkle made a very good thing indeed out of him for Lady Wondershoot, consuming as he did scarcely anything but his food, though that never restrained her denunciation of 'the Creature' as a gigantic parasite upon her charity.

At that time he used to wear a sort of smock of sacking, trousers of patched leather and iron-shod sabots. Over his head was sometimes a queer thing – a worn-out beehive straw chair it was, but usually he went bare-

headed. He would be moving about the pit with a powerful deliberation, and the vicar on his constitutional round would get there about midday to find him shamefully eating his vast need of food with his back to all the world.

His food was brought to him every day, a mess of grain in the husk, in a truck – a small railway truck, like one of the trucks he was perpetually filling with chalk, and this load he used to char in an old limekiln and then devour. Sometimes he would mix with it a bag of sugar. Sometimes he would sit licking a lump of such salt as is given to cows, or eating a huge lump of dates, stones and all, such as one sees in London on barrows. For drink he walked to the rivulet beyond the burnt-out site of the Experimental Farm at Hickleybrow and put down his face to the stream. It was from his drinking in that way after eating that the Food of the Gods did at last get loose, spreading first of all in huge weeds from the riverside, then in big frogs, bigger trout and stranding carp, and at last in a fantastic exuberance of vegetation all over the little valley.

And after a year or so the queer monstrous grub things in the field before the blacksmith's grew so big and developed into such frightful skipjacks and cockchafers – motor cockchafers the boys called them – that they drove Lady Wondershoot abroad.

4

But soon the Food was to enter upon a new phase of its work in him. In spite of the simple instructions of the vicar – instructions intended to round off the modest natural life befitting a giant peasant, in the most complete and final manner – he began to ask questions, to enquire into things, to *think*. As he grew from boyhood to adolescence it became increasingly evident that his mind had processes of its own – out of the vicar's control. The vicar did his best to ignore this distressing phenomenon, but still – he could feel it there.

The young giant's material for thought lay about him. Quite involuntarily, with his spacious views, his constant overlooking of things, he must have seen a good deal of human life, and as it grew clearer to him that he too, save for this clumsy greatness of his, was also human, he must have come to realise more and more just how much was shut against him by his melancholy distinction. The sociable hum of the school, the mystery of religion that was partaken in such finery, and which exhaled so sweet a strain of melody, the jovial chorusing from the inn, the warmly glowing rooms, candlelit and fire-lit, into which he peered out of the darkness, or again the shouting excitement, the vigour of flannelled exercise upon some imperfectly understood issue that centred about the cricket-field – all these things must have cried aloud to his companionable heart. It would seem

that as his adolescence crept upon him, he began to take a very considerable interest in the proceedings of lovers, in those preferences and pairings, those close intimacies that are so cardinal in life.

One Sunday, just about that hour when the stars and the bats and the passions of rural life come out, there chanced to be a young couple 'kissing each other a bit' in Love Lane, the deep hedged lane that runs out back towards the Upper Lodge. They were giving their little emotions play, as secure in the warm still twilight as any lovers could be. The only conceivable interruption they thought possible must come pacing visibly up the lane; the twelve-foot hedge towards the silent downs seemed to them an absolute guarantee.

Then suddenly – incredibly – they were lifted and drawn apart.

They discovered themselves held up, each with a finger and thumb under the armpits, and with the perplexed brown eyes of young Caddles scanning their warm flushed faces. They were naturally dumb with the emotions of their situation.

'*Why* do you like doing that?' asked young Caddles.

I gather the embarrassment continued until the swain, remembering his manhood, vehemently, with loud shouts, threats and virile blasphemies, such as became the occasion, bade young Caddles under penalties put them down. Whereupon young Caddles, remembering his manners, did put them down politely and very carefully, and conveniently near for a resumption of their embraces, and having hesitated above them for a while, vanished again into the twilight . . .

'But I felt precious silly,' the swain confided to me. 'We couldn't 'ardly look at one another – bein' caught like that.

'Kissing we was – *you* know.

'And the cur'ous thing is, she blamed it all on to me,' said the swain. 'Flew out something outrageous, and wouldn't 'ardly speak to me all the way 'ome . . . '

The giant was embarking upon investigations, there could be no doubt. His mind, it became manifest, was throwing up questions. He put them to few people as yet, but they troubled him. His mother, one gathers, sometimes came in for cross-examination.

He used to come into the yard behind his mother's cottage, and, after a careful inspection of the ground for hens and chicks, he would sit down slowly with his back against the barn. In a minute the chicks, who liked him, would be pecking all over him at the mossy chalk-mud in the seams of his clothing, and if it was blowing up for wet, Mrs Caddles's kitten, who never lost her confidence in him, would assume a sinuous form and start scampering into the cottage, up to the kitchen fender, round, out, up his leg, up his body, right up to his shoulder, meditative moment, and then scat! back again, and so on. Sometimes she would stick her claws in his face out of sheer gaiety of heart, but he never dared to touch her because of the

uncertain weight of his hand upon a creature so frail. Besides, he rather liked to be tickled.

And after a time he would put some clumsy questions to his mother. 'Mother,' he would say, 'if it's good to work, why doesn't everyone work?'

His mother would look up at him and answer, 'It's good for the likes of us.'

He would meditate, '*Why?*'

And going unanswered, 'What's work *for*, mother? Why do I cut chalk and you wash clothes, day after day, while Lady Wondershoot goes about in her carriage, mother, and travels off to those beautiful foreign countries you and I mustn't see, mother?'

'She's a lady,' said Mrs Caddles.

'Oh,' said young Caddles, and meditated profoundly.

'If there wasn't gentlefolks to make work for us to do,' said Mrs Caddles, 'how should we poor people get a living?'

This had to be digested.

'Mother,' he tried again; 'if there wasn't any gentlefolks, wouldn't things belong to people like me and you, and if they did – '

'Lord sakes and *drat* the Boy!' Mrs Caddles would say – she had with the help of a good memory become quite a florid and vigorous individuality since Mrs Skinner died. 'Since your poor dear grandma was took, there's no abiding you. Don't you arst no questions and you won't be told no lies. If once I was to start out answerin' you *serious*, y'r father'd 'ave to go and arst someone else for 'is supper – let alone finishin' the washin'.'

'All right, mother,' he would say, after a wondering stare at her. 'I didn't mean to worry.'

And he would go on thinking.

5

He was thinking too four years after, when the vicar, now no longer ripe but overripe, saw him for the last time of all. You figure the old gentleman visibly a little older now, slacker in his girth, a little coarsened and a little weakened in his thought and speech, with a quivering shakiness in his hand and a quivering shakiness in his convictions, but his eye still bright and merry for all the trouble the Food had caused his village and himself. He had been frightened at times and disturbed, but was he not alive still and the same still? and fifteen long years – a fair sample of eternity – had turned the trouble into use and wont.

'It was a disturbance, I admit,' he would say, 'and things are different – different in many ways. There was a time when a boy could weed, but now a man must go out with axe and crowbar – in some places down by the thickets at least. And it's a little strange still to us old-fashioned people for

all this valley, even what used to be the river bed before they irrigated, to be under wheat – as it is this year – twenty-five feet high. They used the old-fashioned scythe here twenty years ago, and they would bring home the harvest on a wain – rejoicing – in a simple honest fashion. A little simple drunkenness, a little innocent dalliance, perhaps, to conclude . . . poor dear Lady Wondershoot – she didn't like these Innovations. Very conservative, poor dear lady! A touch of the eighteenth century about her, I always said. Her language for example . . . Bluff vigour . . .

'She died comparatively poor. These big weeds got into her garden. She was not one of these gardening women, but she liked her garden in order – things growing where they were planted and as they were planted – under control . . . The way things grew was unexpected – upset her ideas . . . She didn't like the perpetual invasion of this young monster – at last she began to fancy he was always gaping at her over her wall . . . She didn't like his being nearly as high as her house . . . Jarred with her sense of proportion. Poor dear lady! I had hoped she would last my time. It was the big cock-chafers we had for a year or so that decided her. They came from the giant larvae – nasty things as big as rats – in the valley turf . . .

'And the ants no doubt weighed with her also.

'Since everything was upset and there was no peace and quietness any-where now, she said she thought she might just as well be at Monte Carlo as anywhere else. And she went.

'She played pretty boldly, I'm told. Died in a hotel there. Very sad end Exile . . . Not – not what one considers meet . . . A natural leader of our English people . . . Uprooted. So I . . .

'Yet after all,' harped the vicar, 'it comes to very little. A nuisance, of course. Children cannot run about so freely as they used to do, what with ant bites and so forth. Perhaps it's as well . . . There used to be talk – as though this stuff would revolutionise everything . . . But there is something that defies all these forces of the new . . . I don't know of course. I'm not one of your modern philosophers – explain everything with ether and atoms. Evolution. Rubbish like that. What I mean is something the 'ologies don't include. Matter of reason – not understanding. Ripe wisdom. Human nature. *Aere perennius*. . . Call it what you will.'

And so at last it came to the last time.

The vicar had no intimation of what lay so close upon him. He did his customary walk, over by Farthing Down, as he had done it for more than a score of years, and so to the place whence he would watch young Caddles. He did the rise over by the chalk-pit crest a little puffily – he had long since lost the muscular Christian stride of early days; but Caddles was not at his work, and then, as he skirted the thicket of giant bracken that was beginning to obscure and overshadow the hanger, he came upon the monster's huge form seated on the hill – brooding as it were upon the world. Caddles's knees were drawn up, his cheek was on his hand, his head a

little aslant. He sat with his shoulder towards the vicar, so that those perplexed eyes could not be seen. He must have been thinking very intently – at any rate he was sitting very still . . .

He never turned round. He never knew that the vicar, who had played so large a part in shaping his life, looked then at him for the very last of innumerable times – did not know even that he was there. (So it is so many partings happen.) The vicar was struck at the time by the fact that, after all, no one on earth had the slightest idea of what this great monster thought about when he saw fit to rest from his labours. But he was too indolent to follow up that new theme that day; he fell back from its suggestion into his older grooves of thought.

'*Aere perennius,*' he whispered, walking slowly homeward by a path that no longer ran straight athwart the turf after its former fashion, but wound circuitously to avoid new-sprung tussocks of giant grass. 'No! nothing is changed. Dimensions are nothing. The simple round, the common way – '

And that night, quite painlessly, and all unknowing, he himself went the common way – out of this Mystery of Change he had spent his life in denying.

They buried him in the churchyard of Cheasing Eyebright, near to the largest yew, and the modest tombstone bearing his epitaph – it ended with: *Ut in principio, nunc est et semper* – was almost immediately hidden from the eye of man by a spread of giant grey tasselled grass too stout for scythe or sheep, that came sweeping like a fog over the village out of the germinating moisture of the valley meadows in which the Food of the Gods had been working.

BOOK THREE

The Harvest of the Food

CHAPTER ONE

The Altered World

Change played in its new fashion with the world for twenty years. To most men the new things came little by little and day by day, remarkably enough, but not so abruptly as to overwhelm. But to one man at least the full accumulation of those two decades of the Food's work was to be revealed suddenly and amazingly in one day. For our purpose it is convenient to take him for that one day and to tell something of the things he saw. This man was a convict, a prisoner for life – his crime is no concern of ours – whom the law saw fit to pardon after twenty years. One summer morning this poor wretch, who had left the world a young man of three-and-twenty, found himself thrust out again from the grey simplicity of toil and discipline that had become his life into a dazzling freedom. They had put unaccustomed clothes upon him; his hair had been growing for some weeks, and he had parted it now for some days, and there he stood, in a sort of shabby and clumsy newness of body and mind, blinking with his eyes and blinking indeed with his soul, *outside* again, trying to realise one incredible thing, that after all he was again for a little while in the world of life, and for all other incredible things, totally unprepared. He was so fortunate as to have a brother who cared enough for their distant common memories to come and meet him and clasp his hand – a brother he had left a little lad, and who was now a bearded prosperous man – whose very eyes were unfamiliar. And together he and this stranger from his kindred came down into the town of Dover, saying little to one another and feeling many things.

They sat for a space in a public-house, the one answering the questions of the other about this person and that, reviving queer old points of view, brushing aside endless new aspects and new perspectives, and then it was time to go to the station and take the London train. Their names and the personal things they had to talk of do not matter to our story, but only the changes and all the strangeness that this poor returning soul found in the once familiar world.

In Dover itself he remarked little except the goodness of beer from pewter – never before had there been such a draught of beer, and it brought tears of gratitude to his eyes. 'Beer's as good as ever,' said he, believing it infinitely better . . .

It was only as the train rattled them past Folkestone that he could look out beyond his more immediate emotions, to see what had happened to the world. He peered out of the window. 'It's sunny,' he said for the twelfth

time. 'I couldn't ha' had better weather.' And then for the first time it dawned upon him that there were novel disproportions in the world. 'Lord sakes,' he cried, sitting up and looking animated for the first time, 'but them's mortal great thissels growing out there on the bank by that broom. If so be they *be* thissels? Or 'ave I been forgetting?' But they were thistles, and what he took for tall bushes of broom was the new grass, and amidst these things a company of British soldiers – red-coated as ever – was skirmishing in accordance with the directions of the drill book that had been partially revised after the Boer War. Then whack! into a tunnel, and then into Sandling Junction, which was now embedded and dark – its lamps were all alight – in a great thicket of rhododendron that had crept out of some adjacent gardens and grown enormously up the valley. There was a train of trucks on the Sandgate siding piled high with rhododendron logs, and here it was the returning citizen heard first of Boomfood.

As they sped out into a country again that seemed absolutely unchanged, the two brothers were hard at their explanations. The one was full of eager, dull questions; the other had never thought, had never troubled to see the thing as a single fact, and he was allusive and difficult to follow. 'It's this here Boomfood stuff,' he said, touching his bottom rock of knowledge. 'Don't you know? 'Aven't they told you – any of 'em? Boomfood! You know – Boomfood. What all the election's about. Scientific sort of stuff. 'Asn't no one ever told you?'

He thought prison had made his brother a fearful duffer not to know that.

They made wide shots at each other by way of question and answer. Between these scraps of talk were intervals of window-gazing. At first the man's interest in things was vague and general. His imagination had been busy with what old so-and-so would say, how so-and-so would look, how he would say to all and sundry certain things that would present his 'putting away' in a mitigated light. This Boomfood came in at first as it were a thing in an odd paragraph of the newspapers, then as a source of intellectual difficulty with his brother. But it came to him presently that Boomfood was persistently coming in upon any topic he began.

In those days the world was a patchwork of transition, so that this great new fact came to him in a series of shocks of contrast. The process of change had not been uniform; it had spread from one centre of distribution here and another centre there. The country was in patches: great areas where the Food was still to come, and areas where it was already in the soil and in the air, sporadic and contagious. It was a bold new motif creeping in among ancient and venerable airs.

The contrast was very vivid indeed along the line from Dover to London at that time. For a space they traversed just such a countryside as he had known since his childhood, the small oblongs of field, hedge-lined, of a size for pigmy horses to plough, the little roads three cart-widths wide, the elms and oaks and poplars dotting these fields about, little thickets of willow

beside the streams; ricks of hay no higher than a giant's knees, dolls' cottages with diamond panes, brickfields and straggling village streets, the larger houses of the petty great, flower-grown railway banks, garden-set stations, and all the little things of the vanished nineteenth century still holding out against Immensity. Here and there would be a patch of wind-sown, wind-tattered giant thistle defying the axe; here and there a ten-foot puff-ball or the ashen stems of some burnt-out patch of monster grass; but that was all there was to hint at the coming of the Food.

For a couple of score of miles there was nothing else to foreshadow in any way the strange bigness of the wheat and of the weeds that were hidden from him not a dozen miles from his route just over the hills in the Cheasing Eyebright valley. And then presently the traces of the Food would begin. The first striking thing was the great new viaduct at Tonbridge, where the swamp of the choked Medway (due to a giant variety of *Chara*) began in those days. Then again the little country, and then, as the petty multitudinous immensity of London spread out under its haze, the traces of man's fight to keep out greatness became abundant and incessant.

In that south-eastern region of London at that time, and all about where Cossar and his children lived, the Food had become mysteriously insurgent at a hundred points; the little life went on amidst daily portents that only the deliberation of their increase, the slow parallel growth of usage to their presence, had robbed of their warning. But this returning citizen peered out to see for the first time the facts of the Food strange and predominant, scarred and blackened areas, big unsightly defences and preparations, barracks and arsenals that this subtle, persistent influence had forced into the life of men.

Here, on an ampler scale, the experience of the first Experimental Farm had been repeated time and again. It had been in the inferior and accidental things of life – under foot and in waste places, irregularly and irrelevantly – that the coming of a new force and new issues had first declared itself. There were great evil-smelling yards and enclosures where some invincible jungle of weed furnished fuel for gigantic machinery (little cockneys came to stare at its clangorous oiliness and tip the men a sixpence); there were roads and tracks for big motors and vehicles – roads made of the interwoven fibres of hypertrophied hemp; there were towers containing steam sirens that could yell at once and warn the world against any new insurgence of vermin, or, what was queerer, venerable church towers conspicuously fitted with a mechanical scream. There were little red-painted refuge huts and garrison shelters, each with its 300-yard rifle range, where the rifle-men practised daily with soft-nosed ammunition at targets in the shape of monstrous rats.

Six times since the day of the Skinners there had been outbreaks of giant rats – each time from the south-west London sewers, and now they were as much an accepted fact there as tigers in the delta by Calcutta.

The man's brother had bought a paper in a heedless sort of way at Sandling, and at last this chanced to catch the eye of the released man. He opened the unfamiliar sheets – they seemed to him to be smaller, more numerous and different in type from the papers of the times before – and he found himself confronted with innumerable pictures about things so strange as to be uninteresting, and with tall columns of printed matter whose headings, for the most part, were as unmeaning as though they had been written in a foreign tongue – 'Great Speech by Mr Caterham'; 'The Boomfood Laws.'

'Who's this here Caterham?' he asked, in an attempt to make conversation.

'*He's* all right,' said his brother.

'Ah! Sort of politician, eh?'

'Goin' to turn out the Government. Jolly well time he did.'

'Ah!' He reflected. 'I suppose all the lot *I* used to know – Chamberlain, Rosebery – all that lot – *What?*'

His brother had grasped his wrist and pointed out of the window.

'That's the Cossars!' The eyes of the released prisoner followed the finger's direction and saw –

'My Gawd!' he cried, for the first time really overcome with amazement. The paper dropped into final forgottenness between his feet. Through the trees he could see very distinctly, standing in an easy attitude, the legs wide apart and the hand grasping a ball as if about to throw it, a gigantic human figure a good forty feet high. The figure glittered in the sunlight, clad in a suit of woven white metal and belted with a broad belt of steel. For a moment it focused all attention, and then the eye was wrested to another more distant giant who stood prepared to catch, and it became apparent that the whole area of that great bay in the hills just north of Sevenoaks had been scarred to gigantic ends.

A hugely banked entrenchment overhung the chalk pit, in which stood the house, a monstrous squat Egyptian shape that Cossar had built for his sons when the Giant Nursery had served its turn, and behind was a great dark shed that might have covered a cathedral, in which a spluttering incandescence came and went, and from out of which came a titanic hammering to beat upon the ear. Then the attention leapt back to the giant as the great ball of iron-bound timber soared up out of his hand.

The two men stood up and stared. The ball seemed as big as a cask.

'Caught!' cried the man from prison, as a tree blotted out the thrower.

The train looked on these things only for the fraction of a minute and then passed behind trees into the Chislehurst tunnel. 'My Gawd!' said the man from prison again, as the darkness closed about them. 'Why! that chap was as 'igh as a 'ouse.'

'That's them young Cossars,' said his brother, jerking his head allusively – 'what all this trouble's about . . . '

They emerged again to discover more siren-surmounted towers, more red huts, and then the clustering villas of the outer suburbs. The art of bill-sticking had lost nothing in the interval, and from countless tall hoardings, from house ends, from palings and a hundred such points of vantage came the polychromatic appeals of the great Boomfood election. 'Caterham', 'Boomfood' and 'Jack the Giant-Killer' again and again and again, and monstrous caricatures and distortions – a hundred varieties of misrepresentations of those great and shining figures they had passed so nearly only a few minutes before.

2

It had been the purpose of the younger brother to do a very magnificent thing, to celebrate this return to life by a dinner at some restaurant of indisputable quality, a dinner that should be followed by all that glittering succession of impressions the Music Halls of those days were so capable of giving. It was a worthy plan to wipe off the more superficial stains of the prison house by this display of free indulgence; but so far as the second item went the plan was changed. The dinner stood, but there was a desire already more powerful than the appetite for shows, already more efficient in turning the man's mind away from his grim prepossession with his past than any theatre could be, and that was an enormous curiosity and per-plexity about this Boomfood and these Boom children – this new portentous giantry that seemed to dominate the world. 'I 'aven't the 'ang of 'em,' he said. 'They disturve me.'

His brother had that fineness of mind that can even set aside a con-templated hospitality. 'It's *your* evening, dear old boy,' he said. 'We'll try to get into the mass meeting at the People's Palace.'

And at last the man from prison had the luck to find himself wedged into a packed multitude and staring from afar at a little brightly lit platform under an organ and a gallery. The organist had been playing something that had set boots tramping as the people swarmed in; but that was over now.

Hardly had the man from prison settled into place and done his quarrel with an importunate stranger who elbowed, before Caterham came. He walked out of a shadow towards the middle of the platform, the most insignificant little pigmy, away there in the distance, a little black figure with a pink dab for a face – in profile one saw his quite distinctive aquiline nose – a little figure that trailed after it most inexplicably – a cheer. A cheer it was that began away there and grew and spread. A little spluttering of voices about the platform at first that suddenly leapt up into a flame of sound and swept athwart the whole mass of humanity within the building and without. How they cheered! Hooray! Hooray!

No one in all those myriads cheered like the man from prison. The tears

poured down his face, and he only stopped cheering at last because the thing had choked him. You must have been in prison as long as he before you can understand, or even begin to understand, what it means to a man to let his lungs go in a crowd. (But for all that he did not even pretend to himself that he knew what all this emotion was about.) Hooray! Oh God! – Hoo-ray!

And then a sort of silence. Caterham had subsided to a conspicuous patience, and subordinate and inaudible persons were saying and doing formal and insignificant things. It was like hearing voices through the noise of leaves in spring. 'Wawawawa – ' What did it matter? People in the audience talked to one another. 'Wawawawawa – ' the thing went on. Would that grey-headed duffer never have done? Interrupting? Of course they were interrupting. 'Wa, wa, wa, wa – ' But shall we hear Caterham any better?

Meanwhile at any rate there was Caterham to stare at, and one could stand and study the distant prospect of the great man's features. He was easy to draw was this man, and already the world had him to study at leisure on lamp chimneys and children's plates, on Anti-Boomfood medals and Anti-Boomfood flags, on the selvedges of Caterham silks and cottons and in the linings of Good Old English Caterham hats. He pervades all the caricature of that time. One sees him as a sailor standing to an old-fashioned gun, a port-fire labelled 'New Boomfood Laws' in his hand, while in the sea wallows that huge, ugly, threatening monster, 'Boomfood'; or he is cap-à-pie in armour, St George's cross on shield and helm, and a cowardly titanic Caliban sitting amidst desecrations at the mouth of a horrid cave declines his gauntlet of the 'New Boomfood Regulations'; or he comes flying down as Perseus and rescues a chained and beautiful Andromeda (labelled distinctly about her belt as 'Civilisation') from a wallowing waste of sea monster bearing upon its various necks and claws 'Irreligion', 'Trampling Egotism', 'Mechanism', 'Monstrosity', and the like. But it was as 'Jack the Giant-Killer' that the popular imagination considered Caterham most correctly cast, and it was in the vein of a Jack the Giant-Killer poster that the man from prison enlarged that distant miniature.

The 'Wawawawa' came abruptly to an end.

He's done. He's sitting down. Yes! No! Yes! It's Caterham! 'Caterham!' 'Caterham!' And then came the cheers.

It takes a multitude to make such a stillness as followed that disorder of cheering. A man alone in a wilderness – it's stillness of a sort no doubt, but he hears himself breathe, he hears himself move, he hears all sorts of things. Here the voice of Caterham was the one single thing heard, a thing very bright and clear, like a little light burning in a black velvet recess. Hear indeed! One heard him as though he spoke at one's elbow.

It was stupendously effective to the man from prison, that gesticulating

little figure in a halo of light, in a halo of rich and swaying sounds; behind it, partially effaced as it were, sat its supporters on the platform, and in the foreground was a wide perspective of innumerable backs and profiles, a vast multitudinous attention. That little figure seemed to have absorbed the substance from them all.

Caterham spoke of our ancient institutions. 'Earearear,' roared the crowd. 'Ear! ear!' said the man from prison. He spoke of our ancient spirit of order and justice. 'Earearear!' roared the crowd. 'Ear! Ear!' cried the man from prison, deeply moved. He spoke of the wisdom of our forefathers, of the slow growth of venerable institutions, of moral and social traditions, that fitted our English national characteristics as the skin fits the hand. 'Ear! Ear!' groaned the man from prison, with tears of excitement on his cheeks. And now all these things were to go into the melting pot. Yes, into the melting pot! Because three men in London twenty years ago had seen fit to mix something indescribable in a bottle, all the order and sanctity of things – Cries of 'No! No!' – Well, if it was not to be so, they must exert themselves, they must say goodbye to hesitation – Here there came a gust of cheering. They must say goodbye to hesitation and half measures.

'We have heard, gentlemen,' cried Caterham, 'of nettles that become giant nettles. At first they are no more than other nettles – little plants that a firm hand may grasp and wrench away; but if you leave them – if you leave them, they grow with such a power of poisonous expansion that at last you must needs have axe and rope, you must needs have danger to life and limb, you must needs have toil and distress – men may be killed in their felling, men may be killed in their felling –'

There came a stir and interruption, and then the man from prison heard Caterham's voice again, ringing clear and strong: 'Learn about Boomfood from Boomfood itself and –' He paused – '*Grasp your nettle before it is too late!*'

He stopped and stood wiping his lips. 'A crystal,' cried someone, 'a crystal,' and then came that same strange swift growth to thunderous tumult, until the whole world seemed cheering ...

The man from prison came out of the hall at last, marvellously stirred, and with that in his face that marks those who have seen a vision. He knew, everyone knew; his ideas were no longer vague. He had come back to a world in crisis, to the immediate decision of a stupendous issue. He must play his part in the great conflict like a man – like a free, responsible man. The antagonism presented itself as a picture. On the one hand those easy gigantic mail-clad figures of the morning – one saw them now in a different light – on the other this little black-clad gesticulating creature under the limelight, that pigmy thing with its ordered flow of melodious persuasion, its little, marvellously penetrating voice, John Caterham – 'Jack the Giant-Killer'. They must all unite to 'grasp the nettle' before it was 'too late'.

The tallest and strongest and most regarded of all the children of the Food were the three sons of Cossar. The mile or so of land near Sevenoaks in which their boyhood passed became so trenched, so dug out and twisted about, so covered with sheds and huge working models and all the play of their developing powers, it was like no other place on earth. And long since it had become too little for the things they sought to do. The eldest son was a mighty schemer of wheeled engines; he had made himself a sort of giant bicycle that no road in the world had room for, no bridge could bear. There it stood, a great thing of wheels and engines, capable of two hundred and fifty miles an hour, useless save that now and then he would mount it and fling himself backwards and forwards across that cumbered work-yard. He had meant to go around the little world with it; he had made it with that intention, while he was still no more than a dreaming boy. Now its spokes were rusted deep red like wounds, wherever the enamel had been chipped away.

'You must make a road for it first, Sonnie,' Cossar had said, 'before you can do that.'

So one morning about dawn the young giant and his brothers had set to work to make a road about the world. They seem to have had an inkling of opposition impending, and they had worked with remarkable vigour. The world had discovered them soon enough, driving that road as straight as the flight of a bullet towards the English Channel, already some miles of it levelled and made and stamped hard. They had been stopped before midday by a vast crowd of excited people, owners of land, land agents, local authorities, lawyers, policemen, soldiers even.

'We're making a road,' the biggest boy had explained.

'Make a road by all means,' said the leading lawyer on the ground, 'but please respect the rights of other people. You have already infringed the private rights of twenty-seven private proprietors; let alone the special privileges and property of an urban district board, nine parish councils, a county council, two gasworks and a railway company . . .'

'Goodney!' said the elder boy Cossar.

'You will have to stop it.'

'But don't you want a nice straight road in the place of all these rotten rutty little lanes?'

'I won't say it wouldn't be advantageous, but – '

'It isn't to be done,' said the eldest Cossar boy, picking up his tools.

'Not in this way,' said the lawyer, 'certainly.'

'How is it to be done?'

The leading lawyer's answer had been complicated and vague.

Cossar had come down to see the mischief his children had done, and reproved them severely and laughed enormously and seemed to be extremely happy over the affair. 'You boys must wait a bit,' he shouted up to them, 'before you can do things like that.'

'The lawyer told us we must begin by preparing a scheme, and getting special powers and all sorts of rot. Said it would take us years.'

'*We'll* have a scheme before long, little boy,' cried Cossar, hands to his mouth as he shouted, 'never fear. For a bit you'd better play about and make models of the things you want to do.'

They did as he told them like obedient sons.

But for all that the Cossar lads brooded a little.

'It's all very well,' said the second to the first, 'but I don't always want just to play about and plan, I want to do something *real*, you know. We didn't come into this world so strong as we are, just to play about in this messy little bit of ground, you know, and take little walks and keep out of the towns' – for by that time they were forbidden all boroughs and urban districts. 'Doing nothing's just wicked. Can't we find out something the little people *want* done and do it for them – just for the fun of doing it?

'Lots of them haven't houses fit to live in,' said the second boy, 'Let's go and build 'em a house close up to London that will hold heaps and heaps of them and be ever so comfortable and nice, and let's make 'em a nice little road to where they all go and do business – nice straight little road, and make it all as nice as nice. We'll make it all so clean and pretty that they won't any of them be able to live grubby and beastly like most of them do now. Water enough for them to wash with, we'll have – you know they're so dirty now that nine out of ten of their houses haven't even baths in them, the filthy little skunks! You know, the ones that have baths spit insults at the ones that haven't, instead of helping them to get them – and call 'em the Great Unwashed. *You* know. We'll alter all that. And we'll make electricity light and cook and clean up for them, and all. Fancy! They make their women – women who are going to be mothers – crawl about and scrub floors!

'We could make it all beautifully. We could bank up a valley in that range of hills over there and make a nice reservoir, and we could make a big place here to generate our electricity and have it all simply lovely. Couldn't we, brother? And then perhaps they'd let us do some other things.'

'Yes,' said the eldest brother, 'we could do it *very* nice for them.'

'Then *let's*,' said the second brother.

'*I* don't mind,' said the eldest brother, and looked about for a handy tool. And that led to another dreadful bother.

Agitated multitudes were at them in no time, telling them for a thousand reasons to stop, telling them to stop for no reason at all – babbling, confused and varied multitudes. The place they were building was too high – it couldn't possibly be safe. It was ugly; it interfered with the letting

of proper-sized houses in the neighbourhood; it ruined the tone of the neighbourhood; it was unneighbourly; it was contrary to the local Building Regulations; it infringed the right of the local authority to muddle about with a minute expensive electric supply of its own; it interfered with the concerns of the local water company.

Local Government Board clerks roused themselves to judicial obstruction. The little lawyer turned up again to represent about a dozen threatened interests; local landowners appeared in opposition; people with mysterious claims demanded to be bought off at exorbitant rates; the Trades Unions of all the building trades lifted up collective voices; and a ring of dealers in all sorts of building materials became a bar. Extra-ordinary associations of people with prophetic visions of aesthetic horrors rallied to protect the scenery of the place where they would build the great house, of the valley where they would bank up the water. These last people were absolutely the worst asses of the lot, the Cossar boys considered. That beautiful house of the Cossar boys was just like a walking-stick thrust into a wasps' nest, in no time.

'I never did!' said the eldest boy.

'We can't go on,' said the second brother.

'Rotten little beasts they are,' said the third of the brothers; 'we can't do *anything!*'

'Even when it's for their own comfort. Such a *nice* place we'd have made for them too.'

'They seem to spend their silly little lives getting in each other's way,' said the eldest boy. 'Rights and laws and regulations and rascalities; it's like a game of spellicans . . . Well, anyhow, they'll have to live in their grubby, dirty, silly little houses for a bit longer. It's very evident *we* can't go on with this.'

And the Cossar children left that great house unfinished, a mere hole for foundations and the beginnings of a wall, and sulked back to their big enclosure. After a time the hole was filled with water and with stagnation, and weeds and vermin, and the Food, either dropped there by the sons of Cossar or blowing thither as dust, set growth going in its usual fashion. Water voles came out over the country and did infinite havoc, and one day a farmer caught his pigs drinking there, and instantly and with great presence of mind – for he knew of the great hog of Oakham – slew them all. And from that deep pool it was the mosquitoes came, quite terrible mosquitoes, whose only virtue was that the sons of Cossar, after being bitten for a little, could stand the thing no longer, but chose a moonlight night when law and order were abed and drained the water clean away into the river by Brook.

But they left the big weeds and the big water voles and all sorts of big undesirable things still living and breeding on the site they had chosen – the site on which the fair great house of the little people might have towered to heaven . . .

That had been in the boyhood of the sons, but now they were nearly men. And the chains had been tightening upon them and tightening with every year of growth. Each year they grew, and the Food spread and great things multiplied, each year the stress and tension rose. The Food had been at first for the great mass of mankind a distant marvel, and now It was coming home to every threshold, and threatening, pressing against and distorting the whole order of life. It blocked this, it overturned that; it changed natural products, and by changing natural products it stopped employments and threw men out of work by the hundred thousands; it swept over boundaries and turned the world of trade into a world of cataclysms; no wonder mankind hated it.

And since it is easier to hate animate than inanimate things, animals more than plants, and one's fellow men more completely than any animals, the fear and trouble engendered by giant nettles and six-foot grass blades, awful insects and tiger-like vermin, grew all into one great power of detestation that aimed itself with a simple directness at that scattered band of great human beings, the Children of the Food. That hatred had become the central force in political affairs. The old party lines had been traversed and effaced altogether under the insistence of these newer issues, and the conflict lay now with the party of the temporisers, who were for putting little political men to control and regulate the Food, and the party of reaction for whom Caterham spoke, speaking always with a more sinister ambiguity, crystallising his intention first in one threatening phrase and then another, now that men must 'prune the bramble growths', now that they must find a 'cure for elephantiasis', and at last upon the eve of the election that they must 'grasp the nettle'.

One day the three sons of Cossar, who were now no longer boys but men, sat among the masses of their futile work and talked together after their fashion of all these things. They had been working all day at one of a series of great and complicated trenches their father had bid them make, and now it was sunset, and they sat in the little garden space before the great house and looked at the world and rested, until the little servants within should say their food was ready.

You must figure these mighty forms, forty feet high the least of them was, reclining on a patch of turf that would have seemed a stubble of reeds to a common man. One sat up and chipped earth from his huge boots with an iron girder he grasped in his hand; the second rested on his elbow; the third whittled a pine tree into shape and made a smell of resin in the air. They were clothed not in cloth but in undergarments of woven rope and outer clothes of felted aluminium wire; they were shod with timber and

iron, and the links and buttons and belts of their clothing were all of plated steel. The great single-storeyed house they lived in, Egyptian in its massiveness, half built of monstrous blocks of chalk and half excavated from the living rock of the hill, had a front a full hundred feet in height, and beyond, the chimneys and wheels, the cranes and covers of their work sheds rose marvellously against the sky. Through a circular window in the house there was visible a spout from which some white-hot metal dripped and dripped in measured drops into a receptacle out of sight. The place was enclosed and rudely fortified by monstrous banks of earth, backed with steel both over the crests of the downs above and across the dip of the valley. It needed something of common size to mark the nature of the scale. The train that came rattling from Sevenoaks athwart their vision, and presently plunged into the tunnel out of their sight, looked by contrast with them like some small-sized automatic toy.

'They have made all the woods this side of Ightham out of bounds,' said one, 'and moved the board that was out by Knockholt two miles and more this way.'

'It is the least they could do,' said the youngest, after a pause. 'They are trying to take the wind out of Caterham's sails.'

'It's not enough for that, and – it is almost too much for us,' said the third.

'They are cutting us off from Brother Redwood. Last time I went to him the red notices had crept a mile in, either way. The road to him along the downs is no more than a narrow lane.'

The speaker thought. 'What has come to our brother Redwood?'

'Why?' said the eldest brother.

The speaker hacked a bough from his pine. 'He was like – as though he wasn't awake. He didn't seem to listen to what I had to say. And he said something of – love.'

The youngest tapped his girder on the edge of his iron sole and laughed. 'Brother Redwood,' he said, 'has dreams.'

Neither spoke for a space. Then the eldest brother said, 'This cooping up and cooping up grows more than I can bear. At last, I believe, they will draw a line round our boots and tell us to live on that.'

The middle brother swept aside a heap of pine boughs with one hand and shifted his attitude. 'What they do now is nothing to what they will do when Caterham has power.'

'If he gets power,' said the youngest brother, smiting the ground with his girder.

'As he will,' said the eldest, staring at his feet.

The middle brother ceased his lopping, and his eye went to the great banks that sheltered them about. 'Then, brothers,' he said, 'our youth will be over, and, as Father Redwood said to us long ago, we must quit ourselves like men.'

'Yes,' said the eldest brother; 'but what exactly does that mean? Just what does it mean – when that day of trouble comes?'

He too glanced at those rude vast suggestions of entrenchment about them, looking not so much at them as through them and over the hills to the innumerable multitudes beyond. Something of the same sort came into all their minds – a vision of little people coming out to war, in a flood, the little people, inexhaustible, incessant, malignant . . .

'They are little,' said the youngest brother; 'but they have numbers beyond counting, like the sands of the sea.'

'They have arms – they have weapons even, that our brothers in Sunderland have made.'

'Besides, brothers, except for vermin, except for little accidents with evil things, what have we seen of killing?'

'I know,' said the eldest brother. 'For all that – we are what we are. When the day of trouble comes we must do the thing we have to do.'

He closed his knife with a snap – the blade was the length of a man – and used his new pine staff to help himself rise. He stood up and turned towards the squat grey immensity of the house. The crimson of the sunset caught him as he rose, caught the mail and clasps about his neck and the woven metal of his arms, and to the eyes of his brothers it seemed as though he was suddenly suffused with blood.

As the young giant rose a little black figure became visible to him against that western incandescence on the top of the embankment that towered above the summit of the down. The black limbs waved in ungainly gestures. Something in the fling of the limbs suggested haste to the young giant's mind. He waved his pine mast in reply, filled the whole valley with his vast Hello! threw a 'Something's up!' to his brothers, and set off in twenty-foot strides to meet and help his father.

5

It chanced too that a young man who was not a giant was delivering his soul about these sons of Cossar just at that same time. He had come over the hills beyond Sevenoaks, he and his friend, and he it was did the talking. In the hedge as they came along they had heard a pitiful squealing, and had intervened to rescue three nestling tits from the attack of a couple of giant ants. That adventure it was had set him talking.

'Reactionary!' he was saying, as they came within sight of the Cossar encampment. 'Who wouldn't be reactionary? Look at that square of ground, that space of God's earth that was once sweet and fair, torn, desecrated, disembowelled! Those sheds! That great wind-wheel! That monstrous wheeled machine! Those dykes! Look at those three monsters squatting there, plotting some ugly devilment or other! Look – look at all the land!'

His friend glanced at his face. 'You have been listening to Caterham,' he said.

'Using my eyes. Looking a little into the peace and order of the past we leave behind. This foul Food is the last shape of the Devil, still set as ever upon the ruin of our world. Think what the world must have been before our days, what it was still when our mothers bore us, and see it now! Think how these slopes once smiled under the golden harvest, how the hedges, full of sweet little flowers, parted the modest portion of this man from that, how the ruddy farmhouses dotted the land, and the voice of the church bells from yonder tower stilled the whole world each Sabbath into Sabbath prayer. And now, every year, still more and more of monstrous weeds, of monstrous vermin, and these giants growing all about us, straddling over us, blundering against all that is subtle and sacred in our world. Why here – Look!'

He pointed, and his friend's eyes followed the line of his white finger.

'One of their footmarks. See! It has smashed itself three feet deep and more, a pitfall for horse and rider, a trap to the unwary. There is a briar rose smashed to death; there is grass uprooted and a teazle crushed aside, a farmer's drainpipe snapped and the edge of the pathway broken down. Destruction! So they are doing all over the world, all over the order and decency the world of men has made. Trampling on all things. Reaction! What else?'

'But – reaction. What do you hope to do?'

'Stop it!' cried the young man from Oxford. 'Before it is too late.'

'But – '

'It's *not* impossible,' cried the young man from Oxford, with a jump in his voice. 'We want the firm hand; we want the subtle plan, the resolute mind. We have been mealy-mouthed and weak-handed; we have trifled and temporised and the Food has grown and grown. Yet even now – '

He stopped for a moment. 'This is the echo of Caterham,' said his friend.

'Even now. Even now there is hope – abundant hope, if only we make sure of what we want and what we mean to destroy. The mass of people are with us, much more with us than they were a few years ago; the law is with us, the constitution and order of society, the spirit of the established religions, the customs and habits of mankind are with us – and against the Food. Why should we temporise? Why should we lie? We hate it, we don't want it; why then should we have it? Do you mean to just grizzle and obstruct passively and do nothing – till the sands are out?'

He stopped short and turned about. 'Look at that grove of nettles there. In the midst of them are homes – deserted – where once clean families of simple men played out their honest lives!

'And there!' he swung round to where the young Cossars muttered to one another of their wrongs.

'Look at them! And I know their father, a brute, a sort of brute beast

with an intolerant loud voice, a creature who has ran amuck in our all-too-merciful world for the last thirty years and more. An engineer! To him all that we hold dear and sacred is nothing. Nothing! The splendid traditions of our race and land, the noble institutions, the venerable order, the broad slow march from precedent to precedent that has made our English people great and this sunny island free – it is all an idle tale, told and done with. Some claptrap about the Future is worth all these sacred things . . . The sort of man who would run a tramway over his mother's grave if he thought that was the cheapest line the tramway could take . . . And you think to temporise, to make some scheme of compromise, that will enable you to live in your way while that – that machinery – lives in its. I tell you it is hopeless – hopeless. As well make treaties with a tiger! They want things monstrous – we want them sane and sweet. It is one thing or the other.'

'But what can you do?'

'Much! All! Stop the Food! They are still scattered, these giants; still immature and disunited. Chain them, gag them, muzzle them. At any cost stop them. It is their world or ours! Stop the Food. Shut up these men who make it. Do anything to stop Cossar! You don't seem to remember – one generation – only one generation needs holding down, and then – Then we could level those mounds there, fill up their footsteps, take the ugly sirens from our church towers, smash all our elephant guns, and turn our faces again to the old order, the ripe old civilisation for which the soul of man is fitted.'

'It's a mighty effort.'

'For a mighty end. And if we don't? Don't you see the prospect before us clear as day? Everywhere the giants will increase and multiply; everywhere they will make and scatter the Food. The grass will grow gigantic in our fields, the weeds in our hedges, the vermin in the thickets, the rats in the drains. More and more and more. This is only a beginning. The insect world will rise on us, the plant world, the very fishes in the sea, will swamp and drown our ships. Tremendous growths will obscure and hide our houses, smother our churches, smash and destroy all the order of our cities, and we shall become no more than a feeble vermin under the heels of the new race. Mankind will be swamped and drowned in things of its own begetting! And all for nothing! Size! Mere size! Enlargement and *da capo*. Already we go picking our way among the first beginnings of the coming time. And all we do is to say, "How inconvenient!" To grumble and do nothing. *No!*'

He raised his hand.

'Let them do the thing they have to do! So also will I. I am for Reaction – unstinted and fearless Reaction. Unless you mean to take this Food also, what else is there to do in all the world? We have trifled in the middle ways too long. You! Trifling in the middle ways is your habit, your circle of

existence, your space and time. So, not I! I am against the Food, with all my strength and purpose against the Food.'

He turned on his companion's grunt of dissent. 'Where are you?'

'It's a complicated business – '

'Oh! – Driftwood!' said the young man from Oxford, very bitterly, with a fling of all his limbs. 'The middle way is nothingness. It is one thing or the other. Eat or destroy. Eat or destroy! What else is there to do?'

CHAPTER TWO

The Giant Lovers

Now it chanced in the days when Caterham was campaigning against the Boom-children before the General Election that was – amidst the most tragic and terrible circumstances – to bring him into power, that the giant princess, that Serene Highness whose early nutrition had played so great a part in the brilliant career of Dr Winkles, had come from the kingdom of her father to England, on an occasion that was deemed important. She was affianced for reasons of state to a certain prince – and the wedding was to be made an event of international significance. There had arisen mysterious delays. Rumour and Imagination collaborated in the story and many things were said. There were suggestions of a recalcitrant prince who declared he would not be made to look like a fool – at least to this extent. People sympathised with him. That is the most significant aspect of the affair.

Now it may seem a strange thing, but it is a fact that the giant princess, when she came to England, knew of no other giants whatever. She had lived in a world where tact is almost a passion and reservations the air of one's life. They had kept the thing from her; they had hedged her about from sight or suspicion of any gigantic form, until her appointed coming to England was due. Until she met young Redwood she had no inkling that there was such a thing as another giant in the world.

In the kingdom of the father of the princess there were wild wastes of upland and mountains where she had been accustomed to roam freely. She loved the sunrise and the sunset and all the great drama of the open heavens more than anything else in the world, but among a people at once so democratic and so vehemently loyal as the English her freedom was much restricted. People came in brakes, in excursion trains, in organised multitudes to see her; they would cycle long distances to stare at her, and it was necessary to rise betimes if she would walk in peace. It was still near the dawn that morning when young Redwood came upon her.

The great park near the palace where she lodged stretched, for a score of miles and more, west and south of the western palace gates. The chestnut trees of its avenues reached high above her head. Each one as she passed it

seemed to proffer a more abundant wealth of blossom. For a time she was content with sight and scent, but at last she was won over by these offers, and set herself so busily to choose and pick that she did not perceive young Redwood until he was close upon her.

She moved among the chestnut trees, with the destined lover drawing near to her, unanticipated, unsuspected. She thrust her hands in among the branches, breaking them and gathering them. She was alone in the world. Then –

She looked up, and in that moment she was mated.

We must needs put our imaginations to his stature to see the beauty he saw. That unapproachable greatness that prevents our immediate sympathy with her did not exist for him. There she stood, a gracious girl, the first created being that had ever seemed a mate for him, light and slender, lightly clad, the fresh breeze of the dawn moulding the subtly folding robe upon her against the soft strong lines of her form, and with a great mass of blossoming chestnut branches in her hands. The collar of her robe opened to show the whiteness of her neck and a soft shadowed roundness that passed out of sight towards her shoulders. The breeze had stolen a strand or so of her hair too, and strained its red-tipped brown across her cheek. Her eyes were open blue, and her lips rested always in the promise of a smile as she reached among the branches.

She turned upon him with a start, saw him, and for a space they regarded one another. For her, the sight of him was so amazing, so incredible, as to be, for some moments at least, terrible. He came to her with the shock of a supernatural apparition; he broke all the established law of her world. He was a youth of one-and-twenty then, slenderly built, with his father's darkness and his father's gravity. He was clad in close-fitting easy garments of a sober soft brown leather and in brown hose that shaped him bravely. His head went uncovered in all weathers. They stood regarding one another – she incredulously amazed, and he with his heart beating fast. It was a moment without a prelude, the cardinal meeting of their lives.

For him there was less surprise. He had been seeking her, and yet his heart beat fast. He came towards her, slowly, with his eyes upon her face.

'You are the princess,' he said. 'My father has told me. You are the princess who was given the Food of the Gods.'

'I am the princess – yes,' she said, with eyes of wonder. 'But – what are you?'

'I am the son of the man who made the Food of the Gods.'

'The Food of the Gods!'

'Yes, the Food of the Gods.'

'But – '

Her face expressed infinite perplexity.

'What? I don't understand. The Food of the Gods?'

'You have not heard?'

'The Food of the Gods! *No!*'

She found herself trembling violently. The colour left her face. 'I did not know,' she said. 'Do you mean – ?'

He waited for her.

'Do you mean there are other – giants?'

He repeated, 'Did you not know?'

And she answered, with the growing amazement of realisation, '*No!*'

The whole world and all the meaning of the world was changing for her. A branch of chestnut slipped from her hand. 'Do you mean to say,' she repeated stupidly, 'that there are other giants in the world? That some food – ?'

He caught her amazement.

'You know nothing?' he cried. 'You have never heard of us? You, whom the Food has made akin to us!'

There was terror still in the eyes that stared at him. Her hand rose towards her throat and fell again. She whispered, '*No.*'

It seemed to her that she must weep or faint. Then in a moment she had rule over herself and she was speaking and thinking clearly. 'All this has been kept from me,' she said. 'It is like a dream. I have dreamt – have dreamt such things. But waking – No. Tell me! Tell me! What are you? What is this Food of the Gods? Tell me slowly – and clearly. Why have they kept it from me, that I am not alone?'

2

'Tell me,' she said, and young Redwood, tremulous and excited, set himself to tell her – it was poor and broken telling for a time – of the Food of the Gods and the giant children who were scattered over the world.

You must figure them both, flushed and startled in their bearing; getting at one another's meaning through endless half-heard, half-spoken phrases, repeating, making perplexing breaks and new departures – a wonderful talk, in which she awakened from the ignorance of all her life. And very slowly it became clear to her that she was no exception to the order of mankind, but one of a scattered brotherhood, who had all eaten the Food and grown for ever out of the little limits of the folk beneath their feet. Young Redwood spoke of his father, of Cossar, of the Brothers scattered throughout the country, of the great dawn of wider meaning that had come at last into the history of the world. 'We are in the beginning of a beginning,' he said; 'this world of theirs is only the prelude to the world the Food will make.

'My father believes – and I also believe – that a time will come when littleness will have passed altogether out of the world of man – when giants shall go freely about this earth – their earth – doing continually greater and

more splendid things. But that – that is to come. We are not even the first generation of that – we are the first experiments.'

'And of these things,' she said, 'I knew nothing!'

'There are times when it seems to me almost as if we had come too soon. Someone, I suppose, had to come first. But the world was all unprepared for our coming and for the coming of all the lesser great things that drew their greatness from the Food. There have been blunders; there have been conflicts. The little people hate our kind . . .

'They are hard towards us because they are so little . . . And because our feet are heavy on the things that make their lives. But at any rate they hate us now; they will have none of us – only if we could shrink back to the common size of them would they begin to forgive . . .

'They are happy in houses that are prison cells to us; their cities are too small for us; we go in misery along their narrow ways; we cannot worship in their churches . . .

'We see over their walls and over their protections; we look inadvertently into their upper windows; we look over their customs; their laws are no more than a net about our feet . . .

'Every time we stumble we hear them shouting; every time we blunder against their limits or stretch out to any spacious act . . .

'Our easy paces are wild flights to them, and all they deem great and wonderful no more than dolls' pyramids to us. Their pettiness of method and appliance and imagination hampers and defeats our powers. There are no machines to the power of our hands, no helps to fit our needs. They hold our greatness in servitude by a thousand invisible bands. We are stronger, man for man, a hundred times, but we are disarmed; our very greatness makes us debtors; they claim the land we stand upon; they tax our ampler need of food and shelter, and for all these things we must toil with the tools these dwarfs can make us – and to satisfy their dwarfish fancies . . .

'They pen us in, in every way. Even to live one must cross their boundaries. Even to meet you here today I have passed a limit. All that is reasonable and desirable in life they make out of bounds for us. We may not go into the towns; we may not cross the bridges; we may not step on their ploughed fields or into the harbours of the game they kill. I am cut off now from all our Brethren except the three sons of Cossar, and even that way the passage narrows day by day. One could think they sought occasion against us to do some more evil thing . . . '

'But we are strong,' she said.

'We should be strong – yes. We feel, all of us – you too I know must feel – that we have power, power to do great things, power insurgent in us. But before we can do anything – '

He flung out a hand that seemed to sweep away a world.

'Though I thought I was alone in the world,' she said, after a pause, 'I have thought of these things. They have taught me always that strength was

almost a sin, that it was better to be little than great, that all true religion was to shelter the weak and little, encourage the weak and little, help them to multiply and multiply until at last they crawled over one another, to sacrifice all our strength in their cause. But . . . always I have doubted the thing they taught.'

'This life,' he said, 'these bodies of ours, are not for dying.'

'No.'

'Nor to live in futility. But if we would not do that, it is already plain to all our Brethren a conflict must come. I know not what bitterness of conflict must presently come, before the little folks will suffer us to live as we need to live. All the Brethren have thought of that. Cossar, of whom I told you: he too has thought of that.'

'They are very little and weak.'

'In their way. But you know all the means of death are in their hands, and made for their hands. For hundreds of thousands of years these little people, whose world we invade, have been learning how to kill one another. They are very able at that. They are able in many ways. And besides, they can deceive and change suddenly . . . I do not know . . . There comes a conflict. You – you perhaps are different from us. For us, assuredly, the conflict comes . . . The thing they call War. We know it. In a way we prepare for it. But you know – those little people! – we do not know how to kill, at least we do not want to kill – '

'Look,' she interrupted, and he heard a yelping horn.

He turned at the direction of her eyes, and found a bright yellow motor car, with dark goggled driver and fur-clad passengers, whooping, throbbing and buzzing resentfully at his heel. He moved his foot, and the mechanism, with three angry snorts, resumed its fussy way towards the town. 'Filling up the roadway!' floated up to him.

Then someone said, 'Look! Did you see? There is the monster princess over beyond the trees!' and all their goggled faces came round to stare.

'I say,' said another. '*That* won't do . . . '

'All this,' she said, 'is more amazing than I can tell.'

'That they should not have told you – ' he said, and left his sentence incomplete.

'Until you came upon me, I had lived in a world where I was great – alone. I had made myself a life – for that. I had thought I was the victim of some strange freak of nature. And now my world has crumbled down, in half an hour, and I see another world, other conditions, wider possibilities – fellowship – '

'Fellowship,' he answered.

'I want you to tell me more yet, and much more,' she said. 'You know this passes through my mind like a tale that is told. You even . . . In a day perhaps, or after several days, I shall believe in you. Now – Now I am dreaming . . . Listen!'

The first stroke of a clock above the palace offices far away had penetrated to them. Each counted mechanically, 'Seven.'

'This,' she said, 'should be the hour of my return. They will be taking the bowl of my coffee into the hall where I sleep. The little officials and servants – you cannot dream how grave they are – will be stirring about their little duties.'

'They will wonder . . . But I want to talk to you.'

She thought. 'But I want to think too. I want now to think alone, and think out this change in things, think away the old solitude, and think you and those others into my world . . . I shall go. I shall go back today to my place in the castle, and tomorrow, as the dawn comes, I shall come again – here.'

'I shall be here waiting for you.'

'All day I shall dream and dream of this new world you have given me. Even now, I can scarcely believe – '

She took a step back and surveyed him from the feet to the face. Their eyes met and locked for a moment.

'Yes,' she said, with a little laugh that was half a sob. 'You are real. But it is very wonderful! Do you think – indeed – ? Suppose tomorrow I come and find you – a pigmy like the others . . . Yes, I must think. And so for today – as the little people do – '

She held out her hand, and for the first time they touched one another. Their hands clasped firmly and their eyes met again.

'Goodbye,' she said, 'for today. Goodbye! Goodbye, Brother Giant!'

He hesitated with some unspoken thing, and at last he answered her simply, 'Goodbye.'

For a space they held each other's hands, studying each the other's face. And many times after they had parted, she looked back half doubtfully at him, standing still in the place where they had met.

She walked into her apartments across the great yard of the palace like one who walks in a dream, with a vast branch of chestnut trailing from her hand.

3

These two met altogether fourteen times before the beginning of the end. They met in the great park or on the heights and among the gorges of the rusty-roaded, heathery moorland, set with dusky pinewoods, that stretched to the south-west. Twice they met in the great avenue of chestnuts, and five times near the broad ornamental water the king, her great-grandfather, had made. There was a place where a great trim lawn, set with tall conifers, sloped graciously to the water's edge, and there she would sit, and he would lie at her knees and look up in her face and talk, telling of all the things that had been, and of the work his father had set before him, and of the great

and spacious dream of what the giant people should one day be. Commonly they met in the early dawn, but once they met there in the afternoon, and found presently a multitude of peering eavesdroppers about them, cyclists, pedestrians, peeping from the bushes, rustling (as sparrows will rustle about one in the London parks) amidst the dead leaves in the woods behind, gliding down the lake in boats towards a point of view, trying to get nearer to them and hear.

It was the first hint that offered of the enormous interest the countryside was taking in their meetings. And once – it was the seventh time, and it precipitated the scandal – they met out upon the breezy moorland under a clear moonlight, and talked in whispers there, for the night was warm and still.

Very soon they had passed from the realisation that in them and through them a new world of giantry shaped itself in the earth, from the contemplation of the great struggle between big and little, in which they were clearly destined to participate, to interests at once more personal and more spacious. Each time they met and talked and looked on one another, it crept a little more out of their subconscious being towards recognition, that something more dear and wonderful than friendship was between them, and walked between them and drew their hands together. And in a little while they came to the word itself and found themselves lovers, the Adam and Eve of a new race in the world.

They set foot side by side into the wonderful valley of love, with its deep and quiet places. The world changed about them with their changing mood, until presently it had become, as it were, a tabernacular beauty about their meetings, and the stars were no more than flowers of light beneath the feet of their love, and the dawn and sunset the coloured hangings by the way. They ceased to be beings of flesh and blood to one another and themselves; they passed into a bodily texture of tenderness and desire. They gave it first whispers and then silence, and drew close and looked into one another's moonlit and shadowy faces under the infinite arch of the sky. And the still black pine trees stood about them like sentinels.

The beating steps of time were hushed into silence, and it seemed to them the universe hung still. Only their hearts were audible, beating. They seemed to be living together in a world where there is no death, and indeed so it was with them then. It seemed to them that they sounded, and indeed they sounded, such hidden splendours in the very heart of things as none have ever reached before. Even for mean and little souls, love is the revelation of splendours. And these were giant lovers who had eaten the Food of the Gods . . .

* * *

You may imagine the spreading consternation in this ordered world when it became known that the princess who 'was affianced to the prince,

the princess, Her Serene Highness! with royal blood in her veins! met –
frequently met – the hypertrophied offspring of a common professor of
chemistry, a creature of no rank, no position, no wealth, and talked to him
as though there were no kings and princes, no order, no reverence –
nothing but giants and pigmies in the world, talked to him and, it was only
too certain, held him as her lover.

'If those newspaper fellows get hold of it!' gasped Sir Arthur Poodle
Bootlick . . .

'I am told – ' whispered the old Bishop of Frumps.

'New story upstairs,' said the first footman, as he nibbled among the
dessert things. 'So far as I can make out this here giant princess – '

'They say – ' said the lady who kept the stationer's shop by the main
entrance to the palace, where the little Americans get their tickets for the
State Apartments . . .

And then: 'We are authorised to deny – ' said 'Picaroon' in *Gossip*.

And so the whole trouble came out.

4

'They say that we must part,' the princess said to her lover.

'But why?' he cried. 'What new folly have these people got into their
heads?'

'Do you know,' she asked, 'that to love me – is high treason?'

'My dear,' he cried; 'but does it matter? What is their right – right
without a shadow of reason – and their treason and their loyalty to us?'

'You shall hear,' she said, and told him of the things that had been told to
her.

'It was the queerest little man who came to me with a soft, beautifully
modulated voice, a softly moving little gentleman who sidled into the room
like a cat and put his pretty white hand up so, whenever he had anything
significant to say. He is bald, but not of course nakedly bald, and his nose
and face are chubby rosy little things, and his beard is trimmed to a point in
quite the loveliest way. He pretended to have emotions several times and
made his eyes shine. You know he is quite a friend of the real royal family
here, and he called me his dear young lady and was perfectly sympathetic
even from the beginning. "My dear young lady," he said, "you know – *you
mustn't*," several times, and then, "You owe a duty." '

'Where do they make such men?'

'He likes it,' she said.

'But I don't see – '

'He told me serious things.'

'You don't think,' he said, turning on her abruptly, 'that there's anything
in the sort of thing he said?'

'There's something in it quite certainly,' said she.

'You mean – ?'

'I mean that without knowing it we have been trampling on the most sacred conceptions of the little folks. We who are royal are a class apart. We are worshipped prisoners, processional toys. We pay for worship by losing – our elementary freedom. And I was to have married that prince – You know nothing of him though. Well, a pigmy prince. He doesn't matter . . . It seems it would have strengthened the bonds between my country and another. And this country also was to profit. Imagine it! – strengthening the bonds!'

'And now?'

'They want me to go on with it – as though there was nothing between us two.'

'Nothing!'

'Yes. But that isn't all. He said – '

'Your specialist in Tact?'

'Yes. He said it would be better for you, better for all the giants, if we two – abstained from conversation. That was how he put it.'

'But what can they do if we don't?'

'He said you might have your freedom.'

'*I!*'

'He said, with a stress, "My dear young lady, it would be better, it would be more dignified, if you parted, willingly." That was all he said. With a stress on willingly.'

'But – ! What business is it of these little wretches where we love, how we love? What have they and their world to do with us?'

'They do not think that.'

'Of course,' he said, 'you disregard all this.'

'It seems utterly foolish to me.'

'That their laws should fetter us! That we, at the first spring of life, should be trapped by their old engagements, their aimless institutions! Oh – ! We disregard it.'

'I am yours. So far – yes.'

'So far? Isn't that all?'

'But they – If they want to part us – '

'What can they do?'

'I don't know. What *can* they do?'

'Who cares what they can do, or what they will do? I am yours and you are mine. What is there more than that? I am yours and you are mine – for ever. Do you think I will stop for their little rules, for their little prohibitions, their scarlet boards indeed! – and keep from *you*?'

'Yes. But still, what can they do?'

'You mean,' he said, 'what are we to do?'

'Yes.'

'We? We can go on.'

'But if they seek to prevent us?'

He clenched his hands. He looked round as if the little people were already coming to prevent them. Then turned away from her and looked about the world. 'Yes,' he said. 'Your question was the right one. What can they do?'

'Here in this little land – ' she said, and stopped.

He seemed to survey it all. 'They are everywhere.'

'But we might – '

'Whither?'

'We could go. We could swim the seas together. Beyond the seas – '

'I have never been beyond the seas.'

'There are great and desolate mountains amidst which we should seem no more than little people, there are remote and deserted valleys, there are hidden lakes and snow-girdled uplands untrodden by the feet of men. *There* – '

'But to get there we must fight our way day after day through millions and millions of mankind.'

'It is our only hope. In this crowded land there is no fastness, no shelter. What place is there for us among these multitudes? They who are little can hide from one another, but where are we to hide? There is no place where we could eat, no place where we could sleep. If we fled – night and day they would pursue our footsteps.'

A thought came to him.

'There is one place,' he said, 'even in this island.'

'Where?'

'The place our Brothers have made over beyond there. They have made great banks about their house, north and south and east and west; they have made deep pits and hidden places, and even now – one came over to me quite recently. He said – I did not altogether heed what he said then. But he spoke of arms. It may be – there – we should find shelter . . .

'For many days,' he said, after a pause, 'I have not seen our Brothers. Dear! I have been dreaming, I have been forgetting! The days have passed, and I have done nothing but look to see you again . . . I must go to them and talk to them, and tell them of you and of all the things that hang over us. If they will help us, they can help us. Then indeed we might hope. I do not know how strong their place is, but certainly Cossar will have made it strong. Before all this – before you came to me, I remember now – there was trouble brewing. There was an election – when all the little people settle things by counting heads. It must be over now. There were threats against all our race – against all our race, that is, but you. I must see our Brothers. I must tell them all that has happened between us, and all that threatens now.'

He did not come to their next meeting until she had waited some time. They were to meet that day about midday in a great space of park that fitted into a bend of the river, and as she waited, looking ever southward under her hand, it came to her that the world was very still, that indeed it was broodingly still. And then she perceived that, spite of the lateness of the hour, her customary retinue of voluntary spies had failed her. Left and right, when she came to look, there was no one in sight, and there was never a boat upon the silver curve of the Thames. She tried to find a reason for this strange stillness in the world . . .

Then, a grateful sight for her, she saw young Redwood far away over a gap in the tree masses that bounded her view.

Immediately the trees hid him, and presently he was thrusting through them and in sight again. She could see there was something different, and then she saw that he was hurrying unusually and then that he limped. He gestured to her, and she walked towards him. His face became clearer, and she saw with infinite concern that he winced at every stride.

She ran towards him, her mind full of questions and vague fear. He drew near to her and spoke without a greeting.

'Are we to part?' he panted.

'No,' she answered. 'Why? What is the matter?'

'But if we do not part – ! It is *now*.'

'What is the matter?'

'I do not want to part,' he said. 'Only – ' He broke off abruptly to ask, 'You will not part from me?'

She met his eyes with a steadfast look. 'What has happened?' she pressed.

'Not for a time?'

'What time?'

'Years perhaps.'

'Part! No!'

'You have thought?' he insisted.

'I will not part.' She took his hand. 'If this meant death, *now*, I would not let you go.'

'If it meant death,' he said, and she felt his grip upon her fingers.

He looked about him as if he feared to see the little people coming as he spoke. And then: 'It may mean death.'

'Now tell me,' she said.

'They tried to stop my coming.'

'How?'

'And as I came out of my workshop where I make the Food of the Gods for the Cossars to store in their camp, I found a little officer of police – a

man in blue with white clean gloves – who beckoned me to stop. "This way is closed!" said he. I thought little of that; I went round my workshop to where another road runs west, and there was another officer. "This road is closed!" he said, and added: "All the roads are closed!" '

'And then?'

'I argued with him a little. "They are public roads!" I said.

' "That's it," said he. "You spoil them for the public."

' "Very well," said I, "I'll take the fields," and then, up leapt others from behind a hedge and said, "These fields are private."

' "Curse your public and private," I said, "I'm going to my princess," and I stooped down and picked him up very gently – kicking and shouting – and put him out of my way. In a minute all the fields about me seemed alive with running men. I saw one on horseback galloping beside me and reading something as he rode – shouting it. He finished and turned and galloped away from me – head down. I couldn't make it out. And then behind me I heard the crack of guns.'

'Guns!'

'Guns – just as they shoot at the rats. The bullets came through the air with a sound like things tearing: one stung me in the leg.'

'And you?'

'Came on to you here and left them shouting and running and shooting behind me. And now – '

'Now?'

'It is only the beginning. They mean that we shall part. Even now they are coming after me.'

'We will not.'

'No. But if we will not part – then you must come with me to our Brothers.'

'Which way?' she said.

'To the east. Yonder is the way my pursuers will be coming. This then is the way we must go. Along this avenue of trees. Let me go first, so that if they are waiting – '

He made a stride, but she had seized his arm.

'No,' cried she. 'I come close to you, holding you. Perhaps I am royal, perhaps I am sacred. If I hold you – Would God we could fly with my arms about you! – it may be, they will not shoot at you – '

She clasped his shoulder and seized his hand as she spoke; she pressed herself nearer to him. 'It may be they will not shoot you,' she repeated, and with a sudden passion of tenderness he took her into his arms and kissed her cheek. For a space he held her.

'Even if it is death,' she whispered.

She put her hands about his neck and lifted her face to his.

'Dearest, kiss me once more.'

He drew her to him. Silently they kissed one another on the lips, and for

another moment clung to one another. Then hand in hand, and she striving always to keep her body near to his, they set forward if haply they might reach the camp of refuge the sons of Cossar had made, before the pursuit of the little people overtook them.

And as they crossed the great spaces of the park behind the castle there came horsemen galloping out from among the trees and vainly seeking to keep pace with their giant strides. And presently ahead of them were houses, and men with guns running out of the houses. At the sight of that, though he sought to go on and was even disposed to fight and push through, she made him turn aside towards the south.

As they fled a bullet whipped by them overhead.

CHAPTER THREE

Young Caddles in London

All unaware of the trend of events, unaware of the laws that were closing in upon all the Brethren, unaware indeed that there lived a Brother for him on the earth, young Caddles chose this time to come out of his chalk pit and see the world. His brooding came at last to that. There was no answer to all his questions in Cheasing Eyebright; the new vicar was less luminous even than the old, and the riddle of his pointless labour grew at last to the dimensions of exasperation. 'Why should I work in this pit day after day?' he asked. 'Why should I walk within bounds and be refused all the wonders of the world beyond there? What have I done, to be condemned to this?'

And one day he stood up, straightened his back, and said in a loud voice, 'No!

'I won't,' he said, and then with great vigour cursed the pit.

Then, having few words, he sought to express his thought in acts. He took a truck half filled with chalk, lifted it and flung it, smash, against another. Then he grasped a whole row of empty trucks and spun them down a bank. He sent a huge boulder of chalk bursting among them, and then ripped up a dozen yards of rail with a mighty plunge of his foot. So he commenced the conscientious wrecking of the pit.

'Work all my days,' he said, 'at this!'

It was an astonishing five minutes for the little geologist he had, in his preoccupation, overlooked. This poor little creature having dodged two boulders by a hair's breadth, got out by the westward corner and fled athwart the hill, with flapping rucksack and twinkling knicker-bockered legs, leaving a trail of Cretaceous echinoderms behind him; while young Caddles, satisfied with the destruction he had achieved, came striding out to fulfil his purpose in the world.

'Work in that old pit until I die and rot and stink! . . . What worm did they think was living in my giant body? Dig chalk for God knows what foolish purpose! Not *I*!'

The trend of road and railway perhaps, or mere chance it was, turned his face to London, and thither he came striding; over the downs and athwart the meadows through the hot afternoon, to the infinite amazement of the world. It signified nothing to him that torn posters in red and white bearing various names flapped from every wall and barn; he knew nothing of the electoral revolution that had flung Caterham, 'Jack the Giant-Killer', into power. It signified nothing to him that every police station along his route had what was known as Caterham's ukase upon its noticeboard that afternoon, proclaiming that no giant, no person whatever over eight feet in height, should go more than five miles from his 'place of location' without a special permission. It signified nothing to him that in his wake belated police officers, not a little relieved to find themselves belated, shook warning handbills at his retreating back. He was going to see what the world had to show him, poor incredulous blockhead, and he did not mean that occasional spirited persons shouting 'Hi!' at him should stay his course. He came on down by Rochester and Greenwich towards an ever-thickening aggregation of houses, walking rather slowly now, staring about him and swinging his huge chopper.

People in London had heard something of him before, how that he was idiotic but gentle, and wonderfully managed by Lady Wondershoot's agent and the vicar; how in his dull way he revered these authorities and was grateful to them for their care of him, and so forth. So that when they learnt from the newspaper placards that afternoon that he also was 'on strike', the thing appeared to many of them as a deliberate, concerted act.

'They mean to try our strength,' said the men in the trains going home from business.

'Lucky we have Caterham.'

'It's in answer to his proclamation.'

The men in the clubs were better informed. They clustered round the tape or talked in groups in their smoking-rooms.

'He has no weapons. He would have gone to Sevenoaks if he had been put up to it.'

'Caterham will handle him . . .'

The shopmen told their customers. The waiters in restaurants snatched a moment for an evening paper between the courses. The cabmen read it immediately after the betting news . . .

The placards of the chief government evening paper were conspicuous with 'Grasping the Nettle'. Others relied for effect on: 'Giant Redwood continues to meet the Princess'. The *Echo* struck a line of its own with: 'Rumoured Revolt of Giants in the North of England. The Sunderland Giants start for Scotland'. The *Westminster Gazette* sounded its usual

warning note. 'Giants Beware', said the *Westminster Gazette*, and tried to make a point out of it that might perhaps serve towards uniting the Liberal party – at that time greatly torn between seven intensely egotistical leaders. The later newspapers dropped into uniformity. 'The Giant in the New Kent Road', they proclaimed.

'What I want to know,' said the pale young man in the tea shop, 'is why we aren't getting any news of the young Cossars. You'd think they'd be in it most of all . . .'

'They tell me there's another of them young giants got loose,' said the barmaid, wiping out a glass. 'I've always said they was dangerous things to 'ave about. Right away from the beginning . . . It ought to be put a stop to. Any 'ow, I 'ope 'e won't come along 'ere.'

'I'd like to 'ave a look at 'im,' said the young man at the bar recklessly, and added, 'I *seen* the princess.'

'D'you think they'll 'urt 'im?' said the barmaid.

'May 'ave to,' said the young man at the bar, finishing his glass.

Amidst a hum of ten million such sayings young Caddles came to London . . .

2

I think of young Caddles always as he was seen in the New Kent Road, the sunset warm upon his perplexed and staring face. The road was thick with its varied traffic, omnibuses, trams, vans, carts, trolleys, cyclists, motors, and a marvelling crowd – loafers, women, nursemaids, shopping women, children, venturesome hobbledehoys – gathered behind his gingerly moving feet. The hoardings were untidy everywhere with the tattered election paper. A babblement of voices surged about him. One sees the customers and shopmen crowding in the doorways of the shops, the faces that came and went at the windows, the little street boys running and shouting, the policemen taking it all quite stiffly and calmly, the workmen knocking off upon scaffoldings, the seething miscellany of the little folks. They shouted to him, vague encouragement, vague insults, the imbecile catchwords of the day, and he stared down at them, at such a multitude of living creatures as he had never before imagined in the world.

Now that he had fairly entered London he had had to slacken his pace more and more, the little folks crowded so mightily upon him. The crowd grew denser at every step, and at last, at a corner where two great ways converged, he came to a stop, and the multitude flowed about him and closed him in.

There he stood, with his feet a little apart, his back to a big corner gin palace that towered twice his height and ended in a sky sign, staring down at the pigmies and wondering – trying, I doubt not, to collate it all with the

other things of his life, with the valley among the downlands, the nocturnal lovers, the singing in the church, the chalk he hammered daily, and with instinct and death and the sky, trying to see it all together coherent and significant. His brows were knit. He put up his huge paw to scratch his coarse hair, and groaned aloud.

'I don't see it,' he said.

His accent was unfamiliar. A great babblement went across the open space – a babblement amidst which the gongs of the trams, ploughing their obstinate way through the mass, rose like red poppies amidst corn. 'What did he say?' 'Said he didn't see.' 'Said, where is the sea?' 'Said, where is a seat?' 'He wants a seat.' 'Can't the brasted fool sit on a 'ouse or somethin'?'

'What are ye for, ye swarming little people? What are ye all doing, what are ye all for?

'What are ye doing up here, ye swarming little people, while I'm a-cuttin' chalk for ye, down in the chalk pits there?'

His queer voice, the voice that had been so bad for school discipline at Cheasing Eyebright, smote the multitude to silence while it sounded and splashed them all to tumult at the end. Some wit was audible screaming, 'Speech, speech!' 'What's he saying?' was the burthen of the public mind, and an opinion was abroad that he was drunk. 'Hi, hi, hi,' bawled the omnibus-drivers, threading a dangerous way. A drunken American sailor wandered about tearfully enquiring, 'What's he want anyhow?' A leathery-faced rag-dealer upon a little pony-drawn cart soared up over the tumult by virtue of his voice. 'Garn 'ome, you Brasted Giant!' he brawled. 'Garn 'ome! you Brasted Great Dangerous Thing! Can't you see you're a-frightening the 'orses? Go *'ome* with you! 'Asn't anyone 'ad the sense to tell you the law?' And over all this uproar young Caddles stared, perplexed, expectant, saying no more.

Down a side road came a little string of solemn policemen, and threaded itself ingeniously into the traffic. 'Stand back,' said the little voices; 'keep moving, please.'

Young Caddles became aware of a little dark blue figure thumping at his shin. He looked down, and perceived two white hands gesticulating. '*What*?' he said, bending forward.

'Can't stand about here,' shouted the inspector. 'No! You can't stand about here,' he repeated.

'But where am I to go?'

'Back to your village. Place of location. Anyhow, now – you've got to move on. You're obstructing the traffic.'

'What traffic?'

'Along the road.'

'But where is it going? Where does it come from? What does it mean? They're all round me. What do they want? What are they doin'? I want to understand. I'm tired of cuttin' chalk and bein' all alone. What are they

doin' for me while I'm a-cuttin' chalk? I may just as well understand here and now as anywhere.'

'Sorry. But we aren't here to explain things of that sort. I must arst you to move on.'

'Don't you know?'

'I must arst you to move on – *if* you please . . . I'd strongly advise you to get off 'ome. We've 'ad no special instructions yet – but it's against the law . . . Clear away there. Clear away.'

The pavement to his left became invitingly bare, and young Caddles went slowly on his way. But now his tongue was loosened.

'I don't understand,' he muttered. 'I don't understand.' He would appeal brokenly to the changing crowd that ever trailed beside him and behind. 'I didn't know there were such places as this. What are all you people doing with yourselves? What's it all for? What is it all for, and where do I come in?'

He had already begotten a new catchword. Young men of wit and spirit addressed each other in this manner, ' 'Ello, 'Arry, ol' cock. Wot's it all *for*? Eh? Wot's it all bloomin' well *for*?'

To which there sprang up a competing variety of repartees, for the most part impolite. The most popular and best adapted for general use appears to have been, '*Shut* it,' or, in a voice of scornful detachment, '*Garn!*'

There were others almost equally popular.

3

What was he seeking? He wanted something the pigmy world did not give, some end which the pigmy world prevented his attaining, prevented even his seeing clearly, which he was never to see clearly. It was the whole gigantic social side of this lonely dumb monster crying out for his race, for the things akin to him, for something he might love and something he might serve, for a purpose he might comprehend and a command he could obey. And, you know, all this was *dumb*, raged dumbly within him, could not even, had he met a fellow giant, have found outlet and expression in speech. All the life he knew was the dull round of the village, all the speech he knew was the talk of the cottage, that failed and collapsed at the bare outline of his least gigantic need. He knew nothing of money, this monstrous simpleton, nothing of trade, nothing of the complex pretences upon which the social fabric of the little folks was built. He needed, he needed – Whatever he needed, he never found his need.

All through the day and the summer night he wandered, growing hungry but as yet untired, marking the varied traffic of the different streets, the inexplicable businesses of all these infinitesimal beings. In the aggregate it had no other colour than confusion for him . . .

He is said to have plucked a lady from her carriage in Kensington, a lady

in evening dress of the smartest sort, to have scrutinised her closely, train and shoulder blades, and to have replaced her – a little carelessly – with the profoundest sigh. For that I cannot vouch. For an hour or so he watched people fighting for places in the omnibuses at the end of Piccadilly. He was seen looming over Kennington Oval for some moments in the afternoon, but when he saw these dense thousands were engaged with the mystery of cricket and quite regardless of him he went his way with a groan.

He came back to Piccadilly Circus between eleven and twelve at nights and found a new sort of multitude. Clearly they were very intent: full of things they, for inconceivable reasons, might do, and of others they might not do. They stared at him and jeered at him and went their way. The cabmen, vulture-eyed, followed one another continually along the edge of the swarming pavement. People emerged from the restaurants or entered them, grave, intent, dignified, or gently and agreeably excited, or keen and vigilant – beyond the cheating of the sharpest waiter born. The great giant, standing at his corner, peered at them all. 'What is it all for?' he murmured in a mournful vast undertone, 'What is it all for? They are all so earnest. What is it I do not understand?'

And none of them seemed to see, as he could do, the drink-sodden wretchedness of the painted women at the corner, the ragged misery that sneaked along the gutters, the infinite futility of all this employment. The infinite futility! None of them seemed to feel the shadow of that giant's need, that shadow of the future, that lay athwart their paths . . .

Across the road high up mysterious letters flamed and went, that might, could he have read them, have measured for him the dimensions of human interest, have told him of the fundamental needs and features of life as the little folks conceived it. First would come a flaming

T;

Then U would follow,

T U;

Then P,

T U P;

Until at last there stood complete, across the sky, this cheerful message to all who felt the burthen of life's earnestness:

TUPPER'S TONIC WINE FOR VIGOUR

Snap! and it had vanished into night, to be followed in the same slow development by a second universal solicitude:

BEAUTY SOAP

Not, you remark, mere cleansing chemicals, but something, as they say, 'ideal'; and then, completing the tripod of the little life:

YANKER'S YELLOW PILLS

After that there was nothing for it but Tupper again, in flaming crimson letters, snap, snap, across the void. T U P P . . .

Early in the small hours it would seem that young Caddles came to the shadowy quiet of Regent's Park, stepped over the railings and lay down on a grassy slope near where the people skate in wintertime, and there he slept an hour or so. And about six o'clock in the morning, he was talking to a draggled woman he had found sleeping in a ditch near Hampstead Heath, asking her very earnestly what she thought she was for . . .

4

The wandering of Caddles about London came to a head on the second day in the morning. For then his hunger overcame him. He hesitated where the hot-smelling loaves were being tossed into a cart, and then very quietly knelt down and commenced robbery. He emptied the cart while the baker's man fled for the police, and then his great hand came into the shop and cleared counter and cases. Then with an armful, still eating, he went his way looking for another shop to go on with his meal. It happened to be one of those seasons when work is scarce and food dear, and the crowd in that quarter was sympathetic even with a giant who took the food they all desired. They applauded the second phase of his meal, and laughed at his stupid grimace at the policeman.

'I woff hungry,' he said, with his mouth full.

'Brayvo!' cried the crowd. 'Brayvo!'

Then, when he was beginning his third baker's shop, he was stopped by half a dozen policemen hammering with truncheons at his shins. 'Look here, my fine giant, you come along o' me,' said the officer in charge. 'You ain't allowed away from home like this. You come off home with me.' They did their best to arrest him. There was a trolley, I am told, chasing up and down streets at that time, bearing rolls of chain and ship's cable to play the part of handcuffs in that great arrest. There was no intention then of killing him. 'He is no party to the plot,' Caterham had said. 'I will not have innocent blood upon my hands.' And added: ' – until everything else has been tried.'

At first Caddles did not understand the import of these attentions. When he did, he told the policemen not to be fools, and set off in great strides that left them all behind. The bakers' shops had been in the Harrow Road, and he followed the canal to St John's Wood and sat down in a private garden there to pick his teeth and be speedily assailed by another posse of constables.

'You lea' me alone,' he growled, and slouched through the gardens – spoiling several lawns and kicking down a fence or so, while the energetic little policemen followed him up, some through the gardens, some along

the road in front of the houses. Here there were one or two with guns, but they made no use of them. When he came out into the Edgware Road there was a new note and a new movement in the crowd, and a mounted policeman rode over his foot and got upset for his pains.

'You lea' me alone,' said Caddles, facing the breathless crowd. 'I ain't done anything to you.' At that time he was unarmed, for he had left his chalk chopper in Regent's Park. But now, poor wretch, he seems to have felt the need of some weapon. He turned back towards the goods yard of the Great Western Railway, wrenched up the standard of a tall arc light, a formidable mace for him, and flung it over his shoulder. And finding the police still turning up to pester him, he went back along the Edgware Road, towards Cricklewood, and struck off sullenly to the north.

He wandered as far as Waltham, and then turned back westward and then again towards London, and came by the cemeteries and over the crest of Highgate about midday into view of the greatness of the city again. He turned aside and sat down in a garden, with his back to a house that overlooked all London. He was breathless, and his face was lowering, and now the people no longer crowded upon him as they had done when first he came to London, but lurked in the adjacent garden, and peeped from cautious securities. They knew by now the thing was grimmer than they had thought. 'Why can't they lea' me alone?' growled young Caddles. 'I *mus'* eat. Why can't they lea' me alone?'

He sat with a darkling face, gnawing at his knuckles and looking down over London. All the fatigue, worry, perplexity and impotent wrath of his wanderings was coming to a head in him. 'They mean nothing,' he whispered. 'They mean nothing. And they *won't* let me alone, and they *will* get in my way.' And again, over and over to himself, 'Meanin' nothing.

'Ugh! the little people!'

He bit harder at his knuckles and his scowl deepened. 'Cuttin' chalk for 'em,' he whispered. 'And all the world is theirs! *I* don't come in – nowhere.'

Presently with a spasm of sick anger he saw the now familiar form of a policeman astride the garden wall.

'Lea' me alone,' grunted the giant. 'Lea' me alone.'

'I got to do my duty,' said the little policeman, with a face that was white and resolute.

'You lea' me alone. I got to live as well as you. I got to think. I got to eat. You lea' me alone.'

'It's the Law,' said the little policeman, coming no farther. 'We never made the Law.'

'Nor me,' said young Caddles. 'You little people made all that before I was born. You and your Law! What I must and what I mustn't! No food for me to eat unless I work a slave, no rest, no shelter, nothin', and you tell me – '

'I ain't got no business with that,' said the policeman. 'I'm not one to

argue. All I got to do is to carry out the Law.' And he brought his second leg over the wall and seemed disposed to get down. Other policemen appeared behind him.

'I got no quarrel with *you* – mind,' said young Caddles, with his grip tight upon his huge mace of iron, his face pale, and a lank explanatory great finger to the policeman. 'I got no quarrel with you. But – *You lea' me alone.'*

The policeman tried to be calm and commonplace, with a monstrous tragedy clear before his eyes. 'Give me the proclamation,' he said to some unseen follower, and a little white paper was handed to him.

'Lea' me alone,' said Caddles, scowling, tense and drawn together.

'This means,' said the policeman before he read, 'go 'ome. Go 'ome to your chalk pit. If not, you'll be hurt.'

Caddles gave an inarticulate growl.

Then when the proclamation had been read, the officer made a sign. Four men with rifles came into view and took up positions of affected ease along the wall. They wore the uniform of the rat police. At the sight of the guns, young Caddles blazed into anger. He remembered the sting of the Wreckstone farmers' shotguns. 'You going to shoot off those at me?' he said, pointing, and it seemed to the officer he must be afraid.

'If you don't march back to your pit – '

Then in an instant the officer had slung himself back over the wall, and sixty feet above him the great electric standard whirled down to his death. Bang, bang, bang, went the heavy guns, and smash! the shattered wall, the soil and subsoil of the garden flew. Something flew with it, that left red drops on one of the shooter's hands. The riflemen dodged this way and that and turned valiantly to fire again. But young Caddles, already shot twice through the body, had spun about to find who it was had hit him so heavily in the back. Bang! Bang! He had a vision of houses and greenhouses and gardens, of people dodging at windows, the whole swaying fearfully and mysteriously. He seems to have made three stumbling strides, to have raised and dropped his huge mace, and to have clutched his chest. He was stung and wrenched by pain.

What was this, warm and wet, on his hand?

One man peering from a bedroom window saw his face, saw him staring, with a grimace of weeping dismay, at the blood upon his hand, and then his knees bent under him and he came crashing to the earth, the first of the giant nettles to fall to Caterham's resolute clutch, the very last that he had reckoned would come into his hand.

CHAPTER FOUR

Redwood's Two Days

So soon as Caterham knew the moment for grasping his nettle had come, he took the law into his own hands and sent to arrest Cossar and Redwood.

Redwood was there for the taking. He had been undergoing an operation in the side, and the doctors had kept all disturbing things from him until his convalescence was assured. Now they had released him. He was just out of bed, sitting in a fire-warmed room, with a heap of newspapers about him, reading for the first time of the agitation that had swept the country into the hands of Caterham, and of the trouble that was darkening over the princess and his son. It was in the morning of the day when young Caddles died, and when the policeman tried to stop young Redwood on his way to the princess. The latest newspapers Redwood had did but vaguely prefigure these imminent things. He was rereading these first adumbrations of disaster with a sinking heart, reading the shadow of death more and more perceptibly into them, reading to occupy his mind until further news should come. When the officers followed the servant into his room, he looked up eagerly.

'I thought it was an early evening paper,' he said. Then standing up, and with a swift change of manner: 'What's this?'

After that Redwood had no news of anything for two days.

They had come with a vehicle to take him away, but when it became evident that he was ill, it was decided to leave him for a day or so until he could be safely removed, and his house was taken over by the police and converted into a temporary prison. It was the same house in winch Giant Redwood had been born and in which Herakleophorbia had for the first time been given to a human being, and Redwood had now been a widower and had lived alone in it eight years.

He had become an iron-grey man, with a little pointed grey beard and still active brown eyes. He was slender and soft-voiced, as he had ever been, but his features had now that indefinable quality that comes of brooding over mighty things. To the arresting officer his appearance was in impressive contrast to the enormity of his offences. 'Here's this feller,' said the officer in command to his next subordinate, 'has done his level best to bust up everything, and 'e's got a face like a quiet country gentleman; and here's Judge Hangbrow keepin' everything nice and in order for everyone, and 'e's got a 'ead like a 'og. Then their manners! One all consideration and the other snort and grunt. Which just shows you, doesn't it, that appearances aren't to be gone upon, whatever else you do.'

But his praise of Redwood's consideration was presently dashed. The

officers found him troublesome at first until they had made it clear that it was useless for him to ask questions or beg for papers. They made a sort of inspection of his study indeed, and cleared away even the papers he had. Redwood's voice was high and expostulatory. 'But don't you see,' he said over and over again, 'it's my son, my only son, that is in this trouble. It isn't the Food I care for, but my son.'

'I wish indeed I could tell you, sir,' said the officer. 'But our orders are strict.'

'Who gave the orders?' cried Redwood.

'Ah! *that*, sir – ' said the officer, and moved towards the door . . .

' 'E's going up and down 'is room,' said the second officer, when his superior came down. 'That's all right. He'll walk it off a bit.'

'I hope 'e will,' said the chief officer. 'The fact is I didn't see it in that light before, but this here Giant what's been going on with the princess, you know, is this man's son.'

The two regarded one another and the third policeman for a space.

'Then it is a bit rough on him,' the third policeman said.

It became evident that Redwood had still imperfectly apprehended the fact that an iron curtain had dropped between him and the outer world. They heard him go to the door, try the handle and rattle the lock, and then the voice of the officer who was stationed on the landing telling him it was no good to do that. Then afterwards they heard him at the windows and saw the men outside looking up. 'It's no good that way,' said the second officer. Then Redwood began upon the bell. The senior officer went up and explained very patiently that it could do no good to ring the bell like that, and if it was rung for nothing now it might have to be disregarded presently when he had need of something. 'Any reasonable attendance, sir,' the officer said. 'But if you ring it just by way of protest we shall be obliged, sir, to disconnect.'

The last word the officer heard was Redwood's high-pitched, 'But at least you might tell me if my son – '

2

After that Redwood spent most of his time at the windows.

But the windows offered him little of the march of events outside. It was a quiet street at all times, and that day it was unusually quiet: scarcely a cab, scarcely a tradesman's cart passed all that morning. Now and then men went by – without any distinctive air of events – now and then a little group of children, a nursemaid and a woman going shopping, and so forth. They came on to the stage right or left, up or down the street, with an exasperating suggestion of indifference to any concerns more spacious than their own; they would discover the police-guarded house with

amazement and exit in the opposite direction, where the great trusses of a giant hydrangea hung across the pavement, staring back or pointing. Now and then a man would come and ask one of the policemen a question and get a curt reply.

Opposite the houses seemed dead. A housemaid appeared once at a bedroom window and stared for a space, and it occurred to Redwood to signal to her. For a time she watched his gestures as if with interest and made a vague response to them, then looked over her shoulder suddenly and turned and went away. An old man hobbled out of Number 37 and came down the steps and went off to the right, altogether without looking up. For ten minutes the only occupant of the road was a cat . . .

With such events that interminable momentous morning lengthened out.

About twelve there came a bawling of news-vendors from the adjacent road; but it passed. Contrary to their wont they left Redwood's street alone, and a suspicion dawned upon him that the police were guarding the end of the street. He tried to open the window, but this brought a policeman into the room forthwith.

The clock of the parish church struck twelve, and after an abyss of time – one.

They mocked him with lunch.

He ate a mouthful and tumbled the food about a little in order to get it taken away, drank freely of whisky, and then took a chair and went back to the window. The minutes expanded into grey immensities, and for a time perhaps he slept . . .

He woke with a vague impression of remote concussions. He perceived a rattling of the windows, like the quiver of an earthquake, that lasted for a minute or so and died away. Then after a silence it returned . . . Then it died away again. He fancied it might be merely the passage of some heavy vehicle along the main road. What else could it be?

After a time he began to doubt whether he had heard this sound.

He began to reason interminably with himself. Why, after all, was he seized? Caterham had been in office two days – just long enough – to grasp his nettle! Grasp his Nettle! Grasp his Giant Nettle! The refrain, once started, sang through his mind and would not be dismissed.

What, after all, could Caterham do? He was a religious man. He was bound in a sort of way by that not to do violence without a cause.

Grasp his Nettle! Perhaps, for example, the princess was to be seized and sent abroad. There might be trouble with his son. In which case – ! But why had he been arrested? Why was it necessary to keep him in ignorance of a thing like that? The thing suggested – something more extensive.

Perhaps, for example – they meant to lay all the giants by the heels! They were all to be arrested together. There had been hints of that in the election speeches. And then?

No doubt they had got Cossar also?

Caterham was a religious man. Redwood clung to that. The back of his mind was a black curtain, and on that curtain there came and went a word – a word written in letters of fire. He struggled perpetually against that word. It was always as it were beginning to get written on the curtain and never getting completed.

He faced it at last. 'Massacre!' There was the word in its full brutality.

No! No! No! It was impossible! Caterham was a religious man, a civilised man. And besides after all these years, after all these hopes!

Redwood sprang up; he paced the room. He spoke to himself; he shouted, '*No!*'

Mankind was surely not so mad as that – surely not! It was impossible, it was incredible, it could not be. What good would it do to kill the giant human when the gigantic in all the lower things had now inevitably come? They could not be so mad as that! 'I must dismiss such an idea,' he said aloud; 'dismiss such an idea! Absolutely!'

He pulled up short. What was that?

Certainly the windows had rattled. He went to look out into the street. Opposite he saw the instant confirmation of his ears. At a bedroom at Number 35 was a woman, towel in hand, and at the dining-room of Number 37 a man was visible behind a great vase of hypertrophied maidenhair fern, both staring out and up, both disquieted and curious. He could see now too, quite clearly, that the policeman on the pavement had heard it also. The thing was not his imagination.

He turned to the darkling room.

'Guns,' he said.

He brooded. 'Guns?'

They brought him in strong tea, such as he was accustomed to have. It was evident his housekeeper had been taken into consultation. After drinking it, he was too restless to sit any longer at the window, and he paced the room. His mind became more capable of consecutive thought.

The room had been his study for four-and-twenty years. It had been furnished at his marriage, and all the essential equipment dated from then, the large complex writing-desk, the rotating chair, the easy chair at the fire, the rotating bookcase, the fixture of indexed pigeonholes that filled the farther recess. The vivid Turkey carpet, the later Victorian rugs and curtains had mellowed now to a rich dignity of effect, and copper and brass shone warm about the open fire. Electric lights had replaced the lamp of former days; that was the chief alteration in the original equipment. But among these things his connection with the Food had left abundant traces. Along one wall, above the dado, ran a crowded array of black-framed photographs and photogravures, showing his son and Cossar's sons and others of the Boom-children at various ages and amidst various surroundings. Even young Caddles's vacant visage had its place in that

collection. In the corner stood a sheaf of the tassels of gigantic meadow grass from Cheasing Eyebright, and on the desk there lay three empty poppy heads as big as hats. The curtain rods were grass stems. And the tremendous skull of the great hog of Oakham hung, a portentous ivory overmantel, with a Chinese jar in either eye socket, snout down above the fire.

It was to the photographs that Redwood went, and in particular to the photographs of his son.

They brought back countless memories of things that had passed out of his mind, of the early days of the Food, of Bensington's timid presence, of his cousin Jane, of Cossar and the night work at the Experimental Farm. These things came to him now very little and bright and distinct, like things seen through a telescope on a sunny day. And then there was the giant nursery, the giant childhood, the young giant's first efforts to speak, his first clear signs of affection.

Guns?

It flowed in on him, irresistibly, overwhelmingly, that outside there, outside this accursed silence and mystery, his son and Cossar's sons, and all these glorious first-fruits of a greater age were even now – fighting. Fighting for life! Even now his son might be in some dismal quandary, cornered, wounded, overcome . . .

He swung away from the pictures and went up and down the room gesticulating. 'It cannot be,' he cried, 'it cannot be. It cannot end like that!'

'What was that?'

He stopped, stricken rigid.

The trembling of the windows had begun again, and then had come a thud – a vast concussion that shook the house. The concussion seemed to last for an age. It must have been very near. For a moment it seemed that something had struck the house above him – an enormous impact that broke into a tinkle of falling glass, and then a stillness that ended at last with a minute clear sound of running feet in the street below.

Those feet released him from his rigor. He turned towards the window, and saw it starred and broken.

His heart beat high with a sense of crisis, of conclusive occurrence, of release. And then again, his realisation of impotent confinement fell about him like a curtain!

He could see nothing outside except that the small electric lamp opposite was not lighted; he could hear nothing after the first suggestion of a wide alarm. He could add nothing to interpret or enlarge that mystery except that presently there came a reddish fluctuating brightness in the sky towards the south-east.

This light waxed and waned. When it waned he doubted if it had ever waxed. It had crept upon him very gradually with the darkling. It became the predominant fact in his long night of suspense. Sometimes it seemed to

him it had the quiver one associates with dancing flames, at others he fancied it was no more than the normal reflection of the evening lights. It waxed and waned through the long hours, and only vanished at last when it was submerged altogether under the rising tide of dawn. Did it mean – ? What could it mean? Almost certainly it was some sort of fire, near or remote, but he could not even tell whether it was smoke or cloud drift that streamed across the sky. But about one o'clock there began a flickering of searchlights athwart that ruddy tumult, a flickering that continued for the rest of the night. That too might mean many things? What could it mean? What did it mean? Just this stained unrestful sky he had and the suggestion of a huge explosion to occupy his mind. There came no further sounds, no further running, nothing but a shouting that might have been only the distant efforts of drunken men . . .

He did not turn up his lights; he stood at his draughty broken window, a distressful, slight black outline to the officer who looked ever and again into the room and exhorted him to rest.

All night Redwood remained at his window peering up at the ambiguous drift of the sky, and only with the coming of the dawn did he obey his fatigue and lie down upon the little bed they had prepared for him between his writing-desk and the sinking fire in the fireplace under the great hog's skull.

3

For thirty-six long hours did Redwood remain imprisoned, closed in and shut off from the great drama of the Two Days, while the little people in the dawn of greatness fought against the Children of the Food. Then abruptly the iron curtain rose again, and he found himself near the very centre of the struggle. That curtain rose as unexpectedly as it fell. In the late afternoon he was called to the window by the clatter of a cab, that stopped without. A young man descended, and in another minute stood before him in the room, a slightly built young man of thirty perhaps, clean shaven, well dressed, well mannered.

'Mr Redwood, sir,' he began, 'would you be willing to come to Mr Caterham? He needs your presence very urgently.'

'Needs my presence!' There leapt a question into Redwood's mind that for a moment he could not put. He hesitated. Then in a voice that broke he asked: 'What has he done to my son?' and stood breathless for the reply.

'Your son, sir? Your son is doing well. So at least we gather.'

'Doing well?'

'He was wounded, sir, yesterday. Have you not heard?'

Redwood smote these pretences aside. His voice was no longer coloured by fear, but by anger. 'You know I have not heard. You know I have heard nothing.'

'Mr Caterham feared, sir – It was a time of upheaval. Everyone – taken by surprise. He arrested you to save you, sir, from any misadventure – '

'He arrested me to prevent my giving any warning or advice to my son. Go on. Tell me what has happened. Have you succeeded? Have you killed them all?'

The young man made a pace or so towards the window, and turned.

'No, sir,' he said concisely.

'What have you to tell me?'

'It's our proof, sir, that this fighting was not planned by us. They found us . . . totally unprepared.'

'You mean?'

'I mean, sir, the Giants have – to a certain extent – held their own.'

The world changed, for Redwood. For a moment something like hysteria had the muscles of his face and throat. Then he gave vent to a profound 'Ah!' His heart bounded towards exultation. 'The Giants have held their own!'

'There has been terrible fighting – terrible destruction. It is all a most hideous misunderstanding . . . In the north and midlands Giants have been killed . . . Everywhere.'

'They are fighting now?'

'No, sir. There was a flag of truce.'

'From them?'

'No, sir. Mr Caterham sent a flag of truce. The whole thing is a hideous misunderstanding. That is why he wants to talk to you, and put his case before you. They insist, sir, that you should intervene – '

Redwood interrupted. 'Do you know what happened to my son?' he asked.

'He was wounded.'

'Tell me! Tell me!'

'He and the princess came before the movement to surround the Cossar camp was complete – the Cossar pit at Chislehurst. They came suddenly, sir, crashing through a dense thicket of giant oats, near River, upon a column of infantry . . . Soldiers had been very nervous all day, and this produced a panic.'

'They shot him?'

'No, sir. They ran away. Some shot at him – wildly – against orders.'

Redwood gave a note of denial.

'It's true, sir. Not on account of your son, I won't pretend, but on account of the princess.'

'Yes. That's true.'

'The two Giants ran shouting towards the encampment. The soldiers ran this way and that, and then some began firing. They say they saw him stagger – '

'Ugh!'

'Yes, sir. But we know he is not badly hurt.'

'How?'

'He sent the message, sir, that he was doing well!'

'To me?'

'Who else, sir?'

Redwood stood for nearly a minute with his arms tightly folded, taking this in. Then his indignation found a voice.

'Because you were fools in doing the thing, because you miscalculated and blundered, you would like me to think you are not murderers in intention. And besides – The rest?'

The young man looked interrogation.

'The other Giants?'

The young man made no further pretence of misunderstanding. His tone fell. 'Thirteen, sir, are dead.'

'And others wounded?'

'Yes, sir.'

'And Caterham,' he gasped, 'wants to meet me! Where are the others?'

'Some got to the encampment during the fighting, sir . . . They seem to have known – '

'Well, of course they did. If it hadn't been for Cossar – Cossar is there?'

'Yes, sir. And all the surviving Giants are there – the ones who didn't get to the camp in the fighting have gone, or are going now under the flag of trace.'

'That means,' said Redwood, 'that you are beaten.'

'We are not beaten. No, sir. You cannot say we are beaten. But your sons have broken the rules of war. Once last night, and now again. After our attack had been withdrawn. This afternoon they began to bombard London – '

'That's legitimate!'

'They have been firing shells filled with – poison.'

'Poison?'

'Yes. Poison. The Food – '

'Herakleophorbia?'

'Yes, sir. Mr Caterham, sir – '

'You are beaten! Of course that beats you. It's Cossar! What can you hope to do now? What good is it to do anything now? You will breathe it in the dust of every street. What is there to fight for more? Rules of war, indeed! And now Caterham wants to humbug me to help him bargain. Good heavens, man! Why should I come to your exploded windbag? He has played his game . . . murdered and muddled. Why should I?'

The young man stood with an air of vigilant respect.

'It is a fact, sir,' he interrupted, 'that the Giants insist that they shall see you. They will have no ambassador but you. Unless you come to them, I am afraid, sir, there will be more bloodshed.'

'On *your* side, perhaps.'

'No, sir – on both sides. The world is resolved the thing must end.'

Redwood looked about the study. His eyes rested for a moment on the photograph of his boy. He turned and met the expectation of the young man. 'Yes,' he said at last, 'I will come.'

4

His encounter with Caterham was entirely different from his anticipation. He had seen the man only twice in his life, once at dinner and once in the lobby of the House, and his imagination had been active not with the man but with the creation of the newspapers and caricaturists, the legendary Caterham, Jack the Giant-Killer, Perseus, and all the rest of it. The element of a human personality came in to disorder all that.

Here was not the face of the caricatures and portraits, but the face of a worn and sleepless man, lined and drawn, yellow in the whites of the eyes, a little weakened about the mouth. Here, indeed, were the red-brown eyes, the black hair, the distinctive aquiline profile of the great demagogue, but here was also something else that smote any premeditated scorn and rhetoric aside. This man was suffering; he was suffering acutely; he was under enormous stress. From the beginning he had an air of impersonating himself. Presently, with a single gesture, the slightest movement, he revealed to Redwood that he was keeping himself up with drugs. He moved a thumb to his waistcoat pocket, and then, after a few sentences more, threw concealment aside and slipped the little tabloid to his lips.

Moreover, in spite of the stresses upon him, in spite of the fact that he was in the wrong, and Redwood's junior by a dozen years, that strange quality in him, the something – personal magnetism one may call it for want of a better name – that had won his way for him to this eminence of disaster was with him still. On that also Redwood had failed to reckon. From the first, so far as the course and conduct of their speech went, Caterham prevailed over Redwood. All the quality of the first phase of their meeting was determined by him, all the tone and procedure were his. That happened as if it was a matter of course. All Redwood's expectations vanished at his presence. He shook hands before Redwood remembered that he meant to parry that familiarity; he pitched the note of their conference from the outset, sure and clear, as a search for expedients under a common catastrophe.

If he made any mistake it was when ever and again his fatigue got the better of his immediate attention, and the habit of the public meeting carried him away. Then he drew himself up – through all their interview both men stood – and looked away from Redwood, and began to fence and justify. Once even he said, 'Gentlemen!'

Quietly, expandingly, he began to talk . . .

There were moments when Redwood ceased even to feel himself an interlocutor, when he became the mere auditor of a monologue. He became the privileged spectator of an extraordinary phenomenon. He perceived something almost like a specific difference between himself and this being whose beautiful voice enveloped him, who was talking, talking. This mind before him was so powerful and so limited. From its driving energy, its personal weight, its invincible oblivion to certain things, there sprang up in Redwood's mind the most grotesque and strange of images. Instead of an antagonist who was a fellow-creature, a man one could hold morally responsible, and to whom one could address reasonable appeals, he saw Caterham as something, something like a monstrous rhinoceros, as it were, a civilised rhinoceros begotten of the jungle of democratic affairs, a monster of irresistible onset and invincible resistance. In all the crashing conflicts of that tangle he was supreme. And beyond? This man was a being supremely adapted to make his way through multitudes of men. For him there was no fault so important as self-contradiction, no science so significant as the reconciliation of 'interests'. Economic realities, topographical necessities, the barely touched mines of scientific expedients, existed for him no more than railways or rifled guns or geographical literature exist for his animal prototype. What did exist were gatherings, and caucuses, and votes – above all, votes. He was votes incarnate – millions of votes.

And now in the great crisis, with the Giants broken but not beaten, this vote-monster talked.

It was so evident that even now he had everything to learn. He did not know there were physical laws and economic laws, quantities and reactions that all humanity voting *nemine contradicente* cannot vote away, and that are disobeyed only at the price of destruction. He did not know there are moral laws that cannot be bent by any force of glamour, or are bent only to fly back with vindictive violence. In the face of shrapnel or the Judgement Day, it was evident to Redwood that this man would have sheltered behind some curiously dodged vote of the House of Commons.

What most concerned his mind now was not the powers that held the fastness away there to the south, not defeat and death, but the effect of these things upon his Majority, the cardinal reality in his life. He had to defeat the Giants or go under. He was by no means absolutely despairful. In this hour of his utmost failure, with blood and disaster upon his hands, and the rich promise of still more horrible disaster, with the gigantic destinies of the world towering and toppling over him, he was capable of a belief that by sheer exertion of his voice, by explaining and qualifying and restating, he might yet reconstitute his power. He was puzzled and distressed no doubt, fatigued and suffering, but if only he could keep up, if only he could keep talking –

As he talked he seemed to Redwood to advance and recede, to dilate and

contract. Redwood's share of the talk was of the most subsidiary sort, wedges as it were suddenly thrust in. 'That's all nonsense.' 'No.' 'It's no use suggesting that.' 'Then why did you begin?'

It is doubtful if Caterham really heard him at all. Round such interpolations Caterham's speech flowed indeed like some swift stream about a rock. There this incredible man stood, on his official hearthrug, talking, talking with enormous power and skill, talking as though a pause in his talk, his explanations, his presentation of standpoints and lights, of considerations and expedients, would permit some antagonistic influence to leap into being – into vocal being, the only being he could comprehend. There he stood amidst the slightly faded splendours of that official room in which one man after another had succumbed to the belief that a certain power of intervention was the creative control of an empire . . .

The more he talked the more certain Redwood's sense of stupendous futility grew. Did this man realise that while he stood and talked there, the whole great world was moving, that the invincible tide of growth flowed and flowed, that there were any hours but parliamentary hours, or any weapons in the hands of the Avengers of Blood? Outside, darkling the whole room, a single leaf of giant Virginian creeper tapped unheeded on the pane.

Redwood became anxious to end this amazing monologue, to escape to sanity and judgement, to that beleaguered camp, the fastness of the future, where, at the very nucleus of greatness, the Sons were gathered together. For that this talking was endured. He had a curious impression that unless this monologue ended he would presently find himself carried away by it, that he must fight against Caterham's voice as one fights against a drug. Facts had altered and were altering beneath that spell.

What was the man saying?

Since Redwood had to report it to the Children of the Food, in a sort of way he perceived it did matter. He would have to listen and guard his sense of realities as well as he could.

Much about blood guiltiness. That was eloquence. That didn't matter. Next?

He was suggesting a convention!

He was suggesting that the surviving Children of the Food should capitulate and go apart and form a community of their own. There were precedents, he said, for this. 'We would assign them territory – '

'Where?' interjected Redwood, stooping to argue.

Caterham snatched at that concession. He turned his face to Redwood's, and his voice fell to a persuasive reasonableness. That could be determined. That, he contended, was a quite subsidiary question. Then he went on to stipulate: 'And except for them and where they are we must have absolute control, the Food and all the Fruits of the Food must be stamped out – '

Redwood found himself bargaining: 'The princess?'

'She stands apart.'

'No,' said Redwood, struggling to get back to the old footing. 'That's absurd.'

'That afterwards. At any rate we are agreed that the making of the Food must stop – '

'I have agreed to nothing. I have said nothing – '

'But on one planet, to have two races of men, one great, one small! Consider what has happened! Consider that is but a little foretaste of what might presently happen if this Food has its way! Consider all you have already brought upon this world! If there is to be a race of Giants, increasing and multiplying – '

'It is not for me to argue,' said Redwood. 'I must go to our sons. I want to go to my son. That is why I have come to you. Tell me exactly what you offer.'

Caterham made a speech upon his terms.

The Children of the Food were to be given a great reservation – in North America perhaps or Africa – in which they might live out their lives in their own fashion.

'But it's nonsense,' said Redwood. 'There are other Giants now abroad. All over Europe – here and there!'

'There could be an international convention. It's *not* impossible. Something of the sort indeed has already been spoken of . . . But in this reservation they can live out their own lives in their own way. They may do what they like; they may make what they like. We shall be glad if they will make us things. They may be happy. Think!'

'Provided there are no more Children.'

'Precisely. The children are for us. And so, sir, we shall save the world, we shall save it absolutely from the fruits of your terrible discovery. It is not too late for us. Only we are eager to temper expediency with mercy. Even now we are burning and searing the places their shells hit yesterday. We can get it under. Trust me we shall get it under. But in that way, without cruelty, without injustice – '

'And suppose the Children do not agree?'

For the first time Caterham looked Redwood fully in the face.

'They must!'

'I don't think they will.'

'Why should they not agree?' he asked, in richly toned amazement.

'Suppose they don't?'

'What can it be but war? We cannot have the thing go on. We cannot. sir. Have you scientific men *no* imagination? Have you no mercy? We cannot have our world trampled under a growing herd of such monsters and monstrous growths as your Food has made. We cannot and we cannot! I ask you, sir, what can it be but war? And remember – this that has happened is only a beginning! *This* was a skirmish. A mere affair of

police. Believe me, a mere affair of police. Do not be cheated by per-
spective, by the immediate bigness of these newer things. Behind us is the
nation – is humanity. Behind the thousands who have died there are
millions. Were it not for the fear of bloodshed, sir, behind our first attacks
there would be forming other attacks, even now. Whether we can kill this
Food or not, most assuredly we can kill your sons! You reckon too much
on the things of yesterday, on the happenings of a mere score of years, on
one battle. You have no sense of the slow course of history. I offer this
convention for the sake of lives, not because it can change the inevitable
end. If you think that your poor two dozen of Giants can resist all the
forces of our people and of all the alien peoples who will come to our aid;
if you think you can change Humanity at a blow, in a single generation,
and alter the nature and stature of Man – '

He flung out an arm. 'Go to them now, sir. I see them, for all the evil
they have done, crouching among their wounded – '

He stopped, as though he had glanced at Redwood's son by chance.

There came a pause.

'Go to them,' he said.

'That is what I want to do.'

'Then go now . . . '

He turned and pressed the button of a bell; without, in immediate
response, came a sound of opening doors and hastening feet.

The talk was at an end. The display was over. Abruptly Caterham
seemed to contract, to shrivel up into a yellow-faced, fagged-out, middle-
sized, middle-aged man. He stepped forward, as if he were stepping out
of a picture, and, with a complete assumption of that friendliness that
lies behind all the public conflicts of our race, he held out his hand to
Redwood. As if it were a matter of course, Redwood shook hands with him
for the second time.

CHAPTER FIVE

The Giant Leaguer

Presently Redwood found himself in a train going south over the Thames.
He had a brief vision of the river shining under its lights, and of the smoke
still going up from the place where the shell had fallen on the north
bank, and where a vast multitude of men had been organised to burn the
Herakleophorbia out of the ground. The southern bank was dark, for some
reason even the streets were not lit, all that was clearly visible were the
outlines of the tall alarm-towers and the dark bulks of flats and schools, and
after a minute of peering scrutiny he turned his back on the window and

sank into thought. There was nothing more to see or do until he saw the Sons . . .

He was fatigued by the stresses of the last two days; it seemed to him that his emotions must needs be exhausted, but he had fortified himself with strong coffee before starting, and his thoughts ran thin and clear. His mind touched many things. He reviewed again, but now in the enlightenment of accomplished events, the manner in which the Food had entered and unfolded itself in the world.

'Bensington thought it might be an excellent food for infants,' he whispered to himself, with a faint smile. Then there came into his mind as vivid as if they were still unsettled his own horrible doubts after he had committed himself by giving it to his own son. From that, with a steady unfaltering expansion, in spite of every effort of men to help and hinder, the Food had spread through the whole world of man. And now?

'Even if they kill them all,' Redwood whispered, 'the thing is done.'

The secret of its making was known far and wide. That had been his own work. Plants, animals, a multitude of distressful growing children would conspire irresistibly to force the world to revert again to the Food, whatever happened in the present struggle. 'The thing is done,' he said, with his mind swinging round beyond all his controlling to rest upon the present fate of the Children and his son. Would he find them exhausted by the efforts of the battle, wounded, starving, on the verge of defeat, or would he find them still stout and hopeful, ready for the still grimmer conflict of the morrow? His son was wounded! But he had sent a message!

His mind came back to his interview with Caterham.

He was roused from his thoughts by the stopping of his train in Chisle-hurst station. He recognised the place by the huge rat alarm-tower that crested Camden Hill, and the row of blossoming giant hemlocks that lined the road . . .

Caterham's private secretary came to him from the other carriage and told him that half a mile farther the line had been wrecked, and that the rest of the journey was to be made in a motor car. Redwood descended upon a platform lit only by a hand lantern and swept by the cool night breeze. The quiet of that derelict, wood-set, weed-embedded suburb – for all the inhabitants had taken refuge in London at the outbreak of yesterday's conflict – became instantly impressive. His conductor took him down the steps to where a motor car was waiting with blazing lights – the only lights to be seen, handed him over to the care of the driver and bade him farewell.

'You will do your best for us,' he said, with an imitation of his master's manner, as he held Redwood's hand.

So soon as Redwood could be wrapped about they started out into the night. At one moment they stood still, and then the motor car was rushing softly and swiftly down the station incline. They turned one corner and another, followed the windings of a lane of villas, and then before them

stretched the road. The motor droned up to its topmost speed, and the black night swept past them. Everything was very dark under the starlight, and the whole world crouched mysteriously and was gone without a sound. Not a breath stirred the flying things by the wayside; the deserted, pallid white villas on either hand, with their black unlit windows, reminded him of a noiseless procession of skulls. The driver beside him was a silent man, or stricken into silence by the conditions of his journey. He answered Redwood's brief questions in monosyllables, and gruffly. Athwart the southern sky the beams of searchlights waved noiseless passes; the sole strange evidences of life they seemed in all that derelict world about the hurrying machine.

The road was presently bordered on either side by gigantic blackthorn shoots that made it very dark, and by tail grass and big campions, huge giant dead-nettles as high as trees, flickering past darkly in silhouette overhead. Beyond Keston they came to a rising hill, and the driver went slow. At the crest he stopped. The engine throbbed and became still. 'There,' he said, and his big gloved finger pointed, a black misshapen thing before Redwood's eyes.

Far away as it seemed, the great embankment, crested by the blaze from which the searchlights sprang, rose up against the sky. Those beams went and came among the clouds and the hilly land about them as if they traced mysterious incantations.

'I don't know,' said the driver at last, and it was clear he was afraid to go on.

Presently a searchlight swept down the sky to them, stopped as it were with a start, scrutinised them, a blinding stare confused rather than mitigated by an intervening monstrous weed stem or so. They sat with their gloves held over their eyes, trying to look under them and meet that light.

'Go on,' said Redwood after a while.

The driver still had his doubts; he tried to express them, and died down to 'I don't know' again.

At last he ventured on. 'Here goes,' he said, and roused his machinery to motion again, followed intently by that great white eye.

To Redwood it seemed for a long time they were no longer on earth but passing in a state of palpitating hurry through a luminous cloud. Teuf, teuf, teuf, teuf, went the machine, and ever and again – obeying I know not what nervous impulse – the driver sounded his horn.

They passed into the welcome darkness of a high-fenced lane, and down into a hollow and past some houses into that blinding stare again. Then for a space the road ran naked across a down, and they seemed to hang throbbing in immensity. Once more giant weeds rose about them and whirled past. Then quite abruptly close upon them loomed the figure of a giant, shining brightly where the searchlight caught him below, and black against the sky above. 'Hello there!' he cried, and, 'stop! There's no more road beyond . . . Is that Father Redwood?'

Redwood stood up and gave a vague shout by way of answer, and then Cossar was in the road beside him, gripping both hands with both of his and pulling him out of the car.

'What of my son?' asked Redwood.

'He's all right,' said Cossar. 'They've hurt nothing serious in *him*.'

'And your lads?'

'Well. All of them, well. But we've had to make a fight for it.'

The Giant was saying something to the motor driver. Redwood stood aside as the machine wheeled round, and then suddenly Cossar vanished, everything vanished, and he was in absolute darkness for a space. The glare was following the motor back to the crest of the Keston hill. He watched the little conveyance receding in that white halo. It had a curious effect, as though it was not moving at all and the halo was. A group of war-blasted giant trees flashed into gaunt scarred gesticulations and were swallowed again by the night . . . Redwood turned to Cossar's dim outline again and clasped his hand. 'I have been shut up and kept in ignorance,' he said, 'for two whole days.'

'We fired the Food at them,' said Cossar. 'Obviously! Thirty shots. Eh!'

'I come from Caterham.'

'I know you do.' He laughed with a note of bitterness. 'I suppose he's wiping it up.'

2

'Where is my son?' said Redwood.

'He is all right. The Giants are waiting for your message.'

'Yes, but my son – '

He passed with Cossar down a long slanting tunnel that was lit red for a moment and then became dark again, and came out presently into the great pit of shelter the Giants had made.

Redwood's first impression was of an enormous arena bounded by very high cliffs and with its floor greatly encumbered. It was in darkness save for the passing reflections of the watchman's searchlights that whirled perpetually high overhead, and for a red glow that came and went from a distant corner where two Giants worked together amidst a metallic clangour. Against the sky, as the glare came about, his eye caught the familiar outlines of the old worksheds and playsheds that were made for the Cossar boys. They were hanging now, as it were, at a cliff brow, and strangely twisted and distorted with the guns of Caterham's bombardment. There were suggestions of huge gun emplacements above there, and nearer were piles of mighty cylinders that were perhaps ammunition. All about the wide space below, the forms of great engines and incomprehensible bulks were scattered in vague disorder. The Giants appeared and vanished among

these masses and in the uncertain light; great shapes they were, not dis-
proportionate to the things amidst which they moved. Some were actively
employed, some sitting and lying as if they courted sleep, and one near at
hand, whose body was bandaged, lay on a rough litter of pine boughs and
was certainly asleep. Redwood peered at these dim forms; his eyes went
from one stirring outline to another.

'Where is my son, Cossar?'

Then he saw him.

His son was sitting under the shadow of a great wall of steel. He
presented himself as a black shape recognisable only by his pose – his
features were invisible. He sat chin upon hand, as though weary or lost in
thought. Beside him Redwood discovered the figure of the princess, the
dark suggestion of her merely, and then, as the glow from the distant iron
returned, he saw for an instant, red-lit and tender, the infinite kindliness of
her shadowed face. She stood looking down upon her lover with her hand
resting against the steel. It seemed that she whispered to him.

Redwood would have gone towards them.

'Presently,' said Cossar. 'First there is your message.'

'Yes,' said Redwood, 'but – '

He stopped. His son was now looking up and speaking to the princess,
but in too low a tone for them to hear. Young Redwood raised his face, and
she bent down towards him, and glanced aside before she spoke.

'But if we are beaten,' they heard the whispered voice of young Redwood.

She paused, and the red blaze showed her eyes bright with unshed tears.
She bent nearer him and spoke still lower. There was something so intimate
and private in their bearing, in their soft tones, that Redwood – Redwood
who had thought for two whole days of nothing but his son – felt himself
intrusive there. Abruptly he was checked. For the first time in his life
perhaps he realised how much more a son may be to his father than a father
can ever be to a son; he realised the full predominance of the future over the
past. Here between these two he had no part. His part was played. He
turned to Cossar, in the instant realisation. Their eyes met. His voice was
changed to the tone of a grey resolve.

'I will deliver my message now,' he said. 'Afterwards – . . . It will be soon
enough then.'

The pit was so enormous and so encumbered that it was a long and
tortuous route to the place from which Redwood could speak to them all.

He and Cossar followed a steeply descending way that passed beneath an
arch of interlocking machinery, and so came into a vast deep gangway that
ran athwart the bottom of the pit. This gangway, wide and vacant, and yet
relatively narrow, conspired with everything about it to enhance Redwood's
sense of his own littleness. It became, as it were, an excavated gorge. High
overhead, separated from him by cliffs of darkness, the searchlights wheeled
and blazed, and the shining shapes went to and fro. Giant voices called to

one another above there, calling the Giants together to the Council of War, to hear the terms that Caterham had sent. The gangway still inclined downward towards black vastnesses, towards shadows and mysteries and inconceivable things, into which Redwood went slowly with reluctant footsteps and Cossar with a confident stride.

Redwood's thoughts were busy. The two men passed into the completest darkness, and Cossar took his companion's wrist. They went now slowly perforce.

Redwood was moved to speak. 'All this,' he said, 'is strange.'

'Big,' said Cossar.

'Strange. And strange that it should be strange to me – I, who am, in a sense, the beginning of it all. It's – '

He stopped, wrestling with his elusive meaning, and threw an unseen gesture at the cliff.

'I have not thought of it before. I have been busy, and the years have passed. But here I see. It is a new generation, Cossar, and new emotions and new needs. All this, Cossar – ' Cossar saw now his dim gesture to the things about them. 'All this is Youth.'

Cossar made no answers and his irregular footfalls went striding on.

'It isn't *our* youth, Cossar. They are taking things over. They are beginning upon their own emotions, their own experiences, their own way. We have made a new world, and it isn't ours. It isn't even – sympathetic. This great place – '

'I planned it,' said Cossar, his face close.

'But now?'

'Ah! I have given it to my sons.'

Redwood could feel the loose wave of the arm that he could not see.

'That is it. We are over – or almost over.'

'Your message!'

'Yes. And then – '

'We're over.'

'Well – ?'

'Of course we are out of it, we two old men,' said Cossar, with his familiar note of sudden anger. 'Of course we are. Obviously. Each man for his own time. And now – it's *their* time beginning. That's all right. Excavator's gang. We do our job and go. See? That is what Death is for. We work out all our little brains and all our little emotions, and then this lot begins afresh. Fresh and fresh! Perfectly simple. What's the trouble?'

He paused to guide Redwood to some steps.

'Yes,' said Redwood, 'but one feels – '

He left his sentence incomplete.

'That is what Death is for.' He heard Cossar below him insisting, 'How else could the thing be done? That is what Death is for.'

After devious windings and ascents they came out upon a projecting ledge from which it was possible to see over the greater extent of the Giants' pit, and from which Redwood might make himself heard by the whole of their assembly. The Giants were already gathered below and about him at different levels, to hear the message he had to deliver. The eldest son of Cossar stood on the bank overhead watching the revelations of the searchlights, for they feared a breach of the truce. The workers at the great apparatus in the corner stood out clear in their own light; they were near stripped; they turned their faces towards Redwood, but with a watchful reference ever and again to the castings that they could not leave. He saw these nearer figures with a fluctuating indistinctness by lights that came and went, and the remoter ones still less distinctly. They came from and vanished again into the depths of great obscurities. For these Giants had no more light than they could help in the pit, that their eyes might be ready to see effectually any attacking force that might spring upon them out of the darknesses around.

Ever and again some chance glare would pick out and display this group or that of tall and powerful forms, the Giants from Sunderland clothed in overlapping metal plates, and the others clad in leather, in woven rope or in woven metal, as their conditions had determined. They sat amidst or rested their hands upon or stood erect among machines and weapons as mighty as themselves, and all their faces, as they came and went from visible to invisible, had steadfast eyes.

He made an effort to begin and did not do so.

Then for a moment his son's face glowed out in a hot insurgence of the fire, his son's face looking up to him, tender as well as strong; and at that he found a voice to reach them all, speaking across a gulf, as it were, to his son.

'I come from Caterham,' he said. 'He sent me to you, to tell you the terms he offers.'

He paused. 'They are impossible terms, I know, now that I see you here all together; they are impossible terms, but I brought them to you, because I wanted to see you all – and my son. Once more . . . I wanted to see my son . . .'

'Tell them the terms,' said Cossar.

'This is what Caterham offers. He wants you to go apart and leave his world!'

'Where?'

'He does not know. Vaguely somewhere in the world a great region is to be set apart . . . And you are to make no more of the Food, to have no

children of your own, to live in your own way for your own time, and then to end for ever.'

He stopped.

'And that is all?'

'That is all.'

There followed a great stillness. The darkness that veiled the Giants seemed to look thoughtfully at him.

He felt a touch at his elbow, and Cossar was holding a chair for him – a queer fragment of doll's furniture amidst these piled immensities. He sat down and crossed his legs, and then put one across the knee of the other, and clutched his boot nervously, and felt small and self-conscious and acutely visible and absurdly placed.

Then at the sound of a voice he forgot himself again.

'You have heard, Brothers,' said this voice out of the shadows.

And another answered, 'We have heard.'

'And the answer, Brothers?'

'To Caterham? Is No!'

'And then?'

There was a silence for the space of some seconds.

Then a voice said: 'These people are right. After their lights, that is. They have been right in killing all that grew larger than its kind – beast and plant and all manner of great things that arose. They were right in trying to massacre us. They are right now in saying we must not marry our kind. According to their lights they are right. They know – it is time that we also knew – that you cannot have pigmies and giants in one world together. Caterham has said that again and again – clearly – their world or ours.'

'We are not half a hundred now,' said another, 'and they are endless millions.'

'So it may be. But the thing is as I have said.'

Then another long silence.

'And are we to die then?'

'God forbid!'

'Are they?'

'No.'

'But that is what Caterham says! He would have us live out our lives, die one by one, till only one remains, and that one at last would die also, and they would cut down all the giant plants and weeds, kill all the giant underlife, burn out the traces of the Food – make an end to us and to the Food for ever. Then the little pigmy world would be safe. They would go on – safe for ever, living their little pigmy lives, doing pigmy kindnesses and pigmy cruelties each to the other; they might even perhaps attain a sort of pigmy millennium, make an end to war, make an end to over-population, sit down in a worldwide city to practise pigmy arts, worshipping one another till the world begins to freeze . . .'

In the corner a sheet of iron fell in thunder to the ground.

'Brothers, we know what we mean to do.'

In a spluttering of light from the searchlights, Redwood saw earnest youthful faces turning to his son.

'It is easy now to make the Food. It would be easy for us to make Food for all the world.'

'You mean, Brother Redwood,' said a voice out of the darkness, 'that it is for the little people to eat the Food.'

'What else is there to do?'

'We are not half a hundred and they are many millions.'

'But we held our own.'

'So far.'

'If it is God's will, we may still hold our own.'

'Yes. But think of the dead!'

Another voice took up the strain. 'The dead?' it said. 'Think of the unborn . . .'

'Brothers,' came the voice of young Redwood, 'what can we do but fight them, and if we beat them, make them take the Food? They cannot help but take the Food now. Suppose we were to resign our heritage and do this folly that Caterham suggests! Suppose we could! Suppose we give up this great thing that stirs within us, repudiate this thing our fathers did for us – that *you*, father, did for us – and pass, when our time has come, into decay and nothingness! What then? Will this little world of theirs be as it was before? They may fight against greatness in us who are the children of men, but can they conquer? Even if they should destroy us every one, what then? Would it save them? No! For greatness is abroad, not only in us, not only in the Food, but in the purpose of all things! It is in the nature of all things; it is part of space and time. To grow and still to grow: from first to last that is Being – that is the law of life. What other law can there be?'

'To help others?'

'To grow. It is still, to grow. Unless we help them to fail . . .'

'They will fight hard to overcome us,' said a voice.

And another, 'What of that?'

'They will fight,' said young Redwood. 'If we refuse these terms, I doubt not they will fight. Indeed I hope they will be open and fight. If after all they offer peace, it will be only the better to catch us unawares. Make no mistake, Brothers; in some way or other they will fight. The war has begun, and we must fight, to the end. Unless we are wise, we may find presently we have lived only to make them better weapons against our children and our kind. This, so far, has been only the dawn of battle. All our lives will be a battle. Some of us will be killed in battle, some of us will be waylaid. There is no easy victory – no victory whatever that is not more than half defeat for us. Be sure of that. What of that? If only we keep a foothold, if only we leave behind us a growing host to fight when we are gone!'

'And tomorrow?'

'We will scatter the Food; we will saturate the world with the Food.'

'Suppose they come to terms?'

'Our terms are the Food. It is not as though little and great could live together in any perfection of compromise. It is one thing or the other. What right have parents to say, My child shall have no light but the light I have had, shall grow no greater than the greatness to which I have grown? Do I speak for you, Brothers?'

Assenting murmurs answered him.

'And to the children who will be women as well as to the children who will be men . . . ' said a voice from the darkness.

'Even more so – to be mothers of a new race . . . '

'But for the next generation there must be great and little,' said Redwood, with his eyes on his son's face.

'For many generations. And the little will hamper the great and the great press upon the little. So it must needs be, father.'

'There will be conflict.'

'Endless conflict. Endless misunderstanding. All life is that. Great and little cannot understand one another. But in every child born of man, Father Redwood, lurks some seed of greatness – waiting for the Food.'

'Then I am to go to Caterham again and tell him – '

'You will stay with us, Father Redwood. Our answer goes to Caterham at dawn.'

'He says that he will fight . . . '

'So be it,' said young Redwood, and his brethren murmured assent.

'*The iron waits*,' cried a voice, and the two Giants who were working in the corner began a rhythmic hammering that made a mighty music to the scene. The metal glowed out far more brightly than it had done before, and gave Redwood a clearer view of the encampment than had yet come to him. He saw the oblong space to its full extent, with the great engines of warfare ranged ready to hand. Beyond, and at a higher level, the house of the Cossars stood. About him were the young Giants, huge and beautiful, glittering in their mail, amidst the preparations for the morrow. The sight of them lifted his heart. They were so easily powerful! They were so tall and gracious! They were so steadfast in their movements! There was his son among them, and the first of all giant women, the princess . . .

There leapt into his mind the oddest contrast, a memory of Bensington, very bright and little – Bensington with his hand amid the soft breast feathers of that first great chick, standing in that conventionally furnished room of his, peering over his spectacles dubiously as Cousin Jane banged the door . . .

It had all happened in a yesterday of one-and-twenty years.

Then suddenly a strange doubt took hold of him: that this place and present greatness were but the texture of a dream; that he was dreaming,

and would in an instant wake to find himself in his study again, the Giants slaughtered, the Food suppressed, and himself a prisoner locked in. What else indeed was life but that – always to be a prisoner locked in! This was the culmination and end of his dream. He would wake, through bloodshed and battle, to find his Food the most foolish of fancies, and his hopes and faith of a greater world to come no more than the coloured film upon a pool of bottomless decay. Littleness invincible!

So strong and deep was this wave of despondency, this suggestion of impending disillusionment, that he started to his feet. He stood and pressed his clenched fists into his eyes, and so for a moment remained, fearing to open them again and see, lest the dream should already have passed away . . .

The voice of the giant children spoke to one another, an undertone to that clangorous melody of the smiths. His tide of doubt ebbed. He heard the giant voices; he heard their movements about him still. It was real, surely it was real – as real as spiteful acts! More real, for these great things, it may be, are the coming things, and the littleness, bestiality and infirmity of men are the things that go. He opened his eyes.

'Done,' cried one of the two ironworkers, and they flung their hammers down.

A voice sounded above. The son of Cossar, standing on the great embankment, had turned and was now speaking to them all.

'It is not that we would oust the little people from the world,' he said, 'in order that we, who are no more than one step upwards from their littleness, may hold their world for ever. It is the step we fight for and not ourselves . . . We are here, Brothers, to what end? To serve the spirit and the purpose that has been breathed into our lives. We fight not for ourselves – for we are but the momentary hands and eyes of the Life of the World. So you, Father Redwood, taught us. Through us and through the little folk the Spirit looks and learns. From us by word and birth and act it must pass – to still greater lives. This earth is no resting place; this earth is no playing place, else indeed we might put our throats to the little people's knife, having no greater right to live than they. And they in their turn might yield to the ants and vermin. We fight not for ourselves but for growth – growth that goes on for ever. Tomorrow, whether we live or die, growth will conquer through us. That is the law of the spirit for ever more. To grow according to the will of God! To grow out of these cracks and crannies, out of these shadows and darknesses, into greatness and the light! Greater,' he said, speaking with slow deliberation, 'greater, my Brothers! And then – still greater. To grow, and again – to grow. To grow at last into the fellowship and understanding of God. Growing . . . Till the earth is no more than a footstool . . . Till the spirit shall have driven fear into nothingness, and spread . . . ' he swung his arm heavenward – '*there!*'

His voice ceased. The white glare of one of the searchlights wheeled

about, and for a moment fell upon him, standing out gigantic with hand upraised against the sky.

For one instant he shone, looking up fearlessly into the starry deeps, mail-clad, young and strong, resolute and still. Then the light had passed, and he was no more than a great black outline against the starry sky – a great black outline that threatened with one mighty gesture the firmament of heaven and all its multitude of stars.

from the thunderstorm the night of the catastrophe. Our muddy footsteps I saw still went up the stairs.

I followed them to my study, and found lying on my writing-table still, with the selenite paperweight upon it, the sheet of work I had left on the afternoon of the opening of the cylinder. For a space I stood reading over my abandoned arguments. It was a paper on the probable development of Moral Ideas with the development of the civilising process, and the last sentence was the opening of a prophecy: 'In about two hundred years,' I had written, 'we may expect – ' The sentence ended abruptly. I remembered my inability to fix my mind that morning, scarcely a month gone by, and how I had broken off to get my *Daily Chronicle* from the newsboy. I remembered how I went down to the garden gate as he came along, and how I had listened to his odd story of 'Men from Mars'.

I came down and went into the dining room. There were the mutton and the bread, both far gone now in decay, and a beer bottle overturned, just as I and the artilleryman had left them. My home was desolate. I perceived the folly of the faint hope I had cherished so long. And then a strange thing occurred. 'It is no use,' said a voice. 'The house is deserted. No one has been here these ten days. Do not stay here to torment yourself. No one escaped but you.'

I was startled. Had I spoken my thought aloud? I turned, and the French window was open behind me. I made a step to it, and stood looking out.

And there, amazed and afraid, even as I stood amazed and afraid, were my cousin and my wife – my wife white and tearless. She gave a faint cry.

'I came,' she said. 'I knew – knew – '

She put her hand to her throat – swayed. I made a step forward, and caught her in my arms.

The Epilogue

I cannot but regret, now that I am concluding my story, how little I am able to contribute to the discussion of the many debatable questions which are still unsettled. In one respect I shall certainly provoke criticism. My particular province is speculative philosophy. My knowledge of comparative physiology is confined to a book or two, but it seems to me that Carver's suggestions as to the reason of the rapid death of the Martians is

so probable as to be regarded almost as a proven conclusion. I have assumed that in the body of my narrative.

At any rate, in all the bodies of the Martians that were examined after the war, no bacteria except those already known as terrestrial species were found. That they did not bury any of their dead, and the reckless slaughter they perpetrated, point also to an entire ignorance of the putrefactive process. But probable as this seems, it is by no means a proven conclusion.

Neither is the composition of the Black Smoke known, which the Martians used with such deadly effect, and the generator of the Heat-Rays remains a puzzle. The terrible disasters at the Ealing and South Kensington laboratories have disinclined analysts for further investigations upon the latter. Spectrum analysis of the black powder points unmistakably to the presence of an unknown element with a brilliant group of three lines in the green, and it is possible that it combines with argon to form a compound which acts at once with deadly effect upon some constituent in the blood. But such unproven speculations will scarcely be of interest to the general reader, to whom this story is addressed. None of the brown scum that drifted down the Thames after the destruction of Shepperton was examined at the time, and now none is forthcoming.

The results of an anatomical examination of the Martians, so far as the prowling dogs had left such an examination possible, I have already given. But everyone is familiar with the magnificent and almost complete specimen in spirits at the Natural History Museum, and the countless drawings that have been made from it; and beyond that the interest of their physiology and structure is purely scientific.

A question of graver and universal interest is the possibility of another attack from the Martians. I do not think that nearly enough attention is being given to this aspect of the matter. At present the planet Mars is in conjunction, but with every return to opposition I, for one, anticipate a renewal of their adventure. In any case, we should be prepared. It seems to me that it should be possible to define the position of the gun from which the shots are discharged, to keep a sustained watch upon this part of the planet, and to anticipate the arrival of the next attack.

In that case the cylinder might be destroyed with dynamite or artillery before it was sufficiently cool for the Martians to emerge, or they might be butchered by means of guns so soon as the screw opened. It seems to me that they have lost a vast advantage in the failure of their first surprise. Possibly they see it in the same light.

Lessing has advanced excellent reasons for supposing that the Martians have actually succeeded in effecting a landing on the planet Venus. Seven months ago now, Venus and Mars were in alignment with the sun; that is to say, Mars was in opposition from the point of view of an observer on Venus. Subsequently a peculiar luminous and sinuous marking appeared on the unillumined half of the inner planet, and almost simultaneously a faint dark

mark of a similar sinuous character was detected upon a photograph of the Martian disk. One needs to see the drawings of these appearances in order to appreciate fully their remarkable resemblance in character.

At any rate, whether we expect another invasion or not, our views of the human future must be greatly modified by these events. We have learned now that we cannot regard this planet as being fenced in and a secure abiding place for Man; we can never anticipate the unseen good or evil that may come upon us suddenly out of space. It may be that in the larger design of the universe this invasion from Mars is not without its ultimate benefit for men; it has robbed us of that serene confidence in the future which is the most fruitful source of decadence, the gifts to human science it has brought are enormous, and it has done much to promote the conception of the commonweal of mankind. It may be that across the immensity of space the Martians have watched the fate of these pioneers of theirs and learned their lesson, and that on the planet Venus they have found a securer settlement. Be that as it may, for many years yet there will certainly be no relaxation of the eager scrutiny of the Martian disk, and those fiery darts of the sky, the shooting stars, will bring with them as they fall an unavoidable apprehension to all the sons of men.

The broadening of men's views that has resulted can scarcely be exaggerated. Before the cylinder fell there was a general persuasion that through all the deep of space no life existed beyond the petty surface of our minute sphere. Now we see further. If the Martians can reach Venus, there is no reason to suppose that the thing is impossible for men, and when the slow cooling of the sun makes this earth uninhabitable, as at last it must do, it may be that the thread of life that has begun here will have streamed out and caught our sister planet within its toils.

Dim and wonderful is the vision I have conjured up in my mind of life spreading slowly from this little seed bed of the solar system throughout the inanimate vastness of sidereal space. But that is a remote dream. It may be, on the other hand, that the destruction of the Martians is only a reprieve. To them, and not to us, perhaps, is the future ordained.

The War of the Worlds

A novel first published in 1898

Contents

BOOK ONE

The Coming of the Martians

BOOK TWO

The Earth Under the Martians

BOOK ONE

The Coming of the Martians

The War of the Worlds was first published in Great Britain
in serial form in 1897 by *Pearson's Magazine* and
in the United States by *Cosmopolitan*.
The casebound edition was first published in 1898
by William Heinemann in London
and by Harper & Brothers in New York.

CHAPTER ONE

The Eve of the War

N O ONE WOULD HAVE BELIEVED in the last years of the nineteenth century that this world was being watched keenly and closely by intelligences greater than man's and yet as mortal as his own; that as men busied themselves about their various concerns they were scrutinised and studied, perhaps almost as narrowly as a man with a microscope might scrutinise the transient creatures that swarm and multiply in a drop of water. With infinite complacency men went to and fro over this globe about their little affairs, serene in their assurance of their empire over matter. It is possible that the infusoria under the microscope do the same. No one gave a thought to the older worlds of space as sources of human danger, or thought of them only to dismiss the idea of life upon them as impossible or improbable. It is curious to recall some of the mental habits of those departed days. At most terrestrial men fancied there might be other men upon Mars, perhaps inferior to themselves and ready to welcome a missionary enterprise. Yet across the gulf of space, minds that are to our minds as ours are to those of the beasts that perish, intellects vast and cool and unsympathetic, regarded this earth with envious eyes, and slowly and surely drew their plans against us. And early in the twentieth century came the great disillusionment.

The planet Mars, I scarcely need remind the reader, revolves about the sun at a mean distance of 140,000,000 miles, and the light and heat it receives from the sun is barely half of that received by this world. It must be, if the nebular hypothesis has any truth, older than our world; and long before this earth ceased to be molten, life upon its surface must have begun its course. The fact that it is scarcely one-seventh of the volume of the earth must have accelerated its cooling to the temperature at which life could begin. It has air and water and all that is necessary for the support of animated existence.

Yet so vain is man, and so blinded by his vanity, that no writer, up to the very end of the nineteenth century, expressed any idea that intelligent life might have developed there far, or indeed at all, beyond its earthly level. Nor was it generally understood that since Mars is older than our earth, with scarcely a quarter of the superficial area and remoter from the sun, it necessarily follows that it is not only more distant from time's beginning but nearer its end.

The secular cooling that must someday overtake our planet has already gone far indeed with our neighbour. Its physical condition is still largely a

mystery, but we know now that even in its equatorial region the midday temperature barely approaches that of our coldest winter. Its air is much more attenuated than ours, its oceans have shrunk until they cover but a third of its surface, and as its slow seasons change huge snowcaps gather and melt about either pole and periodically inundate its temperate zones. That last stage of exhaustion, which to us is still incredibly remote, has become a present-day problem for the inhabitants of Mars. The immediate pressure of necessity has brightened their intellects, enlarged their powers, and hardened their hearts. And looking across space with instruments, and intelligences such as we have scarcely dreamed of, they see, at its nearest distance only 35,000,000 of miles sunward of them, a morning star of hope, our own warmer planet, green with vegetation and grey with water, with a cloudy atmosphere eloquent of fertility, with glimpses through its drifting cloud wisps of broad stretches of populous country and narrow, navy crowded seas.

And we men, the creatures who inhabit this earth, must be to them at least as alien and lowly as are the monkeys and lemurs to us. The intellectual side of man already admits that life is an incessant struggle for existence, and it would seem that this too is the belief of the minds upon Mars. Their world is far gone in its cooling and this world is still crowded with life, but crowded only with what they regard as inferior animals. To carry warfare sunward is, indeed, their only escape from the destruction that, generation after generation, creeps upon them.

And before we judge of them too harshly we must remember what ruthless and utter destruction our own species has wrought, not only upon animals, such as the vanished bison and the dodo, but upon its inferior races. The Tasmanians, in spite of their human likeness, were entirely swept out of existence in a war of extermination waged by European immigrants, in the space of fifty years. Are we such apostles of mercy as to complain if the Martians warred in the same spirit?

The Martians seem to have calculated their descent with amazing subtlety – their mathematical learning is evidently far in excess of ours – and to have carried out their preparations with a well-nigh perfect unanimity. Had our instruments permitted it, we might have seen the gathering trouble far back in the nineteenth century. Men like Schiaparelli watched the red planet – it is odd, by the by, that for countless centuries Mars has been the star of war – but failed to interpret the fluctuating appearances of the markings they mapped so well. All that time the Martians must have been getting ready.

During the opposition of 1894 a great light was seen on the illuminated part of the disk, first at the Lick Observatory, then by Perrotin of Nice, and then by other observers. English readers heard of it first in the issue of *Nature* dated August 2. I am inclined to think that this blaze may have been the casting of the huge gun, in the vast pit sunk into their planet, from

which their shots were fired at us. Peculiar markings, as yet unexplained, were seen near the site of that outbreak during the next two oppositions.

The storm burst upon us six years ago now. As Mars approached opposition, Lavelle of Java set the wires of the astronomical exchange palpitating with the amazing intelligence of a huge outbreak of incandescent gas upon the planet. It had occurred towards midnight of the twelfth; and the spectroscope, to which he had at once resorted, indicated a mass of flaming gas, chiefly hydrogen, moving with an enormous velocity towards this earth. This jet of fire had become invisible about a quarter past twelve. He compared it to a colossal puff of flame suddenly and violently squirted out of the planet, 'as flaming gases rushed out of a gun'.

A singularly appropriate phrase it proved. Yet the next day there was nothing of this in the papers except a little note in the *Daily Telegraph*, and the world went in ignorance of one of the gravest dangers that ever threatened the human race. I might not have heard of the eruption at all had I not met Ogilvy, the well-known astronomer, at Ottershaw. He was immensely excited at the news, and in the excess of his feelings invited me up to take a turn with him that night in a scrutiny of the red planet.

In spite of all that has happened since, I still remember that vigil very distinctly: the black and silent observatory, the shadowed lantern throwing a feeble glow upon the floor in the corner, the steady ticking of the clockwork of the telescope, the little slit in the roof – an oblong profundity with the stardust streaked across it. Ogilvy moved about, invisible but audible. Looking through the telescope, one saw a circle of deep blue and the little round planet swimming in the field. It seemed such a little thing, so bright and small and still, faintly marked with transverse stripes, and slightly flattened from the perfect round. But so little it was, so silvery warm – a pin's-head of light! It was as if it quivered, but really this was the telescope vibrating with the activity of the clockwork that kept the planet in view.

As I watched, the planet seemed to grow larger and smaller and to advance and recede, but that was simply that my eye was tired. Forty millions of miles it was from us – more than forty millions of miles of void. Few people realise the immensity of vacancy in which the dust of the material universe swims.

Near it in the field, I remember, were three faint points of light, three telescopic stars infinitely remote, and all around it was the unfathomable darkness of empty space. You know how that blackness looks on a frosty starlight night. In a telescope it seems far profounder. And invisible to me because it was so remote and small, flying swiftly and steadily towards me across that incredible distance, drawing nearer every minute by so many thousands of miles, came the Thing they were sending us, the Thing that was to bring so much struggle and calamity and death to the earth. I never dreamed of it then as I watched; no one on earth dreamed of that unerring missile.

That night, too, there was another jetting out of gas from the distant planet. I saw it. A reddish flash at the edge, the slightest projection of the outline just as the chronometer struck midnight; and at that I told Ogilvy and he took my place. The night was warm and I was thirsty, and I went stretching my legs clumsily and feeling my way in the darkness, to the little table where the siphon stood, while Ogilvy exclaimed at the streamer of gas that came out towards us.

That night another invisible missile started on its way to the earth from Mars, just a second or so under twenty-four hours after the first one. I remember how I sat on the table there in the blackness, with patches of green and crimson swimming before my eyes. I wished I had a light to smoke by, little suspecting the meaning of the minute gleam I had seen and all that it would presently bring me. Ogilvy watched till one, and then gave it up; and we lit the lantern and walked over to his house. Down below in the darkness were Ottershaw and Chertsey and all their hundreds of people, sleeping in peace.

He was full of speculation that night about the condition of Mars, and scoffed at the vulgar idea of its having inhabitants who were signalling us. His idea was that meteorites might be falling in a heavy shower upon the planet, or that a huge volcanic explosion was in progress. He pointed out to me how unlikely it was that organic evolution had taken the same direction in the two adjacent planets.

'The chances against anything manlike on Mars are a million to one,' he said.

Hundreds of observers saw the flame that night and the night after about midnight, and again the night after; and so for ten nights, a flame each night. Why the shots ceased after the tenth no one on earth has attempted to explain. It may be the gases of the firing caused the Martians inconvenience. Dense clouds of smoke or dust, visible through a powerful telescope on earth as little grey, fluctuating patches, spread through the clearness of the planet's atmosphere and obscured its more familiar features.

Even the daily papers woke up to the disturbances at last, and popular notes appeared here, there, and everywhere concerning the volcanoes upon Mars. The serio-comic periodical *Punch*, I remember, made a happy use of it in the political cartoon. And, all unsuspected, those missiles the Martians had fired at us drew earthward, rushing now at a pace of many miles a second through the empty gulf of space, hour by hour and day by day, nearer and nearer. It seems to me now almost incredibly wonderful that, with that swift fate hanging over us, men could go about their petty concerns as they did. I remember how jubilant Markham was at securing a new photograph of the planet for the illustrated paper he edited in those days. People in these latter times scarcely realise the abundance and enterprise of our nineteenth-century papers. For my own part, I was much

occupied in learning to ride the bicycle, and busy upon a series of papers discussing the probable developments of moral ideas as civilisation progressed.

One night (the first missile then could scarcely have been 10,000,000 miles away) I went for a walk with my wife. It was starlight and I explained the Signs of the Zodiac to her, and pointed out Mars, a bright dot of light creeping zenithward, towards which so many telescopes were pointed. It was a warm night. Coming home, a party of excursionists from Chertsey or Isleworth passed us singing and playing music. There were lights in the upper windows of the houses as the people went to bed. From the railway station in the distance came the sound of shunting trains, ringing and rumbling, softened almost into melody by the distance. My wife pointed out to me the brightness of the red, green, and yellow signal lights hanging in a framework against the sky. It seemed so safe and tranquil.

CHAPTER TWO

The Falling Star

Then came the night of the first falling star. It was seen early in the morning, rushing over Winchester eastward, a line of flame high in the atmosphere. Hundreds must have seen it, and taken it for an ordinary falling star. Albin described it as leaving a greenish streak behind it that glowed for some seconds. Denning, our greatest authority on meteorites, stated that the height of its first appearance was about ninety or one hundred miles. It seemed to him that it fell to earth about one hundred miles east of him.

I was at home at that hour and writing in my study; and although my French windows face towards Ottershaw and the blind was up (for I loved in those days to look up at the night sky), I saw nothing of it. Yet this strangest of all things that ever came to earth from outer space must have fallen while I was sitting there, visible to me had I only looked up as it passed. Some of those who saw its flight say it travelled with a hissing sound. I myself heard nothing of that. Many people in Berkshire, Surrey, and Middlesex must have seen the fall of it, and, at most, have thought that another meteorite had descended. No one seems to have troubled to look for the fallen mass that night.

But very early in the morning poor Ogilvy, who had seen the shooting star and who was persuaded that a meteorite lay somewhere on the common between Horsell, Ottershaw, and Woking, rose early with the idea of finding it. Find it he did, soon after dawn, and not far from the sand pits. An enormous hole had been made by the impact of the projectile, and the sand and gravel had been flung violently in every direction over the heath,

forming heaps visible a mile and a half away. The heather was on fire eastward, and a thin blue smoke rose against the dawn.

The Thing itself lay almost entirely buried in sand, amidst the scattered splinters of a fir tree it had shivered to fragments in its descent. The uncovered part had the appearance of a huge cylinder, caked over and its outline softened by a thick scaly dun-coloured incrustation. It had a diameter of about thirty yards. He approached the mass, surprised at the size and more so at the shape, since most meteorites are rounded more or less completely. It was, however, still so hot from its flight through the air as to forbid his near approach. A stirring noise within its cylinder he ascribed to the unequal cooling of its surface; for at that time it had not occurred to him that it might be hollow.

He remained standing at the edge of the pit that the Thing had made for itself, staring at its strange appearance, astonished chiefly at its unusual shape and colour, and dimly perceiving even then some evidence of design in its arrival. The early morning was wonderfully still, and the sun, just clearing the pine trees towards Weybridge, was already warm. He did not remember hearing any birds that morning, there was certainly no breeze stirring, and the only sounds were the faint movements from within the cindery cylinder. He was all alone on the common.

Then suddenly he noticed with a start that some of the grey clinker, the ashy incrustation that covered the meteorite, was falling off the circular edge of the end. It was dropping off in flakes and raining down upon the sand. A large piece suddenly came off and fell with a sharp noise that brought his heart into his mouth.

For a minute he scarcely realised what this meant, and, although the heat was excessive, he clambered down into the pit close to the bulk to see the Thing more clearly. He fancied even then that the cooling of the body might account for this, but what disturbed that idea was the fact that the ash was falling only from the end of the cylinder.

And then he perceived that, very slowly, the circular top of the cylinder was rotating on its body. It was such a gradual movement that he discovered it only through noticing that a black mark that had been near him five minutes ago was now at the other side of the circumference. Even then he scarcely understood what this indicated, until he heard a muffled grating sound and saw the black mark jerk forward an inch or so. Then the thing came upon him in a flash. The cylinder was artificial – hollow – with an end that screwed out! Something within the cylinder was unscrewing the top!

'Good heavens!' said Ogilvy. 'There's a man in it – men in it! Half roasted to death! Trying to escape!'

At once, with a quick mental leap, he linked the Thing with the flash upon Mars.

The thought of the confined creature was so dreadful to him that he forgot the heat and went forward to the cylinder to help turn. But luckily

the dull radiation arrested him before he could burn his hands on the still-glowing metal. At that he stood irresolute for a moment, then turned, scrambled out of the pit, and set off running wildly into Woking. The time then must have been somewhere about six o'clock. He met a waggoner and tried to make him understand, but the tale he told and his appearance were so wild - his hat had fallen off in the pit - that the man simply drove on. He was equally unsuccessful with the potman who was just unlocking the doors of the public-house by Horsell Bridge. The fellow thought he was a lunatic at large and made an unsuccessful attempt to shut him into the taproom. That sobered him a little; and when he saw Henderson, the London journalist, in his garden, he called over the palings and made himself understood.

'Henderson,' he called, 'you saw that shooting star last night?'

'Well?' said Henderson.

'It's out on Horsell Common now.'

'Good Lord!' said Henderson. 'Fallen meteorite! That's good.'

'But it's something more than a meteorite. It's a cylinder - an artificial cylinder, man! And there's something inside.'

Henderson stood up with his spade in his hand.

'What's that?' he said. He was deaf in one ear.

Ogilvy told him all that he had seen. Henderson was a minute or so taking it in. Then he dropped his spade, snatched up his jacket, and came out into the road. The two men hurried back at once to the common, and found the cylinder still lying in the same position. But now the sounds inside had ceased, and a thin circle of bright metal showed between the top and the body of the cylinder. Air was either entering or escaping at the rim with a thin, sizzling sound.

They listened, rapped on the scaly burnt metal with a stick, and, meeting with no response, they both concluded the man or men inside must be insensible or dead.

Of course the two were quite unable to do anything. They shouted consolation and promises, and went off back to the town again to get help. One can imagine them, covered with sand, excited and disordered, running up the little street in the bright sunlight just as the shop folks were taking down their shutters and people were opening their bedroom windows. Henderson went into the railway station at once, in order to telegraph the news to London. The newspaper articles had prepared men's minds for the reception of the idea.

By eight o'clock a number of boys and unemployed men had already started for the common to see the 'dead men from Mars'. That was the form the story took. I heard of it first from my newspaper boy about a quarter to nine when I went out to get my *Daily Chronicle*. I was naturally startled, and lost no time in going out and across the Ottershaw bridge to the sand pits.

CHAPTER THREE

On Horsell Common

I found a little crowd of perhaps twenty people surrounding the huge hole in which the cylinder lay. I have already described the appearance of that colossal bulk, embedded in the ground. The turf and gravel about it seemed charred as if by a sudden explosion. No doubt its impact had caused a flash of fire. Henderson and Ogilvy were not there. I think they perceived that nothing was to be done for the present, and had gone away to breakfast at Henderson's house.

There were four or five boys sitting on the edge of the pit, with their feet dangling, and amusing themselves – until I stopped them – by throwing stones at the giant mass. After I had spoken to them about it, they began playing at 'touch' in and out of the group of bystanders.

Among these were a couple of cyclists, a jobbing gardener I employed sometimes, a girl carrying a baby, Gregg the butcher and his little boy, and two or three loafers and golf caddies who were accustomed to hang about the railway station. There was very little talking. Few of the common people in England had anything but the vaguest astronomical ideas in those days. Most of them were staring quietly at the big table-ike end of the cylinder, which was still as Ogilvy and Henderson had left it. I fancy the popular expectation of a heap of charred corpses was disappointed at this inanimate bulk. Some went away while I was there, and other people came. I clambered into the pit and fancied I heard a faint movement under my feet. The top had certainly ceased to rotate.

It was only when I got thus close to it that the strangeness of this object was at all evident to me. At the first glance it was really no more exciting than an overturned carriage or a tree blown across the road. Not so much so, indeed. It looked like a rusty gas float. It required a certain amount of scientific education to perceive that the grey scale of the Thing was no common oxide, that the yellowish-white metal that gleamed in the crack between the lid and the cylinder had an unfamiliar hue. 'Extraterrestrial' had no meaning for most of the onlookers.

At that time it was quite clear in my own mind that the Thing had come from the planet Mars, but I judged it improbable that it contained any living creature. I thought the unscrewing might be automatic. In spite of Ogilvy, I still believed that there were men in Mars. My mind ran fancifully on the possibilities of its containing manuscript, on the difficulties in translation that might arise, whether we should find coins and models in it, and so forth. Yet it was a little too large for assurance on this idea. I felt an impatience to see it opened. About eleven, as nothing seemed happening, I

walked back, full of such thought, to my home in Maybury. But I found it difficult to get to work upon my abstract investigations.

In the afternoon the appearance of the common had altered very much. The early editions of the evening papers had startled London with enormous headlines:

A MESSAGE RECEIVED FROM MARS.

REMARKABLE STORY FROM WOKING,

and so forth. In addition, Ogilvy's wire to the Astronomical Exchange had roused every observatory in the three kingdoms.

There were half a dozen flys or more from the Woking station standing in the road by the sand pits, a basket-chaise from Chobham, and a rather lordly carriage. Besides that, there was quite a heap of bicycles. In addition, a large number of people must have walked, in spite of the heat of the day, from Woking and Chertsey, so that there was altogether quite a considerable crowd – one or two gaily dressed ladies among the others.

It was glaringly hot, not a cloud in the sky nor a breath of wind, and the only shadow was that of the few scattered pine trees. The burning heather had been extinguished, but the level ground towards Ottershaw was blackened as far as one could see, and still giving off vertical streamers of smoke. An enterprising sweet-stuff dealer in the Chobham Road had sent up his son with a barrow-load of green apples and ginger beer.

Going to the edge of the pit, I found it occupied by a group of about half a dozen men – Henderson, Ogilvy, and a tall, fair-haired man that I afterwards learned was Stent, the Astronomer Royal, with several workmen wielding spades and pickaxes. Stent was giving directions in a clear, high-pitched voice. He was standing on the cylinder, which was now evidently much cooler; his face was crimson and streaming with perspiration, and something seemed to have irritated him.

A large portion of the cylinder had been uncovered, though its lower end was still embedded. As soon as Ogilvy saw me among the staring crowd on the edge of the pit he called to me to come down, and asked me if I would mind going over to see Lord Hilton, the lord of the manor.

The growing crowd, he said, was becoming a serious impediment to their excavations, especially the boys. They wanted a light railing put up, and help to keep the people back. He told me that a faint stirring was occasionally still audible within the case, but that the workmen had failed to unscrew the top, as it afforded no grip to them. The case appeared to be enormously thick, and it was possible that the faint sounds we heard represented a noisy tumult in the interior.

I was very glad to do as he asked, and so become one of the privileged spectators within the contemplated enclosure. I failed to find Lord Hilton at his house, but I was told he was expected from London by the six o'clock

train from Waterloo; and as it was then about a quarter past five, I went home, had some tea, and walked up to the station to waylay him.

CHAPTER FOUR

The Cylinder Opens

When I returned to the common the sun was setting. Scattered groups were hurrying from the direction of Woking, and one or two persons were returning. The crowd about the pit had increased, and stood out black against the lemon yellow of the sky – a couple of hundred people, perhaps. There were raised voices, and some sort of struggle appeared to be going on about the pit. Strange imaginings passed through my mind. As I drew nearer I heard Stent's voice: 'Keep back! Keep back!'

A boy came running towards me.

'It's a-movin',' he said to me as he passed; 'a-screwin' and a-screwin' out. I don't like it. I'm a-goin' 'ome, I am.'

I went on to the crowd. There were really, I should think, two or three hundred people elbowing and jostling one another, the one or two ladies there being by no means the least active.

'He's fallen in the pit!' cried someone.

'Keep back!' said several.

The crowd swayed a little, and I elbowed my way through. Everyone seemed greatly excited. I heard a peculiar humming sound from the pit.

'I say!' said Ogilvy; 'help keep these idiots back. We don't know what's in the confounded thing, you know!'

I saw a young man, a shop assistant in Woking I believe he was, standing on the cylinder and trying to scramble out of the hole again. The crowd had pushed him in.

The end of the cylinder was being screwed out from within. Nearly two feet of shining screw projected. Somebody blundered against me, and I narrowly missed being pitched on to the top of the screw. I turned, and as I did so the screw must have come out, for the lid of the cylinder fell upon the gravel with a ringing concussion. I stuck my elbow into the person behind me, and turned my head towards the Thing again. For a moment that circular cavity seemed perfectly black. I had the sunset in my eyes.

I think everyone expected to see a man emerge – possibly something a little unlike us terrestrial men, but in all essentials a man. I know I did. But, looking, I presently saw something stirring within the shadow: greyish billowy movements, one above another, and then two luminous disks – like eyes. Then something resembling a little grey snake, about the thickness of a walking stick, coiled up out of the writhing middle, and wriggled in the air towards me – and then another.

A sudden chill came over me. There was a loud shriek from a woman behind. I half turned, keeping my eyes fixed upon the cylinder still, from which other tentacles were now projecting, and began pushing my way back from the edge of the pit. I saw astonishment giving place to horror on the faces of the people about me. I heard inarticulate exclamations on all sides. There was a general movement backwards. I saw the shopman struggling still on the edge of the pit. I found myself alone, and saw the people on the other side of the pit running off, Stent among them. I looked again at the cylinder, and ungovernable terror gripped me. I stood petrified and staring.

A big greyish rounded bulk, the size, perhaps, of a bear, was rising slowly and painfully out of the cylinder. As it bulged up and caught the light, it glistened like wet leather.

Two large dark-coloured eyes were regarding me steadfastly. The mass that framed them, the head of the thing, was rounded, and had, one might say, a face. There was a mouth under the eyes, the lipless brim of which quivered and panted, and dropped saliva. The whole creature heaved and pulsated convulsively. A lank tentacular appendage gripped the edge of the cylinder, another swayed in the air.

Those who have never seen a living Martian can scarcely imagine the strange horror of its appearance. The peculiar V-shaped mouth with its pointed upper lip, the absence of brow ridges, the absence of a chin beneath the wedgelike lower lip, the incessant quivering of this mouth, the Gorgon groups of tentacles, the tumultuous breathing of the lungs in a strange atmosphere, the evident heaviness and painfulness of movement due to the greater gravitational energy of the earth – above all, the extraordinary intensity of the immense eyes – were at once vital, intense, inhuman, crippled and monstrous. There was something fungoid in the oily brown skin, something in the clumsy deliberation of the tedious movements unspeakably nasty. Even at this first encounter, this first glimpse, I was overcome with disgust and dread.

Suddenly the monster vanished. It had toppled over the brim of the cylinder and fallen into the pit, with a thud like the fall of a great mass of leather. I heard it give a peculiar thick cry, and forthwith another of these creatures appeared darkly in the deep shadow of the aperture.

I turned and, running madly, made for the first group of trees, perhaps a hundred yards away; but I ran slantingly and stumbling, for I could not avert my face from these things.

There, among some young pine trees and furze bushes, I stopped, panting, and waited further developments. The common round the sand pits was dotted with people, standing like myself in a half-fascinated terror, staring at these creatures, or rather at the heaped gravel at the edge of the pit in which they lay. And then, with a renewed horror, I saw a round, black object bobbing up and down on the edge of the pit. It was the head of the shopman who had fallen in, but showing as a little black object against the

hot western sun. Now he got his shoulder and knee up, and again he seemed to slip back until only his head was visible. Suddenly he vanished, and I could have fancied a faint shriek had reached me. I had a momentary impulse to go back and help him that my fears overruled.

Everything was then quite invisible, hidden by the deep pit and the heap of sand that the fall of the cylinder had made. Anyone coming along the road from Chobham or Woking would have been amazed at the sight – a dwindling multitude of perhaps a hundred people or more standing in a great irregular circle, in ditches, behind bushes, behind gates and hedges, saying little to one another and that in short, excited shouts, and staring, staring hard at a few heaps of sand. The barrow of ginger beer stood, a queer derelict, black against the burning sky, and in the sand pits was a row of deserted vehicles with their horses feeding out of nosebags or pawing the ground.

CHAPTER FIVE

The Heat-Ray

After the glimpse I had had of the Martians emerging from the cylinder in which they had come to the earth from their planet, a kind of fascination paralysed my actions. I remained standing knee-deep in the heather, staring at the mound that hid them. I was a battleground of fear and curiosity.

I did not dare to go back towards the pit, but I felt a passionate longing to peer into it. I began walking, therefore, in a big curve, seeking some point of vantage and continually looking at the sand heaps that hid these new-comers to our earth. Once a leash of thin black whips, like the arms of an octopus, flashed across the sunset and was immediately withdrawn, and afterwards a thin rod rose up, joint by joint, bearing at its apex a circular disk that spun with a wobbling motion. What could be going on there?

Most of the spectators had gathered in one or two groups – one a little crowd towards Woking, the other a knot of people in the direction of Chobham. Evidently they shared my mental conflict. There were few near me. One man I approached – he was, I perceived, a neighbour of mine, though I did not know his name – and accosted. But it was scarcely a time for articulate conversation.

'What ugly *brutes*!' he said. 'Good God! What ugly brutes!' He repeated this over and over again.

'Did you see a man in the pit?' I said; but he made no answer to that. We became silent, and stood watching for a time side by side, deriving, I fancy, a certain comfort in one another's company. Then I shifted my position to a little knoll that gave me the advantage of a yard or more of elevation and when I looked for him presently he was walking towards Woking.

The sunset faded to twilight before anything further happened. The crowd far away on the left, towards Woking, seemed to grow, and I heard now a faint murmur from it. The little knot of people towards Chobham dispersed. There was scarcely an intimation of movement from the pit.

It was this, as much as anything, that gave people courage, and I suppose the new arrivals from Woking also helped to restore confidence. At any rate, as the dusk came on a slow, intermittent movement upon the sand pits began, a movement that seemed to gather force as the stillness of the evening about the cylinder remained unbroken. Vertical black figures in twos and threes would advance, stop, watch, and advance again, spreading out as they did so in a thin irregular crescent that promised to enclose the pit in its attenuated horns. I, too, on my side began to move towards the pit.

Then I saw some cabmen and others had walked boldly into the sand pits, and heard the clatter of hoofs and the gride of wheels. I saw a lad trundling off the barrow of apples. And then, within thirty yards of the pit, advancing from the direction of Horsell, I noted a little black knot of men, the foremost of whom was waving a white flag.

This was the Deputation. There had been a hasty consultation, and since the Martians were evidently, in spite of their repulsive forms, intelligent creatures, it had been resolved to show them, by approaching them with signals, that we too were intelligent.

Flutter, flutter, went the flag, first to the right, then to the left. It was too far for me to recognise anyone there, but afterwards I learned that Ogilvy, Stent, and Henderson were with others in this attempt at communication. This little group had in its advance dragged inward, so to speak, the circumference of the now almost complete circle of people, and a number of dim black figures followed it at discreet distances.

Suddenly there was a flash of light, and a quantity of luminous greenish smoke came out of the pit in three distinct puffs, which drove up, one after the other, straight into the still air.

This smoke (or flame, perhaps, would be the better word for it) was so bright that the deep blue sky overhead and the hazy stretches of brown common towards Chertsey, set with black pine trees, seemed to darken abruptly as these puffs arose, and to remain the darker after their dispersal. At the same time a faint hissing sound became audible.

Beyond the pit stood the little wedge of people with the white flag at its apex, arrested by these phenomena, a little knot of small vertical black shapes upon the black ground. As the green smoke arose, their faces flashed out pallid green, and faded again as it vanished. Then slowly the hissing passed into a humming, into a long, loud, droning noise. Slowly a humped shape rose out of the pit, and the ghost of a beam of light seemed to flicker out from it.

Forthwith flashes of actual flame, a bright glare leaping from one to another, sprang from the scattered group of men. It was as if some invisible

jet impinged upon them and flashed into white flame. It was as if each man were suddenly and momentarily turned to fire.

Then, by the light of their own destruction, I saw them staggering and falling, and their supporters turning to run.

I stood staring, not as yet realising that this was death leaping from man to man in that little distant crowd. All I felt was that it was something very strange. An almost noiseless and blinding flash of light, and a man fell headlong and lay still; and as the unseen shaft of heat passed over them, pine trees burst into fire, and every dry furze bush became with one dull thud a mass of flames. And far away towards Knaphill I saw the flashes of trees and hedges and wooden buildings suddenly set alight.

It was sweeping round swiftly and steadily, this flaming death, this invisible, inevitable sword of heat. I perceived it coming towards me by the flashing bushes it touched, and was too astounded and stupefied to stir. I heard the crackle of fire in the sand pits and the sudden squeal of a horse that was as suddenly stilled. Then it was as if an invisible yet intensely heated finger were drawn through the heather between me and the Martians, and all along a curving line beyond the sand pits the dark ground smoked and crackled. Something fell with a crash far away to the left where the road from Woking station opens out on the common. Forthwith the hissing and humming ceased, and the black, domelike object sank slowly out of sight into the pit.

All this had happened with such swiftness that I had stood motionless, dumbfounded and dazzled by the flashes of light. Had that death swept through a full circle, it must inevitably have slain me in my surprise. But it passed and spared me, and left the night about me suddenly dark and unfamiliar.

The undulating common seemed now dark almost to blackness, except where its roadways lay grey and pale under the deep blue sky of the early night. It was dark, and suddenly void of men. Overhead the stars were mustering, and in the west the sky was still a pale, bright, almost greenish blue. The tops of the pine trees and the roofs of Horsell came out sharp and black against the western afterglow. The Martians and their appliances were altogether invisible, save for that thin mast upon which their restless mirror wobbled. Patches of bush and isolated trees here and there smoked and glowed still, and the houses towards Woking station were sending up spires of flame into the stillness of the evening air.

Nothing was changed save for that and a terrible astonishment. The little group of black specks with the flag of white had been swept out of existence, and the stillness of the evening, so it seemed to me, had scarcely been broken.

It came to me that I was upon this dark common, helpless, unprotected, and alone. Suddenly, like a thing falling upon me from without, came – fear.

With an effort I turned and began a stumbling run through the heather.

The fear I felt was no rational fear, but a panic terror not only of the Martians, but of the dusk and stillness all about me. Such an extraordinary effect in unmanning me it had that I ran weeping silently as a child might do. Once I had turned, I did not dare to look back.

I remember I felt an extraordinary persuasion that I was being played with, that presently, when I was upon the very verge of safety, this mysterious death – as swift as the passage of light – would leap after me from the pit about the cylinder and strike me down.

CHAPTER SIX

The Heat-Ray in the Chobham Road

It is still a matter of wonder how the Martians are able to slay men so swiftly and so silently. Many think that in some way they are able to generate an intense heat in a chamber of practically absolute non-conductivity. This intense heat they project in a parallel beam against any object they choose, by means of a polished parabolic mirror of unknown composition, much as the parabolic mirror of a lighthouse projects a beam of light. But no one has absolutely proved these details. However it is done, it is certain that a beam of heat is the essence of the matter. Heat, and invisible, instead of visible, light. Whatever is combustible flashes into flame at its touch, lead runs like water, it softens iron, cracks and melts glass, and when it falls upon water, incontinently that explodes into steam.

That night nearly forty people lay under the starlight about the pit, charred and distorted beyond recognition, and all night long the common from Horsell to Maybury was deserted and brightly ablaze.

The news of the massacre probably reached Chobham, Woking, and Ottershaw about the same time. In Woking the shops had closed when the tragedy happened, and a number of people, shop people and so forth, attracted by the stories they had heard, were walking over the Horsell Bridge and along the road between the hedges that runs out at last upon the common. You may imagine the young people brushed up after the labours of the day, and making this novelty, as they would make any novelty, the excuse for walking together and enjoying a trivial flirtation. You may figure to yourself the hum of voices along the road in the gloaming . . .

As yet, of course, few people in Woking even knew that the cylinder had opened, though poor Henderson had sent a messenger on a bicycle to the post office with a special wire to an evening paper.

As these folks came out by twos and threes upon the open, they found little knots of people talking excitedly and peering at the spinning mirror over the sand pits, and the newcomers were, no doubt, soon infected by the excitement of the occasion.

By half-past eight, when the Deputation was destroyed, there may have been a crowd of three hundred people or more at this place, besides those who had left the road to approach the Martians nearer. There were three policemen too, one of whom was mounted, doing their best, under instructions from Stent, to keep the people back and deter them from approaching the cylinder. There was some booing from those more thoughtless and excitable souls to whom a crowd is always an occasion for noise and horseplay.

Stent and Ogilvy, anticipating some possibilities of a collision, had telegraphed from Horsell to the barracks as soon as the Martians emerged, for the help of a company of soldiers to protect these strange creatures from violence. After that they returned to lead that ill-fated advance. The description of their death, as it was seen by the crowd, tallies very closely with my own impressions: the three puffs of green smoke, the deep humming note, and the flashes of flame.

But that crowd of people had a far narrower escape than mine. Only the fact that a hummock of heathery sand intercepted the lower part of the Heat-Ray saved them. Had the elevation of the parabolic mirror been a few yards higher, none could have lived to tell the tale. They saw the flashes and the men falling and an invisible hand, as it were, lit the bushes as it hurried towards them through the twilight. Then, with a whistling note that rose above the droning of the pit, the beam swung close over their heads, lighting the tops of the beech trees that line the road, and splitting the bricks, smashing the windows, firing the window frames, and bringing down in crumbling ruin a portion of the gable of the house nearest the corner.

In the sudden thud, hiss, and glare of the igniting trees, the panic-stricken crowd seems to have swayed hesitatingly for some moments. Sparks and burning twigs began to fall into the road, and single leaves like puffs of flame. Hats and dresses caught fire. Then came a crying from the common. There were shrieks and shouts, and suddenly a mounted policeman came galloping through the confusion with his hands clasped over his head, screaming.

'They're coming!' a woman shrieked, and incontinently everyone was turning and pushing at those behind, in order to clear their way to Woking again. They must have bolted as blindly as a flock of sheep. Where the road grows narrow and black between the high banks the crowd jammed, and a desperate struggle occurred. All that crowd did not escape; three persons at least, two women and a little boy, were crushed and trampled there, and left to die amid the terror and the darkness.

CHAPTER SEVEN

How I Reached Home

For my own part, I remember nothing of my flight except the stress of blundering against trees and stumbling through the heather. All about me gathered the invisible terrors of the Martians; that pitiless sword of heat seemed whirling to and fro, flourishing overhead before it descended and smote me out of life. I came into the road between the crossroads and Horsell, and ran along this to the crossroads.

At last I could go no further; I was exhausted with the violence of my emotion and of my flight, and I staggered and fell by the wayside. That was near the bridge that crosses the canal by the gasworks. I fell and lay still.

I must have remained there some time.

I sat up, strangely perplexed. For a moment, perhaps, I could not clearly understand how I came there. My terror had fallen from me like a garment. My hat had gone, and my collar had burst away from its fastener. A few minutes before, there had only been three real things before me – the immensity of the night and space and nature, my own feebleness and anguish, and the near approach of death. Now it was as if something turned over, and the point of view altered abruptly. There was no sensible transition from one state of mind to the other. I was immediately the self of every day again – a decent, ordinary citizen. The silent common, the impulse of my flight, the starting flames, were as if they had been in a dream. I asked myself had these latter things indeed happened? I could not credit it.

I rose and walked unsteadily up the steep incline of the bridge. My mind was blank wonder. My muscles and nerves seemed drained of their strength. I dare say I staggered drunkenly. A head rose over the arch, and the figure of a workman carrying a basket appeared. Beside him ran a little boy. He passed me, wishing me good-night. I was minded to speak to him, but did not. I answered his greeting with a meaningless mumble and went on over the bridge.

Over the Maybury arch a train, a billowing tumult of white, firelit smoke, and a long caterpillar of lighted windows, went flying south – clatter, clatter, clap, rap, and it had gone. A dim group of people talked in the gate of one of the houses in the pretty little row of gables that was called Oriental Terrace. It was all so real and so familiar. And that behind me! It was frantic, fantastic! Such things, I told myself, could not be.

Perhaps I am a man of exceptional moods. I do not know how far my experience is common. At times I suffer from the strangest sense of detachment from myself and the world about me; I seem to watch it all from

the outside, from somewhere inconceivably remote, out of time, out of space, out of the stress and tragedy of it all. This feeling was very strong upon me that night. Here was another side to my dream.

But the trouble was the blank incongruity of this serenity and the swift death flying yonder, not two miles away. There was a noise of business from the gasworks, and the electric lamps were all alight. I stopped at the group of people.

'What news from the common?' said I.

There were two men and a woman at the gate.

'Eh?' said one of the men, turning.

'What news from the common?' I said.

' 'Ain't yer just *been* there?' asked the men.

'People seem fair silly about the common,' said the woman over the gate. 'What's it all abart?'

'Haven't you heard of the men from Mars?' said I; 'the creatures from Mars?'

'Quite enough,' said the woman over the gate. 'Thenks'; and all three of them laughed.

I felt foolish and angry. I tried and found I could not tell them what I had seen. They laughed again at my broken sentences.

'You'll hear more yet,' I said, and went on to my home.

I startled my wife at the doorway, so haggard was I. I went into the dining room, sat down, drank some wine, and so soon as I could collect myself sufficiently I told her the things I had seen. The dinner, which was a cold one, had already been served, and remained neglected on the table while I told my story.

'There is one thing,' I said, to allay the fears I had aroused; 'they are the most sluggish things I ever saw crawl. They may keep the pit and kill people who come near them, but they cannot get out of it . . . But the horror of them!'

'Don't, dear!' said my wife, knitting her brows and putting her hand on mine.

'Poor Ogilvy!' I said. 'To think he may be lying dead there!'

My wife at least did not find my experience incredible. When I saw how deadly white her face was, I ceased abruptly.

'They may come here,' she said again and again.

I pressed her to take wine, and tried to reassure her.

'They can scarcely move,' I said.

I began to comfort her and myself by repeating all that Ogilvy had told me of the impossibility of the Martians establishing themselves on the earth. In particular I laid stress on the gravitational difficulty. On the surface of the earth the force of gravity is three times what it is on the surface of Mars. A Martian, therefore, would weigh three times more than on Mars, albeit his muscular strength would be the same. His own

body would be a cope of lead to him. That, indeed, was the general opinion. Both *The Times* and the *Daily Telegraph*, for instance, insisted on it the next morning, and both overlooked, just as I did, two obvious modifying influences.

The atmosphere of the earth, we now know, contains far more oxygen or far less argon (whichever way one likes to put it) than does Mars. The invigorating influences of this excess of oxygen upon the Martians indisputably did much to counterbalance the increased weight of their bodies. And, in the second place, we all overlooked the fact that such mechanical intelligence as the Martian possessed was quite able to dispense with muscular exertion at a pinch.

But I did not consider these points at the time, and so my reasoning was dead against the chances of the invaders. With wine and food, the confidence of my own table, and the necessity of reassuring my wife, I grew by insensible degrees courageous and secure.

'They have done a foolish thing,' said I, fingering my wineglass. 'They are dangerous because, no doubt, they are mad with terror. Perhaps they expected to find no living things – certainly no intelligent living things.'

'A shell in the pit,' said I, 'if the worst comes to the worst, will kill them all.'

The intense excitement of the events had no doubt left my perceptive powers in a state of erethism. I remember that dinner table with extra-ordinary vividness even now. My dear wife's sweet anxious face peering at me from under the pink lampshade, the white cloth with its silver and glass table furniture – for in those days even philosophical writers had many little luxuries – the crimson-purple wine in my glass, are photographically distinct. At the end of it I sat, tempering nuts with a cigarette, regretting Ogilvy's rashness, and denouncing the short-sighted timidity of the Martians.

So some respectable dodo in the Mauritius might have lorded it in his nest, and discussed the arrival of that shipful of pitiless sailors in want of animal food. 'We will peck them to death tomorrow, my dear.'

I did not know it, but that was the last civilised dinner I was to eat for very many strange and terrible days.

CHAPTER EIGHT

Friday Night

The most extraordinary thing to my mind, of all the strange and wonderful things that happened upon that Friday, was the dovetailing of the commonplace habits of our social order with the first beginnings of the series of events that was to topple that social order headlong. If on Friday night you had taken a pair of compasses and drawn a circle with a radius of

five miles round the Woking sand pits, I doubt if you would have had one human being outside it, unless it were some relation of Stent or of the three or four cyclists or London people lying dead on the common, whose emotions or habits were at all affected by the new-comers. Many people had heard of the cylinder, of course, and talked about it in their leisure, but it certainly did not make the sensation that an ultimatum to Germany would have done.

In London that night poor Henderson's telegram describing the gradual unscrewing of the shot was judged to be a canard, and his evening paper, after wiring for authentication from him and receiving no reply – the man was killed – decided not to print a special edition.

Even within the five-mile circle the great majority of people were inert. I have already described the behaviour of the men and women to whom I spoke. All over the district people were dining and supping; working men were gardening after the labours of the day, children were being put to bed, young people were wandering through the lanes love-making, students sat over their books.

Maybe there was a murmur in the village streets, a novel and dominant topic in the public-houses, and here and there a messenger, or even an eye-witness of the later occurrences, caused a whirl of excitement, a shouting, and a running to and fro; but for the most part the daily routine of working, eating, drinking, sleeping, went on as it had done for countless years – as though no planet Mars existed in the sky. Even at Woking station and Horsell and Chobham that was the case.

In Woking junction, until a late hour, trains were stopping and going on, others were shunting on the sidings, passengers were alighting and waiting, and everything was proceeding in the most ordinary way. A boy from the town, trenching on Smith's monopoly, was selling papers with the after-noon's news. The ringing impact of trucks, the sharp whistle of the engines from the junction, mingled with their shouts of 'Men from Mars!' Excited men came into the station about nine o'clock with incredible tidings, and caused no more disturbance than drunkards might have done. People rattling Londonwards peered into the darkness outside the carriage windows, and saw only a rare, flickering, vanishing spark dance up from the direction of Horsell, a red glow and a thin veil of smoke driving across the stars, and thought that nothing more serious than a heath fire was happening. It was only round the edge of the common that any disturbance was perceptible. There were half a dozen villas burning on the Woking border. There were lights in all the houses on the common side of the three villages, and the people there kept awake till dawn.

A curious crowd lingered restlessly, people coming and going but the crowd remaining, both on the Chobham and Horsell bridges. One or two adventurous souls, it was afterwards found, went into the darkness and crawled quite near the Martians; but they never returned, for now and again

a light-ray, like the beam of a warship's searchlight, swept the common, and the Heat-Ray was ready to follow. Save for such, that big area of common was silent and desolate, and the charred bodies lay about on it all night under the stars, and all the next day. A noise of hammering from the pit was heard by many people.

So you have the state of things on Friday night. In the centre, sticking into the skin of our old planet Earth like a poisoned dart, was this cylinder. But the poison was scarcely working yet. Around it was a patch of silent common, smouldering in places, and with a few dark, dimly seen objects lying in contorted attitudes here and there. Here and there was a burning bush or tree. Beyond was a fringe of excitement, and farther than that fringe the inflammation had not crept as yet. In the rest of the world the stream of life still flowed as it had flowed for immemorial years. The fever of war that would presently clog vein and artery, deaden nerve and destroy brain, had still to develop.

All night long the Martians were hammering and stirring, sleepless, indefatigable, at work upon the machines they were making ready, and ever and again a puff of greenish-white smoke whirled up to the starlit sky.

About eleven a company of soldiers came through Horsell, and deployed along the edge of the common to form a cordon. Later a second company marched through Chobham to deploy on the north side of the common. Several officers from the Inkerman barracks had been on the common earlier in the day, and one, Major Eden, was reported to be missing. The colonel of the regiment came to the Chobham bridge and was busy questioning the crowd at midnight. The military authorities were certainly alive to the seriousness of the business. About eleven, the next morning's papers were able to say, a squadron of hussars, two Maxims, and about four hundred men of the Cardigan regiment started from Aldershot.

A few seconds after midnight the crowd in the Chertsey road, Woking, saw a star fall from heaven into the pine woods to the north-west. It had a greenish colour, and caused a silent brightness like summer lightning. This was the second cylinder.

CHAPTER NINE

The Fighting Begins

Saturday lives in my memory as a day of suspense. It was a day of lassitude too, hot and close, with, I am told, a rapidly fluctuating barometer. I had slept but little, though my wife had succeeded in sleeping, and I rose early. I went into my garden before breakfast and stood listening, but towards the common there was nothing stirring but a lark.

The milkman came as usual. I heard the rattle of his chariot and I went

round to the side gate to ask the latest news. He told me that during the night the Martians had been surrounded by troops, and that guns were expected. Then – a familiar, reassuring note – I heard a train running towards Woking.

'They aren't to be killed,' said the milkman, 'if that can possibly be avoided.'

I saw my neighbour gardening, chatted with him for a time, and then strolled in to breakfast. It was a most unexceptional morning. My neighbour was of opinion that the troops would be able to capture or to destroy the Martians during the day.

'It's a pity they make themselves so unapproachable,' he said. 'It would be curious to know how they live on another planet; we might learn a thing or two.'

He came up to the fence and extended a handful of strawberries, for his gardening was as generous as it was enthusiastic. At the same time he told me of the burning of the pine woods about the Byfleet Golf Links.

'They say,' said he, 'that there's another of those blessed things fallen there – number two. But one's enough, surely. This lot'll cost the insurance people a pretty penny before everything's settled.' He laughed with an air of the greatest good humour as he said this. The woods, he said, were still burning, and pointed out a haze of smoke to me. 'They will be hot under foot for days, on account of the thick soil of pine needles and turf,' he said, and then grew serious over 'poor Ogilvy'.

After breakfast, instead of working, I decided to walk down towards the common. Under the railway bridge I found a group of soldiers – sappers, I think, men in small round caps, dirty red jackets unbuttoned, and showing their blue shirts, dark trousers, and boots coming to the calf. They told me no one was allowed over the canal, and, looking along the road towards the bridge, I saw one of the Cardigan men standing sentinel there. I talked with these soldiers for a time; I told them of my sight of the Martians on the previous evening. None of them had seen the Martians, and they had but the vaguest ideas of them, so that they plied me with questions. They said that they did not know who had authorised the movements of the troops; their idea was that a dispute had arisen at the Horse Guards. The ordinary sapper is a great deal better educated than the common soldier, and they discussed the peculiar conditions of the possible fight with some acuteness. I described the Heat-Ray to them, and they began to argue among themselves.

'Crawl up under cover and rush 'em, say I,' said one.

'Get aht!' said another. 'What's cover against this 'ere 'eat? Sticks to cook yer! What we got to do is to go as near as the ground'll let us, and then drive a trench.'

'Blow yer trenches! You always want trenches; you ought to ha' been born a rabbit, Snippy.'

' 'Ain't they got any necks, then?' said a third, abruptly – a little, contemplative, dark man, smoking a pipe.

I repeated my description.

'Octopuses,' said he, 'that's what I calls 'em. Talk about fishers of men – fighters of fish it is this time!'

'It ain't no murder killing beasts like that,' said the first speaker.

'Why not shell the darned things strite off and finish 'em?' said the little dark man. 'You carn tell what they might do.'

'Where's your shells?' said the first speaker. 'There ain't no time. Do it in a rush, that's my tip, and do it at once.'

So they discussed it. After a while I left them, and went on to the railway station to get as many morning papers as I could.

But I will not weary the reader with a description of that long morning and of the longer afternoon. I did not succeed in getting a glimpse of the common, for even Horsell and Chobham church towers were in the hands of the military authorities. The soldiers I addressed didn't know anything; the officers were mysterious as well as busy. I found people in the town quite secure again in the presence of the military, and I heard for the first time from Marshall, the tobacconist, that his son was among the dead on the common. The soldiers had made the people on the outskirts of Horsell lock up and leave their houses.

I got back to lunch about two, very tired for, as I have said, the day was extremely hot and dull; and in order to refresh myself I took a cold bath in the afternoon. About half-past four I went up to the railway station to get an evening paper, for the morning papers had contained only a very inaccurate description of the killing of Stent, Henderson, Ogilvy, and the others. But there was little I didn't know. The Martians did not show an inch of themselves. They seemed busy in their pit, and there was a sound of hammering and an almost continuous streamer of smoke. Apparently they were busy getting ready for a struggle. 'Fresh attempts have been made to signal, but without success,' was the stereotyped formula of the papers. A sapper told me it was done by a man in a ditch with a flag on a long pole. The Martians took as much notice of such advances as we should of the lowing of a cow.

I must confess the sight of all this armament, all this preparation, greatly excited me. My imagination became belligerent, and defeated the invaders in a dozen striking ways; something of my schoolboy dreams of battle and heroism came back. It hardly seemed a fair fight to me at that time. They seemed very helpless in that pit of theirs.

About three o'clock there began the thud of a gun at measured intervals from Chertsey or Addlestone. I learned that the smouldering pine wood into which the second cylinder had fallen was being shelled, in the hope of destroying that object before it opened. It was only about five, however, that a field gun reached Chobham for use against the first body of Martians.

About six in the evening, as I sat at tea with my wife in the summerhouse talking vigorously about the battle that was lowering upon us, I heard a muffled detonation from the common, and immediately after a gust of firing. Close on the heels of that came a violent rattling crash, quite close to us, that shook the ground; and, starting out upon the lawn, I saw the tops of the trees about the Oriental College burst into smoky red flame, and the tower of the little church beside it slide down into ruin. The pinnacle of the mosque had vanished, and the roof line of the college itself looked as if a hundred-ton gun had been at work upon it. One of our chimneys cracked as if a shot had hit it, flew, and a piece of it came clattering down the tiles and made a heap of broken red fragments upon the flower bed by my study window.

I and my wife stood amazed. Then I realised that the crest of Maybury Hill must be within range of the Martians' Heat-Ray now that the college was cleared out of the way.

At that I gripped my wife's arm, and without ceremony ran her out into the road. Then I fetched out the servant, telling her I would go upstairs myself for the box she was clamouring for.

'We can't possibly stay here,' I said; and as I spoke the firing reopened for a moment upon the common.

'But where are we to go?' said my wife in terror.

I thought perplexed. Then I remembered her cousins at Leatherhead.

'Leatherhead!' I shouted above the sudden noise.

She looked away from me downhill. The people were coming out of their houses, astonished.

'How are we to get to Leatherhead?' she said.

Down the hill I saw a bevy of hussars ride under the railway bridge; three galloped through the open gates of the Oriental College; two others dismounted, and began running from house to house. The sun, shining through the smoke that drove up from the tops of the trees, seemed blood red, and threw an unfamiliar lurid light upon everything.

'Stop here,' said I; 'you are safe here'; and I started off at once for the Spotted Dog, for I knew the landlord had a horse and dogcart. I ran, for I perceived that in a moment everyone upon this side of the hill would be moving. I found him in his bar, quite unaware of what was going on behind his house. A man stood with his back to me, talking to him.

'I must have a pound,' said the landlord, 'and I've no one to drive it.'

'I'll give you two,' said I, over the stranger's shoulder.

'What for?'

'And I'll bring it back by midnight,' I said.

'Lord!' said the landlord; 'what's the hurry? I'm selling my bit of a pig. Two pounds, and you bring it back? What's going on now?'

I explained hastily that I had to leave my home, and so secured the dog cart. At the time it did not seem to me nearly so urgent that the landlord

should leave his. I took care to have the cart there and then, drove it off down the road, and, leaving it in charge of my wife and servant, rushed into my house and packed a few valuables, such plate as we had, and so forth. The beech trees below the house were burning while I did this, and the palings up the road glowed red. While I was occupied in this way, one of the dismounted hussars came running up. He was going from house to house, warning people to leave. He was going on as I came out of my front door, lugging my treasures, done up in a tablecloth. I shouted after him: 'What news?'

He turned, stared, bawled something about 'crawling out in a thing like a dish cover', and ran on to the gate of the house at the crest. A sudden whirl of black smoke driving across the road hid him for a moment. I ran to my neighbour's door and rapped to satisfy myself of what I already knew, that his wife had gone to London with him and had locked up their house. I went in again, according to my promise, to get my servant's box, lugged it out, clapped it beside her on the tail of the dog cart, and then caught the reins and jumped up into the driver's seat beside my wife. In another moment we were clear of the smoke and noise, and spanking down the opposite slope of Maybury Hill towards Old Woking.

In front was a quiet sunny landscape, a wheat field ahead on either side of the road, and the Maybury Inn with its swinging sign. I saw the doctor's cart ahead of me. At the bottom of the hill I turned my head to look at the hillside I was leaving. Thick streamers of black smoke shot with threads of red fire were driving up into the still air, and throwing dark shadows upon the green treetops eastward. The smoke already extended far away to the east and west – to the Byfleet pine woods eastward, and to Woking on the west. The road was dotted with people running towards us. And very faint now, but very distinct through the hot, quiet air, one heard the whirr of a machine-gun that was presently stilled, and an intermittent cracking of rifles. Apparently the Martians were setting fire to everything within range of their Heat-Ray.

I am not an expert driver, and I had immediately to turn my attention to the horse. When I looked back again the second hill had hidden the black smoke. I slashed the horse with the whip, and gave him a loose rein until Woking and Send lay between us and that quivering tumult. I overtook and passed the doctor between Woking and Send.

CHAPTER TEN

In the Storm

Leatherhead is about twelve miles from Maybury Hill. The scent of hay was in the air through the lush meadows beyond Pyrford, and the hedges on either side were sweet and gay with multitudes of dog-roses. The heavy firing that had broken out while we were driving down Maybury Hill ceased as abruptly as it began, leaving the evening very peaceful and still. We got to Leatherhead without misadventure about nine o'clock, and the horse had an hour's rest while I took supper with my cousins and commended my wife to their care.

My wife was curiously silent throughout the drive, and seemed oppressed with forebodings of evil. I talked to her reassuringly, pointing out that the Martians were tied to the pit by sheer heaviness, and at the utmost could but crawl a little out of it; but she answered only in monosyllables. Had it not been for my promise to the innkeeper, she would, I think, have urged me to stay in Leatherhead that night. Would that I had! Her face, I remember, was very white as we parted.

For my own part, I had been feverishly excited all day. Something very like the war fever that occasionally runs through a civilised community had got into my blood, and in my heart I was not so very sorry that I had to return to Maybury that night. I was even afraid that that last fusillade I had heard might mean the extermination of our invaders from Mars. I can best express my state of mind by saying that I wanted to be in at the death.

It was nearly eleven when I started to return. The night was unexpectedly dark; to me, walking out of the lighted passage of my cousins' house, it seemed indeed black, and it was as hot and close as the day. Overhead the clouds were driving fast, albeit not a breath stirred the shrubs about us. My cousins' man lit both lamps. Happily, I knew the road intimately. My wife stood in the light of the doorway, and watched me until I jumped up into the dog cart. Then abruptly she turned and went in, leaving my cousins side by side wishing me good hap.

I was a little depressed at first with the contagion of my wife's fears, but very soon my thoughts reverted to the Martians. At that time I was absolutely in the dark as to the course of the evening's fighting. I did not know even the circumstances that had precipitated the conflict. As I came through Ockham (for that was the way I returned, and not through Send and Old Woking) I saw along the western horizon a blood-red glow, which as I drew nearer, crept slowly up the sky. The driving clouds of the gathering thunderstorm mingled there with masses of black and red smoke.

Ripley Street was deserted, and except for a lighted window or so the

village showed not a sign of life; but I narrowly escaped an accident at the corner of the road to Pyrford, where a knot of people stood with their backs to me. They said nothing to me as I passed. I do not know what they knew of the things happening beyond the hill, nor do I know if the silent houses I passed on my way were sleeping securely, or deserted and empty, or harassed and watching against the terror of the night.

From Ripley until I came through Pyrford I was in the valley of the Wey, and the red glare was hidden from me. As I ascended the little hill beyond Pyrford Church the glare came into view again, and the trees about me shivered with the first intimation of the storm that was upon me. Then I heard midnight pealing out from Pyrford Church behind me, and then came the silhouette of Maybury Hill, with its treetops and roofs black and sharp against the red.

Even as I beheld this a lurid green glare lit the road about me and showed the distant woods towards Addlestone. I felt a tug at the reins. I saw that the driving clouds had been pierced as it were by a thread of green fire, suddenly lighting their confusion and falling into the field to my left. It was the third falling star!

Close on its apparition, and blindingly violet by contrast, danced out the first lightning of the gathering storm, and the thunder burst like a rocket overhead. The horse took the bit between his teeth and bolted.

A moderate incline runs towards the foot of Maybury Hill, and down this we clattered. Once the lightning had begun, it went on in as rapid a succession of flashes as I have ever seen. The thunderclaps, treading one on the heels of another and with a strange crackling accompaniment, sounded more like the working of a gigantic electric machine than the usual detonating reverberations. The flickering light was blinding and confusing, and a thin hail smote gustily at my face as I drove down the slope.

At first I regarded little but the road before me, and then abruptly my attention was arrested by something that was moving rapidly down the opposite slope of Maybury Hill. At first I took it for the wet roof of a house, but one flash following another showed it to be in swift rolling movement. It was an elusive vision – a moment of bewildering darkness, and then, in a flash like daylight, the red masses of the Orphanage near the crest of the hill, the green tops of the pine trees, and this problematical object came out clear and sharp and bright.

And this Thing I saw! How can I describe it? A monstrous tripod, higher than many houses, striding over the young pine trees, and smashing them aside in its career; a walking engine of glittering metal, striding now across the heather; articulate ropes of steel dangling from it, and the clattering tumult of its passage mingling with the riot of the thunder. A flash, and it came out vividly, heeling over one way with two feet in the air, to vanish and reappear almost instantly as it seemed, with the next flash, a hundred yards nearer. Can you imagine a milking stool tilted and bowled violently

along the ground? That was the impression those instant flashes gave. But instead of a milking stool imagine it a great body of machinery on a tripod stand.

Then suddenly the trees in the pine wood ahead of me were parted, as brittle reeds are parted by a man thrusting through them; they were snapped off and driven headlong, and a second huge tripod appeared, rushing, as it seemed, headlong towards me. And I was galloping hard to meet it! At the sight of the second monster my nerve went altogether. Not stopping to look again, I wrenched the horse's head hard round to the right and in another moment the dog cart had heeled over upon the horse; the shafts smashed noisily, and I was flung sideways and fell heavily into a shallow pool of water.

I crawled out almost immediately, and crouched, my feet still in the water, under a clump of furze. The horse lay motionless (his neck was broken, poor brute!) and by the lightning flashes I saw the black bulk of the overturned dog cart and the silhouette of the wheel still spinning slowly. In another moment the colossal mechanism went striding by me, and passed uphill towards Pyrford.

Seen nearer, the Thing was incredibly strange, for it was no mere insensate machine driving on its way. Machine it was, with a ringing metallic pace, and long, flexible, glittering tentacles (one of which gripped a young pine tree) swinging and rattling about its strange body. It picked its road as it went striding along, and the brazen hood that surmounted it moved to and fro with the inevitable suggestion of a head looking about. Behind the main body was a huge mass of white metal like a gigantic fisherman's basket, and puffs of green smoke squirted out from the joints of the limbs as the monster swept by me. And in an instant it was gone.

So much I saw then, all vaguely for the flickering of the lightning, in blinding highlights and dense black shadows.

As it passed it set up an exultant deafening howl that drowned the thunder – 'Aloo! Aloo!' – and in another minute it was with its companion, half a mile away, stooping over something in the field. I have no doubt this Thing in the field was the third of the ten cylinders they had fired at us from Mars.

For some minutes I lay there in the rain and darkness watching, by the intermittent light, these monstrous beings of metal moving about in the distance over the hedge tops. A thin hail was now beginning, and as it came and went their figures grew misty and then flashed into clearness again. Now and then came a gap in the lightning, and the night swallowed them up.

I was soaked with hail above and puddle water below. It was some time before my blank astonishment would let me struggle up the bank to a drier position, or think at all of my imminent peril.

Not far from me was a little one-roomed squatter's hut of wood, surrounded by a patch of potato garden. I struggled to my feet at last, and,

crouching and making use of every chance of cover, I made a run for this. I hammered at the door, but I could not make the people hear (if there were any people inside), and after a time I desisted, and, availing myself of a ditch for the greater part of the way, succeeded in crawling, unobserved by these monstrous machines, into the pine woods towards Maybury.

Under cover of this I pushed on, wet and shivering now, towards my own house. I walked among the trees trying to find the footpath. It was very dark indeed in the wood, for the lightning was now becoming infrequent, and the hail, which was pouring down in a torrent, fell in columns through the gaps in the heavy foliage.

If I had fully realised the meaning of all the things I had seen I should have immediately worked my way round through Byfleet to Street Cobham, and so gone back to rejoin my wife at Leatherhead. But that night the strangeness of things about me, and my physical wretchedness, prevented me, for I was bruised, weary, wet to the skin, deafened and blinded by the storm.

I had a vague idea of going on to my own house, and that was as much motive as I had. I staggered through the trees, fell into a ditch and bruised my knees against a plank, and finally splashed out into the lane that ran down from the College Arms. I say splashed, for the storm water was sweeping the sand down the hill in a muddy torrent. There in the darkness a man blundered into me and sent me reeling back.

He gave a cry of terror, sprang sideways, and rushed on before I could gather my wits sufficiently to speak to him. So heavy was the stress of the storm just at this place that I had the hardest task to win my way up the hill. I went close up to the fence on the left and worked my way along its palings.

Near the top I stumbled upon something soft, and, by a flash of lightning, saw between my feet a heap of black broadcloth and a pair of boots. Before I could distinguish clearly how the man lay, the flicker of light had passed. I stood over him waiting for the next flash. When it came, I saw that he was a sturdy man, cheaply but not shabbily dressed; his head was bent under his body, and he lay crumpled up close to the fence, as though he had been flung violently against it.

Overcoming the repugnance natural to one who had never before touched a dead body, I stooped and turned him over to feel for his heart. He was quite dead. Apparently his neck had been broken. The lightning flashed for a third time, and his face leaped upon me. I sprang to my feet. It was the landlord of the Spotted Dog, whose conveyance I had taken.

I stepped over him gingerly and pushed on up the hill. I made my way by the police station and the College Arms towards my own house. Nothing was burning on the hillside, though from the common there still came a red glare and a rolling tumult of ruddy smoke beating up against the drenching hail. So far as I could see by the flashes, the houses about me were mostly uninjured. By the College Arms a dark heap lay in the road.

Down the road towards Maybury Bridge there were voices and the sound of feet, but I had not the courage to shout or to go to them. I let myself in with my latchkey, closed, locked and bolted the door, staggered to the foot of the staircase, and sat down. My imagination was full of those striding metallic monsters, and of the dead body smashed against the fence.

I crouched at the foot of the staircase with my back to the wall, shivering violently.

CHAPTER ELEVEN

At the Window

I have already said that my storms of emotion have a trick of exhausting themselves. After a time I discovered that I was cold and wet, and with little pools of water about me on the stair carpet. I got up almost mechanically, went into the dining room and drank some whisky, and then I was moved to change my clothes.

After I had done that I went upstairs to my study, but why I did so I do not know. The window of my study looks over the trees and the railway towards Horsell Common. In the hurry of our departure this window had been left open. The passage was dark, and, by contrast with the picture the window frame enclosed, the side of the room seemed impenetrably dark. I stopped short in the doorway.

The thunderstorm had passed. The towers of the Oriental College and the pine trees about it had gone, and very far away, lit by a vivid red glare, the common about the sand pits was visible. Across the light huge black shapes, grotesque and strange, moved busily to and fro.

It seemed indeed as if the whole country in that direction was on fire – a broad hillside set with minute tongues of flame, swaying and writhing with the gusts of the dying storm, and throwing a red reflection upon the cloud-scud above. Every now and then a haze of smoke from some nearer con-flagration drove across the window and hid the Martian shapes. I could not see what they were doing, nor the clear form of them, nor recognise the black objects they were busied upon. Neither could I see the nearer fire, though the reflections of it danced on the wall and ceiling of the study. A sharp, resinous tang of burning was in the air.

I closed the door noiselessly and crept towards the window. As I did so, the view opened out until, on the one hand, it reached to the houses about Woking station, and on the other to the charred and blackened pine woods of Byfleet. There was a light down below the hill, on the railway, near the arch, and several of the houses along the Maybury road and the streets near the station were glowing ruins. The light upon the railway puzzled me at first; there were a black heap and a vivid glare, and to the right of that a row

of yellow oblongs. Then I perceived this was a wrecked train, the fore part smashed and on fire, the hinder carriages still upon the rails.

Between these three main centres of light – the houses, the train, and the burning county towards Chobham – stretched irregular patches of dark country, broken here and there by intervals of dimly glowing and smoking ground. It was the strangest spectacle, that black expanse set with fire. It reminded me, more than anything else, of the Potteries at night. At first I could distinguish no people at all, though I peered intently for them. Later I saw against the light of Woking station a number of black figures hurrying one after the other across the line.

And this was the little world in which I had been living securely for years, this fiery chaos! What had happened in the last seven hours I still did not know; nor did I know, though I was beginning to guess, the relation between these mechanical colossi and the sluggish lumps I had seen disgorged from the cylinder. With a queer feeling of impersonal interest I turned my desk chair to the window, sat down, and stared at the blackened country, and particularly at the three gigantic black things that were going to and fro in the glare about the sand pits.

They seemed amazingly busy. I began to ask myself what they could be. Were they intelligent mechanisms? Such a thing I felt was impossible. Or did a Martian sit within each, ruling, directing, using, much as a man's brain sits and rules in his body? I began to compare the things to human machines, to ask myself for the first time in my life how an ironclad or a steam engine would seem to an intelligent lower animal.

The storm had left the sky clear, and over the smoke of the burning land the little fading pinpoint of Mars was dropping into the west, when a soldier came into my garden. I heard a slight scraping at the fence, and rousing myself from the lethargy that had fallen upon me, I looked down and saw him dimly, clambering over the palings. At the sight of another human being my torpor passed, and I leaned out of the window eagerly.

'Hist!' said I, in a whisper.

He stopped astride of the fence in doubt. Then he came over and across the lawn to the corner of the house. He bent down and stepped softly.

'Who's there?' he said, also whispering, standing under the window and peering up.

'Where are you going?' I asked.

'God knows.'

'Are you trying to hide?'

'That's it.'

'Come into the house,' I said.

I went down, unfastened the door, and let him in, and locked the door again. I could not see his face. He was hatless, and his coat was unbuttoned.

'My God!' he said, as I drew him in.

'What has happened?' I asked.

'What hasn't?' In the obscurity I could see he made a gesture of despair. 'They wiped us out – simply wiped us out,' he repeated again and again.

He followed me, almost mechanically, into the dining room.

'Take some whisky,' I said, pouring out a stiff dose.

He drank it. Then abruptly he sat down before the table, put his head on his arms, and began to sob and weep like a little boy, in a perfect passion of emotion, while I, with a curious forgetfulness of my own recent despair, stood beside him, wondering.

It was a long time before he could steady his nerves to answer my questions, and then he answered perplexingly and brokenly. He was a driver in the artillery, and had only come into action about seven. At that time firing was going on across the common, and it was said the first party of Martians were crawling slowly towards their second cylinder under cover of a metal shield.

Later this shield staggered up on tripod legs and became the first of the fighting-machines I had seen. The gun he drove had been unlimbered near Horsell, in order to command the sand pits, and its arrival it was that had precipitated the action. As the limber gunners went to the rear, his horse trod in a rabbit hole and came down, throwing him into a depression of the ground. At the same moment the gun exploded behind him, the ammunition blew up, there was fire all about him, and he found himself lying under a heap of charred dead men and dead horses.

'I lay still,' he said, 'scared out of my wits, with the fore quarter of a horse atop of me. We'd been wiped out. And the smell – good God! Like burnt meat! I was hurt across the back by the fall of the horse, and there I had to lie until I felt better. Just like parade it had been a minute before – then stumble, bang, swish!

'Wiped out!' he said.

He had hid under the dead horse for a long time, peeping out furtively across the common. The Cardigan men had tried a rush, in skirmishing order, at the pit, simply to be swept out of existence. Then the monster had risen to its feet and had begun to walk leisurely to and fro across the common among the few fugitives, with its headlike hood turning about exactly like the head of a cowled human being. A kind of arm carried a complicated metallic case, about which green flashes scintillated, and out of the funnel of this there smoked the Heat-Ray.

In a few minutes there was, so far as the soldier could see, not a living thing left upon the common, and every bush and tree upon it that was not already a blackened skeleton was burning. The hussars had been on the road beyond the curvature of the ground, and he saw nothing of them. He heard the Martians rattle for a time and then become still. The giant saved Woking station and its cluster of houses until the last; then in a moment the Heat-Ray was brought to bear, and the town became a heap of fiery ruins. Then the Thing shut off the Heat-Ray, and turning its back upon the

artilleryman, began to waddle away towards the smouldering pine woods that sheltered the second cylinder. As it did so a second glittering Titan built itself up out of the pit.

The second monster followed the first, and at that the artilleryman began to crawl very cautiously across the hot heather ash towards Horsell. He managed to get alive into the ditch by the side of the road, and so escaped to Woking. There his story became ejaculatory. The place was impassable. It seems there were a few people alive there, frantic for the most part and many burned and scalded. He was turned aside by the fire, and hid among some almost scorching heaps of broken wall as one of the Martian giants returned. He saw this one pursue a man, catch him up in one of its steely tentacles, and knock his head against the trunk of a pine tree. At last, after nightfall, the artilleryman made a rush for it and got over the railway embankment.

Since then he had been skulking along towards Maybury, in the hope of getting out of danger Londonward. People were hiding in trenches and cellars, and many of the survivors had made off towards Woking village and Send. He had been consumed with thirst until he found one of the water mains near the railway arch smashed, and the water bubbling out like a spring upon the road.

That was the story I got from him, bit by bit. He grew calmer telling me and trying to make me see the things he had seen. He had eaten no food since midday, he told me early in his narrative, and I found some mutton and bread in the pantry and brought it into the room. We lit no lamp for fear of attracting the Martians, and ever and again our hands would touch upon bread or meat. As he talked, things about us came darkly out of the darkness, and the trampled bushes and broken rose trees outside the window grew distinct. It would seem that a number of men or animals had rushed across the lawn. I began to see his face, blackened and haggard, as no doubt mine was also.

When we had finished eating we went softly upstairs to my study, and I looked again out of the open window. In one night the valley had become a valley of ashes. The fires had dwindled now. Where flames had been there were now streamers of smoke; but the countless ruins of shattered and gutted houses and blasted and blackened trees that the night had hidden stood out now gaunt and terrible in the pitiless light of dawn. Yet here and there some object had had the luck to escape – a white railway signal here, the end of a greenhouse there, white and fresh amid the wreckage. Never before in the history of warfare had destruction been so indiscriminate and so universal. And shining with the growing light of the east, three of the metallic giants stood about the pit, their cowls rotating as though they were surveying the desolation they had made.

It seemed to me that the pit had been enlarged, and ever and again puffs of vivid green vapour streamed up and out of it towards the brightening dawn – streamed up, whirled, broke, and vanished.

Beyond were the pillars of fire about Chobham. They became pillars of bloodshot smoke at the first touch of day.

CHAPTER TWELVE

What I Saw of the Destruction of Weybridge and Shepperton

As the dawn grew brighter we withdrew from the window from which we had watched the Martians, and went very quietly downstairs.

The artilleryman agreed with me that the house was no place to stay in. He proposed, he said, to make his way Londonward, and thence rejoin his battery – No. 12, of the Horse Artillery. My plan was to return at once to Leatherhead; and so greatly had the strength of the Martians impressed me that I had determined to take my wife to Newhaven, and go with her out of the country forthwith. For I already perceived clearly that the country about London must inevitably be the scene of a disastrous struggle before such creatures as these could be destroyed.

Between us and Leatherhead, however, lay the third cylinder, with its guarding giants. Had I been alone, I think I should have taken my chance and struck across country. But the artilleryman dissuaded me: 'It's no kindness to the right sort of wife,' he said, 'to make her a widow'; and in the end I agreed to go with him, under cover of the woods, northward as far as Street Cobham before I parted with him. Thence I would make a big detour by Epsom to reach Leatherhead.

I should have started at once, but my companion had been in active service and he knew better than that. He made me ransack the house for a flask, which he filled with whisky; and we lined every available pocket with packets of biscuits and slices of meat. Then we crept out of the house, and ran as quickly as we could down the ill-made road by which I had come overnight. The houses seemed deserted. In the road lay a group of three charred bodies close together, struck dead by the Heat-Ray; and here and there were things that people had dropped – a clock, a slipper, a silver spoon, and the like poor valuables. At the corner turning up towards the post office a little cart, filled with boxes and furniture, and horseless, heeled over on a broken wheel. A cash box had been hastily smashed open and thrown under the debris.

Except the lodge at the Orphanage, which was still on fire, none of the houses had suffered very greatly here. The Heat-Ray had shaved the chimney tops and passed. Yet, save ourselves, there did not seem to be a living soul on Maybury Hill. The majority of the inhabitants had escaped, I suppose, by way of the Old Woking road – the road I had taken when I drove to Leatherhead – or they had hidden.

We went down the lane, by the body of the man in black, sodden now

from the overnight hail, and broke into the woods at the foot of the hill. We pushed through these towards the railway without meeting a soul. The woods across the line were but the scarred and blackened ruins of woods; for the most part the trees had fallen, but a certain proportion still stood, dismal grey stems, with dark brown foliage instead of green.

On our side the fire had done no more than scorch the nearer trees; it had failed to secure its footing. In one place the woodmen had been at work on Saturday; trees, felled and freshly trimmed, lay in a clearing, with heaps of sawdust by the sawing-machine and its engine. Hard by was a temporary hut, deserted. There was not a breath of wind this morning, and everything was strangely still. Even the birds were hushed, and as we hurried along I and the artilleryman talked in whispers and looked now and again over our shoulders. Once or twice we stopped to listen.

After a time we drew near the road, and as we did so we heard the clatter of hoofs and saw through the tree stems three cavalry soldiers riding slowly towards Woking. We hailed them, and they halted while we hurried towards them. It was a lieutenant and a couple of privates of the 8th Hussars, with a stand like a theodolite, which the artilleryman told me was a heliograph.

'You are the first men I've seen coming this way this morning,' said the lieutenant. 'What's brewing?'

His voice and face were eager. The men behind him stared curiously. The artilleryman jumped down the bank into the road and saluted.

'Gun destroyed last night, sir. Have been hiding. Trying to rejoin battery, sir. You'll come in sight of the Martians, I expect, about half a mile along this road.'

'What the dickens are they like?' asked the lieutenant.

'Giants in armour, sir. Hundred feet high. Three legs and a body like 'luminium, with a mighty great head in a hood, sir.'

'Get out!' said the lieutenant. 'What confounded nonsense!'

'You'll see, sir. They carry a kind of box, sir, that shoots fire and strikes you dead.'

'What d'ye mean – a gun?'

'No, sir,' and the artilleryman began a vivid account of the Heat-Ray. Halfway through, the lieutenant interrupted him and looked up at me. I was still standing on the bank by the side of the road.

'It's perfectly true,' I said.

'Well,' said the lieutenant, 'I suppose it's my business to see it too. Look here' – to the artilleryman – 'we're detailed here clearing people out of their houses. You'd better go along and report yourself to Brigadier-General Marvin, and tell him all you know. He's at Weybridge. Know the way?'

'I do,' I said; and he turned his horse southward again.

'Half a mile, you say?' said he.

'At most,' I answered, and pointed over the treetops southward. He thanked me and rode on, and we saw them no more.

Farther along we came upon a group of three women and two children in the road, busy clearing out a labourer's cottage. They had got hold of a little hand truck, and were piling it up with unclean-looking bundles and shabby furniture. They were all too assiduously engaged to talk to us as we passed.

By Byfleet station we emerged from the pine trees, and found the country calm and peaceful under the morning sunlight. We were far beyond the range of the Heat-Ray there, and had it not been for the silent desertion of some of the houses, the stirring movement of packing in others, and the knot of soldiers standing on the bridge over the railway and staring down the line towards Woking, the day would have seemed very like any other Sunday.

Several farm waggons and carts were moving creakily along the road to Addlestone, and suddenly through the gate of a field we saw, across a stretch of flat meadow, six twelve-pounders standing neatly at equal distances pointing towards Woking. The gunners stood by the guns waiting, and the ammunition waggons were at a businesslike distance. The men stood almost as if under inspection.

'That's good!' said I. 'They will get one fair shot, at any rate.'

The artilleryman hesitated at the gate.

'I shall go on,' he said.

Farther on towards Weybridge, just over the bridge, there were a number of men in white fatigue jackets throwing up a long rampart, and more guns behind.

'It's bows and arrows against the lightning, anyhow,' said the artilleryman. 'They 'aven't seen that fire-beam yet.'

The officers who were not actively engaged stood and stared over the treetops south-westward, and the men digging would stop every now and again to stare in the same direction.

Byfleet was in a tumult; people packing, and a score of hussars, some of them dismounted, some on horseback, were hunting them about. Three or four black government waggons, with crosses in white circles, and an old omnibus, among other vehicles, were being loaded in the village street. There were scores of people, most of them sufficiently sabbatical to have assumed their best clothes. The soldiers were having the greatest difficulty in making them realise the gravity of their position. We saw one shrivelled old fellow with a huge box and a score or more of flower pots containing orchids, angrily expostulating with the corporal who would leave them behind. I stopped and gripped his arm.

'Do you know what's over there?' I said, pointing at the pine tops that hid the Martians.

'Eh?' said he, turning. 'I was explainin' these is vallyble.'

'Death!' I shouted. 'Death is coming! Death!' and leaving him to digest

that if he could, I hurried on after the artilleryman. At the corner I looked back. The soldier had left him, and he was still standing by his box, with the pots of orchids on the lid of it, and staring vaguely over the trees.

No one in Weybridge could tell us where the headquarters were established; the whole place was in such confusion as I had never seen in any town before. Carts, carriages everywhere, the most astonishing miscellany of conveyances and horseflesh. The respectable inhabitants of the place, men in golf and boating costumes, wives prettily dressed, were packing, riverside loafers energetically helping, children excited, and, for the most part, highly delighted at this astonishing variation of their Sunday experiences. In the midst of it all the worthy vicar was very pluckily holding an early celebration, and his bell was jangling out above the excitement.

I and the artilleryman, seated on the step of the drinking fountain, made a very passable meal upon what we had brought with us. Patrols of soldiers – here no longer hussars, but grenadiers in white – were warning people to move now or to take refuge in their cellars as soon as the firing began. We saw as we crossed the railway bridge that a growing crowd of people had assembled in and about the railway station, and the swarming platform was piled with boxes and packages. The ordinary traffic had been stopped, I believe, in order to allow of the passage of troops and guns to Chertsey, and I have heard since that a savage struggle occurred for places in the special trains that were put on at a later hour.

We remained at Weybridge until midday, and at that hour we found ourselves at the place near Shepperton Lock where the Wey and Thames join. Part of the time we spent helping two old women to pack a little cart. The Wey has a treble mouth, and at this point boats are to be hired, and there was a ferry across the river. On the Shepperton side was an inn with a lawn, and beyond that the tower of Shepperton Church – it has been replaced by a spire – rose above the trees.

Here we found an excited and noisy crowd of fugitives. As yet the flight had not grown to a panic, but there were already far more people than all the boats going to and fro could enable to cross. People came panting along under heavy burdens; one husband and wife were even carrying a small outhouse door between them, with some of their household goods piled thereon. One man told us he meant to try to get away from Shepperton station.

There was a lot of shouting, and one man was even jesting. The idea people seemed to have here was that the Martians were simply formidable human beings, who might attack and sack the town, to be certainly destroyed in the end. Every now and then people would glance nervously across the Wey, at the meadows towards Chertsey, but everything over there was still.

Across the Thames, except just where the boats landed, everything was quiet, in vivid contrast with the Surrey side. The people who landed there from the boats went tramping off down the lane. The big ferryboat had just

made a journey. Three or four soldiers stood on the lawn of the inn, staring and jesting at the fugitives, without offering to help. The inn was closed, as it was now within prohibited hours.

'What's that?' cried a boatman, and 'Shut up, you fool!' said a man near me to a yelping dog. Then the sound came again, this time from the direction of Chertsey, a muffled thud – the sound of a gun.

The fighting was beginning. Almost immediately unseen batteries across the river to our right, unseen because of the trees, took up the chorus, firing heavily one after the other. A woman screamed. Everyone stood arrested by the sudden stir of battle, near us and yet invisible to us. Nothing was to be seen save flat meadows, cows feeding unconcernedly for the most part, and silvery pollard willows motionless in the warm sunlight.

'The sojers'll stop 'em,' said a woman beside me, doubtfully. A haziness rose over the treetops.

Then suddenly we saw a rush of smoke far away up the river, a puff of smoke that jerked up into the air and hung; and forthwith the ground heaved underfoot and a heavy explosion shook the air, smashing two or three windows in the houses near, and leaving us astonished.

'Here they are!' shouted a man in a blue jersey. 'Yonder! D'yer see them? Yonder!'

Quickly, one after the other, one, two, three, four of the armoured Martians appeared, far away over the little trees, across the flat meadows that stretched towards Chertsey, and striding hurriedly towards the river. Little cowled figures they seemed at first, going with a rolling motion and as fast as flying birds.

Then, advancing obliquely towards us, came a fifth. Their armoured bodies glittered in the sun as they swept swiftly forward upon the guns, growing rapidly larger as they drew nearer. One on the extreme left, the remotest that is, flourished a huge case high in the air, and the ghostly, terrible Heat-Ray I had already seen on Friday night smote towards Chertsey, and struck the town.

At sight of these strange, swift, and terrible creatures the crowd near the water's edge seemed to me to be for a moment horror-struck. There was no screaming or shouting, but a silence. Then a hoarse murmur and a movement of feet – a splashing from the water. A man, too frightened to drop the portmanteau he carried on his shoulder, swung round and sent me staggering with a blow from the corner of his burden. A woman thrust at me with her hand and rushed past me. I turned with the rush of the people, but I was not too terrified for thought. The terrible Heat-Ray was in my mind. To get under water! That was it!

'Get under water!' I shouted, unheeded.

I faced about again, and rushed towards the approaching Martian, rushed right down the gravelly beach and headlong into the water. Others did the same. A boatload of people putting back came leaping out as I

rushed past. The stones under my feet were muddy and slippery, and the river was so low that I ran perhaps twenty feet scarcely waist-deep. Then, as the Martian towered overhead scarcely a couple of hundred yards away, I flung myself forward under the surface. The splashes of the people in the boats leaping into the river sounded like thunderclaps in my ears. People were landing hastily on both sides of the river. But the Martian machine took no more notice for the moment of the people running this way and that than a man would of the confusion of ants in a nest against which his foot has kicked. When, half suffocated, I raised my head above water, the Martian's hood pointed at the batteries that were still firing across the river, and as it advanced it swung loose what must have been the generator of the Heat-Ray.

In another moment it was on the bank, and in a stride wading halfway across. The knees of its foremost legs bent at the farther bank, and in another moment it had raised itself to its full height again, close to the village of Shepperton. Forthwith the six guns which, unknown to anyone on the right bank, had been hidden behind the outskirts of that village, fired simultaneously. The sudden near concussion, the last close upon the first, made my heart jump. The monster was already raising the case generating the Heat-Ray as the first shell burst six yards above the hood.

I gave a cry of astonishment. I saw and thought nothing of the other four Martian monsters; my attention was riveted upon the nearer incident. Simultaneously two other shells burst in the air near the body as the hood twisted round in time to receive, but not in time to dodge, the fourth shell.

The shell burst clean in the face of the Thing. The hood bulged, flashed, was whirled off in a dozen tattered fragments of red flesh and glittering metal.

'Hit!' shouted I, with something between a scream and a cheer.

I heard answering shouts from the people in the water about me. I could have leaped out of the water with that momentary exultation.

The decapitated colossus reeled like a drunken giant; but it did not fall over. It recovered its balance by a miracle, and, no longer heeding its steps and with the camera that fired the Heat-Ray now rigidly upheld, it reeled swiftly upon Shepperton. The living intelligence, the Martian within the hood, was slain and splashed to the four winds of heaven, and the Thing was now but a mere intricate device of metal whirling to destruction. It drove along in a straight line, incapable of guidance. It struck the tower of Shepperton Church, smashing it down as the impact of a battering ram might have done, swerved aside, blundered on and collapsed with tremendous force into the river out of my sight.

A violent explosion shook the air, and a spout of water, steam, mud, and shattered metal shot far up into the sky. As the camera of the Heat-Ray hit the water, the latter had immediately flashed into steam. In another moment a huge wave, like a muddy tidal bore but almost scaldingly hot,

came sweeping round the bend upstream. I saw people struggling shore-wards, and heard their screaming and shouting faintly above the seething and roar of the Martian's collapse.

For a moment I heeded nothing of the heat, forgot the patent need of self-preservation. I splashed through the tumultuous water, pushing aside a man in black to do so, until I could see round the bend. Half a dozen deserted boats pitched aimlessly upon the confusion of the waves. The fallen Martian came into sight downstream, lying across the river, and for the most part submerged.

Thick clouds of steam were pouring off the wreckage, and through the tumultuously whirling wisps I could see, intermittently and vaguely, the gigantic limbs churning the water and flinging a splash and spray of mud and froth into the air. The tentacles swayed and struck like living arms, and, save for the helpless purposelessness of these movements, it was as if some wounded thing were struggling for its life amid the waves. Enormous quantities of a ruddy-brown fluid were spurting up in noisy jets out of the machine.

My attention was diverted from this death flurry by a furious yelling, like that of the thing called a siren in our manufacturing towns. A man, knee-deep near the towing path, shouted inaudibly to me and pointed. Looking back, I saw the other Martians advancing with gigantic strides down the riverbank from the direction of Chertsey. The Shepperton guns spoke this time unavailingly.

At that I ducked at once under water, and, holding my breath until movement was an agony, blundered painfully ahead under the surface as long as I could. The water was in a tumult about me, and rapidly growing hotter.

When for a moment I raised my head to take breath and throw the hair and water from my eyes, the steam was rising in a whirling white fog that at first hid the Martians altogether. The noise was deafening. Then I saw them dimly, colossal figures of grey, magnified by the mist. They had passed by me, and two were stooping over the frothing, tumultuous ruins of their comrade.

The third and fourth stood beside him in the water, one perhaps two hundred yards from me, the other towards Laleham. The generators of the Heat-Rays waved high, and the hissing beams smote down this way and that.

The air was full of sound, a deafening and confusing conflict of noises – the clangorous din of the Martians, the crash of falling houses, the thud of trees, fences, sheds flashing into flame, and the crackling and roaring of fire. Dense black smoke was leaping up to mingle with the steam from the river, and as the Heat-Ray went to and fro over Weybridge its impact was marked by flashes of incandescent white, that gave place at once to a smoky dance of lurid flames. The nearer houses still stood intact, awaiting their

fate, shadowy, faint and pallid in the steam, with the fire behind them going to and fro.

For a moment perhaps I stood there, breast-high in the almost boiling water, dumbfounded at my position, hopeless of escape. Through the reek I could see the people who had been with me in the river scrambling out of the water through the reeds, like little frogs hurrying through grass from the advance of a man, or running to and fro in utter dismay on the towing path.

Then suddenly the white flashes of the Heat-Ray came leaping towards me. The houses caved in as they dissolved at its touch, and darted out flames; the trees changed to fire with a roar. The Ray flickered up and down the towing path, licking off the people who ran this way and that, and came down to the water's edge not fifty yards from where I stood. It swept across the river to Shepperton, and the water in its track rose in a boiling weal crested with steam. I turned shoreward.

In another moment the huge wave, well-nigh at the boiling-point, had rushed upon me. I screamed aloud, and scalded, half blinded, agonised, I staggered through the leaping, hissing water towards the shore. Had my foot stumbled, it would have been the end. I fell helplessly, in full sight of the Martians, upon the broad, bare gravelly spit that runs down to mark the angle of the Wey and Thames. I expected nothing but death.

I have a dim memory of the foot of a Martian coming down within a score of yards of my head, driving straight into the loose gravel, whirling it this way and that and lifting again; of a long suspense, and then of the four carrying the debris of their comrade between them, now clear and then presently faint through a veil of smoke, receding interminably, as it seemed to me, across a vast space of river and meadow. And then, very slowly, I realised that by a miracle I had escaped.

CHAPTER THIRTEEN

How I Fell in with the Curate

After getting this sudden lesson in the power of terrestrial weapons, the Martians retreated to their original position upon Horsell Common; and in their haste, and encumbered with the debris of their smashed companion, they no doubt overlooked many such a stray and negligible victim as myself. Had they left their comrade and pushed on forthwith, there was nothing at that time between them and London but batteries of twelve-pounder guns, and they would certainly have reached the capital in advance of the tidings of their approach; as sudden, dreadful, and destructive their advent would have been as the earthquake that destroyed Lisbon a century ago.

But they were in no hurry. Cylinder followed cylinder on its inter-

planetary flight; every twenty-four hours brought them reinforcement. And meanwhile the military and naval authorities, now fully alive to the tremendous power of their antagonists, worked with furious energy. Every minute a fresh gun came into position until, before twilight, every copse, every row of suburban villas on the hilly slopes about Kingston and Richmond, masked an expectant black muzzle. And through the charred and desolated area – perhaps twenty square miles altogether – that encircled the Martian encampment on Horsell Common, through charred and ruined villages among the green trees, through the blackened and smoking arcades that had been but a day ago pine spinneys, crawled the devoted scouts with the heliographs that were presently to warn the gunners of the Martian approach. But the Martians now understood our command of artillery and the danger of human proximity, and not a man ventured within a mile of either cylinder, save at the price of his life.

It would seem that these giants spent the earlier part of the afternoon in going to and fro, transferring everything from the second and third cylinders – the second in Addlestone Golf Links and the third at Pyrford – to their original pit on Horsell Common. Over that, above the blackened heather and ruined buildings that stretched far and wide, stood one as sentinel, while the rest abandoned their vast fighting-machines and descended into the pit. They were hard at work there far into the night, and the towering pillar of dense green smoke that rose therefrom could be seen from the hills about Merrow, and even, it is said, from Banstead and Epsom Downs.

And while the Martians behind me were thus preparing for their next sally, and in front of me Humanity gathered for the battle, I made my way with infinite pains and labour from the fire and smoke of burning Weybridge towards London.

I saw an abandoned boat, very small and remote, drifting downstream; and throwing off the most of my sodden clothes, I went after it, gained it, and so escaped out of that destruction. There were no oars in the boat, but I contrived to paddle, as well as my parboiled hands would allow, down the river towards Halliford and Walton, going very tediously and continually looking behind me, as you may well understand. I followed the river, because I considered that the water gave me my best chance of escape should these giants return.

The hot water from the Martian's overthrow drifted downstream with me, so that for the best part of a mile I could see little of either bank. Once, however, I made out a string of black figures hurrying across the meadows from the direction of Weybridge. Halliford, it seemed, was deserted, and several of the houses facing the river were on fire. It was strange to see the place quite tranquil, quite desolate under the hot blue sky, with the smoke and little threads of flame going straight up into the heat of the afternoon. Never before had I seen houses burning without the accompaniment of an

obstructive crowd. A little farther on the dry reeds up the bank were smoking and glowing, and a line of fire inland was marching steadily across a late field of hay.

For a long time I drifted, so painful and weary was I after the violence I had been through, and so intense the heat upon the water. Then my fears got the better of me again, and I resumed my paddling. The sun scorched my bare back. At last, as the bridge at Walton was coming into sight round the bend, my fever and faintness overcame my fears, and I landed on the Middlesex bank and lay down, deadly sick, amid the long grass. I suppose the time was then about four or five o'clock. I got up presently, walked perhaps half a mile without meeting a soul, and then lay down again in the shadow of a hedge. I seem to remember talking, wanderingly, to myself during that last spurt. I was also very thirsty, and bitterly regretful I had drunk no more water. It is a curious thing that I felt angry with my wife; I cannot account for it, but my impotent desire to reach Leatherhead worried me excessively.

I do not clearly remember the arrival of the curate, so that probably I dozed. I became aware of him as a seated figure in soot-smudged shirt sleeves, and with his upturned, clean-shaven face staring at a faint flickering that danced over the sky. The sky was what is called a mackerel sky – rows and rows of faint down-plumes of cloud, just tinted with the midsummer sunset.

I sat up, and at the rustle of my motion he looked at me quickly.

'Have you any water?' I asked abruptly.

He shook his head.

'You have been asking for water for the last hour,' he said.

For a moment we were silent, taking stock of each other. I dare say he found me a strange enough figure, naked, save for my water-soaked trousers and socks, scalded, and my face and shoulders blackened by the smoke. His face was a fair weakness, his chin retreated, and his hair lay in crisp, almost flaxen curls on his low forehead; his eyes were rather large, pale blue, and blankly staring. He spoke abruptly, looking vacantly away from me.

'What does it mean?' he said. 'What do these things mean?'

I stared at him and made no answer.

He extended a thin white hand and spoke in almost a complaining tone.

'Why are these things permitted? What sins have we done? The morning service was over, I was walking through the roads to clear my brain for the afternoon, and then – fire, earthquake, death! As if it were Sodom and Gomorrah! All our work undone, all the work – What are these Martians?'

'What are we?' I answered, clearing my throat.

He gripped his knees and turned to look at me again. For half a minute, perhaps, he stared silently.

'I was walking through the roads to clear my brain,' he said. 'And suddenly – fire, earthquake, death!'

He relapsed into silence, with his chin now sunken almost to his knees. Presently he began waving his hand.

'All the work – all the Sunday schools – What have we done – what has Weybridge done? Everything gone – everything destroyed. The church! We rebuilt it only three years ago. Gone! Swept out of existence! Why?'

Another pause, and he broke out again like one demented.

'The smoke of her burning goeth up for ever and ever!' he shouted.

His eyes flamed, and he pointed a lean finger in the direction of Weybridge.

By this time I was beginning to take his measure. The tremendous tragedy in which he had been involved – it was evident he was a fugitive from Weybridge – had driven him to the very verge of his reason.

'Are we far from Sunbury?' I said, in a matter-of-fact tone.

'What are we to do?' he asked. 'Are these creatures everywhere? Has the earth been given over to them?'

'Are we far from Sunbury?'

'Only this morning I officiated at early celebration – '

'Things have changed,' I said, quietly. 'You must keep your head. There is still hope.'

'Hope!'

'Yes. Plentiful hope – for all this destruction!'

I began to explain my view of our position. He listened at first, but as I went on the interest dawning in his eyes gave place to their former stare, and his regard wandered from me.

'This must be the beginning of the end,' he said, interrupting me. 'The end! The great and terrible day of the Lord! When men shall call upon the mountains and the rocks to fall upon them and hide them – hide them from the face of Him that sitteth upon the throne!'

I began to understand the position. I ceased my laboured reasoning, struggled to my feet, and, standing over him, laid my hand on his shoulder.

'Be a man!' said I. 'You are scared out of your wits! What good is religion if it collapses under calamity? Think of what earthquakes and floods, wars and volcanoes, have done before to men! Did you think God had exempted Weybridge? He is not an insurance agent.'

For a time he sat in blank silence.

'But how can we escape?' he asked, suddenly. 'They are invulnerable, they are pitiless.'

'Neither the one nor, perhaps, the other,' I answered. 'And the mightier they are the more sane and wary should we be. One of them was killed yonder not three hours ago.'

'Killed!' he said, staring about him. 'How can God's ministers be killed?'

'I saw it happen.' I proceeded to tell him. 'We have chanced to come in for the thick of it,' said I, 'and that is all.'

'What is that flicker in the sky?' he asked abruptly.

I told him it was the heliograph signalling – that it was the sign of human help and effort in the sky.

'We are in the midst of it,' I said, 'quiet as it is. That flicker in the sky tells of the gathering storm. Yonder, I take it, are the Martians, and Londonward, where those hills rise about Richmond and Kingston and the trees give cover, earthworks are being thrown up and guns are being placed. Presently the Martians will be coming this way again.'

And even as I spoke he sprang to his feet and stopped me by a gesture.

'Listen!' he said.

From beyond the low hills across the water came the dull resonance of distant guns and a remote weird crying. Then everything was still. A cockchafer came droning over the hedge and past us. High in the west the crescent moon hung faint and pale above the smoke of Weybridge and Shepperton and the hot, still splendour of the sunset.

'We had better follow this path,' I said, 'northward.'

CHAPTER FOURTEEN

In London

My younger brother was in London when the Martians fell on Woking. He was a medical student working for an imminent examination, and he heard nothing of the arrival until Saturday morning. The morning papers on Saturday contained, in addition to lengthy special articles on the planet Mars, on life in the planets, and so forth, a brief and vaguely worded telegram, all the more striking for its brevity.

The Martians, alarmed by the approach of a crowd, had killed a number of people with a quick-firing gun, so the story ran. The telegram concluded with the words: 'Formidable as they seem to be, the Martians have not moved from the pit into which they have fallen, and, indeed, seem incapable of doing so. Probably this is due to the relative strength of the earth's gravitational energy.' On that last text their leader-writer expanded very comfortingly.

Of course all the students in the crammer's biology class, to which my brother went that day, were intensely interested, but there were no signs of any unusual excitement in the streets. The afternoon papers puffed scraps of news under big headlines. They had nothing to tell beyond the movements of troops about the common, and the burning of the pine woods between Woking and Weybridge, until eight. Then the *St James's Gazette*, in an extra-special edition, announced the bare fact of the interruption of telegraphic communication. This was thought to be due to the falling of burning pine trees across the line. Nothing more of the fighting was known that night, the night of my drive to Leatherhead and back.

My brother felt no anxiety about us, as he knew from the description in

the papers that the cylinder was a good two miles from my house. He made up his mind to run down that night to me, in order, as he says, to see the Things before they were killed. He dispatched a telegram, which never reached me, about four o'clock, and spent the evening at a music hall.

In London, also, on Saturday night there was a thunderstorm, and my brother reached Waterloo in a cab. On the platform from which the midnight train usually starts he learned, after some waiting, that an accident prevented trains from reaching Woking that night. The nature of the accident he could not ascertain; indeed, the railway authorities did not clearly know at that time. There was very little excitement in the station, as the officials, failing to realise that anything further than a breakdown between Byfleet and Woking junction had occurred, were running the theatre trains which usually passed through Woking round by Virginia Water or Guildford. They were busy making the necessary arrangements to alter the route of the Southampton and Portsmouth Sunday League excursions. A nocturnal newspaper reporter, mistaking my brother for the traffic manager, to whom he bears a slight resemblance, waylaid and tried to interview him. Few people, excepting the railway officials, connected the breakdown with the Martians.

I have read, in another account of these events, that on Sunday morning 'all London was electrified by the news from Woking'. As a matter of fact, there was nothing to justify that very extravagant phrase. Plenty of Londoners did not hear of the Martians until the panic of Monday morning. Those who did took some time to realise all that the hastily worded telegrams in the Sunday papers conveyed. The majority of people in London do not read Sunday papers.

The habit of personal security, moreover, is so deeply fixed in the Londoner's mind, and startling intelligence so much a matter of course in the papers, that they could read without any personal tremors: 'About seven o'clock last night the Martians came out of the cylinder, and, moving about under an armour of metallic shields, have completely wrecked Woking station with the adjacent houses, and massacred an entire battalion of the Cardigan Regiment. No details are known. Maxims have been absolutely useless against their armour; the field guns have been disabled by them. Flying hussars have been galloping into Chertsey. The Martians appear to be moving slowly towards Chertsey or Windsor. Great anxiety prevails in West Surrey, and earthworks are being thrown up to check the advance Londonward.' That was how the *Sunday Sun* put it, and a clever and remarkably prompt 'handbook' article in the *Referee* compared the affair to a menagerie suddenly let loose in a village.

No one in London knew positively of the nature of the armoured Martians, and there was still a fixed idea that these monsters must be sluggish: 'crawling', 'creeping painfully' – such expressions occurred in almost all the earlier reports. None of the telegrams could have been

written by an eyewitness of their advance. The Sunday papers printed separate editions as further news came to hand, some even in default of it. But there was practically nothing more to tell people until late in the afternoon, when the authorities gave the press agencies the news in their possession. It was stated that the people of Walton and Weybridge, and all the district were pouring along the roads Londonward, and that was all.

My brother went to church at the Foundling Hospital in the morning, still in ignorance of what had happened on the previous night. There he heard allusions made to the invasion, and a special prayer for peace. Coming out, he bought a *Referee*. He became alarmed at the news in this, and went again to Waterloo station to find out if communication were restored. The omnibuses, carriages, cyclists, and innumerable people walking in their best clothes seemed scarcely affected by the strange intelligence that the news vendors were disseminating. People were interested, or, if alarmed, alarmed only on account of the local residents. At the station he heard for the first time that the Windsor and Chertsey lines were now interrupted. The porters told him that several remarkable telegrams had been received in the morning from Byfleet and Chertsey stations, but that these had abruptly ceased. My brother could get very little precise detail out of them. 'There's fighting going on about Weybridge' was the extent of their information.

The train service was now very much disorganised. Quite a number of people who had been expecting friends from places on the South-Western network were standing about the station. One grey-headed old gentleman came and abused the South-Western Company bitterly to my brother. 'It wants showing up,' he said.

One or two trains came in from Richmond, Putney, and Kingston, containing people who had gone out for a day's boating and found the locks closed and a feeling of panic in the air. A man in a blue and white blazer addressed my brother, full of strange tidings.

'There's hosts of people driving into Kingston in traps and carts and things, with boxes of valuables and all that,' he said. 'They come from Molesey and Weybridge and Walton, and they say there's been guns heard at Chertsey, heavy firing, and that mounted soldiers have told them to get off at once because the Martians are coming. We heard guns firing at Hampton Court station, but we thought it was thunder. What the dickens does it all mean? The Martians can't get out of their pit, can they?'

My brother could not tell him.

Afterwards he found that the vague feeling of alarm had spread to the clients of the underground railway, and that the Sunday excursionists began to return from all over the South-Western 'lungs' – Barnes, Wimbledon, Richmond Park, Kew, and so forth – at unnaturally early hours; but not a soul had anything more than vague hearsay to tell of. Everyone connected with the terminus seemed ill-tempered.

About five o'clock the gathering crowd in the station was immensely excited by the opening of the line of communication, which is almost invariably closed, between the South-Eastern and the South-Western stations, and the passage of carriage trucks bearing huge guns and carriages crammed with soldiers. These were the guns that were brought up from Woolwich and Chatham to cover Kingston. There was an exchange of pleasantries: 'You'll get eaten!' 'We're the beast-tamers!' and so forth. A little while after that a squad of police came into the station and began to clear the public off the platforms, and my brother went out into the street again.

The church bells were ringing for evensong, and a squad of Salvation Army lassies came singing down Waterloo Road. On the bridge a number of loafers were watching a curious brown scum that came drifting down the stream in patches. The sun was just setting, and the Clock Tower and the Houses of Parliament rose against one of the most peaceful skies it is possible to imagine, a sky of gold, barred with long transverse stripes of reddish-purple cloud. There was talk of a floating body. One of the men there, a reservist he said he was, told my brother he had seen the heliograph flickering in the west.

In Wellington Street my brother met a couple of sturdy roughs who had just been rushed out of Fleet Street with still-wet newspapers and staring placards. 'Dreadful catastrophe!' they bawled one to the other down Wellington Street. 'Fighting at Weybridge! Full description! Repulse of the Martians! London in Danger!' He had to give threepence for a copy of that paper.

Then it was, and then only, that he realised something of the full power and terror of these monsters. He learned that they were not merely a handful of small sluggish creatures, but that they were minds swaying vast mechanical bodies; and that they could move swiftly and smite with such power that even the mightiest guns could not stand against them.

They were described as 'vast spiderlike machines, nearly a hundred feet high, capable of the speed of an express train, and able to shoot out a beam of intense heat'. Masked batteries, chiefly of field guns, had been planted in the country about Horsell Common, and especially between the Woking district and London. Five of the machines had been seen moving towards the Thames, and one, by a happy chance, had been destroyed. In the other cases the shells had missed, and the batteries had been at once annihilated by the Heat-Rays. Heavy losses of soldiers were mentioned, but the tone of the dispatch was optimistic.

The Martians had been repulsed; they were not invulnerable. They had retreated to their triangle of cylinders again, in the circle about Woking. Signallers with heliographs were pushing forward upon them from all sides. Guns were in rapid transit from Windsor, Portsmouth, Aldershot, Woolwich – even from the north; among others, long wire-guns of ninety-

five tons from Woolwich. Altogether one hundred and sixteen were in position or being hastily placed, chiefly covering London. Never before in England had there been such a vast or rapid concentration of military material.

Any further cylinders that fell, it was hoped, could be destroyed at once by high explosives, which were being rapidly manufactured and distributed. No doubt, ran the report, the situation was of the strangest and gravest description, but the public was exhorted to avoid and discourage panic. No doubt the Martians were strange and terrible in the extreme, but at the outside there could not be more than twenty of them against our millions.

The authorities had reason to suppose, from the size of the cylinders, that at the outside there could not be more than five in each cylinder – fifteen altogether. And one at least was disposed of – perhaps more. The public would be fairly warned of the approach of danger, and elaborate measures were being taken for the protection of the people in the threatened south-western suburbs. And so, with reiterated assurances of the safety of London and the ability of the authorities to cope with the difficulty, this quasi-proclamation closed.

This was printed in enormous type on paper so fresh that it was still wet, and there had been no time to add a word of comment. It was curious, my brother said, to see how ruthlessly the usual contents of the paper had been hacked and taken out to give this place.

All down Wellington Street people could be seen fluttering out the pink sheets and reading, and the Strand was suddenly noisy with the voices of an army of hawkers following these pioneers. Men came scrambling off buses to secure copies. Certainly this news excited people intensely, whatever their previous apathy. The shutters of a map shop in the Strand were being taken down, my brother said, and a man in his Sunday raiment, lemon-yellow gloves even, was visible inside the window hastily fastening maps of Surrey to the glass.

Going on along the Strand to Trafalgar Square, the paper in his hand, my brother saw some of the fugitives from West Surrey. There was a man with his wife and two boys and some articles of furniture in a cart such as greengrocers use. He was driving from the direction of Westminster Bridge; and close behind him came a hay waggon with five or six respectable-looking people in it, and some boxes and bundles. The faces of these people were haggard, and their entire appearance contrasted conspicuously with the Sabbath-best appearance of the people on the omnibuses. People in fashionable clothing peeped at them out of cabs. They stopped at the Square as if undecided which way to take, and finally turned eastward along the Strand. Some way behind these came a man in workday clothes, riding one of those old-fashioned tricycles with a small front wheel. He was dirty and white in the face.

My brother turned down towards Victoria, and met a number of such

people. He had a vague idea that he might see something of me. He noticed an unusual number of police regulating the traffic. Some of the refugees were exchanging news with the people on the omnibuses. One was professing to have seen the Martians. 'Boilers on stilts, I tell you, striding along like men.' Most of them were excited and animated by their strange experience.

Beyond Victoria the public-houses were doing a lively trade with these arrivals. At all the street corners groups of people were reading papers, talking excitedly, or staring at these unusual Sunday visitors. They seemed to increase as night drew on, until at last the roads, my brother said, were like Epsom High Street on a Derby Day. My brother addressed several of these fugitives and got unsatisfactory answers from most.

None of them could tell him any news of Woking except one man, who assured him that Woking had been entirely destroyed on the previous night.

'I come from Byfleet,' he said; 'a man on a bicycle came through the place in the early morning, and ran from door to door warning us to come away. Then came soldiers. We went out to look, and there were clouds of smoke to the south – nothing but smoke, and not a soul coming that way. Then we heard the guns at Chertsey, and folks coming from Weybridge. So I've locked up my house and come on.'

At the time there was a strong feeling in the streets that the authorities were to blame for their incapacity to dispose of the invaders without all this inconvenience.

About eight o'clock a noise of heavy firing was distinctly audible all over the south of London. My brother could not hear it for the traffic in the main thoroughfares, but by striking through the quiet back streets to the river he was able to distinguish it quite plainly.

He walked from Westminster to his apartments near Regent's Park, about two. He was now very anxious on my account, and disturbed at the evident magnitude of the trouble. His mind was inclined to run, even as mine had run on Saturday, on military details. He thought of all those silent, expectant guns, of the suddenly nomadic countryside; he tried to imagine 'boilers on stilts' a hundred feet high.

There were one or two cartloads of refugees passing along Oxford Street, and several in the Marylebone Road, but so slowly was the news spreading that Regent Street and Portland Place were full of their usual Sunday-night promenaders, albeit they talked in groups, and along the edge of Regent's Park there were as many silent couples 'walking out' together under the scattered gas lamps as ever there had been. The night was warm and still, and a little oppressive; the sound of guns continued intermittently, and after midnight there seemed to be sheet lightning in the south.

He read and reread the paper, fearing the worst had happened to me. He was restless, and after supper prowled out again aimlessly. He returned and

tried in vain to divert his attention to his examination notes. He went to bed a little after midnight, and was awakened from lurid dreams in the small hours of Monday by the sound of door knockers, feet running in the street, distant drumming, and a clamour of bells. Red reflections danced on the ceiling. For a moment he lay astonished, wondering whether day had come or the world gone mad. Then he jumped out of bed and ran to the window.

His room was an attic and as he thrust his head out, up and down the street there were a dozen echoes to the noise of his window sash, and heads in every kind of night disarray appeared. Enquiries were being shouted. 'They are coming!' bawled a policeman, hammering at the door; 'the Martians are coming!' and hurried to the next door.

The sound of drumming and trumpeting came from the Albany Street Barracks, and every church within earshot was hard at work killing sleep with a vehement disorderly tocsin. There was a noise of doors opening, and window after window in the houses opposite flashed from darkness into yellow illumination.

Up the street came galloping a closed carriage, bursting abruptly into noise at the corner, rising to a clattering climax under the window, and dying away slowly in the distance. Close on the rear of this came a couple of cabs, the forerunners of a long procession of flying vehicles, going for the most part to Chalk Farm station, where the North-Western special trains were loading up, instead of coming down the gradient into Euston.

For a long time my brother stared out of the window in blank astonishment, watching the policemen hammering at door after door, and delivering their incomprehensible message. Then the door behind him opened, and the man who lodged across the landing came in, dressed only in shirt, trousers, and slippers, his braces loose about his waist, his hair disordered from his pillow.

'What the devil is it?' he asked. 'A fire? What a devil of a row!'

They both craned their heads out of the window, straining to hear what the policemen were shouting. People were coming out of the side streets, and standing in groups at the corners talking.

'What the devil is it all about?' said my brother's fellow lodger.

My brother answered him vaguely and began to dress, running with each garment to the window in order to miss nothing of the growing excitement. And presently men selling unnaturally early newspapers came bawling into the street: 'London in danger of suffocation! The Kingston and Richmond defences forced! Fearful massacres in the Thames Valley!'

And all about him – in the rooms below, in the houses on each side and across the road, and behind in the Park Terraces and in the hundred other streets of that part of Marylebone, and the Westbourne Park district and St Pancras, and westward and northward in Kilburn and St John's Wood and Hampstead, and eastward in Shoreditch and Highbury and Haggerston and Hoxton, and, indeed, through all the vastness of London from Ealing to

East Ham – people were rubbing their eyes, and opening windows to stare out and ask aimless questions, dressing hastily as the first breath of the coming storm of Fear blew through the streets. It was the dawn of the great panic. London, which had gone to bed on Sunday night oblivious and inert, was awakened, in the small hours of Monday morning, to a vivid sense of danger.

Unable from his window to learn what was happening, my brother went down and out into the street, just as the sky between the parapets of the houses grew pink with the early dawn. The flying people on foot and in vehicles grew more numerous every moment. 'Black smoke!' he heard people crying, and again 'Black smoke!' The contagion of such a unanimous fear was inevitable. As my brother hesitated on the doorstep, he saw another news vendor approaching, and got a paper forthwith. The man was running away with the rest, and selling his papers for a shilling each as he ran – a grotesque mingling of profit and panic.

And from this paper my brother read that catastrophic dispatch of the Commander-in-Chief:

> The Martians are able to discharge enormous clouds of a black and poisonous vapour by means of rockets. They have smothered our batteries, destroyed Richmond, Kingston, and Wimbledon, and are advancing slowly towards London, destroying everything on the way. It is impossible to stop them. There is no safety from the Black Smoke but in instant flight.

That was all, but it was enough. The whole population of the great six-million city was stirring, slipping, running; presently it would be pouring *en masse* northward.

'Black smoke!' the voices cried. 'Fire!'

The bells of the neighbouring church made a jangling tumult, a cart carelessly driven smashed, amid shrieks and curses, against the water trough up the street. Sickly yellow lights went to and fro in the houses, and some of the passing cabs flaunted unextinguished lamps. And overhead the dawn was growing brighter, clear and steady and calm.

He heard footsteps running to and fro in the rooms, and up and down stairs behind him. His landlady came to the door, loosely wrapped in dressing gown and shawl; her husband followed ejaculating.

As my brother began to realise the import of all these things, he turned hastily to his own room, put all his available money – some ten pounds altogether – into his pockets, and went out again into the streets.

CHAPTER FIFTEEN

What Happened in Surrey

It was while the curate had sat and talked so wildly to me under the hedge in the flat meadows near Halliford, and while my brother was watching the fugitives stream over Westminster Bridge, that the Martians had resumed the offensive. So far as one can ascertain from the conflicting accounts that have been put forth, the majority of them remained busied with preparations in the Horsell pit until nine that night, hurrying on some operation that disengaged huge volumes of green smoke.

But three certainly came out about eight o'clock and, advancing slowly and cautiously, made their way through Byfleet and Pyrford towards Ripley and Weybridge, and so came in sight of the expectant batteries against the setting sun. These Martians did not advance in a body, but in a line, each perhaps a mile and a half from his nearest fellow. They communicated with one another by means of siren-like howls, running up and down the scale from one note to another.

It was this howling and firing of the guns at Ripley and St George's Hill that we had heard at Upper Halliford. The Ripley gunners, unseasoned artillery volunteers who ought never to have been placed in such a position, fired one wild, premature, ineffectual volley, and bolted on horse and foot through the deserted village, while the Martian, without using his Heat-Ray, walked serenely over their guns, stepped gingerly among them, passed in front of them, and so came unexpectedly upon the guns in Painshill Park, which he destroyed.

The St George's Hill men, however, were better led or of a better mettle. Hidden by a pine wood as they were, they seem to have been quite unsuspected by the Martian nearest to them. They laid their guns as deliberately as if they had been on parade, and fired at about a thousand yards' range.

The shells flashed all round him, and he was seen to advance a few paces, stagger, and go down. Everybody yelled together, and the guns were reloaded in frantic haste. The overthrown Martian set up a pro-longed ululation, and immediately a second glittering giant, answering him, appeared over the trees to the south. It would seem that a leg of the tripod had been smashed by one of the shells. The whole of the second volley flew wide of the Martian on the ground, and, simultaneously, both his companions brought their Heat-Rays to bear on the battery. The ammunition blew up, the pine trees all about the guns flashed into fire, and only one or two of the men who were already running over the crest of the hill escaped.

After this it would seem that the three took counsel together and halted, and the scouts who were watching them report that they remained absolutely stationary for the next half-hour. The Martian who had been overthrown crawled tediously out of his hood, a small brown figure, oddly suggestive from that distance of a speck of blight, and apparently engaged in the repair of his support. About nine he had finished, for his cowl was then seen above the trees again.

It was a few minutes past nine that night when these three sentinels were joined by four other Martians, each carrying a thick black tube. A similar tube was handed to each of the three, and the seven proceeded to distribute themselves at equal distances along a curved line between St George's Hill, Weybridge, and the village of Send, south-west of Ripley.

A dozen rockets sprang out of the hills before them so soon as they began to move, and warned the waiting batteries about Ditton and Esher. At the same time four of their fighting machines, similarly armed with tubes, crossed the river, and two of them, black against the western sky, came into sight of myself and the curate as we hurried wearily and painfully along the road that runs northward out of Halliford. They moved, as it seemed to us, upon a cloud, for a milky mist covered the fields and rose to a third of their height.

At this sight the curate cried faintly in his throat, and began running; but I knew it was no good running from a Martian, and I turned aside and crawled through dewy nettles and brambles into the broad ditch by the side of the road. He looked back, saw what I was doing, and turned to join me.

The two halted, the nearer to us standing and facing Sunbury, the remoter being a grey indistinctness towards the evening star, away towards Staines.

The occasional howling of the Martians had ceased; they took up their positions in the huge crescent about their cylinders in absolute silence. It was a crescent with twelve miles between its horns. Never since the devising of gunpowder was the beginning of a battle so still. To us and to an observer about Ripley it would have had precisely the same effect – the Martians seemed in solitary possession of the darkling night, lit only as it was by the slender moon, the stars, the afterglow of the daylight, and the ruddy glare from St George's Hill and the woods of Painshill.

But facing that crescent everywhere – at Staines, Hounslow, Ditton, Esher, Ockham, behind hills and woods south of the river, and across the flat grass meadows to the north of it, wherever a cluster of trees or village houses gave sufficient cover – the guns were waiting. The signal rockets burst and rained their sparks through the night and vanished, and the spirit of all those watching batteries rose to a tense expectation. The Martians had but to advance into the line of fire, and instantly those motionless black forms of men, those guns glittering so darkly in the early night, would explode into a thunderous fury of battle.

No doubt the thought that was uppermost in a thousand of those vigilant minds, even as it was uppermost in mine, was the riddle – how much they understood of us. Did they grasp that we in our millions were organised, disciplined, working together? Or did they interpret our spurts of fire, the sudden stinging of our shells, our steady investment of their encampment, as we should the furious unanimity of onslaught in a disturbed hive of bees? Did they dream they might exterminate us? (At that time no one knew what food they needed.) A hundred such questions struggled together in my mind as I watched that vast sentinel shape. And in the back of my mind was the sense of all the huge unknown and hidden forces Londonward. Had they prepared pitfalls? Were the powder mills at Hounslow ready as a snare? Would the Londoners have the heart and courage to make a greater Moscow of their mighty province of houses?

Then, after an interminable time, as it seemed to us, crouching and peering through the hedge, came a sound like the distant concussion of a gun. Another nearer, and then another. And then the Martian beside us raised his tube on high and discharged it, gunwise, with a heavy report that made the ground heave. The one towards Staines answered him. There was no flash, no smoke, simply that loaded detonation.

I was so excited by these heavy minute-guns following one another that I so far forgot my personal safety and my scalded hands as to clamber up into the hedge and stare towards Sunbury. As I did so a second report followed, and a big projectile hurtled overhead towards Hounslow. I expected at least to see smoke or fire, or some such evidence of its work. But all I saw was the deep blue sky above, with one solitary star, and the white mist spreading wide and low beneath. And there had been no crash, no answering explosion. The silence was restored; the minute lengthened to three.

'What has happened?' said the curate, standing up beside me.

'Heaven knows!' said I.

A bat flickered by and vanished. A distant tumult of shouting began and ceased. I looked again at the Martian, and saw he was now moving eastward along the riverbank, with a swift, rolling motion.

Every moment I expected the fire of some hidden battery to spring upon him; but the evening calm was unbroken. The figure of the Martian grew smaller as he receded, and presently the mist and the gathering night had swallowed him up. By a common impulse we clambered higher. Towards Sunbury was a dark appearance, as though a conical hill had suddenly come into being there, hiding our view of the farther country; and then, remoter across the river, over Walton, we saw another such summit. These hill-like forms grew lower and broader even as we stared.

Moved by a sudden thought, I looked northward, and there I perceived a third of these cloudy black kopjes had risen.

Everything had suddenly become very still. Far away to the south-east,

marking the quiet, we heard the Martians hooting to one another, and then the air quivered again with the distant thud of their guns. But the earthly artillery made no reply.

Now at the time we could not understand these things, but later I was to learn the meaning of these ominous kopjes that gathered in the twilight. Each of the Martians, standing in the great crescent I have described, had discharged, by means of the gunlike tube he carried, a huge canister over whatever hill, copse, cluster of houses, or other possible cover for guns, chanced to be in front of him. Some fired only one of these, some two – as in the case of the one we had seen; the one at Ripley is said to have discharged no fewer than five at that time. These canisters smashed on striking the ground – they did not explode – and incontinently disengaged an enormous volume of heavy, inky vapour, coiling and pouring upward in a huge and ebony cumulus cloud, a gaseous hill that sank and spread itself slowly over the surrounding country. And the touch of that vapour, the inhaling of its pungent wisps, was death to all that breathes.

It was heavy, this vapour, heavier than the densest smoke, so that, after the first tumultuous uprush and outflow of its impact, it sank down through the air and poured over the ground in a manner rather liquid than gaseous, abandoning the hills, and streaming into the valleys and ditches and watercourses even as I have heard the carbonic-acid gas that pours from volcanic clefts is wont to do. And where it came upon water some chemical action occurred, and the surface would be instantly covered with a powdery scum that sank slowly and made way for more. The scum was absolutely insoluble, and it is a strange thing, seeing the instant effect of the gas, that one could drink without hurt the water from which it had been strained. The vapour did not diffuse as a true gas would do. It hung together in banks, flowing sluggishly down the slope of the land and driving reluctantly before the wind, and very slowly it combined with the mist and moisture of the air, and sank to the earth in the form of dust. Save that an unknown element giving a group of four lines in the blue of the spectrum is concerned, we are still entirely ignorant of the nature of this substance.

Once the tumultuous upheaval of its dispersion was over, the Black Smoke clung so closely to the ground, even before its precipitation, that fifty feet up in the air, on the roofs and upper storeys of high houses and on great trees, there was a chance of escaping its poison altogether, as was proved even that night at Street Cobham and Ditton.

The man who escaped at the former place tells a wonderful story of the strangeness of its coiling flow, and how he looked down from the church spire and saw the houses of the village rising like ghosts out of its inky nothingness. For a day and a half he remained there, weary, starving and sun-scorched, the earth under the blue sky and against the prospect of the distant hills a velvet-black expanse, with red roofs, green trees, and, later,

black-veiled shrubs and gates, barns, outhouses, and walls, rising here and there into the sunlight.

But that was at Street Cobham, where the black vapour was allowed to remain until it sank of its own accord into the ground. As a rule the Martians, when it had served its purpose, cleared the air of it again by wading into it and directing a jet of steam upon it.

This they did with the vapour banks near us, as we saw in the starlight from the window of a deserted house at Upper Halliford, whither we had returned. From there we could see the searchlights on Richmond Hill and Kingston Hill going to and fro, and about eleven the windows rattled, and we heard the sound of the huge siege guns that had been put in position there. These continued intermittently for the space of a quarter of an hour, sending chance shots at the invisible Martians at Hampton and Ditton, and then the pale beams of the electric light vanished, and were replaced by a bright red glow.

Then the fourth cylinder fell – a brilliant green meteor – as I learned afterwards, in Bushey Park. Before the guns on the Richmond and Kingston line of hills began, there was a fitful cannonade far away in the south-west, due, I believe, to guns being fired haphazard before the black vapour could overwhelm the gunners.

So, setting about it as methodically as men might smoke out a wasps' nest, the Martians spread this strange stifling vapour over the Londonward country. The horns of the crescent slowly moved apart, until at last they formed a line from Hanwell to Coombe and Malden. All night through their destructive tubes advanced. Never once, after the Martian at St George's Hill was brought down, did they give the artillery the ghost of a chance against them. Wherever there was a possibility of guns being laid for them unseen, a fresh canister of the black vapour was discharged, and where the guns were openly displayed the Heat-Ray was brought to bear.

By midnight the blazing trees along the slopes of Richmond Park and the glare of Kingston Hill threw their light upon a network of Black Smoke, blotting out the whole valley of the Thames and extending as far as the eye could reach. And through this two Martians slowly waded, and turned their hissing steam jets this way and that.

They were sparing of the Heat-Ray that night, either because they had but a limited supply of material for its production or because they did not wish to destroy the country but only to crush and overawe the opposition they had aroused. In the latter aim they certainly succeeded. Sunday night was the end of the organised opposition to their movements. After that no body of men would stand against them, so hopeless was the enterprise. Even the crews of the torpedo-boats and destroyers that had brought their quick-firers up the Thames refused to stop, mutinied, and went down again. The only offensive operation men ventured upon after that night was the preparation of mines and pitfalls, and even in that their energies were frantic and spasmodic.

One has to imagine, as well as one may, the fate of those batteries towards Esher, waiting so tensely in the twilight. Survivors there were none. One may picture the orderly expectation, the officers alert and watchful, the gunners ready, the ammunition piled to hand, the limber gunners with their horses and waggons, the groups of civilian spectators standing as near as they were permitted, the evening stillness, the ambulances and hospital tents with the burned and wounded from Weybridge; then the dull resonance of the shots the Martians fired, and the clumsy projectile whirling over the trees and houses and smashing amid the neighbouring fields.

One may picture, too, the sudden shifting of the attention, the swiftly spreading coils and bellyings of that blackness advancing headlong, towering heavenward, turning the twilight to a palpable darkness, a strange and horrible antagonist of vapour striding upon its victims, men and horses near it seen dimly, running, shrieking, falling headlong, shouts of dismay, the guns suddenly abandoned, men choking and writhing on the ground, and the swift broadening-out of the opaque cone of smoke. And then night and extinction – nothing but a silent mass of impenetrable vapour hiding its dead.

Before dawn the black vapour was pouring through the streets of Richmond, and the disintegrating organism of government was, with a last expiring effort, rousing the population of London to the necessity of flight.

CHAPTER SIXTEEN

The Exodus from London

So you understand the roaring wave of fear that swept through the greatest city in the world just as Monday was dawning – the stream of flight rising swiftly to a torrent, lashing in a foaming tumult round the railway stations, banked up into a horrible struggle about the shipping in the Thames, and hurrying by every available channel northward and eastward. By ten o'clock the police organisation, and by midday even the railway organisations, were losing coherency, losing shape and efficiency, guttering, softening, running at last in that swift liquefaction of the social body.

All the railway lines north of the Thames and the South-Eastern people at Cannon Street had been warned by midnight on Sunday, and trains were being filled. People were fighting savagely for standing-room in the carriages even at two o'clock. By three, people were being trampled and crushed even in Bishopsgate Street, a couple of hundred yards or more from Liverpool Street station; revolvers were fired, people stabbed, and the policemen who had been sent to direct the traffic, exhausted and infuriated, were breaking the heads of the people they were called out to protect.

And as the day advanced and the engine drivers and stokers refused to return to London, the pressure of the flight drove the people in an ever-thickening multitude away from the stations and along the northward-running roads. By midday a Martian had been seen at Barnes, and a cloud of slowly sinking black vapour drove along the Thames and across the flats of Lambeth, cutting off all escape over the bridges in its sluggish advance. Another bank drove over Ealing, and surrounded a little island of survivors on Castle Hill, alive, but unable to escape.

After a fruitless struggle to get aboard a North-Western train at Chalk Farm – the engines of the trains that had loaded in the goods yard there *ploughed* through shrieking people, and a dozen stalwart men fought to keep the crowd from crushing the driver against his furnace – my brother emerged upon the Chalk Farm road, dodged across through a hurrying swarm of vehicles, and had the luck to be foremost in the sack of a cycle shop. The front tire of the machine he got was punctured in dragging it through the window, but he got up and off, notwithstanding, with no further injury than a cut wrist. The steep foot of Haverstock Hill was impassable owing to several overturned horses, and my brother struck into Belsize Road.

So he got out of the fury of the panic, and, skirting the Edgware Road, reached Edgware about seven, fasting and wearied, but well ahead of the crowd. Along the road people were standing in the roadway, curious, wondering. He was passed by a number of cyclists, some horsemen, and two motor cars. A mile from Edgware the rim of the wheel broke, and the machine became unridable. He left it by the roadside and trudged through the village. There were shops half opened in the main street of the place, and people crowded on the pavement and in the doorways and windows, staring astonished at this extraordinary procession of fugitives that was beginning. He succeeded in getting some food at an inn.

For a time he remained in Edgware not knowing what next to do. The flying people increased in number. Many of them, like my brother, seemed inclined to loiter in the place. There was no fresh news of the invaders from Mars.

At that time the road was crowded, but as yet far from congested. Most of the fugitives at that hour were mounted on cycles, but there were soon motor cars, hansom cabs, and carriages hurrying along, and the dust hung in heavy clouds along the road to St Albans.

It was perhaps a vague idea of making his way to Chelmsford, where some friends of his lived, that at last induced my brother to strike into a quiet lane running eastward. Presently he came upon a stile, and, crossing it, followed a footpath north-eastward. He passed near several farmhouses and some little places whose names he did not learn. He saw few fugitives until, in a grass lane towards High Barnet, he happened upon two ladies who became his fellow travellers. He came upon them just in time to save them.

He heard their screams, and, hurrying round the corner, saw a couple of men struggling to drag them out of the little pony-chaise in which they had been driving, while a third with difficulty held the frightened pony's head. One of the ladies, a short woman dressed in white, was simply screaming; the other, a dark, slender figure, slashed at the man who gripped her arm with a whip she held in her disengaged hand.

My brother immediately grasped the situation, shouted, and hurried towards the struggle. One of the men desisted and turned towards him, and my brother, realising from his antagonist's face that a fight was unavoidable, and being an expert boxer, went into him forthwith and sent him down against the wheel of the chaise.

It was no time for pugilistic chivalry and my brother laid him quiet with a kick, and gripped the collar of the man who pulled at the slender lady's arm. He heard the clatter of hoofs, the whip stung across his face, a third antagonist struck him between the eyes, and the man he held wrenched himself free and made off down the lane in the direction from which he had come.

Partly stunned, he found himself facing the man who had held the horse's head, and became aware of the chaise receding from him down the lane, swaying from side to side, and with the women in it looking back. The man before him, a burly rough, tried to close, and he stopped him with a blow in the face. Then, realising that he was deserted, he dodged round and made off down the lane after the chaise, with the sturdy man close behind him, and the fugitive, who had turned now, following remotely.

Suddenly he stumbled and fell; his immediate pursuer went headlong, and he rose to his feet to find himself with a couple of antagonists again. He would have had little chance against them had not the slender lady very pluckily pulled up and returned to his help. It seems she had had a revolver all this time, but it had been under the seat when she and her companion were attacked. She fired at six yards' distance, narrowly missing my brother. The less courageous of the robbers made off, and his companion followed him, cursing his cowardice. They both stopped in sight down the lane, where the third man lay insensible.

'Take this!' said the slender lady, and she gave my brother her revolver.

'Go back to the chaise,' said my brother, wiping the blood from his split lip.

She turned without a word – they were both panting – and they went back to where the lady in white struggled to hold back the frightened pony.

The robbers had evidently had enough of it. When my brother looked again they were retreating.

'I'll sit here,' said my brother, 'if I may'; and he got upon the empty front seat. The lady looked over her shoulder.

'Give me the reins,' she said, and laid the whip along the pony's side. In another moment a bend in the road hid the three men from my brother's eyes.

So, quite unexpectedly, my brother found himself, panting, with a cut mouth, a bruised jaw, and bloodstained knuckles, driving along an unknown lane with these two women.

He learned they were the wife and the younger sister of a surgeon living at Stanmore, who had come in the small hours from a dangerous case at Pinner, and heard at some railway station on his way of the Martian advance. He had hurried home, roused the women – their servant had left them two days before – packed some provisions, put his revolver under the seat – luckily for my brother – and told them to drive on to Edgware, with the idea of getting a train there. He stopped behind to tell the neighbours. He would overtake them, he said, at about half-past four in the morning, and now it was nearly nine and they had seen nothing of him. They could not stop in Edgware because of the growing traffic through the place, and so they had come into this side lane.

That was the story they told my brother in fragments when presently they stopped again, nearer to New Barnet. He promised to stay with them, at least until they could determine what to do, or until the missing man arrived, and professed to be an expert shot with the revolver – a weapon strange to him – in order to give them confidence.

They made a sort of encampment by the wayside, and the pony became happy in the hedge. He told them of his own escape out of London, and all that he knew of these Martians and their ways. The sun crept higher in the sky, and after a time their talk died out and gave place to an uneasy state of anticipation. Several wayfarers came along the lane, and of these my brother gathered such news as he could. Every broken answer he had deepened his impression of the great disaster that had come on humanity, deepened his persuasion of the immediate necessity for prosecuting this flight. He urged the matter upon them.

'We have money,' said the slender woman, and hesitated.

Her eyes met my brother's, and her hesitation ended.

'So have I,' said my brother.

She explained that they had as much as thirty pounds in gold, besides a five-pound note, and suggested that with that they might get upon a train at St Albans or New Barnet. My brother thought that was hopeless, seeing the fury of the Londoners to crowd upon the trains, and broached his own idea of striking across Essex towards Harwich and thence escaping from the country altogether.

Mrs Elphinstone – that was the name of the woman in white – would listen to no reasoning, and kept calling upon 'George'; but her sister-in-law was astonishingly quiet and deliberate, and at last agreed to my brother's suggestion. So, designing to cross the Great North Road, they went on towards Barnet, my brother leading the pony to save it as much as possible. As the sun crept up the sky the day became excessively hot, and under foot a thick, whitish sand grew burning and blinding, so that they travelled only

very slowly. The hedges were grey with dust. And as they advanced towards Barnet a tumultuous murmuring grew stronger.

They began to meet more people. For the most part these were staring before them, murmuring indistinct questions, jaded, haggard, unclean. One man in evening dress passed them on foot, his eyes on the ground. They heard his voice, and, looking back at him, saw one hand clutched in his hair and the other beating invisible things. His paroxysm of rage over, he went on his way without once looking back.

As my brother's party went on towards the crossroads to the south of Barnet they saw a woman approaching the road across some fields on their left, carrying a child and with two other children; and then passed a man in dirty black, with a thick stick in one hand and a small portmanteau in the other. Then round the corner of the lane, from between the villas that guarded it at its confluence with the high road, came a little cart drawn by a sweating black pony and driven by a sallow youth in a bowler hat, grey with dust. There were three girls, East End factory girls, and a couple of little children crowded in the cart.

'This'll tike us rahnd Edgware?' asked the driver, wild-eyed, white-faced; and when my brother told him it would if he turned to the left, he whipped up at once without the formality of thanks.

My brother noticed a pale grey smoke or haze rising among the houses in front of them, and veiling the white façade of a terrace beyond the road that appeared between the backs of the villas. Mrs Elphinstone suddenly cried out at a number of tongues of smoky red flame leaping up above the houses in front of them against the hot, blue sky. The tumultuous noise resolved itself now into the disorderly mingling of many voices, the gride of many wheels, the creaking of waggons, and the staccato of hoofs. The lane came round sharply not fifty yards from the crossroads.

'Good heavens!' cried Mrs Elphinstone. 'What is this you are driving us into?'

My brother stopped.

For the main road was a boiling stream of people, a torrent of human beings rushing northward, one pressing on another. A great bank of dust, white and luminous in the blaze of the sun, made everything within twenty feet of the ground grey and indistinct and was perpetually renewed by the hurrying feet of a dense crowd of horses and of men and women on foot, and by the wheels of vehicles of every description.

'Way!' my brother heard voices crying. 'Make way!'

It was like riding into the smoke of a fire to approach the meeting point of the lane and road; the crowd roared like a fire, and the dust was hot and pungent. And, indeed, a little way up the road a villa was burning and sending rolling masses of black smoke across the road to add to the confusion.

Two men came past them. Then a dirty woman, carrying a heavy bundle

and weeping. A lost retriever dog, with hanging tongue, circled dubiously round them, scared and wretched, and fled at my brother's threat.

So much as they could see of the road Londonward between the houses to the right was a tumultuous stream of dirty, hurrying people, pent in between the villas on either side; the black heads, the crowded forms, grew into distinctness as they rushed towards the corner, hurried past, and merged their individuality again in a receding multitude that was swallowed up at last in a cloud of dust.

'Go on! Go on!' cried the voices. 'Way! Way!'

One man's hands pressed on the back of another. My brother stood at the pony's head. Irresistibly attracted, he advanced slowly, pace by pace, down the lane.

Edgware had been a scene of confusion, Chalk Farm a riotous tumult, but this was a whole population in movement. It is hard to imagine that host. It had no character of its own. The figures poured out past the corner, and receded with their backs to the group in the lane. Along the margin came those who were on foot threatened by the wheels, stumbling in the ditches, blundering into one another.

The carts and carriages crowded close upon one another, making little way for those swifter and more impatient vehicles that darted forward every now and then when an opportunity showed itself of doing so, sending the people scattering against the fences and gates of the villas.

'Push on!' was the cry. 'Push on! They are coming!'

In one cart stood a blind man in the uniform of the Salvation Army, gesticulating with his crooked fingers and bawling, 'Eternity! Eternity!' His voice was hoarse and very loud so that my brother could hear him long after he was lost to sight in the dust. Some of the people who crowded in the carts whipped stupidly at their horses and quarrelled with other drivers; some sat motionless, staring at nothing with miserable eyes; some gnawed their hands with thirst, or lay prostrate in the bottoms of their conveyances. The horses' bits were covered with foam, their eyes bloodshot.

There were cabs, carriages, shop cars, waggons, beyond counting; a mail cart, a road-cleaner's cart marked 'Vestry of St Pancras', a huge timber waggon crowded with roughs. A brewer's dray rumbled by with its two near wheels splashed with fresh blood.

'Clear the way!' cried the voices. 'Clear the way!'

'Eter—nity! Eter—nity!' came echoing down the road.

There were sad, haggard women tramping by, well dressed, with children that cried and stumbled, their dainty clothes smothered in dust, their weary faces smeared with tears. With many of these came men, sometimes helpful, sometimes lowering and savage. Fighting side by side with them pushed some weary street outcast in faded black rags, wide-eyed, loud-voiced, and foul-mouthed. There were sturdy workmen thrusting their way along, wretched, unkempt men, clothed like clerks or shopmen, struggling

spasmodically; a wounded soldier my brother noticed, men dressed in the clothes of railway porters, one wretched creature in a nightshirt with a coat thrown over it.

But varied as its composition was, certain things all that host had in common. There were fear and pain on their faces, and fear behind them. A tumult up the road, a quarrel for a place in a waggon, sent the whole host of them quickening their pace; even a man so scared and broken that his knees bent under him was galvanised for a moment into renewed activity. The heat and dust had already been at work upon this multitude. Their skins were dry, their lips black and cracked. They were all thirsty, weary, and footsore. And amid the various cries one heard disputes, reproaches, groans of weariness and fatigue; the voices of most of them were hoarse and weak. Through it all ran a refrain: 'Way! Way! The Martians are coming!'

Few stopped and came aside from that flood. The lane opened slantingly into the main road with a narrow opening, and had a delusive appearance of coming from the direction of London. Yet a kind of eddy of people drove into its mouth; weaklings elbowed out of the stream, who for the most part rested but a moment before plunging into it again. A little way down the lane, with two friends bending over him, lay a man with a bare leg, wrapped about with bloody rags. He was a lucky man to have friends.

A little old man, with a grey military moustache and a filthy black frock coat, limped out and sat down beside the trap, removed his boot – his sock was blood-stained – shook out a pebble, and hobbled on again; and then a little girl of eight or nine, all alone, threw herself under the hedge close by my brother, weeping.

'I can't go on! I can't go on!'

My brother woke from his torpor of astonishment and lifted her up, speaking gently to her, and carried her to Miss Elphinstone. So soon as my brother touched her she became quite still, as if frightened.

'Ellen!' shrieked a woman in the crowd, with tears in her voice – 'Ellen!' And the child suddenly darted away from my brother, crying 'Mother!'

'They are coming,' said a man on horseback, riding past along the lane.

'Out of the way, there!' bawled a coachman, towering high; and my brother saw a closed carriage turning into the lane.

The people crushed back on one another to avoid the horse. My brother pushed the pony and chaise back into the hedge, and the man drove by and stopped at the turn of the way. It was a carriage, with a pole for a pair of horses, but only one was in the traces. My brother saw dimly through the dust that two men lifted out something on a white stretcher and put it gently on the grass beneath the privet hedge.

One of the men came running to my brother.

'Where is there any water?' he said. 'He is dying fast, and very thirsty. It is Lord Garrick.'

'Lord Garrick!' said my brother – 'the Chief Justice?'

'The water?' he said.

'There may be a tap,' said my brother, 'in some of the houses. We have no water. I dare not leave my people.'

The man pushed against the crowd towards the gate of the corner house.

'Go on!' said the people, thrusting at him. 'They are coming! Go on!'

Then my brother's attention was distracted by a bearded, eagle-faced man lugging a small handbag, which split even as my brother's eyes rested on it and disgorged a mass of sovereigns that seemed to break up into separate coins as it struck the ground. They rolled hither and thither among the struggling feet of men and horses. The man stopped and looked stupidly at the heap, and the shaft of a cab struck his shoulder and sent him reeling. He gave a shriek and dodged back, and a cartwheel shaved him narrowly.

'Way!' cried the men all about him. 'Make way!'

So soon as the cab had passed, he flung himself, with both hands open, upon the heap of coins, and began thrusting handfuls in his pocket. A horse rose close upon him, and in another moment, half rising, he had been borne down under the horse's hoofs.

'Stop!' screamed my brother, and pushing a woman out of his way, tried to clutch the bit of the horse.

Before he could get to it, he heard a scream under the wheels, and saw through the dust the rim passing over the poor wretch's back. The driver of the cart slashed his whip at my brother, who ran round behind the cart. The multitudinous shouting confused his ears. The man was writhing in the dust among his scattered money, unable to rise, for the wheel had broken his back, and his lower limbs lay limp and dead. My brother stood up and yelled at the next driver, and a man on a black horse came to his assistance.

'Get him out of the road,' said he; and, clutching the man's collar with his free hand, my brother lugged him sideways. But he still clutched after his money, and regarded my brother fiercely, hammering at his arm with a handful of gold. 'Go on! Go on!' shouted angry voices behind. 'Way! Way!'

There was a smash as the pole of a carriage crashed into the cart that the man on horseback stopped. My brother looked up, and the man with the gold twisted his head round and bit the wrist that held his collar. There was a concussion, and the black horse came staggering sideways, and the carthorse pushed beside it. A hoof missed my brother's foot by a hair's breadth. He released his grip on the fallen man and jumped back. He saw anger change to terror on the face of the poor wretch on the ground, and in a moment he was hidden and my brother was borne backward and carried past the entrance of the lane, and had to fight hard in the torrent to recover it.

He saw Miss Elphinstone covering her eyes, and a little child, with all a child's want of sympathetic imagination, staring with dilated eyes at a dusty something that lay black and still, ground and crushed under the rolling

wheels. 'Let us go back!' he shouted, and began turning the pony round. 'We cannot cross this – hell,' he said; and they went back a hundred yards the way they had come, until the fighting crowd was hidden. As they passed the bend in the lane my brother saw the face of the dying man in the ditch under the privet, deadly white and drawn, and shining with perspiration. The two women sat silent, crouching in their seat and shivering.

Then beyond the bend my brother stopped again. Miss Elphinstone was white and pale, and her sister-in-law sat weeping, too wretched even to call upon 'George'. My brother was horrified and perplexed. So soon as they had retreated he realised how urgent and unavoidable it was to attempt this crossing. He turned to Miss Elphinstone, suddenly resolute.

'We must go that way,' he said, and led the pony round again.

For the second time that day this girl proved her quality. To force their way into the torrent of people, my brother plunged into the traffic and held back a cab horse, while she drove the pony across its head. A waggon locked wheels for a moment and ripped a long splinter from the chaise. In another moment they were caught and swept forward by the stream. My brother, with the cabman's whip marks red across his face and hands, scrambled into the chaise and took the reins from her.

'Point the revolver at the man behind,' he said, giving it to her, 'if he presses us too hard. No! – point it at his horse.'

Then he began to look out for a chance of edging to the right across the road. But once in the stream he seemed to lose volition, to become a part of that dusty rout. They swept through Chipping Barnet with the torrent; they were nearly a mile beyond the centre of the town before they had fought across to the opposite side of the way. It was din and confusion indescribable; but in and beyond the town the road forks repeatedly, and this to some extent relieved the stress.

They struck eastward through Hadley, and there on either side of the road, and at another place farther on they came upon a great multitude of people drinking at the stream, some fighting to come at the water. And farther on, from a lull near East Barnet, they saw two trains running slowly one after the other without signal or order – trains swarming with people, with men even among the coals behind the engines – going northward along the Great Northern Railway. My brother supposes they must have filled outside London, for at that time the furious terror of the people had rendered the central termini impossible.

Near this place they halted for the rest of the afternoon, for the violence of the day had already utterly exhausted all three of them. They began to suffer the beginnings of hunger; the night was cold, and none of them dared to sleep. And in the evening many people came hurrying along the road nearby their stopping place, fleeing from unknown dangers before them, and going in the direction from which my brother had come.

The Thunder Child

Had the Martians aimed only at destruction, they might on Monday have annihilated the entire population of London, as it spread itself slowly through the home counties. Not only along the road through Barnet, but also through Edgware and Waltham Abbey, and along the roads eastward to Southend and Shoeburyness, and south of the Thames to Deal and Broadstairs, poured the same frantic rout. If one could have hung that June morning in a balloon in the blazing blue above London every northward and eastward road running out of the tangled maze of streets would have seemed stippled black with the streaming fugitives, each dot a human agony of terror and physical distress. I have set forth at length in the last chapter my brother's account of the road through Chipping Barnet, in order that my readers may realise how that swarming of black dots appeared to one of those concerned. Never before in the history of the world had such a mass of human beings moved and suffered together. The legendary hosts of Goths and Huns, the hugest armies Asia has ever seen, would have been but a drop in that current. And this was no disciplined march; it was a stampede – a stampede gigantic and terrible – without order and without a goal, six million people unarmed and unprovisioned, driving headlong. It was the beginning of the rout of civilisation, of the massacre of mankind.

Directly below him the balloonist would have seen the network of streets far and wide, houses, churches, squares, crescents, gardens – already derelict – spread out like a huge map, and in the southward *blotted*. Over Ealing, Richmond, Wimbledon, it would have seemed as if some monstrous pen had flung ink upon the chart. Steadily, incessantly, each black splash grew and spread, shooting out ramifications this way and that, now banking itself against rising ground, now pouring swiftly over a crest into a new-found valley, exactly as a gout of ink would spread itself upon blotting paper.

And beyond, over the blue hills that rise southward of the river, the glittering Martians went to and fro, calmly and methodically spreading their poison cloud over this patch of country and then over that, laying it again with their steam jets when it had served its purpose, and taking possession of the conquered country. They do not seem to have aimed at extermination so much as at complete demoralisation and the destruction of any opposition. They exploded any stores of powder they came upon, cut every telegraph, and wrecked the railways here and there. They were hamstringing mankind. They seemed in no hurry to extend the field of their operations, and did not come beyond the central part of London all

that day. It is possible that a very considerable number of people in London stuck to their houses through Monday morning. Certain it is that many died at home suffocated by the Black Smoke.

Until about midday the Pool of London was an astonishing scene. Steamboats and shipping of all sorts lay there, tempted by the enormous sums of money offered by fugitives, and it is said that many who swam out to these vessels were thrust off with boathooks and drowned. About one o'clock in the afternoon the thinning remnant of a cloud of the black vapour appeared between the arches of Blackfriars Bridge. At that the Pool became a scene of mad confusion, fighting, and collision, and for some time a multitude of boats and barges jammed in the northern arch of the Tower Bridge, and the sailors and lightermen had to fight savagely against the people who swarmed upon them from the riverfront. People were actually clambering down the piers of the bridge from above.

When, an hour later, a Martian appeared beyond the Clock Tower and waded down the river, nothing but wreckage floated above Limehouse.

Of the falling of the fifth cylinder I have presently to tell. The sixth star fell at Wimbledon. My brother, keeping watch beside the women in the chaise in a meadow, saw the green flash of it far beyond the hills. On Tuesday the little party, still set upon getting across the sea, made its way through the swarming country towards Colchester. The news that the Martians were now in possession of the whole of London was confirmed. They had been seen at Highgate, and even, it was said, at Neasden. But they did not come into my brother's view until the morrow.

That day the scattered multitudes began to realise the urgent need of provisions. As they grew hungry the rights of property ceased to be regarded. Farmers were out to defend their cattle-sheds, granaries, and ripening root crops with arms in their hands. A number of people now, like my brother, had their faces eastward, and there were some desperate souls even going back towards London to get food. These were chiefly people from the northern suburbs, whose knowledge of the Black Smoke came by hearsay. He heard that about half the members of the government had gathered at Birmingham, and that enormous quantities of high explosives were being prepared to be used in automatic mines across the Midland counties.

He was also told that the Midland Railway Company had replaced the desertions of the first day's panic, had resumed traffic, and was running northward trains from St Albans to relieve the congestion of the home counties. There was also a placard in Chipping Ongar announcing that large stores of flour were available in the northern towns and that within twenty-four hours bread would be distributed among the starving people in the neighbourhood. But this intelligence did not deter him from the plan of escape he had formed, and the three pressed eastward all day, and heard no more of the bread distribution than this promise. Nor, as a matter of fact,

did anyone else hear more of it. That night fell the seventh star, falling upon Primrose Hill. It fell while Miss Elphinstone was watching, for she took that duty alternately with my brother. She saw it.

On Wednesday the three fugitives – they had passed the night in a field of unripe wheat – reached Chelmsford, and there a body of the inhabitants, calling itself the Committee of Public Supply, seized the pony as provisions, and would give nothing in exchange for it but the promise of a share in it the next day. Here there were rumours of Martians at Epping, and news of the destruction of Waltham Abbey Powder Mills in a vain attempt to blow up one of the invaders.

People were watching for Martians here from the church towers. My brother, very luckily for him as it chanced, preferred to push on at once to the coast rather than wait for food, although all three of them were very hungry. By midday they passed through Tillingham, which, strangely enough, seemed to be quite silent and deserted, save for a few furtive plunderers hunting for food. Near Tillingham they suddenly came in sight of the sea, and the most amazing crowd of shipping of all sorts that it is possible to imagine.

For after the sailors could no longer come up the Thames, they came on to the Essex coast, to Harwich and Walton and Clacton, and afterwards to Foulness and Shoebury, to bring off the people. They lay in a huge sickle-shaped curve that vanished into mist at last towards the Naze. Close inshore was a multitude of fishing smacks – English, Scotch, French, Dutch, and Swedish; steam launches from the Thames, yachts, electric boats; and beyond were ships of large burden, a multitude of filthy colliers, trim merchantmen, cattle ships, passenger boats, petroleum tanks, ocean tramps, an old white transport even, neat white and grey liners from Southampton and Hamburg; and along the blue coast across the Blackwater my brother could make out dimly a dense swarm of boats chaffering with the people on the beach, a swarm which also extended up the Blackwater almost to Maldon.

About a couple of miles out lay an ironclad, very low in the water, almost, to my brother's perception, like a waterlogged ship. This was the ram *Thunder Child*. It was the only warship in sight, but far away to the right over the smooth surface of the sea – for that day there was a dead calm – lay a serpent of black smoke to mark the next ironclads of the Channel Fleet, which hovered in an extended line, steam up and ready for action, across the Thames estuary during the course of the Martian conquest, vigilant and yet powerless to prevent it.

At the sight of the sea, Mrs Elphinstone, in spite of the assurances of her sister-in-law, gave way to panic. She had never been out of England before, she would rather die than trust herself friendless in a foreign country, and so forth. She seemed, poor woman, to imagine that the French and the Martians might prove very similar. She had been growing increasingly

hysterical, fearful, and depressed during the two days' journeyings. Her great idea was to return to Stanmore. Things had been always well and safe at Stanmore. They would find George at Stanmore.

It was with the greatest difficulty they could get her down to the beach, where presently my brother succeeded in attracting the attention of some men on a paddle steamer from the Thames. They sent a boat and drove a bargain for thirty-six pounds for the three. The steamer was going, these men said, to Ostend.

It was about two o'clock when my brother, having paid their fares at the gangway, found himself safely aboard the steamboat with his charges. There was food aboard, albeit at exorbitant prices, and the three of them contrived to eat a meal on one of the seats forward.

There were already a couple of score of passengers aboard, some of whom had expended their last money in securing a passage, but the captain lay off the Blackwater until five in the afternoon, picking up passengers until the seated decks were even dangerously crowded. He would probably have remained longer had it not been for the sound of guns that began about that hour in the south. As if in answer, the ironclad seaward fired a small gun and hoisted a string of flags. A jet of smoke sprang out of her funnels.

Some of the passengers were of opinion that this firing came from Shoeburyness, until it was noticed that it was growing louder. At the same time, far away in the south-east the masts and upperworks of three ironclads rose one after the other out of the sea, beneath clouds of black smoke. But my brother's attention speedily reverted to the distant firing in the south. He fancied he saw a column of smoke rising out of the distant grey haze.

The little steamer was already flapping her way eastward of the big crescent of shipping, and the low Essex coast was growing blue and hazy, when a Martian appeared, small and faint in the remote distance, advancing along the muddy coast from the direction of Foulness. At that the captain on the bridge swore at the top of his voice with fear and anger at his own delay, and the paddles seemed infected with his terror. Every soul aboard stood at the bulwarks or on the seats of the steamer and stared at that distant shape, higher than the trees or church towers inland, and advancing with a leisurely parody of a human stride.

It was the first Martian my brother had seen, and he stood, more amazed than terrified, watching this Titan advancing deliberately towards the shipping, wading farther and farther into the water as the coast fell away. Then, far away beyond the Crouch, came another, striding over some stunted trees, and then yet another, still farther off, wading deeply through a shiny mudflat that seemed to hang halfway up between sea and sky. They were all stalking seaward, as if to intercept the escape of the multitudinous vessels that were crowded between Foulness and the Naze.

In spite of the throbbing exertions of the engines of the little paddle-boat, and the pouring foam that her wheels flung behind her, she receded with terrifying slowness from this ominous advance.

Glancing north-westward, my brother saw the large crescent of shipping already writhing with the approaching terror; one ship passing behind another, another coming round from broadside to end on, steamships whistling and giving off volumes of steam, sails being let out, launches rushing hither and thither. He was so fascinated by this and by the creeping danger away to the left that he had no eyes for anything seaward. And then a swift movement of the steamboat (she had suddenly come round to avoid being run down) flung him headlong from the seat upon which he was standing. There was a shouting all about him, a trampling of feet, and a cheer that seemed to be answered faintly. The steamboat lurched and rolled him over upon his hands.

He sprang to his feet and saw to starboard, and not a hundred yards from their heeling, pitching boat, a vast iron bulk like the blade of a plough tearing through the water, tossing it on either side in huge waves of foam that leaped towards the steamer, flinging her paddles helplessly in the air, and then sucking her deck down almost to the waterline.

A douche of spray blinded my brother for a moment. When his eyes were clear again he saw the monster had passed and was rushing landward. Big iron upperworks rose out of this headlong structure, and from that twin funnels projected and spat a smoking blast shot with fire. It was the torpedo ram, *Thunder Child*, steaming headlong, coming to the rescue of the threatened shipping.

Keeping his footing on the heaving deck by clutching the bulwarks, my brother looked past this charging leviathan at the Martians again, and he saw the three of them now close together, and standing so far out to sea that their tripod supports were almost entirely submerged. Thus sunken, and seen in remote perspective, they appeared far less formidable than the huge iron bulk in whose wake the steamer was pitching so helplessly. It would seem they were regarding this new antagonist with astonishment. To their intelligence, it may be, the giant was even such another as themselves. The *Thunder Child* fired no gun, but simply drove full speed towards them. It was probably her not firing that enabled her to get so near the enemy as she did. They did not know what to make of her. One shell, and they would have sent her to the bottom forthwith with the Heat-Ray.

She was steaming at such a pace that in a minute she seemed halfway between the steamboat and the Martians – a diminishing black bulk against the receding horizontal expanse of the Essex coast.

Suddenly the foremost Martian lowered his tube and discharged a canister of the black gas at the ironclad. It hit her larboard side and glanced off in an inky jet that rolled away to seaward, an unfolding torrent of Black Smoke, from which the ironclad drove clear. To the watchers from the

steamer, low in the water and with the sun in their eyes, it seemed as though she were already among the Martians.

They saw the gaunt figures separating and rising out of the water as they retreated shoreward, and one of them raised the camera-like generator of the Heat-Ray. He held it pointing obliquely downward, and a bank of steam sprang from the water at its touch. It must have driven through the iron of the ship's side like a white-hot iron rod through paper.

A flicker of flame went up through the rising steam, and then the Martian reeled and staggered. In another moment he was cut down, and a great body of water and steam shot high in the air. The guns of the *Thunder Child* sounded through the reek, going off one after the other, and one shot splashed the water high close by the steamer, ricocheted towards the other flying ships to the north, and smashed a smack to matchwood.

But no one heeded that very much. At the sight of the Martian's collapse the captain on the bridge yelled inarticulately, and all the crowding passengers on the steamer's stern shouted together. And then they yelled again. For, surging out beyond the white tumult, drove something long and black, the flames streaming from its middle parts, its ventilators and funnels spouting fire.

She was alive still; the steering gear, it seems, was intact and her engines working. She headed straight for a second Martian, and was within a hundred yards of him when the Heat-Ray came to bear. Then with a violent thud, a blinding flash, her decks, her funnels, leaped upward. The Martian staggered with the violence of her explosion, and in another moment the flaming wreckage, still driving forward with the impetus of its pace, had struck him and crumpled him up like a thing of cardboard. My brother shouted involuntarily. A boiling tumult of steam hid everything again.

'Two!' yelled the captain.

Everyone was shouting. The whole steamer from end to end rang with frantic cheering that was taken up first by one and then by all in the crowding multitude of ships and boats that was driving out to sea.

The steam hung upon the water for many minutes, hiding the third Martian and the coast altogether. And all this time the boat was paddling steadily out to sea and away from the fight; and when at last the confusion cleared, the drifting bank of black vapour intervened, and nothing of the *Thunder Child* could be made out, nor could the third Martian be seen. But the ironclads to seaward were now quite close and standing in towards shore past the steamboat.

The little vessel continued to beat its way seaward, and the ironclads receded slowly towards the coast, which was hidden still by a marbled bank of vapour, part steam, part black gas, eddying and combining in the strangest way. The fleet of refugees was scattering to the north-east; several smacks were sailing between the ironclads and the steamboat. After a time, and before they reached the sinking cloud bank, the warships

turned northward, and then abruptly went about and passed into the thickening haze of evening southward. The coast grew faint, and at last indistinguishable amid the low banks of clouds that were gathering about the sinking sun.

Then suddenly out of the golden haze of the sunset came the vibration of guns, and a form of black shadows moving. Everyone struggled to the rail of the steamer and peered into the blinding furnace of the west, but nothing was to be distinguished clearly. A mass of smoke rose slanting and barred the face of the sun. The steamboat throbbed on its way through an interminable suspense.

The sun sank into grey clouds, the sky flushed and darkened, the evening star trembled into sight. It was deep twilight when the captain cried out and pointed. My brother strained his eyes. Something rushed up into the sky out of the greyness – rushed slantingly upward and very swiftly into the luminous clearness above the clouds in the western sky; something flat and broad, and very large, that swept round in a vast curve, grew smaller, sank slowly, and vanished again into the grey mystery of the night. And as it flew it rained down darkness upon the land.

BOOK TWO

The Earth Under the Martians

CHAPTER ONE

Under Foot

In the first book I have wandered so much from my own adventures to tell of the experiences of my brother that all through the last two chapters I and the curate have been lurking in the empty house at Halliford whither we fled to escape the Black Smoke. There I will resume. We stopped there all Sunday night and all the next day – the day of the panic – in a little island of daylight, cut off by the Black Smoke from the rest of the world. We could do nothing but wait in aching inactivity during those two weary days.

My mind was occupied by anxiety for my wife. I figured her at Leatherhead, terrified, in danger, mourning me already as a dead man. I paced the rooms and cried aloud when I thought of how I was cut off from her, of all that might happen to her in my absence. My cousin I knew was brave enough for any emergency, but he was not the sort of man to realise danger quickly, to rise promptly. What was needed now was not bravery, but circumspection. My only consolation was to believe that the Martians were moving Londonward and away from her. Such vague anxieties keep the mind sensitive and painful. I grew very weary and irritable with the curate's perpetual ejaculations; I tired of the sight of his selfish despair. After some ineffectual remonstrance I kept away from him, staying in a room – evidently a children's schoolroom – containing globes, forms, and copybooks. When he followed me thither, I went to a box room at the top of the house and, in order to be alone with my aching miseries, locked myself in.

We were hopelessly hemmed in by the Black Smoke all that day and the morning of the next. There were signs of people in the next house on Sunday evening – a face at a window and moving lights, and later the slamming of a door. But I do not know who these people were, nor what became of them. We saw nothing of them next day. The Black Smoke drifted slowly riverward all through Monday morning, creeping nearer and nearer to us, driving at last along the roadway outside the house that hid us.

A Martian came across the fields about midday, laying the stuff with a jet of superheated steam that hissed against the walls, smashed all the windows it touched, and scalded the curate's hand as he fled out of the front room. When at last we crept across the sodden rooms and looked out again, the country northward was as though a black snowstorm had passed over it. Looking towards the river, we were astonished to see an unaccountable redness mingling with the black of the scorched meadows.

For a time we did not see how this change affected our position, save that we were relieved of our fear of the Black Smoke. But later I perceived that we were no longer hemmed in, that now we might get away. So soon as I realised that the way of escape was open, my dream of action returned. But the curate was lethargic, unreasonable.

'We are safe here,' he repeated; 'safe here.'

I resolved to leave him – would that I had! Wiser now for the artillery-man's teaching, I sought out food and drink. I had found oil and rags for my burns, and I also took a hat and a flannel shirt that I found in one of the bedrooms. When it was clear to him that I meant to go alone – had reconciled myself to going alone – he suddenly roused himself to come. And all being quiet throughout the afternoon, we started about five o'clock, as I should judge, along the blackened road to Sunbury.

In Sunbury, and at intervals along the road, were dead bodies lying in contorted attitudes, horses as well as men, overturned carts and luggage, all covered thickly with black dust. That pall of cindery powder made me think of what I had read of the destruction of Pompeii. We got to Hampton Court without misadventure, our minds full of strange and unfamiliar appearances, and at Hampton Court our eyes were relieved to find a patch of green that had escaped the suffocating drift. We went through Bushey Park, with its deer going to and fro under the chestnuts, and some men and women hurrying in the distance towards Hampton, and so we came to Twickenham. These were the first people we saw.

Away across the road the woods beyond Ham and Petersham were still afire. Twickenham was uninjured by either Heat-Ray or Black Smoke, and there were more people about here, though none could give us news. For the most part they were like ourselves, taking advantage of a lull to shift their quarters. I have an impression that many of the houses here were still occupied by scared inhabitants, too frightened even for flight. Here too the evidence of a hasty rout was abundant along the road. I remember most vividly three smashed bicycles in a heap, pounded into the road by the wheels of subsequent carts. We crossed Richmond Bridge about half-past eight. We hurried across the exposed bridge, of course, but I noticed floating down the stream a number of red masses, some many feet across. I did not know what these were – there was no time for scrutiny – and I put a more horrible interpretation on them than they deserved. Here again on the Surrey side were black dust that had once been smoke, and dead bodies – a heap near the approach to the station; but we had no glimpse of the Martians until we were some way towards Barnes.

We saw in the blackened distance a group of three people running down a side street towards the river, but otherwise it seemed deserted. Up the hill Richmond town was burning briskly; outside the town of Richmond there was no trace of the Black Smoke.

Then suddenly, as we approached Kew, came a number of people

running, and the upperworks of a Martian fighting-machine loomed in sight over the housetops, not a hundred yards away from us. We stood aghast at our danger, and had the Martian looked down we must immediately have perished. We were so terrified that we dared not go on, but turned aside and hid in a shed in a garden. There the curate crouched, weeping silently, and refusing to stir again.

But my fixed idea of reaching Leatherhead would not let me rest, and in the twilight I ventured out again. I went through a shrubbery, and along a passage beside a big house standing in its own grounds, and so emerged upon the road towards Kew. The curate I left in the shed, but he came hurrying after me.

That second start was the most foolhardy thing I ever did. For it was manifest the Martians were about us. No sooner had the curate overtaken me than we saw either the fighting-machine we had seen before or another, far away across the meadows in the direction of Kew Lodge. Four or five little black figures hurried before it across the green-grey of the field, and in a moment it was evident this Martian pursued them. In three strides he was among them, and they ran radiating from his feet in all directions. He used no Heat-Ray to destroy them, but picked them up one by one. Apparently he tossed them into the great metallic carrier which projected behind him, much as a workman's basket hangs over his shoulder.

It was the first time I realised that the Martians might have any other purpose than destruction with defeated humanity. We stood for a moment petrified, then turned and fled through a gate behind us into a walled garden, fell into, rather than found, a fortunate ditch, and lay there, scarce daring to whisper to each other until the stars were out.

I suppose it was nearly eleven o'clock before we gathered courage to start again, no longer venturing into the road, but sneaking along hedgerows and through plantations, and watching keenly through the darkness, he on the right and I on the left, for the Martians, who seemed to be all about us. In one place we blundered upon a scorched and blackened area, now cooling and ashen, and a number of scattered dead bodies of men, burned horribly about the heads and trunks but with their legs and boots mostly intact; and of dead horses, fifty feet, perhaps, behind a line of four ripped guns and smashed gun carriages.

Sheen, it seemed, had escaped destruction, but the place was silent and deserted. Here we happened on no dead, though the night was too dark for us to see into the side roads of the place. In Sheen my companion suddenly complained of faintness and thirst, and we decided to try one of the houses.

The first house we entered, after a little difficulty with the window, was a small semi-detached villa, and I found nothing eatable left in the place but some mouldy cheese. There was, however, water to drink; and I took a hatchet, which promised to be useful in our next housebreaking.

We then crossed to a place where the road turns towards Mortlake. Here

there stood a white house within a walled garden, and in the pantry of this domicile we found a store of food – two loaves of bread in a pan, an uncooked steak, and the half of a ham. I give this catalogue so precisely because, as it happened, we were destined to subsist upon this store for the next fortnight. Bottled beer stood under a shelf, and there were two bags of haricot beans and some limp lettuces. This pantry opened into a kind of wash-up kitchen, and in this was firewood; there was also a cupboard, in which we found nearly a dozen of burgundy, tinned soups and salmon, and two tins of biscuits.

We sat in the adjacent kitchen in the dark – for we dared not strike a light – and ate bread and ham, and drank beer out of the same bottle. The curate, who was still timorous and restless, was now, oddly enough, for pushing on, and I was urging him to keep up his strength by eating when the thing happened that was to imprison us.

'It can't be midnight yet,' I said, and then came a blinding glare of vivid green light. Everything in the kitchen leaped out, clearly visible in green and black, and vanished again. And then followed such a concussion as I have never heard before or since. So close on the heels of this as to seem instantaneous came a thud behind me, a clash of glass, a crash and rattle of falling masonry all about us, and the plaster of the ceiling came down upon us, smashing into a multitude of fragments upon our heads. I was knocked headlong across the floor against the oven handle and stunned. I was insensible for a long time, the curate told me, and when I came to we were in darkness again, and he, with a face wet, as I found afterwards, with blood from a cut forehead, was dabbing water over me.

For some time I could not recollect what had happened. Then things came to me slowly. A bruise on my temple asserted itself.

'Are you better?' asked the curate in a whisper.

At last I answered him. I sat up.

'Don't move,' he said. 'The floor is covered with smashed crockery from the dresser. You can't possibly move without making a noise, and I fancy *they* are outside.'

We both sat quite silent, so that we could scarcely hear each other breathing. Everything seemed deadly still, but once something near us, some plaster or broken brickwork, slid down with a rumbling sound. Outside and very near was an intermittent, metallic rattle.

'That!' said the curate, when presently it happened again.

'Yes,' I said. 'But what is it?'

'A Martian!' said the curate.

I listened again.

'It was not like the Heat-Ray,' I said, and for a time I was inclined to think one of the great fighting-machines had stumbled against the house, as I had seen one stumble against the tower of Shepperton Church.

Our situation was so strange and incomprehensible that for three or four

hours, until the dawn came, we scarcely moved. And then the light filtered in, not through the window, which remained black, but through a triangular aperture between a beam and a heap of broken bricks in the wall behind us. The interior of the kitchen we now saw greyly for the first time.

The window had been burst in by a mass of garden mould, which flowed over the table upon which we had been sitting and lay about our feet. Outside, the soil was banked high against the house. At the top of the window frame we could see an uprooted drainpipe. The floor was littered with smashed hardware; the end of the kitchen towards the house was broken into, and since the daylight shone in there, it was evident the greater part of the house had collapsed. Contrasting vividly with this ruin was the neat dresser, stained in the fashion, pale green, and with a number of copper and tin vessels below it, the wallpaper imitating blue and white tiles, and a couple of coloured supplements fluttering from the walls above the kitchen range.

As the dawn grew clearer, we saw through the gap in the wall the body of a Martian, standing sentinel, I suppose, over the still glowing cylinder. At the sight of that we crawled as circumspectly as possible out of the twilight of the kitchen into the darkness of the scullery.

Abruptly the right interpretation dawned upon my mind.

'The fifth cylinder,' I whispered, 'the fifth shot from Mars, has struck this house and buried us under the ruins!'

For a time the curate was silent, and then he whispered: 'God have mercy upon us!'

I heard him presently whimpering to himself.

Save for that sound we lay quite still in the scullery; I for my part scarce dared breathe, and sat with my eyes fixed on the faint light of the kitchen door. I could just see the curate's face, a dim, oval shape, and his collar and cuffs. Outside there began a metallic hammering, then a violent hooting, and then again, after a quiet interval, a hissing like the hissing of an engine. These noises, for the most part problematical, continued intermittently, and seemed if anything to increase in number as time wore on. Presently a measured thudding and a vibration that made everything about us quiver and the vessels in the pantry ring and shift, began and continued. Once the light was eclipsed, and the ghostly kitchen doorway became absolutely dark. For many hours we must have crouched there, silent and shivering, until our tired attention failed . . .

At last I found myself awake and very hungry. I am inclined to believe we must have spent the greater portion of a day before that awakening. My hunger was at a stride so insistent that it moved me to action. I told the curate I was going to seek food, and felt my way towards the pantry. He made me no answer, but so soon as I began eating the faint noise I made stirred him up and I heard him crawling after me.

CHAPTER TWO

What We Saw from the Ruined House

After eating we crept back to the scullery, and there I must have dozed again, for when presently I looked round I was alone. The thudding vibration continued with wearisome persistence. I whispered for the curate several times, and at last felt my way to the door of the kitchen. It was still daylight, and I perceived him across the room, lying against the triangular hole that looked out upon the Martians. His shoulders were hunched, so that his head was hidden from me.

I could hear a number of noises almost like those in an engine shed; and the place rocked with that beating thud. Through the aperture in the wall I could see the top of a tree touched with gold and the warm blue of a tranquil evening sky. For a minute or so I remained watching the curate, and then I advanced, crouching and stepping with extreme care amid the broken crockery that littered the floor.

I touched the curate's leg, and he started so violently that a mass of plaster went sliding down outside and fell with a loud impact. I gripped his arm, fearing he might cry out, and for a long time we crouched motionless. Then I turned to see how much of our rampart remained. The detachment of the plaster had left a vertical slit open in the debris, and by raising myself cautiously across a beam I was able to see out of this gap into what had been overnight a quiet suburban roadway. Vast, indeed, was the change that we beheld.

The fifth cylinder must have fallen right into the midst of the house we had first visited. The building had vanished, completely smashed, pulverised, and dispersed by the blow. The cylinder lay now far beneath the original foundations – deep in a hole, already vastly larger than the pit I had looked into at Woking. The earth all round it had splashed under that tremendous impact – 'splashed' is the only word – and lay in heaped piles that hid the masses of the adjacent houses. It had behaved exactly like mud under the violent blow of a hammer. Our house had collapsed backward; the front portion, even on the ground floor, had been destroyed completely; by a chance the kitchen and scullery had escaped, and stood buried now under soil and ruins, closed in by tons of earth on every side save towards the cylinder. Over that aspect we hung now on the very edge of the great circular pit the Martians were engaged in making. The heavy beating sound was evidently just behind us, and ever and again a bright green vapour drove up like a veil across our peephole.

The cylinder was already opened in the centre of the pit, and on the farther edge of the pit, amid the smashed and gravel-heaped shrubbery, one

of the great fighting-machines, deserted by its occupant, stood stiff and tall against the evening sky. At first I scarcely noticed the pit and the cylinder, although it has been convenient to describe them first, on account of the extraordinary glittering mechanism I saw busy in the excavation, and on account of the strange creatures that were crawling slowly and painfully across the heaped mould near it.

The mechanism it certainly was that held my attention first. It was one of those complicated fabrics that have since been called handling-machines, and the study of which has already given such an enormous impetus to terrestrial invention. As it dawned upon me first, it presented a sort of metallic spider with five jointed, agile legs, and with an extraordinary number of jointed levers, bars, and reaching and clutching tentacles about its body. Most of its arms were retracted, but with three long tentacles it was fishing out a number of rods, plates, and bars which lined the covering and apparently strengthened the walls of the cylinder. These, as it extracted them, were lifted out and deposited upon a level surface of earth behind it.

Its motion was so swift, complex, and perfect that at first I did not see it as a machine, in spite of its metallic glitter. The fighting-machines were coordinated and animated to an extraordinary pitch, but nothing to compare with this. People who have never seen these structures, and have only the ill-imagined efforts of artists or the imperfect descriptions of such eye-witnesses as myself to go upon, scarcely realise that living quality.

I recall particularly the illustration of one of the first pamphlets to give a consecutive account of the war. The artist had evidently made a hasty study of one of the fighting-machines, and there his knowledge ended. He presented them as tilted, stiff tripods, without either flexibility or subtlety, and with an altogether misleading monotony of effect. The pamphlet containing these renderings had a considerable vogue, and I mention them here simply to warn the reader against the impression they may have created. They were no more like the Martians I saw in action than a Dutch doll is like a human being. To my mind, the pamphlet would have been much better without them.

At first, I say, the handling-machine did not impress me as a machine, but as a crablike creature with a glittering integument, the controlling Martian whose delicate tentacles actuated its movements seeming to be simply the equivalent of the crab's cerebral portion. But then I perceived the resemblance of its grey-brown, shiny, leathery integument to that of the other sprawling bodies beyond, and the true nature of this dexterous workman dawned upon me. With that realisation my interest shifted to those other creatures, the real Martians. Already I had a transient impression of these, and the first nausea no longer obscured my observation. Moreover, I was concealed and motionless, and under no urgency of action.

They were, I now saw, the most unearthly creatures it is possible to

conceive. They were huge round bodies – or, rather, heads – about four feet in diameter, each body having in front of it a face. This face had no nostrils – indeed, the Martians do not seem to have had any sense of smell, but it had a pair of very large dark-coloured eyes, and just beneath this a kind of fleshy beak. In the back of this head or body – I scarcely know how to speak of it – was the single tight tympanic surface, since known to be anatomically an ear, though it must have been almost useless in our dense air. In a group round the mouth were sixteen slender, almost whiplike tentacles, arranged in two bunches of eight each. These bunches have since been named rather aptly, by that distinguished anatomist, Professor Howes, the *hands*. Even as I saw these Martians for the first time they seemed to be endeavouring to raise themselves on these hands, but of course, with the increased weight of terrestrial conditions, this was impossible. There is reason to suppose that on Mars they may have progressed upon them with some facility.

The internal anatomy, I may remark here, as dissection has since shown, was almost equally simple. The greater part of the structure was the brain, sending enormous nerves to the eyes, ear, and tactile tentacles. Besides this were the bulky lungs, into which the mouth opened, and the heart and its vessels. The pulmonary distress caused by the denser atmosphere and greater gravitational attraction was only too evident in the convulsive movements of the outer skin.

And this was the sum of the Martian organs. Strange as it may seem to a human being, all the complex apparatus of digestion, which makes up the bulk of our bodies, did not exist in the Martians. They were heads – merely heads. Entrails they had none. They did not eat, much less digest. Instead, they took the fresh, living blood of other creatures, and *injected* it into their own veins. I have myself seen this being done, as I shall mention in its place. But, squeamish as I may seem, I cannot bring myself to describe what I could not endure even to continue watching. Let it suffice to say, blood obtained from a still living animal, in most cases from a human being, was run directly by means of a little pipette into the recipient canal . . .

The bare idea of this is no doubt horribly repulsive to us, but at the same time I think that we should remember how repulsive our carnivorous habits would seem to an intelligent rabbit.

The physiological advantages of the practice of injection are undeniable, if one thinks of the tremendous waste of human time and energy occasioned by eating and the digestive process. Our bodies are half made up of glands and tubes and organs, occupied in turning heterogeneous food into blood. The digestive processes and their reaction upon the nervous system sap our strength and colour our minds. Men go happy or miserable as they have healthy or unhealthy livers, or sound gastric glands. But the Martians were lifted above all these organic fluctuations of mood and emotion.

Their undeniable preference for men as their source of nourishment is

partly explained by the nature of the remains of the victims they had brought with them as provisions from Mars. These creatures, to judge from the shrivelled remains that have fallen into human hands, were bipeds with flimsy, silicious skeletons (almost like those of the silicious sponges) and feeble musculature, standing about six feet high and having round, erect heads, and large eyes in flinty sockets. Two or three of these seem to have been brought in each cylinder, and all were killed before earth was reached. It was just as well for them, for the mere attempt to stand upright upon our planet would have broken every bone in their bodies.

And while I am engaged in this description, I may add in this place certain further details which, although they were not all evident to us at the time, will enable the reader who is unacquainted with them to form a clearer picture of these offensive creatures.

In three other points their physiology differed strangely from ours. Their organisms did not sleep, any more than the heart of man sleeps. Since they had no extensive muscular mechanism to recuperate, that periodical extinction was unknown to them. They had little or no sense of fatigue, it would seem. On earth they could never have moved without effort, yet even to the last they kept in action. In twenty-four hours they did twenty-four hours of work, as even on earth is perhaps the case with the ants.

In the next place, wonderful as it seems in a sexual world, the Martians were absolutely without sex, and therefore without any of the tumultuous emotions that arise from that difference among men. A young Martian, there can now be no dispute, was really born upon earth during the war, and it was found attached to its parent, partially *budded* off, just as young lily-bulbs bud off, or like the young animals in the freshwater polyp.

In man, in all the higher terrestrial animals, such a method of increase has disappeared; but even on this earth it was certainly the primitive method. Among the lower animals, up even to those first cousins of the vertebrated animals, the Tunicates, the two processes occur side by side, but finally the sexual method superseded its competitor altogether. On Mars, however, just the reverse has apparently been the case.

It is worthy of remark that a certain speculative writer of quasi-scientific repute, writing long before the Martian invasion, did forecast for man a final structure not unlike the actual Martian condition. His prophecy, I remember, appeared in November or December 1893, in a long-defunct publication, the *Pall Mall Budget*, and I recall a caricature of it in a pre-Martian periodical called *Punch*. He pointed out – writing in a foolish, facetious tone – that the perfection of mechanical appliances must ultimately supersede limbs; the perfection of chemical devices, digestion; that such organs as hair, external nose, teeth, ears, and chin were no longer essential parts of the human being, and that the tendency of natural selection would lie in the direction of their steady diminution through the coming ages. The brain alone remained a cardinal necessity. Only one

other part of the body had a strong case for survival, and that was the hand, 'teacher and agent of the brain'. While the rest of the body dwindled, the hands would grow larger.

There is many a true word written in jest, and here in the Martians we have beyond dispute the actual accomplishment of such a suppression of the animal side of the organism by the intelligence. To me it is quite credible that the Martians may be descended from beings not unlike ourselves, by a gradual development of brain and hands (the latter giving rise to the two bunches of delicate tentacles at last) at the expense of the rest of the body. Without the body the brain would, of course, become a mere selfish intelligence, without any of the emotional substratum of the human being.

The last salient point in which the systems of these creatures differed from ours was in what one might have thought a very trivial particular. Micro-organisms, which cause so much disease and pain on earth, have either never appeared upon Mars or Martian sanitary science eliminated them ages ago. A hundred diseases, all the fevers and contagions of human life, consumption, cancers, tumours and such morbidities, never enter the scheme of their life. And speaking of the differences between the life on Mars and terrestrial life, I may allude here to the curious suggestions of the red weed.

Apparently the vegetable kingdom in Mars, instead of having green for a dominant colour, is of a vivid blood-red tint. At any rate, the seeds which the Martians (intentionally or accidentally) brought with them gave rise in all cases to red-coloured growths. Only that known popularly as the red weed, however, gained any footing in competition with terrestrial forms. The red creeper was quite a transitory growth, and few people have seen it growing. For a time, however, the red weed grew with astonishing vigour and luxuriance. It spread up the sides of the pit by the third or fourth day of our imprisonment, and its cactus-like branches formed a carmine fringe to the edges of our triangular window. And afterwards I found it broadcast throughout the country, and especially wherever there was a stream of water.

The Martians had what appears to have been an auditory organ, a single round drum at the back of the head-body, and eyes with a visual range not very different from ours except that, according to Philips, blue and violet were as black to them. It is commonly supposed that they communicated by sounds and tentacular gesticulations; this is asserted, for instance, in the able but hastily compiled pamphlet (written evidently by someone not an eye-witness of Martian actions) to which I have already alluded, and which, so far, has been the chief source of information concerning them. Now no surviving human being saw so much of the Martians in action as I did. I take no credit to myself for an accident, but the fact is so. And I assert that I watched them closely time after time, and that I have seen four, five, and (once) six of them sluggishly performing the most elaborately complicated

operations together without either sound or gesture. Their peculiar hooting invariably preceded feeding; it had no modulation, and was, I believe, in no sense a signal, but merely the expiration of air preparatory to the suctional operation. I have a certain claim to at least an elementary knowledge of psychology, and in this matter I am convinced – as firmly as I am convinced of anything – that the Martians interchanged thoughts without any physical intermediation. And I have been convinced of this in spite of strong preconceptions. Before the Martian invasion, as an occasional reader here or there may remember, I had written with some little vehemence against the telepathic theory.

The Martians wore no clothing. Their conceptions of ornament and decorum were necessarily different from ours; and not only were they evidently much less sensible of changes of temperature than we are, but changes of pressure do not seem to have affected their health at all seriously. Yet though they wore no clothing, it was in the other artificial additions to their bodily resources that their great superiority over man lay. We men, with our bicycles and road-skates, our Lilienthal soaring-machines, our guns and sticks and so forth, are just in the beginning of the evolution that the Martians have worked out. They have become practically mere brains, wearing different bodies according to their needs just as men wear suits of clothes and take a bicycle in a hurry or an umbrella in the wet. And of their appliances, perhaps nothing is more wonderful to a man than the curious fact that what is the dominant feature of almost all human devices in mechanism is absent – the *wheel* is absent; among all the things they brought to earth there is no trace or suggestion of their use of wheels. One would have at least expected it in locomotion. And in this connection it is curious to remark that even on this earth Nature has never hit upon the wheel, or has preferred other expedients to its development. And not only did the Martians either not know of (which is incredible), or abstain from, the wheel, but in their apparatus singularly little use is made of the fixed pivot or relatively fixed pivot, with circular motions thereabout confined to one plane. Almost all the joints of the machinery present a complicated system of sliding parts moving over small but beautifully curved friction bearings. And while upon this matter of detail, it is remarkable that the long leverages of their machines are in most cases actuated by a sort of sham musculature of the disks in an elastic sheath; these disks become polarised and drawn closely and powerfully together when traversed by a current of electricity. In this way the curious parallelism to animal motions, which was so striking and disturbing to the human beholder, was attained. Such quasi-muscles abounded in the crablike handling-machine which, on my first peeping out of the slit, I watched unpacking the cylinder. It seemed infinitely more alive than the actual Martians lying beyond it in the sunset light, panting, stirring ineffectual tentacles, and moving feebly after their vast journey across space.

While I was still watching their sluggish motions in the sunlight, and noting each strange detail of their form, the curate reminded me of his presence by pulling violently at my arm. I turned to a scowling face, and silent, eloquent lips. He wanted the slit, which permitted only one of us to peep through; and so I had to forgo watching them for a time while he enjoyed that privilege.

When I looked again, the busy handling-machine had already put together several of the pieces of apparatus it had taken out of the cylinder into a shape having an unmistakable likeness to its own; and down on the left a busy little digging mechanism had come into view, emitting jets of green vapour and working its way round the pit, excavating and embanking in a methodical and discriminating manner. This it was which had caused the regular beating noise, and the rhythmic shocks that had kept our ruinous refuge quivering. It piped and whistled as it worked. So far as I could see, the thing was without a directing Martian at all.

CHAPTER THREE

The Days of Imprisonment

The arrival of a second fighting-machine drove us from our peephole into the scullery, for we feared that from his elevation the Martian might see down upon us behind our barrier. At a later date we began to feel less in danger of their eyes, for to an eye in the dazzle of the sunlight outside our refuge must have been blank blackness, but at first the slightest suggestion of approach drove us into the scullery in heart-throbbing retreat. Yet terrible as was the danger we incurred, the attraction of peeping was for both of us irresistible. And I recall now with a sort of wonder that, in spite of the infinite danger in which we were between starvation and a still more terrible death, we could yet struggle bitterly for that horrible privilege of sight. We would race across the kitchen in a grotesque way between eagerness and the dread of making a noise, and strike each other, and thrust and kick, within a few inches of exposure.

The fact is that we had absolutely incompatible dispositions and habits of thought and action, and our danger and isolation only accentuated the incompatibility. At Halliford I had already come to hate the curate's trick of helpless exclamation, his stupid rigidity of mind. His endless muttering monologue vitiated every effort I made to think out a line of action, and drove me at times, thus pent up and intensified, almost to the verge of craziness. He was as lacking in restraint as a silly woman. He would weep for hours together, and I verily believe that to the very end this spoiled child of life thought his weak tears in some way efficacious. And I would sit in the darkness unable to keep my mind off him by reason of his importunities. He

ate more than I did, and it was in vain I pointed out that our only chance of life was to stop in the house until the Martians had done with their pit, that in that long patience a time might presently come when we should need food. He ate and drank impulsively in heavy meals at long intervals. He slept little.

As the days wore on, his utter carelessness of any consideration so intensified our distress and danger that I had, much as I loathed doing it, to resort to threats, and at last to blows. That brought him to reason for a time. But he was one of those weak creatures, void of pride, timorous, anaemic, hateful souls, full of shifty cunning, who face neither God nor man, who face not even themselves.

It is disagreeable for me to recall and write these things, but I set them down that my story may lack nothing. Those who have escaped the dark and terrible aspects of life will find my brutality, my flash of rage in our final tragedy, easy enough to blame; for they know what is wrong as well as any, but not what is possible to tortured men. But those who have been under the shadow, who have gone down at last to elemental things, will have a wider charity.

And while within we fought out our dark, dim contest of whispers, snatched food and drink, and gripping hands and blows, without, in the pitiless sunlight of that terrible June, was the strange wonder, the unfamiliar routine of the Martians in the pit. Let me return to those first new experiences of mine. After a long time I ventured back to the peephole, to find that the new-comers had been reinforced by the occupants of no fewer than three of the fighting-machines. These last had brought with them certain fresh appliances that stood in an orderly manner about the cylinder. The second handling-machine was now completed, and was busied in serving one of the novel contrivances the big machine had brought. This was a body resembling a milk can in its general form, above which oscillated a pear-shaped receptacle, and from which a stream of white powder flowed into a circular basin below.

The oscillatory motion was imparted to this by one tentacle of the handling-machine. With two spatulate hands the handling-machine was digging out and flinging masses of clay into the pear-shaped receptacle above, while with another arm it periodically opened a door and removed rusty and blackened clinkers from the middle part of the machine. Another steely tentacle directed the powder from the basin along a ribbed channel towards some receiver that was hidden from me by the mound of bluish dust. From this unseen receiver a little thread of green smoke rose vertically into the quiet air. As I looked, the handling-machine, with a faint and musical clinking, extended, telescopic fashion, a tentacle that had been a moment before a mere blunt projection, until its end was hidden behind the mound of clay. In another second it had lifted a bar of white aluminium into sight, untarnished as yet, and shining dazzlingly, and deposited it in a

growing stack of bars that stood at the side of the pit. Between sunset and starlight this dexterous machine must have made more than a hundred such bars out of the crude clay, and the mound of bluish dust rose steadily until it topped the side of the pit.

The contrast between the swift and complex movements of these contrivances and the inert panting clumsiness of their masters was acute, and for days I had to tell myself repeatedly that these latter were indeed the living of the two things.

The curate had possession of the slit when the first men were brought to the pit. I was sitting below, huddled up, listening with all my ears. He made a sudden movement backward, and I, fearful that we were observed, crouched in a spasm of terror. He came sliding down the rubbish and crept beside me in the darkness, inarticulate, gesticulating, and for a moment I shared his panic. His gesture suggested a resignation of the slit, and after a little while my curiosity gave me courage, and I rose up, stepped across him, and clambered up to it. At first I could see no reason for his frantic behaviour. The twilight had now come, the stars were little and faint, but the pit was illuminated by the flickering green fire that came from the aluminium-making. The whole picture was a flickering scheme of green gleams and shifting rusty black shadows, strangely trying to the eyes. Over and through it all went the bats, heeding it not at all. The sprawling Martians were no longer to be seen, the mound of blue-green powder had risen to cover them from sight, and a fighting-machine, with its legs contracted, crumpled, and abbreviated, stood across the corner of the pit. And then, amid the clangour of the machinery, came a drifting suspicion of human voices, that I entertained at first only to dismiss.

I crouched, watching this fighting-machine closely, satisfying myself now for the first time that the hood did indeed contain a Martian. As the green flames lifted I could see the oily gleam of his integument and the brightness of his eyes. And suddenly I heard a yell, and saw a long tentacle reaching over the shoulder of the machine to the little cage that hunched upon its back. Then something – something struggling violently – was lifted high against the sky, a black, vague enigma against the starlight; and as this black object came down again, I saw by the green brightness that it was a man. For an instant he was clearly visible. He was a stout, ruddy, middle-aged man, well dressed; three days before, he must have been walking the world, a man of considerable consequence. I could see his staring eyes and gleams of light on his studs and watch chain. He vanished behind the mound, and for a moment there was silence. And then began a shrieking and a sustained and cheerful hooting from the Martians.

I slid down the rubbish, struggled to my feet, clapped my hands over my ears, and bolted into the scullery. The curate, who had been crouching silently with his arms over his head, looked up as I passed, cried out quite loudly at my desertion of him, and came running after me.

That night, as we lurked in the scullery, balanced between our horror and the terrible fascination this peeping had, although I felt an urgent need of action I tried in vain to conceive some plan of escape; but afterwards, during the second day, I was able to consider our position with great clearness. The curate, I found, was quite incapable of discussion; this new and culminating atrocity had robbed him of all vestiges of reason or forethought. Practically he had already sunk to the level of an animal. But as the saying goes, I gripped myself with both hands. It grew upon my mind, once I could face the facts, that terrible as our position was, there was as yet no justification for absolute despair. Our chief chance lay in the possibility of the Martians making the pit nothing more than a temporary encampment. Or even if they kept it permanently, they might not consider it necessary to guard it, and a chance of escape might be afforded us. I also weighed very carefully the possibility of our digging a way out in a direction away from the pit, but the chances of our emerging within sight of some sentinel fighting-machine seemed at first too great. And I should have had to do all the digging myself. The curate would certainly have failed me.

It was on the third day, if my memory serves me right, that I saw the lad killed. It was the only occasion on which I actually saw the Martians feed. After that experience I avoided the hole in the wall for the better part of a day. I went into the scullery, removed the door, and spent some hours digging with my hatchet as silently as possible; but when I had made a hole about a couple of feet deep the loose earth collapsed noisily, and I did not dare continue. I lost heart, and lay down on the scullery floor for a long time, having no spirit even to move. And after that I abandoned altogether the idea of escaping by excavation.

It says much for the impression the Martians had made upon me that at first I entertained little or no hope of our escape being brought about by their overthrow through any human effort. But on the fourth or fifth night I heard a sound like heavy guns.

It was very late in the night, and the moon was shining brightly. The Martians had taken away the excavating-machine, and, save for a fighting-machine that stood in the remoter bank of the pit and a handling-machine that was buried out of my sight in a corner of the pit immediately beneath my peephole, the place was deserted by them. Except for the pale glow from the handling-machine and the bars and patches of white moonlight the pit was in darkness, and, except for the clinking of the handling-machine, quite still. That night was a beautiful serenity; save for one planet, the moon seemed to have the sky to herself. I heard a dog howling, and that familiar sound it was that made me listen. Then I heard quite distinctly a booming exactly like the sound of great guns. Six distinct reports I counted, and after a long interval six again. And that was all.

CHAPTER FOUR

The Death of the Curate

It was on the sixth day of our imprisonment that I peeped for the last time, and presently found myself alone. Instead of keeping close to me and trying to oust me from the slit, the curate had gone back into the scullery. I was struck by a sudden thought. I went back quickly and quietly into the scullery. In the darkness I heard the curate drinking. I snatched in the darkness, and my fingers caught a bottle of burgundy.

For a few minutes there was a tussle. The bottle struck the floor and broke, and I desisted and rose. We stood panting and threatening each other. In the end I planted myself between him and the food, and told him of my determination to begin a discipline. I divided the food in the pantry, into rations to last us ten days. I would not let him eat any more that day. In the afternoon he made a feeble effort to get at the food. I had been dozing, but in an instant I was awake. All day and all night we sat face to face, I weary but resolute, and he weeping and complaining of his immediate hunger. It was, I know, a night and a day, but to me it seemed – it seems now – an interminable length of time.

And so our widened incompatibility ended at last in open conflict. For two vast days we struggled in undertones and wrestling contests. There were times when I beat and kicked him madly, times when I cajoled and persuaded him, and once I tried to bribe him with the last bottle of burgundy, for there was a rainwater pump from which I could get water. But neither force nor kindness availed; he was indeed beyond reason. He would neither desist from his attacks on the food nor from his noisy babbling to himself. The rudimentary precautions to keep our imprisonment endurable he would not observe. Slowly I began to realise the complete overthrow of his intelligence, to perceive that my sole companion in this close and sickly darkness was a man insane.

From certain vague memories I am inclined to think my own mind wandered at times. I had strange and hideous dreams whenever I slept. cIt sounds paradoxical, but I am inclined to think that the weakness and insanity of the curate warned me, braced me, and kept me a sane man.

On the eighth day he began to talk aloud instead of whispering, and nothing I could do would moderate his speech.

'It is just, O God!' he would say, over and over again. 'It is just. On me and mine be the punishment laid. We have sinned, we have fallen short. There was poverty, sorrow; the poor were trodden in the dust, and I held my peace. I preached acceptable folly – my God, what folly! – when I should have stood up, though I died for it, and called upon them to

repent – repent! . . . Oppressors of the poor and needy . . . ! The wine press of God!'

Then he would suddenly revert to the matter of the food I withheld from him, praying, begging, weeping, at last threatening. He began to raise his voice – I prayed him not to. He perceived a hold on me – he threatened he would shout and bring the Martians upon us. For a time that scared me; but any concession would have shortened our chance of escape beyond estimating. I defied him, although I felt no assurance that he might not do this thing. But that day, at any rate, he did not. He talked with his voice rising slowly, through the greater part of the eighth and ninth days – threats, entreaties, mingled with a torrent of half-sane and always frothy repentance for his vacant sham of God's service, such as made me pity him. Then he slept awhile, and began again with renewed strength, so loudly that I must needs make him desist.

'Be still!' I implored.

He rose to his knees, for he had been sitting in the darkness near the copper.

'I have been still too long,' he said, in a tone that must have reached the pit, 'and now I must bear my witness. Woe unto this unfaithful city! Woe! Woe! Woe! Woe! Woe! To the inhabitants of the earth by reason of the other voices of the trumpet – '

'Shut up!' I said, rising to my feet, and in a terror lest the Martians should hear us. 'For God's sake – '

'Nay,' shouted the curate, at the top of his voice, standing likewise and extending his arms. 'Speak! The word of the Lord is upon me!'

In three strides he was at the door leading into the kitchen.

'I must bear my witness! I go! It has already been too long delayed.'

I put out my hand and felt the meat chopper hanging to the wall. In a flash I was after him. I was fierce with fear. Before he was halfway across the kitchen I had overtaken him. With one last touch of humanity I turned the blade back and struck him with the butt. He went headlong forward and lay stretched on the ground. I stumbled over him and stood panting. He lay still.

Suddenly I heard a noise without, the run and smash of slipping plaster, and the triangular aperture in the wall was darkened. I looked up and saw the lower surface of a handling-machine coming slowly across the hole. One of its gripping limbs curled amid the debris; another limb appeared, feeling its way over the fallen beams. I stood petrified, staring. Then I saw through a sort of glass plate near the edge of the body the face, as we may call it, and the large dark eyes of a Martian, peering, and then a long metallic snake of tentacle came feeling slowly through the hole.

I turned by an effort, stumbled over the curate, and stopped at the scullery door. The tentacle was now some way, two yards or more, in the room, and twisting and turning, with queer sudden movements, this way

and that. For a while I stood fascinated by that slow, fitful advance. Then, with a faint, hoarse cry, I forced myself across the scullery. I trembled violently; I could scarcely stand upright. I opened the door of the coal cellar, and stood there in the darkness staring at the faintly lit doorway into the kitchen, and listening. Had the Martian seen me? What was it doing now?

Something was moving to and fro there, very quietly; every now and then it tapped against the wall, or started on its movements with a faint metallic ringing, like the movements of keys on a split-ring. Then a heavy body – I knew too well what – was dragged across the floor of the kitchen towards the opening. Irresistibly attracted, I crept to the door and peeped into the kitchen. In the triangle of bright outer sunlight I saw the Martian, in its Briareus of a handling-machine, scrutinising the curate's head. I thought at once that it would infer my presence from the mark of the blow I had given him.

I crept back to the coal cellar, shut the door, and began to cover myself up as much as I could, and as noiselessly as possible in the darkness, among the firewood and coal therein. Every now and then I paused, rigid, to hear if the Martian had thrust its tentacles through the opening again.

Then the faint metallic jingle returned. I traced it slowly feeling over the kitchen. Presently I heard it nearer – in the scullery, as I judged. I thought that its length might be insufficient to reach me. I prayed copiously. It passed, scraping faintly across the cellar door. An age of almost intolerable suspense intervened; then I heard it fumbling at the latch! It had found the door! The Martians understood doors!

It worried at the catch for a minute, perhaps, and then the door opened.

In the darkness I could just see the thing – like an elephant's trunk more than anything else – waving towards me and touching and examining the wall, coals, wood and ceiling. It was like a black worm swaying its blind head to and fro.

Once, even, it touched the heel of my boot. I was on the verge of screaming; I bit my hand. For a time the tentacle was silent. I could have fancied it had been withdrawn. Presently, with an abrupt click, it gripped something – I thought it had me! – and seemed to go out of the cellar again. For a minute I was not sure. Apparently it had taken a lump of coal to examine.

I seized the opportunity of slightly shifting my position, which had become cramped, and then listened. I whispered passionate prayers for safety.

Then I heard the slow, deliberate sound creeping towards me again. Slowly, slowly it drew near, scratching against the walls and tapping the furniture.

While I was still doubtful, it rapped smartly against the cellar door and closed it. I heard it go into the pantry, and the biscuit-tins rattled and a

bottle smashed, and then came a heavy bump against the cellar door. Then silence that passed into an infinity of suspense.

Had it gone?

At last I decided that it had.

It came into the scullery no more; but I lay all the tenth day in the close darkness, buried among coals and firewood, not daring even to crawl out for the drink for which I craved. It was the eleventh day before I ventured so far from my security.

CHAPTER FIVE

The Stillness

My first act before I went into the pantry was to fasten the door between the kitchen and the scullery. But the pantry was empty; every scrap of food had gone. Apparently, the Martian had taken it all on the previous day. At that discovery I despaired for the first time. I took no food, or no drink either, on the eleventh or the twelfth day.

At first my mouth and throat were parched, and my strength ebbed sensibly. I sat about in the darkness of the scullery, in a state of despondent wretchedness. My mind ran on eating. I thought I had become deaf, for the noises of movement I had been accustomed to hear from the pit had ceased absolutely. I did not feel strong enough to crawl noiselessly to the peephole, or I would have gone there.

On the twelfth day my throat was so painful that, taking the chance of alarming the Martians, I attacked the creaking rainwater pump that stood by the sink, and got a couple of glassfuls of blackened and tainted rain-water. I was greatly refreshed by this, and emboldened by the fact that no enquiring tentacle followed the noise of my pumping.

During these days, in a rambling, inconclusive way, I thought much of the curate and of the manner of his death.

On the thirteenth day I drank some more water, and dozed and thought disjointedly of eating and of vague impossible plans of escape. Whenever I dozed I dreamt of horrible phantasms, of the death of the curate, or of sumptuous dinners; but, asleep or awake, I felt a keen pain that urged me to drink again and again. The light that came into the scullery was no longer grey, but red. To my disordered imagination it seemed the colour of blood.

On the fourteenth day I went into the kitchen, and I was surprised to find that the fronds of the red weed had grown right across the hole in the wall, turning the half-light of the place into a crimson-coloured obscurity.

It was early on the fifteenth day that I heard a curious, familiar sequence of sounds in the kitchen, and, listening, identified it as the snuffing and

scratching of a dog. Going into the kitchen, I saw a dog's nose peering in through a break among the ruddy fronds. This greatly surprised me. At the scent of me he barked shortly.

I thought if I could induce him to come into the place quietly I should be able, perhaps, to kill and eat him; and in any case, it would be advisable to kill him, lest his actions attracted the attention of the Martians.

I crept forward, saying 'Good dog!' very softly; but he suddenly withdrew his head and disappeared.

I listened – I was not deaf – but certainly the pit was still. I heard a sound like the flutter of a bird's wings, and a hoarse croaking, but that was all.

For a long while I lay close to the peephole, but not daring to move aside the red plants that obscured it. Once or twice I heard a faint pitter-patter like the feet of the dog going hither and thither on the sand far below me, and there were more birdlike sounds, but that was all. At length, encouraged by the silence, I looked out.

Except in the corner, where a multitude of crows hopped and fought over the skeletons of the dead the Martians had consumed, there was not a living thing in the pit.

I stared about me, scarcely believing my eyes. All the machinery had gone. Save for the big mound of greyish-blue powder in one corner, certain bars of aluminium in another, the black birds, and the skeletons of the killed, the place was merely an empty circular pit in the sand.

Slowly I thrust myself out through the red weed, and stood upon the mound of rubble. I could see in any direction save behind me, to the north, and neither Martians nor sign of Martians were to be seen. The pit dropped sheerly from my feet, but a little way along the rubbish afforded a practicable slope to the summit of the ruins. My chance of escape had come. I began to tremble.

I hesitated for some time, and then, in a gust of desperate resolution, and with a heart that throbbed violently, I scrambled to the top of the mound in which I had been buried so long.

I looked about again. To the northward, too, no Martian was visible.

When I had last seen this part of Sheen in the daylight it had been a straggling street of comfortable white and red houses, interspersed with abundant shady trees. Now I stood on a mound of smashed brickwork, clay, and gravel, over which spread a multitude of red cactus-shaped plants, knee-high, without a solitary terrestrial growth to dispute their footing. The trees near me were dead and brown, but a further network of red thread scaled the still living stems.

The neighbouring houses had all been wrecked, but none had been burned; their walls stood, sometimes to the second storey, with smashed windows and shattered doors. The red weed grew tumultuously in their roofless rooms. Below me was the great pit, with the crows struggling for its refuse. A number of other birds hopped about among the ruins. Far

away I saw a gaunt cat slink crouchingly along a wall, but traces of men there were none.

The day seemed, by contrast with my recent confinement, dazzlingly bright, the sky a glowing blue. A gentle breeze kept the red weed that covered every scrap of unoccupied ground gently swaying. And oh! the sweetness of the air!

CHAPTER SIX

The Work of Fifteen Days

For some time I stood tottering on the mound regardless of my safety. Within that noisome den from which I had emerged I had thought with a narrow intensity only of our immediate security. I had not realised what had been happening to the world, had not anticipated this startling vision of unfamiliar things. I had expected to see Sheen in ruins – I found about me the landscape, weird and lurid, of another planet.

For that moment I touched an emotion beyond the common range of men, yet one that the poor brutes we dominate know only too well. I felt as a rabbit might feel returning to his burrow and suddenly confronted by the work of a dozen busy navvies digging the foundations of a house. I felt the first inkling of a thing that presently grew quite clear in my mind, that oppressed me for many days, a sense of dethronement, a persuasion that I was no longer a master, but an animal among the animals, under the Martian heel. With us it would be as with them, to lurk and watch, to run and hide; the fear and empire of man had passed away.

But so soon as this strangeness had been realised it passed, and my dominant motive became the hunger of my long and dismal fast. In the direction away from the pit I saw, beyond a red-covered wall, a patch of garden ground unburied. This gave me a hint, and I went knee-deep, and sometimes neck-deep, in the red weed. The density of the weed gave me a reassuring sense of hiding. The wall was some six feet high, and when I attempted to clamber it I found I could not lift my feet to the crest. So I went along by the side of it, and came to a corner and a rockwork that enabled me to get to the top, and tumble into the garden I coveted. Here I found some young onions, a couple of gladiolus bulbs, and a quantity of immature carrots, all of which I secured, and, scrambling over a ruined wall, went on my way through scarlet and crimson trees towards Kew – it was like walking through an avenue of gigantic blood drops – possessed with two ideas: to get more food, and to limp, as soon and as far as my strength permitted, out of this accursed unearthly region of the pit.

Some way farther, in a grassy place, was a group of mushrooms which also I devoured, and then I came upon a brown sheet of flowing shallow

water, where meadows used to be. These fragments of nourishment served only to whet my hunger. At first I was surprised at this flood in a hot, dry summer, but afterwards I discovered that it was caused by the tropical exuberance of the red weed. Directly this extraordinary growth encountered water it straightway became gigantic and of unparalleled fecundity. Its seeds were simply poured down into the water of the Wey and Thames, and its swiftly growing and Titanic water fronds speedily choked both those rivers.

At Putney, as I afterwards saw, the bridge was almost lost in a tangle of this weed, and at Richmond, too, the Thames water poured in a broad and shallow stream across the meadows of Hampton and Twickenham. As the water spread the weed followed them, until the ruined villas of the Thames valley were for a time lost in this red swamp, whose margin I explored, and much of the desolation the Martians had caused was concealed.

In the end the red weed succumbed almost as quickly as it had spread. A cankering disease, due, it is believed, to the action of certain bacteria, presently seized upon it. Now by the action of natural selection, all terrestrial plants have acquired a resisting power against bacterial diseases – they never succumb without a severe struggle, but the red weed rotted like a thing already dead. The fronds became bleached, and then shrivelled and brittle. They broke off at the least touch, and the waters that had stimulated their early growth carried their last vestiges out to sea.

My first act on coming to this water was, of course, to slake my thirst. I drank a great deal of it and, moved by an impulse, gnawed some fronds of red weed; but they were watery, and had a sickly, metallic taste. I found the water was sufficiently shallow for me to wade securely, although the red weed impeded my feet a little; but the flood evidently got deeper towards the river, and I turned back to Mortlake. I managed to make out the road by means of occasional ruins of its villas and fences and lamps, and so presently I got out of this spate and made my way to the hill going up towards Roehampton and came out on Putney Common.

Here the scenery changed from the strange and unfamiliar to the wreckage of the familiar: patches of ground exhibited the devastation of a cyclone, and in a few score yards I would come upon perfectly undisturbed spaces, houses with their blinds trimly drawn and doors closed, as if they had been left for a day by the owners, or as if their inhabitants slept within. The red weed was less abundant; the tall trees along the lane were free from the red creeper. I hunted for food among the trees, finding nothing, and I also raided a couple of silent houses, but they had already been broken into and ransacked. I rested for the remainder of the daylight in a shrubbery, being, in my enfeebled condition, too fatigued to push on.

All this time I saw no human beings, and no signs of the Martians. I encountered a couple of hungry-looking dogs, but both hurried circuitously away from the advances I made them. Near Roehampton I had seen two

human skeletons – not bodies, but skeletons, picked clean – and in the wood by me I found the crushed and scattered bones of several cats and rabbits and the skull of a sheep. But though I gnawed parts of these in my mouth, there was nothing to be got from them.

After sunset I struggled on along the road towards Putney, where I think the Heat-Ray must have been used for some reason. And in the garden beyond Roehampton I got a quantity of immature potatoes, sufficient to stay my hunger. From this garden one looked down upon Putney and the river. The aspect of the place in the dusk was singularly desolate: blackened trees, blackened, desolate ruins, and down the hill the sheets of the flooded river, red-tinged with the weed. And over all – silence. It filled me with indescribable terror to think how swiftly that desolating change had come.

For a time I believed that mankind had been swept out of existence, and that I stood there alone, the last man left alive. Hard by the top of Putney Hill I came upon another skeleton, with the arms dislocated and removed several yards from the rest of the body. As I proceeded I became more and more convinced that the extermination of mankind was, save for such stragglers as myself, already accomplished in this part of the world. The Martians, I thought, had gone on and left the country desolated, seeking food elsewhere. Perhaps even now they were destroying Berlin or Paris, or it might be they had gone northward.

CHAPTER SEVEN

The Man on Putney Hill

I spent that night in the inn that stands at the top of Putney Hill, sleeping in a made bed for the first time since my flight to Leatherhead. I will not tell the needless trouble I had breaking into that house – afterwards I found the front door was on the latch – nor how I ransacked every room for food, until just on the verge of despair, in what seemed to me to be a servant's bedroom, I found a rat-gnawed crust and two tins of pineapple. The place had been already searched and emptied. In the bar I afterwards found some biscuits and sandwiches that had been overlooked. The latter I could not eat, they were too rotten, but the former not only stayed my hunger, but filled my pockets. I lit no lamps, fearing some Martian might come beating that part of London for food in the night. Before I went to bed I had an interval of restlessness, and prowled from window to window, peering out for some sign of these monsters. I slept little. As I lay in bed I found myself thinking consecutively – a thing I do not remember to have done since my last argument with the curate. During all the intervening time my mental condition had been a hurrying succession of vague emotional states or a sort

of stupid receptivity. But in the night my brain, reinforced, I suppose, by the food I had eaten, grew clear again, and I thought.

Three things struggled for possession of my mind: the killing of the curate, the whereabouts of the Martians, and the possible fate of my wife. The former gave me no sensation of horror or remorse to recall; I saw it simply as a thing done, a memory infinitely disagreeable but quite without the quality of remorse. I saw myself then as I see myself now, driven step by step towards that hasty blow, the creature of a sequence of accidents leading inevitably to that. I felt no condemnation; yet the memory, static, un-progressive, haunted me. In the silence of the night, with that sense of the nearness of God that sometimes comes into the stillness and the darkness, I stood my trial, my only trial, for that moment of wrath and fear. I retraced every step of our conversation from the moment when I had found him crouching beside me, heedless of my thirst, and pointing to the fire and smoke that streamed up from the ruins of Weybridge. We had been in-capable of co-operation – grim chance had taken no heed of that. Had I foreseen, I should have left him at Halliford. But I did not foresee; and crime is to foresee and do. And I set this down as I have set all this story down, as it was. There were no witnesses – all these things I might have concealed. But I set it down, and the reader must form his judgement as he will.

And when, by an effort, I had set aside that picture of a prostrate body, I faced the problem of the Martians and the fate of my wife. For the former I had no data; I could imagine a hundred things, and so, unhappily, I could for the latter. And suddenly that night became terrible. I found myself sitting up in bed, staring at the dark. I found myself praying that the Heat-Ray might have suddenly and painlessly struck her out of being. Since the night of my return from Leatherhead I had not prayed. I had uttered prayers, fetish prayers, had prayed as heathens mutter charms when I was in extremity; but now I prayed indeed, pleading steadfastly and sanely, face to face with the darkness of God. Strange night! Strangest in this, that so soon as dawn had come, I, who had talked with God, crept out of the house like a rat leaving its hiding place – a creature scarcely larger, an inferior animal, a thing that for any passing whim of our masters might be hunted and killed. Perhaps they also prayed confidently to God. Surely, if we have learned nothing else, this war has taught us pity – pity for those witless souls that suffer our dominion.

The morning was bright and fine, and the eastern sky glowed pink, and was fretted with little golden clouds. In the road that runs from the top of Putney Hill to Wimbledon was a number of poor vestiges of the panic torrent that must have poured Londonward on the Sunday night after the fighting began. There was a little two-wheeled cart inscribed with the name of Thomas Lobb, Greengrocer, New Malden, with a smashed wheel and an abandoned tin trunk; there was a straw hat trampled into the now hardened mud, and at the top of West Hill a lot of blood-stained glass about the

overturned water trough. My movements were languid, my plans of the vaguest. I had an idea of going to Leatherhead, though I knew that there I had the poorest chance of finding my wife. Certainly, unless death had overtaken them suddenly, my cousins and she would have fled thence; but it seemed to me I might find or learn there whither the Surrey people had fled. I knew I wanted to find my wife, that my heart ached for her and the world of men, but I had no clear idea how the finding might be done. I was also sharply aware now of my intense loneliness. From the corner I went, under cover of a thicket of trees and bushes, to the edge of Wimbledon Common, stretching wide and far.

That dark expanse was lit in patches by yellow gorse and broom; there was no red weed to be seen, and as I prowled, hesitating, on the verge of the open, the sun rose, flooding it all with light and vitality. I came upon a busy swarm of little frogs in a swampy place among the trees. I stopped to look at them, drawing a lesson from their stout resolve to live. And presently, turning suddenly, with an odd feeling of being watched, I beheld something crouching amid a clump of bushes. I stood regarding this. I made a step towards it, and it rose up and became a man armed with a cutlass. I approached him slowly. He stood silent and motionless, regarding me.

As I drew nearer I perceived he was dressed in clothes as dusty and filthy as my own; he looked, indeed, as though he had been dragged through a culvert. Nearer, I distinguished the green slime of ditches mixing with the pale drab of dried clay and shiny, coaly patches. His black hair fell over his eyes, and his face was dark and dirty and sunken, so that at first I did not recognise him. There was a red cut across the lower part of his face.

'Stop!' he cried, when I was within ten yards of him, and I stopped. His voice was hoarse. 'Where do you come from?' he said.

I thought, surveying him.

'I come from Mortlake,' I said. 'I was buried near the pit the Martians made about their cylinder. I have worked my way out and escaped.'

'There is no food about here,' he said. 'This is my country. All this hill down to the river, and back to Clapham, and up to the edge of the common. There is only food for one. Which way are you going?'

I answered slowly.

'I don't know,' I said. 'I have been buried in the ruins of a house thirteen or fourteen days. I don't know what has happened.'

He looked at me doubtfully, then started, and looked with a changed expression.

'I've no wish to stop about here,' said I. 'I think I shall go to Leatherhead, for my wife was there.'

He shot out a pointing finger.

'It is you,' said he; 'the man from Woking. And you weren't killed at Weybridge?'

I recognised him at the same moment.

'You are the artilleryman who came into my garden.'

'Good luck!' he said. 'We are lucky ones! Fancy *you!*' He put out a hand, and I took it. 'I crawled up a drain,' he said. 'But they didn't kill everyone. And after they went away I got off towards Walton across the fields. But – It's not sixteen days altogether – and your hair is grey.' He looked over his shoulder suddenly. 'Only a rook,' he said. 'One gets to know that birds have shadows these days. This is a bit open. Let us crawl under those bushes and talk.'

'Have you seen any Martians?' I said. 'Since I crawled out – '

'They've gone away across London,' he said. 'I guess they've got a bigger camp there. Of a night, all over there, Hampstead way, the sky is alive with their lights. It's like a great city, and in the glare you can just see them moving. By daylight you can't. But nearer – I haven't seen them – ' (he counted on his fingers) 'five days. Then I saw a couple across Hammersmith way carrying something big. And the night before last' – he stopped and spoke impressively – 'it was just a matter of lights, but it was something up in the air. I believe they've built a flying-machine, and are learning to fly.'

I stopped, on hands and knees, for we had come to the bushes.

'Fly!'

'Yes,' he said, 'fly.'

I went on into a little bower, and sat down.

'It is all over with humanity,' I said. 'If they can do that they will simply go round the world.'

He nodded.

'They will. But – It will relieve things over here a bit. And besides – ' He looked at me. 'Aren't you satisfied it *is* up with humanity? I am. We're down; we're beat.'

I stared. Strange as it may seem, I had not arrived at this fact – a fact perfectly obvious so soon as he spoke. I had still held a vague hope; rather, I had kept a lifelong habit of mind. He repeated his words, 'We're beat.' They carried absolute conviction.

'It's all over,' he said. 'They've lost *one* – just *one*. And they've made their footing good and crippled the greatest power in the world. They've walked over us. The death of that one at Weybridge was an accident. And these are only pioneers. They kept on coming. These green stars – I've seen none these five or six days, but I've no doubt they're falling somewhere every night. Nothing's to be done. We're under! We're beat!'

I made him no answer. I sat staring before me, trying in vain to devise some countervailing thought.

'This isn't a war,' said the artilleryman. 'It never was a war, any more than there's war between man and ants.'

Suddenly I recalled the night in the observatory.

'After the tenth shot they fired no more – at least, until the first cylinder came.'

'How do you know?' said the artilleryman. I explained. He thought. 'Something wrong with the gun,' he said. 'But what if there is? They'll get it right again. And even if there's a delay, how can it alter the end? It's just men and ants. There's the ants builds their cities, live their lives, have wars, revolutions, until the men want them out of the way, and then they go out of the way. That's what we are now – just ants. Only – '

'Yes,' I said.

'We're eatable ants.'

We sat looking at each other.

'And what will they do with us?' I said.

'That's what I've been thinking,' he said; 'that's what I've been thinking. After Weybridge I went south – thinking. I saw what was up. Most of the people were hard at it squealing and exciting themselves. But I'm not so fond of squealing. I've been in sight of death once or twice; I'm not an ornamental soldier, and at the best and worst, death – it's just death. And it's the man that keeps on thinking comes through. I saw everyone tracking away south. Says I, "Food won't last this way," and I turned right back. I went for the Martians like a sparrow goes for man. All round' – he waved a hand to the horizon – 'they're starving in heaps, bolting, treading on each other . . . '

He saw my face, and halted awkwardly.

'No doubt lots who had money have gone away to France,' he said. He seemed to hesitate whether to apologise, met my eyes, and went on: 'There's food all about here. Canned things in shops; wines, spirits, mineral waters; and the water mains and drains are empty. Well, I was telling you what I was thinking. "Here's intelligent things," I said, "and it seems they want us for food. First, they'll smash us up – ships, machines, guns, cities, all the order and organisation. All that will go. If we were the size of ants we might pull through. But we're not. It's all too bulky to stop. That's the first certainty." Eh?'

I assented.

'It is; I've thought it out. Very well, then – next; at present we're caught as we're wanted. A Martian has only to go a few miles to get a crowd on the run. And I saw one, one day, out by Wandsworth, picking houses to pieces and routing among the wreckage. But they won't keep on doing that. So soon as they've settled all our guns and ships, and smashed our railways, and done all the things they are doing over there, they will begin catching us systematic, picking the best and storing us in cages and things. That's what they will start doing in a bit. Lord! They haven't begun on us yet. Don't you see that?'

'Not begun!' I exclaimed.

'Not begun. All that's happened so far is through our not having the sense to keep quiet – worrying them with guns and such foolery. And losing our heads, and rushing off in crowds to where there wasn't any more safety

than where we were. They don't want to bother us yet. They're making their things – making all the things they couldn't bring with them, getting things ready for the rest of their people. Very likely that's why the cylinders have stopped for a bit, for fear of hitting those who are here. And instead of our rushing about blind, on the howl, or getting dynamite on the chance of busting them up, we've got to fix ourselves up according to the new state of affairs. That's how I figure it out. It isn't quite according to what a man wants for his species, but it's about what the facts point to. And that's the principle I acted upon. Cities, nations, civilisation, progress – it's all over. That game's up. We're beat.'

'But if that is so, what is there to live for?'

The artilleryman looked at me for a moment.

'There won't be any more blessed concerts for a million years or so; there won't be any Royal Academy of Arts, and no nice little feeds at restaurants. If it's amusement you're after, I reckon the game is up. If you've got any drawing-room manners or a dislike to eating peas with a knife or dropping aitches, you'd better chuck 'em away. They ain't no further use.'

'You mean – '

'I mean that men like me are going on living – for the sake of the breed. I tell you, I'm grim set on living. And if I'm not mistaken, you'll show what insides *you've* got, too, before long. We aren't going to be exterminated. And I don't mean to be caught either, and tamed and fattened and bred like a thundering ox. Ugh! Fancy those brown creepers!'

'You don't mean to say – '

'I do. I'm going on, under their feet. I've got it planned; I've thought it out. We men are beat. We don't know enough. We've got to learn before we've got a chance. And we've got to live and keep independent while we learn. See! That's what has to be done.'

I stared, astonished, and stirred profoundly by the man's resolution.

'Great God!' cried I. 'But you are a man indeed!' And suddenly I gripped his hand.

'Eh!' he said, with his eyes shining. 'I've thought it out, eh?'

'Go on,' I said.

'Well, those who mean to escape their catching must get ready. I'm getting ready. Mind you, it isn't all of us that are made for wild beasts; and that's what it's got to be. That's why I watched you. I had my doubts. You're slender. I didn't know that it was you, you see, or just how you'd been buried. All these – the sort of people that lived in these houses, and all those damn little clerks that used to live down that way – they'd be no good. They haven't any spirit in them – no proud dreams and no proud lusts; and a man who hasn't one or the other – Lord! What is he but funk and precautions? They just used to skedaddle off to work – I've seen hundreds of 'em, bit of breakfast in hand, running wild and shining to catch their little season-ticket train, for fear they'd get dismissed if they didn't; working at

businesses they were afraid to take the trouble to understand; skedaddling back for fear they wouldn't be in time for dinner; keeping indoors after dinner for fear of the back streets, and sleeping with the wives they married, not because they wanted them, but because they had a bit of money that would make for safety in their one little miserable skedaddle through the world. Lives insured and a bit invested for fear of accidents. And on Sundays – fear of the hereafter. As if hell was built for rabbits! Well, the Martians will just be a godsend to these. Nice roomy cages, fattening food, careful breeding, no worry. After a week or so chasing about the fields and lands on empty stomachs, they'll come and be caught cheerful. They'll be quite glad after a bit. They'll wonder what people did before there were Martians to take care of them. And the bar loafers, and mashers, and singers – I can imagine them. I can imagine them,' he said, with a sort of sombre gratification. 'There'll be any amount of sentiment and religion loose among them. There's hundreds of things I saw with my eyes that I've only begun to see clearly these last few days. There's lots will take things as they are – fat and stupid; and lots will be worried by a sort of feeling that it's all wrong, and that they ought to be doing something. Now whenever things are so that a lot of people feel they ought to be doing something, the weak, and those who go weak with a lot of complicated thinking, always make for a sort of do-nothing religion, very pious and superior, and submit to persecution and the will of the Lord. Very likely you've seen the same thing. It's energy in a gale of funk, and turned clean inside out. These cages will be full of psalms and hymns and piety. And those of a less simple sort will work in a bit of – what is it? – eroticism.'

He paused.

'Very likely these Martians will make pets of some of them; train them to do tricks – who knows? – get sentimental over the pet boy who grew up and had to be killed. And some, maybe, they will train to hunt us.'

'No,' I cried, 'that's impossible! No human being – '

'What's the good of going on with such lies?' said the artilleryman. 'There's men who'd do it cheerful. What nonsense to pretend there isn't!'

And I succumbed to his conviction.

'If they come after me,' he said; 'Lord, if they come after me!' and subsided into a grim meditation.

I sat contemplating these things. I could find nothing to bring against this man's reasoning. In the days before the invasion no one would have questioned my intellectual superiority to his – I, a professed and recognised writer on philosophical themes, and he, a common soldier; and yet he had already formulated a situation that I had scarcely realised.

'What are you doing?' I said presently. 'What plans have you made?'

He hesitated.

'Well, it's like this,' he said. 'What have we to do? We have to invent a sort of life where men can live and breed, and be sufficiently secure to bring

the children up. Yes – wait a bit, and I'll make it clearer what I think ought to be done. The tame ones will go like all tame beasts; in a few generations they'll be big, beautiful, rich-blooded, stupid – rubbish! The risk is that we who keep wild will go savage – degenerate into a sort of big, savage rat . . . You see, how I mean to live is underground. I've been thinking about the drains. Of course those who don't know drains think horrible things; but under this London are miles and miles – hundreds of miles – and a few days' rain and London empty will leave them sweet and clean. The main drains are big enough and airy enough for anyone. Then there's cellars, vaults, stores, from which bolting passages may be made to the drains. And the railway tunnels and subways. Eh? You begin to see? And we form a band – able-bodied, clean-minded men. We're not going to pick up any rubbish that drifts in. Weaklings go out again.'

'As you meant me to go?'

'Well – I parleyed, didn't I?'

'We won't quarrel about that. Go on.'

'Those who stop obey orders. Able-bodied, clean-minded women we want also – mothers and teachers. No lackadaisical ladies – no blasted rolling eyes. We can't have any weak or silly. Life is real again, and the useless and cumbersome and mischievous have to die. They ought to die. They ought to be willing to die. It's a sort of disloyalty, after all, to live and taint the race. And they can't be happy. Moreover, dying's none so dreadful; it's the funking makes it bad. And in all those places we shall gather. Our district will be London. And we may even be able to keep a watch, and run about in the open when the Martians keep away. Play cricket, perhaps. That's how we shall save the race. Eh? It's a possible thing? But saving the race is nothing in itself. As I say, that's only being rats. It's saving our knowledge and adding to it is the thing. There men like you come in. There's books, there's models. We must make great safe places down deep, and get all the books we can; not novels and poetry swipes, but ideas, science books. That's where men like you come in. We must go to the British Museum and pick all those books through. Especially we must keep up our science – learn more. We must watch these Martians. Some of us must go as spies. When it's all working, perhaps I will. Get caught, I mean. And the great thing is, we must leave the Martians alone. We mustn't even steal. If we get in their way, we clear out. We must show them we mean no harm. Yes, I know. But they're intelligent things, and they won't hunt us down if they have all they want, and think we're just harmless vermin.'

The artilleryman paused and laid a brown hand upon my arm.

'After all, it may not be so much we may have to learn before – Just imagine this: four or five of their fighting-machines suddenly starting off – Heat-Rays right and left, and not a Martian in 'em. Not a Martian in 'em, but men – men who have learned the way how. It may be in my time, even – those men. Fancy having one of them lovely things, with its Heat-Ray wide

and free! Fancy having it in control! What would it matter if you smashed to smithereens at the end of the run, after a bust like that? I reckon the Martians'll open their beautiful eyes! Can't you see them, man? Can't you see them hurrying, hurrying – puffing and blowing and hooting to their other mechanical affairs? Something out of gear in every case. And swish, bang, rattle, swish! Just as they are fumbling over it, *swish* comes the Heat-Ray, and, behold! man has come back to his own.'

For a while the imaginative daring of the artilleryman, and the tone of assurance and courage he assumed, completely dominated my mind. I believed unhesitatingly both in his forecast of human destiny and in the practicability of his astonishing scheme, and the reader who thinks me susceptible and foolish must contrast his position, reading steadily with all his thoughts about his subject, and mine, crouching fearfully in the bushes and listening, distracted by apprehension. We talked in this manner through the early morning time, and later crept out of the bushes, and, after scanning the sky for Martians, hurried precipitately to the house on Putney Hill where he had made his lair. It was the coal cellar of the place, and when I saw the work he had spent a week upon – it was a burrow scarcely ten yards long, which he designed to reach to the main drain on Putney Hill – I had my first inkling of the gulf between his dreams and his powers. Such a hole I could have dug in a day. But I believed in him sufficiently to work with him all that morning until past midday at his digging. We had a garden barrow and shot the earth we removed against the kitchen range. We refreshed ourselves with a tin of mock-turtle soup and wine from the neighbouring pantry. I found a curious relief from the aching strangeness of the world in this steady labour. As we worked, I turned his project over in my mind, and presently objections and doubts began to arise; but I worked there all the morning, so glad was I to find myself with a purpose again. After working an hour I began to speculate on the distance one had to go before the cloaca was reached, the chances we had of missing it altogether. My immediate trouble was why we should dig this long tunnel, when it was possible to get into the drain at once down one of the manholes, and work back to the house. It seemed to me, too, that the house was inconveniently chosen, and required a needless length of tunnel. And just as I was beginning to face these things, the artilleryman stopped digging, and looked at me.

'We're working well,' he said. He put down his spade. 'Let us knock off a bit,' he said. 'I think it's time we reconnoitred from the roof of the house.'

I was for going on, and after a little hesitation he resumed his spade; and then suddenly I was struck by a thought. I stopped, and so did he at once.

'Why were you walking about the common,' I said, 'instead of being here?'

'Taking the air,' he said. 'I was coming back. It's safer by night.'

'But the work?'

'Oh, one can't always work,' he said, and in a flash I saw the man plain. He hesitated, holding his spade. 'We ought to reconnoitre now,' he said, 'because if any come near they may hear the spades and drop upon us unawares.'

I was no longer disposed to object. We went together to the roof and stood on a ladder peeping out of the roof door. No Martians were to be seen, and we ventured out on the tiles, and slipped down under shelter of the parapet.

From this position a shrubbery hid the greater portion of Putney, but we could see the river below, a bubbly mass of red weed, and the low parts of Lambeth flooded and red. The red creeper swarmed up the trees about the old palace, and their branches stretched gaunt and dead, and set with shrivelled leaves, from amid its clusters. It was strange how entirely dependent both these things were upon flowing water for their propagation. About us neither had gained a footing; laburnums, pink mays, snowballs, and trees of arbor-vitae, rose out of laurels and hydrangeas, green and brilliant into the sunlight. Beyond Kensington dense smoke was rising, and that and a blue haze hid the northward hills.

The artilleryman began to tell me of the sort of people who still remained in London.

'One night last week,' he said, 'some fools got the electric light in order, and there was all Regent Street and the Circus ablaze, crowded with painted and ragged drunkards, men and women, dancing and shouting till dawn. A man who was there told me. And as the day came they became aware of a fighting-machine standing near by the Langham and looking down at them. Heaven knows how long he had been there. It must have given some of them a nasty turn. He came down the road towards them, and picked up nearly a hundred too drunk or frightened to run away.'

Grotesque gleam of a time no history will ever fully describe!

From that, in answer to my questions, he came round to his grandiose plans again. He grew enthusiastic. He talked so eloquently of the possibility of capturing a fighting-machine that I more than half believed in him again. But now that I was beginning to understand something of his quality, I could divine the stress he laid on doing nothing precipitately. And I noted that now there was no question that he personally was to capture and fight the great machine.

After a time we went down to the cellar. Neither of us seemed disposed to resume digging, and when he suggested a meal, I was nothing loath. He became suddenly very generous, and when we had eaten he went away and returned with some excellent cigars. We lit these, and his optimism glowed. He was inclined to regard my coming as a great occasion.

'There's some champagne in the cellar,' he said.

'We can dig better on this Thames-side burgundy,' said I.

'No,' said he; 'I am host today. Champagne! Great God! We've a heavy

enough task before us! Let us take a rest and gather strength while we may. Look at these blistered hands!'

And pursuant to this idea of a holiday, he insisted upon playing cards after we had eaten. He taught me euchre, and after dividing London between us, I taking the northern side and he the southern, we played for parish points. Grotesque and foolish as this will seem to the sober reader, it is absolutely true, and what is more remarkable, I found the card game and several others we played extremely interesting.

Strange mind of man! that, with our species upon the edge of extermination or appalling degradation, with no clear prospect before us but the chance of a horrible death, we could sit following the chance of this painted pasteboard, and playing the 'joker' with vivid delight. Afterwards he taught me poker, and I beat him at three tough chess games. When dark came we decided to take the risk, and lit a lamp.

After an interminable string of games, we supped, and the artilleryman finished the champagne. We went on smoking the cigars. He was no longer the energetic regenerator of his species I had encountered in the morning. He was still optimistic, but it was a less kinetic, a more thoughtful optimism. I remember he wound up with my health, proposed in a speech of small variety and considerable intermittence. I took a cigar, and went upstairs to look at the lights of which he had spoken that blazed so greenly along the Highgate hills.

At first I stared unintelligently across the London valley. The northern hills were shrouded in darkness; the fires near Kensington glowed redly, and now and then an orange-red tongue of flame flashed up and vanished in the deep blue night. All the rest of London was black. Then, nearer, I perceived a strange light, a pale, violet-purple fluorescent glow, quivering under the night breeze. For a space I could not understand it, and then I knew that it must be the red weed from which this faint irradiation proceeded. With that realisation my dormant sense of wonder, my sense of the proportion of things, awoke again. I glanced from that to Mars, red and clear, glowing high in the west, and then gazed long and earnestly at the darkness of Hampstead and Highgate.

I remained a very long time upon the roof, wondering at the grotesque changes of the day. I recalled my mental states from the midnight prayer to the foolish card-playing. I had a violent revulsion of feeling. I remember I flung away the cigar with a certain wasteful symbolism. My folly came to me with glaring exaggeration. I seemed a traitor to my wife and to my kind; I was filled with remorse. I resolved to leave this strange undisciplined dreamer of great things to his drink and gluttony, and to go on into London. There, it seemed to me, I had the best chance of learning what the Martians and my fellow men were doing. I was still upon the roof when the late moon rose.

CHAPTER EIGHT

Dead London

After I had parted from the artilleryman, I went down the hill, and by the High Street across the bridge to Fulham. The red weed was tumultuous at that time, and nearly choked the bridge roadway; but its fronds were already whitened in patches by the spreading disease that presently removed it so swiftly.

At the corner of the lane that runs to Putney Bridge station I found a man lying. He was as black as a sweep with the black dust, alive, but helplessly and speechlessly drunk. I could get nothing from him but curses and furious lunges at my head. I think I should have stayed by him but for the brutal expression of his face.

There was black dust along the roadway from the bridge onwards, and it grew thicker in Fulham. The streets were horribly quiet. I got food – sour, hard, and mouldy, but quite eatable – in a baker's shop here. Some way towards Walham Green the streets became clear of powder, and I passed a white terrace of houses on fire; the noise of the burning was an absolute relief. Going on towards Brompton, the streets were quiet again.

Here I came once more upon the black powder in the streets and upon dead bodies. I saw altogether about a dozen in the length of the Fulham Road. They had been dead many days, so that I hurried quickly past them. The black powder covered them over, and softened their outlines. One or two had been disturbed by dogs.

Where there was no black powder, it was curiously like a Sunday in the City, with the closed shops, the houses locked up and the blinds drawn, the desertion, and the stillness. In some places plunderers had been at work, but rarely at other than the provision and wine shops. A jeweller's window had been broken open in one place, but apparently the thief had been disturbed, and a number of gold chains and a watch lay scattered on the pavement. I did not trouble to touch them. Farther on was a tattered woman in a heap on a doorstep; the hand that hung over her knee was gashed and bled down her rusty brown dress, and a smashed magnum of champagne formed a pool across the pavement. She seemed asleep, but she was dead.

The farther I penetrated into London, the profounder grew the stillness. But it was not so much the stillness of death – it was the stillness of suspense, of expectation. At any time the destruction that had already singed the north-western borders of the metropolis, and had annihilated Ealing and Kilburn, might strike among these houses and leave them smoking ruins. It was a city condemned and derelict . . .

In South Kensington the streets were clear of dead and of black powder.

It was near South Kensington that I first heard the howling. It crept almost imperceptibly upon my senses. It was a sobbing alternation of two notes, 'Ulla, ulla, ulla, ulla,' keeping on perpetually. When I passed streets that ran northward it grew in volume, and houses and buildings seemed to deaden and cut it off again. It came in a full tide down Exhibition Road. I stopped, staring towards Kensington Gardens, wondering at this strange, remote wailing. It was as if that mighty desert of houses had found a voice for its fear and solitude.

'Ulla, ulla, ulla, ulla,' wailed that superhuman note – great waves of sound sweeping down the broad, sunlit roadway, between the tall buildings on each side. I turned northwards, marvelling, towards the iron gates of Hyde Park. I had half a mind to break into the Natural History Museum and find my way up to the summits of the towers, in order to see across the park. But I decided to keep to the ground, where quick hiding was possible, and so went on up the Exhibition Road. All the large mansions on each side of the road were empty and still, and my footsteps echoed against the sides of the houses. At the top, near the park gate, I came upon a strange sight – a bus overturned, and the skeleton of a horse picked clean. I puzzled over this for a time, and then went on to the bridge over the Serpentine. The voice grew stronger and stronger, though I could see nothing above the housetops on the north side of the park, save a haze of smoke to the north-west.

'Ulla, ulla, ulla, ulla,' cried the voice, coming, as it seemed to me, from the district about Regent's Park. The desolating cry worked upon my mind. The mood that had sustained me passed. The wailing took possession of me. I found I was intensely weary, footsore, and now again hungry and thirsty.

It was already past noon. Why was I wandering alone in this city of the dead? Why was I alone when all London was lying in state, and in its black shroud? I felt intolerably lonely. My mind ran on old friends that I had forgotten for years. I thought of the poisons in the chemists' shops, of the liquors the wine merchants stored; I recalled the two sodden creatures of despair, who so far as I knew, shared the city with myself . . .

I came into Oxford Street by the Marble Arch, and here again were black powder and several bodies, and an evil, ominous smell from the gratings of the cellars of some of the houses. I grew very thirsty after the heat of my long walk. With infinite trouble I managed to break into a public-house and get food and drink. I was weary after eating, and went into the parlour behind the bar, and slept on a black horsehair sofa I found there.

I awoke to find that dismal howling still in my ears, 'Ulla, ulla, ulla, ulla.' It was now dusk, and after I had routed out some biscuits and a cheese in the bar – there was a meat safe, but it contained nothing but maggots – I wandered on through the silent residential squares to Baker Street – Portman Square is the only one I can name – and so came out at last upon Regent's Park. And as I emerged from the top of Baker Street, I

saw far away over the trees in the clearness of the sunset the hood of the Martian giant from which this howling proceeded. I was not terrified. I came upon him as if it were a matter of course. I watched him for some time, but he did not move. He appeared to be standing and yelling, for no reason that I could discover.

I tried to formulate a plan of action. That perpetual sound of 'Ulla, ulla, ulla, ulla,' confused my mind. Perhaps I was too tired to be very fearful. Certainly I was more curious to know the reason of this monotonous crying than afraid. I turned back away from the park and struck into Park Road, intending to skirt the park, went along under the shelter of the terraces, and got a view of this stationary, howling Martian from the direction of St John's Wood. A couple of hundred yards out of Baker Street I heard a yelping chorus, and saw, first a dog with a piece of putrescent red meat in his jaws coming headlong towards me, and then a pack of starving mongrels in pursuit of him. He made a wide curve to avoid me, as though he feared I might prove a fresh competitor. As the yelping died away down the silent road, the wailing sound of 'Ulla, ulla, ulla, ulla,' reasserted itself.

I came upon the wrecked handling-machine halfway to St John's Wood station. At first I thought a house had fallen across the road. It was only as I clambered among the ruins that I saw, with a start, this mechanical Samson lying, with its tentacles bent and smashed and twisted, among the ruins it had made. The forepart was shattered. It seemed as if it had driven blindly straight at the house, and had been overwhelmed in its overthrow. It seemed to me then that this might have happened by a handling-machine escaping from the guidance of its Martian. I could not clamber among the ruins to see it, and the twilight was now so far advanced that the blood with which its seat was smeared, and the gnawed gristle of the Martian that the dogs had left, were invisible to me.

Wondering still more at all that I had seen, I pushed on towards Primrose Hill. Far away, through a gap in the trees, I saw a second Martian, as motionless as the first, standing in the park towards the Zoological Gardens, and silent. A little beyond the ruins about the smashed handling-machine I came upon the red weed again, and found the Regent's Canal, a spongy mass of dark-red vegetation.

As I crossed the bridge, the sound of 'Ulla, ulla, ulla, ulla,' ceased. It was, as it were, cut off. The silence came like a thunderclap.

The dusky houses about me stood faint and tall and dim; the trees towards the park were growing black. All about me the red weed clambered among the ruins, writhing to get above me in the dimness. Night, the mother of fear and mystery, was coming upon me. But while that voice sounded the solitude, the desolation, had been endurable; by virtue of it London had still seemed alive, and the sense of life about me had upheld me. Then suddenly a change, the passing of something – I knew not what – and then a stillness that could be felt. Nothing but this gaunt quiet.

London about me gazed at me spectrally. The windows in the white houses were like the eye sockets of skulls. About me my imagination found a thousand noiseless enemies moving. Terror seized me, a horror of my temerity. In front of me the road became pitchy black as though it was tarred, and I saw a contorted shape lying across the pathway. I could not bring myself to go on. I turned down St John's Wood Road, and ran headlong from this unendurable stillness towards Kilburn. I hid from the night and the silence, until long after midnight, in a cabmen's shelter in Harrow Road. But before the dawn my courage returned, and while the stars were still in the sky I turned once more towards Regent's Park. I missed my way among the streets, and presently saw down a long avenue, in the half-light of the early dawn, the curve of Primrose Hill. On the summit, towering up to the fading stars, was a third Martian, erect and motionless like the others.

An insane resolve possessed me. I would die and end it. And I would save myself even the trouble of killing myself. I marched on recklessly towards this Titan, and then, as I drew nearer and the light grew, I saw that a multitude of black birds was circling and clustering about the hood. At that my heart gave a bound, and I began running along the road.

I hurried through the red weed that choked St Edmund's Terrace (I waded breast-high across a torrent of water that was rushing down from the waterworks towards the Albert Road), and emerged upon the grass before the rising of the sun. Great mounds had been heaped about the crest of the hill, making a huge redoubt of it – it was the final and largest place the Martians had made – and from behind these heaps there rose a thin smoke against the sky. Against the skyline an eager dog ran and disappeared. The thought that had flashed into my mind grew real, grew credible. I felt no fear, only a wild, trembling exultation, as I ran up the hill towards the motionless monster. Out of the hood hung lank shreds of brown, at which the hungry birds pecked and tore.

In another moment I had scrambled up the earthen rampart and stood upon its crest, and the interior of the redoubt was below me. A mighty space it was, with gigantic machines here and there within it, huge mounds of material and strange shelter places. And scattered about it, some in their overturned war-machines, some in the now rigid handling-machines, and a dozen of them stark and silent and laid in a row, were the Martians – *dead!* – slain by the putrefactive and disease bacteria against which their systems were unprepared; slain as the red weed was being slain; slain, after all man's devices had failed, by the humblest things that God, in his wisdom, has put upon this earth.

For so it had come about, as indeed I and many men might have foreseen had not terror and disaster blinded our minds. These germs of disease have taken toll of humanity since the beginning of things – taken toll of our prehuman ancestors since life began here. But by virtue of this natural

selection of our kind we have developed resisting power; to no germs do we succumb without a struggle, and to many – those that cause putrefaction in dead matter, for instance – our living frames are altogether immune. But there are no bacteria in Mars, and directly these invaders arrived, directly they drank and fed, our microscopic allies began to work their overthrow. Already when I watched them they were irrevocably doomed, dying and rotting even as they went to and fro. It was inevitable. By the toll of a billion deaths man has bought his birthright of the earth, and it is his against all comers; it would still be his were the Martians ten times as mighty as they are. For neither do men live nor die in vain.

Here and there they were scattered, nearly fifty altogether, in that great gulf they had made, overtaken by a death that must have seemed to them as incomprehensible as any death could be. To me also at that time this death was incomprehensible. All I knew was that these things that had been alive and so terrible to men were dead. For a moment I believed that the destruction of Sennacherib had been repeated, that God had repented, that the Angel of Death had slain them in the night.

I stood staring into the pit, and my heart lightened gloriously, even as the rising sun struck the world to fire about me with his rays. The pit was still in darkness; the mighty engines, so great and wonderful in their power and complexity, so unearthly in their tortuous forms, rose weird and vague and strange out of the shadows towards the light. A multitude of dogs, I could hear, fought over the bodies that lay darkly in the depth of the pit, far below me. Across the pit on its farther lip, flat and vast and strange, lay the great flying-machine with which they had been experimenting upon our denser atmosphere when decay and death arrested them. Death had come not a day too soon. At the sound of a cawing overhead I looked up at the huge fighting-machine that would fight no more for ever, at the tattered red shreds of flesh that dripped down upon the overturned seats on the summit of Primrose Hill.

I turned and looked down the slope of the hill to where, enhaloed now in birds, stood those other two Martians that I had seen overnight, just as death had overtaken them. The one had died, even as it had been crying to its companions; perhaps it was the last to die, and its voice had gone on perpetually until the force of its machinery was exhausted. They glittered now, harmless tripod towers of shining metal, in the brightness of the rising sun.

All about the pit, and saved as by a miracle from everlasting destruction, stretched the great Mother of Cities. Those who have only seen London veiled in her sombre robes of smoke can scarcely imagine the naked clearness and beauty of the silent wilderness of houses.

Eastward, over the blackened ruins of the Albert Terrace and the splintered spire of the church, the sun blazed dazzling in a clear sky, and here and there some facet in the great wilderness of roofs caught the light and glared with a white intensity.

Northward were Kilburn and Hampsted, blue and crowded with houses; westward the great city was dimmed; and southward, beyond the Martians, the green waves of Regent's Park, the Langham Hotel, the dome of the Albert Hall, the Imperial Institute, and the giant mansions of the Brompton Road came out clear and little in the sunrise, the jagged ruins of Westminster rising hazily beyond. Far away and blue were the Surrey hills, and the towers of the Crystal Palace glittered like two silver rods. The dome of St Paul's was dark against the sunrise, and injured, I saw for the first time, by a huge gaping cavity on its western side.

And as I looked at this wide expanse of houses and factories and churches, silent and abandoned; as I thought of the multitudinous hopes and efforts, the innumerable hosts of lives that had gone to build this human reef, and of the swift and ruthless destruction that had hung over it all; when I realised that the shadow had been rolled back, and that men might still live in the streets, and this dear vast dead city of mine be once more alive and powerful, I felt a wave of emotion that was near akin to tears.

The torment was over. Even that day the healing would begin. The survivors of the people scattered over the country – leaderless, lawless, foodless, like sheep without a shepherd – the thousands who had fled by sea, would begin to return; the pulse of life, growing stronger and stronger, would beat again in the empty streets and pour across the vacant squares. Whatever destruction was done, the hand of the destroyer was stayed. All the gaunt wrecks, the blackened skeletons of houses that stared so dismally at the sunlit grass of the hill, would presently be echoing with the hammers of the restorers and ringing with the tapping of their trowels. At the thought I extended my hands towards the sky and began thanking God. In a year, thought I – in a year. . .

With overwhelming force came the thought of myself, of my wife, and the old life of hope and tender helpfulness that had ceased for ever.

CHAPTER NINE

Wreckage

And now comes the strangest thing in my story. Yet, perhaps, it is not altogether strange. I remember, clearly and coldly and vividly, all that I did that day until the time that I stood weeping and praising God upon the summit of Primrose Hill. And then I forget.

Of the next three days I know nothing. I have learned since that, so far from my being the first discoverer of the Martian overthrow, several such wanderers as myself had already discovered this on the previous night. One man – the first – had gone to St Martin's-le-Grand, and, while I sheltered in the cabmen's hut, had contrived to telegraph to Paris. Thence the joyful

news had flashed all over the world; a thousand cities, chilled by ghastly apprehensions, suddenly flashed into frantic illuminations; they knew of it in Dublin, Edinburgh, Manchester, Birmingham, at the time when I stood upon the verge of the pit. Already men, weeping with joy, as I have heard, shouting and staying their work to shake hands and shout, were making up trains, even as near as Crewe, to descend upon London. The church bells that had ceased a fortnight since suddenly caught the news, until all England was bell-ringing. Men on cycles, lean-faced, unkempt, scorched along every country lane shouting of unhoped deliverance, shouting to gaunt, staring figures of despair. And for the food! Across the Channel, across the Irish Sea, across the Atlantic, corn, bread, and meat were tearing to our relief. All the shipping in the world seemed going Londonward in those days. But of all this I have no memory. I drifted – a demented man. I found myself in a house of kindly people, who had found me on the third day wandering, weeping, and raving through the streets of St John's Wood. They have told me since that I was singing some insane doggerel about 'The Last Man Left Alive! Hurrah! The Last Man Left Alive!' Troubled as they were with their own affairs, these people, whose name, much as I would like to express my gratitude to them, I may not even give here, nevertheless cumbered themselves with me, sheltered me, and protected me from myself. Apparently they had learned something of my story from me during the days of my lapse.

Very gently, when my mind was assured again, did they break to me what they had learned of the fate of Leatherhead. Two days after I was imprisoned it had been destroyed, with every soul in it, by a Martian. He had swept it out of existence, as it seemed, without any provocation, as a boy might crush an ant hill, in the mere wantonness of power.

I was a lonely man, and they were very kind to me. I was a lonely man and a sad one, and they bore with me. I remained with them four days after my recovery. All that time I felt a vague, a growing craving to look once more on whatever remained of the little life that seemed so happy and bright in my past. It was a mere hopeless desire to feast upon my misery. They dissuaded me. They did all they could to divert me from this morbidity. But at last I could resist the impulse no longer, and, promising faithfully to return to them, and parting, as I will confess, from these four-day friends with tears, I went out again into the streets that had lately been so dark and strange and empty.

Already they were busy with returning people; in places even there were shops open, and I saw a drinking fountain running water.

I remember how mockingly bright the day seemed as I went back on my melancholy pilgrimage to the little house at Woking, how busy the streets and vivid the moving life about me. So many people were abroad every-where, busied in a thousand activities, that it seemed incredible that any great proportion of the population could have been slain. But then I noticed

how yellow were the skins of the people I met, how shaggy the hair of the men, how large and bright their eyes, and that every other man still wore his dirty rags. Their faces seemed all with one of two expressions – a leaping exultation and energy or a grim resolution. Save for the expression of the faces, London seemed a city of tramps. The vestries were indiscriminately distributing bread sent us by the French government. The ribs of the few horses showed dismally. Haggard special constables with white badges stood at the corners of every street. I saw little of the mischief wrought by the Martians until I reached Wellington Street, and there I saw the red weed clambering over the buttresses of Waterloo Bridge.

At the corner of the bridge, too, I saw one of the common contrasts of that grotesque time – a sheet of paper flaunting against a thicket of the red weed, transfixed by a stick that kept it in place. It was the placard of the first newspaper to resume publication – the *Daily Mail*. I bought a copy for a blackened shilling I found in my pocket. Most of it was in blank, but the solitary compositor who did the thing had amused himself by making a grotesque scheme of advertisement stereo on the back page. The matter he printed was emotional; the news organisation had not as yet found its way back. I learned nothing fresh except that already in one week the examination of the Martian mechanisms had yielded astonishing results. Among other things, the article assured me what I did not believe at the time, that the 'Secret of Flying' was discovered. At Waterloo I found the free trains that were taking people to their homes. The first rush was already over. There were few people in the train, and I was in no mood for casual conversation. I got a compartment to myself, and sat with folded arms, looking greyly at the sunlit devastation that flowed past the windows. And just outside the terminus the train jolted over temporary rails, and on either side of the railway the houses were blackened ruins. To Clapham Junction the face of London was grimy with powder of the Black Smoke, in spite of two days of thunderstorms and rain, and at Clapham Junction the line had been wrecked again; there were hundreds of out-of-work clerks and shopmen working side by side with the customary navvies, and we were jolted over a hasty relaying.

All down the line from there the aspect of the country was gaunt and unfamiliar; Wimbledon particularly had suffered. Walton, by virtue of its unburned pine woods, seemed the least hurt of any place along the line. The Wandle, the Mole, every little stream, was a heaped mass of red weed, in appearance between butcher's meat and pickled cabbage. The Surrey pine woods were too dry, however, for the festoons of the red climber. Beyond Wimbledon, within sight of the line, in certain nursery grounds, were the heaped masses of earth about the sixth cylinder. A number of people were standing about it, and some sappers were busy in the midst of it. Over it flaunted a Union Jack, flapping cheerfully in the morning breeze. The nursery grounds were everywhere crimson with the weed, a wide

expanse of livid colour cut with purple shadows, and very painful to the eye. One's gaze went with infinite relief from the scorched greys and sullen reds of the foreground to the blue-green softness of the eastward hills.

The line on the London side of Woking station was still undergoing repair, so I descended at Byfleet station and took the road to Maybury, past the place where I and the artilleryman had talked to the hussars, and on by the spot where the Martian had appeared to me in the thunderstorm. Here, moved by curiosity, I turned aside to find, among a tangle of red fronds, the warped and broken dog cart with the whitened bones of the horse scattered and gnawed. For a time I stood regarding these vestiges . . .

Then I returned through the pine wood, neck-high with red weed here and there, to find the landlord of the Spotted Dog had already found burial, and so came home past the College Arms. A man standing at an open cottage door greeted me by name as I passed.

I looked at my house with a quick flash of hope that faded immediately. The door had been forced; it was unfast and was opening slowly as I approached.

It slammed again. The curtains of my study fluttered out of the open window from which I and the artilleryman had watched the dawn. No one had closed it since. The smashed bushes were just as I had left them nearly four weeks ago. I stumbled into the hall, and the house felt empty. The stair carpet was ruffled and discoloured where I had crouched, soaked to the skin from the thunderstorm the night of the catastrophe. Our muddy footsteps I saw still went up the stairs.

I followed them to my study, and found lying on my writing-table still, with the selenite paperweight upon it, the sheet of work I had left on the afternoon of the opening of the cylinder. For a space I stood reading over my abandoned arguments. It was a paper on the probable development of Moral Ideas with the development of the civilising process; and the last sentence was the opening of a prophecy: 'In about two hundred years,' I had written, 'we may expect – ' The sentence ended abruptly. I remembered my inability to fix my mind that morning, scarcely a month gone by, and how I had broken off to get my *Daily Chronicle* from the newsboy. I remembered how I went down to the garden gate as he came along, and how I had listened to his odd story of 'Men from Mars'.

I came down and went into the dining room. There were the mutton and the bread, both far gone now in decay, and a beer bottle overturned, just as I and the artilleryman had left them. My home was desolate. I perceived the folly of the faint hope I had cherished so long. And then a strange thing occurred. 'It is no use,' said a voice. 'The house is deserted. No one has been here these ten days. Do not stay here to torment yourself. No one escaped but you.'

I was startled. Had I spoken my thought aloud? I turned, and the French window was open behind me. I made a step to it, and stood looking out.

And there, amazed and afraid, even as I stood amazed and afraid, were my cousin and my wife – my wife white and tearless. She gave a faint cry.

'I came,' she said. 'I knew – knew – '

She put her hand to her throat – swayed. I made a step forward, and caught her in my arms.

CHAPTER TEN

The Epilogue

I cannot but regret, now that I am concluding my story, how little I am able to contribute to the discussion of the many debatable questions which are still unsettled. In one respect I shall certainly provoke criticism. My particular province is speculative philosophy. My knowledge of comparative physiology is confined to a book or two, but it seems to me that Carver's suggestions as to the reason of the rapid death of the Martians is so probable as to be regarded almost as a proven conclusion. I have assumed that in the body of my narrative.

At any rate, in all the bodies of the Martians that were examined after the war, no bacteria except those already known as terrestrial species were found. That they did not bury any of their dead, and the reckless slaughter they perpetrated, point also to an entire ignorance of the putrefactive process. But probable as this seems, it is by no means a proven conclusion.

Neither is the composition of the Black Smoke known, which the Martians used with such deadly effect, and the generator of the Heat-Rays remains a puzzle. The terrible disasters at the Ealing and South Kensington laboratories have disinclined analysts for further investigations upon the latter. Spectrum analysis of the black powder points unmistakably to the presence of an unknown element with a brilliant group of three lines in the green, and it is possible that it combines with argon to form a compound which acts at once with deadly effect upon some constituent in the blood. But such unproven speculations will scarcely be of interest to the general reader, to whom this story is addressed. None of the brown scum that drifted down the Thames after the destruction of Shepperton was examined at the time, and now none is forthcoming.

The results of an anatomical examination of the Martians, so far as the prowling dogs had left such an examination possible, I have already given. But everyone is familiar with the magnificent and almost complete specimen in spirits at the Natural History Museum, and the countless drawings that have been made from it; and beyond that the interest of their physiology and structure is purely scientific.

A question of graver and universal interest is the possibility of another attack from the Martians. I do not think that nearly enough attention is

being given to this aspect of the matter. At present the planet Mars is in conjunction, but with every return to opposition I, for one, anticipate a renewal of their adventure. In any case, we should be prepared. It seems to me that it should be possible to define the position of the gun from which the shots are discharged, to keep a sustained watch upon this part of the planet, and to anticipate the arrival of the next attack.

In that case the cylinder might be destroyed with dynamite or artillery before it was sufficiently cool for the Martians to emerge, or they might be butchered by means of guns so soon as the screw opened. It seems to me that they have lost a vast advantage in the failure of their first surprise. Possibly they see it in the same light.

Lessing has advanced excellent reasons for supposing that the Martians have actually succeeded in effecting a landing on the planet Venus. Seven months ago now, Venus and Mars were in alignment with the sun; that is to say, Mars was in opposition from the point of view of an observer on Venus. Subsequently a peculiar luminous and sinuous marking appeared on the unillumined half of the inner planet, and almost simultaneously a faint dark mark of a similar sinuous character was detected upon a photograph of the Martian disk. One needs to see the drawings of these appearances in order to appreciate fully their remarkable resemblance in character.

At any rate, whether we expect another invasion or not, our views of the human future must be greatly modified by these events. We have learned now that we cannot regard this planet as being fenced in and a secure abiding place for Man; we can never anticipate the unseen good or evil that may come upon us suddenly out of space. It may be that in the larger design of the universe this invasion from Mars is not without its ultimate benefit for men; it has robbed us of that serene confidence in the future which is the most fruitful source of decadence, the gifts to human science it has brought are enormous, and it has done much to promote the conception of the commonweal of mankind. It may be that across the immensity of space the Martians have watched the fate of these pioneers of theirs and learned their lesson, and that on the planet Venus they have found a securer settlement. Be that as it may, for many years yet there will certainly be no relaxation of the eager scrutiny of the Martian disk, and those fiery darts of the sky, the shooting stars, will bring with them as they fall an unavoidable apprehension to all the sons of men.

The broadening of men's views that has resulted can scarcely be exaggerated. Before the cylinder fell there was a general persuasion that through all the deep of space no life existed beyond the petty surface of our minute sphere. Now we see further. If the Martians can reach Venus, there is no reason to suppose that the thing is impossible for men, and when the slow cooling of the sun makes this earth uninhabitable, as at last it must do, it may be that the thread of life that has begun here will have streamed out and caught our sister planet within its toils.

Dim and wonderful is the vision I have conjured up in my mind of life spreading slowly from this little seed bed of the solar system throughout the inanimate vastness of sidereal space. But that is a remote dream. It may be, on the other hand, that the destruction of the Martians is only a reprieve. To them, and not to us, perhaps, is the future ordained.

I must confess the stress and danger of the time have left an abiding sense of doubt and insecurity in my mind. I sit in my study writing by lamplight, and suddenly I see again the healing valley below set with writhing flames, and feel the house behind and about me empty and desolate. I go out into the Byfleet Road, and vehicles pass me, a butcher boy in a cart, a cabful of visitors, a workman on a bicycle, children going to school, and suddenly they become vague and unreal, and I hurry again with the artilleryman through the hot, brooding silence. Of a night I see the black powder darkening the silent streets, and the contorted bodies shrouded in that layer; they rise upon me tattered and dog-bitten. They gibber and grow fiercer, paler, uglier, mad distortions of humanity at last, and I wake, cold and wretched, in the darkness of the night.

I go to London and see the busy multitudes in Fleet Street and the Strand, and it comes across my mind that they are but the ghosts of the past, haunting the streets that I have seen silent and wretched, going to and fro, phantasms in a dead city, the mockery of life in a galvanised body. And strange, too, it is to stand on Primrose Hill, as I did but a day before writing this last chapter, to see the great province of houses, dim and blue through the haze of the smoke and mist, vanishing at last into the vague lower sky, to see the people walking to and fro among the flower beds on the hill, to see the sight-seers about the Martian machine that stands there still, to hear the tumult of playing children, and to recall the time when I saw it all bright and clear-cut, hard and silent, under the dawn of that last great day . . .

And strangest of all is it to hold my wife's hand again, and to think that I have counted her, and that she has counted me, among the dead.

Kipps
The Story of a Simple Soul

A novel first published in 1905

Contents

The Making of Kipps

The History of Mr Polly was first published in Great Britain
in 1910 by Thomas Nelson & Sons, London,
and in the United States in 1909 by
Grosset & Dunlap, New York

CHAPTER ONE

The Little Shop at New Romney

UNTIL HE WAS NEARLY ARRIVED at adolescence it did not become clear to Kipps how it was that he was under the care of an aunt and uncle instead of having a father and mother like other boys. Yet he had vague memories of a somewhere else that was not New Romney – of a dim room, a window looking down on white buildings – and of a some one else who talked to forgotten people, and who was his mother. He could not recall her features very distinctly, but he remembered with extreme definition a white dress she wore, with a pattern of little sprigs of flowers and little bows of ribbon upon it, and a girdle of straight-ribbed white ribbon about the waist. Linked with this, he knew not how, were clouded half-obliterated recollections of scenes in which there was weeping, weeping in which he was inscrutably moved to join. Some terrible tall man with a loud voice played a part in these scenes, and either before or after them there were impressions of looking for interminable periods out of the windows of railway trains in the company of these two people –

He knew, though he could not remember that he had ever been told, that a certain faded, wistful face, that looked at him from a plush and gilt framed daguerreotype above the mantel of the 'sitting-room', was the face of his mother. But that knowledge did not touch his dim memories with any elucidation. In that photograph she was a girlish figure, leaning against a photographer's stile, and with all the self-conscious shrinking natural to that position. She had curly hair and a face far younger and prettier than any other mother in his experience. She swung a Dolly Varden hat by the string, and looked with obedient respectful eyes on the photographer-gentleman who had commanded the pose. She was very slight and pretty. But the phantom mother that haunted his memory so elusively was not like that, though he could not remember how she differed. Perhaps she was older, or a little less shrinking, or, it may be, only dressed in a different way . . .

It is clear she handed him over to his aunt and uncle at New Romney with explicit directions and a certain endowment. One gathers she had something of that fine sense of social distinctions that subsequently played so large a part in Kipps's career. He was not to go to a 'common' school, she provided, but to a certain seminary in Hastings that was not only a 'middle-class academy', with mortar boards and every evidence of a higher social tone, but also remarkably cheap. She seems to have been animated

by the desire to do her best for Kipps, even at a certain sacrifice of herself, as though Kipps were in some way a superior sort of person. She sent pocket-money to him from time to time for a year or more after Hastings had begun for him, but her face he never saw in the days of his lucid memory.

His aunt and uncle were already high on the hill of life when first he came to them. They had married for comfort in the evening or at any rate in the late afternoon of their days. They were at first no more than vague figures in the background of proximate realities, such realities as familiar chairs and tables, quiet to ride and drive, the newel of the staircase, kitchen furniture, pieces of firewood, the boiler tap, old newspapers, the cat, the High Street, the back yard and the flat fields that are always so near in that little town. He knew all the stones in the yard individually, the creeper in the corner, the dustbin and the mossy wall, better than many men know the faces of their wives. There was a corner under the ironing-board which by means of a shawl could, under propitious gods, be made a very decent cubby-house, a corner that served him for several years as the indisputable hub of the world; and the stringy places in the carpet, the knots upon the dresser, and the several corners of the rag hearthrug his uncle had made, became essential parts of his mental foundations. The shop he did not know so thoroughly – it was a forbidden region to him; yet somehow he managed to know it very well.

His aunt and uncle were, as it were, the immediate gods of this world; and, like the gods of the world of old, occasionally descended right into it, with arbitrary injunctions and disproportionate punishments. And, un-happily, one rose to their Olympian level at meals. Then one had to say one's 'grace', hold one's spoon and fork in mad, unnatural ways called 'properly', and refrain from eating even nice sweet things 'too fast'. If he 'gobbled' there was trouble, and at the slightest *abandon* with knife, fork and spoon, his aunt rapped his knuckles, albeit his uncle always finished up his gravy with his knife. Sometimes, moreover, his uncle would come, pipe in hand, out of a sedentary remoteness in the most disconcerting way, when a little boy was doing the most natural and attractive things, with 'Drat and drabbit that young rascal! What's he a-doing of now?' And his aunt would appear at door or window to interrupt interesting conversation with children who were upon unknown grounds considered 'low' and undesirable, and call him in. The pleasantest little noises, however softly you did them – drumming on tea-trays, trumpeting your fists, whistling on keys, ringing chimes with a couple of pails, or playing tunes on the window-panes – brought down the gods in anger. Yet what noise is fainter than your finger on the window – gently done? Sometimes, however, these gods gave him broken toys out of the shop, and then one loved them better – for the shop they kept was, among other things, a toy shop. (The other things included books to read and books to give away and local photographs; it had

some pretensions also to be a china shop, and the fascia spoke of glass; it was also a stationer's shop with a touch of haberdashery about it, and in the windows and odd corners were mats and terracotta dishes, and milking-stools for painting; and there was a hint of picture-frames, and fire-screens, and fishing tackle, and air-guns, and bathing suits, and tents: various things, indeed, but all cruelly attractive to a small boy's fingers.) Once his aunt gave him a trumpet if he would *promise* faithfully not to blow it, and afterwards took it away again. And his aunt made him say his catechism and something she certainly called the 'Colic for the Day' every Sunday in the year.

As the two grew old while he grew up, and as his impression of them modified insensibly from year to year, it seemed to him at last that they had always been as they were when, in his adolescent days, his impression of things grew fixed. His aunt he thought of as always lean, rather worried-looking, and prone to a certain obliquity of cap, and his uncle massive, many-chinned and careless about his buttons. They neither visited nor received visitors. They were always very suspicious about their neighbours and other people generally; they feared the 'low' and they hated and despised the 'stuck-up', and so they 'kept themselves *to* themselves', according to the English ideal. Consequently little Kipps had no playmates, except through the sin of disobedience. By inherent nature he had a sociable disposition. When he was in the High Street he made a point of saying 'Hello!' to passing cyclists, and he would put his tongue out at the Quodling children whenever their nursemaid was not looking. And he began a friendship with Sid Pornick, the son of the haberdasher next door, that, with wide intermissions, was destined to last his lifetime through.

Pornick, the haberdasher, I may say at once, was, according to old Kipps, a 'blaring jackass'; he was a teetotaller, a 'nyar, nyar, 'im-singing Methodis' ', and altogether distasteful and detrimental, he and his together, to true Kipps ideals, so far as little Kipps could gather them. This Pornick certainly possessed an enormous voice, and he annoyed old Kipps greatly by calling 'You – Arn' and 'Siddee' up and down his house. He annoyed old Kipps by private choral services on Sunday, all his family 'nyar, nyar-ing'; and by mushroom culture; by behaving as though the pilaster between the two shops was common property; by making a noise of hammering in the afternoon, when old Kipps wanted to be quiet after his midday meal; by going up and down uncarpeted stairs in his boots; by having a black beard; by attempting to be friendly; and by – all that sort of thing. In fact, he annoyed old Kipps. He annoyed him especially with his shop doormat. Old Kipps never beat his mat, preferring to let sleeping dust lie; and, seeking a motive for a foolish proceeding, he held that Pornick waited until there was a suitable wind in order that the dust disengaged in that operation might defile his neighbour's shop. These issues would frequently develop into loud and vehement quarrels, and on one occasion came so near to violence as to be subsequently described by Pornick (who read his newspaper) as a

'Disgraceful Frackass'. On that occasion he certainly went into his own shop with extreme celerity.

But it was through one of these quarrels that the friendship of little Kipps and Sid Pornick came about. The two small boys found themselves one day looking through the gate at the doctor's goats together; they exchanged a few contradictions about which goat could fight which, and then young Kipps was moved to remark that Sid's father was a 'blaring jackass'. Sid said he wasn't, and Kipps repeated that he was, and quoted his authority. Then Sid, flying off at a tangent rather alarmingly, said he could fight young Kipps with one hand, an assertion young Kipps with a secret want of confidence denied. There were some vain repetitions, and the incident might have ended there, but happily a sporting butcher boy chanced on the controversy at this stage, and insisted upon seeing fair play.

The two small boys under his pressing encouragement did at last button up their jackets, square and fight an edifying drawn battle, until it seemed good to the butcher boy to go on with Mrs Holyer's mutton. Then, according to his directions and under his experienced stage management, they shook hands and made it up. Subsequently, a little tear-stained perhaps, but flushed with the butcher boy's approval ('tough little kids'), and with cold stones down their necks as he advised, they sat side by side on the doctor's gate, projecting very much behind, staunching an honourable bloodshed, and expressing respect for one another. Each had a bloody nose and a black eye – three days later they matched to a shade – neither had given in, and, though this was tacit, neither wanted any more.

It was an excellent beginning. After this first encounter the attributes of their parents and their own relative value in battle never rose between them, and if anything was wanted to complete the warmth of their regard it was found in a joint dislike of the eldest Quodling. The eldest Quodling lisped, had a silly sort of straw hat and a large pink face (all covered over with self-satisfaction) and he went to the National School with a green-baize bag – a contemptible thing to do. They called him names and threw stones at him, and when he replied by threatenings ('Look 'ere, young Art Kipth, you better *thtoppit!*') they were moved to attack and put him to flight.

And after that they broke the head of Ann Pornick's doll, so that she went home weeping loudly – a wicked and endearing proceeding. Sid was whacked, but, as he explained, he wore a newspaper tactically adjusted during the transaction, and really it didn't hurt him at all . . . And Mrs Pornick put her head out of the shop door suddenly, and threatened Kipps as he passed.

'Cavendish Academy', the school that had won the limited choice of Kipps's vanished mother, was established in a battered private house in the part of Hastings remotest from the sea; it was called an Academy for Young Gentlemen, and many of the young gentlemen had parents in 'India', and other unverifiable places. Others were the sons of credulous widows, anxious, as Kipps's mother had been, to get something a little 'superior' to a board-school education as cheaply as possible; and others again were sent to demonstrate the dignity of their parents and guardians. And of course there were boys from France.

Its 'principal' was a lean, long creature of indifferent digestion and temper, who proclaimed himself on a gilt-lettered board in his front garden George Garden Woodrow, F.S.Sc., letters indicating that he had paid certain guineas for a bogus diploma. A bleak whitewashed outhouse constituted his schoolroom, and the scholastic quality of its carved and worn desks and forms was enhanced by a slippery blackboard and two large yellow out-of-date maps, one of Africa and the other of Wiltshire, that he had picked up cheap at a sale. There were other maps and globes in his study, where he interviewed enquiring parents, but these his pupils never saw. And in a glass cupboard in the passage were several-shillingsworth of test tubes and chemicals, a tripod, a glass retort and a damaged Bunsen burner, manifesting that the 'Scientific Laboratory' mentioned in the pro-spectus was no idle boast.

This prospectus, which was in dignified but incorrect English, laid particular stress on the sound preparation for a commercial career given at the Academy, but the army, navy and civil service were glanced at in an ambiguous sentence. There was something vague in the prospectus about 'examinational successes' – though Woodrow, of course, disapproved of 'cram' – and a declaration that the curriculum included 'art', 'modern foreign languages' and 'a sound technical and scientific training'. Then came insistence upon the 'moral well-being' of the pupils, and an emphatic boast of the excellence of the religious instruction, 'so often neglected nowadays even in schools of wide repute'. 'That's bound to fetch 'em,' Mr Woodrow had remarked when he drew up the prospectus. And in conjunction with the mortar boards it certainly did. Attention was directed to the 'motherly' care of Mrs Woodrow – in reality a small partially effaced woman with a plaintive face and a mind above cookery; and the prospectus concluded with a phrase intentionally vague, 'Fare unrestricted, and our own milk and produce.'

The memories Kipps carried from that school into afterlife were set in an atmosphere of stuffiness and mental muddle; and included countless

pictures of sitting on creaking forms bored and idle, of blot licking and the taste of ink, of torn books with covers that set one's teeth on edge, of the slimy surface of the laboured slates, of furtive marble-playing, whispered storytelling, and of pinches, blows and a thousand such petty annoyances being perpetually 'passed on' according to the custom of the place; of standing up in class and being hit suddenly and unreasonably for imaginary misbehaviour; of Mr Woodrow's raving days, when a scarcely sane injustice prevailed; of the cold vacuity of the hour of preparation before the bread-and-butter breakfast; and of horrible headaches and queer, unprecedented, internal feelings resulting from Mrs Woodrow's motherly rather than intelligent cookery. There were dreary walks, when the boys marched two by two, all dressed in the mortar-board caps that so impressed the widowed mothers; there were dismal half-holidays when the weather was wet and the spirit of evil temper and evil imagination had the pent boys to work its will on; there were unfair, dishonourable fights and miserable defeats and victories, there was bullying and being bullied. A coward boy Kipps particularly afflicted, until at last he was goaded to revolt by incessant persecution and smote Kipps to tolerance with whirling fists. There were memories of sleeping three in a bed, of the dense leathery smell of the schoolroom when one returned thither after ten minutes' play, of a playground of mud and incidental sharp flints. And there was much furtive foul language.

'Our Sundays are our happiest days,' was one of Woodrow's formulae with the enquiring parent, but Kipps was not called in evidence. They were to him terrible gaps of inanity – no work, no play, a drear expanse of time with the mystery of church twice and plum duff once in the middle. The afternoon was given up to furtive relaxations, among which 'Torture Chamber' games with the less agreeable, weaker boys figured. It was from the difference between this day and common days that Kipps derived his first definite conceptions of the nature of God and Heaven. His instinct was to evade any closer acquaintance as long as he could.

The school work varied, according to the prevailing mood of Mr Woodrow. Sometimes that was a despondent lethargy; copybooks were distributed or sums were 'set', or the great mystery of bookkeeping was declared in being, and beneath these superficial activities lengthy conversations and interminable guessing games with marbles went on while Mr Woodrow sat inanimate at his desk heedless of school affairs, staring in front of him at unseen things. At times his face was utterly inane; at times it had an expression of stagnant amazement, as if he saw before his eyes with pitiless clearness the dishonour and mischief of his being . . .

At other times the F.S.Sc. roused himself to action, and would stand up a wavering class and teach it, goading it with bitter mockery and blows through a chapter of Ahn's *First French Course*, or *France and the French*, or a dialogue about a traveller's washing or the parts of an opera-house. His

own knowledge of French had been obtained years ago in another English private school, and he had refreshed it by occasional weeks of loafing and mean adventure in Dieppe. He would sometimes in their lessons hit upon some reminiscence of these brighter days, and then he would laugh inexplicably and repeat French phrases of an unfamiliar type.

Among the commoner exercises he prescribed the learning of long passages of poetry from a 'Potry Book', which he would delegate an elder boy to 'hear', and there was reading aloud from the Holy Bible, verse by verse – it was none of your 'godless' schools! – so that you counted the verses up to your turn and then gave yourself to conversation; and sometimes one read from a cheap History of this land. They did, as Kipps reported, 'loads of catechism'. Also there was much learning of geographical names and lists, and sometimes Woodrow in an outbreak of energy would see these names were actually found on a map. And once, just once, there was a chemistry lesson – a lesson of indescribable excitement – glass things of the strangest shape, a smell like bad eggs, something bubbling in something, a smash and stench, and Mr Woodrow saying quite distinctly – they thrashed it out in the dormitory afterwards – 'Damn!' followed by the whole school being kept in, with extraordinary severities, for an hour . . .

But interspersed with the memories of this grey routine were certain patches of brilliant colour – the holidays, his holidays, which in spite of the feud between their seniors, he spent as much as possible with Sid Pornick, the son of the irascible black-bearded haberdasher next door. They seemed to be memories of a different world. There were glorious days of 'mucking about' along the beach, the siege of unresisting Martello towers, the incessant interest of the mystery and motion of windmills, the windy excursions with boarded feet over the yielding shingle to Dungeness lighthouse – Sid Pornick and he far adrift from reality, smugglers and armed men from the moment they left Great Stone behind them – wanderings in the hedgeless reedy marsh, long excursions reaching even to Hythe, where the machine-guns of the Empire are forever whirling and tapping, and to Rye and Winchelsea, perched like dream-cities on their little hills. The sky in these memories was the blazing hemisphere of the marsh heaven in summer, or its wintry tumult of sky and sea; and there were wrecks, real wrecks, in it (near Dymchurch pitched high and blackened and rotting were the ribs of a fishing smack flung aside like an empty basket when the sea had devoured its crew); and there was bathing all naked in the sea, bathing to one's armpits and even trying to swim in the warm sea-water (spite of his aunt's prohibition), and (with her indulgence) the rare eating of dinner from a paper parcel miles away from home. Cake and cold ground-rice puddin' with plums it used to be – there is no better food at all. And for the background, in the place of Woodrow's mean, fretting rule, were his aunt's spare but frequently quite amiable figure – for though she insisted on

his repeating the English Church Catechism every Sunday, she had an easy way over dinners that one wanted to take abroad – and his uncle, corpulent and irascible, but sedentary and easily escaped. And freedom!

The holidays were indeed very different from school. They were free, they were spacious, and though he never knew it in these words – they had an element of beauty. In his memory of his boyhood they shone like strips of stained-glass window in a dreary waste of scholastic wall, they grew brighter and brighter as they grew remoter. There came a time at last and moods when he could look back to them with a feeling akin to tears.

The last of these windows was the brightest, and instead of the kaleidoscopic effects of its predecessors its glory was a single figure. For in the last of his holidays, before the Moloch of Retail Trade got hold of him, Kipps made his first tentative essays at the mysterious shrine of Love. Very tentative they were, for he had become a boy of subdued passions, and potential rather than actual affectionateness.

And the object of these first stirrings of the great desire was no other than Ann Pornick, the head of whose doll he and Sid had broken long ago, and rejoiced over long ago, in the days when he had yet to learn the meaning of a heart.

3

Negotiations were already on foot to make Kipps into a draper before he discovered the lights that lurked in Ann Pornick's eyes. School was over, absolutely over, and it was chiefly present to him that he was never to go to school again. It was high summer. The 'breaking up' of school had been hilarious; and the excellent maxim, 'Last Day's Pay Day', had been observed by him with a scrupulous attention to his honour. He had punched the heads of all his enemies, wrung wrists and kicked shins; he had distributed all his unfinished copybooks, all his schoolbooks, his collection of marbles and his mortar-board cap among such as loved him; and he had secretly written in obscure pages of their books, 'remember Art Kipps'. He had also split the anaemic Woodrow's cane, carved his own name deeply in several places about the premises, and broken the scullery window. He had told everybody so often that he was to learn to be a sea captain that he had come almost to believe the thing himself. And now he was home, and school was at an end for him for evermore.

He was up before six on the day of his return, and out in the hot sunlight of the yard. He set himself to whistle a peculiarly penetrating arrangement of three notes supposed by the boys of the Hastings Academy and himself and Sid Pornick, for no earthly reason whatever, to be the original Huron war-cry. As he did this he feigned not to be doing it because of the hatred between his uncle and the Pornicks, but to be examining with respect and

admiration a new wing of the dustbin recently erected by his uncle – a pretence that would not have deceived a nestling tomtit.

Presently there came a familiar echo from the Pornick hunting-ground. Then Kipps began to sing, 'Ar pars eight tra-la, in the lane be'ind the church.' To which an unseen person answered, 'Ar pars eight it is, in the lane be'ind the church.' The 'tra-la' was considered to render this sentence incomprehensible to the uninitiated. In order to conceal their operations still more securely, both parties to this duet then gave vent to a vocalisation of the Huron war-cry again, and after a lingering repetition of the last and shrillest note, dispersed severally, as became boys in the enjoyment of holidays, to light the house fires for the day.

Half-past eight found Kipps sitting on the sunlit gate at the top of the long lane that runs towards the sea, clashing his boots in a slow rhythm, and whistling with great violence all that he knew of an excruciatingly pathetic air. There appeared along by the churchyard wall a girl in a short frock, brown-haired, quick-coloured, and with dark-blue eyes. She had grown so that she was a little taller than Kipps, and her colour had improved. He scarcely remembered her, so changed was she since last holidays – if indeed he had seen her last holidays, a thing he could not clearly remember. Some vague emotion arose at the sight of her. He stopped whistling and regarded her, oddly tongue-tied.

'He can't come,' said Ann, advancing boldly. 'Not yet.'

'What – not Sid?'

'No. Father's made him dust all his boxes again.'

'What for?'

'I dunno. Father's in a stew 'smorning.'

'Oh!'

Pause. Kipps looked at her, and then was unable to look at her again. She regarded him with interest. 'You left school?' she remarked after a pause.

'Yes.'

'So's Sid.'

The conversation languished. Ann put her hands on the top of the gate, and began a stationary hopping, a sort of ineffectual gymnastic experiment.

'Can you run?' she said presently.

'Run you any day,' said Kipps.

'Gimme a start?'

'Where for?' said Kipps.

Ann considered, and indicated a tree. She walked towards it, and turned. 'Gimme to here?' she called.

Kipps, standing now and touching the gate, smiled to express conscious superiority. 'Farther!' he said.

'Here?'

'Bit more!' said Kipps, and then, repenting of his magnanimity, said 'Orf!' suddenly, and so recovered his lost concession.

They arrived abreast at the tree, flushed and out of breath.

'Tie!' said Ann, throwing her hair back from her face with her hand.

'I won,' panted Kipps.

They disputed firmly but quite politely.

'Run it again, then,' said Kipps. 'I don't mind.'

They returned towards the gate.

'You don't run bad,' said Kipps, temperately expressing sincere admiration. 'I'm pretty good, you know.'

Ann sent her hair back by an expert toss of the head. 'You give me a start,' she allowed.

They became aware of Sid approaching them.

'You better look out, young Ann,' said Sid, with that irreverent want of sympathy usual in brothers. 'You been out nearly 'arf-hour. Nothing ain't been done upstairs. Father said he didn't know where you was, but when he did he'd warm y'r young ear.'

Ann prepared to go.

'How about that race?' asked Kipps.

'Lor!' cried Sid, quite shocked. 'You ain't been racing *her*!'

Ann swung herself round the end of the gate with her eyes on Kipps, and then turned away suddenly and ran off down the lane.

Kipps's eyes tried to go after her, and came back to Sid's.

'I give her a lot of start,' said Kipps apologetically. 'It wasn't a proper race.' And so the subject was dismissed. But Kipps was *distrait* for some seconds, perhaps, and the mischief had begun in him.

4

They proceeded to the question of how two accomplished Hurons might most satisfactorily spend the morning. Manifestly their line lay straight along the lane to the sea.

'There's a new wreck,' said Sid, 'and my! – don't it stink just!'

'Stink?'

'Fair make you sick. It's rotten wheat.'

They fell to talking of wrecks, and so came to ironclads and wars and suchlike manly matters.

Halfway to the wreck Kipps made a casual irrelevant remark. 'Your sister ain't a bad sort,' he said offhandedly.

'I clout her a lot,' said Sidney modestly, and after a pause the talk reverted to more suitable topics.

The new wreck was full of rotting grain, and smelt abominably, even as Sid had said. This was excellent. They had it all to themselves. They took possession of it in force, at Sid's suggestion, and had speedily to defend it against enormous numbers of imaginary 'natives', who were at last driven

off by loud shouts of *bang*, *bang*, and vigorous thrusting and shoving of sticks. Then, also at Sid's direction, they sailed with it into the midst of a combined French, German and Russian fleet, demolishing the combination unassisted, and, having descended to the beach, clambered up the side and cut out their own vessel in brilliant style, they underwent a magnificent shipwreck (with vocalised thunder) and floated '*waterlogged*' – so Sid insisted – upon an exhausted sea.

These things drove Ann out of mind for a time. But at last, as they drifted without food or water upon a stagnant ocean, haggard-eyed, chins between their hands, looking in vain for a sail, she came to mind again abruptly.

'It's rather nice 'aving sisters,' remarked one perishing mariner.

Sid turned round and regarded him thoughtfully. 'Not it!' he said.

'No?'

'Not a bit of it.' He grinned confidentially. 'Know too much,' he said; and afterwards, 'Get out of things.'

He resumed his gloomy scrutiny of the hopeless horizon. Presently he fell to spitting jerkily between his teeth, as he had read was the way with such ripe manhood as chews its quid.

'Sisters,' he said, 'is rot. That's what sisters are. Girls if you like, but sisters – no!'

'But ain't sisters girls?'

'*N–eaow!*' said Sid, with unspeakable scorn.

And Kipps answered, 'Of course. I didn't mean – I wasn't thinking of that.'

'You got a girl?' asked Sid, spitting very cleverly again.

Kipps admitted his deficiency. He felt compunction.

'You don't know who *my* girl is, Art Kipps – I bet.'

'Who *is*, then?' asked Kipps, still chiefly occupied by his own poverty.

'Ah!'

Kipps let a moment elapse before he did his duty. 'Tell us!'

Sid eyed him and hesitated. 'Secret?' he said.

'Secret.'

'Dying solemn?'

'Dying solemn!' Kipps's self-concentration passed into curiosity.

Sid administered a terrible oath. Even after that precaution he adhered lovingly to his facts. 'It begins with a Nem,' he said, doling them out parsimoniously. 'M-A-U-D,' he spelt, with a stern eye on Kipps, 'C-H-A-R-T-E-R-I-S.'

Now, Maud Charteris was a young person of eighteen and the daughter of the vicar of St Bavon's – besides which she had a bicycle – so that as her name unfolded the face of Kipps lengthened with respect. 'Get out!' he gasped incredulously. 'She ain't your girl, Sid Pornick.'

'She is!' answered Sid, stoutly.

'What – truth?'

'*Truth.*'

Kipps scrutinised his face. 'Reely?'

Sid touched wood, whistled, and repeated a binding doggerel with great solemnity.

Kipps still struggled with the amazing new light on the world about him. 'D'you mean – she knows?'

Sid flushed deeply, and his aspect became stern and gloomy. He resumed his wistful scrutiny of the sunlit sea. 'I'd die for that girl, Art Kipps,' he said presently, and Kipps did not press a question he felt to be ill timed. 'I'd do anything she asked me to do,' said Sid – 'just anything. If she was to ask me to chuck myself into the sea,' he met Kipps's eye, 'I *would*,' he said.

They were pensive for a space, and then Sid began to discourse in fragments of Love, a theme upon which Kipps had already in a furtive way meditated a little, but which, apart from badinage, he had never yet heard talked about in the light of day. Of course many and various aspects of life had come to light in the muffled exchange of knowledge that went on under the shadow of Woodrow, but this of Sentimental Love was not among them. Sid, who was a boy with an imagination, having once broached this topic, opened his heart, or at any rate a new wing of his heart, to Kipps, and found no fault with Kipps for a lack of return. He produced a thumbed novelette that had played a part in his sentimental awakening; he proffered it to Kipps, and confessed there was a character in it, a baronet, singularly like himself. This baronet was a person of volcanic passions which he concealed beneath a demeanour of 'icy cynicism'. The utmost expression he permitted himself was to grit his teeth; and now his attention was called to it, Kipps remarked that Sid also had a habit of gritting his teeth – and indeed had had all the morning. They read for a time, and presently Sid talked again. The conception of love Sid made evident was compact of devotion and much spirited fighting and a touch of mystery; but through all that cloud of talk there floated before Kipps a face that was flushed and hair that was tossed aside.

So they budded, sitting on the blackening old wreck in which men had lived and died, looking out to sea, talking of that other sea upon which they must presently embark –

They ceased to talk, and Sid read; but Kipps falling behind with the reading and not wishing to admit that he read slowlier than Sid, whose education was of the inferior elementary school brand, lapsed into meditation.

'I *would* like to 'ave a girl,' said Kipps. 'I mean just to talk to and all that . . .'

A floating object distracted them at last from this obscure topic. They abandoned the wreck and followed the new interest a mile along the beach, bombarding it with stones until it came to land. They had inclined to a view

that it would contain romantic mysteries, but it was simply an ill-preserved kitten – too much even for them. And at last they were drawn dinnerward and went home hungry and pensive side by side.

5

But Kipps's imagination had been warmed by that talk of love, and in the afternoon, when he saw Ann Pornick in the High Street and said 'Hello!' it was a different 'hello' from that of their previous intercourse. And when they had passed they both looked back and caught each other doing so. Yes, he *did* want a girl badly. . .

Afterwards he was distracted by a traction engine going through the town, and his aunt had got some sprats for supper. When he was in bed, however, sentiment came upon him again in a torrent quite abruptly and abundantly, and he put his head under the pillow and whispered very softly, 'I love Ann Pornick,' as a sort of supplementary devotion.

In his subsequent dreams he ran races with Ann, and they lived in a wreck together, and always her face was flushed and her hair about her face. They just lived in a wreck and ran races, and were very, very fond of one another. And their favourite food was rock-chocolate, dates, such as one buys off barrows, and sprats – fried sprats . . .

In the morning he could hear Ann singing in the scullery next door. He listened to her for some time, and it was clear to him that he must put things before her.

Towards dusk that evening they chanced on one another at the gate by the church; but though there was much in his mind, it stopped there with a resolute shyness until he and Ann were out of breath catching cockchafers, and were sitting on that gate of theirs again. Ann sat up upon the gate, dark against vast masses of flaming crimson and darkling purple, and her eyes looked at Kipps from a shadowed face. There came a stillness between them, and quite abruptly he was moved to tell his love.

'Ann,' he said, 'I *do* like you. I wish you was my girl . . . I say, Ann: will you *be* my girl?'

Ann made no pretence of astonishment. She weighed the proposal for a moment with her eyes on Kipps. 'If you like, Artie,' she said lightly. '*I* don't mind if I am.'

'All right,' said Kipps, breathless with excitement, 'then you are.'

'All right,' said Ann.

Something seemed to fall between them, and they no longer looked openly at one another. 'Lor'!' cried Ann suddenly, 'see that one!' and jumped down and darted after a cockchafer that had boomed within a yard of her face. And with that they were girl and boy again . . .

They avoided their new relationship painfully.

They did not recur to it for several days, though they met twice. Both felt that there remained something before this great experience was complete, but there was an infinite diffidence about the next step. Kipps talked in fragments of all sorts of matters, telling particularly of the great things that were being done to make a man and a draper of him; how he had two new pairs of trousers and a black coat and four new shirts. And all the while his imagination was urging him to that unknown next step, and when he was alone and in the dark he became even an enterprising wooer. It became evident to him that it would be nice to take Ann by the hand; even the decorous novelettes Sid affected egged him on to that greater nearness of intimacy.

Then a great idea came to him, in a paragraph called 'Lovers' Tokens' that he read in a torn fragment of *Tit-Bits*. It fell into the measure of his courage – a divided sixpence! He secured his aunt's best scissors, fished a sixpence out of his jejune tin money-box, and jabbed his finger in a varied series of attempts to get it in half. When they met again the sixpence was still undivided. He had not intended to mention the matter to her at that stage, but it came up spontaneously. He endeavoured to explain the theory of broken sixpences and his unexpected failure to break one.

'But what you break it for?' said Ann. 'It's no good if it's broke.'

'It's a Token,' said Kipps.

'Like – ?'

'Oh, you keep half and I keep half, and when we're sep'rated you look at your half and I look at mine – see! Then we think of each other.'

'Oh!' said Ann, and appeared to assimilate this information.

'Only *I* can't get it in 'arf nohow,' said Kipps.

They discussed this difficulty for some time without illumination. Then Ann had a happy thought. 'Tell you what,' she said, starting away from him abruptly and laying a hand on his arm, 'you let *me* 'ave it, Artie. I know where father keeps his file.'

Kipps handed her the sixpence, and they came upon a pause.

'I'll easy do it,' said Ann.

In considering the sixpence side by side, his head had come near her cheek. Quite abruptly he was moved to take his next step into the unknown mysteries of love.

'Ann,' he said, and gulped at his temerity, 'I *do* love you. Straight. I'd do anything for you, Ann. Reely – I would.'

He paused for breath. She answered nothing, but she was no doubt enjoying herself. He came yet closer to her – his shoulder touched hers. 'Ann, I wish you'd – '

He stopped.

'What?' said Ann.

'Ann – lemme kiss you.'

Things seemed to hang for a space; his tone, the drop of his courage,

made the thing incredible as he spoke. Kipps was not of that bold order of wooers who impose conditions.

Ann perceived that she was not prepared for kissing after all. Kissing, she said, was silly, and when Kipps would have displayed a belated enterprise, she flung away from him. He essayed argument. He stood afar off, as it were – the better part of a yard – and said she *might* let him kiss her, and then that he didn't see what good it was for her to be his girl if he couldn't kiss her.

She repeated that kissing was silly. A certain estrangement took them homeward. They arrived in the dusky High Street not exactly together, and not exactly apart, but struggling. They had not kissed, but all the guilt of kissing was between them. When Kipps saw the portly contours of his uncle standing dimly in the shop doorway, his footsteps faltered, and the space between our young couple increased. Above, the window over Pornick's shop was open, and Mrs Pornick was visible, taking the air. Kipps assumed an expression of extreme innocence. He found himself face to face with his uncle's advanced outposts of waistcoat buttons.

'Where ye bin, my boy?'

'Bin for a walk, uncle.'

'Not along of that brat of Pornick's?'

'Along of who?'

'That gell' – indicating Ann with his pipe.

'Oh, no, uncle!' – very faintly.

'Run in, my boy.'

Old Kipps stood aside, with an oblique glance upward, and his nephew brushed clumsily by him and vanished out of sight of the street into the vague obscurity of the little shop. The door closed behind old Kipps with a nervous jangle of its bell, and he set himself to light the single oil lamp that illuminated his shop at nights. It was an operation requiring care and watching, or else it flared and 'smelt'. Often it smelt after all. Kipps for some reason found the dusky living-room with his aunt in it too populous for his feelings, and went upstairs.

'That brat of Pornick's!' It seemed to him that a horrible catastrophe had occurred. He felt he had identified himself inextricably with his uncle, and cut himself off from her for ever by saying 'Oh, no!' At supper he was so visibly depressed that his aunt asked him if he wasn't feeling well. Under this imminent threat of medicine he assumed an unnatural cheerfulness . . .

He lay awake for nearly half an hour that night, groaning because things had all gone wrong – because Ann wouldn't let him kiss her, and because his uncle had called her a brat. It seemed to Kipps almost as though he himself had called her a brat –

There came an interval during which Ann was altogether inaccessible. One, two, three days passed, and he did not see her. Sid he met several times; they went fishing, and twice they bathed; but though Sid lent and received back two further love stories, they talked no more of love. They

kept themselves in accord, however, agreeing that the most flagrantly sentimental story was 'proper'. Kipps was always wanting to speak of Ann, but never daring to do so. He saw her on Sunday evening going off to chapel. She was more beautiful than ever in her Sunday clothes, but she pretended not to see him because her mother was with her. But he thought she pretended not to see him because she had given him up for ever. Brat! – who could be expected ever to forgive that? He abandoned himself to despair, he ceased even to haunt the places where she might be found . . .

6

With paralysing unexpectedness came the end.

Mr Shalford, the draper at Folkestone to whom he was to be bound apprentice, had expressed a wish to 'shape the lad a bit' before the autumn sale. Kipps became aware that his box was being packed, and gathered the full truth of things on the evening before his departure. He became feverishly eager to see Ann just once more. He made silly and needless excuses to go out into the yard, he walked three times across the street without any excuse at all, to look up at the Pornick windows. Still she was hidden. He grew desperate. It was within half an hour of his departure that he came on Sid.

'Hello!' he said; 'I'm orf!'

'Business?'

'Yes.'

Pause.

'I say, Sid. You going 'ome?'

'Straight now.'

'D'you mind? Ask Ann about that.'

'About what?'

'She'll know.'

And Sid said he would. But even that, it seemed, failed to evoke Ann.

At last the Folkestone bus rumbled up, and he ascended. His aunt stood in the doorway to see him off. His uncle assisted with the box and portmanteau. Only furtively could he glance up at the Pornick windows, and still it seemed Ann hardened her heart against him. 'Get up!' said the driver, and the hoofs began to clatter. No – she would not come out even to see him off. The bus was in motion, and old Kipps was going back into his shop. Kipps stared in front of him, assuring himself that he did not care.

He heard a door slam, and instantly craned out his neck to look back. He knew that slam so well. Behold! out of the haberdasher's door a small, untidy figure in homely pink print had shot resolutely into the road and was sprinting in pursuit. In a dozen seconds she was abreast of the bus. At the sight of her Kipps's heart began to beat very quickly, but he made no immediate motion of recognition.

'Artie!' she cried breathlessly. 'Artie! Artie! You know! I got *that*!'

The bus was already quickening its pace, and leaving her behind again, when Kipps realised what 'that' meant. He became animated, he gasped, and, gathering his courage together, he mumbled an incoherent request to the driver to 'stop jest a jiff for sunthin' '. The driver grunted, as the disparity of their years demanded, and then the bus had pulled up, and Ann was below.

She leapt up upon the wheel. Kipps looked down into Ann's face, and it was foreshortened and resolute. He met her eyes just for one second as their hands touched. He was not a reader of eyes. Something passed quickly from hand to hand, something that the driver, alert at the corner of his eye, was not allowed to see. Kipps hadn't a word to say, and all she said was, 'I done it, 'smorning.' It was like a blank space in which something pregnant should have been written and wasn't. Then she dropped down, and the bus moved forward.

After the lapse of about ten seconds it occurred to him to stand and wave his new bowler hat at her over the corner of the bus top, and to shout hoarsely, 'Goo'bye, Ann! Don' forget me – while I'm away!'

She stood in the road looking after him, and presently she waved her hand.

He remained standing unstably, his bright, flushed face looking back at her, and his hair fluffing in the wind, and he waved his hat until at last the bend of the road hid her from his eyes. Then he turned about and sat down, and presently he began to put the half sixpence he held clenched in his hand into his trouser pocket. He looked sideways at the driver, to judge how much he had seen.

Then he fell a-thinking. He resolved that, come what might, when he came back to New Romney at Christmas, he would by hook or by crook kiss Ann.

Then everything would be perfect and right, and he would be perfectly happy.

CHAPTER TWO

The Emporium

When Kipps left New Romney, with a small yellow tin box, a still smaller portmanteau, a new umbrella and a keepsake half-sixpence, to become a draper, he was a youngster of fourteen, thin, with whimsical drakes' tails at the poll of his head, smallish features and eyes that were sometimes very light and sometimes very dark, gifts those of his birth; and by the nature of his training he was indistinct in his speech, confused in his mind and retreating in his manners. Inexorable fate had appointed him to serve his country in commerce, and the same national bias towards private

enterprise and leaving bad alone, which entrusted his general education to Mr Woodrow, now indentured him firmly into the hands of Mr Shalford, of the Folkestone Drapery Bazaar. Apprenticeship is still the recognised English way to the distributing branch of the social service. If Mr Kipps had been so unfortunate as to have been born a German he might have been educated in an elaborate and costly special school ('over-educated – crammed up' – old Kipps) to fit him for his end – such being their pedagogic way. He might . . . But why make unpatriotic reflections in a novel? There was nothing pedagogic about Mr Shalford.

He was an irascible, energetic little man with hairy hands, for the most part under his coat-tails, a long, shiny, bald head, a pointed aquiline nose a little askew, and a neatly trimmed beard. He walked lightly and with a confident jerk, and he was given to humming. He had added to exceptional business 'push', bankruptcy under the old dispensation and judicious matrimony. His establishment was now one of the most considerable in Folkestone, and he insisted on every inch of frontage by alternate stripes of green and yellow down the houses over the shops. His shops were numbered 3, 5 and 7 on the street, and on his billheads '3 to 7'. He encountered the abashed and awestricken Kipps with the praises of his System and himself. He spread himself out behind his desk with a grip on the lapels of his coat and made Kipps a sort of speech. 'We expect y'r to work, y'r know, and we expect y'r to study our interests,' explained Mr Shalford in the regal and commercial plural. 'Our System here is the best system y'r could have. I made it, and I ought to know. I began at the very bottom of the ladder when I was fourteen, and there isn't a step in it I don't know. Not a step. Mr Booch in the desk will give y'r the card of rules and fines. Jest wait a minute.' He pretended to be busy with some dusty memoranda under a paperweight, while Kipps stood in a sort of paralysis of awe regarding his new master's oval baldness. 'Two thous'n' three forty-seven pounds,' whispered Mr Shalford audibly, feigning forgetfulness of Kipps. Clearly a place of great transactions!

Mr Shalford rose, and handing Kipps a blotting-pad and an inkpot to carry – mere symbols of servitude, for he made no use of them – emerged into a counting-house where three clerks had been feverishly busy ever since his door handle had turned. 'Booch,' said Mr Shalford, ' 'ave y'r copy of the rules?' and a downtrodden, shabby little old man, with a ruler in one hand and a quill pen in his mouth, silently held out a small book with green and yellow covers, mainly devoted, as Kipps presently discovered, to a voracious system of fines. He became acutely aware that his hands were full, and that everybody was staring at him. He hesitated a moment before putting the inkpot down to free a hand.

'Mustn't fumble like *that*,' said Mr Shalford as Kipps pocketed the rules. 'Won't do here. Come along, come along,' and he cocked his coat-tails high, as a lady might hold up her dress, and led the way into the shop.

A vast interminable place it seemed to Kipps, with unending shining counters and innumerable faultlessly dressed young men and presently houri-like young women staring at him. Here there was a long vista of gloves dangling from overhead rods, there ribbons and baby-linen. A short young lady in black mittens was making out the account of a customer, and was clearly confused in her addition by Shalford's eagle eye.

A thickset young man with a bald head and a round, very wise face, who was profoundly absorbed in adjusting all the empty chairs down the counter to absolutely equal distances, awoke out of his preoccupation and answered respectfully to a few Napoleonic and quite unnecessary remarks from his employer. Kipps was told that this young man's name was Mr Buggins, and that he was to do whatever Mr Buggins told him to do.

They came round a corner into a new smell, which was destined to be the smell of Kipps's life for many years, the vague, distinctive smell of Manchester goods. A fat man with a large nose jumped – actually jumped – at their appearance, and began to fold a pattern of damask in front of him exactly like an automaton that is suddenly set going.

'Carshot, see to this boy tomorrow,' said the master. 'See he don't fumble. Smart'n 'im up.'

'Yussir,' said Carshot fatly, glanced at Kipps, and resumed his pattern-folding with extreme zeal.

'Whatever Mr Carshot says y'r to do, ye *do*,' said Mr Shalford, trotting onward; and Carshot blew out his face with an appearance of relief.

They crossed a large room full of the strangest things Kipps had ever seen. Ladylike figures, surmounted by black wooden knobs in the place of the refined heads one might have reasonably expected, stood about with a lifelike air of conscious fashion.

'Costume room,' said Shalford.

Two voices engaged in some sort of argument – 'I can assure you, Miss Mergle, you are entirely mistaken – entirely, in supposing I should do anything so unwomanly' – sank abruptly, and they discovered two young ladies, taller and fairer than any of the other young ladies, and with black trains to their dresses, who were engaged in writing at a little table. Whatever they told him to do, Kipps gathered he was to do. He was also, he understood, to do whatever Carshot and Booch told him to do. And there were also Buggins and Mr Shalford. And not to forget or fumble!

They descended into a cellar called 'The Warehouse', and Kipps had an optical illusion of errand boys fighting. Some aerial voice said, 'Teddy!' and the illusion passed. He looked again, and saw quite clearly that they were packing parcels and always would be, and that the last thing in the world that they would or could possibly do was to fight. Yet he gathered from the remarks Mr Shalford addressed to their busy backs that they had been fighting – no doubt at some past period of their lives.

Emerging in the shop again among a litter of toys and what are called

'fancy articles', Shalford withdrew a hand from beneath his coat-tails to indicate an overhead change-carrier. He entered into elaborate calculations to show how many minutes in one year were saved thereby, and lost himself among the figures. 'Seven tums eight seven nine – was it? Or seven eight nine? Now, *now*! Why, when I was a boy your age I c'd do a sum like that as soon as hear it. We'll soon get y'r into better shape than that. Make you Fishent. Well, y'r must take my word it comes to pounds and pounds saved in the year – pounds and pounds. System! System everywhere. Fishency.' He went on murmuring 'Fishency' and 'System' at intervals for some time.

They passed into a yard, and Mr Shalford waved his hand at his three delivery vans all striped green and yellow – 'uniform – green, yell'r – System.' All over the premises were pinned absurd little cards, 'This door locked after 7:30. By order, Edwin Shalford', and the like.

Mr Shalford always wrote 'By order', though it conveyed no earthly meaning to him. He was one of those people who collect technicalities upon them as the Reduvius bug collects dirt. He was the sort of man who is not only ignorant, but absolutely incapable of English. When he wanted to say he had a sixpenny-ha'penny longcloth to sell, he put it thus to startled customers: 'Can DO you one six half, if y' like.' He always omitted pronouns and articles and so forth; it seemed to him the very essence of the efficiently businesslike. His only preposition was 'as' or the compound 'as per'. He abbreviated every word he could; he would have considered himself the laughing-stock of Wood Street if he had chanced to spell *socks* in any way but 'sox'. But, on the other hand, if he saved words here, he wasted them there: he never acknowledged an order that was not an esteemed favour, nor sent a pattern without begging to submit it. He never stipulated for so many months' credit, but bought in November 'as Jan'. It was not only words he abbreviated in his London communications. In paying his wholesalers his 'System' admitted of a constant error in the discount of a penny or twopence, and it 'facilitated business', he alleged, to ignore odd pence in the cheques he wrote. His ledger clerk was so struck with the beauty of this part of the System, that he started a private one on his own account with the stamp box that never came to Shalford's knowledge.

This admirable British merchant would glow with a particular pride of intellect when writing his London orders.

'Ah! do y'r think *you'll* ever be able to write London orders?' he would say with honest pride to Kipps, waiting impatiently long after closing time to take these triumphs of commercial efficiency to post, and so end the interminable day.

Kipps shook his head, anxious for Mr Shalford to get on.

'Now, here, f'example, I've written – see? – "1 piece 1 in cott blkelas 1/ or". What do I mean by that *or*, eh? – d'ye know?'

Kipps promptly hadn't the faintest idea.

'And then, "2 ea silk net as per patts herewith"; *ea*, eh?'

'Dunno, sir.'

It was not Mr Shalford's way to explain things. 'Dear, dear! Pity you couldn't get some c'mercial education at your school. 'Stid of all this lit'ry stuff. Well, my boy, if y'r not a bit sharper y'll never write London orders, *that's* pretty plain. Jest stick stamps on all those letters, and mind y'r stick 'em right way up, and try and profit a little more by the opportunities your aunt and uncle have provided ye. Can't say *what*'ll happen t'ye if ye don't.'

And Kipps, tired, hungry and belated, set about stamping with vigour and despatch.

'Lick the *envelope*,' said Mr Shalford, 'lick the *envelope*,' as though he grudged the youngster the postage-stamp gum. 'It's the little things mount up,' he would say; and, indeed, that was his philosophy of life – to bustle and save, always to bustle and save. His political creed linked Reform, which meant nothing, with Efficiency, which meant a sweated service, and Economy, which meant a sweated expenditure, and his conception of a satisfactory municipal life was to 'keep down the rates'. Even his religion was to save his soul, and to preach a similar cheese-paring to the world.

2

The indentures that bound Kipps to Mr Shalford were antique and complex: they insisted on the latter gentleman's parental privileges; they forbade Kipps to dice and game; they made him over body and soul to Mr Shalford for seven long years, the crucial years of his life. In return there were vague stipulations about teaching the whole art and mystery of the trade to him; but as there was no penalty attached to negligence, Mr Shalford, being a sound, practical businessman, considered this a mere rhetorical flourish, and set himself assiduously to get as much out of Kipps and to put as little into him as he could in the seven years of their intercourse.

What he put into Kipps was chiefly bread and margarine, infusions of chicory and tea-dust, colonial meat by contract at threepence a pound, potatoes by the sack and watered beer. If, however, Kipps chose to buy any supplementary material for growth, Mr Shalford had the generosity to place his kitchen resources at his disposal free – if the fire chanced to be going. He was also allowed to share a bedroom with eight other young Englishmen, and to sleep in a bed which, except in very severe weather, could be made with the help of his overcoat and private underlinen, not to mention newspapers, quite sufficiently warm for any reasonable soul. In addition, Kipps was taught the list of fines; and how to tie up parcels; to know where goods were kept in Mr Shalford's systematised shop; to hold his hands extended upon the counter and to repeat such phrases as, 'What

can I have the pleasure . . . ?' 'No trouble, I 'ssure you,' and the like; to block, fold and measure materials of all sorts; to lift his hat from his head when he passed Mr Shalford abroad, and to practise a servile obedience to a large number of people. But he was not, of course, taught the 'cost' mark of the goods he sold, nor anything of the method of buying such goods. Nor was his attention directed to the unfamiliar social habits and fashions to which his trade ministered. The use of half the goods he saw sold and was presently to assist in selling he did not understand: materials for hangings, cretonnes, chintzes, and the like; serviettes and all the bright, hard white-wear of a well-ordered house; pleasant dress materials, linings, stiffenings – they were to him from first to last no more than things heavy and difficult to handle in bulk, that one folded up, unfolded, cut in lengths and saw dwindle and pass away out into that mysterious happy world in which the Customer dwells. Kipps hurried from piling linen tablecloths, that were collectively as heavy as lead, to eat off oilcloth in a gas-lit dining-room underground; and he dreamt of combing endless blankets beneath his over-coat, spare undershirt and three newspapers. So he had at least the chance of learning the beginnings of philosophy.

In return for these benefits he worked so that he commonly went to bed exhausted and footsore. His round began at half-past six in the morning, when he would descend unwashed and shirtless, in old clothes and a scarf, and dust boxes and yawn, and take down wrappers and clean the windows until eight. Then in half an hour he would complete his toilet and take an austere breakfast of bread and margarine and what only an Imperial Englishman would admit to be coffee, after which refreshment he ascended to the shop for the labours of the day.

Commonly these began with a mighty running to and fro with planks and boxes and goods for Carshot, the window-dresser, who, whether he worked well or ill, nagged persistently by reason of a chronic indigestion, until the window was done. Sometimes the costume window had to be dressed, and then Kipps staggered down the whole length of the shop from the costume room with one after another of those ladylike shapes grasped firmly, but shamefully, each about her single ankle of wood. Such days as there was no window-dressing, there was a mighty carrying and lifting of blocks and bales of goods into piles and stacks. After this there were terrible exercises, at first almost despairfully difficult: certain sorts of goods that came in folded had to be rolled upon rollers, and for the most part refused absolutely to be rolled, at any rate by Kipps; and certain other sorts of goods that came from the wholesalers rolled had to be measured and folded, which folding makes young apprentices wish they were dead. All of it, too, quite avoidable trouble, you know, that is not avoided because of the cheapness of the genteeler sorts of labour and the dearness of forethought in the world. And then consignments of new goods had to be marked off and packed into proper parcels; and Carshot packed like

conjuring tricks, and Kipps packed like a boy with tastes in some other direction – not ascertained. And always Carshot nagged . . .

He had a curious formula of appeal to his visceral economy, had Carshot, that the refinement of the times and the earnest entreaties of my friends oblige me to render by an etiolated paraphrase.

'My Heart and Liver! I never see such a boy,' so I present Carshot's refrain; and even when he was within a foot or so of the customer's face the disciplined ear of Kipps would still at times develop a featureless, inter-calary murmur into – well, 'My Heart and Liver!'

There came a blessed interval when Kipps was sent abroad 'matching'. This consisted chiefly in supplying unexpected defects in buttons, ribbon, lining, and so forth in the dressmaking department. He was given a written paper of orders with patterns pinned thereto, and discharged into the sunshine and interest of the street. Then, until he thought it wise to return and stand the racket of his delay, he was a free man, clear of all reproach.

He made remarkable discoveries in topography, as, for example, that the most convenient way from the establishment of Mr Adolphus Davis to the establishment of Messrs Plummer, Roddis & Tyrrel, two of his principal places of call, is not as is generally supposed down the Sandgate Road, but up the Sandgate Road, round by West Terrace and along the Leas to the lift, watch the lift up and down *twice*, but not longer, because that wouldn't do, back along the Leas, watch the harbour for a short time, and then round by the churchyard, and so (hurrying) into Church Street and Rendezvous Street. But on some exceptionally fine days the route lay through Radnor Park to the pond where the little boys sail ships and there are interesting swans.

He would return to find the shop settling down to the business of serving customers. And now he had to stand by to furnish any help that was necessary to the seniors who served, to carry parcels and bills about the shop, to clear away 'stuff' after each engagement, to hold up curtains until his arms ached, and, what was more difficult than all, to do nothing, and not stare disconcertingly at customers when there was nothing for him to do. He plumbed an abyss of boredom, or stood a mere carcass, with his mind far away fighting the enemies of the Empire, or steering a dream ship perilously into unknown seas. To be recalled sharply to our higher civilisation by some bustling senior's, 'Nar then, Kipps. *Look* alive! Ketch 'old. (My Heart and Liver!)'

At half-past seven o'clock – except on late nights – a feverish activity of 'straightening up' began, and when the last shutter was up outside, Kipps with the speed of an arrow leaving a bow would start hanging wrappers over the fixtures and over the piles of wares upon the counters, preparatory to a vigorous scattering of wet sawdust and the sweeping out of the shop.

Sometimes people would stay long after the shop was closed – 'They don't mind a bit at Shalford's,' these ladies used to say – it is always ladies do

this sort of thing – and while they loitered it was forbidden to touch a wrapper, or take any measures to conclude the day until the doors closed behind them.

Mr Kipps would watch these later customers from the shadow of a stack of goods, and death and disfigurement was the least he wished for them. Rarely much later than nine, a supper of bread and cheese and watered beer awaited him upstairs, and, that consumed, the rest of the day was entirely at his disposal for reading, recreation and the improvement of his mind . . .

The front door was locked at half-past ten, and the gas in the dormitory extinguished at eleven.

3

On Sundays he was obliged to go to church once, and commonly he went twice, for there was nothing else to do. He sat in the free seats at the back; he was too shy to sing, and not always clever enough to keep his place in the Prayer Book, and he rarely listened to the sermon. But he had developed a sort of idea that going to church had a tendency to alleviate life. His aunt wanted to have him confirmed, but he evaded this ceremony for some years.

In the intervals between services he walked about Folkestone with an air of looking for something. Folkestone was not so interesting on Sundays as on weekdays, because the shops were shut; but on the other hand there was a sort of confusing brilliance along the front of the Leas in the afternoon. Sometimes the apprentice next above him would condescend to go with him; but when the apprentice next but one above him condescended to go with the apprentice next above him, then Kipps, being habited as yet in ready-made clothes without tails, and unsuitable therefore to appear in such company, went alone.

Sometimes he would strike out into the country – still as if looking for something he missed – but the rope of meal-times haled him home again; and sometimes he would invest the major portion of the weekly allowance of a shilling that old Booch handed out to him in a sacred concert on the pier. He would sometimes walk up and down the Leas between twenty and thirty times after supper, desiring much the courage to speak to some other person in the multitude similarly employed. Almost invariably he ended his Sunday footsore.

He never read a book; there were none for him to read, and besides, in spite of Mr Woodrow's guidance through a cheap and cheaply annotated edition of *The Tempest* (English Literature), he had no taste that way; he never read any newspapers, except occasionally *Tit-Bits* or a ha'penny 'comic'. His chief intellectual stimulus was an occasional argy-bargy that sprang up between Carshot and Buggins at dinner. Kipps listened as if to unparalleled wisdom and wit, and treasured all the gems of repartee in his

heart against the time when he, too, should be a Buggins and have the chance and courage for speech.

At times there came breaks in this routine – sale times, darkened by extra toil and work past midnight, but brightened by a sprat supper and some shillings in the way of 'premiums'. And every year – not now and then, but every year – Mr Shalford, with parenthetic admiration of his own generosity and glancing comparisons with the austerer days when *he* was apprenticed, conceded Kipps no less than ten days' holiday – ten whole days every year! Many a poor soul at Portland might well envy the fortunate Kipps. Insatiable heart of man! but how those days were grudged and counted as they snatched themselves away from him one after another!

Once a year came stocktaking and at intervals gusts of 'marking off' goods newly arrived. Then the splendours of Mr Shalford's being shone with oppressive brilliancy. 'System!' he would say, 'system. Come! *'ussel!*' and issue sharp, confusing, contradictory orders very quickly. Carshot trotted about, confused, perspiring, his big nose up in the air, his little eye on Mr Shalford, his forehead crinkled, his lips always going to the formula, 'Oh, my Heart and Liver!' The smart junior and the second apprentice vied with one another in obsequious alacrity. The smart junior aspired to Carshot's position, and that made him almost violently subservient to Shalford. They all snapped at Kipps. Kipps held the blotting-pad and the safety inkpot and a box of tickets, and ran and fetched things. If he put the ink down before he went to fetch things Mr Shalford usually knocked it over, and if he took it away Mr Shalford wanted it before he returned. 'You make my tooth ache, Kipps,' Mr Shalford would say. 'You gimme n'ralgia. You got no more System in you than a bad potato.' And at the times when Kipps carried off the inkpot, Mr Shalford would become purple in the face and jab round with his dry pen at imaginary inkpots and swear, and Carshot would stand and vociferate, and the smart junior would run to the corner of the department and vociferate, and the second apprentice would pursue Kipps, vociferating, 'Look Alive, Kipps! Look Alive! Ink, Man! Ink!'

A vague self-disgust, that shaped itself as an intense hate of Shalford and all his fellow creatures, filled the soul of Kipps during these periods of storm and stress. He felt that the whole business was unjust and idiotic, but the why and the wherefore were too much for his unfortunate brain. His mind was a welter. One desire, the desire to dodge some at least of a pelting storm of disagreeable comment, guided him through a fumbling performance of his duties. His disgust was infinite! It was not decreased by the inflamed ankles and sore feet that form a normal incident in the business of making an English draper; and the senior apprentice, Minton, a gaunt, sullen-faced youngster with close-cropped, wiry, black hair, a loose, ugly mouth, and a moustache like a smudge of ink, directed his attention to deeper aspects of the question and sealed his misery.

'When you get too old to work they chuck you away,' said Minton. 'Lor!

you find old drapers everywhere – tramps, beggars, dock labourers, bus conductors – Quod. Anywhere but in a crib.'

'Don't they get shops of their own?'

'Lord! '*Ow* are they to get shops of their own? They 'aven't any capital! How's a draper's shopman to save up five hundred pounds even? I tell you it can't be done. You got to stick to cribs until it's over. I tell you we're in a blessed drainpipe, and we've got to crawl along it till we die.'

The idea that fermented perpetually in the mind of Minton was to 'hit the little beggar slap in the eye' – the little beggar being Mr Shalford – 'and see how his blessed System met that.'

The threat filled Kipps with splendid anticipations whenever Shalford went marking off in Minton's department. He would look at Minton and look at Shalford, and decide where he would best like Shalford hit . . . But for reasons known to himself Shalford never pished and tushed with Minton as he did at the harmless Carshot, and this interesting experiment upon the System was never attempted.

4

There were times when Kipps would lie awake, all others in the dormitory asleep and snoring, and think dismally of the outlook Minton pictured. Dimly he perceived the thing that had happened to him – how the great, stupid machine of retail trade had caught his life into its wheels, a vast, irresistible force which he had neither strength of will nor knowledge to escape. This was to be his life until his days should end. No adventures, no glory, no change, no freedom. Neither – though the force of that came home to him later – might he dream of effectual love and marriage. And there was a terrible something called the 'swap', or 'the key of the street', and 'crib hunting', of which the talk was scanty but sufficient. Night after night he would resolve to enlist, to run away to sea, to set fire to the warehouse, or drown himself; and morning after morning he rose up and hurried downstairs in fear of a sixpenny fine. He would compare his dismal round of servile drudgery with those windy, sunlit days at Littlestone, those windows of happiness shining ever brighter as they receded. The little figure of Ann seemed in all these windows now.

She, too, had happened on evil things. When Kipps went home for the first Christmas after he was bound, that great suspended resolve of his to kiss her flared up to hot determination, and he hurried out and whistled in the yard. There was a still silence, and then old Kipps appeared behind him.

'It's no good your whistling there, my boy,' said old Kipps in a loud, clear tone, designed to be audible over the wall. 'They've cleared out all you 'ad any truck with. *She*'s gone as help to Ashford, my boy. *Help!* Slavey is what

we used to call 'em, but times are changed. Wonder they didn't say lady-'elp while they was about it. It 'ud be like 'em.'

And Sid? Sid had gone, too. 'Arrand boy or somethink,' said old Kipps. 'To one of these here brasted bicycle shops.'

'*Has* 'e!' said Kipps, with a feeling that he had been gripped about the chest, and he turned quickly and went indoors.

Old Kipps, still supposing him present, went on to further observations of an anti-Pornick tendency.

When Kipps got upstairs safe in his own bedroom, he sat down on the bed and stared at nothing. They were caught – they were all caught. All life took on the hue of one perpetual, dismal Monday morning. The Hurons were scattered, the wrecks and the beach had passed away from him, the sun of those warm evenings at Littlestone had set for evermore . . .

The only pleasure left for the brief remainder of his holiday after that was to think he was not in the shop. Even that was transient. Two more days – one more day – half a day. When he went back there were one or two very dismal nights indeed. He went so far as to write home some vague intimation of his feelings about business and his prospects, quoting Minton. But Mrs Kipps answered him, 'Did he want the Pornicks to say he wasn't good enough to be a draper?' This dreadful possibility was of course conclusive in the matter. No, he resolved they should not say he failed at that.

He derived much help from a 'manly' sermon delivered in an enormous voice by a large, fat, sun-red clergyman, just home from a colonial bishopric he had resigned on the plea of ill-health, exhorting him that whatever his hand found to do, he was to do with all his might; and the revision of his catechism preparatory to his confirmation reminded him that it behoved him to do his duty in that state of life into which it had pleased God to call him.

After a time the sorrows of Kipps grew less acute, and save for a miracle the brief tragedy of his life was over. He subdued himself to his position even as his Church required of him, seeing moreover no way out of it.

The earliest mitigation of his lot was that his soles and ankles became indurated to the perpetual standing. The next was an unexpected weekly whiff of freedom that came every Thursday. Mr Shalford, after a brave stand for what he called 'Innyvishal lib'ty' and the 'Idea of my System', a stand which he explained he made chiefly on patriotic grounds, was at last, under pressure of certain of his customers, compelled to fall in line with the rest of the local Early Closing Association, and Mr Kipps could emerge in daylight and go where he listed for long, long hours. Moreover, Minton, the pessimist, reached the end of his appointed time and left – to enlist in a cavalry regiment and go about this planet leading an insubordinate but interesting life, that ended at last in an intimate, vivid and really, you know, by no means painful or tragic night grapple in the Terah Valley. In a little

while Kipps cleaned windows no longer; he was serving customers (of the less important sort) and taking goods out on approval; and presently he was third apprentice, and his moustache was visible, and there were three apprentices whom he might legally snub and cuff. But one was (most dishonestly) too big to cuff in spite of his greener years . . .

5

There came still other distractions, the natural distractions of adolescence, to take his mind off the inevitable. His costume, for example, began to interest him more; he began to realise himself as a visible object, to find an interest in the costume-room mirrors and the eyes of the girl apprentices.

In this he was helped by counsel and example. Pierce, his immediate senior, was by way of being what was called a Masher, and preached his cult. During slack times grave discussions about collars, ties, the cut of trouser legs and the proper shape of a boot-toe, were held in the Manchester department. In due course, Kipps went to a tailor, and his short jacket was replaced by a morning coat with tails. Stirred by this, he purchased at his own expense three stand-up collars to replace his former turndown ones. They were nearly three inches high, higher than those Pierce wore, and they made his neck quite sore and left a red mark under his ears . . . So equipped, he found himself fit company even for this fashionable apprentice, who had now succeeded Minton in his seniority.

Most potent help of all in the business of forgetting his cosmic disaster was this, that so soon as he was in tail coats the young ladies of the establishment began to discover that he was no longer a 'horrid little boy'. Hitherto they had tossed heads at him and kept him in his place. Now they discovered that he was a 'nice boy', which is next door at least to being a 'feller', and in some ways even preferable. It is painful to record that his fidelity to Ann failed at their first onset. I am fully sensible how entirely better this story would be from a sentimental point of view if he had remained true to that early love. Only then it would have been a different story altogether. And at least Kipps was thus far true, that with none of these later loves was there any of that particular quality that linked Ann's flushed face and warmth and the inner things of life so inseparably together. Though they were not without emotions of various sorts.

It was one of the young ladies in the costume-room who first showed by her manner that he was a visible object and capable of exciting interest. She talked to him, she encouraged him to talk to her, she lent him a book she possessed, and darned a sock for him, and said she would be his elder sister. She allowed him to escort her to church with a great air of having induced him to go. Then she investigated his eternal welfare, overcame a certain affectation of virile indifference to religion and extorted a promise that

he would undergo 'confirmation'. This excited the other young lady in the costumes, her natural rival, and she set herself with great charm and subtlety to the capture of the ripening heart of Kipps. She took a more worldly line. She went for a walk with him to the pier on Sunday afternoon, and explained to him how a gentleman must always walk 'outside' a lady on a pavement, and how all gentlemen wore, or at least carried, gloves, and generally the broad beginnings of the British social ideal. Afterwards the ladies exchanged 'words', upon Sabbatical grounds. In this way was the *toga virilis* bestowed on Kipps, and he became recognised as a suitable object for that Platonic Eros whose blunted darts devastate even the very highest-class establishments. In this way, too, did that pervading ambition of the British young man to be if not a 'gentleman' at least mistakably like one, take root in his heart.

He took to these new interests with quite natural and personal zest. He became initiated into the mysteries of 'flirting', and – at a slightly later stage, and with some leading hints from Pierce, who was of a communicative disposition in these matters – of the milder forms of 'spooning'. Very soon he was engaged. Before two years were out he had been engaged six times, and was beginning to be rather a desperate fellow, so far as he could make out. Desperate, but quite gentlemanly, be it understood, and without let or hindrance to the fact that he was, in four brief lessons, 'prepared' by a distant-mannered and gloomy young curate and 'confirmed' a member of the Established Church.

The engagements in drapery establishments do not necessarily involve a subsequent marriage. They are essentially more refined, less coarsely practical, and altogether less binding than the engagements of the vulgar rich. These young ladies do not like not to be engaged – it is so unnatural; and Mr Kipps was as easy to get engaged to as one could wish. There are, from the young lady's point of view, many conveniences in being engaged. You get an escort for church and walks and so forth. It is not quite the thing to walk abroad with a 'feller', much more to 'spoon' with him, when he is neither one's fiancé nor an adopted brother; it is considered either a little *fast*, or else as savouring of the 'walking-out' habits of the servant girls. Now, such is the sweetness of human charity, that the shop young lady in England has just the same horror of doing anything that savours of the servant girl as the lady journalist, let us say, has of anything savouring of the shop girl, or the really quite nice young lady has of anything savouring of any sort of girl who has gone down into the economic battlefield to earn herself a living . . . But the very deepest of these affairs was still among the shallow places of love; at best it was paddling where it is decreed that men must sink or swim. Of the deep and dangerous places, and of the huge buoyant lift of its waves, he tasted nothing. Affairs of clothes and vanities they were, jealousies about a thing said, flatteries and mutual boastings, climaxes in the answering grasp of hands, the temerarious use of Christian

names, culminations in a walk, or a near confidence, or a little pressure more or less. Close-sitting on a seat after twilight, with some little fondling, was indeed the boldest of a lover's adventures, the utmost limit of his enterprises in the service of that stark Great Lady, who is daughter of Uranus and the sea. The 'young ladies' who reigned in his heart came and went like people in an omnibus: there was the vehicle, so to speak, upon the road, and they entered and left it without any cataclysm of emotion. For all that, this development of the sex interest was continuously very interesting to Kipps, and kept him going as much as anything through all these servile years . . .

6

For a tailpiece to this chapter one may vignette one of those little affairs.

It is a bright Sunday afternoon; the scene is a secluded little seat halfway down the front of the Leas, and Kipps is four years older than when he parted from Ann. There is a quite perceptible down upon his upper lip, and his costume is just as tremendous a 'mash' as lies within his means. His collar is so high that it scars his unaggressive jawbone, and his hat has a curly brim, his tie shows taste, his trousers are modestly brilliant, and his boots have light cloth uppers that button at the side. He jabs at the gravel before him with a cheap cane, and glances sideways at Flo Bates, the young lady from the cash desk. She is wearing a brilliant blouse and a gaily trimmed hat. There is an air of fashion about her that might disappear under the analysis of a woman of the world, but which is quite sufficient to make Kipps very proud to be distinguished as her particular 'feller', and to be allowed at temperate intervals to use her Christian name.

The conversation is light and gay in the modern style, and Flo keeps on smiling, good temper being her special charm.

'Ye see, you don' mean what *I* mean,' he is saying.

'Well, what do *you* mean?'

'Not what you mean!'

'Well, tell me.'

'*Ah!* That's another story.'

Pause. They look meaningly at one another.

'You *are* a one for being roundabout,' says the lady.

'Well, you're not so plain, you know.'

'Not plain?'

'No.'

'You don't mean to say I'm roundabout?'

'No. I mean to say . . . though – '

Pause.

'Well?'

'You're not a bit plain – you're' (his voice jumps up to a squeak) 'pretty. See?'

'Oh, get *out!*' her voice lifts also – with pleasure.

She strikes at him with her glove, then glances suddenly at a ring upon her finger. Her smile disappears momentarily. Another pause. Eyes meet and the smile returns.

'I wish I knew – ' says Kipps.

'Knew – ?'

'Where you got that ring.'

She lifts the hand with the ring until her eyes just show (very prettily) over it. 'You'd just *like* to know,' she says slowly, and smiles still more brightly with the sense of successful effect.

'I des say I could guess.'

'I des say you couldn't.'

'Couldn't I?'

'No!'

'Guess it in three.'

'Not the name.'

'Ah!'

'*Ah!*'

'Well, anyhow, lemme look at it.'

He looks at it.

Pause. Giggles, slight struggle, and a slap on Kipps's coat-sleeve. A passer-by appears down the path, and she hastily withdraws her hand.

She glances at the face of the approaching man. They maintain a bashful silence until he has passed . . .

CHAPTER THREE

The Wood-Carving Class

Though these services to Venus Epipontia, the seaside Venus, and these studies in the art of dress, did much to distract his thoughts and mitigate his earlier miseries, it would be mere optimism to present Kipps as altogether happy. A vague dissatisfaction with life drifted about him and every now and again enveloped him like a sea fog. During these periods it was greyly evident that there was something, something vital in life, lacking. For no earthly reason that Kipps could discover, he was haunted by a suspicion that life was going wrong or had already gone wrong in some irrevocable way. The ripening self-consciousness of adolescence developed this into a clearly felt insufficiency. It was all very well to carry gloves, open doors, never say 'Miss' to a girl, and walk 'outside', but were there not other things, conceivably even deeper things, before the complete thing was attained?

For example, certain matters of knowledge. He perceived great bogs of ignorance about him, fumbling traps, where other people, it was alleged, *real* gentlemen and ladies, for example, and the clergy, had knowledge and assurance, bogs which it was sometimes difficult to elude. A girl arrived in the millinery department who could, she said, *speak* French and German. She snubbed certain advances, and a realisation of inferiority blistered Kipps. But he tried to pass the thing off as a joke by saying, 'Parlez-vous Francey,' whenever he met her, and inducing the junior apprentice to say the same.

He even made some dim half-secret experiments towards remedying the deficiencies he suspected. He spent five shillings on five serial numbers of a *Home Educator*, and bought (and even thought of reading) a Shakespeare and a Bacon's *Advancement of Learning* and the poems of Herrick from a chap who was hard up. He battled with Shakespeare all one Sunday afternoon, and found the 'English Literature' with which Mr Woodrow had equipped him had vanished down some crack in his mind. He had no doubt it was very splendid stuff, but he couldn't quite make out what it was all about. There was an occult meaning, he knew, in literature, and he had forgotten it. Moreover, he discovered one day, while taunting the junior apprentice with ignorance, that his 'rivers of England' had also slipped his memory, and he laboriously restored that fabric of rote learning: 'Ty Wear Tees 'Umber . . . '

I suppose some such phase of discontent is a normal thing in every adolescence. The ripening mind seeks something upon which its will may crystallise, upon which its discursive emotions, growing more abundant with each year of life, may concentrate. For many, though not for all, it takes a religious direction, but in those particular years the mental atmosphere of Folkestone was exceptionally free from any revivalistic disturbance that might have reached Kipps's mental being. Sometimes they fall in love. I have known this uneasiness end in different cases in a vow to read one book (not a novel) every week, to read the Bible through in a year, to pass in the Honours division of the London Matriculation examination, to become an accomplished chemist, and never more to tell a lie. It led Kipps finally into Technical Education as we understand it in the south of England.

It was in the last year of his apprenticeship that he had pursued his researches after that missing qualification into the Folkestone Young Men's Association, where Mr Chester Coote prevailed. Mr Chester Coote was a young man of semi-independent means who inherited a share in a house agency, read Mrs Humphry Ward, and took an interest in social work. He was a whitish-faced young man with a prominent nose, pale blue eyes, and a quivering quality in his voice. He was very active upon committees; he was very prominent and useful on all social occasions, in evidence upon platforms and upon all those semi-public occasions when the Great descend.

He lived with an only sister. To Kipps and his kind in the Young Men's Association he read a stimulating paper on 'Self-Help'. He said it was the noblest of all our distinctive English characteristics, and he was very much down upon the 'over-educated' Germans. At the close a young German hairdresser made a few commendatory remarks which developed somehow into an oration on Hanoverian politics. As he became excited he became guttural and obscure; the meeting sniggered cheerfully at such ridiculous English, and Kipps was so much amused that he forgot a private project to ask this Chester Coote how he might set about a little self-help on his own private account in such narrow margins of time as the System of Mr Shalford spared him. But afterwards in the night-time it came to him again.

It was a few months later, and after his apprenticeship was over and Mr Shalford had with depreciatory observations taken him on as an improver at twenty pounds a year, that this question was revived by a casual article on Technical Education in a morning paper that a commercial traveller had left behind him. It played the role of the word in season. Something in the nature of conversion, a faint sort of concentration of purpose, really occurred in him then. The article was written with penetrating vehemence, and it stimulated him to the pitch of enquiring about the local Science and Art Classes, and after he had told everybody in the shop about it and taken the advice of all who supported his desperate resolution, he joined. At first he attended the class in Freehand, that being the subject taught on early-closing night; and he had already made some progress in that extraordinary routine of reproducing freehand 'copies' which for two generations had passed with English people for instruction in art, when the dates of the classes were changed. Thereby just as the March winds were blowing he was precipitated into the wood-carving class, and his mind diverted first to this useful and broadening pursuit, and then to its teacher.

2

The class in wood-carving was an extremely select class, conducted at that time by a young lady named Walshingham, and as this young lady was destined by fortune to teach Kipps a great deal more than wood carving, it will be well if the reader gets the picture of her correctly in mind. She was only a year or so older than he was; she had a pale, intellectual face, dark grey eyes and black hair, which she wore over her forehead in an original and striking way that she had adopted from a picture by Rossetti in the South Kensington Museum. She was slender, so that without ungainliness she had an effect of being tall, and her hands were shapely and white when they came into contrast with hands much exercised in rolling and blocking. She dressed in those loose and pleasant forms and those soft and tempered shades that arose in England in the socialistic-aesthetic epoch and remain to

this day among us as the badge of those who read Turgenev's novels, scorn current fiction, and think on higher planes. I think she was as beautiful as most beautiful people, and to Kipps she was altogether beautiful. She had, Kipps learnt, matriculated at London University, an astounding feat to his imagination; and the masterly way in which she demonstrated how to prod and worry honest pieces of wood into useless and unedifying patterns in relief extorted his utmost admiration.

At first, when Kipps had learnt he was to be taught by a 'girl', he was inclined to resent it, the more so as Buggins had recently been very strong on the gross injustice of feminine employment.

'We have to keep wives,' said Buggins (though as a matter of fact he did not keep even one), 'and how are we to do it with a lot of girls coming in to take the work out of our mouths?'

Afterwards Kipps, in conjunction with Pierce, looked at it from another point of view, and thought it would be rather a 'lark'. Finally, when he saw her, and saw her teaching and coming nearer to him with an impressive deliberation, he was breathless with awe and the quality of her dark, slender femininity.

The class consisted of two girls and a maiden lady of riper years, friends of Miss Walshingham's, and anxious rather to support her in an interesting experiment than to become really expert wood-carvers; an oldish young man with spectacles and a black beard, who never spoke to anyone, and who was evidently too short-sighted to see his work as a whole; a small boy who was understood to have a 'gift' for wood-carving; and a lodging-house keeper who 'took classes' every winter, she told Mr Kipps, as though they were a tonic, and 'found they did her good'. And occasionally Mr Chester Coote – refined and gentlemanly – would come into the class, with or without papers, ostensibly on committee business, but in reality to talk to the less attractive one of the two girl students; and sometimes a brother of Miss Walshingham's, a slender, dark young man with a pale face, and fluctuating resemblances to the young Napoleon, would arrive just at the end of the class-time to see his sister home.

All these personages impressed Kipps with a sense of inferiority that in the case of Miss Walshingham became positively abysmal. The ideas and knowledge they appeared to have, their personal capacity and freedom, opened a new world to his imagination. These people came and went, with a sense of absolute assurance, against an overwhelming background of plaster casts, diagrams and tables, benches and a blackboard – a background that seemed to him to be saturated with recondite knowledge and the occult and jealously guarded tips and secrets that constitute Art and the Higher Life. They went home, he imagined, to homes where the piano was played with distinction and freedom, and books littered the tables, and foreign languages were habitually used. They had complicated meals, no doubt – with serviettes. They 'knew etiquette', and how to avoid all the errors for

which Kipps bought penny manuals, *What to Avoid*, *Common Errors in Speaking*, and the like. He knew nothing about it all – nothing whatever; he was a creature of the outer darkness blinking in an unsuspected light.

He heard them speak easily and freely to one another of examinations, of books and paintings, of 'last year's Academy' – a little contemptuously; and once, just at the end of the class-time, Mr Chester Coote and young Walshingham and the two girls argued about something or other called, he fancied, 'Vagner' or 'Vargner' – they seemed to say it both ways – which presently shaped itself more definitely as the name of a man who made up music. (Carshot and Buggins weren't in it with them.) Young Walshingham, it appeared, said something or other that was an 'epigram', and they all applauded him. Kipps, I say, felt himself a creature of outer darkness, an inexcusable intruder in an altitudinous world. When the epigram happened, he first of all smiled, to pretend he understood, and instantly suppressed the smile to show he did not listen. Then he became extremely hot and uncomfortable, though nobody had noticed either phase.

It was clear his only chance of concealing his bottomless baseness was to hold his tongue, and meanwhile he chipped with earnest care, and abased his soul before the very shadow of Miss Walshingham. She used to come and direct and advise him, with, he felt, an effort to conceal the scorn she had for him; and, indeed, it is true that at first she thought of him chiefly as the clumsy young man with the red ears.

And as soon as he emerged from the first effect of pure and awestricken humility – he was greatly helped to emerge from that condition to a perception of human equality by the need the lodging-house keeper was under to talk while she worked, and as she didn't like Miss Walshingham and her friends very much, and the young man with spectacles was deaf, she naturally talked to Kipps – he perceived that he was in a state of adoration for Miss Walshingham that it seemed almost a blasphemous familiarity to speak of as being in love.

This state, you must understand, had nothing to do with 'flirting' or 'spooning' and that superficial passion that flashes from eye to eye upon the leas and pier – absolutely nothing. That he knew from the first. Her rather pallid, intelligent young face, beneath those sombre clouds of hair, put her in a class apart; towards her the thought of 'attentions' paled and vanished. To approach such a being, to perform sacrifices and to perish obviously for her, seemed the limit he might aspire to, he or any man. For if his love was abasement, at any rate it had this much of manliness, that it covered all his sex. It had not yet come to Kipps to acknowledge any man as his better in his heart of hearts. When one does that the game is played and one grows old indeed.

The rest of his sentimental interests vanished altogether in this great illumination. He meditated about her when he was blocking cretonne; her image was before his eyes at teatime, and blotted out the more immediate

faces, and made him silent and preoccupied, and so careless in his bearing that the junior apprentice, sitting beside him, mocked at and parodied his enormous bites of bread and butter unreproved. He became conspicuously less popular on the 'fancy' side, 'costumes' was chilly with him and 'millinery' cutting. But he did not care. An intermittent correspondence with Flo Bates, that had gone on since she left Mr Shalford's desk for a position at Tunbridge 'nearer home', and which had roused Kipps in its earlier stages to unparalleled heights of epistolatory effort, died out altogether by reason of his neglect. He heard with scarcely a pang that, as a consequence perhaps of his neglect, Flo was 'carrying on with a chap who managed a farm'.

Every Thursday he jabbed and gouged at his wood, jabbing and gouging intersecting circles and diamond traceries, and that laboured inane which our mad world calls ornament, and he watched Miss Walshingham furtively whenever she turned away. The circles in consequence were jabbed crooked, and his panels, losing their symmetry, became comparatively pleasing to the untrained eye – and once he jabbed his finger. He would cheerfully have jabbed all his fingers if he could have found some means of using the opening to express himself of the vague emotions that possessed him. But he shirked conversation just as earnestly as he desired it; he feared that profound general ignorance of his might appear.

3

There came a time when she could not open one of the classroom windows. The man with the black beard pored over his chipping heedlessly . . .

It did not take Kipps a moment to grasp his opportunity. He dropped his gouge and stepped forward. 'Lem *me*,' he said . . .

He could not open the window either!

'Oh, please don't trouble,' she said.

' 'Sno trouble,' he gasped.

Still the sash stuck. He felt his manhood was at stake. He gathered himself together for a tremendous effort, and the pane broke with a snap, and he thrust his hand into the void beyond.

'*There!*' said Miss Walshingham, and the glass fell ringing into the courtyard below.

Then Kipps made to bring his hand back, and felt the keen touch of the edge of the broken glass at his wrist. He turned dolefully. 'I'm tremendously sorry,' he said in answer to the accusation in Miss Walshingham's eyes. 'I didn't think it would break like that' – as if he had expected it to break in some quite different and entirely more satisfactory manner. The boy with the gift for wood-carving, having stared at Kipps's face for a moment, became involved in a Laocoön struggle with a giggle.

'You've cut your wrist,' said one of the girl friends, standing up and pointing. She was a pleasant-faced, greatly freckled girl, with a helpful disposition, and she said, 'You've cut your wrist,' as brightly as if she had been a trained nurse.

Kipps looked down, and saw a swift line of scarlet rush down his hand. He perceived the other man student regarding this with magnified eyes. 'You *have* cut your wrist,' said Miss Walshingham, and Kipps regarded his damage with greater interest.

'He's cut his wrist,' said the maiden lady to the lodging-house keeper, and seemed in doubt what a lady should do. 'It's – ' she hesitated at the word 'bleeding', and nodded to the lodging-house keeper instead.

'Dreadfully,' said the maiden lady, and tried to look and tried not to look at the same time.

'Of *course* he's cut his wrist,' said the lodging-house keeper, momentarily quite annoyed at Kipps; and the other young lady, who thought Kipps rather common, went on quietly with her wood-cutting with an air of its being the proper thing to do – though nobody else seemed to know it.

'You must tie it up,' said Miss Walshingham.

'We must tie it up,' said the freckled girl.

'I 'adn't the slightest idea that window was going to break like that,' said Kipps, with candour. 'Nort the slightest.'

He glanced again at the blood on his wrist, and it seemed to him that it was on the very point of dropping on the floor of that cultured classroom. So he very neatly licked it off, feeling at the same time for his handkerchief. 'Oh, *don't!*' said Miss Walshingham as he did so, and the girl with the freckles made a movement of horror. The giggle got the better of the boy with the gift, and celebrated its triumph by unseemly noises; in spite of which it seemed to Kipps at the moment that the act that had made Miss Walshingham say, 'Oh, *don't!*' was rather a desperate and manly treatment of what was after all a creditable injury.

'It ought to be tied up,' said the lodging-house keeper, holding her chisel upright in her hand. 'It's a bad cut to bleed like that.'

'We must tie it up,' said the freckled girl, and hesitated in front of Kipps. 'Have you got a handkerchief?' she said.

'I dunno 'ow I managed *not* to bring one,' said Kipps. 'I – Not 'aving a cold I suppose some'ow I didn't think – '

He checked a further flow of blood.

The girl with the freckles caught Miss Walshingham's eye, and held it for a moment. Both glanced at Kipps's injury. The boy with the gift, who had reappeared with a chastened expression from some noisy pursuit beneath his desk, made the neglected motions of one who proffers shyly. Miss Walshingham under the spell of the freckled girl's eye produced a handkerchief. The voice of the maiden lady could be heard in the background. 'I've been through all the technical education ambulance classes

twice, and I know you go *so* if it's a vein, and *so* if it's an artery – at least you go *so* for one and *so* for the other, whichever it may be; but . . . '

'If you will give me your hand,' said the freckled girl, and proceeded with Miss Walshingham's assistance to bandage Kipps in a most businesslike way. Yes, they actually bandaged Kipps. They pulled up his cuff – happily his cuffs were not a very frayed pair – and held his wrist, and wrapped the soft handkerchief round it, and tightened the knot together. And Miss Walshingham's face, the face of that almost divine Over-human, came close to the face of Kipps.

'We're not hurting you, are we?' she said.

'Not a bit,' said Kipps, as he would have said if they had been sawing his arm off.

'We're not experts, you know,' said the freckled girl.

'I'm sure it's a dreadful cut,' said Miss Walshingham.

'It ain't much reely,' said Kipps; 'and you're taking a lot of trouble. I'm sorry I broke that window. I can't think what I could have been doing.'

'It isn't so much the cut at the time, it's the poisoning afterwards,' came the voice of the maiden lady.

'Of course I'm quite willing to pay for the window,' panted Kipps opulently.

'We must make it just as tight as possible, to stop the bleeding,' said the freckled girl.

'I don't think it's much reely,' said Kipps. 'I'm awful sorry I broke that window, though.'

'Put your finger on the knot, dear,' said the freckled girl.

'Eh?' said Kipps; 'I mean – '

Both the young ladies became very intent on the knot, and Mr Kipps was very red and very intent upon the two young ladies.

'Mortified, and had to be sawn off,' said the maiden lady.

'Sawn off?' said the lodging-house keeper.

'Sawn *right* off,' said the maiden lady, and jabbed at her mangled design.

'*There*,' said the freckled girl, 'I think that ought to do. You're sure it's not too tight?'

'Not a bit,' said Kipps.

He met Miss Walshingham's eye, and smiled to show how little he cared for wounds and pain. 'It's only a little cut,' he added.

The maiden lady appeared as an addition to their group. 'You should have washed the wound, dear,' she said. 'I was just telling Miss Collis.' She peered through her glasses at the bandage. 'That doesn't look *quite* right,' she remarked critically. 'You should have taken the ambulance classes. But I suppose it will have to do. Are you hurting?'

'Not a bit,' said Kipps, and he smiled at them all with the air of a brave soldier in hospital.

'I'm sure it *must* hurt,' said Miss Walshingham.

'Anyhow, you're a very good patient,' said the girl with the freckles.

Mr Kipps became quite pink. 'I'm only sorry I broke the window – that's all,' he said. 'But who would have thought it was going to break like that?'

Pause.

'I'm afraid you won't be able to go on carving tonight,' said Miss Walshingham.

'I'll try,' said Kipps. 'It reelly doesn't hurt – not anything to matter.'

Presently Miss Walshingham came to him as he carved heroically with his hand bandaged in her handkerchief. There was a touch of novel interest in her eyes. 'I'm afraid you're not getting on very fast,' she said.

The freckled girl looked up and regarded Miss Walshingham.

'I'm doing a little, anyhow,' said Kipps. 'I don't want to waste any time. A feller like me hasn't much time to spare.'

It struck the girls that there was a quality of modest disavowal about that 'feller like me'. It gave them a light into this obscure person, and Miss Walshingham ventured to commend his work as 'promising' and to ask whether he meant to follow it up. Kipps didn't 'altogether know' – 'things depended on so much', but if he was in Folkestone next winter he certainly should. It did not occur to Miss Walshingham at the time to ask why his progress in art depended upon his presence in Folkestone. There were some more questions and answers – they continued to talk to him for a little time, even when Mr Chester Coote had come into the room – and when at last the conversation had died out it dawned upon Kipps just how much his cut wrist had done for him –

He went to sleep that night revising that conversation for the twentieth time, treasuring this and expanding that, and inserting things he might have said to Miss Walshingham, things he might still say about himself – in relation, more or less explicit, to her. He wasn't quite sure if he wouldn't like his arm to mortify a bit, which would make him interesting, or to heal up absolutely, which would show the exceptional purity of his blood . . .

4

The affair of the broken window happened late in April, and the class came to an end in May. In that interval there were several small incidents and great developments of emotion. I have done Kipps no justice if I have made it seem that his face was unsightly. It was, as the freckled girl pointed out to Helen Walshingham, an 'interesting' face, and that aspect of him which presented chiefly erratic hair and glowing ears ceased to prevail.

They talked him over, and the freckled girl discovered there was something 'wistful' in his manner. They detected a 'natural delicacy', and the freckled girl set herself to draw him out from that time forth. The freckled girl was nineteen, and very wise and motherly and benevolent, and really

she greatly preferred drawing out Kipps to wood-carving. It was quite evident to her that Kipps was in love with Helen Walshingham, and it struck her as a queer and romantic and pathetic and extremely interesting phenomenon. And as at that time she regarded Helen as 'simply lovely', it seemed only right and proper that she should assist Kipps in his modest efforts to place himself in a state of absolute *abandon* upon her altar.

Under her sympathetic management the position of Kipps was presently defined quite clearly. He was unhappy in his position – misunderstood. He told her he 'didn't seem to get on like' with customers, and she translated this for him as his being 'too sensitive'. The discontent with his fate in life, the dreadful feeling that education was slipping by him, troubles that time and usage were glazing over a little, revived to their old acuteness but not to their old hopelessness. As a basis for sympathy, indeed, they were even a source of pleasure.

And one day at dinner it happened that Carshot and Buggins fell to talking of 'these here writers', and how Dickens had been a labeller of blacking and Thackeray 'an artist who couldn't sell a drawing', and how Samuel Johnson had walked to London without any boots, having thrown away his only pair 'out of pride'.

'It's luck,' said Buggins, 'to a very large extent. They just happen to hit on something that catches on, and there you are!'

'Nice easy life they have of it, too,' said Miss Mergle. 'Write just an hour or so, and done for the day! Almost like gentlefolks.'

'There's more work in it than you'd think,' said Carshot, stooping to a mouthful.

'I wouldn't mind changing, for all that,' said Buggins. 'I'd like to see one of these here authors marking off with Jimmy.'

'I think they copy from each other a good deal,' said Miss Mergle.

'Even then (chup, chup, chup),' said Carshot, 'there's writing it out in their own hands.'

They proceeded to enlarge upon the literary life, on its ease and dignity, on the social recognition accorded to those who led it, and on the ample gratifications their vanity achieved. 'Pictures everywhere – never get a new suit without being photographed – almost like Royalty,' said Miss Mergle.

And all this talk impressed the imagination of Kipps very greatly. Here was a class that seemed to bridge the gulf. On the one hand essentially Low, but by factitious circumstances capable of entering upon those levels of social superiority to which all true Englishmen aspire, those levels from which one may tip a butler, scorn a tailor, and even commune with those who lead 'men' into battle. 'Almost like gentlefolks' – that was it! He brooded over these things in the afternoon, until they blossomed into daydreams. Suppose, for example, he had chanced to write a book, a well-known book, under an assumed name, and yet kept on being a draper all the time . . . Impossible, of course; but *suppose* – it made quite a long dream.

And at the next wood-carving class he let it be drawn from him that his real choice in life was to be a Nawther – 'only one doesn't get a chance'.

After that there were times when Kipps had that pleasant sense that comes of attracting interest. He was a mute, inglorious Dickens, or at any rate something of that sort, and they were all taking him at that. The discovery of this indefinable 'something' in him, the development of which was now painfully restricted and impossible, did much to bridge the gulf between himself and Miss Walshingham. He was unfortunate, he was futile, but he was not 'common'. Even now with help . . . ? The two girls, and the freckled girl in particular, tried to 'stir him up' to some effort to do his imputed potentialities justice. They were still young enough to believe that to nice and niceish members of the male sex – more especially when under the stimulus of feminine encouragement – nothing is finally impossible.

The freckled girl was, I say, the stage manager of this affair, but Miss Walshingham was the presiding divinity. A touch of proprietorship came into her eyes at times when she looked at him. He was hers – unconditionally – and she knew it.

To her directly Kipps scarcely ever made a speech. The enterprising things that he was continually devising to say to her, he usually did not say, or he said them in a suitably modified form to the girl with the freckles. And one day the girl with the freckles smote him to the heart. She said to him, with the faintest indication of her head across the classroom to where her friend reached a cast from the shelf, 'I do think Helen Walshingham is sometimes the most lovely person in the world. Look at her now!'

Kipps gasped for a moment. The moment lengthened, and she regarded him as an intelligent young surgeon might regard an operation without anaesthetics.

'You're right,' he said, and then looked at her with an entire abandonment of visage. She coloured under his glare of silent avowal, and he blushed brightly. 'I think so, too,' he said hoarsely, cleared his throat, and after a meditative moment proceeded sacramentally with his wood-carving.

'You *are* wonderful,' said the freckled girl to Miss Walshingham, apropos of nothing, as they went on their way home together. 'He simply adores you.'

'But, my dear, what have I done?' said Helen.

'That's just it,' said the freckled girl. 'What *have* you done?'

And then with a terrible swiftness came the last class of the course, to terminate this relationship altogether. Kipps was careless of dates, and the thing came upon him with an effect of abrupt surprise. Just as his petals were expanding so hopefully, 'Finis', and the thing was at an end. But Kipps did not fully appreciate that the end was indeed and really and truly the end, until he was back in the Emporium after the end was over.

The end began practically in the middle of the last class, when the freckled girl broached the topic of terminations. She developed the

question of just how he was going on after the class ended. She hoped he would stick to certain resolutions of self-improvement he had breathed. She said quite honestly that he owed it to himself to develop his possibilities. He expressed firm resolve, but dwelt on difficulties. He had no books. She instructed him how to get books from the public library. He was to get a form of application for a ticket signed by a ratepayer; and he said 'of course', when she said Mr Shalford would do that, though all the time he knew perfectly well it would 'never do' to ask Mr Shalford for anything of the sort. She explained that she was going to North Wales for the summer, information he received without immediate regret. At intervals he expressed his intention of going on with wood-carving when the summer was over, and once he added, 'if – '

She considered herself extremely delicate not to press for the completion of that 'if – '

After that talk there was an interval of languid wood carving and watching Miss Walshingham.

Then presently there came a bustle of packing, a great ceremony of hand-shaking all round by Miss Collis and the maiden lady of ripe years, and then Kipps found himself outside the classroom, on the landing with his two friends. It seemed to him he had only just learnt that this was the last class of all. There came a little pause, and the freckled girl suddenly went back into the classroom, and left Kipps and Miss Walshingham alone together for the first time. Kipps was instantly breathless. She looked at his face with a glance that mingled sympathy and curiosity, and held out her white hand.

'Well, goodbye, Mr Kipps,' she said.

He took her hand and held it. 'I'd do anything,' said Kipps, and had not the temerity to add, 'for you.' He stopped awkwardly. He shook her hand and said, 'Goodbye.'

There was a little pause.

'I hope you will have a pleasant holiday,' she said.

'I shall come back to the class next year, anyhow,' said Kipps valiantly, and turned abruptly to the stairs.

'I hope you will,' said Miss Walshingham.

He turned back towards her. 'Reelly?' he said.

'I hope everybody will come back.'

'I will – anyhow,' said Kipps. 'You may count on that,' and he tried to make his tones significant.

They looked at one another through a little pause.

'Goodbye,' she said.

Kipps lifted his hat. She turned towards the classroom.

'Well?' said the freckled girl, coming back towards her.

'Nothing,' said Helen. 'At least – presently.' And she became very energetic about some scattered tools on a desk.

The freckled girl went out and stood for a moment at the head of the stairs. When she came back she looked very hard at her friend. The incident struck her as important – wonderfully important. It was unassimilable, of course, and absurd, but there it was, the thing that is so cardinal to a girl, the emotion, the subservience, the crowning triumph of her sex. She could not help feeling that Helen took it, on the whole, a little too hardly.

CHAPTER FOUR

Chitterlow

The hour of the class on the following Thursday found Kipps in a state of nearly incredible despondency. He was sitting with his eyes on the reading-room clock, his chin resting on his fists and his elbows on the accumulated comic papers that were comic, alas, in vain! He paid no heed to the little man in spectacles glaring opposite to him, famishing for *Fun*. In this place it was he had sat night after night, each night more blissful than the last, waiting until it should be time to go to Her! And then – bliss! And now the hour had come and there was no class! There would be no class now until next October; it might be there would never be a class so far as he was concerned again.

It might be there would never be a class again, for Shalford, taking exception to a certain absent-mindedness that led to mistakes and more particularly to the ticketing of several articles in Kipps's Manchester window upside down, had been 'on to' him for the past few days in an exceedingly onerous manner.

He sighed profoundly, pushed the comic papers back – they were rent away from him instantly by the little man in spectacles – and tried the old engravings of Folkestone in the past that hung about the room. But these, too, failed to minister to his bruised heart. He wandered about the corridors for a time and watched the library indicator for awhile. Wonderful thing that! But it did not hold him for long. People came and laughed near him and that jarred with him dreadfully. He went out of the building and a beastly cheerful barrel-organ mocked him in the street. He was moved to a desperate resolve to go down to the beach. There it might be he would be alone. The sea might be rough – and attuned to him. It would certainly be dark.

'If I 'ad a penny I'm blest if I wouldn't go and chuck myself off the end of the pier . . . *She*'d never miss me . . . ' He followed a deepening vein of thought.

'Penny though! It's tuppence,' he said after a space.

He went down Dover Street in a state of profound melancholia – at the pace and mood, as it were, of his own funeral procession – and he crossed at

the corner of Tontine Street heedless of all mundane things. And there it was that Fortune came upon him, in disguise and with a loud shout, the shout of a person endowed with an unusually rich, full voice, followed immediately by a violent blow in the back.

His hat was over his eyes and an enormous weight rested on his shoulders and something kicked him in the back of his calf.

Then he was on all fours in some mud that Fortune, in conjunction with the Folkestone corporation and in the pursuit of equally mysterious ends, had heaped together even lavishly for his reception.

He remained in that position for some seconds awaiting further developments and believing almost anything broken before his heart. Gathering at last that this temporary violence of things in general was over, and being perhaps assisted by a clutching hand, he arose, and found himself confronting a figure holding a bicycle and thrusting forward a dark face in anxious scrutiny.

'You aren't hurt, matey?' gasped the figure.

'Was that *you* 'it me?' said Kipps.

'It's these handles, you know,' said the figure with an air of being a fellow sufferer. 'They're too *low*. And when I go to turn, if I don't remember, Bif! – and I'm *in*to something.'

'Well – you give me a oner in the back – anyhow,' said Kipps, taking stock of his damages.

'I was coming downhill, you know,' explained the bicyclist. 'These little Folkestone hills are a Fair Treat. It isn't as though I'd been on the level. I came rather a whop.'

'You did *that*,' said Kipps.

'I was back-pedalling for all I was worth anyhow,' said the bicyclist. 'Not that I *am* worth much back-pedalling.'

He glanced round and made a sudden movement almost as if to mount his machine. Then he turned as rapidly to Kipps again, who was now stooping down, pursuing the tale of his injuries.

'Here's the back of my trouser leg all tore down,' said Kipps, 'and I believe I'm bleeding. You reely ought to be more careful – '

The stranger investigated the damage with a rapid movement. 'Holy Smoke, so you are!' He laid a friendly hand on Kipps's arm. 'I say – look here! Come up to my diggings and sew it up. I'm –Of course I'm to blame, and I say – ' his voice sank to a confidential friendliness. 'Here's a slop. Don't let on I ran you down. Haven't a lamp, you know. Might be a bit awkward, for *me*.'

Kipps looked up towards the advancing policeman. The appeal to his generosity was not misplaced. He immediately took sides with his assailant. He stood up as the representative of the law drew nearer. He assumed an air which he considered highly suggestive of an accident not having happened.

'All right,' he said, 'go on!'

'Right you are,' said the cyclist promptly, and led the way, and then, apparently with some idea of deception, called over his shoulder, 'I'm tremendous glad to have met you, old chap.

'It really isn't a hundred yards,' he said after they had passed the police-man, 'it's just round the corner.'

'Of course,' said Kipps, limping slightly, 'I don't want to get a chap into trouble. Accidents *will* happen. Still – '

'Oh! *rather*! I believe you. Accidents *will* happen. Especially when you get *me* on a bicycle.' He laughed. 'You aren't the first I've run down, not by any manner of means! I don't think you can be hurt much either. It isn't as though I was scorching. You didn't see me coming. I was back-pedalling like anything. Only naturally it seems to you I must have been coming fast. And I did all I could to ease off the bump as I hit you. It was just the treadle I think came against your calf. But it was All Right of you about that policeman, you know. That was a Fair Bit of All Right. Under the Circs, if you'd told him I was riding it might have been forty bob! Forty bob! I'd have had to tell 'em Time is Money just now for Mr H. C.

'I shouldn't have blamed you either, you know. Most men after a bump like that might have been spiteful. The least I can do is to stand you a needle and thread. And a clothes brush. It isn't everyone who'd have taken it like you.

'Scorching! Why if I'd been scorching you'd have – coming as we did – you'd have been knocked silly.

'But I tell you, the way you caught on about that slop was something worth seeing. When I asked you, I didn't half expect it. Bif! Right off. Cool as a cucumber. Had your line at once. I tell you that there isn't many men would have acted as you have done, I *will* say that. You acted like a gentle-man over that slop.'

Kipps's first sense of injury disappeared. He limped along a pace or so behind, making depreciatory noises in response to these flattering remarks and taking stock of the very appreciative person who uttered them.

As they passed the lamps he was visible as a figure with a slight anterior plumpness, progressing buoyantly on knickerbockered legs, with quite enormous calves, legs that, contrasting with Kipps's own narrow practice, were even exuberantly turned out at the knees and toes. A cycling cap was worn very much on one side, and from beneath it protruded carelessly straight wisps of dark red hair, and ever and again an ample nose came into momentary view round the corner. The muscular cheeks of this person and a certain generosity of chin he possessed were blue shaven and he had no moustache. His carriage was spacious and confident, his gestures up and down the narrow deserted back street they traversed were irresistibly suggestive of ownership; a succession of broadly gesticulating shadows were born squatting on his feet, and grew and took possession of the road, and reunited at last with the shadows of the infinite as lamp after lamp was

passed. Kipps saw by the flickering light of one of them that they were in Little Fenchurch Street, and then they came round a corner sharply into a dark court and stopped at the door of a particularly ramshackle looking little house, held up between two larger ones, like a drunken man between policemen.

The cyclist propped his machine carefully against the window, produced a key and blew down it sharply. 'The lock's a bit tricky,' he said, and devoted himself for some moments to the task of opening the door. Some mechanical catastrophe ensued and the door was open.

'You'd better wait here a bit while I get the lamp,' he remarked to Kipps; 'very likely it isn't filled,' and vanished into the blackness of the passage. 'Thank God for matches!' he said, and Kipps had an impression of a passage in the transitory pink flare and the bicyclist disappearing into a farther room. Kipps was so much interested by these things that for the time he forgot his injuries altogether.

An interval and Kipps was dazzled by a pink shaded kerosene lamp. 'You go in,' said the red-haired man, 'and I'll bring in the bike,' and for a moment Kipps was alone in the lamp-lit room. He took in rather vaguely the shabby ensemble of the little apartment, the round table covered with a torn, red, glass-stained cover on which the lamp stood, a mottled looking-glass over the fireplace reflecting this, a disused gas bracket, an extinct fire, a number of dusty postcards and memoranda stuck round the glass, a dusty, crowded paper-rack on the mantel with a number of cabinet photographs, a table littered with papers and cigarette ash and a syphon of soda water. Then the cyclist reappeared and Kipps saw his blue-shaved, rather animated face and bright reddish-brown eyes for the first time. He was a man perhaps ten years older than Kipps, but his beardless face made them in a way contemporary.

'You behaved all right about that policeman – anyhow,' he repeated as he came forward.

'I don't see 'ow else I could 'ave done,' said Kipps quite modestly. The cyclist scanned his guest for the first time and decided upon hospitable details.

'We'd better let that mud dry a bit before we brush it. Whisky there is, good Old Methusaleh, Canadian Rye, and there's some brandy that's all right. Which'll you have?'

'*I* dunno,' said Kipps, taken by surprise, and then seeing no other course but acceptance, 'well – whisky, then.'

'Right you are, old boy, and if you'll take my advice you'll take it neat. I may not be a particular judge of this sort of thing, but I do know Old Methusaleh pretty well. Old Methusaleh – three stars. That's me! Good old Harry Chitterlow and good Old Methusaleh. Leave 'em together. Bif! He's gone!'

He laughed loudly, looked about him, hesitated and retired, leaving

Kipps in possession of the room and free to make a more precise examination of its contents.

2

He particularly remarked the photographs that adorned the apartment. They were chiefly photographs of ladies, in one case in tights, which Kipps thought a 'bit 'ot', but one represented the bicyclist in the costume of some remote epoch. It did not take Kipps long to infer that the others were probably actresses and that his host was an actor, and the presence of the half of a large, coloured playbill seemed to confirm this. A note framed in an Oxford frame that was a little too large for it he presently demeaned himself to read. 'Dear Mr Chitterlow,' it ran its brief course, 'if after all you will send the play you spoke of I will endeavour to read it,' followed by a stylish but absolutely illegible signature, and across this was written in pencil, 'What price, Harry, now?' And in the shadow by the window was a rough and rather able sketch of the bicyclist in chalk on brown paper, calling particular attention to the curvature of the forward lines of his hull and calves and the jaunty carriage of his nose, and labelled unmistakably 'Chitterlow'. Kipps thought it 'rather a take-off'. The papers on the table by the syphon were in manuscript, Kipps observed, manuscript of a particularly convulsive and blottesque sort and running obliquely across the page.

Presently he heard the metallic clamour as if of a series of irreparable breakages with which the lock of the front door discharged its function, and then Chitterlow reappeared, a little out of breath as if from running and with a starry labelled bottle in his large, freckled hand.

'Sit down, old chap,' he said, 'sit down. I had to go out for it after all. Wasn't a solitary bottle left. However, it's all right now we're here. No, don't sit on that chair, there's sheets of my play on that. That's the one – with the broken arm. I think this glass is clean, but anyhow wash it out with a squizz of syphon and shy it in the fireplace. Here! I'll do it! Lend it here!'

As he spoke Mr Chitterlow produced a corkscrew from a table drawer, attached and overcame good Old Methusaleh's cork in a style a bartender might envy, washed out two tumblers in his simple, effectual manner, and poured a couple of inches of the ancient fluid into each. Kipps took his tumbler, said 'Thenks' in an offhand way, and after a momentary hesitation whether he should say, 'Here's to you!' or not, put it to his lips without that ceremony. For a space fire in his throat occupied his attention to the exclusion of other matters, and then he discovered Mr Chitterlow with an intensely bulldog pipe alight, seated on the opposite side of the empty fireplace and pouring himself out a second dose of whisky.

'After all,' said Mr Chitterlow, with his eye on the bottle and a little smile

wandering to hide amidst his larger features, 'this accident might have been worse. I wanted someone to talk to a bit, and I didn't want to go to a pub, leastways not a Folkestone pub, because as a matter of fact I'd promised Mrs Chitterlow, who's away, not to, for various reasons – though of course if I'd wanted to I'm just that sort that should have all the same – and here we are! It's curious how one runs up against people out bicycling!'

'Isn't it!' said Kipps, feeling that the time had come for him to say something.

'Here we are, sitting and talking like old friends, and half an hour ago we didn't know we existed. Leastways we didn't know each other existed. I might have passed you in the street perhaps and you might have passed me, and how was I to tell that, put to the test, you would have behaved as decently as you have behaved. Only it happened otherwise, that's all. You're not smoking!' he said. 'Have a cigarette?'

Kipps made a confused reply that took the form of not minding if he did, and drank another sip of Old Methusaleh in his confusion. He was able to follow the subsequent course of that sip for quite a long way. It was as though the old gentleman was brandishing a burning torch through his vitals, lighting him here and lighting him there until at last his whole being was in a glow. Chitterlow produced a tobacco pouch and cigarette papers and, with an interesting parenthesis that was a little difficult to follow about some lady named Kitty something or other who had taught him the art when he was as yet only what you might call a nice boy, made Kipps a cigarette, and with a consideration that won Kipps's gratitude suggested that after all he might find a little soda water an improvement with the whisky. 'Some people like it that way,' said Chitterlow, and then with voluminous emphasis, '*I don't.*'

Emboldened by the weakened state of his enemy, Kipps promptly swallowed the rest of him and had his glass at once hospitably replenished. He began to feel he was of a firmer consistency than he commonly believed, and turned his mind to what Chitterlow was saying with the resolve to play a larger part in the conversation than he had hitherto done. Also he smoked through his nose quite successfully, an art he had only very recently acquired.

Meanwhile Chitterlow explained that he was a playwright, and the tongue of Kipps was unloosened to respond that he knew a chap, or rather one of their fellows knew a chap, or at least to be perfectly correct this fellow's brother did, who had written a play. In response to Chitterlow's enquiries, he could not recall the title of the play, nor where it had appeared, nor the name of the manager who produced it, though he thought the title was something about 'Love's Ransom', or something like that.

'He made five 'undred pounds by it, though,' said Kipps. 'I know that.'

'That's nothing,' said Chitterlow, with an air of experience that was

extremely convincing. 'Nothing. May seem a big sum to *you*, but *I* can assure you it's just what one gets any day. There's any amount of money, an-ny amount, in a good play.'

'I des say,' said Kipps, drinking.

'Any amount of money!'

Chitterlow began a series of illustrative instances. He was clearly a person of quite unequalled gift for monologue. It was as though some conversational dam had burst upon Kipps, and in a little while he was drifting along upon a copious rapid of talk about all sorts of theatrical things by one who knows all about them, and quite incapable of anticipating whither that rapid meant to carry him. Presently somehow they had got to anecdotes about well-known theatrical managers – little Teddy Bletherskite, artful old Chumps and the magnificent Behemoth, 'petted to death, you know, fair sickened, by all these society women'. Chitterlow described various personal encounters with these personages, always with modest self-depreciation, and gave Kipps a very amusing imitation of old Chumps in a state of intoxication. Then he took two more stiff doses of Old Methusaleh in rapid succession.

Kipps reduced the hither end of his cigarette to a pulp as he sat 'des saying' and 'quite believing' Chitterlow in the sagest manner and admiring the easy way in which he was getting on with this very novel and entertaining personage. He had another cigarette made for him, and then Chitterlow, assuming by insensible degrees more and more of the manner of a rich and successful playwright being interviewed by a young admirer, set himself to answer questions which sometimes Kipps asked and sometimes Chitterlow, about the particulars and methods of his career. He undertook this self-imposed task with great earnestness and vigour, treating the matter indeed with such fullness that at times it seemed lost altogether under a thicket of parentheses, footnotes and episodes that branched and budded from its stem. But it always emerged again, usually by way of illustration to its own degressions. Practically it was a mass of material for the biography of a man who had been everywhere and done everything (including the Hon. Thomas Norgate, which was a record), and in particular had acted with great distinction and profit (he dated various anecdotes, 'when I was getting thirty, or forty, or fifty dollars a week') throughout America and the entire civilised world.

And as he talked on and on in that full, rich, satisfying voice he had, and as Old Methusaleh, indisputably a most drunken old reprobate of a whisky, busied himself throughout Kipps, lighting lamp after lamp until the entire framework of the little draper was illuminated and glowing like some public building on a festival, behold Chitterlow and Kipps with him and the room in which they sat were transfigured! Chitterlow became in very truth that ripe, full man of infinite experience and humour and genius, fellow of Shakespeare and Ibsen and Maeterlinck (three names he placed together

quite modestly far above his own), and no longer ambiguously dressed in a sort of yachting costume with cycling knickerbockers but elegantly if unconventionally attired, and the room ceased to be a small and shabby room in a Folkestone slum, and grew larger and more richly furnished, and the fly-blown photographs were curious old pictures, and the rubbish on the walls the most rare and costly bric-à-brac, and the indisputable paraffin lamp, a soft and splendid light. A certain youthful heat that to many minds might have weakened Old Methusaleh's starry claim to a ripe antiquity vanished in that glamour, two burnt holes and a claimant darn in the tablecloth, moreover, became no more than the pleasing contradictions natural in the house of genius, and as for Kipps! – Kipps was a bright young man of promise, distinguished by recent quick, courageous proceedings not too definitely insisted upon, and he had been rewarded by admission to a sanctum and confidences for which the common prosperous, for which 'society women' even, were notoriously sighing in vain. 'Don't *want* them, my boy; they'd simply play old Harry with the work, you know! Chaps outside, bank clerks and university fellows, think the life's all *that* sort of thing. Don't you believe 'em. Don't you believe 'em.'

And then – !

'Boom . . . Boom . . . Boom . . . Boom . . . ' right in the middle of a most entertaining digression on flats who join touring companies under the impression that they are actors, Kipps much amused at their flatness as exposed by Chitterlow.

'Lor'!' said Kipps like one who awakens, 'that's not eleven!'

'Must be,' said Chitterlow. 'It was nearly ten when I got that whisky. It's early yet – '

'All the same I must be going,' said Kipps, and stood up. 'Even now – maybe. Fact is – I 'ad *no* idea. The 'ouse door shuts at 'arf-past ten, you know. I ought to 'ave thought before.'

'Well, if you *must* go! I tell you what. I'll come, too . . . Why! There's your leg, old man! Clean forgot it! You can't go through the streets like that. I'll sew up the tear. And meanwhile have another whisky.'

'I ought to be getting on *now*,' protested Kipps feebly; and then Chitterlow was showing him how to kneel on a chair in order that the rent trouser leg should be attainable, and Old Methusaleh on his third round was busy repairing the temporary eclipse of Kipps's arterial glow. Then suddenly Chitterlow was seized with laughter and had to leave off sewing to tell Kipps that the scene wouldn't make a bad bit of business in a farcical comedy, and then he began to sketch out the farcical comedy and that led him to a digression about another farcical comedy of which he had written a ripping opening scene which wouldn't take ten minutes to read. It had something in it that had never been done on the stage before, and was yet perfectly legitimate, namely, a man with a live beetle down the back of his neck trying to seem at his ease in a roomful of people –

'*They* won't lock you out,' he said, in a singularly reassuring tone, and began to read and act what he explained to be (not because he had written it, but simply because he knew it was so on account of his exceptional experience of the stage) and what Kipps also quite clearly saw to be, one of the best opening scenes that had ever been written.

When it was over Kipps, who rarely swore, was inspired to say the scene was 'damned fine' about six times over, whereupon, as if by way of recognition, Chitterlow took a simply enormous portion of the inspiring antediluvian, declaring at the same time that he had rarely met a '*finer*' intelligence than Kipps's (stronger there might be, *that* he couldn't say with certainty as yet, seeing how little after all they had seen of each other, but a finer *never*); that it was a shame such a gallant and discriminating intelligence should be nightly either locked up or locked out at ten – well, ten-thirty then – and that he had half a mind to recommend old somebody or other (apparently the editor of a London daily paper) to put on Kipps forthwith as a dramatic critic in the place of the current incapable.

'I don't think I've ever made up anything for print,' said Kipps; 'ever. I'd have a thundering good try, though, if ever I got a chance. I would that! I've written window tickets orfen enough. Made 'em up and everything. But that's different.'

'You'd come to it all the fresher for not having done it before. And the way you picked up every point in that scene, my boy, was a Fair Treat! I tell you, you'd knock William Archer into fits. Not so literary, of course, you'd be, but I don't believe in literary critics any more than in literary play-wrights. Plays *aren't* literature – that's just the point they miss. Plays are plays. No! That won't hamper you anyhow. You're wasted down here, I tell you. Just as I was, before I took to acting. I'm hanged if I wouldn't like your opinion on these first two acts of that tragedy I'm on to. I haven't told you about that. It wouldn't take me more than an hour to read . . . '

3

Then so far as he could subsequently remember, Kipps had 'another', and then it would seem that suddenly, regardless of the tragedy, he insisted that he 'reelly *must* be getting on', and from that point his memory became irregular. Certain things have remained quite clearly, and as it is a matter of common knowledge that intoxicated people forget what happens to them, it follows that he was not intoxicated. Chitterlow came with him partly to see him home and partly for a freshener before turning in. Kipps recalled afterwards very distinctly how in Little Fenchurch Street he discovered that he could not walk straight and also that Chitterlow's needle and thread in his still unmended trouser leg was making an annoying little noise on the pavement behind him. He tried to pick up the needle suddenly by surprise,

and somehow tripped and fell, and then Chitterlow, laughing uproariously, helped him up. 'It wasn't a bicycle this time, old boy,' said Chitterlow, and that appeared to them both at the time as being a quite extraordinarily good joke indeed. They punched each other about on the strength of it.

For a time after that Kipps certainly pretended to be quite desperately drunk and unable to walk and Chitterlow entered into the pretence and supported him. After that Kipps remembered being struck with the extremely laughable absurdity of going downhill to Tontine Street in order to go uphill again to the Emporium, and trying to get that idea into Chitterlow's head and being unable to do so on account of his own merriment or Chitterlow's evident intoxication, and his next memory after that was of the exterior of the Emporium, shut and darkened, and, as it were, frowning at him with all its stripes of yellow and green. The chilly way in which SHALFORD glittered in the moonlight printed itself with particular vividness on his mind. It appeared to Kipps that that establishment was closed to him for evermore. Those gilded letters, in spite of appearances, spelt FINIS for him and exile from Folkestone. He would never do wood-carving, never see Miss Walshingham again. Not that he had ever hoped to see her again. But this was the knife, this was final. He had stayed out, he had got drunk, there had been that row about the Manchester window-dressing only three days ago . . . In the retrospect he was quite sure that he was perfectly sober then and at bottom extremely unhappy, but he kept a brave face on the matter nevertheless, and declared stoutly he didn't care if he *was* locked out.

Whereupon Chitterlow slapped him on the back very hard and told him that was a 'Bit of All Right', and assured him that when he himself had been a clerk in Sheffield before he took to acting he had been locked out sometimes for six nights running.

'What's the result?' said Chitterlow. 'I could go back to that place now, and they'd be glad to have me . . . Glad to have me,' he repeated, and then added, 'that is to say, if they remember me – which isn't very likely.'

Kipps asked a little weakly, 'What am I to do?'

'Keep out,' said Chitterlow. 'You can't knock 'em up now – that would give you away *Right* away. You'd better try and sneak in in the morning with the cat. That'll do you. You'll probably get in all right in the morning if nobody gives you away.'

Then for a time – perhaps as the result of that slap in the back – Kipps felt decidedly queer, and acting on Chitterlow's advice went for a bit of a freshener upon the Leas. After a time he threw off the temporary queerness and found Chitterlow patting him on the shoulder and telling him that he'd be all right now in a minute and all the better for it – which he was. And the wind having dropped and the night being now a really very beautiful moonlight night indeed, and all before Kipps to spend as he liked and with only a very little tendency to spin round now and again to mar its splendour, they

set out to walk the whole length of the Leas to the Sandgate lift and back, and as they walked Chitterlow spoke first of moonlight transfiguring the sea and then of moonlight transfiguring faces, and so at last he came to the topic of Love, and upon that he dwelt a great while, and with a wealth of experience and illustrative anecdote that seemed remarkably pungent and material to Kipps. He forgot his lost Miss Walshingham and his outraged employer again. He became as it were a desperado by reflection.

Chitterlow had had adventures, a quite astonishing variety of adventures in this direction; he was a man with a past, a really opulent past, and he certainly seemed to like to look back and see himself amidst its opulence.

He made no consecutive history, but he gave Kipps vivid, momentary pictures of relations and entanglements. One moment he was in flight – only too worthily in flight – before the husband of a Malay woman in Cape Town. At the next he was having passionate complications with the daughter of a clergyman in York. Then he passed to a remarkable grouping at Seaford.

'They say you can't love two women at once,' said Chitterlow. 'But I tell you – ' He gesticulated and raised his ample voice. 'It's *Rot*! *Rot!*'

'I know that,' said Kipps.

'Why, when I was in the smalls with Bessie Hopper's company there were three.' He laughed and decided to add, 'Not counting Bessie, that is.'

He set out to reveal Life as it is lived in touring companies, a quite amazing jungle of interwoven 'affairs' it appeared to be, a mere amorous winepress for the crushing of hearts.

'People say this sort of thing's a nuisance and interferes with Work. I tell you it isn't. The Work couldn't go on without it. They *must* do it. They haven't the Temperament if they don't. If they hadn't the Temperament they wouldn't want to act; if they have – Bif!'

'You're right,' said Kipps. 'I see that.'

Chitterlow proceeded to a close criticism of certain historical indiscretions of Mr Clement Scott respecting the morals of the stage. Speaking in confidence and not as one who addresses the public, he admitted regretfully the general truth of these comments. He proceeded to examine various typical instances that had almost forced themselves upon him personally, and with especial regard to the contrast between his own character towards women and that of the Hon. Thomas Norgate, with whom it appeared he had once been on terms of great intimacy . . .

Kipps listened with emotion to these extraordinary recollections. They were wonderful to him, they were incredibly credible. The tumultuous, passionate, irregular course was the way life ran – except in high-class establishments! Such things happened in novels, in plays – only he had been fool enough not to understand they happened. His share in the conversation was now indeed no more than faint writing in the margin; Chitterlow was talking quite continuously. He expanded his magnificent

voice into huge guffaws, he drew it together into a confidential intensity, it became drawlingly reminiscent, he was frank, frank with the effect of a revelation, reticent also with the effect of a revelation, a stupendously gesticulating moonlit black figure, wallowing in itself, preaching Adventure and the Flesh to Kipps. Yet withal shot with something of sentiment, with a sort of sentimental refinement very coarsely and egotistically done. The Times he had had! – even before he was as old as Kipps he had had innumerable Times.

Well, he said with a sudden transition, he had sown his wild oats – one had to somewhen – and now, he fancied he had mentioned it earlier in the evening, he was happily married. She was, he indicated, a 'born lady'. Her father was a prominent lawyer, a solicitor in Kentish Town, 'done a lot of public-house business'; her mother was second cousin to the wife of Abel Jones, the fashionable portrait painter – 'almost Society people in a way'. That didn't count with Chitterlow. He was no snob. What *did* count was that she possessed what, he ventured to assert without much fear of contradiction, was the very finest, completely untrained contralto voice in all the world. ('But to hear it properly,' said Chitterlow, 'you want a Big Hall.') He became rather vague and jerked his head about to indicate when and how he had entered matrimony. She was, it seemed, 'away with her people'. It was clear that Chitterlow did not get on with these people very well. It would seem they failed to appreciate his playwriting, regarding it as an unremunerative pursuit, whereas, as he and Kipps knew, wealth beyond the dreams of avarice would presently accrue. Only patience and persistence were needful.

He went off at a tangent to hospitality. Kipps must come down home with him. They couldn't wander about all night, with a bottle of the right sort pining at home for them. 'You can sleep on the sofa. You won't be worried by broken springs anyhow, for I took 'em all out myself two or three weeks ago. I don't see what they ever put 'em in for. It's a point I know about. I took particular notice of it when I was with Bessie Hopper. Three months we were and all over England, North Wales and the Isle of Man, and I never struck a sofa in diggings anywhere that hadn't a broken spring. Not once – all the time.'

He added almost absently: 'It happens like that at times.'

They descended the slant road towards Harbour Street and went on past the Pavilion Hotel.

4

They came into the presence of Old Methusaleh again, and that worthy under Chitterlow's direction at once resumed the illumination of Kipps's interior with the conscientious thoroughness that distinguished

him. Chitterlow took a tall portion to himself with an air of asbestos, lit the bulldog pipe again, and lapsed for a space into meditation, from which Kipps roused him by remarking that he expected 'a nacter 'as a lot of ups and downs like, now and then'.

At which Chitterlow seemed to bestir himself. 'Ra-ther,' he said. 'And sometimes it's his own fault and sometimes it isn't. Usually it is. If it isn't one thing it's another. If it isn't the manager's wife it's bar-bragging. I tell you things happen at times. I'm a fatalist. The fact is Character has you. You can't get away from it. You may think you do, but you don't.'

He reflected for a moment. 'It's that what makes tragedy. Psychology really. It's the Greek irony – Ibsen and – all that. Up to date.'

He emitted this exhaustive summary of high-toned modern criticism as if he was repeating a lesson while thinking of something else, but it seemed to rouse him as it passed his lips by including the name of Ibsen.

He became interested in telling Kipps, who was indeed open to any information whatever about this quite novel name, exactly where he thought Ibsen fell short, points where it happened that Ibsen was defective just where it chanced that he, Chitterlow, was strong. Of course he had no desire to place himself in any way on an equality with Ibsen; still the fact remained that his own experience in England and America and the colonies was altogether more extensive than that of Ibsen. Ibsen had probably never seen 'one decent bar scrap' in his life. That, of course, was not Ibsen's fault or his own merit, but there the thing was. Genius, he knew, was supposed to be able to do anything or to do without anything; still he was now inclined to doubt that. He had a play in hand that might perhaps not please William Archer – whose opinion, after all, he did not value as he valued Kipps's opinion – but which he thought was at any rate as well constructed as anything Ibsen ever did.

So with infinite deviousness Chitterlow came at last to his play. He decided he would not read it to Kipps, but tell him about it. This was the simpler because much of it was still unwritten. He began to explain his plot. It was a complicated plot and all about a nobleman who had seen everything and done everything and knew practically all that Chitterlow knew about women, that is to say 'all about women', and suchlike matters. It warmed and excited Chitterlow. Presently he stood up to act a situation which could not be explained. It was an extremely vivid situation.

Kipps applauded the situation vehemently. 'Tha's dam' fine,' said the new dramatic critic, quite familiar with his part now, striking the table with his fist and almost upsetting his third portion (in the second series) of Old Methusaleh. 'Tha's dam' fine, Chit'low!'

'You see it?' said Chitterlow, with the last vestiges of that incidental gloom disappearing. 'Good, old boy! I thought you'd see it. But it's just the sort of thing the literary critic can't see. However, it's only a beginning – '

He replenished Kipps and proceeded with his exposition.

In a little while it was no longer necessary to give that over-advertised Ibsen the purely conventional precedence he had hitherto had. Kipps and Chitterlow were friends and they could speak frankly and openly of things not usually admitted. 'Any'ow,' said Kipps, a little irrelevantly and speaking over the brim of the replenishment, 'what you read jus' now was dam' fine. Nothing can't alter that.'

He perceived a sort of faint, buzzing vibration about things that was very nice and pleasant, and with a little care he had no difficulty whatever in putting his glass back on the table. Then he perceived Chitterlow was going on with the scenario, and then that Old Methusaleh had almost entirely left his bottle. He was glad there was so little more Methusaleh to drink because that would prevent his getting drunk. He knew that he was not now drunk, but he knew that he had had enough. He was one of those who always know when they have had enough. He tried to interrupt Chitterlow to tell him this, but he could not get a suitable opening. He doubted whether Chitterlow might not be one of those people who did not know when they had had enough. He discovered that he disapproved of Chitterlow. Highly. It seemed to him that Chitterlow went on and on like a river. For a time he was inexplicably and quite unjustly cross with Chitterlow and wanted to say to him, 'you got the gift of the gab', but he only got so far as to say 'the gift', and then Chitterlow thanked him and said he was better than Archer any day. So he eyed Chitterlow with a baleful eye until it dawned upon him that a most extraordinary thing was taking place. Chitterlow kept mentioning someone named Kipps. This presently began to perplex Kipps very greatly. Dimly but decidedly he perceived this was wrong.

'Look 'ere,' he said suddenly, '*what* Kipps?'

'This chap Kipps I'm telling you about.'

'What chap Kipps you're telling which about?'

'I told you.'

Kipps struggled with a difficulty in silence for a space. Then he reiterated firmly, '*What* chap Kipps?'

'This chap in my play – man who kisses the girl.'

'Never kissed a girl,' said Kipps; 'leastwise – ' and subsided for a space. He could not remember whether he had kissed Ann or not – he knew he had meant to. Then suddenly in a tone of great sadness and addressing the hearth he said, '*My* name's Kipps.'

'Eh?' said Chitterlow.

'Kipps,' said Kipps, smiling a little cynically.

'What about him?'

'He's me.' He tapped his breastbone with his middle finger to indicate his essential self.

He leant forward very gravely towards Chitterlow. 'Look 'ere, Chit'low,' he said, 'you haven't no business putting my name into play. You mustn't do things like that. You'd lose me my crib, right away.' And they had a little

argument – so far as Kipps could remember. Chitterlow entered upon a general explanation of how he got his names. These, he had for the most part got out of a newspaper that was still, he believed, 'lying about'. He even made to look for it, and while he was doing so Kipps went on with the argument, addressing himself more particularly to the photograph of the girl in tights. He said that at first her costume had not commended her to him, but now he perceived she had an extremely sensible face. He told her she would like Buggins if she met him; he could see she was just that sort. She would admit, all sensible people would admit, that using names in plays was wrong. You could, for example, have the law on him.

He became confidential. He explained that he was already in sufficient trouble for stopping out all night, without having his name put in plays. He was certain to be in the deuce of a row, the deuce of a row. Why had he done it? Why hadn't he gone at ten? Because one thing leads to another. One thing, he generalised, always does lead to another . . .

He was trying to tell her that he was utterly unworthy of Miss Walshing-ham, when Chitterlow gave up the search and suddenly accused him of being drunk and talking 'Rot – '

CHAPTER FIVE

'Swapped'

He awoke on the thoroughly comfortable sofa that had had all its springs removed, and although he had certainly not been intoxicated, he awoke with what Chitterlow pronounced to be, quite indisputably, a Head and a Mouth. He had slept in his clothes and he felt stiff and uncomfortable all over, but the head and mouth insisted that he must not bother over little things like that. In the head was one large, angular idea that it was physically painful to have there. If he moved his head the angular idea shifted about in the most agonising way. This idea was that he had lost his situation and was utterly ruined and that it really mattered very little. Shalford was certain to hear of his escapade, and that, coupled with that row about the Manchester window – !

He raised himself into a sitting position under Chitterlow's urgent encouragement.

He submitted apathetically to his host's attentions. Chitterlow, who admitted being a 'bit off it' himself and in need of an egg-cupful of brandy, just an egg-cupful neat, dealt with that Head and Mouth as a mother might deal with the fall of an only child. He compared it with other Heads and Mouths that he had met, and in particular to certain experienced by the Hon. Thomas Norgate. 'Right up to the last,' said Chitterlow, 'he couldn't stand his liquor. It happens like that at times.' And after Chitterlow had

pumped on the young beginner's head and given him some anchovy paste piping hot on buttered toast, which he preferred to all the other remedies he had encountered, Kipps resumed his crumpled collar, brushed his clothes, tacked up his trouser-leg and prepared to face Mr Shalford and the reckoning for this wild, unprecedented night – the first 'night out' that ever he had taken.

Acting on Chitterlow's advice to have a bit of a freshener before returning to the Emporium, Kipps walked some way along the Leas and back and then went down to a shop near the Harbour to get a cup of coffee. He found that extremely reinvigorating, and he went on up the High Street to face the inevitable terrors of the office, a faint touch of pride in his depravity tempering his extreme self-abasement. After all, it was not an unmanly headache; he had been out all night, and he had been drinking and his physical disorder was there to witness the fact. If it wasn't for the thought of Shalford he would have been even a proud man to discover himself at last in such a condition. But the thought of Shalford was very dreadful. He met two of the apprentices snatching a walk before shop began. At the sight of them he pulled his spirits together, put his hat back from his pallid brow, thrust his hands into his trouser pockets and adopted an altogether more dissipated carriage; he met their innocent faces with a wan smile. Just for a moment he was glad that the rent in his trousers was, after all, visible and that some at least of the mud on his clothes had refused to move at Chitterlow's brushing. What wouldn't they think he had been up to? He passed them without speaking. He could imagine how they regarded his back. Then he recollected Mr Shalford . . .

The deuce of a row certainly and perhaps – ! He tried to think of plausible versions of the affair. He could explain he had been run down by rather a wild sort of fellow who was riding a bicycle, almost stunned for the moment (even now he felt the effects of the concussion in his head) and had been given whisky to restore him, and 'the fact is, sir' – with an upward inflection of the voice, an upward inflection of the eyebrows and an air of its being the last thing one would have expected whisky to do, the manifestation indeed of a practically unique physiological weakness – 'it got into my 'ed!' . . .

Put like that it didn't look so bad.

He got to the Emporium a little before eight and the housekeeper with whom he was something of a favourite ('There's no harm in Mr Kipps,' she used to say) seemed to like him if anything better for having broken the rules and gave him a piece of dry toast and a good hot cup of tea.

'I suppose the G. V. – ' began Kipps.

'He knows,' said the housekeeper.

He went down to the shop a little before time, and presently Booch summoned him to the presence.

He emerged from the private office after an interval of ten minutes.

The junior clerk scrutinised his visage. Buggins put the frank question. Kipps answered with one word.

'Swapped!' said Kipps.

2

Kipps leant against the fixtures with his hands in his pockets and talked to the two apprentices under him.

'I don't care if I *am* swapped,' said Kipps. 'I been sick of Teddy and his System some time. I was a good mind to chuck it when my time was up. Wish I 'ad now.'

Afterwards Pierce came round and Kipps repeated this.

'What's it for?' said Pierce. 'That row about the window tickets?'

'No fear!' said Kipps and sought to convey a perspective of splendid depravity. 'I wasn't in las' night,' he said and made even Pierce, 'man about town' Pierce, open his eyes.

'Why! where did you get to?' asked Pierce.

He conveyed that he had been 'fair round the town'. 'With a Nactor chap, I know.'

'One can't *always* be living like a curit,' he said.

'No fear,' said Pierce, trying to play up to him.

But Kipps had the top place in that conversation.

'My Lor'!' said Kipps, when Pierce had gone, 'but wasn't my mouth and 'ed bad this morning before I 'ad a pick-me-up!'

'Whad jer 'ave?'

'Anchovy on 'ot buttered toast. It's the very best pick-me-up there is. You trust me, Rodgers. I never take no other and I don't advise you to. See?'

And when pressed for further particulars, he said again he had been 'fair all *round* the town, with a Nactor chap' he knew. They asked curiously all he had done and he said, 'Well, what do *you* think?' And when they pressed for still further details he said there were things little boys ought not to know and laughed darkly and found them some huckaback to roll.

And in this manner for a space did Kipps fend off the contemplation of the 'key of the street' that Shalford had presented him.

3

This sort of thing was all very well when junior apprentices were about, but when Kipps was alone with himself it served him not at all. He was uncomfortable inside and his skin was uncomfortable, and the Head and Mouth, palliated perhaps but certainly not cured, were still with him. He

felt, to tell the truth, nasty and dirty and extremely disgusted with himself. To work was dreadful and to stand still and think still more dreadful. His torn trouser-leg reproached him. These were the second best of his three pairs of trousers, and they had cost him thirteen and sixpence. Practically ruined they were. His dusting pair were unfit for shop and he would have to degrade his best. When he was under inspection he affected the slouch of a desperado, but directly he found himself alone, this passed insensibly into the droop.

The financial aspect of things grew large before him. His whole capital in the world was the sum of five pounds in the Post Office Savings Bank and four and sixpence cash. Besides there would be two months' screw. His little tin box upstairs was no longer big enough for his belongings; he would have to buy another, let alone that it was not calculated to make a good impression in a new 'crib'. Then there would be paper and stamps needed in some abundance for answering advertisements and railway fares when he went 'crib hunting'. He would have to write letters, and he never wrote letters. There was spelling, for example, to consider. Probably if nothing turned up before his month was up he would have to go home to his uncle and aunt.

How would they take it? . . .

For the present at any rate he resolved not to write to them.

Such disagreeable things as these they were that lurked below the fair surface of Kipps's assertion, 'I've been wanting a change. If 'e 'adn't swapped me, I should very likely 'ave swapped 'im.'

In the perplexed privacies of his own mind he could not understand how everything had happened. He had been the Victim of Fate, or at least of one as inexorable – Chitterlow. He tried to recall the successive steps that had culminated so disastrously. They were difficult to recall . . .

Buggins that night abounded in counsel and reminiscence.

'Curious thing,' said Buggins, 'but every time I've had the swap I've never believed I should get another crib – never. But I have,' said Buggins. 'Always. So don't lose heart, whatever you do –

'Whatever you do,' said Buggins, 'keep hold of your collars and cuffs – shirts if you can, but collars anyhow. Spout them last. And anyhow, it's summer! – you won't want your coat . . . You got a good umbrella . . .

'You'll no more get a shop from New Romney, than – anything. Go straight up to London, get the cheapest room you can find – and hang out. Don't eat too much. Many a chap's put his prospects in his stomach. Get a cup o' coffee and a slice – egg if you like – but remember you got to turn up at the Warehouse tidy. The best places *now*, I believe, are the old cabmen's eating houses. Keep your watch and chain as long as you can . . .

'There's lots of shops going,' said Buggins. 'Lots!'

And added reflectively, 'But not this time of year perhaps.'

He began to recall his own researches. ' 'Stonishing lot of chaps you see,'

he said. 'All sorts. Look like dukes some of 'em. High hat. Patent boots. Frock coat. All there. All right for a West End crib. Others – Lord! It's a caution, Kipps. Boots been inked in some reading rooms – *I* used to write in a Reading Room in Fleet Street, regular penny club – hat been wetted, collar frayed, tail coat buttoned up, black chest-plaster tie – spread out. Shirt, you know, gone – ' Buggins pointed upward with a pious expression.

'No shirt, I expect?'

'Ate it,' said Buggins.

Kipps meditated. 'I wonder where old Merton is,' he said at last. 'I often wondered about 'im.'

4

It was the morning following Kipps's notice of dismissal that Miss Walshingham came into the shop. She came in with a dark, slender lady, rather faded, rather tightly dressed, whom Kipps was to know someday as her mother. He discovered them in the main shop at the counter of the ribbon department. He had come to the opposite glove counter with some goods enclosed in a parcel that he had unpacked in his own department. The two ladies were both bent over a box of black ribbon.

He had a moment of tumultuous hesitations. The etiquette of the situation was incomprehensible. He put down his goods very quietly and stood hands on counter, staring at these two ladies. Then, as Miss Walshingham sat back, the instinct of flight seized him . . .

He returned to his Manchester shop wildly agitated. Directly he was out of sight of her he wanted to see her. He fretted up and down the counter, and addressed some snappish remarks to the apprentice in the window. He fumbled for a moment with a parcel, untied it needlessly, began to tie it up again and then bolted back again into the main shop. He could hear his own heart beating.

The two ladies were standing in the manner of those who have completed their purchases and are waiting for their change. Mrs Walshingham regarded some remnants with impersonal interest; Helen's eyes searched the shop. They distinctly lit up when they discovered Kipps.

He dropped his hands to the counter by habit and stood for a moment regarding her awkwardly. What would she do? Would she cut him? She came across the shop to him.

'How are *you*, Mr Kipps?' she said, in her clear, distinct tones, and she held out her hand.

'Very well, thank you,' said Kipps; 'how are you?'

She said she had been buying some ribbon.

He became aware of Mrs Walshingham very much surprised. This checked something allusive about the class and he said instead that he

supposed she was glad to be having her holidays now. She said she was, it gave her more time for reading and that sort of thing. He supposed that she would be going abroad and she thought that perhaps they *would* go to Knocke or Bruges for a time.

Then came a pause and Kipps's soul surged within him. He wanted to tell her he was leaving and would never see her again. He could find neither words nor voice to say it. The swift seconds passed. The girl in the ribbons was handing Mrs Walshingham her change. 'Well,' said Miss Walshingham, 'Goodbye,' and gave him her hand again.

Kipps bowed over her hand. His manners, his counter manners, were the easiest she had ever seen upon him. She turned to her mother. It was no good now, no good. Her mother! You couldn't say a thing like that before her mother! All was lost but politeness. Kipps rushed for the door. He stood at the door bowing with infinite gravity, and she smiled and nodded as she went out. She saw nothing of the struggle within him, nothing but a gratifying emotion. She smiled like a satisfied goddess as the incense ascends.

Mrs Walshingham bowed stiffly and a little awkwardly.

He remained holding the door open for some seconds after they had passed out, then rushed suddenly to the back of the 'costume' window to watch them go down the street. His hands tightened on the window rack as he stared. Her mother appeared to be asking discreet questions. Helen's bearing suggested the offhand replies of a person who found the world a satisfactory place to live in. 'Really, Mumsie, you cannot expect me to cut my own students dead,' she was in fact saying . . .

They vanished round Henderson's corner.

Gone! And he would never see her again – never!

It was as though someone had struck his heart with a whip. Never! Never! Never! And she didn't know! He turned back from the window and the department with its two apprentices was impossible. The whole glaring world was insupportable.

He hesitated and made a rush head down for the cellar that was his Manchester warehouse. Rodgers asked him a question that he pretended not to hear.

The Manchester warehouse was a small cellar apart from the general basement of the building and dimly lit by a small gas flare. He did not turn that up, but rushed for the darkest corner, where on the lowest shelf the sale window-tickets were stored. He drew out the box of these with trembling hands and upset them on the floor, and so having made himself a justifiable excuse for being on the ground with his head well in the dark, he could let his poor bursting little heart have its way with him for a space.

And there he remained until the cry of 'Kipps! Forward!' summoned him once more to face the world.

CHAPTER SIX

The Unexpected

Now in the slack of that same day, after the midday dinner and before the coming of the afternoon customers, this disastrous Chitterlow descended upon Kipps with the most amazing coincidence in the world. He did not call formally, entering and demanding Kipps, but privately, in a confidential and mysterious manner.

Kipps was first aware of him as a dark object bobbing about excitedly outside the hosiery window. He was stooping and craning and peering in the endeavour to see into the interior between and over the socks and stockings. Then he transferred his attention to the door, and after a hovering scrutiny, tried the baby-linen display. His movements and gestures suggested a suppressed excitement.

Seen by daylight, Chitterlow was not nearly such a magnificent figure as he had been by the subdued nocturnal lightings and beneath the glamour of his own interpretation. The lines were the same indeed, but the texture was different. There was a quality about the yachting cap, an indefinable finality of dustiness, a shiny finish on all the salient surfaces of the reefer coat. The red hair and the profile, though still forcible and fine, were less in the quality of Michelangelo and more in that of the merely picturesque. But it was a bright brown eye still that sought amidst the interstices of the baby-linen.

Kipps was by no means anxious to interview Chitterlow again. If he had felt sure that Chitterlow would not enter the shop he would have hid in the warehouse until the danger was past, but he had no idea of Chitterlow's limitations. He decided to keep up the shop in the shadows until Chitterlow reached the side window of the Manchester department and then to go outside as if to inspect the condition of the window and explain to him that things were unfavourable to immediate intercourse. He might tell him he had already lost his situation . . .

' 'Ello, Chit'low,' he said, emerging.

'Very man I want to see,' said Chitterlow, shaking with vigour. 'Very man I want to see.' He laid a hand on Kipps's arm. 'How *old* are you, Kipps?'

'One-and-twenty,' said Kipps. 'Why?'

'Talk about coincidences! And your name now? Wait a minute.' He held out a finger. '*Is* it Arthur?'

'Yes,' said Kipps.

'You're the man,' said Chitterlow.

'What man?'

'It's about the thickest coincidence I ever struck,' said Chitterlow, plunging his extensive hand into his breast coat pocket. 'Half a jiff and I'll tell you your mother's Christian name.' He laughed and struggled with his coat for a space, produced a washing book and two pencils, which he deposited in his side pocket; then in one capacious handful, a bent but by no means finally disabled cigar, the rubber proboscis of a bicycle pump, some twine and a lady's purse, and finally a small pocket book, and from this, after dropping and recovering several visiting cards, he extracted a carelessly torn piece of newspaper. 'Euphemia', he read and brought his face close to Kipps's. 'Eh?' He laughed noisily. 'It's about as fair a Bit of All Right as anyone *could* have – outside a coincidence play. Don't say her name wasn't Euphemia, Kipps, and spoil the whole blessed show.'

'Whose name – Euphemia?' asked Kipps.

'Your mother's.'

'Lemme see what it says on the paper.'

Chitterlow handed him the fragment and turned away. 'You may say what you like,' he said, addressing a vast, deep laugh to the street generally.

Kipps attempted to read. ' "WADDY or KIPPS. If Arthur Waddy or Arthur Kipps, the son of Margaret Euphemia Kipps, who – " '

Chitterlow's finger swept over the print. 'I went down the column and every blessed name that seemed to fit my play I took. I don't believe in made-up names. As I told you. I'm all with Zola on that. Documents whenever you can. I like 'em hot and real. See? Who was Waddy?'

'Never heard his name.'

'Not Waddy?'

'No!'

Kipps tried to read again and abandoned the attempt. 'What does it mean?' he said. 'I don't understand.'

'It means,' said Chitterlow, with a momentary note of lucid exposition, 'so far as I can make out that you're going to strike it Rich. Never mind about the Waddy – that's a detail. What does it usually mean? You'll hear of something to your advantage – very well. I took that newspaper up to get my names by the merest chance. Directly I saw it again and read that – I knew it was you. I believe in coincidences. People say they don't happen. *I* say they do. Everything's a coincidence. Seen properly. Here you are. Here's one! Incredible? Not a bit of it! See? It's you! Kipps! Waddy be damned! It's a Mascot. There's luck in my play. Bif! You're there. *I'm* there. Fair *in* it! Snap!' And he discharged his fingers like a pistol. 'Never you mind about the "Waddy". '

'Eh?' said Kipps, with a nervous eye on Chitterlow's fingers.

'You're all right,' said Chitterlow; 'you may bet the seat of your only breeches on that! Don't you worry about the Waddy – that's as clear as day. You're about as right side up as a billiard ball – whatever you do. Don't stand there gaping, man! Read the paper if you don't believe me. Read it!'

He shook it under Kipps's nose.

Kipps became aware of the second apprentice watching them from the shop. His air of perplexity gave place to a more confident bearing.

' – "who was born at East Grinstead". I certainly was born there. I've 'eard my aunt say – '

'I knew it,' said Chitterlow, taking hold of one edge of the paper and bringing his face close alongside Kipps's.

' " – on September the first, eighteen hundred and seventy-eight" – '

'*That's* all right,' said Chitterlow. 'It's all, all right, and all you have to do is write to Watson and Bean and get it – '

'Get what?'

'Whatever it is.'

Kipps sought his moustache. 'You'd write?' he asked.

'Ra-ther.'

'But what d'you think it is?'

'That's the fun of it!' said Chitterlow, taking three steps in some as yet uninvented dance. 'That's where the joke comes in. It may be anything – it may be a million. If so! Where does little Harry come in? Eh?'

Kipps was trembling slightly. 'But – ' he said, and thought. 'If you was me – ' he began. 'About that Waddy – ?'

He glanced up and saw the second apprentice disappear with amazing swiftness from behind the goods in the window.

'*What?*' asked Chitterlow, but he never had an answer.

'Lor'! There's the guv'nor!' said Kipps, and made a prompt dive for the door.

He dashed in only to discover that Shalford, with the junior apprentice in attendance, had come to mark off remnants of Kipps's cotton dresses and was demanding him. 'Hello, Kipps,' he said, 'outside – ?'

'Seein' if the window was straight, sir,' said Kipps.

'Umph!' said Shalford.

For a space Kipps was too busily employed to think at all of Chitterlow or the crumpled bit of paper in his trouser pocket. He was, however, painfully aware of a suddenly disconnected excitement at large in the street. There came one awful moment when Chitterlow's nose loomed interrogatively over the ground glass of the department door, and his bright little red-brown eye sought for the reason for Kipps's disappearance, and then it became evident that he saw the high light of Shalford's baldness and grasped the situation and went away. And then Kipps (with that advertisement in his pocket) was able to come back to the business in hand.

He became aware that Shalford had asked a question. 'Yessir, nosir, rightsir. I'm sorting up zephyrs tomorrow, sir,' said Kipps.

Presently he had a moment to himself again, and, taking up a safe position behind a newly unpacked pile of summer lace curtains, he straightened out

the piece of paper and reperused it. It was a little perplexing. That 'Arthur Waddy or Arthur Kipps' – did that imply two persons or one? He would ask Pierce or Buggins. Only –

It had always been impressed upon him that there was something demanding secrecy about his mother.

'Don't you answer no questions about your mother,' his aunt had been wont to say. 'Tell them you don't know, whatever it is they ask you.'

'Now this – ?'

Kipps's face became portentously careful and he tugged at his moustache, such as it was, hard.

He had always represented his father as being a 'gentleman farmer'. 'It didn't pay,' he used to say with a picture in his own mind of a penny-magazine aristocrat prematurely worn out by worry. 'I'm a Norfan, both sides,' he would explain, with the air of one who had seen trouble. He said he lived with his uncle and aunt, but he did not say that they kept a toy shop, and to tell anyone that his uncle had been a butler – *a servant!* – would have seemed the maddest of indiscretions. Almost all the assistants in the Emporium were equally reticent and vague, so great was their horror of 'Lowness' of any sort. To ask about this 'Waddy or Kipps' would upset all these little fictions. He was not, as a matter of fact, perfectly clear about his real status in the world (he was not, as a matter of fact, perfectly clear about anything), but he knew that there was a quality about his status that was – detrimental.

Under the circumstances – ?

It occurred to him that it would save a lot of trouble to destroy the advertisement there and then.

In which case he would have to explain to Chitterlow!

'Eng!' said Mr Kipps.

'Kipps,' cried Carshot, who was shopwalking; 'Kipps, Forward!'

He thrust back the crumpled paper into his pocket and sallied forth to the customer.

'I want,' said the customer, looking vaguely about her through glasses, 'a little bit of something to cover a little stool I have. Anything would do – a remnant or anything – '

The matter of the advertisement remained in abeyance for half an hour, and at the end the little stool was still a candidate for covering and Kipps had a thoroughly representative collection of the textile fabrics in his department to clear away. He was so angry about the little stool that the crumpled advertisement lay for a space in his pocket absolutely forgotten.

Kipps sat on his tin box under the gas bracket that evening, and looked up the name Euphemia and learnt what it meant in the *Enquire Within About Everything* that constituted Buggins's reference library. He hoped Buggins, according to his habit, would ask him what he was looking for, but Buggins was busy turning out his week's washing. 'Two collars,' said Buggins, 'half pair socks, two dickeys. Shirt? . . . M'm. There ought to be another collar somewhere.'

'Euphemia,' said Kipps at last, unable altogether to keep to himself this suspicion of a high origin that floated so delightfully about him, 'Euphemia; it isn't a name *common* people would give to a girl, is it?'

'It isn't the name any decent people would give to a girl,' said Buggins, ' – common or not.'

'Lor'!' said Kipps. 'Why?'

'It's giving girls names like that,' said Buggins, 'that nine times out of ten makes 'em go wrong. It unsettles 'em. If ever I was to have a girl, if ever I was to have a dozen girls, I'd call 'em all Jane. Every one of 'em. You couldn't have a better name than that. Euphemia indeed! What next? . . . Good Lord! . . . That isn't one of my collars there, is it? under your bed?' . . .

Kipps got him the collar.

'I don't see no great 'arm in Euphemia,' he said as he did so.

After that he became restless. 'I'm a good mind to write that letter,' he said; and then, finding Buggins preoccupied wrapping his washing up in the 'half sox', added to himself, 'a thundering good mind.'

So he got his penny bottle of ink, borrowed the pen from Buggins and with no very serious difficulty in spelling or composition, did as he had resolved.

He came back into the bedroom about an hour afterwards a little out of breath and pale. 'Where you been?' said Buggins, who was now reading the *Daily World Manager*, which came to him in rotation from Carshot.

'Out to post some letters,' said Kipps, hanging up his hat.

'Crib hunting?'

'Mostly,' said Kipps. 'Rather,' he added, with a nervous laugh; 'what else?'

Buggins went on reading. Kipps sat on his bed and regarded the back of the *Daily World Manager* thoughtfully.

'Buggins,' he said at last.

Buggins lowered his paper and looked.

'I say, Buggins, what do these here advertisements mean that say so-and-so will hear of something greatly to his advantage?'

'Missin' people,' said Buggins, making to resume reading.

'How d'yer mean?' asked Kipps. 'Money left and that sort of thing?'

Buggins shook his head. 'Debts,' he said, 'more often than not.'

'But that ain't to his advantage.'

'They put that to get 'old of 'em,' said Buggins. 'Often it's wives.'

'What you mean?'

'Deserted wives, try and get their husbands back that way.'

'I suppose it *is* legacies sometimes, eh? Perhaps if someone was left a hundred pounds by someone – '

'Hardly ever,' said Buggins.

'Well, 'ow – ?' began Kipps and hesitated.

Buggins resumed reading. He was very much excited by a leader on Indian affairs. 'By Jove!' he said, 'it won't do to give these here Blacks votes.'

'No fear,' said Kipps.

'They're different altogether,' said Buggins. 'They 'aven't the sound sense of Englishmen, and they 'aven't the character. There's a sort of tricky dishonesty about 'em – false witness and all that – of which an Englishman has no idea. Outside their courts of law – it's a pos'tive fact, Kipps – there's witnesses waitin' to be 'ired. Reg'lar trade. Touch their 'ats as you go in. Englishmen 'ave no idea, I tell you – not ord'nary Englishmen. It's in their blood. They're too timid to be honest. Too slavish. They aren't used to being free like we are, and if you gave 'em freedom they wouldn't make a proper use of it. Now *we* – Oh, *damn*!'

For the gas had suddenly gone out and Buggins had the whole column of Society Club Chat still to read.

Buggins could talk of nothing after that but Shalford's meanness in turning off the gas, and after being extremely satirical indeed about their employer, undressed in the dark, hit his bare toe against a box and subsided after unseemly ejaculations into silent ill-temper.

Though Kipps tried to get to sleep before the affair of the letter he had just posted resumed possession of his mind he could not do so. He went over the whole thing again, quite exhaustively. Now that his first terror was abating he couldn't quite determine whether he was glad or sorry that he had posted that letter. If it *should* happen to be a hundred pounds!

It *must* be a hundred pounds!

If it was he could hold out for a year, for a couple of years even, before he got a Crib.

Even if it was fifty pounds – !

Buggins was already breathing regularly when Kipps spoke again. '*Buggins*,' he said.

Buggins pretended to be asleep, and thickened his regular breathing (a little too hastily) to a snore.

'I say Buggins,' said Kipps after an interval.

'*What's* up now?' said Buggins unamiably.

' 'Spose *you* saw an advertisement in a paper, with your name in it, see, asking you to come and see someone, like, so as to hear of something very much to your – '

'Hide,' said Buggins shortly.

'But – '

'I'd hide.'

'Er?'

'Goo'-night, o' man,' said Buggins, with convincing earnestness. Kipps lay still for a long time, then blew profoundly, turned over and stared at the other side of the dark.

He had been a fool to post that letter!

Lord! *Hadn't* he been a fool!

3

It was just five days and a half after the light had been turned out while Buggins was reading, that a young man with a white face and eyes bright and wide-open emerged from a side road upon the Leas front. He was dressed in his best clothes, and, although the weather was fine, he carried his umbrella, just as if he had been to church. He hesitated and turned to the right. He scanned each house narrowly as he passed it, and presently came to an abrupt stop. 'Hughenden', said the gateposts in firm, black letters, and the fanlight in gold repeated 'Hughenden'. It was a stucco house fit to take your breath away, and its balcony was painted a beautiful sea-green, enlivened with gilding. He stood looking up at it.

'Gollys!' he said at last in an awestricken whisper.

It had rich-looking crimson curtains to all the lower windows and brass railed blinds above. There was a splendid tropical plant in a large, artistic pot in the drawing-room window. There was a splendid bronzed knocker (ring also) and two bells – one marked 'servants'.

'Gollys! *Servants*, eh?'

He walked past away from it, with his eyes regarding it, and then turned and came back. He passed through a further indecision, and finally drifted away to the seafront and sat down on a seat a little way along the Leas and put his arm over the back and regarded 'Hughenden'. He whistled an air very softly to himself, put his head first on one side and then on the other. Then for a space he scowled fixedly at it.

A very stout old gentleman, with a very red face and very protuberant eyes, sat down beside Kipps, removed a Panama hat of the most abandoned desperado cut, and mopped his brow and blew. Then he began mopping the inside of his hat. Kipps watched him for a space, wondering how much he might have a year, and where he bought his hat. Then 'Hughenden' reasserted itself.

An impulse overwhelmed him. 'I say,' he said, leaning forward to the old gentleman.

The old gentleman started and stared.

'*Whad* d'you say?' he asked fiercely.

'You wouldn't think,' said Kipps, indicating with his forefinger, 'that that 'ouse there belongs to me.'

The old gentleman twisted his neck round to look at 'Hughenden'. Then he came back to Kipps, looked at his mean, little garments with apoplectic intensity and blew at him by way of reply.

'It does,' said Kipps, a little less confidently.

'Don't be a Fool,' said the old gentleman, and put his hat on and wiped out the corners of his eyes. 'It's hot enough,' panted the old gentleman indignantly, 'without Fools.' Kipps looked from the old gentleman to the house and back to the old gentleman. The old gentleman looked at Kipps and snorted and looked out to sea, and again, snorting very contemptuously, at Kipps.

'Mean to say it doesn't belong to me?' said Kipps.

The old gentleman just glanced over his shoulder at the house in dispute and then fell to pretending Kipps didn't exist. 'It's been lef' me this very morning,' said Kipps. 'It ain't the only one that's been lef' me, neither.'

'Aw!' said the old gentleman, like one who is sorely tried. He seemed to expect the passers-by presently to remove Kipps.

'It 'as,' said Kipps. He made no further remark to the old gentleman for a space, but looked with a little less certitude at the house . . .

'I got – ' he said and stopped. 'It's no good telling you if you don't believe,' he said.

The old gentleman, after a struggle with himself, decided not to have a fit. 'Try that game on with me,' he panted. 'Give you in charge.'

'What game?'

'Wasn't born yesterday,' said the old gentleman, and blew. 'Besides,' he added, '*look* at you! I know you,' and the old gentleman coughed shortly and nodded to the horizon and coughed again.

Kipps looked dubiously from the house to the old gentleman and back to the house. Their conversation, he gathered, was over. Presently he got up and went slowly across the grass to its stucco portal again. He stood and his mouth shaped the precious word, 'Hughenden'. It was all *right*! He looked over his shoulder as if in appeal to the old gentleman, then turned and went his way. The old gentleman was so evidently past all reason!

He hung for a moment some distance along the parade, as though some invisible string was pulling him back. When he could no longer see the house from the pavement he went out into the road. Then with an effort he snapped the string.

He went on down a quiet side street, unbuttoned his coat furtively, took out three bank notes in an envelope, looked at them and replaced them.

Then he fished up five new sovereigns from his trouser pocket and examined them. To such a confidence had his exact resemblance to his dead mother's portrait carried Messrs Watson and Bean.

It was right enough.

It really was *all* right.

He replaced the coins with grave precaution and went his way with a sudden briskness. It was all right – he had it now – he was a rich man at large. He went up a street and round a corner and along another street, and started towards the Pavilion and changed his mind and came round back, resolved to go straight to the Emporium and tell them all.

He was aware of someone crossing a road far off ahead of him, someone curiously relevant to his present extraordinary state of mind. It was Chitterlow. Of course it was Chitterlow who had told him first of the whole thing! The playwright was marching buoyantly along a cross street. His nose was in the air, the yachting cap was on the back of his head and the large freckled hand grasped two novels from the library, a morning newspaper, a new hat done up in paper and a lady's net bag full of onions and tomatoes –

He passed out of sight behind the wine merchant's at the corner, as Kipps decided to hurry forward and tell him of the amazing change in the Order of the Universe that had just occurred.

Kipps uttered a feeble shout, arrested as it began, and waved his umbrella. Then he set off at a smart pace in pursuit. He came round the corner and Chitterlow had gone; he hurried to the next and there was no Chitterlow; he turned back unavailingly and his eyes sought some other possible corner. His hand fluttered to his mouth and he stood for a space at the pavement edge, staring about him. No good!

But the sight of Chitterlow was a wholesome thing, it connected events together, joined him on again to the past at a new point, and that was what he so badly needed –

It was all right – all right.

He became suddenly very anxious to tell everybody at the Emporium, absolutely everybody, all about it. That was what wanted doing. He felt that telling was the thing to make this business real. He gripped his umbrella about the middle and walked very eagerly.

He entered the Emporium through the Manchester department. He flung open the door (over whose ground glass he had so recently, in infinite apprehension, watched the nose of Chitterlow) and discovered the second apprentice and Pierce in conversation. Pierce was prodding his hollow tooth with a pin and talking in fragments about the distinctive characteristics of Good Style.

Kipps came up in front of the counter.

'I say,' he said; 'what d'yer think?'

'What?' said Pierce over the pin.

'Guess.'

'You've slipped out because Teddy's in London.'

'Something more.'

'What?'

'Been left a fortune.'

'Garn!'

'I 'ave.'

'Get out!'

'Straight. I been lef' twelve 'undred pounds – twelve 'undred pounds a year!'

He moved towards the little door out of the department into the house, moving, as heralds say, *regardant passant*. Pierce stood with mouth wide open and pin poised in air. 'No!' he said at last.

'It's right,' said Kipps, 'and I'm going.'

And he fell over the doormat into the house.

<p style="text-align:center">4</p>

It happened that Mr Shalford was in London buying summer sale goods – and no doubt also interviewing aspirants to succeed Kipps.

So that there was positively nothing to hinder a wild rush of rumour from end to end of the Emporium. All the masculine members began their report with the same formula: 'Heard about Kipps?'

The new girl in the cashdesk had had it from Pierce and had dashed out into the fancy shop to be the first with the news on the fancy side. Kipps had been left a thousand pounds a year, twelve thousand pounds a year. Kipps had been left twelve hundred thousand pounds. The figures were uncertain, but the essential facts they had correct. Kipps had gone upstairs. Kipps was packing his box. He said he wouldn't stop another day in the old Emporium, not for a thousand pounds! It was said that he was singing ribaldry about old Shalford.

He had come down! He was in the counting house. There was a general movement thither. Poor old Buggins had a customer and couldn't make out what the deuce it was all about! Completely out of it was Buggins.

There was a sound of running to and fro and voices saying this, that and the other thing about Kipps. Ring-a-dinger, ring-a-dinger went the dinner bell all unheeded. The whole of the Emporium was suddenly bright-eyed, excited, hungry to tell somebody, to find at any cost somebody who didn't know and be first to tell them, 'Kipps has been left thirty – forty – fifty thousand pounds!'

'*What!*' cried the senior porter. 'Him!' and ran up to the counting house as eagerly as though Kipps had broken his neck.

'One of our chaps just been left sixty thousand pounds,' said the first apprentice, returning after a great absence to his customer.

'Unexpectedly?' said the customer.

'Quite,' said the first apprentice . . .

'I'm sure if Anyone deserves it, it's Mr Kipps,' said Miss Mergle, and her train rustled as she hurried to the counting house.

There stood Kipps amidst a pelting shower of congratulations. His face was flushed and his hair disordered. He still clutched his hat and best umbrella in his left hand. His right hand was anyone's to shake rather than his own. (Ring-a-dinger, ring-a-dinger, ding, ding, ding, dang you! went the neglected dinner bell.)

'Good old Kipps,' said Pierce, shaking; 'Good old Kipps.'

Booch rubbed one anaemic hand upon the other. 'You're sure it's all right, Mr Kipps,' he said in the background.

'I'm sure we all congratulate him,' said Miss Mergle.

'Great Scott!' said the new young lady in the glove department. 'Twelve hundred a year! Great Scott! You aren't thinking of marrying anyone, are you, Mr Kipps?'

'Three pounds five and ninepence a day,' said Mr Booch, working in his head almost miraculously . . .

Everyone, it seemed, was saying how glad they were it was Kipps, except the junior apprentice, upon whom – he being the only son of a widow and used to having the best of everything as a right – an intolerable envy, a sense of unbearable wrong, had cast its gloomy shade. All the rest were quite honestly and simply glad – gladder perhaps at that time than Kipps because they were not so overpowered . . .

Kipps went downstairs to dinner, emitting fragmentary, disconnected statements. 'Never expected anything of the sort . . . When this here old Bean told me, you could have knocked me down with a feather . . . He says, "You b'en lef' money." Even then I didn't expect it'd be mor'n a hundred pounds perhaps. Something like that.'

With the sitting down to dinner and the handing of plates, the excitement assumed a more orderly quality. The housekeeper emitted congratulations as she carved and the maidservant became dangerous to clothes with the plates – she held them anyhow, one expected to see one upside down even – she found Kipps so fascinating to look at. Everyone was the brisker and hungrier for the news (except the junior apprentice) and the housekeeper carved with unusual liberality. It was High Old Times there under the gaslight, High Old Times. 'I'm sure if Anyone deserves it,' said Miss Mergle – 'pass the salt, please – it's Kipps.'

The babble died away a little as Carshot began barking across the table at Kipps. 'You'll be a bit of a Swell, Kipps,' he said. 'You won't hardly know yourself.'

'Quite the gentleman,' said Miss Mergle.

'Many real gentlemen's families,' said the housekeeper, 'have to do with less.'

'See you on the Leas,' said Carshot. 'My gu – !' He met the house-keeper's eye. She had spoken about that before. 'My eye!' he said tamely, lest words should mar the day.

'You'll go to London, I reckon,' said Pierce. 'You'll be a man about town. We shall see you mashing 'em, with violets in your button'ole, down the Burlington Arcade.

'One of these West End flats. That'd be *my* style,' said Pierce. 'And a first-class club.'

'Aren't these clubs a bit 'ard to get into?' asked Kipps, open-eyed, over a mouthful of potato.

'No fear. Not for Money,' said Pierce. And the girl in the laces who had acquired a cynical view of Modern Society from the fearless exposures of Miss Marie Corelli, said, 'Money goes everywhere nowadays, Mr Kipps.'

But Carshot showed the true British strain.

'If I was Kipps,' he said, pausing momentarily for a knifeful of gravy, 'I should go to the Rockies and shoot bears.'

'I'd certainly 'ave a run over to Boulogne,' said Pierce, 'and look about a bit. I'm going to do that next Easter myself, anyhow – see if I don't.'

'Go to Oireland, Mr Kipps,' came the soft insistence of Biddy Murphy, who managed the big workroom, flushed and shining in the Irish way as she spoke. 'Go to Oireland. Ut's the loveliest country in the world. Outside Currrs. Fishin', shootin', huntin'. An' pretty gals! Eh! You should see the Lakes of Killarney, Mr Kipps!' And she expressed ecstasy by a facial pantomime and smacked her lips.

And presently they crowned the event.

It was Pierce who said, 'Kipps, you ought to stand Sham!'

And it was Carshot who found the more poetical word, 'Champagne.'

'Rather!' said Kipps hilariously, and the rest was a question of detail and willing emissaries. 'Here it comes!' they said as the apprentice came down the staircase. 'How about the shop?' said someone. 'Oh! *bang* the shop!' said Carshot and made gruntulous demands for a corkscrew with a thing to cut the wire. Pierce, the dog! had a wire-cutter in his pocket knife. How Shalford would have stared at the gold-tipped bottles if he had chanced to take an early train! Bang went the corks, and bang! Gluck, gluck, gluck, and sizzle!

When Kipps found them all standing about him under the gas flare, saying almost solemnly, 'Kipps!' with tumblers upheld – 'Have it in tumblers,' Carshot had said; 'have it in tumblers. It isn't a wine like you have in glasses. Not like port and sherry. It cheers you up, but you don't get drunk. It isn't hardly stronger than lemonade. They drink it at dinner, some of 'em, every day.'

'What! At three and six a bottle!' said the housekeeper incredulously.

'*They* don't stick at *that*,' said Carshot; 'not the champagne sort.'

The housekeeper pursed her lips and shook her head . . .

When Kipps, I say, found them all standing up to toast him in that manner, there came such a feeling in his throat and face that for the life of him he scarcely knew for a moment whether he was not going to cry. 'Kipps!' they all said, with kindly eyes. It was very good of them, it was very good of them, and hard there wasn't a stroke of luck for them all!

But the sight of upturned chins and glasses pulled him together again . . .

They did him honour. Unenviously and freely they did him honour.

For example, Carshot, being subsequently engaged in serving cretonne and desiring to push a number of rejected blocks up the counter in order to have space for measuring, swept them by a powerful and ill-calculated movement of the arm, with a noise like thunder, partly on to the floor and partly on to the foot of the still gloomily preoccupied junior apprentice. And Buggins, whose place it was to shopwalk while Carshot served, shopwalked with quite unparalleled dignity, dangling a new season's sunshade with a crooked handle on one finger. He arrested each customer who came down the shop with a grave and penetrating look. 'Showing very 'tractive line new sheason's shunshade,' he would remark, and, after a suitable pause, ' 'Markable thing, one our 'sistant leg'sy twelve 'undred a year. V'ry 'tractive. Nothing more today, mum? No!' And he would then go and hold the door open for them with perfect decorum and with the sunshade dangling elegantly from his left hand . . .

And the second apprentice, serving a customer with cheap ticking, and being asked suddenly if it was strong, answered remarkably, 'Oo! *no*, mum! Strong! Why it ain't 'ardly stronger than lemonade . . . '

The head porter, moreover, was filled with a virtuous resolve to break the record as a lightning packer and make up for lost time. Mr Swaffenham, of the Sandgate Riviera, for example, who was going out to dinner that night at seven, received at half-past six, instead of the urgently needed dress shirt he expected, a corset specially adapted to the needs of persons inclined to embonpoint. A parcel of summer underclothing selected by the elder Miss Waldershawe was somehow distributed in the form of gratis additions throughout a number of parcels of a less intimate nature, and a box of millinery on approval to Lady Pamshort (at Wampachs) was enriched by the addition of the junior porter's cap . . .

These little things, slight in themselves, witness perhaps none the less eloquently to the unselfish exhilaration felt throughout the Emporium at the extraordinary and unexpected enrichment of Mr Kipps.

5

The bus that plies between New Romney and Folkestone is painted a British red and inscribed on either side with the word 'Tip-top' in gold amidst voluptuous scrolls. It is a slow and portly bus; even as a young bus it

must have been slow and portly. Below it swings a sort of hold, hung by chains between the wheels, and in the summertime the top has garden seats. The front over the two dauntless unhurrying horses rises in tiers like a theatre: there is first a seat for the driver and his company, and above that a seat, and above that, unless my memory plays me false, a seat. You sit in a sort of composition by some Italian painter – a celestial group of you. There are days when this bus goes and days when it doesn't go – you have to find out. And so you get to New Romney. So you will continue to get to New Romney for many years, for the light-railway concession along the coast is happily in the South Eastern Railway Company's keeping and the peace of the Marsh is kept inviolate except for the bicycle bells of such as Kipps and I.

This bus it was, this ruddy, venerable and immortal bus, that came down the Folkestone hill with unflinching deliberation, and trundled through Sandgate and Hythe, and out into the windy spaces of the Marsh, with Kipps and all his fortunes on its brow. You figure him there. He sat on the highest seat diametrically above the driver and his head was spinning and spinning with champagne and this stupendous Tomfoolery of Luck, and his heart was swelling, swelling indeed at times as though it would burst him, and his face towards the sunlight was transfigured. He said never a word, but ever and again as he thought of this or that, he laughed. He seemed full of chuckles for a time, detached and independent chuckles, chuckles that rose and burst in him like bubbles in a wine . . . He held a banjo sceptre-fashion and restless on his knee. He had always wanted a banjo, and now he had got one at Malchior's while he was waiting for the bus.

There sat beside him a young servant who was sucking peppermint and a little boy with a sniff, whose flitting eyes showed him curious to know why ever and again Kipps laughed, and beside the driver were two young men in gaiters talking about 'tegs'. And there sat Kipps, all unsuspected, twelve hundred a year, as it were, except for the protrusion of the banjo, disguised as a common young man. And the young man in gaiters to the left of the driver eyed Kipps and his banjo, and especially his banjo, ever and again as if he found it and him, with his rapt face, an insoluble enigma. And many a king has ridden into a conquered city with a lesser sense of splendour than Kipps.

Their shadows grew long behind them and their faces were trans-figured in gold as they rumbled on towards the splendid West. The sun set before they had passed Dymchurch, and as they came lumbering into New Romney past the windmill the dusk had come.

The driver handed down the banjo and the portmanteau, and Kipps having paid him – 'That's aw right,' he said to the change, as a gentleman should – turned about and ran the portmanteau smartly into old Kipps, whom the sound of the stopping of the bus had brought to the door of the shop in an aggressive mood and with his mouth full of supper.

' 'Ello, uncle, didn't see you,' said Kipps.

'Blunderin' ninny,' said old Kipps. 'What's brought *you* here? Ain't early closing, is it? Not Toosday?'

'Got some news for you, uncle,' said Kipps, dropping the portmanteau.

'Ain't lost your situation, 'ave you? What's that you got there? I'm blowed if it ain't a banjo. Goo' Lord! Spendin' your money on banjoes! Don't put down your portmanty there – anyhow. Right in the way of everybody. I'm blowed if ever I saw such a boy as you've got lately. Here! Molly! And, look here! What you got a portmanty for? Why! Goo' Lord! You ain't *really* lost your place, 'ave you?'

'Somethin's happened,' said Kipps slightly dashed. 'It's all right, uncle. I'll tell you in a minute.'

Old Kipps took the banjo as his nephew picked up the portmanteau again.

The living-room door opened quickly, showing a table equipped with elaborate simplicity for supper, and Mrs Kipps appeared.

'If it ain't young Artie,' she said. 'Why! Whatever's brought *you* 'ome?'

' 'Ello aunt,' said Artie. 'I'm coming in. I got somethin' to tell you. I've 'ad a bit of Luck.'

He wouldn't tell them all at once. He staggered with the portmanteau round the corner of the counter, set a bundle of children's tin pails into clattering oscillation, and entered the little room. He deposited his luggage in the corner beside the tall clock, and turned to his aunt and uncle again. His aunt regarded him doubtfully; the yellow light from the little lamp on the table escaped above the shade and lit her forehead and the tip of her nose. It would be all right in a minute. He wouldn't tell them all at once. Old Kipps stood in the shop door with the banjo in his hand, breathing noisily. 'The fact is, aunt, I've 'ad a bit of Luck.'

'You ain't been backin' gordless 'orses, Artie?' she asked.

'No fear.'

'It's a draw he's been in,' said old Kipps, still panting from the impact of the portmanteau; 'it's a dratted draw. Jest look here, Molly. He's won this 'ere trashy banjer and throwed up his situation on the strength of it – that's what he's done. Goin' about singing. Dash and plunge! Jest the very fault poor Pheamy always 'ad. Blunder right in and no one mustn't stop 'er!'

'You ain't thrown up your place, Artie, 'ave you?' said Mrs Kipps.

Kipps perceived his opportunity. 'I 'ave,' he said; 'I've throwed it up.'

'What for?' said old Kipps.

'So's to learn the banjo!'

'Goo' *Lord*!' said old Kipps, in horror to find himself verified.

'I'm going about playing!' said Kipps with a giggle. 'Goin' to black my face, aunt, and sing on the beach. I'm going to 'ave a most tremenjous lark and earn any amount of money – you see. Twenty-six fousand pounds I'm going to earn just as easy as nothing!'

'Kipps,' said Mrs Kipps, 'he's been drinking!'

They regarded their nephew across the supper table with long faces. Kipps exploded with laughter and broke out again when his Aunt shook her head very sadly at him. Then suddenly he fell grave. He felt he could keep it up no longer. 'It's all right, aunt. Reely. I ain't mad and I ain't been drinking. I been lef' money. I been left twenty-six fousand pounds.'

Pause.

'And you thrown up your place?' said old Kipps.

'Yes,' said Kipps. 'Rather!'

'And bort this banjer, put on your best noo trousers and come right on 'ere?'

'Well,' said Mrs Kipps, '*I* never did.'

'These ain't my noo trousers, aunt,' said Kipps regretfully. 'My noo trousers wasn't done.'

'I shouldn't ha' thought that *even you* could ha' been such a fool as that,' said old Kipps.

Pause.

'It's *all* right,' said Kipps, a little disconcerted by their distrustful solemnity. 'It's all right – reely! Twenny-six fousan' pounds. And a 'ouse – '

Old Kipps pursed his lips and shook his head.

'A 'ouse on the Leas. I could have gone there. Only I didn't. I didn't care to. I didn't know what to say. I wanted to come and tell you.'

'How d'yer know the 'ouse – ?'

'They told me.'

'Well,' said old Kipps, and nodded his head portentously towards his nephew, with the corners of his mouth pulled down in a portentous, discouraging way. 'Well, you *are* a young Gaby.'

'I didn't *think* it of you, Artie!' said Mrs Kipps.

'Wadjer mean?' asked Kipps faintly, looking from one to the other with a withered face.

Old Kipps closed the shop door. 'They been 'avin' a lark with you,' said old Kipps in a mournful undertone. 'That's what I mean, my boy. They jest been seein' what a Gaby like you 'ud do.'

'I des say that young Quodling was in it,' said Mrs Kipps. ' 'E's jest that sort.'

(For Quodling of the green-baize bag had grown up to be a fearful dog, the terror of New Romney.)

'It's somebody after your place very likely,' said old Kipps.

Kipps looked from one sceptical, reproving face to the other, and round him at the familiar shabby little room, with his familiar cheap portmanteau on the mended chair, and that banjo amidst the supper things like some irrevocable deed. Could he be rich indeed? Could it be that these things had really happened? Or had some insane fancy whirled him hither?

Still – perhaps a hundred pounds –

'But,' he said. 'It's all right, reely, uncle. You don't think – ? I 'ad a letter.'

'Got up,' said old Kipps.

'But I answered it and went to a norfis.'

Old Kipps felt staggered for a moment, but he shook his head and chins sagely from side to side. As the memory of old Bean revived, the confidence of Kipps came back to him.

'I saw a nold gent, uncle – perfect gentleman. And 'e told me all about it. Mos' respectable 'e was. Said 'is name was Watson and Bean – leastways 'e was Bean. Said it was lef' me – ' Kipps suddenly dived into his breast pocket – 'by my grandfather – '

The old people started.

Old Kipps uttered an exclamation and wheeled round towards the mantelshelf above which the daguerreotype of his lost younger sister smiled its fading smile upon the world.

'Waddy 'is name was,' said Kipps, with his hand still deep in his pocket. 'It was '*is* son was my father – '

'Waddy!' said old Kipps.

'Waddy!' said Mrs Kipps.

'She'd never say,' said old Kipps.

There was a long silence.

Kipps fumbled with a letter, a crumpled advertisement and three bank notes. He hesitated between these items.

'Why! That young chap what was arsting questions – ' said old Kipps, and regarded his wife with an eye of amazement.

'Must 'ave been,' said Mrs Kipps.

'Must 'ave been,' said old Kipps.

'James,' said Mrs Kipps, in an awestricken voice, 'after all – perhaps – it's true!'

"*Ow* much did you say?' asked old Kipps. ' 'Ow much did you say 'e'd lef' you, me b'y?'

It was thrilling, though not quite in the way Kipps had expected. He answered almost meekly across the meagre supper things, with his documentary evidence in his hand: 'Twelve 'undred pounds. 'Proximately, he said. Twelve 'undred pounds a year. 'E made 'is will, jest before 'e died – not more'n a month ago. When 'e was dying, 'e seemed to change like, Mr Bean said. 'E'd never forgiven 'is son, never – not till then. 'Is son 'ad died in Australia, years and years ago, and *then* 'e 'adn't forgiven 'im. You know – 'is son what was my father. But jest when 'e was ill and dying 'e seemed to get worried like and longing for someone of 'is own. And 'e told Mr Bean it was 'im that had prevented them marrying. So 'e thought. That's 'ow it all come about . . . '

At last Kipps's flaring candle went up the narrow uncarpeted staircase to the little attic that had been his shelter and refuge during all the days of his childhood and youth. His head was whirling. He had been advised, he had been warned, he had been flattered and congratulated, he had been given whisky and hot water and lemon and sugar, and his health had been drunk in the same. He had also eaten two Welsh rarebits – an unusual supper. His uncle was chiefly for his going into Parliament, his aunt was consumed with a great anxiety. 'I'm afraid he'll go and marry beneath 'im.'

'Y'ought to 'ave a bit o' shootin' somewheer,' said old Kipps.

'It's your *duty* to marry into a county family, Artie. Remember that.'

'There's lots of young noblemen'll be glad to 'ang on to you,' said old Kipps. 'You mark my words. And borry your money. And then, good-day to ye.'

'I got to be precious Careful,' said Kipps. 'Mr Bean said that.'

'And you got to be precious careful of this old Bean,' said old Kipps. 'We may be out of the world in Noo Romney, but I've 'eard a bit about s'licitors, for all that. You keep your eye on old Bean, me b'y.

' 'Ow do we know what 'e's up to, with your money, even now?' said old Kipps, pursuing this uncomfortable topic.

' 'E *looked* very respectable,' said Kipps –

Kipps undressed with great deliberation, and with vast gaps of pensive margin. Twenty-six thousand pounds!

His aunt's solicitude had brought back certain matters into the foreground that his 'twelve 'undred a year!' had for a time driven away altogether. His thoughts went back to the wood-carving class. Twelve Hundred a Year. He sat on the edge of the bed in profound meditation and his boots fell 'whop' and 'whop' upon the floor, with a long interval between each 'whop'. Twenty-six thousand pounds. 'By gum!' He dropped the remainder of his costume about him on the floor, got into bed, pulled the patchwork quilt over him and put his head on the pillow that had been first to hear of Ann Pornick's accession to his heart. But he did not think of Ann Pornick now.

It was about everything in the world except Ann Pornick that he seemed to be trying to think of – simultaneously. All the vivid happenings of the day came and went in his overtaxed brain: 'that old Bean' explaining and explaining, the fat man who wouldn't believe, an overpowering smell of peppermint, the banjo, Miss Mergle saying he deserved it, Chitterlow's vanishing round a corner, the wisdom and advice and warnings of his aunt and uncle. She was afraid he would marry beneath him, *was* she? She didn't know . . .

His brain made an excursion into the wood-carving class and presented Kipps with the picture of himself amazing that class by a modest yet clearly audible remark, 'I been left twenty-six thousand pounds.'

Then he told them all quietly but firmly that he had always loved Miss Walshingham, always, and so he had brought all his twenty-six thousand pounds with him to give to her there and then. He wanted nothing in return . . . Yes, he wanted nothing in return. He would give it to her all in an envelope and go. Of course he would keep the banjo – and a little present for his aunt and uncle – and a new suit perhaps – and one or two other things she would not miss. He went off at a tangent. He might buy a motor car, he might buy one of these here things that will play you a piano – that would make old Buggins sit up! He could pretend he had learnt to play – he might buy a bicycle and a cyclist suit . . .

A terrific multitude of plans of what he might do and in particular of what he might buy, came crowding into his brain, and he did not so much fall asleep as pass into a disorder of dreams in which he was driving a four-horse Tip-Top coach down Sandgate Hill ('I shall have to be precious careful'), wearing innumerable suits of clothes, and through some terrible accident wearing them all wrong. Consequently he was being laughed at. The coach vanished in the interest of the costume. He was wearing golfing suits and a silk hat. This passed into a nightmare that he was promenading on the Leas in a Highland costume, with a kilt that kept shrinking, and Shalford was following him with three policemen. 'He's my assistant,' Shalford kept repeating; 'he's escaped. He's an escaped Improver. Keep by him and in a minute you'll have to run him in. I know 'em. We say they wash, but they won't.' . . . He could feel the kilt creeping up his legs. He would have tugged at it to pull it down only his arms were paralysed. He had an impression of giddy crisis. He uttered a shriek of despair. '*Now!*' said Shalford. He woke in horror, his quilt had slipped off the bed.

He had a fancy he had just been called, that he had somehow overslept himself and missed going down for dusting. Then he perceived it was still night and light by reason of the moonlight, and that he was no longer in the Emporium. He wondered where he could be. He had a curious fancy that the world had been swept and rolled up like a carpet and that he was nowhere. It occurred to him that perhaps he was mad. 'Buggins!' he said. There was no answer, not even the defensive snore. No room, no Buggins, nothing!

Then he remembered better. He sat on the edge of his bed for some time. Could anyone have seen his face they would have seen it white and drawn with staring eyes. Then he groaned weakly. 'Twenty-six thousand pounds!' he whispered.

Just then it presented itself in an almost horribly overwhelming mass.

He remade his bed and returned to it. He was still dreadfully wakeful. It was suddenly clear to him that he need never trouble to get up punctually

at seven again. That fact shone out upon him like a star through clouds. He was free to lie in bed as long as he liked, get up when he liked, go where he liked, have eggs every morning for breakfast or rashers or bloater paste or . . . Also he was going to astonish Miss Walshingham . . .

Astonish her and astonish her . . .

* * *

He was awakened by a thrush singing in the fresh dawn. The whole room was flooded with warm, golden sunshine. 'I say!' said the thrush. 'I say! I say! Twelve 'undred a year! Twelve 'Undred a Year! Twelve 'UNDRED a Year! I say! I say! I say!'

He sat up in bed and rubbed the sleep from his eyes with his knuckles. Then he jumped out of bed and began dressing very eagerly. He did not want to lose any time in beginning the new life.

BOOK TWO

Mr Coote, the Chaperon

CHAPTER ONE

The New Conditions

There comes a gentlemanly figure into these events who for a space takes a leading part therein; a Good Influence, a refined and amiable figure, Mr Chester Coote. You must figure him as about to enter our story, walking with a curious rectitude of bearing through the evening dusk towards the Public Library, erect, large-headed – he had a great, big head full of the suggestion of a powerful mind well under control – with a large, official-looking envelope in his white and knuckly hand. In the other he carries a gold-handled cane. He wears a silken grey jacket suit, buttoned up, and anon he coughs behind the official envelope. He has a prominent nose, slatey grey eyes and a certain heaviness about the mouth. His mouth hangs breathing open, with a slight protrusion of the lower jaw. His straw hat is pulled down a little in front, and he looks each person he passes in the eye, and directly his look is answered looks away.

Thus Mr Chester Coote, as he was on the evening when he came upon Kipps. He was a local house agent and a most active and gentlemanly person, a conscious gentleman, equally aware of society and the serious side of life. From amateur theatricals of a nice refined sort to science classes, few things were able to get along without him. He supplied a fine, full bass, a little flat and quavery perhaps, but very abundant, to the St Stylites' choir . . .

He passes on towards the Public Library, lifts the envelope in salutation to a passing curate, smiles and enters . . .

It was in the Public Library that he came upon Kipps.

By that time Kipps had been rich a week or more, and the change in his circumstances was visible upon his person. He was wearing a new suit of drab flannels, a Panama hat and a red tie for the first time, and he carried a silver-mounted stick with a tortoiseshell handle. He felt extraordinarily different, perhaps more different than he really was, from the meek Improver of a week ago. He felt as he felt dukes must feel, yet at bottom he was still modest. He was leaning on his stick and regarding the indicator with a respect that never palled. He faced round to meet Mr Coote's overflowing smile.

'What are you doang hea?' said Mr Chester Coote.

Kipps was momentarily abashed. 'Oh,' he said slowly, and then, 'Mooching round a bit.'

That Coote should address him with this easy familiarity was a fresh reminder of his enhanced social position. 'Jes' mooching round,' he said. 'I been back in Folkestone free days now. At my 'ouse, you know.'

'Ah!' said Mr Coote. 'I haven't yet had an opportunity of congratulating you on your good fortune.'

Kipps held out his hand. 'It was the cleanest surprise that ever was,' he said. 'When Mr Bean told me of it – you could have knocked me down with a feather.'

'It must mean a tremendous change for you.'

'O-o. Rather. Change? Why, I'm like the chap in the song they sing, I don't 'ardly know where I are. *You* know.'

'An extraordinary change,' said Mr Coote. 'I can quite believe it. Are you stopping in Folkestone?'

'For a bit. I got a 'ouse, you know. What my gran'father 'ad. I'm stopping there. His housekeeper was kep' on. Fancy – being in the same town and everything!'

'Precisely,' said Mr Coote. 'That's it!' and coughed like a sheep behind four straight fingers.

'Mr Bean got me to come back to see to things. Else I was out in New Romney, where my uncle and aunt live. But It's a Lark coming back. In a way . . .'

The conversation hung for a moment.

'Are you getting a book?' asked Coote.

'Well, I 'aven't got a ticket yet. But I shall get one all right, and have a go in at reading. I've often wanted to. Rather. I was just 'aving a look at this Indicator. First-class idea. Tells you all you want to know.'

'It's simple,' said Coote, and coughed again, keeping his eyes fixed on Kipps. For a moment they hung, evidently disinclined to part. Then Kipps jumped at an idea he had cherished for a day or more – not particularly in relation to Coote, but in relation to anyone.

'You doing anything?' he asked.

'Just called with a papah about the classes.'

'Because – Would you care to come up and look at my 'ouse and 'ave a smoke and a chat? Eh?' He made indicative back jerks of the head, and was smitten with a horrible doubt whether possibly this invitation might not be some hideous breach of etiquette. Was it, for example, the correct hour? 'I'd be awfully glad if you would,' he added.

Mr Coote begged for a moment while he handed the official-looking envelope to the librarian and then declared himself quite at Kipps's service. They muddled a moment over precedence at each door they went through and so emerged to the street.

'It feels awful rum to me at first, all this,' said Kipps ' 'Aving a 'ouse of my own and all that. It's strange, you know. 'Aving all day. Reely I don't 'ardly know what to do with my time.

'D'ju smoke?' he said suddenly, proffering a magnificent gold-decorated pigskin cigarette case, which he produced from nothing, almost as though it was some sort of trick. Coote hesitated and declined, and then, with great liberality, 'Don't let me hinder you . . .'

They walked a little way in silence, Kipps being chiefly concerned to

affect ease in his new clothes and keeping a wary eye on Coote.

'It's rather a big windfall,' said Coote presently. 'It yields you an income – ?'

'Twelve 'undred a year,' said Kipps. 'Bit over – if anything.'

'Do you think of living in Folkestone?'

'Don't know 'ardly yet. I *may*. Then again, I may not. I got a furnished 'ouse, but I may let it.'

'Your plans are undecided?'

'That's jest it,' said Kipps.

'Very beautiful sunset it was tonight,' said Coote, and Kipps said, 'Wasn't it?' and they began to talk of the merits of sunsets. Did Kipps paint? Not since he was a boy. He didn't believe he could now. Coote said his sister was a painter and Kipps received this intimation with respect. Coote sometimes wished he could find time to paint himself – but one couldn't do everything, and Kipps said that was 'jest it'.

They came out presently upon the end of the Leas and looked down to where the squat dark masses of the harbour and harbour station, gemmed with pinpoint lights, crouched against the twilit grey of the sea. 'If one could do *that*,' said Coote, and Kipps was inspired to throw his head back, cock it on one side, regard the harbour with one eye shut and say that it would take some doing. Then Coote said something about 'Abend', which Kipps judged to be in a foreign language and got over by lighting another cigarette from his by no means completed first one. 'You're right, *puff, puff*.'

He felt that so far he had held up his end of the conversation in a very creditable manner, but that extreme discretion was advisable.

They turned away and Coote remarked that the sea was good for crossing, and asked Kipps if he had been over the water very much. Kipps said he hadn't been – 'much', but he thought very likely he'd have a run over to Boulogne soon, and Coote proceeded to talk of the charms of foreign travel, mentioning quite a number of unheard-of places by name. He had been to them! Kipps remained on the defensive, but behind his defences his heart sank. It was all very well to pretend, but presently it was bound to come out. *He* didn't know anything of all this . . .

So they drew near the house. At his own gate Kipps became extremely nervous. It was a fine, impressive door. He knocked neither a single knock nor a double, but about one and a half – an apologetic half. They were admitted by an irreproachable housemaid, with a steady eye, before which Kipps cringed dreadfully. He hung up his hat and fell about over hall chairs and things. 'There's a fire in the study, Mary?' he had the audacity to ask, though evidently he knew, and led the way upstairs panting. He tried to shut the door and discovered the housemaid behind him coming to light his lamp. This enfeebled him further. He said nothing until the door closed behind her. Meanwhile to show his *sang froid* he hummed and flitted towards the window, and here and there.

Coote went to the big hearthrug and turned and surveyed his host. His hand went to the back of his head and patted his occiput – a gesture frequent with him.

' 'Ere we are,' said Kipps, hands in his pockets and glancing round him.

It was a gaunt Victorian room with a heavy, dirty cornice, and the ceiling enriched by the radiant plaster ornament of an obliterated gas chandelier. It held two large glass-fronted bookcases, one of which was surmounted by a stuffed terrier encased in glass. There was a mirror over the mantel and hangings and curtains of magnificent crimson patternings. On the mantel were a huge black clock of classical design, vases in the Burslem Etruscan style, spills and toothpicks in large receptacles of carved rock, large lava ashtrays and an exceptionally big box of matches. The fender was very great and brassy. In a favourable position, under the window, was a spacious rosewood writing desk, and all the chairs and other furniture were of rosewood and well stuffed.

'This,' said Kipps, in something near an undertone, 'was the o' gentleman's study – my grandfather that was. 'E used to sit at that desk and write.'

'Books?'

'No. Letters to *The Times*, and things like that. 'E's got 'em all cut out – stuck in a book . . . Leastways, he *'ad*. It's in that bookcase . . . Won't you sit down?'

Coote did, bowing very slightly, and Kipps secured his vacated position on the extensive black skin rug. He spread out his legs compass-fashion and tried to appear at his ease. The rug, the fender, the mantel and mirror conspired with great success to make him look a trivial and intrusive little creature amidst their commonplace hauteur, and his own shadow on the opposite wall seemed to think everything a great lark and mocked and made tremendous fun of him . . .

2

For a space Kipps played a defensive game and Coote drew the lines of the conversation. They kept away from the theme of Kipps's change of fortune, and Coote made remarks upon local and social affairs. 'You must take an interest in these things now,' was as much as he said in the way of personalities. But it speedily became evident that he was a person of wide and commanding social relationships. He spoke of 'society' being mixed in the neighbourhood and of the difficulty of getting people to work together, and 'do' things; they were cliquish. Incidentally he alluded quite familiarly to men with military titles, and once even to someone with a title, a Lady Punnet. Not snobbishly, you understand, nor deliberately, but quite in passing. He had, it appeared, talked to Lady Punnet about private theatricals! In connection with the Hospitals. She had been unreasonable

and he had put her right, gently of course, but firmly. 'If you stand up to these people,' said Coote, 'they like you all the better.' It was also very evident he was at his ease with the clergy; 'My friend, Mr Densemore – a curate, you know, and rather curious, the Reverend *and* Honourable.' Coote grew visibly in Kipps's eyes as he said these things: he became not only the exponent of 'Vagner or Vargner', the man whose sister had painted a picture to be exhibited at the Royal Academy, the type of the hidden thing called culture, but a delegate, as it were, or at least an intermediary from that great world 'up there', where there were men-servants, where there were titles, where people dressed for dinner, drank wine at meals, wine costing very often as much as three and sixpence the bottle, and followed through a maze of etiquette the most stupendous practices . . .

Coote sat back in the armchair smoking luxuriously and expanding pleasantly, with the delightful sense of *Savoir Faire*; Kipps sat forward, his elbows on his chair arm, alert, and his head a little on one side. You figure him as looking little and cheap and feeling smaller and cheaper amidst his new surroundings. But it was a most stimulating and interesting con-versation. And soon it became less general and more serious and intimate. Coote spoke of people who had got on, and of people who hadn't, of people who seemed to be *in* everything and people who seemed to be *out* of everything, and then he came round to Kipps.

'You'll have a good time,' he said abruptly, with a smile that would have interested a dentist.

'I dunno,' said Kipps.

'There's mistakes, of course.'

'That's jest it.'

Coote lit a new cigarette. 'One can't help being interested in what you will do,' he remarked. 'Of course – for a young man of spirit, come suddenly into wealth – there's temptations.'

'I got to go careful,' said Kipps. 'O' Bean told me that at the very first.'

Coote went on to speak of pitfalls – of Betting, of Bad Companions.

'I know,' said Kipps, 'I know.'

'There's Doubt again,' said Coote. 'I know a young fellow – a solicitor – handsome, gifted. And yet, you know – utterly sceptical. Practically altogether a Sceptic.'

'Lor'!' said Kipps, 'not a Natheist?'

'I fear so,' said Coote. 'Really, you know, an awfully fine young fellow – Gifted! But full of this dreadful Modern Spirit – Cynical! All this Overman stuff. Nietzsche and all that . . . I wish I could do something for him.'

'Ah!' said Kipps and knocked the ash off his cigarette. 'I know a chap – one of our apprentices he was – once. Always scoffing . . . He lef'!' He paused. 'Never wrote for his refs,' he said, in the deep tone proper to a moral tragedy, and then, after a pause – 'Enlisted!'

'Ah!' said Coote.

'And often,' he said, after a pause, 'it's just the most spirited chaps, just the chaps one likes best, who Go Wrong.'

'It's temptation,' Kipps remarked.

He glanced at Coote, leant forward, knocked the ash from his cigarette into the mighty fender. 'That's jest it,' he said; 'you get tempted. Before you know where you are.'

'Modern life,' said Coote, 'is so – complex. It isn't everyone is Strong. Half the young fellows who go wrong, aren't really bad.'

'That's jest it,' said Kipps.

'One gets a tone from one's surroundings – '

'That's exactly it,' said Kipps.

He meditated. '*I* picked up with a chap,' he said. 'A Nacter. Leastways he writes plays. Clever fellow. But – '

He implied extensive moral obloquy by a movement of his head. 'Of course it's seeing life,' he added.

Coote pretended to understand the full implications of Kipps's remark. 'Is it *worth* it?' he asked.

'That's jest it,' said Kipps.

He decided to give some more. 'One gets talking,' he said. 'Then it's " 'ave a drink!" Old Methusaleh three stars – and where *are* you? *I* been drunk,' he said in a tone of profound humility, and added, 'lots of times.'

'Tut-tut,' said Coote.

'Dozens of times,' said Kipps, smiling sadly, and added, 'lately.'

His imagination became active and seductive. 'One thing leads to another. Cards, p'r'aps. Girls – '

'I know,' said Coote; 'I know.'

Kipps regarded the fire and flushed slightly. He borrowed a sentence that Chitterlow had recently used. 'One can't tell tales out of school,' he said.

'I can imagine it,' said Coote.

Kipps looked with a confidential expression into Coote's face. 'It was bad enough when money was limited,' he remarked. 'But now – ' he spoke with raised eyebrows, 'I got to steady down.'

'You *must*,' said Coote, protruding his lips into a sort of whistling concern for a moment.

'I must,' said Kipps, nodding his head slowly with raised eyebrows. He looked at his cigarette end and threw it into the fender. He was beginning to think he was holding his own in this conversation rather well, after all.

Kipps was never a good liar. He was the first to break silence. 'I don't mean to say I been reely bad or reely bad drunk. A 'eadache perhaps – three or four times, say. But there it is!'

'I have never tasted alcohol in my life,' said Coote, with an immense frankness, 'never!'

'No?'

'Never. I don't feel *I* should be likely to get drunk at all – it isn't that. And I don't go so far as to say even that in small quantities – at meals – it does one harm. But if I take it, someone else who doesn't know where to stop – you see?'

'That's jest it,' said Kipps, with admiring eyes.

'I smoke,' admitted Coote. 'One doesn't want to be a Pharisee.'

It struck Kipps what a tremendously Good chap this Coote was, not only tremendously clever and educated and a gentleman and one knowing Lady Punnet, but Good. He seemed to be giving all his time and thought to doing good things to other people. A great desire to confide certain things to him arose. At first Kipps hesitated whether he should confide an equal desire for Benevolent activities or for further Depravity – either was in his mind. He rather affected the pose of the Good Intentioned Dog. Then suddenly his impulses took quite a different turn, fell indeed into what was a far more serious rut in his mind. It seemed to him Coote might be able to do for him something he very much wanted done.

'Companionship accounts for so much,' said Coote.

'That's jest it,' said Kipps. 'Of course, you know, in my new position – That's just the difficulty.'

He plunged boldly at his most secret trouble. He knew that he wanted refinement – culture. It was all very well – but he knew. But how was one to get it? He knew no one, knew no people – He rested on the broken sentence. The shop chaps were all very well, very good chaps and all that, but not what one wanted. 'I feel be'ind,' said Kipps. 'I feel out of it. And consequently I feel it's no good. And then if temptation comes along . . . '

'Exactly,' said Coote.

Kipps spoke of his respect for Miss Walshingham and her freckled friend. He contrived not to look too self-conscious. 'You know, I'd like to talk to people like that, but I can't. A chap's afraid of giving himself away.'

'Of course,' said Coote, 'of course.'

'I went to a middle-class school, you know. You mustn't fancy I'm one of these here board-school chaps, but you know it reely wasn't a first-class affair. Leastways he didn't take pains with us. If you didn't want to learn you needn't – I don't believe it was *much* better than one of these here national schools. We wore mortar boards, o' course. But what's *that*?

'I'm a regular fish out of water with this money. When I got it – it's a week ago – reely I thought I'd got everything I wanted. But I dunno what to *do*.' His voice went up into a squeak. 'Practically,' he said, 'it's no good shuttin' my eyes to things – I'm a gentleman.'

Coote indicated a serious assent. 'And there's the responsibilities of a gentleman,' he remarked.

'That's jest it,' said Kipps.

'There's calling on people,' said Kipps. 'If you want to go on knowing

Someone you knew before like. People that's refined.' He laughed nervously. 'I'm a regular fish out of water,' he said, with expectant eyes on Coote.

But Coote only nodded for him to go on.

'This actor chap,' he meditated, 'is a good sort of chap. But 'e isn't what *I* call a gentleman. I got to 'old myself in with 'im. 'E'd make me go it wild in no time. 'E's pretty near the on'y chap I know. Except the shop chaps. They've come round to 'ave supper once already and a bit of a sing-song afterwards. I sang. I got a banjo, you know, and I vamp a bit. Vamping – you know. Haven't got far in the book – *'Ow to Vamp* – but still I'm getting on. Jolly, of course, in a way, but what does it *lead* to? . . . Besides that, there's my aunt and uncle. *They*'re very good old people – very – jest a bit interfering p'r'aps and thinking one isn't grown up, but Right enough. Only – It isn't what I *want*. I feel I've got be'ind with everything. I want to make it up again. I want to get with educated people who know 'ow to do things – in the regular, proper way.'

His beautiful modesty awakened nothing but benevolence in the mind of Chester Coote.

'If I had someone like you,' said Kipps, 'that I knew regular like – '

From that point their course ran swift and easy. 'If I *could* be of any use to you,' said Coote . . .

'But you're so busy and all that.'

'Not *too* busy. You know, your case is a very interesting one. It was partly that made me speak to you and draw you out. Here you are with all this money and no experience, a spirited young chap – '

'That's jest it,' said Kipps.

'I thought I'd see what you were made of, and I must confess I've rarely talked to anyone that I've found quite so interesting as you have been – '

'I seem able to say things to you like, somehow,' said Kipps.

'I'm glad. I'm tremendously glad.'

'I want a Friend. That's it – straight.'

'My dear chap, if I – '

'Yes, but – '

'*I* want a Friend, too.'

'Reely?'

'Yes. You know, my dear Kipps – if I may call you that.'

'Go on,' said Kipps.

'I'm rather a lonely dog myself. *This* tonight – I've not had anyone I've spoken to so freely of my Work for months.'

'No?'

'Yes. And, my dear chap, if I can do anything to guide or help you – ' Coote displayed all his teeth in a kindly tremulous smile and his eyes were shiny.

'Shake 'ands,' said Kipps, deeply moved, and he and Coote rose and clasped with mutual emotion.

'It's reely too good of you,' said Kipps.

'Whatever I can do I will,' said Coote.

And so their compact was made. From that moment they were Friends, intimate, confidential, high-thinking, *sotto voce* friends. All the rest of their talk (and it inclined to be interminable) was an expansion of that. For that night Kipps wallowed in self-abandonment and Coote behaved as one who had received a great trust. That sinister passion for pedagogy to which the Good Intentioned are so fatally liable, that passion of infinite presumption that permits one weak human being to arrogate the direction of another weak human being's affairs, had Coote in its grip. He was to be a sort of lay confessor and director of Kipps, he was to help Kipps in a thousand ways, he was in fact to chaperon Kipps into the higher and better sort of English life. He was to tell him his faults, advise him about the right thing to do –

'It's all these things I don't know,' said Kipps. 'I don't know, for instance, what's the right sort of dress to wear – I don't even know if I'm dressed right now – '

'All these things' – Coote stuck out his lips and nodded rapidly to show he understood – 'Trust me for that,' he said, 'trust me.'

As the evening wore on Coote's manner changed, became more and more the manner of a proprietor. He began to take up his role, to survey Kipps with a new, with a critical affection. It was evident the thing fell in with his ideas. 'It will be awfully interesting,' he said. 'You know, Kipps, you're really good stuff.' (Every sentence now he said 'Kipps' or 'my dear Kipps' with a curiously authoritative intonation.)

'I know,' said Kipps, 'only there's such a lot of things I don't seem to be up to some'ow. That's where the trouble comes in.'

They talked and talked, and now Kipps was talking freely. They rambled over all sorts of things. Among others Kipps's character was dealt with at length. Kipps gave valuable lights on it. 'When I'm reely excited,' he said, 'I don't seem to care *what* I do. I'm like that.' And again, 'I don't like to do anything under'and. I *must* speak out . . . '

He picked a piece of cotton from his knee, the fire grimaced behind his back, and his shadow on the wall and ceiling was disrespectfully convulsed.

3

Kipps went to bed at last with an impression of important things settled, and he lay awake for quite a long time. He felt he was lucky. He had known – in fact Buggins and Carshot and Pierce had made it very clear indeed – that his status in life had changed and that stupendous adaptations had to be achieved, but the problem of their achievement had driven them into the realm of the incredible. Here in the simplest, easiest

way was the adapter. The thing had become possible. Not of course easy, but possible.

There was much to learn through sheer intellectual toil – methods of address, bowing, an enormous complexity of laws. One broken, you are an outcast. How, for example, would one encounter Lady Punnet? It was quite possible some day he might really have to do that. Coote might introduce him. 'Lord!' he said aloud to the darkness between grinning and dismay. He figured himself going into the Emporium to buy a tie, for example, and there in the face of Buggins, Carshot, Pierce and the rest of them, meeting 'my friend, Lady Punnet!' It might not end with Lady Punnet! His imagination plunged and bolted with him, galloped, took wings and soared to romantic, to poetical altitudes . . .

Suppose some day one met Royalty. By accident, say! He soared to that! After all – twelve hundred a year is a lift, a tremendous lift. How did one address Royalty? 'Your Majesty's Goodness,' it would be, no doubt – something like that – and on the knees. He became impersonal. Over a thousand a year made him an Esquire, didn't it? He thought that was it. In which case, wouldn't he have to be presented at court? Velvet breeches like you wear cycling, and a sword! What a curious place a court must be! Kneeling and bowing, and what was it Miss Mergle used to talk about? Of course! – ladies with long trains walking about backwards. Everybody walked about backwards at court, he knew, when not actually on their knees. Perhaps, though, some people regular stood up to the King! Talked to him, just as one might talk to Buggins, say. Cheek, of course! Dukes, it might be, did that – by permission? Millionnaires? . . .

From such thoughts this free citizen of our Crowned Republic passed insensibly into dreams, turgid dreams of that vast ascent which constitutes the true-born Briton's social scheme, which terminates with retrogressive progression and a bending back.

4

The next morning he came down to breakfast looking grave – a man with much before him in the world.

Kipps made a very special thing of his breakfast. Daily once-hopeless dreams came true then. It had been customary in the Emporium to supplement Shalford's generous, indeed unlimited, supply of bread and butter-substitute by private purchases, and this had given Kipps very broad, artistic conceptions of what the meal might be. Now there would be a cutlet or so or a mutton chop – this splendour Buggins had reported from the great London clubs – haddock, kipper, whiting or fish-balls, eggs, boiled or scrambled, or eggs and bacon, kidney also frequently and sometimes liver. Amidst a garland of such themes, sausages, black and white puddings,

bubble-and-squeak, fried cabbage and scallops came and went. Always as camp followers came potted meat in all varieties, cold bacon, German sausage, brawn, marmalade and two sorts of jam, and when he had finished these he would sit among his plates and smoke a cigarette and look at all these dishes crowded round him with a beatific approval. It was his principal meal. He was sitting with his cigarette regarding his apartment with that complacency begotten of a generous plan of feeding successfully realised, when newspapers and post arrived.

There were several things by the post, tradesmen's circulars and cards and two pathetic begging letters – his luck had got into the papers – and there was a letter from a literary man and a book to enforce his request for ten shillings to put down Socialism. The book made it very clear that prompt action on the part of property owners was becoming urgent, if property was to last out the year. Kipps dipped in it and was seriously perturbed. And there was a letter from old Kipps saying it was difficult to leave the shop and come over and see him again just yet, but that he had been to a sale at Lydd the previous day and bought a few good old books and things it would be difficult to find the equal of in Folkestone. 'They don't know the value of these things out here,' wrote old Kipps, 'but you may depend upon it they are valuable,' and a brief financial statement followed. 'There is an engraving someone might come along and offer you a lot of money for one of these days. Depend upon it, these old things are about the best investment you could make . . . '

Old Kipps had long been addicted to sales, and his nephew's good fortune had converted what had once been but a looking and a craving – he had rarely even bid for anything in the old days except the garden tools or the kitchen gallipots or things like that, things one gets for sixpence and finds a use for – into a very active pleasure. Sage and penetrating inspection, a certain mystery of bearing, tactical bids and Purchase! – Purchase! – the old man had had a good time.

While Kipps was rereading the begging letters and wishing he had the sound, clear common sense of Buggins to help him a little, the Parcels Post brought along the box from his uncle. It was a large, insecure-looking case, held together by a few still loyal nails, and by what the British War Office would have recognised at once as an Army Corps of string, rags and odds and ends tied together. Kipps unpacked it with a table knife, assisted at a critical point by the poker, and found a number of books and other objects of an antique type.

There were three bound volumes of early issues of *Chambers's Journal*, a copy of *Punch's Pocket Book* for 1875, Sturm's *Reflections*, an early version of Gill's *Geography* (slightly torn), an illustrated work on Spinal Curvature, an early edition of Kirke's *Human Physiology*, *The Scottish Chiefs* and a little volume on *The Language of Flowers*. There was a fine steel engraving, oak-framed and with some rusty spots, done in the Colossal style and

representing the Handwriting on the Wall. There were also a copper kettle, a pair of candle snuffers, a brass shoehorn, a tea caddy to lock, two decanters (one stoppered) and what was probably a portion of an eighteenth-century child's rattle.

Kipps examined these objects one by one and wished he knew more about them. Turning over the pages of the *Physiology* again he came upon a striking plate in which a youth of agreeable profile displayed his interior in an unstinted manner to the startled eye. It was a new view of humanity altogether for Kipps, and it arrested his mind.

'Chubes,' he whispered. 'Chubes.'

This anatomised figure made him forget for a space that he was 'practically a gentleman' altogether, and he was still surveying its extraordinary complications when another reminder of a world quite outside those spheres of ordered gentility into which his dreams had carried him overnight, arrived (following the servant) in the person of Chitterlow.

5

' 'El–*lo*!' said Kipps, rising.

'Not busy?' said Chitterlow, enveloping Kipps's hand for a moment in one of his own and tossing the yachting cap upon the monumental carved-oak sideboard.

'Only a bit of reading,' said Kipps.

'Reading, eh?' Chitterlow cocked the red eye at the books and other properties for a moment and then, 'I've been expecting you round again one night.'

'I been coming round,' said Kipps. 'On'y there's a chap 'ere – I was coming round last night on'y I met 'im.'

He walked to the hearthrug. Chitterlow drifted around the room for a time, glancing at things as he talked. 'I've altered that play tremendously since I saw you,' he said. 'Pulled it all to pieces.'

'What play's that, Chit'low?'

'The one we were talking about. You know. You said something – I don't know if you meant it – about buying half of it. Not the tragedy. I wouldn't sell my own twin brother a share in that. That's my investment. That's my Serious Work. No! I mean that new farce I've been on to. Thing with the business about a beetle.'

'Oo yes,' said Kipps. '*I* remember.'

'I thought you would. Said you'd take a fourth share for a hundred pounds. *You* know.'

'I seem to remember something – '

'Well, it's all different. Every bit of it. I'll tell you. You remember what you said about a butterfly? You got confused, you know – Old Meth. Kept

calling the beetle a butterfly and that set me off. I've made it quite different. Quite different. Instead of Popplewaddle – thundering good farce name that, you know; for all that it came from a Visitors' List – instead of Popplewaddle getting a beetle down his neck and rushing about, I've made him a collector – collects butterflies, and this one you know's a rare one. Comes in at window, centre.' Chitterlow began to illustrate with appropriate gestures. 'Pop rushes about after it. Forgets he mustn't let on he's in the house. After that – Tells 'em. Rare butterfly, worth lots of money. Some are, you know. Everyone's on to it after that. Butterfly can't get out of room; every time it comes out to have a try, rush and scurry. Well, I've worked on that. Only – '

He came very close to Kipps. He held up one hand horizontally and tapped it in a striking and confidential manner with the fingers of the other. 'Something else,' he said. 'That's given me a Real Ibsenish Touch – like the *Wild Duck*. You know that woman – I've made her lighter – and she sees it. When they're chasing the butterfly the third time, she's on! She looks. "That's me!" she says. Bif! Pestered Butterfly. *She's* the Pestered Butterfly. It's legitimate. Much more legitimate than the *Wild Duck* – where there isn't a duck!

'Knock 'em! The very title ought to knock 'em. I've been working like a horse at it . . . You'll have a gold mine in that quarter share, Kipps . . . *I* don't mind. It's suited me to sell it, and suited you to buy. Bif!'

Chitterlow interrupted his discourse to ask, 'You haven't any brandy in the house, have you? Not to drink, you know. But I want just an eggcupful to pull me steady. My liver's a bit queer . . . It doesn't matter, if you haven't. Not a bit. I'm like that. Yes, whisky'll do. Better!'

Kipps hesitated for a moment, then turned and fumbled in the cupboard of his sideboard. Presently he disinterred a bottle of whisky and placed it on the table. Then he put out first one bottle of soda water and after the hesitation of a moment another. Chitterlow picked up the bottle and read the label. 'Good Old Methusaleh,' he said. Kipps handed him the corkscrew and then his hand fluttered up to his mouth. 'I'll have to ring now,' he said, 'to get glasses.' He hesitated for a moment before doing so, leaning doubtfully as it were towards the bell.

When the housemaid appeared he was standing on the hearthrug with his legs wide apart, with the bearing of a desperate fellow. And after they had both had whiskies – 'You know a decent whisky,' Chitterlow remarked, and took another 'just to drink' – Kipps produced cigarettes and the conversation flowed again.

Chitterlow paced the room. He was, he explained, taking a day off; that was why he had come around to see Kipps. Whenever he thought of any extensive change in a play he was writing he always took a day off. In the end it saved time to do so. It prevented his starting rashly upon work that might have to be rewritten. There was no good in doing work when you might have to do it over again, none whatever.

Presently they were descending the steps by the Parade *en route* for The Warren, with Chitterlow doing the talking and going with a dancing drop from step to step . . .

They had a great walk, not a long one, but a great one. They went up by the Sanatorium and over the East Cliff and into that queer little wilderness of slippery and tumbling clay and rock under the chalk cliffs, a wilderness of thorn and bramble, wild rose and wayfaring tree, that adds so greatly to Folkestone's charm. They traversed its intricacies and clambered up to the crest of the cliffs at last by a precipitous path that Chitterlow endowed in some mysterious way with suggestions of Alpine adventure. Every now and then he would glance aside at sea and cliffs with a fresh boyishness of imagination that brought back New Romney and the stranded wrecks to Kipps's memory; but mostly he bored on with his great obsession of plays and playwriting, and that empty absurdity that is so serious to his kind, his Art. That was a thing that needed a monstrous lot of explaining. Along they went, sometimes abreast, sometimes in single file, up the little paths and down the little paths, and in among the bushes and out along the edge above the beach, and Kipps went along trying ever and again to get an insignificant word in edgeways, and the gestures of Chitterlow flew wide and far and his great voice rose and fell, and he said this and he said that and he biffed and banged into the circumambient Inane.

It was assumed that they were embarked upon no more trivial enterprise than the Reform of the British Stage, and Kipps found himself classed with many opulent and even royal and noble amateurs – the Honourable Thomas Norgate came in here – who had interested themselves in the practical realisation of high ideals about the Drama. Only he had a finer understanding of these things, and instead of being preyed upon by the common professional – 'and they *are* a lot,' said Chitterlow; 'I haven't toured for nothing' – he would have Chitterlow. Kipps gathered few details. It was clear he had bought the quarter of a farcical comedy – practically a gold mine – and it would appear it would be a good thing to buy the half. A suggestion, or the suggestion of a suggestion, floated out that he should buy the whole play and produce it forthwith. It seemed he was to produce the play upon a royalty system of a new sort, whatever a royalty system of any sort might be. Then there was some doubt, after all, whether that farcical comedy was in itself sufficient to revolutionise the present lamentable state of the British Drama. Better perhaps for such a purpose was that tragedy – as yet unfinished – which was to display all that Chitterlow knew about women, and which was to centre about a Russian nobleman embodying the fundamental Chitterlow personality. Then it became clearer that Kipps was to produce several plays. Kipps was to produce a great number of plays. Kipps was to found a National Theatre . . .

It is probable that Kipps would have expressed some sort of disavowal, if he had known how to express it. Occasionally his face assumed an

expression of whistling meditation, but that was as far as he got towards protest.

In the clutch of Chitterlow and the Incalculable, Kipps came round to the house in Fenchurch Street and was there made to participate in the midday meal. He came to the house forgetting certain confidences, and was reminded of the existence of a Mrs Chitterlow (with the finest completely untrained contralto voice in England) by her appearance. She had an air of being older than Chitterlow, although probably she wasn't, and her hair was a reddish brown, streaked with gold. She was dressed in one of those complaisant garments that are dressing gowns or tea gowns or bathing wraps or rather original evening robes according to the exigencies of the moment – from the first Kipps was aware that she possessed a warm and rounded neck, and her well-moulded arms came and vanished from the sleeves – and she had large, expressive brown eyes that he discovered ever and again fixed in an enigmatical manner upon his own.

A simple but sufficient meal had been distributed with careless spontaneity over the little round table in the room with the photographs and looking glass; and when a plate had by Chitterlow's direction been taken from under the marmalade in the cupboard and the kitchen fork and a knife that was not loose in its handle had been found for Kipps, they began and made a tumultuous repast. Chitterlow ate with quiet enormity, but it did not interfere with the flow of his talk. He introduced Kipps to his wife very briefly; she had evidently heard of Kipps before, and he made it vaguely evident that the production of the comedy was the thing chiefly settled. His reach extended over the table, and he troubled nobody. When Mrs Chitterlow, who for a little while seemed socially self-conscious, reproved him for taking a potato with a jab of his fork, he answered, 'Well, you shouldn't have married a man of Genius,' and from a subsequent remark it was perfectly clear that Chitterlow's standing in this respect was made no secret of in his household.

They drank Old Methusaleh and syphon soda, and there was no clearing away; they just sat among the plates and things, and Mrs Chitterlow took her husband's tobacco pouch and made a cigarette and smoked and blew smoke and looked at Kipps with her large brown eyes. Kipps had seen cigarettes smoked by ladies before, 'for fun', but this was real smoking. It frightened him rather. He felt he must not encourage this lady – at any rate in Chitterlow's presence.

They became very cheerful after the repast, and as there was now no waste to deplore, such as one experiences in the windy open air, Chitterlow gave his voice full vent. He fell to praising Kipps very highly and loudly. He said he had known Kipps was the right sort, he had seen it from the first, almost before he got up out of the mud on that memorable night. 'You can,' he said, 'sometimes. That was why – ' he stopped, but he seemed on the verge of explaining that it was his certainty of Kipps being the right sort had

led him to confer this great Fortune upon him. He left that impression. He threw out a number of long sentences and material for sentences of a highly philosophical and incoherent character about Coincidences. It became evident he considered dramatic criticism in a perilously low condition . . .

About four Kipps found himself stranded, as it were, by a receding Chitterlow on a seat upon the Leas.

He was chiefly aware that Chitterlow was an overwhelming personality. He puffed his cheeks and blew.

No doubt this was seeing life, but had he particularly wanted to see life that day? In a way Chitterlow had interrupted him. The day he had designed for himself was altogether different from this. He had been going to read through a precious little volume called *Don't* that Coote had sent round for him, a book of invaluable hints, a summary of British deportment that had only the one defect of being at points a little out of date.

That reminded him he had intended to perform a difficult exercise called an Afternoon Call upon the Cootes, as a preliminary to doing it in deadly earnest upon the Walshinghams. It was no good today, anyhow, now.

He came back to Chitterlow. He would have to explain to Chitterlow he was taking too much for granted, he would have to do that. It was so difficult to do in Chitterlow's presence though; in his absence it was easy enough. This half share, and taking a theatre and all of it, was going too far.

The quarter share was right enough, he supposed, but even that – ! A hundred pounds! What wealth is there left in the world after one has paid out a hundred pounds from it?

He had to recall that in a sense Chitterlow had indeed brought him his fortune before he could face even that.

You must not think too hardly of him. To Kipps, you see, there was as yet no such thing as proportion in these matters. A hundred pounds went to his horizon. A hundred pounds seemed to him just exactly as big as any other large sum of money.

CHAPTER TWO

The Walshinghams

The Cootes live in a little house in Bouverie Square with a tangle of Virginia creeper up the verandah.

Kipps had been troubled in his mind about knocking double or single – it is these things show what a man is made of – but happily there was a bell.

A queer little maid with a big cap admitted Kipps and took him through a bead curtain and a door into a little drawing-room, with a black and gold piano, a glazed bookcase, a Moorish cosy corner and a draped looking-

glass overmantel bright with Regent Street ornaments and photographs of various intellectual lights. A number of cards of invitation to meetings and the match list of a Band of Hope cricket club were stuck into the looking-glass frame, with Coote's name as a vice-president. There was a bust of Beethoven over the bookcase and the walls were thick with conscientiously executed but carelessly selected 'views' in oil and watercolours in gilt frames. At the end of the room facing the light was a portrait that struck Kipps at first as being Coote in spectacles and feminine costume and that he afterwards decided must be Coote's mother. Then the original appeared and he discovered that it was Coote's elder and only sister who kept house for him. She wore her hair in a knob behind, and the sight of the knob suggested to Kipps an explanation for a frequent gesture of Coote's, a patting exploratory movement to the back of his head. And then it occurred to him that this was quite an absurd idea altogether.

She said, 'Mr Kipps, I believe,' and Kipps laughed pleasantly and said, 'That's it!' and then she told him that 'Chester' had gone down to the art school to see about sending off some drawings or other and that he would be back soon. Then she asked Kipps if he painted, and showed him the pictures on the wall. Kipps asked her where each one was 'of', and when she showed him some of the Leas slopes he said he never would have recognised them. He said it was funny how things looked in a picture very often. 'But they're awfully *good*,' he said. 'Did you do them?' He would look at them with his neck arched like a swan's, his head back and on one side, and then suddenly peer closely into them. 'They *are* good. I wish I could paint.'

'That's what Chester says,' she answered. 'I tell him he has better things to do.'

Kipps seemed to get on very well with her.

Then Coote came in and they left her and went upstairs together and had a good talk about reading and the Rules of Life. Or rather Coote talked, and the praises of thought and reading were in his mouth . . .

You must figure Coote's study, a little bedroom put to studious uses, and over the mantel an array of things he had been led to believe indicative of culture and refinement: an autotype of Rossetti's *Annunciation*, an autotype of Watts's *Minotaur*, a Swiss carved pipe with many joints and a photograph of Amiens Cathedral (these two the spoils of travel), a phrenological bust and some broken fossils from The Warren. A rotating bookshelf carried the *Encyclopaedia Britannica* (tenth edition), and on the top of it a large official-looking, age-grubby envelope bearing the mystic words 'On His Majesty's Service', a number or so of the *Bookman* and a box of cigarettes were lying. A table under the window bore a little microscope, some dust in a saucer, some grimy glass slips and broken cover glasses; for Coote had 'gone in for' biology a bit. The longer side of the room was given over to bookshelves, neatly edged with pinked American cloth, and with an array of books – no

worse an array of books than you find in any public library; an almost
haphazard accumulation of obsolete classics, contemporary successes, the
Hundred Best Books (including Samuel Warren's *Ten Thousand a Year*), old
school books, directories, *The Times Atlas*, Ruskin in bulk, Tennyson
complete in one volume, Longfellow, Charles Kingsley, Smiles and Mrs
Humphry Ward, a guide book or so, several medical pamphlets, odd
magazine numbers, and much indescribable rubbish – in fact, a com-
pendium of the contemporary British mind. And in front of this array
stood Kipps, ill-taught and untrained, respectful, awestricken and, for a
moment at any rate, willing to learn, while Coote, the exemplary Coote,
talked to him like a bishop of reading and the virtue in books.

'Nothing enlarges the mind,' said Coote, 'like Travel and Books . . . And
they're both so easy nowadays, and so cheap!'

'I've often wanted to 'ave a good go in at reading,' Kipps replied.

'You'd hardly believe,' Coote said, 'how much you can get out of books.
Provided you avoid trashy reading, that is. You ought to make a rule, Kipps,
and read one Serious Book a week. Of course, we can Learn even from
Novels, Nace Novels that is, but it isn't the same thing as serious reading. I
made a rule, One Serious Book and One Novel – no more. There are some
of the serious books I've been reading lately – on that table: *Sartor Resartus*,
Mrs Twaddletome's *Pond Life*, the *Scottish Chiefs*, *Life and Letters of Dean
Farrar* . . . '

2

There came at last the sound of a gong and Kipps descended to tea in that
state of nervous apprehension at the difficulties of eating and drinking that
his aunt's knuckle rappings had implanted in him for ever. Over Coote's
shoulder he became aware of a fourth person in the Moorish cosy corner,
and he turned, leaving incomplete something incoherent he was saying to
Miss Coote about his modest respect and desire for literature, to discover
this fourth person was Miss Helen Walshingham, hatless and looking very
much at home.

She rose at once with an extended hand to meet his hesitation.

'You're stopping in Folkestone, Mr Kipps?'

' 'Ere on a bit of business,' said Kipps. 'I thought you was away in
Bruges.'

'That's later,' said Miss Walshingham. 'We're stopping until my
brother's holiday begins and we're trying to let our house. Where are you
staying in Folkestone?'

'I got a 'ouse of mine – on the Leas.'

'I've heard all about your good fortune – this afternoon.'

'Isn't it a Go!' said Kipps. 'I 'aven't nearly got to believe its reely

'appened yet. When that Mr Bean told me of it you could 'ave knocked me down with a feather . . . It's a tremenjous change for me.'

He discovered Miss Coote was asking him whether he took milk and sugar. '*I* don't mind,' said Kipps. 'Just as you like.'

Coote became active handing tea and bread and butter. It was thinly cut, and the bread was rather new, and half of the slice that Kipps took fell upon the floor. He had been holding it by the edge, for he was not used to this migratory method of taking tea without plates or table. This little incident ruled him out of the conversation for a time, and when he came to attend to it again they were talking about something or other prodigious – a performer of some sort – that was coming, called, it seemed, 'Padrooski'. So Kipps, who had quietly dropped into a chair, ate his bread and butter, said 'no, thank you' to any more, and by this discreet restraint got more freedom with his cup and saucer.

Apart from the confusion natural to tea, he was in a state of tremulous excitement on account of the presence of Miss Walshingham. He glanced from Miss Coote to her brother and then at Helen. He regarded her over the top of his cup as he drank. Here she was, solid and real. It was wonderful. He remarked, as he had done at times before, the easy flow of the dark hair back from her brow over her ears, the shapeliness of the white hands that came out from her simple white cuffs, the delicate pencilling of her brow.

Presently she turned her face to him almost suddenly, and smiled with the easiest assurance of friendship.

'You will go, I suppose,' she said, and added, 'to the Recital.'

'If I'm in Folkestone I shall,' said Kipps, clearing away a little hoarseness. 'I don't *know* much about music, but what I do know I like.'

'I'm sure you'll like Paderewski,' she said.

'If you do,' he said, 'I des say I shall.'

He found Coote very kindly taking his cup.

'Do you think of living in Folkestone?' asked Miss Coote, in a tone of proprietorship, from the hearthrug.

'No,' said Kipps, 'that's jest it – I hardly know.' He also said that he wanted to look around a bit before doing anything.

'There's so much to consider,' said Coote, smoothing the back of his head.

'I may go back to New Romney for a bit,' said Kipps. 'I got an uncle and aunt there. I reely don't know.'

Helen regarded him thoughtfully for a moment. 'You must come and see us,' she said, 'before we go to Bruges.'

'Oo, rather!' said Kipps. 'If I may.'

'Yes, do,' she said, and suddenly stood up before Kipps could formulate an enquiry when he should call.

'You're sure you can spare that drawing board?' she said to Miss Coote, and the conversation passed out of range.

And when he had said goodbye to Miss Walshingham and she had repeated her invitation to call, he went upstairs again with Coote to look out certain initiatory books they had had under discussion. And then Kipps, blowing very resolutely, went back to his own place, bearing under his arm (1) *Sesame and Lilies*, (2) *Sir George Tressady*, (3) an anonymous book on *Vitality* that Coote particularly esteemed. And, having got to his own sitting-room, he opened *Sesame and Lilies* and read it with ruthless determination for some time.

3

Presently he leant back and gave himself up to the business of trying to imagine just exactly what Miss Walshingham could have thought of him when she saw him. Doubts about the precise effect of the grey-flannel suit began to trouble him. He turned to the mirror over the mantel, and then got on to a chair to study the hang of the trousers. It looked all right. Luckily, she had not seen the Panama hat. He knew that he had the brim turned up wrong, but he could not find out which way the brim was right. However, that she had not seen. He might perhaps ask at the shop where he bought it.

He meditated for awhile on his reflected face – doubtful whether he liked it or not – and then got down again and flitted across to the sideboard where there lay two little books, one in a cheap magnificent cover of red and gold and the other in green canvas. The former was called, as its cover witnessed, *Manners and Rules of Good Society, by a Member of the Aristocracy*, and after the cover had indulged in a band of gilded decoration, light-hearted but natural under the circumstances, it added 'TWENTY-FIRST EDITION'. The second was that admirable classic *The Art of Conversing*. Kipps returned with these to his seat, placed the two before him, opened the latter with a sigh and flattened it under his hand.

Then with knitted brows he began to read onward from a mark, his lips moving.

Having thus acquired possession of an idea, the little ship should not be abruptly launched into deep waters, but should be first permitted to glide gently and smoothly into the shallows, that is to say, the conversation should not be commenced by broadly and roundly stating a fact, or didactically expressing an opinion, as the subject would be thus virtually or summarily disposed of, or perhaps be met with a 'Really' or 'Indeed', or some equally brief monosyllabic reply. If an opposite opinion were held by the person to whom the remark were addressed, he might not, if a stranger, care to express it in the form of a direct contradiction, or actual dissent. To glide imperceptibly into conversation is the object to be attained.

At this point Mr Kipps rubbed his fingers through his hair with an expression of some perplexity and went back to the beginning.

4

When Kipps made his call on the Walshinghams, it all happened so differently from the *Manners and Rules* prescription ('Paying Calls') that he was quite lost from the very outset. Instead of the footman or maidservant proper in these cases, Miss Walshingham opened the door to him herself. 'I'm so glad you've come,' she said, with one of her rare smiles.

She stood aside for him to enter the rather narrow passage.

'I thought I'd call,' he said, retaining his hat and stick.

She closed the door and led the way to a little drawing-room, which impressed Kipps as being smaller and less emphatically coloured than that of the Cootes, and in which at first only a copper bowl of white poppies upon the brown tablecloth caught his particular attention.

'You won't think it unconventional to come in, Mr Kipps, will you?' she remarked. 'Mother is out.'

'I don't mind,' he said, smiling amiably, 'if you don't.'

She walked around the table and stood regarding him across it, with that same look between speculative curiosity and appreciation that he remembered from the last of the art-class meetings.

'I wondered whether you would call or whether you wouldn't before you left Folkestone.'

'I'm not leaving Folkestone for a bit, and any'ow, I should have called on you.'

'Mother will be sorry she was out. I've told her about you, and she wants, I know, to meet you.'

'I saw 'er – if that was 'er – in the shop,' said Kipps.

'Yes – you did, didn't you! . . . She has gone out to make some duty calls, and I didn't go. I had something to write. I write a little, you know.'

'Reely!' said Kipps.

'It's nothing much,' she said, 'and it comes to nothing.' She glanced at a little desk near the window, on which there lay some paper. 'One must do something.' She broke off abruptly. 'Have you seen our outlook?' she asked and walked to the window, and Kipps came and stood beside her. 'We look on the square. It might be worse, you know. That out-porter's truck there is horrid – and the railings, but it's better than staring one's social replica in the face, isn't it? It's pleasant in early spring – bright green, laid on with a dry brush – and it's pleasant in autumn.'

'I like it,' said Kipps. 'That laylock there is pretty, isn't it?'

'Children come and pick it at times,' she remarked.

'I dessay they do,' said Kipps.

He rested on his hat and stick and looked appreciatively out of the window, and she glanced at him for one swift moment. A suggestion that might have come from *The Art of Conversing* came into his head. 'Have you a garden?' he said.

She shrugged her shoulders. 'Only a little one,' she said, and then, 'Perhaps you would like to see it.'

'I like gardenin',' said Kipps, with memories of a pennyworth of nasturtiums he had once trained over his uncle's dustbin.

She led the way with a certain relief.

They emerged through a four-seasons coloured-glass door to a little iron verandah that led by iron steps to a minute walled garden. There was just room for a patch of turf and a flower-bed; one sturdy variegated euonymus grew in the corner. But the early June flowers – the big narcissus, snow-upon-the-mountains and a fine show of yellow wallflowers – shone gay.

'That's our garden,' said Helen. 'It's not a very big one, is it?'

'I like it,' said Kipps.

'It's small,' she said, 'but this is the day of small things.'

Kipps didn't follow that.

'If you were writing when I came,' he remarked, 'I'm interrupting you.'

She turned round with her back to the railing and rested, leaning on her hands. 'I had finished,' she said. 'I couldn't get on.'

'Were you making up something?' asked Kipps.

There was a little interval before she smiled. 'I try – quite vainly – to write stories,' she said. 'One must do something. I don't know whether I shall ever do any good – at that – anyhow. It seems so hopeless. And, of course, one must study the popular taste. But, now my brother has gone to London, I get a lot of leisure.'

'I seen your brother, 'aven't I?'

'He came to the class once or twice. Very probably you have. He's gone to London to pass his examinations and become a solicitor. And then, I suppose, he'll have a chance. Not much, perhaps, even then. But he's luckier than I am.'

'You got your classes and things.'

'They ought to satisfy me. But they don't. I suppose I'm ambitious. We both are. And we hadn't much of a springboard.' She glanced over his shoulder at the cramped little garden with an air of reference in her gesture.

'I should think you could do anything if you wanted to,' said Kipps.

'As a matter of fact I can't do anything I want to.'

'You done a good deal.'

'What?'

'Well, didn't you pass one of these here University things?'

'Oh! I matriculated!'

'I should think I was no end of a swell if *I* did, I know that.'

'Mr Kipps, do you know how many people matriculate into London University every year?'

'How many then?'

'Between two and three thousand.'

'Well, just think how many don't!'

Her smile came again, and broke into a laugh. 'Oh, *they* don't count,' she said, and then, realising that might penetrate Kipps if he was left with it, she hurried on to, 'The fact is, I'm a discontented person, Mr Kipps. Folkestone, you know, is a Sea Front, and it values people by sheer vulgar prosperity. We're not prosperous, and we live in a back street. We have to live here because this is our house. It's a mercy we haven't to "let". One feels one hasn't opportunities. If one had, I suppose one wouldn't use them. Still – '

Kipps felt he was being taken tremendously into her confidence. 'That's jest it,' he said, very sagely.

He leant forward on his stick and said, very earnestly, 'I believe you could do anything you wanted to, if you tried.'

She threw out her hands in disavowal.

'I know,' said he, very sagely and nodding his head. 'I watched you once or twice when you were teaching that wood-carving class.'

For some reason this made her laugh – a rather pleasant laugh, and that made Kipps feel a very witty and successful person. 'It's very evident,' she said, 'that you're one of those rare people who believe in me, Mr Kipps,' to which he answered, 'Oo, I *do*!' and then suddenly they became aware of Mrs Walshingham coming along the passage. In another moment she appeared through the four-seasons door, bonneted and ladylike, and a little faded, exactly as Kipps had seen her in the shop. Kipps felt a certain apprehension at her appearance, in spite of the reassurances he had had from Coote.

'Mr Kipps has called on us,' said Helen, and Mrs Walshingham said it was very kind of him, and added that new people didn't call on them very much nowadays. There was nothing of the scandalised surprise Kipps had seen in the shop; she had heard, perhaps, he was a gentleman now. In the shop he had thought her rather jaded and haughty, but he had scarcely taken her hand, which responded to his touch with a friendly pressure, before he knew how mistaken he had been. She then told her daughter that someone called Mrs Wace had been out, and turned to Kipps again to ask him if he had had tea. Kipps said he had not, and Helen moved towards some mysterious interior. 'But *I* say,' said Kipps; 'don't you on my account – !'

Helen vanished, and he found himself alone with Mrs Walshingham, which, of course, made him breathless and Boreas-looking for a moment.

'You were one of Helen's pupils in the wood-carving class?' asked Mrs Walshingham, regarding him with the quiet watchfulness proper to her position.

'Yes,' said Kipps, 'that's 'ow I 'ad the pleasure – '

'She took a great interest in her wood-carving class. She is so energetic, you know, and it gives her an Outlet.'

'I thought she taught something splendid.'

'Everyone says she did very well. Helen, I think, would do anything well that she undertook to do. She's so very clever. And she throws herself into things so.'

She untied her bonnet strings with a pleasant informality.

'She has told me all about her class. She used to be full of it. And about your cut hand.'

'Lor'!' said Kipps; 'fancy, telling that!'

'Oh, yes! And how brave you were.' (Though, indeed, Helen's chief detail had been his remarkable expedient for checking bloodshed.)

Kipps became bright pink.

'She said you didn't seem to feel it a bit.'

Kipps felt he would have to spend weeks over *The Art of Conversing*.

While he still hung fire Helen returned with the apparatus for afternoon tea upon a tray.

'Do you mind pulling out the table?' asked Mrs Walshingham.

That, again, was very homelike. Kipps put down his hat and stick in the corner and, amidst an iron thunder, pulled out a little rusty, green-painted table, and then in the easiest manner followed Helen in to get chairs.

So soon as he had got rid of his teacup – he refused all food, of course, and they were merciful – he became wonderfully at his ease. Presently he was talking. He talked quite modestly and simply about his changed condition and his difficulties and plans. He spread what indeed had an air of being all his simple little soul before their eyes. In a little while his clipped, defective accent had become less perceptible to their ears, and they began to realise, as the girl with the freckles had long since realised, that there were passable aspects of Kipps. He confided, he submitted; and for both of them he had the realest, the most seductively flattering undertone of awe and reverence.

He remained about two hours, having forgotten how terribly incorrect it is to stay at such a length. They did not mind at all.

CHAPTER THREE

Engaged

Within two months, within a matter of three and fifty days, Kipps had clambered to the battlements of Heart's Desire.

It all became possible by the Walshinghams – it would seem at Coote's instigation – deciding, after all, not to spend the holidays at Bruges. Instead, they remained in Folkestone, and this happy chance gave Kipps just all those opportunities of which he stood in need.

His crowning day was at Lympne, and long before the summer warmth began to break, while, indeed, August still flamed on high. They had organised – no one seemed to know who suggested it first – a water party on the still reaches of the old military canal at Hythe, the canal that was to have stopped Napoleon if the sea failed us, and they were to picnic by the brick bridge, and afterwards to clamber to Lympne Castle. The host of the gathering, it was understood very clearly, was Kipps.

They went, a merry party. The canal was weedy, with only a few inches of water at the shallows, and so they went in three Canadian canoes. Kipps had learned to paddle – it had been his first athletic accomplishment, and his second – with the last three or four of ten private lessons still to come – was to be cycling. But Kipps did not paddle at all badly; muscles hardened by lifting pieces of cretonne could cut a respectable figure by the side of Coote's executions, and the girl with the freckles, the girl who understood him, came in his canoe. They raced the Walshinghams, brother and sister; and Coote, in a liquefying state and blowing mightily, but still persistent and always quite polite and considerate, toiled behind with Mrs Walshingham. She could not be expected to paddle (though, of course, she 'offered') and she reclined upon specially adjusted cushions under a black and white sunshade and watched Kipps and her daughter, and feared at intervals that Coote was getting hot.

They were all more or less in holiday costume, the eyes of the girls looked out under the shade of wide-brimmed hats; even the freckled girl was unexpectedly pretty, and Helen, swinging sunlit to her paddle, gave Kipps, almost for the first time, the suggestion of a graceful body. Kipps was arrayed in the completest boating costume, and when his fashionable Panama was discarded and his hair blown into disorder he became, in his white flannels, as sightly as most young men. His complexion was a notable asset.

Things favoured him, the day favoured him, everyone favoured him. Young Walshingham, the girl with the freckles, Coote and Mrs Walshingham, were playing up to him in the most benevolent way, and between the landing place and Lympne, Fortune, to crown their efforts, had placed a

small, convenient field entirely at the disposal of an adolescent bull. Not a big, real, resolute bull, but, on the other hand, no calf; a young bull, in the same stage of emotional development as Kipps, 'standing where the two rivers meet'. Detachedly our party drifted towards him.

When they landed, young Walshingham, with the simple directness of a brother, abandoned his sister to Kipps and secured the freckled girl, leaving Coote to carry Mrs Walshingham's light wool wrap. He started at once, in order to put an effectual distance between himself and his companions, on the one hand, and a certain pervasive chaperonage that went with Coote, on the other. Young Walshingham, I think I have said, was dark, with a Napoleonic profile, and it was natural for him, therefore, to be a bold thinker and an epigrammatic speaker, and he had long ago discovered great possibilities of appreciation in the freckled girl. He was in a very happy frame that day because he had just been entrusted with the management of Kipps's affairs (old Bean inexplicably dismissed), and that was not a bad beginning for a solicitor of only a few months' standing, and, moreover, he had been reading Nietzsche, and he thought that in all probability he was the Non-Moral Overman referred to by that writer. He wore fairly large-sized hats. He wanted to expand the theme of the Non-Moral Overman in the ear of the freckled girl, to say it over, so to speak, and in order to seclude his exposition they went aside from the direct path and trespassed through a coppice, avoiding the youthful bull. They escaped to these higher themes but narrowly, for Coote and Mrs Walshingham, subtle chaperones both, and each indisposed for excellent reasons to encumber Kipps and Helen, were hot upon their heels. These two kept direct route to the stile of the bull's field, and the sight of the animal at once awakened Coote's innate aversion to brutality in any shape or form. He said the stiles were too high, and that they could do better by going around by the hedge, and Mrs Walshingham, nothing loath, agreed.

This left the way clear for Kipps and Helen, and they encountered the bull. Helen did not observe the bull, but Kipps did; but, that afternoon at any rate, he was equal to facing a lion. And the bull really came at them. It was not an affair of the bullring exactly, no desperate rushes and gorings; but he came; he regarded them with a large, wicked, bluish eye, opened a mouth below his moistly glistening nose and booed, at any rate, if he did not exactly bellow, and he shook his head wickedly and showed that tossing was in his mind. Helen was frightened, without any loss of dignity, and Kipps went extremely white. But he was perfectly calm, and he seemed to her to have lost the last vestiges of his accent and his social shakiness. He directed her to walk quietly towards the stile, and made an oblique advance towards the bull.

'You be orf!' he said.

When Helen was well over the stile Kipps withdrew in good order. He got over the stile under cover of a feint, and the thing was done – a small thing, no doubt, but just enough to remove from Helen's mind an incorrect

deduction that a man who was so terribly afraid of a teacup as Kipps must necessarily be abjectly afraid of everything else in the world. In her moment of reaction she went perhaps too far in the opposite direction. Hitherto Kipps had always had a certain flimsiness of effect for her. Now suddenly he was discovered solid. He was discovered possible in many new ways. Here, after all, was the sort of back a woman can get behind! . . .

As these heirs of the immemorial ages went past the turf-crowned mass of Portus Lemanus up the steep slopes towards the mediaeval castle on the crest, the thing was also manifest in her eyes.

2

Everyone who stays in Folkestone gets, sooner or later, to Lympne. The castle became a farmhouse long ago, and the farmhouse, itself now ripe and venerable, wears the walls of the castle as a little man wears a big man's coat. The kindliest of farm ladies entertains a perpetual stream of visitors and shows her vast mangle, and her big kitchen, and takes you out upon the sunniest little terrace garden in all the world, and you look down the sheep-dotted slopes to where, beside the canal and under the trees, the crumpled memories of Rome sleep for ever. For hither to this lonely spot the galleys once came, the legions, the emperors, masters of the world. The castle is but a thing of yesterday, King Stephen's time or thereabouts, in that retrospect. One climbs the keep, up a tortuous spiral of stone, worn now to the pitch of perforation, and there one is lifted to the centre of far more than a hemisphere of view. Away below one's feet, almost at the bottom of the hill, the Marsh begins, and spreads and spreads in a mighty crescent that sweeps about the sea, the Marsh dotted with the church towers of forgotten mediaeval towns and breaking at last into the low blue hills of Winchelsea and Hastings; east hangs France, between the sea and the sky, and round the north, bounding the wide prospectives of farms and houses and woods, the Downs, with their hangers and chalk pits, sustain the passing shadows of the sailing clouds.

And here it was, high out of the world of everyday, and in the presence of spacious beauty, that Kipps and Helen found themselves agreeably alone. All six, it had seemed, had been coming for the Keep, but Mrs Walshingham had hesitated at the horrid little stairs, and then suddenly felt faint, and so she and the freckled girl had remained below, walking up and down in the shadow of the house and Coote had remembered they were all out of cigarettes, and had taken off young Walshingham into the village. There had been shouting to explain between ground and parapet, and then Helen and Kipps turned again to the view, and commended it and fell silent.

Helen sat fearlessly in an embrasure, and Kipps stood beside her.

'I've always been fond of scenery,' Kipps repeated, after an interval.

Then he went off at a tangent. 'D'you reely think that was right what Coote was saying?'

She looked interrogation.

'About my name?'

'Being really C-U-Y-P-S? I have my doubts. I thought at first –What makes Mr Coote add an S to Cuyp?'

'*I* dunno,' said Kipps, foiled. 'I was jest thinking . . . '

She shot one wary glance at him and then turned her eyes to the sea.

Kipps was out for a space. He had intended to lead from this question to the general question of surnames and change of names; it had seemed a light and witty way of saying something he had in mind, and suddenly he perceived that this was an unutterably vulgar and silly project. The hitch about that S had saved him. He regarded her profile for a moment, framed in weather-beaten stone, and backed by the blue elements.

He dropped the question of his name out of existence and spoke again of the view. 'When I see scenery – and things that – that are beautiful, it makes me feel – '

She looked at him suddenly, and saw him fumbling for his words.

'Silly like,' he said.

She took him in with her glance, the old look of proprietorship it was, touched with a certain warmth. She spoke in a voice as unambiguous as her eyes. 'You needn't,' she said. 'You know, Mr Kipps, you hold yourself too cheap.'

Her eyes and words smote him with amazement. He stared at her like a man who awakens. She looked down.

'You mean – ' he said; and then, 'don't you hold me cheap?'

She glanced up again and shook her head.

'But – for instance – you don't think of me – as an equal like.'

'Why not?'

'Oo! But reely – '

His heart beat very fast.

'If I thought – ' he said; and then, 'You know so much.'

'That's nothing,' she said.

Then, for a long time, as it seemed to them, both kept silence, a silence that said and accomplished many things.

'I know what I am,' he said, at length . . . 'If I thought it was possible . . . If I thought *you* . . . I believe I could do anything – '

He stopped, and she sat downcast and strikingly still.

'Miss Walshingham,' he said, 'is it possible that you . . . could care for me enough to – to 'elp me? Miss Walshingham, do you care for me at all?'

It seemed she was never going to answer. She looked up at him. 'I think,' she said, 'you are the most generous – look at what you have done for my brother! – the most generous and the most modest of men. And this afternoon – I thought you were the bravest.'

She turned her head, glanced down, waved her hand to someone on the terrace below, and stood up.

'Mother is signalling,' she said. 'We must go down.'

Kipps became polite and deferential by habit, but his mind was a tumult that had nothing to do with that.

He moved before her towards the little door that opened on the winding stairs – 'always precede a lady down or up stairs' – and then on the second step he turned resolutely. 'But – ' he said, looking up out of the shadow, flannel-clad and singularly like a man.

She looked down on him, with her hand upon the stone lintel.

He held out his hand as if to help her. 'Can you tell me?' he said. 'You must know – '

'What?'

'If you care for me?'

She did not answer for a long time. It was as if everything in the world had drawn to the breaking point, and in a minute must certainly break.

'Yes,' she said, at last, 'I know.'

Abruptly, by some impalpable sign, he knew what the answer would be, and he remained still.

She bent down over him and softened to her wonderful smile.

'Promise me,' she insisted.

He promised with his still face.

'If *I* do not hold you cheap! you will never hold yourself cheap – '

'If you do not hold me cheap! You mean – ?'

She bent down quite close beside him. 'I hold you,' she said, and then whispered, '*dear.*'

'Me?'

She laughed aloud.

He was astonished beyond measure. He stipulated, lest there might be some misconception, 'You will marry me?'

She was laughing, inundated by the sense of bountiful power, of possession and success. He looked quite a nice little man to have. 'Yes,' she laughed. 'What else could I mean?' and, 'Yes.'

He felt as a praying hermit might have felt, snatched from the midst of his quiet devotions, his modest sackcloth and ashes, and hurled neck and crop over the glittering gates of Paradise, smack among the iridescent wings, the bright-eyed Cherubim. He felt like some lowly and righteous man dynamited into Bliss . . .

His hand tightened upon the rope that steadied one upon the stairs of stone. He was for kissing her hand and did not.

He said not a word more. He turned about, and with something very like a scared expression on his face led the way into the obscurity of their descent . . .

Everyone seemed to understand. Nothing was said, nothing was explained, the merest touch of the eyes sufficed. As they clustered in the castle gateway Coote, Kipps remembered afterwards, laid hold of his arm as if by chance and pressed it. It was quite evident he knew. His eyes, his nose, shone with benevolent congratulations, shone, too, with the sense of a good thing conducted to its climax. Mrs Walshingham, who had seemed a little fatigued by the hill, recovered, and was even obviously stirred by affection for her daughter. There was, in passing, a motherly caress. She asked Kipps to give her his arm in walking down the steep. Kipps in a sort of dream obeyed. He found himself trying to attend to her, and soon he was attending.

She and Kipps talked like sober, responsible people and went slowly, while the others drifted down the hill together, a loose little group of four. He wondered momentarily what they would talk about and then sank into his conversation with Mrs Walshingham. He conversed, as it were, out of his superficial personality, and his inner self lay stunned in unsuspected depths within. It had an air of being an interesting and friendly talk, almost their first long talk together. Hitherto he had had a sort of fear of Mrs Walshingham, as of a person possibly satirical, but she proved a soul of sense and sentiment, and Kipps, for all of his abstraction, got on with her unexpectedly well. They talked a little upon scenery and the inevitable melancholy attaching to the old ruins and the thought of vanished generations.

'Perhaps they jousted here,' said Mrs Walshingham.

'They was up to all sorts of things,' said Kipps, and then the two came round to Helen. She spoke of her daughter's literary ambitions. 'She will do something, I feel sure. You know, Mr Kipps, it's a great responsibility to a mother to feel her daughter is – exceptionally clever.'

'I dessay it is,' said Kipps. 'There's no mistake about that.'

She spoke, too, of her son – almost like Helen's twin – alike, yet different. She made Kipps feel quite fatherly. 'They are so quick, so artistic,' she said, 'so full of ideas. Almost they frighten me. One feels they need opportunities – as other people need air.'

She spoke of Helen's writing. 'Even when she was quite a little dot she wrote verse.'

(Kipps, sensation.)

'Her father had just the same tastes – ' Mrs Walshingham turned a little beam of half-pathetic reminiscence on the past. 'He was more artist than businessman. That was the trouble . . . He was misled by his partner, and when the crash came everyone blamed him . . . Well, it doesn't do to dwell

on horrid things – especially today. There are bright days, Mr Kipps, and dark days. And mine have not always been bright.'

Kipps presented a face of Coote-like sympathy.

She diverged to talk of flowers, and Kipps's mind was filled with the picture of Helen bending down towards him in the Keep . . .

They spread the tea under the trees before the little inn, and at a certain moment Kipps became aware that everyone in the party was simultaneously and furtively glancing at him. There might have been a certain tension had it not been first of all for Coote and his tact, and afterwards for a number of wasps. Coote was resolved to make this memorable day pass off well, and displayed an almost boisterous sense of fun. Then young Walshingham began talking of the Roman remains below Lympne, intending to lead up to the Overman. 'These old Roman chaps – ' he said, and then the wasps arrived. They killed three in the jam alone.

Kipps killed wasps, as if it were in a dream, and handed things to the wrong people, and maintained a thin surface of ordinary intelligence with the utmost difficulty. At times he became aware, aware with an extraordinary vividness, of Helen. Helen was carefully not looking at him and behaving with amazing coolness and ease. But just for that one time there was the faintest suggestion of pink beneath the ivory of her cheeks . . .

Tacitly the others conceded to Kipps the right to paddle back with Helen; he helped her into the canoe and took his paddle, and, paddling slowly, dropped behind the others. And now his inner self stirred again. He said nothing to her. How could he ever say anything to her again? She spoke to him at rare intervals about reflections and the flowers and the trees, and he nodded in reply. But his mind moved very slowly forward now from the point at which it had fallen stunned in the Lympne Keep, moving forward to the beginnings of realisation. As yet he did not say even in the recesses of his heart that she was his. But he perceived that the goddess had come from her altar amazingly, and had taken him by the hand!

The sky was a vast splendour, and then close to them were the dark, protecting trees and the shining, smooth, still water. He was an erect, black outline to her; he plied his paddle with no unskilful gesture, the water broke to snaky silver and glittered far behind his strokes. Indeed, he did not seem so bad to her. Youth calls to youth the wide world through, and her soul rose in triumph over his subjection. And behind him was money and opportunity, freedom and London, a great background of seductively indistinct hopes. To him her face was a warm dimness. In truth, he could not see her eyes, but it seemed to his love-witched brain he did and that they shone out at him like dusky stars.

All the world that evening was no more than a shadowy frame of darkling sky and water and dipping bows about Helen. He seemed to see through things with an extraordinary clearness; she was revealed to him certainly, as the cause and essence of it all.

He was indeed at his Heart's Desire. It was one of those times when there seems to be no future, when Time has stopped and we are at an end. Kipps, that evening, could not have imagined a tomorrow; all that his imagination had pointed towards was attained. His mind stood still and took the moments as they came.

4

About nine that night Coote came around to Kipps's new apartmentin the Upper Sandgate Road – the house on the Leas had been let furnished – and Kipps made an effort towards realisation. He was discovered sitting at the open window and without a lamp, quite still. Coote was deeply moved, and he pressed Kipps's palm and laid a knobby white hand on his shoulder and displayed the sort of tenderness becoming in a crisis. Kipps too was moved that night, and treated Coote like a very dear brother.

'She's splendid,' said Coote, coming to it abruptly.

'Isn't she?' said Kipps.

'I couldn't help noticing her face,' said Coote . . . 'You know, my dear Kipps, this is better than a legacy.'

'I don't deserve it,' said Kipps.

'You can't say that.'

'I don't. I can't 'ardly believe it. I can't believe it at all. No!'

There followed an expressive stillness.

'It's wonderful,' said Kipps. 'It takes me like that.'

Coote made a faint blowing noise, and so again they came for a time on silence.

'And it began – before your money?'

'When I was in 'er class,' said Kipps, solemnly.

Coote, speaking out of a darkness which he was illuminating strangely with efforts to strike a match, said that it was beautiful. He could not have *wished* Kipps a better fortune –

He lit a cigarette, and Kipps was moved to do the same, with a sacramental expression. Presently speech flowed more freely.

Coote began to praise Helen and her mother and brother. He talked of when 'it' might be; he presented the thing as concrete and credible. 'It's a county family, you know,' he said. 'She is connected, you know, with the Beauprés family – you know Lord Beauprés.'

'No!' said Kipps, 'reely!'

'Distantly, of course,' said Coote. 'Still – '

He smiled a smile that glimmered in the twilight.

'It's too much,' said Kipps, overcome. 'It's so all like that.'

Coote exhaled. For a time Kipps listened to Helen's praises and matured a point of view.

'I say, Coote,' he said. 'What ought I to do now?'

'What do you mean?' said Coote.

'I mean about calling on 'er and all that.'

He reflected. 'Naturally, I want to do it all right.'

'Of course,' said Coote.

'It would be awful to go and do something – now – all wrong.'

Coote's cigarette glowed as he meditated. 'You must call, of course,' he decided. 'You'll have to speak to Mrs Walshingham.'

' 'Ow?' said Kipps.

'Tell her you mean to marry her daughter.'

'I dessay she knows,' said Kipps, with defensive penetration.

Coote's head was visible, shaking itself judiciously.

'Then there's the ring,' said Kipps. 'What 'ave I to do about that?'

'What ring do you mean?'

' 'Ngagement Ring. There isn't anything at all about that in *Manners and Rules of Good Society* – not a word.'

'Of course you must get something – tasteful. Yes.'

'What sort of a ring?'

'Something nace. They'll show you in the shop.'

'Of course. I 'spose I got to take it to 'er, eh? Put it on her finger.'

'Oh, no! Send it. Much better.'

'Ah!' said Kipps, for the first time with a note of relief.

'Then, 'ow about this call – on Mrs Walshingham, I mean. 'Ow ought one to go?'

'Rather a ceremonial occasion,' reflected Coote.

'Wadyer mean? Frock coat?'

'I *think* so,' said Coote, with discrimination.

'Light trousers and all that?'

'Yes.'

'Rose?'

'I think it might run to a buttonhole.'

The curtain that hung over the future became less opaque to the eyes of Kipps. Tomorrow, and then other days, became perceptible at least as existing. Frock coat, silk hat and a rose! With a certain solemnity he contemplated himself in the process of slow transformation into an English gentleman, Arthur Cuyps, frock-coated on occasions of ceremony, the familiar acquaintance of Lady Punnet, the recognised wooer of a distant connection of the Earl of Beauprés.

Something like awe at the magnitude of his own fortune came upon him. He felt the world was opening out like a magic flower in a transformation scene at the touch of this wand of gold. And Helen, nestling beautiful in the red heart of the flower. Only ten weeks ago he had been no more than the shabbiest of improvers and shamefully dismissed for dissipation, the mere soil-buried seed, as it were, of these glories. He resolved the engagement

ring should be of expressively excessive quality and appearance, in fact, the very best they had.

'Ought I to send 'er flowers?' he speculated.

'Not necessarily,' said Coote. 'Though, of course, it's an attention . . . '

Kipps meditated on flowers.

'When you see her,' said Coote, 'you'll have to ask her to name the day.'

Kipps started. 'That won't be just yet a bit, will it?'

'Don't know any reason for delay.'

'Oo, but – a year, say.'

'Rather a long taime,' said Coote.

'Is it?' said Kipps, turning his head sharply. 'But – '

There was quite a long pause.

'I say,' he said, at last, and in an altered voice, 'you'll 'ave to 'elp me about the wedding.'

'Only too happy,' said Coote.

'Of course,' said Kipps, 'I didn't think – ' He changed his line of thought. 'Coote,' he asked, 'wot's a "tate-eh-tate"?'

'A "tate-ah-tay"!' said Coote, improvingly, 'is a conversation alone together.'

'Lor'!' said Kipps, 'but I thought – It says *strictly* we oughtn't to enjoy a tater-tay, not sit together, walk together, ride together, or meet during any part of the day. That don't leave much time for meeting, does it?'

'The books says that?' asked Coote.

'I jest learnt it by 'eart before you came. I thought that was a bit rum, but I s'pose it's all right.'

'You won't find Miss Walshingham so strict as all that,' said Coote. 'I think that's a bit extreme. They'd only do that now in very strict old aristocratic families. Besides, the Walshinghams are so modern – advanced, you might say. I expect you'll get plenty of chances of talking together.'

'There's a tremendous lot to think about,' said Kipps, blowing a profound sigh. 'D'you mean – p'r'aps we might be married in a few months or so?'

'You'll *have* to be,' said Coote. 'Why not?' . . .

Midnight found Kipps alone, looking a little tired and turning over the leaves of the red-covered textbook with a studious expression. He paused for a moment on page 233, his eye caught by the words: 'FOR AN AUNT OR UNCLE BY MARRIAGE the period is six weeks black, with jet trimmings.'

'No,' said Kipps, after a vigorous mental effort. 'That's not it.' The pages rustled again. He stopped and flattened out the little book decisively at the beginning of the chapter on 'Weddings'.

He became pensive. He stared at the lamp-wick. 'I suppose I ought to go over and tell them,' he said, at last.

Kipps called on Mrs Walshingham attired in the proper costume for ceremonial Occasions in the Day. He carried a silk hat, and he wore a deep-skirted frock coat, his boots were patent leather and his trousers dark grey. He had generous white cuffs with gold links, and his grey gloves, one thumb of which had burst when he put them on, he held loosely in his hand. He carried a small umbrella rolled to an exquisite tightness. A sense of singular correctness pervaded his being and warred with the enormity of the occasion for possession of his soul. Anon he touched his silk cravat. The world smelt of his rosebud.

He seated himself on a new re-covered chintz armchair and stuck out the elbow of the arm that held his hat.

'I know,' said Mrs Walshingham, 'I know everything,' and helped him out most amazingly. She deepened the impression he had already received of her sense and refinement. She displayed an amount of tenderness that touched him.

'This is a great thing,' she said, 'to a mother,' and her hand rested for a moment on his impeccable coat sleeve.

'A daughter, Arthur,' she explained, 'is so much more than a son.'

Marriage, she said, was a lottery, and without love and toleration there was much unhappiness. Her life had not always been bright – there had been dark days and bright days. She smiled rather sweetly. 'This is a bright one,' she said.

She said very kind and flattering things to Kipps, and she thanked him for his goodness to her son. ('That wasn't anything,' said Kipps.) And then she expanded upon the theme of her two children. 'Both so accomplished,' she said, 'so clever. I call them my Twin Jewels.'

She was repeating a remark that she had made at Lympne, that she always said her children needed opportunities, as other people needed air, when she was abruptly arrested by the entry of Helen. They hung on a pause, Helen perhaps surprised by Kipps's weekday magnificence. Then she advanced with outstretched hand.

Both the young people were shy. 'I jest called round,' began Kipps, and became uncertain how to end.

'Won't you have some tea?' asked Helen.

She walked to the window, looked out at the familiar out-porter's barrow, turned, surveyed Kipps for a moment ambiguously, said 'I will get some tea,' and so departed again.

Mrs Walshingham and Kipps looked at one another and the lady smiled indulgently. 'You two young people mustn't be shy of each other,' said Mrs Walshingham, which damaged Kipps considerably.

She was explaining how sensitive Helen always had been, even about quite little things, when the servant appeared with the tea things, and then Helen followed, and taking up a secure position behind the little banboo tea table, broke the ice with officious tea-cup clattering. Then she introduced the topic of a forthcoming open-air performance of *As You Like It*, and steered past the worst of the awkwardness. They discussed stage illusion. 'I mus' say,' said Kipps, 'I don't quite like a play in a theayter. It seems sort of unreal, some'ow.'

'But most plays are written for the stage,' said Helen, looking at the sugar.

'I know,' admitted Kipps.

They finished tea. 'Well,' said Kipps, and rose.

'You mustn't go yet,' said Mrs Walshingham, rising and taking his hand. 'I'm sure you two must have heaps to say to each other,' and so she escaped towards the door.

6

Among other projects that seemed almost equally correct to Kipps at that exalted moment was one of embracing Helen with ardour as soon as the door closed behind her mother, and one of headlong flight through the open window. Then he remembered he ought to hold the door open for Mrs Walshingham, and turned from that duty to find Helen still standing, beautifully inaccessible, behind the tea things. He closed the door and advanced towards her with his arms akimbo and his hands upon his coat skirts. Then, feeling angular, he moved his right hand to his moustache. Anyhow, he was dressed all right. Somewhere at the back of his mind, dim and mingled with doubt and surprise, appeared the perception that he felt now quite differently towards her, that something between them had been blown from Lympne Keep to the four winds of heaven . . .

She regarded him with an eye of critical proprietorship.

'Mother has been making up to you,' she said, smiling slightly.

She added, 'It was nice of you to come around to see her.'

They stood through a brief pause, as though each had expected something different in the other and was a little perplexed at its not being there. Kipps found he was at the corner of the brown-covered table, and he picked up a little flexible book that lay upon it to occupy his mind.

'I bought you a ring today,' he said, bending the book and speaking for the sake of saying something, and then he was moved to genuine speech. 'You know,' he said, 'I can't 'ardly believe it.'

Her face relaxed slightly again. 'No?' she said, and may have breathed, 'Nor I.'

'No,' he went on. 'It's as though everything 'ad changed. More even than

when I got my money. 'Ere we are going to marry. It's like being someone else. What I feel is – '

He turned a flushed and earnest face to her. He seemed to come alive to her with one natural gesture. 'I don't *know* things. I'm not good enough. I'm not refined. The more you'll see of me the more you'll find me out.'

'But I'm going to help you.'

'You'll 'ave to 'elp me a fearful lot.'

She walked to the window, glanced out of it, made up her mind, turned and came towards him, with her hands clasped behind her back.

'All these things that trouble you are very little things. If you don't mind – if you will let me tell you things – '

'I wish you would.'

'Then I will.'

'They're little things to you, but they aren't to me.'

'It all depends, if you don't mind being told.'

'By you?'

'I don't expect you to be told by strangers.'

'Oo!' said Kipps, expressing much.

'You know, there are just a few little things. For instance, you know, you are careless with your pronunciation . . . You don't mind my telling you?'

'I like it,' said Kipps.

'There are aitches.'

'I know,' said Kipps, and then, endorsingly, 'I been told. Fact is, I know a chap, a Nacter, *he's* told me. He's told me, and he's going to give me a lesson or so.'

'I'm glad of that. It only requires a little care.'

'Of course. On the stage they got to look out. They take regular lessons.'

'Of course,' said Helen, a little absently.

'I dessay I shall soon get into it,' said Kipps.

'And then there's dress,' said Helen, taking up her thread again.

Kipps became pink, but he remained respectfully attentive.

'You don't mind?' she said.

'Oo, no.'

'You mustn't be too – too dressy. It's possible to be over-conventional, over-elaborate. It makes you look like a shop – like a common, well-off person. There's a sort of easiness that is better. A real gentleman looks right, without looking as though he had tried to be right.'

'Jest as though 'e'd put on what came first?' said the pupil, in a faded voice.

'Not exactly that, but a sort of ease.'

Kipps nodded his head intelligently. In his heart he was kicking his silk hat about the room in an ecstasy of disappointment.

'And you must accustom yourself to be more at your ease when you are with people,' said Helen. 'You've only got to forget yourself a little and not be anxious – '

'I'll try,' said Kipps, looking rather hard at the teapot. 'I'll do my best to try.'

'I know you will,' she said, and laid a hand for an instant upon his shoulder and withdrew it.

He did not perceive her caress. 'One has to learn,' he said. His attention was distracted by the strenuous efforts that were going on in the back of his head to translate, 'I say, didn't you ought to name the day?' into easy as well as elegant English, a struggle that was still undecided when the time came for them to part . . .

He sat for a long time at the open window of his sitting-room with an intent face, recapitulating that interview. His eyes rested at last almost reproachfully on the silk hat beside him. ' 'Ow *is* one to know?' he asked. His attention was caught by a rubbed place in the nap, and, still thoughtful, he rolled up his handkerchief skilfully into a soft ball and began to smooth this down.

His expression changed slowly.

' 'Ow the Juice is one to know?' he said, putting down the hat with some emphasis.

He rose up, went across the room to the sideboard, and, standing there, opened and began to read *Manners and Rules*.

CHAPTER FOUR

The Bicycle Manufacturer

So Kipps embarked upon his engagement, steeled himself to the high enterprise of marrying above his breeding. The next morning found him dressing with a certain quiet severity of movement, and it seemed to his landlady's housemaid that he was unusually dignified at breakfast. He meditated profoundly over his kipper and his kidney and bacon. He was going to New Romney to tell the old people what had happened and where he stood. And the love of Helen had also given him courage to do what Buggins had once suggested to him as a thing he would do were he in Kipps's place, and that was to hire a motor car for the afternoon. He had an early cold lunch, and then, with an air of quiet resolution, assumed a cap and coat he had purchased to this end, and thus equipped strolled around, blowing slightly, to the motor shop. The transaction was unexpectedly easy, and within the hour Kipps, spectacled and wrapped about, was tootling through Dymchurch.

They came to a stop smartly and neatly outside the little toy shop. 'Make that thing 'oot a bit, will you,' said Kipps. 'Yes, that's it.'

'Whup,' said the motor car. 'Whurrup!'

Both his aunt and uncle came out on the pavement. 'Why, it's Artie,' cried his aunt, and Kipps had a moment of triumph.

He descended to hand claspings, removed wraps and spectacles, and the motor driver retired to take 'an hour off'. Old Kipps surveyed the machinery and disconcerted Kipps for a moment by asking him in a knowing tone what they asked him for a thing like that. The two men stood inspecting the machine and impressing the neighbours for a time, and then they strolled through the shop into the little parlour for a drink.

'They ain't settled,' old Kipps had said to the neighbours. 'They ain't got no further than experiments. There's a bit of take-in about each. You take my advice and wait, me boy, even if it's a year or two, before you buy one for your own use.'

(Though Kipps had said nothing of doing anything of the sort.)

' 'Ow d'you like that whisky I sent?' asked Kipps, dodging the old familiar bunch of children's pails.

Old Kipps became tactful. 'It's a very good whisky, my boy,' said old Kipps. 'I 'aven't the slightest doubt it's a very good whisky and cost you a tidy price. But – dashed if it soots me! They put this here Foozle Ile in it, my boy, and it ketches me jest 'ere.' He indicated his centre of figure. 'Gives me the heartburn,' he said, and shook his head rather sadly.

'It's a very good whisky,' said Kipps. 'It's what the actor manager chaps drink in London, I 'appen to know.'

'I des say they do, my boy,' said old Kipps, 'but then they've 'ad their livers burnt out, and I 'aven't. They ain't dellicat like me. My stummik always *as* been extrey dellicat. Sometimes it's almost been as though nothing would lay on it. But that's in passing. I liked those segars. You can send me some more of them segars . . . '

You cannot lead a conversation straight from the gastric consequences of Foozle Ile to Love, and so Kipps, after a friendly inspection of a rare old engraving after Morland (perfect except for a hole kicked through the centre) that his uncle had recently purchased by private haggle, came to the topic of the old people's removal.

At the outset of Kipps's great fortunes there had been much talk of some permanent provision for them. It had been conceded they were to be provided for comfortably, and the phrase 'retire from business' had been very much in the air. Kipps had pictured an ideal cottage, with a creeper always in exuberant flower about the door, where the sun shone for ever and the wind never blew and a perpetual welcome hovered in the doorway. It was an agreeable dream, but when it came to the point of deciding upon this particular cottage or that, and on this particular house or that, Kipps was surprised by an unexpected clinging to the little home, which he had always understood to be the worst of all possible houses.

'We don't want to move in a 'urry,' said Mrs Kipps.

'When we want to move, we want to move for life. I've had enough moving about in my time,' said old Kipps.

'We can do here a bit more, now we done here so long,' said Mrs Kipps.

'You lemme look about a bit *fust*,' said old Kipps.

And in looking about old Kipps found perhaps a finer joy than any mere possession could have given. He would shut his shop more or less effectually against the intrusion of customers, and toddle abroad seeking new matter for his dream; no house was too small and none too large for his knowing enquiries. Occupied houses took his fancy more than vacant ones, and he would remark, 'You won't be a-livin' 'ere for ever, even if you think you will,' when irate householders protested against the unsolicited examination of their more intimate premises –

Remarkable difficulties arose of a totally unexpected sort.

'If we 'ave a larger 'ouse,' said Mrs Kipps with sudden bitterness, 'we shall want a servant, and I don't want no gells in the place larfin' at me, sniggerin' and larfin' and prancin' and trapesin', lardy da! If we 'ave a smaller 'ouse, there won't be room to swing a cat.'

Room to swing a cat it seemed was absolutely essential. It was an infrequent but indispensable operation.

'When we *do* move,' said old Kipps, 'if we could get a bit of shootin' – I don't want to sell off all this here stock for nothin'. It's took years to 'cumulate. I put a ticket in the winder sayin' "sellin' orf", but it 'asn't brought nothing like a roosh. One of these 'ere dratted visitors pretendin' to want an airgun, was all we 'ad in yesterday. Jest an excuse for spyin' round and then go away and larf at you. No-thanky to everything, it didn't matter what . . . That's 'ow *I* look at it, Artie.'

They pursued meandering fancies about the topic of their future settlement for a space and Kipps became more and more hopeless of any proper conversational opening that would lead to his great announcement, and more and more uncertain how such an opening should be taken. Once, indeed, old Kipps, anxious to get away from this dangerous subject of removals, began: 'And what are you a-doin' of in Folkestone? I shall have to come over and see you one of these days,' but before Kipps could get in upon that, his uncle had passed into a general exposition of the proper treatment of landladies and their humbugging, cheating ways, and so the opportunity vanished. It seemed to Kipps the only thing to do was to go out into the town for a stroll, compose an effectual opening at leisure, and then come back and discharge it at them in its consecutive completeness. And even out of doors and alone he found his mind distracted by irrelevant thoughts.

2

His steps led him out of the High Street towards the church, and he leant for a time over the gate that had once been the winning-post of his race with Ann Pornick, and presently found himself in a sitting position on the

top rail. He had to get things smooth again, he knew; his mind was like a mirror of water after a breeze. The image of Helen and his great future was broken and mingled into fragmentary reflections of remoter things, of the good name of Old Methusaleh Three Stars, of long dormant memories the High Street saw fit, by some trick of light and atmosphere, to arouse that afternoon . . .

Abruptly a fine, full voice from under his elbow shouted, 'What-o, Art!' and, behold, Sid Pornick was back in his world, leaning over the gate beside him, and holding out a friendly hand.

He was oddly changed and yet oddly like the Sid that Kipps had known. He had the old broad face and mouth, abundantly freckled, the same short nose and the same blunt chin, the same odd suggestion of his sister Ann without a touch of her beauty; but he had quite a new voice, loud and a little hard, and his upper lip carried a stiff and very fair moustache.

Kipps shook hands. 'I was jest thinking of *you*, Sid,' he said, 'jest this very moment and wondering if ever I should see you again, ever. And 'ere you are!'

'One likes a look round at times,' said Sid. 'How are *you*, old chap?'

'All right,' said Kipps. 'I just been lef' – '

'You aren't changed much,' interrupted Sid.

'Ent I?' said Kipps, foiled.

'I knew your back directly I came round the corner. Spite of that 'at you got on. Hang it, I said, that's Art Kipps or the devil. And so it was.'

Kipps made a movement of his neck as if he would look at his back and judge. Then he looked Sid in the face. 'You got a moustache, Sid,' he said.

'I s'pose you're having your holidays?' said Sid.

'Well, partly. But I just been lef' – '

'*I'm* taking a bit of a holiday,' Sid went on. 'But the fact is, I have to give *myself* holidays nowadays. I've set up for myself.'

'Not down here?'

'No fear! I'm not a turnip. I've started in Hammersmith, manufacturing.' Sid spoke offhand as though there was no such thing as pride.

'Not drapery?'

'No fear! Engineer. Manufacture bicycles.' He clapped his hand to his breast pocket and produced a number of pink handbills. He handed one to Kipps and prevented him reading it by explanations and explanatory dabs of a pointing finger. 'That's our make, my make to be exact, The Red Flag, see? – I got a transfer with my name – Pantocrat tyres, eight pounds – yes, *there* – Clinchers ten, Dunlop's eleven, Ladies' one pound more – that's the lady's. Best machine at a democratic price in London. No guineas and no discounts – honest trade. I build 'em – to order. I've built,' he reflected, looking away seaward – 'seventeen. Counting orders in 'and . . . Come down to look at the old place a bit. Mother likes it at times.'

'Thought you'd all gone away – '

'What! after my father's death? No! My mother's come back, and she's living at Muggett's cottages. The sea air suits 'er. She likes the old place better than Hammersmith . . . and I can afford it. Got an old crony or so here . . . Gossip . . . have tea . . . S'pose *you* ain't married, Kipps?'

Kipps shook his head, 'I – ' he began.

'*I* am,' said Sid. 'Married these two years and got a nipper. Proper little chap.'

Kipps got his word in at last. 'I got engaged day before yesterday,' he said.

'Ah!' said Sid airily. 'That's all right. Who's the fortunate lady?'

Kipps tried to speak in an offhand way. He stuck his hands in his pockets as he spoke. 'She's a solicitor's daughter,' he said, 'in Folkestone. Rather'r nice set. County family. Related to the Earl of Beauprés – '

'Steady on!' cried Sid.

'You see, I've 'ad a bit of luck, Sid. Been lef' money.'

Sid's eye travelled instinctively to mark Kipps's garments. 'How much?' he asked.

' 'Bout twelve 'undred a year,' said Kipps, more offhandedly than ever.

'Lord!' said Sid, with a note of positive dismay, and stepped back a pace or two.

'My granfaver it was,' said Kipps, trying hard to be calm and simple. ' 'Ardly knew I '*ad* a granfaver. And then – bang! When o' Bean, the solicitor, told me of it, you could 'ave knocked me down – '

''*Ow* much?' demanded Sid, with a sharp note in his voice.

'Twelve 'undred pound a year – 'proximately, that is . . . '

Sid's attempt at genial unenvious congratulation did not last a minute. He shook hands with an unreal heartiness and said he was jolly glad. 'It's a bloomin' stroke of Luck,' he said.

'It's a bloomin' stroke of Luck,' he repeated; 'that's what it is,' with the smile fading from his face. 'Of course, better you 'ave it than me, o' chap. So I don't envy you, anyhow. *I* couldn't keep it, if I did 'ave it.'

' 'Ow's that?' said Kipps, a little hipped by Sid's patent chagrin.

'I'm a Socialist, you see,' said Sid. 'I don't 'old with Wealth. What *is* Wealth? Labour robbed out of the poor. At most it's only yours in Trust. Leastways, that 'ow *I* should take it.' He reflected. 'The Present distribution of Wealth,' he said and stopped.

Then he let himself go, with unmasked bitterness. 'It's no sense at all. It's jest damn foolishness. Who's going to work and care in a muddle like this? Here first you do – something anyhow – of the world's work, and it pays you hardly anything, and then it invites you to do nothing, nothing whatever, and pays you twelve hundred pounds a year. Who's going to respect laws and customs when they come to damn silliness like that?' He repeated, 'Twelve hundred pounds a year!'

At the sight of Kipps's face he relented slightly.

'It's not you I'm thinking of, o' man; it's the system. Better you than most people. Still – '

He laid both hands on the gate and repeated to himself, 'Twelve 'undred a year . . . Gee-whizz, Kipps! You'll be a swell!'

'I shan't,' said Kipps with imperfect conviction. 'No fear.'

'You can't 'ave money like that and not swell out. You'll soon be too big to speak to – 'ow do they put it? – a mere mechanic like me.'

'No fear, Siddee,' said Kipps with conviction. 'I ain't that sort.'

'Ah!' said Sid, with a sort of unwilling scepticism, 'money'll be too much for you. Besides – you're caught by a swell already.'

' 'Ow d'you mean?'

'That girl you're going to marry. Masterman says – '

'Oo's Masterman?'

'Rare good chap I know – takes my first-floor front room. Masterson says it's always the wife pitches the key. Always. There's no social differences – till women come in.'

'Ah!' said Kipps profoundly. 'You don't know.'

Sid shook his head. 'Fancy!' he reflected, 'Art Kipps! . . . Twelve 'Undred a Year!'

Kipps tried to bridge that opening gulf. 'Remember the Hurons, Sid?'

'Rather,' said Sid.

'Remember that wreck?'

'I can smell it now – sort of sour smell.'

Kipps was silent for a moment with reminiscent eyes on Sid's still troubled face.

'I say, Sid, 'ow's Ann?'

'*She's* all right,' said Sid.

'Where is she now?'

'In a place . . . Ashford.'

'Oh!'

Sid's face had become a shade sulkier than before.

'The fact is,' he said, 'we don't get on very well together. *I* don't hold with service. We're common people, I suppose, but I don't like it. I don't see why a sister of mine should wait at other people's tables. No. Not even if they got Twelve 'Undred a Year.'

Kipps tried to change the point of application. 'Remember 'ow you came out once when we were racing here? . . . She didn't run bad for a girl.'

And his own words raised an image brighter than he could have supposed, so bright it seemed to breathe before him and did not fade altogether even when he was back in Folkestone an hour or so later.

But Sid was not to be deflected from that other rankling theme by any reminiscences of Ann.

'I wonder what you will do with all that money,' he speculated. 'I wonder if you will do any good at all. I wonder what you *could* do. You should hear

Masterman. He'd tell you things. Suppose it came to me, what should I do? It's no good giving it back to the state as things are. Start an Owenite profit-sharing factory perhaps. Or a new Socialist paper. We want a new Socialist paper.'

He tried to drown his personal chagrin in elaborate exemplary suggestions . . .

3

'I must be gettin' on to my motor,' said Kipps at last, having to a large extent heard him out.

'What! Got a motor?'

'No!' said Kipps apologetically. 'Only jobbed for the day.'

' 'Ow much?'

'Five pounds.'

'Keep five families for a week! Good Lord!' That seemed to crown Sid's disgust.

Yet drawn by a sort of fascination he came with Kipps and assisted at the mounting of the motor. He was pleased to note it was not the most modern of motors, but that was the only grain of comfort. Kipps mounted at once, after one violent agitation of the little shop-door to set the bell a-jingle and warn his uncle and aunt. Sid assisted with the great fur-lined overcoat and examined the spectacles.

'Goodbye, o' chap!' said Kipps.

'Goodbye, o' chap!' said Sid.

The old people came out to say goodbye.

Old Kipps was radiant with triumph. ' 'Pon my Sammy, Artie! I'm a goo' mind to come with you,' he shouted, and then, 'I got something you might take with you!'

He dodged back into the shop and returned with the perforated engraving after Morland.

'You stick to this, my boy,' he said. 'You get it repaired by someone who knows. It's the most vallyble thing I got you so far, you take my word.'

'Warrup!' said the motor, and tuff, tuff, tuff, and backed and snorted while old Kipps danced about on the pavement as if foreseeing complex catastrophes, and told the driver, 'That's all right.'

He waved his stout stick to his receding nephew. Then he turned to Sid. 'Now, if you could make something like that, young Pornick, you *might* blow a bit!'

'I'll make a doocid sight better than *that* before I'm done,' said Sid, hands deep in his pockets.

'Not *you*,' said old Kipps.

The motor set up a prolonged sobbing moan and vanished around the

corner. Sid stood motionless for a space, unheeding some further remark from old Kipps. The young mechanic had just discovered that to have manufactured seventeen bicycles, including orders in hand, is not so big a thing as he had supposed, and such discoveries try one's manhood –

'Oh well!' said Sid at last, and turned his face towards his mother's cottage.

She had got a hot teacake for him, and she was a little hurt that he was dark and preoccupied as he consumed it. He had always been such a boy for teacake, and then when one went out specially and got him one – !

He did not tell her – he did not tell anyone – he had seen young Kipps. He did not want to talk about Kipps for a bit to anyone at all.

CHAPTER FIVE

The Pupil Lover

When Kipps came to reflect upon his afternoon's work he had his first inkling of certain comprehensive incompatibilities lying about the course of true love in his particular case. He had felt without understanding the incongruity between the announcement he had failed to make and the circle of ideas of his aunt and uncle. It was this rather than the want of a specific intention that had silenced him, the perception that when he travelled from Folkestone to New Romney he travelled from an atmosphere where his engagement to Helen was sane and excellent to an atmosphere where it was only to be regarded with incredulous suspicion. Coupled and associated with this jar was his sense of the altered behaviour of Sid Pornick, the evident shock to that ancient alliance caused by the fact of his enrichment, the touch of hostility in his 'You'll soon be swelled too big to speak to a poor mechanic like me.' Kipps was unprepared for the unpleasant truth that the path of social advancement is and must be strewn with broken friendships. This first protrusion of that fact caused a painful confusion in his mind. It was speedily to protrude in a far more serious fashion in relation to the 'hands' from the Emporium, and Chitterlow.

From the day at Lympne Castle his relations with Helen had entered upon a new footing. He had prayed for Helen as good souls pray for Heaven, with as little understanding of what it was he prayed for. And now that period of standing humbly in the shadows before the shrine was over, and the goddess, her veil of mystery flung aside, had come down to him and taken hold of him, a good, strong, firm hold, and walked by his side . . . She liked him. What was singular was that very soon she had kissed him thrice, whimsically upon the brow, and he had never kissed her at all. He could not analyse his feelings, only he knew the world was wonderfully changed about them; but the truth was that, though he still worshipped

and feared her, though his pride in his engagement was ridiculously vast, he loved her now no more. That subtle something. woven of the most delicate strands of self-love and tenderness and desire, had vanished imperceptibly and was gone now for ever. But that she did not suspect in him, nor as a matter of fact did he.

She took him in hand in perfect good faith. She told him things about his accent, she told him things about his bearing, about his costume and his way of looking at things. She thrust the blade of her intelligence into the tenderest corners of Kipps's secret vanity, she slashed his most intimate pride to bleeding tatters. He sought very diligently to anticipate some at least of these informing thrusts by making great use of Coote. But the unanticipated made a brave number –

She found his simple willingness a very lovable thing.

Indeed she liked him more and more. There was a touch of motherliness in her feelings towards him. But his upbringing and his associations had been, she diagnosed, 'awful'. At New Romney she glanced but little; that was remote. But in her inventory – she went over him as one might go over a newly taken house, with impartial thoroughness – she discovered more proximate influences: surprising intimations of nocturnal 'sing-songs' – she pictured it as almost shocking that Kipps should sing to the banjo – much low-grade wisdom treasured from a person called Buggins – 'Who *is* Buggins?' said Helen – vague figures of indisputable vulgarity, Pierce and Carshot – and more particularly, a very terrible social phenomenon, Chitterlow.

Chitterlow blazed upon them with unheralded oppressive brilliance the first time they were abroad together.

They were going along the front of the Leas to see a school play in Sandgate – at the last moment Mrs Walshingham had been unable to come with them – when Chitterlow loomed up into the new world. He was wearing the suit of striped flannel and the straw hat that had followed Kipps's payment in advance for his course in elocution, his hands were deep in his side pockets and animated the corners of his jacket, and his attentive gaze at the passing loungers, the faint smile under his boldly drawn nose, showed him engaged in studying character – no doubt for some forth-coming play.

'What-HO!' said he, at the sight of Kipps, and swept off the straw hat with so ample a clutch of his great, flat hand that it suggested to Helen's startled mind a conjurer about to palm a halfpenny.

' 'Ello, Chitt'low,' said Kipps a little awkwardly and not saluting.

Chitterlow hesitated. 'Half a mo', my boy,' he said, and arrested Kipps by extending a large hand over his chest. 'Excuse me, my dear,' he said, bowing like his Russian count by way of apology to Helen, and with a smile that would have killed at a hundred yards. He affected a semi-confidential grouping of himself and Kipps, while Helen stood in white amazement.

'About that play,' he said.

' 'Ow about it?' asked Kipps, acutely aware of Helen.

'It's all right,' said Chitterlow. 'There's a strong smell of syndicate in the air, I may tell you – Strong.'

'That's aw right,' said Kipps.

'You needn't tell everybody,' said Chitterlow, with a transitory confidential hand to his mouth which pointed the application of the 'everybody' just a trifle too strongly, 'but I think it's coming off. However –I mustn't detain you now. So long. You'll come round, eh?'

'Right you are,' said Kipps.

'Tonight?'

'At eight.'

And then, and more in the manner of a Russian prince than any common count, Chitterlow bowed and withdrew. Just for a moment he allowed a conquering eye to challenge Helen's, and noted her for a girl of quality.

There was a silence between our lovers for a space.

'That,' said Kipps with an allusive movement of the head, 'was Chitterlow.'

'Is he – a friend of yours?'

'In a way . . . You see – I met 'im. Leastways 'e met me. Run into me with a bicycle, 'e did, and so we got talking together.'

He tried to appear at his ease.

The young lady scrutinised his profile. 'What is he?'

' 'E's a Nacter chap,' said Kipps. 'Leastways 'e writes plays.'

'And sells them?'

'Partly.'

'Whom to?'

'Different people. Shares he sells . . . It's all right, reely – I meant to tell you about him before.'

Helen looked over her shoulder to catch a view of Chitterlow's retreating aspect. It did not compel her complete confidence.

She turned to her lover and said in a tone of quiet authority, 'You must tell me all about Chitterlow. Now.'

The explanation began . . .

The school play came almost as a relief to Kipps. In the flusterment of going in he could almost forget for a time his Laocoön struggle to explain, and in the intervals he did his best to keep forgetting. But Helen, with a gentle insistence, resumed the explanation of Chitterlow as they returned towards Folkestone.

Chitterlow was confoundedly difficult to explain. You could hardly imagine!

There was an almost motherly anxiety in Helen's manner, blended with the resolution of a schoolmistress to get to the bottom of the affair. Kipps's ears were soon quite brightly red.

'Have you seen one of his plays?'

' 'E's tole me about one.'

'But on the stage.'

'No. He 'asn't 'ad any on the stage yet. That's all coming . . . '

'Promise me,' she said in conclusion, 'you won't do anything without consulting me.'

And, of course, Kipps promised. 'Oo – no!'

They went on their way in silence.

'One can't know everybody,' said Helen in general.

'Of course,' said Kipps; 'in a sort of way it was him that helped me to my money.' And he indicated in a confused manner the story of the advertisement. 'I don't like to drop 'im all at once,' he added.

Helen was silent for a space, and when she spoke she went off at a tangent. 'We shall live in London – soon,' she remarked. 'It's only while we are here.'

It was the first intimation she gave him of their post-nuptial prospects.

'We shall have a nice little flat somewhere, not too far west, and there we shall build up a circle of our own.'

<div align="center">2</div>

All that declining summer Kipps was the pupil lover. He made an extraordinarily open secret of his desire for self-improvement; indeed Helen had to hint once or twice that his modest frankness was excessive, and all this new circle of friends did, each after his or her manner, everything that was possible to supplement Helen's efforts and help him to ease and skill in the more cultivated circles to which he had come. Coote was still the chief teacher, the tutor – there are so many little difficulties that a man may take to another man that he would not care to propound to the woman he loves – but they were all, so to speak, upon the staff. Even the freckled girl said to him once in a pleasant way, 'You mustn't say "contre temps", you must say "contraytom",' when he borrowed that expression from *Manners and Rules*, and she tried at his own suggestion to give him clear ideas upon the subject of 'as' and 'has'. A certain confusion between these words was becoming evident, the first fruits of a lesson from Chitterlow on the aspirate. Hitherto he had discarded that dangerous letter almost altogether, but now he would pull up at words beginning with 'h' and draw a sawing breath – rather like a startled kitten – and then aspirate with vigour.

Said Kipps one day, ' '*As* 'e? – I should say, ah – Has 'e? Ye know I got a lot of difficulty over them two words, which is which?'

'Well, "as" is a conjunction and "has" is a verb.'

'I know,' said Kipps, 'but when is "has" a conjunction and when is "as" a verb?'

'Well,' said the freckled girl, preparing to be very lucid. 'It's *has* when it means one has, meaning having, but if it isn't it's *as*. As for instance one says 'e – I mean *he* – He has. But one says "as he has".'

'I see,' said Kipps. 'So I ought to say "as 'e?"'

'No, if you are asking a question you say *has* 'e – I mean he – 'as he?' She blushed quite brightly, but still clung to her air of lucidity.

'I see,' said Kipps. He was about to say something further, but he desisted. 'I got it much clearer now. *Has* 'e? *Has* 'e as. Yes.'

'If you remember about having.'

'Oo, I will,' said Kipps . . .

Miss Coote specialised in Kipps's artistic development. She had early formed an opinion that he had considerable artistic sensibility, his remarks on her work had struck her as decidedly intelligent, and whenever he called around to see them she would show him some work of art – now an illustrated book, now perhaps a colour print of a Botticelli, now the *Hundred Best Paintings*, now 'Academy Pictures', now a German art hand-book and now some magazine of furniture and design. 'I know you like these things,' she used to say, and Kipps said, 'Oo, I *do*.' He soon acquired a little armoury of appreciative sayings. When presently the Walshinghams took him up to the Arts and Crafts, his deportment was intelligent in the extreme. For a time he kept a wary silence until suddenly he pitched upon a colour print. 'That's rather nace,' he said to Mrs Walshingham. 'That lill' thing. There.' He always said things like that by preference to the mother rather than the daughter unless he was perfectly sure.

He quite took to Mrs Walshingham. He was impressed by her con-spicuous tact and refinement; it seemed to him that the ladylike could go no further. She was always dressed with a delicate fussiness that was never disarranged and even a sort of faded quality about her hair and face and bearing and emotions contributed to her effect. Kipps was not a big man, and commonly he did not feel a big man, but with Mrs Walshingham he always felt enormous and distended, as though he was a navvy who had taken some disagreeable poison which puffed him up inside his skin as a preliminary to bursting. He felt, too, as though he had been rolled in clay and his hair dressed with gum. And he felt that his voice was strident and his accent like somebody swinging a crowded pig's pail in a free and careless manner. All this increased and enforced his respect for her. Her hand, which flitted often and again to his hand and arm, was singularly well shaped and cool. 'Arthur,' she called him from the very beginning.

She did not so much positively teach and tell him as tactfully guide and infect him. Her conversation was not so much didactic as exemplary. She would say, 'I *do* like people to do' so and so. She would tell him anecdotes of nice things done, of gentlemanly feats of graceful consideration; she would record her neat observations of people in trains and omnibuses; how, for example, a man had passed her change to the conductor, 'quite a common

man he looked', but he had lifted his hat. She stamped Kipps so deeply with the hat-raising habit that he would uncover if he found himself in the same railway ticket-office with a lady and so had to stand ceremoniously until the difficulties of change drove him to an apologetic provisional oblique resumption of his headgear . . . And robbing these things of any air of personal application, she threw about them an abundant talk about her two children – she called them her Twin Jewels quite frequently – about their gifts, their temperaments, their ambition, their need of opportunity. They needed opportunity, she would say, as other people needed air . . .

In his conversations with her Kipps always assumed, and she seemed to assume, that she was to join that home in London Helen foreshadowed, but he was surprised one day to gather that this was not to be the case. 'It wouldn't do,' said Helen, with decision. 'We want to make a circle of our own.'

'But won't she be a bit lonely down here?' asked Kipps.

'There's the Waces, and Mrs Prebble, and Mrs Bindon Botting and – lots of people she knows.' And Helen dismissed this possibility . . .

Young Walshingham's share in the educational syndicate was smaller. But he shone out when they went to London on that Arts and Crafts expedition. Then this rising man of affairs showed Kipps how to buy the more theatrical weeklies for consumption in the train, how to buy and what to buy in the way of cigarettes with gold tips and shilling cigars, and how to order hock for lunch and sparkling Moselle for dinner, how to calculate the fare of a hansom cab – penny a minute while he goes – how to look intelligently at a hotel tape, and how to sit still in a train like a thoughtful man instead of talking like a fool and giving yourself away. And he, too, would glance at the good time coming when they were to be in London for good and all.

That prospect expanded and developed particulars. It presently took up a large part of Helen's conversation. Her conversations with Kipps were never of a grossly sentimental sort; there was a shyness of speech in that matter with both of them, but these new adumbrations were at least as interesting and not so directly disagreeable as the clear-cut intimations of personal defect that for a time had so greatly chastened Kipps's delight in her presence. The future presented itself with an almost perfect frankness as a joint campaign of Mrs Walshingham's Twin Jewels upon the Great World, with Kipps in the capacity of baggage and supply. They would still be dreadfully poor, of course – this amazed Kipps, but he said nothing – until 'Brudderkins' began to succeed, but if they were clever and lucky they might do a great deal.

When Helen spoke of London, a brooding look, as of one who contemplates a distant country, came into her eyes. Already it seemed they had the nucleus of a set. Brudderkins was a member of the Theatrical Judges, an excellent and influential little club of journalists and literary people, and he

knew Shimer and Stargate and Whiffle, of the 'Red Dragon'; and besides these were the Revels. They knew the Revels quite well. Sidney Revel, before his rapid rise to prominence as a writer of epigrammatic essays that were quite above the ordinary public, had been an assistant master at one of the best Folkestone schools. Brudderkins had brought him home to tea several times, and it was he had first suggested Helen should try and write. 'It's perfectly easy,' Sidney had said. He had been writing occasional things for the evening papers and for the weekly reviews even at that time. Then he had gone up to London and had almost unavoidably become a dramatic critic. Those brilliant essays had followed, and then *Red Hearts a-Beating*, the romance that had made him. It was a tale of spirited adventure, full of youth and beauty and naïve passion and generous devotion, bold, as the *Bookman* said, and frank in places, but never in the slightest degree morbid. He had met and married an American widow with quite a lot of money, and they had made a very distinct place for themselves, Kipps learnt, in the literary and artistic society of London. Helen seemed to dwell on the Revels a great deal; it was her exemplary story, and when she spoke of Sidney – she often called him Sidney – she would become thoughtful. She spoke most of him naturally because she had still to meet Mrs Revel . . . Certainly they would be in the world in no time, even if the distant connection with the Beauprés family came to nothing.

Kipps gathered that with his marriage and the movement to London they were to undergo that subtle change of name Coote had first adumbrated. They were to become 'Cuyps', Mr and Mrs Cuyps. Or, was it Cuyp?

'It'll be rum at first,' said Kipps. 'I dessay I shall soon get into it . . .'

So in their several ways they all contributed to enlarge and refine and exercise the intelligence of Kipps. And behind all these other influences, and, as it were, presiding over and correcting these influences, was Kipps's nearest friend, Coote, a sort of master of the ceremonies. You figure his face, blowing slightly with solicitude, his slate-coloured, projecting but not unkindly eye intent upon our hero. The thing, he thought, was going off admirably. He studied Kipps's character immensely. He would discuss him with his sister, with Mrs Walshingham, with the freckled girl, with anyone who would stand it. 'He is an interesting character,' he would say, 'likable – a sort of gentleman by instinct. He takes to all these things. He improves every day. He'll soon get *Sang Froid*. We took him up just in time. He wants now – well – Next year, perhaps, if there is a good Extension Literature course he might go in for it. He wants to go in for something like that.'

'He's going in for his bicycle now,' said Mrs Walshingham.

'That's all right for summer,' said Coote, 'but he wants to go in for some serious, intellectual interest, something to take him out of himself a little more. *Savoir Faire* and self-forgetfulness are more than half the secret of *Sang Froid*.'

The world as Coote presented it was in part an endorsement, in part an amplification and in part a rectification of the world of Kipps, the world that derived from the old couple in New Romney and had been developed in the Emporium; the world, in fact, of common British life. There was the same subtle sense of social graduation that had moved Mrs Kipps to prohibit intercourse with labourers' children and the same dread of any-thing 'common' that had kept the personal quality of Mr Shalford's establishment so high. But now a certain disagreeable doubt about Kipps's own position was removed and he stood with Coote inside the sphere of gentlemen assured. Within the sphere of gentlemen there are distinctions of rank indeed, but none of class; there are the Big People and the modest, refined, gentlemanly little people like Coote, who may even dabble in the professions and counterless trades; there are lords and magnificences, and there are gentlefolk who have to manage; but they can all call on one another, they preserve a general equality of deportment throughout, they constitute that great state within the state, Society.

'But reely,' said the Pupil, 'not what you call being in Society?'

'Yes,' said Coote. 'Of course, down here one doesn't see much of it, but there's local society. It has the same rules.'

'Calling and all that?'

'Precisely,' said Coote.

Kipps thought, whistled a bar, and suddenly broached a question of conscience. 'I often wonder,' he said, 'whether I oughtn't to dress for dinner – when I'm alone 'ere.'

Coote protruded his lips and reflected. 'Not full dress,' he adjudicated; 'that would be a little excessive. But you should *change*, you know. Put on a mess jacket and that sort of thing – easy dress. That is what *I* should do, certainly, if I wasn't in harness – and poor.'

He coughed modestly and patted his hair behind.

And after that the washing bill of Kipps quadrupled, and he was to be seen at times by the bandstand with his light summer overcoat unbuttoned to give a glimpse of his nice white tie. He and Coote would be smoking the gold-tipped cigarettes young Walshingham had prescribed as *chic*, and appreciating the music highly. 'That's – puff – a very nice bit,' Kipps would say; or better, 'That's nace.' And at the first grunts of the loyal anthem up they stood with religiously uplifted hats. Whatever else you might call them, you could never call them disloyal.

The boundary of Society was admittedly very close to Coote and Kipps, and a leading solicitude of the true gentleman was to detect clearly those 'beneath' him, and to behave towards them in a proper spirit. 'It's jest there

it's so 'ard for me,' said Kipps. He had to cultivate a certain 'distance', to acquire altogether the art of checking the presumption of bounders and old friends. It was difficult, Coote admitted.

'I got mixed up with this lot 'ere,' said Kipps. 'That's what, so harkward – I mean awkward.'

'You could give them a hint,' said Coote.

' 'Ow?'

'Oh! – the occasion will suggest something.'

The occasion came one early-closing night when Kipps was sitting in a canopy chair near the bandstand, with his summer overcoat fully open and a new Gibus pulled slightly forward over his brow, waiting for Coote. They were to hear the band for an hour and then go down to assist Miss Coote and the freckled girl in trying over some of Beethoven's duets, if they remembered them, that is, sufficiently well. And as Kipps lounged back in his chair and occupied his mind with his favourite amusement on such evenings, which consisted chiefly in supposing that everyone about him was wondering who he was, there came a rude rap at the canvas back and the voice of Pierce.

'It's nice to be a gentleman,' said Pierce, and swung a penny chair into position while Buggins appeared smiling agreeably on the other side and leant upon his stick. *He was smoking a common briar pipe!*

Two real ladies, very fashionably dressed and sitting close at hand, glanced quickly at Pierce, and then away again, and it was evident *their* wonder was at an end.

'*He*'s all right,' said Buggins, removing his pipe and surveying Kipps.

' 'Ello, Buggins!' said Kipps, not too cordially. ' 'Ow goes it?'

'All right. Holiday's next week. If you don't look out, Kipps, I shall be on the Continong before you. Eh?'

'You going t' Boologne?'

'Ra-ther. Parley vous Francey. You bet.'

'*I* shall 'ave a bit of a run over there one of these days,' said Kipps.

There came a pause. Pierce applied the top of his stick to his mouth for a space and regarded Kipps. Then he glanced at the people about them.

'I say, Kipps,' he said in a distinct, loud voice, 'see 'er Ladyship lately?'

Kipps perceived the audience was to be impressed, but he responded half-heartedly, 'No, I 'aven't,' he said.

'She was along of Sir William the other night,' said Pierce, still loud and clear, 'and she asked to be remembered to you.'

It seemed to Kipps that one of the two ladies smiled faintly and said something to the other, and then certainly they glanced at Pierce. Kipps flushed scarlet. '*Did* she?' he answered.

Buggins laughed good-humouredly over his pipe.

'Sir William suffers a lot from his gout,' Pierce continued unabashed.

(Buggins much amused with his pipe between his teeth.)

Kipps became aware of Coote at hand.

Coote nodded rather distantly to Pierce. 'Hope I haven't kept you waiting, Kipps,' he said.

'I kep' a chair for you,' said Kipps and removed a guardian foot.

'But you've got your friends,' said Coote.

'Oh! *we* don't mind,' said Pierce cordially, 'the more the merrier,' and, 'Why don't you get a chair, Buggins?' Buggins shook his head in a sort of aside to Pierce and Coote coughed behind his hand.

'Been kep' late at business?' asked Pierce.

Coote turned quite pale and pretended not to hear. His eyes sought in space for a time and with a convulsive movement he recognised a distant acquaintance and raised his hat.

Pierce had also become a little pale. He addressed himself to Kipps in an undertone.

'Mr Coote, isn't he?' he asked.

Coote addressed himself to Kipps directly and exclusively His manner had the calm of extreme tension.

'I'm rather late,' he said. 'I think we ought almost to be going on *now*.'

Kipps stood up. 'That's all right,' he said.

'Which way are you going?' said Pierce, standing also, and brushing some crumbs of cigarette ash from his sleeve.

For a moment Coote was breathless. 'Thank you,' he said, and gasped. Then he delivered the necessary blow: 'I don't think we're in need of your society, you know,' and turned away.

Kipps found himself falling over chairs and things in the wake of Coote, and then they were clear of the crowd.

For a space Coote said nothing; then he remarked abruptly and quite angrily for him, 'I think that was *awful* Cheek!'

Kipps made no reply . . .

The whole thing was an interesting little object lesson in distance, and it stuck in the front of Kipps's mind for a long time. He had particularly vivid the face of Pierce, with an expression between astonishment and anger. He felt as though he had struck Pierce in the face under circumstances that gave Pierce no power to reply. He did not attend very much to the duets and even forgot at the end of one of them to say how perfectly lovely it was.

4

But you must not imagine that the national ideal of a gentleman, as Coote developed it, was all a matter of deportment and selectness, a mere isolation from debasing associations. There is a Serious Side, a deeper aspect of the True Gentleman. But it is not vocal. The True Gentleman does not wear his heart on his sleeve. He is a polished surface above deeps. For example, he is deeply religious, as Coote was, as Mrs Walshingham was, but outside

the walls of a church it never appears, except perhaps now and then in a pause, in a profound look, in a sudden avoidance. In quite a little while Kipps also had learnt the pause, the profound look, the sudden avoidance, that final refinement of spirituality, impressionistic piety.

And the True Gentleman is patriotic also. When one saw Coote lifting his hat to the National Anthem, then perhaps one got a glimpse of what patriotic emotions, what worship, the polish of a gentleman may hide. Or singing out his deep notes against the Hosts of Midian, in the St Stylites choir; then indeed you plumbed his spiritual side.

> Christian, dost thou heed them,
> On the holy ground,
> How the hosts of Mid-i-an,
> Prowl and prowl around!
> Christian, up and smai–it them . . .

But these were but gleams. For the rest, Religion, Nationality, Passion, Money, Politics, much more so those cardinal issues, Birth and Death, the True Gentleman skirted about, and became facially rigid towards, and ceased to speak and panted and blew.

'One doesn't talk of that sort of thing,' Coote would say with a gesture of the knuckly hand.

'O' course,' Kipps would reply, with an equal significance.

Profundities. Deep, as it were, blowing too deep.

One does not talk, but on the other hand one is punctilious to do. Actions speak. Kipps – in spite of the fact that the Walshinghams were more than a little lax – Kipps, who had formerly flitted Sunday after Sunday from one Folkestone church to another, had now a sitting of his own, paid for duly at Saint Stylites. There he was to be seen, always at the surplice evening service, and sometimes of a morning, dressed with a sober precision, and with an eye on Coote in the chancel. No difficulties now about finding the place in his book. He became a communicant again – he had lapsed soon after his confirmation when the young lady in the costume-room, who was his adopted sister, left the Emporium – and he would sometimes go around to the vestry for Coote after the service. One evening he was introduced to the Hon. and Revd Densemore. He was much too confused to say anything, and the noble cleric had nothing to say, but indisputably they were introduced –

No! you must not imagine our national ideal of a gentleman is without its 'serious side', without even its stern and uncompromising side. The imagination no doubt refuses to see Coote displaying extraordinary refinements of courage upon the stricken field, but in the walks of peace there is sometimes sore need of sternness. Charitable as one may be, one must admit there are people who *do* things, impossible things; people who place themselves 'out of it' in countless ways; people, moreover, who are by a sort of pre-destination out of it from the beginning, and against these Society has

invented a terrible protection for its Cootery, the Cut. The cut is no joke for anyone. It is excommunication. You may be cut by an individual, you may be cut by a set or you may be – and this is so tragic that beautiful romances have been written about it – 'Cut by the County'. One figures Coote discharging this last duty and cutting somebody – Coote, erect and pale, never speaking, going past with eyes of pitiless slate, lower jaw protruding a little, face pursed up and cold and stiff . . .

It never dawned upon Kipps that he would one day have to face this terrible front, to be to Coote not only as one dead, but as one gone more than a stage or so in decay, cut and passed, banned and outcast for ever. It never dawned upon either of them.

Yet so it was to be!

One cannot hide any longer that all this fine progress of Kipps is doomed to end in collapse. So far indeed you have seen him ascend. You have seen him becoming more refined and careful day by day, more carefully dressed, less clumsy in the uses of social life. You have seen the gulf widening between himself and his former low associates. I have brought you at last to the vision of him, faultlessly dressed and posed, in an atmosphere of candlelight and chanting, in his own sitting in one of the most fashionable churches in Folkestone . . . All the time I have refrained from the lightest touch upon the tragic note that must now creep into my tale. Yet the net of his low connections has been about his feet, and moreover there was something interwoven in his being . . .

CHAPTER SIX

Discords

One day Kipps set out upon his newly-mastered bicycle to New Romney to break the news of his engagement to his uncle and aunt – this time positively. He was now a finished cyclist, but as yet an unseasoned one; the south-west wind, even in its summer guise, as one meets it in the Marsh, is the equivalent of a reasonable hill, and ever and again he got off and refreshed himself by a spell of walking. He was walking just outside New Romney preparatory to his triumphal entry (one hand off) when abruptly he came upon Ann Pornick.

It chanced he was thinking about her at the time. He had been thinking curious things; whether, after all, the atmosphere of New Romney and the Marsh had not some difference, some faint impalpable quality that was missing in the great and fashionable world of Folkestone behind there on the hill. Here there was a homeliness, a familiarity. He had noted as he passed that old Mr Cliffordown's gate had been mended with a fresh piece of string. In Folkestone he didn't take notice and he didn't care if they built

three hundred houses. Come to think of it, that was odd. It was fine and grand to have twelve hundred a year; it was fine to go about on trams and omnibuses and think not a person aboard was as rich as oneself; it was fine to buy and order this and that and never have any work to do and to be engaged to a girl distantly related to the Earl of Beauprés, but yet there had been a zest in the old time out here, a rare zest in the holidays, in sunlight, on the sea beach and in the High Street, that failed from these new things. He thought of those bright windows of holiday that had seemed so glorious to him in the retrospect from his apprentice days. It was strange that now, amidst his present splendours, they were glorious still!

All those things were over now – perhaps that was it! Something had happened to the world and the old light had been turned out. He himself was changed, and Sid was changed, terribly changed, and Ann no doubt was changed.

He thought of her with the hair blown about her flushed cheeks as they stood together after their race . . .

Certainly she must be changed, and all the magic she had been fraught with to the very hem of her short petticoats gone no doubt for ever. And as he thought that, or before and while he thought it, for he came to all these things in his own vague and stumbling way, he looked up and there was Ann!

She was seven years older and greatly altered; yet for the moment it seemed to him that she had not changed at all. 'Ann!' he said, and she, with a lifting note, 'It's Art Kipps!'

Then he became aware of changes – improvements. She was as pretty as she had promised to be, her blue eyes as dark as his memory of them, and with a quick, high colour, but now Kipps by several inches was the taller again. She was dressed in a simple grey dress that showed her very clearly as a straight and healthy little woman, and her hat was Sundayfied with pink flowers. She looked soft and warm and welcoming. Her face was alight to Kipps with her artless gladness at their encounter.

'It's Art Kipps!' she said.

'Rather,' said Kipps.

'You got your holidays?'

It flashed upon Kipps that Sid had not told her of his great fortune. Much regretful meditation upon Sid's behaviour had convinced him that he himself was to blame for exasperating boastfulness in that affair, and this time he took care not to err in that direction. He erred in the other.

'I'm taking a bit of a 'oliday,' he said.

'So'm I,' said Ann.

'You been for a walk?' asked Kipps.

Ann showed him a bunch of wayside flowers.

'It's a long time since I seen you, Ann. Why, 'ow long must it be? Seven – eight years nearly.'

'It don't do to count,' said Ann.

'It don't look like it,' said Kipps, with the slightest emphasis.

'You got a moustache,' said Ann, smelling her flowers and looking at him over them, not without admiration.

Kipps blushed . . . Presently they came to the bifurcation of the roads.

'I'm going down this way to mother's cottage,' said Ann.

'I'll come a bit your way if I may.'

In New Romney social distinctions that are primary realities in Folkestone are absolutely non-existent, and it seemed quite permissible for him to walk with Ann, for all that she was no more than a servant. They talked with remarkable ease to one another; they slipped into a vein of intimate reminiscence in the easiest manner.

In a little while Kipps was amazed to find Ann and himself at this: 'You r'ember that half sixpence? What you cut for me?'

'Yes.'

'I got it still.'

She hesitated. 'Funny, wasn't it?' she said; and then, 'You got yours, Artie?'

'Rather,' said Kipps. 'What do *you* think?' and wondered in his heart of hearts why he had never looked at that sixpence for so long.

Ann smiled at him frankly.

'I didn't expect you'd keep it,' she said. 'I thought often – it was silly to keep mine. Besides,' she reflected, 'it didn't mean anything really.'

She glanced at him as she spoke and met his eye.

'Oh, didn't it!' said Kipps, a little late with his response, and realising his infidelity to Helen even as he spoke.

'It didn't mean much anyhow,' said Ann. 'You still in the drapery?'

'I'm living at Folkestone,' began Kipps and decided that that sufficed. 'Didn't Sid tell you he met me?'

'No! Here?'

'Yes. The other day. 'Bout a week or more ago.'

'That was before I came.'

'Ah! that was it,' said Kipps.

' 'E's got on,' said Ann. 'Got 'is own shop now, Artie.'

' 'E tole me.'

They found themselves outside Muggett's cottages. 'You going in?' said Kipps.

'I s'pose so,' said Ann.

They both hung upon the pause. Ann took a plunge.

'D'you often come to New Romney?' she said.

'I ride over a bit at times,' said Kipps.

Another pause. Ann held out her hand. 'I'm glad I seen you,' she said.

Extraordinary impulses arose in neglected parts of Kipps's being. 'Ann – ' he said and stopped.

'Yes,' said she, and was bright to him.

They looked at one another.

All and more than all of those first emotions of his adolescence had come back to him. Her presence banished a multitude of countervaling considerations. It was Ann more than ever. She stood breathing close to him, with her soft-looking lips a little apart and gladness in her eyes.

'I'm awful glad to see you again,' he said; 'it brings back old times.'

'Doesn't it?'

Another pause. He would have liked to have had a long talk to her, to have gone for a walk with her or something, to have drawn nearer to her in any conceivable way, and, above all, to have had some more of the appreciation that shone in her eyes, but a vestige of Folkestone still clinging to him told him it 'wouldn't do'.

'Well,' he said, 'I must be getting on,' and turned away reluctantly, with a will under compulsion . . .

When he looked back from the corner she was still at the gate. She was perhaps a little disconcerted by his retreat. He felt that. He hesitated for a moment, half turned, stood and suddenly did great things with his hat. That hat! The wonderful hat of our civilisation! . . .

In another minute he was engaged in a singularly absent-minded conversation with his uncle about the usual topics.

His uncle was very anxious to buy him a few upright clocks as an investment for subsequent sale. And there were also some very nice globes, one terrestrial and the other celestial, in a shop at Lydd, that would look well in a drawing-room and inevitably increase in value . . . Kipps either did or did not agree to this purchase; he was unable to recollect.

The south-west wind perhaps helped him back; at any rate he found himself through Dymchurch without having noticed the place. There came an odd effect as he drew near Hythe. The hills on the left and the trees on the right seemed to draw together and close in upon him until his way was straight and narrow. He could not turn around on that treacherous, half-tamed machine, but he knew that behind him, he knew so well, spread the wide, vast flatness of the Marsh shining under the afternoon sky. In some way this was material to his thoughts. And as he rode through Hythe he came upon the idea that there was a considerable amount of incompatibility between the existence of one who was practically a gentleman and of Ann.

In the neighbourhood of Seabrook he began to think he had, in some subtle way, lowered himself by walking along by the side of Ann . . . After all, she was only a servant.

Ann!

She called out all the least gentlemanly instincts of his nature. There had been a moment in their conversation when he had quite distinctly thought it would really be an extremely nice thing for someone to kiss her lips . . . There was something warming about Ann – at least for Kipps. She impressed him as having somewhen during their vast interval of separation contrived to make herself in some distinctive way his.

Fancy keeping that half sixpence all this time!

It was the most flattering thing that had ever happened to Kipps.

2

He found himself presently sitting over *The Art of Conversing*, lost in the strangest musings. He got up, walked about, became stagnant at the window for a space, roused himself and by way of something lighter tried *Sesame and Lilies*. From that, too, his attention wandered. He sat back. Anon he smiled, anon sighed. He arose, pulled his keys from his pocket, looked at them, decided and went upstairs. He opened the little yellow box that had been the nucleus of all his possessions in the world and took out a small 'escritoire', the very humblest sort of present, and opened it – kneeling. And there, in the corner, was a little packet of paper, sealed as a last defence against any prying invader with red sealing wax. It had gone untouched for years. He held this little packet between finger and thumb for a moment, regarding it, and then put down the escritoire and broke the seal . . .

As he was getting into bed that night he remembered something for the first time! 'Dash it!' he said. 'Dashed if I told 'em *this* time . . . *Well!* I shall 'ave to go over to New Romney again!'

He got into bed and remained sitting pensively on the pillow for a space. 'It's a rum world,' he reflected after a vast interval.

Then he recalled that she had noticed his moustache and embarked upon a sea of egotistical musings.

He imagined himself telling Ann how rich he was. What a surprise that would be for her!

Finally he sighed profoundly, blew out his candle and snuggled down, and in a little while he was asleep.

But the next morning and at intervals afterwards he found himself thinking of Ann – Ann, the bright, the desirable, the welcoming, and with an extraordinary streakiness he wanted quite badly to go and then as badly not to go over to New Romney again.

Sitting on the Leas in the afternoon, he had an idea. 'I ought to 'ave told 'er, I suppose, about my being engaged.

'Ann!'

All sorts of dreams and impressions that had gone clean out of his mental existence came back to him, changed and brought up to date to fit her altered presence. He thought of how he had gone back to New Romney for his Christmas holidays, determined to kiss her, and of the awful blankness of the discovery that she had gone away.

It seemed incredible now, and yet not wholly incredible, that he had cried real tears for her – how many years was it ago?

Daily I should thank my Maker that He did not appoint me Censor of the world of men. I should temper a fierce injustice with a spasmodic indecision that would prolong rather than mitigate the bitterness of the Day. For human dignity, for all conscious human superiority, I should lack the beginnings of charity; for bishops, prosperous schoolmasters, judges and all large respect-pampered souls. And more especially bishops, towards whom I bear an atavistic Viking grudge, dreaming not infrequently and with invariable zest of galleys and landings and well-known living ornaments of the episcopal bench sprinting inland on twinkling gaiters before my thirsty blade – all these people, I say, I should treat below their deserts; but, on the other hand, for such as Kipps – There the exasperating indecisions would come in. The Judgement would be arrested at Kipps. Everyone and everything would wait. *You* would wait. The balance would sway and sway, and whenever it heeled towards an adverse decision, my finger would set it swaying again. Kings, warriors, statesmen, brilliant women of our first families, 'personalities' panting with indignation, headline humanity in general, would stand undamned, unheeded, or be damned in the most casual manner for their importunity, while my eye went about for anything possible that could be said on behalf of Kipps . . . Albeit I fear nothing can save him from condemnation upon this present score, that within two days he was talking to Ann again.

One seeks excuses. Overnight there had been an encounter of Chitterlow and young Walshingham in his presence that had certainly warped his standards. They had called within a few minutes of each other, and the two, swayed by virile attentions to Old Methuselah Three Stars, had talked against each other, over and at the hospitable presence of Kipps. Walshingham had seemed to win at the beginning, but finally Chitterlow had made a magnificent display of vociferation and swept him out of existence. At the beginning Chitterlow had opened upon the great profits of playwrights and young Walshingham had capped him at once with a cynical, but impressive, display of knowledge of High Finance. If Chitterlow boasted his thousands, young Walshingham boasted his hundreds of thousands, and was for a space left in sole possession of the stage, juggling with the wealth of nations. He was going on by way of Financial Politics to the Overman, before Chitterlow recovered from his first check and came back to victory. 'Talking of Women,' said Chitterlow, coming in abruptly upon some things not generally known beyond Walshingham's more immediate circle about a recently departed Empire-builder; 'Talking of Women and the way they Get at a man – '

(Though as a matter of fact they had been talking of the Corruption of Society by Speculation.)

Upon this new topic Chitterlow was soon manifestly invincible. He knew so much, he had known so many. Young Walshingham did his best with epigrams and reservations, but even to Kipps it was evident that this was a book-learned depravity. One felt Walshingham had never known the inner realities of passion. But Chitterlow convinced and amazed. He had run away with girls, he had been run away with by girls, he had been in love with several at a time – 'not counting Bessie' – he had loved and lost, he had loved and refrained, and he had loved and failed. He threw remarkable lights upon the moral state of America – in which country he had toured with great success. He set his talk to the tune of one of Mr Kipling's best-known songs. He told an incident of simple romantic passion, a delirious dream of love and beauty in a Saturday-to-Monday steamboat trip up the Hudson, and tagged his end with, 'I learnt about women from 'er!' After that he adopted the refrain, and then lapsed into the praises of Kipling. 'Little Kipling,' said Chitterlow, with the familiarity of affection, '*he* knows,' and broke into quotation:

> "I've taken my fun where I've found it;
> I've rogued and I've ranged in my time;
> I've 'ad my picking of sweet'earts,
> An' four of the lot was Prime." '

(These things, I say, affect the moral standards of the best of us.)

'*I'd* have liked to have written that,' said Chitterlow. 'That's Life, that is! But go and put it on the Stage, put even a bit of the Realities of Life on the Stage, and see what they'll do to you! Only Kipling could venture on a job like that. That Poem KNOCKED me! I don't say Kipling hasn't knocked me before and since, but that was a Fair Knock Out.

'And yet – you know – there's one thing in it . . . this:

> "I've taken my fun where I've found it,
> And now I must pay for my fun,
> For the more you 'ave known o' the others,
> The less will you settle to one – "

Well. In my case anyhow – I don't know how much that proves, seeing I'm exceptional in so many things and there's no good denying it – but so far as I'm concerned – I tell you two, but of course you needn't let it go any further – I've been perfectly faithful to Muriel ever since I married her – ever since . . . Not once. Not even by accident have I ever said or done anything in the slightest – ' His little brown eye became pensive after this flattering intimacy and the gorgeous draperies of his abundant voice fell into graver folds. '*I learnt about women from 'er,*' he said impressively.

'Yes,' said Walshingham, getting into the hinder spaces of that splendid pause, 'a man must know about women. And the only sound way of learning is the experimental method.'

'If you want to know about the experimental method, my boy,' said Chitterlow, resuming . . .

So they talked. *Ex pede Herculem*, as Coote, that cultivated polyglot, would have put it. And in the small hours Kipps went to bed, with his brain whirling with words and whisky, and sat for an unconscionable time upon his bed edge, musing sadly upon the unmanly monogamy that had cast its shadow upon his career, musing with his thoughts pointing around more and more certainly to the possibility of at least duplicity with Ann.

4

For a whole day he had refrained with some insistence from going off to New Romney again . . .

I do not know if this may count in palliation of his misconduct. Men, real Strong-Souled, Healthy Men, should be, I suppose, impervious to conversational atmospheres, but I have never claimed for Kipps a place at these high levels. The unquenchable fact remains that the next day he spent the afternoon with Ann and found no scruple in displaying himself a budding lover.

He had met her in the High Street, had stopped her, and almost on the spur of the moment had boldly proposed a walk, 'for the sake of old times'.

'*I* don't mind,' said Ann.

Her consent almost frightened Kipps. His imagination had not carried him to that. 'It would be a lark,' said Kipps, and looked up the street and down. 'Now?' he said.

'I don't mind a bit, Artie. I was just going for a walk along towards St Mary's.'

'Let's go that way be'ind the church,' said Kipps, and presently they found themselves drifting seaward in a mood of pleasant commonplace. For a while they talked of Sid. It went clean out of Kipps's head at that early stage even that Ann was a 'girl' according to the exposition of Chitterlow, and for a time he remembered only that she was Ann. But afterwards, with the reek of that talk in his head, he lapsed a little from that personal relation. They came out upon the beach and sat down in a tumbled pebbly place, where a meagre grass and patches of sea poppy were growing, and Kipps reclined on his elbow and tossed pebbles in his hand, and Ann sat up, sunlit, regarding him. They talked in fragments. They exhausted Sid, they exhausted Ann, and Kipps was chary of his riches.

He declined to a faint lovemaking. 'I got that 'arf sixpence still,' he said.

'Reely?'

That changed the key. 'I always kept mine, some'ow,' said Ann, and there was a pause.

They spoke of how often they had thought of each other during those

intervening years. Kipps may have been untruthful, but Ann perhaps was not. 'I met people here and there,' said Ann; 'but I never met anyone quite like you, Artie.'

'It's jolly our meeting again, anyhow,' said Kipps. 'Look at that ship out there. She's pretty close in . . . '

He had a dull period, became indeed almost pensive, and then he was enterprising for a while. He tossed up his pebbles so that as if by accident they fell on Ann's hand. Then, very penitently, he stroked the place. That would have led to all sorts of coquetries on the part of Flo Banks, for example, but it disconcerted and checked Kipps to find Ann made no objection, smiled pleasantly down on him, with eyes half shut because of the sun. She was taking things very much for granted.

He began to talk, and Chitterlow standards resuming possession of him he said he had never forgotten her.

'I never forgotten you either, Artie,' she said. 'Funny, isn't it?'

It impressed Kipps also as funny.

He became reminiscent, and suddenly a warm summer's evening came back to him. 'Remember them cockchafers, Ann?' he said. But the reality of the evening he recalled was not the chase of cockchafers. The great reality that had suddenly arisen between them was that he had never kissed Ann in his life. He looked up and there were her lips.

He had wanted to very badly, and his memory leaped and annihilated an interval. That old resolution came back to him and all sorts of new resolutions passed out of mind. And he had learnt something since those boyish days. This time he did not ask. He went on talking, his nerves began very faintly to quiver and his mind grew bright.

Presently, having satisfied himself that there was no one to see, he sat up beside her and remarked upon the clearness of the air, and how close Dungeness seemed to them. Then they came upon a pause again.

'Ann,' he whispered, and put an arm that quivered about her.

She was mute and unresisting, and, as he was to remember, solemn.

He turned her face towards him, and kissed her lips, and she kissed him back again – kisses frank and tender as a child's.

5

It was curious that in the retrospect he did not find nearly the satisfaction in this infidelity he had imagined was there. It was no doubt desperately doggish, doggish to an almost Chitterlowesque degree, to recline on the beach at Littlestone with a 'girl', to make love to her and to achieve the triumph of kissing her, when he was engaged to another 'girl' at Folkestone, but somehow these two people were not 'girls', they were Ann and Helen. Particularly Helen declined to be considered as a 'girl'. And there was

something in Ann's quietly friendly eyes, in her frank smile, in the naïve pressure of her hand, there was something undefended and welcoming that imparted a flavour to the business upon which he had not counted. He had learnt about women from her. That refrain ran through his mind and deflected his thoughts, but as a matter of fact he had learnt about nothing but himself.

He wanted very much to see Ann some more and explain. He did not clearly know what it was he wanted to explain.

He did not clearly know anything. It is the last achievement of the intelligence to get all of one's life into one coherent scheme, and Kipps was only in a measure more aware of himself as a whole than is a tree. His existence was an affair of dissolving and recurring moods. When he thought of Helen or Ann or any of his friends, he thought sometimes of this aspect and sometimes of that – and often one aspect was finally incongruous with another. He loved Helen, he revered Helen. He was also beginning to hate her with some intensity. When he thought of that expedition to Lympne, profound, vague, beautiful emotions flooded his being; when he thought of paying calls with her perforce, or of her latest comment on his bearing, he found himself rebelliously composing fierce and pungent insults, couched in the vernacular. But Ann, whom he had seen so much less of, was a simpler memory. She was pretty, she was almost softly feminine, and she was possible to his imagination just exactly where Helen was impossible. More than anything else, she carried the charm of respect for him, the slightest glance of her eyes was balm for his perpetually wounded self-conceit.

Chance suggestions it was set the tune of his thoughts, and his state of health and repletion gave the colour. Yet somehow he had this at least almost clear in his mind, that to have gone to see Ann a second time, to have implied that she had been in possession of his thoughts through all this interval, and, above all, to have kissed her, was shabby and wrong. Only unhappily this much of lucidity had come now just a few hours after it was needed.

6

Four days after this it was that Kipps got up so late. He got up late, cut his chin while shaving, kicked a slipper into his sponge bath and said, 'Desh!'

Perhaps you know those intolerable mornings, dear Reader, when you seem to have neither the heart nor the strength to rise, and your nervous adjustments are all wrong, and your fingers thumbs, and you hate the very birds for singing. You feel inadequate to any demand whatever. Often such awakenings follow a poor night's rest, and commonly they mean indiscriminate eating, or those subtle mental influences old Kipps ascribed to 'Foozle Ile' in the system, or worry. And with Kipps – albeit Chitterlow had again been his guest overnight – assuredly worry had played a leading

role. Troubles had been gathering upon him for days, there had been a sort of concentration of these hosts of Midian overnight, and in the grey small hours Kipps had held his review.

The predominating trouble marched under this banner:

Mr Kipps

Mrs Bindon Botting
At Home
Thursday, September 16th

Anagrams, 4 to 6:30　　　　*R. S. V. P.*

a banner that was the facsimile of a card upon his looking glass in the room below. And in relation to this terribly significant document, things had come to a pass with Helen that he could only describe in his own expressive idiom as 'words'.

It had long been a smouldering issue between them that Kipps was not availing himself with any energy or freedom of the opportunities he had of social exercises, much less was he seeking additional opportunities. He had, it was evident, a peculiar dread of that universal afternoon enjoyment, the Call, and Helen made it unambiguously evident that this dread was 'silly' and had to be overcome. His first display of this unmanly weakness occurred at the Cootes' on the day before he kissed Ann. They were all there, chatting very pleasantly, when the little servant with the big cap announced the younger Miss Wace.

Whereupon Kipps manifested a lively horror and rose partially from his chair. 'O Gum!' he protested. 'Carn't I go upstairs?'

Then he sank back, for it was too late. Very probably the younger Miss Wace had heard him as she came in.

Helen said nothing of that, though her manner may have shown her surprise, but afterwards she told Kipps he must get used to seeing people, and suggested that he should pay a series of calls with Mrs Walshingham and herself. Kipps gave a reluctant assent at the time and afterwards displayed a talent for evasion that she had not suspected in him. At last she did succeed in securing him for a call upon Miss Punchafer, of Radnor Park – a particularly easy call because Miss Punchafer being so deaf one could say practically what one liked – and then outside the gate he shirked again. 'I can't go in,' he said in a faded voice.

'You *must*,' said Helen, beautiful as ever, but even more than a little hard and forbidding.

'I can't.'

He produced his handkerchief hastily, thrust it to his face, and regarded her over it with rounded, hostile eyes.

' 'Possible,' he said in a hoarse, strange voice out of the handkerchief. 'Nozzez bleedin' . . .'

But that was the end of his power of resistance, and when the rally for the Anagram Tea occurred she bore down his feeble protests altogether. She insisted. She said frankly, 'I am going to give you a good talking to about this,' and she did . . .

From Coote he gathered something of the nature of Anagrams and Anagram parties. An anagram, Coote explained, was a word spelt the same way as another, only differently arranged, as, for instance, TOCOE would be an anagram for his own name, Coote.

'TOCOE,' repeated Kipps very carefully.

'Or TOCOE,' said Coote.

'Or TOCOE,' said Kipps, assisting his poor head by nodding it at each letter.

'Toe Company like,' he said in his efforts to comprehend.

When Kipps was clear what an anagram meant, Coote came to the second heading – the Tea. Kipps gathered there might be from thirty to sixty people present, and that each one would have an anagram pinned on. 'They give you a card to put your guesses on, rather like a dance programme, and then, you know, you go around and guess,' said Coote. 'It's rather good fun.'

'Oo rather!' said Kipps, with simulated gusto.

'It shakes everybody up together,' said Coote.

Kipps smiled and nodded . . .

In the small hours all his painful meditations were threaded by the vision of that Anagram Tea; it kept marching to and fro and in and out of all his other troubles; from thirty to sixty people, mostly ladies and callers, and a great number of the letters of the alphabet, and more particularly PIKPS and TOCOE, and he was trying to make one word out of the whole interminable procession . . .

This word, as he finally gave it with some emphasis to the silence of the night, was, '*Demn!*'

Then, wreathed as it were in this lettered procession, was the figure of Helen as she had appeared at the moment of 'words'; her face a little hard, a little irritated, a little disappointed. He imagined himself going around and guessing under her eye . . .

He tried to think of other things, without lapsing upon a still deeper uneasiness that was wreathed with yellow sea poppies; and the figures of Buggins, Pierce and Carshot, three murdered Friendships, rose reproachfully in the stillness and changed horrible apprehensions into unspeakable remorse. Last night had been their customary night for the banjo, and Kipps, with a certain tremulous uncertainty, had put Old Methuselah amidst a retinue of glasses on the table and opened a box of choice cigars. In vain. They were in no need, it seemed, of *his* society. But instead Chitterlow had

come, anxious to know if it was all right about that syndicate plan. He had declined anything but a very weak whisky and soda, 'just to drink', at least until business was settled, and had then opened the whole affair with an effect of great orderliness to Kipps. Soon he was taking another whisky by sheer inadvertency, and the complex fabric of his conversation was running more easily from the broad loom of his mind. Into that pattern had been interwoven a narrative of extensive alterations in The Pestered Butterfly' – the neck and beetle business was to be restored – the story of a grave difference of opinion with Mrs Chitterlow, where and how to live after the play had succeeded, the reasons why the Hon. Thomas Norgate had never financed a syndicate, and much matter also about the syndicate now under discussion. But if the current of their conversation had been vortical and crowded, the outcome was perfectly clear. Kipps was to be the chief participator in the syndicate, and his contribution was to be two thousand pounds. Kipps groaned and rolled over and found Helen, as it were, on the other side. 'Promise me,' she had said, 'you won't do anything without consulting me.'

Kipps at once rolled back to his former position, and for a space lay quite still. He felt like a very young rabbit in a trap.

Then suddenly, with extraordinary distinctness, his heart cried out for Ann, and he saw her as he had seen her at New Romney, sitting amidst the yellow sea poppies with the sunlight on her face. His heart called out for her in the darkness as one calls for rescue. He knew, as though he had known it always, that he loved Helen no more. He wanted Ann, he wanted to hold her and be held by her, to kiss her again and again, to turn his back for ever on all these other things . . .

He rose late, but this terrible discovery was still there, undispelled by cockcrow or the day. He rose in a shattered condition, and he cut himself while shaving, but at last he got into his dining-room and could pull the bell for the hot constituents of his multifarious breakfast. And then he turned to his letters. There were two real letters in addition to the customary electric-belt advertisement, continental lottery circular and betting tout's card. One was in a slight mourning envelope and addressed in an unfamiliar hand. This he opened first and discovered a note:

Mrs Raymond Wace
requests the pleasure of
Mr Kipps's
Company at Dinner
on Tuesday, September 21st, at 8 o'clock

R.S.V.P.

With a hasty movement Kipps turned his mind to the second letter. It was an unusually long one from his uncle, and ran as follows:

MY DEAR NEPHEW – We are considerably startled by your letter, though expecting something of the sort and disposed to hope for the best. If the young lady is a relation to the Earl of Beaupres well and good but take care you are not being imposed upon for there are many who will be glad enough to snap you up now your circumstances are altered – I waited on the old Earl once while in service and he was remarkably close with his tips and suffered from corns. A hasty old gent and hard to please – I dare say he has forgotten me altogether – and anyhow there is no need to rake up bygones. Tomorrow is bus day and as you say the young lady is living near by we shall shut up shop for there is really nothing doing now what with all the visitors bringing everything with them down to their very children's pails and say how de do to her and give her a bit of a kiss and encouragement if we think her suitable – she will be pleased to see your old uncle – We wish we could have had a look at her first but still there is not much mischief done and hoping that all will turn out well yet I am

 Your affectionate Uncle

 EDWARD GEORGE KIPPS

My heartburn still very bad. I shall bring over a few bits of rhubub I picked up, a sort you won't get in Folkestone, and if possible a good bunch of flowers for the young lady.

'Comin' over today,' said Kipps, standing helplessly with the letter in his hand.
' 'Ow, the Juice – ?
'I carn't.
'Kiss 'er!'
A terrible anticipation of that gathering framed itself in his mind – a hideous, impossible disaster.
'I carn't even face 'er – !' His voice went up to a note of despair. 'And it's too late to telegrarf and stop 'em!'

7

About twenty minutes after this, an out-porter in Castle Hill Avenue was accosted by a young man with a pale, desperate face, an exquisitely rolled umbrella and a heavy Gladstone bag.
'Carry this to the station, will you?' said the young man. 'I want to ketch the nex' train to London . . . You'll 'ave to look sharp – I 'aven't very much time.'

CHAPTER SEVEN

London

London was Kipps's third world. There were no doubt other worlds, but Kipps knew only these three: first, New Romney and the Emporium, constituting his primary world, his world of origin, which also contained Ann; secondly, the world of culture and refinement, the world of which Coote was chaperon and into which Kipps was presently to marry, a world it was fast becoming evident absolutely incompatible with the first; and, thirdly, a world still to a large extent unexplored, London. London presented itself as a place of great grey spaces and incredible multitudes of people, centring about Charing Cross Station and the Royal Grand Hotel, and containing at unexpected arbitrary points shops of the most amazing sort, statuary, squares, restaurants – where it was possible for clever people like Walshingham to order a lunch item by item, to the waiters' evident respect and sympathy – exhibitions of incredible things – the Walshinghams had taken him to the Arts and Crafts and to a picture gallery – and theatres. London, moreover, is rendered habitable by hansom cabs. Young Walshingham was a natural cab-taker; he was an all-round large-minded young man, and he had in the course of their two days' stay taken Kipps into no less than nine, so that Kipps was singularly not afraid of these vehicles. He knew that wherever you were, so soon as you were thoroughly lost you said, 'Hi!' to a cab, and then, 'Royal Grand Hotel.' Day and night these trusty conveyances are returning the strayed Londoner back to his point of departure, and were it not for their activity, in a little while the whole population, so vast and incomprehensible is the intricate complexity of this great city, would be hopelessly lost for ever. At any rate, that is how the thing presented itself to Kipps, and I have heard much the same from visitors from America.

His train was composed of corridor carriages, and he forgot his trouble for a time in the wonders of this modern substitute for railway compartments. He went from the non-smoking to the smoking carriage and smoked a cigarette, and strayed from his second-class carriage to a first and back. But presently Black Care got aboard the train and came and sat beside him. The exhilaration of escape had evaporated now, and he was presented with a terrible picture of his aunt and uncle arriving at his lodgings and finding him fled. He had left a hasty message that he was called away suddenly on business, 'ver' important business', and they were to be sumptuously entertained. His immediate motive had been his passionate dread of an encounter between these excellent but unrefined old people and the Walshinghams, but now that end was secured, he could see how thwarted and exasperated they would be.

How to explain to them?

He ought never to have written to tell them!

He ought to have got married and told them afterwards.

He ought to have consulted Helen.

'Promise me,' she had said.

'Oh, *desh!*' said Kipps, and got up and walked back into the smoking car and began to consume cigarettes.

Suppose, after all, they found out the Walshinghams' address and went there!

At Charing Cross, however, there were distractions again. He took a cab in an entirely Walshingham manner, and was pleased to note the enhanced respect of the cabman when he mentioned the Royal Grand. He followed Walshingham's routine on their previous visit with perfect success. They were very nice in the office, and gave him an excellent room at fourteen shillings the night.

He went up and spent a considerable time in examining the furniture of his room, scrutinising himself in its various mirrors and sitting on the edge of the bed whistling. It was a vast and splendid apartment, and cheap at fourteen shillings. But, finding the figure of Ann inclined to resume possession of his mind, he roused himself and descended by the staircase, after a momentary hesitation before the lift. He had thought of lunch, but he drifted into the great drawing-room and read a guide to the Hotels of Europe for a space, until a doubt whether he was entitled to use this palatial apartment without extra charge arose in his mind. He would have liked something to eat very much now, but his inbred terror of the table was very strong. He did at last get by a porter in uniform towards the dining-room, but at the sight of a number of waiters and tables, with remarkable complications of knives and glasses, terror seized him, and he backed out again, with a mumbled remark to the waiter in the doorway about this not being the way.

He hovered in the hall and lounge until he thought the presiding porter regarded him with suspicion, and then went up to his room again by the staircase, got his hat and umbrella and struck boldly across the courtyard. He would go to a restaurant instead.

He had a moment of elation in the gateway. He felt all the Strand must notice him as he emerged through the great gate of the Hotel. 'One of these here rich swells,' they would say. 'Don't they do it just!' A cabman touched his hat. 'No fear,' said Kipps, pleasantly . . .

Then he remembered he was hungry.

Yet he decided he was in no great hurry for lunch, in spite of an internal protest, and turned eastward along the Strand in a leisurely manner. He would find a place to suit him soon enough. He tried to remember the sort of things Walshingham had ordered. Before all things he didn't want to go into a place and look like a fool. Some of these places rook you dreadful,

besides making fun of you. There was a place near Essex Street where there was a window brightly full of chops, tomatoes and lettuce. He stopped at this and reflected for a time, and then it occurred to him that you were expected to buy these things raw and cook them at home. Anyhow, there was sufficient doubt in the matter to stop him. He drifted on to a neat window with champagne bottles, a dish of asparagus and a framed menu for a two-shilling lunch. He was about to enter, when fortunately he perceived two waiters looking at him over the back screen of the window with a most ironical expression, and he sheered off at once. There was a wonderful smell of hot food halfway down Fleet Street and a nice-looking tavern with several doors, but he could not decide which door. His nerve was going under the strain.

He hesitated at Farringdon Street and drifted up to St Paul's and round the churchyard, full chiefly of dead bargains in the shop windows, to Cheapside. But now Kipps was getting demoralised, and each house of refreshment seemed to promise still more complicated obstacles to food. He didn't know how you went in and what was the correct thing to do with your hat; he didn't know what you said to the waiter or what you called the different things; he was convinced absolutely he would 'fumble', as Shalford would have said, and look like a fool. Somebody might laugh at him! The hungrier he got the more unendurable was the thought that anyone should laugh at him. For a time he considered an extraordinary expedient to account for his ignorance. He would go in and pretend to be a foreigner and not know English. Then they might understand . . . Presently he had drifted into a part of London where there did not seem to be any refreshment places at all.

'Oh, *desh*!' said Kipps, in a sort of agony of indecisiveness. 'The very nex' place I see, in I go.'

The next place was a fried fish shop in a little side street, where there were also sausages on a gas-lit grill.

He would have gone in, but suddenly a new scruple came to him, that he was too well dressed for the company he could see dimly through the steam sitting at the counter and eating with a sort of nonchalant speed.

2

He was half minded to resort to a hansom and brave the terrors of the dining-room of the Royal Grand – they wouldn't know why he had gone out really – when the only person he knew in London appeared (as the only person one does know will do in London) and slapped him on the shoulder. Kipps was hovering at a window at a few yards from the fish shop, pretending to examine some really strikingly cheap pink baby linen, and trying to settle finally about those sausages.

'Hello, Kipps!' cried Sid; 'spending the millions?'

Kipps turned, and was glad to perceive no lingering vestige of the chagrin that had been so painful at New Romney. Sid looked grave and important, and he wore a quite new silk hat that gave a commercial touch to a generally socialistic costume. For a moment the sight of Sid uplifted Kipps wonderfully. He saw him as a friend and helper, and only presently did it come clearly into his mind that this was the brother of Ann.

He made amiable noises.

'I've just been up this way,' Sid explained, 'buying a second-hand 'namelling stove . . . I'm going to 'namel myself.'

'Lor'!' said Kipps.

'Yes. Do me a lot of good. Let the customer choose his colour. See? What brings *you* up?'

Kipps had a momentary vision of his foiled uncle and aunt. 'Jest a bit of a change,' he said.

Sid came to a swift decision. 'Come down to my little show. I got someone I'd like to see talking to you.'

Even then Kipps did not think of Ann in this connection.

'Well,' he said, trying to invent an excuse on the spur of the moment. 'Fact is,' he explained, 'I was jest looking round to get a bit of lunch.'

'Dinner, we call it,' said Sid. 'But that's all right. You can't get anything to eat hereabout. If you're not too haughty to do a bit of slumming, there's some mutton spoiling for me now – '

The word 'mutton' affected Kipps greatly.

'It won't take us 'arf an hour,' said Sid, and Kipps was carried.

He discovered another means of London locomotion in the Underground Railway, and recovered his self-possession in that interest. 'You don't mind going third?' asked Sid, and Kipps said, 'Nort a *bit* of it.' They were silent in the train for a time, on account of strangers in the carriage, and then Sid began to explain who it was that he wanted Kipps to meet. 'It's a chap named Masterman – do you no end of good.

'He occupies our first-floor front room, you know. It isn't so much for gain I let as company. We don't *want* the whole 'ouse, that's one thing ,and another is, I knew the man before. Met him at our Sociological, and after a bit he said he wasn't comfortable where he was. That's how it came about. He's a first-class chap – first-class. Science! You should see his books!

'Properly he's a sort of journalist. He's written a lot of things, but he's been too ill lately to do very much. Poetry he's written, all sorts. He writes for the *Commonweal* sometimes, and sometimes he reviews books. 'E's got 'eaps of books – 'eaps. Besides selling a lot.

'He knows a regular lot of people, and all sorts of things. He's been a dentist, and he's a qualified chemist, an' I seen him often reading German and French. Taught 'imself. He was here – '

Sid indicated South Kensington, which had come opportunely outside

the carriage windows, with a nod of his head, ' – three years. Studying science. But you'll see 'im. When he really gets to talking – he *pours* it out.'

'Ah!' said Kipps, nodding sympathetically, with his two hands on his umbrella knob.

'He'll do big things some day,' said Sid. 'He's written a book on science already. *Physiography*, it's called. *Elementary Physiography*! Some day he'll write an Advanced – when he gets time.'

He let this soak into Kipps.

'I can't introduce you to lords and swells,' he went on, 'but I *can* show you a Famous Man, that's going to be. I *can* do that. Leastways – unless – '

Sid hesitated.

'He's got a frightful cough,' he said.

'He won't care to talk with me,' weighed Kipps.

'That's all right; *he* won't mind. He's fond of talking. He'd talk to anyone,' said Sid, reassuringly, and added a perplexing bit of Londonised Latin. 'He doesn't *pute* anything, *non alienum*. You know.'

'*I* know,' said Kipps, intelligently, over his umbrella knob, though of course that was altogether untrue.

3

Kipps found Sid's shop a practical-looking establishment, stocked with the most remarkable collection of bicycles and pieces of bicycle that he had ever beheld. 'My hiring stock,' said Sid, with a wave to this ironmongery, 'and there's the best machine at a democratic price in London, The Red-Flag, built by *me*. See?' He indicated a graceful, grey-brown framework in the window. 'And there's my stock of accessories – store prices.'

'Go in for motors a bit,' added Sid.

'Mutton?' said Kipps, not hearing him distinctly.

'Motors, I *said* . . . 'Owever, Mutton Department 'ere,' and he opened a door that had a curtain-guarded window in its upper panel, to reveal a little room with red walls and green furniture and a white-clothed table and the generous promise of a meal. 'Fanny!' he shouted. 'Here's Art Kipps.'

A bright-eyed young woman of five- or six-and-twenty in a pink print appeared, a little flushed from cooking, and wiped a hand on an apron and shook hands and smiled, and said it would all be ready in a minute. She went on to say she had heard of Kipps and his luck, and meanwhile Sid vanished to draw the beer, and returned with two glasses for himself and Kipps.

'Drink that,' said Sid, and Kipps felt all the better for it.

'I give Mr Masterman '*is* upstairs a hour ago,' said Mrs Sid. 'I didn't think 'e ought to wait.'

A rapid succession of brisk movements on the part of everyone, and they

were all four at dinner – the fourth person being Master Walt Whitman Pornick, a cheerful young gentleman of one and a half, who was given a spoon to hammer on the table with to keep him quiet, and who got 'Kipps' right at the first effort and kept it all through the meal, combining it first with this previous acquisition and then that. 'Peacock Kipps,' said Master Walt, at which there was great laughter, and also, 'More Mutton, Kipps.'

'He's a regular oner,' said Mrs Sid, 'for catching up words. You can't say a word but what 'e's on to it.'

There were no serviettes and less ceremony, and Kipps thought he had never enjoyed a meal so much. Everyone was a little excited by the meeting and chatting, and disposed to laugh, and things went off easily from the very beginning. If there was a pause Master Walt filled it in. Mrs Sid, who tempered her enormous admiration for Sid's intellect and his socialism and his severe business methods by a motherly sense of her sex and seniority, spoke of them both as 'you boys', and dilated – when she was not urging Kipps to have some more of this or that – on the disparity between herself and her husband.

'Shouldn't ha' thought there was a year between you,' said Kipps; 'you seem jest a match.'

'I'm *his* match, anyhow,' said Mrs Sid, and no epigram of young Walshingham's was ever better received.

'Match,' said young Walt, coming in on the trail of the joke and getting a round for himself.

Any sense of superior fortune had long vanished from Kipps's mind, and he found himself looking at host and hostess with enormous respect. Really, old Sid was a wonderful chap, here in his own house at two and twenty, carving his own mutton and lording it over wife and child. No legacies needed by him! And Mrs Sid, so kind and bright and hearty! And the child, old Sid's child! Old Sid had jumped round a bit. It needed the sense of his fortune at the back of his mind to keep Kipps from feeling abject. He resolved he'd buy young Walt something tremendous in toys at the first opportunity.

'Drop more beer, Art?'

'Right you are, old man.'

'Cut Mr Kipps a bit more bread, Sid.'

'Can't I pass *you* a bit?' . . .

Sid was all right, Sid was, and there was no mistake about that. It was growing up in his mind that Sid was the brother of Ann, but he said nothing about her for excellent reasons. After all, Sid's irritation at her name when they had met in New Romney seemed to show a certain separation. They didn't tell each other much . . . He didn't know how things might be between Ann and Sid, either.

Still, for all that, Sid was Ann's brother.

The furniture of the room did not assert itself very much above the

cheerful business at the table, but Kipps was impressed with the idea that it was pretty. There was a dresser at the end with a number of gay plates and a mug or so, a Labour Day poster, by Walter Crane, on the wall, and through the glass and over the blind of the shop door one had a glimpse of the bright-coloured advertisement cards of bicycle dealers, and a shelf full of boxes labelled, The Paragon Bell, The Scarum Bell, and The Patent Omi! Horn . . .

It seemed incredible that he had been in Folkestone that morning, and even now his aunt and uncle – !

B-r-r-r. It didn't do to think of his aunt and uncle.

4

When Sid repeated his invitation to come and see Masterman, Kipps, now flushed with beer and Irish stew, said he didn't mind if he did, and after a preliminary shout from Sid that was answered by a voice and a cough, the two went upstairs.

'Masterman's a rare one,' said Sid over his arm and in an undertone. 'You should hear him speak at a meeting . . . If he's in form, that is.'

He rapped and went into a large, untidy room.

'This is Kipps,' he said. 'You know. The chap I told you of. With twelve 'undred a year.'

Masterman sat gnawing at an empty pipe and as close to the fire as though it was alight and the season midwinter. Kipps concentrated upon him for a space, and only later took in something of the frowsy furniture, the little bed half behind – and evidently supposed to be wholly behind – a careless screen, the spittoon by the fender, the remains of a dinner on the chest of drawers and the scattered books and papers. Masterman's face showed him a man of forty or more, with curious hollows at the sides of his forehead and about his eyes. His eyes were very bright; there was a spot of red in each cheek, and the wiry black moustache under his short red nose had been trimmed with scissors into a sort of brush along his upper lip. His teeth were darkened ruins. His jacket collar was turned up about a knitted white neck wrap, and his sleeves betrayed no cuffs. He did not rise to greet Kipps, but held out a thin-wristed hand and pointed with the other to a bedroom armchair.

'Glad to see you,' he said. 'Sit down and make yourself at home. Will you smoke?'

Kipps said he would, and produced his store. He was about to take one, and then, with a civil afterthought, handed the packet first to Masterman and Sid. Masterman pretended surprise to find his pipe out before he took one. There was an interlude of matches. Sid pushed the end of the screen out of his way, sat down on the bed thus frankly admitted, and prepared,

with a certain quiet satisfaction of manner, to witness Masterman's treatment of Kipps.

'And how does it feel to have twelve hundred a year?' asked Masterman, holding his cigarette to his nose tip in a curious manner.

'It's rum,' confided Kipps, after a reflective interval. 'It feels juiced rum.'

'I've never felt it,' said Masterman.

'It takes a bit of getting into,' said Kipps. 'I can tell you that.'

Masterman smoked and regarded Kipps with curious eyes.

'I expect it does,' he said presently.

'And has it made you perfectly happy?' he asked, abruptly.

'I couldn't 'ardly say *that*,' said Kipps.

Masterman smiled. 'No,' he said. 'Has it made you much happier?'

'It did at first.'

'Yes. But you got used to it. How long, for example, did the real delirious excitement last?'

'Oo, *that*! Perhaps a week,' said Kipps.

Masterman nodded his head. 'That's what discourages *me* from amassing wealth,' he said to Sid. 'You adjust yourself. It doesn't last. I've always had an inkling of that, and it's interesting to get it confirmed. I shall go on sponging for a bit longer on *you*, I think.'

'You don't,' said Sid. 'No fear.'

'Twenty-six thousand pounds,' said Masterman, and blew a cloud of smoke. 'Lord! Doesn't it worry you?'

'It is a bit worrying at times . . . Things 'appen.'

'Going to marry?'

'Yes.'

'H'm. Lady, I guess, of a superior social position?'

'Rather,' said Kipps. 'Cousin to the Earl of Beauprés.'

Masterman readjusted his long body with an air of having accumulated all the facts he needed. He snuggled his shoulder-blades down into the chair and raised his angular knees. 'I doubt,' he said, flicking cigarette ash into the atmosphere, 'if any great gain or loss of money does – as things are at present – make more than the slightest difference in one's happiness. It ought to – if money was what it ought to be, the token for given service; one ought to get an increase in power and happiness for every pound one got. But the plain fact is the times are out of joint, and money – money, like everything else, is a deception and a disappointment.'

He turned his face to Kipps and enforced his next words with the index finger of his lean, lank hand. 'If I thought otherwise,' he said, 'I should exert myself to get some. But, if one sees things clearly, one is so discouraged. So confoundedly discouraged . . . When you first got your money, you thought that it meant you might buy just anything you fancied?'

'I was a bit that way,' said Kipps.

'And you found that you couldn't. You found that for all sorts of things it

was a question of where to buy and how to buy, and what you didn't know how to buy with your money, straight away this world planted something else upon you – '

'I got rather done over a banjo first day,' said Kipps. 'Leastways, my uncle says so.'

'Exactly,' said Masterman.

Sid began to speak from the bed. 'That's all very well, Masterman,' he said, 'but, after all, money *is* Power, you know. You can do all sorts of things – '

'I'm talking of happiness,' said Masterman. 'You can do all sorts of things with a loaded gun in the Hammersmith Broadway, but nothing – practically – that will make you or anyone else very happy. Nothing. Power's a different matter altogether. As for happiness, you want a world in order before money or property or any of those things have any real value; and this world, I tell you, is hopelessly out of joint. Man is a social animal with a mind nowadays that goes around the globe, and a community cannot be happy in one part and unhappy in another. It's all or nothing, no patching any more for ever. It is the standing mistake of the world not to understand that. Consequently people think there is a class or order somewhere, just above them or just below them, or a country or place somewhere, that is really safe and happy. The fact is, Society is one body, and it is either well or ill. That's the law. This society we live in is ill. It's a fractious, feverish invalid, gouty, greedy and ill-nourished. You can't have a happy left leg with neuralgia, or a happy throat with a broken leg. That's my position, and that's the knowledge you'll come to. I'm so satisfied of it that I sit here and wait for my end quite calmly, sure that I can't better things by bothering – in my time, and so far as I am concerned, that is. I'm not even greedy any more – my egotism's at the bottom of a pond, with a philosophical brick around its neck. The world is ill, my time is short and my strength is small. I'm as happy here as anywhere.'

He coughed and was silent for a moment, then brought the index finger around to Kipps again. 'You've had the opportunity of sampling two grades of society, and you don't find the new people you're among much better or any happier than the old?'

'No,' said Kipps, reflectively. 'No. I 'aven't seen it quite like that before, but – no. They're not.'

'And you might go all up the scale and down the scale and find the same thing. Man's a gregarious beast, a gregarious beast, and no money will buy you out of your own time – any more than out of your own skin. All the way up and all the way down the scale there's the same discontent. No one is quite sure where they stand, and everyone's fretting. The herd's uneasy and feverish. All the old tradition goes or has gone, and there's no one to make a new tradition. Where are your nobles now? Where are your gentlemen?

They vanished directly the peasant found out he wasn't happy and ceased to be a peasant. There's big men and little men mixed up together, that's all. None of us know where we are. Your cads in a bank-holiday train and your cads in a two-thousand-pound motor – except for a difference in scale, there's not a pin to choose between them. Your smart society is as low and vulgar and uncomfortable for a balanced soul as a gin palace, no more and no less; there's no place or level of honour or fine living left in the world; so what's the good of climbing?'

' 'Ear, 'ear!' said Sid.

'It's true,' said Kipps.

'*I* don't climb,' said Masterman, and accepted Kipps's silent offer of another cigarette.

'No,' he said. 'This world is out of joint. It's broken up, and I doubt if it will heal. I doubt very much if it'll heal. We're in the beginning of the Sickness of the World.'

He rolled his cigarette in his lean fingers and repeated with satisfaction: 'The Sickness of the World.'

'It's we've got to make it better,' said Sid, and looked at Kipps.

'Ah, Sid's an optimist,' said Masterman.

'So are you, most times,' said Sid.

Kipps lit another cigarette with an air of intelligent participation.

'Frankly,' said Masterman, recrossing his legs and expelling a jet of smoke luxuriously, 'frankly, I think this civilisation of ours is on the topple.'

'There's Socialism,' said Sid.

'There's no imagination to make use of it.'

'We've got to *make* one,' said Sid.

'In a couple of centuries perhaps,' said Masterman. 'But meanwhile we're going to have a pretty acute attack of confusion. Universal confusion. Like one of those crushes when men are killed and maimed for no reason at all, going into a meeting or crowding for a train. Commercial and Industrial Stresses. Political Exploitation. Tariff Wars. Revolutions. All the bloodshed that will come of some fools calling half the white world yellow. These things alter the attitude of everybody to everybody. Everybody's going to feel 'em. Every fool in the world panting and shoving. We're all going to be as happy and comfortable as a household during a removal. What else can we expect?'

Kipps was moved to speak, but not in answer to Masterman's enquiry. 'I've never rightly got the 'eng of this Socialism,' he said. 'What's it going to do, like?'

They had been imagining that he had some elementary idea in the matter, but as soon as he had made it clear that he hadn't, Sid plunged at exposition, and in a little while Masterman, abandoning his pose of the detached man ready to die, joined in. At first he joined in only to correct Sid's version, but afterwards he took control. His manner changed. He sat

up and rested his elbow on his knees, and his cheek flushed a little. He expanded his case against Property and the property class with such vigour that Kipps was completely carried away, and never thought of asking for a clear vision of the thing that would fill the void this abolition might create. For a time he quite forgot his own private opulence. And it was as if something had been lit in Masterman. His languor passed. He enforced his words by gestures of his long thin hands. And as he passed swiftly from point to point of his argument it was evident he grew angry.

'Today,' he said, 'the world is ruled by rich men; they may do almost anything they like with the world. And what are they doing? Laying it waste!'

'Hear, hear!' said Sid, very sternly.

Masterman stood up, gaunt and long, thrust his hands in his pockets and turned his back to the fireplace.

'Collectively, the rich today have neither heart nor imagination No! They own machinery, they have knowledge and instruments and powers beyond all previous dreaming, and what are they doing with them? Think what they are doing with them, Kipps, and think what they might do. God gives them a power like the motor car, and all they can do with it is to go careering about the roads in goggled masks killing children and making machinery hateful to the soul of man! ['True,' said Sid, 'true.'] God gives them means of communication, power unparalleled of every sort, time and absolute liberty! They waste it all in folly! Here under their feet [and Kipps's eyes followed the direction of a lean index finger to the hearthrug], under their accursed wheels, the great mass of men festers and breeds in darkness, darkness those others make by standing in the light. The darkness breeds and breeds. It knows no better . . . Unless you can crawl or pander or rob you must stay in the stew you are born in. And those rich beasts above claw and clutch as though they had nothing! They grudge us our schools, they grudge us a gleam of light and air, they cheat us and then seek to forget us . . . There is no rule, no guidance, only accidents and happy flukes . . . Our multitudes of poverty increase, and this crew of rulers makes no provision, foresees nothing, anticipates nothing . . . '

He paused and made a step, and stood over Kipps in a white heat of anger. Kipps nodded in a non-committal manner and looked hard and rather gloomily at his host's slipper as he talked.

'It isn't as though they had something to show for the waste they make of us, Kipps. They haven't. They are ugly and cowardly and mean. Look at their women! Painted, dyed and drugged, hiding their ugly shapes under a load of dress! There isn't a woman in the swim of society at the present time wouldn't sell herself, body and soul, who wouldn't lick the boots of a Jew or marry a nigger, rather than live decently on a hundred a year! On what would be wealth for you and me! They know it. They know we know it . . . No one believes in them. No one believes in nobility any more.

Nobody believes in kingship any more. Nobody believes there is justice in the law . . . But people have habits, people go on in the old grooves, as long as there's work, as long as there's weekly money . . . It won't last, Kipps.'

He coughed and paused. 'Wait for the lean years,' he cried. 'Wait for the lean years.' And suddenly he fell into a struggle with his cough and spat a gout of blood. 'It's nothing,' he said to Kipps's note of startled horror.

He went on talking, and the protests of his cough interlaced with his words, and Sid beamed in an ecstasy of painful admiration.

'Look at the fraud they have let life become, the miserable mockery of the hope of one's youth. What have *I* had? I found myself at thirteen being forced into a factory like a rabbit into a chloroformed box. Thirteen! – when *their* children are babies. But even a child of that age could see what it meant, that hell of a factory! Monotony and toil and contempt and dishonour! And then death. So I fought – at thirteen!'

Minton's 'crawling up a drainpipe until you die' echoed in Kipps's mind, but Masterman, instead of Minton's growl, spoke in a high, indignant tenor.

'I got out at last – somehow,' he said, quietly, suddenly plumping back in his chair. He went on after a pause. 'For a bit. Some of us get out by luck, some by cunning, and crawl on to the grass, exhausted and crippled, to die. That's a poor man's success, Kipps. Most of us don't get out at all. I worked all day and studied half the night, and here I am with the common consequences. Beaten! And never once have I had a fair chance, never once!' His lean, clenched fist flew out in a gust of tremulous anger. 'These Skunks shut up all the university scholarships at nineteen for fear of men like me. And then – do *nothing* . . . We're wasted for nothing. By the time I'd learnt something the doors were locked. I thought knowledge would do it – I did think that! I've fought for knowledge as other men fight for bread. I've starved for knowledge. I've turned my back on women; I've done even that. I've burst my accursed lung . . . ' His voice rose with impotent anger. 'I'm a better man than any ten princes alive! And I'm beaten and wasted. I've been crushed, trampled and defiled by a drove of hogs. I'm no use to myself or the world. I've thrown my life away to make myself too good for use in this huckster's scramble. If I had gone in for business, if I had gone in for plotting to cheat my fellow men – ah, well! It's too late. It's too late for that, anyhow. It's too late for anything now! And I couldn't have done it . . . And over in New York now there's a pet of society making a corner in wheat!

'By God!' he cried hoarsely, with a clutch of the lean hand. 'By God! If I had his throat! Even now I might do something for the world.'

He glared at Kipps, his face flushed deep, his sunken eyes glowing with passion, and then suddenly he changed altogether.

There was a sound of tea things rattling upon a tray outside the door, and Sid rose to open it.

'All of which amounts to this,' said Masterman, suddenly quiet and again talking against time. 'The world is out of joint, and there isn't a soul alive

who isn't half waste or more. You'll find it the same with you in the end, wherever your luck may take you . . . I suppose you won't mind my having another cigarette?'

He took Kipps's cigarette with a hand that trembled so violently it almost missed its object, and stood up, with something of guilt in his manner, as Mrs Sid came into the room.

Her eye met his and marked the flush upon his face.

'Been talking Socialism?' said Mrs Sid, a little severely.

5

Six o'clock that day found Kipps drifting eastward along the southward margin of Rotten Row. You figure him a small, respectably attired figure going slowly through a sometimes immensely difficult and always immense world. At times he becomes pensive and whistles softly. At times he looks about him. There are a few riders in the Row, a carriage flashes by every now and then along the roadway, and among the great rhododendrons and laurels and upon the greensward there are a few groups and isolated people dressed in the style Kipps adopted to call upon the Walshinghams when first he was engaged. Amid the complicated confusion of Kipps's mind was a regret that he had not worn his other things . . .

Presently he perceived that he would like to sit down; a green chair tempted him. He hesitated at it, took possession of it, and leant back and crossed one leg over the other.

He rubbed his underlip with his umbrella handle and reflected upon Masterman and his denunciation of the world.

'Bit orf 'is 'ead, poor chap,' said Kipps; and added: 'I wonder – '

He thought intently for a space.

'I wonder what he meant by the lean years?'

The world seemed a very solid and prosperous concern just here, and well out of reach of Masterman's dying clutch. And yet –

It was curious he should have been reminded of Minton.

His mind turned to a far more important matter. Just at the end Sid had said to him, 'Seen Ann?' and as he was about to answer, 'You'll see a bit more of her now. She's got a place in Folkestone.'

It had brought him back from any concern about the world being out of joint or anything of that sort.

Ann!

One might run against her any day.

He tugged at his little moustache.

He would like to run against Ann very much . . .

'And it would be juiced awkward if I did!'

In Folkestone! It was a jolly sight too close . . .

Then, at the thought that he might run against Ann in his beautiful evening dress on the way to the band, he fluttered into a momentary dream that jumped abruptly into a nightmare.

Suppose he met her when he was out with Helen! 'Oh, Lor'!' said Kipps. Life had developed a new complication that would go on and go on. For some time he wished with the utmost fervour that he had not kissed Ann, that he had not gone to New Romney the second time. He marvelled at his amazing forgetfulness of Helen on that occasion. Helen took possession of his mind. He would have to write to Helen, an easy, offhand letter, to say that he had come to London for a day or so. He tried to imagine her reading it. He would write just such another letter to the old people, and say he had had to come up on business. That might do for *them* all right, but Helen was different. She would insist on explanations.

He wished he could never go back to Folkestone again. That would settle the whole affair.

A passing group attracted his attention, two faultlessly dressed gentlemen and a radiantly expensive lady. They were talking, no doubt, very brilliantly. His eyes followed them. The lady tapped the arm of the left-hand gentleman with a daintily tinted glove. Swells! No end . . .

His soul looked out upon life in general as a very small nestling might peep out of its nest. What an extraordinary thing life was, to be sure, and what a remarkable variety of people there were in it!

He lit a cigarette and speculated upon that receding group of three, and blew smoke and watched them. They seemed to do it all right. Probably they all had incomes of very much over twelve hundred a year. Perhaps not. Probably none of them suspected, as they went past, that he, too, was a gentleman of independent means, dressed, as he was, without distinction. Of course things were easier for them. They were brought up always to dress well and do the right thing from their very earliest years; they started clear of all his perplexities; they had never got mixed up with all sorts of different people who didn't go together. If, for example, that lady there got engaged to that gentleman, she would be quite safe from any encounter with a corpulent, osculatory uncle, or Chitterlow, or the dangerously significant eye of Pierce.

His thoughts came round to Helen.

When they were married and Cuyps – or Cuyp, Coote had failed to justify his 's' – and in that West End flat and shaken free of all these low-class associations, would he and she parade here of an afternoon dressed like that? It would be rather fine to do so. If one's dress was all right.

Helen!

She was difficult to understand at times.

He blew extensive clouds of cigarette smoke.

There would be teas, there would be dinners, there would be calls. Of course he would get into the way of it.

But Anagrams were a bit stiff to begin with!

It was beastly confusing at first to know when to use your fork at dinner, and all that. Still –

He felt an extraordinary doubt whether he would get into the way of it. He was interested for a space by a girl and groom on horseback, and then he came back to his personal preoccupations.

He would have to write to Helen. What could he say to explain his absence from the Anagram Tea? She had been pretty clear she wanted him to come. He recalled her resolute face without any great tenderness. He *knew* he would look like a silly ass at that confounded tea! Suppose he shirked it and went back in time for the dinner! Dinners were beastly difficult, too, but not as bad as Anagrams. The very first thing that might happen when he got back to Folkestone would be to run against Ann. Suppose, after all, he did meet Ann when he was with Helen!

What queer encounters were possible in the world!

Thank goodness, they were going to live in London!

But that brought him around to Chitterlow. The Chitterlows were coming to London, too. If they didn't get money they'd come after it; they weren't the sort of people to be choked off easily; and if they did they'd come to London to produce their play. He tried to imagine some seemly social occasion invaded by Chitterlow and his rhetoric, by his torrential thunder of self-assertion, the whole company flattened thereunder like wheat under a hurricane.

Confound and hang Chitterlow! Yet, somehow, somewhen, one would have to settle accounts with him! And there was Sid! Sid was Ann's brother. He realised with sudden horror the social indiscretion of accepting Sid's invitation to dinner.

Sid wasn't the sort of chap one could snub or cut, and besides – Ann's brother! He didn't want to cut him. It would be worse than cutting Buggins and Pierce – a sight worse. And after that lunch!

It would be the next thing to cutting Ann herself. And even as to Ann –

Suppose he was with Helen or Coote! . . .

'Oh, Blow!' he said, at last, and then, viciously, '*Blow!*' and so rose and flung away his cigarette end and pursued his reluctant, dubitating way towards the really quite uncongenial splendours of the Royal Grand –

And it is vulgarly imagined that to have money is to have no troubles at all!

Kipps endured splendour at the Royal Grand Hotel for three nights and days, and then he retreated in disorder. The Royal Grand defeated and overcame and routed Kipps, not of intention, but by sheer royal grandeur, grandeur combined with an organisation for his comfort carried to excess. On his return he came upon a difficulty: he had lost his circular piece of cardboard with the number of his room, and he drifted about the hall and passages in a state of perplexity for some time, until he thought all the porters and officials in gold-lace caps must be watching him and jesting to one another about him. Finally, in a quiet corner, down below the hairdresser's shop, he found a kindly-looking personage in bottle green, to whom he broached his difficulty. 'I say,' he said, with a pleasant smile, 'I can't find my room nohow.' The personage in bottle green, instead of laughing in a nasty way, as he might well have done, became extremely helpful, showed Kipps what to do, got his key, and conducted him by lift and passage to his chamber. Kipps tipped him half a crown.

Safe in his room, Kipps pulled himself together for dinner. He had learnt enough from young Walshingham to bring his dress clothes, and now he began to assume them. Unfortunately, in the excitement of his flight from his aunt and uncle, he had forgotten to put in his other boots, and he was some time deciding between his purple cloth slippers, with a golden marigold, and the prospect of cleaning the boots he was wearing with the towel, but finally, being a little footsore, he took the slippers.

Afterwards, when he saw the porters and waiters and the other guests catch a sight of the slippers, he was sorry he had not chosen the boots. However, to make up for any want of style at that end, he had his crush hat under his arm.

He found the dining-room without excessive trouble. It was a vast and splendidly decorated place, and a number of people, evidently quite *au fait*, were dining there at little tables lit with electric red-shaded candles, gentlemen in evening dress and ladies with dazzling, astonishing necks. Kipps had never seen evening dress in full vigour before, and he doubted his eyes. And there were also people not in evening dress, who no doubt wondered what noble family Kipps represented. There was a band in a decorated recess, and the band looked collectively at the purple slippers, and so lost any chance they may have had of a donation so far as Kipps was concerned. The chief drawback to this magnificent place was the excessive space of floor that had to be crossed before you got your purple slippers hidden under a table.

He selected a little table – not the one where a rather impudent looking waiter held a chair, but another – sat down, and finding his gibus in his

hand, decided after a moment of thought to rise slightly and sit on it. (It was discovered in his abandoned chair at a late hour by a supper party, and restored to him next day.)

He put the napkin carefully on one side, selected his soup without difficulty, 'Clear, please,' but he was rather floored by the presentation of a quite splendidly bound wine card. He turned it over, discovered a section devoted to whisky, and had a bright idea.

' 'Ere,' he said to the waiter, with an encouraging movement of his head, and then in a confidential manner, 'you haven't any Old Methuselah Three Stars, 'ave you?'

The waiter went away to enquire, and Kipps went on with his soup with an enhanced self-respect. Finally, Old Methuselah being unobtainable, he ordered a claret from about the middle of the list. 'Let's 'ave some of this,' he said. He knew claret was a good sort of wine.

'A half-bottle?' said the waiter.

'Right you are,' said Kipps.

He felt he was getting on. He leant back after his soup, a man of the world, and then slowly brought his eyes around to the ladies in evening dress on his right . . .

He couldn't have thought it!

They were scorchers. Jest a bit of black velvet over the shoulders!

He looked again. One of them was laughing, with a glass of wine half raised – wicked-looking woman she was – the other, the black velvet one, was eating bits of bread with nervous quickness and talking fast.

He wished old Buggins could see them.

He found a waiter regarding him and blushed deeply. He did not look again for some time, and became confused about his knife and fork over the fish. Presently he remarked a lady in pink to the left of him eating the fish with an entirely different implement.

It was over the *vol-au-vent* that he began to go to pieces. He took a knife to it; then saw the lady in pink was using a fork only, and hastily put down his knife, with a considerable amount of rich creaminess on the blade, upon the cloth. Then he found that a fork in his inexperienced hand was an instrument of chase rather than capture. His ears became violently red, and then he looked up to discover the lady in pink glancing at him and then smiling as she spoke to the man beside her.

He hated the lady in pink very much.

He stabbed a large piece of the *vol-au-vent* at last, and was too glad of his luck not to make a mouthful of it. But it was an extensive fragment, and pieces escaped him. Shirt front! 'Desh it!' he said, and had resort to his spoon. His waiter went and spoke to two other waiters, no doubt jeering at him. He became very fierce suddenly. ' 'Ere!' he said, gesticulating, and then, 'clear this away!'

The entire dinner party on his right, the party of the ladies in advanced

evening dress, looked at him . . . He felt that everyone was watching him and making fun of him, and the injustice of this angered him. After all, they had every advantage he hadn't. And then, when they got him there doing his best, what must they do but glance and sneer and nudge one another. He tried to catch them at it, and then took refuge in a second glass of wine.

Suddenly and extraordinarily he found himself a Socialist. He did not care how close it was to the lean years when all these things would end.

Lamb came with peas. He arrested the hand of the waiter. 'No peas,' he said. He knew something of the difficulty and danger of eating peas. Then, when the peas went away he was embittered again . . . Echoes of Masterman's burning rhetoric began to reverberate in his mind. Nice lot of people these were to laugh at anyone! Women half undressed! It was that made him so beastly uncomfortable. How could one eat one's dinner with people about him like that? Nice lot they were. He was glad he wasn't one of them, anyhow. Yes, they might look. He resolved if they looked at him again he would ask one of the men who he was staring at. His perturbed and angry face would have concerned anyone. The band by an unfortunate accident was playing truculent military music. The mental change Kipps underwent was, in its way, what psychologists call a conversion. In a few moments all Kipps's ideals were changed. He who had been 'practically a gentleman', the sedulous pupil of Coote, the punctilious raiser of hats, was instantly a rebel, an outcast, the hater of everything 'stuck up', the foe of Society and the social order of today. Here they were among the profits of their robbery, these people who might do anything with the world . . .

'No, thanks,' he said to a dish.

He addressed a scornful eye at the shoulders of the lady to his left.

Presently he was refusing another dish. He didn't like it – fussed up food! Probably cooked by some foreigner. He finished up his wine and his bread . . .

'No, thanks.'

'No, thanks . . . '

He discovered the eye of a diner fixed curiously upon his flushed face. He responded with a glare. Couldn't he go without things if he liked?

'What's this?' said Kipps to a great green cone.

'Ice,' said the waiter.

'I'll 'ave some,' said Kipps.

He seized a fork and spoon and assailed the bombe. It cut rather stiffly. 'Come up!' said Kipps, with concentrated bitterness, and the truncated summit of the bombe flew off suddenly, travelling eastward with remarkable velocity. Flop, it went upon the floor a yard away, and for a while time seemed empty.

At the adjacent table they were laughing together.

Shy the rest of the bombe at them?

Flight?

At any rate a dignified withdrawal.

'No!' said Kipps, 'no more,' arresting the polite attempt of the waiter to serve him with another piece. He had a vague idea he might carry off the affair as though he had meant the ice to go on the floor – not liking ice, for example, and being annoyed at the badness of his dinner. He put both hands on the table, thrust back his chair, disengaged a purple slipper from his napkin, and rose. He stepped carefully over the prostrate ice, kicked the napkin under the table, thrust his hands deep into his pockets, and marched out – shaking the dust of the place, as it were, from his feet. He left behind him a melting fragment of ice upon the floor, his gibus hat, warm and compressed in his chair, and, in addition, every social ambition he had ever entertained in the world.

7

Kipps went back to Folkestone in time for the Anagram Tea. But you must not imagine that the change of heart that came to him in the dining-room of the Royal Grand Hotel involved any change of attitude towards this promised social and intellectual treat. He went back because the Royal Grand was too much for him.

Outwardly calm, or at most a little flushed and ruffled, inwardly Kipps was a horrible, tormented battleground of scruples, doubts, shames and self-assertions during that three days of silent, desperate grappling with the big hotel. He did not intend the monstrosity should beat him without a struggle, but at last he had sullenly to admit himself overcome. The odds were terrific. On the one hand himself – with, among other things, only one pair of boots; on the other a vast wilderness of rooms, covering several acres, and with over a thousand people, staff and visitors, all chiefly occupied in looking queerly at Kipps, in laughing at him behind his back, in watching for difficult corners at which to confront and perplex him and inflict humiliations upon him. For example, the hotel scored over its electric light. After the dinner the chambermaid, a hard, unsympathetic young woman with a superior manner, was summoned by a bell Kipps had rung under the impression the button was the electric light switch. 'Look 'ere,' said Kipps, rubbing a shin that had suffered during his search in the dark, 'why aren't there any candles or matches?' The hotel explained and scored heavily.

'It isn't everyone is up to these things,' said Kipps.

'No, it isn't,' said the chambermaid, with ill-concealed scorn, and slammed the door at him.

'S'pose I ought to have tipped her,' said Kipps.

After that Kipps cleaned his boots with a pocket-handkerchief and went for a long walk and got home in a hansom, but the hotel scored again by his

not putting out his boots and so having to clean them again in the morning. The hotel also snubbed him by bringing him hot water when he was fully dressed and looking surprised at his collar, but he got a breakfast, I must admit, with scarcely any difficulty.

After that the hotel scored heavily by the fact that there are twenty-four hours in the day and Kipps had nothing to do in any of them. He was a little footsore from his previous day's pedestrianism, and he could make up his mind for no long excursions. He flitted in and out of the hotel several times, and it was the polite porter who touched his hat every time that first set Kipps tipping.

'What 'e wants is a tip,' said Kipps.

So at the next opportunity he gave the man an unexpected shilling, and having once put his hand in his pocket, there was no reason why he should not go on. He bought a newspaper at the bookstall and tipped the boy the rest of the shilling, and then went up by the lift and tipped the man a sixpence, leaving his newspaper inadvertently in the lift. He met his chambermaid in the passage and gave her half a crown. He resolved to demonstrate his position to the entire establishment in this way. He didn't like the place; he disapproved of it politically, socially, morally, but he resolved no taint of meanness should disfigure his sojourn in its luxurious halls. He went down by the lift (tipping again), and, being accosted by a waiter with his gibus, tipped the finder half a crown. He had a vague sense that he was making a flank movement upon the hotel and buying over its staff. They would regard him as a character. They would get to like him. He found his stock of small silver diminishing, and replenished it at a desk in the hall. He tipped a man in bottle green who looked like the man who had shown him his room the day before, and then he saw a visitor eyeing him, and doubted whether he was in this instance doing right. Finally he went out and took chance buses to their destinations, and wandered a little in remote, wonderful suburbs and returned. He lunched at a chop house in Islington, and found himself back in the Royal Grand, now unmistakably footsore and London weary, about three. He was attracted to the drawing-room by a neat placard about afternoon tea.

It occurred to him that the campaign of tipping upon which he had embarked was perhaps after all a mistake. He was confirmed in this by observing that the hotel officials were watching him, not respectfully, but with a sort of amused wonder, as if to see whom he would tip next. However, if he backed out now, they would think him an awful fool. Everyone wasn't so rich as he was. It was his way to tip. Still –

He grew more certain the hotel had scored again.

He pretended to be lost in thought and so drifted by, and having put hat and umbrella in the cloakroom went into the drawing-room for afternoon tea.

There he did get what for a time he held to be a point in his favour. The

room was large and quiet at first, and he sat back restfully until it occurred to him that his attitude brought his extremely dusty boots too prominently into the light, so instead he sat up, and then people of the upper and upper-middle classes began to come and group themselves about him and have tea likewise, and so revive the class animosities of the previous day.

Presently a fluffy, fair-haired lady came into prominent existence a few yards away. She was talking to a respectful, low-voiced clergyman, whom she was possibly entertaining at tea. 'No,' she said, 'dear Lady Jane wouldn't like that!'

'Mumble, mumble, mumble,' from the clergyman.

'Poor dear Lady Jane was always so sensitive,' the voice of the lady sang out clear and emphatic.

A fat, hairless, important-looking man joined this group, took a chair and planted it firmly with its back in the face of Kipps, a thing that offended Kipps mightily. 'Are you telling him,' gurgled the fat, hairless man, 'about dear Lady Jane's affliction?' A young couple, lady brilliantly attired and the man in a magnificently-cut frock coat, arranged themselves to the right, also with an air of exclusion towards Kipps. 'I've told him,' said the gentleman in a flat, abundant voice. 'My!' said the young lady, with an American smile. No doubt they all thought Kipps was out of it. A great desire to assert himself in some way surged up in his heart. He felt he would like to cut in on the conversation in some dramatic way. A monologue something in the manner of Masterman? At any rate, abandoning that as impossible, he would like to appear self-centred and at ease. His eyes, wandering over the black surfaces of a noble architectural mass close by, discovered a slot and an enamelled plaque of directions.

It was some sort of musical box! As a matter of fact, it was the very best sort of harmonicon and specially made to the scale of the hotel.

He scrutinised the plaque with his head at various angles and glanced about him at his neighbours.

It occurred to Kipps that he would like some music, that to inaugurate some would show him a man of taste and at his ease at the same time. He rose, read over a list of tunes, selected one haphazard, pressed his sixpence – it was sixpence! – home, and prepared for a confidential, refined little melody.

Considering the high social tone of the Royal Grand, it was really a very loud instrument indeed. It gave vent to three deafening brays and so burst the dam of silence that had long pent it in. It seemed to be chiefly full of the great-uncles of trumpets, megalo-trombones and railway brakes. It made sounds like shunting trains. It did not so much begin as blow up your counter-scarp and rush forward to storm under cover of melodious shrapnel. It had not so much an air as a ricochet. The music had, in short, the inimitable quality of Sousa. It swept down upon the friend of Lady Jane and carried away something socially striking into the eternal night of the

unheard; the American girl to the left of it was borne shrieking into the inaudible. 'HIGH cockalorum Tootletootle tootle loo. HIGH cockalorum tootle lootle loo. BUMP, bump, bump – BUMP.' Joyous, exorbitant music it was from the gigantic nursery of the Future, bearing the hearer along upon its torrential succession of sounds, as if he was in a cask on Niagara. Whiroo! Yah and have at you! The strenuous Life! Yaha! Stop! A Reprieve! A Reprieve! No! Bang! Bump!

Everybody looked around, conversation ceased and gave place to gestures.

The friend of Lady Jane became terribly agitated.

'Can't it be stopped?' she vociferated, pointing a gloved finger and saying something to the waiter about 'that dreadful young man'.

'Ought not to be working,' said the clerical friend of Lady Jane.

The waiter shook his head at the fat, hairless gentleman. People began to move away. Kipps leant back luxurious, and then tipped with a half-crown to pay. He paid, tipped like a gentleman, rose with an easy gesture and strolled towards the door. His retreat evidently completed the indignation of the friend of Lady Jane, and from the door he could still discern her gestures as asking, 'Can't it be stopped?' The music followed him into the passage and pursued him to the lift and only died away completely in the quiet of his own room, and afterwards from his window he saw the friend of Lady Jane and her party having their tea carried out to a little table in the court. Certainly that was a point to him. But it was his only score; all the rest of the game lay in the hands of the upper classes and the big hotel. And presently he was doubting whether even this was really a point. It seemed a trifle vulgar, come to think it over, to interrupt people when they were talking.

He saw a clerk peering at him from the office, and suddenly it occurred to him that the place might get back at him tremendously over the bill.

They would probably take it out on him by charging pounds and pounds. Suppose they charged more than he had!

The clerk had a particularly nasty face, just the face to take advantage of a vacillating Kipps.

He became aware of a man in a cap touching it, and produced his shilling automatically, but the strain was beginning to tell. It was a deuce and all of an expense – this tipping.

If the hotel chose to stick it on to the bill something tremendous what was Kipps to do? Refuse to pay? Make a row?

If he did he couldn't fight all these men in bottle green.

He went out about seven and walked for a long time and dined at last upon a chop in the Euston Road; then he walked along to the Edgeware Road and sat and rested in the Metropolitan Music Hall for a time until a trapeze performance unnerved him and finally he came back to bed. He tipped the lift-man sixpence and wished him good-night. In the silent

watches of the night he reviewed the tale of the day's tipping, went over the horrors of the previous night's dinner, and heard again the triumphant bray of the harmonicon devil released from its long imprisonment. Everyone would be told about him tomorrow. He couldn't go on! He admitted his defeat. Never in their whole lives had any of these people seen such a Fool as he! Ugh . . . !

His method of announcing his withdrawal to the clerk was touched with bitterness.

'I'm going to get out of this,' said Kipps, blowing windily. 'Let's see what you got on my bill.'

'One breakfast?' asked the clerk.

'Do I *look* as if I'd ate two?' . . .

At his departure Kipps, with a hot face, convulsive gestures and an embittered heart, tipped everyone who did not promptly and actively resist, including an absent-minded South African diamond merchant, who was waiting in the hall for his wife and succumbed to old habit. He paid his cabman a four-shilling piece at Charing Cross, having no smaller change, and wished he could burn him alive. Then, in a sudden reaction of economy, he refused the proffered help of a porter and carried his bag quite violently to the train.

CHAPTER EIGHT

Kipps Enters Society

Submission to Inexorable Fate took Kipps to the Anagram Tea.

At any rate he would meet Helen there in the presence of other people and be able to carry off the worst of the difficulty of explaining his little jaunt to London. He had not seen her since his last portentous visit to New Romney. He was engaged to her, he would have to marry her, and the sooner he faced her again the better. Before wild plans of turning socialist, defying the world and repudiating all calling for ever, his heart on second thoughts sank. He felt Helen would never permit anything of the sort. As for the Anagrams, he could do no more than his best, and that he was resolved to do. What had happened at the Royal Grand, what had happened at New Romney, he must bury in his memory and begin again at the reconstruction of his social position. Ann, Buggins, Chitterlow, all these, seen in the matter-of-fact light of the Folkestone train, stood just as they stood before; people of an inferior social position who had to be eliminated from his world. It was a bother about Ann, a bother and a pity. His mind rested so for a space on Ann until the memory of these Anagrams drew him away. If he could see Coote that evening he might, he thought, be able to arrange some sort of connivance about the Anagrams, and his mind was

chiefly busy sketching proposals for such an arrangement. It would not, of course, be ungentlemanly cheating, but only a little mystification. Coote very probably might drop him a hint of the solution of one or two of the things, not enough to win a prize, but enough to cover his shame. Or failing that he might take a humorous, quizzical line and pretend he was pretending to be very stupid. There were plenty of ways out of it if one kept a sharp lookout . . .

The costume Kipps wore to the Anagram Tea was designed as a compromise between the strict letter of high fashion and seaside laxity, a sort of easy, semi-state for afternoon. Helen's first reproof had always lingered in his mind. He wore a frock coat, but mitigated it by a Panama hat of romantic shape with a black band, grey gloves, but for relaxation brown button boots. The only other man besides the clergy present, a new doctor with an attractive wife, was in full afternoon dress. Coote was not there.

Kipps was a little pale, but quite self-possessed, as he approached Mrs Bindon Botting's door. He took a turn while some people went in and then faced it manfully. The door opened and revealed – Ann!

In the background through a draped doorway, behind a big fern in a great art pot, the elder Miss Botting was visible talking to two guests; the auditory background was a froth of feminine voices . . .

Our two young people were much too amazed to give one another any formula of greeting, though they had parted warmly enough. Each was already in a state of extreme tension to meet the demands of this great and unprecedented occasion, an Anagram Tea. 'Lor'!' said Ann, her sole remark, and then the sense of Miss Botting's eye ruled her straight again. She became very pale, but she took his hat mechanically, and he was already removing his gloves. 'Ann,' he said in a low tone, and then, 'Fency!' The elder Miss Botting knew Kipps was the sort of guest who requires nursing, and she came forward vocalising charm. She said it was 'awfully jolly of him to come, awfully jolly. It was awfully difficult to get any good men!'

She handed Kipps forward, mumbling and in a dazed condition, to the drawing-room, and there he encountered Helen looking unfamiliar in an unfamiliar hat. It was as if he had not met her for years.

She astonished him. She didn't seem to mind in the least his going to London. She held out a shapely hand, and smiled encouragingly. 'You've faced the anagrams?' she said.

The second Miss Botting accosted them, a number of oblong pieces of paper in her hand, mysteriously inscribed. 'Take an anagram,' she said; 'take an anagram,' and boldly pinned one of these brief documents to Kipps's lapel. The letters were 'Cypshi', and Kipps from the very beginning suspected this was an anagram for Cuyps. She also left a thing like a long dance programme, from which dangled a little pencil, in his hand. He found himself being introduced to people, and then he was in a corner with the

short lady in a big bonnet, who was pelting him with gritty little bits of small talk that were gone before you could take hold of them and reply.

'Very hot,' said this lady. 'Very hot, indeed – hot all the summer – remarkable year – all the years remarkable now – don't know what we're coming to – don't you think so, Mr Kipps?'

'Oo, rather,' said Kipps, and wondered if Ann was still in the hall. Ann!

He ought not to have stared at her like a stuck fish and pretended not to know her. That couldn't be right. But what *was* right?

The lady in the big bonnet proceeded to a second discharge. 'Hope you're fond of anagrams, Mr Kipps – difficult exercise – still one must do something to bring people together – better than Ludo anyhow. Don't you think so, Mr Kipps?'

Ann fluttered past the open door. Her eyes met his in amazed enquiry. Something had got dislocated in the world for both of them . . .

He ought to have told her he was engaged. He ought to have explained things to her. Perhaps even now he might be able to drop her a hint.

'Don't you think so, Mr Kipps?'

'Oo, rather,' said Kipps for the third time.

A lady with a tired smile, who was labelled conspicuously 'Wogdelenk', drifted towards Kipps's interlocutor and the two fell into conversation. Kipps found himself socially aground. He looked about him. Helen was talking to a curate and laughing. Kipps was overcome by a vague desire to speak to Ann. He was for sidling doorward.

'What are *you*, please?' said an extraordinarily bold, tall girl, and arrested him while she took down 'Cypshi'.

'I'm sure I don't know what it means,' she explained. 'I'm Sir Bubh. Don't you think anagrams are something chronic?'

Kipps made stockish noises, and the young lady suddenly became the nucleus of a party of excited friends who were forming a syndicate to guess and barred his escape. She took no further notice of him. He found himself jammed against an occasional table and listening to the conversation of Mrs 'Wogdelenk' and his lady with the big bonnet.

'She packed her two beauties off together,' said the lady in the big bonnet. 'Time enough, too. Don't think much of this girl she's got as housemaid now. Pretty, of course, but there's no occasion for a housemaid to be pretty – none whatever. And she doesn't look particularly up to her work either. Kind of 'mazed expression.'

'You never can tell,' said the lady labelled 'Wogdelenk'; 'you never can tell. My wretches are big enough, heaven knows, and do they work? Not a bit of it!' . . .

Kipps felt dreadfully out of it with regard to all these people, and dreadfully in it with Ann.

He scanned the back of the big bonnet and concluded it was an extremely ugly bonnet indeed. It went jerking forward as each short dry sentence was

snapped off at the end; and a plume of osprey on it jerked excessively. 'She hasn't guessed even one!' followed by a shriek of girlish merriment, came from the group about the tall, bold girl. They'd shriek at him presently, perhaps. Beyond thinking his own anagram might be Cuyps, he hadn't a notion. What a chatter they were all making! It was just like a summer sale! Just the sort of people who'd give a lot of trouble and swap you! And suddenly the smouldering fires of rebellion leapt to flame again. These were a rotten lot of people, and the anagrams were rotten nonsense, and he, Kipps, had been a rotten fool to come. There was Helen away there, still laughing, with her curate. Pity she couldn't marry a curate and leave him (Kipps) alone! Then he'd know what to do. He disliked the whole gathering collectively and in detail. Why were they all trying to make him one of themselves? He perceived unexpected ugliness everywhere about him. There were two great pins jabbed through the tall girl's hat, and the swirls of her hair below the brim with the minutest piece of tape tie-up showing did not repay close examination. Mrs 'Wogdelenk' wore a sort of mumps bandage of lace, and there was another lady perfectly dazzling with beads and jewels and bits of trimming. They were all flaps and angles and flounces – these women. Not one of them looked as neat and decent a shape as Ann's clean, trim little figure. Echoes of Masterman woke up in him again. Ladies indeed! Here were all these chattering people, with money, with leisure, with every chance in the world, and all they could do was to crowd like this into a couple of rooms and jabber nonsense about anagrams.

'Could Cypshi really mean Cuyps?' floated like a dissolving wreath of mist across his mind.

Abruptly resolution stood armed in his heart. He was going to get out of this!

' 'Scuse me,' he said, and began to wade neck deep through the bubbling tea party.

He was going to get out of it all!

He found himself close by Helen. 'I'm orf,' he said, but she gave him the briefest glance. She did not appear to hear him. 'Still, Mr Spratlingdown, you *must* admit there's a limit even to conformity,' she was saying . . .

He was in a curtained archway, and Ann was before him carrying a tray supporting several small sugar bowls.

He was moved to speech. '*What* a Lot!' he said, and then mysteriously, 'I'm engaged to *her*.' He indicated Helen's new hat, and became aware of a skirt he had stepped upon.

Ann stared at him helplessly, borne past in the grip of incomprehensible imperatives.

Why shouldn't they talk together?

He was in a small room, and then at the foot of the staircase in the hall. He heard the rustle of a dress, and what was conceivably his hostess was upon him.

'But you're not going, Mr Kipps?' she said.

'I must,' he said; 'I got to.'

'But, Mr Kipps!'

'I must,' he said. 'I'm not well.'

'But before the guessing! Without any tea!'

Ann appeared and hovered behind him.

'I got to go,' said Kipps.

If he parleyed with her Helen might awake to his desperate attempt.

'Of course if you *must* go.'

'It's something I've forgotten,' said Kipps, beginning to feel regrets. 'Reely I must.'

Mrs Botting turned with a certain offended dignity, and Ann in a state of flushed calm that evidently concealed much came forward to open the door.

'I'm very sorry,' he said; 'I'm very sorry,' half to his hostess and half to her, and was swept past her by superior social forces – like a drowning man in a millrace – and into the Upper Sandgate Road. He half turned upon the step, and then slam went the door. . .

He retreated along the Leas, a thing of shame and perplexity – Mrs Botting's aggrieved astonishment uppermost in his mind.

Something – reinforced by the glances of the people he was passing – pressed its way to his attention through the tumultuous disorder of his mind.

He became aware that he was still wearing his little placard with the letters 'Cypshi'.

'Desh it!' he said, clutching off this abomination. In another moment its several letters, their task accomplished, were scattering gleefully before the breeze down the front of the Leas.

2

Kipps was dressed for Mrs Wace's dinner half an hour before it was time to start, and he sat waiting until Coote should come to take him round. *Manners and Rules of Good Society* lay before him neglected. He had read the polished prose of the Member of the Aristocracy on page 96, as far as

> the acceptance of an invitation is, in the eyes of diners out, a binding obligation which only ill-health, family bereavement or some other all-important reason justifies being set on one side or otherwise evaded . . .

and then he had lapsed into gloomy thoughts.

That afternoon he had had a serious talk with Helen.

He had tried to express something of the change of heart that had happened to him. But to broach the real state of the matter had been altogether too terrible for him. He had sought a minor issue. 'I don't like all this Society,' he had said.

'But you must *see* people,' said Helen.

'Yes, but – it's the sort of people you see.' He nerved himself. 'I didn't think much of that lot at the Enegram Tea.'

'You have to see all sorts of people if you want to see the world,' said Helen.

Kipps was silent for a space and a little short of breath.

'My dear Arthur,' she began, almost kindly, 'I shouldn't ask you to go to these affairs if I didn't think it good for you, should I?'

Kipps acquiesced in silence.

'You will find the benefit of it all when we get to London. You learn to swim in a tank before you go out into the sea. These people here are good enough to learn upon. They're stiff and rather silly and dreadfully narrow and not an idea in a dozen of them, but it really doesn't matter at all. You'll soon get *Savoir Faire*.'

He made to speak again, and found his powers of verbal expression lacking. Instead he blew a sigh.

'You'll get used to it all very soon,' said Helen helpfully –

As he sat meditating over that interview and over the vistas of London that opened before him, on the little flat, and teas and occasions and the constant presence of Brudderkins and all the bright prospect of his new and better life, and how he would never see Ann any more, the housemaid entered with a little package, a small square envelope to 'Arthur Kipps, Esquire'.

'A young woman left this, sir,' said the housemaid, a little severely.

'Eh?' said Kipps; 'what young woman?' and then suddenly began to understand.

'She looked an ordinary young woman,' said the housemaid coldly.

'Ah!' said Kipps. '*That*'s orlright.'

He waited till the door had closed behind the girl, staring at the envelope in his hand, and then, with a curious feeling of increasing tension, tore it open. As he did so, some quicker sense than sight or touch told him its contents. It was Ann's half-sixpence. And, besides, not a word!

Then she must have heard him – !

She had kept the half-sixpence all these years!

He was standing with the envelope in his hand, trying to get on from that last inference, when Coote became audible without.

Coote appeared in evening dress, a clean and radiant Coote, with large greenish-white gloves and a particularly large white tie, edged with black. 'For a third cousin,' he presently explained. 'Nace, isn't it?' He could see Kipps was pale and disturbed and put this down to the approaching social trial. 'You keep your nerve up, Kipps, my dear chap, and you'll be all right,' said Coote, with a big, brotherly glove on Kipps's sleeve.

The dinner came to a crisis, so far as Kipps's emotions were concerned, with Mrs Bindon Botting's talk about servants, but before that there had been several things of greater or smaller magnitude to perturb and disarrange his social front. One little matter that was mildly insurgent throughout the entire meal was, if I may be permitted to mention so intimate a matter, the behaviour of his left brace. The webbing – which was of a cheerful scarlet silk – had slipped away from its buckle, fastened no doubt in agitation, and had developed a strong tendency to place itself obliquely, in the manner rather of an official decoration, athwart his spotless front. It first asserted itself before they went in to dinner. He replaced this ornament by a dexterous thrust when no one was looking, and thereafter the suppression of his novel innovation upon the stereotyped sombreness of evening dress became a standing preoccupation. On the whole, he was inclined to think his first horror excessive; at any rate no one remarked upon it. However, you imagine him constantly throughout the evening with one eye and one hand, whatever the rest of him might be doing, predominantly concerned with the weak corner.

But this, I say, was a little matter. What exercised him much more was to discover Helen quite terribly in evening dress.

The young lady had let her imagination rove Londonward, and this costume was perhaps an anticipation of that clever little flat not too far west which was to become the centre of so delightful a literary and artistic set. It was, of all the feminine costumes present, most distinctly an evening dress. One was advised Miss Walshingham had arms and shoulders of a type by no means despicable, one was advised Miss Walshingham was capable not only of dignity but charm, even a certain glow of charm. It was, you know, her first evening dress, a tribute paid by Walshingham finance to her brightening future. Had she wanted keeping in countenance, she would have had to have fallen back upon her hostess, who was resplendent in black and steel. The other ladies had to a certain extent compromised. Mrs Walshingham had dressed with just a refined little V, and Mrs Bindon Botting, except for her dear mottled arms, confided scarcely more of her plump charm to the world. The elder Miss Botting stopped short of shoulders, and so did Miss Wace. But Helen didn't. She was – had Kipps had eyes to see it – a quite beautiful human figure; she knew it and she met him with a radiant smile that had forgotten all the little difference of the afternoon. But to Kipps her appearance was the last release. With that, she had become as remote, as foreign, as incredible as a wife and mate, as though the Cnidian Venus herself, in all her simple elegance, was before witnesses, declared to be his. If, indeed, she had ever been credible as a wife and mate.

She ascribed his confusion to modest reverence, and having blazed smiling upon him for a moment turned a shapely shoulder towards him and exchanged a remark with Mrs Bindon Botting. Ann's poor little half-sixpence came against Kipps's fingers in his pocket and he clutched at it suddenly as though it was a talisman. Then he abandoned it to suppress his Order of the Brace. He was affected by a cough. 'Miss Wace tells me Mr Revel is coming,' Mrs Botting was saying.

'Isn't it delightful?' said Helen. 'We saw him last night. He's stopped on his way to Paris. He's going to meet his wife there.'

Kipps's eyes rested for a moment on Helen's dazzling deltoid, and then went enquiringly, accusingly almost, to Coote's face. Where, in the presence of this terrible emergence, was the gospel of suppression now – that Furtive treatment of Religion and Politics and Birth and Death and Bathing and Babies and 'all those things' which constitutes your True Gentleman? He had been too modest even to discuss this question with his Mentor, but surely, surely this quintessence of all that is good and nice could regard these unsolicited confidences only in one way. With something between relief and the confirmation of his worst fears he perceived, by a sort of twitching of the exceptionally abundant muscles about Coote's lower jaw, in a certain deliberate avoidance of one particular direction by those pale, but resolute, grey eyes, by the almost convulsive grip of the ample, greenish-white gloves behind him, a grip broken at times for controlling pats at the black-bordered tie and the back of that spacious head, and by a slight but increasing disposition to cough, that *Coote did not approve!*

To Kipps Helen had once supplied a delicately beautiful dream, a thing of romance and unsubstantial mystery. But this was her final materialisation, and the last thin wreath of glamour about her was dispelled. In some way (he had forgotten how and it was perfectly incomprehensible) he was bound to this dark, solid and determined young person whose shadow and suggestion he had once loved. He had to go through with the thing as a gentleman should. Still –

And when he was sacrificing Ann!

He wouldn't stand this sort of thing, whatever else he stood . . . Should he say something about her dress to her – tomorrow?

He could put his foot down firmly. He could say, 'Look 'ere. I don't care. I ain't going to stand it. See?'

She'd say something unexpected, of course. She always did say something unexpected.

Suppose for once he overrode what she said? Simply repeated his point?

He found these thoughts battling with certain conversational aggressions from Mrs Wace, and then Revel arrived and took the centre of the stage.

The author of that brilliant romance *Red Hearts a-Beating* was a less imposing man than Kipps had anticipated, but he speedily effaced that

disappointment by his predominating manners. Although he lived habitually in the vivid world of London, his collar and tie were in no way remarkable, and he was neither brilliantly handsome nor curly nor long-haired. His personal appearance suggested armchairs, rather than the equestrian exercises and amorous toyings and passionate intensities of his masterpiece; he was inclined to be fat, with whitish flesh and muddy-coloured straight hair, he had a rather shapeless and truncated nose and his chin was asymmetrical. One eye was more inclined to stare than the other. He might have been esteemed a little undistinguished-looking were it not for his beeswaxed moustache, which came amidst his features with a pleasing note of incongruity, and the whimsical wrinkles above and about his greater eye. His regard sought and found Helen's as he entered the room and they shook hands presently with an air of intimacy Kipps, for no clear reason, found objectionable. He saw them clasp hands, heard Coote's characteristic cough – a sound rather more like a very, very old sheep, a quarter of a mile away, being blown to pieces by a small charge of gunpowder than anything else in the world – did some confused beginnings of a thought, and then they were all going in to dinner and Helen's shining bare arm lay along his sleeve. Kipps was in no state for conversation. She glanced at him, and, though he did not know it, very slightly pressed his elbow. He struggled with strange respiratory dislocations. Before them went Coote, discoursing in amiable reverberations to Mrs Walshingham, and at the head of the procession was Mrs Bindon Botting talking fast and brightly beside the erect military figure of little Mr Wace. (He was not a soldier really, but he had caught a martinet bearing by living so close to Shorncliffe.) Revel came last, in charge of Mrs Wace's queenly black and steel, politely admiring in a flutelike cultivated voice the mellow wallpaper of the staircase. Kipps marvelled at everybody's self-possession.

From the earliest spoonful of soup it became evident that Revel considered himself responsible for the table talk. And before the soup was over it was almost as manifest that Mrs Bindon Botting inclined to consider his sense of responsibility excessive. In her circle Mrs Bindon Botting was esteemed an agreeable rattle, her manner and appearance were conspicuously vivacious for one so plump, and she had an almost Irish facility for humorous description. She would keep people amused all through an afternoon call with the story of how her jobbing gardener had got himself married and what his home was like, or how her favourite butt, Mr Stigson Warder, had had all his unfortunate children taught almost every conceivable instrument because they had the phrenological bump of music abnormally large. 'They got to trombones, my dear!' she would say, with her voice coming to a climax. Usually her friends conspired to draw her out, but on this occasion they neglected to do so, a thing that militated against her keen desire to shine in Revel's eyes. After a time she perceived that the only thing for her to do was to cut in on the talk on her own account, and

this she began to do. She made several ineffectual snatches at the general attention and then Revel drifted towards a topic she regarded as particularly her own, the ordering of households.

They came to the thing through talk about localities. 'We are leaving our house in The Boltons,' said Revel, 'and taking a little place at Wimbledon, and I think of having rooms in Dane's Inn. It will be more convenient in many ways. My wife is furiously addicted to golf and exercise of all sorts, and I like to sit about in clubs – I haven't the strength necessary for these hygienic proceedings – and the old arrangement suited neither of us. And, besides, no one could imagine the demoralisation the domestics of West London have undergone during the last three years.'

'It's the same everywhere,' said Mrs Bindon Botting.

'Very possibly it is. A friend of mine calls it the servile tradition in decay and regards it all as a most hopeful phenomenon – '

'He ought to have had my last two criminals,' said Mrs Bindon Botting.

She turned to Mrs Wace while Revel came again a little too late with a 'Possibly – '

'And I haven't told you, my dear,' she said, speaking with voluble rapidity, 'I'm in trouble again.'

'The last girl?'

'The last girl. Before I can get a cook, my hard-won housemaid' – she paused – 'chucks it.'

'Panic?' asked young Walshingham.

'Mysterious grief! Everything merry as a marriage bell until my Anagram Tea! Then in the evening a portentous rigour of bearing, a word or so from my aunt, and immediately – Floods of Tears and Notice!' For a moment her eye rested thoughtfully on Kipps, as she said: 'Is there anything heartrending about Anagrams?'

'I find them so,' said Revel. 'I – '

But Mrs Bindon Botting got away again. 'For a time it made me quite uneasy – '

Kipps jabbed his lip with his fork rather painfully, and was recalled from a fascinated glare at Mrs Botting to the immediate facts of dinner.

' – whether anagrams might not have offended the good domestic's Moral Code – you never can tell. We made enquiries. No. No. No. She *must* go and that's all!'

'One perceives,' said Revel, 'in these disorders, dimly and distantly, the last dying glow of the age of Romance. Let us suppose, Mrs Botting, let us at least try to suppose – it is Love.'

Kipps clattered with his knife and fork.

'It's love,' said Mrs Botting; 'what else can it be? Beneath the orderly humdrum of our lives these romances are going on, until at last they bust up and give Notice and upset our humdrum altogether. Some fatal, wonderful soldier – '

'The passions of the common or house domestic,' said Revel, and recovered possession of the table.

Upon the troubled disorder of Kipps's table manners there had supervened a quietness, an unusual calm. For once in his life he had distinctly made up his mind on his own account. He listened no more to Revel. He put down his knife and fork and refused anything that followed. Coote regarded him with tactful concern and Helen flushed a little.

4

About half-past nine that night came a violent pull at the bell of Mrs Bindon Botting, and a young man in a dress suit, a gibus and other marks of exalted social position stood without. Athwart his white expanse of breast lay a ruddy bar of patterned silk that gave him a singular distinction and minimised the glow of a few small stains of burgundy. His gibus was thrust back and exposed a disorder of hair that suggested a reckless desperation. He had, in fact, burnt his boats and refused to join the ladies. Coote, in the subsequent conversation, had protested quietly, 'You're going on all right, you know,' to which Kipps had answered he didn't care a 'Eng' about that, and so, after a brief tussle with Walshingham's detaining arm, had got away. 'I got something to do,' he said. ' 'Ome.' And here he was – panting an extraordinary resolve. The door opened, revealing the pleasantly furnished hall of Mrs Bindon Botting, lit by rose-tinted lights, and in the centre of the picture, neat and pretty in black and white, stood Ann. At the sight of Kipps her colour vanished.

'Ann,' said Kipps, 'I want to speak to you. I got something to say to you right away. See? I'm – '

'This ain't the door to speak to me at,' said Ann.

'But, Ann! It's something special.'

'You spoke enough,' said Ann.

'Ann!'

'Besides. That's my door, down there. Basement. If I was caught talking at *this* door – !'

'But, Ann, *I'm* – '

'Basement after nine. Them's my hours. I'm a servant and likely to keep one. If you're calling here, what name, please? But you got your friends and I got mine, and you mustn't go talking to *me*.'

'But, Ann, I want to ask you – '

Someone appeared in the hall behind Ann.

'Not here,' said Ann. 'Don't know anyone of that name,' and incontinently slammed the door in his face.

'What was that, Ann?' said Mrs Bindon Botting's invalid aunt.

'Ge'm a little intoxicated, ma'am – asking for the wrong name, ma'am.'

'What name did he want?' asked the lady, doubtfully.

'No name that *we* know, ma'am,' said Ann, hustling along the hall towards the kitchen stairs.

'I hope you weren't too short with him, Ann.'

'No shorter than he deserved, considering 'ow he be'aved,' said Ann, with her bosom heaving.

And Mrs Bindon Botting's invalid aunt, perceiving suddenly that this call had some relation to Ann's private and sentimental trouble, turned, after one moment of hesitating scrutiny, away.

She was an extremely sympathetic lady, was Mrs Bindon Botting's invalid aunt; she took an interest in the servants, imposed piety, extorted confessions and followed human nature, blushing and lying defensively, to its reluctantly revealed recesses; but Ann's sense of privacy was strong and her manner, under drawing out and encouragement, sometimes even alarming . . .

So the poor old lady went upstairs again.

5

The basement door opened and Kipps came into the kitchen. He was flushed and panting.

He struggled for speech.

' 'Ere,' he said, and held out two half-sixpences.

Ann stood behind the kitchen table – face pale and eyes round, and now – and it simplified Kipps very much – he could see she had indeed been crying.

'Well?' she said.

'Don't you see?'

Ann moved her head slightly.

'I kep' it all these years.'

'You kep' it too long.'

His mouth closed and his flush died away. He looked at her. The amulet, it seemed, had failed to work.

'Ann!' he said.

'Well?'

'Ann.'

The conversation still hung fire.

'Ann,' he said, made a movement with his hands that suggested appeal, and advanced a step.

Ann shook her head more defiantly, and became defensive.

'Look here, Ann,' said Kipps. 'I been a fool.'

They stared into each other's miserable eyes.

'Ann,' he said. 'I want to marry you.'

Ann clutched the table edge. 'You can't,' she said faintly.

He made as if to approach her around the table, and she took a step that restored their distance.

'I must,' he said.

'You can't.'

'I must. You *got* to marry me, Ann.'

'You can't go marrying everybody. You got to marry 'er.'

'I shan't.'

Ann shook her head. 'You're engaged to that girl. Lady, rather. You can't be engaged to me.'

'I don't want to be engaged to you. I *been* engaged. I want to be married to you. See? Rightaway.'

Ann turned a shade paler. 'But what d'you mean?' she asked.

'Come right off to London and marry me. Now.'

'What d'you mean?'

Kipps became extremely lucid and earnest.

'I mean come right off and marry me now before anyone else can. *See?*'

'In London?'

'In London.'

They stared at one another again. They took things for granted in the most amazing way.

'I couldn't,' said Ann. 'For one thing, my month's not up for mor'n free weeks yet.'

They hung before that for a moment as though it was insurmountable.

'Look 'ere, Ann! Arst to go. Arst to go!'

'*She* wouldn't,' said Ann.

'Then come without arsting,' said Kipps.

'She'll keep my box – '

'She won't.'

'She will.'

'She won't.'

'You don't know 'er.'

'Well, desh 'er – let 'er! LET 'ER! Who cares? I'll buy you a 'undred boxes if you'll come.'

'It wouldn't be right towards Her.'

'It isn't Her you got to think about, Ann. It's me.'

'And you 'aven't treated me properly,' she said. 'You 'aven't treated me properly, Artie. You didn't ought to 'ave – '

'I didn't say I '*ad*,' he interrupted, 'did I? Ann,' he appealed, 'I didn't come to arguefy. I'm all wrong. I never said I wasn't. It's yes or no. Me or not . . . I been a fool. There! See? I been a fool. Ain't that enough? I got myself all tied up with everyone and made a fool of myself all round . . . '

He pleaded, 'It isn't as if we didn't care for one another, Ann.'

She seemed impassive and he resumed his discourse.

'I thought I wasn't likely ever to see you again, Ann. I reely did. It isn't as though I was seein' you all the time. I didn't know what I wanted, and I went and be'aved like a fool – jest as anyone might. I know what I want and I know what I don't want now.

'Ann!'

'Well?'

'Will you come? . . . Will you come? . . . '

Silence.

'If you don't answer me, Ann – I'm desprit – if you don't answer me now, if you don't say you'll come, I'll go right out now – '

He turned doorward passionately as he spoke, with his threat incomplete.

'I'll go,' he said; 'I 'aven't a friend in the world! I been and throwed everything away. I don't know why I done things and why I 'aven't. All I know is I can't stand nothing in the world any more.' He choked. 'The pier – ' he said.

He fumbled with the door latch, grumbling some inarticulate self-pity, as if he sought a handle, and then he had it open.

Clearly he was going.

'Artie!' said Ann, sharply.

He turned about and the two hung, white and tense.

'I'll do it,' said Ann.

His face began to work; he shut the door and came a step back to her, staring; his face became pitiful and then suddenly they moved together. 'Artie!' she cried, 'don't go!' and held out her arms, weeping.

They clung close to one another . . .

'Oh! I *been* so mis'bel,' cried Kipps, clinging to this lifebuoy; and suddenly his emotion, having no further serious work in hand, burst its way to a loud *boohoo*! His fashionable and expensive gibus flopped off and fell and rolled and lay neglected on the floor.

'I been so mis'bel,' said Kipps, giving himself vent. 'Oh! I *been* so mis'bel, Ann.'

'Be quiet,' said Ann, holding his poor, blubbering head tightly to her heaving shoulder, and herself all a-quiver; 'be quiet. She's there! Listenin'. She'll 'ear you, Artie, on the stairs . . . '

6

Ann's last words when, an hour later, they parted, Mrs and Miss Bindon Botting having returned very audibly upstairs, deserve a section to themselves.

'I wouldn't do this for everyone, mind you,' whispered Ann.

The Labyrinthodon

You imagine them fleeing through our complex and difficult social system as it were for life, first on foot and severally to the Folkestone Central Station, then in a first-class carriage, with Kipps's bag as sole chaperone, to Charing Cross, and then in a four-wheeler, a long, rumbling, palpitating, slow flight through the multitudinous swarming London streets to Sid. Kipps kept peeping out of the window. 'It's the next corner after this, I believe,' he would say. For he had a sort of feeling that at Sid's he would be immune from the hottest pursuit. He paid the cabman in a manner adequate to the occasion and turned to his prospective brother-in-law. 'Me and Ann,' he said, 'we're going to marry.'

'But I thought – ' began Sid.

Kipps motioned him towards explanations in the shop –

'It's no good, my arguing with you,' said Sid, smiling delightedly as the case unfolded. 'You done it now.' And Masterman, being apprised of the nature of the affair, descended slowly in a state of flushed congratulation.

'I thought you might find the Higher Life a bit difficult,' said Masterman, projecting a bony hand. 'But I never thought you'd have the originality to clear out . . . Won't the young lady of the superior classes swear! Never mind – it doesn't matter anyhow.

'You were starting a climb,' he said at dinner, 'that doesn't lead any-where. You would have clambered from one refinement of vulgarity to another and never got to any satisfactory top. There isn't a top. It's a squirrel's cage. Things are out of joint, and the only top there is is a lot of blazing card-playing women and betting men, seasoned with archbishops and officials and all that sort of glossy, pandering Tosh . . . You'd have hung on, a disconsolate, dismal little figure somewhere up the ladder, far below even the motor-car class, while your wife larked about – or fretted because she wasn't a bit higher than she was . . . I found it all out long ago. I've seen women of that sort. And I don't climb any more.'

'I often thought about what you said last time I saw you,' said Kipps.

'I wonder what I said,' said Masterman in parenthesis. 'Anyhow, you're doing the right and sane thing, and that's a rare spectacle. You're going to marry your equal, and you're going to take your own line, quite in-dependently of what people up there, or people down there, think you ought or ought not to do. That's about the only course one can take nowadays with everything getting more muddled and upside down every day. Make your own little world and your own house first of all, keep that right side up whatever you do, and marry your mate . . . That, I suppose, is

what *I* should do – if *I* had a mate . . . But people of my sort, luckily for the world, don't get made in pairs. No!

'Besides – ! However – ' And abruptly, taking advantage of an interruption by Master Walt, he lapsed into thought.

Presently he came out of his musings.

'After all,' he said, 'there's hope.'

'What about?' said Sid.

'Everything,' said Masterman.

'Where there's life there's hope,' said Mrs Sid. 'But none of you aren't eating anything like you ought to.'

Masterman lifted his glass.

'Here's to Hope!' he said. 'The Light of the World!'

Sid beamed at Kipps as who should say, 'You don't meet a character like *this* every dinner time.'

'Here's to Hope,' repeated Masterman. 'The best thing one can have. Hope of life – yes.'

He imposed his moment of magnificent self-pity on them all. Even young Walt was impressed.

2

They spent the days before their marriage in a number of agreeable excursions together. One day they went to Kew by steamboat, and admired the house full of paintings of flowers extremely; and one day they went early to have a good long day at the Crystal Palace, and enjoyed themselves very much indeed. They got there so early that nothing was open inside, all the stalls were wrappered up and all the minor exhibitions locked and barred; they seemed the minutest creatures even to themselves in that enormous empty aisle and their echoing footsteps indecently loud. They contemplated realistic groups of plaster savages, and Ann thought they'd be queer people to have about. She was glad there were none in this country. They meditated upon replicas of classical statuary without excessive comment. Kipps said, at large, it must have been a queer world then, but Ann very properly doubted if they really went about like that. But the place at that early hour was really lonely. One began to fancy things. So they went out into the October sunshine of the mighty terraces, and wandered amidst miles of stucco tanks and about those quiet Gargantuan grounds. A great, grey emptiness it was, and it seemed marvellous to them, but not nearly so marvellous as it might have seemed. 'I never see a finer place, never,' said Kipps, turning to survey the entirety of the enormous glass front with Paxton's vast image in the centre.

'What it must 'ave cost to build!' said Ann, and left her sentence eloquently incomplete.

Presently they came to a region of caves and waterways, and amidst these waterways strange reminders of the possibilities of the Creator. They passed under an arch made of a whale's jaws, and discovered amidst herbage, as if they were browsing or standing unoccupied and staring as if amazed at themselves, huge effigies of iguanodons and deinotheria and mastodons and suchlike cattle, gloriously done in green and gold.

'They got everything,' said Kipps. 'Earl's Court isn't a patch on it.'

His mind was very greatly exercised by these monsters, and he hovered about them and returned to them. 'You'd wonder 'ow they ever got enough to eat,' he said several times.

3

It was later in the day, and upon a seat in the presence of the green-and-gold Labyrinthodon that looms so splendidly above the lake, that the Kippses fell into talk about their future. They had made a sufficient lunch in the palace, they had seen pictures and no end of remarkable things, and that and the amber sunlight made a mood for them, quiet and philosophical, a haven mood. Kipps broke a contemplative silence with an abrupt allusion to one principal preoccupation. 'I shall offer an 'pology and I shall offer 'er brother damages. If she likes to bring an action for Breach after that, well – I done all I can . . . They can't get much out of reading my letters in court, because I didn't write none. I dessay a thousan' or two'll settle all that, anyhow. I ain't much worried about that. That don't worry me very much, Ann – No.'

And then, 'It's a lark, our marrying. It's curious 'ow things come about. If I 'adn't run against you, where should I 'ave been now? Eh? . . . Even after we met, I didn't seem to see it like – not marrying you, I mean – until that night I came. I didn't – reely.'

'I didn't neither,' said Ann, with thoughtful eyes on the water.

For a time Kipps's mind was occupied by the prettiness of her thinking face. A faint, tremulous network of lights, reflected from the ripples of a passing duck, played subtly over her cheek and faded away.

Ann reflected. 'I s'pose things 'ad to be,' she said.

Kipps mused. 'It's curious 'ow ever I got on to be engaged to 'er.'

'She wasn't suited to you,' said Ann.

'Suited. No fear! That's jest it. 'Ow did it come about?'

'I expect she led you on,' said Ann.

Kipps was half-minded to assent. Then he had a twinge of conscience. 'It wasn't that, Ann,' he said. 'It's curious. I don't know what it was, but it wasn't that. I don't recollect . . . No . . . Life's jolly rum; that's one thing any'ow. And I suppose I'm a rum sort of feller. I get excited sometimes, and then I don't seem to care *what* I do. That's about what it was reely. Still – '

They meditated, Kipps with his arms folded and pulling at his scanty moustache. Presently a faint smile came over his face.

'We'll get a nice little 'ouse out 'Ythe way.'

'It's 'omelier than Folkestone,' said Ann.

'Jest a nice little 'ouse,' said Kipps. 'There's Hughenden, of course. But that's let. Besides being miles too big. And I wouldn't live in Folkestone again some'ow – not for anything.'

'I'd like to 'ave a 'ouse of my own,' said Ann. 'I've often thought, being in service, 'ow much I'd like to manage a 'ouse of my own.'

'You'd know all about what the servants was up to, anyhow,' said Kipps, amused.

'Servants! We don't want no servants,' said Ann, startled.

'You'll 'ave to 'ave a servant,' said Kipps. 'If it's only to do the 'eavy work of the 'ouse.'

'What! and not be able 'ardly to go into my own kitchen?' said Ann.

'You ought to 'ave a servant,' said Kipps.

'One could easy 'ave a woman in for anything that's 'eavy,' said Ann. 'Besides – If I 'ad one of the girls one sees about nowadays, I should want to be taking the broom out of 'er 'and and doing it all over myself. I'd manage better without 'er.'

'We ought to 'ave one servant anyhow,' said Kipps, 'else 'ow should we manage if we wanted to go out together or anything like that?'

'I might get a *young* girl,' said Ann, 'and bring 'er up in my own way.'

Kipps left the matter at that and came back to the house.

'There's little 'ouses going into Hythe, just the sort we want, not too big and not too small. We'll 'ave a kitching and a dining-room and a little room to sit in of a night.'

'It mustn't be a 'ouse with a basement,' said Ann.

'What's a basement?'

'It's a downstairs, where there's not arf enough light and everything got to be carried – up and down, up and down, all day – coals and everything. And it's got to 'ave a water-tap and sink and things upstairs. You'd 'ardly believe, Artie, if you 'adn't been in service, 'ow cruel and silly some 'ouses are built – you'd think they 'ad a spite against servants the way the stairs are made.'

'We won't 'ave one of that sort,' said Kipps . . . 'We'll 'ave a quiet little life. Now go out a bit – now come 'ome again. Read a book perhaps if we got nothing else to do. 'Ave old Buggins in for an evening at times. 'Ave Sid down. There's bicycles – '

'I don't fancy myself on a bicycle,' said Ann.

' 'Ave a trailer,' said Kipps, 'and sit like a lady. I'd take you out to New Romney easy as anything, jest to see the old people.'

'I wouldn't mind that,' said Ann.

'We'll jest 'ave a sensible little 'ouse, and sensible things. No art or

anything of that sort, nothing stuck-up or anything, but jest sensible. We'll be as right as anything, Ann.'

'No Socialism,' said Ann, starting a lurking doubt.

'No Socialism,' said Kipps; 'just sensible, that's all.'

'I dessay it's all right for them that understand it, Artie, but I don't agree with this Socialism.'

'I don't neither, reely,' said Kipps. 'I can't argue about it, but it don't seem real like to me. All the same, Masterman's a clever fellow, Ann.'

'I didn't like 'im at first, Artie, but I do now – in a way. You don't understand 'im all at once.'

' 'E's so clever,' said Kipps. 'Arf the time I can't make out what 'e's up to. 'E's the cleverest chap I ever met. I never 'eard such talking. 'E ought to write a book . . . It's a rum world, Ann, when a chap like that isn't 'ardly able to earn a living.'

'It's 'is 'ealth,' said Ann.

'I expect it is,' said Kipps, and ceased to talk for a little while.

Then he spoke with deliberation, 'Sea air might be the saving of 'im, Ann.'

He glanced doubtfully at Ann, and she was looking at him even fondly.

'You think of other people a lot,' said Ann. 'I been looking at you sittin' there and thinking.'

'I suppose I do. I suppose when one's 'appy one does.'

'*You* do,' said Ann.

'We shall be 'appy in that little 'ouse, Ann. Don't y' think?'

She met his eyes and nodded.

'I seem to see it,' said Kipps, 'sort of cosy like. 'Bout tea time and muffins, kettle on the 'ob, cat on the 'earthrug – we must get a cat, Ann – and *you* there. Eh?'

They regarded each other with appreciative eyes and Kipps became irrelevant.

'I don't believe, Ann,' he said, 'I 'aven't kissed you not for 'arf an hour. Leastways not since we was in those caves.'

For kissing had already ceased to be a matter of thrilling adventure for them.

Ann shook her head. 'You be sensible and go on talking about Mr Masterman,' she said.

But Kipps had wandered to something else. 'I like the way your 'air turns back just there,' he said, with an indicative finger. 'It was like that, I remember, when you was a girl. Sort of wavy. I've often thought of it . . . 'Member when we raced that time – out be'ind the church?'

Then for a time they sat idly, each following out agreeable meditations.

'It's rum,' said Kipps.

'What's rum?'

' 'Ow everything's 'appened,' said Kipps. 'Who'd 'ave thought of our

being 'ere like this six weeks ago? . . . Who'd 'ave thought of my ever 'aving any money?'

His eyes went to the big Labyrinthodon. He looked first carelessly and then suddenly with a growing interest in its vast face.

'I'm deshed,' he murmured. Ann became interested. He laid a hand on her arm and pointed. Ann scrutinised the Labyrinthodon and then came around to Kipps's face in mute interrogation.

'Don't you see it?' said Kipps.

'See what?'

' 'E's *jest* like old Coote.'

'It's extinct,' said Ann, not clearly apprehending.

'I dessay 'e is. But 'e's jest like old Coote all the same for that.'

Kipps meditated on the monstrous shapes in sight. 'I wonder 'ow all these old antediluvium animals *got* extinct,' he asked. 'No one couldn't possibly 'ave killed 'em.'

'Why! *I* know that,' said Ann. 'They was overtook by the Flood . . . '

Kipps meditated for a while. 'But I thought they had to take two of everything there was – '

'Within reason they 'ad,' said Ann . . .

The Kippses left it at that.

The great green-and-gold Labyrinthodon took no notice of their conversation. It gazed with its wonderful eyes over their heads into the infinite – inflexibly calm. It might indeed have been Coote himself there, Coote, the unassuming, cutting them dead.

4

And in due course these two simple souls married, and Venus Urania, the Goddess of Wedded Love, the Goddess of Tolerant Kindliness or Meeting Halfway, to whom all young couples should pray and offer sacrifices of self, who is indeed a very great and noble and kindly goddess, was in some manner propitiated and bent down and blessed them in their union.

BOOK THREE

Kippses

CHAPTER ONE

The Housing Problem

Honeymoons and all things come to an end, and you see at last Mr and Mrs Arthur Kipps descending upon the Hythe platform – coming to Hythe to find that nice *little* house – to realise that bright dream of a home they had first talked about in the grounds of the Crystal Palace. They are a valiant couple, you perceive, but small; and the world is a large incongruous system of complex and difficult things. Kipps wears a grey suit, with a wing-poke collar and a neat, smart tie. Mrs Kipps is the same bright and healthy little girl-woman you saw in the Marsh; not an inch has been added to her stature in all my voluminous narrative. Only now she wears a hat.

It is a hat very unlike the hats she used to wear on her Sundays out, a flourishing hat with feathers and buckle and bows and things. The price of that hat would take many people's breath away – it cost two guineas! Kipps chose it. Kipps paid for it. They left the shop with flushed cheeks and smarting eyes, glad to be out of range of the condescending saleswoman.

'Artie,' said Ann, 'you didn't ought to 'ave – '

That was all. And you know, the hat didn't suit Ann a bit. Her clothes did not suit her at all. The simple, cheap, clean brightness of her former style had given place not only to this hat, but to several other things in the same key. And out from among these things looked her pretty face, the face of a wise little child – an artless wonder struggling through a preposterous dignity.

They had bought that hat one day when they had gone to see the shops in Bond Street. Kipps had looked at the passers-by and it had suddenly occurred to him that Ann was dowdy. He had noted the hat of a very proud-looking lady passing in an electric brougham and had resolved to get Ann the nearest thing to that.

The railway porters perceived some subtle incongruity in Ann, the knot of cabmen in the station doorway, the two golfers and the lady with daughters, who had also got out of the train. And Kipps, a little pale, blowing a little, not in complete possession of himself, knew that they noticed her and him. And Ann – It is hard to say just what Ann observed of these things.

' 'Ere!' said Kipps to a cabman, and regretted too late a vanished 'H'.

'I got a trunk up there,' he said to a ticket inspector, 'marked A. K.'

'Ask a porter,' said the inspector, turning his back.

'Demn!' said Kipps, not altogether inaudibly.

It is all very well to sit in the sunshine and talk of the house you will have, and another altogether to achieve it. We English – all the world indeed today – live in a strange atmosphere of neglected great issues, of insistent, triumphant petty things; we are given up to the fine littlenesses of inter-course; table manners and small correctitudes are the substance of our lives. You do not escape these things for long even by so catastrophic a pro-ceeding as flying to London with a young lady of no wealth and inferior social position. The mists of noble emotion swirl and pass and there you are divorced from all your deities and grazing in the meadows under the Argus eyes of the social system, the innumerable mean judgements you feel raining upon you, upon your clothes and bearing, upon your pretensions and movements.

Our world today is a meanly conceived one – it is only an added meanness to conceal that fact. For one consequence, it has very few nice little houses, such things do not come for the asking, they are not to be bought with money during ignoble times. Its houses are built on the ground of monstrously rich, shabbily extortionate landowners, by poor, parsimonious, greedy people in a mood of elbowing competition. What can you expect from such ridiculous conditions? To go house-hunting is to spy out the nakedness of this pretentious world, to see what our civilisation amounts to when you take away curtains and flounces and carpets and all the fluster and distraction of people and fittings. It is to see mean plans meanly executed for mean ends, the conventions torn aside, the secrets stripped, the substance underlying all such Chester Cootery soiled and worn and left.

So you see our poor dear Kippses going to and fro, in Hythe, in Sandgate, in Ashford and Canterbury and Deal and Dover – at last even in Folkestone, with 'orders to view', pink and green and white and yellow orders to view, and labelled keys in Kipps's hand and frowns and perplexity upon their faces . . . They did not clearly know what they wanted, but whatever it was they saw, they knew they did not want that. Always they found a confusing multitude of houses they could not take, and none they could. Their dreams began to turn mainly on empty, abandoned-looking rooms, with unfaded patches of paper to mark the place of vanished pictures and doors that had lost their keys. They saw rooms floored with boards that yawned apart and were splintered, skirtings eloquent of the industrious mouse, kitchens with a dead black-beetle in the empty cupboard and a hideous variety of coal-holes and dark cupboards under the stairs. They stuck their little heads through roof trap-doors and gazed at disorganised ball taps, at the bleak filthiness of unstopped roofs. There were occasions

when it seemed to them that they must be the victims of an elaborate conspiracy of house agents, so bleak and cheerless is a second-hand empty house in comparison with the humblest of inhabited dwellings.

Commonly the houses were too big. They had huge windows that demanded vast curtains in mitigation, countless bedrooms, acreage of stone steps to be cleaned, kitchens that made Ann protest. She had come so far towards a proper conception of Kipps's social position as to admit the prospect of one servant – 'but lor'!' she would say, 'you'd want a manservant in this 'ouse.' When the houses were not too big, then they were almost invariably the product of speculative building, of that multitudinous hasty building for the extravagant multitude of new births that was the essential disaster of the nineteenth century. The new houses Ann refused as damp, and even the youngest of these that had been in use showed remarkable signs of a sickly constitution, the plaster flaked away, the floors gaped, the paper mouldered and peeled, the doors dropped, the bricks scaled and the railings rusted. Nature in the form of spiders, earwigs, cockroaches, mice, rats, fungi and remarkable smells, was already fighting her way back . . .

And the plan was invariably inconvenient, invariably. All the houses they saw had a common quality for which she could find no word, but for which the proper word is incivility. 'They build these 'ouses,' she said, 'as though girls wasn't 'uman beings.' Sid's social democracy had got into her blood perhaps, and anyhow they went about discovering the most remarkable inconsiderateness in the contemporary house. 'There's kitching stairs to go up, Artie!' Ann would say. 'Some poor girl's got to go up and down, up and down, and be tired out, jest because they haven't the sense to leave enough space to give their steps a proper rise – and no water upstairs anywhere – every drop got to be carried! It's 'ouses like this wear girls out.

'It's 'aving 'ouses built by men, I believe, makes all the work and trouble,' said Ann . . .

The Kippses, you see, thought they were looking for a reasonably simple little contemporary house, but they were in fact looking either for dreamland or 1975 AD or thereabouts, and it hadn't come.

3

But it was a foolish thing of Kipps to begin building a house.

He did that out of an extraordinary animosity for house agents he had conceived.

Everybody hates house agents just as everybody loves sailors. It is no doubt a very wicked and unjust hatred, but the business of a novelist is not ethical principle but facts. Everybody hates house agents because they have everybody at a disadvantage. All other callings have a certain amount of give and take; the house agent simply takes. All other callings want you: your

solicitor is afraid you may change him, your doctor cannot go too far, your novelist – if only you knew it – is mutely abject towards your unspoken wishes, and as for your tradespeople, milkmen will fight outside your front door for you and greengrocers call in tears if you discard them suddenly; but who ever heard of a house agent struggling to serve anyone? You want to get a house; you go to him, you dishevelled and angry from travel, anxious, enquiring; he calm, clean, inactive, reticent, quietly doing nothing. You beg him to reduce rents, whitewash ceilings, produce other houses, combine the summer-house of No. 6 with the conservatory of No. 4 – much he cares! You want to dispose of a house; then he is just the same, serene, indifferent – on one occasion I remember he was picking his teeth all the time he answered me. Competition is a mockery among house agents, they are all alike; you cannot wound them by going to the opposite office, you cannot dismiss them, you can at most dismiss yourself. They are invulnerably placed behind mahogany and brass, too far usually even for a sudden swift lunge with an umbrella, and to throw away the keys they lend you instead of returning them is larceny and punishable as such.

It was a house agent in Dover who finally decided Kipps to build. Kipps, with a certain faltering in his voice, had delivered his ultimatum, no basement, not more than eight rooms, hot and cold water upstairs, coal cellar in the house but with intervening doors to keep dust from the scullery and so forth. He stood blowing. 'You'll have to build a house,' said the house agent, sighing wearily, 'if you want all that.' It was rather for the sake of effective answer than with any intention at the time that Kipps mumbled, 'That's about what I shall do if this goes on.'

Whereupon the house agent smiled. He smiled!

When Kipps came to turn the thing over in his mind he was surprised to find quite a considerable intention had germinated and was growing up in him. After all, lots of people *have* built houses. How could there be so many if they hadn't? Suppose he 'reely' did! Then he would go to the house agent and say, ' 'Ere, while you been getting me a sootable 'ouse, blowed if I 'aven't built one!' Go round to all of them; all the house agents in Folkestone, in Dover, Ashford, Canterbury, Margate, Ramsgate, saying that! Perhaps then they might be sorry. It was in the small hours that he awoke to a realisation that he had made up his mind in the matter.

'Ann,' he said, 'Ann,' and also used the sharp of his elbow.

Ann was at last awakened to the pitch of an indistinct enquiry what was the matter.

'I'm going to build a house, Ann.'

'Eh?' said Ann, suddenly, as if awake.

'Build a house.'

Ann said something incoherent about he'd better wait until the morning before he did anything of the sort, and immediately with a fine trustfulness went fast asleep again.

But Kipps lay awake for a long while building his house, and in the morning at breakfast he made his meaning clear. He had smarted under the indignities of house agents long enough, and this seemed to promise revenge – a fine revenge. 'And, you know, we might reely make rather a nice little 'ouse out of it – like we want.'

So resolved, it became possible for them to take a house for a year, with a basement, no service lift, black-leading to do everywhere, no water upstairs, no bathroom, vast sash windows to be cleaned from the sill, stone steps with a twist and open to the rain into the coal cellar, insufficient cupboards, unpaved path to the dustbin, no fireplace in the servant's bedroom, no end of splintery wood to scrub – in fact, a very typical English middle-class house. And having added to this house some furniture, and a languid young person with unauthentic golden hair named Gwendolen, who was engaged to a sergeant-major and had formerly been in a hotel, having 'moved in' and spent some sleepless nights varied by nocturnal explorations in search of burglars, because of the strangeness of being in a house for which they were personally responsible, Kipps settled down for a time and turned himself with considerable resolution to the project of building a home.

4

At first Kipps had gathered advice, finding an initial difficulty in how to begin. He went into a builder's shop at Seabrook one day, and told the lady in charge that he wanted a house built; he was breathless but quite determined, and he was prepared to give his order there and then, but she temporised with him and said her husband was out, and he left without giving his name. Also he went and talked to a man in a cart who was pointed out to him by a workman as the builder of a new house near Saltwood, but he found him first sceptical and then overpoweringly sarcastic. 'I suppose you build a 'ouse every 'oliday,' he said, and turned from Kipps with every symptom of contempt.

Afterwards Carshot told alarming stories about builders, and shook Kipps's expressed resolution a good deal, and then Pierce raised the question whether one ought to go in the first instance to a builder at all and not rather to an architect. Pierce knew a man at Ashford whose brother was an architect and, as it is always better in these matters to get someone you know, the Kippses decided, before Pierce had gone and Carshot's warnings had resumed their sway, to apply to him. They did so – rather dubiously.

The architect who was brother of Pierce's friend appeared as a small, alert individual with a black bag and a cylindrical silk hat, and he sat at the dining-room table, with his hat and his bag exactly equidistant right and left of him, and maintained a demeanour of impressive woodenness, while

Kipps on the hearthrug, with a quaking sense of gigantic enterprise, vacillated answers to his enquiries. Ann held a watching brief for herself, in a position she had chosen as suitable to the occasion beside the corner of the carved oak sideboard. They felt, in a sense, at bay.

The architect began by asking for the site, and seemed a little discomposed to discover this had still to be found. 'I thought of building just anywhere,' said Kipps. 'I 'aven't made up my mind about that yet.' The architect remarked that he would have preferred to see the site in order to know where to put what he called his 'ugly side', but it was quite possible of course to plan a house 'in the air', on the level, 'simply with back and front assumed' – if they would like to do that. Kipps flushed slightly, and secretly hoping it would make no great difference in the fees, said a little doubtfully that he thought that would be all right.

The architect then marked off, as it were, the first section of his subject with a single dry cough, opened his bag, took out a spring tape measure, some hard biscuits, a metal flask, a new pair of dogskin gloves, a clockwork motor car partially wrapped in paper, a bunch of violets, a paper of small brass screws and, finally, a large distended notebook; he replaced the other objects carefully, opened his notebook, put a pencil to his lips and said: 'And what accommodation will you require?' To which Ann, who had followed his every movement with the closest attention and a deepening dread, replied with the violent suddenness of one who has long lain in wait, 'Cubbuds!

'Anyhow,' she added, catching her husband's eye.

The architect wrote it down.

'And how many rooms?' he said, coming to secondary matters.

The young people regarded one another. It was dreadfully like giving an order.

'How many bedrooms, for example?' asked the architect.

'One?' suggested Kipps, inclined now to minimise at any cost.

'There's Gwendolen,' said Ann.

'Visitors perhaps,' said the architect, and temperately, 'You never know.'

'Two, p'r'aps?' said Kipps. 'We don't want no more than a *little* 'ouse, you know.'

'But the merest shooting-box – ' said the architect . . .

They got to six; he beat them steadily from bedroom to bedroom; the word 'nursery' played across their imaginative skies – he mentioned it as the remotest possibility – and then six being reluctantly conceded, Ann came forward to the table, sat down and delivered herself of one of her prepared conditions: ' 'Ot and cold water,' she said, 'laid on to each room – any'ow.'

It was an idea long since acquired from Sid.

'Yes,' said Kipps, on the hearthrug, ' 'Ot and cold water laid on to each bedroom – we've settled on that.'

It was the first intimation to the architect that he had to deal with a

couple of exceptional originality, and as he had spent the previous after-
noon in finding three large houses in the *Builder*, which he intended to
combine into an original and copyright design of his own, he naturally
struggled against these novel requirements. He enlarged on the extreme
expensiveness of plumbing, on the extreme expensiveness of everything
not already arranged for in his scheme, and only when Ann declared she'd
as soon not have the house as not have her requirements, and Kipps,
blenching the while, had said he didn't mind what a thing cost him so long
as he got what he wanted, did he allow a kindred originality of his own to
appear beneath the acquired professionalism of his methods. He dismissed
their previous talk with his paragraphic cough. 'Of course,' he said, 'if you
don't mind being unconventional – '

He explained that he had been thinking of a Queen Anne style of
architecture (Ann directly she heard her name shook her head at Kipps in
an aside) so far as the exterior went. For his own part, he said, he liked to
have the exterior of a house in a style, not priggishly in a style, but mixed,
with one style uppermost; and the gables and dormers and casements of the
Queen Anne style, with a little roughcast and sham timbering here and
there and perhaps a bit of an overhang, diversified a house and made it
interesting. The advantage of what he called a Queen Anne style was that
it had such a variety of features . . . Still, if they were prepared to be
unconventional it could be done. A number of houses were now built in the
unconventional style and were often very pretty. In the unconventional
style one frequently had what perhaps he might call Internal Features – for
example, an Old English oak staircase and gallery. White roughcast and
green paint were a good deal favoured in houses of this type.

He indicated that this excursus on style was finished by a momentary use
of his cough, and reopened his notebook, which he had closed to wave
about in a moment of descriptive enthusiasm while expatiating on the
unbridled wealth of External Features associated with Queen Anne. 'Six
bedrooms,' he said, moistening his pencil. 'One with barred windows
suitable for a nursery if required.'

Kipps endorsed this huskily and reluctantly.

There followed a most interesting discussion upon house building, in
which Kipps played a minor part. They passed from bedrooms to the
kitchen and scullery, and there Ann displayed an intelligent exactingness
that won the expressed admiration of the architect. They were particularly
novel upon the position of the coal cellar, which Ann held to be altogether
too low in the ordinary house, necessitating much heavy carrying. They
dismissed as impracticable the idea of having coal cellar and kitchen at the
top of the house, because that would involve carrying all the coal through
the house, and therewith much subsequent cleaning, and for a time they
dealt with a conception of a coal cellar on the ground floor with a light
staircase running up outside to an exterior shoot. 'It might be made a

Feature,' said the architect, a little doubtfully, jotting down a note of it. 'It would be apt to get black, you know.'

Thence they passed to the alternative of service lifts, and then by an inspiration of the architect to the possibilities of gas heating. Kipps did a complicated verbal fugue on the theme 'gas heating heats the air', with variable aspirates; he became very red and was lost to the discussion altogether for a time, though his lips kept silently moving.

Subsequently the architect wrote to say that he found in his notebook very full and explicit directions for bow windows to all rooms, for bedrooms, for water supply, lift, height of stairs and absence of twists therein, for a well-ventilated kitchen twenty feet square, with two dressers and a large box-window seat, for scullery and outhouses and offices, but nothing whatever about drawing-room, dining-room, library or study, or approximate cost, and he awaited further instructions. He presumed there would be a breakfast-room, dining-room, drawing-room, and study for Mr Kipps, at least that was his conception, and the young couple discussed this matter long and ardently.

Ann was distinctly restrictive in this direction. 'I don't see what you want a drawin'-room and a dinin' *and* a kitchen for. If we was going to let in summer – well and good. But we're not going to let. Consequently we don't want so many rooms. Then there's a 'all. What use is a 'all? It only makes work. And a study!'

Kipps had been humming and stroking his moustache since he had read the architect's letter. 'I think I'd like a little bit of a study – not a big one, of course, but one with a desk and bookshelves, like there was in Hughenden. I'd like that.'

It was only after they had talked to the architect again and seen how scandalised he was at the idea of not having a drawing-room that they consented to that Internal Feature. They consented to please him. 'But we shan't never use it,' said Ann.

Kipps had his way about a study. 'When I get that study,' said Kipps, 'I shall do a bit of reading I've long wanted to do. I shall make a habit of going in there and reading something an hour every day. There's Shakespeare and a lot of things a man like me ought to read. Besides, we got to 'ave *somewhere* to put the *Encyclopaedia*. I've always thought a study was about what I've wanted all along. You can't 'elp reading if you got a study. If you 'aven't, there's nothing for it, so far's *I* can see, but treshy novels.'

He looked down at Ann and was surprised to see a joyless thoughtfulness upon her face.

'Fency, Ann!' he said, not too buoyantly, ' 'aving a little 'ouse of our own!'

'It won't be a little 'ouse,' said Ann, 'not with all them rooms.'

Any lingering doubt in that matter was dispelled when it came to plans.

The architect drew three sets of plans on a transparent bluish sort of paper that smelt abominably. He painted them very nicely; brick-red and ginger, and arsenic green and a leaden sort of blue, and brought them over to show our young people. The first set were very simple, with practically no External Features – 'a plain style', he said it was – but it looked a big sort of house nevertheless; the second had such extras as a conservatory, bay windows of various sorts, one roughcast gable and one half-timbered ditto in plaster, and a sort of overhung verandah, and was much more imposing; and the third was quite fungoid with External Features, and honeycombed with Internal ones; it was, he said, 'practically a mansion', and altogether a very noble fruit of the creative mind of man. It was, he admitted, perhaps almost too good for Hythe; his art had run away with him and produced a modern mansion in the 'best Folkestone style'; it had a central hall with a staircase, a Moorish gallery and Tudor stained-glass window, crenelated battlements to the leading over the portico, an octagonal bulge with octagonal bay windows, surmounted by an oriental dome of metal, lines of yellow bricks to break up the red and many other richnesses and attractions. It was the sort of house, ornate and in its dignified way voluptuous, that a city magnate might build, but it seemed excessive to the Kippses. The first plan had seven bedrooms, the second eight, the third eleven; they had, the architect explained, 'worked in' as if they were pebbles in a mountaineer's boot.

'They're big 'ouses,' said Ann directly the elevations were unrolled.

Kipps listened to the architect with round eyes and an exuberant caution in his manner, anxious not to commit himself further than he had done to the enterprise, and the architect pointed out the Features and other objects of interest with the scalpel belonging to a pocket manicure set that he carried. Ann watched Kipps's face and communicated with him furtively over the architect's head. '*Not so big*,' said Ann's lips.

'It's a bit big for what I meant,' said Kipps, with a reassuring eye on Ann.

'You won't think it big when you see it up,' said the architect; 'you take my word for that.'

'We don't want no more than six bedrooms,' said Kipps.

'Make this one a boxroom, then,' said the architect.

A feeling of impotence silenced Kipps for a time.

'Now which,' said the architect, spreading them out, 'is it to be?'

He flattened down the plans of the most ornate mansion to show it to better effect.

Kipps wanted to know how much each would cost 'at the outside', which

led to much alarmed signalling from Ann. But the architect could estimate only in the most general way.

They were not really committed to anything when the architect went away; Kipps had promised to think it over, that was all.

'We can't 'ave that 'ouse,' said Ann.

'They're miles too big – all of them,' agreed Kipps.

'You'd want –Four servants wouldn't be 'ardly enough,' said Ann.

Kipps went to the hearthrug and spread himself. His tone was almost offhand. 'Nex' time 'e comes,' said Kipps, 'I'll 'splain to him. It isn't at all the sort of thing we want. It's – it's a misunderstanding. You got no occasion to be anxious 'bout it, Ann.'

'I don't see much good reely in building an 'ouse at all,' said Ann.

'Oo, we *got* to build a 'ouse now we begun,' said Kipps. 'But now supposin' we 'ad – '

He spread out the most modest of the three plans and scratched his cheek.

6

It was unfortunate that old Kipps came over the next day.

Old Kipps always produced peculiar states of mind in his nephew, a rash assertiveness, a disposition towards display unlike his usual self. There had been great difficulty in reconciling both the old people to the Pornick *mésalliance*, and at times the controversy echoed in old Kipps's expressed thoughts. This perhaps it was, and no ignoble vanity, that set the note of florid successfulness going in Kipps's conversation whenever his uncle appeared. Mrs Kipps was, as a matter of fact, not reconciled at all; she had declined all invitations to come over on the bus, and was a taciturn hostess on the one occasion when the young people called at the toy shop *en route* for Mrs Pornick. She displayed a tendency to sniff that was clearly due to pride rather than catarrh, and except for telling Ann she hoped she would not feel too 'stuck up' about her marriage, confined her conversation to her nephew or the infinite. The call was a brief one and made up chiefly of pauses, no refreshment was offered or asked for, and Ann departed with a singularly high colour. For some reason she would not call at the toy shop when they found themselves again in New Romney.

But old Kipps, having adventured over and tried the table of the new *ménage* and found it to his taste, showed many signs of softening towards Ann. He came again and then again. He would come over by the bus, and, except when his mouth was absolutely full, he would give his nephew one solid and continuous mass of advice of the most subtle and disturbing description, until it was time to toddle back to the High Street for the afternoon bus. He would walk with him to the sea front, and commence

pourparlers with boatmen for the purchase of one of their boats – 'You ought to keep a boat of your own,' he said, though Kipps was a singularly poor sailor – or he would pursue a plan that was forming in his mind in which he should own and manage what he called 'weekly' property in the less conspicuous streets of Hythe. The cream of that was to be a weekly collection of rents in person, the nearest approach to feudal splendour left in this democratised country. He gave no hint of the source of the capital he designed for this investment and at times it would appear he intended it as an occupation for his nephew rather than himself.

But there remained something in his manner towards Ann, in the glances of scrutiny he gave her unawares, that kept Kipps alertly expansive whenever he was about. And in all sorts of ways. It was on account of old Kipps, for example, that our Kipps plunged one day, a golden plunge, and brought home a box of cummerbundy ninepenny cigars and substituted blue-label Old Methusaleh Four Stars for the common and generally satisfactory white brand.

'Some of this is whisky, my boy,' said old Kipps when he tasted it, smacking critical lips.

'Saw a lot of young officery fellers coming along,' said old Kipps. 'You ought to join the volunteers, my boy, and get to know a few.'

'I dessay I shall,' said Kipps. 'Later.'

'They'd make you an officer, you know, 'n no time. They want officers,' said old Kipps. 'It isn't everyone can afford it. They'd be regular glad to 'ave you . . . Ain't bort a dog yet?'

'Not yet, uncle. 'Ave a segar?'

'Not a moty car?'

'Not yet, uncle.'

'There's no 'urry 'bout that. And don't get one of these 'ere trashy cheap ones when you do get it, my boy. Get one as'll last a lifetime . . . I'm surprised you don't 'ire a bit more.'

'Ann don't seem to fency a moty car,' said Kipps.

'Ah!' said old Kipps, 'I expect not,' and glanced a comment at the door. 'She ain't used to going out,' he said. 'More at 'ome indoors.'

'Fact is,' said Kipps, hastily, 'we're thinking of building a 'ouse.'

'I wouldn't do that, my boy,' began old Kipps, but his nephew was rooting in the cheffonier drawer amidst the plans. He got them in time to check some further comment on Ann. 'Um,' said the old gentleman, a little impressed by the extraordinary odour and the unusual transparency of the tracing paper Kipps put into his hands. 'Thinking of building a 'ouse, are you?'

Kipps began with the most modest of the three projects.

Old Kipps read slowly through his silver-rimmed spectacles: 'Plan of a 'ouse for Arthur Kipps Esquire – Um.'

He didn't warm to the project all at once, and Ann drifted into the room to find him still scrutinising the architect's proposals a little doubtfully.

'We couldn't find a decent 'ouse anywhere,' said Kipps, leaning against the table and assuming an offhand note. 'I didn't see why we shouldn't run up one for ourselves.'

Old Kipps could not help liking the tone of that.

'We thought we might see – ' said Ann.

'It's a spekerlation, of course,' said old Kipps, and held the plan at a distance of two feet or more from his glasses and frowned. 'This isn't exactly the 'ouse I should expect you to 'ave thought of, though,' he said. 'Practically it's a villa. It's the sort of 'ouse a bank clerk might 'ave. 'Tisn't what I should call a gentleman's 'ouse, Artie.'

'It's plain, of course,' said Kipps, standing beside his uncle and looking down at this plan, which certainly did seem a little less magnificent now than it had at the first encounter.

'You mustn't 'ave it too plain,' said old Kipps.

'If it's comfortable – ' Ann hazarded.

Old Kipps glanced at her over his spectacles. 'You ain't comfortable, my gal, in this world, not if you don't live up to your position,' so putting compactly into contemporary English that fine old phrase *noblesse oblige*. 'A 'ouse of this sort is what a retired tradesman might 'ave, or some little whippersnapper of a s'liciter. But *you* – '

'Course that isn't the o'ny plan,' said Kipps, and tried the middle one.

But it was the third one which won over old Kipps. 'Now that's a *'ouse*, my boy,' he said at the sight of it.

Ann came and stood just behind her husband's shoulder while old Kipps expanded upon the desirability of the largest scheme. 'You ought to 'ave a billiard-room,' he said; 'I don't see that, but all the rest's all right. A lot of these 'ere officers 'ere 'ud be glad of a game of billiards . . .

'What's all these dots?' said old Kipps.

'S'rubbery,' said Kipps. 'Flow'ing s'rubs.'

'There's eleven bedrooms in that 'ouse,' said Ann. 'It's a bit of a lot, ain't it, uncle?'

'You'll want 'em, my girl. As you get on, you'll be 'aving visitors. Friends of your 'usband, p'r'aps, from the School of Musketry, what you want 'im to get on with. You can't never tell.'

'If we 'ave a great s'rubbery,' Ann ventured, 'we shall 'ave to keep a gardener.'

'If you don't 'ave a s'rubbery,' said old Kipps, with a note of patient reasoning, ' 'ow are you to prevent every jackanapes that goes by starin' into your drorin'-room winder – p'r'aps when you get someone a bit special to entertain?'

'We ain't *used* to a s'rubbery,' said Ann, mulishly; 'we get on very well 'ere.'

'It isn't what you're used to,' said old Kipps, 'it's what you ought to 'ave now.' And with that Ann dropped out of the discussion.

'Study and lib'ry,' old Kipps read. 'That's right. I see a tantalus the other

day over Brookland, the very thing for a gentleman's study. I'll try and get over and bid for it . . . '

By bus time old Kipps was quite enthusiastic about the house building, and it seemed to be definitely settled that the largest plan was the one decided upon. But Ann had said nothing further in the matter.

7

When Kipps returned from seeing his uncle into the bus – there always seemed a certain doubt whether that portly figure would go into the little red 'Tip-Top' box – he found Ann still standing by the table, looking with an expression of comprehensive disapproval at the three plans.

'There don't seem much the matter with uncle,' said Kipps, assuming the hearthrug, 'spite of 'is 'eartburn. 'E 'opped up them steps like a bird.'

Ann remained staring at the plans.

'You don't like them plans?' hazarded Kipps.

'No, I don't, Artie.'

'We got to build somethin' now.'

'But – it's a gentleman's 'ouse, Artie!'

'It's – it's a decent size, o' course.'

Kipps took a flirting look at the drawing and went to the window.

'Look at the cleanin'. Free servants'll be lost in that 'ouse, Artie.'

'We must 'ave servants,' said Kipps.

Ann looked despondently at her future residence.

'We got to keep up our position, any'ow,' said Kipps, turning towards her. 'It stands to reason, Ann, we got a position. Very well! I can't 'ave you scrubbin' floors. You got to 'ave a servant and you got to manage a 'ouse. You wouldn't 'ave me ashamed – '

Ann opened her lips and did not speak.

'What?' asked Kipps.

'Nothing,' said Ann, 'only I did want it to be a *little* 'ouse, Artie. I wanted it to be a 'andy little 'ouse, jest for us.'

Kipps's face was suddenly flushed and mulish. He took up the curiously smelling tracings again. 'I'm not a-going to be looked down upon,' he said. 'It's not only uncle I'm thinking of!'

Ann stared at him.

Kipps went on. 'I won't 'ave that young Walshingham f'r instance, sneering and sniffling at me. Making out as if we was all wrong. I see 'im yesterday . . . Nor Coote neether. I'm as good – we're as good – whatever's 'appened.'

Silence and the rustle of plans.

He looked up and saw Ann's eyes bright with tears. For a moment the two stared at one another.

'We'll 'ave the big 'ouse,' said Ann, with a gulp. 'I didn't think of that, Artie.'

Her aspect was fierce and resolute, and she struggled with emotion. 'We'll 'ave the big 'ouse,' she repeated. 'They shan't say I dragged you down wiv' me – none of them shan't say that. I've thought – I've always been afraid of that.'

Kipps looked again at the plan, and suddenly the grand house had become very grand indeed. He blew.

'No, Artie, none of them shan't say that,' and with something blind in her motions, Ann tried to turn the plan round to her . . .

After all, Kipps thought, there might be something to say for the milder project . . . But he had gone so far that now he did not know how to say it.

And so the plans went out to the builders, and in a little while Kipps was committed to two thousand five hundred pounds' worth of building. But then, you know, he had an income of twelve hundred a year.

8

It is extraordinary what minor difficulties cluster about house building.

'I say, Ann,' remarked Kipps one day, 'we shall 'ave to call this little 'ouse by a name. I was thinking of 'Ome Cottage. But I dunno whether 'Ome Cottage is quite the thing like. All these little fishermen's places are called Cottages.'

'I like "Cottage",' said Ann.

'It's got eleven bedrooms, y'see,' said Kipps. 'I don't see 'ow you can call it a cottage with more bedrooms than four. Prop'ly speaking, it's a Large Villa. Prop'ly, it's almost a Big 'Ouse. Leastways a 'Ouse.'

'Well,' said Ann, 'if you must call it Villa – Home Villa . . . I wish it wasn't.'

Kipps meditated.

' 'Ow about Eureka Villa?' he said, raising his voice.

'What's Eureka?'

'It's a name,' he said. 'There used to be Eureka Dress Fasteners. There's lots of names, come to think of it, to be got out of a shop. There's Pyjama Villa. I remember that in the hosiery. No, come to think, that wouldn't do. But Maraposa – sort of oatmeal cloth, that was . . . No! Eureka's better.'

Ann meditated. 'It seems silly like to 'ave a name that don't mean much.'

'Perhaps it does,' said Kipps. 'Though it's what people 'ave to do.'

He became meditative. 'I got it!' he cried.

'Not Oreeka!' said Ann.

'No! There used to be a 'ouse at Hastings opposite our school – quite a big 'ouse it was – St Ann's. Now *that* –'

'No,' said Mrs Kipps with decision. 'Thanking you kindly, but I won't have no butcher boys making game of me . . . '

They consulted Carshot, who suggested, after some days of reflection, Waddycombe, as a graceful reminder of Kipps's grandfather; old Kipps, who was for 'Upton Manor House', where he had once been second footman; Buggins, who favoured either a stern simple number, 'Number One' – if there were no other houses there – or something patriotic, as 'Empire Villa'; and Pierce, who inclined to 'Sandringham'; but in spite of all this help they were still undecided when, amidst violent perturbations of the soul, and after the most complex and difficult hagglings, wranglings, fears, muddles and goings to and fro, Kipps became the joyless owner of a freehold plot of three-eighths of an acre, and saw the turf being wheeled away from the site that should one day be his home.

CHAPTER TWO

The Callers

The Kippses sat at their midday dinner-table amidst the vestiges of rhubarb pie and discussed two postcards the one o'clock post had brought. It was a rare bright moment of sunshine in a wet and windy day in the March that followed their marriage. Kipps was attired in a suit of brown, with a tie of fashionable green, while Ann wore one of those picturesque loose robes that are usually associated with sandals and advanced ideas. But there weren't any sandals on Ann or any advanced ideas, and the robe had come quite recently through the counsels of Mrs Sid Pornick. 'It's Art-like,' said Kipps, but giving way. 'It's more comfortable,' said Ann. The room looked out by French windows upon a little patch of green and the Hythe parade. The parade was all shiny wet with rain, and the green-grey sea tumbled and tumbled between parade and sky.

The Kippes's furniture, except for certain chromo-lithographs of Kipps's incidental choice that struck a quiet note amidst the wallpaper, had been tactfully forced by an expert salesman, and it was in a style of mediocre elegance. There was a sideboard of carved oak that had only one fault, it reminded Kipps at times of wood-carving, and its panel of bevelled glass now reflected the back of his head. On its shelf were two books from Parsons' Library, each with a 'place' marked by a slip of paper; neither of the Kippses could have told you the title of either book they read, much less the author's name. There was an ebonised overmantel set with phials and pots of brilliant colour, each duplicated by looking-glass, and bearing also a pair of Chinese jars made in Birmingham, a wedding present from Mr and Mrs Sidney Pornick, and several sumptuous Japanese fans. And there was a Turkey carpet of great richness. In addition to these modern exploits of

Messrs Bunt and Bubble, there were two inactive tall clocks, whose extreme dilapidation appealed to the connoisseur; a terrestrial and a celestial globe, the latter deeply indented; a number of good old iron-moulded and dusty books; and a stuffed owl wanting one (easily replaceable) glass eye, obtained by the exertions of Uncle Kipps. The table equipage was as much as possible like Mrs Bindon Botting's, only more costly, and in addition there were green and crimson wine glasses – though the Kippses never drank wine.

Kipps turned to the more legible of his two postcards again.

' "Unavoidably prevented from seein' me today", 'e says. I like 'is cheek. After I give 'im 'is start and everything.'

He blew.

' 'E certainly treats you a bit orf'and,' said Ann.

Kipps gave vent to his dislike of young Walshingham. 'He's getting too big for 'is britches,' he said. 'I'm beginning to wish she *'ad* brought an action for breach. Ever since 'e said she wouldn't, 'e's seemed to think I've got no right to spend my own money.'

' 'E's never liked your building the 'ouse,' said Ann.

Kipps displayed wrath. 'What the goodness 'as it got to do wiv' 'im? Overman indeed!' he added. 'Overmantel! . . . 'E tries that on with me, I'll tell 'im something 'e won't like.'

He took up the second card. 'Dashed if I can read a word of it. I can jest make out Chit'low at the end and that's all.'

He scrutinised it. 'It's like someone in a fit writing. This here might be w-h-a-t – *what*. P-r-i-c-e – *I* got it! What price Harry now? It was a sort of saying of 'is. I expect 'e's either done something or not done something towards starting that play, Ann.'

'I expect that's about it,' said Ann.

Kipps grunted with effort. 'I can't read the rest,' he said at last, 'nohow.'

A thoroughly annoying post. He pitched the card on the table, stood up and went to the window, where Ann, after a momentary reconnaissance at Chitterlow's hieroglyphics, came to join him.

'Wonder what I shall do this afternoon,' said Kipps, with his hands deep in his pockets.

He produced and lit a cigarette.

'Go for a walk, I s'pose,' said Ann.

'I *been* for a walk this morning . . . S'pose I must go for another,' he added, after an interval.

They regarded the windy waste of sea for a space.

'Wonder why it is 'e won't see me,' said Kipps, returning to the problem of young Walshingham. 'It's all lies about 'is being too busy.'

Ann offered no solution.

'Rain again!' said Kipps, as the lash of the little drops stung the window.

'Oo, bother!' said Kipps, 'you got to do something. Look 'ere, Ann! I'll go orf for a reg'lar tramp through the rain, up by Saltwood, round by

Newington, over the camp, and so round and back, and see 'ow they're getting on about the 'ouse. See? And look 'ere! You get Gwendolen to go out a bit before I come back. If it's still rainy, she can easy go round and see 'er sister. Then we'll 'ave a bit of tea, with teacake – all buttery, see? Toce it ourselves, p'r'aps. Eh?'

'I dessay I can find something to do in the 'ouse,' said Ann, considering. 'You'll take your mackintosh and leggin's, I s'pose. You'll get wet without your mackintosh over those roads.'

'Righ-o,' said Kipps, and went to ask Gwendolen for his brown leggings and his other pair of boots.

2

Things conspired to demoralise Kipps that afternoon.

When he got outside the house everything looked so wet under the drive of the south-wester that he abandoned the prospect of the clay lanes towards Newington altogether, and turned east to Folkestone along the Seabrook digue. His mackintosh flapped about him, the rain stung his cheek; for a time he felt a hardy man. And then as abruptly the rain ceased and the wind fell, and before he was through Sandgate High Street it was a bright spring day. And there was Kipps in his mackintosh and squeaky leggings, looking like a fool!

Inertia carried him another mile to the Leas, and there the whole world was pretending there had never been such a thing as rain – ever. There wasn't a cloud in the sky; except for an occasional puddle the asphalt paths looked as dry as a bone. A smartly dressed man in one of those overcoats that look like ordinary cloth and are really most deceitfully and unfairly waterproof, passed him and glanced at the stiff folds of his mackintosh. 'Demn!' said Kipps. His mackintosh swished against his leggings, his leggings piped and whistled over his boot-tops.

'Why do I never get anything right?' Kipps asked of a bright implacable universe.

Nice old ladies passed him, refined people with tidy umbrellas, bright, beautiful, supercilious-looking children. Of course! the right thing for such a day as this was a light overcoat and an umbrella. A child might have known that. He had them at home, but how could one explain that? He decided to turn down by the Harvey monument and escape through Clifton Gardens towards the hills. And thereby he came upon Coote.

He already felt the most abject and propitiatory of social outcasts when he came upon Coote, and Coote finished him. He passed within a yard of Coote. Coote was coming along towards the Leas, and when Kipps saw him his legs hesitated about their office and he seemed to himself to stagger about all over the footpath. At the sight of him Coote started visibly. Then

a sort of *rigor vitae* passed through his frame, his jaw protruded and errant bubbles of air seemed to escape and run about beneath his loose skin. (Seemed, I say – I am perfectly well aware that there is really connective tissue in Coote as in all of us to prevent anything of the sort.) His eyes fixed themselves on the horizon and glazed. As he went by Kipps could hear his even, resolute breathing. He went by, and Kipps staggered on into a universe of dead cats and dust heaps, rind and ashes – *cut!*

It was part of the inexorable decrees of Providence that almost immediately afterwards the residuum of Kipps had to pass a very, very long and observant-looking girls' school.

Kipps recovered consciousness again on the road between Shorncliffe Station and Cheriton, though he cannot remember, indeed to this day he has never attempted to remember, how he got there. And he was back at certain thoughts suggested by his last night's novel reading that linked up directly with the pariah-like emotions of these last encounters. The novel lay at home upon the chiffonier; it was one of society and politics – there is no need whatever to give the title or name the author – written with a heavy-handed thoroughness that overrode any possibility of resistance on the part of the Kipps mind. It had crushed all his poor little edifice of ideals, his dreams of a sensible, unassuming existence, of snugness, of not caring what people said and all the rest of it, to dust; it had reinstated, squarely and strongly again, the only proper conception of English social life. There was a character in the book who trifled with Art, who was addicted to reading French novels, who dressed in a loose, careless way, who was a sorrow to his dignified, silvery-haired, politico-religious mother, and met the admonitions of bishops with a front of brass. He treated a 'nice girl', to whom they had got him engaged, badly; he married beneath him – some low thing or other. And sank –

Kipps could not escape the application of the case. He was enabled to see how this sort of thing looked to decent people; he was enabled to gauge the measure of the penalties due. His mind went from that to the frozen marble of Coote's visage.

He deserved it!

That day of remorse! Later it found him coming upon the site of his building operations and surveying the disorder of preparation in a mood near to despair, his mackintosh over his arm.

Hardly anyone was at work that day – no doubt the builders were having him in some obscure manner – and the whole place seemed a dismal and depressing litter. The builder's shed, black-lettered WILKINS, BUILDER, HYTHE, looked like a stranded thing amidst a cast-up disorder of wheel-barrows and wheeling planks, and earth and sand and bricks. The foundations of the walls were trenches full of damp concrete, drying in patches; the rooms – it was incredible they could ever be rooms – were shaped out as squares and oblongs of coarse wet grass and sorrel. They looked absurdly

small – dishonestly small. What could you expect? Of course the builders were having him, building too small, building all wrong, using bad materials! Old Kipps had told him a wrinkle or two. The builders were having him, young Walshingham was having him, everybody was having him! They were having him and laughing at him because they didn't respect him. They didn't respect him because he couldn't do things right. Who could respect him . . . ?

He was an outcast, he had no place in the society of mankind. He had had his chance in the world and turned his back on it. He had 'behaved badly' – that was the phrase . . .

Here a great house was presently to arise, a house to be paid for, a house neither he nor Ann could manage – with eleven bedrooms, and four disrespectful servants having them all the time!

How had it all happened exactly?

This was the end of his great fortune! What a chance he had had! If he had really carried out his first intentions and stuck to things, how much better everything might have been! If he had got a tutor – that had been in his mind originally – a special sort of tutor to show him everything right; a tutor for gentlemen of neglected education. If he had read more and attended better to what Coote had said!

Coote, who had just cut him!

Eleven bedrooms! What had possessed him? No one would ever come to see them, no one would ever have anything to do with them. Even his aunt cut him! His uncle treated him with a half-contemptuous sufferance. He had not a friend worth counting in the world! Buggins, Carshot, Pierce – shop assistants! The Pornicks – a low socialist lot! He stood among his foundations like a lonely figure among ruins; he stood among the ruins of his future, and owned himself a foolish and mistaken man. He saw himself and Ann living out their shameful lives in this great crazy place – as it would be – with everybody laughing secretly at them and their eleven bedrooms, and nobody approaching them – nobody nice and right that is, for ever. And Ann!

What was the matter with Ann? She'd given up going for walks lately, got touchy and tearful, been fitful with her food. Just when she didn't ought to. It was all a part of the judgement upon wrongdoing, it was all part of the social penalties that Juggernaut of a novel had brought home to his mind.

3

He let himself in with his latchkey. He went moodily into the dining-room and got out the plans to look at them. He had a vague hope that there would prove to be only ten bedrooms. But he found there were still eleven. He became aware of Ann standing over him. 'Look 'ere, Artie!' said Ann.

He looked up and found her holding a number of white oblongs. His eyebrows rose.

'It's Callers,' said Ann.

He put his plans aside slowly and took and read the cards in silence, with a sort of solemnity. Callers! Then perhaps he wasn't to be left out of the world after all. Mrs G. Porrett Smith, Miss Porrett Smith, Miss Mabel Porrett Smith, and two smaller cards of the Revd G. Porrett Smith. 'Lor'!' he said. '*Clergy!*'

'There was a lady,' said Ann, 'and two growed-up gals – all dressed up!'

'And 'im?'

'There wasn't no '*im*.'

'Not – ?' He held out the little cards.

'No; there was a lady and two young ladies.'

'But – these cards! Wad they go and leave these two little cards with the Revd G. Smith on for? Not if 'e wasn't with 'em.'

' 'E wasn't with 'em.'

'Not a little chap – dodgin' about be'ind the others? And didn't come in?'

'I didn't see no gentleman with them at all,' said Ann.

'Rum!' said Kipps. A half-forgotten experience came back to him. '*I* know,' he said, waving the reverend gentleman's card; ' 'e give 'em the slip, that's what he'd done. Gone off while they was rapping before you let 'em in. It's a fair call, any'ow.' He felt a momentary base satisfaction at his absence. 'What did they talk about, Ann?'

There was a pause. 'I didn't let 'em in,' said Ann.

He looked up suddenly and perceived that something unusual was the matter with Ann. Her face was flushed, her eyes were red and hard.

'Didn't let 'em in?'

'No! They didn't come in at all.'

He was too astonished for words.

'I answered the door,' said Ann; 'I'd been upstairs 'namelling the floor. 'Ow was I to think about Callers, Artie? We ain't never 'ad Callers all the time we been 'ere. I'd sent Gwendolen out for a bref of fresh air, and there I was upstairs 'namelling that floor she done so bad, so's to get it done before she came back. I thought I'd 'namel that floor and then get tea and 'ave it quiet with you, toce and all, before she came back. 'Ow was I to think about Callers?'

She paused. 'Well,' said Kipps, 'what then?'

'They came and rapped. 'Ow was I to know? I thought it was a tradesman or something. Never took my apron off, never wiped the 'namel off my 'ands – nothing. There they was!'

She paused again. She was getting to the disagreeable part.

'Wad they say?' said Kipps.

'She says, "Is Mrs Kipps at home?" See? To me.'

'Yes.'

'And me all painty and no cap on and nothing, neither missis nor servant like. There, Artie, I could 'a sunk through the floor with shame, I really

could. I could 'ardly get my voice. I couldn't think of nothing to say but just, "Not at 'Ome," and out of 'abit like I 'eld the tray. And they give me the cards and went, and 'ow I shall ever look that lady in the face again I don't know . . . And that's all about it, Artie! They looked me up and down, they did, and then I shut the door on 'em.'

'Goo!' said Kipps.

Ann went and poked the fire needlessly with a passion-quivering hand.

'I wouldn't 'ave 'ad that 'appen for five pounds,' said Kipps. 'A clergyman and all!'

Ann dropped the poker into the fender with some *éclat* and stood up and looked at her hot face in the glass. Kipps's disappointment grew. 'You did ought to 'ave known better than that, Ann! You reely did.'

He sat forward, cards in hand, with a deepening sense of social disaster. The plates were laid upon the table, toast sheltered under a cover at mid-fender, the teapot warmed beside it, and the kettle, just lifted from the hob, sang amidst the coals. Ann glanced at him for a moment, then stooped with the kettle-holder to wet the tea.

'Tcha!' said Kipps, with his mental state developing.

'I don't see it's any use getting in a state about it now,' said Ann.

'Don't you? I do. See? 'Ere's these people, good people, want to 'sociate with us, and 'ere you go and slap 'em in the face!'

'I didn't slap 'em in the face.'

'You do – practically. You slams the door in their face, and that's all we see of 'em ever. I wouldn't 'ave 'ad this 'appen not for a ten-pound note.'

He rounded his regrets with a grunt. For a while there was silence, save for the little stir of Ann's movements preparing the tea.

'Tea, Artie,' said Ann, handing him a cup.

Kipps took it.

'I put sugar *once*,' said Ann.

'Oo, dash it! Oo cares?' said Kipps, taking an extraordinarily large additional lump with fury-quivering fingers, and putting his cup with a slight excess of force on the recess cupboard. 'Oo cares?

'I wouldn't 'ave 'ad that 'appen,' he said, bidding steadily against accomplished things, 'for twenty pounds.'

He gloomed in silence through a long minute or so. Then Ann said the fatal thing that exploded him. 'Artie!' she said.

'What?'

'There's Buttud Toce down there! By your foot!' There was a pause, husband and wife regarded one another.

'Buttud Toce!' he said. 'You go and mess up them callers and then you try and stuff me up with Buttud Toce! Buttud Toce indeed! 'Ere's our first chance of knowing anyone that's at all fit to 'sociate with –Look 'ere, Ann! Tell you what it is – you got to return that call.'

'Return that call!'

'Yes, you got to return that call. That's what you got to do! I know – ' He waved his arm vaguely towards the miscellany of books in the recess. 'It's in *Manners and Rools of Good S'ity*. You got to find jest 'ow many cards to leave and you got to go and leave 'em. See?'

Ann's face expressed terror. 'But, Artie, 'ow *can* I?'

' 'Ow *can* you? 'Ow *could* you? You got to do it, any'ow. They won't know you – not in your Bond Street 'at! If they do, they won't say nothing.'

His voice assumed a note of entreaty. 'You mus', Ann.'

'I can't.'

'You mus'.'

'I can't and I won't. Anything in reason I'll do, but face those people again I can't – after what 'as 'appened.'

'You won't?'

'No!'

'So there they go – orf! And we never see them again! And so it goes on! So it goes on! We don't know nobody and we *shan't* know anybody! And you won't put yourself out not a little bit, or take the trouble to find out anything 'ow it ought to be done.'

Terrible pause.

'I never ought to 'ave married you, Artie, that's the troof.'

'Oh! *don't* go into that.'

'I never ought to 'ave married you, Artie. I'm not equal to the position. If you 'adn't said you'd drown yourself – ' She choked.

'I don' see why you shouldn't *try*, Ann. *I've* improved. Why don't you? 'Stead of which you go sending out the servant and 'namelling floors, and then when visitors come – '

' 'Ow was *I* to know about y'r old visitors?' cried Ann in a wail, and suddenly got up and fled from amidst their ruined tea, the tea of which 'toce, all buttery' was to be the crown and glory.

Kipps watched her with a momentary consternation. Then he hardened his heart. 'Ought to 'ave known better,' he said, 'goin' on like that!' He remained for a space rubbing his knees and muttering. He emitted scornfully: 'I carn't an' I won't.' He saw her as the source of all his shames.

Presently, quite mechanically, he stooped down and lifted the flowery china cover. 'Ter dash 'er Buttud Toce!' he shouted at the sight of it, and clapped the cover down again hard –

When Gwendolen came back she perceived things were in a slightly unusual poise. Kipps sat by the fire in a rigid attitude reading a casually selected volume of the *Encyclopaedia Britannica*, and Ann was upstairs and inaccessible – to reappear at a later stage with reddened eyes. Before the fire and still in a perfectly assimilable condition was what was evidently an untouched supply of richly buttered toast under a cracked cover.

'They've 'ad a bit of a tiff,' said Gwendolen, attending to her duties in

the kitchen, with her outdoor hat still on and her mouth full. 'They're rummuns – if ever! My eye!'

And she took another piece of Ann's generously buttered toast.

4

The Kippses spoke no more that day to one another.

The squabble about cards and buttered toast was as serious to them as the most rational of differences. It was all rational to them. Their sense of wrong burnt within them; their sense of what was owing to themselves, the duty of implacability, the obstinacy of pride. In the small hours Kipps lay awake at the nadir of unhappiness and came near groaning. He saw life as an extraordinarily desolating muddle: his futile house, his social discredit, his bad behaviour to Helen, his low marriage to Ann . . .

He became aware of something irregular in Ann's breathing –

He listened. She was awake and quietly and privately sobbing!

He hardened his heart; resolutely he hardened his heart.

And presently Ann lay still.

5

The stupid little tragedies of these clipped and limited lives!

What is the good of keeping up the idyllic sham and pretending that ill-educated, misdirected people 'get along very well', and that all this is harmlessly funny and nothing more? You think I'm going to write fat, silly, grinning novels about half-educated, under-trained people and keep it up all the time, that the whole thing's nothing but funny!

As I think of them lying unhappily there in the darkness, my vision pierces the night. See what I can see! Above them, brooding over them, I tell you, there is a monster, a lumpish monster, like some great, clumsy griffin thing, like the Crystal Palace labyrinthodon, like Coote, like the leaden goddess of *The Dunciad*, like some fat, proud flunkey, like pride, like indolence, like all that is darkening and heavy and obstructive in life. It is matter and darkness, it is the anti-soul, it is the ruling power of this land, Stupidity. My Kippses live in its shadow. Shalford and his apprenticeship system, the Hastings Academy, the ideas of Coote, the ideas of the old Kippses, all the ideas that have made Kipps what he is, all these are a part of its shadow. But for that monster they might not be groping among false ideas and hurt one another so sorely; but for that, the glowing promise of childhood and youth might have had a happier fruition, thought might have awakened in them to meet the thought of the world, the quickening sunshine of literature pierced to the substance of their souls, their lives

might not have been divorced, as now they are divorced, from the apprehension of beauty that we favoured ones are given – the vision of the Grail that makes life fine for ever. I have laughed, and I laugh at these two people; I have sought to make you laugh . . .

But I see through the darkness the souls of my Kippses as they are, as little pink strips of quivering living stuff, as things like the bodies of little, ill-nourished, ailing, ignorant children, children who feel pain, who are naughty and muddled and suffer and do not understand why. And the claw of this Beast rests upon them!

CHAPTER THREE

Terminations

Next morning came a remarkable telegram from Folkestone. 'Please come at once, urgent, Walshingham,' said the telegram, and Kipps, after an agitated but still ample breakfast, departed . . .

When he returned his face was very white and his countenance disordered. He let himself in with his latchkey and came into the dining-room where Ann sat, affecting to work at a little thing she called a bib. She heard his hat fall in the hall before he entered, as though he had missed the peg. 'I got something to tell you, Ann,' he said, disregarding their overnight quarrel, and went to the hearthrug and took hold of the mantel, and stared at Ann as though the sight of her was novel.

'Well?' said Ann, not looking up and working a little faster.

' 'E's gone!'

Ann looked up sharply and her hands stopped. '*Who*'s gone?'

For the first time she perceived Kipps's pallor.

'Young Walshingham – I saw 'er and she tole me.'

'Gone? What d'you mean?'

'Cleared out! Gone off for good!'

'What for?'

'For 'is 'ealth,' said Kipps, with sudden bitterness. ' 'E's been speckylating. He's speckylated our money and 'e's speckylated their money, and now 'e's took 'is 'ook. That's all about it, Ann.'

'You mean – ?'

'I mean 'e's orf and our twenty-four thousand's orf too! And 'ere we are! Smashed up! That's all about it, Ann.' He panted.

Ann had no vocabulary for such an occasion. 'Oh, Lor'!' she said, and sat still.

Kipps came about and stuck his hands deeply in his trouser pockets. 'Speckylated every penny – lorst it all – and gorn.'

Even his lips were white.

'You mean we ain't got nothin' left, Artie?'

'Not a penny! Not a bloomin' penny, Ann. No!'

A gust of passion whirled across the soul of Kipps. He flung out a knuckly fist. 'If I 'ad 'im 'ere,' he said, 'I'd – I'd – I'd wring 'is neck for 'im. I'd – I'd – ' His voice rose to a shout. He thought of Gwendolen in the kitchen and fell to, 'Ugh!'

'But, Artie,' said Ann, trying to grasp it, 'd'you mean to say he's took our money?'

'Speckylated it!' said Kipps, with an illustrative flourish of the arm that failed to illustrate. 'Bort things dear and sold 'em cheap, and played the 'anky-panky jackass with everything we got. That's what I mean 'e's done, Ann.' He repeated this last sentence with the addition of violent adverbs.

'D'you mean to say our money's *gone*, Artie?'

'Ter dash it, *Yes*, Ann!' swore Kipps, exploding in a shout. 'Ain't I tellin' you?'

He was immediately sorry. 'I didn't mean to 'oller at you, Ann,' he said, 'but I'm all shook up. I don't 'ardly know what I'm sayin'. Ev'ry penny.' . . .

'But, Artie – '

Kipps grunted. He went to the window and stared for a moment at a sunlit sea. 'Gord!' he swore.

'I mean,' he said, coming back to Ann and with an air of exasperation, 'that he's 'bezzled and 'ooked it. That's what I mean, Ann.'

Ann put down the bib. 'But wot are we going to *do*, Artie?'

Kipps indicated ignorance, wrath and despair with one comprehensive gesture of his hands. He caught an ornament from the mantel and replaced it. 'I'm going to bang about,' he said, 'if I ain't precious careful.'

'You saw 'er, you say?'

'Yes.'

'What did she say 'xactly?' said Ann.

'Told me to see a s'licitor – tole me to get someone to 'elp me at once. She was there in black – like she used to be – and speaking cool and careful-like. 'Elen! . . . She's precious 'ard, is 'Elen. She looked at me straight. "It's my fault," she said, "I ought to 'ave warned you . . . Only under the circumstances it was a little difficult." Straight as anything. I didn't 'ardly say anything to 'er. I didn't seem to begin to take it in until she was showing me out. I 'adn't anything to say. Jest as well, perhaps. She talked – like a Call a'most. She said – what *was* it she said about her mother? "My mother's overcome with grief," she said, "so naturally everything comes on me." '

'And she told you to get someone to 'elp you?'

'Yes. I been to old Bean.'

'O' Bean?'

'Yes. What I took my business away from!'

'What did he say?'

'He was a bit off 'and at first, but then 'e come round. He couldn't tell me

anything till 'e knew the facts. What I know of young Walshingham, there won't be much 'elp in the facts. No!'

He reflected for a space. 'It's a smash-up, Ann. More likely than not, Ann, 'e's left us over'ead in debt. We got to get out of it just 'ow we can . . .

'We got to begin again,' he went on. ''*Ow*, I don't know. All the way 'ome my 'ead's been going. We got to get a living some'ow or other. 'Aving time to ourselves, and a bit of money to spend, and no hurry and worry, it's all over for ever, Ann. We was fools, Ann. We didn't know our benefits. We been caught. Gord! . . . Gord!'

He was on the verge of 'banging about' again.

They heard a jingle in the passage, the large soft impact of a servant's indoor boots. As if she were a part, a mitigatory part, of Fate, came Gwendolen to lay the midday meal. Kipps displayed self-control forthwith. Ann picked up the hib again and bent over it, and the Kippses bore themselves gloomily perhaps, but not despairfully, while their dependant was in the room. She spread the cloth and put out the cutlery with a slow inaccuracy, and Kipps, after a whisper to himself, went again to the window. Ann got up and put away her work methodically in the chiffonier.

'When I think,' said Kipps, as soon as the door closed again behind Gwendolen, 'when I think of the ole people and 'aving to tell 'em of it all – I want to smesh my 'ead against the nearest wall. Smesh my silly brains out! And Buggins – Buggins what I'd 'arf promised to start in a lill' outfitting shop in Rendezvous Street.' . . .

Gwendolen returned and restored dignity.

The midday meal spread itself slowly before them. Gwendolen, after her custom, left the door open and Kipps closed it carefully before sitting down.

He stood for a moment, regarding the meal doubtfully.

'I don't feel as if I could swaller a moufful,' he said.

'You got to eat,' said Ann . . .

For a time they said little, and once swallowing was achieved, ate on with a sort of melancholy appetite. Each was now busy thinking.

'After all,' said Kipps, presently, 'whatever 'appens, they can't turn us out or sell us up before nex' quarter-day. I'm pretty sure about that.'

'Sell us up!' said Ann.

'I dessey we're bankrup',' said Kipps, trying to say it easily and helping himself with a trembling hand to unnecessary potatoes.

Then a long silence. Ann ceased to eat, and there were silent tears.

'More potatoes, Artie?' choked Ann.

'I couldn't,' said Kipps. 'No.'

He pushed back his plate, which was indeed replete with potatoes, got up and walked about the room. Even the dinner-table looked distraught and unusual.

'What to do, I *don't* know,' he said.

'Oh, *Lord!*' he ejaculated, and picked up and slapped down a book.

Then his eye fell upon another postcard that had come from Chitterlow by the morning's post, and which now lay by him on the mantelshelf. He took it up, glanced at its imperfectly legible message, and put it down.

'Delayed!' he said, scornfully. 'Not prodooced in the smalls. Or is it smells 'e says? 'Ow can one understand that? Any'ow 'e's 'umbugging again . . . Somefing about the Strand. No! Well, 'e's 'ad all the money 'e'll ever get out of me! . . . I'm done.'

He seemed to find a momentary relief in the dramatic effect of his announcement. He came near to a swagger of despair upon the hearthrug, and then suddenly came and sat down next to Ann and rested his chin on the knuckles of his two clenched hands.

'I been a fool, Ann,' he said in a gloomy monotone. 'I been a brasted fool. But it's 'ard on us, all the same. It's 'ard.'

' 'Ow was you to know?' said Ann.

'I ought to 'ave known. I did in a sort of way know. And 'ere we are! I wouldn't care so much if it was myself, but it's *you*, Ann! 'Ere we are! Regular smashed up! And you – ' He checked at an unspeakable aggravation of their disaster. 'I knew 'e wasn't to be depended upon and there I left it! And you got to pay . . . What's to 'appen to us all, I don't know.'

He thrust out his chin and glared at fate.

' 'Ow do you know 'e's speckylated everything?' said Ann, after a silent survey of him.

' 'E 'as,' said Kipps, irritably, holding firm to disaster.

'She say so?'

'She don't know, of course, but you depend upon it that's it. She told me she knew something was on, and when she found 'im gone and a note lef' for her she knew it was up with 'im. 'E went by the night boat. She wrote that telegrarf off to me straight away.'

Ann surveyed his features with tender, perplexed eyes; she had never seen him so white and drawn before, and her hand rested an inch or so away from his arm. The actual loss was still, as it were, afar from her. The immediate thing was his enormous distress.

' 'Ow do you know – ?' she said and stopped. It would irritate him too much.

Kipps's imagination was going headlong.

'Sold up!' he emitted presently, and Ann flinched. 'Going back to work, day after day – I can't stand it, Ann, I can't. And you – '

'It don't do to think of it,' said Ann.

Presently he came upon a resolve. 'I keep on thinking of it, and thinking of it, and what's to be done and what's to be done. I shan't be any good 'ome s'arfernoon. It keeps on going round and round in my 'ead, and round and round. I better go for a walk or something. I'd be no comfort to you, Ann. I should want to 'owl and 'ammer things if I 'ung about 'ome. My fingers 'rall

atwitch. I shall keep on thinking 'ow I might 'ave stopped it and callin' myself a fool . . . '

He looked at her between pleading and shame. It seemed like deserting her.

Ann regarded him with tear-dimmed eyes.

'You'd better do what's good for you, Artie,' she said . . . '*I'll* be best cleaning. It's no use sending off Gwendolen before her month, and the top room wants turning out.' She added with a sort of grim humour: 'May as well turn it out now while I got it.'

'I *better* go for a walk,' said Kipps . . .

And presently our poor exploded Kipps was marching out to bear his sudden misery. Habit turned him up the road towards his growing house, and then suddenly he perceived his direction – 'Oh, Lor'!' – and turned aside and went up the steep way to the hill crest and the Sandling Road, and over the line by that tree-embowered Junction, and athwart the wide fields towards Postling – a little, black, marching figure – and so up the Downs and over the hills, whither he had never gone before . . .

2

He came back long after dark, and Ann met him in the passage.

'Where you been, Artie?' she asked, with a strained note in her voice.

'I been walking and walking – trying to tire myself out. All the time I been thinking what shall I do? Trying to fix something up all out of nothing.'

'I didn't know you meant to be out all this time.'

Kipps was gripped by compunction . . .

'I can't think what we ought to do,' he said, presently.

'You can't do anything much, Artie, not till you hear from Mr Bean.'

'No; I can't do anything much. That's jest it. And all this time I keep feelin' if I don't do something the top of my 'ead'll bust . . . Been trying to make up advertisements 'arf the time I been out – 'bout finding a place; good salesman and stock-keeper, and good Manchester dresses, window-dressing – Lor'! Fancy that all beginning again! . . . If you went to stay with Sid a bit – if I sent every penny I got to you – I dunno! I dunno!'

When they had gone to bed there was an elaborate attempt to get to sleep . . . In one of their great waking pauses Kipps remarked in a muffled tone: 'I didn't mean to frighten you, Ann, being out so late. I kep' on walking and walking, and some'ow it seemed to do me good. I went out to the 'illtop ever so far beyond Stanford, and sat there ever so long, and it seemed to make me better. Just looking over the Marsh like, and seeing the sun set . . . '

'Very likely,' said Ann, after a long interval, 'it isn't so bad as you think it is, Artie.'

'It's bad,' said Kipps.

'Very likely, after all, it isn't quite so bad. If there's only a little – '

There came another long silence.

'Ann,' said Kipps in the quiet darkness.

'Yes,' said Ann.

'Ann,' said Kipps, and stopped as though he had hastily shut a door upon speech.

'I kep' thinking,' he said, trying again, 'I kep' thinking – after all – I been cross with you and a fool about things – about them cards, Ann; but' – his voice shook to pieces – 'we 'ave been 'appy, Ann . . . some'ow . . . togever.'

And with that he and then she fell into a passion of weeping. They clung very tightly together – closer than they had been since ever the first brightness of their married days turned to the grey of common life again.

All the disaster in the world could not prevent their going to sleep at last with their poor little troubled heads close together on one pillow. There was nothing more to be done, there was nothing more to be thought. Time might go on with his mischiefs, but for a little while at least they still had one another.

3

Kipps returned from his second interview with Mr Bean in a state of strange excitement. He let himself in with his latchkey and slammed the door.

'Ann!' he shouted, in an unusual note; 'Ann!'

Ann replied distantly.

'Something to tell you,' said Kipps; 'something noo!'

Ann appeared apprehensive from the kitchen.

'Ann,' he said, going before her into the little dining-room, for his news was too dignified for the passage, 'very likely, Ann, o' Bean says, we shall 'ave – ' He decided to prolong the suspense. 'Guess!'

'I can't, Artie.'

'Think of a lot of money!'

'A 'undred pounds p'r'aps?'

He spoke with immense deliberation. '*Over a fousand pounds!*'

Ann stared and said nothing, only went a shade whiter.

'Over, he said. A'most certainly over.'

He shut the dining-room door and came forward hastily, for Ann, it was clear, meant to take this mitigation of their disaster with a complete abandonment of her self-control. She came near flopping; she fell into his arms.

'Artie,' she got to at last and began to weep, clinging tightly to him.

'Pretty near certain,' said Kipps, holding her. 'A fousand pounds!'

'I *said*, Artie,' she wailed on his shoulder with the note of accumulated wrongs, 'very likely it wasn't so bad . . . '

'There's things,' he said, when presently he came to particulars, ' 'e couldn't touch. The noo place! It's freehold and paid for, and with the bit of building on it, there's five or six 'undred pound p'r'aps – say worf free 'undred, for safety. We can't be sold up to finish it, like we thought. O' Bean says we can very likely sell it and get money. 'E says you often get a chance to sell a 'ouse lessen 'arf done, specially free'old. *Very* likely, 'e say. Then there's Hughenden. Hughenden 'asn't been mortgaged not for more than 'arf its value. There's a 'undred or so to be got on that, and the furniture and the rent for the summer still coming in. 'E says there's very likely other things. A fousand pounds, that's what 'e said. 'E said it might even be more . . . '

They were sitting now at the table.

'It alters everything,' said Ann.

'I been thinking that, Ann, all the way 'ome. I came in the motor car. First ride I've 'ad since the smash. We needn't send off Gwendolen, leastways not till *after*. You know. We needn't turn out of 'ere – not for a long time. What we been doing for the o' people we can go on doing a'most as much. And your mother! . . . I wanted to 'oller, coming along. I pretty near run coming down the road by the hotel.'

'Oh, I *am* glad we can stop 'ere and be comfortable a bit,' said Ann. 'I *am* glad for that.'

'I pretty near told the driver on the motor – only 'e was the sort won't talk . . . You see, Ann, we'll be able to start a shop, we'll be able to get *into* something like. All about our 'aving to go back to places and that; all that doesn't matter any more.'

For a while they abandoned themselves to ejaculating transports. Then they fell talking to shape an idea to themselves of the new prospect that opened before them.

'We must start a sort of shop,' said Kipps, whose imagination had been working. 'It'll 'ave to be a shop.'

'Drapery?' said Ann.

'You want such a lot of capital for the drapery; mor'n a thousand pounds you want by a long way – to start it anything like proper.'

'Well, outfitting. Like Buggins was going to do.'

Kipps glanced at that for a moment, because the idea had not occurred to him. Then he came back to his prepossession.

'Well, I thought of something else, Ann,' he said. 'You see, I've always thought a little bookshop – It isn't like the drapery – 'aving to be learnt. I thought – even before this smash-up – 'ow I'd like to 'ave something to do, instead of always 'aving 'olidays always like we 'ave been 'aving.'

She reflected.

'You don't know *much* about books, do you, Artie?'

'You don't want to.' He illustrated. 'I noticed when we used to go to that lib'ry at Folkestone, ladies weren't anything like what they was in a

draper's – if you 'aven't got *just* what they want it's "Oh, no!" and out they go. But in a bookshop it's different. One book's very like another – after all, what is it? Something to read and be done with. It's not a thing that matters like print dresses or serviettes – where you either like 'em or don't, and people judge you by. They take what you give 'em in bookshops and lib'ries, and glad to be told *what* to take. See 'ow we was – up at that lib'ry . . . '

He paused. 'You see, Ann –

'Well, I read 'n 'dvertisement the other day – I been asking Mr Bean. It said – five 'undred pounds.'

'What did?'

'Branches,' said Kipps.

Ann failed to understand. 'It's a sort of thing that gets up bookshops all over the country,' said Kipps 'I didn't tell you, but I arst about it a bit. On'y I dropped it again. Before this smash, I mean. I'd thought I'd like to keep a shop for a lark, on'y then I thought it silly. Besides it 'ud 'ave been beneath me.'

He blushed vividly. 'It was a sort of projek of mine, Ann.

'On'y it wouldn't 'ave done,' he added.

It was a tortuous journey when the Kippses set out to explain anything to each other. But through a maze of fragmentary elucidations and questions, their minds did presently begin to approximate to a picture of a compact, bright, little shop as a framework for themselves.

'I thought of it one day when I was in Folkestone. I thought of it one day when I was looking in at a window. I see a chap dressin' a window and he was whistlin' reg'lar light-'arted . . . I thought then I'd like to keep a bookshop, any'ow, jest for something to do. And when people weren't about, then you could sit and read the books. See? It wouldn't be 'arf bad . . . '

They mused, each with elbows on table and knuckles to lips, looking with speculative eyes at each other.

'Very likely we'll be 'appier than we should 'ave been with more money,' said Kipps presently.

'We wasn't 'ardly suited – ' reflected Ann, and left her sentence incomplete.

'Fish out of water like,' said Kipps . . .

'You won't 'ave to return that call now,' said Kipps, opening a new branch of the question. 'That's one good thing.'

'Lor'!' said Ann, visibly brightening, 'no more I shan't!'

'I don't s'pose they'd want you to, even if you did – with things as they are.'

A certain added brightness came into Ann's face. 'Nobody won't be able to come leaving cards on us, Artie, now, any more. We are out of *that*!'

'There isn't no necessity for us to be stuck up,' said Kipps, 'any more for ever! 'Ere we are, Ann, common people, with jest no position at all, as you

might say, to keep up. No se'v'nts, not if you don't like. No dressin' better than other people. If it wasn't we been robbed – dashed if I'd care a rap about losing that money. I b'lieve' – his face shone with the rare pleasure of paradox – 'I reely b'lieve, Ann, it'll prove a savin' in the end.'

<div align="center">4</div>

The remarkable advertisement which had fired Kipps's imagination with this dream of a bookshop opened out in the most alluring way. It was one little facet in a comprehensive scheme of transatlantic origin, which was to make our old-world methods of bookselling 'sit up', and it displayed an imaginative briskness, a lucidity and promise, that aroused the profoundest scepticism in the mind of Mr Bean. To Kipps's renewed investigations it presented itself in an expository illustrated pamphlet (far too well printed, Mr Bean thought, for a reputable undertaking) of the most convincing sort. Mr Bean would not let him sink his capital in shares in its projected company that was to make all things new in the world of books, but he could not prevent Kipps becoming one of their associated booksellers. And so when presently it became apparent that an epoch was not to be made, and the 'Associated Booksellers' Trading Union (Limited)' receded and dissolved and liquidated (a few drops) and vanished and went away to talk about something else, Kipps remained floating undamaged in this interestingly uncertain universe as an independent bookseller.

Except that it failed, the Associated Booksellers' Trading Union had all the stigmata of success. Its fault, perhaps, was that it had them all instead of only one or two. It was to buy wholesale for all its members and associates and exchange stock, having a common books-in-stock list and a common lending library, and it was to provide a uniform registered shopfront to signify all these things to the intelligent passer-by. Except that it was controlled by buoyant young Overmen with a touch of genius in their arithmetic, it was, I say, a most plausible and hopeful project. Kipps went several times to London and an agent came to Hythe; Mr Bean made some timely interventions, and then behind a veil of planks and an announcement in the High Street, the uniform registered shopfront came rapidly into being. 'Associated Booksellers' Trading Union' said this shopfront, in a refined, artistic lettering that bookbuyers were going to value as wise men over forty value the proper label for Berncasteler Doctor, and then, 'Arthur Kipps'.

Next to starting a haberdasher's shop, I doubt if Kipps could have been more truly happy than during those weeks of preparation.

There is, of course, nothing on earth, and I doubt at times if there is a joy in heaven, like starting a small haberdasher's shop. Imagine, for example, having a drawerful of tapes (one whole piece most exquisitely blocked of

every possible width of tape), or, again, an army of neat, large packages, each displaying one sample of hooks and eyes. Think of your cottons, your drawer of coloured silks, the little, less, least of the compartments and thin packets of your needle drawer! Poor princes and wretched gentlefolk mysteriously above retail trade, may taste only the faint unsatisfactory shadow of these delights with trays of stamps or butterflies. I write, of course, for those to whom these things appeal; there are clods alive who see nothing, or next to nothing, in spools of mercerised cotton and endless bands of paper-set pins. I write for the wise, and as I write I wonder that Kipps resisted haberdashery. He did. Yet even starting a bookshop is at least twenty times as interesting as building your own house to your own design in unlimited space and time, or any possible thing people with indisputable social position and sound securities can possibly find to do. Upon that I rest.

You figure Kipps 'going to have a look to see how the little shop is getting on', the shop that is not to be a loss and a spending of money, but a gain. He does not walk too fast towards it; as he comes into view of it his paces slacken and his head goes to one side. He crosses to the pavement opposite in order to inspect the fascia better; already his name is adumbrated in faint white lines; stops in the middle of the road and scrutinises imaginary details for the benefit of his future next-door neighbour, the curiosity-shop man, and so at last, in . . . A smell of paint and of the shavings of imperfectly seasoned pinewood! The shop is already glazed and a carpenter is busy over the fittings for adjustable shelves in the side windows. A painter is busy on the fixtures round about (shelving above and drawers below), which are to accommodate most of the stock, and the counter – the counter and desk are done. Kipps goes inside the desk, the desk which is to be the strategic centre of the shop, brushes away some sawdust, and draws out the marvellous till: here gold is to be, here silver, here copper – notes locked up in a cashbox in the well below. Then he leans his elbows on the desk, rests his chin on his fist and fills the shelves with imaginary stock; books beyond reading. Every day a man who cares to wash his hands and read uncut pages artfully may have his cake and eat it, among that stock. Under the counter to the right, paper and string are to lurk, ready to leap up and embrace goods sold; on the table to the left, art publications, whatever they may prove to be! He maps it out, serves an imaginary customer, receives a dream seven and six-pence, packs, bows out. He wonders how it was he ever came to fancy a shop a disagreeable place.

'It's different,' he says at last, after musing on that difficulty, 'being your own.'

It *is* different –

Or, again, you figure Kipps with something of the air of a young sacristan, handling his brightly virginal account-books, and looking, and looking again, and then still looking, at an unparalleled specimen of copperplate engraving, ruled money below and above bearing the words

'In Account with ARTHUR KIPPS' (loud flourishes), 'The Booksellers' Trading Union' (temperate decoration). You figure Ann sitting and stitching at one point of the circumference of the light of the lamp, stitching queer little garments for some unknown stranger, and over against her sits Kipps. Before him is one of those engraved memorandum forms, a moist pad, wet with some thick and greasy greenish-purple ink that is also spreading quietly but steadily over his fingers, a cross-nibbed pen for first-aid surgical assistance to the patient in his hand, a dating rubber stamp. At intervals he brings down this latter with great care and emphasis upon the paper, and when he lifts it there appears a beautiful oval design of which 'Paid, Arthur Kipps, The Associated Booksellers' Trading Union' and a date are the essential ingredients, stamped in purple ink.

Anon he turns his attention to a box of small, round, yellow labels, declaring, 'This book was bought from the Associated Booksellers' Trading Union.' He licks one with deliberate care, sticks it on the paper before him and defaces it with great solemnity. 'I can do it, Ann,' he says, looking up brightly. For the Associated Booksellers' Trading Union, among other brilliant notions and inspirations, devised an ingenious system of taking back its books again in part payment for new ones within a specified period. When it failed, all sorts of people were left with these unredeemed pledges in hand.

5

Amidst all this bustle and interest, all this going to and fro before they 'moved in' to the High Street, came the great crisis that hung over the Kippses, and one morning in the small hours Ann's child was born . . .

Kipps was coming to manhood swiftly now. The once rabbit-like soul that had been so amazed by the discovery of 'chubes' in the human interior and so shocked by the sight of a woman's shoulder-blades, that had found shame and anguish in a mislaid Gibus and terror in an Anagram Tea, was at last facing the greater realities. He came suddenly upon the master thing in life, birth. He passed through hours of listening, hours of impotent fear in the night and in the dawn, and then there was put into his arms something most wonderful, a weak and wailing creature, incredibly, heart-stirringly soft and pitiful, with minute appealing hands that it wrung his heart to see. He held this miracle in his arms and touched its tender cheek as if he feared his lips might injure it. And this marvel was his Son!

And there was Ann, with a greater strangeness and a greater familiarity in her quality than he had ever found before. There were little beads of perspiration on her temples and her lips, and her face was flushed, not pale as he had feared to see it. She had the look of one who emerges from some strenuous and invigorating act. He bent down and kissed her, and he had no

words to say. She wasn't to speak much yet, but she stroked his arm with her hand and had to tell him one thing: 'He's over nine pounds, Artie,' she whispered. 'Bessie's – Bessie's wasn't no more than eight.'

To have given Kipps a pound of triumph over Sid seemed to her almost to justify Nunc Dimittis. She watched his face for a moment, then closed her eyes in a kind of blissful exhaustion as the nurse, with something motherly in her manner, pushed Kipps out of the room.

6

Kipps was far too much preoccupied with his own life to worry about the further exploits of Chitterlow. The man had got his two thousand; on the whole Kipps was glad he had had it rather than young Walshingham, and there was an end to the matter. As for the complicated transactions he achieved and proclaimed by mainly illegible and always incomprehensible postcards, they were like passing voices heard in the street as one goes about one's urgent concerns. Kipps put them aside and they got in between the pages of the stock and were lost for ever and sold in with the goods to customers who puzzled over them mightily.

Then one morning as our bookseller was dusting round before breakfast, Chitterlow returned, appeared suddenly in the shop doorway.

Kipps was overcome with amazement.

It was the most unexpected thing in the world. The man was in evening dress, evening dress in that singularly crumpled state it assumes after the hour of dawn, and above his dishevelled red hair, a smallish gibus had tilted remarkably forward. He opened the door and stood, tall and spread, with one vast white glove flung out as if to display how burst a glove might be, his eyes bright, such wrinkling of brow and mouth as only an experienced actor can produce, and a singular radiance of emotion upon his whole being; an altogether astonishing spectacle.

It was amazing beyond the powers of Kipps. The bell jangled for a bit and then gave it up and was silent. For a long second everything was quietly attentive. Kipps was amazed to his uttermost; had he had ten times the capacity he would still have been fully amazed. 'It's Chit'low!' he said at last, standing duster in hand.

But he doubted whether it was not a dream.

'Tzit!' gasped that most excitable and extraordinary person, still in an incredibly expanded attitude, and then with a slight forward jerk of the starry split glove, 'Bif!'

He could say no more. The tremendous speech he had had ready vanished from his mind. Kipps stared at his extraordinary facial changes, vaguely conscious of the truth of the teachings of Nisbet and Lombroso concerning men of genius.

Then suddenly Chitterlow's features were convulsed, the histrionic fell from him like a garment, and he was weeping. He said something indistinct about 'Old Kipps! *Good* old Kipps! Oh, old Kipps!' and somehow he managed to mix a chuckle and a sob in the most remarkable way. He emerged from somewhere near the middle of his original attitude, a merely life-size creature. 'My play, boo-hoo!' he sobbed, clutching at his friend's arm. 'My play, Kipps (sob)! You know?'

'Well?' cried Kipps, with his heart sinking in sympathy. 'It ain't – '

'No,' howled Chitterlow; 'no. It's a Success! My dear chap! my dear boy! Oh! It's a – bu – boo-hoo! – a Big Success!' He turned away and wiped streaming tears with the back of his hand. He walked a pace or so and turned. He sat down on one of the specially designed artistic chairs of the Associated Booksellers' Trading Union and produced an exiguous lady's handkerchief, extraordinarily belaced. He choked, '*My* play,' and covered his face here and there.

He made an unsuccessful effort to control himself, and shrank for a space to the dimensions of a small and pathetic creature. His great nose suddenly came through a careless place in the handkerchief.

'I'm knocked,' he said in a muffled voice, and so remained for a space – wonderful – veiled.

He made a gallant effort to wipe his tears away. 'I had to tell you,' he said, gulping. 'Be all right in a minute,' he added. 'Calm!' and sat still –

Kipps stared in commiseration of such success. Then he heard footsteps and went quickly to the house doorway. 'Jest a minute,' he said. 'Don't go in the shop, Ann, for a minute. It's Chitterlow. He's a bit essited. But he'll be better in a minute. It's knocked him over a bit. You see' – his voice sank to a hushed note as one who announces death – ' 'e's made a success with his play.'

He pushed her back lest she should see the scandal of another male's tears . . .

Soon Chitterlow felt better, but for a little while his manner was even alarmingly subdued. 'I *had* to come and tell you,' he said. 'I *had* to astonish someone. Muriel – she'll be first-rate, of course. But she's over at Dymchurch.' He blew his nose with enormous noise, and emerged instantly a merely garrulous optimist.

'I expect she'll be precious glad.'

'She doesn't know yet, my dear boy. She's at Dymchurch – with a friend. She's seen some of my first nights before . . . Better out of it . . . I'm going to her now. I've been up all night – talking to the boys and all that. I'm a bit off it just for a bit. But – it Knocked 'em. It Knocked everybody.'

He stared at the floor and went on in a monotone. 'They laughed a bit at the beginning – but nothing like a settled laugh – not until the second act – you know – the chap with the beetle down his neck. Little Chisholme did that bit to rights. Then they began – *to* rights.' His voice warmed and

increased. 'Laughing! It made *me* laugh! We jumped 'em into the third act before they had time to cool. Everybody was on it. I never saw a first night go so fast. Laugh, laugh, laugh, LAUGH, LAUGH, LAUGH' (he howled the last repetition with stupendous violence). 'Everything they laughed at. They laughed at things that we hadn't meant to be funny – not for one moment. Bif! Bizz! Curtain. A Fair Knock-Out! . . . I went on – but I didn't say a word. Chisholme did the patter. Shouting! It was like walking under Niagara – going across that stage. It was like never having seen an audience before . . .

'Then afterwards – the Boys!'

His emotion held him for a space. 'Dear old Boys!' he murmured.

His words multiplied, his importance increased. In a little while he was restored to something of his old self. He was enormously excited. He seemed unable to sit down anywhere. He came into the breakfast-room so soon as Kipps was sure of him, shook hands with Mrs Kipps parenthetically, sat down and immediately got up again. He went to the bassinette in the corner and looked absent-mindedly at Kipps junior, and said he was glad if only for the youngster's sake. He immediately resumed the thread of his discourse . . . He drank a cup of coffee noisily and walked up and down the room talking, while they attempted breakfast amidst the gale of his excitement. The infant slept marvellously through it all.

'You won't mind my sitting down, Mrs Kipps. I couldn't sit down for anyone, or I'd do it for you. It's you I'm thinking of more than anyone, you and Muriel, and all Old Pals and Good Friends. It means wealth, it means money – hundreds and thousands . . . If you'd heard 'em, *you'd know.*'

He was silent through a portentous moment while topics battled for him and finally he burst and talked of them all together. It was like the rush of water when a dam bursts and washes out a fair-sized provincial town; all sorts of things floated along on the swirl. For example, he was discussing his future behaviour. 'I'm glad it's come now. Not before. I've had my lesson. I shall be very discreet now, trust me. We've learnt the value of money.' He discussed the possibility of a country house, of taking a Martello tower as a swimming-box (as one might say a shooting-box), of living in Venice because of its artistic associations and scenic possibilities, of a flat in West-minster or a house in the West End. He also raised the question of giving up smoking and drinking, and what classes of drink were especially noxious to a man of his constitution. But discourses on all this did not prevent a parenthetical computation of the probable profits on the supposition of a thousand nights here and in America, nor did it ignore the share Kipps was to have, nor the gladness with which Chitterlow would pay that share, nor the surprise and regret with which he had learnt, through an indirect source which awakened many associations, of the turpitude of young Walshing-ham, nor the distaste Chitterlow had always felt for young Walshingham and men of his type. An excursus upon Napoleon had got into the torrent

somehow and kept bobbing up and down. The whole thing was thrown into the form of a single complex sentence, with parenthetical and subordinate clauses fitting one into the other like Chinese boxes, and from first to last it never even had an air of approaching anything in the remotest degree partaking of the nature of a full stop.

Into this deluge came the *Daily News*, like the gleam of light in Watts's picture, the waters were assuaged while its sheet was opened, and it had a column, a whole column, of praise. Chitterlow held the paper and Kipps read over his left hand, and Ann under his right. It made the affair more real to Kipps; it seemed even to confirm Chitterlow against lurking doubts he had been concealing. But it took him away. He departed in a whirl, to secure a copy of every morning paper, every blessed rag there was, and take them all to Dymchurch and Muriel forthwith. It had been the send-off the Boys had given him that had prevented his doing as much at Charing Cross – let alone that he only caught it by the skin of his teeth . . . Besides which the bookstall wasn't open. His white face, lit by a vast excitement, bid them a tremendous farewell, and he departed through the sunlight, with his buoyant walk, buoyant almost to the tottering pitch. His hair, as one got it sunlit in the street, seemed to have grown in the night.

They saw him stop a newsboy.

'Every blessed rag' floated to them on the notes of that gorgeous voice.

The newsboy, too, had happened on luck. Something like a faint cheer from the newsboy came down the air to terminate that transaction.

Chitterlow went on his way swinging a great budget of papers, a figure of merited success. The newsboy recovered from his emotion with a jerk, examined something in his hand again, transferred it to his pocket, watched Chitterlow for a space, and then in a sort of hushed silence resumed his daily routine . . .

Ann and Kipps watched that receding happiness in silence, until he vanished round the bend of the road.

'I *am* glad,' said Ann at last, speaking with a little sigh.

'So'm I,' said Kipps, with emphasis. 'For if ever a feller 'as worked and waited – it's 'im.' . . .

They went back through the shop rather thoughtfully, and after a peep at the sleeping baby, resumed their interrupted breakfast. 'If ever a feller 'as worked and waited, it's 'im,' said Kipps, cutting bread.

'Very likely it's true,' said Ann, a little wistfully.

'What's true?'

'About all that money coming.'

Kipps meditated. 'I don't see why it shouldn't be,' he decided, and handed Ann a piece of bread on the tip of his knife.

'But we'll keep on the shop,' he said after an interval for further reflection, 'all the same . . . I 'aven't much trust in money after the things we've seen.'

That was two years ago, and as the whole world knows, the *Pestered Butterfly* is running still. It *was* true. It has made the fortune of a once declining little theatre in the Strand, night after night the great beetle scene draws happy tears from a house packed to repletion, and Kipps – for all that Chitterlow is not what one might call a businessman – is almost as rich as he was in the beginning. People in Australia, people in Lancashire, Scotland, Ireland, in New Orleans, in Jamaica, in New York and Montreal, have crowded through doorways to Kipps's enrichment, lured by the hitherto unsuspected humours of the entomological drama. Wealth rises like an exhalation all over our little planet, and condenses, or at least some of it does, in the pockets of Kipps.

'It's rum,' said Kipps.

He sat in the little kitchen out behind the bookshop and philosophised and smiled, while Ann gave Arthur Waddy Kipps his evening tub before the fire. Kipps was always present at this ceremony unless customers prevented; there was something in the mixture of the odours of tobacco, soap and domesticity that charmed him unspeakably.

'Chuckerdee, o' man,' he said, affably, wagging his pipe at his son, and thought incidentally, after the manner of all parents, that very few children could have so straight and clean a body.

'Dadda's got a cheque,' said Arthur Waddy Kipps, emerging for a moment from the towel.

' E gets 'old of everything,' said Ann. 'You can't say a word – '

'Dadda got a cheque,' this marvellous child repeated.

'Yes, o' man, I got a cheque. And it's got to go into a bank for you, against when you got to go to school. See? So's you'll grow up knowing your way about a bit.'

'Dadda's got a cheque,' said the wonder son, and then gave his mind to making mighty splashes with his foot. Every time he splashed, laughter overcame him, and he had to be held up for fear he should tumble out of the tub in his merriment. Finally he was towelled to his toe-tips, wrapped up in warm flannel, and kissed, and carried off to bed by Ann's cousin and lady help, Emma. And then after Ann had carried away the bath into the scullery, she returned to find her husband with his pipe extinct and the cheque still in his hand.

'Two fousand pounds,' he said. 'It's dashed rum. Wot 'ave *I* done to get two fousand pounds, Ann?'

'What 'aven't you – not to?' said Ann.

He reflected upon this view of the case.

'I shan't never give up this shop,' he said at last.

'We're very 'appy 'ere,' said Ann.

'Not if I 'ad *fifty* fousand pounds.'

'No fear,' said Ann.

'You got a shop,' said Kipps, 'and you come along in a year's time and there it is. But money – look 'ow it come and goes! There's no sense in money. You may kill yourself trying to get it, and then it comes when you aren't looking. There's my 'riginal money! Where is it now? Gone! And it's took young Walshingham with it, and 'e's gone, too. It's like playing skittles. 'Long comes the ball, right and left you fly, and there it is rolling away and not changed a bit. No sense in it! 'E's gone, and she's gone – gone off with that chap Revel, that sat with me at dinner. Married man! And Chit'low rich! Lor'! – what a fine place that Gerrik Club is, to be sure, where I 'ad lunch wiv' 'im! Better'n *any* 'otel. Footmen in powder they got – not waiters, Ann – footmen! 'E's rich and me rich – in a sort of way . . . Don't seem much sense in it, Ann, 'owever you look at it.' He shook his head.

'I know one thing,' said Kipps.

'What?'

'I'm going to put it in jest as many different banks as I can. See? Fifty 'ere, fifty there. 'Posit. I'm not going to 'nvest it – no fear.'

'It's only frowing money away,' said Ann.

'I'm 'arf a mind to bury some of it under the shop. Only I expect one 'ud always be coming down at nights to make sure it was there . . . I don't seem to trust anyone – not with money.' He put the cheque on the table corner and smiled and tapped his pipe on the grate, with his eyes on that wonderful document.

'S'pose old Bean started orf,' he reflected . . . 'One thing, 'e *is* a bit lame.'

' 'E wouldn't,' said Ann; 'not 'im.'

'I was only joking like.'

He stood up, put his pipe among the candlesticks on the mantel, took up the cheque and began folding it carefully to put it back in his pocketbook.

A little bell jangled.

'Shop!' said Kipps. 'That's right. Keep a shop and the shop'll keep you. That's 'ow I look at it, Ann.'

He drove his pocketbook securely into his breast pocket before he opened the living-room door . . .

But whether indeed it is the bookshop that keeps Kipps or whether it is Kipps who keeps the bookshop is just one of those commercial mysteries people of my unarithmetical temperament are never able to solve. They do very well, the dears, anyhow, thank heaven!

The bookshop of Kipps is on the left-hand side of the Hythe High Street coming from Folkestone, between the yard of the livery stable and the shop-window full of old silver and suchlike things – it is quite easy to find – and there you may see him for yourself and speak to him and buy this book

of him if you like. He has it in stock, I know. Very delicately I've seen to that. His name is not Kipps, of course, you must understand that, but everything else is exactly as I have told you. You can talk to him about books, about politics, about going to Boulogne, about life, and the ups and downs of life. Perhaps he will quote you Buggins – from whom, by the by, one can now buy everything a gentleman's wardrobe should contain at the little shop in Rendezvous Street, Folkestone. If you are fortunate to find Kipps in a good mood he may even let you know how he inherited a fortune 'once'. 'Run froo it,' he'll say with a not unhappy smile. 'Got another afterwards – speckylating in plays. Needn't keep this shop if I didn't like. But it's something to do . . . '

Or he may be even more intimate. 'I seen some things,' he said to me once. 'Raver! Life! Why! once I – I *'loped*! I did – reely!'

(Of course you will not tell Kipps that he *is* 'Kipps', or that I have put him in this book. He has not the remotest suspicion of that. And you know, you never can tell how people are going to take that sort of thing. I am an old and trusted customer now, and for many amiable reasons I should prefer that things remained exactly on their present footing.)

8

One early-closing evening in July they left the baby to the servant cousin, and Kipps took Ann for a row on the Hythe canal. It was a glorious evening, and the sun set in a mighty blaze and left a world warm, and very still. The twilight came. And there was the water, shining bright, and the sky a deepening blue, and the great trees that dipped their boughs towards the water, exactly as it had been when he paddled home with Helen, when her eyes had seemed to him like dusky stars. He had ceased from rowing and rested on his oars, and suddenly he was touched by the wonder of life; the strangeness that is a presence stood again by his side.

Out of the darknesses beneath the shallow, weedy stream of his being rose a question, a question that looked up dimly and never reached the surface. It was the question of the wonder of the beauty, the purposeless, inconsecutive beauty, that falls so strangely among the happenings and memories of life. It never reached the surface of his mind, it never took to itself substance or form; it looked up merely as the phantom of a face might look, out of deep waters, and sank again to nothingness.

'Artie,' said Ann.

He woke up and pulled a stroke. 'What?' he said.

'Penny for your thoughts, Artie.'

He considered.

'I reely don't think I was thinking of anything,' he said at last with a smile. 'No.'

He still rested on his oars.

'I expect,' he said, 'I was thinking jest what a Rum Go everything is. I expect it was something like that.'

'Queer old Artie!'

'Ain't I? I don't suppose there ever was a chap quite like me before.'

He reflected for just another minute.

'Oo! I dunno,' he said, and roused himself to pull.

The History of Mr Polly

A novel first published in 1909

Contents

The History of Mr Polly was first published in Great Britain
in 1910 by Thomas Nelson & Sons following its
publication in the United States the previous year
by Grosset & Dunlap.

Beginnings, and the Bazaar

'HOLE!' SAID MR POLLY, and then for a change, and with greatly increased emphasis: ' '*Ole!*' He paused, and then broke out with one of his private and peculiar idioms. 'Oh! *Beastly* Silly Wheeze of a Hole!'

He was sitting on a stile between two threadbare-looking fields, and suffering acutely from indigestion

He suffered from indigestion now nearly every afternoon of his life, but as he lacked introspection he projected the associated discomfort upon the world. Every afternoon he discovered afresh that life as a whole and every aspect of life that presented itself was 'beastly'. And this afternoon, lured by the delusive blueness of a sky that was blue because the wind was in the east, he had come out in the hope of snatching something of the joyousness of spring. The mysterious alchemy of mind and body refused, however, to permit any joyousness whatever in the spring.

He had had a little difficulty in finding his cap before he came out. He wanted his cap – the new golf cap – and Mrs Polly must needs fish out his old soft brown felt hat. ' '*Ere*'s your 'at,' she said in a tone of insincere encouragement.

He had been routing among the piled newspapers under the kitchen dresser, and had turned quite hopefully and taken the thing. He put it on. But it didn't feel right. Nothing felt right. He put a trembling hand upon the crown of the thing and pressed it on his head, and tried it askew to the right and then askew to the left.

Then the full sense of the indignity offered him came home to him. The hat masked the upper sinister quarter of his face, and he spoke with a wrathful eye regarding his wife from under the brim. In a voice thick with fury he said: 'I s'pose you'd like me to wear that silly Mud Pie for ever, eh? I tell you I won't. I'm sick of it. I'm pretty near sick of everything, comes to that . . . Hat!'

He clutched it with quivering fingers. 'Hat!' he repeated. Then he flung it to the ground and kicked it with extraordinary fury across the kitchen. It flew up against the door and dropped to the ground with its ribbon-band half off.

'Shan't go out!' he said, and sticking his hands into his jacket pockets discovered the missing cap in the right one.

There was nothing for it but to go straight upstairs without a word, and out, slamming the shop door hard.

'Beauty!' said Mrs Polly at last to a tremendous silence, picking up and dusting the rejected headdress. 'Tantrums,' she added. 'I 'aven't patience.' And moving with the slow reluctance of a deeply offended woman, she began to pile together the simple apparatus of their recent meal, for transportation to the scullery sink.

The repast she had prepared for him did not seem to her to justify his ingratitude. There had been the cold pork from Sunday and some nice cold potatoes, and Rashdall's Mixed Pickles, of which he was inordinately fond. He had eaten three gherkins, two onions, a small cauliflower head and several capers with every appearance of appetite, and indeed with avidity; and then there had been cold suet pudding to follow, with treacle, and then a nice bit of cheese. It was the pale, hard sort of cheese he liked; red cheese he declared was indigestible. He had also had three big slices of greyish baker's bread, and had drunk the best part of the jugful of beer . . . But there seems to be no pleasing some people.

'Tantrums!' said Mrs Polly at the sink, struggling with the mustard on his plate and expressing the only solution of the problem that occurred to her.

And Mr Polly sat on the stile and hated the whole scheme of life – which was at once excessive and inadequate as a solution. He hated Foxbourne, he hated Foxbourne High Street, he hated his shop and his wife and his neighbours – every blessed neighbour – and with indescribable bitterness he hated himself.

'Why did I ever get in this silly Hole?' he said. 'Why did I ever?'

He sat on the stile, and looked with eyes that seemed blurred with impalpable flaws at a world in which even the spring buds were wilted, the sunlight metallic and the shadows mixed with blue-black ink.

To the moralist I know he might have served as a figure of sinful discontent, but that is because it is the habit of moralists to ignore material circumstances – if indeed one may speak of a recent meal as a circumstance rendering Mr Polly circum. Drink, indeed, our teachers will criticise nowadays both as regards quantity and quality, but neither church nor state nor school will raise a warning finger between a man and his hunger and his wife's catering. So on nearly every day in his life Mr Polly fell into a violent rage and hatred against the outer world in the afternoon, and never suspected that it was this inner world to which I am with such masterly delicacy alluding that was thus reflecting its sinister disorder upon the things without. It is a pity that some human beings are not more transparent. If Mr Polly, for example, had been transparent or even passably translucent, then perhaps he might have realised from the Laocoön struggle he would have glimpsed that indeed he was not so much a human being as a civil war.

Wonderful things must have been going on inside Mr Polly. Oh! wonderful things. It must have been like a badly managed industrial city

during a period of depression: agitators, acts of violence, strikes, the forces of law and order doing their best, rushings to and fro, upheavals, the *Marseillaise*, tumbrils, the rumble and the thunder of the tumbrils –

I do not know why the east wind aggravates life to unhealthy people. It made Mr Polly's teeth seem loose in his head, and his skin feel like a misfit, and his hair a dry, stringy exasperation –

Why cannot doctors give us an antidote to the east wind?

'Never have the sense to get your hair cut till it's too long,' said Mr Polly, catching sight of his shadow, 'you blighted, degenerated Paintbrush! Ugh!' and he flattened down the projecting tails with an urgent hand.

2

Mr Polly's age was exactly thirty-five years and a half. He was a short, compact figure, and a little inclined to a localised *embonpoint*. His face was not unpleasing; the features fine, but a trifle too pointed about the nose to be classically perfect. The corners of his sensitive mouth were depressed. His eyes were ruddy brown and troubled, and the left one was round with more of wonder in it than its fellow. His complexion was dull and yellowish – that, as I have explained, on account of those civil disturbances. He was, in the technical sense of the word, clean shaved, with a small sallow patch under the right ear and a cut on the chin. His brow had the little puckerings of a thoroughly discontented man, little wrinklings and lumps, particularly over his right eye, and he sat with his hands in his pockets, a little askew on the stile, and swung one leg. 'Hole!' he repeated presently.

He broke into a quavering song. 'Ro–o–o–tten Be–e–astly Silly Hole!'

His voice thickened with rage, and the rest of his discourse was marred by an unfortunate choice of epithets.

He was dressed in a shabby black morning coat and waistcoat; the braid that bound these garments was a little loose in places; his collar was chosen from stock and had projecting corners; it was what was called in those days a 'wing-poke'; that and his tie, which was new and loose and rich in colouring, had been selected to encourage and stimulate customers – for he dealt in gentlemen's outfitting. His golf cap, which was also from stock and aslant over his eye, gave his misery a desperate touch. He wore brown leather boots – because he hated the smell of blacking.

Perhaps after all it was not simply indigestion that troubled him.

Behind the superficialities of Mr Polly's being, moved a larger and vaguer distress. The elementary education he had acquired had left him with the impression that arithmetic was a fluky science and best avoided in practical affairs, but even the absence of bookkeeping and a total inability to distinguish between capital and interest could not blind him for ever to the fact that the little shop in the High Street was not paying. An absence of

returns, a constriction of credit, a depleted till, the most valiant resolves to keep smiling, could not prevail for ever against these insistent phenomena. One might bustle about in the morning before dinner and in the afternoon after tea and forget that huge dark cloud of insolvency that gathered and spread in the background, but it was part of the desolation of these afternoon periods, these grey spaces of time after meals, when all one's courage had descended to the unseen battles of the pit, that life seemed stripped to the bone and one saw with a hopeless clearness.

Let me tell the history of Mr Polly from the cradle to these present difficulties. 'First the infant, mewling and puking in its nurse's arms.'

There had been a time when two people had thought Mr Polly the most wonderful and adorable thing in the world, had kissed his toenails, saying 'myum, myum,' and marvelled at the exquisite softness and delicacy of his hair, had called to one another to remark the peculiar distinction with which he bubbled, had disputed whether the sound he had made was *just da da*, or truly and intentionally dadda, had washed him in the utmost detail, and wrapped him up in soft, warm blankets, and smothered him with kisses. A regal time that was, and four and thirty years ago; and a merciful forgetfulness barred Mr Polly from ever bringing its careless luxury, its autocratic demands and instant obedience, into contrast with his present condition of life. These two people had worshipped him from the crown of his head to the soles of his exquisite feet. And also they had fed him rather unwisely, for no one had ever troubled to teach his mother anything about the mysteries of a child's upbringing – though of course the monthly nurse and her charwoman gave some valuable hints – and by his fifth birthday the perfect rhythms of his nice new interior were already darkened with perplexity . . .

His mother died when he was seven.

He began only to have distinctive memories of himself in the time when his education had already begun.

I remember seeing a picture of Education – in some place. I think it was Education, but quite conceivably it represented the Empire teaching her Sons, and I have a strong impression that it was a wall painting upon some public building in Manchester or Birmingham or Glasgow, but very possibly I am mistaken about that. It represented a glorious woman with a wise and fearless face stooping over her children and pointing them to far horizons. The sky displayed the pearly warmth of a summer dawn, and all the painting was marvellously bright as if with the youth and hope of the delicately beautiful children in the foreground. She was telling them, one felt, of the great prospect of life that opened before them, of the spectacle of the world, the splendours of sea and mountain they might travel and see, the joys of skill they might acquire, of effort and the pride of effort and the devotions and nobilities it was theirs to achieve. Perhaps even she whispered of the warm triumphant mystery of love that comes at last to

those who have patience and unblemished hearts . . . She was reminding them of their great heritage as English children, rulers of more than one-fifth of mankind, of the obligation to do and be the best that such a pride of empire entails, of their essential nobility and knighthood and the restraints and the charities and the disciplined strength that is becoming in knights and rulers . . .

The education of Mr Polly did not follow this picture very closely. He went for some time to a National School, which was run on severely economical lines to keep down the rates by a largely untrained staff, he was set sums to do that he did not understand, and that no one made him understand, he was made to read the catechism and Bible with the utmost industry and an entire disregard of punctuation or significance, and caused to imitate writing copies and drawing copies, and given object lessons upon scaling wax and silkworms and potato bugs and ginger and iron and such-like things, and taught various other subjects his mind refused to entertain, and afterwards, when he was about twelve, he was jerked by his parent to 'finish off' in a private school of dingy aspect and still dingier pretensions, where there were no object lessons, and the studies of bookkeeping and French were pursued (but never effectually overtaken) under the guidance of an elderly gentleman who wore a nondescript gown and took snuff, wrote copperplate, explained nothing and used a cane with remarkable dexterity and gusto.

Mr Polly went into the National School at six and he left the private school at fourteen, and by that time his mind was in much the same state that you would be in, dear reader, if you were operated upon for appendicitis by a well-meaning, boldly enterprising, but rather over-worked and underpaid butcher boy, who was superseded towards the climax of the operation by a left-handed clerk of high principles but intemperate habits – that is to say, it was in a thorough mess. The nice little curiosities and willingnesses of a child were in a jumbled and thwarted condition, hacked and cut about – the operators had left, so to speak, all their sponges and ligatures in the mangled confusion – and Mr Polly had lost much of his natural confidence, so far as figures and sciences and languages and the possibilities of learning things were concerned. He thought of the present world no longer as a wonderland of experiences, but as geography and history, as the repeating of names that were hard to pronounce and lists of products and populations and heights and lengths, and as lists and dates – oh! and boredom in-describable. He thought of religion as the recital of more or less incomprehensible words that were hard to remember, and of the Divinity as of a limitless Being having the nature of a schoolmaster and making infinite rules, known and unknown rules, that were always ruthlessly enforced, and with an infinite capacity for punishment and, most horrible of all to think of! limitless powers of espial. (So to the best of his ability he did not think of that unrelenting eye.) He was uncertain about the spelling and pro-

nunciation of most of the words in our beautiful but abundant and per-
plexing tongue – that especially was a pity because words attracted him, and
under happier conditions he might have used them well – he was always
doubtful whether it was eight sevens or nine eights that were sixty-three (he
knew no method for settling the difficulty) and he thought the merit of a
drawing consisted in the care with which it was 'lined in'. 'Lining in' bored
him beyond measure.

But the indigestions of mind and body that were to play so large a part in
his subsequent career were still only beginning. His liver and his gastric
juice, his wonder and imagination kept up a fight against the things that
threatened to overwhelm soul and body together. Outside the regions
devastated by the school curriculum he was still intensely curious. He had
cheerful phases of enterprise, and at about thirteen he suddenly discovered
reading and its joys. He began to read stories voraciously, and books of
travel, provided they were also adventurous. He got these chiefly from the
local institute, and he also 'took in', irregularly but thoroughly, one of those
inspiring weeklies that dull people used to call 'penny dreadfuls', admirable
weeklies crammed with imagination that the cheap boys' 'comics' of today
have replaced. At fourteen, when he emerged from the valley of the shadow
of education, there survived something, indeed it survived still, obscured
and thwarted, at five and thirty, that pointed – not with a visible and
prevailing finger like the finger of that beautiful woman in the picture, but
pointed nevertheless – to the idea that there was interest and happiness in
the world. Deep in the being of Mr Polly, deep in that darkness, like a
creature which has been beaten about the head and left for dead but still
lives, crawled a persuasion that over and above the things that were jolly
and 'bits of all right', there was beauty, there was delight, that somewhere –
magically inaccessible perhaps, but still somewhere – were pure and easy
and joyous states of body and mind.

He would sneak out on moonless winter nights and stare up at the stars,
and afterwards find it difficult to tell his father where he had been.

He would read tales about hunters and explorers, and imagine himself
riding mustangs as fleet as the wind across the prairies of Western America,
or coming as a conquering and adored white man into the swarming villages
of Central Africa. He shot bears with a revolver – a cigarette in the other
hand – and made a necklace of their teeth and claws for the chief's beautiful
young daughter. Also he killed a lion with a pointed stake, stabbing through
the beast's heart as it stood over him.

He thought it would be splendid to be a diver and go down into the dark
green mysteries of the sea.

He led stormers against well-nigh impregnable forts, and died on the
ramparts at the moment of victory. (His grave was watered by a nation's
tears.)

He rammed and torpedoed ships, one against ten.

He was beloved by queens in barbaric lands, and reconciled whole nations to the Christian faith.

He was martyred, and took it very calmly and beautifully – but only once or twice after the Revivalist week. It did not become a habit with him.

He explored the Amazon, and found, newly exposed by the fall of a great tree, a rock of gold.

Engaged in these pursuits he would neglect the work immediately in hand, sitting somewhat slackly on the form and projecting himself in a manner tempting to a schoolmaster with a cane . . . And twice he had books confiscated.

Recalled to the realities of life, he would rub himself or sigh deeply as the occasion required, and resume his attempts to write as good as copperplate. He hated writing; the ink always crept up his fingers and the smell of ink offended him. And he was filled with unexpressed doubts. *Why* should writing slope down from right to left? *Why* should down strokes be thick and up strokes thin? *Why* should the handle of one's pen point over one's right shoulder?

His copy books towards the end foreshadowed his destiny and took the form of commercial documents. '*Dear Sir*,' they ran, '*Referring to your esteemed order of the 26th ult., we beg to inform you*,' and so on.

The compression of Mr Polly's mind and soul in the educational institutions of his time was terminated abruptly by his father between his fourteenth and fifteenth birthdays. His father – who had long since forgotten the time when his son's little limbs seemed to have come straight from God's hand, and when he had kissed five minute toenails in a rapture of loving tenderness – remarked: 'It's time that dratted boy did something for a living.'

And a month or so later Mr Polly began that career in business that led him at last to the sole proprietorship of a bankrupt outfitter's shop – and to the stile on which he was sitting.

3

Mr Polly was not naturally interested in hosiery and gentlemen's outfitting. At times, indeed, he urged himself to a spurious curiosity about that trade, but presently something more congenial came along and checked the effort. He was apprenticed in one of those large, rather low-class establishments which sell everything from pianos and furniture to books and millinery, a department store in fact – the Port Burdock Drapery Bazaar at Port Burdock, one of the three townships that are grouped around the Port Burdock naval dockyards. There he remained six years. He spent most of the time inattentive to business, in a sort of uncomfortable happiness, increasing his indigestion.

On the whole he preferred business to school; the hours were longer but the tension was not nearly so great. The place was better aired, you were not kept in for no reason at all, and the cane was not employed. You watched the growth of your moustache with interest and impatience, and mastered the beginnings of social intercourse. You talked, and found there were things amusing to say. Also you had regular pocket money, and a voice in the purchase of your clothes, and presently a small salary. And there were girls. And friendship! In the retrospect Port Burdock sparkled with the facets of quite a cluster of remembered jolly times.

('Didn't save much money though,' said Mr Polly.)

The first-apprentices' dormitory was a long bleak room with six beds, six chests of drawers and looking glasses and a number of boxes of wood or tin; it opened into a still longer and bleaker room of eight beds, and this into a third apartment with yellow-grained paper and American-cloth tables, which was the dining-room by day and the men's sitting-and smoking-room after nine. Here Mr Polly, who had been an only child, first tasted the joys of social intercourse. At first there were attempts to bully him on account of his refusal to consider face-washing a diurnal duty, but two fights with the apprentices next above him established a useful reputation for choler, and the presence of girl apprentices in the shop somehow raised his standard of cleanliness to a more acceptable level. He didn't, of course, have very much to do with the feminine staff in his department, but he spoke to them casually as he traversed foreign parts of the Bazaar, or got out of their way politely, or helped them to lift down heavy boxes, and on such occasions he felt their scrutiny. Except in the course of business or at meal times the men and women of the establishment had very little opportunity of meeting; the men were in their rooms and the girls in theirs. Yet these feminine creatures, at once so near and so remote, affected him profoundly. He would watch them going to and fro, and marvel secretly at the beauty of their hair or the roundness of their necks or the warm softness of their cheeks or the delicacy of their hands. He would fall into passions for them at dinner time, and try and show devotion by his manner of passing the bread and margarine at tea. There was a very fair-haired, fair-skinned apprentice in the adjacent haberdashery to whom he said 'good-morning' every morning, and for a period it seemed to him the most significant event in his day. When she said, 'I *do* hope it will be fine tomorrow,' he felt it marked an epoch. He had had no sisters, and was innately disposed to worship womankind. But he did not betray as much to Platt and Parsons.

To Platt and Parsons he affected an attitude of seasoned depravity towards womankind. Platt and Parsons were his contemporary apprentices in departments of the drapery shop, and the three were drawn together into a close friendship by the fact that all their names began with P. They decided they were the Three Ps, and went about together of an evening with the bearing of desperate dogs. Sometimes, when they had money, they

went into public houses and had drinks. Then they would become more desperate than ever, and walk along the pavement under the gas lamps arm in arm singing. Platt had a good tenor voice and had been in a church choir, and so he led the singing; Parsons had a serviceable bellow, which roared and faded and roared again very wonderfully; Mr Polly's share was an extraordinary lowing noise, a sort of flat recitative which he called 'singing seconds'. They would have sung catches if they had known how to do it, but as it was they sang melancholy music-hall songs about dying soldiers and the old folks far away.

They would sometimes go into the quieter residential quarters of Port Burdock, where policemen and other obstacles were infrequent, and really let their voices soar like hawks and feel very happy. The dogs of the district would be stirred to hopeless emulation, and would keep it up for long after the Three Ps had been swallowed up by the night. One jealous brute of an Irish terrier made a gallant attempt to bite Parsons, but was beaten by numbers and solidarity.

The Three Ps took the utmost interest in each other and found no other company so good. They talked about everything in the world, and would go on talking in their dormitory after the gas was out until the other men were reduced to throwing boots; they skulked from their departments in the slack hours of the afternoon to gossip in the packing-room of the warehouse; on Sundays and Bank Holidays they went for long walks together, talking.

Platt was white-faced and dark, and disposed to undertones and mystery and a curiosity about society and the *demi-monde*. He kept himself *au courant* by reading a penny paper of infinite suggestion called *Modern Society*. Parsons was of an ampler build, already promising fatness, with curly hair and a lot of rolling, rollicking, curly features, and a large blob-shaped nose. He had a great memory and a real interest in literature. He knew great portions of Shakespeare and Milton by heart, and would recite them at the slightest provocation. He read everything he could get hold of, and if he liked it he read it aloud. It did not matter who else liked it. At first Mr Polly was disposed to be suspicious of this literature, but was carried away by Parsons's enthusiasm. The Three Ps went to a performance of *Romeo and Juliet* at the Port Burdock Theatre Royal, and hung over the gallery fascinated. After that they made a sort of password of: 'Do you bite your thumbs at us, sir?' To which the countersign was: 'We bite our thumbs.'

For weeks the glory of Shakespeare's Verona lit Mr Polly's life. He walked as though he carried a sword at his side, and swung a mantle from his shoulders. He went through the grimy streets of Port Burdock with his eye on the first-floor windows – looking for balconies. A ladder in the yard flooded his mind with romantic ideas. Then Parsons discovered an Italian writer, whose name Mr Polly rendered as 'Bocashieu', and after some

excursions into that author's remains the talk of Parsons became infested with the word '*amours*', and Mr Polly would stand in front of his hosiery fixtures trifling with paper and string and thinking of perennial picnics under dark olive trees in the everlasting sunshine of Italy.

And about that time it was that all three Ps adopted turndown collars and large, loose, artistic silk ties, which they tied very much on one side and wore with an air of defiance. And a certain swashbuckling carriage.

And then came the glorious revelation of that great Frenchman whom Mr Polly called 'Rabooloose'. The Three Ps thought the birth feast of Gargantua the most glorious piece of writing in the world, and I am not certain they were wrong, and on wet Sunday evenings when there was danger of hymn singing they would get Parsons to read it aloud.

Towards the several members of the YMCA who shared the dormitory, the Three Ps always maintained a sarcastic and defiant attitude.

'We got a perfect right to do what we like in our corner,' Platt maintained. 'You do what you like in yours.'

'But the language!' objected Morrison, the white-faced, earnest-eyed improver, who was leading a profoundly religious life under great difficulties.

'*Language*, man!' roared Parsons, 'why, it's *Literature*!'

'Sunday isn't the time for Literature.'

'It's the only time we've got. And besides – '

The horrors of religious controversy would begin . . .

Mr Polly stuck loyally to the Three Ps, but in the secret places of his heart he was torn. A fire of conviction burnt in Morrison's eyes and spoke in his urgent persuasive voice; he lived the better life manifestly, chaste in word and deed, industrious, studiously kindly. When the junior apprentice had sore feet and homesickness Morrison washed the feet and comforted the heart, and he helped other men to get through with their work when he might have gone early, a superhuman thing to do. Polly was secretly a little afraid to be left alone with this man and the power of the spirit that was in him. He felt watched.

Platt, also struggling with things his mind could not contrive to reconcile, said 'that confounded hypocrite'.

'He's no hypocrite,' said Parsons, 'he's no hypocrite, o' man. But he's got no blessed *Joy de Vive*; that's what's wrong with him. Let's go down to the Harbour Arms and see some of those blessed old captains getting drunk.'

'Short of sugar, o' man,' said Mr Polly, slapping his trouser pocket.

'Oh, *carm* on,' said Parsons. 'Always do it on tuppence for a bitter.'

'Lemme get my pipe on,' said Platt, who had recently taken to smoking with great ferocity. 'Then I'm with you.'

Pause and struggle.

'Don't ram it down, o' man,' said Parsons, watching with knitted brows. 'Don't ram it down. Give it Air. Seen my stick, o' man? Right-o.'

And leaning on his cane he composed himself in an attitude of sympathetic patience towards Platt's incendiary efforts.

4

Jolly days of companionship they were for the incipient bankrupt on the stile to look back upon.

The interminable working hours of the Bazaar had long since faded from his memory – except for one or two conspicuous rows and one or two larks – but the rare Sundays and holidays shone out like diamonds among pebbles. They shone with the mellow splendour of evening skies reflected in calm water, and athwart them all went old Parsons bellowing an interpretation of life, gesticulating, appreciating and making appreciate, expounding books, talking of that mystery of his, the '*Joy de Vive*'.

There were some particularly splendid walks on Bank Holidays. The Three Ps would start on Sunday morning early and find a room in some modest inn and talk themselves asleep, and return singing through the night, or having an 'argy bargy' about the stars, on Monday evening. They would come over the hills out of the pleasant English countryside in which they had wandered, and see Port Burdock spread out below, a network of interlacing street lamps and shifting tram lights against the black, beacon-gemmed immensity of the harbour waters.

'Back to the collar, o' man,' Parsons would say. There is no satisfactory plural to o' man, so he always used it in the singular.

'Don't mention it,' said Platt.

And once they got a boat for the whole summer day, and rowed up past the moored ironclads and the black old hulks and the various shipping of the harbour, past a white troopship and past the trim front and the ships and interesting vistas of the dockyard to the shallow channels and rocky weedy wildernesses of the upper harbour. And Parsons and Mr Polly had a great dispute and quarrel that day as to how far a big gun could shoot.

The country over the hills behind Port Burdock is all that an old-fashioned, scarcely disturbed English countryside should be. In those days the bicycle was still rare and costly and the motor car had yet to come and stir up rural serenities. The Three Ps would take footpaths haphazard across fields, and plunge into unknown winding lanes between high hedges of honeysuckle and dog rose. Greatly daring, they would follow green bridle paths through primrose-studded undergrowths, or wander waist deep in the bracken of beech woods. About twenty miles from Port Burdock there came a region of hop gardens and hoast-crowned farms, and farther on, to be reached only by cheap tickets at Bank Holiday times, was a sterile ridge of very clean roads and red sand pits and pines and gorse and heather. The Three Ps could not afford to buy bicycles and they found boots the

greatest item of their skimpy expenditure. They threw appearances to the winds at last and got ready-made workingmen's hobnails. There was much discussion and strong feeling over this step in the dormitory.

There is no countryside like the English countryside for those who have learnt to love it. Its firm yet gentle lines of hill and dale, its ordered confusion of features, its deer parks and downland, its castles and stately houses, its hamlets and old churches, its farms and ricks and great barns and ancient trees, its pools and ponds and shining threads of rivers; its flower-starred hedgerows, its orchards and woodland patches, its village greens and kindly inns. Other countrysides have their pleasant aspects, but none such variety, none that shine so steadfastly throughout the year. Picardy is pink and white and pleasant in the blossom time; Burgundy goes on with its sunshine and wide hillsides and cramped vineyards, a beautiful tune repeated and repeated; Italy gives salitas and wayside chapels and chestnuts and olive orchards; the Ardennes has its woods and gorges; Touraine and the Rhineland, the wide Campagna with its distant Apennines, and the neat prosperities and mountain backgrounds of South Germany, all clamour their especial merits at one's memory. And there are the hills and fields of Virginia, like an England grown very big and slovenly, the woods and big river sweeps of Pennsylvania, the trim New England landscape, a little bleak and rather fine like the New England mind, and the wide rough country roads and hills and woodland of New York State. But none of these change scene and character in three miles of walking, nor have so mellow a sunlight nor so diversified a cloudland, nor confess the perpetual refreshment of the strong soft winds that blow from off the sea, as our Mother England does.

It was good for the Three Ps to walk through such a land and forget for a time that indeed they had no footing in it all, that they were doomed to toil behind counters in such places as Port Burdock for the better part of their lives. They would forget the customers and shopwalkers and department buyers and everything and become just happy wanderers in a world of pleasant breezes and songbirds and shady trees.

The arrival at the inn was a great affair. No one, they were convinced, would take them for drapers, and there might be a pretty serving girl or a jolly old lady, or what Parsons called a 'bit of character' drinking in the bar.

There would always be weighty enquiries as to what they could have, and it would work out always at cold beef and pickles, or fried ham and eggs and shandygaff, two pints of beer and two bottles of ginger beer foaming in a huge round-bellied jug.

The glorious moment of standing lordly in the inn doorway, and staring out at the world, the swinging sign, the geese upon the green, the duck-pond, a waiting waggon, the church tower, a sleepy cat, the blue heavens, with the sizzle of the frying audible behind one! The keen smell of the bacon! The trotting of feet bearing the repast; the click and clatter as the tableware is finally arranged! A clean white cloth!

'Ready, sir!' or 'Ready, gentlemen.' Better hearing that than 'Forward Polly! look sharp!'

The going in! The sitting down! The falling to!

'Bread, o' man?'

'Right-o! Don't bag all the crust, o' man.'

Once a simple-mannered girl in a pink print dress stayed and talked with them as they ate; led by the gallant Parsons they professed to be all desperately in love with her, and courted her to say which she preferred of them, it was so manifest she did prefer one and so impossible to say which it was held her there, until a distant maternal voice called her away. Afterwards as they left the inn she waylaid them at the orchard corner and gave them, a little shyly, three keen yellow-green apples – and wished them to come again some day, and vanished, and reappeared looking after them as they turned the corner waving a white handkerchief. All the rest of that day they disputed over the signs of her favour, and the next Sunday they went there again.

But she had vanished, and a mother of forbidding aspect afforded no explanations.

If Platt and Parsons and Mr Polly live to be a hundred, they will none of them forget that girl as she stood with a pink flush upon her, faintly smiling and yet earnest, parting the branches of the hedgerows and reaching down apple in hand.

And once they went along the coast, following it as closely as possible, and so came at last to Foxbourne, that easternmost suburb of Brayling and Hampsted-on-the-Sea.

Foxbourne seemed a very jolly little place to Mr Polly that afternoon. It has a clean sandy beach instead of the mud and pebbles and coaly defilements of Port Burdock, a row of six bathing-machines, and a shelter on the parade in which the Three Ps sat after a satisfying but rather expensive lunch that had included celery. Rows of verandahed villas proffered apartments; they had feasted in a hotel with a porch painted white and gay with geraniums above: and the High Street, with the old church at the head, had been full of an agreeable afternoon stillness.

'Nice little place for business,' said Platt sagely from behind his big pipe.

It stuck in Mr Polly's memory.

5

Mr Polly was not so picturesque a youth as Parsons. He lacked richness in his voice, and went about in those days with his hands in his pockets looking quietly speculative.

He specialised in slang and the misuse of English, and he played the role of an appreciative stimulant to Parsons. Words attracted him curiously,

words rich in suggestion, and he loved a novel and striking phrase. His school training had given him little or no mastery of the mysterious pronunciation of English and no confidence in himself. His schoolmaster indeed had been both unsound and variable. New words had terror and fascination for him; he did not acquire them, he could not avoid them, and so he plunged into them. His only rule was not to be misled by the spelling. That was no guide anyhow. He avoided every recognised phrase in the language and mispronounced everything in order that he should be suspected of whim rather than ignorance

'Sesquippledan,' he would say. 'Sesquippledan verboojuice.'

'Eh?' said Platt.

'Eloquent Rapsodooce.'

'Where?' asked Platt.

'In the warehouse, o' man. All among the tablecloths and blankets. Carlyle. He's reading aloud. Doing the High Froth. Spuming! Windmilling! Waw, waw! It's a sight worth seeing. He'll bark his blessed knuckles one of these days on the fixtures, o' man.'

He held an imaginary book in one hand and waved an eloquent gesture. 'So too shall every Hero inasmuch as notwithstanding for evermore come back to Reality,' he parodied the enthusiastic Parsons, 'so that in fashion and thereby, upon things and not *under* things articulariously He stands.'

'I should laugh if the Governor dropped on him,' said Platt. 'He'd never hear him coming.'

'The o' man's drunk with it – fair drunk,' said Polly. 'I never did. It's worse than when he got on to Rabooloose.'

CHAPTER TWO

The Dismissal of Parsons

Suddenly Parsons got himself dismissed.

He got himself dismissed under circumstances of peculiar violence that left a deep impression on Mr Polly's mind. He wondered about it for years afterwards, trying to get the rights of the case.

Parsons's apprenticeship was over; he had reached the status of an Improver, and he dressed the window of the Manchester department. By all the standards available he dressed it very well. By his own standards he dressed it wonderfully. 'Well, o' man,' he used to say, 'there's one thing about my position here– I *can* dress a window.'

And when trouble was under discussion he would hold that 'little Fluffums' – which was the apprentices' name for Mr Garvace, the senior partner and managing director of the Bazaar – would think twice before

he got rid of the only man in the place who could make a windowful of Manchester goods *tell*.

Then like many a fellow artist he fell a prey to theories.

'The art of window-dressing is in its Infancy, o' man – in its blooming Infancy. All balance and stiffness like a blessed Egyptian picture. No Joy in it, no blooming Joy! Conventional. A shop window ought to get hold of people, *grip* 'em as they go along. It stands to reason. Grip!'

His voice would sink to a kind of quiet bellow. '*Do* they grip?'

Then after a pause, a savage roar: '*Naw!*'

'He's got a Heavy on,' said Mr Polly. 'Go it, o' man; let's have some more of it.'

'Look at old Morrison's dress-stuff windows! Tidy, tasteful, correct, I grant you, but Bleak!' He let out the word reinforced to a shout: 'Bleak!'

'Bleak!' echoed Mr Polly.

'Just pieces of stuff in rows, rows of tidy little putts, perhaps one bit just unrolled, quiet tickets.'

'Might as well be in church, o' man,' said Mr Polly.

'A window ought to be exciting,' said Parsons; 'it ought to make you say: " 'El-*lo*!" when you see it.'

He paused, and Platt watched him over a snorting pipe.

'Rockcockyo,' said Mr Polly.

'We want a new school of window-dressing,' said Parsons, regardless of the comment. 'A New School! The Port Burdock School. Day after tomorrow I change the Fitzallan Street stuff. This time, it's going to be a change. I mean to have a crowd or bust!'

And as a matter of fact he did both.

His voice dropped to a note of self-reproach. 'I've been timid, o' man. I've been holding myself in. I haven't done myself Justice. I've kept down the simmering, seething, teeming ideas . . . All that's over now.'

'Over,' gulped Polly.

'Over for good and all, o' man.'

2

Platt came to Polly, who was sorting up collar boxes. 'o' man's doing his Blooming Window.'

'What window?'

'What he said.'

Polly remembered.

He went on with his collar boxes with his eye on his senior, Mansfield. Mansfield was presently called away to the counting house, and instantly Polly shot out by the street door, and made a rapid transit along the street front past the Manchester window, and so into the silk-room door. He

could not linger long, but he gathered joy, a swift and fearful joy, from his brief inspection of Parsons's unconscious back. Parsons had his tail coat off and was working with vigour; his habit of pulling his waistcoat straps to the utmost brought out all the agreeable promise of corpulence in his youthful frame. He was blowing excitedly and running his fingers through his hair, and then moving with all the swift eagerness of a man inspired. All about his feet and knees were scarlet blankets, not folded, not formally unfolded, but – the only phrase is – shied about. And a great bar sinister of roller towelling stretched across the front of the window on which was a ticket, and the ticket said in bold black letters: 'LOOK!'

So soon as Mr Polly got into the silk department and met Platt he knew he had not lingered nearly long enough outside. 'Did you see the boards at the back?' said Platt.

He hadn't. 'The High Egrugious is fairly On,' he said, and dived down to return by devious subterranean routes to the outfitting department.

Presently the street door opened and Platt, with an air of intense devotion to business assumed to cover his adoption of that unusual route, came in and made for the staircase down to the warehouse. He rolled up his eyes at Polly. 'Oh, *Lor!*' he said and vanished.

Irresistible curiosity seized Polly. Should he go through the shop to the Manchester department, or risk a second transit outside?

He was impelled to make a dive at the street door.

'Where are you going?' asked Mansfield.

'Li'le dog,' said Polly with an air of lucid explanation, and left him to get any meaning he could from it.

Parsons was worth the subsequent trouble. Parsons really was extremely rich. This time Polly stopped to take it in.

Parsons had made a huge asymmetrical pile of thick white and red blankets twisted and rolled to accentuate their woolly richness, heaped up in a warm disorder, with large window tickets inscribed in blazing red letters: 'Cosy Comfort at Cut Prices', and 'Curl up and Cuddle below Cost'. Regardless of the daylight he had turned up the electric light on that side of the window to reflect a warm glow upon the heap, and behind, in pursuit of contrasted bleakness, he was now hanging long strips of grey silesia and chilly-coloured linen dusterings.

It was wonderful, but –

Mr Polly decided that it was time he went in. He found Platt in the silk department, apparently on the verge of another plunge into the exterior world. 'Cosy Comfort at Cut Prices,' said Polly. 'Allittritions Artful Aid.'

He did not dare go into the street for the third time, and he was hovering feverishly near the window when he saw the governor, Mr Garvace, that is to say, the managing director of the Bazaar, walking along the pavement after his manner to assure himself all was well with the establishment he guided.

Mr Garvace was a short stout man, with that air of modest pride that so

often goes with corpulence, choleric and decisive in manner, and with hands that looked like bunches of fingers. He was red-haired and ruddy, and after the custom of such complexions, hairs sprang from the tip of his nose. When he wished to bring the power of the human eye to bear upon an assistant, he projected his chest, knitted one brow and partially closed the left eyelid.

An expression of speculative wonder overspread the countenance of Mr Polly. He felt he must *see*. Yes, whatever happened, he must *see*. 'Want to speak to Parsons, sir,' he said to Mr Mansfield, and deserted his post hastily, dashed through the intervening departments and was in position behind a pile of Bolton sheeting as the governor came in out of the street.

'What on earth do you think you are doing with that window, Parsons?' began Mr Garvace.

Only the legs of Parsons and the lower part of his waistcoat and an intervening inch of shirt were visible. He was standing inside the window on the steps, hanging up the last strip of his background from the brass rail along the ceiling. Within, the Manchester shop window was cut off by a partition rather like the partition of an old-fashioned church pew from the general space of the shop. There was a panelled barrier, that is to say, with a little door like a pew door in it. Parsons's face appeared, staring with round eyes at his employer.

Mr Garvace had to repeat his question.

'Dressing it, sir – on new lines.'

'Come out of it,' said Mr Garvace.

Parsons stared, and Mr Garvace had to repeat his command.

Parsons, with a dazed expression, began to descend the steps slowly.

Mr Garvace turned about. 'Where's Morrison? Morrison!'

Morrison appeared.

'Take this window over,' said Mr Garvace, pointing his bunch of fingers at Parsons. 'Take all this muddle out and dress it properly.'

Morrison advanced and hesitated.

'I beg your pardon, sir,' said Parsons with an immense politeness, 'but this is *my* window.'

'Take it all out,' said Mr Garvace, turning away.

Morrison advanced. Parsons shut the door with a click that arrested Mr Garvace.

'Come out of that window,' he said. 'You can't dress it. If you want to play the fool with a window – '

'This window's All Right,' said the genius in window-dressing, and there was a little pause.

'Open the door and go right in,' said Mr Garvace to Morrison.

'You leave that door alone, Morrison,' said Parsons.

Polly was no longer even trying to hide behind the stack of Bolton sheeting. He realised he was in the presence of forces too stupendous to heed him.

'Get him out,' said Mr Garvace.

Morrison seemed to be thinking out the ethics of his position. The idea of loyalty to his employer prevailed with him. He laid his hand on the door to open it; Parsons tried to disengage his hand. Mr Garvace joined his effort to Morrison's. Then the heart of Polly leapt and the world blazed up to wonder and splendour. Parsons disappeared behind the partition for a moment and reappeared instantly, gripping a thin cylinder of rolled huckaback. With this he smote at Morrison's head. Morrison's head ducked under the resounding impact, but he clung on and so did Mr Garvace. The door came open, and then Mr Garvace was staggering back, hand to head; his autocratic, his sacred baldness, smitten. Parsons was beyond all control – a strangeness, a marvel. Heaven knows how the artistic struggle had strained that richly endowed temperament. 'Say I can't dress a window, you thundering old Humbug,' he said, and hurled the huckaback at his master. He followed this up by hurling first a blanket, then an armful of silesia, then a window support out of the window into the shop. It leapt into Polly's mind that Parsons hated his own effort and was glad to demolish it. For a crowded second Polly's mind was concentrated upon Parsons, infuriated, active, like a figure of earthquake with its coat off, shying things headlong.

Then he perceived the back of Mr Garvace and heard his gubernatorial voice crying to no one in particular and everybody in general: 'Get him out of the window. He's mad. He's dangerous. Get him out of the window.'

Then a crimson blanket was for a moment over the head of Mr Garvace, and his voice, muffled for an instant, broke out into unwonted expletive.

Then people had arrived from all parts of the Bazaar. Luck, the ledger clerk, blundered against Polly and said, 'Help him!' Somerville from the silks vaulted the counter, and seized a chair by the back. Polly lost his head. He clawed at the Bolton sheeting before him, and if he could have detached a piece he would certainly have hit somebody with it. As it was he simply upset the pile. It fell away from Polly, and he had an impression of somebody squeaking as it went down. It was the sort of impression one disregards. The collapse of the pile of goods just sufficed to end his subconscious efforts to get something to hit somebody with, and his whole attention focused itself upon the struggle in the window. For a splendid instant Parsons towered up over the active backs that clustered about the shop-window door, an active whirl of gesture, tearing things down and throwing them, and then he went under. There was an instant's furious struggle, a crash, a second crash and the crack of broken plate glass. Then a stillness and heavy breathing.

Parsons was overpowered . . .

Polly, stepping over scattered pieces of Bolton sheeting, saw his transfigured friend with a dark cut, that was not at present bleeding, on the forehead, one arm held by Somerville and the other by Morrison.

'You – you – you – you annoyed me,' said Parsons, sobbing for breath.

There are events that detach themselves from the general stream of occurrences and seem to partake of the nature of revelations. Such was this Parsons affair. It began by seeming grotesque; it ended disconcertingly. The fabric of Mr Polly's daily life was torn, and beneath it he discovered depths and terrors.

Life was not altogether a lark.

The calling in of a policeman seemed at the moment a pantomime touch. But when it became manifest that Mr Garvace was in a fury of vindictiveness, the affair took on a different complexion. The way in which the policeman made a note of everything and aspirated nothing impressed the sensitive mind of Polly profoundly. Polly presently found himself straightening up ties to the refrain of, ' 'E then 'it you on the 'ed – 'ard.'

In the dormitory that night Parsons had become heroic. He sat on the edge of the bed with his head bandaged, packing very slowly and insisting over and over again: 'He ought to have left my window alone, o' man. He didn't ought to have touched my window.'

Polly was to go to the police court in the morning as a witness. The terror of that ordeal almost overshadowed the tragic fact that Parsons was not only summoned for assault, but 'swapped' and packing his box. Polly knew himself well enough to know he would make a bad witness. He felt sure of one fact only, namely, that ' 'E then 'it 'im on the 'ed –'ard. All the rest danced about in his mind now, and how it would dance about on the morrow heaven only knew. Would there be a cross-examination? Is it perjoocery to make a slip? People did sometimes perjuice themselves. Serious offence.

Platt was doing his best to help Parsons, and inciting public opinion against Morrison. But Parsons would not hear of anything against Morrison. 'He was all right, o' man – according to his lights,' said Parsons. 'It isn't him I complain of.'

He speculated on the morrow. 'I shall 'ave to pay a fine,' he said. 'No good trying to get out of it. It's true I hit him. I hit him' – he paused and seemed to be seeking an exquisite accuracy; his voice sank to a confidential note – 'on the head – about here.'

He answered the suggestion of a bright junior apprentice in a corner of the dormitory. 'What's the good of a cross summons?' he replied; 'with old Corks, the chemist, and Mottishead, the house agent, and all that lot on the Bench? Humble Pie, that's my meal tomorrow, o' man. Humble Pie.'

Packing went on for a time.

'But Lord! what a Life it is!' said Parsons, giving his deep notes scope. 'Ten-thirty-five a man trying to do his Duty, mistaken perhaps, but trying

his best; ten-forty – Ruined! Ruined!' He lifted his voice to a shout. 'Ruined!' and dropped it to, 'Like an earthquake.'

'Heated altaclation,' said Polly.

'Like a blooming earthquake!' said Parsons, with the notes of a rising wind.

He meditated gloomily upon his future and a colder chill invaded Polly's mind. 'Likely to get another crib, ain't I? – with assaulted the guv'nor on my reference. I suppose, though, he won't give me refs. Hard enough to get a crib at the best of times,' said Parsons.

'You ought to go round with a show, o' man,' said Mr Polly.

Things were not so dreadful in the police court as Mr Polly had expected. He was given a seat with other witnesses against the wall of the court, and after an interesting larceny case Parsons appeared and stood not in the dock but at the table. By that time Mr Polly's legs, which had been tucked up at first under his chair out of respect to the court, were extended straight before him and his hands were in his trouser pockets. He was inventing names for the four magistrates on the bench, and had got to 'the Grave and Reverend Signor with the palatial Boko', when his thoughts were recalled to gravity by the sound of his name. He rose with alacrity and was fielded by an expert policeman from a brisk attempt to get into the vacant dock. The clerk to the Justices repeated the oath with incredible rapidity.

'Right-o,' said Mr Polly, but quite respectfully, and kissed the book.

His evidence was simple and quite audible after one warning from the superintendent of police to 'speak up'. He tried to put in a good word for Parsons by saying he was 'naturally of a choleraic disposition', but the start and the slow grin of enjoyment upon the face of the grave and Reverend Signor with the palatial Boko suggested that the word was not so good as he had thought it. The rest of the bench was frankly puzzled and there were hasty consultations.

'You mean 'e 'as a 'ot temper,' said the presiding magistrate.

'I mean 'e 'as a 'ot temper,' replied Polly, magically incapable of aspirates for the moment.

'You don't mean 'e ketches cholera.'

'I mean – he's easily put out.'

'Then why can't you say so?' said the presiding magistrate.

Parsons was bound over.

He came for his luggage while everyone was in the shop, and Garvace would not let him invade the business to say goodbye. When Mr Polly went upstairs for margarine and bread and tea, he slipped on into the dormitory at once to see what was happening further in the Parsons case. But Parsons had vanished. There was no Parsons, no trace of Parsons. His cubicle was swept and garnished. For the first time in his life Polly had a sense of irreparable loss.

A minute or so after Platt dashed in.

'Ugh!' he said, and then discovered Polly. Polly was leaning out of the window and did not look around. Platt went up to him.

'He's gone already,' said Platt. 'Might have stopped to say goodbye to a chap.'

There was a little pause before Polly replied. He thrust his finger into his mouth and gulped.

'Bit on that beastly tooth of mine,' he said, still not looking at Platt. 'It's made my eyes water, something chronic. Anyone might think I'd been doing a blooming Pipe, by the look of me.'

CHAPTER THREE

Cribs

Port Burdock was never the same place for Mr Polly after Parsons had left it. There were no chest notes in his occasional letters, and little of the '*Joy de Vive*' got through by them. Parsons had gone, he said, to London, and found a place as warehouseman in a cheap outfitting shop near St Paul's Churchyard, where references were not required. It became apparent as time passed that new interests were absorbing him. He wrote of Socialism and the rights of man, things that had no appeal for Mr Polly. He felt strangers had got hold of his Parsons, were at work upon him, making him into someone else, something less picturesque . . . Port Burdock became a dreariness, full of faded memories of Parsons, and work a bore. Platt revealed himself alone as a tiresome companion, obsessed by romantic ideas about intrigues and vices and 'society women'.

Mr Polly's depression manifested itself in a general slackness. A certain impatience in the manner of Mr Garvace presently got upon his nerves. Relations were becoming strained. He asked for a rise of salary to test his position, and gave notice to leave when it was refused.

It took him two months to place himself in another situation, and during that time he had quite a disagreeable amount of loneliness, disappointment, anxiety and humiliation.

He went at first to stay with a married cousin who had a house at Easewood. His widowed father had recently given up the music and bicycle shop (with the post of organist at the parish church) that had sustained his home, and was living upon a small annuity as a guest with this cousin, and growing a little tiresome on account of some mysterious internal discomfort that the local practitioner diagnosed as imagination. He had aged with mysterious rapidity and become excessively irritable, but the cousin's wife was a born manager, and contrived to get along with him. Our Mr Polly's status was that of a guest pure and simple, but after a fortnight of congested hospitality in which he wrote nearly a hundred letters beginning:

Sir – Refferring to your advt. in the *Christian World* for an Improver in Gents' outfitting, I beg to submit myself for the situation. Have had six years' experience . . .

and upset a penny bottle of ink over a toilet cover and the bedroom carpet, his cousin took him for a walk and pointed out the superior advantages of apartments in London from which to swoop upon the briefly yawning vacancy.

'Helpful,' said Mr Polly; 'very helpful, o' man, indeed. I might have gone on here for weeks,' and packed.

He got a room in an institution that was partly a benevolent hostel for men in his circumstances and partly a high-minded but forbidding coffee house and a centre for pleasant Sunday afternoons. Mr Polly spent a critical but pleasant Sunday afternoon in a back seat, inventing such phrases as: 'Soulful Owner of the Exorbiant Largenial Development' – an Adam's Apple being in question; 'Earnest Joy'; 'Exultant, Urgent Loogoobuosity'.

A manly young curate, marking and misunderstanding his preoccupied face and moving lips, came and sat by him and entered into conversation with the idea of making him feel more at home. The conversation was awkward and disconnected for a minute or so, and then suddenly a memory of the Port Burdock Bazaar occurred to Mr Polly, and with a baffling whisper of 'Li'le dog', and a reassuring nod, he rose up and escaped, to wander out relieved and observant into the varied London streets.

He found the collection of men he met waiting about in wholesale establishments in Wood Street and St Paul's Churchyard (where they interview the buyers who have come up from the country) interesting and stimulating, but far too strongly charged with the suggestion of his own fate to be really joyful. There were men in all degrees between confidence and distress, and in every stage between extravagant smartness and the last stages of decay. There were sunny young men full of an abounding and elbowing energy, before whom the soul of Polly sank in hate and dismay. 'Smart Juniors,' said Polly to himself, 'full of Smart Juniosity. The Shoveacious Cult.' There were hungry-looking individuals of thirty-five or so that he decided must be 'Proletelerians' – he had often wanted to find someone who fitted that attractive word. Middle-aged men, 'too old at forty', discoursed in the waiting-rooms on the outlook in the trade; it had never been so bad, they said, while Mr Polly wondered if 'Dejuiced' was a permissible epithet. There were men with an overweening sense of their importance, manifestly annoyed and angry to find themselves still disengaged, and inclined to suspect a plot, and men so faint-hearted one was terrified to imagine their behaviour when it came to an interview. There was a fresh-faced young man with an unintelligent face who seemed to think himself equipped against the world beyond all misadventure by a collar of exceptional height, and another who introduced a note of gaiety by

wearing a flannel shirt and a check suit of remarkable virulence. Every day
Mr Polly looked round to mark how many of the familiar faces had gone,
and the deepening anxiety (reflecting his own) on the faces that remained,
and every day some new type joined the drifting shoal. He realised how
small a chance his poor letter from Easewood ran against this hungry
cluster of competitors at the fountain head.

At the back of Mr Polly's mind while he made his observations was a
disagreeable flavour of dentist's parlour. At any moment his name might be
shouted, and he might have to haul himself into the presence of some fresh
specimen of employer, and to repeat once more his passionate protestation of
interest in the business, his possession of a capacity for zeal – zeal on behalf
of anyone who would pay him a yearly salary of twenty-six pounds a year.

The prospective employer would unfold his ideals of the employee. 'I
want a smart, willing young man, thoroughly willing – who won't object to
take trouble. I don't want a slacker, the sort of fellow who has to be pushed
up to his work and held there. I've got no use for him.'

At the back of Mr Polly's mind, and quite beyond his control, the
insubordinate phrasemaker would be proffering such combinations as
'Chubby Chops', or 'Chubby Charmer', as suitable for the gentleman,
very much as a hat salesman proffers hats.

'I don't think you'd find much slackness about *me*, sir,' said Mr Polly
brightly, trying to disregard his deeper self.

'I want a young man who means getting on.'

'Exactly, sir. Excelsior.'

'I beg your pardon?'

'I said excelsior, sir. It's a sort of motto of mine. From Longfellow.
Would you want me to serve through?'

The chubby gentleman explained and reverted to his ideals, with a faint
air of suspicion. 'Do *you* mean getting on?' he asked.

'I hope so, sir,' said Mr Polly.

'Get on or get out, eh?'

Mr Polly made a rapturous noise, nodded appreciation, and said
indistinctly, '*Quite* my style.'

'Some of my people have been with me twenty years,' said the employer.
'My Manchester buyer came to me as a boy of twelve. You're a Christian?'

'Church of England,' said Mr Polly.

'H'm,' said the employer a little checked. 'For good all-round business
work I should have preferred a Baptist. Still – '

He studied Mr Polly's tie, which was severely neat and businesslike, as
became an aspiring outfitter. Mr Polly's conception of his own pose and
expression was rendered by that uncontrollable phrasemonger at the back
as 'Obsequies Deference'.

'I am inclined,' said the prospective employer in a conclusive manner, 'to
look up your reference.'

Mr Polly stood up abruptly.

'Thank you,' said the employer and dismissed him.

'Chump chops! How about chump chops?' said the phrasemonger with an air of inspiration.

'I hope then to hear from you, sir,' said Mr Polly in his best salesman manner.

'If everything is satisfactory,' said the prospective employer.

2

A man whose brain devotes its hinterland to making odd phrases and nicknames out of ill-conceived words, whose conception of life is a lump of auriferous rock to which all the value is given by rare veins of unbusinesslike joy, who reads Boccaccio and Rabelais and Shakespeare with gusto, and uses 'Stertoraneous Shover' and 'Smart Junior' as terms of bitterest opprobrium, is not likely to make a great success under modern business conditions. Mr Polly dreamt always of picturesque and mellow things, and had an instinctive hatred of the strenuous life. He would have resisted the spell of ex-President Roosevelt, or General Baden Powell, or Mr Peter Keary, or the late Dr Samuel Smiles, quite easily; and he loved Falstaff and Hudibras and coarse laughter, and the old England of Washington Irving and the memory of Charles the Second's courtly days. His progress was necessarily slow. He did not get rises; he lost situations; there was something in his eye employers did not like; he would have lost his places oftener if he had not been at times an exceptionally brilliant salesman, rather carefully neat, and a slow but very fair window-dresser.

He went from situation to situation, he invented a great wealth of nicknames, he conceived enmities and made friends – but none so richly satisfying as Parsons. He was frequently but mildly and discursively in love, and sometimes he thought of that girl who had given him a yellow-green apple. He had an idea, amounting to a flattering certainty, whose youthful freshness it was had stirred her to self-forgetfulness. And sometimes he thought of Foxbourne sleeping prosperously in the sun. And he began to have moods of discomfort and lassitude and ill-temper due to the beginnings of indigestion.

Various forces and suggestions came into his life and swayed him for longer and shorter periods.

He went to Canterbury and came under the influence of Gothic architecture. There was a blood affinity between Mr Polly and the Gothic; in the Middle Ages he would no doubt have sat upon a scaffolding and carved out penetrating and none too flattering portraits of church dignitaries upon the capitals, and when he strolled, with his hands behind his back, along the cloisters behind the cathedral, and looked at the rich

grass plot in the centre, he had the strangest sense of being at home – far more than he had ever been at home before. 'Portly capons,' he used to murmur to himself, under the impression that he was naming a characteristic type of mediaeval churchman.

He liked to sit in the nave during the service, and look through the great gates at the candles and choristers, and listen to the organ-sustained voices, but the transepts he never penetrated because of the charge for admission. The music and the long vista of the fretted roof filled him with a vague and mystical happiness that he had no words, even mispronounceable words, to express. But some of the smug monuments in the aisles got a wreath of epithets: 'Metrorious urnfuls', 'funererial claims', 'dejected angelosity', for example. He wandered about the precincts and speculated about the people who lived in the ripe and cosy houses of grey stone that cluster there so comfortably. Through green doors in high stone walls he caught glimpses of level lawns and blazing flower beds; mullioned windows revealed shaded reading-lamps and disciplined shelves of brown-bound books. Now and then a dignitary in gaiters would pass him, 'Portly capon', or a drift of white-robed choir boys cross a distant arcade and vanish in a doorway, or the pink and cream of some girlish dress flit like a butterfly across the cool still spaces of the place. Particularly he responded to the ruined arches of the Benedictines' Infirmary and the view of Bell Harry Tower from the school buildings. He was stirred to read the *Canterbury Tales*, but he could not get on with Chaucer's old-fashioned English; it fatigued his attention, and he would have given all the storytelling very readily for a few adventures on the road. He wanted these nice people to live more and yarn less. He liked the Wife of Bath very much. He would have liked to have known that woman.

At Canterbury, too, he first to his knowledge saw Americans.

His shop did a good-class trade in Westgate Street, and he would see them go by on the way to stare at Chaucer's Chequers and then turn down Mercery Lane to Prior Goldstone's gate. It impressed him that they were always in a kind of quiet hurry, and very determined and methodical people – much more so than any English he knew.

'Cultured Rapacicity,' he tried.

'Vorocious Return to the Heritage.'

He would expound them incidentally to his attendant apprentices. He had overheard a little lady putting her view to a friend near the Christ-church gate. The accent and intonation had hung in his memory, and he would reproduce them more or less accurately. 'Now does this Marlowe monument really and truly *matter*?' he had heard the little lady enquire. 'We've no time for side shows and second-rate stunts, Mamie. We want just the Big Simple Things of the place, just the Broad Elemental Canterbury praposition. What is it saying to us? I want to get right hold of that, and then have tea in the very room that Chaucer did, and hustle to get that four-eighteen train back to London . . .'

He would go over these precious phrases, finding them full of an indescribable flavour. 'Just the Broad Elemental Canterbury praposition,' he would repeat . . .

He would try to imagine Parsons confronted with Americans. For his own part he knew himself to be altogether inadequate . . .

Canterbury was the most congenial situation Mr Polly ever found during these wander years, albeit a very desert so far as companionship went.

3

It was after Canterbury that the universe became really disagreeable to Mr Polly. It was brought home to him, not so much vividly as with a harsh and ungainly insistence, that he was a failure in his trade. It was not the trade he ought to have chosen, though what trade he ought to have chosen was by no means clear.

He made great but irregular efforts and produced a forced smartness that, like a cheap dye, refused to stand sunshine. He acquired a sort of parsimony also, in which acquisition he was helped by one or two phases of absolute impecuniosity. But he was hopeless in competition against the naturally gifted, the born hustlers, the young men who meant to get on.

He left the Canterbury place very regretfully. He and another commercial gentleman took a boat one Sunday afternoon at Sturry-on-the-Stour, when the wind was in the west, and sailed it very happily eastward for an hour. They had never sailed a boat before and it seemed simple and wonderful. When they turned they found the river too narrow for tacking and the tide running out like a sluice. They battled back to Sturry in the course of six hours (at a shilling the first hour and sixpence for each hour afterwards) rowing a mile in an hour and a half or so, until the turn of the tide came to help them, and then they had a night walk to Canterbury, and found themselves remorselessly locked out.

The Canterbury employer was an amiable, religious-spirited man and he would probably not have dismissed Mr Polly if that unfortunate tendency to phrase things had not shocked him. 'A Tide's a Tide, sir,' said Mr Polly, feeling that things were not so bad. 'I've no lune-attic power to alter *that*.'

It proved impossible to explain to the Canterbury employer that this was not a highly disrespectful and blasphemous remark.

'And besides, what good are you to me this morning, do you think?' said the Canterbury employer, 'with your arms pulled out of their sockets?'

So Mr Polly resumed his observations in the Wood Street warehouses once more, and had some dismal times. The shoal of fish waiting for the crumbs of employment seemed larger than ever.

He took counsel with himself. Should he 'chuck' the outfitting? It wasn't any good for him now, and presently when he was older and his youthful

smartness had passed into the dullness of middle age it would be worse. What else could he do?

He could think of nothing. He went one night to a music hall and developed a vague idea of a comic performance; the comic men seemed violent rowdies and not at all funny; but when he thought of the great pit of the audience yawning before him he realised that his was an altogether too delicate talent for such a use. He was impressed by the charm of selling vegetables by auction in one of those open shops near London Bridge, but admitted upon reflection his general want of technical knowledge. He made some enquiries about emigration, but none of the colonies were in want of shop assistants without capital. He kept up his attendance in Wood Street.

He subdued his ideal of salary by the sum of five pounds a year, and was taken at that into a driving establishment in Clapham, which dealt chiefly in ready-made suits, fed its assistants in an underground dining-room and kept them until twelve on Saturdays. He found it hard to be cheerful there. His fits of indigestion became worse, and he began to lie awake at night and think. Sunshine and laughter seemed things lost for ever; picnics and shouting in the moonlight.

The chief shopwalker took a dislike to him and nagged him. 'Nar then, Polly!' 'Look alive, Polly!' became the burthen of his days. 'As smart a chap as you could have,' said the chief shopwalker, 'but no *Zest*. No *Zest*! No *Vim*! What's the matter with you?'

During his night vigils Mr Polly had a feeling – A young rabbit must have very much the feeling when, after a youth of gambolling in sunny woods and furtive jolly raids upon the growing wheat and exciting triumphant bolts before ineffectual casual dogs, it finds itself at last for a long night of floundering effort and perplexity in a net – for the rest of its life.

He could not grasp what was wrong with him. He made enormous efforts to diagnose his case. Was he really just a 'lazy slacker' who ought to 'buck up'? He couldn't find it in him to believe it. He blamed his father a good deal – it is what fathers are for – for putting him to a trade he wasn't happy to follow, but he found it impossible to say what he ought to have followed. He felt there had been something stupid about his school, but just where that came in he couldn't say. He made some perfectly sincere efforts to 'buck up' and 'shove' ruthlessly. But that was infernal – impossible. He had to admit himself miserable, with all the misery of a social misfit and with no clear prospect of more than the most incidental happiness ahead of him. And for all his attempts at self-reproach or self-discipline he felt at bottom that he wasn't at fault.

As a matter of fact all the elements of his troubles had been adequately diagnosed by a certain high-browed, spectacled gentleman living at Highbury, wearing a gold *pince-nez* and writing for the most part in the beautiful library of the Reform Club. This gentleman did not know Mr Polly personally, but he had dealt with him generally as 'one of those ill-adjusted

units that abound in a society that has failed to develop a collective intelligence and a collective will for order, commensurate with its complexities'.

But phrases of that sort had no appeal for Mr Polly.

CHAPTER FOUR

Mr Polly an Orphan

Then a great change was brought about in the life of Mr Polly by the death of his father. His father had died suddenly – the local practitioner still clung to his theory that it was imagination he suffered from, but compromised in the certificate with the appendicitis that was then so fashionable and Mr Polly found himself heir to a debateable number of pieces of furniture in the house of his cousin near Easewood Junction, a family Bible, an engraved portrait of Garibaldi and a bust of Mr Gladstone, an invalid gold watch, a gold locket formerly belonging to his mother, some minor jewellery and bric-à-brac, a quantity of nearly valueless old clothes and an insurance policy and money in the bank amounting altogether to the sum of three hundred and ninety-five pounds.

Mr Polly had always regarded his father as an immortal, as an eternal fact, and his father being of a reserved nature in his declining years had said nothing about the insurance policy. Both wealth and bereavement therefore took Mr Polly by surprise and found him a little inadequate. His mother's death had been a childish grief and long forgotten, and the strongest affection in his life had been for Parsons. An only child of sociable tendencies necessarily turns his back a good deal upon home, and the aunt who had succeeded his mother was an economist and furniture polisher, a knuckle rapper and sharp silencer, no friend for a slovenly little boy. He had loved other little boys and girls transitorily, none had been frequent and familiar enough to strike deep roots in his heart, and he had grown up with a tattered and dissipated affectionateness that was becoming wildly shy. His father had always been a stranger, an irritable stranger with exceptional powers of intervention and comment, and an air of being disappointed about his offspring. It was shocking to lose him; it was like an unexpected hole in the universe, the writing of 'Death' upon the sky, but it did not tear Mr Polly's heartstrings at first so much as rouse him to a pitch of vivid attention.

He came down to the cottage at Easewood in response to an urgent telegram, and found his father already dead. His cousin Johnson received him with much solemnity and ushered him upstairs, to look at a stiff, straight, shrouded form, with a face unwontedly quiet and, as it seemed by reason of its pinched nostrils, scornful.

'Looks peaceful,' said Mr Polly, disregarding the scorn to the best of his ability.

'It was a merciful relief,' said Mr Johnson.

There was a pause.

'Second – second Departed I've ever seen. Not counting mummies,' said Mr Polly, feeling it necessary to say something.

'We did all we could.'

'No doubt of it, o' man,' said Mr Polly.

A second long pause followed, and then, much to Mr Polly's great relief, Johnson moved towards the door.

Afterwards Mr Polly went for a solitary walk in the evening light, and as he walked, suddenly his dead father became real to him. He thought of things far away down the perspective of memory, of jolly moments when his father had skylarked with a wildly excited little boy; of a certain annual visit to the Crystal Palace pantomime, full of trivial glittering incidents and wonders; of his father's dread back while customers were in the old, minutely known shop. It is curious that the memory which seemed to link him nearest to the dead man was the memory of a fit of passion. His father had wanted to get a small sofa up the narrow winding staircase from the little room behind the shop to the bedroom above, and it had jammed. For a time his father had coaxed, and then groaned like a soul in torment and given way to blind fury; had sworn, kicked and struck at the offending piece of furniture and finally wrenched it upstairs, with considerable incidental damage to lath and plaster and one of the castors. That moment when self-control was altogether torn aside, the shocked discovery of his father's perfect humanity, had left a singular impression on Mr Polly's queer mind. It was as if something extravagantly vital had come out of his father and laid a warmly passionate hand upon his heart. He remembered that now very vividly, and it became a clue to endless other memories that had else been dispersed and confusing.

A weakly wilful being struggling to get obdurate things round impossible corners – in that symbol Mr Polly could recognise himself and all the trouble of humanity.

He hadn't had a particularly good time, poor old chap, and now it was all over. Finished . . .

Johnson was the sort of man who derives great satisfaction from a funeral; a melancholy, serious, practical-minded man of five and thirty, with great powers of advice. He was the up-line ticket clerk at Easewood Junction, and felt the responsibilities of his position. He was naturally thoughtful and reserved, and greatly sustained in that by an innate rectitude of body and an overhanging and forward inclination of the upper part of his face and head. He was pale but freckled, and his dark grey eyes were deeply set. His lightest interest was cricket, but he did not take that lightly. His chief holiday was to go to a cricket match, which he did as if he was going to

church, and he watched critically, applauded sparingly, and was darkly offended by any unorthodox play. His convictions upon all subjects were taciturnly inflexible. He was an obstinate player of draughts and chess, and an earnest and persistent reader of the *British Weekly*. His wife was a pink, short, wilfully smiling, managing, ingratiating, talkative woman, who was determined to be pleasant and to take a bright hopeful view of everything, even when it was not really bright and hopeful. She had large blue expressive eyes and a round face, and she always spoke of her husband as Harold. She addressed sympathetic and considerate remarks about the deceased to Mr Polly in notes of brisk encouragement. 'He was really quite cheerful at the end,' she said several times, with congratulatory gusto, 'quite cheerful.'

She made dying seem almost agreeable.

Both these people were resolved to treat Mr Polly very well, and to help his exceptional incompetence in every possible way, and after a simple supper of ham and bread and cheese and pickles and cold apple tart and small beer had been cleared away, they put him into the armchair almost as though he was an invalid, and sat on chairs that made them look down on him, and opened a directive discussion of the arrangements for the funeral. After all a funeral is a distinct social opportunity, and rare when you have no family and few relations, and they did not want to see it spoilt and wasted.

'You'll have a hearse, of course,' said Mrs Johnson. 'Not one of them combinations with the driver sitting on the coffin. Disrespectful I think they are. I can't fancy how people can bring themselves to be buried in combinations.' She flattened her voice in a manner she used to intimate aesthetic feeling. 'I *do* like them glass hearses,' she said. 'So refined and nice they are.'

'Podger's hearse you'll have,' said Johnson conclusively. 'It's the best in Easewood.'

'Everything that's right and proper,' said Mr Polly.

'Podger's ready to come and measure at any time,' said Johnson.

'Then you'll want a mourners' carriage or two, according as to whom you're going to invite,' said Mr Johnson.

'Didn't think of inviting anyone,' said Mr Polly.

'Oh! you'll *have* to ask a few friends,' said Mrs Johnson. 'You can't let your father go to his grave without asking a few friends.'

'Funerial baked meats like,' said Mr Polly.

'Not baked, but of course you'll have to give them something. Ham and chicken's very suitable. You don't want a lot of cooking with the ceremony coming into the middle of it. I wonder who Alfred ought to invite, Harold. Just the immediate relations; one doesn't want a Great Crowd of People and one doesn't want not to show respect.'

'But he hated our relations – most of them.'

'He's not hating them *now*,' said Mr Johnson, 'you may be sure of that.

It's just because of that I think they ought to come – all of them – even your Aunt Mildred.'

'Bit vulturial, isn't it?' said Mr Polly unheeded.

'Wouldn't be more than twelve or thirteen people if they *all* came,' said Mr Johnson.

'We could have everything put out ready in the back room and the gloves and whisky in the front room, and while we were all at the ceremony, Bessie could bring it all into the front room on a tray and put it out nice and proper. There'd have to be whisky and sherry or port for the ladies . . . '

'Where'll you get your mourning?' asked Johnson abruptly.

Mr Polly had not yet considered this by-product of sorrow. 'Haven't thought of it yet, o' man.'

A disagreeable feeling spread over his body as though he was blackening as he sat. He hated black garments.

'I suppose I must have mourning,' he said.

'Well!' said Johnson with a solemn smile.

'Got to see it through,' said Mr Polly indistinctly.

'If I were you,' said Johnson, 'I should get ready-made trousers. That's all you really want. And a black satin tie and a top hat with a deep mourning band. And gloves.'

'Jet cuff links he ought to have – as chief mourner,' said Mrs Johnson.

'Not obligatory,' said Johnson.

'It shows respect,' said Mrs Johnson.

'It shows respect of course,' said Johnson.

And then Mrs Johnson went on with the utmost gusto to the details of the 'casket', while Mr Polly sat more and more deeply and droopingly into the armchair, assenting with a note of protest to all they said. After he had retired for the night he remained for a long time perched on the edge of the sofa which was his bed, staring at the prospect before him. 'Chasing the o' man about to the last,' he said.

He hated the thought and elaboration of death as a healthy animal must hate it. His mind struggled with unwonted social problems.

'Got to put 'em away somehow, I suppose,' said Mr Polly. 'Wish I'd looked him up a bit more while he was alive.'

2

Bereavement came to Mr Polly before the realisation of opulence and its anxieties and responsibilities. That only dawned upon him on the morrow – which chanced to be Sunday – as he walked with Johnson before church time about the tangle of struggling building enterprise that constituted the rising urban district of Easewood. Johnson was off duty that morning, and

devoted the time very generously to the admonitory discussion of Mr Polly's worldly outlook.

'Don't seem to get the hang of the business somehow,' said Mr Polly. 'Too much blooming humbug in it for my way of thinking.'

'If I were you,' said Mr Johnson, 'I should push for a first-class place in London – take almost nothing and live on my reserves. That's what I should do.'

'Come the Heavy,' said Mr Polly.

'Get a better-class reference.'

There was a pause. 'Think of investing your money?' asked Johnson.

'Hardly got used to the idea of having it yet, o' man.'

'You'll have to do something with it. Give you nearly twenty pounds a year if you invest it properly.'

'Haven't seen it yet in that light,' said Mr Polly defensively.

'There's no end of things you could put it into.'

'It's getting it out again I shouldn't feel sure of. I'm no sort of Fiancianier. Sooner back horses.'

'I wouldn't do that if I were you.'

'Not my style, o' man.'

'It's a nest egg,' said Johnson.

Mr Polly made an indeterminate noise.

'There's building societies,' Johnson threw out in a speculative tone. Mr Polly, with detached brevity, admitted there were.

'You might lend it on mortgage,' said Johnson. 'Very safe form of investment.'

'Shan't think anything about it – not till the o' man's underground,' said Mr Polly with an inspiration.

They turned a corner that led towards the junction.

'Might do worse,' said Johnson, 'than put it into a small shop.'

At the moment this remark made very little appeal to Mr Polly. But afterwards it developed. It fell into his mind like some small obscure seed, and germinated.

'These shops aren't in a bad position,' said Johnson.

The row he referred to gaped in the late painful stage in building before the healing touch of the plasterer assuages the roughness of the brickwork. The space for the shop yawned an oblong gap below, framed above by an iron girder: 'Windows and fittings to suit tenant' a board at the end of the row promised; and behind was the door space and a glimpse of stairs going up to the living-rooms above. 'Not a bad position,' said Johnson, and led the way into the establishment. 'Room for fixtures there,' he said, pointing to the blank wall. The two men went upstairs to the little sitting-room (or best bedroom it would have to be) above the shop. Then they descended to the kitchen below.

'Rooms in a new house always look a bit small,' said Johnson.

They came out of the house again by the prospective back door, and picked their way through builders' litter across the yard space to the road again. They drew nearer the junction where a pavement and shops already open and active formed the commercial centre of Easewood. On the opposite side of the way the side door of a flourishing little establishment opened, and a man and his wife and a little boy in a sailor suit came into the street. The wife was a pretty woman in brown with a floriferous straw hat, and the group was altogether very Sundayfied and shiny and spick and span. The shop itself had a large plate-glass window whose contents were now veiled by a buff blind on which was inscribed in scrolly letters: 'Rymer, Pork Butcher and Provision Merchant', and then with voluptuous elaboration: 'The World-Famed Easewood Sausage'.

Greetings were exchanged between Mr Johnson and this distinguished comestible.

'Off to church already?' said Johnson.

'Walking across the fields to Little Dorington,' said Mr Rymer.

'Very pleasant walk,' said Johnson.

'Very,' said Mr Rymer.

'Hope you'll enjoy it,' said Mr Johnson.

'That chap's done well,' said Johnson *sotto voce* as they went on. 'Came here with nothing – practically, four years ago. And as thin as a lath. Look at him now!'

'He's worked hard of course,' added Johnson, improving the occasion.

Thought fell between the cousins for a space.

'Some men can do one thing,' said Johnson, 'and some another . . . For a man who sticks to it there's a lot to be done in a shop.'

3

All the preparations for the funeral ran easily and happily under Mrs Johnson's skilful hands. On the eve of the sad event she produced a reserve of black sateen, the kitchen steps and a box of tin-tacks, and decorated the house with festoons and bows of black in the best possible taste. She tied up the knocker with black crape, and put a large bow over the corner of the steel engraving of Garibaldi, and swathed the bust of Mr Gladstone that had belonged to the deceased with inky swathings. She turned the two vases that had views of Tivoli and the Bay of Naples round, so that these rather brilliant landscapes were hidden and only the plain blue enamel showed, and she anticipated the long-contemplated purchase of a tablecloth for the front room, and substituted a violet purple cover for the now very worn and faded raptures and roses in plushette that had hitherto done duty there. Everything that loving consideration could do to impart a dignified solemnity to her little home was done.

She had released Mr Polly from the irksome duty of issuing invitations, and as the moments of assembly drew near she sent him and Mr Johnson out into the narrow long strip of garden at the back of the house, to be free to put a finishing touch or so to her preparations. She sent them out together because she had a queer little persuasion at the back of her mind that Mr Polly wanted to bolt from his sacred duties, and there was no way out of the garden except through the house.

Mr Johnson was a steady, successful gardener, and particularly good with celery and peas. He walked slowly along the narrow path down the centre pointing out to Mr Polly a number of interesting points in the management of peas, wrinkles neatly applied and difficulties wisely overcome, and all that he did for the comfort and propitiation of that fitful but rewarding vegetable.

Presently a sound of nervous laughter and raised voices from the house proclaimed the arrival of the earlier guests, and the worst of that anticipatory tension was over.

When Mr Polly re-entered the house he found three entirely strange young women with pink faces, demonstrative manners and emphatic mourning engaged in an incoherent conversation with Mrs Johnson. All three kissed him with great gusto after the ancient English fashion. 'These are your cousins Larkins,' said Mrs Johnson; 'that's Annie (unexpected hug and smack), that's Miriam (resolute hug and smack), and that's Minnie (prolonged hug and smack).'

'Right-o,' said Mr Polly, emerging a little crumpled and breathless from this hearty introduction. 'I see.'

'Here's Aunt Larkins,' said Mrs Johnson, as an elderly and stouter edition of the three young women appeared in the doorway.

Mr Polly backed rather faint-heartedly, but Aunt Larkins was not to be denied. Having hugged and kissed her nephew resoundingly, she gripped him by the wrists and scanned his features. She had a round, sentimental, freckled face. 'I should 'ave known 'im anywhere,' she said with fervour.

'Hark at mother!' said the cousin called Annie. 'Why, she's never set eyes on him before!'

'I should 'ave known 'im anywhere,' said Mrs Larkins, 'for Lizzie's child. You've got her eyes! It's a Resemblance! And as for *never seeing 'im* – I've *dandled* him, Miss Imperence. I've dandled him.'

'You couldn't dandle him now, ma!' Miss Annie remarked with a shriek of laughter.

All the sisters laughed at that. 'The things you say, Annie!' said Miriam, and for a time the room was full of mirth.

Mr Polly felt it incumbent upon him to say something. '*My* dandling days are over,' he said.

The reception of this remark would have convinced a far more modest character than Mr Polly that it was extremely witty.

Mr Polly followed it up by another one almost equally good. 'My turn to dandle,' he said, with a sly look at his aunt, and convulsed everyone.

'Not me,' said Mrs Larkins, taking his point, '*thank* you,' and achieved a climax.

It was queer, but they seemed to be easy people to get on with anyhow. They were still picking little ripples and giggles of mirth from the idea of Mr Polly dandling Aunt Larkins when Mr Johnson, who had answered the door, ushered in a stooping figure, who was at once hailed by Mrs Johnson as 'Why! Uncle Pentstemon!' Uncle Pentstemon was rather a shock. His was an aged rather than venerable figure; Time had removed the hair from the top of his head and distributed a small dividend of the plunder in little bunches carelessly and impartially over the rest of his features; he was dressed in a very big old frock coat and a long cylindrical top hat, which he had kept on; he was very much bent, and he carried a rush basket from which protruded coy intimations of the lettuces and onions he had brought to grace the occasion. He hobbled into the room, resisting the efforts of Johnson to divest him of his various encumbrances, halted and surveyed the company with an expression of profound hostility, breathing hard. Recognition quickened in his eyes.

'*You* here,' he said to Aunt Larkins and then; 'You *would* be . . . These your gals?'

'They are,' said Aunt Larkins, 'and better gals – '

'That Annie?' asked Uncle Pentstemon, pointing a horny thumbnail.

'Fancy your remembering her name!'

'She mucked up my mushroom bed, the baggage!' said Uncle Pentstemon ungenially, 'and I give it to her to rights. Trounced her I did – fairly. I remember her. Here's some green stuff for you, Grace. Fresh it is and wholesome. I shall be wanting the basket back and mind you let me have it . . . Have you nailed him down yet? You always was a bit in front of what was needful.'

His attention was drawn inward by a troublesome tooth, and he sucked at it spitefully. There was something potent about this old man that silenced everyone for a moment or so. He seemed a fragment from the ruder agricultural past of our race, like a lump of soil among things of paper. He put his basket of vegetables very deliberately on the new violet tablecloth, removed his hat carefully and dabbled his brow, and wiped out his hat brim with an abundant crimson and yellow pocket handkerchief.

'I'm glad you were able to come, uncle,' said Mrs Johnson.

'Oh, I *came*' said Uncle Pentstemon. 'I *came*.'

He turned on Mrs Larkins. 'Gals in service?' he asked.

'They aren't and they won't be,' said Mrs Larkins.

'No,' he said with infinite meaning, and turned his eye on Mr Polly.

'You Lizzie's boy?' he said.

Mr Polly was spared much self-exposition by the tumult occasioned by further arrivals.

'Ah! here's May Punt!' said Mrs Johnson, and a small woman dressed in the borrowed mourning of a large woman and leading a very small long-haired observant little boy – it was his first funeral – appeared, closely followed by several friends of Mrs Johnson who had come to swell the display of respect and made only vague, confused impressions upon Mr Polly's mind. (Aunt Mildred, who was an unexplained family scandal, had declined Mrs Johnson's hospitality.)

Everybody was in profound mourning, of course, mourning in the modern English style, with the dyer's handiwork only too apparent, and hats and jackets of the current cut. There was very little crape, and the costumes had none of the goodness and specialisation and genuine enjoyment of mourning for mourning's sake that a similar Continental gathering would have displayed. Still that congestion of strangers in black sufficed to stun and confuse Mr Polly's impressionable mind. It seemed to him much more extraordinary than anything he had expected.

'Now, gals,' said Mrs Larkins, 'see if you can help,' and the three daughters became confusingly active between the front room and the back.

'I hope everyone'll take a glass of sherry and a biscuit,' said Mrs Johnson. 'We don't stand on ceremony,' and a decanter appeared in the place of Uncle Pentstemon's vegetables.

Uncle Pentstemon had refused to be relieved of his hat; he sat stiffly down on a chair against the wall with that venerable headdress between his feet, watching the approach of anyone jealously. 'Don't you go squashing my hat,' he said. Conversation became confused and general. Uncle Pentstemon addressed himself to Mr Polly. 'You're a little chap,' he said, 'a puny little chap. I never did agree to Lizzie marrying him, but I suppose bygones must be bygones now. I suppose they made you a clerk or something.'

'Outfitter,' said Mr Polly.

'I remember. Them girls pretend to be dressmakers.'

'They *are* dressmakers,' said Mrs Larkins across the room.

'I *will* take a glass of sherry. They 'old to it, you see.'

He took the glass Mrs Johnson handed him, and poised it critically between a horny finger and thumb. 'You'll be paying for this,' he said to Mr Polly. 'Here's *to* you . . . Don't you go treading on my hat, young woman. You brush your skirts against it and you take a shillin' off its value. It ain't the sort of 'at you see nowadays.'

He drank noisily.

The sherry presently loosened everybody's tongue, and the early coldness passed.

'There ought to have been a post-mortem,' Polly heard Mrs Punt remarking to one of Mrs Johnson's friends, and Miriam and another were lost in admiration of Mrs Johnson's decorations. 'So very nice and refined,' they were both repeating at intervals.

The sherry and biscuits were still being discussed when Mr Podger the

undertaker arrived, a broad, cheerfully sorrowful, clean-shaven little man, accompanied by a melancholy-faced assistant. He conversed for a time with Johnson in the passage outside; the sense of his business stilled the rising waves of chatter and carried off everyone's attention in the wake of his heavy footsteps to the room above.

4

Things crowded upon Mr Polly. Everyone, he noticed, took sherry with a solemn avidity, and a small portion even was administered sacramentally to the Punt boy. There followed a distribution of black kid gloves, and much trying on and humouring of fingers. '*Good* gloves,' said one of Mrs Johnson's friends. 'There's a little pair there for Willie,' said Mrs Johnson triumphantly. Everyone seemed gravely content with the amazing procedure of the occasion. Presently Mr Podger was picking Mr Polly out as Chief Mourner to go with Mrs Johnson, Mrs Larkins and Annie in the first mourning carriage.

'Right-o,' said Mr Polly, and repented instantly of the alacrity of the phrase.

'There'll have to be a walking party,' said Mrs Johnson cheerfully. 'There's only two coaches. I dare say we can put in six in each, but that leaves three over.'

There was a generous struggle to be pedestrian, and the two other Larkins girls, confessing coyly to tight new boots and displaying a certain eagerness, were added to the contents of the first carriage.

'It'll be a squeeze,' said Annie.

'*I* don't mind a squeeze,' said Mr Polly.

He decided privately that the proper phrase for the result of that remark was 'hysterial catechunations'.

Mr Podger re-entered the room from a momentary supervision of the bumping business that was now proceeding down the staircase.

'Bearing up,' he said cheerfully, rubbing his hands together. 'Bearing up!'

That stuck very vividly in Mr Polly's mind, and so did the close-wedged drive to the churchyard, bunched in between two young women in confused dull and shiny black, and the fact that the wind was bleak and that the officiating clergyman had a cold and sniffed between his sentences. The wonder of life! The wonder of everything! What had he expected that this should all be so astoundingly different?

He found his attention converging more and more upon the Larkins cousins. The interest was reciprocal. They watched him with a kind of suppressed excitement and became risible with his every word and gesture. He was more and more aware of their personal quality. Annie had blue eyes and a red, attractive mouth, a harsh voice and a habit of extreme liveliness

that even this occasion could not suppress; Minnie was fond, extremely free about the touching of hands and suchlike endearments; Miriam was dark and quieter than her sisters and regarded him earnestly. Mrs Larkins was very happy in her daughters, and they had the naïve affectionateness of those who see few people and find a strange cousin a wonderful outlet. Mr Polly had never been very much kissed, and it made his mind swim. He did not know for the life of him whether he liked or disliked all or any of the Larkins cousins. It was rather attractive to make them laugh; they laughed at anything.

There they were tugging at his mind, and the funeral tugging at his mind, too, and the sense of himself as Chief Mourner in a brand new silk hat with a broad mourning band. He watched the ceremony and missed his responses, and strange feelings twisted at his heartstrings.

5

Mr Polly walked back to the house because he wanted to be alone. Miriam and Minnie would have accompanied him, but finding Uncle Pentstemon beside the Chief Mourner they went on in front.

'You're wise,' said Uncle Pentstemon.

'Glad you think so,' said Mr Polly, rousing himself to talk.

'I likes a bit of walking before a meal,' said Uncle Pentstemon, and made a kind of large hiccup. 'That sherry rises,' he remarked. 'Grocer's stuff, I expect.'

He went on to ask how much the funeral might be costing, and seemed pleased to find Mr Polly didn't know.

'In that case,' he said impressively, 'it's pretty certain to cost more'n you expect, my boy.'

He meditated for a time. 'I've seen a mort of undertakers,' he declared; 'a mort of undertakers.'

The Larkins girls attracted his attention.

'Let's lodgin's and chars,' he commented. 'Leastways she goes out to cook dinners. And look at 'em! Dressed up to the nines. If it ain't borryd clothes, that is. And they goes out to work at a factory!'

'Did you know my father much, Uncle Pentstemon?' asked Mr Polly.

'Couldn't stand Lizzie throwin' herself away like that,' said Uncle Pentstemon, and repeated his hiccup on a larger scale.

'That *weren't* good sherry,' said Uncle Pentstemon with the first note of pathos Mr Polly had detected in his quavering voice.

The funeral in the rather cold wind had proved wonderfully appetising, and every eye brightened at the sight of the cold collation that was now spread in the front room. Mrs Johnson was very brisk, and Mr Polly, when he re-entered the house found everybody sitting down. 'Come along,

Alfred,' cried the hostess cheerfully. 'We can't very well begin without you. Have you got the bottled beer ready to open, Bessie? Uncle, you'll have a drop of whisky, I expect.'

'Put it where I can mix for myself,' said Uncle Pentstemon, placing his hat very carefully out of harm's way on the bookcase.

There were two cold boiled chickens, which Johnson carved with great care and justice, and a nice piece of ham, some brawn and a steak-and-kidney pie, a large bowl of salad and several sorts of pickles, and afterwards came cold apple tart, jam roll and a good piece of Stilton cheese, lots of bottled beer, some lemonade for the ladies and milk for Master Punt; a very bright and satisfying meal. Mr Polly found himself seated between Mrs Punt, who was much preoccupied with Master Punt's table manners, and one of Mrs Johnson's school friends, who was exchanging reminiscences of school days and news of how various common friends had changed and married with Mrs Johnson. Opposite him was Miriam and another of the Johnson circle, and also he had brawn to carve and there was hardly room for the helpful Bessie to pass behind his chair, so that altogether his mind would have been amply distracted from any mortuary broodings, even if a wordy warfare about the education of the modern young woman had not sprung up between Uncle Pentstemon and Mrs Larkins and threatened for a time, in spite of a word or so in season from Johnson, to wreck all the harmony of the sad occasion.

The general effect was after this fashion: First an impression of Mrs Punt on the right speaking in a refined undertone: 'You didn't, I suppose, Mr Polly, think to 'ave your poor dear father post-mortemed – '

Lady on the left side breaking in: 'I was just reminding Grace of the dear dead days beyond recall – '

Attempted reply to Mrs Punt: 'Didn't think of it for a moment. Can't give you a piece of this brawn, can I?'

Fragment from the left: 'Grace and Beauty they used to call us and we used to sit at the same desk – '

Mrs Punt, breaking out suddenly: 'Don't *swaller* your fork, Willy. You see, Mr Polly, I used to 'ave a young gentleman, a medical student, lodging with me – '

Voice from down the table: ' 'Am, Alfred? I didn't give you very much.'

Bessie became evident at the back of Mr Polly's chair, struggling wildly to get past. Mr Polly did his best to be helpful. 'Can you get past? Lemme sit forward a bit. Urr–oo! Right-o.'

Lady to the left going on valiantly and speaking to everyone who cares to listen, while Mrs Johnson beams beside her: 'There she used to sit as bold as brass, and the fun she used to make of things no one *could* believe – knowing her now. She used to make faces at the mistress through the – '

Mrs Punt keeping steadily on: 'The contents of the stummik at any rate *ought* to be examined.'

Voice of Mr Johnson. 'Elfrid, pass the mustid down.'

Miriam leaning across the table: 'Elfrid!'

'Once she got us all kept in. The whole school!'

Miriam, more insistently: 'Elfrid!'

Uncle Pentstemon, raising his voice defiantly: 'Trounce 'er again I would if she did as much now. That I would! Dratted mischief!'

Miriam, catching Mr Polly's eye: 'Elfrid! This lady knows Canterbury. I been telling her you been there.'

Mr Polly: 'Glad you know it.'

The lady shouting: 'I like it.'

Mrs Larkins, raising her voice: 'I won't 'ave my girls spoken of, not by nobody, old or young.'

Pop! imperfectly located.

Mr Johnson at large: 'Ain't the beer up! It's the 'eated room.'

Bessie: ' 'Scuse me, sir, passing so soon again, but – ' Rest inaudible. Mr Polly, accommodating himself: 'Urr–oo! Right? Right-o.'

The knives and forks, probably by some secret common agreement, clash and clatter together and drown every other sound.

'Nobody 'ad the least idea 'ow 'e died – nobody . . . Willie, don't *golp* so. You ain't in a 'urry, are you? You don't want to ketch a train or anything – golping like that!'

'D'you remember, Grace, 'ow one day we 'ad writing lesson . . . '

'Nicer girls no one ever 'ad – though I say it who shouldn't.'

Mrs Johnson in a shrill clear hospitable voice: 'Harold, won't Mrs Larkins 'ave a teeny bit more fowl?'

Mr Polly rising to the situation. 'Or some brawn, Mrs Larkins?' Catching Uncle Pentstemon's eye: 'Can't send *you* some brawn, sir?'

'Elfrid!'

Loud hiccup from Uncle Pentstemon, momentary consternation followed by giggle from Annie.

The narration at Mr Polly's elbow pursued a quiet but relentless course. 'Directly the new doctor came in he said: "Everything must be took out and put in spirits – everything." '

Willie – audible ingurgitation.

The narration on the left was flourishing up to a climax. ' "Ladies," she sez, "dip their pens *in* their ink and keep their noses out of it!" '

'Elfrid!' – persuasively.

'Certain people may cast snacks at other people's daughters, never having had any of their own, though two poor souls of wives dead and buried through their goings on – '

Johnson ruling the storm: 'We don't want old scores dug up on such a day as this – '

'Old scores you may call them, but worth a dozen of them that put them to their rest, poor dears.'

'Elfrid!' – with a note of remonstrance.

'If you choke yourself, my lord, not another mouthful do you 'ave. No nice puddin'! Nothing!'

'And kept us in, she did, every afternoon for a week!'

It seemed to be the end, and Mr Polly replied with an air of being profoundly impressed: 'Really!'

'Elfrid!' – a little disheartened.

'And then they 'ad it! They found he'd swallowed the very key to unlock the drawer – '

'Then don't let people go casting snacks!'

'*Who's* casting snacks!'

'Elfrid! This lady wants to know, 'ave the Prossers left Canterbury?'

'No wish to make myself disagreeable, not to God's 'umblest worm – '

'Alf, you aren't very busy with that brawn up there!'

And so on for the hour.

The general effect upon Mr Polly at the time was at once confusing and exhilarating; but it led him to eat copiously and carelessly, and long before the end, when after an hour and a quarter a movement took the party and it pushed away its cheese plates and rose sighing and stretching from the remains of the repast, little streaks and bands of dyspeptic irritation and melancholy were darkening the serenity of his mind.

He stood between the mantel shelf and the window – the blinds were up now – and the Larkins sisters clustered about him. He battled with the oncoming depression and forced himself to be extremely facetious about two noticeable rings on Annie's hand. 'They ain't real,' said Annie coquettishly. 'Got 'em out of a prize packet.'

'Prize packet in trousers, I expect,' said Mr Polly, and awakened inextinguishable laughter.

'Oh! the Things you say!' said Minnie, slapping his shoulder.

Suddenly something he had quite extraordinarily forgotten came into his head.

'Bless my heart!' he cried, suddenly serious.

'What's the matter?' asked Johnson.

'Ought to have gone back to the shop – three days ago. They'll make no end of a row!'

'Lor, you *are* a Treat!' said cousin Annie, and screamed with laughter at a delicious idea. 'You'll get the Chuck,' she said.

Mr Polly made a convulsing grimace at her.

'I'll die!' she said. 'I don't believe you care a bit!'

Feeling a little disorganised by her hilarity and a shocked expression that had come to the face of cousin Miriam, he made some indistinct excuse and went out through the back room and scullery into the little garden. The cool air and a very slight drizzle of rain was a relief – anyhow. But the black mood of the replete dyspeptic had come upon him. His soul darkened

hopelessly. He walked with his hands in his pockets down the path between the rows of exceptionally cultured peas, and unreasonably, overwhelmingly, he was smitten by sorrow for his father. The heady noise and muddle and confused excitement of the feast passed from him like a curtain drawn away. He thought of that hot and angry and struggling creature who had tugged and sworn so foolishly at the sofa upon the twisted staircase, and who was now lying still and hidden, at the bottom of a wall-sided oblong pit beside the heaped gravel that would presently cover him. The stillness of it! the wonder of it! the infinite reproach! Hatred for all these people – all of them – possessed Mr Polly's soul.

'Hen-witted gigglers,' said Mr Polly.

He went down to the fence, and stood with his hands on it staring away at nothing. He stayed there for what seemed a long time. From the house came a sound of raised voices that subsided, and then Mrs Johnson calling for Bessie.

'Gowlish gusto,' said Mr Polly. 'Jumping it in. Funererial Games. Don't hurt *him* of course. Doesn't matter to *him* . . .'

Nobody missed Mr Polly for a long time.

When at last he reappeared among them his eye was almost grim, but nobody noticed his eye. They were looking at watches, and Johnson was being omniscient about trains. They seemed to discover Mr Polly afresh just at the moment of parting, and said a number of more or less appropriate things. But Uncle Pentstemon was far too worried about his rush basket, which had been carelessly mislaid, he seemed to think with larcenous intentions, to remember Mr Polly at all. Mrs Johnson had tried to fob him off with a similar but inferior basket – his own had one handle mended with string according to a method of peculiar virtue and inimitable distinction known only to himself – and the old gentleman had taken her attempt as the gravest reflection upon his years and intelligence. Mr Polly was left very largely to the Larkins trio. Cousin Minnie became shameless and kept kissing him goodbye – and then finding out it wasn't time to go. Cousin Miriam seemed to think her silly, and caught Mr Polly's eye sympathetically. Cousin Annie ceased to giggle and lapsed into a nearly sentimental state. She said with real feeling that she had enjoyed the funeral more than words could tell.

Mr Polly Takes a Vacation

Mr Polly returned to Clapham from the funeral celebration prepared for trouble, and took his dismissal in a manly spirit.

'You've merely antiseparated me by a hair,' he said politely.

And he told them in the dormitory that he meant to take a little holiday before his next crib, though a certain inherited reticence suppressed the fact of the legacy.

'You'll do that all right,' said Ascough, the head of the boot shop. 'It's quite the fashion just at present. Six Weeks in Wonderful Wood Street. They're running excursions . . . '

'A little holiday'; that was the form his sense of wealth took first, that it made a little holiday possible. Holidays were his life, and the rest merely adulterated living. And now he might take a little holiday and have money for railway fares and money for meals and money for inns. But – he wanted someone to take the holiday with.

For a time he cherished a design of hunting up Parsons, getting him to throw up his situation, and going with him to Stratford-on-Avon and Shrewsbury and the Welsh mountains and the Wye and a lot of places like that, for a really gorgeous, careless, illimitable old holiday of a month. But alas! Parsons had gone from the St Paul's Churchyard outfitter's long ago, and left no address.

Mr Polly tried to think he would be almost as happy wandering alone, but he knew better. He had dreamt of casual encounters with delightfully interesting people by the wayside – even romantic encounters. Such things happened in Chaucer and 'Bocashiew'; they happened with extreme facility in Mr Richard Le Gallienne's very detrimental book *The Quest of the Golden Girl*, which he had read at Canterbury, but he had no confidence they would happen in England – to him.

When, a month later, he came out of the Clapham side door at last into the bright sunshine of a fine London day, with a dazzling sense of limitless freedom upon him, he did nothing more adventurous than order the cabman to drive to Waterloo and there take a ticket for Easewood.

He wanted – what *did* he want most in life? I think his distinctive craving is best expressed as fun – fun in companionship. He had already spent a pound or two upon three select feasts to his fellow assistants, sprat suppers they were, and there had been a great and very successful Sunday pilgrimage to Richmond, by Wandsworth and Wimbledon's open common, a trailing garrulous company walking about a solemnly happy host, to wonderful cold meat and salad at the Roebuck, a bowl of punch,

punch! and a bill to correspond; but now it was a weekday, and he went down to Easewood with his bag and portmanteau in a solitary compartment, and looked out of the window upon a world in which every possible congenial soul seemed either toiling in a situation or else looking for one with a gnawing and hopelessly preoccupying anxiety. He stared out of the window at the exploitation roads of suburbs, and rows of houses all very much alike, either emphatically and impatiently To Let or full of rather busy unsocial people. Near Wimbledon he had a glimpse of golf links, and saw two elderly gentlemen who, had they chosen, might have been gentlemen of grace and leisure, addressing themselves to smite little hunted white balls great distances with the utmost bitterness and dexterity. Mr Polly could not understand them.

Every road he remarked, as freshly as though he had never observed it before, was bordered by inflexible palings or iron fences or severely disciplined hedges. He wondered if perhaps abroad there might be beautifully careless, unenclosed high roads. Perhaps after all the best way of taking a holiday is to go abroad.

He was haunted by the memory of what was either a half-forgotten picture or a dream: a carriage was drawn up by the wayside and four beautiful people, two men and two women graciously dressed, were dancing a formal ceremonious dance, full of bows and curtseys, to the music of a wandering fiddler they had encountered. They had been driving one way and he walking another – a happy encounter with this obvious result. They might have come straight out of happy Theleme, whose motto is: 'Do what thou wilt.' The driver had taken his two sleek horses out; they grazed unchallenged; and he sat on a stone clapping time with his hands while the fiddler played. The shade of the trees did not altogether shut out the sunshine, the grass in the wood was lush and full of still daffodils, the turf they danced on was starred with daisies.

Mr Polly, dear heart! firmly believed that things like that could and did happen – somewhere. Only it puzzled him that morning that he never saw them happening. Perhaps they happened south of Guildford. Perhaps they happened in Italy. Perhaps they ceased to happen a hundred years ago. Perhaps they happened just round the corner – on weekdays when all good Mr Pollys are safely shut up in shops. And so dreaming of delightful impossibilities until his heart ached for them, he was rattled along in the suburban train to Johnson's discreet home and the briskly stimulating welcome of Mrs Johnson.

Mr Polly translated his restless craving for joy and leisure into Harold Johnsonese by saying that he meant to look about him for a bit before going into another situation. It was a decision Johnson very warmly approved. It was arranged that Mr Polly should occupy his former room and board with the Johnsons in consideration of a weekly payment of eighteen shillings. And the next morning Mr Polly went out early and reappeared with a purchase, a safety bicycle, which he proposed to study and master in the sandy lane below the Johnsons' house. But over the struggles that preceded his mastery it is humane to draw a veil.

And also Mr Polly bought a number of books: Rabelais for his own, and *The Arabian Nights*, the works of Sterne, a pile of *Tales from Blackwood*, cheap in a second-hand bookshop, the plays of William Shakespeare, a second-hand copy of Belloc's *Path to Rome*, an odd volume of *Purchas his Pilgrimes* and *The Life and Death of Jason*.

'Better get yourself a good book on bookkeeping,' said Johnson, turning over perplexing pages.

A belated spring was now advancing with great strides to make up for lost time. Sunshine and a stirring wind were poured out over the land, fleets of towering clouds sailed upon urgent tremendous missions across the blue seas of heaven, and presently Mr Polly was riding a little unstably along unfamiliar Surrey roads, wondering always what was round the next corner, and marking the blackthorn and looking out for the first white flower-buds of the may. He was perplexed and distressed, as indeed are all right-thinking souls, that there is no may in early May.

He did not ride at the even pace sensible people use who have marked out a journey from one place to another, and settled what time it will take them. He rode at variable speeds, and always as though he was looking for something that, missing, left life attractive still, but a little wanting in significance. And sometimes he was so unreasonably happy he had to whistle and sing, and sometimes he was incredibly, but not at all painfully, sad. His indigestion vanished with air and exercise, and it was quite pleasant in the evening to stroll about the garden with Johnson and discuss plans for the future. Johnson was full of ideas. Moreover, Mr Polly had marked the road that led to Stamton, that rising populous suburb; and as his bicycle legs grew strong his wheel with a sort of inevitableness carried him towards the row of houses in a back street in which his Larkins cousins made their home together.

He was received with great enthusiasm.

The street was a dingy little street, a cul-de-sac of very small houses in a row, each with an almost flattened bow window and a blistered brown door

with a black knocker. He poised his bright new bicycle against the window and knocked and stood waiting; he felt himself in his straw hat and black serge suit a very pleasant and prosperous-looking figure. The door was opened by cousin Miriam. She was wearing a bluish print dress that brought out a kind of sallow warmth in her skin, and although it was nearly four o'clock in the afternoon, her sleeves were tucked up, as if for some domestic work, above the elbows, showing her rather slender but very shapely yellowish arms. The loosely pinned bodice confessed a delicately rounded neck.

For a moment she regarded him with suspicion and a faint hostility, and then recognition dawned in her eyes.

'Why!' she said, 'it's cousin Elfrid!'

'Thought I'd look you up,' he said.

'Fancy you coming to see us like this!' she answered.

They stood confronting one another for a moment, while Miriam collected herself for the unexpected emergency.

'Exploratious menanderings,' said Mr Polly, indicating the bicycle.

Miriam's face betrayed no appreciation of the remark.

'Wait a moment,' she said, coming to a rapid decision, 'and I'll tell ma.'

She closed the door on him abruptly, leaving him a little surprised in the street. 'Ma!' he heard her calling, and swift speech followed, the import of which he didn't catch. Then she reappeared. It seemed but an instant, but she was changed; the arms had vanished into sleeves, the apron had gone, a certain pleasing disorder of the hair had been at least reproved.

'I didn't mean to shut you out,' she said, coming out upon the step. 'I just told ma. How are you, Elfrid? You *are* looking well. I didn't know you rode a bicycle. Is it a new one?'

She leaned upon his bicycle. 'Bright it is!' she said. 'What a trouble you must have to keep it clean!'

Mr Polly was aware of a rustling transit along the passage, and of the house suddenly full of hushed but strenuous movement.

'It's plated mostly,' said Mr Polly.

'What do you carry in that little bag thing?' she asked, and then branched off to: 'We're all in a mess today, you know. It's my cleaning up day today. I'm not a bit tidy I know, but I *do* like to 'ave a go in at things now and then. You got to take us as you find us, Elfrid. Mercy we wasn't all out.' She paused. She was talking against time. 'I *am* glad to see you again,' she repeated.

'Couldn't keep away,' said Mr Polly gallantly. 'Had to come over and see my pretty cousins again.'

Miriam did not answer for a moment. She coloured deeply. 'You *do say* things!' she said.

She stared at Mr Polly, and his unfortunate sense of fitness made him nod his head towards her, regard her firmly with a round brown eye, and add impressively: 'I don't say *which* of them.'

Her answering expression made him realise in an instant the terrible dangers he trifled with. Avidity flared up in her eyes. Minnie's voice came happily to dissolve the situation.

' 'Ello, Elfrid!' she said from the doorstep.

Her hair was just passably tidy, and she was a little effaced by a red blouse, but there was no mistaking the genuine brightness of her welcome.

He was to come in to tea, and Mrs Larkins, exuberantly genial in a floriferous but dingy flannel dressing gown, appeared to confirm that. He brought in his bicycle and put it in the narrow, empty passage, and everyone crowded into a small untidy kitchen, whose table had been hastily cleared of the debris of the midday repast.

'You must come in 'ere,' said Mrs Larkins, 'for Miriam's turning out the front room. I never did see such a girl for cleanin' up. Miriam's 'oliday's a scrub. You've caught us on the 'Op, as the sayin' is, but Welcome all the same. Pity Annie's at work today; she won't be 'ome till seven.'

Miriam put chairs and attended to the fire; Minnie edged up to Mr Polly and said: 'I *am* glad to see you again, Elfrid,' with a warm contiguous intimacy that betrayed a broken tooth. Mrs Larkins got out tea things, and descanted on the noble simplicity of their lives, and how he 'mustn't mind our simple ways'. They enveloped Mr Polly with a geniality that intoxicated his amiable nature; he insisted upon helping lay the things, and created enormous laughter by pretending not to know where plates and knives and cups ought to go. 'Who'm I going to sit next?' he said, and developed voluminous amusement by attempts to arrange the plates so that he could rub elbows with all three. Mrs Larkins had to sit down in the windsor chair by the grandfather clock (which was dark with dirt and not going) to laugh at her ease at his well-acted perplexity.

They got seated at last, and Mr Polly struck a vein of humour in telling them how he learnt to ride the bicycle. He found the mere repetition of the word 'wobble' sufficient to produce almost inextinguishable mirth.

'No foreseeing little accidentulous misadventures,' he said, 'none whatever.'

(Giggle from Minnie.)

'Stout elderly gentleman – shirt sleeves – large straw waste-paper-basket sort of hat – starts to cross the road – going to the oil shop – prodic refreshment of oil can – '

'Don't say you run 'im down,' said Mrs Larkins, gasping. 'Don't say you run 'im down, Elfrid!'

'Run 'im down! Not me, madam. I never run anything down. Wobble. Ring the bell. Wobble, wobble – '

(Laughter and tears.)

'No one's going to run him down. Hears the bell! Wobble. Gust of wind. Off comes the hat smack into the wheel. Wobble. *Lord! what's* going to happen? Hat across the road, old gentleman after it, bell, shriek. He ran

into me. Didn't ring his bell, hadn't *got* a bell – just ran into me. Over I went clinging to his venerable head. Down he went with me clinging to him. Oil can blump, blump into the road.'

(Interlude while Minnie is attended to for crumb in the windpipe.)

'Well, what happened to the old man with the oil can?' said Mrs Larkins.

'We sat about among the debreece and had a bit of an argument. I told him he oughtn't to come out wearing such a dangerous hat – flying at things. Said if he couldn't control his hat he ought to leave it at home. High old jawbacious argument we had, I tell you. "I tell you, sir – " "I tell *you*, sir." Waw-waw-waw. Infuriacious. But that's the sort of thing that's constantly happening, you know – on a bicycle. People run into you, hens and cats and dogs and things. Everything seems to have its mark on you; everything.'

'*You* never run into anything.'

'Never. Swelpme,' said Mr Polly very solemnly.

'Never, 'e say!' squealed Minnie. 'Hark at 'im!' and relapsed into a condition that urgently demanded back thumping.

'Don't be so silly,' said Miriam, thumping hard.

Mr Polly had never been such a social success before. They hung upon his every word – and laughed. What a family they were for laughter! And he loved laughter. The background he apprehended dimly; it was very much the sort of background his life had always had. There was a threadbare tablecloth on the table, and the slop basin and teapot did not go with the cups and saucers, the plates were different again, the knives worn down, the butter lived in a greenish glass dish of its own. Behind was a dresser hung with spare and miscellaneous crockery, with a workbox and an untidy workbasket; there was an ailing musk plant in the window, and the tattered and blotched wallpaper was covered by bright-coloured grocers' almanacs. Feminine wrappings hung from pegs upon the door, and the floor was covered with a varied collection of fragments of oilcloth. The Windsor chair he sat in was unstable – which presently afforded material for humour. 'Steady, old nag,' he said; 'whoa, my friskiacious palfry!'

'The things he says! You never know what he won't say next!'

3

'You ain't talkin' of goin'!' cried Mrs Larkins.

'Supper at eight.'

'Stay to supper with *us*, now you 'ave come over,' said Mrs Larkins, with corroborating cries from Minnie. ' 'Ave a bit of a walk with the gals, and then come back to supper. You might all go and meet Annie while I straighten up and lay things out.'

'You're not to go touching the front room mind,' said Miriam.

'*Who's* going to touch yer front room?' said Mrs Larkins, apparently forgetful for a moment of Mr Polly.

Both girls dressed with some care while Mrs Larkins sketched the better side of their characters, and then the three young people went out to see something of Stamton. In the streets their risible mood gave way to a self-conscious propriety that was particularly evident in Miriam's bearing. They took Mr Polly to the Stamton Wreckeryation ground – that at least was what they called it – with its handsome custodian's cottage, its asphalt paths, its Jubilee drinking fountain, its clumps of wallflowers and daffodils, its charmingly artistic noticeboards with green borders and 'art' lettering, and so to the new cemetery and a distant view of the Surrey hills, and round by the gasworks to the canal and to the factory that presently disgorged a surprised and radiant Annie.

'El-*lo*,' said Annie.

It is very pleasant to every properly constituted mind to be a centre of amiable interest for one's fellow creatures; and when one is a young man conscious of becoming mourning and a certain wit, and the fellow creatures are three young and ardent and sufficiently expressive young women who dispute for the honour of walking by one's side, one may be excused a secret exaltation. They did dispute.

'I'm going to 'ave 'im now,' said Annie. 'You two've been 'aving 'im all the afternoon. Besides, I've got something to say to him.'

She had something to say to him. It came presently.

'I say,' she said abruptly. 'I *did* get them rings out of a prize packet.'

'What rings?' asked Mr Polly.

'What you saw at your poor father's funeral. You made out they meant something. They didn't – straight.'

'Then some people have been very remiss about their chances,' said Mr Polly, understanding.

'They haven't had any chances,' said Annie. 'I don't believe in making oneself too free with people.'

'Nor me,' said Mr Polly.

'I may be a bit larky and cheerful in my manner,' Annie admitted. 'But it don't *mean* anything. I ain't that sort.'

'Right-o,' said Mr Polly.

4

It was past ten when Mr Polly found himself riding back towards Easewood in a broad moonlight with a little Japanese lantern dangling from his handlebar and making a fiery circle of pinkish light on and round about his front wheel. He was mightily pleased with himself and the day. There had been four-ale to drink at supper mixed with ginger beer, very free and jolly

in a jug. No shadow fell upon the agreeable excitement of his mind until he faced the anxious and reproachful face of Johnson, who had been sitting up for him, smoking and trying to read the odd volume of *Purchas his Pilgrimes* – about the monk who went into Sarmatia and saw the Tartar carts.

'Not had an accident, Elfrid?' said Johnson.

The weakness of Mr Polly's character came out in his reply. 'Not much,' he said. 'Pedal got a bit loose in Stamton, o' man. Couldn't ride it. So I looked up the cousins while I waited.'

'Not the Larkins lot?'

'Yes.'

Johnson yawned hugely and asked for and was given friendly particulars. 'Well,' he said, 'better get to bed. I have been reading that book of yours – rum stuff. Can't make it out quite. Quite out of date I should say if you asked me.'

'That's all right, o' man,' said Mr Polly.

'Not a bit of use for anything I can see.'

'Not a bit.'

'See any shops in Stamton?'

'Nothing to speak of,' said Mr Polly. 'Good-night, o' man.'

Before and after this brief conversation his mind ran on his cousins very warmly and prettily in the vein of high spring. Mr Polly had been drinking at the poisoned fountains of English literature, fountains so unsuited to the needs of a decent clerk or shopman, fountains charged with the dangerous suggestion that it becomes a man of gaiety and spirit to make love, gallantly and rather carelessly. It seemed to him that evening to be handsome and humorous and practicable to make love to all his cousins. It wasn't that he liked any of them particularly, but he liked something about them. He liked their youth and femininity, their resolute high spirits and their interest in him.

They laughed at nothing and knew nothing, and Minnie had lost a tooth and Annie screamed and shouted, but they were interesting, intensely interesting.

And Miriam wasn't so bad as the others. He had kissed them all and had been kissed in addition several times by Minnie – 'oscoolatory exercises'.

He buried his nose in his pillow and went to sleep – to dream of anything rather than getting on in the world, as a sensible young man in his position ought to have done.

5

And now Mr Polly began to lead a divided life. With the Johnsons he professed to be inclined, but not so conclusively inclined as to be in-convenient, to get a shop for himself – to be, to use the phrase he preferred,

'looking for an opening'. He would ride off in the afternoon upon that research, remarking that he was going to 'cast a strategetical eye' on Chertsey or Weybridge. But if not all roads still a great majority of them led by however devious ways to Stamton, and to laughter and increasing familiarity. Relations developed with Annie and Minnie and Miriam. Their various characters were increasingly interesting. The laughter became perceptibly less abundant, something of the fizz had gone from the first opening, still these visits remained wonderfully friendly and upholding. Then back he would come to grave but evasive discussions with Johnson.

Johnson was really anxious to get Mr Polly 'into something'. His was a reserved, honest character, and he would really have preferred to see his lodger doing things for himself than receive his money for housekeeping. He hated waste, anybody's waste, much more than he desired profit. But Mrs Johnson was all for Mr Polly's loitering. She seemed much the more human and likeable of the two to Mr Polly.

He tried at times to work up enthusiasm for the various avenues to wellbeing his discussion with Johnson opened. But they remained disheartening prospects. He imagined himself wonderfully smartened up, acquiring style and value in a London shop, but the picture was stiff and unconvincing. He tried to rouse himself to enthusiasm by the idea of his property increasing by leaps and bounds, by twenty pounds a year or so, let us say, each year, in a well-placed little shop, the corner shop Johnson favoured. There was a certain picturesque interest in imagining cut-throat economies, but his heart told him there would be little in practising them.

And then it happened to Mr Polly that real Romance came out of dreamland into life, and intoxicated and gladdened him with sweetly beautiful suggestions – and left him. She came and left him as that dear lady leaves so many of us, alas! not sparing him one jot or one tittle of the hollowness of her retreating aspect.

It was all the more to Mr Polly's taste that the thing should happen as things happen in books.

In a resolute attempt not to get to Stamton that day, he had turned due southward from Easewood towards a country where the abundance of bracken jungles, lady's smock, stitchwort, bluebells and grassy stretches by the wayside under shady trees does much to compensate the lighter type of mind for the absence of promising 'openings'. He turned aside from the road and wheeled his machine along a faintly marked attractive trail through bracken until he came to a heap of logs against a high old stone wall with damaged coping and wallflower plants already gone to seed. He sat down, balanced the straw hat on a convenient lump of wood, lit a cigarette, and abandoned himself to agreeable musings and the friendly observation of a cheerful little brown and grey bird his stillness presently encouraged to approach him. 'This is All Right,' said Mr Polly softly to the little brown and grey bird. 'Business – later.'

He reflected that he might go on this way for four or five years, and then be scarcely worse off than he had been in his father's lifetime.

'Vile Business,' said Mr Polly.

Then Romance appeared. Or, to be exact, Romance became audible.

Romance began as a series of small but increasingly vigorous movements on the other side of the wall, then as a voice murmuring, then as a falling of little fragments on the hither side and as ten pink fingertips, scarcely apprehended before Romance became startling and emphatically a leg, remained for a time a fine, slender, actively struggling limb, brown stockinged and wearing a brown toe-worn shoe, and then – A handsome red-haired girl wearing a short dress of blue linen was sitting astride the wall, panting, considerably disarranged by her climbing, and as yet unaware of Mr Polly . . .

His fine instincts made him turn his head away and assume an attitude of negligent contemplation, with his ears and mind alive to every sound behind him.

'Goodness!' said a voice with a sharp note of surprise.

Mr Polly was on his feet in an instant. 'Dear me! Can I be of any assistance?' he said with deferential gallantry.

'I don't know,' said the young lady, and regarded him calmly with clear blue eyes. 'I didn't know there was anyone here,' she added.

'Sorry,' said Mr Polly, 'if I am intrudaceous. I didn't know you didn't want me to be here.'

She reflected for a moment on the word. 'It isn't that,' she said, surveying him.

'I oughtn't to get over the wall,' she explained. 'It's out of bounds. At least in term time. But this being holidays – '

Her manner placed the matter before him.

'Holidays is different,' said Mr Polly.

'I don't want to actually *break* the rules,' she said.

'Leave them behind you,' said Mr Polly with a catch of the breath, 'where they are safe;' and marvelling at his own wit and daring, and indeed trembling within himself, he held out a hand for her.

She brought another brown leg from the unknown, and arranged her skirt with a dexterity altogether feminine. 'I think I'll stay on the wall,' she decided. 'So long as some of me's in bounds – '

She continued to regard him with eyes that presently danced in an irresistible smile of satisfaction. Mr Polly smiled in return.

'You bicycle?' she said.

Mr Polly admitted the fact, and she said she did too.

'All my people are in India,' she explained. 'It's beastly rot – I mean it's frightfully dull being left here alone.'

'All *my* people,' said Mr Polly, 'are in heaven!'

'I say!'

'Fact!' said Mr Polly. 'Got nobody.'

'And that's why – ' she checked her artless comment on his mourning. 'I say,' she said in a sympathetic voice, 'I *am* sorry. I really am. Was it a fire or a ship – or something?'

Her sympathy was very delightful. He shook his head. 'The ordinary tables of mortality,' he said. 'First one and then another.'

Behind his outward melancholy, delight was dancing wildly.

'Are *you* lonely?' asked the girl.

Mr Polly nodded.

'I was just sitting there in melancholy rectrospectatiousness,' he said, indicating the logs; and again a swift thoughtfulness swept across her face.

'There's no harm in our talking,' she reflected.

'It's a kindness. Won't you get down?'

She reflected, and surveyed the turf below and the scene around and him.

'I'll stay on the wall,' she said. 'If only for bounds' sake.'

She certainly looked quite adorable on the wall. She had a fine neck and pointed chin that was particularly admirable from below, and pretty eyes and fine eyebrows are never so pretty as when they look down upon one. But no calculation of that sort, thank heaven, was going on beneath her ruddy shock of hair.

6

'Let's talk,' she said, and for a time they were both tongue-tied.

Mr Polly's literary proclivities had taught him that under such circumstances a strain of gallantry was demanded. And something in his blood repeated that lesson.

'You make me feel like one of those old knights,' he said, 'who rode about the country looking for dragons and beautiful maidens and chivalresque adventures.'

'Oh!' she said. 'Why?'

'Beautiful maiden,' he said.

She flushed under her freckles with the quick bright flush those pretty red-haired people have. 'Nonsense!' she said.

'You are. I'm not the first to tell you that. A beautiful maiden imprisoned in an enchanted school.'

'*You* wouldn't think it enchanted!'

'And here am I – clad in steel. Well, not exactly, but my fiery war horse is anyhow. Ready to absquatulate all the dragons and rescue you.'

She laughed, a jolly laugh that showed delightfully gleaming teeth. 'I wish you could *see* the dragons,' she said with great enjoyment. Mr Polly felt they were a sun's distance from the world of everyday.

'Fly with me!' he dared.

She stared for a moment, and then went off into peals of laughter. 'You *are* funny!' she said. 'Why, I haven't known you five minutes.'

'One doesn't – in this medevial world. My mind is made up, anyhow.' He was proud and pleased with his joke, and quick to change his key neatly. 'I wish one could,' he said.

'I wonder if people ever did!'

'If there were people like you.'

'We don't even know each other's names,' she remarked, with a descent to matters of fact.

'Yours is the prettiest name in the world.'

'How do you know?'

'It must be – anyhow.'

'It *is* rather pretty you know – it's Christabel.'

'What did I tell you?'

'And yours?'

'Poorer than I deserve. It's Alfred.'

'*I* can't call you Alfred.'

'Well, Polly.'

'It's a girl's name!'

For a moment he was out of tune. 'I wish it was!' he said, and could have bitten out his tongue at the Larkins sound of it.

'I shan't forget it,' she remarked consolingly.

'I say,' she said in the pause that followed. 'Why are you riding about the country on a bicycle?'

'I'm doing it because I like it.'

She sought to estimate his social status on her limited basis of experience. He stood leaning with one hand against the wall, looking up at her and tingling with daring thoughts. He was a littleish man, you must remember, but neither mean-looking nor unhandsome in those days, sunburnt by his holiday and now warmly flushed. He had an inspiration to simple speech that no practised trifler with love could have bettered. 'There *is* love at first sight,' he said, and said it sincerely.

She stared at him with eyes round and big with excitement.

'I think,' she said slowly, and without any signs of fear or retreat, 'I ought to get back over the wall.'

'It needn't matter to you,' he said. 'I'm just a nobody. But I know you are the best and most beautiful thing I've ever spoken to.' His breath caught against something. 'No harm in telling you that,' he said.

'I should have to go back if I thought you were serious,' she said after a pause, and they both smiled together.

After that they talked in a fragmentary way for some time. The blue eyes surveyed Mr Polly with kindly curiosity from under a broad, finely modelled brow, much as an exceptionally intelligent cat might survey a new sort of dog. She meant to find out all about him. She asked questions

that riddled the honest knight in armour below, and probed ever nearer to the hateful secret of the shop and his normal servitude. And when he made a flourish and mispronounced a word a thoughtful shade passed like the shadow of a cloud across her face.

'Boom!' came the sound of a gong.

'Lordy!' cried the girl and flashed a pair of brown legs at him and was gone.

Then her pink fingertips reappeared, and the top of her red hair. 'Knight!' she cried from the other side of the wall. 'Knight there!'

'Lady!' he answered.

'Come again tomorrow!'

'At your command. But – '

'Yes?'

'Just one finger.'

'What do you mean?'

'To kiss.'

The rustle of retreating footsteps and silence . . .

But after he had waited next day for twenty minutes she reappeared, a little out of breath with the effort to surmount the wall – and head first this time. And it seemed to him she was lighter and more daring and altogether prettier than the dreams and enchanted memories that had filled the interval.

<div style="text-align:center">

7

</div>

From first to last their acquaintance lasted ten days, but into that time Mr Polly packed ten years of dreams.

'He don't seem,' said Johnson, 'to take a serious interest in anything. That shop at the corner's bound to be snapped up if he don't look out.'

The girl and Mr Polly did not meet on every one of those ten days; one was Sunday and she could not come, and on the eighth the school reassembled and she made vague excuses. All their meetings amounted to this, that she sat on the wall, more or less in bounds as she expressed it, and let Mr Polly fall in love with her and try to express it below. She sat in a state of irresponsible exaltation, watching him and at intervals prodding a vivisecting point of encouragement into him – with that strange passive cruelty which is natural to her sex and age.

And Mr Polly fell in love, as though the world had given way beneath him and he had dropped through into another, into a world of luminous clouds and of a desolate hopeless wilderness of desiring and of wild valleys of unreasonable ecstasies, a world whose infinite miseries were finer and in some inexplicable way sweeter than the purest gold of the daily life, whose joys – they were indeed but the merest remote glimpses of joy – were

brighter than a dying martyr's vision of heaven. Her smiling face looked down upon him out of heaven, her careless pose was the living body of life. It was senseless, it was utterly foolish, but all that was best and richest in Mr Polly's nature broke like a wave and foamed up at that girl's feet, and died, and never touched her. And she sat on the wall and marvelled at him and was amused, and once, suddenly moved and wrung by his pleading, she bent down rather shamefacedly and gave him a freckled, tennis-blistered little paw to kiss. And she looked into his eyes and suddenly felt a perplexity, a curious swimming of the mind that made her recoil and stiffen, and wonder afterwards and dream . . .

And then, with some dim instinct of self-protection, she went and told her three best friends, great students of character all, of this remarkable phenomenon she had discovered on the other side of the wall.

'Look here,' said Mr Polly, 'I'm wild for the love of you! I can't keep up this gesticulatious game any more! I'm not a Knight. Treat me as a human man. You may sit up there smiling, but I'd die in torments to have you mine for an hour. I'm nobody and nothing. But look here! Will you wait for me for five years? You're just a girl yet, and it wouldn't be hard.'

'Shut up!' said Christabel, in an aside he did not hear, and something he did not see touched her hand.

'I've always been just dilletentytating about till now, but I could work. I've just woke up. Wait till I've got a chance with the money I've got.'

'But you haven't got much money!'

'I've got enough to take a chance with, some sort of a chance. I'd find a chance. I'll do that anyhow. I'll go away. I mean what I say – I'll stop trifling and shirking. If I don't come back it won't matter. If I do – '

Her expression had become uneasy. Suddenly she bent down towards him.

'Don't!' she said in an undertone.

'Don't – what?'

'Don't go on like this! You're different! Go on being the knight who wants to kiss my hand as his – what did you call it?' The ghost of a smile curved her face. 'Gurdrum!'

'But – !'

Then through a pause they both stared at each other, listening.

A muffled tumult on the other side of the wall asserted itself.

'Shut *up*, Rosie!' said a voice.

'I tell you I will see! I can't half hear. Give me a leg up!'

'You Idiot! He'll see you. You're spoiling everything.'

The bottom dropped out of Mr Polly's world. He felt as people must feel who are going to faint.

'You've got someone – ' he said aghast.

She found life inexpressible to Mr Polly. She addressed some unseen hearers. 'You filthy little Beasts!' she cried with a sharp note of agony in her

voice, and swung herself back over the wall and vanished. There was a squeal of pain and fear, and a swift, fierce altercation.

For a couple of seconds he stood agape.

Then a wild resolve to confirm his worst sense of what was on the other side of the wall made him seize a log, put it against the stones, clutch the parapet with insecure fingers, and lug himself to a momentary balance on the wall.

Romance and his goddess had vanished.

A red-haired girl with a pigtail was wringing the wrist of a schoolfellow who shrieked with pain and cried: 'Mercy! mercy! Ooo! Christabel!'

'You idiot!' cried Christabel. 'You giggling Idiot!'

Two other young ladies made off through the beech trees from this outburst of savagery.

Then the grip of Mr Polly's fingers gave, and he hit his chin against the stones and slipped clumsily to the ground again, scraping his cheek against the wall and hurting his shin against the log by which he had reached the top. Just for a moment he crouched against the wall.

He swore, staggered to the pile of logs and sat down.

He remained very still for some time, with his lips pressed together.

'Fool,' he said at last; 'you Blithering Fool!' and began to rub his shin as though he had just discovered its bruises.

Afterwards he found his face was wet with blood – which was none the less red stuff from the heart because it came from slight abrasions.

CHAPTER SIX

Miriam

It is an illogical consequence of one human being's ill-treatment that we should fly immediately to another, but that is the way with us. It seemed to Mr Polly that only a human touch could assuage the smart of his humiliation. Moreover it had for some undefined reason to be a feminine touch, and the number of women in his world was limited.

He thought of the Larkins family – the Larkins whom he had not been near now for ten long days. Healing people they seemed to him now – healing, simple people. They had good hearts, and he had neglected them for a mirage. If he rode over to them he would be able to talk nonsense and laugh and forget the whirl of memories and thoughts that was spinning round and round so unendurably in his brain.

'Law!' said Mrs Larkins, 'come in! You're quite a stranger, Elfrid!'

'Been seeing to business,' said the unveracious Polly.

'None of 'em ain't at 'ome, but Miriam's just out to do a bit of shopping. Won't let me shop, she won't, because I'm so keerless. She's a wonderful

manager, that girl. Minnie's got some work at the carpet place. 'Ope it won't make 'er ill again. She's a loving delikit sort, is Minnie . . . Come into the front parlour. It's a bit untidy, but you got to take us as you find us. Wot you been doing to your face?'

'Bit of a scrase with the bicycle,' said Mr Polly.

' 'Ow?'

'Trying to pass a carriage on the wrong side, and he drew up and ran me against a wall.'

Mrs Larkins scrutinised it. 'You ought to 'ave someone look after your scrases,' she said. 'That's all red and rough. It ought to be cold-creamed. Bring your bicycle into the passage and come in.'

She 'straightened up a bit', that is to say she increased the dislocation of a number of scattered articles, put a workbasket on the top of several books, swept two or three dog-eared numbers of the *Lady's Own Novelist* from the table into the broken armchair, and proceeded to sketch together the tea things with various such interpolations as: 'Law, if I ain't forgot the butter!' All the while she talked of Annie's good spirits and cleverness with her millinery, and of Minnie's affection and Miriam's relative love of order and management. Mr Polly stood by the window uneasily and thought how good and sincere was the Larkins tone. It was well to be back again.

'You're a long time finding that shop of yours,' said Mrs Larkins.

'Don't do to be precipitous,' said Mr Polly.

'No,' said Mrs Larkins, 'once you got it you got it. Like choosing a 'usband. You better see you got it good. I kept Larkins 'esitating two years I did, until I felt sure of him. A 'ansom man 'e was as you can see by the looks of the girls, but 'ansom is as 'ansom does. You'd like a bit of jam to your tea, I expect? I 'ope they'll keep *their* men waiting when the time comes. I tell them if they think of marrying it only shows they don't know when they're well off. Here's Miriam!'

Miriam entered with several parcels in a net, and a peevish expression. 'Mother,' she said, 'you might 'ave prevented my going out with the net with the broken handle. I've been cutting my fingers with the string all the way 'ome.' Then she discovered Mr Polly and her face brightened.

' 'Ello, Elfrid!' she said. 'Where you been all this time?'

'Looking round,' said Mr Polly.

'Found a shop?'

'One or two likely ones. But it takes time.'

'You've got the wrong cups, mother.'

She went into the kitchen, disposed of her purchases, and returned with the right cups. 'What you done to your face, Elfrid?' she asked, and came and scrutinised his scratches. 'All rough it is.'

He repeated his story of the accident, and she was sympathetic in a pleasant homely way.

'You *are* quiet today,' she said as they sat down to tea.

'Meditatious,' said Mr Polly.

Quite by accident he touched her hand on the table, and she answered his touch.

'Why not?' thought Mr Polly, and looking up, caught Mrs Larkins's eye and flushed guiltily. But Mrs Larkins, with unusual restraint, said nothing. She merely made a grimace, enigmatical but in its essence friendly.

Presently Minnie came in with some vague grievance against the manager of the carpet-making place about his method of estimating piece-work. Her account was redundant, defective and highly technical, but redeemed by a certain earnestness. 'I'm never within sixpence of what I reckon to be,' she said. 'It's a bit too 'ot.' Then Mr Polly, feeling that he was being conspicuously dull, launched into a description of the shop he was looking for and the shops he had seen. His mind warmed up as he talked.

'Found your tongue again,' said Mrs Larkins.

He had. He began to embroider the subject and work upon it. For the first time it assumed picturesque and desirable qualities in his mind. It stimulated him to see how readily and willingly they accepted his sketches. Bright ideas appeared in his mind from nowhere. He was suddenly enthusiastic.

'When I get this shop of mine I shall have a cat. Must make a home for a cat, you know.'

'What, to catch the mice?' said Mrs Larkins.

'No – sleep in the window. A venerable signor of a cat. Tabby. Cat's no good if it isn't tabby. Cat I'm going to have, and a canary! Didn't think of that before, but a cat and a canary seem to go, you know. Summer weather I shall sit at breakfast in the little room behind the shop, sun streaming in the window to rights, cat on a chair, canary singing and – Mrs Polly . . . '

' 'Ello!' said Mrs Larkins.

'Mrs Polly frying an extra bit of bacon. Bacon singing, cat singing, canary singing. Kettle singing. Mrs Polly – '

'But who's Mrs Polly going to be?' said Mrs Larkins.

'Figment of the imagination, ma'am,' said Mr Polly. 'Put in to fill up picture. No face to figure as yet. Still, that's how it will be, I can assure you. I think I must have a bit of garden. Johnson's the man for a garden of course,' he said, going off at a tangent, 'but I don't mean a fierce sort of garden. Earnest industry. Anxious moments. Fervous digging. Shan't go in for that sort of garden, ma'am. No! Too much backache for me. My garden will be just a patch of 'sturtiums and sweet pea. Red-brick yard, clothes-line. Trellis put up in odd time. Humorous wind vane. Creeper up the back of the house.'

'Virginia creeper?' asked Miriam.

'Canary creeper,' said Mr Polly.

'You *will* 'ave it nice,' said Miriam, desirously.

'Rather,' said Mr Polly. 'Ting-a-ling-a-ling. *Shop!*'

He straightened himself up and then they all laughed.

'Smart little shop,' he said. 'Counter. Desk. All complete. Umbrella stand. Carpet on the floor. Cat asleep on the counter. Ties and hose on a rail over the counter. All right.'

'I wonder you don't set about it right off,' said Miriam.

'Mean to get it exactly right, ma'am,' said Mr Polly.

'Have to have a tomcat,' said Mr Polly, and paused for an expectant moment. 'Wouldn't do to open shop one morning, you know, and find the window full of kittens. Can't sell kittens . . .'

When tea was over he was left alone with Minnie for a few minutes, and an odd intimation of an incident occurred that left Mr Polly rather scared and shaken. A silence fell between them – an uneasy silence. He sat with his elbows on the table looking at her. All the way from Easewood to Stamton his erratic imagination had been running upon neat ways of proposing marriage. I don't know why it should have done, but it had. It was a kind of secret exercise that had not had any definite aim at the time, but which now recurred to him with extraordinary force. He couldn't think of anything in the world that wasn't the gambit to a proposal. It was almost irresistibly fascinating to think how immensely a few words from him would excite and revolutionise Minnie. She was sitting at the table with a workbasket among the tea things, mending a glove in order to avoid her share of clearing away.

'I like cats,' said Minnie after a thoughtful pause. 'I'm always saying to mother, "I wish we 'ad a cat." But we couldn't 'ave a cat 'ere – not with no yard.'

'Never had a cat myself,' said Mr Polly. 'No!'

'I'm fond of them,' said Minnie.

'I like the look of them,' said Mr Polly. 'Can't exactly call myself fond.'

'I expect I shall get one someday. When about you get your shop.'

'I shall have my shop all right before long,' said Mr Polly. 'Trust me. Canary bird and all.'

She shook her head. 'I shall get a cat first,' she said. 'You never mean anything you say.'

'Might get 'em together,' said Mr Polly, with his sense of a neat thing outrunning his discretion.

'Why! 'ow d'you mean?' said Minnie, suddenly alert.

'Shop and cat thrown in,' said Mr Polly in spite of himself, and his head swam and he broke out into a cold sweat as he said it.

He found her eyes fixed on him with an eager expression. 'Mean to say –' she began as if for verification.

He sprang to his feet, and turned to the window. 'Little dog!' he said, and moved doorward hastily. 'Eating my bicycle tyre, I believe,' he explained. And so escaped.

He saw his bicycle in the hall and cut it dead.

He heard Mrs Larkins in the passage behind him as he opened the front door.

He turned to her. 'Thought my bicycle was on fire,' he said. 'Outside. Funny fancy! All right, reely. Little dog outside . . . Miriam ready?'

'What for?'

'To go and meet Annie.'

Mrs Larkins stared at him. 'You're stopping for a bit of supper?'

'If I may,' said Mr Polly.

'You're a rum un,' said Mrs Larkins, and called: 'Miriam!'

Minnie appeared at the door of the room looking infinitely perplexed. 'There ain't a little dog anywhere, Elfrid,' she said.

Mr Polly passed his hand over his brow. 'I had a most curious sensation. Felt exactly as though something was up somewhere. That's why I said Little Dog All right now.'

He bent down and pinched his bicycle tyre.

'You was saying something about a cat, Elfrid,' said Minnie.

'Give you one,' he answered without looking up. 'The very day my shop is opened.'

He straightened himself up and smiled reassuringly. 'Trust me,' he said.

2

When, after imperceptible manoeuvres by Mrs Larkins, he found himself starting circuitously through the inevitable recreation ground with Miriam to meet Annie, he found himself quite unable to avoid the topic of the shop that had now taken such a grip upon him. A sense of danger only increased the attraction. Minnie's persistent disposition to accompany them had been crushed by a novel and violent and urgently expressed desire on the part of Mrs Larkins to see her do something in the house sometimes –

'You really think you'll open a shop?' asked Miriam.

'I hate cribs,' said Mr Polly, adopting a moderate tone. 'In a shop there's this drawback and that, but one is one's own master.'

'That wasn't all talk?'

'Not a bit of it.

'After all,' he went on, 'a little shop needn't be so bad.'

'It's a 'ome,' said Miriam.

'It's a home.'

Pause.

'There's no need to keep accounts and that sort of thing if there's no assistant. I dare say I could run a shop all right if I wasn't interfered with.'

'I should like to see you in your shop,' said Miriam. 'I expect you'd keep everything tremendously neat.'

The conversation flagged.

'Let's sit down on one of those seats over there,' said Miriam. 'Where we can see those blue flowers.'

They did as she suggested, and sat down in a corner where a triangular bed of stock and delphinium brightened the asphalted traceries of the recreation ground.

'I wonder what they call those flowers,' she said. 'I always like them. They're handsome.'

'Delphicums and larkspurs,' said Mr Polly. 'They used to be in the park at Port Burdock.

'Floriferous corner,' he added approvingly.

He put an arm over the back of the seat, and assumed a more comfortable attitude. He glanced at Miriam, who was sitting in a lax, thoughtful pose with her eyes on the flowers. She was wearing her old dress – she had not had time to change - and the blue tones of her old dress brought out a certain warmth in her skin, and her pose exaggerated whatever was feminine in her rather lean and insufficient body, and rounded her flat chest delusively. A little line of light lay along her profile. The afternoon was full of transfiguring sunshine; children were playing noisily in the adjacent sandpit, some Judas trees were brightly a-bloom in the villa gardens that bordered the recreation ground, and all the place was bright with touches of young summer colour. It all merged with the effect of Miriam in Mr Polly's mind.

Her thoughts found speech. 'One did ought to be happy in a shop,' she said with a note of unusual softness in her voice.

It seemed to him that she was right. One did ought to be happy in a shop. Folly not to banish dreams that made one ache, dreams of townless woods and bracken tangles and red-haired linen-clad figures sitting in dappled sunshine upon grey and crumbling walls and looking queenly down on one with clear blue eyes. Cruel and foolish dreams they were, that ended in one's being laughed at and made a mock of. There was no mockery here.

'A shop's such a respectable thing to be,' said Miriam thoughtfully.

'*I* could be happy in a shop,' he said.

His sense of effect made him pause.

'If I had the right company,' he added.

She became very still.

Mr Polly swerved a little from the conversational ice-run upon which he had embarked.

'I'm not such a blooming Geezer,' he said, 'as not to be able to sell goods a bit. One has to be nosy over one's buying of course. But I shall do all right.'

He stopped, and felt falling, falling through the aching silence that followed.

'If you get the right company,' said Miriam.

'I shall get that all right.'

'You don't mean you've got someone – '

He found himself plunging.

'I've got someone in my eye, this minute,' he said.

'Elfrid!' she said, turning on him. 'You don't mean – '

Well, *did* he mean? 'I do!' he said.

'Not reely!' She clenched her hands to keep still.

He took the conclusive step.

'Well, you and me, Miriam, in a little shop – with a cat and a canary – '
He tried too late to get back to a hypothetical note. 'Just suppose it!'

'You mean,' said Miriam, 'you're in love with me, Elfrid?'

What possible answer can a man give to such a question but 'Yes!'

Regardless of the public park, the children in the sandpit and everyone,
she bent forward and seized his shoulder and kissed him on the lips. Some-
thing lit up in Mr Polly at the touch. He put an arm about her and kissed
her back, and felt an irrevocable act was sealed. He had a curious feeling
that it would be very satisfying to marry and have a wife – only somehow he
wished it wasn't Miriam. Her lips were very pleasant to him, and the feel of
her in his arm.

They recoiled a little from each other and sat for a moment, flushed and
awkwardly silent. His mind was altogether incapable of controlling its
confusion.

'I didn't dream,' said Miriam, 'you cared – Sometimes I thought it was
Annie, sometimes Minnie – '

'Always liked you better than them,' said Mr Polly.

'I loved you, Elfrid,' said Miriam, 'since ever we met at your poor father's
funeral. Leastways I *would* have done, if I had thought – You didn't seem to
mean anything you said.

'I *can't* believe it!' she added.

'Nor I,' said Mr Polly.

'You mean to marry me and start that little shop – '

'Soon as ever I find it,' said Mr Polly.

'I had no more idea when I came out with you – '

'Nor me!'

'It's like a dream.'

They said no more for a little while.

'I got to pinch myself to think it's real,' said Miriam. 'What they'll do
without me at 'ome I can't imagine. When I tell them – '

For the life of him Mr Polly could not tell whether he was fullest of
tender anticipations or regretful panic.

'Mother's no good at managing – not a bit. Annie don't care for 'ousework
and Minnie's got no 'ed for it. What they'll do without me I can't imagine.'

'They'll have to do without you,' said Mr Polly, sticking to his guns.

A clock in the town began striking.

'Lor'!' said Miriam, 'we shall miss Annie – sitting 'ere and lovemaking!'

She rose and made as if to take Mr Polly's arm. But Mr Polly felt that

their condition must be nakedly exposed to the ridicule of the world by such a linking, and evaded her movement.

Annie was already in sight before a flood of hesitation and terrors assailed Mr Polly.

'Don't tell anyone yet a bit,' he said.

'Only mother,' said Miriam firmly.

3

Figures are the most shocking things in the world. The prettiest little squiggles of black looked at in the right light, and yet consider the blow they can give you upon the heart. You return from a little careless holiday abroad, and turn over the page of a newspaper, and against the name of that distant, vague-conceived railway in mortgages upon which you have embarked the bulk of your capital you see instead of the familiar, persistent 95-6 (varying at most to 93 *ex. div.*) this slightly richer arrangement of marks: 76/2 – 78/2.

It is like the opening of a pit just under your feet!

So, too, Mr Polly's happy sense of limitless resources was obliterated suddenly by a vision of this tracery:

'298'

instead of the

'350'

he had come to regard as the fixed symbol of his affluence.

It gave him a disagreeable feeling about the diaphragm, akin in a remote degree to the sensation he had when the perfidy of the red-haired schoolgirl became plain to him. It made his brow moist.

'Going down a vortex!' he whispered.

By a characteristic feat of subtraction he decided that he must have spent sixty-two pounds.

'Funererial baked meats,' he said, recalling possible items.

The happy dream in which he had been living, of long warm days, of open roads, of limitless unchecked hours, of infinite time to look about him, vanished like a thing enchanted. He was suddenly back in the hard old economic world, that exacts work, that limits range, that discourages phrasing and dispels laughter. He saw Wood Street and its fearful suspenses yawning beneath his feet.

And also he had promised to marry Miriam, and on the whole rather wanted to.

He was distraught at supper. Afterwards, when Mrs Johnson had gone to bed with a slight headache, he opened a conversation with Johnson.

'It's about time, o' man, I saw about doing something,' he said. 'Riding

about and looking at shops, all very debonnairious, o' man, but it's time I took one for keeps.'

'What did I tell you?' said Johnson.

'How do you think that corner shop of yours will figure out?' Mr Polly asked.

'You're really meaning it?'

'If it's a practable proposition, o' man. Assuming it's practable, what's your idea of the figures?'

Johnson went to the chiffonier, got out a letter and tore off the back sheet. 'Let's figure it out,' he said with solemn satisfaction. 'Let's see the lowest you could do it on.'

He squared himself to the task, and Mr Polly sat beside him like a pupil, watching the evolution of the grey, distasteful figures that were to dispose of his little hoard.

'What running expenses have we got to provide for?' said Johnson, wetting his pencil. 'Let's have them first. Rent? . . . '

At the end of an hour of hideous speculations, Johnson decided: 'It's close. But you'll have a chance.'

'M'm,' said Mr Polly. 'What more does a brave man want?'

'One thing you can do quite easily. I've asked about it.'

'What's that, o' man?' said Mr Polly.

'Take the shop without the house above it.'

'I suppose I might put my head in to mind it,' said Mr Polly, 'and get a job with my body.'

'Not exactly that. But I thought you'd save a lot if you stayed on here – being all alone as you are.'

'Never thought of that, o' man,' said Mr Polly, and reflected silently upon the needlessness of Miriam.

'We were talking of eighty pounds for stock,' said Johnson. 'Of course seventy-five is five pounds less, isn't it? Not much else we can cut.'

'No,' said Mr Polly.

'It's very interesting, all this,' said Johnson, folding up the half-sheet of paper and unfolding it. 'I wish sometimes I had a business of my own instead of a fixed salary. You'll have to keep books of course.'

'One wants to know where one is.'

'I should do it all by double entry,' said Johnson. 'A little troublesome at first, but far the best in the end.'

'Lemme see that paper,' said Mr Polly, and took it with the feeling of a man who takes a nauseating medicine, and scrutinised his cousin's neat figures with listless eyes.

'Well,' said Johnson, rising and stretching. 'Bed! Better sleep on it, o' man.'

'Right-o,' said Mr Polly, without moving; but indeed he could as well have slept upon a bed of thorns.

He had a dreadful night. It was like the end of the annual holiday, only infinitely worse. It was like a newly arrived prisoner's backward glance at the trees and heather through the prison gates. He had to go back to harness, and he was as fitted to go in harness as the ordinary domestic cat. All night, Fate, with the quiet complacency, and indeed at times the very face and gestures, of Johnson, guided him towards that undesired establishment at the corner near the station. 'O Lord!' he cried, 'I'd rather go back to cribs. I should keep my money anyhow.' Fate never winced.

'Run away to sea,' whispered Mr Polly, but he knew he wasn't man enough.

'Cut my blooming throat.'

Some braver strain urged him to think of Miriam, and for a little while he lay still . . .

'Well, o' man?' said Johnson, when Mr Polly came down to breakfast, and Mrs Johnson looked up brightly. Mr Polly had never felt breakfast so unattractive before.

'Just a day or so more, o' man – to turn it over in my mind,' he said.

'You'll get the place snapped up,' said Johnson.

There were times in those last few days of coyness with his destiny when his engagement seemed the most negligible of circumstances, and times – and these happened for the most part at nights after Mrs Johnson had indulged everybody in a Welsh rarebit – when it assumed so sinister and portentous an appearance as to make him think of suicide. And there were times too when he very distinctly desired to be married, now that the idea had got into his head, at any cost. Also he tried to recall all the circumstances of his proposal, time after time, and never quite succeeded in recalling what had brought the thing off. He went over to Stamton with a becoming frequency, and kissed all his cousins, and Miriam especially, a great deal, and found it very stirring and refreshing. They all appeared to know; and Minnie was tearful, but resigned. Mrs Larkins met him, and indeed enveloped him, with unwonted warmth, and there was a big pot of household jam for tea. But he could not make up his mind to sign his name to anything about the shop, though it crawled nearer and nearer to him, though the project had materialised now to the extent of a draft agreement with the place for his signature indicated in pencil.

One morning, just after Mr Johnson had gone to the station, Mr Polly wheeled his bicycle out into the road, went up to his bedroom, packed his long white nightshirt, a comb and a toothbrush in a manner that was as offhand as he could make it, informed Mrs Johnson, who was manifestly curious, that he was 'off for a day or two to clear his head', and fled forthright into the road; mounting, he turned his wheel towards the tropics and the equator and the south coast of England, and indeed more particularly to where the little village of Fishbourne slumbers and sleeps.

When he returned four days later, he astonished Johnson beyond

measure by remarking so soon as the shop project was reopened: 'I've took a little contraption at Fishbourne, o' man, that I fancy suits me better.'

He paused, and then added in a manner, if possible, even more offhand: 'Oh! and I'm going to have a bit of a nuptial over at Stamton with one of the Larkins cousins.'

'Nuptial!' said Johnson.

'Wedding bells, o' man. Benedictine collapse.'

On the whole Johnson showed great self-control. 'It's your own affair, o' man,' he said, when things had been more clearly explained, 'and I hope you won't feel sorry when it's too late.'

But Mrs Johnson was first of all angrily silent, and then reproachful. 'I don't see what we've done to be made fools of like this,' she said. 'After all the trouble we've 'ad to make you comfortable and see after you. Out late and sitting up and everything. And then you go off as sly as sly without a word, and get a shop behind our backs as though you thought we meant to steal your money. I 'aven't patience with such deceitfulness, and I didn't think it of you, Elfrid. And now the letting season's 'arf gone by, and what I shall do with that room of yours I've no idea. Frank is frank, and fair play fair play; so *I* was told any'ow when I was a girl. Just as long as it suits you to stay 'ere you stay 'ere, and then it's off and no thank you whether we like it or not. Johnson's too easy with you. 'E sits there and doesn't say a word, and night after night 'e's been addin' and thinkin' for you, instead of seeing to his own affairs – '

She paused for breath.

'Unfortunate amoor,' said Mr Polly, apologetically and indistinctly. 'Didn't expect it myself.'

4

Mr Polly's marriage followed with a certain inevitableness.

He tried to assure himself that he was acting upon his own forceful initiative, but at the back of his mind was the completest realisation of his powerlessness to resist the gigantic social forces he had set in motion. He had got to marry under the will of society, even as in times past it has been appointed for other sunny souls under the will of society that they should be led out by serious and unavoidable fellow-creatures and ceremoniously drowned or burnt or hanged. He would have preferred infinitely a more observant and less conspicuous role, but the choice was no longer open to him. He did his best to play his part, and he procured some particularly neat check trousers to do it in. The rest of his costume, except for some bright-yellow gloves, a grey-and-blue-mixture tie and that the broad crape hat-band was changed for a livelier piece of silk, were the things he had worn at the funeral of his father. So nearly akin are human joy and sorrow.

The Larkins sisters had done wonders with grey sateen. The idea of orange blossom and white veils had been abandoned reluctantly on account of the expense of cabs. A novelette in which the heroine had stood at the altar in 'a modest going-away dress' had materially assisted this decision. Miriam was frankly tearful, and so indeed was Annie, but with laughter as well to carry it off. Mr Polly heard Annie say something vague, about never getting a chance because of Miriam always sticking about at home like a cat at a mouse-hole, that became, as people say, food for thought. Mrs Larkins was from the first flushed, garrulous, and wet and smeared by copious weeping; an incredibly soaked and crumpled and used-up pocket handkerchief never left the clutch of her plump red hand. 'Goo' girls, all of them,' she kept on saying in a tremulous voice; 'such-goo-goo-goo-girls!' She wetted Mr Polly dreadfully when she kissed him. Her emotion affected the buttons down the back of her bodice, and almost the last filial duty Miriam did before entering on her new life was to close that gaping orifice for the eleventh time. Her bonnet was small and ill-balanced, black adorned with red roses, and first it got over her right eye until Annie told her of it, and then she pushed it over her left eye and looked ferocious for a space, and after that baptismal kissing of Mr Polly the delicate millinery took fright and climbed right up to the back part of her head and hung on there by a pin, and flapped piteously at all the larger waves of emotion that filled the gathering. Mr Polly became more and more aware of that bonnet as time went on, until he felt for it like a thing alive. Towards the end it had yawning fits.

The company did not include Mrs Johnson, but Johnson came with a manifest surreptitiousness and backed against walls and watched Mr Polly with doubt and speculation in his large grey eyes and whistled noiselessly and doubtful on the edge of things. He was, so to speak, to be best man *sotto voce*. A sprinkling of girls in gay hats from Miriam's place of business appeared in church, great nudgers all of them, but only two came on afterwards to the house. Mrs Punt brought her son with his ever-widening mind – it was his first wedding – and a Larkins uncle, a Mr Voules, a licensed victualler, very kindly drove over in a gig from Sommershill with a plump, well-dressed wife to give the bride away. One or two total strangers drifted into the church and sat down observantly far away.

This sprinkling of people seemed only to enhance the cool brown emptiness of the church, the rows and rows of empty pews, disengaged prayer-books and abandoned hassocks. It had the effect of a preposterous misfit. Johnson consulted with a thin-legged, short-skirted verger about the disposition of the party. The officiating clergy appeared distantly in the doorway of the vestry, putting on his surplice, and relapsed into a contemplative cheek-scratching that was manifestly habitual. Before the bride arrived Mr Polly's sense of the church found an outlet in whispered criticisms of ecclesiastical architecture with Johnson. 'Early Norman arches, eh?' he said, 'or Perpendicular.'

'Can't say,' said Johnson.

'Telessated pavements, all right.'

'It's well laid anyhow.'

'Can't say I admire the altar. Scrappy rather with those flowers.'

He coughed behind his hand and cleared his throat. At the back of his mind he was speculating whether flight at this eleventh hour would be criminal or merely reprehensible bad taste. A murmur from the nudgers announced the arrival of the bridal party.

The little procession from a remote door became one of the enduring memories of Mr Polly's life. The verger had bustled to meet it, and arrange it according to tradition and morality. In spite of Mrs Larkins's 'Don't take her from me yet!' he made Miriam go first with Mr Voules and the bridesmaids followed – as did he himself, hopelessly unable to disentangle himself from the whispering maternal anguish of Mrs Larkins. Mrs Voules, a compact, rounded woman with a square, expressionless face, imperturbable dignity, and a dress of considerable fashion, completed the procession.

Mr Polly's eye fell first upon the bride; the sight of her filled him with a curious stir of emotion. Alarm, desire, affection, respect – and a queer element of reluctant dislike all played their part in that complex eddy. The grey dress made her a stranger to him, made her stiff and commonplace; she was not even the rather drooping form that had caught his facile sense of beauty when he had proposed to her in the recreation ground. There was something too that did not please him in the angle of her hat; it was indeed an ill-conceived hat with large aimless rosettes of pink and grey. Then his mind passed to Mrs Larkins and the bonnet that was to gain such a hold upon him – it seemed to be flag-signalling as she advanced – and to the two eager, unrefined sisters he was acquiring.

A freak of fancy set him wondering where and when in the future a beautiful girl with red hair might march along some splendid aisle. Never mind! He became aware of Mr Voules.

He became aware of Mr Voules as a watchful, blue eye of intense forcefulness. It was the eye of a man who has got hold of a situation. He was a fat, short, red-faced man clad in a tight-fitting tail coat of black and white check with a coquettish bow tie under the lowest of a number of crisp little red chins. He held the bride under his arm with an air of invincible championship, and his free arm flourished a grey top hat of an equestrian type. Mr Polly instantly learnt from the eye that Mr Voules knew all about his longing for flight. Its azure pupil glowed with disciplined resolution. It said: 'I've come to give this girl away, and give her away I will. I'm here now and things have to go on all right. So don't think of it any more' – and Mr Polly didn't. A faint phantom of a certain 'li'le dog' that had hovered just beneath the threshold of consciousness vanished into black impossibility. Until the conclusive moment of the service was attained the eye of Mr Voules

watched Mr Polly relentlessly, and then instantly he relieved guard, and blew his nose into a voluminous and richly patterned handkerchief, and sighed and looked round for the approval and sympathy of Mrs Voules, and nodded to her brightly like one who has always foretold a successful issue to things. Mr Polly felt then like a marionette that has just dropped off its wire. But it was long before that release arrived.

He became aware of Miriam breathing close to him.

'Hello!' he said, and feeling that was clumsy and would meet the eye's disapproval: 'Grey dress – suits you no end.'

Miriam's eyes shone under her hat-brim.

'Not reely!' she whispered.

'You're all right,' he said, with the feeling of the eye's observation and criticism stiffening his lips. He cleared his throat.

The verger's hand pushed at him from behind. Someone was driving Miriam towards the altar rail and the clergyman. 'We're in for it,' said Mr Polly to her sympathetically. 'Where? Here? Right-o.'

He was interested for a moment or so in something indescribably habitual in the clergyman's pose. What a lot of weddings he must have seen! Sick he must be of them!

'Don't let your attention wander,' said the eye.

'Got the ring?' whispered Johnson.

'Pawned it yesterday,' answered Mr Polly, and then had a dreadful moment under that pitiless scrutiny while he felt in the wrong waistcoat pocket . . .

The officiating clergy sighed deeply, began, and married them wearily and without any hitch.

'D' b'loved, we gath'd 'gether sight o' Gard 'n face this con'gation join 'gether Man Wom' Holy Mat'mony which is a 'bl state 'stooted by Gard in times man's innocency . . . '

Mr Polly's thoughts wandered wide and far, and once again something like a cold hand touched his heart, and he saw a sweet face in sunshine under the shadow of trees.

Someone was nudging him. It was Johnson's finger diverted his eyes to the crucial place in the Prayer Book to which they had come.

'Wiltou lover, cumfer, oner, keeper sickness and health . . . '

'Say, "I will." '

Mr Polly moistened his lips. 'I will,' he said hoarsely.

Miriam, nearly inaudible, answered some similar demand.

Then the clergyman said: 'Who gi's wom mar'd t' this man?'

'Well, *I'm* doing that,' said Mr Voules in a refreshingly full voice and looking round the church. 'You see, me and Martha Larkins being cousins – '

He was silenced by the clergyman's rapid grip directing the exchange of hands.

'Pete arf me,' said the clergyman to Mr Polly. 'Take thee Mirum wed' wife – '

'Take thee Mirum wed' wife,' said Mr Polly.

'Have hold this day ford.'

'Have hold this day ford.'

'Betworse, richpoo' – '

'Betworse, richpoo' . . . '

Then came Miriam's turn.

'Lego hands,' said the clergyman; 'got the ring? No! On the book. So! Here! Pete arf me, "Wi'is ring Ivy wed." '

'Wi'is ring Ivy wed – '

So it went on, blurred and hurried, like the momentary vision of an utterly beautiful thing seen through the smoke of a passing train –

'Now, my boy,' said Mr Voules at last, gripping Mr Polly's elbow tightly, 'you've got to sign the registry, and there you are! Done!'

Before him stood Miriam, a little stiffly, the hat with a slight rake across her forehead, and a kind of questioning hesitation in her face. Mr Voules urged him past her.

It was astounding. She was his wife!

And for some reason Miriam and Mrs Larkins were sobbing, and Annie was looking grave. Hadn't they after all wanted him to marry her? Because if that was the case – !

He became aware for the first time of the presence of Uncle Pentstemon, in the background but approaching, wearing a tie of a light mineral-blue colour, and grinning and sucking enigmatically and judiciously round his principal tooth.

5

It was in the vestry that the force of Mr Voules's personality began to show at its true value. He seemed to open out, like the fisherman's Ginn from the pot, and spread over things directly the restraints of the ceremony were at an end.

'Everything,' he said to the clergyman, 'excellent.' He also shook hands with Mrs Larkins, who clung to him for a space, and kissed Miriam on the cheek. 'First kiss for me,' he said, 'anyhow.'

He led Mr Polly to the register by the arm, and then got chairs for Mrs Larkins and his wife. He then turned on Miriam. 'Now, young people,' he said. 'One! or *I* shall again.

'That's right!' said Mr Voules. 'Same again, miss.'

Mr Polly was overcome with modest confusion, and turning, found a refuge from this publicity in the arms of Mrs Larkins. Then in a state of profuse moisture he was assaulted and kissed by Annie and Minnie, who were immediately kissed upon some indistinctly stated grounds by Mr Voules, who then kissed the entirely impassive Mrs Voules and smacked his lips and

remarked: 'Home again safe and sound!' Then with a strange harrowing cry Mrs Larkins seized upon and bedewed Miriam with kisses, Annie and Minnie kissed each other, and Johnson went abruptly to the door of the vestry and stared into the church – no doubt with ideas of sanctuary in his mind. 'Like a bit of a kiss round sometimes,' said Mr Voules, and made a kind of hissing noise with his teeth, and suddenly smacked his hands together with great *éclat* several times. Meanwhile the clergyman scratched his cheek with one hand and fiddled the pen with the other and the verger coughed protestingly.

'The dog cart's just outside,' said Mr Voules. 'No walking home today for the bride, ma'am.'

'Not going to drive us?' cried Annie.

'The happy pair, miss. *Your* turn soon.'

'Get out!' said Annie. 'I shan't marry – ever.'

'You won't be able to help it. You'll have to do it – just to disperse the crowd.' Mr Voules laid his hand on Mr Polly's shoulder. 'The bridegroom gives his arm to the bride. Hands across and down the middle. Prump, Prump, Perump-pump-pump-pump-perump.'

Mr Polly found himself and the bride leading the way towards the western door.

Mrs Larkins passed close to Uncle Pentstemon, sobbing too earnestly to be aware of him. 'Such a goo-goo-goo-girl!' she sobbed.

'Didn't think *I'd* come, did you?' said Uncle Pentstemon, but she swept past him, too busy with the expression of her feelings to observe him.

'She didn't think I'd come, I lay,' said Uncle Pentstemon, a little foiled, but effecting an auditory lodgement upon Johnson.

'I don't know,' said Johnson uncomfortably. 'I suppose you were asked. How are you getting on?'

'I was *arst*,' said Uncle Pentstemon, and brooded for a moment.

'I goes about seeing wonders,' he added, and then in a sort of enhanced undertone: 'One of 'er girls gettin' married. That's what I mean by wonders. Lord's goodness! Wow!'

'Nothing the matter?' asked Johnson.

'Got it in the back for a moment. Going to be a change of weather, I suppose,' said Uncle Pentstemon. 'I brought 'er a nice present, too, what I got in this passel. Vallyble old tea caddy that uset' be my mother's. What I kep' my baccy in for years and years – till the hinge at the back got broke. It ain't been no use to me particular since, so thinks I, drat it! I may as well give it 'er as not . . . '

Mr Polly found himself emerging from the western door.

Outside, a crowd of half a dozen adults and about fifty children had collected, and hailed the approach of the newly wedded couple with a faint, indeterminate cheer. All the children were holding something in little bags, and his attention was caught by the expression of vindictive concentration upon the face of a small big-eared boy in the foreground.

He didn't for the moment realise what these things might import. Then he received a stinging handful of rice in the ear, and a great light shone.

'Not yet, you young fool!' he heard Mr Voules saying behind him, and then a second handful spoke against his hat.

'Not yet,' said Mr Voules with increasing emphasis, and Mr Polly became aware that he and Miriam were the focus of two crescents of small boys, each with the light of massacre in his eyes and a grubby fist clutching into a paper bag for rice; and that Mr Voules was warding off probable discharges with a large red hand.

The dog cart was in charge of a loafer, and the horse and the whip were adorned with white favours, and the back seat was confused, but not untenable, with hampers. 'Up we go,' said Mr Voules, 'old birds in front and young ones behind.' An ominous group of ill-restrained rice-throwers followed them up as they mounted.

'Get your handkerchief for your face,' said Mr Polly to his bride, and taking the place next the pavement with considerable heroism, held on, gripped his hat, shut his eyes and prepared for the worst. 'Off!' said Mr Voules, and a concentrated fire came stinging Mr Polly's face.

The horse shied, and when the bridegroom could look at the world again it was manifest the dog cart had just missed an electric tram by a hair's breadth, and far away outside the church railings the verger and Johnson were battling with an active crowd of small boys for the life of the rest of the Larkins family. Mrs Punt and her son had escaped across the road, the son trailing and stumbling at the end of a remorseless arm, but Uncle Pentstemon, encumbered by the tea-caddy, was the centre of a little circle of his own, and appeared to be dratting them all very heartily. Remoter, a policeman approached with an air of tranquil unconsciousness.

'Steady, you idiot. Stead-y!' cried Mr Voules, and then over his shoulder: 'I brought that rice! I like old customs! Whoa! Stead-y.'

The dog cart swerved violently, and then, evoking a shout of groundless alarm from a cyclist, took a corner, and the rest of the wedding party was hidden from Mr Polly's eyes.

6

'We'll get the stuff into the house before the old gal comes along,' said Mr Voules, 'if you'll hold the hoss.'

'How about the key?' asked Mr Polly.

'I got the key, coming.'

And while Mr Polly held the sweating horse and dodged the foam that dripped from its bit, the house absorbed Miriam and Mr Voules altogether. Mr Voules carried in the various hampers he had brought with him, and finally closed the door behind him.

For some time Mr Polly remained alone with his charge in the little blind alley outside the Larkins's house, while the neighbours scrutinised him from behind their blinds. He reflected that he was a married man, that he must look very like a fool, that the head of a horse is a silly shape and its eye a bulger; he wondered what the horse thought of him, and whether it really liked being held and patted on the neck or whether it only submitted out of contempt. Did it know he was married? Then he wondered if the clergy-man had thought him much of an ass, and then whether the individual lurking behind the lace curtains of the front room next door was a man or a woman. A door opened over the way, and an elderly gentleman in a kind of embroidered fez appeared smoking a pipe with a quiet satisfied expression. He regarded Mr Polly for some time with mild but sustained curiosity. Finally he called: 'Hi!'

'Hello!' said Mr Polly.

'You needn't 'old that 'orse,' said the old gentleman.

'Spirited beast,' said Mr Polly. 'And' – with some faint analogy to ginger beer in his mind – 'he's up today.'

' 'E won't turn 'isself round,' said the old gentleman, 'any'ow. And there ain't no way through for 'im to go.'

'*Verbum sap*,' said Mr Polly, and abandoned the horse and turned to the door. It opened to him just as Mrs Larkins on the arm of Johnson, followed by Annie, Minnie, two friends, Mrs Punt and her son and at a slight distance Uncle Pentstemon, appeared round the corner.

'They're coming,' he said to Miriam, and put an arm about her and gave her a kiss.

She was kissing him back when they were startled violently by the shying of two empty hampers into the passage. Then Mr Voules appeared holding a third.

'Here! you'll 'ave plenty of time for that presently,' he said, 'get these hampers away before the old girl comes. I got a cold collation here to make her sit up. My eye!'

Miriam took the hampers, and Mr Polly under compulsion from Mr Voules went into the little front room. A profuse pie and a large ham had been added to the modest provision of Mrs Larkins, and a number of select-looking bottles shouldered the bottle of sherry and the bottle of port she had got to grace the feast. They certainly went better with the iced wedding cake in the middle. Mrs Voules, still impassive, stood by the window regarding these things with a faint approval.

'Makes it look a bit thicker, eh?' said Mr Voules, and blew out both his cheeks and smacked his hands together violently several times. 'Surprise the old girl no end.'

He stood back and smiled and bowed with arms extended as the others came clustering at the door.

'Why, *Un-cle* Voules!' cried Annie, with a rising note.

It was his reward.

And then came a great wedging and squeezing and crowding into the little room. Nearly everyone was hungry, and eyes brightened at the sight of the pie and the ham and the convivial array of bottles. 'Sit down everyone,' cried Mr Voules. 'Leaning against anything counts as sitting, and makes it easier to shake down the grub!'

The two friends from Miriam's place of business came into the room among the first, and then wedged themselves so hopelessly against Johnson in an attempt to get out again and take off their things upstairs that they abandoned the attempt. Amid the struggle Mr Polly saw Uncle Pentstemon relieve himself of his parcel by giving it to the bride. 'Here!' he said and handed it to her. 'Weddin' present,' he explained, and added with a confidential chuckle, '*I* never thought I'd 'ave to give you one – ever.'

'Who says steak-and-kidney pie?' bawled Mr Voules. 'Who says steak-and-kidney pie? You 'ave a drop of old Tommy, Martha. That's what you want to steady you . . . Sit down everyone and don't all speak at once. Who says steak-and-kidney pie? . . . '

'Vociferatious,' whispered Mr Polly. 'Convivial vociferations.'

'Bit of 'am with it?' shouted Mr Voules, poising a slice of ham on his knife. 'Anyone 'ave a bit of 'am with it? Won't that little man of yours, Mrs Punt – won't 'e 'ave a bit of 'am . . . ?

'And now, ladies and gentlemen,' said Mr Voules, still standing and dominating the crammed roomful, 'now you got your plates filled and something I can warrant you good in your glasses, wot about drinking the 'ealth of the bride?'

'Eat a bit fust,' said Uncle Pentstemon, speaking with his mouth full, amidst murmurs of applause. 'Eat a bit fust.'

So they did, and the plates clattered and the glasses chinked.

Mr Polly stood shoulder to shoulder with Johnson for a moment.

'In for it,' said Mr Polly cheeringly. 'Cheer up, o' man, and peck a bit. No reason why *you* shouldn't eat, you know.'

The Punt boy stood on Mr Polly's boots for a minute, struggling violently against the compunction of Mrs Punt's grip.

'Pie,' said the Punt boy, 'Pie!'

'You sit 'ere and 'ave 'am, my lord!' said Mrs Punt, prevailing. 'Pie you can't 'ave and you won't.'

'Lor' bless my heart, Mrs Punt!' protested Mr Voules, 'let the boy 'ave a bit if he wants it – wedding and all!'

'You 'aven't 'ad 'im sick on your 'ands, Uncle Voules,' said Mrs Punt. 'Else you wouldn't want to humour his fancies as you do . . . '

'I can't help feeling it's a mistake, o' man,' said Johnson, in a confidential undertone. 'I can't help feeling you've been Rash. Let's hope for the best.'

'Always glad of good wishes, o' man,' said Mr Polly. 'You'd better have a drink of something. Anyhow, sit down to it.'

Johnson subsided gloomily, and Mr Polly secured some ham and carried it off and sat himself down on the sewing machine on the floor in the corner to devour it. He was hungry, and a little cut off from the rest of the company by Mrs Voules's hat and back, and he occupied himself for a time with ham and his own thoughts. He became aware of a series of jangling concussions on the table. He craned his neck and discovered that Mr Voules was standing up and leaning forward over the table in the manner distinctive of after-dinner speeches, tapping upon the table with a black bottle. 'Ladies and gentlemen,' said Mr Voules, raising his glass solemnly in the empty desert of sound he had made, and paused for a second or so. 'Ladies and gentlemen – the Bride.' He searched his mind for some suitable wreath of speech, and brightened at last with discovery. 'Here's luck to her!' he said at last.

'Here's luck!' said Johnson hopelessly but resolutely, and raised his glass. Everybody murmured: 'Here's luck.'

'Luck!' said Mr Polly, unseen in his corner, lifting a forkful of ham.

'That's all right,' said Mr Voules with a sigh of relief at having brought off a difficult operation. 'And now, who's for a bit more pie?'

For a time conversation was fragmentary again. But presently Mr Voules rose from his chair again; he had subsided with a contented smile after his first oratorical effort, and produced a silence by renewed hammering. 'Ladies and gents,' he said, 'fill up for the second toast – the happy Bridegroom!' He stood for half a minute searching his mind for the apt phrase that came at last in a rush. 'Here's (hic) luck to *him*,' said Mr Voules.

'Luck to him!' said everyone, and Mr Polly, standing up behind Mrs Voules, bowed amiably, amidst enthusiasm.

'He may say what he likes,' said Mrs Larkins, 'he's *got* luck. That girl's a treasure of treasures, and always has been ever since she tried to nurse her own little sister, being but three at the time, and fell the full flight of stairs from top to bottom; no hurt that any outward eye 'as even seen, but always ready and helpful, always tidying and busy. A treasure, I must say, and a treasure I will say, giving no more than her due . . . '

She was silenced altogether by a rapping sound that would not be denied. Mr Voules had been struck by a fresh idea and was standing up and hammering with the bottle again.

'The third toast, ladies and gentlemen,' he said; 'fill up, please. The Mother of the Bride. I – er . . . Uoo . . . Ere! . . . Ladies and gents, 'ere's luck to 'er! . . . '

The dingy little room was stuffy and crowded to its utmost limit, and Mr Polly's skies were dark with the sense of irreparable acts. Everybody seemed noisy and greedy and doing foolish things. Miriam, still in that unbecoming hat – for presently they had to start off to the station together – sat just beyond Mrs Punt and her son, doing her share in the hospitalities, and ever and again glancing at him with a deliberately encouraging smile. Once she leant over the back of the chair to him and whispered cheeringly: 'Soon be together now.' Next to her sat Johnson, profoundly silent, and then Annie, talking vigorously to a friend. Uncle Pentstemon was eating voraciously opposite, but with a kindling eye for Annie. Mrs Larkins sat next to Mr Voules. She was unable to eat a mouthful, she declared, it would choke her, but ever and again Mr Voules wooed her to swallow a little drop of liquid refreshment.

There seemed a lot of rice upon everybody, in their hats and hair and the folds of their garments.

Presently Mr Voules was hammering the table for the fourth time in the interests of the Best Man . . .

All feasts come to an end at last, and the break-up of things was precipitated by alarming symptoms on the part of Master Punt. He was taken out hastily after a whispered consultation, and since he had got into the corner between the fireplace and the cupboard, that meant everyone moving to make way for him. Johnson took the opportunity to say, 'Well – so long,' to anyone who might be listening, and disappear. Mr Polly found himself smoking a cigarette and walking up and down outside in the company of Uncle Pentstemon, while Mr Voules replaced bottles in hampers and prepared for departure, and the womenkind of the party crowded upstairs with the bride. Mr Polly felt taciturn, but the events of the day had stirred the mind of Uncle Pentstemon to speech. And so he spoke, discursively and disconnectedly, a little heedless of his listener as wise old men will.

'They do say,' said Uncle Pentstemon, 'one funeral makes many. This time it's a wedding. But it's all very much of a muchness . . .

' 'Am *do* get in my teeth nowadays,' said Uncle Pentstemon, 'I can't understand it. 'Tisn't like there was nubblicks or strings or such in 'am. It's a plain food, sure-ly.

'You *got* to get married,' said Uncle Pentstemon, resuming his discourse. 'That's the way of it. Some has. Some hain't. I done it long before I was your age. It hain't for me to blame you. You can't 'elp being the marrying sort any more than me. It's nat'ral – like poaching or drinking or wind on the stummik. You can't 'elp it and there you are! As for the good of it, there

ain't no particular good in it as I can see. It's a toss up. The hotter come, the sooner cold; but they all gets tired of it sooner or later . . . I hain't no grounds to complain. Two I've 'ad and berried, and might 'ave 'ad a third, and never no worrit with kids – never . . .

'You done well not to 'ave the big gal. I will say that for ye. She's a gadabout grinny, she is, if ever was. A gadabout grinny. Mucked up my mushroom bed to rights, she did, and I 'aven't forgot it. Got the feet of a centipede, she 'as – all over everything and neither with your leave nor by your leave. Like a stray 'en in a pea patch. Cluck! cluck! Trying to laugh it off. *I* laughed 'er off, I did. Dratted lumpin baggage! . . . '

For a while he mused malevolently upon Annie, and routed out a reluctant crumb from some coy sitting-out place in his tooth.

'Wimmin's a toss up,' said Uncle Pentstemon. 'Prize packets they are, and you can't tell what's in 'em till you took 'em 'ome and undone 'em. Never was a bachelor married yet that didn't buy a pig in a poke. Never. Marriage seems to change the very natures in 'em through and through. You can't tell what they won't turn into – nohow.

'I seen the nicest girls go wrong,' said Uncle Pentstemon, and added with unusual thoughtfulness, 'Not that I mean *you* got one of that sort.'

He sent another crumb on to its long home with a sucking, encouraging noise.

'The *wust* sort's the grizzler,' Uncle Pentstemon resumed. 'If ever I'd 'ad a grizzler I'd up and 'it 'er on the 'ed with sumpthin' pretty quick. I don't think I could abide a grizzler,' said Uncle Pentstemon. 'I'd liefer 'ave a lump-about like that other gal. I would indeed. I lay I'd make 'er stop laughing after a bit for all 'er airs. And mind where her clumsy great feet went . . .

'A man's got to tackle 'em, whatever they be,' said Uncle Pentstemon, summing up the shrewd observation of an old-world lifetime. 'Good or bad,' said Uncle Pentstemon, raising his voice fearlessly, 'a man's got to tackle 'em.'

8

At last it was time for the two young people to catch the train for Waterloo *en route* for Fishbourne. They had to hurry, and as a concluding glory of matrimony they travelled second-class, and were seen off by all the rest of the party except the Punts, Master Punt being now beyond any question unwell.

'Off!' The train moved out of the station.

Mr Polly remained waving his hat and Mrs Polly her handkerchief until they were hidden under the bridge. The dominating figure to the last was Mr Voules. He had followed them along the platform waving the equestrian grey hat and kissing his hand to the bride.

They subsided into their seats.

'Got a compartment to ourselves anyhow,' said Mrs Polly after a pause.

Silence for a moment.

'The rice 'e must 'ave bought. Pounds and pounds!'

Mr Polly felt round his collar at the thought.

'Ain't you going to kiss me, Elfrid, now we're alone together?'

He roused himself to sit forward, hands on knees, cocked his hat over one eye, and assumed an expression of avidity becoming to the occasion.

'Never!' he said. 'Ever!' and feigned to be selecting a place to kiss with great discrimination.

'Come here,' he said, and drew her to him.

'Be careful of my 'at,' said Mrs Polly, yielding awkwardly.

CHAPTER SEVEN

The Little Shop at Fishbourne

For fifteen years Mr Polly was a respectable shopkeeper in Fishbourne.

Years they were in which every day was tedious, and when they were gone it was as if they had gone in a flash. But now Mr Polly had good looks no more, he was as I have described him in the beginning of this story, thirty-seven and fattish in a not very healthy way, dull and yellowish about the complexion, and with discontented wrinklings round his eyes. He sat on the stile above Fishbourne and cried to the heavens above him: 'Oh! Ro-o-o-tten Be-e-astly Silly Hole!' And he wore a rather shabby black morning coat and waistcoat, and his tie was richly splendid, being from stock, and his golf cap aslant over one eye.

Fifteen years ago, and it might have seemed to you that the queer little flower of Mr Polly's imagination must be altogether withered and dead, and with no living seed left in any part of him. But indeed it still lived as an insatiable hunger for bright and delightful experiences, for the gracious aspects of things, for beauty. He still read books when he had a chance, books that told of glorious places abroad and glorious times, that wrung a rich humour from life and contained the delight of words freshly and expressively grouped. But alas! there are not many such books, and for the newspapers and the cheap fiction that abounded more and more in the world Mr Polly had little taste. There was no epithet in them. And there was no one to talk to, as he loved to talk. And he had to mind his shop.

It was a reluctant little shop from the beginning.

He had taken it to escape the doom of Johnson's choice and because Fishbourne had a hold upon his imagination. He had disregarded the ill-built cramped rooms behind it in which he would have to lurk and live, the relentless limitations of its dimensions, the inconvenience of an

underground kitchen that must necessarily be the living-room in winter, the narrow yard behind giving upon the yard of the Royal Fishbourne Hotel, the tiresome sitting and waiting for custom, the restricted prospects of trade. He had visualised himself and Miriam first as at breakfast on a clear bright winter morning amidst a tremendous smell of bacon, and then as having muffins for tea. He had also thought of sitting on the beach on Sunday afternoons and of going for a walk in the country behind the town and picking marguerites and poppies. But, in fact, Miriam and he were extremely cross at breakfast, and it didn't run to muffins at tea. And she didn't think it looked well, she said, to go trapesing about the country on Sundays.

It was unfortunate that Miriam never took to the house from the first. She did not like it when she saw it, and liked it less as she explored it. 'There's too many stairs,' she said, 'and the coal being indoors will make a lot of work.'

'Didn't think of that,' said Mr Polly, following her round.

'It'll be a hard house to keep clean,' said Miriam.

'White paint's all very well in its way,' said Miriam, 'but it shows the dirt something fearful. Better 'ave 'ad it nicely grained.'

'There's a kind of place here,' said Mr Polly, 'where we might have some flowers in pots.'

'Not me,' said Miriam. 'I've 'ad trouble enough with Minnie and 'er musk . . . '

They stayed for a week in a cheap boarding house before they moved in. They had bought some furniture in Stamton, mostly second-hand, but with new cheap cutlery and china and linen, and they had supplemented this from the Fishbourne shops. Miriam, relieved from the hilarious associations of home, developed a meagre and serious quality of her own, and went about with knitted brows pursuing some ideal of ' 'aving everything right'. Mr Polly gave himself to the arrangement of the shop with a certain zest, and whistled a good deal until Miriam appeared and said that it went through her head. So soon as he had taken the shop he had filled the window with aggressive posters announcing in no measured terms that he was going to open, and now he was getting his stuff put out he was resolved to show Fishbourne what window-dressing could do. He meant to give them boater straws, imitation Panamas, bathing dresses with novelties in stripes, light flannel shirts, summer ties, and ready-made flannel trousers for men, youths and boys. Incidentally he watched the small fishmonger over the way, and had a glimpse of the china dealer next door, and wondered if a friendly nod would be out of place. And on the first Sunday in this new life he and Miriam arrayed themselves with great care, he in his wedding-funeral hat and coat and she in her going-away dress, and went processionally to church – a more respectable-looking couple you could hardly imagine – and looked about them.

Things began to settle down next week into their places. A few customers came, chiefly for bathing suits and hat guards, and on Saturday night the cheapest straw hats and ties, and Mr Polly found himself more and more drawn towards the shop door and the social charm of the street. He found the china dealer unpacking a crate at the edge of the pavement, and remarked that it was a fine day. The china dealer gave a reluctant assent, and plunged into the crate in a manner that presented no encouragement to a loquacious neighbour.

'Zealacious commerciality,' whispered Mr Polly to that unfriendly back view . . .

2

Miriam combined earnestness of spirit with great practical incapacity. The house was never clean nor tidy, but always being frightfully disarranged for cleaning or tidying up, and she cooked because food had to be cooked and with a sound moralist's entire disregard of the quality of the consequences. The food came from her hands done rather than improved, and looking as uncomfortable as savages clothed under duress by a missionary with a stock of outsizes. Such food is too apt to behave resentfully, rebel and work Obi. She ceased to listen to her husband's talk from the day she married him, and ceased to unwrinkle the kink in her brow at his presence, giving herself up to mental states that had a quality of secret preoccupation. And she developed an idea, for which perhaps there was legitimate excuse, that he was lazy. He seemed to stand about in the shop a great deal, to read – an indolent habit – and presently to seek company for talking. He began to attend the bar parlour of the God's Providence Inn with some frequency, and would have done so regularly in the evening if cards, which bored him to death, had not arrested conversation. But the perpetual foolish variation of the permutations and combinations of two and fifty cards taken five at a time, and the meagre surprises and excitements that ensue, had no charms for Mr Polly's mind, which was at once too vivid in its impressions and too easily fatigued.

It was soon manifest the shop paid only in the least exacting sense, and Miriam did not conceal her opinion that he ought to bestir himself and 'do things', though what he was to do was hard to say. You see, when you have once sunk your capital in a shop you do not very easily get it out again. If customers will not come to you cheerfully and freely, the law sets limits upon the compulsion you may exercise. You cannot pursue people about the streets of a watering place, compelling them either by threats or importunity to buy flannel trousers. Additional sources of income for a tradesman are not always easy to find. Wintershed, at the bicycle and gramophone shop to the right, played the organ in the church, and Clamp

of the toy shop was pew opener and so forth; Gambell, the greengrocer, waited at table and his wife cooked, and Carter, the watchmaker, left things to his wife while he went about the world winding clocks; but Mr Polly had none of these arts, and wouldn't, in spite of Miriam's quietly persistent protests, get any other. And on summer evenings he would ride his bicycle about the country, and if he discovered a sale where there were books he would as often as not waste half the next day in going again to acquire a job lot of them haphazard, and bring them home tied about with a string, and hide them from Miriam under the counter in the shop. That is a heart-breaking thing for any wife with a serious investigatory turn of mind to discover. She was always thinking of burning these finds, but her natural turn for economy prevailed with her.

The books he read during those fifteen years! He read everything he – got except theology, and as he read his little unsuccessful circumstances vanished and the wonder of life returned to him, the routine of reluctant getting up, opening shop, pretending to dust it with zest, breakfasting with a shop egg underdone or overdone or a herring raw or charred, and coffee made Miriam's way and full of little particles, the return to the shop, the morning paper, the standing, standing at the door saying, 'How do!' to passers-by, or getting a bit of gossip, or watching unusual visitors, all these things vanished as the auditorium of a theatre vanishes when the stage is lit. He acquired hundreds of books at last, old dusty books, books with torn covers and broken covers, fat books whose backs were naked string and glue – an inimical litter to Miriam.

There was, for example, *The Voyage of La Perouse*, with many careful, explicit woodcuts and the frankest revelations of the ways of the eight-eenth-century sailorman, homely, adventurous, drunken, incontinent and delightful, until he floated, smooth and slow, with all sails set and mirrored in the glassy water, until his head was full of the thought of shining, kindly, brown-skinned women, who smiled at him and wreathed his head with unfamiliar flowers. He had, too, a piece of a book about the lost palaces of Yucatan, those vast terraces buried in primordial forest, of whose makers there is now no human memory. With La Perouse he linked *The Island Nights' Entertainments*, and it never palled upon him that in the dusky stabbing of the 'Island of Voices' something poured over the stabber's hands 'like warm tea'. Queer incommunicable joy it is, the joy of the vivid phrase that turns the statement of the horridest fact to beauty!

And another book which had no beginning for him was the second volume of the travels of the Abbés Huc and Gabet. He followed those two sweet souls from their lessons in Tibetan under Sandura the Bearded (who called them donkeys, to their infinite benefit, and stole their store of butter) through a hundred misadventures to the very heart of Lhassa; and it was a thirst in him that was never quenched to find the other volume, and whence they came, and who in fact they were. He read Fenimore Cooper and *Tom*

Cringle's Log side by side with Joseph Conrad, and dreamt of the many-hued humanity of the East and West Indies until his heart ached to see those sun-soaked lands before he died. Conrad's prose had a pleasure for him that he was never able to define, a peculiar deep-coloured effect. He found too one day among a pile of soiled sixpenny books at Port Burdock, to which place he sometimes rode on his ageing bicycle, Bart Kennedy's *A Sailor Tramp*, all written in livid jerks, and had for ever after a kindlier and more understanding eye for every burly rough who slouched through Fishbourne High Street. Sterne he read with a wavering appreciation and some perplexity, but, except for the *Pickwick Papers*, for some reason that I do not understand he never took at all kindly to Dickens. Yet he liked Lever, and Thackeray's *Catherine*, and all Dumas until he got to *The Vicomte de Bragelonne*. I am puzzled by his insensibility to Dickens, and I record it as a good historian should, with an admission of my perplexity. It is much more understandable that he had no love for Scott. And I suppose it was because of his ignorance of the proper pronunciation of words that he infinitely preferred any prose to any metrical writing.

A book he browsed over with a recurrent pleasure was Waterton's *Wanderings in South America*. He would even amuse himself by inventing descriptions of other birds in the Watertonian manner, new birds that he invented, birds with peculiarities that made him chuckle when they occurred to him. He tried to make Rusper, the ironmonger, share this joy with him. He read Bates, too, about the Amazon, but when he discovered that you could not see one bank from the other, he lost, through some mysterious action of the soul that again I cannot understand, at least a tithe of the pleasure he had taken in that river. But he read all sorts of things; a book of old Celtic stories collected by Joyce charmed him and Mitford's *Tales of Old Japan*, and a number of paper-covered volumes, *Tales from Blackwood*, he had acquired at Easewood remained a stand-by. He developed a quite considerable acquaintance with the plays of William Shakespeare, and in his dreams he wore cinque cento or Elizabethan clothes, and walked about a stormy, ruffling, taverning, teeming world. Great land of sublimated things, thou World of Books, happy asylum, refreshment and refuge from the world of everyday . . . !

The essential thing of those fifteen long years of shopkeeping is Mr Polly, well athwart the counter of his rather ill-lit shop, lost in a book or rousing himself with a sigh to attend to business.

Meanwhile he got little exercise; indigestion grew with him until it ruled all his moods; he fattened and deteriorated physically, great moods of distress invaded and darkened his skies, little things irritated him more and more, and casual laughter ceased in him. His hair began to come off until he had a large bald space at the back of his head. Suddenly one day it came to him – forgetful of those books and all he had lived and seen through them – that he had been in his shop for exactly fifteen years, that he would soon be

forty, and that his life during that time had not been worth living, that it had been in apathetic and feebly hostile and critical company, ugly in detail and mean in scope – and that it had brought him at last to an outlook utterly hopeless and grey.

3

I have already had occasion to mention, indeed I have quoted, a certain high-browed gentleman living at Highbury, wearing a golden *pince-nez* and writing for the most part in that beautiful room, the library of the Reform Club. There he wrestles with what he calls 'social problems' in a bloodless but at times, I think one must admit, an extremely illuminating manner. He has a fixed idea that something called a 'collective intelligence' is wanted in the world, which means in practice that you and I and everyone have to think about things frightfully hard and pool the results, and oblige ourselves to be shamelessly and persistently clear and truthful and support and respect (I suppose) a perfect horde of professors and writers and artists and ill-groomed difficult people, instead of using our brains in a moderate, sensible manner to play golf and bridge (pretending a sense of humour prevents our doing anything else with them) and generally taking life in a nice, easy, gentlemanly way, confound him! Well, this dome-headed monster of intellect alleges that Mr Polly was unhappy entirely through that.

A rapidly complicating society [he writes], which as a whole declines to contemplate its future or face the intricate problems of its organisation, is in exactly the position of a man who takes no thought of dietary or regimen, who abstains from baths and exercise and gives his appetites free play. It accumulates useless and aimless lives as a man accumulates fat and morbid products in his blood, it declines in its collective efficiency and vigour and secretes discomfort and misery. Every phase of its evolution is accompanied by a maximum of avoidable distress and inconvenience and human waste . . .

Nothing can better demonstrate the collective dullness of our community, the crying need for a strenuous intellectual renewal, than the consideration of that vast mass of useless, uncomfortable, under-educated, under-trained and altogether pitiable people we contemplate when we use that inaccurate and misleading term, the Lower-Middle Class. A great proportion of the lower-middle class should properly be assigned to the unemployed and the un-employable. They are only not that because the possession of some small hoard of money, savings during a period of wage earning, an insurance policy or suchlike capital, prevents a direct appeal to the rates. But they are doing little or nothing for the community in return for what they consume; they have no understanding of any relation of service to the community, they have never been trained nor their imaginations touched to any social purpose. A

great proportion of small shopkeepers, for example, are people who have, through the inefficiency that comes from inadequate training and sheer aimlessness, or improvements in machinery or the drift of trade, been thrown out of employment, and who set up in needless shops as a method of eking out the savings upon which they count. They contrive to make sixty or seventy per cent of their expenditure, the rest is drawn from the shrinking capital. Essentially their lives are failures, not the sharp and tragic failure of the labourer who gets out of work and starves, but a slow, chronic process of consecutive small losses which may end if the individual is exceptionally fortunate in an impoverished deathbed before actual bankruptcy or destitution supervenes. Their chances of ascendant means are less in their shops than in any lottery that was ever planned. The secular development of transit and communications has made the organisation of distributing businesses upon large and economical lines inevitable; except in the chaotic confusions of newly opened countries, the day when a man might earn an independent living by unskilled or practically unskilled retailing has gone for ever. Yet every year sees the melancholy procession towards petty bankruptcy and imprisonment for debt go on, and there is no statesmanship in us to avert it. Every issue of every trade journal has its four or five columns of abridged bankruptcy proceedings, nearly every item in which means the final collapse of another struggling family upon the resources of the community, and continually a fresh supply of superfluous artisans and shop assistants, coming out of employment with savings or 'help' from relations, of widows with a husband's insurance money, of the ill-trained sons of parsimonious fathers, replaces the fallen in the ill-equipped, jerry-built shops that everywhere abound . . .

I quote these fragments from a gifted, if unpleasant, contemporary for what they are worth. I feel this has come in here as the broad aspect of this *History*. I come back to Mr Polly sitting upon his gate and swearing in the east wind, and I so returning have a sense of floating across unbridged abysses between the General and the Particular. There, on the one hand, is the man of understanding, seeing clearly – I suppose he sees clearly – the big process that dooms millions of lives to thwarting and discomfort and unhappy circumstances, and giving us no help, no hint, by which we may get that better 'collective will and intelligence' which would dam the stream of human failure, and, on the other hand, Mr Polly sitting on his gate, untrained, unwarned, confused, distressed, angry, seeing nothing except that he is, as it were, netted in greyness and discomfort – with life dancing all about him; Mr Polly with a capacity for joy and beauty at least as keen and subtle as yours or mine.

I have hinted that our Mother England had equipped Mr Polly for the management of his internal concerns no whit better than she had for the direction of his external affairs. With a careless generosity she affords her children a variety of foods unparalleled in the world's history, including many condiments and preserved preparations novel to the human economy. And Miriam did the cooking. Mr Polly's system, like a confused and ill-governed democracy, had been brought to a state of perpetual clamour and disorder, demanding now evil and unsuitable internal satisfactions, such as pickles and vinegar and the crackling on pork, and now vindictive external expression, war and bloodshed throughout the world. So that Mr Polly had been led into hatred and a series of disagreeable quarrels with his landlord, his wholesalers, and most of his neighbours.

Rumbold, the china dealer next door, seemed hostile from the first for no apparent reason, and always unpacked his crates with a full back to his new neighbour, and from the first Mr Polly resented and hated that uncivil breadth of expressionless humanity, wanted to prod it, kick it, satirise it. But you cannot satirise a back, if you have no friend to nudge while you do it.

At last Mr Polly could stand it no longer. He approached and prodded Rumbold.

' 'Ello!' said Rumbold, suddenly erect and turned about.

'Can't we have some other point of view?' said Mr Polly. 'I'm tired of the end elevation.'

'Eh?' said Mr Rumbold, frankly puzzled.

'Of all the vertebracious animals man alone raises his face to the sky, o' man. Well, why invert it?'

Rumbold shook his head with a helpless expression.

'Don't like so much Arreary Pensy.'

Rumbold distressed in utter obscurity.

'In fact, I'm sick of your turning your back on me, see?'

A great light shone on Rumbold. '*That*'s what you're talking about!' he said.

'That's it,' said Polly.

Rumbold scratched his ear with the three strawy jampots he held in his hand. 'Way the wind blows, I expect,' he said. 'But what's the fuss?'

'No fuss!' said Mr Polly. 'Passing Remark. I don't like it, o' man, that's all.'

'Can't help it, if the wind blows my stror,' said Mr Rumbold, still far from clear about it.

'It isn't ordinary civility,' said Mr Polly.

'Got to unpack 'ow it suits me. Can't unpack with the stror blowing into one's eyes.'

'Needn't unpack like a pig rooting for truffles, need you?'

'Truffles?'

'Needn't unpack like a pig.'

Mr Rumbold apprehended something.

'Pig!' he said, impressed. 'You calling me a pig?'

'It's the side I seem to get of you.'

' 'Ere,' said Mr Rumbold, suddenly fierce and shouting and marking his point with gesticulated jampots, 'you go indoors. I don't want no row with you, and I don't want you to row with me. I don't know what you're after, but I'm a peaceable man – teetotaller, too, and a good thing if *you* was. See? You go indoors!'

'You mean to say – I'm asking you civilly to stop unpacking with your back to me.'

'Pig ain't civil, and you ain't sober. You go indoors and lemme go on unpacking. You – you're excited.'

'D'you mean – !' Mr Polly was foiled.

He perceived an immense solidity about Rumbold.

'Get back to your shop and lemme get on with my business,' said Mr Rumbold. 'Stop calling me pigs. See? Sweep your pavemint.'

'I came here to make a civil request.'

'You came 'ere to make a row. I don't want no truck with you. See? I don't like the looks of you. See? And I can't stand 'ere all day arguing. See?'

Pause of mutual inspection.

It occurred to Mr Polly that probably he was to some extent in the wrong.

Mr Rumbold, blowing heavily, walked past him, deposited the jampots in his shop with an immense affectation that there was no Mr Polly in the world, returned, turned a scornful back on Mr Polly and dived to the interior of the crate. Mr Polly stood baffled. Should he kick this solid mass before him? Should he administer a resounding kick?

No!

He plunged his hands deeply into his trouser pockets, began to whistle and returned to his own doorstep with an air of profound unconcern. There for a time, to the tune of 'Men of Harlech', he contemplated the receding possibility of kicking Mr Rumbold hard. It would be splendid – and for the moment satisfying. But he decided not to do it. For indefinable reasons he could not do it. He went indoors and straightened up his dress ties very slowly and thoughtfully. Presently he went to the window and regarded Mr Rumbold obliquely. Mr Rumbold was still unpacking. . .

Mr Polly had no human intercourse thereafter with Rumbold for fifteen years. He kept up a Hate.

There was a time when it seemed as if Rumbold might go, but he had a meeting of his creditors and then went on unpacking as obtusely as ever.

Hinks, the saddler, two shops farther down the street, was a different case. Hinks was the aggressor – practically.

Hinks was a sporting man in his way, with that taste for checks in costume and tight trousers which is, under Providence, so mysteriously and invariably associated with equestrian proclivities. At first Mr Polly took to him as a character, became frequent in the God's Providence Inn under his guidance, stood and was stood drinks and concealed a great ignorance of horses until Hinks became urgent for him to play billiards or bet.

Then Mr Polly took to evading him, and Hinks ceased to conceal his opinion that Mr Polly was in reality a softish sort of flat.

He did not, however, discontinue conversation with Mr Polly; he would come along to him whenever he appeared at his door, and converse about sport and women and fisticuffs and the pride of life with an air of extreme initiation, until Mr Polly felt himself the faintest underdeveloped intimation of a man that had ever hovered on the verge of non-existence.

So he invented phrases for Hinks's clothes and took Rusper, the ironmonger, into his confidence upon the weaknesses of Hinks. He called him the 'chequered Careerist', and spoke of his patterned legs as 'shivery shakys'. Good things of this sort are apt to get round to people.

He was standing at his door one day, feeling bored, when Hinks appeared down the street, stood still and regarded him with a strange malignant expression for a space.

Mr Polly waved a hand in a rather belated salutation.

Mr Hinks spat on the pavement and appeared to reflect. Then he came towards Mr Polly portentously and paused, and spoke between his teeth in an earnest confidential tone.

'You been flapping your mouth about me, I'm told,' he said.

Mr Polly felt suddenly spiritless. 'Not that I know of,' he answered.

'Not that you know of, be blowed! You been flapping your mouth.'

'Don't see it,' said Mr Polly.

'Don't see it, be blowed! You go flapping your silly mouth about me and I'll give you a poke in the eye. See?'

Mr Hinks regarded the effect of this coldly but firmly, and spat again.

'Understand me?' he enquired.

'Don't recollect – ' began Mr Polly.

'Don't recollect, be blowed! You flap your mouth a damn sight too much. This place gets more of your mouth than it wants . . . Seen this?'

And Mr Hinks, having displayed a freckled fist of extraordinary size and pugginess in an ostentatiously familiar manner to Mr Polly's close inspection by sight and smell, turned it about this way and that and shaken it gently for a

moment or so, replaced it carefully in his pocket as if for future use, receded slowly and watchfully for a pace, and then turned away as if to other matters, and ceased to be, even in outward seeming, a friend . . .

6

Mr Polly's intercourse with all his fellow tradesmen was tarnished sooner or later by some such adverse incident, until not a friend remained to him, and loneliness made even the shop door terrible. Shops bankrupted all about him and fresh people came and new acquaintances sprang up, but sooner or later a discord was inevitable; the tension under which these badly fed, poorly housed, bored and bothered neighbours lived made it inevitable. The mere fact that Mr Polly had to see them every day, that there was no getting away from them, was in itself sufficient to make them almost unendurable to his frettingly active mind.

Among other shopkeepers in the High Street there was Chuffles, the grocer, a small, hairy, silently intent polygamist, who was given rough music by the youth of the neighbourhood because of a scandal about his wife's sister, but who was nevertheless totally uninteresting, and Tonks, the second grocer, an old man with an older, very enfeebled wife, both submerged by piety. Tonks went bankrupt, and was succeeded by a branch of the National Provision Company, with a young manager exactly like a fox, except that he barked. The toy and sweetstuff shop was kept by an old woman of repellent manners, and so was the little fish shop at the end of the street. The Berlin wool shop, having gone bankrupt, became a newspaper shop, then fell to a haberdasher in consumption, and finally to a stationer; the three shops at the end of the street wallowed in and out of insolvency in the hands of a bicycle repairer and dealer, a gramophone dealer, a tobacconist, a sixpenny-halfpenny bazaar-keeper, a shoemaker, a green-grocer, and the exploiter of a cinematograph peep-show – but none of them supplied friendship to Mr Polly.

These adventurers in commerce were all more or less distraught souls, driving without intelligible comment before the gale of fate. The two milkmen of Fishbourne were brothers who had quarrelled about their father's will, and started up in opposition to each other; one was stone deaf and no use to Mr Polly, and the other was a sporting man with a natural dread of epithet who sided with Hinks. So it was all about him; on every hand it seemed were uncongenial people, uninteresting people or people who conceived the deepest distrust and hostility towards him, a magic circle of suspicious, preoccupied and dehumanised humanity. So the poison in his system poisoned the world without.

(But Boomer, the wine merchant, and Tashingford, the chemist, be it noted, were fraught with pride and held themselves to be a cut above Mr

Polly. They never quarrelled with him, preferring to bear themselves from the outset as though they had already done so.)

As his internal malady grew upon Mr Polly and he became more and more a battleground of fermenting foods and warring juices, he came to hate the very sight, as people say, of every one of these neighbours. There they were, every day and all the days, just the same, echoing his own stagnation. They pained him all round the top and back of his head; they made his legs and arms weary and spiritless. The air was tasteless by reason of them. He lost his human kindliness.

In the afternoons he would hover in the shop, bored to death with his business and his home and Miriam, and yet afraid to go out because of his inflamed and magnified dislike and dread of these neighbours. He could not bring himself to go out and run the gauntlet of the observant windows and the cold estranged eyes.

One of his last friendships was with Rusper, the ironmonger. Rusper took over Worthington's shop about three years after Mr Polly opened. He was a tall, lean, nervous, convulsive man, with an upturned, back-thrown, oval head, who read newspapers and the *Review of Reviews* assiduously, had belonged to a Literary Society somewhere once, and had some defect of the palate that at first gave his lightest word a charm and interest for Mr Polly. It caused a peculiar clicking sound, as though he had something between a giggle and a gas-meter at work in his neck.

His literary admirations were not precisely Mr Polly's literary admirations; he thought books were written to enshrine Great Thoughts, and that art was pedagogy in fancy dress, he had no sense of phrase or epithet or richness of texture, but still he knew there were books. He did know there were books and he was full of large windy ideas of the sort he called 'Modern (kik) Thought', and seemed needlessly and helplessly concerned about '(kik) the Welfare of the Race'.

Mr Polly would dream about that (kik) at nights.

It seemed to that undesirable mind of his that Rusper's head was the most egg-shaped head he had ever seen; the similarity weighed upon him, and when he found an argument growing warm with Rusper he would say: 'Boil it some more, o' man; boil it harder!' or, 'Six minutes at least,' allusions Rusper could never make head or tail of, and got at last to disregard as a part of Mr Polly's general eccentricity. For a long time that little tendency threw no shadow over their intercourse, but it contained within it the seeds of an ultimate disruption.

Often during the days of this friendship Mr Polly would leave his shop and walk over to Mr Rusper's establishment, and stand in his doorway and enquire: 'Well, o' man, how's the Mind of the Age working?' and get quite an hour of it, and sometimes Mr Rusper would come into the outfitter's shop with, 'Heard the (kik) latest?' and spend the rest of the morning.

Then Mr Rusper married, and he married very inconsiderately a woman

who was totally uninteresting to Mr Polly. A coolness grew between them from the first intimation of her advent. Mr Polly couldn't help thinking when he saw her that she drew her hair back from her forehead a great deal too tightly, and that her elbows were angular. His desire not to mention these things in the apt terms that welled up so richly in his mind made him awkward in her presence, and that gave her an impression that he was hiding some guilty secret from her. She decided he must have a bad influence upon her husband, and she made it a point to appear whenever she heard him talking to Rusper.

One day they became a little heated about the German peril.

'I lay (kik) they'll invade us,' said Rusper.

'Not a bit of it. William's not the Xerxiacious sort.'

'You'll see, o' man.'

'Just what I shan't do.'

'Before (kik) five years are out.'

'Not it.'

'Yes.'

'No.'

'Yes.'

'Oh! Boil it hard!' said Mr Polly.

Then he looked up and saw Mrs Rusper standing behind the counter half hidden by a trophy of spades and garden shears and a knife-cleaning machine, and by her expression he knew instantly that she understood.

The conversation paled and presently Mr Polly withdrew.

After that, estrangement increased steadily.

Mr Rusper ceased altogether to come over to the outfitter's, and Mr Polly called upon the ironmonger only with the completest air of casuality. And everything they said to each other led now to flat contradiction and raised voices. Rusper had been warned in vague and alarming terms that Mr Polly insulted and made game of him; he couldn't discover exactly where; and so it appeared to him now that every word of Mr Polly's might be an insult meriting his resentment, meriting it none the less because it was masked and cloaked.

Soon Mr Polly's calls upon Mr Rusper ceased also, and then Mr Rusper, pursuing incomprehensible lines of thought, became afflicted with a specialised short-sightedness that applied only to Mr Polly. He would look in other directions when Mr Polly appeared, and his large oval face assumed an expression of conscious serenity and deliberate happy unawareness that would have maddened a far less irritable person than Mr Polly. It evoked a strong desire to mock and ape, and produced in his throat a cough of singular scornfulness, more particularly when Mr Rusper also assisted, with an assumed unconsciousness that was all his own.

Then one day Mr Polly had a bicycle accident.

His bicycle was now very old, and it is one of the concomitants of a

bicycle's senility that its free wheel should one day obstinately cease to be free. It corresponds to that epoch in human decay when an old gentleman loses an incisor tooth. It happened just as Mr Polly was approaching Mr Rusper's shop, and the untoward chance of a motor car trying to pass a waggon on the wrong side gave Mr Polly no choice but to get on to the pavement and dismount. He was always accustomed to take his time and step off his left pedal at its lowest point, but the jamming of the free wheel gear made that lowest moment a transitory one, and the pedal was lifting his foot for another revolution before he realised what had happened. Before he could dismount according to his habit the pedal had to make a revolution, and before it could make a revolution Mr Polly found himself among the various sonorous things with which Mr Rusper adorned the front of his shop – zinc dustbins, household pails, lawn mowers, rakes, spades and all manner of clattering things. Before he got among them he had one of those agonising moments of helpless wrath and suspense that seem to last ages, in which one seems to perceive everything and think of nothing but words that are better forgotten. He sent a column of pails thundering across the doorway and dismounted with one foot in a sanitary dustbin amidst an enormous uproar of falling ironmongery.

'Put all over the place!' he cried, and found Mr Rusper emerging from his shop with the large tranquillities of his countenance puckered to anger, like the frowns in the brow of a reefing sail. He gesticulated speechlessly for a moment.

'(kik) Jer doing?' he said at last.

'Tin mantraps!' said Mr Polly.

'Jer (kik) doing?'

'Dressing all over the pavement as though the blessed town belonged to you! Ugh!'

And Mr Polly in attempting a dignified movement realised his entanglement with the dustbin for the first time. With a low embittering expression, he kicked his foot about in it for a moment very noisily, and finally sent it thundering to the kerb. On its way it struck a pail or so. Then Mr Polly picked up his bicycle and proposed to resume his homeward way. But the hand of Mr Rusper arrested him.

'Put it (kik) all (kik kik) back (kik).'

'Put it (kik) back yourself.'

'You got (kik) t'put it back.'

'Get out of the (kik) way.'

Mr Rusper laid one hand on the bicycle handle, and the other gripped Mr Polly's collar urgently. Whereupon Mr Polly said: 'Leggo!' and again, 'D'you *hear*! Leggo!' and then drove his elbow with considerable force into the region of Mr Rusper's midriff. Whereupon Mr Rusper, with a loud impassioned cry, resembling 'Woo (kik)' more than any other combination of letters, released the bicycle handle, seized Mr Polly by the cap and hair,

and bore his head and shoulders downward. Thereat Mr Polly, emitting such words as everyone knows and nobody prints, butted his utmost into the concavity of Mr Rusper, entwined a leg about him and, after terrific moments of swaying instability, fell headlong beneath him amidst the bicycle and pails. There on the pavement these inexpert children of a pacific age, untrained in arms and uninured to violence, abandoned themselves to amateurish and absurd efforts to hurt and injure one another – of which the most palpable consequences were dusty backs, ruffled hair and torn and twisted collars. Mr Polly, by accident, got his finger into Mr Rusper's mouth, and strove earnestly for some time to prolong that aperture in the direction of Mr Rusper's ear before it occurred to Mr Rusper to bite him (and even then he didn't bite very hard), while Mr Rusper concentrated his mind almost entirely on an effort to rub Mr Polly's face on the pavement. (And their positions bristled with chances of the deadliest sort!) They didn't, from first to last, draw blood.

Then it seemed to each of them that the other had become endowed with many hands and several voices and great accessions of strength. They submitted to fate and ceased to struggle. They found themselves torn apart and held up by outwardly scandalised and inwardly delighted neighbours, and invited to explain what it was all about.

'Got to (kik) puttem all back!' panted Mr Rusper, in the expert grasp of Hinks. 'Merely asked him to (kik) puttem all back.'

Mr Polly was under restraint of little Clamp, of the toy shop, who was holding his hands in a complex and uncomfortable manner that he afterwards explained to Wintershed was a combination of something romantic called 'Ju-jitsu' and something else still more romantic called the 'Police Grip'.

'Pails,' explained Mr Polly in breathless fragments. 'All over the road. Pails. Bungs up the street with his pails. Look at them!'

'Deliber (kik) lib (kik) liberately rode into my goods (kik). Constantly (kik) annoying me (kik)!' said Mr Rusper.

They were both tremendously earnest and reasonable in their manner. They wished everyone to regard them as responsible and intellectual men acting for the love of right and the enduring good of the world. They felt they must treat this business as a profound and publicly significant affair. They wanted to explain and orate and show the entire necessity of everything they had done. Mr Polly was convinced he had never been so absolutely correct in all his life as when he planted his foot in the sanitary dustbin, and Mr Rusper considered his clutch at Mr Polly's hair as the one faultless impulse in an otherwise undistinguished career. But it was clear in their minds they might easily become ridiculous if they were not careful, if for a second they stepped over the edge of the high spirit and pitiless dignity they had hitherto maintained. At any cost they perceived they must not become ridiculous.

Mr Chuffles, the scandalous grocer, joined the throng about the principal combatants, mutely as became an outcast, and with a sad, distressed, helpful expression picked up Mr Polly's bicycle. Gambell's summer errand boy, moved by example, restored the dustbin and pails to their self-respect.

' 'E ought – 'e ought (kik) t'pick them up,' protested Mr Rusper.

'What's it all about?' said Mr Hinks for the third time, shaking Mr Rusper gently. 'As 'e been calling you names?'

'Simply ran into his pails – as anyone might,' said Mr Polly, 'and out he comes and scrags me!'

'(kik) Assault!' said Mr Rusper.

'He assaulted *me*,' said Mr Polly.

'Jumped (kik) into my dus'bin!' said Mr Rusper. 'That assault? Or isn't it?'

'You better drop it,' said Mr Hinks.

'Great pity they can't be'ave better, both of 'em,' said Mr Chuffles, glad for once to find himself morally unassailable.

'Anyone see it begin?' said Mr Wintershed.

'*I* was in the shop,' said Mrs Rusper suddenly from the doorstep, piercing the little group of men and boys with the sharp horror of an unexpected woman's voice. 'If a witness is wanted, I suppose I've got a tongue. I suppose I got a voice in seeing my own 'usband injured. My husband went out and spoke to Mr Polly, who was jumping off his bicycle all among our pails and things, and immediately 'e butted him in the stomach – immediately – most savagely – butted him. Just after his dinner too, and him far from strong. I could have screamed. But Rusper caught hold of him right away, I will say that for Rusper . . .'

'I'm going,' said Mr Polly suddenly, releasing himself from the Anglo-Japanese grip and holding out his hands for his bicycle.

'Teach you (kik) to leave things alone,' said Mr Rusper, with an air of one who has given a lesson.

The testimony of Mrs Rusper continued relentlessly in the background.

'You'll hear of me through a summons,' said Mr Polly, preparing to wheel his bicycle.

'(kik) Me too,' said Mr Rusper.

Someone handed Mr Polly a collar. 'This yours?'

Mr Polly investigated his neck. 'I suppose it is. Anyone seen a tie?'

A small boy produced a grimy strip of spotted blue silk.

'Human life isn't safe with you,' said Mr Polly as a parting shot.

'(kik) Yours isn't,' said Mr Rusper.

And they got small satisfaction out of the Bench, which refused altogether to perceive the relentless correctitude of the behaviour of either party, and reproved the eagerness of Mrs Rusper – speaking to her gently, firmly but exasperatingly as 'My Good Woman' and telling her to 'Answer the Question! Answer the Question!'

'Seems a Pity,' said the chairman, when binding them over to keep the

peacc, 'you can't behave like Respectable Tradesmen. Seems a Great Pity. Bad Example to the Young and all that. Don't do any Good to the town, don't do any Good to yourselves, don't do any manner of Good to have all the Tradesmen in the Place scrapping about the Pavement of an Afternoon. Think we're letting you off very easily this time, and hope it will be a Warning to you. Don't expect Men of your Position to come up before us. Very Regrettable Affair. Eh?'

He addressed the latter enquiry to his two colleagues.

'Exactly, exactly,' said the colleague to the right.

'Er – (kik),' said Mr Rusper.

7

But the disgust that overshadowed Mr Polly's being as he sat upon the stile had other and profounder justification than his quarrel with Rusper and the indignity of appearing before the county bench. He was for the first time in his business career short with his rent for the approaching quarter day, and, so far as he could trust his own handling of figures, he was sixty or seventy pounds on the wrong side of solvency. And that was the outcome of fifteen years of passive endurance of dullness throughout the best years of his life! What would Miriam say when she learnt this, and was invited to face the prospect of exile – heaven knows what sort of exile! – from their present home? She would grumble and scold and become limply unhelpful, he knew, and none the less so because he could not help things. She would say he ought to have worked harder, and a hundred such exasperating pointless things. Such thoughts as these require no aid from undigested cold pork and cold potatoes and pickles to darken the soul, and with these aids his soul was black indeed.

'May as well have a bit of a walk,' said Mr Polly at last, after nearly intolerable meditations, and sat round and put a leg over the stile.

He remained still for some time before he brought over the other leg.

'Kill myself,' he murmured at last.

It was an idea that came back to his mind nowadays with a continually increasing attractiveness – more particularly after meals. Life he felt had no further happiness to offer him. He hated Miriam, and there was no getting away from her whatever might betide. And for the rest there was toil and struggle, toil and struggle with a failing heart and dwindling courage, to sustain that dreary duologue. 'Life's insured,' said Mr Polly; 'place is insured. I don't see it does any harm to her or anyone.'

He stuck his hands in his pockets. 'Needn't hurt much,' he said. He began to elaborate a plan.

He found it quite interesting elaborating his plan. His countenance became less miserable and his pace quickened.

There is nothing so good in all the world for melancholia as walking, and the exercise of the imagination in planning something presently to be done, and soon the wrathful wretchedness had vanished from Mr Polly's face. He would have to do the thing secretly and elaborately, because otherwise there might be difficulties about the life insurance. He began to scheme how he could circumvent that difficulty . . .

He took a long walk, for after all what is the good of hurrying back to shop when you are not only insolvent but very soon to die? His dinner and the east wind lost their sinister hold upon his soul, and when at last he came back along the Fishbourne High Street, his face was unusually bright and the craving hunger of the dyspeptic was returning. So he went into the grocer's and bought a ruddily decorated tin of a brightly pink fishlike substance known as 'Deep Sea Salmon'. This he was resolved to consume, regardless of cost, with vinegar and salt and pepper as a relish to his supper.

He did, and since he and Miriam rarely talked, and Miriam thought honour and his recent behaviour demanded a hostile silence, he ate fast and copiously and soon gloomily. He ate alone, for she refrained, to mark her sense of his extravagance. Then he prowled into the High Street for a time, thought it an infernal place, tried his pipe and found it foul and bitter, and retired wearily to bed.

He slept for an hour or so and then woke up to the contemplation of Miriam's hunched back and the riddle of life – and this bright attractive idea of ending for ever and ever and ever all the things that were locking him in, this bright idea that shone like a baleful star above all the reek and darkness of his misery . . .

CHAPTER EIGHT

Making an End to Things

Mr Polly designed his suicide with considerable care, and a quite remarkable altruism. His passionate hatred for Miriam vanished directly the idea of getting away from her for ever became clear in his mind. He found himself full of solicitude then for her welfare. He did not want to buy his release at her expense. He had not the remotest intention of leaving her unprotected with a painfully dead husband and a bankrupt shop on her hands. It seemed to him that he could contrive to secure for her the full benefit of both his life insurance and his fire insurance if he managed things in a tactful manner. He felt happier than he had done for years scheming out this undertaking, albeit it was perhaps a larger and somberer kind of happiness than had fallen to his lot before. It amazed him to think he had endured his monotony of misery and failure for so long.

But there were some queer doubts and questions in the dim, half-lit

background of his mind that he had very resolutely to ignore. 'Sick of it,' he had to repeat to himself aloud, to keep his determination clear and firm. His life was a failure, there was nothing more to hope for but unhappiness. Why shouldn't he?

His project was to begin the fire with the stairs that led from the ground floor to the underground kitchen and scullery. These he would soak with paraffin, and assist with firewood and paper and a brisk fire in the coal cellar underneath. He would smash a hole or so in the stairs to ventilate the blaze, and have a good pile of boxes and paper, and a convenient chair or so, in the shop above. He would have the paraffin can upset and the shop lamp, as if awaiting refilling, at a convenient distance in the scullery ready to catch. Then he would smash the house lamp on the staircase – a fall with that in his hand was to be the ostensible cause of the blaze – and then he would cut his throat at the top of the kitchen stairs, which would then become his funeral pyre. He would do all this on Sunday evening while Miriam was at church, and it would appear that he had fallen downstairs with the lamp and been burnt to death. There was really no flaw whatever that he could see in the scheme. He was quite sure he knew how to cut his throat, deep at the side and not to saw at the windpipe, and he was reasonably sure it wouldn't hurt him very much. And then everything would be at an end.

There was no particular hurry to get the thing done, of course, and meanwhile he occupied his mind with possible variations of the scheme . . .

It needed a particularly dry and dusty east wind, a Sunday dinner of exceptional virulence, a conclusive letter from Konk, Maybrick, Ghool and Gabbitas, his principal and most urgent creditors, and a conversation with Miriam arising out of arrears of rent and leading on to mutual character sketching, before Mr Polly could be brought to the necessary pitch of despair to carry out his plans. He went for an embittering walk, and came back to find Miriam in a bad temper over the tea things, with the brewings of three-quarters of an hour in the pot, and hot buttered muffin gone leathery. He sat eating in silence with his resolution made.

'Coming to church?' said Miriam after she had cleared away.

'Rather. I got a lot to be grateful for,' said Mr Polly.

'You got what you deserve,' said Miriam.

'Suppose I have,' said Mr Polly, and went and stared out of the back window at a despondent horse in the hotel yard.

He was still standing there when Miriam came downstairs dressed for church. Something in his immobility struck home to her. 'You'd better come to church than mope,' she said.

'I shan't mope,' he answered.

She remained still for a moment. Her presence irritated him. He felt that in another moment he should say something absurd to her, make some last appeal for that understanding she had never been able to give.

'Oh! *go* to church!' he said.

In another moment the outer door slammed upon her. 'Good riddance!' said Mr Polly.

He turned about. 'I've had my whack,' he said.

He reflected. 'I don't see she'll have any cause to holler,' he said. 'Beastly Home! Beastly Life!'

For a space he remained thoughtful. 'Here goes!' he said at last.

2

For twenty minutes Mr Polly busied himself about the house, making his preparations very neatly and methodically.

He opened the attic windows in order to make sure of a good draught through the house, and drew down the blinds at the back and shut the kitchen door to conceal his arrangements from casual observation. At the end he would open the door on the yard and so make a clean clear draught right through the house. He hacked at, and wedged off, the tread of a stair. He cleared out the coals from under the staircase, and built a neat fire of firewood and paper there, he splashed about paraffin and arranged the lamps and can even as he had designed, and made a fine inflammable pile of things in the little parlour behind the shop. 'Looks pretty arsonical,' he said as he surveyed it all. 'Wouldn't do to have a caller now. Now for the stairs!'

'Plenty of time,' he assured himself, and took the lamp which was to explain the whole affair and went to the head of the staircase between the scullery and the parlour. He sat down in the twilight with the unlit lamp beside him and surveyed things. He must light the fire in the coal cellar under the stairs, open the back door, then come up them very quickly and light the paraffin puddles on each step, then sit down here again and cut his throat.

He drew his razor from his pocket and felt the edge. It wouldn't hurt much, and in ten minutes he would be indistinguishable ashes in the blaze.

And this was the end of life for him!

The end! And it seemed to him now that life had never begun for him, never! It was as if his soul had been cramped and his eyes bandaged from the hour of his birth. Why had he lived such a life? Why had he submitted to things, blundered into things? Why had he never insisted on the things he thought beautiful and the things he desired, never sought them, fought for them, taken any risk for them, died rather than abandon them? They were the things that mattered. Safety did not matter. A living did not matter unless there were things to live for . . .

He had been a fool, a coward and a fool; he had been fooled, too, for no one had ever warned him to take a firm hold upon life, no one had ever told him of the littleness of fear, or pain, or death; but what was the good of going through it now again? It was over and done with.

The clock in the back parlour pinged the half hour.

'Time!' said Mr Polly, and stood up.

For an instant he battled with an impulse to put it all back, hastily, guiltily, and abandon this desperate plan of suicide for ever.

But Miriam would smell the paraffin!

'No way out this time, o' man,' said Mr Polly; and he went slowly downstairs, matchbox in hand.

He paused for five seconds, perhaps, to listen to noises in the yard of the Royal Fishbourne Hotel before he struck his match. It trembled a little in his hand. The paper blackened, and an edge of blue flame ran outward and spread. The fire burnt up readily, and in an instant the wood was crackling cheerfully.

Someone might hear. He must hurry.

He lit a pool of paraffin on the scullery floor, and instantly a nest of snaky, wavering blue flame became agog for prey. He went up the stairs three steps at a time with one eager blue flicker in pursuit of him. He seized the lamp at the top. 'Now!' he said and flung it smashing. The chimney broke, but the glass receiver stood the shock and rolled to the bottom, a potential bomb. Old Rumbold would hear that and wonder what it was! . . . He'd know soon enough!

Then Mr Polly stood hesitating, razor in hand, and then sat down. He was trembling violently, but quite unafraid.

He drew the blade lightly under one ear. 'Lord!' but it stung like a nettle!

Then he perceived a little blue thread of flame running up his leg. It arrested his attention, and for a moment he sat, razor in hand, staring at it. It must be paraffin on his trousers that had caught fire on the stairs. Of course his legs were wet with paraffin! He smacked the flicker with his hand to put it out, and felt his leg burn as he did so. But his trousers still charred and glowed. It seemed to him necessary that he must put this out before he cut his throat. He put down the razor beside him to smack with both hands very eagerly. And as he did so a thin tall red flame came up through the hole in the stairs he had made and stood still, quite still as it seemed, and looked at him. It was a strange-looking flame, a flattish salmon colour, redly streaked. It was so queer and quiet-mannered that the sight of it held Mr Polly agape.

'Whuff!' went the can of paraffin below, and boiled over with stinking white fire. At the outbreak the salmon-coloured flames shivered and ducked and then doubled and vanished, and instantly all the staircase was noisily ablaze.

Mr Polly sprang up and backwards, as though the uprushing tongues of fire were a pack of eager wolves.

'Good Lord!' he cried like a man who wakes up from a dream.

He swore sharply and slapped again at a recrudescent flame upon his leg.

'What the deuce shall I do? I'm soaked with the confounded stuff!'

He had nerved himself for throat-cutting, but this was fire!

He wanted to delay things, to put them off for a moment while he did his business. The idea of arresting all this hurry with water occurred to him.

There was no water in the little parlour and none in the shop. He hesitated for a moment whether he should not run upstairs to the bedrooms and get a ewer of water to throw on the flames. At this rate Rumbold's would be ablaze in five minutes! Things were going all too fast for Mr Polly. He ran towards the staircase door, and its hot breath pulled him up sharply. Then he dashed out through his shop. The catch of the front door was sometimes obstinate; it was now, and instantly he became frantic. He rattled and stormed and felt the parlour already ablaze behind him. In another moment he was in the High Street with the door wide open.

The staircase behind him was crackling now like horsewhips and pistol shots.

He had a vague sense that he wasn't doing as he had proposed, but the chief thing was his sense of that uncontrolled fire within. What was he going to do? There was the fire brigade station next door but one.

The Fishbourne High Street had never seemed so empty.

Far off at the corner by the God's Providence Inn a group of three stiff hobbledehoys in their black, best clothes, conversed intermittently with Taplow, the policeman.

'Hi!' bawled Mr Polly to them. 'Fire! Fire!' and struck by a horrible thought, the thought of Rumbold's deaf mother-in-law upstairs, began to bang and kick and rattle with the utmost fury at Rumbold's shop door.

'Hi!' he repeated. 'Fire!'

3

That was the beginning of the great Fishbourne fire, which burnt its way sideways into Mr Rusper's piles of crates and straw, and backwards to the petrol and stabling of the Royal Fishbourne Hotel, and spread from that basis until it seemed half Fishbourne would be ablaze. The east wind, which had been gathering in strength all that day, fanned the flames; everything was dry and ready, and the little shed beyond Rumbold's in which the local fire brigade kept its manual was alight before the Fishbourne fire hose could be saved from disaster. In marvellously little time a great column of black smoke, shot with red streamers, rose out of the middle of the High Street, and all Fishbourne was alive with excitement.

Much of the more respectable elements of Fishbourne society was in church or chapel; many, however, had been tempted by the blue sky and the hard freshness of spring to take walks inland, and there had been the usual disappearance of loungers and conversationalists from the beach and the back streets when at the hour of six the drawing of bolts and the turning of

keys had ended the British Ramadan, that weekly interlude of drought our law imposes. The youth of the place were scattered on the beach or playing in backyards, under threat if their clothes were dirtied, and the adolescent were disposed in pairs among the more secluded corners to be found upon the outskirts of the place. Several godless youths, seasick but fishing steadily, were tossing upon the sea in old Tarbold the infidel's boat, and the Clamps were entertaining cousins from Port Burdock. Such few visitors as Fishbourne could boast in the spring were at church or on the beach. To all these that column of smoke did in a manner address itself. 'Look here!' it said, 'this, within limits, is your affair; what are you going to do?'

The three hobbledehoys, had it been a weekday and they in working clothes, might have felt free to act, but the stiffness of black was upon them and they simply moved to the corner by Rusper's to take a better view of Mr Polly beating at the door. The policeman was a young, inexpert constable with far too lively a sense of the public house. He put his head inside the Private Bar to the horror of everyone there. But there was no breach of the law, thank heaven! 'Polly's and Rumbold's on fire!' he said, and vanished again. A window in the top storey over Boomer's shop opened, and Boomer, captain of the fire brigade, appeared, staring out with a blank expression. Still staring, he began to fumble with his collar and tie; manifestly he had to put on his uniform. Hinks's dog, which had been lying on the pavement outside Wintershed's, woke up, and having regarded Mr Polly suspiciously for some time, growled nervously and went round the corner into Granville Alley. Mr Polly continued to beat and kick at Rumbold's door.

Then the public houses began to vomit forth the less desirable elements of Fishbourne society; boys and men were moved to run and shout, and more windows went up as the stir increased. Tashingford, the chemist, appeared at his door in shirtsleeves and an apron, with his photographic plate holders in his hand. And then, like a vision of purpose, came Mr Gambell, the greengrocer, running out of Clayford's Alley and buttoning on his jacket as he ran. His great brass fireman's helmet was on his head, hiding it all but the sharp nose, the firm mouth, the intrepid chin. He ran straight to the fire station and tried the door, and turned about and met the eye of Boomer still at his upper window. 'The key!' cried Mr Gambell, 'the key!'

Mr Boomer made some inaudible explanation about his trousers and half a minute.

'Seen old Rumbold?' cried Mr Polly, approaching Mr Gambell.

'Gone over Downford for a walk,' said Mr Gambell. 'He told me! But look 'ere! We 'aven't got the key!'

'Lord!' said Mr Polly, and regarded the china shop with open eyes. He knew the old woman must be there alone. He went back to the shop front and stood surveying it in infinite perplexity. The other activities in the street did not interest him. A deaf old lady somewhere upstairs there!

Precious moments passing! Suddenly he was struck by an idea and vanished from public vision into the open door of the Royal Fishbourne Tap.

And now the street was getting crowded and people were laying their hands to this and that.

Mr Rusper had been at home reading a number of tracts upon Tariff Reform, during the quiet of his wife's absence in church, and trying to work out the application of the whole question to ironmongery. He heard a clattering in the street and for a time disregarded it, until a cry of 'Fire!' drew him to the window. He pencil-marked the tract of Chiozza Money's that he was reading side by side with one by Mr Holt Schooling, made a hasty note: 'Bal. of Trade say 12,000,000', and went to look out. Instantly he opened the window and ceased to believe the Fiscal Question the most urgent of human affairs.

'Good (kik) Gud!' said Mr Rusper.

For now the rapidly spreading blaze had forced the partition into Mr Rumbold's premises, swept across his cellar, clambered his garden wall by means of his well-tarred mushroom shed, and assailed the engine house. It stayed not to consume, but ran as a thing that seeks a quarry. Polly's shop and upper parts were already a furnace, and black smoke was coming out of Rumbold's cellar gratings. The fire in the engine house showed only as a sudden rush of smoke from the back, like something suddenly blown up. The fire brigade, still much under strength, were now hard at work in the front of the latter building; they had got the door open all too late, they had rescued the fire escape and some buckets, and were now lugging out their manual, with the hose already a dripping mass of molten, flaring, stinking rubber. Boomer was dancing about and swearing and shouting; this direct attack upon his apparatus outraged his sense of chivalry. The rest of the brigade hovered in a disheartened state about the rescued fire escape, and tried to piece Boomer's comments into some tangible instructions.

'Hi!' said Rusper from the window. '(kik)! What's up?'

Gambell answered him out of his helmet. 'Hose!' he cried. 'Hose gone!'

'I (kik) got hose!' cried Rusper.

He had. He had a stock of several thousand feet of garden hose, of various qualities and calibres, and now he felt was the time to use it. In another moment his shop door was open and he was hurling pails, garden syringes and rolls of garden hose out upon the pavement. '(kik) Undo it,' he cried, to the gathering crowd in the roadway.

They did. Presently a hundred ready hands were unrolling and spreading and tangling up and twisting and hopelessly involving Mr Rusper's stock of hose, sustained by an unquenchable assurance that presently it would in some manner contain and convey water, and Mr Rusper, on his knees, (kiking) violently, became incredibly busy with wire and brass junctions and all sorts of mysteries.

'Fix it to the (kik) bathroom tap!' said Mr Rusper.

Next door to the fire station was Mantell and Throbson's, the little Fishbourne branch of that celebrated firm, and Mr Boomer, seeking in a teeming mind for a plan of action, had determined to save this building. 'Someone telephone to the Port Burdock and Hampstead-on-Sea fire brigades,' he cried to the crowd and then to his fellows: 'Cut away the woodwork of the fire station!' and so led the way into the blaze with a whirling hatchet that effected wonders in ventilation in no time.

But it was not, after all, such a bad idea of his. Mantell and Throbson's was separated from the fire station in front by a glass-covered passage, and at the back the roof of a big outhouse sloped down to the fire station leads. The sturdy longshoremen, who made up the bulk of the fire brigade, assailed the glass roof of the passage with extraordinary gusto, and made a smashing of glass that drowned for a time the rising uproar of the flames.

A number of willing volunteers started off to the new telephone office in obedience to Mr Boomer's request, only to be told with cold official politeness by the young lady at the exchange that all that had been done on her own initiative ten minutes ago. She parleyed with these heated enthusiasts for a space, and then returned to the window.

And indeed the spectacle was well worth looking at. The dusk was falling, and the flames were showing brilliantly at half a dozen points. The Royal Fishbourne Hotel Tap, which adjoined Mr Polly to the west, was being kept wet by the enthusiastic efforts of a string of volunteers with buckets of water, and above at a bathroom window the little German waiter was busy with the garden hose. But Mr Polly's establishment looked more like a house afire than most houses on fire contrive to look from start to finish. Every window showed eager flickering flames, and flames like serpents' tongues were licking out of three large holes in the roof, which was already beginning to fall in. Behind, larger and abundantly spark-shot gusts of fire rose from the fodder that was now getting alight in the Royal Fishbourne Hotel stables. Next door to Mr Polly, Mr Rumbold's house was disgorging black smoke from the gratings that protected its underground windows, and smoke and occasional shivers of flame were also coming out of its first-floor windows. The fire station was better alight at the back than in front, and its woodwork burnt pretty briskly with peculiar greenish flickerings and a pungent flavour. In the street an unaggressively disorderly crowd clambered over the rescued fire escape and resisted the attempts of the three local constables to get it away from the danger of Mr Polly's tottering façade; a cluster of busy forms danced and shouted and advised on the noisy and smashing attempt to cut off Mantell and Throbson's from the fire station that was still in ineffectual progress. Further a number of people appeared to be destroying interminable red and grey snakes under the heated direction of Mr Rusper; it was as if the High Street had a plague of worms; and beyond again the more timid and less active crowded in front of an accumulation of arrested traffic. Most of the men were in sabbatical

black, and this and the white and starched quality of the women and children in their best clothes gave a note of ceremony to the whole affair.

For a moment the attention of the telephone clerk was held by the activities of Mr Tashingford, the chemist, who, regardless of everyone else, was rushing across the road hurling fire grenades into the fire station and running back for more, and then her eyes lifted to the slanting outhouse roof that went up to a ridge behind the parapet of Mantell and Throbson's. An expression of incredulity came into the telephone operator's eyes and gave place to hard activity. She flung up the window and screamed out: 'Two people on the roof up there! Two people on the roof!'

4

Her eyes had not deceived her. Two figures which had emerged from the upper staircase window of Mr Rumbold's and had got, after a perilous paddle in his cistern, on to the fire station, were now slowly but resolutely clambering up the outhouse roof towards the back of the main premises of Messrs Mantell and Throbson. They clambered slowly and one urged and helped the other, slipping and pausing ever and again, amidst a constant trickle of fragments of broken tile.

One was Mr Polly, with his hair wildly disordered, his face covered with black smudges and streaked with perspiration, and his trouser legs scorched and blackened; the other was an elderly lady, quietly but becomingly dressed in black, with small white frills at her neck and wrists and a Sunday cap of ecru lace enlivened with a black velvet bow. Her hair was brushed back from her wrinkled brow and plastered down tightly, meeting in a small knob behind; her wrinkled mouth bore that expression of supreme resolution common with the toothless aged. She was shaky, not with fear, but with the vibrations natural to her years, and she spoke with the slow quavering firmness of the very aged.

'I don't mind scrambling,' she said with piping inflexibility, 'but I can't jump and I *wunt* jump.'

'Scramble, old lady, then – scramble!' said Mr Polly, pulling her arm. 'It's one up and two down on these blessed tiles.'

'It's not what I'm used to,' she said.

'Stick to it!' said Mr Polly, 'live and learn,' and got to the ridge and grasped at her arm to pull her after him.

'I can't jump, mind ye,' she repeated, pressing her lips together. 'And old ladies like me mustn't be hurried.'

'Well, let's get as high as possible anyhow!' said Mr Polly, urging her gently upward. 'Shinning up a waterspout in your line? Near as you'll get to heaven.'

'I *can't* jump,' she said. 'I can do anything but jump.'

'Hold on!' said Mr Polly, 'while I give you a boost. That's – wonderful.'

'So long as it isn't jumping . . . '

The old lady grasped the parapet above, and there was a moment of intense struggle.

'Urup!' said Mr Polly. 'Hold on! Gollys! where's she gone to. . . ?'

Then an ill-mended, wavering, yet very reassuring spring-sided boot appeared for an instant.

'Thought perhaps there wasn't any roof there!' he explained, scrambling up over the parapet beside her.

'I've never been out on a roof before,' said the old lady. 'I'm all disconnected. It's very bumpy. Especially that last bit. Can't we sit here for a bit and rest? I'm not the girl I use to be.'

'You sit here ten minutes,' shouted Mr Polly, 'and you'll pop like a roast chestnut. Don't understand me? *Roast chestnut!* ROAST CHESTNUT! POP! There ought to be a limit to deafness. Come on round to the front and see if we can find an attic window. Look at this smoke!'

'Nasty!' said the old lady, her eyes following his gesture, puckering her face into an expression of great distaste.

'Come on!'

'Can't hear a word you say.'

He pulled her arm. 'Come on!'

She paused for a moment to relieve herself of a series of entirely unexpected chuckles. '*Sich* goings on!' she said, 'I never did! Where's he going now?' and came along behind the parapet to the front of the drapery establishment.

Below, the street was now fully alive to their presence, and encouraged the appearance of their heads by shouts and cheers. A sort of free fight was going on round the fire escape, order represented by Mr Boomer and the very young policeman, and disorder by some partially intoxicated volunteers with views of their own about the manipulation of the apparatus. Two or three lengths of Mr Rusper's garden hose appeared to have twined themselves round the ladder. Mr Polly watched the struggle with a certain impatience, and glanced ever and again over his shoulder at the increasing volume of smoke and steam that was pouring up from the burning fire station. He decided to break an attic window and get in, and so try and get down through the shop. He found himself in a little bedroom, and returned to fetch his charge. For some time he could not make her understand his purpose.

'Got to come at once!' he shouted.

'I hain't 'ad sich a time for years!' said the old lady.

'We'll have to get down through the house!'

'Can't do no jumpin',' said the old lady. 'No!'

She yielded reluctantly to his grasp.

She stared over the parapet. 'Runnin' and scurryin' about like black beetles in a kitchin,' she said.

'We've got to hurry.'

'Mr Rumbold 'e's a very Quiet man. 'E likes everything Quiet. He'll be surprised to see me 'ere! Why! – there 'e is!' She fumbled in her garments mysteriously and at last produced a wrinkled pocket handkerchief and began to wave it.

'Oh, come ON!' cried Mr Polly, and seized her.

He got her into the attic, but the staircase, he found, was full of suffocating smoke, and he dared not venture below the next floor. He took her into a long dormitory, shut the door on those pungent and pervasive fumes, and opened the window – to discover the fire escape was now against the house, and all Fishbourne boiling with excitement as an immensely helmeted and active and resolute little figure ascended. In another moment the rescuer stared over the windowsill, heroic, but just a trifle self-conscious and grotesque.

'Lawks a mussy!' said the old lady. 'Wonders and Wonders! Why! it's Mr Gambell! 'Iding 'is 'ed in that thing! I *never* did!'

'Can we get her out?' said Mr Gambell. 'There's not much time.'

'He might git stuck in it.'

'*You*'ll get stuck in it,' said Mr Polly, 'come along!'

'Not for jumpin' I don't,' said the old lady, understanding his gestures rather than his words. 'Not a bit of it. I bain't no good at jumping and I *wunt*.'

They urged her gently but firmly towards the window.

'You lemme do it my own way,' said the old lady at the sill . . .

'I could do it better if e'd take it off.'

'Oh! *carm* on!'

'It's wuss than Carter's stile,' she said, 'before they mended it. With a cow a-looking at you.'

Mr Gambell hovered protectingly below. Mr Polly steered her aged limbs from above. An anxious crowd below babbled advice and did its best to upset the fire escape. Within, streamers of black smoke were pouring up through the cracks in the floor. For some seconds the world waited while the old lady gave herself up to reckless mirth again. '*Sich* times!' she said, and, '*Poor* Rumbold!'

Slowly they descended, and Mr Polly remained at the post of danger steadying the long ladder until the old lady was in safety below and sheltered by Mr Rumbold (who was in tears) and the young policeman from the urgent congratulations of the crowd. The crowd was full of an impotent passion to participate. Those nearest wanted to shake her hand, those remoter cheered.

'The fust fire I was ever in and likely to be my last. It's a scurryin', 'urryin' business, but I'm real glad I haven't missed it,' said the old lady as she was borne rather than led towards the refuge of the Temperance Hotel.

Also she was heard to remark: ' 'E was saying something about 'ot chestnuts. *I* 'aven't 'ad no 'ot chestnuts.'

Then the crowd became aware of Mr Polly awkwardly negotiating the top rungs of the fire escape. ' 'Ere 'e comes!' cried a voice, and Mr Polly descended into the world again out of the conflagration he had lit to be his funeral pyre, moist, excited, and tremendously alive, amidst a tempest of applause. As he got lower and lower the crowd howled like a pack of dogs at him. Impatient men, unable to wait for him, seized and shook his descending boots, and so brought him to earth with a run. He was rescued with difficulty from an enthusiast who wished to slake at his own expense and to his own accompaniment a thirst altogether heroic. He was hauled into the Temperance Hotel and flung like a sack, breathless and helpless, into the tear-wet embrace of Miriam.

5

With the dusk and the arrival of some county constabulary, and first one and presently two other fire engines from Port Burdock and Hampstead-on-Sea, the local talent of Fishbourne found itself forced back into a secondary, less responsible and more observant role. I will not pursue the story of the fire to its ashes, nor will I do more than glance at the unfortunate Mr Rusper, a modern Laocoön, vainly trying to retrieve his scattered hose amidst the tramplings and rushings of the Port Burdock experts.

In a small sitting-room of the Fishbourne Temperance Hotel a little group of Fishbourne tradesmen sat and conversed in fragments and anon went to the window and looked out upon the smoking desolation of their homes across the way, and anon sat down again. They and their families were the guests of old Lady Bargrave, who had displayed the utmost sympathy and interest in their misfortunes. She had taken several people into her own house at Everdean, had engaged the Temperance Hotel as a temporary refuge, and personally superintended the housing of Mantell and Throbson's homeless assistants. The Temperance Hotel became and remained extremely noisy and congested, with people sitting about anywhere, conversing in fragments and totally unable to get themselves to bed. The manager was an old soldier, and following the best traditions of the service saw that everyone had hot cocoa. Hot cocoa seemed to be about everywhere, and it was no doubt very heartening and sustaining to everyone. When the manager detected anyone disposed to be drooping or pensive, he exhorted that person at once to drink further hot cocoa and maintain a stout heart.

The hero of the occasion, the centre of interest, was Mr Polly. For he had not only caused the fire by upsetting a lighted lamp, scorching his trousers and narrowly escaping death, as indeed he had now explained in detail about twenty times, but he had further thought at once of that

amiable but helpless old lady next door, had shown the utmost decision in making his way to her over the yard wall of the Royal Fishbourne Hotel, and had rescued her with persistence and vigour in spite of the levity natural to her years. Everyone thought well of him and was anxious to show it, more especially by shaking his hand painfully and repeatedly. Mr Rumbold, breaking a silence of nearly fifteen years, thanked him profusely, said he had never understood him properly and declared he ought to have a medal. There seemed to be a widely diffused idea that Mr Polly ought to have a medal. Hinks thought so. He declared, moreover, and with the utmost emphasis, that Mr Polly had a crowded and richly decorated interior – or words to that effect. There was something apologetic in this persistence; it was as if he regretted past intimations that Mr Polly was internally defective and hollow. He also said that Mr Polly was a 'white man', albeit, as he developed it, with a liver of the deepest chromatic satisfactions.

Mr Polly wandered centrally through it all, with his face washed and his hair carefully brushed and parted, looking modest and more than a little absent-minded, and wearing a pair of black dress trousers belonging to the manager of the Temperance Hotel – a larger man than himself in every way.

He drifted upstairs to his fellow-tradesmen, and stood for a time staring into the littered street, with its pools of water and extinguished gas lamps. His companions in misfortune resumed a fragmentary disconnected conversation. They touched now on one aspect of the disaster and now on another, and there were intervals of silence. More or less empty cocoa cups were distributed over the table, mantelshelf and piano, and in the middle of the table was a tin of biscuits, into which Mr Rumbold, sitting round-shoulderedly, dipped ever and again in an absent-minded way, and munched like a distant shooting of coals. It added to the solemnity of the affair that nearly all of them were in their black Sunday clothes; little Clamp was particularly impressive and dignified in a wide open frock coat, a Gladstone-shaped paper collar, and a large white and blue tie. They felt that they were in the presence of a great disaster, the sort of disaster that gets into the papers, and is even illustrated by blurred photographs of the crumbling ruins. In the presence of that sort of disaster all honourable men are lugubrious and sententious.

And yet it is impossible to deny a certain element of elation. Not one of those excellent men but was already realising that a great door had opened, as it were, in the opaque fabric of destiny, that they were to get their money again that had seemed sunk for ever beyond any hope in the deeps of retail trade. Life was already in their imagination rising like a Phoenix from the flames.

'I suppose there'll be a public subscription,' said Mr Clamp.

'Not for those who're insured,' said Mr Wintershed.

'I was thinking of them assistants from Mantell and Throbson's. They must have lost nearly everything.'

'They'll be looked after all right,' said Mr Rumbold. 'Never fear.'

Pause.

'*I'm* insured,' said Mr Clamp, with unconcealed satisfaction. 'Royal Salamander.'

'Same here,' said Mr Wintershed.

'Mine's the Glasgow Sun,' Mr Hinks remarked. 'Very good company.'

'You insured, Mr Polly?'

'He deserves to be,' said Rumbold.

'Ra-ther,' said Hinks. 'Blowed if he don't. Hard lines it *would* be – if there wasn't something for him.'

'Commercial and General,' answered Mr Polly over his shoulder, still staring out of the window. 'Oh! I'm all right.'

The topic dropped for a time, though manifestly it continued to exercise their minds.

'It's cleared me out of a lot of old stock,' said Mr Wintershed; 'that's one good thing.'

The remark was felt to be in rather questionable taste, and still more so was his next comment.

'Rusper's a bit sick it didn't reach '*im*.'

Everyone looked uncomfortable, and no one was willing to point the reason why Rusper should be a bit sick.

'Rusper's been playing a game of his own,' said Hinks. 'Wonder what he thought he was up to! Sittin' in the middle of the road with a pair of tweezers he was, and about a yard of wire – mending somethin'. Wonder he warn't run over by the Port Burdock engine.'

Presently a little chat sprang up upon the causes of fires, and Mr Polly was moved to tell how it had happened for the one and twentieth time. His story had now become as circumstantial and exact as the evidence of a police witness. 'Upset the lamp,' he said. 'I'd just lighted it, I was going upstairs, and my foot slipped against where one of the treads was a bit rotten, and down I went. Thing was aflare in a moment! . . . '

He yawned at the end of the discussion, and moved doorward.

'So long,' said Mr Polly.

'Good-night,' said Mr Rumbold. 'You played a brave man's part! If you don't get a medal – '

He left an eloquent pause.

' 'Ear, 'ear!' said Mr Wintershed and Mr Clamp. 'Goo'night, o' man,' said Mr Hinks.

'Goo'night all,' said Mr Polly . . . ·

He went slowly upstairs. The vague perplexity common to popular heroes pervaded his mind. He entered the bedroom and turned up the electric light. It was quite a pleasant room, one of the best in the Temperance Hotel, with a nice clean flowered wallpaper, and a very large looking-glass. Miriam appeared to be asleep, and her shoulders were

humped up under the clothes in a shapeless, forbidding lump that Mr Polly had found utterly loathsome for fifteen years. He went softly over to the dressing-table and surveyed himself thoughtfully. Presently he hitched up the trousers. 'Miles too big for me,' he remarked. 'Funny not to have a pair of breeches of one's own . . . Like being born again. Naked came I into the world . . .'

Miriam stirred and rolled over, and stared at him.

'Hello!' she said.

'Hello.'

'Come to bed?'

'It's three.'

Pause, while Mr Polly disrobed slowly.

'I been thinking,' said Miriam, 'It isn't going to be so bad after all. We shall get your insurance. We can easy begin all over again.'

'H'm,' said Mr Polly.

She turned her face away from him and reflected.

'Get a better house,' said Miriam, regarding the wallpaper pattern. 'I've always 'ated them stairs.'

Mr Polly removed a boot.

'Choose a better position where there's more doing,' murmured Miriam . . .

'Not half so bad,' she whispered . . .

'You *wanted* stirring up,' she said, half asleep –

It dawned upon Mr Polly for the first time that he had forgotten something.

He ought to have cut his throat!

The fact struck him as remarkable, but as now no longer of any particular urgency. It seemed a thing far off in the past, and he wondered why he had not thought of it before. Odd thing life is! If he had done it he would never have seen this clean and agreeable apartment with the electric light . . . His thoughts wandered into a question of detail. Where could he have put the razor down? Somewhere in the little room behind the shop, he supposed, but he could not think where more precisely. Anyhow it didn't matter now.

He undressed himself calmly, got into bed, and fell asleep almost immediately.

CHAPTER NINE

The Potwell Inn

But when a man has once broken through the paper walls of everyday circumstance, those unsubstantial walls that hold so many of us securely prisoned from the cradle to the grave, he has made a discovery. If the world does not please you *you can change it.* Determine to alter it at any price, and you can change it altogether. You may change it to something sinister and angry, to something appalling, but it may be you will change it to something brighter, something more agreeable, and at the worst something much more interesting. There is only one sort of man who is absolutely to blame for his own misery, and that is the man who finds life dull and dreary. There are no circumstances in the world that determined action cannot alter, unless perhaps they are the walls of a prison cell, and even those will dissolve and change, I am told, into the infirmary compartment at any rate, for the man who can fast with resolution. I give these things as facts and information, and with no moral intimations. And Mr Polly, lying awake at nights, with a renewed indigestion, with Miriam sleeping sonorously beside him and a general air of inevitableness about his situation, saw through it, understood there was no inevitable any more, and escaped his former despair.

He could, for example, 'clear out'.

It became a wonderful and alluring phrase to him: 'Clear out!'

Why had he never thought of clearing out before?

He was amazed and a little shocked at the unimaginative and superfluous criminality in him that had turned old cramped and stagnant Fishbourne into a blaze and new beginnings. (I wish from the bottom of my heart I could add that he was properly sorry.) But something constricting and restrained seemed to have been destroyed by that flare. *Fishbourne wasn't the world.* That was the new, the essential fact of which he had lived so lamentably in ignorance. Fishbourne as he had known it and hated it, so that he wanted to kill himself to get out of it, *wasn't the world.*

The insurance money he was to receive made everything humane and kindly and practicable. He would 'clear out', with justice and humanity. He would take exactly twenty-one pounds, and all the rest he would leave to Miriam. That seemed to him absolutely fair. Without him, she could do all sorts of things – all the sorts of things she was constantly urging him to do . . .

And he would go off along the white road that led to Garchester, and on to Crogate and so to Tunbridge Wells, where there was a Toad Rock he had heard of, but never seen. (It seemed to him this must needs be a

marvel.) And so to other towns and cities. He would walk and loiter by the way, and sleep in inns at night, and get an odd job here and there and talk to strange people. Perhaps he would get quite a lot of work and prosper, and if he did not do so he would lie down in front of a train, or wait for a warm night and then fall into some smooth, broad river. Not so bad as sitting down to a dentist, not nearly so bad. And he would never open a shop any more. Never!

So the possibilities of the future presented themselves to Mr Polly as he lay awake at nights.

It was springtime, and in the woods so soon as one got out of reach of the sea wind, there would be anemones and primroses.

2

A month later a leisurely and dusty tramp, plump equatorially and slightly bald, with his hands in his pockets and his lips puckered to a contemplative whistle, strolled along the river bank between Uppingdon and Potwell. It was a profusely budding spring day and greens such as God had never permitted in the world before in human memory (though indeed they come every year and we forgot), were mirrored vividly in a mirror of equally unprecedented brown. For a time the wanderer stopped and stood still, and even the thin whistle died away from his lips as he watched a water vole run to and fro upon a little headland across the stream. The vole plopped into the water and swam and dived and only when the last ring of its disturbance had vanished did Mr Polly resume his thoughtful course to nowhere in particular.

For the first time in many years he had been leading a healthy human life, living constantly in the open air, walking every day for eight or nine hours, eating sparingly, accepting every conversational opportunity, not even disdaining the discussion of possible work. And beyond mending a hole in his coat that he had made while negotiating barbed wire, with a borrowed needle and thread in a lodging house, he had done no work at all. Neither had he worried about business nor about time and seasons. And for the first time in his life he had seen the Aurora Borealis.

So far the holiday had cost him very little. He had arranged it on a plan that was entirely his own. He had started with four five-pound notes and a pound divided into silver, and he had gone by train from Fishbourne to Ashington. At Ashington he had gone to the post office, obtained a registered letter, and sent his four five-pound notes with a short brotherly note addressed to himself at Gilhampton post office. He sent this letter to Gilhampton for no other reason in the world than that he liked the name of Gilhampton and the rural suggestion of its containing county, which was Sussex; and having so despatched it, he set himself to discover, mark down and walk to Gilhampton, and so recover his resources. And having got to

Gilhampton at last, he changed one five-pound note, bought four pound postal orders, and repeated his manoeuvre with nineteen pounds.

After a lapse of fifteen years he rediscovered this interesting world, about which so many people go incredibly blind and bored. He went along country roads while all the birds were piping and chirruping and cheeping and singing, and looked at fresh new things, and felt as happy and irresponsible as a boy with an unexpected half-holiday. And if ever the thought of Miriam returned to him he controlled his mind. He came to country inns and sat for unmeasured hours talking of this and that to those sage carters who rest for ever in the taps of country inns, while the big sleek brass jingling horses wait patiently outside with their waggons; he got a job with some van people who were wandering about the country with swings and a steam roundabout and remained with them for three days, until one of their dogs took a violent dislike to him and made his duties unpleasant; he talked to tramps and wayside labourers, he snoozed under hedges by day and in outhouses and hayricks at night, and once, but only once, he slept in a casual ward. He felt as the etiolated grass and daisies must do when you move the garden roller away to a new place.

He gathered a quantity of strange and interesting memories.

He crossed some misty meadows by moonlight and the mist lay low on the grass, so low that it scarcely reached above his waist, and houses and clumps of trees stood out like islands in a milky sea, so sharply defined was the upper surface of the mist bank. He came nearer and nearer to a strange thing that floated like a boat upon this magic lake, and behold! something moved at the stern and a rope was whisked at the prow, and it had changed into a pensive cow, drowsy-eyed, regarding him . . .

He saw a remarkable sunset in a new valley near Maidstone, a very red and clear sunset, a wide redness under a pale cloudless heaven, and with the hills all round the edge of the sky a deep purple blue and clear and flat, looking exactly as he had seen mountains painted in pictures. He seemed transported to some strange country, and would have felt no surprise if the old labourer he came upon leaning silently over a gate had addressed him in an unfamiliar tongue . . .

Then one night, just towards dawn, his sleep upon a pile of brushwood was broken by the distant rattle of a racing motor car breaking all the speed regulations, and as he could not sleep again, he got up and walked into Maidstone as the day came. He had never been abroad in a town at half-past two in his life before, and the stillness of everything in the bright sunrise impressed him profoundly. At one corner was a startling policeman, standing in a doorway quite motionless, like a waxen image. Mr Polly wished him 'good-morning' unanswered, and went down to the bridge over the Medway and sat on the parapet very still and thoughtful, watching the town awaken, and wondering what he should do if it didn't, if the world of men never woke again . . .

One day he found himself going along a road with a wide space of sprouting bracken and occasional trees on either side, and suddenly this road became strangely, perplexingly familiar. 'Lord!' he said, and turned about and stood. 'It can't be.'

He was incredulous, then left the road and walked along a scarcely perceptible track to the left, and came in half a minute to an old lichenous stone wall. It seemed exactly the bit of wall he had known so well. It might have been but yesterday he was in that place; there remained even a little pile of wood. It became absurdly the same wood. The bracken perhaps was not so high, and most of its fronds still uncoiled; that was all. Here he had stood, it seemed, and there she had sat and looked down upon him. Where was she now, and what had become of her? He counted the years back and marvelled that beauty should have called to him with so imperious a voice – and signified nothing.

He hoisted himself with some little difficulty to the top of the wall, and saw off under the beech trees two schoolgirls – small, insignificant, pig-tailed creatures, with heads of blond and black, with their arms twined about each other's necks, no doubt telling each other the silliest secrets.

But that girl with the red hair – was she a countess? was she a queen? Children perhaps? Had sorrow dared to touch her?

Had she forgotten altogether? . . .

A tramp sat by the roadside thinking, and it seemed to the man in the passing motor car he must needs be plotting for another pot of beer. But as a matter of fact what the tramp was saying to himself over and over again was a variant upon a well-known Hebrew word.

'Itchabod,' the tramp was saying in the voice of one who reasons on the side of the inevitable. 'It's Fair Itchabod, o' man. There's no going back to it.'

3

It was about two o'clock in the afternoon one hot day in high May when Mr Polly, unhurrying and serene, came to that broad bend of the river to which the little lawn and garden of the Potwell Inn run down. He stopped at the sight of the place with its deep tiled roof, nestling under big trees – you never get a decently big, decently shaped tree by the seaside – its sign towards the roadway, its sun-blistered green bench and tables, its shapely white windows and its row of upshooting hollyhock plants in the garden. A hedge separated it from a buttercup-yellow meadow, and beyond stood three poplars in a group against the sky, three exceptionally tall, graceful and harmonious poplars. It is hard to say what there was about them that made them so beautiful to Mr Polly; but they seemed to him to touch a pleasant scene with a distinction almost divine. He remained admiring

them for a long time. At last the need for coarser aesthetic satisfactions arose in him.

'Provinder,' he whispered, drawing near to the inn. 'Cold sirloin for choice. And nut-brown brew and wheaten bread.'

The nearer he came to the place the more he liked it. The windows on the ground floor were long and low, and they had pleasing red blinds. The green tables outside were agreeably ringed with memories of former drinks, and an extensive grape vine spread level branches across the whole front of the place. Against the wall was a broken oar, two boat-hooks and the stained and faded red cushions of a pleasure boat. One went up three steps to the glass-panelled door and peeped into a broad, low room with a bar and beer engine, behind which were many bright and helpful-looking bottles against mirrors, and great and little pewter measures, and bottles fastened in brass wire upside down with their corks replaced by taps, and a white china cask labelled 'Shrub', and cigar boxes, and boxes of cigarettes, and a couple of toby jugs and a beautifully coloured hunting scene framed and glazed, showing the most elegant and beautiful people taking Piper's Cherry Brandy, and cards such as the law requires about the dilution of spirits and the illegality of bringing children into bars, and satirical verses about swearing and asking for credit, and three very bright red-cheeked wax apples and a round-shaped clock.

But these were the mere background to the really pleasant thing in the spectacle, which was quite the plumpest woman Mr Polly had ever seen, seated in an armchair in the midst of all these bottles and glasses and glittering things, peacefully and tranquilly, and without the slightest loss of dignity, asleep. Many people would have called her a fat woman, but Mr Polly's innate sense of epithet told him from the outset that plump was the word. She had shapely brows and a straight, well-shaped nose, kind lines and contentment about her mouth, and beneath it the jolly chins clustered like chubby little cherubim about the feet of an Assumptioning Madonna. Her plumpness was firm and pink and wholesome, and her hands, dimpled at every joint, were clasped in front of her; she seemed as it were to embrace herself with infinite confidence and kindliness as one who knew herself good in substance, good in essence, and would show her gratitude to God by that ready acceptance of all that He had given her. Her head was a little on one side, not much, but just enough to speak of trustfulness and rob her of the stiff effect of self-reliance. And she slept.

'*My* sort,' said Mr Polly, and opened the door very softly, divided between the desire to enter and come nearer and an instinctive indisposition to break slumbers so manifestly sweet and satisfying.

She awoke with a start, and it amazed Mr Polly to see swift terror flash into her eyes. Instantly it had gone again.

'Law!' she said, her face softening with relief. 'I thought you were Jim.'

'I'm never Jim,' said Mr Polly.

'You've got his sort of hat.'

'Ah!' said Mr Polly, and leant over the bar.

'It just came into my head you was Jim,' said the plump lady, dismissed the topic and stood up. 'I believe I was having forty winks,' she said, 'if all the truth was told. What can I do for you?'

'Cold meat?' said Mr Polly.

'There *is* cold meat,' the plump woman admitted.

'And room for it.'

The plump woman came and leant over the bar and regarded him judicially, but kindly. 'There's some cold boiled beef,' she said, and added: 'A bit of crisp lettuce?'

'New mustard,' said Mr Polly.

'And a tankard!'

'A tankard.'

They understood each other perfectly.

'Looking for work?' asked the plump woman.

'In a way,' said Mr Polly.

They smiled like old friends.

Whatever the truth may be about love, there is certainly such a thing as friendship at first sight. They liked each other's voices, they liked each other's way of smiling and speaking.

'It's such beautiful weather this spring,' said Mr Polly, explaining everything.

'What sort of work do you want?' she asked.

'I've never properly thought that out,' said Mr Polly. 'I've been looking round – for ideas.'

'Will you have your beef in the tap or outside? That's the tap.'

Mr Polly had a glimpse of an oaken settle. 'In the tap will be handier for you,' he said.

'Hear that?' said the plump lady.

'Hear what?'

'Listen.'

Presently the silence was broken by a distant howl – 'Oooooover!'

'Eh?' she said.

He nodded.

'That's the ferry. And there isn't a ferryman.'

'Could I?'

'Can you punt?'

'Never tried.'

'Well – pull the pole out before you reach the end of the punt, that's all. Try.'

Mr Polly went out again into the sunshine.

At times one can tell so much so briefly. Here are the facts then – bare. He found a punt and a pole, got across to the steps on the opposite side, picked up an elderly gentleman in an alpaca jacket and a pith helmet,

cruised with him vaguely for twenty minutes, conveyed him tortuously into the midst of a thicket of forget-me-not-spangled sedges, splashed some water-weed over him, hit him twice with the punt pole, and finally landed him, alarmed but abusive, in treacherous soil at the edge of a hay meadow about forty yards downstream, where he immediately got into difficulties with a noisy, aggressive little white dog that was guarding a jacket.

Mr Polly returned in a complicated manner, but with perfect dignity, to his moorings.

He found the plump woman rather flushed and tearful, and seated at one of the green tables outside.

'I been laughing at you,' she said.

'What for?' asked Mr Polly.

'I ain't 'ad such a laugh since Jim come 'ome. When you 'it 'is 'ed, it 'urt my side.'

'It didn't hurt his head – not particularly.'

She waved her head. 'Did you charge him anything?'

'Gratis,' said Mr Polly. 'I never thought of it.'

The plump woman pressed her hands to her sides and laughed silently for a space. 'You ought to have charged him sumpthing,' she said. 'You better come and have your cold meat, before you do any more puntin'. You and me'll get on together.'

Presently she came and stood watching him eat. 'You eat better than you punt,' she said; and then, 'I dessay you could learn to punt.'

'Wax to receive and marble to retain,' said Mr Polly. 'This beef is a Bit of All Right, ma'am. I could have done differently if I hadn't been punting on an empty stomach. There's a leer feeling as the pole goes in – ?

'I've never held with fasting,' said the plump woman.

'You want a ferryman?'

'I want an odd man about the place.'

'I'm odd, all right. What's your wages?'

'Not much, but you get tips and pickings. I've a sort of feeling it would suit you.'

'I've a sort of feeling it would. What's the duties? Fetch and carry? Ferry? Garden? Wash bottles? *Ceteris paribus?*'

'That's about it,' said the fat woman.

'Give me a trial.'

'I've more than half a mind. Or I wouldn't have said anything about it. I suppose you're all right. You've got a sort of half-respectable look about you. I suppose you 'aven't *done* anything.'

'Bit of Arson,' said Mr Polly, as if he jested.

'So long as you haven't the habit,' said the plump woman.

'My first time, ma'am,' said Mr Polly, munching his way through an excellent big leaf of lettuce. 'And my last.'

'It's all right if you haven't been to prison,' said the plump woman. 'It

isn't what a man's happened to do makes 'im bad. We all happen to do things at times. It's bringing it home to him and spoiling his self-respect does the mischief. You don't *look* a wrong 'un. 'Ave you been to prison?'

'Never.'

'Nor a reformatory? Nor any institution?'

'Not me. Do I *look* reformed?'

'Can you paint and carpenter a bit?'

'Well, I'm ripe for it.'

'Have a bit of cheese?'

'If I might.'

And the way she brought the cheese showed Mr Polly that the business was settled in her mind.

He spent the afternoon exploring the premises of the Potwell Inn and learning the duties that might be expected of him, such as Stockholm-tarring fences, digging potatoes, swabbing out boats, helping people land, embarking, landing and time-keeping for the hirers of two rowing boats and one Canadian canoe, baling out the said vessels and concealing their leaks and defects from prospective hirers, persuading inexperienced hirers to start downstream rather than up, repairing rowlocks and taking inventories of returning boats with a view to supplementary charges, cleaning boots, sweeping chimneys, house-painting, cleaning windows, sweeping out and sanding the tap and bar, cleaning pewter, washing glasses, turpentining woodwork, whitewashing generally, plumbing and engineering, repairing locks and clocks, waiting and tapster's work generally, beating carpets and mats, cleaning bottles and saving corks, taking into the cellar, moving, tapping and connecting beer casks with their engines, blocking and destroying wasps' nests, doing forestry with several trees, drowning superfluous kittens, dog-fancying as required, assisting in the rearing of ducklings and the care of various poultry, bee-keeping, stabling, baiting and grooming horses and asses, cleaning and 'garing' motor cars and bicycles, inflating tyres and repairing punctures, recovering the bodies of drowned persons from the river as required, assisting people in trouble in the water, first-aid and sympathy, improvising and superintending a bathing station for visitors, attending inquests and funerals in the interests of the establishment, scrubbing floors and all the ordinary duties of a scullion, the ferry, chasing hens and goats from the adjacent cottages out of the garden, making up paths and superintending drainage, gardening generally, delivering bottled beer and soda-water syphons in the neighbourhood, running miscellaneous errands, removing drunken and offensive persons from the premises by tact or muscle as occasion required, keeping in with the local policemen, defending the premises in general and the orchard in particular from depredators . . .

'Can but try it,' said Mr Polly towards tea time. 'When there's nothing else on hand I suppose I might do a bit of fishing.'

Mr Polly was particularly charmed by the ducklings.

They were piping about among the vegetables in the company of their foster mother, and as he and the plump woman came down the garden path the little creatures mobbed them, and ran over their boots and in between Mr Polly's legs, and did their best to be trodden upon and killed after the manner of ducklings all the world over. Mr Polly had never been near young ducklings before, and their extreme blondness and the delicate completeness of their feet and beaks filled him with admiration. It is open to question whether there is anything more friendly in the world than a very young duckling. It was with the utmost difficulty that he tore himself away to practise punting, with the plump woman coaching from the bank. Punting he found was difficult, but not impossible, and towards four o'clock he succeeded in conveying a second passenger across the sundering flood from the inn to the unknown.

As he returned, slowly indeed, but now one might almost say surely, to the peg to which the punt was moored, he became aware of a singularly delightful human being awaiting him on the bank. She stood with her legs very wide apart, her hands behind her back, and her head a little on one side, watching his gestures with an expression of disdainful interest. She had black hair and brown legs and a buff short frock and very intelligent eyes. And when he had reached a sufficient proximity she remarked: 'Hello!'

'Hello,' said Mr Polly, and saved himself in the nick of time from disaster.

'Silly,' said the young lady, and Mr Polly lunged nearer.

'What are you called?'

'Polly.'

'Liar!'

'Why?'

'I'm Polly.'

'Then I'm Alfred. But I meant to be Polly.'

'I was first.'

'All right. I'm going to be the ferryman.'

'I see. You'll have to punt better.'

'You should have seen me early in the afternoon.'

'I can imagine it . . . I've seen the others.'

'What others?' Mr Polly had landed now and was fastening up the punt.

'What Uncle Jim has scooted.'

'Scooted?'

'He comes and scoots them. He'll scoot you too, I expect.'

A mysterious shadow seemed to fall athwart the sunshine and pleasantness of the Potwell Inn.

'I'm not a scooter,' said Mr Polly.

'Uncle Jim is.'

She whistled a little flatly for a moment, and threw small stones at a clump of meadow-sweet that sprang from the bank.

Then she remarked: 'When Uncle Jim comes back he'll cut your insides out . . . P'r'aps, very likely, he'll let me see.'

There was a pause.

'*Who's* Uncle Jim?' Mr Polly asked in a faded voice.

'Don't you know who Uncle Jim is? He'll show you. He's a scorcher, is Uncle Jim. He only came back just a little time ago, and he's scooted three men. He don't like strangers about, don't Uncle Jim. He *can* swear. He's going to teach me, soon as I can whissle properly.'

'Teach you to swear!' cried Mr Polly, horrified.

'*And* spit,' said the little girl proudly. 'He says I'm the gamest little beast he ever came across – ever.'

For the first time in his life it seemed to Mr Polly that he had come across something sheerly dreadful. He stared at the pretty thing of flesh and spirit in front of him, lightly balanced on its stout little legs and looking at him with eyes that had still to learn the expression of either disgust or fear.

'I say,' said Mr Polly, 'how old are you?'

'Nine,' said the little girl.

She turned away and reflected. Truth compelled her to add one other statement.

'He's not what I should call handsome, not Uncle Jim,' she said. 'But he's a Scorcher and no Mistake . . . Gramma don't like him.'

5

Mr Polly found the plump woman in the big bricked kitchen lighting a fire for tea. He went to the root of the matter at once.

'I say,' he asked, 'who's Uncle Jim?'

The plump woman blanched and stood still for a moment. A stick fell out of the bundle in her hand unheeded.

'That little granddaughter of mine been saying things?' she asked faintly.

'Bits of things,' said Mr Polly.

'Well, I suppose I must tell you sooner or later. He's – It's Jim. He's the Drorback to this place, that's what he is. The Drorback. I hoped you mightn't hear so soon . . . Very likely he's gone.'

'*She* don't seem to think so.'

' 'E 'asn't been near the place these two weeks and more,' said the plump woman.

'But who is he?'

'I suppose I got to tell you,' said the plump woman.

'She says he scoots people,' Mr Polly remarked after a pause.

'He's my own sister's son.' The plump woman watched the crackling fire for a space. 'I suppose I got to tell you,' she repeated.

She softened towards tears. 'I try not to think of it, but night and day he's haunting me. I try not to think of it. I've been for easy-going all my life. But I'm that worried and afraid, with death and ruin threatened and evil all about me! I don't know what to do! My own sister's son, and me a widow woman and 'elpless against his doin's!'

She put down the sticks she held upon the fender, and felt for her handkerchief. She began to sob and talk quickly.

'I wouldn't mind nothing else half so much if he'd leave that child alone. But he goes talking to her – if I leave her a moment he's talking to her, teaching her words and giving her ideas!'

'That's a Bit Thick,' said Mr Polly.

'Thick!' cried the plump woman; 'it's 'orrible! And what am I to do? He's been here three times now, six days and a week and a part of a week, and I pray to God night and day he may never come again. Praying! Back he's come sure as fate. He takes my money and he takes my things. He won't let no man stay here to protect me or do the boats or work the ferry. The ferry's getting a scandal. They stand and shout and scream and use language . . . If I complain they'll say I'm helpless to manage here, they'll take away my licence, out I shall go – and it's all the living I can get – and he knows it, and he plays on it, and he don't care. And here I am. I'd send the child away, but I got nowhere to send the child. I buys him off when it comes to that, and back he comes, worse than ever, prowling round and doing evil. And not a soul to help me. Not a soul! I just hoped there might be a day or so – before he comes back again. I was just hoping – I'm the sort that hopes.'

Mr Polly was reflecting on the flaws and drawbacks that seem to be inseparable from all the more agreeable things in life.

'Biggish sort of man, I expect?' asked Mr Polly, trying to get the situation in all its bearings.

But the plump woman did not heed him. She was going on with her fire-making, and retailing in disconnected fragments the fearfulness of Uncle Jim.

'There was always something a bit wrong with him,' she said, 'but nothing you mightn't have hoped for, not till they took him and carried him off and reformed him . . .

'He was cruel to the hens and chickings, it's true, and stuck a knife into another boy; but then I've seen him that nice to a cat, nobody could have been kinder. I'm sure he didn't do no 'arm to that cat whatever anyone tries to make out of it. I'd never listen to that . . . It was that Reformatory ruined him. They put him along of a lot of London boys full of ideas of wicked-ness, and because he didn't mind pain – and he don't, I *will* admit, try as I

would – they made him think himself a hero. Them boys laughed at the teachers they set over them, laughed and mocked at them – and I don't suppose they *was* the best teachers in the world; I don't suppose, and I don't suppose anyone sensible does suppose, that everyone who goes to be a teacher or a chapl'in or a warder in a Reformatory Home goes and changes right away into an Angel of Grace from Heaven – and oh, Lord! where was I?'

'What did they send him to the Reformatory for?'

'Playing truant and stealing. He stole right enough – stole the money from an old woman, and what was I to do when it came to the trial but say what I knew. And him like a viper a-looking at me – more like a viper than a human boy. He leans on the bar and looks at me. "All right, Aunt Flo," he says, just that and nothing more. Time after time, I've dreamt of it, and now he's come. "They've Reformed me," he says, "and made me a devil, and a devil I mean to be to you. So out with it," he says.'

'What did you give him last time?' asked Mr Polly.

'Three golden pounds,' said the plump woman.

' "That won't last very long," he says. "But there ain't no hurry. I'll be back in a week about." If I wasn't one of the hoping sort – '

She left the sentence unfinished.

Mr Polly reflected. 'What sort of a size is he?' he asked. 'I'm not one of your Herculaceous sort, if you mean that. Nothing very wonderful bicepitally.'

'You'll scoot,' said the plump woman with conviction rather than bitterness. 'You'd better scoot now, and I'll try and find some money for him to go away again when he comes. It ain't reasonable to expect you to do anything but scoot. But I suppose it's the way of a woman in trouble to try and get help from a man, and hope and hope. I'm the hoping sort.'

'How long's he been about?' asked Mr Polly, ignoring his own outlook.

'Three months it is come the seventh since he come in by that very back door – and I hadn't set eyes on him for seven long years. He stood in the door watchin' me, and suddenly he let off a yelp – like a dog, and there he was grinning at the fright he'd given me. "Good old Aunty Flo," he says, "ain't you dee–lighted to see me?" he says, "now I'm Reformed." '

The plump lady went to the sink and filled the kettle.

'I never did like 'im,' she said, standing at the sink. 'And seeing him there, with his teeth all black and broken – P'r'aps I didn't give him much of a welcome at first. Not what would have been kind to him. "Lord!" I said, "it's Jim." '

' "It's Jim," he said. "Like a bad shillin' – like a damned bad shillin'. Jim and trouble. You all of you wanted me Reformed and now you got me Reformed. I'm a Reformatory Reformed Character, warranted all right and turned out as such. Ain't you going to ask me in, aunty dear?"

' "Come in," I said, "I won't have it said I wasn't ready to be kind to you!"

'He comes in and shuts the door. Down he sits in that chair. "I come to torment you!" he says, "you old Sumpthing!" and begins at me . . . No human being could ever have been called such things before. It made me cry out. "And now," he says, "just to show I ain't afraid of 'urting you," he says, and ups and twists my wrist.'

Mr Polly gasped.

'I could stand even his vi'lence,' said the plump woman, 'if it wasn't for the child.'

Mr Polly went to the kitchen window and surveyed his namesake, who was away up the garden path with her hands behind her back, and whisps of black hair in disorder about her little face, thinking, thinking profoundly, about ducklings.

'You two oughtn't to be left,' he said.

The plump woman stared at his back with hard hope in her eyes.

'I don't see that it's *my* affair,' said Mr Polly.

The plump woman resumed her business with the kettle.

'I'd like to have a look at him before I go,' said Mr Polly, thinking aloud, and added, 'somehow. Not my business, of course.

'Lord!' he cried with a start at a noise in the bar, 'who's that?'

'Only a customer,' said the plump woman.

6

Mr Polly made no rash promises, and thought a great deal.

'It seems a good sort of crib,' he said, and added, 'for a chap who's looking for Trouble.'

But he stayed on and did various things out of the list I have already given, and worked the ferry, and it was four days before he saw anything of Uncle Jim. And so resistant is the human mind to things not yet experienced, that he could easily have believed in that time that there was no such person in the world as Uncle Jim. The plump woman, after her one outbreak of confidence, ignored the subject, and little Polly seemed to have exhausted her impressions in her first communication, and engaged her mind now with a simple directness in the study and subjugation of the new human being heaven had sent into her world. The first unfavourable impression of his punting was soon effaced; he could nickname ducklings very amusingly, create boats out of wooden splinters, and stalk and fly from imaginary tigers in the orchard with a convincing earnestness that was surely beyond the power of any other human being. She conceded at last that he should be called Mr Polly, in honour of her, Miss Polly, even as he desired.

Uncle Jim turned up in the twilight.

Uncle Jim appeared with none of the disruptive violence Mr Polly had

dreaded. He came quite softly. Mr Polly was going down the lane behind the church that led to the Potwell Inn after posting a letter to the lime-juice people at the post office. He was walking slowly, after his habit, and thinking discursively. With a sudden tightening of the muscles he became aware of a figure walking noiselessly beside him. His first impression was of a face singularly broad above and with a wide empty grin as its chief feature below, of a slouching body and dragging feet.

'Arf a mo',' said the figure, as if in response to his start, and speaking in a hoarse whisper. 'Arf a mo', mister. You the noo bloke at the Potwell Inn?'

Mr Polly felt evasive. 'S'pose I am,' he replied hoarsely, and quickened his pace.

'Arf a mo',' said Uncle Jim, taking his arm. 'We ain't doing a (sanguinary) Marathon. It ain't a (decorated) cinder track. I want a word with you, mister. See?'

Mr Polly wriggled his arm free and stopped. 'What is it?' he asked, and faced the terror.

'I jest want a (decorated) word wiv you. See? – just a friendly word or two. Just to clear up any blooming errors. That's all I want. No need to be so (richly decorated) proud, if you *are* the noo bloke at Potwell Inn. Not a bit of it. See?'

Uncle Jim was certainly not a handsome person. He was short, shorter than Mr Polly, with long arms and lean big hands; a thin and wiry neck stuck out of his grey flannel shirt and supported a big head that had something of the snake in the convergent lines of its broad knotty brow, meanly proportioned face and pointed chin. His almost toothless mouth seemed a cavern in the twilight. Some accident had left him with one small and active and one large and expressionless reddish eye, and wisps of straight hair strayed from under the blue cricket cap he wore pulled down obliquely over the latter. He spat between his teeth and wiped his mouth untidily with the soft side of his fist.

'You got to blurry well shift,' he said. 'See?'

'Shift!' said Mr Polly. 'How?'

' 'Cos the Potwell Inn's *my* beat. See?'

Mr Polly had never felt less witty. 'How's it your beat?' he asked.

Uncle Jim thrust his face forward and shook his open hand, bent like a claw, under Mr Polly's nose. 'Not your blooming business,' he said. 'You got to shift.'

'S'pose I don't,' said Mr Polly.

'You got to shift.'

The tone of Uncle Jim's voice became urgent and confidential.

'You don't know who you're up against,' he said. 'It's a kindness I'm doing to warn you. See? I'm just one of those blokes who don't stick at things, see? I don't stick at nuffin'.'

Mr Polly's manner became detached and confidential – as though the

matter and the speaker interested him greatly, but didn't concern him over-much. 'What do you think you'll do?' he asked.

'If you don't clear out?'

'Yes.'

'*Gaw!*' said Uncle Jim. 'You'd better. *'Ere!*'

He gripped Mr Polly's wrist with a grip of steel, and in an instant Mr Polly understood the relative quality of their muscles. He breathed, an uninspiring breath, into Mr Polly's face.

'What *won't* I do?' he said, 'once I start in on you.'

He paused, and the night about them seemed to be listening. 'I'll make a mess of you,' he said in his hoarse whisper. 'I'll do you – injuries. I'll 'urt you. I'll kick you ugly, see? I'll 'urt you in 'orrible ways – 'orrible, ugly ways . . .'

He scrutinised Mr Polly's face.

'You'll cry,' he said, 'to see yourself. See? Cry you will.'

'You got no right,' began Mr Polly.

'Right!' His note was fierce. 'Ain't the old woman me aunt?'

He spoke still closer. 'I'll make a gory mess of you. I'll cut bits orf you – '

He receded a little. 'I got no quarrel with *you*,' he said.

'It's too late to go tonight,' said Mr Polly.

'I'll be round tomorrer – 'bout eleven. See? And if I finds you – '

He produced a blood-curdling oath.

'H'm,' said Mr Polly, trying to keep things light. 'We'll consider your suggestions.'

'You better,' said Uncle Jim, and suddenly, noiselessly, was going.

His whispering voice sank until Mr Polly could hear only the dim fragments of sentences. ' 'Orrible things to you – 'orrible things . . . Kick yer ugly . . . Cut yer – liver out . . . spread it all about, I will . . . See? I don't care a dead rat one way or the uvver.'

And with a curious twisting gesture of the arm, Uncle Jim receded until his face was a still, dim thing that watched, and the black shadows of the hedge seemed to have swallowed up his body altogether.

7

Next morning about half-past ten Mr Polly found himself seated under a clump of fir trees by the roadside and about three miles and a half from the Potwell Inn. He was by no means sure whether he was taking a walk to clear his mind or leaving that threat-marred paradise for good and all. His reason pointed a lean, unhesitating finger along the latter course.

For after all, the thing was not *his* quarrel.

That agreeable plump woman, agreeable, motherly, comfortable as she might be, wasn't his affair; that child with the mop of black hair who

combined so magically the charm of mouse and butterfly and flitting bird, who was daintier than a flower and softer than a peach, was no concern of his. Good heavens! what were they to him? Nothing . . . !

Uncle Jim, of course, *had* a claim, a sort of claim.

If it came to duty and chucking up this attractive, indolent, observant, humorous, tramping life, there were those who had a right to him, a legitimate right, a prior claim on his protection and chivalry.

Why not listen to the call of duty and go back to Miriam now. . . ?

He had had a very agreeable holiday –

And while Mr Polly sat thinking these things as well as he could, he knew that, if only he dared to look up, the heavens had opened and the clear judgement on his case was written across the sky.

He knew – he knew now as much as a man can know of life. He knew he had to fight or perish.

Life had never been so clear to him before. It had always been a confused, entertaining spectacle; he had responded to this impulse and that, seeking agreeable and entertaining things, evading difficult and painful things. Such is the way of those who grow up to a life that has neither danger nor honour in its texture. He had been muddled and wrapped about and entangled, like a creature born in the jungle who has never seen sea or sky. Now he had come out of it suddenly into a great exposed place. It was as if God and heaven waited over him, and all the earth was expectation.

'Not my business,' said Mr Polly, speaking aloud. 'Where the devil do *I* come in?'

And again, with something between a whine and a snarl in his voice, 'Not my blasted business!'

His mind seemed to have divided itself into several compartments, each with its own particular discussion busily in progress, and quite regardless of the others. One was busy with the detailed interpretation of the phrase 'kick you ugly'. There's a sort of French wrestling in which you use and guard against feet. Watch the man's eye, and as his foot comes up, grip and over he goes – at your mercy, if you use the advantage rightly. But how do you use the advantage rightly?

When he thought of Uncle Jim, the inside feeling of his body faded away rapidly to a blank discomfort –

'Old cadger! She hadn't no business to drag me into her quarrels. Ought to go to the police and ask for help! Dragging me into a quarrel that don't concern me.

'Wish I'd never set eyes on the rotten inn!'

The reality of the case arched over him like the vault of the sky, as plain as the sweet blue heavens above and the wide spread of hill and valley about him. Man comes into life to seek and find his sufficient beauty, to serve it, to win and increase it, to fight for it, to face anything and dare anything for it, counting death as nothing so long as the dying eyes still turn to it. And

fear, and dullness and indolence and appetite, which indeed are no more than fear's three crippled brothers, who make ambushes and creep by night, are against him, to delay him, to hold him off, to hamper and beguile and kill him in that quest. He had but to lift his eyes to see all that, as much a part of his world as the driving clouds and the bending grass, but he kept himself downcast, a grumbling, inglorious, fattish little tramp, full of dreads and quivering excuses.

'Why the hell was I ever born?' he said, with the truth almost winning him.

What do you do when a dirty man, who smells, gets you down and under, in the dirt and dust, with a knee below your diaphragm and a large hairy hand squeezing your windpipe tighter and tighter in a quarrel that isn't, properly speaking, yours?

'If I had a chance against him – ' protested Mr Polly.

'It's no Good, you see,' said Mr Polly.

He stood up as though his decision was made, and was for an instant struck still by doubt.

There lay the road before him, going this way to the east and that to the west.

Westward, one hour away now, was the Potwell Inn. Already things might be happening there –

Eastward was the wise man's course, a road dipping between hedges to a hop garden and a wood and presently no doubt reaching an inn, a picturesque church, perhaps, a village and fresh company. The wise man's course. Mr Polly saw himself going along it, and tried to see himself going along it with all the self-applause a wise man feels. But somehow it wouldn't come like that. The wise man fell short of happiness for all his wisdom. The wise man had a paunch and round shoulders and red ears and excuses. It was a pleasant road, and why the wise man should not go along it merry and singing, full of summer happiness, was a miracle to Mr Polly's mind; but, confound it! the fact remained, the figure went slinking – slinking was the only word for it – and would not go otherwise than slinking. He turned his eyes westward as if for an explanation, and if the figure was no longer ignoble, the prospect was appalling.

'One kick in the stummick would settle a chap like me,' said Mr Polly.

'Oh, God!' cried Mr Polly, and lifted his eyes to heaven, and said for the last time in that struggle, 'It–isn't–my–affair!'

And so saying he turned his face towards the Potwell Inn.

He went back neither halting nor hastening in his pace after this last decision, but with a mind feverishly busy.

'If I get killed, I get killed, and if he gets killed I get hung. Don't seem just somehow.

'Don't suppose I shall *frighten* him off.'

The private war between Mr Polly and Uncle Jim for the possession of the Potwell Inn fell naturally into three chief campaigns. There was first of all the great campaign which ended in the triumphant eviction of Uncle Jim from the inn premises; there came next after a brief interval the futile invasions of the premises by Uncle Jim that culminated in the Battle of the Dead Eel; and, after some months of involuntary truce, there was the last supreme conflict of the Night Surprise. Each of these campaigns merits a section to itself.

Mr Polly re-entered the inn discreetly. He found the plump woman seated in her bar, her eyes a-stare, her face white and wet with tears. 'O God!' she was saying over and over again. 'O God!' The air was full of a spirituous reek, and on the sanded boards in front of the bar were the fragments of a broken bottle and an overturned glass.

She turned her despair at the sound of his entry, and despair gave place to astonishment.

'You come back!' she said.

'Ra-ther,' said Mr Polly.

'He's – he's mad drunk and looking for her.'

'Where is she?'

'Locked upstairs.'

'Haven't you sent to the police?'

'No one to send.'

'I'll see to it,' said Mr Polly. 'Out this way?'

She nodded.

He went to the crinkly paned window and peered out. Uncle Jim was coming down the garden path towards the house, his hands in his pockets and singing hoarsely. Mr Polly remembered afterwards with pride and amazement that he felt neither faint nor rigid. He glanced round him, seized a bottle of beer by the neck as an improvised club, and went out by the garden door. Uncle Jim stopped amazed. His brain did not instantly rise to the new posture of things.

'You!' he cried, and stopped for a moment. 'You – *scoot!*'

'*Your* job,' said Mr Polly, and advanced some paces.

Uncle Jim stood swaying with wrathful astonishment and then darted forward with clutching hands. Mr Polly felt that if his antagonist closed he was lost, and smote with all his force at the ugly head before him. Smash went the bottle, and Uncle Jim staggered, half-stunned by the blow and blinded with beer.

The lapses and leaps of the human mind are for ever mysterious. Mr Polly had never expected that bottle to break. In the instant he felt

disarmed and helpless. Before him was Uncle Jim, infuriated and evidently still coming on, and for defence was nothing but the neck of a bottle.

For a time our Mr Polly has figured heroic. Now comes the fall again; he sounded abject terror; he dropped that ineffectual scrap of glass and turned and fled round the corner of the house.

'Bolls!' came the thick voice of the enemy behind him as one who accepts a challenge, and bleeding, but indomitable, Uncle Jim entered the house.

'Bolls!' he said, surveying the bar. 'Fightin' with bolls! I'll show 'im fightin' with bolls!'

Uncle Jim had learnt all about fighting with bottles in the Reformatory Home. Regardless of his terror-stricken aunt he ranged among the bottled beer and succeeded after one or two failures in preparing two bottles to his satisfaction by knocking off the bottoms, and gripping them dagger-wise by the necks. So prepared, he went forth again to destroy Mr Polly.

Mr Polly, freed from the sense of urgent pursuit, had halted beyond the raspberry canes and rallied his courage. The sense of Uncle Jim victorious in the house restored his manhood. He went round by the outhouses to the riverside, seeking a weapon, and found an old paddle boat-hook. With this he smote Uncle Jim as he emerged by the door of the tap. Uncle Jim, blaspheming dreadfully and with dire stabbing intimations in either hand, came through the splintering paddle like a circus rider through a paper hoop, and once more Mr Polly dropped his weapon and fled.

A careless observer watching him sprint round and round the inn in front of the lumbering and reproachful pursuit of Uncle Jim might have formed an altogether erroneous estimate of the issue of the campaign. Certain compensating qualities of the very greatest military value were appearing in Mr Polly even as he ran; if Uncle Jim had strength and brute courage and the rich toughening experience a Reformatory Home affords, Mr Polly was nevertheless sober, more mobile and with a mind now stimulated to an almost incredible nimbleness. So that he not only gained on Uncle Jim, but thought what use he might make of this advantage. The word 'strategious' flamed red across the tumult of his mind. As he came round the house for the third time, he darted suddenly into the yard, swung the door to behind himself and bolted it, seized the zinc pig's pail that stood by the entrance to the kitchen and had it neatly and resonantly over Uncle Jim's head as he came belatedly in round the outhouse on the other side. One of the splintered bottles jabbed Mr Polly's ear – at the time it seemed of no importance – and then Uncle Jim was down and writhing dangerously and noisily upon the yard tiles, with his head still in the pig pail and his bottles gone to splinters, and Mr Polly was fastening the kitchen door against him.

'Can't go on like this for ever,' said Mr Polly, whooping for breath, and selecting a weapon from among the brooms that stood behind the kitchen door.

Uncle Jim was losing his head. He was up and kicking the door and bellowing unamiable proposals and invitations, so that a strategist emerging silently by the tap door could locate him without difficulty, steal upon him unawares and – !

But before that felling blow could be delivered Uncle Jim's ear had caught a footfall, and he turned. Mr Polly quailed and lowered his broom – a fatal hesitation.

'*Now* I got you!' cried Uncle Jim, dancing forward in a disconcerting zigzag.

He rushed to close, and Mr Polly stopped him neatly, as it were by a miracle, with the head of the broom across his chest. Uncle Jim seized the broom with both hands. 'Lea' go!' he said, and tugged. Mr Polly shook his head, tugged and showed pale, compressed lips. Both tugged. Then Uncle Jim tried to get round the end of the broom; Mr Polly circled away. They began to circle about one another, both tugging hard, both intensely watchful of the slightest initiative on the part of the other. Mr Polly wished brooms were longer, twelve or thirteen feet, for example; Uncle Jim was clearly for shortness in brooms. He wasted breath in saying what was to happen shortly – sanguinary, oriental soul-blenching things – when the broom no longer separated them. Mr Polly thought he had never seen an uglier person. Suddenly Uncle Jim flashed into violent activity, but alcohol slows movement, and Mr Polly was equal to him. Then Uncle Jim tried jerks, and for a terrible instant seemed to have the broom out of Mr Polly's hands. But Mr Polly recovered it with the clutch of a drowning man. Then Uncle Jim drove suddenly at Mr Polly's midriff, but again Mr Polly was ready and swept him round in a circle. Then suddenly a wild hope filled Mr Polly. He saw the river was very near, the post to which the punt was tied not three yards away. With a wild yell, he sent the broom home into his antagonist's ribs.

'Woosh!' he cried, as the resistance gave.

'Oh! *Gaw!*' said Uncle Jim, going backward helplessly, and Mr Polly thrust hard and abandoned the broom to the enemy's despairing clutch.

Splash! Uncle Jim was in the water and Mr Polly had leapt like a cat aboard the ferry punt and grasped the pole.

Up came Uncle Jim spluttering and dripping. 'You (unprofitable matter, and printing it would lead to a censorship of novels)! You know I got a weak *chess!*'

The pole took him in the throat and drove him backwards and down-wards.

'Lea' go!' cried Uncle Jim, staggering and with real terror in his once awful eyes.

Splash! Down he fell backwards into a frothing mass of water with Mr Polly jabbing at him. Under water he turned round and came up again as if in flight towards the middle of the river. Directly his head reappeared Mr

Polly had him between the shoulders and under again, bubbling thickly. A hand clutched and disappeared.

It was stupendous! Mr Polly had discovered the heel of Achilles. Uncle Jim had no stomach for cold water. The broom floated away, pitching gently on the swell. Mr Polly, infuriated with victory, thrust Uncle Jim under again, and drove the punt round on its chain in such a manner that when Uncle Jim came up for the fourth time – and now he was nearly out of his depth, too buoyed up to walk and apparently nearly helpless – Mr Polly, fortunately for them both, could not reach him. Uncle Jim made the clumsy gestures of those who struggle insecurely in the water. 'Keep out,' said Mr Polly. Uncle Jim with a great effort got a footing, emerged until his armpits were out of the water, until his waistcoat buttons showed, one by one, till scarcely two remained, and made for the camp sheeting.

'Keep out!' cried Mr Polly, and leapt off the punt and followed the movements of his victim along the shore.

'I tell you I got a weak chess,' said Uncle Jim, moistly. 'This ain't fair fightin'.'

'Keep out!' said Mr Polly.

'This ain't fair fightin',' said Uncle Jim, almost weeping, and all his terrors had gone.

'Keep out!' said Mr Polly, with an accurately poised pole.

'I tell you I got to land, you fool,' said Uncle Jim, with a sort of despairing wrathfulness, and began moving downstream.

'You keep out,' said Mr Polly in parallel movement. 'Don't you ever land on this place again . . . !'

Slowly, argumentatively and reluctantly, Uncle Jim waded downstream. He tried threats, he tried persuasion, he even tried a belated note of pathos; Mr Polly remained inexorable, if in secret a little perplexed as to the outcome of the situation. 'This cold's getting to my *marrer*!' said Uncle Jim.

'You want cooling. You keep out in it,' said Mr Polly.

They came round the bend into sight of Nicholson's ait, where the backwater runs down to the Potwell Mill. And there, after much parley and several feints, Uncle Jim made a desperate effort and struggled into clutch of the overhanging osiers on the island, and so got out of the water with the millstream between them. He emerged dripping and muddy and vindictive. 'By *Gaw*!' he said. 'I'll skin you for this!'

'You keep off or I'll do worse to you,' said Mr Polly.

The spirit was out of Uncle Jim for the time, and he turned away to struggle through the osiers towards the mill, leaving a shining trail of water among the green-grey stems.

Mr Polly returned slowly and thoughtfully to the inn, and suddenly his mind began to bubble with phrases. The plump woman stood at the top of the steps that led up to the inn door to greet him.

'Law!' she cried as he drew near, ' 'asn't 'e killed you?'

'Do I look like it?' said Mr Polly.

'But where's Jim?'

'Gone off.'

' 'E was mad drunk and dangerous!'

'I put him in the river,' said Mr Polly. 'That toned down his alcolaceous frenzy! I gave him a bit of a doing altogether.'

'Hain't he 'urt you?'

'Not a bit of it!'

'Then what's all that blood beside your ear?'

Mr Polly felt. 'Quite a cut! Funny how one overlooks things! Heated moments! He must have done that when he jabbed about with those bottles. Hello, kiddy! You venturing downstairs again?'

'Ain't he killed you?' asked the little girl.

'Well!'

'I wish I'd seen more of the fighting.'

'Didn't you?'

'All I saw was you running round the house and Uncle Jim after you.'

There was a little pause. 'I was leading him on,' said Mr Polly.

'Someone's shouting at the ferry,' she said.

'Right-o. But you won't see any more of Uncle Jim for a bit. We've been having a *conversazione* about that.'

'I believe it *is* Uncle Jim,' said the little girl.

'Then he can wait,' said Mr Polly shortly.

He turned round and listened for the words that drifted across from the little figure on the opposite bank. So far as he could judge, Uncle Jim was making an appointment for the morrow. He replied with a defiant movement of the punt pole. The little figure was convulsed for a moment and then went on its way upstream – fiercely.

So it was the first campaign ended in an insecure victory.

9

The next day was Wednesday and a slack day for the Potwell Inn. It was a hot, close day, full of the murmuring of bees. One or two people crossed by the ferry, an elaborately equipped fisherman stopped for cold meat and dry ginger ale in the bar parlour, some haymakers came and drank beer for an hour, and afterwards sent jars and jugs by a boy to be replenished; that was all. Mr Polly had risen early and was busy about the place meditating upon the probable tactics of Uncle Jim. He was no longer strung up to the desperate pitch of the first encounter. But he was grave and anxious. Uncle Jim had shrunken, as all antagonists that are boldly faced shrink, after the first battle, to the negotiable, the vulnerable. Formidable he was no doubt,

but not invincible. He had, under Providence, been defeated once, and he might be defeated altogether.

Mr Polly went about the place considering the militant possibilities of pacific things – pokers, copper sticks, garden implements, kitchen knives, garden nets, barbed wire, oars, clothes lines, blankets, pewter pots, stockings and broken bottles. He prepared a club with a stocking and a bottle inside, upon the best East End model. He swung it round his head once, broke an outhouse window with a flying fragment of glass, and ruined the stocking beyond all darning. He developed a subtle scheme with the cellar flap as a sort of pitfall, but he rejected it finally because (a) it might entrap the plump woman, and (b) he had no use whatever for Uncle Jim in the cellar. He determined to wire the garden that evening, burglar fashion, against the possibilities of a night attack.

Towards two o'clock in the afternoon three young men arrived in a capacious boat from the direction of Lammam, and asked permission to camp in the paddock. It was given all the more readily by Mr Polly because he perceived in their proximity a possible check upon the self-expression of Uncle Jim. But he did not foresee and no one could have foreseen that Uncle Jim, stealing unawares upon the Potwell Inn in the late afternoon, armed with a large rough-hewn stake, should have mistaken the bending form of one of those campers – who was pulling a few onions by permission in the garden – for Mr Polly's, and crept upon it swiftly and silently and smitten its wide invitation unforgettably and unforgiveably. It was an error impossible to explain; the resounding whack went up to heaven, as did the cry of amazement, and Mr Polly emerged from the inn, armed with the frying-pan he was cleaning, to take this reckless assailant in the rear. Uncle Jim, realising his error, fled blaspheming into the arms of the other two campers, who were returning from the village with butcher's meat and groceries. They caught him, they smacked his face with steak and punched him with a bursting parcel of lump sugar, they held him though he bit them, and their idea of punishment was to duck him. They were hilarious, strong young stockbrokers' clerks, Territorials and seasoned boating men; they ducked him as though it was romping, and all that Mr Polly had to do was to pick up lumps of sugar for them and wipe them on his sleeve and put them on a plate, and explain that Uncle Jim was a notorious bad character and not quite right in his head.

'Got a regular obsession that the missis is his aunt,' said Mr Polly, expanding it. 'Perfect noosance he is.'

But he caught a glance of Uncle Jim's eye as he receded before the campers' urgency that boded ill for him, and in the night he had a disagreeable idea that perhaps his luck might not hold for the third occasion.

That came soon enough. So soon, indeed, as the campers had gone.

Thursday was the early-closing day at Lammam, and next to Sunday the busiest part of the week at the Potwell Inn. Sometimes as many as six boats

all at once would be moored against the ferry punt and hiring rowboats. People could either have a complete but unadorned tea, a complete tea with jam, cake and eggs, a kettle of boiling water and find the rest, or refreshments *à la carte*, as they chose. They sat about, but usually the boiling water–ers had a delicacy about using the tables and grouped themselves humbly on the ground. The complete tea–ers with jam and eggs got the best tablecloth on the table nearest the steps that led up to the glass-panelled door.

The groups about the lawn were very satisfying to Mr Polly's sense of amenity. To the right were the complete tea-ers with everything heart could desire; then a small group of three young men in remarkable green and violet and pale-blue shirts, and two girls in mauve and yellow blouses, with complete but unadorned teas and gooseberry jam at the green clothless table; then, on the grass down by the pollard willow, a small family of hot water-ers with a hamper, a little troubled by wasps in their jam from the nest in the tree, and all in mourning, but happy otherwise; and on the lawn to the right a ginger-beer lot of 'prentices without their collars and very jocular and happy. The young people in the rainbow shirts and blouses formed the centre of interest; they were under the leadership of a gold-spectacled senior with a fluting voice and an air of mystery; he ordered everything, and showed a peculiar knowledge of the qualities of the Potwell jams, preferring gooseberry with much insistence. Mr Polly watched him, christened him the 'benifluous influence', glanced at the 'prentices and went inside and down into the cellar in order to replenish the stock of stone ginger beer which the plump woman had allowed to run low during the preoccupations of the campaign.

It was in the cellar that he first became aware of the return of Uncle Jim. He became aware of him as a voice, a voice not only hoarse, but thick, as voices thicken under the influence of alcohol.

'Where's that muddy-faced mongrel?' cried Uncle Jim. 'Let 'im come out to me! Where's that blighted whisp with the punt pole – I got a word to say to 'im. Come out of it, you pot-bellied chunk of dirtiness, you! Come out and 'ave your ugly face wiped. I got a Thing for you . . . *'Ear* me?'

' 'E's 'iding, that's what 'e's doing,' said the voice of Uncle Jim, dropping for a moment to sorrow, and then with a great increment of wrathfulness: 'Come out of my nest, you blinking cuckoo, you, or I'll cut your silly insides out! Come out of it – you pockmarked Rat! Stealing another man's 'ome away from 'im! Come out and look me in the face, you squinting son of a Skunk! . . . '

Mr Polly took the ginger beer and went thoughtfully upstairs to the bar.

' 'E's back,' said the plump woman as he appeared. 'I knew 'e'd come back.'

'I heard him,' said Mr Polly, and looked about. 'Just gimme the old poker handle that's under the beer engine.'

The door opened softly and Mr Polly turned quickly. But it was only the pointed nose and intelligent face of the young man with the gilt spectacles and discreet manner. He coughed and the spectacles fixed Mr Polly.

'I say,' he said with quiet earnestness. 'There's a chap out here seems to want someone.'

'Why don't he come in?' said Mr Polly.

'He seems to want you out there.'

'What's he want?'

'I *think*,' said the spectacled young man after a thoughtful moment, 'he appears to have brought you a present of fish.'

'Isn't he shouting?'

'He *is* a little boisterous.'

'He'd better come in.'

The manner of the spectacled young man intensified. 'I wish you'd come out and persuade him to go away,' he said. 'His language – isn't quite the thing – ladies.'

'It never was,' said the plump woman, her voice charged with sorrow.

Mr Polly moved towards the door and stood with his hand on the handle. The gold-spectacled face disappeared.

'Now, my man,' came his voice from outside, 'be careful what you're saying – '

'Oo in all the World and Hereafter are you to call me, me man?' cried Uncle Jim, in the voice of one astonished and pained beyond endurance, and added scornfully: 'You gold-eyed Geezer, you!'

'Tut, tut!' said the gentleman in gilt glasses. 'Restrain yourself!'

Mr Polly emerged, poker in hand, just in time to see what followed. Uncle Jim in his shirtsleeves and a state of ferocious décolletage, was holding something – yes! – a dead eel by means of a piece of newspaper about its tail, holding it down and back and a little sideways in such a way as to smite with it upwards and hard. It struck the spectacled gentleman under the jaw with a peculiar dead thud, and a cry of horror came from the two seated parties at the sight. One of the girls shrieked piercingly, 'Horace!' and everyone sprang up. The sense of helping numbers came to Mr Polly's aid.

'Drop it!' he cried, and came down the steps waving his poker and thrusting the spectacled gentleman before him as once heroes were wont to wield the ox-hide shield.

Uncle Jim gave ground suddenly, and trod upon the foot of a young man in a blue shirt, who immediately thrust at him violently with both hands.

'Lea' go!' howled Uncle Jim. 'That's the chap I'm looking for!' and pressing the head of the spectacled gentleman aside, smote hard at Mr Polly.

But at the sight of this indignity inflicted upon the spectacled gentleman a woman's heart was stirred, and a pink parasol drove hard and true at

Uncle Jim's wiry neck, and at the same moment the young man in the blue shirt sought to collar him and lost his grip again.

'Suffragettes,' gasped Uncle Jim with the ferule at his throat. 'Everywhere!' and aimed a second, more successful, blow at Mr Polly.

'Wup!' said Mr Polly.

But now the jam and egg party was joining in the fray. A stout yet still fairly able-bodied gentleman in white and black checks enquired: 'What's the fellow up to? Ain't there no police here?' and it was evident that once more public opinion was rallying to the support of Mr Polly.

'Oh, come on then all the LOT of you!' cried Uncle Jim and, backing dexterously, whirled the eel round in a destructive circle. The pink sunshade was torn from the hand that gripped it and whirled athwart the complete but unadorned tea things on the green table.

'Collar him! Someone get hold of his collar!' cried the gold-spectacled gentleman, coming out of the scrimmage and retreating up the steps to the inn door as if to rally his forces.

'Stand clear, you blessed mantel ornaments!' cried Uncle Jim, 'stand clear!' and retired backing, staving off attack by means of the whirling eel.

Mr Polly, undeterred by a sense of grave damage done to his nose, pressed the attack in front, the two young men in violet and blue skirmished on Uncle Jim's flanks, the man in white and black checks sought still further outflanking possibilities, and two of the apprentice boys ran for oars. The gold-spectacled gentleman, as if inspired, came down the wooden steps again, seized the tablecloth of the jam and egg party, lugged it from under the crockery with inadequate precautions against breakage, and advanced with compressed lips, curious lateral crouching movements, swift flashings of his glasses, and a general suggestion of bullfighting in his pose and gestures. Uncle Jim was kept busy, and unable to plan his retreat with any strategic soundness. He was moreover manifestly a little nervous about the river in his rear. He gave ground in a curve, and so came right across the rapidly abandoned camp of the family in mourning, crunching a teacup under his heel, oversetting the teapot, and finally tripping backwards over the hamper. The eel flew out at a tangent from his hand and became a mere looping relic on the sward.

'Hold him!' cried the gentleman in spectacles. 'Collar him!' and moving forward with extraordinary promptitude wrapped the best tablecloth about Uncle Jim's arms and head. Mr Polly grasped his purpose instantly, the man in checks was scarcely slower, and in another moment Uncle Jim was no more than a bundle of smothered blasphemy and a pair of wildly active legs.

'Duck him!' panted Mr Polly, holding on to the earthquake. 'Bes' thing – duck him.'

The bundle was convulsed by paroxysms of anger and protest. One boot got the hamper and sent it ten yards.

'Go in the house for a clothes-line someone!' said the gentleman in gold spectacles. 'He'll get out of this in a moment.'

One of the apprentices ran.

'Bird nets in the garden,' shouted Mr Polly. 'In the garden!'

The apprentice was divided in his purpose. And then suddenly Uncle Jim collapsed and became a limp, dead-seeming thing under their hands. His arms were drawn inward, his legs bent up under his person, and so he lay.

'Fainted!' said the man in checks, relaxing his grip.

'A fit, perhaps,' said the man in spectacles.

'Keep hold!' said Mr Polly, too late.

For suddenly Uncle Jim's arms and legs flew out like springs released. Mr Polly was tumbled backwards and fell over the broken teapot and into the arms of the father in mourning. Something struck his head – dazzingly. In another second Uncle Jim was on his feet and the tablecloth enshrouded the head of the man in checks. Uncle Jim manifestly considered he had done all that honour required of him, and against overwhelming numbers and the possibility of reiterated duckings, flight is no disgrace.

Uncle Jim fled.

Mr Polly sat up after an interval of an indeterminate length among the ruins of an idyllic afternoon. Quite a lot of things seemed scattered and broken, but it was difficult to grasp it all at once. He stared between the legs of people. He became aware of a voice, speaking slowly and complainingly.

'Someone ought to pay for those tea things,' said the father in mourning. 'We didn't bring them 'ere to be danced on, not by no manner of means.'

10

There followed an anxious peace for three days, and then a rough man in a blue jersey, in the intervals of trying to choke himself with bread and cheese and pickled onions, broke out abruptly into information.

'Jim's lagged again, missus,' he said.

'What!' said the landlady. 'Our Jim?'

'Your Jim,' said the man, and after an absolutely necessary pause for swallowing, added: 'Stealin' a 'atchet.'

He did not speak for some moments, and then he replied to Mr Polly's enquiries: 'Yes, a 'atchet. Down Lammam way – night before last.'

'What'd 'e steal a 'atchet for?' asked the plump woman.

' 'E said 'e wanted a 'atchet.'

'I wonder what he wanted a hatchet for?' said Mr Polly, thoughtfully.

'I dessay 'e 'ad a use for it,' said the gentleman in the blue jersey, and he took a mouthful that amounted to conversational suicide. There was a prolonged pause in the little bar, and Mr Polly did some rapid thinking.

He went to the window and whistled. 'I shall stick it,' he whispered at last. ' 'Atchets or no 'atchets.'

He turned to the man with the blue jersey when he thought him clear for speech again. 'How much did you say they'd given him?' he asked.

'Three munce,' said the man in the blue jersey, and refilled anxiously, as if alarmed at the momentary clearness of his voice.

11

Those three months passed all too quickly; months of sunshine and warmth, of varied novel exertion in the open air, of congenial experiences, of interest and wholesome food and successful digestion, months that browned Mr Polly and hardened him and saw the beginnings of his beard, months marred only by one anxiety, an anxiety Mr Polly did his utmost to suppress. The day of reckoning was never mentioned, it is true, by either the plump woman or himself, but the name of Uncle Jim was written in letters of glaring silence across their intercourse. As the term of that respite drew to an end his anxiety increased, until at last it even trenched upon his well-earned sleep. He had some idea of buying a revolver. At last he compromised upon a small and very foul and dirty rook rifle, which he purchased in Lammam under a pretext of bird scaring, and loaded carefully and concealed under his bed from the plump woman's eye.

September passed away, October came.

And at last came that night in October whose happenings it is so difficult for a sympathetic historian to drag out of their proper nocturnal indistinctness into the clear, hard light of positive statement. A novelist should present characters, not vivisect them publicly.

The best, the kindliest, if not the justest, course is surely to leave untold such things as Mr Polly would manifestly have preferred untold.

Mr Polly had declared that when the cyclist discovered him he was seeking a weapon that should make a conclusive end to Uncle Jim. That declaration is placed before the reader without comment.

The gun was certainly in possession of Uncle Jim at that time and no human being but Mr Polly knows how he got hold of it.

The cyclist was a literary man named Warspite, who suffered from insomnia; he had risen and come out of his house near Lammam just before the dawn, and he discovered Mr Polly partially concealed in the ditch by the Potwell churchyard wall. It is an ordinary dry ditch, full of nettles and overgrown with elder and dog rose, and in no way suggestive of an arsenal. It is the last place in which you would look for a gun. And he says that when he dismounted to see why Mr Polly was allowing only the latter part of his person to show (and that it would seem by inadvertency), Mr Polly merely raised his head and advised him to, 'Look out!' and

added: 'He's let fly at me twice already.' He came out under persuasion and with gestures of extreme caution. He was wearing a white cotton nightgown of the type that has now been so extensively superseded by pyjama sleeping-suits, and his legs and feet were bare and much scratched and torn and very muddy.

Mr Warspite takes that exceptionally lively interest in his fellow-creatures which constitutes so much of the distinctive and complex charm of your novelist all the world over, and he at once involved himself generously in the case. The two men returned at Mr Polly's initiative across the churchyard to the Potwell Inn, and came upon the burst and damaged rook rifle near the new monument to Sir Samuel Harpon at the corner by the yew.

'That must have been his third go,' said Mr Polly. 'It sounded a bit funny.'

The sight inspirited him greatly, and he explained further that he had fled to the churchyard on account of the cover afforded by tombstones from the flight of small shot. He expressed anxiety for the fate of the landlady of the Potwell Inn and her grandchild, and led the way with enhanced alacrity along the lane to that establishment.

They found the doors of the house standing open, the bar in some disorder – several bottles of whisky were afterwards found to be missing – and Blake, the village policeman, rapping patiently at the open door. He entered with them. The glass in the bar had suffered severely, and one of the mirrors was starred from a blow from a pewter pot. The till had been forced and ransacked, and so had the bureau in the minute room behind the bar. An upper window was opened and the voice of the landlady became audible making enquiries. They went out and parleyed with her. She had locked herself upstairs with the little girl, she said, and refused to descend until she was assured that neither Uncle Jim nor Mr Polly's gun were anywhere on the premises. Mr Blake and Mr Warspite proceeded to satisfy themselves with regard to the former condition, and Mr Polly went to his room in search of garments more suited to the brightening dawn. He returned immediately with a request that Mr Blake and Mr Warspite would 'just come and look'. They found the apartment in a state of extraordinary confusion, the bedclothes in a ball in the corner, the drawers all open and ransacked, the chair broken, the lock of the door forced and broken, one door panel slightly scorched and perforated by shot, and the window wide open. None of Mr Polly's clothes were to be seen, but some garments which had apparently once formed part of a stoker's workaday outfit, two brownish-yellow halves of a shirt, and an unsound pair of boots were scattered on the floor. A faint smell of gunpowder still hung in the air, and two or three books Mr Polly had recently acquired had been shied with some violence under the bed.

Mr Warspite looked at Mr Blake, and then both men looked at Mr Polly.

'That's *his* boots,' said Mr Polly.

Blake turned his eye to the window. 'Some of these tiles 'ave just got broken,' he observed.

'I got out of the window and slid down the scullery tiles,' Mr Polly answered, omitting much, they both felt, from his explanation . . .

'Well, we better find 'im and 'ave a word with 'im,' said Blake. 'That's about my business now.'

12

But Uncle Jim had gone altogether . . .

He did not return for some days. That perhaps was not very wonderful. But the days lengthened to weeks and the weeks to months and still Uncle Jim did not recur. A year passed, and the anxiety of him became less acute; a second healing year followed the first. One afternoon about thirty months after the Night Surprise the plump woman spoke of him.

'I wonder what's become of Jim,' she said.

'*I* wonder sometimes,' said Mr Polly.

CHAPTER TEN

Miriam Revisited

One summer afternoon about five years after his first coming to the Potwell Inn Mr Polly found himself sitting under the pollard willow fishing for dace. It was a plumper, browner and healthier Mr Polly altogether than the miserable bankrupt with whose dyspeptic portrait our novel opened. He was fat, but with a fatness more generally diffused, and the lower part of his face was touched to gravity by a small square beard. Also he was balder.

It was the first time he had found leisure to fish, though from the very outset of his Potwell career he had promised himself abundant indulgence in the pleasures of fishing. Fishing, as the golden page of English literature testifies, is a meditative and retrospective pursuit, and the varied page of memory, disregarded so long for sake of the teeming duties I have already enumerated, began to unfold itself to Mr Polly's consideration. A speculation about Uncle Jim died for want of material, and gave place to a reckoning of the years and months that had passed since his coming to Potwell, and that to a philosophical review of his life. He began to think about Miriam, remotely and impersonally. He remembered many things that had been neglected by his conscience during the busier times, as, for example, that he had committed arson and deserted a wife. For the first time he looked these long neglected facts in the face.

It is disagreeable to think one has committed arson, because it is an

action that leads to jail. Otherwise I do not think there was a grain of regret for that in Mr Polly's composition. But deserting Miriam was in a different category. Deserting Miriam was mean.

This is a history and not a glorification of Mr Polly, and I tell of things as they were with him. Apart from the disagreeable twinge arising from the thought of what might happen if he was found out, he had not the slightest remorse about that fire. Arson, after all, is an artificial crime. Some crimes are crimes in themselves, would be crimes without any law, the cruelties, mockery, the breaches of faith that astonish and wound, but the burning of things is in itself neither good nor bad. A large number of houses deserve to be burnt, most modern furniture, an overwhelming majority of pictures and books – one might go on for some time with the list. If our community was collectively anything more than a feeble idiot, it would burn most of London and Chicago, for example, and build sane and beautiful cities in the place of these pestilential heaps of rotten private property. I have failed in presenting Mr Polly altogether if I have not made you see that he was in many respects an artless child of Nature, far more untrained, undisciplined and spontaneous than an ordinary savage. And he was really glad, for all that little drawback of fear, that he had the courage to set fire to his house and fly and come to the Potwell Inn.

But he was not glad he had left Miriam. He had seen Miriam cry once or twice in his life, and it had always reduced him to abject commiseration. He now imagined her crying. He perceived in a perplexed way that he had made himself responsible for her life. He forgot how she had spoilt his own. He had hitherto rested in the faith that she had over a hundred pounds of insurance money, but now, with his eye meditatively upon his float, he realised a hundred pounds does not last for ever. His conviction of her incompetence was unflinching; she was bound to have fooled it away some-how by this time. And then!

He saw her humping her shoulders and sniffing in a manner he had always regarded as detestable at close quarters, but which now became harrowingly pitiful.

'Damn!' said Mr Polly, and down went his float and he flicked up a victim to destruction and took it off the hook.

He compared his own comfort and health with Miriam's imagined distress.

'Ought to have done something for herself,' said Mr Polly, rebaiting his hook. 'She was always talking of doing things. Why couldn't she?'

He watched the float oscillating gently towards quiescence.

'Silly to begin thinking about her,' he said. 'Damn silly!'

But once he had begun thinking about her he had to go on.

'Oh blow!' cried Mr Polly presently, and pulled up his hook to find another fish had just snatched at it in the last instant. His handling must have made the poor thing feel itself unwelcome.

He gathered his things together and turned towards the house.

All the Potwell Inn betrayed his influence now, for here indeed he had found his place in the world. It looked brighter, so bright indeed as to be almost skittish, with the white and green paint he had lavished upon it. Even the garden palings were striped white and green, and so were the boats, for Mr Polly was one of those who find a positive sensuous pleasure in the laying on of paint. Left and right were two large boards which had done much to enhance the inn's popularity with the lighter-minded variety of pleasure-seekers. Both marked innovations. One bore in large letters the single word 'Museum', the other was as plain and laconic with 'Omlets'. The spelling of the latter word was Mr Polly's own, but when he had seen a whole boatload of men, intent on Lammam for lunch, stop open-mouthed, and stare and grin and come in and ask in a marked sarcastic manner for 'omlets', he perceived that his inaccuracy had done more for the place than his utmost cunning could have contrived. In a year or so the inn was known both up and down the river by its new name of 'Omlets', and Mr Polly, after some secret irritation, smiled and was content. And the fat woman's omelettes were things to remember.

(You will note I have changed her epithet. Time works upon us all.)

She stood upon the steps as he came towards the house, and smiled at him richly.

'Caught many?' she asked.

'Got an idea,' said Mr Polly. 'Would it put you out very much if I went off for a day or two for a bit of a holiday? There won't be much doing now until Thursday.'

2

Feeling recklessly secure behind his beard Mr Polly surveyed the Fishbourne High Street once again. The north side was much as he had known it except that Rusper had vanished. A row of new shops replaced the destruction of the great fire. Mantell and Throbson's had risen again upon a more flamboyant pattern, and the new fire station was in the Swiss-Teutonic style and with much red paint. Next door in the place of Rumbold's was a branch of the Colonial Tea Company, and then a Salmon and Gluckstein Tobacco Shop, and then a little shop that displayed sweets and professed a 'Tea Room Upstairs'. He considered this as a possible place in which to prosecute enquiries about his lost wife, wavering a little between it and the God's Providence Inn down the street. Then his eye caught a name over the window, 'Polly,' he read, '& Larkins! Well, I'm – astonished!'

A momentary faintness came upon him. He walked past and down the street, returned and surveyed the shop again.

He saw a middle-aged, rather untidy woman standing behind the counter, who for an instant he thought might be Miriam terribly changed, and then recognised as his sister-in-law Annie, filled out and no longer hilarious. She stared at him without a sign of recognition as he entered the shop.

'Can I have tea?' said Mr Polly.

'Well,' said Annie, 'you *can*. But our Tea Room's upstairs . . . My sister's been cleaning it out – and it's a bit upset.'

'It *would* be,' said Mr Polly softly.

'I beg your pardon?' said Annie.

'I said *I* didn't mind. Up here?'

'I dare say there'll be a table,' said Annie, and followed him up to a room whose conscientious disorder was intensely reminiscent of Miriam.

'Nothing like turning everything upside down when you're cleaning,' said Mr Polly cheerfully.

'It's my sister's way,' said Annie impartially. 'She's gone out for a bit of air, but I dare say she'll be back soon to finish. It's a nice light room when it's tidy. Can I put you a table over there?'

'Let *me*,' said Mr Polly, and assisted. He sat down by the open window and drummed on the table and meditated on his next step while Annie vanished to get his tea. After all, things didn't seem so bad with Miriam. He tried over several gambits in imagination.

'Unusual name,' he said, as Annie laid a cloth before him. Annie looked interrogation.

'Polly. Polly & Larkins. Real, I suppose?'

'Polly's my sister's name. She married a Mr Polly.'

'Widow I presume?' said Mr Polly.

'Yes. This five years – come October.'

'Lord!' said Mr Polly in unfeigned surprise.

'Found drowned he was. There was a lot of talk in the place.'

'Never heard of it,' said Mr Polly. 'I'm a stranger – rather.'

'In the Medway near Maidstone. He must have been in the water for days. Wouldn't have known him, my sister wouldn't, if it hadn't been for the name sewn in his clothes. All whitey and eat away he was.'

'Bless my heart! Must have been rather a shock for her!'

'It *was* a shock,' said Annie, and added darkly: 'But sometimes a shock's better than a long agony.'

'No doubt,' said Mr Polly.

He gazed with a rapt expression at the preparations before him. 'So I'm drowned,' something was saying inside him. 'Life insured?' he asked.

'We started the tea rooms with it,' said Annie.

Why, if things were like this, had remorse and anxiety for Miriam been implanted in his soul? No shadow of an answer appeared.

'Marriage is a lottery,' said Mr Polly.

'*She* found it so,' said Annie. 'Would you like some jam?'

'I'd like an egg,' said Mr Polly. 'I'll have two. I've got a sort of feeling –
As though I wanted keeping up . . . Wasn't particularly good sort, this Mr
Polly?'

'He was a *wearing* husband,' said Annie. 'I've often pitied my sister. He
was one of that sort – '

'Dissolute?' suggested Mr Polly faintly.

'No,' said Annie judiciously; 'not exactly dissolute. Feeble's more the
word. Weak, 'e was. Weak as water. 'Ow long do you like your eggs boiled?'

'Four minutes exactly,' said Mr Polly.

'One gets talking,' said Annie.

'One does,' said Mr-Polly, and she left him to his thoughts.

What perplexed him was his recent remorse and tenderness for Miriam.
Now he was back in her atmosphere all that had vanished, and the old
feeling of helpless antagonism returned. He surveyed the piled furniture,
the economically managed carpet, the unpleasing pictures on the wall. Why
had he felt remorse? Why had he entertained this illusion of a helpless
woman crying aloud in the pitiless darkness for him? He peered into the
unfathomable mysteries of the heart, and ducked back to a smaller issue.
Was he feeble?

The eggs came up. Nothing in Annie's manner invited a resumption of
the discussion.

'Business brisk?' he ventured to ask.

Annie reflected. 'It is,' she said, 'and it isn't. It's like that.'

'Ah!' said Mr Polly, and squared himself to his egg. 'Was there an inquest
on that chap?'

'What chap?'

'What was his name? – Polly!'

'Of course.'

'You're sure it was him?'

'What you mean?'

Annie looked at him hard, and suddenly his soul was black with terror.

'Who else could it have been – in the very clo'es 'e wore?'

'Of course,' said Mr Polly, and began his egg. He was so agitated that he
only realised its condition when he was halfway through it and Annie safely
downstairs.

'Lord!' he said, reaching out hastily for the pepper. 'One of Miriam's!
Management! I haven't tasted such an egg for five years . . . Wonder where
she gets them! Picks them out, I suppose!'

He abandoned it for its fellow.

Except for a slight mustiness the second egg was very palatable indeed.
He was getting to the bottom of it as Miriam came in. He looked up. 'Nice
afternoon,' he said at her stare, and perceived she knew him at once by the
gesture and the voice. She went white and shut the door behind her. She
looked as though she was going to faint. Mr Polly sprang up quickly and

handed her a chair. 'My God!' she whispered, and crumpled up rather than sat down.

'It's *you*' she said.

'No,' said Mr Polly very earnestly. 'It isn't. It just looks like me. That's all.'

'I *knew* that man wasn't you – all along. I tried to think it was. I tried to think perhaps the water had altered your wrists and feet and the colour of your hair.'

'Ah!'

'I'd always feared you'd come back.'

Mr Polly sat down by his egg. 'I haven't come back,' he said very earnestly. 'Don't you think it.'

' 'Ow we'll pay back the insurance now I *don't* know.'

She was weeping. She produced a handkerchief and covered her face.

'Look here, Miriam,' said Mr Polly. 'I haven't come back and I'm not coming back. I'm – I'm a Visitant from Another World. You shut up about me and I'll shut up about myself. I came back because I thought you might be hard up or in trouble or some silly thing like that. Now I see you again – I'm satisfied. I'm satisfied completely. See? I'm going to absquatulate, see? Hey Presto, right away.'

He turned to his tea for a moment, finished his cup noisily, stood up.

'Don't you think you're going to see me again,' he said, 'for you ain't.'

He moved to the door.

'That *was* a tasty egg,' he said, hovered for a second and vanished . . .

Annie was in the shop.

'The missus has had a bit of a shock,' he remarked. 'Got some sort of fancy about a ghost. Can't make it out quite. So long!'

And he had gone.

3

Mr Polly sat beside the fat woman at one of the little green tables at the back of the Potwell Inn, and struggled with the mystery of life. It was one of those evenings, serenely luminous, amply and atmospherically still, when the river bend was at its best. A swan floated against the dark green masses of the farther bank, the stream flowed broad and shining to its destiny, with scarce a ripple – except where the reeds came out from the headland – the three poplars rose clear and harmonious against a sky of green and yellow. And it was as if it was all securely within a great warm friendly globe of crystal sky. It was as safe and enclosed and fearless as a child that has still to be born. It was an evening full of the quality of tranquil, unqualified assurance. Mr Polly's mind was filled with the persuasion that indeed all things whatsoever must needs be satisfying and complete. It was incredible

that life had ever done more than seemed to jar, that there could be any shadow in life save such velvet softnesses as made the setting for that silent swan, or any murmur but the ripple of the water as it swirled round the chained and gently swaying punt. And the mind of Mr Polly, exalted and made tender by this atmosphere, sought gently, but sought, to draw together the varied memories that came drifting, half submerged, across the circle of his mind.

He spoke in words that seemed like a bent and broken stick thrust suddenly into water, destroying the mirror of the shapes they sought. 'Jim's not coming back again ever,' he said. 'He got drowned five years ago.'

'Where?' asked the fat woman, surprised.

'Miles from here. In the Medway. Away in Kent.'

'Lor!' said the fat woman.

'It's right enough,' said Mr Polly.

'How d'you know?'

'I went to my home.'

'Where?'

'Don't matter. I went and found out. He'd been in the water some days. He'd got my clothes and they'd said it was me.'

'They?'

'It don't matter. I'm not going back to them.'

The fat woman regarded him silently for some time. Her expression of scrutiny gave way to a quiet satisfaction. Then her brown eyes went to the river.

'Poor Jim,' she said. ' 'E 'adn't much Tact – ever.'

She added mildly: 'I can't 'ardly say I'm sorry.'

'Nor me,' said Mr Polly, and got a step nearer the thought in him. 'But it don't seem much good his having been alive, does it?'

' 'E wasn't much good,' the fat woman admitted. 'Ever.'

'I suppose there were things that were good to him,' Mr Polly speculated. 'They weren't *our* things.'

His hold slipped again. 'I often wonder about life,' he said weakly.

He tried again. 'One seems to start in life,' he said, 'expecting something. And it doesn't happen. And it doesn't matter. One starts with ideas that things are good and things are bad – and it hasn't much relation to what *is* good and what *is* bad. I've always been the skeptaceous sort, and it's always seemed rot to me to pretend we know good from evil. It's just what I've *never* done. No Adam's apple stuck in *my* throat, ma'am. I don't own to it.'

He reflected. 'I set fire to a house – once.'

The fat woman started.

'I don't feel sorry for it. I don't believe it was a bad thing to do – any more than burning a toy like I did once when I was a baby. I nearly killed myself with a razor. Who hasn't? – anyhow gone as far as thinking of it? Most of my time I've been half dreaming. I married like a dream almost.

I've never really planned my life or set out to live. I happened; things happened to me. It's so with everyone. Jim couldn't help himself. I shot at him and tried to kill him. I dropped the gun and he got it. He very nearly had me. I wasn't a second too soon – ducking . . . Awkward – that night was . . . M'mm . . . But I don't blame him – come to that. Only I don't see what it's all up to . . .

'Like children playing about in a nursery. Hurt themselves at times . . .

'There's something that doesn't mind us,' he resumed presently. 'It isn't what we try to get that we get, it isn't the good we think we do is good. What makes us happy isn't our trying, what makes others happy isn't our trying. There's a sort of character people like and stand up for and a sort they won't. You got to work it out and take the consequences . . . Miriam was always trying.'

'Who was Miriam?' asked the fat woman.

'No one you know. But she used to go about with her brows knit trying not to do whatever she wanted to do – if ever she did want to do anything – '

He lost himself.

'You can't help being fat,' said the fat woman after a pause, trying to get up to his thoughts.

'*You* can't,' said Mr Polly.

'It helps and it hinders.'

'Like my upside down way of talking.'

'The magistrates wouldn't 'ave kept on the licence to me if I 'adn't been fat . . . '

'Then what have we done,' said Mr Polly, 'to get an evening like this? Lord! look at it!' He sent his arm round the great curve of the sky.

'If I was a darkie or an Italian I should come out here and sing. I whistle sometimes, but, bless you, it's singing I've got in my mind. Sometimes I think I live for sunsets.'

'I don't see that it does you any good always looking at sunsets like you do,' said the fat woman.

'Nor me. But I do. Sunsets and things I was made to like.'

'They don't 'elp you,' said the fat woman thoughtfully.

'Who cares?' said Mr Polly.

A deeper strain had come to the fat woman. 'You got to die someday,' she said.

'Some things I can't believe,' said Mr Polly suddenly, 'and one is your being a skeleton . . . ' He pointed his hand towards the neighbour's hedge. 'Look at 'em – against the yellow – and they're just stingin' nettles. Nasty weeds – if you count things by their uses. And no help in the life hereafter. But just look at the look of them!'

'It isn't only looks,' said the fat woman.

'Whenever there's signs of a good sunset and I'm not too busy,' said Mr Polly, 'I'll come and sit out here.'

The fat woman looked at him with eyes in which contentment struggled with some obscure reluctant protest, and at last turned them slowly to the black nettle pagodas against the golden sky.

'I wish we could,' she said.

'I will.'

The fat woman's voice sank nearly to the inaudible.

'Not always,' she said.

Mr Polly was some time before he replied. 'Come here always when I'm a ghost,' he replied.

'Spoil the place for others,' said the fat woman, abandoning her moral solicitudes for a more congenial point of view.

'Not my sort of ghost wouldn't,' said Mr Polly, emerging from another long pause. 'I'd be a sort of diaphalous feeling – just mellowish and warmish like . . .'

They said no more, but sat on in the warm twilight until at last they could scarcely distinguish each other's faces. They were not so much thinking as lost in a smooth still quiet of the mind. A bat flitted by.

'Time we was going in, o' party,' said Mr Polly, standing up. 'Supper to get. It's as you say, we can't sit here for ever.'

The First Men in the Moon

A novel first published in 1901

The First Men in the Moon was first published in Great Britain
by George Newnes Limited in 1901 following
publication of the novel one month earlier in the
United States by the Bowen-Merrill Company of Indianapolis.

Contents

Three thousand stadia from the earth to the moon . . . Marvel not, my comrade, if I appear to be talking to you on super-terrestrial and aerial topics. The long and the short of the matter is that I am running over the order of a Journey I have lately made.

<div align="right">LUCIAN, Icaromenippus</div>

CHAPTER ONE

Mr Bedford Meets Mr Cavor at Lympne

A S I SIT DOWN TO WRITE here amidst the shadows of vine-leaves under the blue sky of southern Italy, it comes to me with a certain quality of astonishment that my participation in these amazing adventures of Mr Cavor was, after all, the outcome of the purest accident. It might have been anyone. I fell into these things at a time when I thought myself removed from the slightest possibility of disturbing experiences. I had gone to Lympne because I had imagined it the most uneventful place in the world. 'Here, at any rate,' said I, 'I shall find peace and a chance to work!'

And this book is the sequel. So utterly at variance is destiny with all the little plans of men.

I may perhaps mention here that very recently I had come an ugly cropper in certain business enterprises. Sitting now surrounded by all the circumstances of wealth, there is a luxury in admitting my extremity. I can admit, even, that to a certain extent my disasters were conceivably of my own making. It may be there are directions in which I have some capacity, but the conduct of business operations is not among these. But in those days I was young, and my youth among other objectionable forms took that of a pride in my capacity for affairs. I am young still in years, but the things that have happened to me have rubbed something of the youth from my mind. Whether they have brought any wisdom to light below it is a more doubtful matter.

It is scarcely necessary to go into the details of the speculations that landed me at Lympne, in Kent. Nowadays even about business transactions there is a strong spice of adventure. I took risks. In these things there is invariably a certain amount of give and take, and it fell to me finally to do the giving. Reluctantly enough. Even when I had got out of everything, one cantankerous creditor saw fit to be malignant. Perhaps you have met that flaming sense of outraged virtue, or perhaps you have only felt it. He ran me hard. It seemed to me, at last, that there was nothing for it but to write a play, unless I wanted to drudge for my living as a clerk. I have a certain imagination, and luxurious tastes, and I meant to make a vigorous fight for it before that fate overtook me. In addition to my belief in my powers as a businessman, I had always in those days had an idea that I was equal to writing a very good play. It is not, I believe, a very uncommon persuasion. I knew there is nothing a man can do outside legitimate business transactions

that has such opulent possibilities, and very probably that biased my opinion. I had, indeed, got into the habit of regarding this unwritten drama as a convenient little reserve put by for a rainy day. That rainy day had come, and I set to work.

I soon discovered that writing a play was a longer business than I had supposed; at first I had reckoned ten days for it, and it was to have a *pied-à-terre* while it was in hand that I came to Lympne. I reckoned myself lucky in getting that little bungalow. I got it on a three years' agreement. I put in a few sticks of furniture, and while the play was in hand I did my own cooking. My cooking would have shocked Mrs Bond. And yet, you know, it had flavour. I had a coffeepot, a saucepan for eggs, and one for potatoes, and a frying-pan for sausages and bacon – such was the simple apparatus of my comfort. One cannot always be magnificent, but simplicity is always a possible alternative. For the rest I laid in an eighteen gallon cask of beer on credit, and a trustful baker came each day. It was not, perhaps, in the style of Sybaris, but I have had worse times. I was a little sorry for the baker, who was a very decent man indeed, but even for him I hoped.

Certainly if anyone wants solitude, the place is Lympne. It is in the clay part of Kent, and my bungalow stood on the edge of an old sea cliff and stared across the flats of Romney Marsh at the sea. In very wet weather the place is almost inaccessible, and I have heard that at times the postman used to traverse the more succulent portions of his route with boards upon his feet. I never saw him doing so, but I can quite imagine it. Outside the doors of the few cottages and houses that make up the present village big birch besoms are stuck, to wipe off the worst of the clay, which will give some idea of the texture of the district. I doubt if the place would be there at all, if it were not a fading memory of things gone for ever. It was the big port of England in Roman times, Portus Lemanus, and now the sea is four miles away. All down the steep hill are boulders and masses of Roman brickwork, and from it old Watling Street, still paved in places, starts like an arrow to the north. I used to stand on the hill and think of it all, the galleys and legions, the captives and officials, the women and traders, the speculators like myself, all the swarm and tumult that came clanking in and out of the harbour. And now just a few lumps of rubble on a grassy slope, and a sheep or two – and me! And where the port had been were the levels of the marsh, sweeping round in a broad curve to distant Dungeness, and dotted here and there with tree clumps and the church towers of old mediaeval towns that are following Lemanus now towards extinction.

That outlook on the marsh was, indeed, one of the finest views I have ever seen. I suppose Dungeness was fifteen miles away; it lay like a raft on the sea, and farther westward were the hills by Hastings under the setting sun. Sometimes they hung close and clear, sometimes they were faded and low, and often the drift of the weather took them clean out of sight. And all the nearer parts of the marsh were laced and lit by ditches and canals.

The window at which I worked looked over the skyline of this crest, and it was from this window that I first set eyes on Cavor. It was just as I was struggling with my scenario, holding down my mind to the sheer hard work of it, and naturally enough he arrested my attention.

The sun had set, the sky was a vivid tranquillity of green and yellow, and against that he came out black – the oddest little figure.

He was a short, round-bodied, thin-legged little man, with a jerky quality in his motions; he had seen fit to clothe his extraordinary mind in a cricket cap, an overcoat, and cycling knickerbockers and stockings. Why he did so I do not know, for he never cycled and he never played cricket. It was a fortuitous concurrence of garments, arising I know not how. He gesticulated with his hands and arms, and jerked his head about and *buzzed*. He buzzed like something electric. You never heard such buzzing. And ever and again he cleared his throat with a most extraordinary noise.

There had been rain, and that spasmodic walk of his was enhanced by the extreme slipperiness of the footpath. Exactly as he came against the sun he stopped, pulled out a watch, hesitated. Then with a sort of convulsive gesture he turned and retreated with every manifestation of haste, no longer gesticulating, but going with ample strides that showed the relatively large size of his feet – they were, I remember, grotesquely exaggerated in size by adhesive clay – to the best possible advantage.

This occurred on the first day of my sojourn, when my play-writing energy was at its height and I regarded the incident simply as an annoying distraction – the waste of five minutes. I returned to my scenario. But when next evening the apparition was repeated with remarkable precision, and again the next evening, and indeed every evening when rain was not falling, concentration upon the scenario became a considerable effort. 'Confound the man,' I said, 'one would think he was learning to be a marionette!' and for several evenings I cursed him pretty heartily.

Then my annoyance gave way to amazement and curiosity. Why on earth should a man do this thing? On the fourteenth evening I could stand it no longer, and so soon as he appeared I opened the french window, crossed the verandah, and directed myself to the point where he invariably stopped.

He had his watch out as I came up to him. He had a chubby, rubicund face with reddish brown eyes – previously I had seen him only against the light. 'One moment, sir,' said I as he turned.

He stared. 'One moment,' he said, 'certainly. Or if you wish to speak to me for longer, and it is not asking too much – your moment is up – would it trouble you to accompany me?'

'Not in the least,' said I, placing myself beside him.

'My habits are regular. My time for intercourse – limited.'

'This, I presume, is your time for exercise?'

'It is. I come here to enjoy the sunset.'

'You don't.'

'Sir?'

'You never look at it.'

'Never look at it?'

'No. I've watched you thirteen nights, and not once have you looked at the sunset – not once.'

He knitted his brows like one who encounters a problem.

'Well, I enjoy the sunlight – the atmosphere – I go along this path, through that gate' – he jerked his head over his shoulder – 'and round – '

'You don't. You never have been. It's all nonsense. There isn't a way. Tonight for instance – '

'Oh! tonight! Let me see. Ah! I just glanced at my watch, saw that I had already been out just three minutes over the precise half-hour, decided there was not time to go round, turned – '

'You always do.'

He looked at me – reflected. 'Perhaps I do, now I come to think of it. But what was it you wanted to speak to me about?'

'Why, this!'

'This?'

'Yes. Why do you do it? Every night you come making a noise – '

'Making a noise?'

'Like this' – I imitated his buzzing noise.

He looked at me, and it was evident the buzzing awakened distaste. 'Do I do *that*?' he asked.

'Every blessed evening.'

'I had no idea.'

He stopped dead. He regarded me gravely. 'Can it be,' he said, 'that I have formed a Habit?'

'Well, it looks like it. Doesn't it?'

He pulled down his lower lip between finger and thumb. He regarded a puddle at his feet.

'My mind is much occupied,' he said. 'And you want to know *why*! Well, sir, I can assure you that not only do I not know why I do these things, but I did not even know I did them. Come to think, it is just as you say; I never *have* been beyond that field . . . And these things annoy you?'

For some reason I was beginning to relent towards him. 'Not *annoy*,' I said. 'But – imagine yourself writing a play!'

'I couldn't.'

'Well, anything that needs concentration.'

'Ah!' he said, 'of course,' and meditated. His expression became so eloquent of distress, that I relented still more. After all, there is a touch of aggression in demanding of a man you don't know why he hums on a public footpath.

'You see,' he said weakly, 'it's a habit.'

'Oh, I recognise that.'

'I must stop it.'

'But not if it puts you out. After all, I had no business – it's something of a liberty.'

'Not at all, sir,' he said, 'not at all. I am greatly indebted to you. I should guard myself against these things. In future I will. Could I trouble you – once again? That noise?'

'Something like this,' I said. 'Zuzzoo, zuzzoo. But really, you know – '

'I am greatly obliged to you. In fact, I know I am getting absurdly absent-minded. You are quite justified, sir – perfectly justified. Indeed, I am indebted to you. The thing shall end. And now, sir, I have already brought you farther than I should have done.'

'I do hope my impertinence – '

'Not at all, sir, not at all.'

We regarded each other for a moment. I raised my hat and wished him a good evening. He responded convulsively, and so we went our ways.

At the stile I looked back at his receding figure. His bearing had changed remarkably, he seemed limp, shrunken. The contrast with his former gesticulating, zuzzoing self took me in some absurd way as pathetic. I watched him out of sight. Then wishing very heartily I had kept to my own business, I returned to my bungalow and my play.

The next evening I saw nothing of him, nor the next. But he was very much in my mind, and it had occurred to me that as a sentimental comic character he might serve a useful purpose in the development of my plot.

The third day he called upon me.

For a time I was puzzled to think what had brought him. He made indifferent conversation in the most formal way, then abruptly he came to business. He wanted to buy me out of my bungalow.

'You see,' he said, 'I don't blame you in the least, but you've destroyed a habit, and it disorganises my day. I've walked past here for years – years. No doubt I've hummed . . . You've made all that impossible!'

I suggested he might try some other direction.

'No. There is no other direction. This is the only one. I've enquired. And now – every afternoon at four – I come to a dead wall.'

'But, my dear sir, if the thing is so important to you . . . '

'It's vital. You see, I'm – I'm an investigator – I am engaged in a scientific research. I live – ' he paused and seemed to think. 'Just over there,' he said, and pointed suddenly dangerously near my eye. 'The house with white chimneys you see just over the trees. And my circumstances are abnormal – abnormal. I am on the point of completing one of the most important – demonstrations – I can assure you one of *the most important* demonstrations that have ever been made. It requires constant thought, constant mental ease and activity. And the afternoon was my brightest time! – effervescing with new ideas – new points of view.'

'But why not come by still?'

'It would be all different. I should be self-conscious. I should think of you at your play – watching me irritated – instead of thinking of my work. No! I must have the bungalow.'

I meditated. Naturally, I wanted to think the matter over thoroughly before anything decisive was said. I was generally ready enough for business in those days, and selling always attracted me; but in the first place it was not my bungalow, and even if I sold it to him at a good price I might get inconvenienced in the delivery of goods if the current owner got wind of the transaction, and in the second I was, well – undischarged. It was clearly a business that required delicate handling. Moreover, the possibility of his being in pursuit of some valuable invention also interested me. It occurred to me that I would like to know more of this research, not with any dishonest intention, but simply with an idea that to know what it was would be a relief from play-writing. I threw out feelers.

He was quite willing to supply information. Indeed, once he was fairly under way the conversation became a monologue. He talked like a man long pent up, who has had it over with himself again and again. He talked for nearly an hour, and I must confess I found it a pretty stiff bit of listening. But through it all there was the undertone of satisfaction one feels when one is neglecting work one has set oneself. During that first interview I gathered very little of the drift of his work. Half his words were technicalities entirely strange to me, and he illustrated one or two points with what he was pleased to call elementary mathematics, computing on an envelope with a copying-ink pencil, in a manner that made it hard even to seem to understand. 'Yes,' I said, 'yes. Go on!' Nevertheless I made out enough to convince me that he was no mere crank playing at discoveries. In spite of his crank-like appearance there was a force about him that made that impossible. Whatever it was, it was a thing with mechanical possibilities. He told me of a work-shed he had, and of three assistants – originally jobbing carpenters – whom he had trained. Now, from the work-shed to the patent office is clearly only one step. He invited me to see those things. I accepted readily, and took care, by a remark or so, to underline that. The proposed transfer of the bungalow remained very conveniently in suspense.

At last he rose to depart, with an apology for the length of his call. Talking over his work was, he said, a pleasure enjoyed only too rarely. It was not often he found such an intelligent listener as myself, he mingled very little with professional scientific men.

'So much pettiness,' he explained; 'so much intrigue! And really, when one has an idea – a novel, fertilising idea – I don't want to be uncharitable, but – '

I am a man who believes in impulses. I made what was perhaps a rash proposition. But you must remember, that I had been alone, play-writing in

Lympne, for fourteen days, and my compunction for his ruined walk still hung about me. 'Why not,' said I, 'make this your new habit? In the place of the one I spoilt? At least, until we can settle about the bungalow. What you want is to turn over your work in your mind. That you have always done during your afternoon walk. Unfortunately that's over – you can't get things back as they were. But why not come and talk about your work to me; use me as a sort of wall against which you may throw your thoughts and catch them again? It's certain I don't know enough to steal your ideas myself – and I know no scientific men – '

I stopped. He was considering. Evidently the thing attracted him. 'But I'm afraid I should bore you,' he said.

'You think I'm too dull?'

'Oh, no; but technicalities – '

'Anyhow, you've interested me immensely this afternoon.'

'Of course it *would* be a great help to me. Nothing clears up one's ideas so much as explaining them. Hitherto – '

'My dear sir, say no more.'

'But really can you spare the time?'

'There is no rest like change of occupation,' I said, with profound conviction.

The affair was over. On my verandah steps he turned. 'I am already greatly indebted to you,' he said.

I made an interrogative noise.

'You have completely cured me of that ridiculous habit of humming,' he explained.

I think I said I was glad to be of any service to him, and he turned away.

Immediately the train of thought that our conversation had suggested must have resumed its sway. His arms began to wave in their former fashion. The faint echo of 'zuzzoo' came back to me on the breeze . . .

Well, after all, that was not my affair . . .

He came the next day, and again the next day after that, and delivered two lectures on physics to our mutual satisfaction. He talked with an air of being extremely lucid about the 'ether' and 'tubes of force', and 'gravitational potential', and things like that, and I sat in my other folding-chair and said, 'Yes,' 'Go on,' 'I follow you,' to keep him going. It was tremendously difficult stuff, but I do not think he ever suspected how much I did not understand him. There were moments when I doubted whether I was well employed, but at any rate I was resting from that confounded play. Now and then things gleamed on me clearly for a space, only to vanish just when I thought I had hold of them. Sometimes my attention failed altogether, and I would give it up and sit and stare at him, wondering whether, after all, it would not be better to use him as a central figure in a good farce and let all this other stuff slide. And then, perhaps, I would catch on again for a bit.

At the earliest opportunity I went to see his house. It was large and carelessly furnished; there were no servants other than his three assistants, and his dietary and private life were characterised by a philosophical simplicity. He was a water-drinker, a vegetarian, and all those logical disciplinary things. But the sight of his equipment settled many doubts. It looked like business from cellar to attic – an amazing little place to find in an out-of-the-way village. The ground-floor rooms contained benches and apparatus, the bakehouse and scullery boiler had developed into respectable furnaces, dynamos occupied the cellar, and there was a gasometer in the garden. He showed it to me with all the confiding zest of a man who has been living too much alone. His seclusion was overflowing now in an excess of confidence, and I had the good luck to be the recipient.

The three assistants were creditable specimens of the class of 'handymen' from which they came. Conscientious if unintelligent, strong, civil, and willing. One, Spargus, who did the cooking and all the metal work, had been a sailor; a second, Gibbs, was a joiner; and the third was an ex-jobbing gardener, and now general assistant. They were the merest labourers. All the intelligent work was done by Cavor. Theirs was the darkest ignorance compared even with my muddled impression.

And now, as to the nature of these enquiries. Here, unhappily, comes a grave difficulty. I am no scientific expert, and if I were to attempt to set forth in the highly scientific language of Mr Cavor the aim to which his experiments tended, I am afraid I should confuse not only the reader but myself, and almost certainly I should make some blunder that would bring upon me the mockery of every up-to-date student of mathematical physics in the country. The best thing I can do therefore is, I think, to give my impressions in my own inexact language, without any attempt to wear a garment of knowledge to which I have no claim.

The object of Mr Cavor's search was a substance that should be 'opaque' – he used some other word I have forgotten, but 'opaque' conveys the idea – to 'all forms of radiant energy'. 'Radiant energy', he made me understand, was anything like light or heat, or those Rontgen Rays there was so much talk about a year or so ago, or the electric waves of Marconi, or gravitation. All these things, he said, *radiate* out from centres, and act on bodies at a distance, whence comes the term 'radiant energy'. Now almost all substances are opaque to some form or other of radiant energy. Glass, for example, is transparent to light, but much less so to heat, so that it is useful as a fire-screen; and alum is transparent to light, but blocks heat completely. A solution of iodine in carbon bisulphide, on the other hand, completely blocks light, but is quite transparent to heat. It will hide a fire from you, but permit all its warmth to reach you. Metals are not only opaque to light and heat, but also to electrical energy, which passes through both iodine solution and glass almost as though they were not interposed. And so on.

Now all known substances are 'transparent' to gravitation. You can use

screens of various sorts to cut off the light or heat, or electrical influence of the sun, or the warmth of the earth from anything; you can screen things by sheets of metal from Marconi's rays, but nothing will cut off the gravitational attraction of the sun or the gravitational attraction of the earth. Yet why there should be nothing is hard to say. Cavor did not see why such a substance should not exist, and certainly I could not tell him. I had never thought of such a possibility before. He showed me by calculations on paper, which Lord Kelvin, no doubt, or Professor Lodge, or Professor Karl Pearson, or any of those great scientific people might have understood, but which simply reduced me to a hopeless muddle, that not only was such a substance possible, but that it must satisfy certain conditions. It was an amazing piece of reasoning. Much as it amazed and exercised me at the time, it would be impossible to reproduce it here. 'Yes,' I said to it all, 'yes; go on!' Suffice it for this story that he believed he might be able to manufacture this possible substance opaque to gravitation out of a complicated alloy of metals and something new – a new element, I fancy – called, I believe, *helium*, which was sent to him from London in sealed stone jars. Doubt has been thrown upon this detail, but I am almost certain it was *helium* he had sent him in sealed stone jars. It was certainly something very gaseous and thin. If only I had taken notes . . .

But then, how was I to foresee the necessity of taking notes?

Anyone with the merest germ of an imagination will understand the extraordinary possibilities of such a substance, and will sympathise a little with the emotion I felt as this understanding emerged from the haze of abstruse phrases in which Cavor expressed himself. Comic relief in a play indeed! It was some time before I would believe that I had interpreted him aright, and I was very careful not to ask questions that would have enabled him to gauge the profundity of misunderstanding into which he dropped his daily exposition. But no one reading the story of it here will sympathise fully, because from my barren narrative it will be impossible to gather the strength of my conviction that this astonishing substance was positively going to be made.

I do not recall that I gave my play an hour's consecutive work at any time after my visit to his house. My imagination had other things to do. There seemed no limit to the possibilities of the stuff; whichever way I tried I came on miracles and revolutions. For example, if one wanted to lift a weight, however enormous, one had only to get a sheet of this substance beneath it, and one might lift it with a straw. My first natural impulse was to apply this principle to guns and ironclads, and all the material and methods of war, and from that to shipping, locomotion, building, every conceivable form of human industry. The chance that had brought me into the very birth-chamber of this new time – it was an epoch, no less – was one of those chances that come once in a thousand years. The thing unrolled, it expanded and expanded. Among other things I saw in it my redemption as a

businessman. I saw a parent company, and daughter companies, applications to right of us, applications to left, rings and trusts, privileges, and concessions spreading and spreading, until one vast, stupendous Cavorite company ran and ruled the world.

And I was in it!

I took my line straight away. I knew I was staking everything, but I jumped there and then.

'We're on absolutely the biggest thing that has ever been invented,' I said, and put the accent on 'we'. 'If you want to keep me out of this, you'll have to do it with a gun. I'm coming down to be your fourth labourer tomorrow.'

He seemed surprised at my enthusiasm, but not a bit suspicious or hostile. Rather, he was self-depreciatory.

He looked at me doubtfully. 'But do you really think – ?' he said. 'And your play! How about that play?'

'It's vanished!' I cried. 'My dear sir, don't you see what you've got? Don't you see what you're going to do?'

That was merely a rhetorical turn, but positively, he didn't. At first I could not believe it. He had not had the beginning of the inkling of an idea. This astonishing little man had been working on purely theoretical grounds the whole time; when he said it was 'the most important' research the world had ever seen, he simply meant it squared up so many theories, settled so much that was in doubt; he had troubled no more about the application of the stuff he was going to turn out than if he had been a machine that makes guns. This was a possible substance, and he was going to make it! *V'la tout*, as the Frenchman says.

Beyond that, he was childish; if he made it, it would go down to posterity as Cavorite or Cavorine, and he would be made an FRS, and his portrait given away as a scientific worthy with *Nature*, and things like that. And that was all he saw! He would have dropped this bombshell into the world as though he had discovered a new species of gnat, if it had not happened that I had come along. And there it would have lain and fizzled, like one or two other little things these scientific people have lit and dropped about us.

When I realised this, it was I did the talking, and Cavor who said, 'Go on!' I jumped up. I paced the room, gesticulating like a boy of twenty. I tried to make him understand his duties and responsibilities in the matter – *our* duties and responsibilities in the matter. I assured him we might make wealth enough to work any sort of social revolution we fancied, we might own and order the whole world. I told him of companies and patents, and the case for secret processes. All these things seemed to take him much as his mathematics had taken me. A look of perplexity came into his ruddy little face. He stammered something about indifference to wealth, but I brushed all that aside. He had got to be rich, and it was no good his

stammering. I gave him to understand the sort of man I was, and that I had had very considerable business experience. I did not tell him I was an undischarged bankrupt at the time, because that was temporary, but I think I reconciled my evident poverty with my financial claims. And quite insensibly, in the way such projects grow, the understanding of a Cavorite monopoly grew up between us. He was to make the stuff, and I was to make the boom.

I stuck like a leech to the 'we' – 'you' and 'I' didn't exist for me.

His idea was that the profits I spoke of might go to endow research, but that, of course, was a matter we had to settle later. 'That's all right,' I shouted, 'that's all right.' The great point, as I insisted, was to get the thing done.

'Here is a substance,' I cried, 'no home, no factory, no fortress, no ship can dare to be without – more universally applicable even than a patent medicine. There isn't a solitary aspect of it, not one of its ten thousand possible uses that will not make us rich, Cavor, beyond the dreams of avarice!'

'No!' he said. 'I begin to see. It's extraordinary how one gets new points of view by talking over things!'

'And as it happens you have just talked to the right man!'

'I suppose no one,' he said, 'is absolutely *averse* to enormous wealth. Of course there is one thing – '

He paused. I stood still.

'It is just possible, you know, that we may not be able to make it after all! It may be one of those things that are a theoretical possibility, but a practical absurdity. Or when we make it, there may be some little hitch – !'

'We'll tackle the hitch when it comes,' said I.

CHAPTER TWO

The First Making of Cavorite

But Cavor's fears were groundless, so far as the actual making was concerned. On the 14th of October, 1899, this incredible substance was made!

Oddly enough, it was made at last by accident, when Mr Cavor least expected it. He had fused together a number of metals and certain other things – I wish I knew the particulars now! – and he intended to leave the mixture a week and then allow it to cool slowly. Unless he had miscalculated, the last stage in the combination would occur when the stuff sank to a temperature of 60°F. But it chanced that, unknown to Cavor, dissension had arisen about the furnace tending. Gibbs, who had previously seen to this, had suddenly attempted to shift it to the man who had been a gardener, on the score that coal was soil, being dug, and therefore could not

possibly fall within the province of a joiner; the man who had been a jobbing gardener alleged, however, that coal was a metallic or ore-like substance, let alone that he was cook. But Spargus insisted on Gibbs doing the coaling, seeing that he was a joiner and that coal is notoriously fossil wood. Consequently Gibbs ceased to replenish the furnace, and no one else did so, and Cavor was too much immersed in certain interesting problems concerning a Cavorite flying machine (neglecting the resistance of the air and one or two other points) to perceive that anything was wrong. And the premature birth of his invention took place just as he was coming across the field to my bungalow for our afternoon talk and tea.

I remember the occasion with extreme vividness. The water was boiling, and everything was prepared, and the sound of his 'zuzzoo' had brought me out upon the verandah. His active little figure was black against the autumnal sunset, and to the right the chimneys of his house just rose above a gloriously tinted group of trees. Remoter rose the Wealden Hills, faint and blue, while to the left the hazy marsh spread out spacious and serene. And then –

The chimneys jerked heavenward, smashing into a string of bricks as they rose, and the roof and a miscellany of furniture followed. Then overtaking them came a huge white flame. The trees about the building swayed and whirled and tore themselves to pieces, that sprang towards the flare. My ears were smitten with a clap of thunder that left me deaf on one side for life, and all about me windows smashed, unheeded.

I took three steps from the verandah towards Cavor's house, and even as I did so came the wind.

Instantly my coat tails were over my head, and I was progressing in great leaps and bounds, and quite against my will, towards him. In the same moment the discoverer was seized, whirled about, and flew through the screaming air. I saw one of my chimney pots hit the ground within six yards of me, leap a score of feet, and so hurry in great strides towards the focus of the disturbance. Cavor, kicking and flapping, came down again, rolled over and over on the ground for a space, struggled up and was lifted and borne forward at an enormous velocity, vanishing at last among the labouring, lashing trees that writhed about his house.

A mass of smoke and ashes, and a square of bluish shining substance rushed up towards the zenith. A large fragment of fencing came sailing past me, dropped edgeways, hit the ground and fell flat, and then the worst was over. The aerial commotion fell swiftly until it was a mere strong gale, and I became once more aware that I had breath and feet. By leaning back against the wind I managed to stop, and could collect such wits as still remained to me.

In that instant the whole face of the world had changed. The tranquil sunset had vanished, the sky was dark with scurrying clouds, everything was flattened and swaying with the gale. I glanced back to see if my bungalow

was still in a general way standing, then staggered forwards towards the trees among which Cavor had vanished, and through whose tall and leaf-denuded branches shone the flames of his burning house.

I entered the copse, dashing from one tree to another and clinging to them, and for a space I sought him in vain. Then amidst a heap of smashed branches and fencing that had banked itself against a portion of his garden wall I perceived something stir. I made a run for this, but before I reached it a brown object separated itself, rose on two muddy legs, and protruded two drooping, bleeding hands. Some tattered ends of garment fluttered out from its middle portion and streamed before the wind.

For a moment I did not recognise this earthy lump, and then I saw that it was Cavor, caked in the mud in which he had rolled. He leant forward against the wind, rubbing the dirt from his eyes and mouth.

He extended a muddy lump of hand, and staggered a pace towards me. His face worked with emotion, little lumps of mud kept falling from it. He looked as damaged and pitiful as any living creature I have ever seen, and his remark therefore amazed me exceedingly. 'Gratulate me,' he gasped; 'gratulate me!'

'Congratulate you! said I. 'Good heavens! What for?'

'I've done it.'

'You *have*. What on earth caused that explosion?'

A gust of wind blew his words away. I understood him to say that it wasn't an explosion at all. The wind hurled me into collision with him, and we stood clinging to one another.

'Try and get back to my bungalow,' I bawled in his ear. He did not hear me, and shouted something about 'three martyrs – science', and also something about 'not much good'. At the time he laboured under the impression that his three attendants had perished in the whirlwind. Happily this was incorrect. Directly he had left for my bungalow they had gone. Off to the public-house in Lympne to discuss the question of the furnaces over some trivial refreshment.

I repeated my suggestion of getting back to my bungalow, and this time he understood. We clung arm-in-arm and started, and managed at last to reach the shelter of as much roof as was left to me. For a space we sat in armchairs and panted. All the windows were broken, and the lighter articles of furniture were in great disorder, but no irrevocable damage was done. Happily the kitchen door had stood the pressure upon it, so that all my crockery and cooking materials had survived. The oil stove was still burning, and I put on the water to boil again for tea. And that prepared, I could turn on Cavor for his explanation.

'Quite correct,' he insisted; 'quite correct. I've done it, and it's all right.'

'But', I protested. 'All right! Why, there can't be a rick standing, or a fence or a thatched roof undamaged for twenty miles round . . . '

'It's all right – *really*. I didn't, of course, foresee this little upset. My mind

was preoccupied with another problem, and I'm apt to disregard these practical side issues. But it's all right – '

'My dear sir,' I cried, 'don't you see you've done thousands of pounds' worth of damage?'

'There, I throw myself on your discretion. I'm not a practical man, of course, but don't you think they will regard it as a cyclone?'

'But the explosion – '

'It was not an explosion. It's perfectly simple. Only, as I say, I'm apt to overlook these little things. Its that zuzzoo business on a larger scale. Inadvertently I made this substance of mine, this Cavorite, in a thin, wide sheet . . . '

He paused. 'You are quite clear that the stuff is opaque to gravitation, that it cuts off things from gravitating towards each other?'

'Yes,' said I. 'Yes.'

'Well, so soon as it reached a temperature of 60°F, and the process of its manufacture was complete, the air above it, the portions of roof and ceiling and floor above it ceased to have weight. I suppose you know – everybody knows nowadays – that, as a usual thing, the air has weight, that it presses on everything at the surface of the earth, presses in all directions, with a pressure of fourteen and a half pounds to the square inch?'

'I know that,' said I. 'Go on.'

'I know that too,' he remarked. 'Only this shows you how useless knowledge is unless you apply it. You see, over our Cavorite this ceased to be the case, the air there ceased to exert any pressure, and the air round it and not over the Cavorite was exerting a pressure of fourteen pounds and a half to the square in upon this suddenly weightless air. Ah! you begin to see! The air all about the Cavorite crushed in upon the air above it with irresistible force. The air above the Cavorite was forced upward violently, the air that rushed in to replace it immediately lost weight, ceased to exert any pressure, followed suit, blew the ceiling through and the roof off . . .

'You perceive,' he said, 'it formed a sort of atmospheric fountain, a kind of chimney in the atmosphere. And if the Cavorite itself hadn't been loose and so got sucked up the chimney, does it occur to you what would have happened?'

I thought. 'I suppose,' I said, 'the air would be rushing up and up over that infernal piece of stuff now.'

'Precisely,' he said. 'A huge fountain – '

'Spouting into space! Good heavens! Why, it would have squirted all the atmosphere of the earth away! It would have robbed the world of air! It would have been the death of all mankind! That little lump of stuff!'

'Not exactly into space,' said Cavor, 'but as bad – practically. It would have whipped the air off the world as one peels a banana, and flung it thousands of miles. It would have dropped back again, of course – but on an asphyxiated world! From our point of view very little better than if it never came back!'

I stared. As yet I was too amazed to realise how all my expectations had been upset. 'What do you mean to do now?' I asked.

'In the first place, if I may borrow a garden trowel I will remove some of this earth with which I am encased, and then if I may avail myself of your domestic conveniences I will have a bath. This done, we will converse more at leisure. It will be wise, I think' – he laid a muddy hand on my arm – 'if nothing were said of this affair beyond ourselves. I know I have caused great damage – probably even dwelling-houses may be ruined here and there upon the countryside. But on the other hand, I cannot possibly pay for the damage I have done, and if the real cause of this is published, it will lead only to heartburning and the obstruction of my work. One cannot foresee *everything*, you know, and I cannot consent for one moment to add the burthen of practical considerations to my theorising. Later on, when you have come in with your practical mind, and Cavorite is floated – floated is the word, isn't it? – and it has realised all you anticipate for it, we may set matters right with these persons. But not now – not now. If no other explanation is offered, people, in the present unsatisfactory state of meteorological science, will ascribe all this to a cyclone; there might be a public subscription, and as my house has collapsed and been burnt, I should in that case receive a considerable share in the compensation, which would be extremely helpful to the prosecution of our researches. But if it is known that *I* caused this, there will be no public subscription, and everybody will be put out. Practically I should never get a chance of working in peace again. My three assistants may or may not have perished. That is a detail. If they have, it is no great loss; they were more zealous than able, and this premature event must be largely due to their joint neglect of the furnace. If they have not perished, I doubt if they have the intelligence to explain the affair. They will accept the cyclone story. And if during the temporary unfitness of my house for occupation, I may lodge in one of the untenanted rooms of this bungalow of yours – '

He paused and regarded me.

A man of such possibilities, I reflected, is no ordinary guest to entertain.

'Perhaps,' said I, rising to my feet, 'we had better begin by looking for a trowel,' and I led the way to the scattered vestiges of the greenhouse.

And while he was having his bath I considered the entire question alone. It was clear there were drawbacks to Mr Cavor's society I had not foreseen. The absent-mindedness that had just escaped depopulating the terrestrial globe, might at any moment result in some other grave inconvenience. On the other hand I was young, my affairs were in a mess, and I was in just the mood for reckless adventure – with a chance of something good at the end of it. I had quite settled in my mind that I was to have half at least in that aspect of the affair. Fortunately I held my bungalow, as I have already explained, on a three-year agreement, without being responsible for repairs; and my furniture, such as there was of it, had been hastily purchased, was

unpaid for, insured, and altogether devoid of associations. In the end I decided to keep on with him, and see the business through.

Certainly the aspect of things had changed very greatly. I no longer doubted at all the enormous possibilities of the substance, but I began to have doubts about the gun-carriage and the patent boots.

We set to work at once to reconstruct his laboratory and proceed with our experiments. Cavor talked more on my level than he had ever done before, when it came to the question of how we should make the stuff next.

'Of course we must make it again,' he said, with a sort of glee I had not expected in him, 'of course we must make it again. We have caught a Tartar, perhaps, but we have left the theoretical behind us for good and all. If we can possibly avoid wrecking this little planet of ours, we will. But – there *must* be risks! There must be. In experimental work there always are. And here, as a practical man, *you* must come in. For my own part it seems to me we might make it edgeways, perhaps, and very thin. Yet I don't know. I have a certain dim perception of another method. I can hardly explain it yet. But curiously enough it came into my mind, while I was rolling over and over in the mud before the wind, and very doubtful how the whole adventure was to end, as being absolutely the thing I ought to have done.'

Even with my aid we found some little difficulty, and meanwhile we kept at work restoring the laboratory. There was plenty to do before it became absolutely necessary to decide upon the precise form and method of our second attempt. Our only hitch was the strike of the three labourers, who objected to my activity as a foreman. But that matter we compromised after two days' delay.

CHAPTER THREE

The Building of the Sphere

I remember the occasion very distinctly when Cavor told me of his idea of the sphere. He had had intimations of it before, but at the time it seemed to come to him in a rush. We were returning to the bungalow for tea, and on the way he fell humming. Suddenly he shouted, 'That's it! That finishes it! A sort of roller blind!'

'Finishes what?' I asked.

'Space – anywhere! The moon.'

'What do you mean?'

'Mean? Why – it must be a sphere! That's what I mean!'

I saw I was out of it, and for a time I let him talk in his own fashion. I hadn't the ghost of an idea then of his drift. But after he had taken tea he made it clear to me.

'It's like this,' he said. 'Last time I ran this stuff that cuts things off from gravitation into a flat tank with an overlap that held it down. And directly it had cooled and the manufacture was completed all that uproar happened, nothing above it weighed anything, the air went squirting up, the house squirted up, and if the stuff itself hadn't squirted up too, I don't know what would have happened! But suppose the substance is loose, and quite free to go up?'

'It will go up at once!'

'Exactly. With no more disturbance than firing a big gun.'

'But what good will that do?'

'I'm going up with it!'

I put down my teacup and stared at him.

'Imagine a sphere,' he explained, 'large enough to hold two people and their luggage. It will be made of steel lined with thick glass; it will contain a proper store of solidified air, concentrated food, water distilling apparatus, and so forth. And enamelled, as it were, on the outer steel – '

'Cavorite?'

'Yes.'

'But how will you get inside?'

'There was a similar problem about a dumpling.'

'Yes, I know. But how?'

'That's perfectly easy. An air-tight manhole is all that is needed. That, of course, will have to be a little complicated; there will have to be a valve, so that things may be thrown out, if necessary, without much loss of air.'

'Like Jules Verne's thing in *A Trip to the Moon*.'

But Cavor was not a reader of fiction.

'I begin to see,' I said slowly. 'And you could get in and screw yourself up while the Cavorite was warm, and as soon as it cooled it would become impervious to gravitation, and off you would fly – '

'At a tangent.'

'You would go off in a straight line – ' I stopped abruptly. 'What is to prevent the thing travelling in a straight line into space for ever?' I asked. 'You're not safe to get anywhere, and if you do – how will you get back?'

'I've just thought of that,' said Cavor. 'That's what I meant when I said the thing is finished. The inner glass sphere can be air-tight, and, except for the manhole, continuous, and the steel sphere can be made in sections, each section capable of rolling up after the fashion of a roller blind. These can easily be worked by springs, and released and checked by electricity conveyed by platinum wires fused through the glass. All that is merely a question of detail. So you see, that except for the thickness of the blind rollers, the Cavorite exterior of the sphere will consist of windows or blinds, whichever you like to call them. Well, when all these windows or blinds are shut, no light, no heat, no gravitation, no radiant energy of any sort will get at the inside of the sphere, it will fly on through space in a straight line, as

you say. But open a window, imagine one of the windows open. Then at once any heavy body that chances to be in that direction will attract us – '

I sat taking it in.

'You see?' he said.

'Oh, I *see*.'

'Practically we shall be able to tack about in space just as we wish. Get attracted by this and that.'

'Oh, yes. *That's* clear enough. Only – '

'Well?'

'I don't quite see what we shall do it for! It's really only jumping off the world and back again.'

'Surely! For example, one might go to the moon.'

'And when one got there? What would you find?'

'We should see – Oh! consider the new knowledge.'

'Is there air there?'

'There may be.'

'It's a fine idea,' I said, 'but it strikes me as a large order all the same. The moon! I'd much rather try some smaller things first.'

'They're out of the question, because of the air difficulty.'

'Why not apply that idea of spring blinds – Cavorite blinds in strong steel cases – to lifting weights?'

'It wouldn't work,' he insisted. 'After all, to go into outer space is not so much worse, if at all, than a polar expedition. Men go on polar expeditions.'

'Not businessmen. And besides, they get paid for polar expeditions. And if anything goes wrong there are relief parties. But this – it's just firing ourselves off the world for nothing.'

'Call it prospecting.'

'You'll have to call it that . . . One might make a book of it perhaps,' I said.

'I have no doubt there will be minerals,' said Cavor.

'For example?'

'Oh! sulphur, ores, gold perhaps, possibly new elements.'

'Cost of carriage,' I said. 'You know you're not a practical man. The moon's a quarter of a million miles away.'

'It seems to me it wouldn't cost much to cart any weight anywhere if you packed it in a Cavorite case.'

I had not thought of that. 'Delivered free on head of purchaser, eh?'

'It isn't as though we were confined to the moon.'

'You mean?'

'There's Mars – clear atmosphere, novel surroundings, exhilarating sense of lightness. It might be pleasant to go there.'

'Is there air on Mars?'

'Oh, yes!'

'Seems as though you might run it as a sanatorium. By the way, how far is Mars?'

'Two hundred million miles at present,' said Cavor airily; 'and you go close by the sun.'

My imagination was picking itself up again. 'After all,' I said, 'there's something in these things. There's travel – '

An extraordinary possibility came rushing into my mind. Suddenly I saw, as in a vision, the whole solar system threaded with Cavorite liners and spheres *de luxe*. 'Rights of pre-emption', came floating into my head – planetary rights of pre-emption. I recalled the old Spanish monopoly in American gold. It wasn't as though it was just this planet or that – it was all of them. I stared at Cavor's rubicund face, and suddenly my imagination was leaping and dancing. I stood up, I walked up and down; my tongue was unloosened.

'I'm beginning to take it in,' I said; 'I'm beginning to take it in.' The transition from doubt to enthusiasm seemed to take scarcely any time at all. 'But this is tremendous!' I cried. 'This is Imperial! I haven't been dreaming of this sort of thing.'

Once the chill of my opposition was removed, his own pent-up excitement had play. He too got up and paced. He too gesticulated and shouted. We behaved like men inspired. We *were* men inspired.

'We'll settle all that!' he said in answer to some incidental difficulty that had pulled me up. 'We'll soon settle that! We'll start the drawings for mouldings this very night.'

'We'll start them now,' I responded, and we hurried off to the laboratory to begin upon this work forthwith.

I was like a child in Wonderland all that night. The dawn found us both still at work – we kept our electric light going heedless of the day. I remember now exactly how these drawings looked. I shaded and tinted while Cavor drew – smudged and haste-marked they were in every line, but wonderfully correct. We got out the orders for the steel blinds and frames we needed from that night's work, and the glass sphere was designed within a week. We gave up our afternoon conversations and our old routine altogether. We worked, and we slept and ate when we could work no longer for hunger and fatigue. Our enthusiasm infected even our three men, though they had no idea what the sphere was for. Through those days the man Gibbs gave up walking, and went everywhere, even across the room, at a sort of fussy run.

And it grew – the sphere. December passed, January – I spent a day with a broom sweeping a path through the snow from bungalow to laboratory – February, March. By the end of March the completion was in sight. In January had come a team of horses, a huge packing-case; we had our thick glass sphere now ready, and in position under the crane we had rigged to sling it into the steel shell. All the bars and blinds of the steel shell – it was not really a spherical shell, but polyhedral, with a roller blind to each facet – had arrived by February, and the lower half was bolted together. The

Cavorite was half made by March, the metallic paste had gone through two of the stages in its manufacture, and we had plastered quite half of it on to the steel bars and blinds. It was astonishing how closely we kept to the lines of Cavor's first inspiration in working out the scheme. When the bolting together of the sphere was finished, he proposed to remove the rough roof of the temporary laboratory in which the work was done, and build a furnace about it. So the last stage of Cavorite making, in which the paste is heated to a dull red glow in a stream of helium, would be accomplished when it was already on the sphere.

And then we had to discuss and decide what provisions we were to take – compressed foods, concentrated essences, steel cylinders containing reserve oxygen, an arrangement for removing carbonic acid and waste from the air and restoring oxygen by means of sodium peroxide, water condensers, and so forth. I remember the little heap they made in the corner – tins, and rolls, and boxes – convincingly matter-of-fact.

It was a strenuous time, with little chance of thinking. But one day, when we were drawing near the end, an odd mood came over me. I had been bricking up the furnace all the morning, and I sat down by these possessions dead beat. Everything seemed dull and incredible.

'But look here, Cavor,' I said. 'After all! What's it all for?'

He smiled. 'The thing now is to go.'

'The moon,' I reflected. 'But what do you expect? I thought the moon was a dead world.'

He shrugged his shoulders.

'We're going to see.'

'*Are* we?' I said, and stared before me.

'You are tired,' he remarked. 'You'd better take a walk this afternoon.'

'No,' I said obstinately; 'I'm going to finish this brickwork.'

And I did, and ensured myself a night of insomnia.

I don't think I have ever had such a night. I had some bad times before my business collapse, but the very worst of those was sweet slumber compared to this infinity of aching wakefulness. I was suddenly in the most enormous funk at the thing we were going to do.

I do not remember before that night thinking at all of the risks we were running. Now they came like that array of spectres that once beleaguered Prague, and camped around me. The strangeness of what we were about to do, the unearthliness of it, overwhelmed me. I was like a man awakened out of pleasant dreams to the most horrible surroundings. I lay, eyes wide open, and the sphere seemed to get more flimsy and feeble, and Cavor more unreal and fantastic, and the whole enterprise madder and madder every moment.

I got out of bed and wandered about. I sat at the window and stared at the immensity of space. Between the stars was the void, the unfathomable darkness! I tried to recall the fragmentary knowledge of astronomy I had

gained in my irregular reading, but it was all too vague to furnish any idea of the things we might expect. At last I got back to bed and snatched some moments of sleep – moments of nightmare rather – in which I fell and fell and fell for evermore into the abyss of the sky.

I astonished Cavor at breakfast. I told him shortly, 'I'm not coming with you in the sphere.'

I met all his protests with a sullen persistence. 'The thing's too mad,' I said, 'and I won't come. The thing's too mad.'

I would not go with him to the laboratory. I fretted about my bungalow for a time, and then took hat and stick and set out alone, I knew not whither. It chanced to be a glorious morning: a warm wind and deep blue sky, the first green of spring abroad, and multitudes of birds singing. I lunched on beef and beer in a little public-house near Elham, and startled the landlord by remarking apropos of the weather, 'A man who leaves the world when days of this sort are about is a fool!'

'That's what I says when I heerd on it!' said the landlord, and I found that for one poor soul at least this world had proved excessive, and there had been a throat-cutting. I went on with a new twist to my thoughts.

In the afternoon I had a pleasant sleep in a sunny place, and went on my way refreshed. I came to a comfortable-looking inn near Canterbury. It was bright with creepers, and the landlady was a clean old woman and took my eye. I found I had just enough money to pay for my lodging with her. I decided to stop the night there. She was a talkative body, and among many other particulars learnt she had never been to London. 'Canterbury's as far as ever I been,' she said. 'I'm not one of your gad-about sort.'

'How would you like a trip to the moon?' I cried.

'I never did hold with them ballooneys,' she said, evidently under the impression that this was a common excursion enough. 'I wouldn't go up in one – not for ever so.'

This struck me as being funny. After I had supped I sat on a bench by the door of the inn and gossiped with two labourers about brick-making, and motor cars, and the cricket of last year. And in the sky a faint new crescent, blue and vague as a distant Alp, sank westward over the sun.

The next day I returned to Cavor. 'I am coming,' I said. 'I've been a little out of order, that's all.'

That was the only time I felt any serious doubt of our enterprise. Nerves purely! After that I worked a little more carefully, and took a trudge for an hour every day. And at last, save for the heating in the furnace, our labours were at an end.

CHAPTER FOUR

Inside the Sphere

'Go on,' said Cavor, as I sat across the edge of the manhole, and looked down into the black interior of the sphere. We two were alone. It was evening, the sun had set, and the stillness of the twilight was upon everything.

I drew my other leg inside and slid down the smooth glass to the bottom of the sphere, then turned to take the cans of food and other impedimenta from Cavor. The interior was warm, the thermometer stood at eighty, and as we should lose little or none of this by radiation, we were dressed in shoes and thin flannels. We had, however, a bundle of thick woollen clothing and several thick blankets to guard against mischance. By Cavor's direction I placed the packages, the cylinders of oxygen, and so forth, loosely about my feet, and soon we had everything in. He walked about the roofless shed for a time seeking anything we had overlooked, and then crawled in after me. I noted something in his hand.

'What have you got there?' I asked.

'Haven't you brought anything to read?'

'Good Lord! No.'

'I forgot to tell you. There are uncertainties – The voyage may last – We may be weeks!'

'But – '

'We shall be floating in this sphere with absolutely no occupation.'

'I wish I'd known – '

He peered out of the manhole. 'Look!' he said. 'There's something there!'

'Is there time?'

'We shall be an hour.'

I looked out. It was an old number of *Tit-Bits* that one of the men must have brought. Farther away in the corner I saw a torn *Lloyd's News*. I scrambled back into the sphere with these things. 'What have you got?' I said.

I took the book from his hand and read, *The Works of William Shakespeare*.

He coloured slightly. 'My education has been so purely scientific – ' he said apologetically.

'Never read him?'

'Never.'

'He knew a little, you know – in an irregular sort of way.'

'Precisely what I am told,' said Cavor.

I assisted him to screw in the glass cover of the manhole, and then he pressed a stud to close the corresponding blind in the outer case. The little oblong of twilight vanished. We were in darkness.

For a time neither of us spoke. Although our case would not be impervious to sound, everything was very still. I perceived there was nothing to grip when the shock of our start should come, and I realised that I should be uncomfortable for want of a chair.

'Why have we no chairs?' I asked.

'I've settled all that,' said Cavor. 'We won't need them.'

'Why not?'

'You will see,' he said, in the tone of a man who refuses to talk.

I became silent. Suddenly it had come to me clear and vivid that I was a fool to be inside that sphere. Even now, I asked myself, is it too late to withdraw? The world outside the sphere, I knew, would be cold and inhospitable enough for me – for weeks I had been living on subsidies from Cavor – but after all, would it be as cold as the infinite zero, as inhospitable as empty space? If it had not been for the appearance of cowardice, I believe that even then I should have made him let me out. But I hesitated on that score, and hesitated, and grew fretful and angry, and the time passed.

There came a little jerk, a noise like champagne being uncorked in another room, and a faint whistling sound. For just one instant I had a sense of enormous tension, a transient conviction that my feet were pressing downward with a force of countless tons. It lasted for an infinitesimal time.

But it stirred me to action. 'Cavor!' I said into the darkness, 'my nerve's in rags . . . I don't think – '

I stopped. He made no answer.

'Confound it!' I cried; 'I'm a fool! What business have I here? I'm not coming, Cavor. The thing's too risky. I'm getting out.'

'You can't,' he said.

'Can't! We'll soon see about that!'

He made no answer for ten seconds. 'It's too late for us to quarrel now, Bedford,' he said. 'That little jerk was the start. Already we are flying as swiftly as a bullet up into the gulf of space.'

'I – ' I said, and then it didn't seem to matter what happened. For a time I was, as it were, stunned; I had nothing to say. It was just as if I had never heard of this idea of leaving the world before. Then I perceived an unaccountable change in my bodily sensations. It was a feeling of lightness, of unreality. Coupled with that was a queer sensation in the head, an apoplectic effect almost, and a thumping of blood vessels at the ears. Neither of these feelings diminished as time went on, but at last I got so used to them that I experienced no inconvenience.

I heard a click, and a little glow lamp came into being.

I saw Cavor's face, as white as I felt my own to be. We regarded one

another in silence. The transparent blackness of the glass behind him made him seem as though he floated in a void.

'Well, we're committed,' I said at last.

'Yes,' he said, 'we're committed.'

'Don't move,' he exclaimed, at some suggestion of a gesture. 'Let your muscles keep quite lax – as if you were in bed. We are in a little universe of our own. Look at those things!'

He pointed to the loose cases and bundles that had been lying on the blankets in the bottom of the sphere. I was astonished to see that they were floating now nearly a foot from the spherical wall. Then I saw from his shadow that Cavor was no longer leaning against the glass. I thrust out my hand behind me, and found that I too was suspended in space, clear of the glass.

I did not cry out nor gesticulate, but fear came upon me. It was like being held and lifted by something – you know not what. The mere touch of my hand against the glass moved me rapidly. I understood what had happened, but that did not prevent my being afraid. We were cut off from all exterior gravitation, only the attraction of objects within our sphere had effect. Consequently everything that was not fixed to the glass was falling – slowly because of the slightness of our masses – towards the centre of gravity of our little world, which seemed to be somewhere about the middle of the sphere, but rather nearer to myself than Cavor, on account of my greater weight.

'We must turn round,' said Cavor, 'and float back to back, with the things between us.'

It was the strangest sensation conceivable, floating thus loosely in space, at first indeed horribly strange, and when the horror passed, not disagreeable at all, exceeding restful; indeed, the nearest thing in earthly experience to it that I know is lying on a very thick, soft feather bed. But the quality of utter detachment and independence! I had not reckoned on things like this. I had expected a violent jerk at starting, a giddy sense of speed. Instead I felt – as if I were disembodied. It was not like the beginning of a journey; it was like the beginning of a dream.

CHAPTER FIVE

The Journey to the Moon

Presently Cavor extinguished the light. He said we had not overmuch energy stored, and that what we had we must economise for reading. For a time, whether it was long or short I do not know, there was nothing but blank darkness.

A question floated up out of the void. 'How are we pointing?' I said. 'What is our direction?'

'We are flying away from the earth at a tangent, and as the moon is near her third quarter we are going somewhere towards her. I will open a blind – '

Came a click, and then a window in the outer case yawned open. The sky outside was as black as the darkness within the sphere, but the shape of the open window was marked by an infinite number of stars.

Those who have only seen the starry sky from the earth cannot imagine its appearance when the vague, half-luminous veil of our air has been withdrawn. The stars we see on earth are the mere scattered survivors that penetrate our misty atmosphere. But now at last I could realise the meaning of the hosts of heaven!

Stranger things we were presently to see, but that airless, star-dusted sky! Of all things, I think that will be one of the last I shall forget.

The little window vanished with a click, another beside it snapped open and instantly closed, and then a third, and for a moment I had to close my eyes because of the blinding splendour of the waning moon.

For a space I had to stare at Cavor and the white-lit things about me to season my eyes to light again, before I could turn them towards that pallid glare.

Four windows were open in order that the gravitation of the moon might act upon all the substances in our sphere. I found I was no longer floating freely in space, but that my feet were resting on the glass in the direction of the moon. The blankets and cases of provisions were also creeping slowly down the glass, and presently came to rest so as to block out a portion of the view. It seemed to me, of course, that I looked 'down' when I looked at the moon. On earth 'down' means earthward, the way things fall, and 'up' the reverse direction. Now the pull of gravitation was towards the moon, and for all I knew to the contrary our earth was overhead. And, of course, when all the Cavorite blinds were closed, 'down' was towards the centre of our sphere, and 'up' towards its outer wall.

It was curiously unlike earthly experience, too, to have the light coming *up* to one. On earth light falls from above, or comes slanting down sideways, but here it came from beneath our feet, and to see our shadows we had to look up.

At first it gave me a sort of vertigo to stand only on thick glass and look down upon the moon through hundreds of thousands of miles of vacant space; but this sickness passed very speedily. And then – the splendour of the sight!

The reader may imagine it best if he will lie on the ground some warm summer's night and look between his up-raised feet at the moon, but for some reason, probably because the absence of air made it so much more luminous, the moon seemed already considerably larger than it does from earth. The minutest details of its surface were acutely clear. And since we did not see it through air, its outline was bright and sharp, there was no

glow or halo about it, and the stardust that covered the sky came right to its very margin, and marked the outline of its unilluminated part. And as I stood and stared at the moon between my feet, that perception of the impossible that had been with me off and on ever since our start, returned again with tenfold conviction.

'Cavor,' I said, 'this takes me queerly. Those companies we were going to run, and all that about minerals?'

'Well?'

'I don't see 'em here.'

'No,' said Cavor; 'but you'll get over all that.'

'I suppose I'm made to turn right side up again. Still, *this* – For a moment I could half believe there never was a world.'

'That copy of *Lloyd's News* might help you.'

I stared at the paper for a moment, then held it above the level of my face, and found I could read it quite easily. I struck a column of mean little advertisements. 'A gentleman of private means is willing to lend money,' I read. I knew that gentleman. Then somebody eccentric wanted to sell a Cutaway bicycle, 'quite new and cost 15 pounds', for five pounds; and a lady in distress wished to dispose of some fish knives and forks, 'a wedding present', at a great sacrifice. No doubt some simple soul was sagely examining these knives and forks, and another triumphantly riding off on that bicycle, and a third trustfully consulting that benevolent gentleman of means even as I read. I laughed, and let the paper drift from my hand.

'Are we visible from the earth?' I asked.

'Why?'

'I knew someone who was rather interested in astronomy. It occurred to me that it would be rather odd if – my friend – chanced to be looking through some telescope.'

'It would need the most powerful telescope on earth even now to see us as the minutest speck.'

For a time I stared in silence at the moon.

'It's a world,' I said; 'one feels that infinitely more than one ever did on earth. People perhaps – '

'People!' he exclaimed. '*No!* Banish all that! Think yourself a sort of ultra-arctic voyager exploring the desolate places of space. Look at it!'

He waved his hand at the shining whiteness below. 'It's dead – dead! Vast extinct volcanoes, lava wildernesses, tumbled wastes of snow, or frozen carbonic acid, or frozen air, and everywhere landslip seams and cracks and gulfs. Nothing happens. Men have watched this planet systematically with telescopes for over two hundred years. How much change do you think they have seen?'

'None.'

'They have traced two indisputable landslips, a doubtful crack, and one slight periodic change of colour, and that's all.'

'I didn't know they'd traced even that.'

'Oh, yes. But as for people!'

'By the way,' I asked, 'how small a thing will the biggest telescopes show upon the moon?'

'One could see a fair-sized church. One could certainly see any towns or buildings, or anything like the handiwork of men. There might perhaps be insects, something in the way of ants, for example, so that they could hide in deep burrows from the lunar light, or some new sort of creatures having no earthly parallel. That is the most probable thing, if we are to find life there at all. Think of the difference in conditions! Life must fit itself to a day as long as fourteen earthly days, a cloudless sun-blaze of fourteen days, and then a night of equal length, growing ever colder and colder under these cold, sharp stars. In that night there must be cold, the ultimate cold, absolute zero, 273°C below the earthly freezing point. Whatever life there is must hibernate through *that*, and rise again each day.'

He mused. 'One can imagine something worm-like,' he said, 'taking its air solid as an earthworm swallows earth, or thick-skinned monsters – '

'By the by,' I said, 'why didn't we bring a gun?'

He did not answer that question. 'No,' he concluded, 'we just have to go. We shall see when we get there.'

I remembered something. 'Of course, there's my minerals, anyhow,' I said; 'whatever the conditions may be.'

Presently he told me he wished to alter our course a little by letting the earth tug at us for a moment. He was going to open one earthward blind for thirty seconds. He warned me that it would make my head swim, and advised me to extend my hands against the glass to break my fall. I did as he directed, and thrust my feet against the bales of food cases and air cylinders to prevent their falling upon me. Then with a click the window flew open. I fell clumsily upon hands and face, and saw for a moment between my black extended fingers our mother earth – a planet in a downward sky.

We were still very near – Cavor told me the distance was perhaps eight hundred miles – and the huge terrestrial disc filled all heaven. But already it was plain to see that the world was a globe. The land below us was in twilight and vague, but westward the vast grey stretches of the Atlantic shone like molten silver under the receding day. I think I recognised the cloud-dimmed coastlines of France and Spain and the south of England, and then, with a click, the shutter closed again, and I found myself in a state of extraordinary confusion sliding slowly over the smooth glass.

When at last things settled themselves in my mind again, it seemed quite beyond question that the moon was 'down' and under my feet, and that the earth was somewhere away on the level of the horizon – the earth that had been 'down' to me and my kindred since the beginning of things.

So slight were the exertions required of us, so easy did the practical annihilation of our weight make all we had to do, that the necessity for

taking refreshment did not occur to us for nearly six hours (by Cavor's chronometer) after our start. I was amazed at that lapse of time. Even then I was satisfied with very little. Cavor examined the apparatus for absorbing carbonic acid and water, and pronounced it to be in satisfactory order, our consumption of oxygen having been extraordinarily slight. And our talk being exhausted for the time, and there being nothing further for us to do, we gave way to a curious drowsiness that had come upon us, and spreading our blankets on the bottom of the sphere in such a manner as to shut out most of the moonlight, wished each other good-night, and almost immediately fell asleep.

And so, sleeping, and sometimes talking and reading a little, and at times eating, although without any keenness of appetite,* but for the most part in a sort of quiescence that was neither waking nor slumber, we fell through a space of time that had neither night nor day in it, silently, softly, and swiftly down towards the moon.

CHAPTER SIX

The Landing on the Moon

I remember how one day Cavor suddenly opened six of our shutters and blinded me so that I cried aloud at him. The whole area was moon, a stupendous scimitar of white dawn with its edge hacked out by notches of darkness, the crescent shore of an ebbing tide of darkness, out of which peaks and pinnacles came glittering into the blaze of the sun. I take it the reader has seen pictures or photographs of the moon and that I need not describe the broader features of that landscape, those spacious ringlike ranges vaster than any terrestrial mountains, their summits shining in the day, their shadows harsh and deep, the grey disordered plains, the ridges, hills, and craterlets, all passing at last from a blazing illumination into a common mystery of black. Athwart this world we were flying scarcely a hundred miles above its crests and pinnacles. And now we could see, what no eye on earth will ever see, that under the blaze of the day the harsh outlines of the rocks and ravines of the plains and crater floor grew grey and indistinct under a thickening haze, that the white of their lit surfaces broke into lumps and patches, and broke again and shrank and vanished, and that here and there strange tints of brown and olive grew and spread.

* It is a curious thing, that while we were in the sphere we felt not the slightest desire for food, nor did we feel the want of it when we abstained. At first we forced our appetites, but afterwards we fasted completely. Altogether we did not consume one-hundredth part of the compressed provisions we had brought with us. The amount of carbonic acid we breathed was also unnaturally low, but why this was, I am quite unable to explain.

But little time we had for watching then. For now we had come to the real danger of our journey. We had to drop ever closer to the moon as we spun about it, to slacken our pace and watch our chance, until at last we could dare to drop upon its surface.

For Cavor that was a time of intense exertion; for me it was an anxious inactivity. I seemed perpetually to be getting out of his way. He leapt about the sphere from point to point with an agility that would have been impossible on earth. He was perpetually opening and closing the Cavorite windows, making calculations, consulting his chronometer by means of the glow lamp during those last eventful hours. For a long time we had all our windows closed and hung silently in darkness hurtling through space.

Then he was feeling for the shutter studs, and suddenly four windows were open. I staggered and covered my eyes, drenched and scorched and blinded by the unaccustomed splendour of the sun beneath my feet. Then again the shutters snapped, leaving my brain spinning in a darkness that pressed against the eyes. And after that I floated in another vast, black silence.

Then Cavor switched on the electric light, and told me he proposed to bind all our luggage together with the blankets about it, against the concussion of our descent. We did this with our windows closed, because in that way our goods arranged themselves naturally at the centre of the sphere. That too was a strange business; we two men floating loose in that spherical space, and packing and pulling ropes. Imagine it if you can! No up nor down, and every effort resulting in unexpected movements. Now I would be pressed against the glass with the full force of Cavor's thrust, now I would be kicking helplessly in a void. Now the star of the electric light would be overhead, now under foot. Now Cavor's feet would float up before my eyes, and now we would be crossways to each other. But at last our goods were safely bound together in a big soft bale, all except two blankets with head holes that we were to wrap about ourselves.

Then for a flash Cavor opened a window moonwards, and we saw that we were dropping towards a huge central crater with a number of minor craters grouped in a sort of cross about it. And then again Cavor flung our little sphere open to the scorching, blinding sun. I think he was using the sun's attraction as a brake. 'Cover yourself with a blanket,' he cried, thrusting himself from me, and for a moment I did not understand.

Then I hauled the blanket from beneath my feet and got it about me and over my head and eyes. Abruptly he closed the shutters again, snapped one open again and closed it, then suddenly began snapping them all open, each safely into its steel roller. There came a jar, and then we were rolling over and over, bumping against the glass and against the big bale of our luggage, and clutching at each other, and outside some white substance splashed as if we were rolling down a slope of snow . . .

Over, clutch, bump, clutch, bump, over . . .

Came a thud, and I was half buried under the bale of our possessions, and

for a space everything was still. Then I could hear Cavor puffing and grunting, and the snapping of a shutter in its sash. I made an effort, thrust back our blanket-wrapped luggage, and emerged from beneath it. Our open windows were just visible as a deeper black set with stars.

We were still alive, and we were lying in the darkness of the shadow of the wall of the great crater into which we had fallen.

We sat getting our breath again, and feeling the bruises on our limbs. I don't think either of us had had a very clear expectation of such rough handling as we had received. I struggled painfully to my feet. 'And now,' said I, 'to look at the landscape of the moon! But – ! It's tremendously dark, Cavor!'

The glass was dewy, and as I spoke I wiped at it with my blanket. 'We're half an hour or so beyond the day,' he said. 'We must wait.'

It was impossible to distinguish anything. We might have been in a sphere of steel for all that we could see. My rubbing with the blanket simply smeared the glass, and as fast as I wiped it, it became opaque again with freshly condensed moisture mixed with an increasing quantity of blanket hairs. Of course I ought not to have used the blanket. In my efforts to clear the glass I slipped upon the damp surface, and hurt my shin against one of the oxygen cylinders that protruded from our bale.

The thing was exasperating – it was absurd. Here we were just arrived upon the moon, amidst we knew not what wonders, and all we could see was the grey and streaming wall of the bubble in which we had come.

'Confound it!' I said, 'but at this rate we might have stopped at home;' and I squatted on the bale and shivered, and drew my blanket closer about me.

Abruptly the moisture turned to spangles and fronds of frost. 'Can you reach the electric heater,' said Cavor. 'Yes – that black knob. Or we shall freeze.'

I did not wait to be told twice. 'And now,' said I, what are we to do?'

'Wait,' he said.

'Wait?'

'Of course. We shall have to wait until our air gets warm again, and then this glass will clear. We can't do anything till then. It's night here yet; we must wait for the day to overtake us. Meanwhile, don't you feel hungry?'

For a space I did not answer him, but sat fretting. I turned reluctantly from the smeared puzzle of the glass and stared at his face. 'Yes,' I said, 'I am hungry. I feel somehow enormously disappointed. I had expected – I don't know what I had expected, but not this.'

I summoned my philosophy, and rearranging my blanket about me sat down on the bale again and began my first meal on the moon. I don't think I finished it – I forget. Presently, first in patches, then running rapidly together into wider spaces, came the clearing of the glass, came the drawing of the misty veil that hid the moon world from our eyes.

We peered out upon the landscape of the moon.

CHAPTER SEVEN

Sunrise on the Moon

As we saw it first it was the wildest and most desolate of scenes. We were in an enormous amphitheatre, a vast circular plain; the floor of the giant crater. Its cliff-like walls closed us in on every side. From the westward the light of the unseen sun fell upon them, reaching to the very foot of the cliff, and showed a disordered escarpment of drab and greyish rock, lined here and there with banks and crevices of snow. This was perhaps a dozen miles away, but at first no intervening atmosphere diminished in the slightest the minutely detailed brilliancy with which these things glared at us. They stood out clear and dazzling against a background of starry blackness that seemed to our earthly eyes rather a gloriously spangled velvet curtain than the spaciousness of the sky.

The eastward cliff was at first merely a starless selvedge to the starry dome. No rosy flush, no creeping pallor, announced the commencing day. Only the Corona, the Zodiacal light, a huge cone-shaped, luminous haze, pointing up towards the splendour of the morning star, warned us of the imminent nearness of the sun.

Whatever light was about us was reflected by the westward cliffs. It showed a huge undulating plain, cold and grey, a grey that deepened eastward into the absolute raven darkness of the cliff shadow. Innumerable rounded grey summits, ghostly hummocks, billows of snowy substance, stretching crest beyond crest into the remote obscurity, gave us our first inkling of the distance of the crater wall. These hummocks looked like snow. At the time I thought they were snow. But they were not – they were mounds and masses of frozen air.

So it was at first, and then, sudden, swift, and amazing, came the lunar day.

The sunlight had crept down the cliff, it touched the drifted masses at its base and incontinently came striding with seven-leagued boots towards us. The distant cliff seemed to shift and quiver, and at the touch of the dawn a reek of grey vapour poured upward from the crater floor, whirls and puffs and drifting wraiths of grey, thicker and broader and denser, until at last the whole westward plain was steaming like a wet handkerchief held before the fire, and the westward cliffs were no more than a refracted glare beyond.

'It is air,' said Cavor. 'It must be air – or it would not rise like this – at the mere touch of a sunbeam. And at this pace . . . '

He peered upwards. 'Look!' he said.

'What?' I asked.

'In the sky. Already. On the blackness – a little touch of blue. See! The

stars seem larger. And the little ones and all those dim nebulosities we saw in empty space – they are hidden!'

Swiftly, steadily, the day approached us. Grey summit after grey summit was overtaken by the blaze, and turned to a smoking white intensity. At last there was nothing to the west of us but a bank of surging fog, the tumultuous advance and ascent of cloudy haze. The distant cliff had receded farther and farther, had loomed and changed through the whirl, and foundered and vanished at last in its confusion.

Nearer came that steaming advance, nearer and nearer, coming as fast as the shadow of a cloud before the south-west wind. About us rose a thin anticipatory haze.

Cavor gripped my arm.

'What?' I said.

'Look! The sunrise! The sun!'

He turned me about and pointed to the brow of the eastward cliff, looming above the haze about us, scarce lighter than the darkness of the sky. But now its line was marked by strange reddish shapes, tongues of vermilion flame that writhed and danced. I fancied it must be spirals of vapour that had caught the light and made this crest of fiery tongues against the sky, but indeed it was the solar prominences I saw, a crown of fire about the sun that is forever hidden from earthly eyes by our atmospheric veil.

And then – the sun!

Steadily, inevitably came a brilliant line, came a thin edge of intolerable effulgence that took a circular shape, became a bow, became a blazing sceptre, and hurled a shaft of heat at us as though it was a spear.

It seemed verily to stab my eyes! I cried aloud and turned about blinded, groping for my blanket beneath the bale.

And with that incandescence came a sound, the first sound that had reached us from without since we left the earth, a hissing and rustling, the stormy trailing of the aerial garment of the advancing day. And with the coming of the sound and the light the sphere lurched, and blinded and dazzled we staggered helplessly against each other. It lurched again, and the hissing grew louder. I had shut my eyes perforce, I was making clumsy efforts to cover my head with my blanket, and this second lurch sent me helplessly off my feet. I fell against the bale, and opening my eyes had a momentary glimpse of the air just outside our glass. It was running – it was boiling – like snow into which a white-hot rod is thrust. What had been solid air had suddenly at the touch of the sun become a paste, a mud, a slushy liquefaction, that hissed and bubbled into gas.

There came a still more violent whirl of the sphere and we had clutched one another. In another moment we were spun about again. Round we went and over, and then I was on all fours. The lunar dawn had hold of us. It meant to show us little men what the moon could do with us.

I caught a second glimpse of things without, puffs of vapour, half-liquid

slush, excavated, sliding, falling, sliding. We dropped into darkness. I went down with Cavor's knees in my chest. Then he seemed to fly away from me, and for a moment I lay with all the breath out of my body staring upward. A toppling crag of the melting stuff had splashed over us, buried us, and now it thinned and boiled off us. I saw the bubbles dancing on the glass above. I heard Cavor exclaiming feebly.

Then some huge landslip in the thawing air had caught us, and spluttering expostulation, we began to roll down a slope, rolling faster and faster, leaping crevasses and rebounding from banks, faster and faster, westward into the white-hot boiling tumult of the lunar day.

Clutching at one another we spun about, pitched this way and that, our bale of packages leaping at us, pounding at us. We collided, we gripped, we were torn asunder – our heads met, and the whole universe burst into fiery darts and stars! On the earth we should have smashed one another a dozen times, but on the moon, luckily for us, our weight was only one-sixth of what it is terrestrially, and we fell very mercifully. I recall a sensation of utter sickness, a feeling as if my brain were upside down within my skull, and then –

* * *

Something was at work upon my face, some thin feelers worried my ears. Then I discovered the brilliance of the landscape around was mitigated by blue spectacles. Cavor bent over me, and I saw his face upside down, his eyes also protected by tinted goggles. His breath came irregularly, and his lip was bleeding from a bruise. 'Better?' he said, wiping the blood with the back of his hand.

Everything seemed swaying for a space, but that was simply my giddiness. I perceived that he had closed some of the shutters in the outer sphere to save me from the direct blaze of the sun. I was aware that everything about us was very brilliant.

'Lord! I gasped. 'But this – !'

I craned my neck to see. I perceived there was a blinding glare outside, an utter change from the gloomy darkness of our first impressions. 'Have I been insensible long?' I asked.

'I don't know – the chronometer is broken. Some little time . . . My dear chap! I have been afraid . . . '

I lay for a space taking this in. I saw his face still bore evidences of emotion. For a while I said nothing. I passed an inquisitive hand over my contusions, and surveyed his face for similar damages. The back of my right hand had suffered most, and was skinless and raw. My forehead was bruised and had bled. He handed me a little measure with some of the restorative – I forget the name of it – he had brought with us. After a time I felt a little better. I began to stretch my limbs carefully. Soon I could talk.

'It wouldn't have done,' I said, as though there had been no interval.

'No! it *wouldn't.*'

He thought, his hands hanging over his knees. He peered through the glass and then stared at me.

'Good Lord!' he said. '*No!*'

'What has happened?' I asked after a pause. 'Have we jumped to the tropics?'

'It was as I expected. This air has evaporated – if it is air. At any rate, it has evaporated, and the surface of the moon is showing. We are lying on a bank of earthy rock. Here and there bare soil is exposed. A queer sort of soil!'

It occurred to him that it was unnecessary to explain. He assisted me into a sitting position, and I could see with my own eyes.

CHAPTER EIGHT

A Lunar Morning

The harsh emphasis, the pitiless black and white of scenery had altogether disappeared. The glare of the sun had taken upon itself a faint tinge of amber; the shadows upon the cliff of the crater wall were deeply purple. To the eastward a dark bank of fog still crouched and sheltered from the sunrise, but to the westward the sky was blue and clear. I began to realise the length of my insensibility.

We were no longer in a void. An atmosphere had arisen about us. The outline of things had gained in character, had grown acute and varied; save for a shadowed space of white substance here and there, white substance that was no longer air but snow, the arctic appearance had gone altogether. Everywhere broad rusty brown spaces of bare and tumbled earth spread to the blaze of the sun. Here and there at the edge of the snowdrifts were transient little pools and eddies of water, the only things stirring in that expanse of barrenness. The sunlight inundated the upper two blinds of our sphere and turned our climate to high summer, but our feet were still in shadow, and the sphere was lying upon a drift of snow.

And scattered here and there upon the slope, and emphasised by little white threads of unthawed snow upon their shady sides, were shapes like sticks, dry twisted sticks of the same rusty hue as the rock upon which they lay. That caught one's thoughts sharply. Sticks! On a lifeless world? Then as my eye grew more accustomed to the texture of their substance, I perceived that almost all this surface had a fibrous texture, like the carpet of brown needles one finds beneath the shade of pine trees.

'Cavor!' I said.

'Yes.'

'It may be a dead world now – but once – '

Something arrested my attention. I had discovered among these needles a number of little round objects. And it seemed to me that one of these had moved.

'Cavor,' I whispered.

'What?'

But I did not answer at once. I stared incredulous. For an instant I could not believe my eyes. I gave an inarticulate cry. I gripped his arm. I pointed. 'Look!' I cried, finding my tongue. 'There! Yes! And there!'

His eyes followed my pointing finger. 'Eh?' he said.

How can I describe the thing I saw? It is so petty a thing to state, and yet it seemed so wonderful, so pregnant with emotion. I have said that amidst the stick-like litter were these rounded bodies, these little oval bodies that might have passed as very small pebbles. And now first one and then another had stirred, had rolled over and cracked, and down the crack of each of them showed a minute line of yellowish green, thrusting outward to meet the hot encouragement of the newly risen sun. For a moment that was all, and then there stirred, and burst a third!

'It is a seed,' said Cavor. And then I heard him whisper very softly, '*Life!*'

'Life!' And immediately it poured upon us that our vast journey had not been made in vain, that we had come to no arid waste of minerals, but to a world that lived and moved! We watched intensely. I remember I kept rubbing the glass before me with my sleeve, jealous of the faintest suspicion of mist.

The picture was clear and vivid only in the middle of the field. All about that centre the dead fibres and seeds were magnified and distorted by the curvature of the glass. But we could see enough! One after another all down the sunlit slope these miraculous little brown bodies burst and gaped apart, like seed-pods, like the husks of fruits; opened eager mouths that drank in the heat and light pouring in a cascade from the newly risen sun.

Every moment more of these seed coats ruptured, and even as they did so the swelling pioneers overflowed their rent-distended seed-cases, and passed into the second stage of growth. With a steady assurance, a swift deliberation, these amazing seeds thrust a rootlet downward to the earth and a queer little bundle-like bud into the air. In a little while the whole slope was dotted with minute plantlets standing at attention in the blaze of the sun.

They did not stand for long. The bundle-like buds swelled and strained and opened with a jerk, thrusting out a coronet of little sharp tips, spreading a whorl of tiny, spiky, brownish leaves, that lengthened rapidly, lengthened visibly even as we watched. The movement was slower than any animal's, swifter than any plant's I have ever seen before. How can I suggest it to you – the way that growth went on? The leaf tips grew so that they moved onward even while we looked at them. The brown seed-case shrivelled and was absorbed with an equal rapidity. Have you ever on a cold day taken a

thermometer into your warm hand and watched the little thread of mercury creep up the tube? These moon plants grew like that.

In a few minutes, as it seemed, the buds of the more forward of these plants had lengthened into a stem and were even putting forth a second whorl of leaves, and all the slope that had seemed so recently a lifeless stretch of litter was now dark with the stunted olive-green herbage of bristling spikes that swayed with the vigour of their growing.

I turned about, and behold! along the upper edge of a rock to the eastward a similar fringe in a scarcely less forward condition swayed and bent, dark against the blinding glare of the sun. And beyond this fringe was the silhouette of a plant mass, branching clumsily like a cactus, and swelling visibly, swelling like a bladder that fills with air.

Then to the westward also I discovered that another such distended form was rising over the scrub. But here the light fell upon its sleek sides, and I could see that its colour was a vivid orange hue. It rose as one watched it; if one looked away from it for a minute and then back, its outline had changed; it thrust out blunt congested branches until in a little time it rose a coralline shape of many feet in height. Compared with such a growth the terrestrial puff-ball, which will sometimes swell a foot in diameter in a single night, would be a hopeless laggard. But then the puff-ball grows against a gravitational pull six times that of the moon. Beyond, out of gullies and flats that had been hidden from us, but not from the quickening sun, over reefs and banks of shining rock, a bristling beard of spiky and fleshy vegetation was straining into view, hurrying tumultuously to take advantage of the brief day in which it must flower and fruit and seed again and die. It was like a miracle, that growth. So, one must imagine, the trees and plants arose at the Creation and covered the desolation of the new-made earth.

Imagine it; imagine that dawn! The resurrection of the frozen air, the stirring and quickening of the soil, and then this silent uprising of vegetation, this unearthly ascent of fleshiness and spikes. Conceive it all lit by a blaze that would make the intensest sunlight of earth seem watery and weak. And still around this stirring jungle, wherever there was shadow, lingered banks of bluish snow. And to have the picture of our impression complete, you must bear in mind that we saw it all through a thick bent glass, distorting it as things are distorted by a lens, acute only in the centre of the picture, and very bright there, and towards the edges magnified and unreal.

CHAPTER NINE

Prospecting Begins

We ceased to gaze. We turned to each other, the same thought, the same question in our eyes. For these plants to grow, there must be some air, however attenuated, air that we also should be able to breathe.

'The manhole?' I said.

'Yes!' said Cavor, 'if it is air we see!'

'In a little while,' I said, 'these plants will be as high as we are. Suppose – suppose after all – Is it certain? How do you know that stuff is air? It may be nitrogen – it may be carbonic acid even!'

'That's easy,' he said, and set about proving it. He produced a big piece of crumpled paper from the bale, lit it, and thrust it hastily through the manhole valve. I bent forward and peered down through the thick glass for its appearance outside, that little flame on whose evidence depended so much!

I saw the paper drop out and lie lightly upon the snow. The pink flame of its burning vanished. For an instant it seemed to be extinguished. And then I saw a little blue tongue upon the edge of it that trembled, and crept, and spread!

Quietly the whole sheet, save where it lay in immediate contact with the snow, charred and shrivelled and sent up a quivering thread of smoke. There was no doubt left to me; the atmosphere of the moon was either pure oxygen or air, and capable therefore – unless its tenuity was excessive – of supporting our alien life. We might emerge – and live!

I sat down with my legs on either side of the manhole and prepared to unscrew it, but Cavor stopped me. 'There is first a little precaution,' he said. He pointed out that although it was certainly an oxygenated atmosphere outside, it might still be so rarefied as to cause us grave injury. He reminded me of mountain sickness, and of the bleeding that often afflicts aeronauts who have ascended too swiftly, and he spent some time in the preparation of a sickly-tasting drink which he insisted on my sharing. It made me feel a little numb, but otherwise had no effect on me. Then he permitted me to begin unscrewing.

Presently the glass stopper of the manhole was so far undone that the denser air within our sphere began to escape along the thread of the screw, singing as a kettle sings before it boils. Thereupon he made me desist. It speedily became evident that the pressure outside was very much less than it was within. How much less it was we had no means of telling.

I sat grasping the stopper with both hands, ready to close it again if, in spite of our intense hope, the lunar atmosphere should after all prove too

rarefied for us, and Cavor sat with a cylinder of compressed oxygen at hand to restore our pressure. We looked at one another in silence, and then at the fantastic vegetation that swayed and grew visibly and noiselessly without. And ever that shrill piping continued.

My blood-vessels began to throb in my ears, and the sound of Cavor's movements diminished. I noted how still everything had become, because of the thinning of the air.

As our air sizzled out from the screw the moisture of it condensed in little puffs.

Presently I experienced a peculiar shortness of breath that lasted indeed during the whole of the time of our exposure to the moon's exterior atmosphere, and a rather unpleasant sensation about the ears and finger-nails and the back of the throat grew upon my attention, and presently passed off again.

But then came vertigo and nausea that abruptly changed the quality of my courage. I gave the lid of the manhole half a turn and made a hasty explanation to Cavor; but now he was the more sanguine. He answered me in a voice that seemed extraordinarily small and remote, because of the thinness of the air that carried the sound. He recommended a nip of brandy, and set me the example, and presently I felt better. I turned the manhole stopper back again. The throbbing in my ears grew louder, and then I remarked that the piping note of the outrush had ceased. For a time I could not be sure that it had ceased.

'Well?' said Cavor, in the ghost of a voice.

'Well?' said I.

'Shall we go on?'

I thought. 'Is this all?'

'If you can stand it.'

By way of answer I went on unscrewing. I lifted the circular operculum from its place and laid it carefully on the bale. A flake or so of snow whirled and vanished as that thin and unfamiliar air took possession of our sphere. I knelt, and then seated myself at the edge of the manhole, peering over it. Beneath, within a yard of my face, lay the untrodden snow of the moon.

There came a little pause. Our eyes met.

'It doesn't distress your lungs too much?' said Cavor.

'No,' I said. 'I can stand this.'

He stretched out his hand for his blanket, thrust his head through its central hole, and wrapped it about him. He sat down on the edge of the manhole, he let his feet drop until they were within six inches of the lunar ground. He hesitated for a moment, then thrust himself forward, dropped these intervening inches, and stood upon the untrodden soil of the moon.

As he stepped forward he was refracted grotesquely by the edge of the glass. He stood for a moment looking this way and that. Then he drew himself together and leapt.

The glass distorted everything, but it seemed to me even then to be an extremely big leap. He had at one bound become remote. He seemed twenty or thirty feet off. He was standing high upon a rocky mass and gesticulating back to me. Perhaps he was shouting – but the sound did not reach me. But how the deuce had he done this? I felt like a man who has just seen a new conjuring trick.

In a puzzled state of mind I too dropped through the manhole. I stood up. Just in front of me the snowdrift had fallen away and made a sort of ditch. I made a step and jumped.

I found myself flying through the air, saw the rock on which he stood coming to meet me, clutched it and clung in a state of infinite amazement.

I gasped a painful laugh. I was tremendously confused. Cavor bent down and shouted in piping tones for me to be careful.

I had forgotten that on the moon, with only an eighth part of the earth's mass and a quarter of its diameter, my weight was barely a sixth what it was on earth. But now that fact insisted on being remembered.

'We are out of Mother Earth's leading-strings now,' he said.

With a guarded effort I raised myself to the top, and moving as cautiously as a rheumatic patient, stood up beside him under the blaze of the sun. The sphere lay behind us on its dwindling snowdrift thirty feet away.

As far as the eye could see over the enormous disorder of rocks that formed the crater floor, the same bristling scrub that surrounded us was starting into life, diversified here and there by bulging masses of a cactus form, and scarlet and purple lichens that grew so fast they seemed to crawl over the rocks. The whole area of the crater seemed to me then to be one similar wilderness up to the very foot of the surrounding cliff.

This cliff was apparently bare of vegetation save at its base, and with buttresses and terraces and platforms that did not very greatly attract our attention at the time. It was many miles away from us in every direction, we seemed to be almost at the centre of the crater, and we saw it through a certain haziness that drove before the wind. For there was even a wind now in the thin air, a swift yet weak wind that chilled exceedingly but exerted little pressure. It was blowing round the crater, as it seemed, to the hot illuminated side from the foggy darkness under the sunward wall. It was difficult to look into this eastward fog; we had to peer with half-closed eyes beneath the shade of our hands, because of the fierce intensity of the motionless sun.

'It seems to be deserted,' said Cavor, 'absolutely desolate.'

I looked about me again. I retained even then a clinging hope of some quasi-human evidence, some pinnacle of building, some house or engine, but everywhere one looked spread the tumbled rocks in peaks and crests, and the darting scrub and those bulging cacti that swelled and swelled, a flat negation as it seemed of all such hope.

'It looks as though these plants had it to themselves,' I said. 'I see no trace of any other creature.'

'No insects – no birds, no! Not a trace, not a scrap nor particle of animal life. If there was – what would they do in the night? . . . No; there's just these plants alone.'

I shaded my eyes with my hand. 'It's like the landscape of a dream. These things are less like earthly land plants than the things one imagines among the rocks at the bottom of the sea. Look at that yonder! One might imagine it a lizard changed into a plant. And the glare!'

'This is only the fresh morning,' said Cavor.

He sighed and looked about him. 'This is no world for men,' he said. 'And yet in a way – it appeals.'

He became silent for a time, then commenced his meditative humming.

I started at a gentle touch, and found a thin sheet of livid lichen lapping over my shoe. I kicked at it and it fell to powder, and each speck began to grow.

I heard Cavor exclaim sharply, and perceived that one of the fixed bayonets of the scrub had pricked him.

He hesitated, his eyes sought among the rocks about us. A sudden blaze of pink had crept up a ragged pillar of crag. It was a most extraordinary pink, a livid magenta.

'Look!' said I, turning, and behold Cavor had vanished.

For an instant I stood transfixed. Then I made a hasty step to look over the verge of the rock. But in my surprise at his disappearance I forgot once more that we were on the moon. The thrust of my foot that I made in striding would have carried me a yard on earth; on the moon it carried me six – a good five yards over the edge. For the moment the thing had something of the effect of those nightmares when one falls and falls. For while one falls sixteen feet in the first second of a fall on earth, on the moon one falls two, and with only a sixth of one's weight. I fell, or rather I jumped down, about ten yards I suppose. It seemed to take quite a long time, five or six seconds, I should think. I floated through the air and fell like a feather, knee-deep in a snowdrift in the bottom of a gully of blue-grey, white-veined rock.

I looked about me. 'Cavor!' I cried; but no Cavor was visible.

'Cavor!' I cried louder, and the rocks echoed me.

I turned fiercely to the rocks and clambered to the summit of them. 'Cavor!' I cried. My voice sounded like the voice of a lost lamb.

The sphere, too, was not in sight, and for a moment a horrible feeling of desolation pinched my heart.

Then I saw him. He was laughing and gesticulating to attract my attention. He was on a bare patch of rock twenty or thirty yards away. I could not hear his voice, but 'jump' said his gestures. I hesitated, the distance seemed enormous. Yet I reflected that surely I must be able to clear a greater distance than Cavor.

I made a step back, gathered myself together, and leapt with all my

might. I seemed to shoot right up in the air as though I should never come down.

It was horrible and delightful, and as wild as a nightmare, to go flying off in this fashion. I realised my leap had been altogether too violent. I flew clean over Cavor's head and beheld a spiky confusion in a gully spreading to meet my fall. I gave a yelp of alarm. I put out my hands and straightened my legs.

I hit a huge fungoid bulk that burst all about me, scattering a mass of orange spores in every direction, and covering me with orange powder. I rolled over spluttering, and came to rest convulsed with breathless laughter.

I became aware of Cavor's little round face peering over a bristling hedge. He shouted some faded enquiry. 'Eh?' I tried to shout, but could not do so for want of breath. He made his way towards me, coming gingerly among the bushes.

'We've got to be careful,' he said. 'This moon has no discipline. She'll let us smash ourselves.'

He helped me to my feet. 'You exerted yourself too much,' he said, dabbing at the yellow stuff with his hand to remove it from my garments.

I stood passive and panting, allowing him to beat off the jelly from my knees and elbows and lecture me upon my misfortunes. 'We don't quite allow for the gravitation. Our muscles are scarcely educated yet. We must practise a little, when you have got your breath.'

I pulled two or three little thorns out of my hand, and sat for a time on a boulder of rock. My muscles were quivering, and I had that feeling of personal disillusionment that comes at the first fall to the learner of cycling on earth.

It suddenly occurred to Cavor that the cold air in the gully, after the brightness of the sun, might give me a fever. So we clambered back into the sunlight. We found that beyond a few abrasions I had received no serious injuries from my tumble, and at Cavor's suggestion we were presently looking round for some safe and easy landing-place for my next leap. We chose a rocky slab some ten yards off, separated from us by a little thicket of olive-green spikes.

'Imagine it there!' said Cavor, who was assuming the airs of a trainer, and he pointed to a spot about four feet from my toes. This leap I managed without difficulty, and I must confess I found a certain satisfaction in Cavor's falling short by a foot or so and tasting the spikes of the scrub. 'One has to be careful you see,' he said, pulling out his thorns, and with that he ceased to be my Mentor and became my fellow-learner in the art of lunar locomotion.

We chose a still easier jump and did it without difficulty, and then leapt back again, and to and fro several times, accustoming our muscles to the new standard. I could never have believed had I not experienced it, how

rapid that adaptation would be. In a very little time indeed, certainly after fewer than thirty leaps, we could judge the effort necessary for a distance with almost terrestrial assurance.

And all this time the lunar plants were growing around us, higher and denser and more entangled, every moment thicker and taller, spiked plants, green cactus masses, fungi, fleshy and lichenous things, strangest radiate and sinuous shapes. But we were so intent upon our leaping, that for a time we gave no heed to their unfaltering expansion.

An extraordinary elation had taken possession of us. Partly, I think, it was our sense of release from the confinement of the sphere. Mainly, however, the thin sweetness of the air, which I am certain contained a much larger proportion of oxygen than our terrestrial atmosphere. In spite of the strange quality of all about us, I felt as adventurous and experimental as a cockney would do placed for the first time among mountains and I do not think it occurred to either of us, face to face though we were with the unknown, to be very greatly afraid.

We were bitten by a spirit of enterprise. We selected a lichenous kopje perhaps fifteen yards away, and landed neatly on its summit one after the other. 'Good!' we cried to each other; 'good!' and Cavor made three steps and went off to a tempting slope of snow a good twenty yards and more beyond. I stood for a moment struck by the grotesque effect of his soaring figure – his dirty cricket cap, and spiky hair, his little round body, his arms and his knickerbockered legs tucked up tightly – against the weird spaciousness of the lunar scene. A gust of laughter seized me, and then I stepped off to follow. Plump! I dropped beside him.

We made a few gargantuan strides, leapt three or four times more, and sat down at last in a lichenous hollow. Our lungs were painful. We sat holding our sides and recovering our breath, looking appreciation to one another. Cavor panted something about 'amazing sensations'. And then came a thought into my head. For the moment it did not seem a particularly appalling thought, simply a natural question arising out of the situation.

'By the way,' I said, 'where exactly is the sphere?'

Cavor looked at me. 'Eh?'

The full meaning of what we were saying struck me sharply.

'Cavor!' I cried, laying a hand on his arm, 'where is the sphere?'

CHAPTER TEN

Lost Men in the Woods

His face caught something of my dismay. He stood up and stared about him at the scrub that fenced us in and rose about us, straining upward in a passion

of growth. He put a dubious hand to his lips. He spoke with a sudden lack of assurance. 'I think,' he said slowly, 'we left it . . . somewhere . . . about *there*.'

He pointed a hesitating finger that wavered in an arc.

'I'm not sure.' His look of consternation deepened. 'Anyhow,' he said, with his eyes on me, 'it can't be far.'

We had both stood up. We made unmeaning ejaculations, our eyes sought in the twining, thickening jungle round about us.

All about us on the sunlit slopes frothed and swayed the darting shrubs, the swelling cactus, the creeping lichens, and wherever the shade remained the snowdrifts lingered. North, south, east, and west spread an identical monotony of unfamiliar forms. And somewhere, buried already among this tangled confusion, was our sphere, our home, our only provision, our only hope of escape from this fantastic wilderness of ephemeral growths into which we had come.

'I think after all,' he said, pointing suddenly, 'it might be over there.'

'No,' I said. 'We have turned in a curve. See! here is the mark of my heels. It's clear the thing must be more to the eastward, much more. No! – the sphere must be over there.'

'I *think*,' said Cavor, 'I kept the sun upon my right all the time.'

'Every leap, it seems to *me*,' I said, 'my shadow flew before me.'

We stared into one another's eyes. The area of the crater had become enormously vast to our imaginations, the growing thickets already impenetrably dense.

'Good heavens! What fools we have been!'

'It's evident that we must find it again,' said Cavor, 'and that soon. The sun grows stronger. We should be fainting with the heat already if it wasn't so dry. And . . . I'm hungry.'

I stared at him. I had not suspected this aspect of the matter before. But it came to me at once – a positive craving. 'Yes,' I said with emphasis. 'I am hungry too.'

He stood up with a look of active resolution. 'Certainly we must find the sphere.'

As calmly as possible we surveyed the interminable reefs and thickets that formed the floor of the crater, each of us weighing in silence the chances of our finding the sphere before we were overtaken by heat and hunger.

'It can't be fifty yards from here,' said Cavor, with indecisive gestures. 'The only thing is to beat round about until we come upon it.'

'That is all we can do,' I said, without any alacrity to begin our hunt. 'I wish this confounded spike bush did not grow so fast!'

'That's just it,' said Cavor. 'But it *was* lying on a bank of snow.'

I stared about me in the vain hope of recognising some knoll or shrub that had been near the sphere. But everywhere was a confusing sameness, everywhere the aspiring bushes, the distending fungi, the dwindling snow banks, steadily and inevitably changed. The sun scorched and stung, the

faintness of an unaccountable hunger mingled with our infinite perplexity. And even as we stood there, confused and lost amidst unprecedented things, we became aware for the first time of a sound upon the moon other than the air of the growing plants, the faint sighing of the wind, or those that we ourselves had made.

Boom . . . Boom . . . Boom . . .

It came from beneath our feet, a sound in the earth. We seemed to hear it with our feet as much as with our ears. Its dull resonance was muffled by distance, thick with the quality of intervening substance. No sound that I can imagine could have astonished us more, or have changed more completely the quality of things about us. For this sound, rich, slow, and deliberate, seemed to us as though it could be nothing but the striking of some gigantic buried clock.

Boom . . . Boom . . . Boom . . .

Sound suggestive of still cloisters, of sleepless nights in crowded cities, of vigils and the awaited hour, of all that is orderly and methodical in life, booming out pregnant and mysterious in this fantastic desert! To the eye everything was unchanged: the desolation of bushes and cacti waving silently in the wind, stretched unbroken to the distant cliffs, the still dark sky was empty overhead, and the hot sun hung and burned. And through it all, a warning, a threat, throbbed this enigma of sound.

Boom . . . Boom . . . Boom . . .

We questioned one another in faint and faded voices.

'A clock?'

'Like a clock!'

'What is it?'

'What can it be?'

'Count,' was Cavor's belated suggestion, and at that word the striking ceased.

The silence, the rhythmic disappointment of the silence, came as a fresh shock. For a moment one could doubt whether one had ever heard a sound. Or whether it might not still be going on. Had I indeed heard a sound?

I felt the pressure of Cavor's hand upon my arm. He spoke in an undertone, as though he feared to wake some sleeping thing. 'Let us keep together,' he whispered, 'and look for the sphere. We must get back to the sphere. This is beyond our understanding.'

'Which way shall we go?'

He hesitated. An intense persuasion of presences, of unseen things about us and near us, dominated our minds. What could they be? Where could they be? Was this arid desolation, alternately frozen and scorched, only the outer rind and mask of some subterranean world? And if so, what sort of world? What sort of inhabitants might it not presently disgorge upon us?

And then, stabbing the aching stillness as vivid and sudden as an

unexpected thunderclap, came a clang and rattle as though great gates of metal had suddenly been flung apart.

It arrested our steps. We stood gaping helplessly. Then Cavor stole towards me.

'I do not understand!' he whispered close to my face. He waved his hand vaguely skyward, the vague suggestion of still vaguer thoughts.

'A hiding-place! If anything came . . . '

I looked about us. I nodded my head in assent to him.

We started off, moving stealthily with the most exaggerated precautions against noise. We went towards a thicket of scrub. A clangour like hammers flung about a boiler hastened our steps. 'We must crawl,' whispered Cavor.

The lower leaves of the bayonet plants, already overshadowed by the newer ones above, were beginning to wilt and shrivel so that we could thrust our way in among the thickening stems without serious injury. A stab in the face or arm we did not heed. At the heart of the thicket I stopped, and stared panting into Cavor's face.

'Subterranean,' he whispered. 'Below.'

'They may come out.'

'We must find the sphere!'

'Yes,' I said; 'but how?'

'Crawl till we come to it.'

'But if we don't?'

'Keep hidden. See what they are like.'

'We will keep together,' said I.

He thought. 'Which way shall we go?'

'We must take our chance.'

We peered this way and that. Then very circumspectly, we began to crawl through the lower jungle, making, so far as we could judge, a circuit, halting now at every waving fungus, at every sound, intent only on the sphere from which we had so foolishly emerged. Ever and again from out of the earth beneath us came concussions, beatings, strange, inexplicable, mechanical sounds; and once, and then again, we thought we heard something, a faint rattle and tumult, borne to us through the air. But fearful as we were we dared essay no vantage-point to survey the crater. For long we saw nothing of the beings whose sounds were so abundant and insistent. But for the faintness of our hunger and the drying of our throats that crawling would have had the quality of a very vivid dream. It was so absolutely unreal. The only element with any touch of reality was these sounds.

Figure it to yourself! About us the dreamlike jungle, with the silent bayonet leaves darting overhead, and the silent, vivid, sun-splashed lichens under our hands and knees, waving with the vigour of their growth as a carpet waves when the wind gets beneath it. Ever and again one of the bladder fungi, bulging and distending under the sun, loomed upon us. Ever

and again some novel shape in vivid colour obtruded. The very cells that built up these plants were as large as my thumb, like beads of coloured glass. And all these things were saturated in the unmitigated glare of the sun, were seen against a sky that was bluish black and spangled still, in spite of the sunlight, with a few surviving stars. Strange! the very forms and texture of the stones were strange. It was all strange, the feeling of one's body was unprecedented, every other movement ended in a surprise. The breath sucked thin in one's throat, the blood flowed through one's ears in a throbbing tide – thud, thud, thud, thud . . .

And ever and again came gusts of turmoil, hammering, the clanging and throb of machinery, and presently – the bellowing of great beasts!

CHAPTER ELEVEN

The Mooncalf Pastures

So we two poor terrestrial castaways, lost in that wild-growing moon jungle, crawled in terror before the sounds that had come upon us. We crawled, as it seemed, a long time before we saw either Selenite or mooncalf, though we heard the bellowing and gruntulous noises of these latter continually drawing nearer to us. We crawled through stony ravines, over snow slopes, amidst fungi that ripped like thin bladders at our thrust, emitting a watery humour, over a perfect pavement of things like puffballs, and beneath interminable thickets of scrub. And ever more helplessly our eyes sought for our abandoned sphere. The noise of the mooncalves would at times be a vast flat calf-like sound, at times it rose to an amazed and wrathy bellowing, and again it would become a clogged bestial sound, as though these unseen creatures had sought to eat and bellow at the same time.

Our first view was but an inadequate transitory glimpse, yet none the less disturbing because it was incomplete. Cavor was crawling in front at the time, and he first was aware of their proximity. He stopped dead, arresting me with a single gesture.

A crackling and smashing of the scrub appeared to be advancing directly upon us, and then, as we squatted close and endeavoured to judge of the nearness and direction of this noise, there came a terrific bellow behind us, so close and vehement that the tops of the bayonet scrub bent before it, and one felt the breath of it hot and moist. And, turning about, we saw indistinctly through a crowd of swaying stems the mooncalf's shining sides, and the long line of its back loomed out against the sky.

Of course it is hard for me now to say how much I saw at that time, because my impressions were corrected by subsequent observation. First of all impressions was its enormous size; the girth of its body was some

fourscore feet, its length perhaps two hundred. Its sides rose and fell with its laboured breathing. I perceived that its gigantic, flabby body lay along the ground, and that its skin was of a corrugated white, dappling into blackness along the backbone. But of its feet we saw nothing. I think also that we saw then the profile at least of the almost brainless head, with its fat-encumbered neck, its slobbering omnivorous mouth, its little nostrils, and tight shut eyes. (For the mooncalf invariably shuts its eyes in the presence of the sun.) We had a glimpse of a vast red pit as it opened its mouth to bleat and bellow again; we had a breath from the pit, and then the monster heeled over like a ship, dragged forward along the ground, creasing all its leathery skin, rolled again, and so wallowed past us, smashing a path amidst the scrub, and was speedily hidden from our eyes by the dense interlacings beyond. Another appeared more distantly, and then another, and then, as though he was guiding these animated lumps of provender to their pasture, a Selenite came momentarily into ken. My grip upon Cavor's foot became convulsive at the sight of him, and we remained motionless and peering long after he had passed out of our range.

By contrast with the mooncalves he seemed a trivial being, a mere ant, scarcely five feet high. He was wearing garments of some leathery substance, so that no portion of his actual body appeared, but of this, of course, we were entirely ignorant. He presented himself, therefore, as a compact, bristling creature, having much of the quality of a complicated insect, with whiplike tentacles and a clanging arm projecting from his shining cylindrical body case. The form of his head was hidden by his enormous many-spiked helmet – we discovered afterwards that he used the spikes for prodding refractory mooncalves – and a pair of goggles of darkened glass, set very much at the side, gave a birdlike quality to the metallic apparatus that covered his face. His arms did not project beyond his body case, and he carried himself upon short legs that, wrapped though they were in warm coverings, seemed to our terrestrial eyes inordinately flimsy. They had very short thighs, very long shanks, and little feet.

In spite of his heavy-looking clothing, he was progressing with what would be, from the terrestrial point of view, very considerable strides, and his clanging arm was busy. The quality of his motion during the instant of his passing suggested haste and a certain anger, and soon after we had lost sight of him we heard the bellow of a mooncalf change abruptly into a short, sharp squeal followed by the scuffle of its acceleration. And gradually that bellowing receded, and then came to an end, as if the pastures sought had been attained.

We listened. For a space the moon world was still. But it was some time before we resumed our crawling search for the vanished sphere.

When next we saw mooncalves they were some little distance away from us in a place of tumbled rocks. The less vertical surfaces of the rocks were thick with a speckled green plant growing in dense mossy clumps, upon

which these creatures were browsing. We stopped at the edge of the reeds amidst which we were crawling at the sight of them, peering out at then and looking round for a second glimpse of a Selenite. They lay against their food like stupendous slugs, huge, greasy hulls, eating greedily and noisily, with a sort of sobbing avidity. They seemed monsters of mere fatness, clumsy and overwhelmed to a degree that would make a Smithfield ox seem a model of agility. Their busy, writhing, chewing mouths, and eyes closed, together with the appetising sound of their munching, made up an effect of animal enjoyment that was singularly stimulating to our empty frames.

'Hogs!' said Cavor, with unusual passion. 'Disgusting hogs!' and after one glare of angry envy crawled off through the bushes to our right. I stayed long enough to see that the speckled plant was quite hopeless for human nourishment, then crawled after him, nibbling a quill of it between my teeth.

Presently we were arrested again by the proximity of a Selenite, and this time we were able to observe him more exactly. Now we could see that the Selenite covering was indeed clothing, and not a sort of crustacean integument. He was quite similar in his costume to the former one we had glimpsed, except that ends of something like wadding were protruding from his neck, and he stood on a promontory of rock and moved his head this way and that, as though he was surveying the crater. We lay quite still, fearing to attract his attention if we moved, and after a time he turned about and disappeared.

We came upon another drove of mooncalves bellowing up a ravine, and then we passed over a place of sounds, sounds of beating machinery as if some huge hall of industry came near the surface there. And while these sounds were still about us we came to the edge of a great open space, perhaps two hundred yards in diameter, and perfectly level. Save for a few lichens that advanced from its margin this space was bare, and presented a powdery surface of a dusty yellow colour. We were afraid to strike out across this space, but as it presented less obstruction to our crawling than the scrub, we went down upon it and began very circumspectly to skirt its edge.

For a little while the noises from below ceased and everything, save for the faint stir of the growing vegetation, was very still. Then abruptly there began an uproar, louder, more vehement, and nearer than any we had so far heard. Of a certainty it came from below. Instinctively we crouched as flat as we could, ready for a prompt plunge into the thicket beside us. Each knock and throb seemed to vibrate through our bodies. Louder grew this throbbing and beating, and that irregular vibration increased until the whole moon world seemed to be jerking and pulsing.

'Cover,' whispered Cavor, and I turned towards the bushes.

At that instant came a thud like the thud of a gun, and then a thing happened – it still haunts me in my dreams. I had turned my head to look at

Cavor's face, and thrust out my hand in front of me as I did so. And my hand met nothing! Plunged suddenly into a bottomless hole!

My chest hit something hard, and I found myself with my chin on the edge of an unfathomable abyss that had suddenly opened beneath me, my hand extended stiffly into the void. The whole of that flat circular area was no more than a gigantic lid, that was now sliding sideways from off the pit it had covered into a slot prepared for it.

Had it not been for Cavor I think I should have remained rigid, hanging over this margin and staring into the enormous gulf below, until at last the edges of the slot scraped me off and hurled me into its depths. But Cavor had not received the shock that had paralysed me. He had been a little distance from the edge when the lid had first opened, and perceiving the peril that held me helpless, gripped my legs and pulled me backward. I came into a sitting position, crawled away from the edge for a space on all fours, then staggered up and ran after him across the thundering, quivering sheet of metal. It seemed to be swinging open with a steadily accelerated velocity, and the bushes in front of me shifted sideways as I ran.

I was none too soon. Cavor's back vanished amidst the bristling thicket, and as I scrambled up after him, the monstrous valve came into its position with a clang. For a long time we lay panting, not daring to approach the pit.

But at last very cautiously and bit by bit we crept into a position from which we could peer down. The bushes about us creaked and waved with the force of a breeze that was blowing down the shaft. We could see nothing at first except smooth vertical walls descending at last into an impenetrable black. And then very gradually we became aware of a number of very faint and little lights going to and fro.

For a time that stupendous gulf of mystery held us so that we forgot even our sphere. In time, as we grew more accustomed to the darkness, we could make out very small, dim, elusive shapes moving about among those needle-point illuminations. We peered amazed and incredulous, understanding so little that we could find no words to say. We could distinguish nothing that would give us a clue to the meaning of the faint shapes we saw.

'What can it be?' I asked; 'what can it be?'

'The engineering! . . . They must live in these caverns during the night, and come out during the day.'

'Cavor!' I said. 'Can they be – *that* – it was something like – men?'

'*That* was not a man.'

'We dare risk nothing!'

'We dare do nothing until we find the sphere!'

'We can do nothing until we find the sphere.'

He assented with a groan and stirred himself to move. He stared about him for a space, sighed, and indicated a direction. We struck out through the jungle. For a time we crawled resolutely, then with diminishing vigour.

Presently among great shapes of flabby purple there came a noise of

trampling and cries about us. We lay close, and for a long time the sounds went to and fro and very near. But this time we saw nothing. I tried to whisper to Cavor that I could hardly go without food much longer, but my mouth had become too dry for whispering.

'Cavor,' I said, 'I must have food.'

He turned a face full of dismay towards me. 'It's a case for holding out,' he said.

'But I *must*,' I said, 'and look at my lips!'

'I've been thirsty some time.'

'If only some of that snow had remained!'

'It's clean gone! We're driving from arctic to tropical at the rate of a degree a minute . . . '

I gnawed my hand.

'The sphere!' he said. 'There is nothing for it but the sphere.'

We roused ourselves to another spurt of crawling. My mind ran entirely on edible things, on the hissing profundity of summer drinks, more particularly I craved for beer. I was haunted by the memory of a sixteen-gallon cask that had swaggered in my Lympne cellar. I thought of the adjacent larder, and especially of steak and kidney pie – tender steak and plenty of kidney, and rich, thick gravy between. Ever and again I was seized with fits of hungry yawning. We came to flat places overgrown with fleshy red things, monstrous coralline growths; as we pushed against them they snapped and broke. I noted the quality of the broken surfaces. The confounded stuff certainly looked of a biteable texture. Then it seemed to me that it smelt rather well.

I picked up a fragment and sniffed at it.

'Cavor,' I said in a hoarse undertone.

He glanced at me with his face screwed up. 'Don't,' he said. I put down the fragment, and we crawled on through this tempting fleshiness for a space.

'Cavor,' I asked, 'why *not?*'

'Poison,' I heard him say, but he did not look round.

We crawled some way before I decided.

'I'll chance it,' said I.

He made a belated gesture to prevent me. I stuffed my mouth full. He crouched watching my face, his own twisted into the oddest expression. 'It's good,' I said.

'O Lord!' he cried.

He watched me munch, his face wrinkled between desire and disapproval, then suddenly succumbed to appetite and began to tear off huge mouthfuls. For a time we did nothing but eat.

The stuff was not unlike a terrestrial mushroom, only it was much laxer in texture, and, as one swallowed it, it warmed the throat. At first we experienced a mere mechanical satisfaction in eating; then our blood began

to run warmer, and we tingled at the lips and fingers, and then new and slightly irrelevant ideas came bubbling up in our minds.

'It's good,' said I. 'Infernally good! What a home for our surplus population! Our poor surplus population,' and I broke off another large portion. It filled me with a curiously benevolent satisfaction that there was such good food in the moon. The depression of my hunger gave way to an irrational exhilaration. The dread and discomfort in which I had been living vanished entirely. I perceived the moon no longer as a planet from which I most earnestly desired the means of escape, but as a possible refuge from human destitution. I think I forgot the Selenites, the mooncalves, the lid, and the noises completely so soon as I had eaten that fungus.

Cavor replied to my third repetition of my 'surplus population' remark with similar words of approval. I felt that my head swam, but I put this down to the stimulating effect of food after a long fast. 'Ess'lent discov'ry yours, Cavor,' said I. 'Se'nd on'y to the 'tato.'

'Whajer mean?' asked Cavor. ' 'Scovery of the moon – se'nd on'y to the 'tato?'

I looked at him, shocked at his suddenly hoarse voice, and by the badness of his articulation. It occurred to me in a flash that he was intoxicated, possibly by the fungus. It also occurred to me that he erred in imagining that he had discovered the moon; he had not discovered it, he had only reached it. I tried to lay my hand on his arm and explain this to him, but the issue was too subtle for his brain. It was also unexpectedly difficult to express. After a momentary attempt to understand me – I remember wondering if the fungus had made my eyes as fishy as his – he set off upon some observations on his own account.

'We are,' he announced with a solemn hiccup, 'the creashurs o' what we eat and drink.'

He repeated this, and as I was now in one of my subtle moods, I determined to dispute it. Possibly I wandered a little from the point. But Cavor certainly did not attend at all properly. He stood up as well as he could, putting a hand on my head to steady himself, which was disrespectful, and stood staring about him, quite devoid now of any fear of the moon beings.

I tried to point out that this was dangerous for some reason that was not perfectly clear to me, but the word 'dangerous' had somehow got mixed with 'indiscreet', and came out rather more like 'injurious' than either; and after an attempt to disentangle them, I resumed my argument, addressing myself principally to the unfamiliar but attentive coralline growths on either side. I felt that it was necessary to clear up this confusion between the moon and a potato at once – I wandered into a long parenthesis on the importance of precision of definition in argument. I did my best to ignore the fact that my bodily sensations were no longer agreeable.

In some way that I have now forgotten, my mind was led back to projects of colonisation. 'We must annex this moon,' I said. 'There must be

no shilly-shally. This is part of the White Man's Burthen. Cavor – we are – *hic* – Satap – mean Satraps! Nempire Caesar never dreamt. B'in all the newspapers. Cavorecia. Bedfordecia. Bedfordecia – hic – Limited. Mean – unlimited! Practically.'

Certainly I was intoxicated.

I embarked upon an argument to show the infinite benefits our arrival would confer on the moon. I involved myself in a rather difficult proof that the arrival of Columbus was, on the whole, beneficial to America. I found I had forgotten the line of argument I had intended to pursue, and continued to repeat 'Similar to C'lumbus', to fill up time.

From that point my memory of the action of that abominable fungus becomes confused. I remember vaguely that we declared our intention of standing no nonsense from any confounded insects, that we decided it ill became men to hide shamefully upon a mere satellite, that we equipped ourselves with huge armfuls of the fungus – whether for missile purposes or not I do not know – and, heedless of the stabs of the bayonet scrub, we started forth into the sunshine.

Almost immediately we must have come upon the Selenites. There were six of them, and they were marching in single file over a rocky place, making the most remarkable piping and whining sounds. They all seemed to become aware of us at once, all instantly became silent and motionless, like animals, with their faces turned towards us.

For a moment I was sobered.

'Insects,' murmured Cavor, 'insects! And they think I'm going to crawl about on my stomach – on my vertebrated stomach!'

'Stomach,' he repeated slowly, as though he chewed the indignity.

Then suddenly, with a shout of fury, he made three vast strides and leapt towards them. He leapt badly; he made a series of somersaults in the air, whirled right over them, and vanished with an enormous splash amidst the cactus bladders. What the Selenites made of this amazing, and to my mind undignified irruption from another planet, I have no means of guessing. I seem to remember the sight of their backs as they ran in all directions, but I am not sure. All these last incidents before oblivion came are vague and faint in my mind. I know I made a step to follow Cavor, and tripped and fell headlong among the rocks. I was, I am certain, suddenly and vehemently ill. I seem to remember, a violent struggle and being gripped by metallic clasps . . .

My next clear recollection is that we were prisoners at we knew not what depths beneath the moon's surface; we were in darkness amidst strange distracting noises; our bodies were covered with scratches and bruises, and our heads racked with pain.

CHAPTER TWELVE

The Selenite's Face

I found myself sitting crouched together in a tumultuous darkness. For a long time I could not understand where I was, nor how I had come to this perplexity. I thought of the cupboard into which I had been thrust at times when I was a child, and then of a very dark and noisy bedroom in which I had slept during an illness. But these sounds about me were not the noises I had known, and there was a thin flavour in the air like the wind of a stable. Then I supposed we must still be at work upon the sphere, and that somehow I had got into the cellar of Cavor's house. I remembered we had finished the sphere, and fancied I must still be in it and travelling through space.

'Cavor,' I said, 'cannot we have some light?'

There came no answer.

'Cavor!' I insisted.

I was answered by a groan. 'My head!' I heard him say; 'my head!'

I attempted to press my hands to my brow, which ached, and discovered they were tied together. This startled me very much. I brought them up to my mouth and felt the cold smoothness of metal. They were chained together. I tried to separate my legs and made out they were similarly fastened, and also that I was fastened to the ground by a much thicker chain about the middle of my body.

I was more frightened than I had yet been by anything in all our strange experiences. For a time I tugged silently at my bonds. 'Cavor!' I cried out sharply. 'Why am I tied? Why have you tied me hand and foot?'

'I haven't tied you,' he answered. 'It's the Selenites.'

The Selenites! My mind hung on that for a space. Then my memories came back to me: the snowy desolation, the thawing of the air, the growth of the plants, our strange hopping and crawling among the rocks and vegetation of the crater. All the distress of our frantic search for the sphere returned to me . . . Finally the opening of the great lid that covered the pit!

Then as I strained to trace our later movements down to our present plight, the pain in my head became intolerable. I came to an insurmountable barrier, an obstinate blank.

'Cavor!'

'Yes?'

'Where are we?'

'How should I know?'

'Are we dead?'

'What nonsense!'

'They've got us, then!'

He made no answer but a grunt. The lingering traces of the poison seemed to make him oddly irritable.

'What do you mean to do?'

'How should I know what to do?'

'Oh, very well!' said I, and became silent. Presently, I was roused from a stupor. 'O *Lord*!' I cried; 'I wish you'd stop that buzzing!'

We lapsed into silence again, listening to the dull confusion of noises like the muffled sounds of a street or factory that filled our ears. I could make nothing of it, my mind pursued first one rhythm and then another, and questioned it in vain. But after a long time I became aware of a new and sharper element, not mingling with the rest but standing out, as it were, against that cloudy background of sound. It was a series of relatively very little definite sounds, tappings and rubbings, like a loose spray of ivy against a window or a bird moving about upon a box. We listened and peered about us, but the darkness was a velvet pall. There followed a noise like the subtle movement of the wards of a well-oiled lock. And then there appeared before me, hanging as it seemed in an immensity of black, a thin bright line.

'Look!' whispered Cavor very softly.

'What is it?'

'I don't know.'

We stared.

The thin bright line became a band, and broader and paler. It took upon itself the quality of a bluish light falling upon a whitewashed wall. It ceased to be parallel-sided; it developed a deep indentation on one side. I turned to remark this to Cavor, and was amazed to see his ear in a brilliant illumination – all the rest of him in shadow. I twisted my head round as well as my bonds would permit. 'Cavor,' I said, 'it's behind!'

His ear vanished – gave place to an eye!

Suddenly the crack that had been admitting the light broadened out, and revealed itself as the space of an opening door. Beyond was a sapphire vista, and in the doorway stood a grotesque outline silhouetted against the glare.

We both made convulsive efforts to turn, and failing, sat staring over our shoulders at this. My first impression was of some clumsy quadruped with lowered head. Then I perceived it was the slender pinched body and short and extremely attenuated bandy legs of a Selenite, with his head depressed between his shoulders. He was without the helmet and body covering they wear upon the exterior.

He was a blank, black figure to us, but instinctively our imaginations supplied features to his very human outline. I, at least, took it instantly that he was somewhat hunchbacked, with a high forehead and long features.

He came forward three steps and paused for a time. His movements seemed absolutely noiseless. Then he came forward again. He walked like a bird, his feet fell one in front of the other. He stepped out of the ray of light

that came through the doorway, and it seemed as though he vanished altogether in the shadow.

For a moment my eyes sought him in the wrong place, and then I perceived him standing facing us both in the full light. Only the human features I had attributed to him were not there at all!

Of course I ought to have expected that, only I didn't. It came to me as an absolute, for a moment an overwhelming shock. It seemed as though it wasn't a face, as though it must needs be a mask, a horror, a deformity, that would presently be disavowed or explained. There was no nose, and the thing had dull bulging eyes at the side – in the silhouette I had supposed they were ears. There were no ears . . . I have tried to draw one of these heads, but I cannot. There was a mouth, downwardly curved, like a human mouth in a face that stares ferociously . . .

The neck on which the head was poised was jointed in three places, almost like the short joints in the leg of a crab. The joints of the limbs I could not see, because of the puttee-like straps in which they were swathed, and which formed the only clothing the being wore.

There the thing was, looking at us!

At the time my mind was taken up by the mad impossibility of the creature. I suppose he also was amazed, and with more reason, perhaps, for amazement than we. Only, confound him! he did not show it. We did at least know what had brought about this meeting of incompatible creatures. But conceive how it would seem to decent Londoners, for example, to come upon a couple of living things, as big as men and absolutely unlike any other earthly animals, careering about among the sheep in Hyde Park! It must have taken him like that.

Figure us! We were bound hand and foot, fagged and filthy; our beards two inches long, our faces scratched and bloody. Cavor you must imagine in his knickerbockers (torn in several places by the bayonet scrub) his Jaegar shirt and old cricket cap, his wiry hair wildly disordered, a tail to every quarter of the heavens. In that blue light his face did not look red but very dark, his lips and the drying blood upon my hands seemed black. If possible I was in a worse plight than he, on account of the yellow fungus into which I had jumped. Our jackets were unbuttoned, and our shoes had been taken off and lay at our feet. And we were sitting with our backs to this queer bluish light, peering at such a monster as Dürer might have invented.

Cavor broke the silence; started to speak, went hoarse, and cleared his throat. Outside began a terrific bellowing, as if a mooncalf were in trouble. It ended in a shriek, and everything was still again.

Presently the Selenite turned about, flickered into the shadow, stood for a moment retrospective at the door, and then closed it on us; and once more we were in that murmurous mystery of darkness into which we had awakened.

CHAPTER THIRTEEN

Mr Cavor Makes Some Suggestions

For a time neither of us spoke. To focus together all the things we had brought upon ourselves, seemed beyond my mental powers.

'They've got us,' I said at last.

'It was that fungus.'

'Well – if I hadn't taken it we should have fainted and starved.'

'We might have found the sphere.'

I lost my temper at his persistence, and swore to myself. For a time we hated one another in silence. I drummed with my fingers on the floor between my knees, and gritted the links of my fetters together. Presently I was forced to talk again.

'What do you make of it, anyhow?' I asked humbly.

'They are reasonable creatures – they can make things and do things. Those lights we saw . . .'

He stopped. It was clear he could make nothing of it.

When he spoke again it was to confess, 'After all, they are more human than we had a right to expect. I suppose – '

He stopped irritatingly.

'Yes?'

'I suppose, anyhow – on any planet where there is an intelligent animal – it will carry its brain case upward, and have hands, and walk erect . . .'

Presently he broke away in another direction.

'We are some way in,' he said. 'I mean – perhaps a couple of thousand feet or more.'

'Why?'

'It's cooler. And our voices are so much louder. That faded quality – it has altogether gone. And the feeling in one's ears and throat.'

I had not noted that, but I did now.

'The air is denser. We must be some depths – a mile even, we may be – inside the moon.'

'We never thought of a world inside the moon.'

'No.'

'How could we?'

'We might have done. Only – one gets into habits of mind.'

He thought for a time.

'*Now*,' he said, 'it seems such an obvious thing.'

'Of course! The moon must be enormously cavernous, with an atmosphere within, and at the centre of its caverns a sea.

'One knew that the moon had a lower specific gravity than the earth, one

knew that it had little air or water outside, one knew, too, that it was sister planet to the earth, and that it was unaccountable that it should be different in composition. The inference that it was hollowed out was as clear as day. And yet one never saw it as a fact. Kepler, of course – '

His voice had the interest now of a man who has discerned a pretty sequence of reasoning.

'Yes,' he said, 'Kepler with his *sub-volvani* was right after all.'

'I wish you had taken the trouble to find that out before we came,' I said.

He answered nothing, buzzing to himself softly, as he pursued his thoughts. My temper was going.

'What do you think has become of the sphere, anyhow?' I asked.

'Lost,' he said, like a man who answers an uninteresting question.

'Among those plants?'

'Unless they find it.'

'And then?'

'How can I tell?'

'Cavor,' I said, with a sort of hysterical bitterness, 'things look bright for my Company . . . '

He made no answer.

'Good Lord!' I exclaimed. 'Just think of all the trouble we took to get into this pickle! What did we come for? What are we after? What was the moon to us or we to the moon? We wanted too much, we tried too much. We ought to have started the little things first. It was you proposed the moon! Those Cavorite spring blinds! I am certain we could have worked them for terrestrial purposes. Certain! Did you really understand what I proposed? A steel cylinder – '

'Rubbish!' said Cavor.

We ceased to converse.

For a time Cavor kept up a broken monologue without much help from me.

'If they find it,' he began, 'if they find it . . . what will they do with it? Well, that's a question. It may be that's *the* question. They won't under-stand it, anyhow. If they understood that sort of thing they would have come long since to the earth. Would they? Why shouldn't they? But they would have sent something – they couldn't keep their hands off such a possibility. No! But they will examine it. Clearly they are intelligent and inquisitive. They will examine it – get inside it – trifle with the studs. Off! . . . That would mean the moon for us for all the rest of our lives. Strange creatures, strange knowledge . . . '

'As for strange knowledge – ' said I, and language failed me.

'Look here, Bedford,' said Cavor, 'you came on this expedition of your own free will.'

'You said to me, "Call it prospecting".'

'There's always risks in prospecting.'

'Especially when you do it unarmed and without thinking out every possibility.'

'I was so taken up with the sphere. The thing rushed on us, and carried us away.'

'Rushed on *me*, you mean.'

'Rushed on me just as much. How was *I* to know when I set to work on molecular physics that the business would bring me here – of all places?'

'It's this accursed science,' I cried. 'It's the very Devil. The mediaeval priests and persecutors were right and the Moderns are all wrong. You tamper with it – and it offers you gifts. And directly you take them it knocks you to pieces in some unexpected way. Old passions and new weapons – now it upsets your religion, now it upsets your social ideas, now it whirls you off to desolation and misery!'

'Anyhow, it's no use your quarrelling with me *now*. These creatures – these Selenites, or whatever we choose to call them – have got us tied hand and foot. Whatever temper you choose to go through with it in, you will have to go through with it . . . We have experiences before us that will need all our coolness.'

He paused as if he required my assent. But I sat sulking. 'Confound your science!' I said.

'The problem is communication. Gestures, I fear, will be different. Pointing, for example. No creatures but men and monkeys point.'

That was too obviously wrong for me. 'Pretty nearly every animal,' I cried, 'points with its eyes or nose.'

Cavor meditated over that. 'Yes,' he said at last, 'and we don't. There's such differences – such differences!'

'One might . . . But how can I tell? There is speech. The sounds they make, a sort of fluting and piping. I don't see how we are to imitate that. Is it their speech, that sort of thing? They may have different senses, different means of communication. Of course they are minds and we are minds; there must be something in common. Who knows how far we may not get to an understanding?'

'The things are outside us,' I said. 'They're more different from us than the strangest animals on earth. They are a different clay. What is the good of talking like this?'

Cavor thought. 'I don't see that. Where there are minds they will have something *similar* – even though they have been evolved on different planets. Of course if it was a question of instincts, if we or they are no more than animals – '

'Well, *are* they? They're much more like ants on their hind legs than human beings, and who ever got to any sort of understanding with ants?'

'But these machines and clothing! No, I don't hold with you, Bedford. The difference is wide – '

'It's insurmountable.'

'The resemblance must bridge it. I remember reading once a paper by the late Professor Galton on the possibility of communication between the planets. Unhappily, at that time it did not seem probable that that would be of any material benefit to me, and I fear I did not give it the attention I should have done – in view of this state of affairs. Yet . . . Now, let me see!

'His idea was to begin with those broad truths that must underlie all conceivable mental existences and establish a basis on those. The great principles of geometry, to begin with. He proposed to take some leading proposition of Euclid's, and show by construction that its truth was known to us, to demonstrate, for example, that the angles at the base of an isosceles triangle are equal, and that if the equal sides be produced the angles on the other side of the base are equal also, or that the square on the hypotenuse of a right-angled triangle is equal to the sum of the squares on the two other sides. By demonstrating our knowledge of these things we should demonstrate our possession of a reasonable intelligence . . . Now, suppose I . . . I might draw the geometrical figure with a wet finger, or even trace it in the air . . . '

He fell silent. I sat meditating his words. For a time his wild hope of communication, of interpretation, with these weird beings held me. Then that angry despair that was a part of my exhaustion and physical misery resumed its sway. I perceived with a sudden novel vividness the extra-ordinary folly of everything I had ever done. 'Ass!' I said; 'oh, ass, unutterable ass . . . I seem to exist only to go about doing preposterous things. Why did we ever leave the thing? . . . Hopping about looking for patents and concessions in the craters of the moon! . . . If only we had had the sense to fasten a handkerchief to a stick to show where we had left the sphere!'

I subsided, fuming.

'It is clear,' meditated Cavor, 'they are intelligent. One can hypotheticate certain things. As they have not killed us at once, they must have ideas of mercy. Mercy! at any rate of restraint. Possibly of intercourse. They may meet us. And this apartment and the glimpses we had of its guardian. These fetters! A high degree of intelligence . . . '

'I wish to heaven,' cried I, 'I'd thought even twice! Plunge after plunge. First one fluky start and then another. It was my confidence in you! *Why* didn't I stick to my play? That was what I was equal to. That was my world and the life I was made for. I could have finished that play. I'm certain . . . it was a good play. I had the scenario as good as done. Then . . . Conceive it! leaping to the moon! Practically – I've thrown my life away! That old woman in the inn near Canterbury had better sense.'

I looked up, and stopped in mid-sentence. The darkness had given place to that bluish light again. The door was opening, and several noiseless Selenites were coming into the chamber. I became quite still, staring at their grotesque faces.

Then suddenly my sense of disagreeable strangeness changed to interest. I perceived that the foremost and second carried bowls. One elemental need at least our minds could understand in common. They were bowls of some metal that, like our fetters, looked dark in that bluish light; and each contained a number of whitish fragments. All the cloudy pain and misery that oppressed me rushed together and took the shape of hunger. I eyed these bowls wolfishly, and, though it returned to me in dreams, at that time it seemed a small matter that at the end of the arms that lowered one towards me were not hands, but a sort of flap and thumb, like the end of an elephant's trunk.

The stuff in the bowl was loose in texture, and whitish brown in colour – rather like lumps of some cold soufflé, and it smelt faintly like mushrooms. From a partially divided carcass of a mooncalf that we presently saw, I am inclined to believe it must have been mooncalf flesh.

My hands were so tightly chained that I could barely contrive to reach the bowl; but when they saw the effort I made, two of them dexterously released one of the turns about my wrist. Their tentacle hands were soft and cold to my skin. I immediately seized a mouthful of the food. It had the same laxness in texture that all organic structures seem to have upon the moon; it tasted rather like a *gauffre* or a damp meringue, but in no way was it disagreeable. I took two other mouthfuls. 'I *wanted* – foo'!' said I, tearing off a still larger piece . . .

For a time we ate with an utter absence of self-consciousness. We ate and presently drank like tramps in a soup kitchen. Never before nor since have I been hungry to the ravenous pitch, and save that I have had this very experience I could never have believed that, a quarter of a million of miles out of our proper world, in utter perplexity of soul, surrounded, watched, touched by beings more grotesque and inhuman than the worst creations of a nightmare, it would be possible for me to eat in utter forgetfulness of all these things. They stood about us watching us, and ever and again making a slight elusive twittering that stood them, I suppose, in the stead of speech. I did not even shiver at their touch. And when the first zeal of my feeding was over, I could note that Cavor, too, had been eating with the same shameless abandon.

CHAPTER FOURTEEN

Experiments in Intercourse

When at last we had made an end of eating, the Selenites linked our hands closely together again, and then untwisted the chains about our feet and rebound them, so as to give us a limited freedom of movement. Then they unfastened the chains about our waists. To do all this they had to handle us

freely, and ever and again one of their queer heads came down close to my face, or a soft tentacle-hand touched my head or neck. I don't remember that I was afraid then or repelled by their proximity. I think that our incurable anthropomorphism made us imagine there were human heads inside their masks. The skin, like everything else, looked bluish, but that was on account of the light; and it was hard and shiny, quite in the beetle-wing fashion, not soft, or moist, or hairy, as a vertebrated animal's would be. Along the crest of the head was a low ridge of whitish spines running from back to front, and a much larger ridge curved on either side over the eyes. The Selenite who untied me used his mouth to help his hands.

'They seem to be releasing us,' said Cavor. 'Remember we are on the moon! Make no sudden movements!'

'Are you going to try that geometry?'

'If I get a chance. But, of course, they may make an advance first.'

We remained passive, and the Selenites, having finished their arrange-ments, stood back from us, and seemed to be looking at us. I say seemed to be, because as their eyes were at the side and not in front, one had the same difficulty in determining the direction in which they were looking as one has in the case of a hen or a fish. They conversed with one another in their reedy tones, that seemed to me impossible to imitate or define. The door behind us opened wider, and, glancing over my shoulder, I saw a vague large space beyond, in which quite a little crowd of Selenites were standing. They seemed a curiously miscellaneous rabble.

'Do they want us to imitate those sounds?' I asked Cavor.

'I don't think so,' he said.

'It seems to me that they are trying to make us understand something.'

'I can't make anything of their gestures. Do you notice this one, who is worrying with his head like a man with an uncomfortable collar?'

'Let us shake our heads at him.'

We did that, and finding it ineffectual, attempted an imitation of the Selenites' movements. That seemed to interest them. At any rate they all set up the same movement. But as that seemed to lead to nothing, we desisted at last and so did they, and fell into a piping argument among themselves. Then one of them, shorter and very much thicker than the others, and with a particularly wide mouth, squatted down suddenly beside Cavor, and put his hands and feet in the same posture as Cavor's were bound, and then by a dexterous movement stood up.

'Cavor,' I shouted, 'they want us to get up!'

He stared open-mouthed. 'That's it!' he said.

And with much heaving and grunting, because our hands were tied together, we contrived to struggle to our feet. The Selenites made way for our elephantine heavings, and seemed to twitter more volubly. As soon as we were on our feet the thick-set Selenite came and patted each of our faces with his tentacles, and walked towards the open doorway. That also was

plain enough, and we followed him. We saw that four of the Selenites standing in the doorway were much taller than the others, and clothed in the same manner as those we had seen in the crater, namely, with spiked round helmets and cylindrical body-cases, and that each of the four carried a goad with spike and guard made of that same dull-looking metal as the bowls. These four closed about us, one on either side of each of us, as we emerged from our chamber into the cavern from which the light had come.

We did not get our impression of that cavern all at once. Our attention was taken up by the movements and attitudes of the Selenites immediately about us, and by the necessity of controlling our motion, lest we should startle and alarm them and ourselves by some excessive stride. In front of us was the short, thick-set being who had solved the problem of asking us to get up, moving with gestures that seemed, almost all of them, intelligible to us, inviting us to follow him. His spout-like face turned from one of us to the other with a quickness that was clearly interrogative. For a time, I say, we were taken up with these things.

But at last the great place that formed a background to our movements asserted itself. It became apparent that the source of much, at least, of the tumult of sounds which had filled our ears ever since we had recovered from the stupefaction of the fungus was a vast mass of machinery in active movement, whose flying and whirling parts were visible indistinctly over the heads and between the bodies of the Selenites who walked about us. And not only did the web of sounds that filled the air proceed from this mechanism, but also the peculiar blue light that irradiated the whole place. We had taken it as a natural thing that a subterranean cavern should be artificially lit, and even now, though the fact was patent to my eyes, I did not really grasp its import until presently the darkness came. The meaning and structure of this huge apparatus we saw I cannot explain, because we neither of us learnt what it was for or how it worked. One after another, big shafts of metal flung out and up from its centre, their heads travelling in what seemed to me to be a parabolic path; each dropped a sort of dangling arm as it rose towards the apex of its flight and plunged down into a vertical cylinder, forcing this down before it. About it moved the shapes of tenders, little figures that seemed vaguely different from the beings about us. As each of the three dangling arms of the machine plunged down, there was a clank and then a roaring, and out of the top of the vertical cylinder came pouring this incandescent substance that lit the place, and ran over as milk runs over a boiling pot, and dripped luminously into a tank of light below. It was a cold blue light, a sort of phosphorescent glow but infinitely brighter, and from the tanks into which it fell it ran in conduits athwart the cavern.

Thud, thud, thud, thud, came the sweeping arms of this unintelligible apparatus, and the light substance hissed and poured. At first the thing seemed only reasonably large and near to us, and then I saw how exceedingly little the Selenites upon it seemed, and I realised the full immensity of

cavern and machine. I looked from this tremendous affair to the faces of the Selenites with a new respect. I stopped, and Cavor stopped, and stared at this thunderous engine.

'But this is stupendous!' I said. 'What can it be for?'

Cavor's blue-lit face was full of an intelligent respect. 'I can't dream! Surely these beings – Men could not make a thing like that! Look at those arms, are they on connecting rods?'

The thick-set Selenite had gone some paces unheeded. He came back and stood between us and the great machine. I avoided seeing him, because I guessed somehow that his idea was to beckon us onward. He walked away in the direction he wished us to go, and turned and came back, and flicked our faces to attract our attention.

Cavor and I looked at one another.

'Cannot we show him we are interested in the machine?' I said.

'Yes,' said Cavor. 'We'll try that.' He turned to our guide and smiled, and pointed to the machine, and pointed again, and then to his head, and then to the machine. By some defect of reasoning he seemed to imagine that broken English might help these gestures. 'Me look 'im,' he said, 'me think 'im very much. Yes.'

His behaviour seemed to check the Selenites in their desire for our progress for a moment. They faced one another, their queer heads moved, the twittering voices came quick and liquid. Then one of them, a lean, tall creature, with a sort of mantle added to the puttee in which the others were dressed, twisted his elephant trunk of a hand about Cavor's waist, and pulled him gently to follow our guide, who again went on ahead.

Cavor resisted. 'We may just as well begin explaining ourselves now. They may think we are new animals, a new sort of mooncalf perhaps! It is most important that we should show an intelligent interest from the outset.'

He began to shake his head violently. 'No, no,' he said, 'me not come on one minute. Me look at 'im.'

'Isn't there some geometrical point you might bring in apropos of that affair?' I suggested, as the Selenites conferred again.

'Possibly a parabolic – ' he began.

He yelled loudly, and leaped six feet or more!

One of the four armed moon-men had pricked him with a goad!

I turned on the goad-bearer behind me with a swift threatening gesture, and he started back. This and Cavor's sudden shout and leap clearly astonished all the Selenites. They receded hastily, facing us. For one of those moments that seem to last for ever, we stood in angry protest, with a scattered semicircle of these inhuman beings about us.

'He pricked me!' said Cavor, with a catching of the voice.

'I saw him,' I answered.

'Confound it!' I said to the Selenites; 'we're not going to stand that! What on earth do you take us for?'

I glanced quickly right and left. Far away across the blue wilderness of cavern I saw a number of other Selenites running towards us; broad and slender they were, and one with a larger head than the others. The cavern spread wide and low, and receded in every direction into darkness. Its roof, I remember, seemed to bulge down as if with the weight of the vast thickness of rocks that prisoned us. There was no way out of it – no way out of it. Above, below, in every direction, was the unknown, and these inhuman creatures, with goads and gestures, confronting us, and we two unsupported men!

CHAPTER FIFTEEN

The Giddy Bridge

Just for a moment that hostile pause endured. I suppose that both we and the Selenites did some very rapid thinking. My clearest impression was that there was nothing to put my back against, and that we were bound to be surrounded and killed. The overwhelming folly of our presence there loomed over me in black, enormous reproach. Why had I ever launched myself on this mad, inhuman expedition?

Cavor came to my side and laid his hand on my arm. His pale and terrified face was ghastly in the blue light.

'We can't do anything,' he said. 'It's a mistake. They don't understand. We must go. As they want us to go.'

I looked down at him, and then at the fresh Selenites who were coming to help their fellows. 'If I had my hands free – '

'It's no use,' he panted.

'No.'

'We'll go.'

And he turned about and led the way in the direction that had been indicated for us.

I followed, trying to look as subdued as possible, and feeling at the chains about my wrists. My blood was boiling. I noted nothing more of that cavern, though it seemed to take a long time before we had marched across it, or if I noted anything I forgot it as I saw it. My thoughts were concentrated, I think, upon my chains and the Selenites, and particularly upon the helmeted ones with the goads. At first they marched parallel with us, and at a respectful distance, but presently they were overtaken by three others, and then they drew nearer, until they were within arm's length again. I winced like a beaten horse as they came near to us. The shorter, thicker Selenite marched at first on our right flank, but presently came in front of us again.

How well the picture of that grouping has bitten into my brain; the back

of Cavor's downcast head just in front of me, and the dejected droop of his shoulders, and our guide's gaping visage, perpetually jerking about him, and the goad-bearers on either side, watchful, yet open-mouthed – a blue monochrome. And after all, I *do* remember one other thing besides the purely personal affair, which is, that a sort of gutter came presently across the floor of the cavern, and then ran along by the side of the path of rock we followed. And it was full of that same bright blue luminous stuff that flowed out of the great machine. I walked close beside it, and I can testify it radiated not a particle of heat. It was brightly shining, and yet it was neither warmer nor colder than anything else in the cavern.

Clang, clang, clang, we passed right under the thumping levers of another vast machine, and so came at last to a wide tunnel, in which we could even hear the pad, pad, of our shoeless feet, and which, save for the trickling thread of blue to the right of us, was quite unlit. The shadows made gigantic travesties of our shapes and those of the Selenites on the irregular wall and roof of the tunnel. Ever and again crystals in the walls of the tunnel scintillated like gems, ever and again the tunnel expanded into a stalactitic cavern, or gave off branches that vanished into darkness.

We seemed to be marching down that tunnel for a long time. 'Trickle, trickle,' went the flowing light very softly, and our footfalls and their echoes made an irregular paddle, paddle. My mind settled down to the question of my chains. If I were to slip off one turn *so*, and then to twist it *so* . . .

If I tried to do it very gradually, would they see I was slipping my wrist out of the looser turn? If they did, what would they do?

'Bedford,' said Cavor, 'it goes down. It keeps on going down.'

His remark roused me from my sullen preoccupation.

'If they wanted to kill us,' he said, dropping back to come level with me, 'there is no reason why they should not have done it.'

'No,' I admitted, 'that's true.'

'They don't understand us,' he said, 'they think we are merely strange animals, some wild sort of mooncalf birth, perhaps. It will be only when they have observed us better that they will begin to think we have minds – '

'When you trace those geometrical problems,' said I.

'It may be that.'

We tramped on for a space.

'You see,' said Cavor, 'these may be Selenites of a lower class.'

'The infernal fools!' said I viciously, glancing at their exasperating faces. 'If we endure what they do to us – '

'We've got to endure it,' said I.

'There may be others less stupid. This is the mere outer fringe of their world. It must go down and down, cavern, passage, tunnel, down at last to the sea – hundreds of miles below.'

His words made me think of the mile or so of rock and tunnel that might

be over our heads already. It was like a weight dropping on my shoulders. 'Away from the sun and air,' I said. 'Even a mine half a mile deep is stuffy.'

'This is not, anyhow. It's probable – Ventilation! The air would blow from the dark side of the moon to the sunlit, and all the carbonic acid would well out there and feed those plants. Up this tunnel, for example, there is quite a breeze. And what a world it must be. The earnest we have in that shaft, and those machines – '

'And the goad,' I said. 'Don't forget the goad!'

He walked a little in front of me for a time.

'Even that goad – ' he said.

'Well?'

'I was angry at the time. But – it was perhaps necessary we should get on. They have different skins, and probably different nerves. They may not understand our objection – Just as a being from Mars might not like our earthly habit of nudging – '

'They'd better be careful how they nudge *me*.'

'And about that geometry. After all, their way is a way of understanding, too. They begin with the elements of life and not of thought. Food. Compulsion. Pain. They strike at fundamentals.'

'There's no doubt about *that*,' I said.

He went on to talk of the enormous and wonderful world into which we were being taken. I realised slowly from his tone, that even now he was not absolutely in despair at the prospect of going ever deeper into this inhuman planet-burrow. His mind ran on machines and invention, to the exclusion of a thousand dark things that beset me. It wasn't that he intended to make any use of these things, he simply wanted to know them.

'After all,' he said, 'this is a tremendous occasion. It is the meeting of two worlds! What are we going to see? Think of what is below us here.'

'We shan't see much if the light isn't better,' I remarked.

'This is only the outer crust. Down below – On this scale – There will be everything. Do you notice how different they seem one from another? The story we shall take back!'

'Some rare sort of animal,' I said, 'might comfort himself in that way while they were bringing him to the Zoo . . . It doesn't follow that we are going to be shown all these things.'

'When they find we have reasonable minds,' said Cavor, 'they will want to learn about the earth. Even if they have no generous emotions, they will teach in order to learn . . . And the things they must know! The unanticipated things!'

He went on to speculate on the possibility of their knowing things he had never hoped to learn on earth, speculating in that way, with a raw wound from that goad already in his skin! Much that he said I forget, for my attention was drawn to the fact that the tunnel along which we had been marching was opening out wider and wider. We seemed, from the feeling of

the air, to be going out into a huge space. But how big the space might really be we could not tell, because it was unlit. Our little stream of light ran in a dwindling thread and vanished far ahead. Presently the rocky walls had vanished altogether on either hand. There was nothing to be seen but the path in front of us and the trickling hurrying rivulet of blue phosphorescence. The figures of Cavor and the guiding Selenite marched before me, the sides of their legs and heads that were towards the rivulet were clear and bright blue, their darkened sides, now that the reflection of the tunnel wall no longer lit them, merged indistinguishably in the darkness beyond.

And soon I perceived that we were approaching a declivity of some sort, because the little blue stream dipped suddenly out of sight.

In another moment, as it seemed, we had reached the edge. The shining stream gave one meander of hesitation and then rushed over. It fell to a depth at which the sound of its descent was absolutely lost to us. Far below was a bluish glow, a sort of blue mist – at an infinite distance below. And the darkness the stream dropped out of became utterly void and black, save that a thing like a plank projected from the edge of the cliff and stretched out and faded and vanished altogether. There was a warm air blowing up out of the gulf.

For a moment I and Cavor stood as near the edge as we dared, peering into a blue-tinged profundity. And then our guide was pulling at my arm.

Then he left me, and walked to the end of that plank and stepped upon it, looking back. Then when he perceived we watched him, he turned about and went on along it, walking as surely as though he was on firm earth. For a moment his form was distinct, then he became a blue blur, and then vanished into the obscurity. I became aware of some vague shape looming darkly out of the black.

There was a pause. 'Surely – !' said Cavor.

One of the other Selenites walked a few paces out upon the plank, and turned and looked back at us unconcernedly. The others stood ready to follow after us. Our guide's expectant figure reappeared. He was returning to see why we had not advanced.

'What is that beyond there?' I asked.

'I can't see.'

'We can't cross this at any price,' said I.

'I could not go three steps on it,' said Cavor, 'even with my hands free.'

We looked at each other's drawn faces in blank consternation.

'They can't know what it is to be giddy!' said Cavor.

'It's quite impossible for us to walk that plank.'

'I don't believe they see as we do. I've been watching them. I wonder if they know this is simply blackness for us. How can we make them understand?'

'Anyhow, we must make them understand.'

I think we said these things with a vague half hope the Selenites might

somehow understand. I knew quite clearly that all that was needed was an explanation. Then as I saw their faces, I realised that an explanation was impossible. Just here it was that our resemblances were not going to bridge our differences. Well, I wasn't going to walk the plank, anyhow. I slipped my wrist very quickly out of the coil of chain that was loose, and then began to twist my wrists in opposite directions. I was standing nearest to the bridge, and as I did this two of the Selenites laid hold of me, and pulled me gently towards it.

I shook my head violently. 'No go,' I said, 'no use. You don't understand.' Another Selenite added his compulsion. I was forced to step forward.

'I've got an idea,' said Cavor; but I knew his ideas.

'Look here!' I exclaimed to the Selenites. 'Steady on! It's all very well for you – '

I sprang round upon my heel. I burst out into curses. For one of the armed Selenites had stabbed me behind with his goad.

I wrenched my wrists free from the little tentacles that held them. I turned on the goad-bearer. 'Confound you!' I cried. 'I've warned you of that. What on earth do you think I'm made of, to stick that into me? If you touch me again – '

By way of answer he pricked me forthwith.

I heard Cavor's voice in alarm and entreaty. Even then I think he wanted to compromise with these creatures. 'I say, Bedford,' he cried, 'I know a way!' But the sting of that second stab seemed to set free some pent-up reserve of energy in my being. Instantly the link of the wrist-chain snapped, and with it snapped all considerations that had held us unresisting in the hands of these moon creatures. For that second, at least, I was mad with fear and anger. I took no thought of consequences. I hit straight out at the face of the thing with the goad. The chain was twisted round my fist . . .

There came another of these beastly surprises of which the moon world is full.

My mailed hand seemed to go clean through him. He smashed like – like some softish sort of sweet with liquid in it! He broke right in! He squelched and splashed. It was like hitting a damp toadstool. The flimsy body went spinning a dozen yards, and fell with a flabby impact. I was astonished. I was incredulous that any living thing could be so flimsy. For an instant I could have believed the whole thing a dream.

Then it had become real and imminent again. Neither Cavor nor the other Selenites seemed to have done anything from the time when I had turned about to the time when the dead Selenite hit the ground. Everyone stood back from us two, everyone alert. That arrest seemed to last at least a second after the Selenite was down. Everyone must have been taking the thing in. I seem to remember myself standing with my arm half retracted, trying also to take it in. 'What next?' clamoured my brain; 'what next?' Then in a moment everyone was moving!

I perceived we must get our chains loose, and that before we could do this these Selenites had to be beaten off. I faced towards the group of the three goad-bearers. Instantly one threw his goad at me. It swished over my head, and I suppose went flying into the abyss behind.

I leaped right at him with all my might as the goad flew over me. He turned to run as I jumped, and I bore him to the ground, came down right upon him, and slipped upon his smashed body and fell. He seemed to wriggle under my foot.

I came into a sitting position, and on every hand the blue backs of the Selenites were receding into the darkness. I bent a link by main force and untwisted the chain that had hampered me about the ankles, and sprang to my feet, with the chain in my hand. Another goad, flung javelin-wise, whistled by me, and I made a rush towards the darkness out of which it had come. Then I turned back towards Cavor, who was still standing in the light of the rivulet near the gulf convulsively busy with his wrists, and at the same time jabbering nonsense about his idea.

'Come on!' I cried.

'My hands!' he answered.

Then, realising that I dared not run back to him, because my ill-calculated steps might carry me over the edge, he came shuffling towards me, with his hands held out before him.

I gripped his chains at once to unfasten them.

'Where are they?' he panted.

'Run away. They'll come back. They're throwing things! Which way shall we go?'

'By the light. To that tunnel. Eh?'

'Yes,' said I, and his hands were free.

I dropped on my knees and fell to work on his ankle bonds. Whack came something – I know not what – and splashed the livid streamlet into drops about us. Far away on our right a piping and whistling began.

I whipped the chain off his feet, and put it in his hand. 'Hit with that!' I said, and without waiting for an answer, set off in big bounds along the path by which we had come. I had a nasty sort of feeling that these things could jump out of the darkness on to my back. I heard the impact of his leaps come following after me.

We ran in vast strides. But that running, you must understand, was an altogether different thing from any running on earth. On earth one leaps and almost instantly hits the ground again, but on the moon, because of its weaker pull, one shot through the air for several seconds before one came to earth. In spite of our violent hurry this gave an effect of long pauses, pauses in which one might have counted seven or eight. 'Step,' and one soared off! All sorts of questions ran through my mind: 'Where are the Selenites? What will they do? Shall we ever get to that tunnel? Is Cavor far behind? Are they likely to cut him off?' Then whack, stride, and off again for another step.

I saw a Selenite running in front of me, his legs going exactly as a man's would go on earth, saw him glance over his shoulder, and heard him shriek as he ran aside out of my way into the darkness. He was, I think, our guide, but I am not sure. Then in another vast stride the walls of rock had come into view on either hand, and in two more strides I was in the tunnel, and tempering my pace to its low roof. I went on to a bend, then stopped and turned back, and plug, plug, plug, Cavor came into view, splashing into the stream of blue light at every stride, and grew larger and blundered into me. We stood clutching each other. For a moment, at least, we had shaken off our captors and were alone.

We were both very much out of breath. We spoke in panting, broken sentences.

'You've spoilt it all!' panted Cavor.

'Nonsense,' I cried. 'It was that or death!'

'What are we to do?'

'Hide.'

'How can we?'

'It's dark enough.'

'But where?'

'Up one of these side caverns.'

'And then?'

'Think.'

'Right – come on.'

We strode on, and presently came to a radiating dark cavern. Cavor was in front. He hesitated, and chose a black mouth that seemed to promise good hiding. He went towards it and turned.

'Its dark,' he said.

'Your legs and feet will light us. You're wet with that luminous stuff.'

'But – '

A tumult of sounds, and in particular a sound like a clanging gong, advancing up the main tunnel, became audible. It was horribly suggestive of a tumultuous pursuit. We made a bolt for the unlit side cavern forthwith. As we ran along it our way was lit by the irradiation of Cavor's legs. 'It's lucky,' I panted, 'they took off our boots, or we should fill this place with clatter.' On we rushed, taking as small steps as we could to avoid striking the roof of the cavern. After a time we seemed to be gaining on the uproar. It became muffled, it dwindled, it died away.

I stopped and looked back, and I heard the pad, pad of Cavor's feet receding. Then he stopped also. 'Bedford,' he whispered, 'there's a sort of light in front of us.'

I looked, and at first could see nothing. Then I perceived his head and shoulders dimly outlined against a fainter darkness. I saw, also, that this mitigation of the darkness was not blue, as all the other light within the moon had been, but a pallid grey, a very vague, faint white, the daylight

colour. Cavor noted this difference as soon, or sooner, than I did, and I think, too, that it filled him with much the same wild hope.

'Bedford,' he whispered, and his voice trembled. 'That light – it is possible – '

He did not dare to say the thing he hoped. Then came a pause. Suddenly I knew by the sound of his feet that he was striding towards that pallor. I followed him with a beating heart.

CHAPTER SIXTEEN

Points of View

The light grew stronger as we advanced. In a little time it was nearly as strong as the phosphorescence on Cavor's legs. Our tunnel was expanding into a cavern, and this new light was at the farther end of it. I perceived something that set my hopes leaping and bounding.

'Cavor,' I said, 'it comes from above! I am certain it comes from above!'

He made no answer, but hurried on.

Indisputably it was a grey light, a silvery light.

In another moment we were beneath it. It filtered down through a chink in the walls of the cavern, and as I stared up, drip, came a drop of water upon my face. I started and stood aside – drip, fell another drop quite audibly on the rocky floor.

'Cavor,' I said, 'if one of us lifts the other, he can reach that crack!'

'I'll lift you,' he said, and incontinently hoisted me as though I was a baby.

I thrust an arm into the crack, and just at my fingertips found a little ledge by which I could hold. I could see the white light was very much brighter now. I pulled myself up by two fingers with scarcely an effort, though on earth I weigh twelve stone, reached to a still higher corner of rock, and so got my feet on the narrow ledge. I stood up and searched up the rocks with my fingers; the cleft broadened out upwardly. 'It's climbable,' I said to Cavor. 'Can you jump up to my hand if I hold it down to you?'

I wedged myself between the sides of the cleft, rested knee and foot on the ledge, and extended a hand. I could not see Cavor, but I could hear the rustle of his movements as he crouched to spring. Then whack and he was hanging to my arm – and no heavier than a kitten! I lugged him up until he had a hand on my ledge, and could release me.

'Confound it!' I said, 'anyone could be a mountaineer on the moon;' and so set myself in earnest to the climbing. For a few minutes I clambered steadily, and then I looked up again. The cleft opened out steadily, and the light was brighter. Only –

It was not daylight after all.

In another moment I could see what it was, and at the sight I could have beaten my head against the rocks with disappointment. For I beheld simply an irregularly sloping open space, and all over its slanting floor stood a forest of little club-shaped fungi, each shining gloriously with that pinkish silvery light. For a moment I stared at their soft radiance, then sprang forward and upward among them. I plucked up half a dozen and flung them against the rocks, and then sat down, laughing bitterly, as Cavor's ruddy face came into view.

'It's phosphorescence again!' I said. 'No need to hurry. Sit down and make yourself at home.' And as he spluttered over our disappointment, I began to lob more of these growths into the cleft.

'I thought it was daylight,' he said.

'Daylight!' cried I. 'Daybreak, sunset, clouds, and windy skies! Shall we ever see such things again?'

As I spoke, a little picture of our world seemed to rise before me, bright and little and clear, like the background of some old Italian picture. 'The sky that changes, and the sea that changes, and the hills and the green trees and the towns and cities shining in the sun. Think of a wet roof at sunset, Cavor! Think of the windows of a westward house!' He made no answer.

'Here we are burrowing in this beastly world that isn't a world, with its inky ocean hidden in some abominable blackness below, and outside that torrid day and that death stillness of night. And all these things that are chasing us now, beastly men of leather – insect men, that come out of a nightmare! After all, they're right! What business have we here smashing them and disturbing their world! For all we know the whole planet is up and after us already. In a minute we may hear them whimpering, and their gongs going. What are we to do? Where are we to go? Here we are as comfortable as snakes from Jamrach's loose in a Surbiton villa!'

'It was your fault,' said Cavor.

'My fault!' I shouted. 'Good Lord!'

'I had an idea!'

'Curse your ideas!'

'If we had refused to budge – '

'Under those goads?'

'Yes. They would have carried us!'

'Over that bridge?'

'Yes. They must have carried us from outside.'

'I'd rather be carried by a fly across a ceiling.'

'Good Heavens!'

I resumed my destruction of the fungi. Then suddenly I saw something that struck me even then.

'Cavor,' I said, 'these chains are of gold!'

He was thinking intently, with his hands gripping his cheeks. He turned

his head slowly and stared at me, and when I had repeated my words, at the twisted chain about his right hand. 'So they are,' he said, 'so they are.' His face lost its transitory interest even as he looked. He hesitated for a moment, then went on with his interrupted meditation. I sat for a space puzzling over the fact that I had only just observed this, until I considered the blue light in which we had been, and which had taken all the colour out of the metal. And from that discovery I also started upon a train of thought that carried me wide and far. I forgot that I had just been asking what business we had in the moon. Gold –

It was Cavor who spoke first. 'It seems to me that there are two courses open to us.'

'Well.'

'Either we can attempt to make our way – fight our way if necessary – out to the exterior again, and then hunt for our sphere until we find it, or the cold of the night comes to kill us, or else – '

He paused. 'Yes?' I said, though I knew what was coming.

'We might attempt once more to establish some sort of understanding with the minds of the people in the moon.'

'So far as I'm concerned – it's the first.'

'I doubt.'

'I don't.'

'You see,' said Cavor, 'I do not think we can judge the Selenites by what we have seen of them. Their central world, their civilised world will be far below in the profounder caverns about their sea. This region of the crust in which we are is an outlying district, a pastoral region. At any rate, that is my interpretation. These Selenites we have seen may be only the equivalent of cowboys and engine-tenders. Their use of goads – in all probability moon-calf goads – the lack of imagination they show in expecting us to be able to do just what they can do, their indisputable brutality, all seem to point to something of that sort. But if we endured – '

'Neither of us could endure a six-inch plank across the bottomless pit for very long.'

'No,' said Cavor; 'but then – '

'I *won't*,' I said.

He discovered a new line of possibilities. 'Well, suppose we got ourselves into some corner, where we could defend ourselves against these hinds and labourers. If, for example, we could hold out for a week or so, it is probable that the news of our appearance would filter down to the more intelligent and populous parts – '

'If they exist.'

'They must exist, or whence came those tremendous machines?'

'That's possible, but it's the worst of the two chances.'

'We might write up inscriptions on walls – '

'How do we know their eyes would see the sort of marks we made?'

'If we cut them – '

'That's possible, of course.'

I took up a new thread of thought. 'After all,' I said, 'I suppose you don't think these Selenites so infinitely wiser than men.'

'They must know a lot more – or at least a lot of different things.'

'Yes, but – ' I hesitated.

'I think you'll quite admit, Cavor, that you're rather an exceptional man.'

'How?'

'Well, you – you're a rather lonely man – have been, that is. You haven't married.'

'Never wanted to. But why – '

'And you never grew richer than you happened to be?'

'Never wanted that either.'

'You've just rooted after knowledge?'

'Well, a certain curiosity is natural – '

'You think so. That's just it. You think every other mind wants to *know*. I remember once, when I asked you why you conducted all these researches, you said you wanted your FRS, and to have the stuff called Cavorite, and things like that. You know perfectly well you didn't do it for that; but at the time my question took you by surprise, and you felt you ought to have something to look like a motive. Really you conducted researches because you *had* to. It's your twist.'

'Perhaps it is – '

'It isn't one man in a million has that twist. Most men want – well, various things, but very few want knowledge for its own sake. *I* don't, I know perfectly well. Now, these Selenites seem to be a driving, busy sort of being, but how do you know that even the most intelligent will take an interest in us or our world? I don't believe they'll even know we have a world. They never come out at night – they'd freeze if they did. They've probably never seen any heavenly body at all except the blazing sun. How are they to know there is another world? What does it matter to them if they do? Well, even if they *have* had a glimpse of a few stars, or even of the earth crescent, what of that? Why should people living *inside* a planet trouble to observe that sort of thing? Men wouldn't have done it except for the seasons and sailing; why should the moon people? . . .

'Well, suppose there are a few philosophers like yourself. They are just the very Selenites who'll never have heard of our existence. Suppose a Selenite had dropped on the earth when you were at Lympne, you'd have been the last man in the world to hear he had come. You never read a newspaper! You see the chances against you. Well, it's for these chances we're sitting here doing nothing while precious time is flying. I tell you we've got into a fix. We've come unarmed, we've lost our sphere, we've got no food, we've shown ourselves to the Selenites, and made them think we're strange, strong, dangerous animals; and unless these Selenites are perfect

fools, they'll set about now and hunt us till they find us, and when they find us they'll try to take us if they can, and kill us if they can't, and that's the end of the matter. If they take us, they'll probably kill us, through some misunderstanding. After we're done for, they may discuss us perhaps, but we shan't get much fun out of that.'

'Go on.'

'On the other hand, here's gold knocking about like cast iron at home. If only we can get some of it back, if only we can find our sphere again before they do, and get back, then – '

'Yes?'

'We might put the thing on a sounder footing. Come back in a bigger sphere with guns.'

'Good Lord!' cried Cavor, as though that was horrible.

I sliced another luminous fungus down the cleft.

'Look here, Cavor,' I said, 'I've half the voting power anyhow in this affair, and this is a case for a practical man. I'm a practical man, and you are not. I'm not going to trust to Selenites and geometrical diagrams if I can help it . . . That's all. Get back. Drop all this secrecy – or most of it. And come again.'

He reflected. 'When I came to the moon,' he said, 'I ought to have come alone.'

'The question before the meeting,' I said, 'is how to get back to the sphere.'

For a time we nursed our knees in silence. Then he seemed to decide for my reasons.

'I think,' he said, 'one can get data. It is clear that while the sun is on this side of the moon the air will be blowing through this planet sponge from the dark side hither. On this side, at any rate, the air will be expanding and flowing out of the moon caverns into the craters . . . Very well, there's a draught here.'

'So there is.'

'And that means that this is not a dead end; somewhere behind us this cleft goes on and up. The draught is blowing up, and that is the way we have to go. If we try to get up any sort of chimney or gully there is, we shall not only get out of these passages where they are hunting for us – '

'But suppose the gully is too narrow?'

'We'll come down again.'

'Ssh!' I said suddenly; 'what's that?'

We listened. At first it was an indistinct murmur, and then one picked out the clang of a gong. 'They must think we are mooncalves,' said I, 'to be frightened at that.'

'They're coming along that passage,' said Cavor.

'They must be.'

'They'll not think of the cleft. They'll go past.'

I listened again for a space. 'This time,' I whispered, 'they're likely to have some sort of weapon.'

Then suddenly I sprang to my feet. 'Good heavens, Cavor!' I cried. 'But they *will*! They'll see the fungi I have been pitching down. They'll – !'

I didn't finish my sentence. I turned about and made a leap over the fungus tops towards the upper end of the cavity. I saw that the space turned upward and became a draughty cleft again, ascending to impenetrable darkness. I was about to clamber up into this, and then with a happy inspiration turned back.

'What are you doing?' asked Cavor.

'Go on!' said I, and went back and got two of the shining fungi, and putting one into the breast pocket of my flannel jacket, so that it stuck out to light our climbing, went back with the other for Cavor. The noise of the Selenites was now so loud that it seemed they must be already beneath the cleft. But it might be they would have difficulty in clambering into it, or might hesitate to ascend it against our possible resistance. At any rate, we had now the comforting knowledge of the enormous muscular superiority our birth in another planet gave us. In other minute I was clambering with gigantic vigour after Cavor's blue-lit heels.

CHAPTER SEVENTEEN

The Fight in the Cave of the Moon Butchers

I do not know how far we clambered before we came to the grating. It may be we ascended only a few hundred feet, but at the time it seemed to me we might have hauled and jammed and hopped and wedged ourselves through a mile or more of vertical ascent. Whenever I recall that time there comes into my head the heavy clank of our golden chains that followed every movement. Very soon my knuckles and knees were raw, and I had a bruise on one cheek. After a time the first violence of our efforts diminished, and our movements became more deliberate and less painful. The noise of the pursuing Selenites had died away altogether. It seemed almost as though they had not traced us up the crack after all, in spite of the tell-tale heap of broken fungi that must have lain beneath it. At times the cleft narrowed so much that we could scarce squeeze up it; at others it expanded into great drusy cavities, studded with prickly crystals or thickly beset with dull, shining fungoid pimples. Sometimes it twisted spirally, and at other times slanted down nearly to the horizontal direction. Ever and again there was the intermittent drip and trickle of water by us. Once or twice it seemed to us that small living things had rustled out of our reach, but what they were we never saw. They may have been venomous beasts for all I know, but they did us no harm, and we were now tuned to a pitch when a weird creeping

thing more or less mattered little. And at last, far above, came the familiar bluish light again, and then we saw that it filtered through a grating that barred our way.

We whispered as we pointed this out to one another, and became more and more cautious in our ascent. Presently we were close under the grating, and by pressing my face against its bars I could see a limited portion of the cavern beyond. It was clearly a large space, and lit no doubt by some rivulet of the same blue light that we had seen flow from the beating machinery. An intermittent trickle of water dropped ever and again between the bars near my face.

My first endeavour was naturally to see what might be upon the floor of the cavern, but our grating lay in a depression whose rim hid all this from our eyes. Our foiled attention then fell back upon the suggestion of the various sounds we heard, and presently my eye caught a number of faint shadows that played across the dim roof far overhead.

Indisputably there were several Selenites, perhaps a considerable number, in this space, for we could hear the noises of their intercourse, and faint sounds that I identified as their footfalls. There was also a succession of regularly repeated sounds – chid, chid, chid – which began and ceased, suggestive of a knife or spade hacking at some soft substance. Then came a clank as if of chains, a whistle and a rumble as of a truck running over a hollowed place, and then again that chid, chid, chid resumed. The shadows told of shapes that moved quickly and rhythmically, in agreement with that regular sound, and rested when it ceased.

We put our heads close together, and began to discuss these things in noiseless whispers.

'They are occupied,' I said, 'they are occupied in some way.'

'Yes.'

'They're not seeking us, or thinking of us.'

'Perhaps they have not heard of us.'

'Those others are hunting about below. If suddenly we appeared here – '

We looked at one another.

'There might be a chance to parley,' said Cavor.

'No,' I said. 'Not as we are.'

For a space we remained, each occupied by his own thoughts.

Chid, chid, chid went the chopping, and the shadows moved to and fro.

I looked at the grating. 'It's flimsy,' I said. 'We might bend two of the bars and crawl through.'

We wasted a little time in vague discussion. Then I took one of the bars in both hands, and got my feet up against the rock until they were almost on a level with my head, and so thrust against the bar. It bent so suddenly that I almost slipped. I clambered about and bent the adjacent bar in the opposite direction, and then took the luminous fungus from my pocket and dropped it down the fissure.

'Don't do anything hastily,' whispered Cavor, as I twisted myself up through the opening I had enlarged. I had a glimpse of busy figures as I came through the grating, and immediately bent down, so that the rim of the depression in which the grating lay hid me from their eyes, and so lay flat, signalling advice to Cavor as he also prepared to come through. Presently we were side by side in the depression, peering over the edge at the cavern and its occupants.

It was a much larger cavern than we had supposed from our first glimpse of it, and we looked up from the lowest portion of its sloping floor. It widened out as it receded from us, and its roof came down and hid the remoter portion altogether. And lying in a line along its length, vanishing at last far away in that tremendous perspective, were a number of huge shapes, huge pallid hulls, upon which the Selenites were busy. At first they seemed big white cylinders of vague import. Then I noted the heads upon them lying towards us, eyeless and skinless like the heads of sheep at a butcher's, and perceived they were the carcasses of mooncalves being cut up, much as the crew of a whaler might cut up a moored whale. They were cutting off the flesh in strips, and on some of the farther trunks the white ribs were showing. It was the sound of their hatchets that made that chid, chid. Some way away a thing like a trolley cable, drawn and loaded with chunks of lax meat, was running up the slope of the cavern floor. This enormous long avenue of hulls that were destined to be food, gave us a sense of the vast populousness of the moon world second only to the effect of our first glimpse down the shaft.

It seemed to me at first that the Selenites must be standing on trestle-supported planks, and then I saw that the planks* and supports and their hatchets were really of the same leaden hue as my fetters had seemed – before white light came to bear on them. A number of very thick-looking crowbars lay about the floor, and had apparently assisted to turn the dead mooncalf over on its side. They were perhaps six feet long, with shaped handles, very tempting-looking weapons. The whole place was lit by three transverse streams of the blue fluid.

We lay for a long time noting all these things in silence. 'Well?' said Cavor at last.

I crouched over and turned to him. I had come upon a brilliant idea. 'Unless they lowered those bodies by a crane,' I said, 'we must be nearer the surface than I thought.'

'Why?'

'The mooncalf doesn't hop, and it hasn't got wings.'

He peered over the edge of the hollow again. 'I wonder now . . . ' he began. 'After all, we have never gone far from the surface – '

I stopped him by a grip on his arm. I had heard a noise from the cleft below us!

We twisted ourselves about, and lay as still as death, with every sense

alert. In a little while I did not doubt that something was quietly ascending the cleft. Very slowly and quite noiselessly I assured myself of a good grip on my chain, and waited for that something to appear.

'Just look at those chaps with the hatchets again,' I said.

'They're all right,' said Cavor.

I took a sort of provisional aim at the gap in the grating. I could hear now quite distinctly the soft twittering of the ascending Selenites, the dab of their hands against the rock, and the falling of dust from their grips as they clambered.

Then I could see that there was something moving dimly in the blackness below the grating, but what it might be I could not distinguish. The whole thing seemed to hang fire just for a moment – then smash! I had sprung to my feet, struck savagely at something that had flashed out at me. It was the keen point of a spear. I have thought since that its length in the narrowness of the cleft must have prevented its being sloped to reach me. Anyhow, it shot out from the grating like the tongue of a snake, and missed and flew back and flashed again. But the second time I snatched and caught it, and wrenched it away, but not before another had darted ineffectually at me.

I shouted with triumph as I felt the hold of the Selenite resist my pull for a moment and give, and then I was jabbing down through the bars, amidst squeals from the darkness, and Cavor had snapped off the other spear, and was leaping and flourishing it beside me, and making inefficient jabs. Clang, clang, came up through the grating, and then an axe hurtled through the air and whacked against the rocks beyond, to remind me of the fleshers at the carcasses up the cavern.

I turned, and they were all coming towards us in open order waving their axes. They were short, thick, little beggars, with long arms, strikingly different from the ones we had seen before. If they had not heard of us before, they must have realised the situation with incredible swiftness. I stared at them for a moment, spear in hand. 'Guard that grating, Cavor,' I cried, howled to intimidate them, and rushed to meet them. Two of them missed with their hatchets, and the rest fled incontinently. Then the two also were sprinting away up the cavern, with hands clenched and heads down. I never saw men run like them!

I knew the spear I had was no good for me. It was thin and flimsy, only effectual for a thrust, and too long for a quick recover. So I only chased the Selenites as far as the first carcass, and stopped there and picked up one of the crowbars that were lying about. It felt comfortingly heavy, and equal to smashing any number of Selenites. I threw away my spear, and picked up a second crowbar for the other hand. I felt five times better than I had with the spear. I shook the two threateningly at the Selenites, who had come to a halt in a little crowd far away up the cavern, and then turned about to look at Cavor.

He was leaping from side to side of the grating, making threatening jabs

with his broken spear. That was all right. It would keep the Selenites down – for a time at any rate. I looked up the cavern again. What on earth were we going to do now?

We were cornered in a sort of way already. But these butchers up the cavern had been surprised, they were probably scared, and they had no special weapons, only those little hatchets of theirs. And that way lay escape. Their sturdy little forms – ever so much shorter and thicker than the mooncalf herds – were scattered up the slope in a way that was eloquent of indecision. I had the moral advantage of a mad bull in a street. But for all that, there seemed a tremendous crowd of them. Very probably there was. Those Selenites down the cleft had certainly some infernally long spears. It might be they had other surprises for us . . . But, confound it! if we charged up the cave we should let them up behind us, and if we didn't those little brutes up the cave would probably get reinforced. Heaven alone knew what tremendous engines of warfare – guns, bombs, terrestrial torpedoes – this unknown world below our feet, this vaster world of which we had only pricked the outer cuticle, might not presently send up to our destruction. It became clear the only thing to do was to charge! It became clearer as the legs of a number of fresh Selenites appeared running down the cavern towards us.

'Bedford!' cried Cavor, and behold! he was halfway between me and the grating.

'Go back!' I cried. 'What are you doing – '

'They've got – it's like a gun!'

And struggling in the grating between those defensive spears appeared the head and shoulders of a singularly lean and angular Selenite, bearing some complicated apparatus.

I realised Cavor's utter incapacity for the fight we had in hand. For a moment I hesitated. Then I rushed past him whirling my crowbars, and shouting to confound the aim of the Selenite. He was aiming in the queerest way with the thing against his stomach. '*Chuzz!*' The thing wasn't a gun; it went off like crossbow more, and dropped me in the middle of a leap.

I didn't fall down, I simply came down a little shorter than I should have done if I hadn't been hit, and from the feel of my shoulder the thing might have tapped me and glanced off. Then my left hand hit again the shaft, and I perceived there was a sort of spear sticking half through my shoulder. The moment after I got home with the crowbar in my right hand, and hit the Selenite fair and square. He collapsed – he crushed and crumpled – his head smashed like an egg.

I dropped a crowbar, pulled the spear out of my shoulder, and began to jab it down the grating into the darkness. At each jab came a shriek and twitter. Finally I hurled the spear down upon them with all my strength, leapt up, picked up the crowbar again, and started for the multitude up the cavern.

'Bedford!' cried Cavor. 'Bedford!' as I flew past him.

I seem to remember his footsteps coming on behind me.

Step, leap . . . whack, step, leap . . . Each leap seemed to last ages. With each, the cave opened out and the number of Selenites visible increased. At first they seemed all running about like ants in a disturbed ant-hill, one or two waving hatchets and coming to meet me, more running away, some bolting sideways into the avenue of carcasses, then presently others came in sight carrying spears, and then others. I saw a most extraordinary thing, all hands and feet, bolting for cover. The cavern grew darker farther up. Flick! something flew over my head. Flick! As I soared in mid-stride I saw a spear hit and quiver in one of the carcasses to my left. Then, as I came down, one hit the ground before me, and I heard the remote chuzz! with which their things were fired. Flick, flick! for a moment it was a shower. They were volleying!

I stopped dead.

I don't think I thought clearly then. I seem to remember a kind of stereotyped phrase running through my mind: 'Zone of fire, seek cover!' I know I made a dash for the space between two of the carcasses, and stood there panting and feeling very wicked.

I looked round for Cavor, and for a moment it seemed as if he had vanished from the world. Then he came out of the darkness between the row of the carcasses and the rocky wall of the cavern. I saw his little face, dark and blue, and shining with perspiration and emotion.

He was saying something, but what it was I did not heed. I had realised that we might work from mooncalf to mooncalf up the cave until we were near enough to charge home. It was charge or nothing. 'Come on!' I said, and led the way.

'Bedford!' he cried unavailingly.

My mind was busy as we went up that narrow alley between the dead bodies and the wall of the cavern. The rocks curved about – they could not enfilade us. Though in that narrow space we could not leap, yet with our earth-born strength we were still able to go very much faster than the Selenites. I reckoned we should presently come right among them. Once we were on them, they would be nearly as formidable as black beetles. Only! – there would first of all be a volley. I thought of a stratagem. I whipped off my flannel jacket as I ran.

'Bedford!' panted Cavor behind me.

I glanced back. 'What?' said I.

He was pointing upward over the carcasses. 'White light!' he said. 'White light again!'

I looked, and it was even so, a faint white ghost of light in the remoter cavern roof. That seemed to give me double strength.

'Keep close,' I said. A flat, long Selenite dashed out of the darkness, and squealed and fled. I halted, and stopped Cavor with my hand. I hung my

jacket over my crowbar, ducked round the next carcass, dropped jacket and crowbar, showed myself, and darted back.

'Chuzz – flick,' just one arrow came. We were close on the Selenites, and they were standing in a crowd, broad, short, and tall together, with a little battery of their shooting implements pointing down the cave. Three or four other arrows followed the first, then their fire ceased.

I stuck out my head, and escaped by a hair's-breadth. This time I drew a dozen shots or more, and heard the Selenites shouting and twittering as if with excitement as they shot. I picked up jacket and crowbar again.

'*Now!*' said I, and thrust out the jacket.

'Chuzz-zz-zz-zz! Chuzz!' In an instant my jacket had grown a thick beard of arrows, and they were quivering all over the carcass behind us. Instantly I slipped the crowbar out of the jacket, dropped the jacket – for all I know to the contrary it is lying up there in the moon now – and rushed out upon them.

For a minute perhaps it was massacre. I was too fierce to discriminate, and the Selenites were probably too scared to fight. At any rate they made no sort of fight against me. I saw scarlet, as the saying is. I remember I seemed to be wading among those leathery, thin things as a man wades through tall grass, mowing and hitting, first right, then left; smash. Little drops of moisture flew about. I trod on things that crushed and piped and went slippery. The crowd seemed to open and close and flow like water. They seemed to have no combined plan whatever. There were spears flew about me, I was grazed over the ear by one. I was stabbed once in the arm and once in the cheek, but I only found that out afterwards, when the blood had had time to run and cool and feel wet.

What Cavor did I do not know. For a space it seemed that this fighting had lasted for an age, and must needs go on for ever. Then suddenly it was all over, and there was nothing to be seen but the backs of heads bobbing up and down as their owners ran in all directions . . . I seemed altogether unhurt. I ran forward some paces, shouting, then turned about. I was amazed.

I had come right through them in vast flying strides, they were all behind me, and running hither and thither to hide.

I felt an enormous astonishment at the evaporation of the great fight into which I had hurled myself, and not a little exultation. It did not seem to me that I had discovered the Selenites were unexpectedly flimsy, but that I was unexpectedly strong. I laughed stupidly. This fantastic moon!

I glanced for a moment at the smashed and writhing bodies that were scattered over the cavern floor, with a vague idea of further violence, then hurried on after Cavor.

CHAPTER EIGHTEEN

In the Sunlight

Presently we saw that the cavern before us opened upon a hazy void. In another moment we had emerged upon a sort of slanting gallery, that projected into a vast circular space, a huge cylindrical pit running vertically up and down. Round this pit the slanting gallery ran without any parapet or protection for a turn and a half, and then plunged high above into the rock again. Somehow it reminded me then of one of those spiral turns of the railway through the St Gothard. It was all tremendously huge. I can scarcely hope to convey to you the Titanic proportion of all that place, the Titanic effect of it. Our eyes followed up the vast declivity of the pit wall, and overhead and far above we beheld a round opening set with faint stars, and half of the lip about it well nigh blinding with the white light of the sun. At that we cried aloud simultaneously.

'Come on!' I said, leading the way.

'But there?' said Cavor, and very carefully stepped nearer the edge of the gallery. I followed his example, and craned forward and looked down, but I was dazzled by that gleam of light above, and I could see only a bottomless darkness with spectral patches of crimson and purple floating therein. Yet if I could not see, I could hear. Out of this darkness came a sound, a sound like the angry hum one can hear if one puts one's ear outside a hive of bees, a sound out of that enormous hollow, it may be, four miles beneath our feet . . .

For a moment I listened, then tightened my grip on my crowbar, and led the way up the gallery.

'This must be the shaft we looked down upon,' said Cavor. 'Under that lid.'

'And below there, is where we saw the lights.'

'The lights!' said he. 'Yes – the lights of the world that now we shall never see.'

'We'll come back,' I said, for now we had escaped so much I was rashly sanguine that we should recover the sphere.

His answer I did not catch.

'Eh?' I asked.

'It doesn't matter,' he answered, and we hurried on in silence.

I suppose that slanting lateral way was four or five miles long, allowing for its curvature, and it ascended at a slope that would have made it almost impossibly steep on earth, but which one strode up easily under lunar conditions. We saw only two Selenites during all that portion of our flight, and directly they became aware of us they ran headlong. It was clear that

the knowledge of our strength and violence had reached them. Our way to the exterior was unexpectedly plain. The spiral gallery straightened into a steeply ascendent tunnel, its floor bearing abundant traces of the moon-calves, and so straight and short in proportion to its vast arch, that no part of it was absolutely dark. Almost immediately it began to lighten, and then far off and high up, and quite blindingly brilliant, appeared its opening on the exterior, a slope of Alpine steepness surmounted by a crest of bayonet shrub, tall and broken down now, and dry and dead, in spiky silhouette against the sun.

And it is strange that we men, to whom this very vegetation had seemed so weird and horrible a little time ago, should now behold it with the emotion a home-coming exile might feel at sight of his native land. We welcomed even the rareness of the air that made us pant as we ran, and which rendered speaking no longer the easy thing that it had been, but an effort to make oneself heard. Larger grew the sunlit circle above us, and larger, and all the nearer tunnel sank into a rim of indistinguishable black. We saw the dead bayonet shrub no longer with any touch of green in it, but brown and dry and thick, and the shadow of its upper branches high out of sight made a densely interlaced pattern upon the tumbled rocks. And at the immediate mouth of the tunnel was a wide trampled space where the mooncalves had come and gone.

We came out upon this space at last into a light and heat that hit and pressed upon us. We traversed the exposed area painfully, and clambered up a slope among the scrub stems, and sat down at last panting in a high place beneath the shadow of a mass of twisted lava. Even in the shade the rock felt hot.

The air was intensely hot, and we were in great physical discomfort, but for all that we were no longer in a nightmare. We seemed to have come to our own province again, beneath the stars. All the fear and stress of our flight through the dim passages and fissures below had fallen from us. That last fight had filled us with an enormous confidence in ourselves so far as the Selenites were concerned. We looked back almost incredulously at the black opening from which we had just emerged. Down there it was, in a blue glow that now in our memories seemed the next thing to absolute darkness, we had met with things like mad mockeries of men, helmet-headed creatures, and had walked in fear before them, and had submitted to them until we could submit no longer. And behold, they had smashed like wax and scattered like chaff, and fled and vanished like the creatures of a dream!

I rubbed my eyes, doubting whether we had not slept and dreamt these things by reason of the fungus we had eaten, and suddenly discovered the blood upon my face, and then that my shirt was sticking painfully to my shoulder and arm.

'Confound it!' I said, gauging my injuries with an investigatory hand, and suddenly that distant tunnel mouth became, as it were, a watching eye.

'Cavor!' I said; 'what are they going to do now? And what are we going to do?'

He shook his head, with his eyes fixed upon the tunnel. 'How can one tell what they will do?'

'It depends on what they think of us, and I don't see how we can begin to guess that. And it depends upon what they have in reserve. It's as you say, Cavor, we have touched the merest outside of this world. They may have all sorts of things inside here. Even with those shooting things they might make it bad for us . . .'

'Yet after all,' I said, 'even if we *don't* find the sphere at once, there is a chance for us. We might hold out. Even through the night. We might go down there again and make a fight for it.'

I stared about me with speculative eyes. The character of the scenery had altered altogether by reason of the enormous growth and subsequent drying of the scrub. The crest on which we sat was high, and commanded a wide prospect of the crater landscape, and we saw it now all sere and dry in the late autumn of the lunar afternoon. Rising one behind the other were long slopes and fields of trampled brown where the mooncalves had pastured, and far away in the full blaze of the sun a drove of them basked slumberously, scattered shapes, each with a blot of shadow against it like sheep on the side of a down. But never a sign of a Selenite was to be seen. Whether they had fled on our emergence from the interior passages, or whether they were accustomed to retire after driving out the mooncalves, I cannot guess. At the time I believed the former was the case.

'If we were to set fire to all this stuff,' I said, 'we might find the sphere among the ashes.'

Cavor did not seem to hear me. He was peering under his hand at the stars, that still, in spite of the intense sunlight, were abundantly visible in the sky. 'How long do you think we've have been here?' he asked at last.

'Been where?'

'On the moon.'

'Two earthly days, perhaps.'

'More nearly ten. Do you know, the sun is past its zenith, and sinking in the west. In four days' time or less it will be night.'

'But – we've only eaten once!'

'I know that. And – But there are the stars!'

'But why should time seem different because we are on a smaller planet?'

'I don't know. There it is!'

'How does one tell time?'

'Hunger – fatigue – all those things are different. Everything is different – everything. To me it seems that since first we came out of the sphere has been only a question of hours – long hours – at most.'

'Ten days,' I said; 'that leaves – ' I looked up at the sun for a moment, and then saw that it was halfway from the zenith to the western edge of things.

'Four days! . . . Cavor, we musn't sit here and dream. How do you think we may begin?'

I stood up. 'We must get a fixed point we can recognise – we might hoist a flag, or a handkerchief, or something – and quarter the ground, and work round that.'

He stood up beside me.

'Yes,' he said, 'there is nothing for it but to hunt the sphere. Nothing. We may find it – certainly we may find it. And if not – '

'We must keep on looking.'

He looked this way and that, glanced up at the sky and down at the tunnel, and astonished me by a sudden gesture of impatience. 'Oh! but we have done foolishly! To have come to this pass! Think how it might have been, and the things we might have done!'

'We might do something yet.'

'Never the thing we might have done. Here below our feet is a world. Think of what that world must be! Think of that machine we saw, and the lid and the shaft! They were just remote outlying things, and those creatures we have seen and fought with no more than ignorant peasants, dwellers in the outskirts, yokels and labourers half akin to brutes. Down below! Caverns beneath caverns, tunnels, structures, ways . . . It must open out, and be greater and wider and more populous as one descends. Assuredly. Right down at the last the central sea that washes round the core of the moon. Think of its inky waters under the spare lights – if, indeed, their eyes need lights! Think of the cascading tributaries pouring down their channels to feed it! Think of the tides upon its surface, and the rush and swirl of its ebb and flow! perhaps they have ships that go upon it, perhaps down there are mighty cities and swarming ways, and wisdom and order passing the wit of man. And we may die here upon it, and never see the masters who *must* be – ruling over these things! We may freeze and die here, and the air will freeze and thaw upon us, and then – ! Then they will come upon us, come on our stiff and silent bodies, and find the sphere we cannot find, and they will understand at last too late all the thought and effort that ended here in vain!'

His voice for all that speech sounded like the voice of someone heard in a telephone, weak and far away.

'But the darkness,' I said.

'One might get over that.'

'How?'

'I don't know. How am I to know? One might carry a torch, one might have a lamp – The others – might understand.'

He stood for a moment with his hands held down and a rueful face, staring out over the waste that defied him. Then with a gesture of renunciation he turned towards me with proposals for the systematic hunting of the sphere.

'We can return,' I said.

He looked about him. 'First of all we shall have to get to earth.'

'We could bring back lamps to carry and climbing irons, and a hundred necessary things.'

'Yes,' he said.

'We can take back an earnest of success in this gold.'

He looked at my golden crowbars, and said nothing for a space. He stood with his hands clasped behind his back, staring across the crater. At last he sighed and spoke. 'It was I found the way here, but to find a way isn't always to be master of a way. If I take my secret back to earth, what will happen? I do not see how I can keep my secret for a year, for even a part of a year. Sooner or later it must come out, even if other men rediscover it. And then . . . Governments and powers will struggle to get hither, they will fight against one another, and against these moon people; it will only spread warfare and multiply the occasions of war. In a little while, in a very little while, if I tell my secret, this planet to its deepest galleries will be strewn with human dead. Other things are doubtful, but that is certain . . . It is not as though man had any use for the moon. What good would the moon be to men? Even of their own planet what have they made but a battleground and theatre of infinite folly? Small as his world is, and short as his time, he has still in his little life down there far more than he can do. No! Science has toiled too long forging weapons for fools to use. It is time she held her hand. Let him find it out for himself again – in a thousand years' time.'

'There are methods of secrecy,' I said.

He looked up at me and smiled. 'After all,' he said, 'why should one worry? There is little chance of our finding the sphere, and down below things are brewing. It's simply the human habit of hoping till we die that makes us think of return. Our troubles are only beginning. We have shown these moon folk violence, we have given them a taste of our quality, and our chances are about as good as a tiger's that has got loose and killed a man in Hyde Park. The news of us must be running down from gallery to gallery, down towards the central parts . . . No sane beings will ever let us take that sphere back to earth after so much as they have seen of us.'

'We aren't improving our chances,' said I, 'by sitting here.'

We stood up side by side.

'After all,' he said, 'we must separate. We must stick up a handkerchief on these tall spikes here and fasten it firmly, and from this as a centre we must work over the crater. You must go westward, moving out in semi-circles to and fro towards the setting sun. You must move first with your shadow on your right until it is at right angles with the direction of your handkerchief, and then with your shadow on your left. And I will do the same to the east. We will look into every gully, examine every skerry of rocks; we will do all we can to find my sphere. If we see the Selenites we will hide from them as well as we can. For drink we must take snow, and if we

feel the need of food, we must kill a mooncalf if we can, and eat such flesh as it has – raw – and so each will go his own way.'

'And if one of us comes upon the sphere?'

'He must come back to the white handkerchief, and stand by it and signal to the other.'

'And if neither – ?'

Cavor glanced up at the sun. 'We go on seeking until the night and cold overtake us.'

'Suppose the Selenites have found the sphere and hidden it?'

He shrugged his shoulders.

'Or if presently they come hunting us?'

He made no answer.

'You had better take a club,' I said.

He shook his head, and stared away from me across the waste.

But for a moment he did not start. He looked round at me shyly, hesitated. '*Au revoir*,' he said.

I felt an odd stab of emotion. A sense of how we had galled each other, and particularly how I must have galled him, came to me. 'Confound it,' thought I, 'we might have done better!' I was on the point of asking him to shake hands – for that, somehow, was how I felt just then – when he put his feet together and leapt away from me towards the north. He seemed to drift through the air as a dead leaf would do, fell lightly, and leapt again. I stood for a moment watching him, then faced westward reluctantly, pulled myself together, and with something of the feeling of a man who leaps into icy water, selected a leaping point, and plunged forward to explore my solitary half of the moon world. I dropped rather clumsily among rocks, stood up and looked about me, clambered on to a rocky slab, and leapt again . . .

When presently I looked for Cavor he was hidden from my eyes, but the handkerchief showed out bravely on its headland, white in the blaze of the sun.

I determined not to lose sight of that handkerchief whatever might betide.

CHAPTER NINETEEN

Mr Bedford Alone

In a little while it seemed to me as though I had always been alone on the moon. I hunted for a time with a certain intentness, but the heat was still very great, and the thinness of the air felt like a hoop about one's chest. I came presently into a hollow basin bristling with tall, brown, dry fronds about its edge, and I sat down under these to rest and cool. I intended to rest for only a little while. I put down my clubs beside me, and sat resting

my chin on my hands. I saw with a sort of colourless interest that the rocks of the basin, where here and there the crackling dry lichens had shrunk away to show them, were all veined and splattered with gold, that here and there bosses of rounded and wrinkled gold projected from among the litter. What did that matter now? A sort of languor had possession of my limbs and mind, I did not believe for a moment that we should ever find the sphere in that vast desiccated wilderness. I seemed to lack a motive for effort until the Selenites should come. Then I supposed I should exert myself, obeying that unreasonable imperative that urges a man before all things to preserve and defend his life, albeit he may preserve it only to die more painfully in a little while.

Why had we come to the moon?

The thing presented itself to me as a perplexing problem. What is this spirit in man that urges him for ever to depart from happiness and security, to toil, to place himself in danger, to risk even a reasonable certainty of death? It dawned upon me up there in the moon as a thing I ought always to have known, that man is not made simply to go about being safe and comfortable and well fed and amused. Almost any man, if you put the thing to him, not in words, but in the shape of opportunities, will show that he knows as much. Against his interest, against his happiness, he is constantly being driven to do unreasonable things. Some force not himself impels him, and go he must. But why? Why? Sitting there in the midst of that useless moon gold, amidst the things of another world, I took count of all my life. Assuming I was to die a castaway upon the moon, I failed altogether to see what purpose I had served. I got no light on that point, but at any rate it was clearer to me than it had ever been in my life before that I was not serving my own purpose, that all my life I had in truth never served the purposes of my private life. Whose purposes, what purposes, was I serving? . . . I ceased to speculate on why we had come to the moon, and took a wider sweep. Why had I come to the earth? Why had I a private life at all? . . . I lost myself at last in bottomless speculations . . .

My thoughts became vague and cloudy, no longer leading in definite directions. I had not felt heavy or weary – I cannot imagine one doing so upon the moon – but I suppose I was greatly fatigued. At any rate I slept.

Slumbering there rested me greatly, I think, and the sun was setting and the violence of the heat abating, through all the time I slumbered. When at last I was roused from my slumbers by a remote clamour, I felt active and capable again. I rubbed my eyes and stretched my arms. I rose to my feet – I was a little stiff – and at once prepared to resume my search. I shouldered my golden clubs, one on each shoulder, and went on out of the ravine of the gold-veined rocks.

The sun was certainly lower, much lower than it had been; the air was very much cooler. I perceived I must have slept some time. It seemed to me that a faint touch of misty blueness hung about the western cliff. I leapt to a

little boss of rock and surveyed the crater. I could see no signs of moon-calves or Selenites, nor could I see Cavor, but I could see my handkerchief far off, spread out on its thicket of thorns. I looked about me, and then leapt forward to the next convenient viewpoint.

I beat my round in a semicircle, and back again in a still remoter crescent. It was very fatiguing and hopeless. The air was really very much cooler, and it seemed to me that the shadow under the westward cliff was growing broad. Ever and again I stopped and reconnoitred, but there was no sign of Cavor, no sign of Selenites; and it seemed to me the mooncalves must have been driven into the interior again – I could see none of them. I became more and more desirous of seeing Cavor. The winged outline of the sun had sunk now, until it was scarcely the distance of its diameter from the rim of the sky. I was oppressed by the idea that the Selenites would presently close their lids and valves, and shut us out under the inexorable onrush of the lunar night. It seemed to me high time that he abandoned his search, and that we took counsel together. I felt how urgent it was that we should decide soon upon our course. We had failed to find the sphere, we no longer had time to seek it, and once these valves were closed with us outside, we were lost men. The great night of space would descend upon us – that blackness of the void which is the only absolute death. All my being shrank from that approach. We must get into the moon again, though we were slain in doing it. I was haunted by a vision of our freezing to death, of our hammering with our last strength on the valve of the great pit.

I took no thought any more of the sphere. I thought only of finding Cavor again. I was half inclined to go back into the moon without him, rather than seek him until it was too late. I was already halfway back towards our handkerchief, when suddenly –

I saw the sphere!

I did not find it so much as it found me. It was lying much farther to the westward than I had gone, and the sloping rays of the sinking sun reflected from its glass had suddenly proclaimed its presence in a dazzling beam. For an instant I thought this was some new device of the Selenites against us, and then I understood.

I threw up my arms, shouted a ghostly shout, and set off in vast leaps towards it. I missed one of my leaps and dropped into a deep ravine and twisted my ankle, and after that I stumbled at almost every leap. I was in a state of hysterical agitation, trembling violently, and quite breathless long before I got to it. Three times at least I had to stop with my hands resting on my side and in spite of the thin dryness of the air, the perspiration was wet upon my face.

I thought of nothing but the sphere until I reached it, I forgot even my trouble of Cavor's whereabouts. My last leap flung me with my hands hard against its glass; then I lay against it panting, and trying vainly to shout, 'Cavor! here is the sphere!' When I had recovered a little I peered through

the thick glass, and the things inside seemed tumbled. I stooped to peer closer. Then I attempted to get in. I had to hoist it over a little to get my head through the manhole. The screw stopper was inside, and I could see now that nothing had been touched, nothing had suffered. It lay there as we had left it when we had dropped out amidst the snow. For a time I was wholly occupied in making and remaking this inventory. I found I was trembling violently. It was good to see that familiar dark interior again! I cannot tell you how good. Presently I crept inside and sat down among the things. I looked through the glass at the moon world and shivered. I placed my gold clubs upon the table, and sought out and took a little food; not so much because I wanted it, but because it was there. Then it occurred to me that it was time to go out and signal for Cavor. But I did not go out and signal for Cavor forthwith. Something held me to the sphere.

After all, everything was coming right. There would be still time for us to get more of the magic stone that gives one mastery over men. Away there, close handy, was gold for the picking up; and the sphere would travel as well half full of gold as though it were empty. We could go back now, masters of ourselves and our world, and then –

I roused myself at last, and with an effort got myself out of the sphere. I shivered as I emerged, for the evening air was growing very cold. I stood in the hollow staring about me. I scrutinised the bushes round me very carefully before I leapt to the rocky shelf hard by, and took once more what had been my first leap in the moon. But now I made it with no effort whatever.

The growth and decay of the vegetation had gone on apace, and the whole aspect of the rocks had changed, but still it was possible to make out the slope on which the seeds had germinated, and the rocky mass from which we had taken our first view of the crater. But the spiky shrub on the slope stood brown and sere now, and thirty feet high, and cast long shadows that stretched out of sight, and the little seeds that clustered in its upper branches were brown and ripe. Its work was done, and it was brittle and ready to fall and crumple under the freezing air, so soon as the nightfall came. And the huge cacti, that had swollen as we watched them, had long since burst and scattered their spores to the four quarters of the moon. Amazing little corner in the universe – the landing place of men!

Some day, thought I, I will have an inscription standing there right in the midst of the hollow. It came to me, if only this teeming world within knew of the full import of the moment, how furious its tumult would become!

But as yet it could scarcely be dreaming of the significance of our coming. For if it did, the crater would surely be an uproar of pursuit, instead of as still as death! I looked about for some place from which I might signal Cavor, and saw that same patch of rock to which he had leapt from my present standpoint, still bare and barren in the sun. For a moment I hesitated at going so far from the sphere. Then with a pang of shame at that hesitation, I leapt . . .

From this vantage point I surveyed the crater again. Far away at the top of the enormous shadow I cast was the little white handkerchief fluttering on the bushes. It was very little and very far, and Cavor was not in sight. It seemed to me that by this time he ought to be looking for me. That was the agreement. But he was nowhere to be seen.

I stood waiting and watching, hands shading my eyes, expecting every moment to distinguish him. Very probably I stood there for quite a long time. I tried to shout, and was reminded of the thinness of the air. I made an undecided step back towards the sphere. But a lurking dread of the Selenites made me hesitate to signal my whereabouts by hoisting one of our sleeping-blankets on to the adjacent scrub. I searched the crater again.

It had an effect of emptiness that chilled me. And it was still; any sound from the Selenites in the world beneath, even had died away. It was as still as death. Save for the faint stir of the shrub about me in the little breeze that was rising, there was no sound nor shadow of a sound. And the breeze blew chill.

Confound Cavor!

I took a deep breath. I put my hands to the sides of my mouth. 'Cavor!' I bawled, and the sound was like some manikin shouting far away.

I looked at the handkerchief, I looked behind me at the broadening shadow of the westward cliff, I looked under my hand at the sun. It seemed to me that almost visibly it was creeping down the sky.

I felt I must act instantly if I was to save Cavor. I whipped off my vest and flung it as a mark on the sere bayonets of the shrubs behind me, and then set off in a straight line towards the handkerchief. Perhaps it was a couple of miles away – a matter of a few hundred leaps and strides. I have already told how one seemed to hang through those lunar leaps. In each suspense I sought Cavor, and marvelled why he should be hidden. In each leap I could feel the sun setting behind me. Each time I touched the ground I was tempted to go back.

A last leap and I was in the depression below our handkerchief, a stride, and I stood on our former vantage point within arms' reach of it. I stood up straight and scanned the world about me, between its lengthening bars of shadow. Far away, down a long declivity, was the opening of the tunnel up which we had fled, and my shadow reached towards it, stretched towards it, and touched it, like a finger of the night.

Not a sign of Cavor, not a sound in all the stillness, only the stir and waving of the scrub and of the shadows increased. And suddenly and violently I shivered. 'Cav – ' I began, and realised once more the uselessness of the human voice in that thin air.

Silence. The silence of death.

Then it was my eye caught something – a little thing lying, perhaps fifty yards away down the slope, amidst a litter of bent and broken branches. What was it? I knew, and yet for some reason I would not know. I went

nearer to it. It was the little cricket-cap Cavor had worn. I did not touch it, I stood looking at it.

I saw then that the scattered branches about it had been forcibly smashed and trampled. I hesitated, stepped forward, and picked it up.

I stood with Cavor's cap in my hand, staring at the trampled reeds and thorns about me. On some of them were little smears of something dark, something that I dared not touch. A dozen yards away, perhaps, the rising breeze dragged something into view, something small and vividly white.

It was a little piece of paper crumpled tightly, as though it had been clutched tightly. I picked it up, and on it were smears of red. My eye caught faint pencil marks. I smoothed it out, and saw uneven and broken writing ending at last in a crooked streak upon the paper.

I set myself to decipher this.

'I have been injured about the knee, I think my kneecap is hurt, and I cannot run or crawl,' it began – pretty distinctly written.

Then less legibly: 'They have been chasing me for some time, and it is only a question of' – the word 'time' seemed to have been written here and erased in favour of something illegible – 'before they get me. They are beating all about me.'

Then the writing became convulsive. 'I can hear them,' I guessed the tracing meant, and then it was quite unreadable for a space. Then came a little string of words that were quite distinct: 'a different sort of Selenite altogether, who appears to be directing the – The writing became a mere hasty confusion again.

'They have larger brain cases – much larger, and slenderer bodies, and very short legs. They make gentle noises, and move with organised deliberation . . .

'And though I am wounded and helpless here, their appearance still gives me hope – ' That was like Cavor. 'They have not shot at me or attempted . . . injury. I intend – '

Then came the sudden streak of the pencil across the paper, and on the back and edges – blood!

And as I stood there stupid, and perplexed, with this dumbfounding relic in my hand, something very soft and light and chill touched my hand for a moment and ceased to be, and then a thing, a little white speck, drifted athwart a shadow. It was a tiny snowflake, the first snowflake, the herald of the night.

I looked up with a start, and the sky had darkened almost to blackness, and was thick with a gathering multitude of coldly watchful stars. I looked eastward, and the light of that shrivelled world was touched with sombre bronze; westward, and the sun robbed now by a thickening white mist of half its heat and splendour, was touching the crater rim, was sinking out of sight, and all the shrubs and jagged and tumbled rocks stood out against it in a bristling disorder of black shapes. Into the great lake of darkness

westward, a vast wreath of mist was sinking. A cold wind set all the crater shivering. Suddenly, for a moment, I was in a puff of falling snow, and all the world about me grey and dim.

And then it was I heard, not loud and penetrating as at first, but faint and dim like a dying voice, that tolling, that same tolling that had welcomed the coming of the day: Boom! . . . Boom! . . . Boom! . . .

It echoed about the crater, it seemed to throb with the throbbing of the greater stars, the blood-red crescent of the sun's disc sank as it tolled out: Boom! . . . Boom! . . . Boom! . . .

What had happened to Cavor? All through that tolling I stood there stupidly, and at last the tolling ceased.

And suddenly the open mouth of the tunnel down below there, shut like an eye and vanished out of sight.

Then indeed was I alone.

Over me, around me, closing in on me, embracing me ever nearer, was the Eternal; that which was before the beginning, and that which triumphs over the end; that enormous void in which all light and life and being is but the thin and vanishing splendour of a falling star, the cold, the stillness, the silence – the infinite and final Night of space.

The sense of solitude and desolation became the sense of an overwhelming presence that stooped towards me, that almost touched me.

'No,' I cried. '*No!* Not yet! not yet! Wait! Wait! Oh, wait!' My voice went up to a shriek. I flung the crumpled paper from me, scrambled back to the crest to take my bearings, and then, with all the will that was in me, leapt out towards the mark I had left, dim and distant now in the very margin of the shadow.

Leap, leap, leap, and each leap was seven ages.

Before me the pale serpent-girdled section of the sun sank and sank, and the advancing shadow swept to seize the sphere before I could reach it. I was two miles away, a hundred leaps or more, and the air about me was thinning out as it thins under an air-pump, and the cold was gripping at my joints. But had I died, I should have died leaping. Once, and then again my foot slipped on the gathering snow as I leapt and shortened my leap; once I fell short into bushes that crashed and smashed into dusty chips and nothingness, and once I stumbled as I dropped and rolled head over heels into a gully, and rose bruised and bleeding and confused as to my direction.

But such incidents were as nothing to the intervals, those awful pauses when one drifted through the air towards that pouring tide of night. My breathing made a piping noise, and it was as though knives were whirling in my lungs. My heart seemed to beat against the top of my brain. 'Shall I reach it? O Heaven! Shall I reach it?'

My whole being became anguish.

'Lie down!' screamed my pain and despair; 'lie down!'

The nearer I struggled, the more awfully remote it seemed. I was numb, I stumbled, I bruised and cut myself and did not bleed.

It was in sight.

I fell on all fours, and my lungs whooped.

I crawled. The frost gathered on my lips, icicles hung from my moustache, I was white with the freezing atmosphere.

I was a dozen yards from it. My eyes had become dim. 'Lie down!' screamed despair; 'lie down!'

I touched it, and halted. 'Too late!' screamed despair; 'lie down!'

I fought stiffly with it. I was on the manhole lip, a stupefied, half-dead being. The snow was all about me. I pulled myself in. There lurked within a little warmer air.

The snowflakes – the air flakes – danced in about me, as I tried with chilling hands to thrust the valve in and spun it tight and hard. I sobbed. 'I will,' I chattered in my teeth. And then, with fingers that quivered and felt brittle, I turned to the shutter studs.

As I fumbled with the switches – for I had never controlled them before – I could see dimly through the steaming glass the blazing red streamers of the sinking sun, dancing and flickering through the snowstorm, and the black forms of the scrub thickening and bending and breaking beneath the accumulating snow. Thicker whirled the snow and thicker, black against the light. What if even now the switches overcame me?

Then something clicked under my hands, and in an instant that last vision of the moon world was hidden from my eyes. I was in the silence and darkness of the interplanetary sphere.

CHAPTER TWENTY

Mr Bedford in Infinite Space

It was almost as though I had been killed. Indeed, I could imagine a man suddenly and violently killed would feel very much as I did. One moment, a passion of agonising existence and fear; the next darkness and stillness, neither light nor life nor sun, moon nor stars, the blank infinite. Although the thing was done by my own act, although I had already tasted this very effect in Cavor's company, I felt astonished, dumbfounded, and over-whelmed. I seemed to be borne upward into an enormous darkness. My fingers floated off the studs, I hung as if I were annihilated, and at last very softly and gently I came against the bale and the golden chain, and the crowbars that had drifted to the middle of the sphere.

I do not know how long that drifting took. In the sphere of course, even more than on the moon, one's earthly time sense was ineffectual. At the touch of the bale it was as if I had awakened from a dreamless sleep. I

immediately perceived that if I wanted to keep awake and alive I must get a light or open a window, so as to get a grip of something with my eyes. And besides, I was cold. I kicked off from the bale, therefore, clawed on to the thin cords within the glass, crawled along until I got to the manhole rim, and so got my bearings for the light and blind studs, took a shove off, and flying once round the bale, and getting a scare from something big and flimsy that was drifting loose, I got my hand on the cord quite close to the studs, and reached them. I lit the little lamp first of all to see what it was I had collided with, and discovered that old copy of *Lloyd's News* had slipped its moorings, and was adrift in the void. That brought me out of the infinite to my own proper dimensions again. It made me laugh and pant for a time, and suggested the idea of a little oxygen from one of the cylinders. After that I lit the heater until I felt warm, and then I took food. Then I set to work in a very gingerly fashion on the Cavorite blinds, to see if I could guess by any means how the sphere was travelling.

The first blind I opened I shut at once, and hung for a time flattened and blinded by the sunlight that had hit me. After thinking a little I started upon the windows at right angles to this one, and got the huge crescent moon and the little crescent earth behind it, the second time. I was amazed to find how far I was from the moon. I had reckoned that not only should I have little or none of the 'kick-off' that the earth's atmosphere had given us at our start, but that the tangential 'fly off' of the moon's spin would be at least twenty-eight times less than the earth's. I had expected to discover myself hanging over our crater, and on the edge of the night, but all that was now only a part of the outline of the white crescent that filled the sky. And Cavor – ?

He was already infinite.

I tried to imagine what could have happened to him. But at that time I could think of nothing but death. I seemed to see him, bent and smashed at the foot of some interminably high cascade of blue. And all about him the stupid insects stared . . .

Under the inspiring touch of the drifting newspaper I became practical again for a while. It was quite clear to me that what I had to do was to get back to earth, but as far as I could see I was drifting away from it. Whatever had happened to Cavor, even if he was still alive, which seemed to me incredible after that bloodstained scrap, I was powerless to help him. There he was, living or dead behind the mantle of that rayless night, and there he must remain at least until I could summon our fellow men to his assistance. Should I do that? Something of the sort I had in my mind; to come back to earth if it were possible, and then as maturer consideration might determine, either to show and explain the sphere to a few discreet persons, and act with them, or else to keep my secret, sell my gold, obtain weapons, provisions, and an assistant, and return with these advantages to deal on equal terms with the flimsy people of the moon, to rescue Cavor, if that

were still possible, and at any rate to procure a sufficient supply of gold to place my subsequent proceedings on a firmer basis. But that was hoping far; I had first to get back.

I set myself to decide just exactly how the return to earth could be contrived. As I struggled with that problem I ceased to worry about what I should do when I got there. At last my only care was to get back.

I puzzled out at last that my best chance would be to drop back towards the moon as near as I dared in order to gather velocity, then to shut my windows, and fly behind it, and when I was past to open my earthward windows, and so get off at a good pace homeward. But whether I should ever reach the earth by that device, or whether I might not simply find myself spinning about it in some hyperbolic or parabolic curve or other, I could not tell. Later I had a happy inspiration, and by opening certain windows to the moon, which had appeared in the sky in front of the earth, I turned my course aside so as to head off the earth, which it had become evident to me I must pass behind without some such expedient. I did a very great deal of complicated thinking over these problems – for I am no mathematician – and in the end I am certain it was much more my good luck than my reasoning that enabled me to hit the earth. Had I known then, as I know now, the mathematical chances there were against me, I doubt if I should have troubled even to touch the studs to make any attempt. And having puzzled out what I considered to be the thing to do, I opened all my moonward windows, and squatted down – the effort lifted me for a time some feet or so into the air, and I hung there in the oddest way – and waited for the crescent to get bigger and bigger until I felt I was near enough for safety. Then I would shut the windows, fly past the moon with the velocity I had got from it – if I did not smash upon it – and so go on towards the earth.

And that is what I did.

At last I felt my moonward start was sufficient. I shut out the sight of the moon from my eyes, and in a state of mind that was, I now recall, incredibly free from anxiety or any distressful quality, I sat down to begin a vigil in that little speck of matter in infinite space that would last until I should strike the earth. The heater had made the sphere tolerably warm, the air had been refreshed by the oxygen, and except for that faint congestion of the head that was always with me while I was away from earth, I felt entire physical comfort. I had extinguished the light again, lest it should fail me in the end; I was in darkness, save for the earth-shine and the glitter of the stars below me. Everything was so absolutely silent and still that I might indeed have been the only being in the universe, and yet, strangely enough, I had no more feeling of loneliness or fear than if I had been lying in bed on earth. Now, this seems all the stranger to me, since during my last hours in that crater of the moon, the sense of my utter loneliness had been an agony . . .

Incredible as it will seem, this interval of time that I spent in space has no sort of proportion to any other interval of time in my life. Sometimes it

seemed as though I sat through immeasurable eternities like some god upon a lotus leaf, and again as though there was a momentary pause as I leapt from moon to earth. In truth, it was altogether some weeks of earthly time. But I had done with care and anxiety, hunger or fear, for that space. I floated, thinking with a strange breadth and freedom of all that we had undergone, and of all my life and motives, and the secret issues of my being. I seemed to myself to have grown greater and greater, to have lost all sense of movement; to be floating amidst the stars, and always the sense of earth's littleness and the infinite littleness of my life upon it, was implicit in my thoughts.

I can't profess to explain the things that happened in my mind. No doubt they could all be traced directly or indirectly to the curious physical conditions under which I was living. I set them down here just for what they are worth, and without any comment. The most prominent quality of it was a pervading doubt of my own identity. I became, if I may so express it, dissociate from Bedford; I looked down on Bedford as a trivial, incidental thing with which I chanced to be connected. I saw Bedford in many relations – as an ass or as a poor beast, where I had hitherto been inclined to regard him with a quiet pride as a very spirited or rather forcible person. I saw him not only as an ass, but as the son of many generations of asses. I reviewed his school-days and his early manhood, and his first encounter with love, very much as one might review the proceedings of an ant in the sand. Something of that period of lucidity I regret still hangs about me, and I doubt if I shall ever recover the full-bodied self-satisfaction of my early days. But at the time the thing was not in the least painful, because I had that extraordinary persuasion that, as a matter of fact, I was no more Bedford than I was anyone else, but only a mind floating in the still serenity of space. Why should I be disturbed about this Bedford's shortcomings? I was not responsible for him or them.

For a time I struggled against this really very grotesque delusion. I tried to summon the memory of vivid moments, of tender or intense emotions to my assistance; I felt that if I could recall one genuine twinge of feeling the growing severance would be stopped. But I could not do it. I saw Bedford rushing down Chancery Lane, hat on the back of his head, coat tails flying out, *en route* for his public examination. I saw him dodging and bumping against, and even saluting, other similar little creatures in that swarming gutter of people. Me? I saw Bedford that same evening in the sitting-room of a certain lady, and his hat was on the table beside him, and it wanted brushing badly, and he was in tears. Me? I saw him with that lady in various attitudes and emotions – I never felt so detached before . . . I saw him hurrying off to Lympne to write a play, and accosting Cavor, and in his shirt sleeves working at the sphere, and walking out to Canterbury because he was afraid to come! Me? I did not believe it.

I still reasoned that all this was hallucination due to my solitude, and the

fact that I had lost all weight and sense of resistance. I endeavoured to recover that sense by banging myself about the sphere, by pinching my hands and clasping them together. Among other things, I lit the light, captured that torn copy of *Lloyd's*, and read those convincingly realistic advertisements about the Cutaway bicycle, and the gentleman of private means, and the lady in distress who was selling those 'forks and spoons'. There was no doubt they existed surely enough, and, said I, 'This is your world, and you are Bedford, and you are going back to live among things like that for all the rest of your life.' But the doubts within me could still argue: 'It is not you that is reading, it is Bedford, but you are not Bedford, you know. That's just where the mistake comes in.'

'Confound it!' I cried; 'and if I am not Bedford, what am I?'

But in that direction no light was forthcoming, though the strangest fancies came drifting into my brain, queer remote suspicions, like shadows seen from faraway. Do you know, I had a sort of idea that really I was something quite outside not only the world, but all worlds, and out of space and time, and that this poor Bedford was just a peephole through which I looked at life? . . .

Bedford! However I disavowed him, there I was most certainly bound up with him, and I knew that wherever or whatever I might be, I must needs feel the stress of his desires, and sympathise with all his joys and sorrows until his life should end. And with the dying of Bedford – what then? . . .

Enough of this remarkable phase of my experiences! I tell it here simply to show how one's isolation and departure from this planet touched not only the functions and feeling of every organ of the body, but indeed also the very fabric of the mind, with strange and unanticipated disturbances. All through the major portion of that vast space journey I hung thinking of such immaterial things as these, hung dissociated and apathetic, a cloudy megalomaniac, as it were, amidst the stars and planets in the void of space; and not only the world to which I was returning, but the blue-lit caverns of the Selenites, their helmet faces, their gigantic and wonderful machines, and the fate of Cavor, dragged helpless into that world, seemed infinitely minute and altogether trivial things to me.

Until at last I began to feel the pull of the earth upon my being, drawing me back again to the life that is real for men. And then, indeed, it grew clearer and clearer to me that I was quite certainly Bedford after all, and returning after amazing adventures to this world of ours, and with a life that I was very likely to lose in this return. I set myself to puzzle out the conditions under which I must fall to earth.

CHAPTER TWENTY-ONE

Mr Bedford at Littlestone

My line of flight was about parallel with the surface as I came into the upper air. The temperature of the sphere began to rise forthwith. I knew it behoved me to drop at once. Far below me, in a darkling twilight, stretched a great expanse of sea. I opened every window I could, and fell – out of sunshine into evening, and out of evening into night. Vaster grew the earth and vaster, swallowing up the stars, and the silvery translucent starlit veil of cloud it wore spread out to catch me. At last the world seemed no longer a sphere but flat, and then concave. It was no longer a planet in the sky, but the world of Man. I shut all but an inch or so of earthward window, and dropped with a slackening velocity. The broadening water, now so near that I could see the dark glitter of the waves, rushed up to meet me. The sphere became very hot. I snapped the last strip of window, and sat scowling and biting my knuckles, waiting for the impact . . .

The sphere hit the water with a huge splash: it must have sent it fathoms high. At the splash I flung the Cavorite shutters open. Down I went, but slower and slower, and then I felt the sphere pressing against my feet, and so drove up again as a bubble drives. And at the last I was floating and rocking upon the surface of the sea, and my journey in space was at an end.

The night was dark and overcast. Two yellow pinpoints far away showed the passing of a ship, and nearer was a red glare that came and went. Had not the electricity of my glow-lamp exhausted itself, I could have got picked up that night. In spite of the inordinate fatigue I was beginning to feel, I was excited now, and for a time hopeful, in a feverish, impatient way, that so my travelling might end.

But at last I ceased to move about, and sat, wrists on knees, staring at a distant red light. It swayed up and down, rocking, rocking. My excitement passed. I realised I had yet to spend another night at least in the sphere. I perceived myself infinitely heavy and fatigued. And so I fell asleep.

A change in my rhythmic motion awakened me. I peered through the refracting glass, and saw that I had come aground upon a huge shallow of sand. Far away I seemed to see houses and trees, and seaward a curve, vague distortion of a ship hung between sea and sky.

I stood up and staggered. My one desire was to emerge. The manhole was upward, and I wrestled with the screw. Slowly I opened the manhole. At last the air was singing in again as once it had sung out. But this time I did not wait until the pressure was adjusted. In another moment I had the weight of the window on my hands, and I was open, wide open, to the old familiar sky of earth.

The air hit me on the chest so that I gasped. I dropped the glass screw. I cried out, put my hands to my chest, and sat down. For a time I was in pain. Then I took deep breaths. At last I could rise and move about again.

I tried to thrust my head through the manhole, and the sphere rolled over. It was as though something had lugged my head down directly it emerged. I ducked back sharply, or I should have been pinned face under water. After some wriggling and shoving I managed to crawl out upon sand, over which the retreating waves still came and went.

I did not attempt to stand up. It seemed to me that my body must be suddenly changed to lead. Mother Earth had her grip on me now – no Cavorite intervening. I sat down heedless of the water that came over my feet.

It was dawn, a grey dawn, rather overcast but showing here and there a long patch of greenish grey. Some way out a ship was lying at anchor, a pale silhouette of a ship with one yellow light. The water came rippling in in long shallow waves. Away to the right curved the land, a shingle bank with little hovels, and at last a lighthouse, a sailing mark and a point. Inland stretched a space of level sand, broken here and there by pools of water, and ending a mile away perhaps in a low shore of scrub. To the north-east some isolated watering-place was visible, a row of gaunt lodging-houses, the tallest things that I could see on earth, dull dabs against the brightening sky. What strange men can have reared these vertical piles in such an amplitude of space I do not know. There they are, like pieces of Brighton lost in the waste.

For a long time I sat there, yawning and rubbing my face. At last I struggled to rise. It made me feel that I was lifting a weight. I stood up.

I stared at the distant houses. For the first time since our starvation in the crater I thought of earthly food. 'Bacon,' I whispered, 'eggs. Good toast and good coffee . . . And how the devil am I going to get all this stuff to Lympne?' I wondered where I was. It was an east shore anyhow, and I had seen Europe before I dropped.

I heard footsteps scrunching in the sand, and a little round-faced, friendly-looking man in flannels, with a bathing towel wrapped about his shoulders, and his bathing dress over his arm, appeared up the beach. I knew instantly that I must be in England. He was staring most intently at the sphere and me. He advanced staring. I dare say I looked a ferocious savage enough – dirty, unkempt, to an indescribable degree; but it did not occur to me at the time. He stopped at a distance of twenty yards. 'Hel-lo, my man!' he said doubtfully.

'Hello yourself!' said I.

He advanced, reassured by that. 'What on earth is that thing?' he asked.

'Can you tell me where I am?' I asked.

'That's Littlestone,' he said, pointing to the houses; 'and that's Dungeness! Have you just landed? What's that thing you've got? Some sort of machine?'

'Yes.'

'Have you floated ashore? Have you been wrecked or something? What is it?'

I meditated swiftly. I made an estimate of the little man's appearance as he drew nearer. 'By Jove!' he said, 'you've had a time of it! I thought you – Well – Where were you cast away? Is that thing a sort of floating thing for saving life?'

I decided to take that line for the present. I made a few vague affirmatives. 'I want help,' I said hoarsely. 'I want to get some stuff up the beach – stuff I can't very well leave about.' I became aware of three other pleasant-looking young men with towels, blazers, and straw hats, coming down the sands towards me. Evidently the early bathing section of this Littlestone.

'Help!' said the young man: 'rather!' He became vaguely active. 'What particularly do you want done?' He turned round and gesticulated. The three young men accelerated their pace. In a minute they were about me, plying me with questions I was indisposed to answer. 'I'll tell all that later,' I said. 'I'm dead beat. I'm a rag.'

'Come up to the hotel,' said the foremost little man. 'We'll look after that thing there.'

I hesitated. 'I can't,' I said. 'In that sphere there's two big bars of gold.'

They looked incredulously at one another, then at me with a new enquiry. I went to the sphere, stooped, crept in, and presently they had the Selenites' crowbars and the broken chain before them. If I had not been so horribly fagged I could have laughed at them. It was like kittens round a beetle. They didn't know what to do with the stuff. The fat little man stooped and lifted the end of one of the bars, and then dropped it with a grunt. Then they all did.

'It's lead, or gold!' said one.

'Oh, it's *gold*!' said another.

'Gold, right enough,' said the third.

Then they all stared at me, and then they all stared at the ship lying at anchor.

'I say!' cried the little man. 'But where did you get that?'

I was too tired to keep up a lie. 'I got it in the moon.'

I saw them stare at one another.

'Look here!' said I, 'I'm not going to argue now. Help me carry these lumps of gold up to the hotel – I guess, with rests, two of you can manage one, and I'll trail this chain thing – and I'll tell you more when I've had some food.'

'And how about that thing?'

'It won't hurt there,' I said. 'Anyhow – confound it! – it must stop there now. If the tide comes up, it will float all right.'

And in a state of enormous wonderment, these young men most

obediently hoisted my treasures on their shoulders, and with limbs that felt like lead I headed a sort of procession towards that distant fragment of 'seafront'. Halfway there we were reinforced by two awestricken little girls with spades, and later a lean little boy, with a penetrating sniff, appeared. He was, I remember, wheeling a bicycle, and he accompanied us at a distance of about a hundred yards on our right flank, and then I suppose, gave us up as uninteresting, mounted his bicycle and rode off over the level sands in the direction of the sphere.

I glanced back after him.

'*He* won't touch it,' said the stout young man reassuringly, and I was only too willing to be reassured.

At first something of the grey of the morning was in my mind, but presently the sun disengaged itself from the level clouds of the horizon and lit the world, and turned the leaden sea to glittering waters. My spirits rose. A sense of the vast importance of the things I had done and had yet to do came with the sunlight into my mind. I laughed aloud as the foremost man staggered under my gold. When indeed I took my place in the world, how amazed the world would be!

If it had not been for my inordinate fatigue, the landlord of the Littlestone hotel would have been amusing, as he hesitated between my gold and my respectable company on the one hand and my filthy appearance on the other. But at last I found myself in a terrestrial bathroom once more with warm water to wash myself with, and a change of raiment, preposterously small indeed, but anyhow clean, that the genial little man had lent me. He lent me a razor too, but I could not screw up my resolution to attack even the outposts of the bristling beard that covered my face.

I sat down to an English breakfast and ate with a sort of languid appetite – an appetite many weeks old and very decrepit – and stirred myself to answer the questions of the four young men. And I told them the truth.

'Well,' said I, 'as you press me – I got it in the moon.'

'The moon?'

'Yes, the moon in the sky.'

'But how do you mean?'

'What I say, confound it!'

'Then you have just come from the moon?'

'Exactly! through space – in that ball.' And I took a delicious mouthful of egg. I made a private note that when I went back to the moon I would take a box of eggs.

I could see clearly that they did not believe one word of what I told them, but evidently they considered me the most respectable liar they had ever met. They glanced at one another, and then concentrated the fire of their eyes on me. I fancy they expected a clue to me in the way I helped myself to salt. They seemed to find something significant in my peppering my egg.

These strangely shaped masses of gold they had staggered under held their minds. There the lumps lay in front of me, each worth thousands of pounds, and as impossible for anyone to steal as a house or a piece of land. As I looked at their curious faces over my coffee-cup, I realised something of the enormous wilderness of explanations into which I should have to wander to render myself comprehensible again.

'You don't *really* mean – ' began the youngest young man, in the tone of one who speaks to an obstinate child.

'Just pass me that toast-rack,' I said, and shut him up completely.

'But look here, I say,' began one of the others. 'We're not going to believe that, you know.'

'Ah, well,' said I, and shrugged my shoulders.

'He doesn't want to tell us,' said the youngest young man in a stage aside; and then, with an appearance of great sang-froid, 'You don't mind if I take a cigarette?'

I waved him a cordial assent, and proceeded with my breakfast. Two of the others went and looked out of the farther window and talked inaudibly. I was struck by a thought. 'The tide,' I said, 'is running out?'

There was a pause, a doubt who should answer me.

'It's near the ebb,' said the fat little man.

'Well, anyhow,' I said, 'it won't float far.'

I decapitated my third egg, and began a little speech. 'Look here,' I said. 'Please don't imagine I'm surly or telling you uncivil lies, or anything of that sort. I'm forced, almost, to be a little short and mysterious. I can quite understand this is as queer as it can be, and that your imaginations must be going it. I can assure you, you're in at a memorable time. But I can't make it clear to you now – it's impossible. I give you my word of honour I've come from the moon, and that's all I can tell you . . . All the same, I'm tremendously obliged to you, you know, tremendously. I hope that my manner hasn't in any way given you offence.'

'Oh, not in the least!' said the youngest young man affably. 'We can quite understand,' and staring hard at me all the time, he heeled his chair back until it very nearly upset, and recovered with some exertion. 'Not a bit of it,' said the fat young man.

'Don't you imagine *that*!' and they all got up and dispersed, and walked about and lit cigarettes, and generally tried to show they were perfectly amiable and disengaged, and entirely free from the slightest curiosity about me and the sphere. 'I'm going to keep an eye on that ship out there all the same,' I heard one of them remarking in an undertone. If only they could have forced themselves to it, they would, I believe, even have gone out and left me. I went on with my third egg.

'The weather,' the fat little man remarked presently, 'has been immense, has it not? I don't know *when* we have had such a summer . . . '

Phoo – whizz! Like a tremendous rocket!

And somewhere a window was broken . . .

'What's that?' said I.

'It isn't – ?' cried the little man, and rushed to the corner window.

All the others rushed to the window likewise. I sat staring at them.

Suddenly I leapt up, knocked over my third egg, rushed for the window also. I had just thought of something. 'Nothing to be seen there,' cried the little man, rushing for the door.

'It's that boy!' I cried, bawling in hoarse fury; 'it's that accursed boy!' and turning about I pushed the waiter aside – he was just bringing me some more toast – and rushed violently out of the room and down and out upon the queer little esplanade in front of the hotel.

The sea, which had been smooth, was rough now with hurrying cat's-paws, and all about where the sphere had been was tumbled water like the wake of a ship. Above, a little puff of cloud whirled like dispersing smoke, and the three or four people on the beach were staring up with interrogative faces towards the point of that unexpected report. And that was all! Boots and waiter and the four young men in blazers came rushing out behind me. Shouts came from windows and doors, and all sorts of worrying people came into sight – agape.

For a time I stood there, too overwhelmed by this new development to think of the people.

At first I was too stunned to see the thing as any definite disaster – I was just stunned, as a man is by some accidental violent blow. It is only afterwards he begins to appreciate his specific injury.

'Good Lord!'

I felt as though somebody was pouring funk out of a can down the back of my neck. My legs became feeble. I had got the first intimation of what the disaster meant for me. There was that confounded boy – sky high! I was utterly 'left'. There was the gold in the coffee-room – my only possession on earth. How would it all work out? The general effect was of a gigantic unmanageable confusion.

'I say,' said the voice of the little man behind. 'I *say*, you know.'

I wheeled about, and there were twenty or thirty people, a sort of irregular investment of people, all bombarding me with dumb inter-rogation, with infinite doubt and suspicion. I felt the compulsion of their eyes intolerably. I groaned aloud.

'I *can't*!' I shouted. 'I tell you I can't! I'm not equal to it! You must puzzle and – and be damned to you!'

I gesticulated convulsively. He receded a step as though I had threatened him. I made a bolt through them into the hotel. I charged back into the coffee-room, rang the bell furiously. I gripped the waiter as he entered. 'D'ye hear?' I shouted. 'Get help and carry these bars up to my room right away.'

He failed to understand me, and I shouted and raved at him. A scared-

looking little old man in a green apron appeared, and further two of the young men in flannels. I made a dash at them and commandeered their services. As soon as the gold was in my room I felt free to quarrel. 'Now get out,' I shouted; 'all of you get out if you don't want to see a man go mad before your eyes!' And I helped the waiter by the shoulder as he hesitated in the doorway. And then, as soon as I had the door locked on them all, I tore off the little man's clothes again, shied them right and left, and got into bed forthwith. And there I lay swearing and panting and cooling for a very long time.

At last I was calm enough to get out of bed and ring up the round-eyed waiter for a flannel nightshirt, a soda and whisky, and some good cigars. And these things being procured me, after an exasperating delay that drove me several times to the bell, I locked the door again and proceeded very deliberately to look the entire situation in the face.

The net result of the great experiment presented itself as an absolute failure. It was a rout, and I was the sole survivor. It was an absolute collapse, and this was the final disaster. There was nothing for it but to save myself, and as much as I could in the way of prospects from our *débâcle*. At one fatal crowning blow all my vague resolutions of return and recovery had vanished. My intention of going back to the moon, of getting a sphereful of gold, and afterwards of having a fragment of Cavorite analysed and so recovering the great secret – perhaps, finally, even of recovering Cavor's body – all these ideas vanished altogether.

I was the sole survivor, and that was all.

I think that going to bed was one of the luckiest ideas I have ever had in an emergency. I really believe I should either have got loose-headed or done some fatal indiscreet thing. But there, locked in and secure from all interruptions, I could think out the position in all its bearings and make my arrangements at leisure.

Of course, it was quite clear to me what had happened to the boy. He had crawled into the sphere, meddled with the studs, shut the Cavorite windows, and gone up. It was highly improbable he had screwed the manhole stopper, and, even if he had, the chances were a thousand to one against his getting back. It was fairly evident that he would gravitate with my bales to somewhere near the middle of the sphere and remain there, and so cease to be a legitimate terrestrial interest, however remarkable he might seem to the inhabitants of some remote quarter of space. I very speedily convinced myself on that point. And as for any responsibility I might have in the matter, the more I reflected upon that, the clearer it became that if only I kept quiet about things, I need not trouble myself about that. If I was faced by sorrowing parents demanding their lost boy, I had merely to demand my lost sphere – or ask them what they meant. At first I had had a vision of weeping parents and guardians, and all sorts of complications; but now I saw that I simply had to keep my mouth shut, and

nothing in that way could arise. And, indeed, the more I lay and smoked and thought, the more evident became the wisdom of impenetrability.

It is within the right of every British citizen, provided he does not commit damage nor indecorum, to appear suddenly wherever he pleases, and as ragged and filthy as he pleases, and with whatever amount of virgin gold he sees fit to encumber himself, and no one has any right at all to hinder and detain him in this procedure. I formulated that at last to myself, and repeated it over as a sort of private Magna Carta of my liberty.

Once I had put that issue on one side, I could take up and consider in an equable manner certain considerations I had scarcely dared to think of before, namely, those arising out of the circumstances of my bankruptcy. But now, looking at this matter calmly and at leisure, I could see that if only I suppressed my identity by a temporary assumption of some less well-known name, and if I retained the two months' beard that had grown upon me, the risks of any annoyance from the spiteful creditor to whom I have already alluded became very small indeed. From that to a definite course of rational worldly action was plain sailing. It was all amazingly petty, no doubt, but what was there remaining for me to do?

Whatever I did I was resolved that I would keep myself level and right side up.

I ordered up writing materials, and addressed a letter to the New Romney Bank – the nearest, the waiter informed me – telling the manager I wished to open an account with him, and requesting him to send two trustworthy persons properly authenticated in a cab with a good horse to fetch some hundredweight of gold with which I happened to be encumbered. I signed the letter 'Blake', which seemed to me to be a thoroughly respectable sort of name. This done, I got a Folkestone Blue Book, picked out an outfitter, and asked him to send a cutter to measure me for a dark tweed suit, ordering at the same time a valise, dressing bag, brown boots, shirts, hat (to fit), and so forth; and from a watchmaker I also ordered a watch. And these letters being despatched, I had up as good a lunch as the hotel could give, and then lay smoking a cigar, as calm and ordinary as possible, until in accordance with my instructions two duly authenticated clerks came from the bank and weighed and took away my gold. After which I pulled the clothes over my ears in order to drown any knocking, and went very comfortably to sleep.

I went to sleep. No doubt it was a prosaic thing for the first man back from the moon to do, and I can imagine that the young and imaginative reader will find my behaviour disappointing. But I was horribly fatigued and bothered, and, confound it! what else was there to do? There certainly was not the remotest chance of my being believed, if I had told my story then, and it would certainly have subjected me to intolerable annoyances. I went to sleep. When at last I woke up again I was ready to face the world as I have always been accustomed to face it since I came to years of discretion.

And so I got away to Italy, and there it is I am writing this story. If the world will not have it as fact, then the world may take it as fiction. It is no concern of mine.

And now that the account is finished, I am amazed to think how completely this adventure is gone and done with. Everybody believes that Cavor was a not very brilliant scientific experimenter who blew up his house and himself at Lympne, and they explain the bang that followed my arrival at Littlestone by a reference to the experiments with explosives that are going on continually at the government establishment of Lydd, two miles away. I must confess that hitherto I have not acknowledged my share in the disappearance of Master Tommy Simmons, which was that little boy's name. That, perhaps, may prove a difficult item of corroboration to explain away. They account for my appearance in rags with two bars of indisputable gold upon the Littlestone beach in various ingenious ways – it doesn't worry me what they think of me. They say I have strung all these things together to avoid being questioned too closely as to the source of my wealth. I would like to see the man who could invent a story that would hold together like this one. Well, they must take it as fiction – there it is.

I have told my story – and now, I suppose, I have to take up the worries of this terrestrial life again. Even if one has been to the moon, one has still to earn a living. So I am working here at Amalfi, on the scenario of that play I sketched before Cavor came walking into my world, and I am trying to piece my life together as it was before ever I saw him. I must confess that I find it hard to keep my mind on the play when the moonshine comes into my room. It is full moon here, and last night I was out on the pergola for hours, staring away at the shining blankness that hides so much. Imagine it! tables and chairs, and trestles and bars of gold! Confound it! – if only one could hit on that Cavorite again! But a thing like that doesn't come twice in a life. Here I am, a little better off than I was at Lympne, and that is all. And Cavor has committed suicide in a more elaborate way than any human being ever did before. So the story closes as finally and completely as a dream. It fits in so little with all the other things of life, so much of it is so utterly remote from all human experience, the leaping, the eating, the breathing, and these weightless times, that indeed there are moments when, in spite of my moon gold, I do more than half believe myself that the whole thing was a dream . . .

The Astonishing Communication of Mr Julius Wendigee

When I had finished my account of my return to the earth at Littlestone, I wrote, 'The End', made a flourish, and threw my pen aside, fully believing that the whole story of the First Men in the Moon was done. Not only had I done this, but I had placed my manuscript in the hands of a literary agent, had permitted it to be sold, had seen the greater portion of it appear in the *Strand Magazine*, and was setting to work again upon the scenario of the play I had commenced at Lympne before I realised that the end was not yet. And then, following me from Amalfi to Algiers, there reached me (it is now about six months ago) one of the most astounding communications I have ever been fated to receive. Briefly, it informed me that Mr Julius Wendigee, a Dutch electrician, who has been experimenting with certain apparatus akin to the apparatus used by Mr Tesla in America, in the hope of discovering some method of communication with Mars, was receiving day by day a curiously fragmentary message in English, which was indisputably emanating from Mr Cavor in the moon.

At first I thought the thing was an elaborate practical joke by someone who had seen the manuscript of my narrative. I answered Mr Wendigee jestingly, but he replied in a manner that put such suspicion altogether aside, and in a state of inconceivable excitement I hurried from Algiers to the little observatory upon the St Gothard in which he was working. In the presence of his record and his appliances – and above all of the messages from Cavor that were coming to hand – my lingering doubts vanished. I decided at once to accept a proposal he made to me to remain with him, assisting him to take down the record from day to day, and endeavouring with him to send a message back to the moon. Cavor, we learnt, was not only alive, but free, in the midst of an almost inconceivable community of these ant-like beings, these ant-men, in the blue darkness of the lunar caves. He was lamed, it seemed, but otherwise in quite good health – in better health, he distinctly said, than he usually enjoyed on earth. He had had a fever, but it had left no bad effects. But curiously enough he seemed to be labouring under a conviction that I was either dead in the moon crater or lost in the deep of space.

His message began to be received by Mr Wendigee when that gentleman was engaged in quite a different investigation. The reader will no doubt recall the little excitement that began the century, arising out an announcement by Mr Nikola Tesla, the American electrical celebrity, that he had received a message from Mars. His announcement renewed attention to a fact that had long been familiar to scientific people, namely: that from some

unknown source in space, waves of electromagnetic disturbance, entirely similar to those used by Signor Marconi for his wireless telegraphy, are constantly reaching the earth. Besides Tesla quite a number of other observers have been engaged in perfecting apparatus for receiving and recording these vibrations, though few would go so far as to consider them actual messages from some extraterrestrial sender. Among that few, however, we must certainly count Mr Wendigee. Ever since 1898 he had devoted himself almost entirely to this subject, and being a man of ample means he had erected an observatory on the flanks of Monte Rosa, in a position singularly adapted in every way for such observations.

My scientific attainments, I must admit, are not great, but so far as they enable me to judge, Mr Wendigee's contrivances for detecting and recording any disturbances in the electromagnetic conditions of space are singularly original and ingenious. And by a happy combination of circumstances they were set up and in operation about two months before Cavor made his first attempt to call up the earth. Consequently we have fragments of his communication even from the beginning. Unhappily, they are only fragments, and the most momentous of all the things that he had to tell humanity – the instructions, that is, for the making of Cavorite, if, indeed, he ever transmitted them – have throbbed themselves away unrecorded into space. We never succeeded in getting a response back to Cavor. He was unable to tell, therefore, what we had received or what we had missed; nor, indeed, did he certainly know that anyone on earth was really aware of his efforts to reach us. And the persistence he displayed in sending eighteen long descriptions of lunar affairs – as they would be if we had them complete – shows how much his mind must have turned back towards his native planet since he left it two years ago.

You can imagine how amazed Mr Wendigee must have been when he discovered his record of electromagnetic disturbances interlaced by Cavor's straightforward English. Mr Wendigee knew nothing of our wild journey moonward, and suddenly – this English out of the void!

It is well the reader should understand the conditions under which it would seem these messages were sent. Somewhere within the moon Cavor certainly had access for a time to a considerable amount of electrical apparatus, and it would seem he rigged up – perhaps furtively – a transmitting arrangement of the Marconi type. This he was able to operate at irregular intervals: sometimes for only half an hour or so, sometimes for three or four hours at a stretch. At these times he transmitted his earthward message, regardless of the fact that the relative position of the moon and points upon the earth's surface is constantly altering. As a consequence of this and of the necessary imperfections of our recording instruments his communication comes and goes in our records in an extremely fitful manner; it becomes blurred; it 'fades out' in a mysterious and altogether exasperating way. And added to this is the fact that he was not an expert

operator; he had partly forgotten, or never completely mastered, the code in general use, and as he became fatigued he dropped words and misspelt in a curious manner.

Altogether we have probably lost quite half of the communications he made, and much we have is damaged, broken, and partly effaced. In the abstract that follows the reader must be prepared therefore for a considerable amount of break, hiatus, and change of topic. Mr Wendigee and I are collaborating in a complete and annotated edition of the Cavor record, which we hope to publish, together with a detailed account of the instruments employed, beginning with the first volume in January next. That will be the full and scientific report, of which this is only the popular transcript. But here we give at least sufficient to complete the story I have told, and to give the broad outlines of the state of that other world so near, so akin, and yet so dissimilar to our own.

CHAPTER TWENTY-THREE

An Abstract of the Six Messages First Received from Mr Cavor

The two earlier messages of Mr Cavor may very well be reserved for that larger volume. They simply tell, with greater brevity and with a difference in several details that is interesting, but not of any vital importance, the bare facts of the making of the sphere and our departure from the world. Throughout, Cavor speaks of me as a man who is dead, but with a curious change of temper as he approaches our landing on the moon. 'Poor Bedford', he says of me, and 'this poor young man'; and he blames himself for inducing a young man, 'by no means well equipped for such adventures', to leave a planet 'on which he was indisputably fitted to succeed' on so precarious a mission. I think he underrates the part my energy and practical capacity played in bringing about the realisation of his theoretical sphere. 'We arrived,' he says, with no more account of our passage through space than if we had made a journey of common occurrence in a railway train.

And then he becomes increasingly unfair to me. Unfair, indeed, to an extent I should not have expected in a man trained in the search for truth. Looking back over my previously written account of these things, I must insist that I have been altogether juster to Cavor than he has been to me. I have extenuated little and suppressed nothing. But his account is:

It speedily became apparent that the entire strangeness of our circumstances and surroundings – great loss of weight, attenuated but highly oxygenated air, consequent exaggeration of the results of muscular effort, rapid develop-

ment of weird plants from obscure spores, lurid sky – was exciting my companion unduly. On the moon his character seemed to deteriorate. He became impulsive, rash, and quarrelsome. In a little while his folly in devouring some gigantic vesicles and his consequent intoxication led to our capture by the Selenites – before we had had the slightest opportunity of properly observing their ways . . .

(He says, you observe, nothing of his own concession to these same 'vesicles'.)

And he goes on from that point to say that 'We came to a difficult passage with them, and Bedford mistaking certain gestures of theirs' – pretty gestures they were! – 'gave way to a panic violence. He ran amuck, killed three, and perforce I had to flee with him after the outrage. Subsequently we fought with a number who endeavoured to bar our way, and slew seven or eight more. It says much for the tolerance of these beings that on my recapture I was not instantly slain. We made our way to the exterior and separated in the crater of our arrival, to increase our chances of recovering our sphere. But presently I came upon a body of Selenites, led by two who were curiously different, even in form, from any of these we had seen hitherto, with larger heads and smaller bodies, and much more elaborately wrapped about. And after evading them for some time I fell into a crevasse, cut my head rather badly, and displaced my patella, and, finding crawling very painful, decided to surrender – if they would still permit me to do so. This they did, and, perceiving my helpless condition, carried me with them again into the moon. And of Bedford I have heard or seen nothing more, nor, so far as I can gather, any Selenite. Either the night overtook him in the crater, or else, which is more probable, he found the sphere, and, desiring to steal a march upon me, made off with it – only, I fear, to find it uncontrollable, and to meet a more lingering fate in outer space.'

And with that Cavor dismisses me and goes on to more interesting topics. I dislike the idea of seeming to use my position as his editor to deflect his story in my own interest, but I am obliged to protest here against the turn he gives these occurrences. He said nothing about that gasping message on the bloodstained paper in which he told, or attempted to tell, a very different story. The dignified self-surrender is an altogether new view of the affair that has come to him, I must insist, since he began to feel secure among the lunar people; and as for the 'stealing a march' conception, I am quite willing to let the reader decide between us on what he has before him. I know I am not a model man – I have made no pretence to be. But am I *that*?

However, that is the sum of my wrongs. From this point I can edit Cavor with an untroubled mind, for he mentions me no more.

It would seem the Selenites who had come upon him carried him to some

point in the interior down 'a great shaft' by means of what he describes as 'a sort of balloon'. We gather from the rather confused passage in which he describes this, and from a number of chance allusions and hints in other and subsequent messages, that this 'great shaft' is one of an enormous system of artificial shafts that run, each from what is called a lunar 'crater', downwards for very nearly a hundred miles towards the central portion of our satellite. These shafts communicate by transverse tunnels, they throw out abysmal caverns and expand into great globular places; the whole of the moon's substance for a hundred miles inward, indeed, is a mere sponge of rock. 'Partly,' says Cavor, 'this sponginess is natural, but very largely it is due to the enormous industry of the Selenites in the past. The enormous circular mounds of the excavated rock and earth it is that form these great circles about the tunnels known to earthly astronomers (misled by a false analogy) as volcanoes.'

It was down this shaft they took him, in this 'sort of balloon' he speaks of, at first into an inky blackness and then into a region of continually increasing phosphorescence. Cavor's despatches show him to be curiously regardless of detail for a scientific man, but we gather that this light was due to the streams and cascades of water – 'no doubt containing some phosphorescent organism' – that flowed ever more abundantly downward towards the Central Sea. And as he descended, he says, 'The Selenites also became luminous.' And at last far below him he saw, as it were, a lake of heatless fire, the waters of the Central Sea, glowing and eddying in strange perturbation, 'like luminous blue milk that is just on the boil'.

'This Lunar Sea,' says Cavor, in a later passage 'is not a stagnant ocean; a solar tide sends it in a perpetual flow around the lunar axis, and strange storms and boilings and rushings of its waters occur, and at times cold winds and thunderings that ascend out of it into the busy ways of the great ant-hill above. It is only when the water is in motion that it gives out light; in its rare seasons of calm it is black. Commonly, when one sees it, its waters rise and fall in an oily swell, and flakes and big rafts of shining, bubbly foam drift with the sluggish, faintly glowing current. The Selenites navigate its cavernous straits and lagoons in little shallow boats of a canoe-like shape; and even before my journey to the galleries about the Grand Lunar, who is Master of the Moon, I was permitted to make a brief excursion on its waters.

'The caverns and passages are naturally very tortuous. A large proportion of these ways are known only to expert pilots among the fishermen, and not infrequently Selenites are lost for ever in their labyrinths. In their remoter recesses, I am told, strange creatures lurk, some of them terrible and dangerous creatures that all the science of the moon has been unable to exterminate. There is particularly the Rapha, an inextricable mass of clutching tentacles that one hacks to pieces only to multiply; and the Tzee, a darting creature that is never seen, so subtly and suddenly does it slay . . . '

He gives us a gleam of description.

'I was reminded on this excursion of what I have read of the Mammoth Caves; if only I had had a yellow flambeau instead of the pervading blue light, and a solid-looking boatman with an oar instead of a scuttle-faced Selenite working an engine at the back of the canoe, I could have imagined I had suddenly got back to earth. The rocks about us were very various, sometimes black, sometimes pale blue and veined, and once they flashed and glittered as though we had come into a mine of sapphires. And below one saw the ghostly phosphorescent fishes flash and vanish in the hardly less phosphorescent deep. Then, presently, a long ultramarine vista down the turgid stream of one of the channels of traffic, and a landing stage, and then, perhaps, a glimpse up the enormous crowded shaft of one of the vertical ways.

'In one great place heavy with glistening stalactites a number of boats were fishing. We went alongside one of these and watched the long-armed Selenites winding in a net. They were little, hunchbacked insects, with very strong arms, short, bandy legs, and crinkled face-masks. As they pulled at it that net seemed the heaviest thing I had come upon in the moon; it was loaded with weights – no doubt of gold – and it took a long time to draw, for in those waters the larger and more edible fish lurk deep. The fish in the net came up like a blue moonrise – a blaze of darting, tossing blue.

'Among their catch was a many-tentaculate, evil-eyed black thing, ferociously active, whose appearance they greeted with shrieks and twitters, and which with quick, nervous movements they hacked to pieces by means of little hatchets. All its dissevered limbs continued to lash and writhe in a vicious manner. Afterwards, when fever had hold of me, I dreamt again and again of that bitter, furious creature rising so vigorous and active out of the unknown sea. It was the most active and malignant thing of all the living creatures I have yet seen in this world inside the moon . . .

* * *

'The surface of this sea must be very nearly two hundred miles (if not more) below the level of the moon's exterior; all the cities of the moon lie, I learnt, immediately above this Central Sea, in such cavernous spaces and artificial galleries as I have described, and they communicate with the exterior by enormous vertical shafts which open invariably in what are called by earthly astronomers the "craters" of the moon. The lid covering one such aperture I had already seen during the wanderings that had preceded my capture.

'Upon the condition of the less central portion of the moon I have not yet arrived at very precise knowledge. There is an enormous system of caverns in which the mooncalves shelter during the night; and there are abattoirs and the like – in one of these it was that I and Bedford fought with the Selenite butchers – and I have since seen balloons laden with meat descending out of the upper dark. I have as yet scarcely learnt as much of these things as a Zulu in London would learn about the British corn supplies in the same time. It is clear, however, that these vertical shafts and

the vegetation of the surface must play an essential role in ventilating and keeping fresh the atmosphere of the moon. At one time, and particularly on my first emergence from my prison, there was certainly a cold wind blowing *down* the shaft, and later there was a kind of sirocco upward that corresponded with my fever. For at the end of about three weeks I fell ill of an indefinable sort of fever, and in spite of sleep and the quinine tabloids that very fortunately I had brought in my pocket, I remained ill and fretting miserably, almost to the time when I was taken into the presence of the Grand Lunar, who is Master of the Moon.

'I will not dilate on the wretchedness of my condition,' he remarks, 'during those days of ill-health.' And he goes on with great amplitude with details I omit here. 'My temperature,' he concludes, 'kept abnormally high for a long time, and I lost all desire for food. I had stagnant waking intervals, and sleep tormented by dreams, and at one phase I was, I remember, so weak as to be earth-sick and almost hysterical. I longed almost intolerably for colour to break the everlasting blue . . . '

He reverts again presently to the topic of this sponge-caught lunar atmosphere. I am told by astronomers and physicists that all he tells is in absolute accordance with what was already known of the moon's condition. Had earthly astronomers had the courage and imagination to push home a bold induction, says Mr Wendigee, they might have foretold almost everything that Cavor has to say of the general structure of the moon. They know now pretty certainly that moon and earth are not so much satellite and primary as smaller and greater sisters, made out of one mass, and consequently made of the same material. And since the density of the moon is only three-fifths that of the earth, there can be nothing for it but that she is hollowed out by a great system of caverns. There was no necessity, said Sir Jabez Flap, FRS, that most entertaining exponent of the facetious side of the stars, that we should ever have gone to the moon to find out such easy inferences, and points the pun with an allusion to Gruyère, but he certainly might have announced his knowledge of the hollowness of the moon before. And if the moon is hollow, then the apparent absence of air and water is, of course, quite easily explained. The sea lies within at the bottom of the caverns, and the air travels through the great sponge of galleries, in accordance with simple physical laws. The caverns of the moon, on the whole, are very windy places. As the sunlight comes round the moon the air in the outer galleries on that side is heated, its pressure increases, some flows out on the exterior and mingles with the evaporating air of the craters (where the plants remove its carbonic acid), while the greater portion flows round through the galleries to replace the shrinking air of the cooling side that the sunlight has left. There is, therefore, a constant eastward breeze in the air of the outer galleries, and an up-flow during the lunar day up the shafts, complicated, of course, very greatly by the varying shape of the galleries, and the ingenious contrivances of the Selenite mind . . .

The Natural History of the Selenites

The messages of Cavor from the sixth up to the sixteenth are for the most part so much broken, and they abound so in repetitions, that they scarcely form a consecutive narrative. They will be given in full, of course, in the scientific report, but here it will be far more convenient to continue simply to abstract and quote as in the former chapter. We have subjected every word to a keen critical scrutiny, and my own brief memories and impressions of lunar things have been of inestimable help in interpreting what would otherwise have been impenetrably dark. And, naturally, as living beings, our interest centres far more upon the strange community of lunar insects in which he was living, it would seem, as an honoured guest than upon the mere physical condition of their world.

I have already made it clear, I think, that the Selenites I saw resembled man in maintaining the erect attitude, and in having four limbs, and I have compared the general appearance of their heads and the jointing of their limbs to that of insects. I have mentioned, too, the peculiar consequence of the smaller gravitation of the moon on their fragile slightness. Cavor confirms me upon all these points. He calls them 'animals', though of course they fall under no division of the classification of earthly creatures, and he points out 'the insect type of anatomy had, fortunately for men, never exceeded a relatively very small size on earth'. The largest terrestrial insects, living or extinct, do not, as a matter of fact, measure six inches in length; 'but here, against the lesser gravitation of the moon, a creature certainly as much an insect as vertebrate seems to have been able to attain to human and ultra-human dimensions'.

He does not mention the ant, but throughout his allusions the ant is continually being brought before my mind, in its sleepless activity, in its intelligence and social organisation, in its structure, and more particularly in the fact that it displays, in addition to the two forms, the male and the female form, that almost all other animals possess, a number of other sexless creatures, workers, soldiers, and the like, differing from one another in structure, character, power, and use, and yet all members of the same species. For these Selenites, also, have a great variety of forms. Of course, they are not only colossally greater in size than ants, but also, in Cavor's opinion at least, in intelligence, morality, and social wisdom are they colossally greater than men. And instead of the four or five different forms of ant that are found, there are almost innumerably different forms of Selenite. I had endeavoured to indicate the very considerable difference observable in such Selenites of the outer crust as I happened to encounter;

the differences in size and proportions were certainly as wide as the differences between the most widely separated races of men. But such differences as I saw fade absolutely to nothing in comparison with the huge distinctions of which Cavor tells. It would seem the exterior Selenites I saw were, indeed, mostly engaged in kindred occupations – mooncalf herds, butchers, fleshers, and the like. But within the moon, practically unsuspected by me, there are, it seems, a number of other sorts of Selenite, differing in size, differing in the relative size of part to part, differing in power and appearance, and yet not different species of creatures, but only different forms of one species, and retaining through all their variations a certain common likeness that marks their specific unity. The moon is, indeed, a sort of vast ant-hill, only, instead of there being only four or five sorts of ant, there are many hundred different sorts of Selenite, and almost every gradation between one sort and another.

It would seem the discovery came upon Cavor very speedily. I infer rather than learn from his narrative that he was captured by the mooncalf herds under the direction of these other Selenites who 'have larger brain cases (heads?) and very much shorter legs'. Finding he would not walk even under the goad, they carried him into darkness, crossed a narrow, plank-like bridge that may have been the identical bridge I had refused, and put him down in something that must have seemed at first to be some sort of lift. This was the balloon – it had certainly been absolutely invisible to us in the darkness – and what had seemed to me a mere plank-walking into the void was really, no doubt, the passage of the gangway. In this he descended towards constantly more luminous caverns of the moon. At first they descended in silence – save for the twitterings of the Selenites – and then into a stir of windy movement. In a little while the profound blackness had made his eyes so sensitive that he began to see more and more of the things about him, and at last the vague took shape.

'Conceive an enormous cylindrical space,' says Cavor, in his seventh message, 'a quarter of a mile across, perhaps; very dimly lit at first and then brighter, with big platforms twisting down its sides in a spiral that vanishes at last below in a blue profundity; and lit even more brightly – one could not tell how or why. Think of the well of the very largest spiral staircase or lift-shaft that you have ever looked down, and magnify that by a hundred. Imagine it at twilight seen through blue glass. Imagine yourself looking down that; only imagine also that you feel extraordinarily light, and have got rid of any giddy feeling you might have on earth, and you will have the first conditions of my impression. Round this enormous shaft imagine a broad gallery running in a much steeper spiral than would be credible on earth, and forming a steep road protected from the gulf only by a little parapet that vanishes at last in perspective a couple of miles below.

'Looking up, I saw the very fellow of the downward vision; it had, of

course, the effect of looking into a very steep cone. A wind was blowing down the shaft, and far above I fancy I heard, growing fainter and fainter, the bellowing of the mooncalves that were being driven down again from their evening pasturage on the exterior. And up and down the spiral galleries were scattered numerous moon people, pallid, faintly luminous beings, regarding our appearance or busied on unknown errands.

'Either I fancied it or a flake of snow came drifting down on the icy breeze. And then, falling like a snowflake, a little figure, a little man-insect, clinging to a parachute, drove down very swiftly towards the central places of the moon.

'The big-headed Selenite sitting beside me, seeing me move my head with the gesture of one who saw, pointed with his trunk-like "hand" and indicated a sort of jetty coming into sight very far below: a little landing-stage, as it were, hanging into the void. As it swept up towards us our pace diminished very rapidly, and in a few moments, as it seemed, we were abreast of it, and at rest. A mooring-rope was flung and grasped, and I found myself pulled down to a level with a great crowd of Selenites, who jostled to see me.

'It was an incredible crowd. Suddenly and violently there was forced upon my attention the vast amount of difference there is among these beings of the moon.

'Indeed, there seemed not two alike in all that jostling multitude. They differed in shape, they differed in size, they rang all the horrible changes on the theme of Selenite form! Some bulged and overhung, some ran about among the feet of their fellows. All of them had a grotesque and disquieting suggestion of an insect that has somehow contrived to mock humanity; but all seemed to present an incredible exaggeration of some particular feature: one had a vast right forelimb, an enormous antennal arm, as it were; one seemed all leg, poised, as it were, on stilts; another protruded the edge of his face mask into a nose-like organ that made him startlingly human until one saw his expressionless gaping mouth. The strange and (except for the want of mandibles and palps) most insect-like head of the mooncalf-minders underwent, indeed, the most incredible transformations: here it was broad and low, here high and narrow; here its leathery brow was drawn out into horns and strange features; here it was whiskered and divided, and there with a grotesquely human profile. One distortion was particularly conspicuous. There were several brain cases distended like bladders to a huge size, with the face mask reduced to quite small proportions. There were several amazing forms, with heads reduced to microscopic proportions and blobby bodies; and fantastic, flimsy things that existed, it would seem, only as a basis for vast, trumpet-like protrusions of the lower part of the mask. And oddest of all, as it seemed to me for the moment, two or three of these weird inhabitants of a subterranean world, a world sheltered by innumerable miles of rock from sun or rain, *carried umbrellas* in their

tentaculate hands – real terrestrial-looking umbrellas! And then I thought of the parachutist I had watched descend.

'These moon people behaved exactly as a human crowd might have done in similar circumstances: they jostled and thrust one another, they shoved one another aside, they even clambered upon one another to get a glimpse of me. Every moment they increased in numbers, and pressed more urgently upon the discs of my ushers' – Cavor does not explain what he means by this – 'every moment fresh shapes emerged from the shadows and forced themselves upon my astounded attention. And presently I was signed and helped into a sort of litter, and lifted up on the shoulders of strong-armed bearers, and so borne through the twilight over this seething multitude towards the apartments that were provided for me in the moon. All about me were eyes, faces, masks, a leathery noise like the rustling of beetle wings, and a great bleating and cricket-like twittering of Selenite voices . . . '

* * *

We gather he was taken to a 'hexagonal apartment', and there for a space he was confined. Afterwards he was given a much more considerable liberty; indeed, almost as much freedom as one has in a civilised town on earth. And it would appear that the mysterious being who is the ruler and master of the moon appointed two Selenites 'with large heads' to guard and study him, and to establish whatever mental communications were possible with him. And, amazing and incredible as it may seem, these two creatures, these fantastic men insects, these beings of other world, were presently communicating with Cavor by means of terrestrial speech.

Cavor speaks of them as Phi-oo and Tsi-puff. Phi-oo, he says, was about five feet high; he had small slender legs about eighteen inches long, and slight feet of the common lunar pattern. On these balanced a little body, throbbing with the pulsations of his heart. He had long, soft, many-jointed arms ending in a tentacled grip, and his neck was many-jointed in the usual way, but exceptionally short and thick. His head, says Cavor – apparently alluding to some previous description that has gone astray in space – 'is of the common lunar type, but strangely modified. The mouth has the usual expressionless gape, but it is unusually small and pointing downward, and the mask is reduced to the size of a large flat nose-flap. On either side are the little eyes.

'The rest of the head is distended into a huge globe and the chitinous leathery cuticle of the mooncalf herds thins out to a mere membrane, through which the pulsating brain movements are distinctly visible. He is a creature, indeed, with a tremendously hypertrophied brain, and with the rest of his organism both relatively and absolutely dwarfed.'

In another passage Cavor compares the back view of him to Atlas supporting the world. Tsi-puff it seems was a very similar insect, but his

'face' was drawn out to a considerable length, and the brain hypertrophy being in different regions, his head was not round but pear-shaped, with the stalk downward. There were also litter-carriers, lopsided beings, with enormous shoulders, very spidery ushers, and a squat foot attendant in Cavor's retinue.

The manner in which Phi-oo and Tsi-puff attacked the problem of speech was fairly obvious. They came into this 'hexagonal cell' in which Cavor was confined, and began imitating every sound he made, beginning with a cough. He seems to have grasped their intention with great quickness, and to have begun repeating words to them and pointing to indicate the application. The procedure was probably always the same. Phi-oo would attend to Cavor for a space, then point also and say the word he had heard.

The first word he mastered was 'man', and the second 'Mooney' – which Cavor on the spur of the moment seems to have used instead of 'Selenite' for the moon race. As soon as Phi-oo was assured of the meaning of a word he repeated it to Tsi-puff, who remembered it infallibly. They mastered over one hundred English nouns at their first session.

Subsequently it seems they brought an artist with them to assist the work of explanation with sketches and diagrams – Cavor's drawings being rather crude. He was, says Cavor, 'a being with an active arm and an arresting eye', and he seemed to draw with incredible swiftness.

The eleventh message is undoubtedly only a fragment of a longer communication. After some broken sentences, the record of which is unintelligible, it goes on:

'But it will interest only linguists, and delay me too long, to give the details of the series of intent parleys of which these were the beginning, and, indeed, I very much doubt if I could give in anything like the proper order all the twistings and turnings that we made in our pursuit of mutual comprehension. Verbs were soon plain sailing – at least, such active verbs as I could express by drawings; some adjectives were easy, but when it came to abstract nouns, to prepositions, and the sort of hackneyed figures of speech, by means of which so much is expressed on earth, it was like diving in cork-jackets. Indeed, these difficulties were insurmountable until to the sixth lesson came a fourth assistant, a being with a huge football-shaped head, whose forte was clearly the pursuit of intricate analogy. He entered in a preoccupied manner, stumbling against a stool, and the difficulties that arose had to be presented to him with a certain amount of clamour and hitting and pricking before they reached his apprehension. But once he was involved his penetration was amazing. Whenever there came a need of thinking beyond Phi-oo's by no means limited scope, this prolate-headed person was in request, but he invariably told the conclusion to Tsi-puff, in order that it might be remembered; Tsi-puff was ever the arsenal for facts. And so we advanced again.

'It seemed long and yet brief – a matter of days – before I was positively talking with these insects of the moon. Of course, at first it was an intercourse infinitely tedious and exasperating, but imperceptibly it has grown to comprehension. And my patience has grown to meet its limitations, Phi-oo it is who does all the talking. He does it with a vast amount of meditative provisional "M'm-M'm" and has caught up one or two phrases, "If I may say", "If you understand", and beads all his speech with them.

'Thus he would discourse. Imagine him explaining his artist.

' "M'm-M'm – he – if I may say – draw. Eat little – drink little – draw. Love draw. No other thing. Hate all who not draw like him. Angry. Hate all who draw like him better. Hate most people. Hate all who not think all world for to draw. Angry. M'm. All things mean nothing to him – only draw. He like you . . . if you understand . . . New thing to draw. Ugly – striking. Eh?

' "He," – turning to Tsi-puff – "love remember words. Remember wonderful more than any. Think no, draw no – remember. Say" – here he referred to his gifted assistant for a word – "histories – all things. He hear once – say ever."

'It is more wonderful to me than I dreamt that anything ever could be again, to hear, in this perpetual obscurity, these extraordinary creatures – for even familiarity fails to weaken the inhuman effect of their appearance – continually piping a nearer approach to coherent earthly speech – asking questions, giving answers. I feel that I am casting back to the fable-hearing period of childhood again, when the ant and the grasshopper talked together and the bee judged between them . . . '

* * *

And while these linguistic exercises were going on Cavor seems to have experienced a considerable relaxation of his confinement. 'The first dread and distrust our unfortunate conflict aroused is being,' he said, 'continually effaced by the deliberate rationality of all I do.' . . . 'I am now able to come and go as I please, or I am restricted only for my own good. So it is I have been able to get at this apparatus, and, assisted by a happy find among the material that is littered in this enormous store-cave, I have contrived to despatch these messages. So far not the slightest attempt has been made to interfere with me in this, though I have made it quite clear to Phi-oo that I am signalling to the earth.

' "You talk to other?" he asked, watching me.

' "Others," said I.

' "Others," he said. "Oh yes, Men?"

'And I went on transmitting.'

* * *

Cavor was continually making corrections in his previous accounts of the

Selenites as fresh facts flowed upon him to modify his conclusions, and accordingly one gives the quotations that follow with a certain amount of reservation. They are quoted from the ninth, thirteenth, and sixteenth messages, and, altogether vague and fragmentary as they are, they probably give as complete a picture of the social life of this strange community as mankind can now hope to have for many generations.

'In the moon,' says Cavor, 'every citizen knows his place. He is born to that place, and the elaborate discipline of training and education and surgery he undergoes fits him at last so completely to it that he has neither ideas nor organs for any purpose beyond it. "Why should he?" Phi-oo would ask. If, for example, a Selenite is destined to be a mathematician, his teachers and trainers set out at once to that end. They check any incipient disposition to other pursuits, they encourage his mathematical bias with a perfect psychological skill. His brain grows, or at least the mathematical faculties of his brain grow, and the rest of him only so much as is necessary to sustain this essential part of him. At last, save for rest and food, his one delight lies in the exercise and display of his facility, his one interest in its application, his sole society with other specialists in his own line. His brain grows continually larger, at least so far as the portions engaging in mathematics are concerned; they bulge ever larger and seem to suck all life and vigour from the rest of his frame. His limbs shrivel, his heart and digestive organs diminish, his insect face is hidden under its bulging contours. His voice becomes a mere stridulation for the stating of formula; he seems deaf to all but properly enunciated problems. The faculty of laughter, save for the sudden discovery of some paradox, is lost to him; his deepest emotion is the evolution of a novel computation. And so he attains his end.

'Or, again, a Selenite appointed to be a minder of mooncalves is from his earliest years induced to think and live mooncalf, to find his pleasure in mooncalf lore, his exercise in their tending and pursuit. He is trained to become wiry and active, his eye is indurated to the tight wrappings, the angular contours that constitute a "smart mooncalfishness". He takes at last no interest in the deeper part of the moon; he regards all Selenites not equally versed in mooncalves with indifference, derision, or hostility. His thoughts are of mooncalf pastures, and his dialect an accomplished mooncalf technique. So also he loves his work, and discharges in perfect happiness the duty that justifies his being. And so it is with all sorts and conditions of Selenites – each is a perfect unit in a world machine . . .

'These beings with big heads, on whom the intellectual labours fall, form a sort of aristocracy in this strange society, and at the head of them, quintessential of the moon, is that marvellous gigantic ganglion the Grand Lunar, into whose presence I am finally to come. The unlimited development of the minds of the intellectual class is rendered possible by the absence of any body skull in the lunar anatomy, that strange box of bone

that clamps about the developing brain of man, imperiously insisting "thus far and no farther" to all his possibilities. They fall into three main classes differing greatly in influence and respect. There are administrators, of whom Phi-oo is one, Selenites of considerable initiative and versatility, responsible each for a certain cubic content of the moon's bulk; the experts like the football-headed thinker, who are trained to perform certain special operations; and the erudite, who are the repositories of all knowledge. To the latter class belongs Tsi-puff, the first lunar professor of terrestrial languages. With regard to these latter, it is a curious little thing to note that the unlimited growth of the lunar brain has rendered unnecessary the invention of all those mechanical aids to brain work which have distinguished the career of man. There are no books, no records of any sort, no libraries or inscriptions. All knowledge is stored in distended brains much as the honey-ants of Texas store honey in their distended abdomens. The lunar Somerset House and the lunar British Museum Library are collections of living brains . . .

'The less specialised administrators, I note, do for the most part take a very lively interest in me whenever they encounter me. They will come out of the way and stare at me and ask questions to which Phi-oo will reply. I see them going hither and thither with a retinue of bearers, attendants, shouters, parachute-carriers, and so forth – queer groups to see. The experts for the most part ignore me completely, even as they ignore each other, or notice me only to begin a clamorous exhibition of their distinctive skill. The erudite for the most part are rapt in an impervious and apoplectic complacency, from which only a denial of their erudition can rouse them. Usually they are led about by little watchers and attendants, and often there are small and active-looking creatures, small females usually, that I am inclined to think are a sort of wife to them; but some of the profounder scholars are altogether too great for locomotion, and are carried from place to place in a sort of sedan tub, wabbling jellies of knowledge that enlist my respectful astonishment. I have just passed one in coming to this place where I am permitted to amuse myself with these electrical toys, a vast, shaven, shaky head, bald and thin-skinned, carried on his grotesque stretcher. In front and behind came his bearers, and curious, almost trumpet-faced, news disseminators shrieked his fame.

'I have already mentioned the retinues that accompany most of the intellectuals: ushers, bearers, valets, extraneous tentacles and muscles, as it were, to replace the abortive physical powers of these hypertrophied minds. Porters almost invariably accompany them. There are also extremely swift messengers with spider-like legs and "hands" for grasping parachutes, and attendants with vocal organs that could well nigh wake the dead. Apart from their controlling intelligence these subordinates are as inert and helpless as umbrellas in a stand. They exist only in relation to the orders they have to obey, the duties they have to perform.

'The bulk of these insects, however, who go to and fro upon the spiral ways, who fill the ascending balloons and drop past me clinging to flimsy parachutes are, I gather, of the operative class. "Machine hands", indeed, some of these are in actual nature – it is not a figure of speech, the single tentacle of the mooncalf herd is profoundly modified for clawing, lifting, guiding, the rest of them no more than necessary subordinate appendages to these important mechanisms, have enormously developed auditory organs; some whose work lies in delicate chemical operations project a vast olfactory organ; others again have flat feet for treadles with anchylosed joints; and others – who I have been told are glass-blowers – seem mere lung-bellows. But every one of these common Selenites I have seen at work is exquisitely adapted to the social need it meets. Fine work is done by fined-down workers, amazingly dwarfed and neat. Some I could hold on the palm of my hand. There is even a sort of turn-spit Selenite, very common, whose duty and only delight it is to apply the motive power for various small appliances. And to rule over these things and order any erring tendency there might be in some aberrant natures are the most muscular beings I have seen in the moon, a sort of lunar police, who must have been trained from their earliest years to give a perfect respect and obedience to the swollen heads.

'The making of these various sorts of operative must be a very curious and interesting process. I am very much in the dark about it, but quite recently I came upon a number of young Selenites confined in jars from which only the forelimbs protruded, who were being compressed to become machine-minders of a special sort. The extended "hand" in this highly developed system of technical education is stimulated by irritants and nourished by injection, while the rest of the body is starved. Phi-oo, unless I misunderstood him, explained that in the earlier stages these queer little creatures are apt to display signs of suffering in their various cramped situations, but they easily become indurated to their lot; and he took me on to where a number of flexible-minded messengers were being drawn out and broken in. It is quite unreasonable, I know, but such glimpses of the educational methods of these beings affect me disagreeably. I hope, however, that may pass off, and I may be able to see more of this aspect of their wonderful social order. That wretched-looking hand-tentacle sticking out of its jar seemed to have a sort of limp appeal for lost possibilities; it haunts me still, although, of course it is really in the end a far more humane proceeding than our earthly method of leaving children to grow into human beings, and then making machines of them.

'Quite recently, too – I think it was on the eleventh or twelfth visit I made to this apparatus – I had a curious light upon the lives of these operatives. I was being guided through a short cut hither, instead of going down the spiral, and by the quays to the Central Sea. From the devious windings of a long, dark gallery, we emerged into a vast, low cavern, pervaded by an earthy

smell, and as things go in this darkness, rather brightly lit. The light came from a tumultuous growth of livid fungoid shapes – some indeed singularly like our terrestrial mushrooms, but standing as high or higher than a man.

' "Mooneys eat these?" said I to Phi-oo.

' "Yes, food."

' "Goodness me!" I cried; "what's that?"

'My eye had just caught the figure of an exceptionally big and ungainly Selenite lying motionless among the stems, face downward. We stopped.

' "Dead?" I asked. (For as yet I have seen no dead on the moon, and I have grown curious.)

' "*No!*" exclaimed Phi-oo. "Him – worker – no work to do. Get little drink then – make sleep – till we him want. What good him wake, eh? No want him walking about."

' "There's another!" cried I.

'And indeed all that huge extent of mushroom ground was, I found, peppered with these prostrate figures sleeping under an opiate until the moon had need of them. There were scores of them of all sorts, and we were able to turn over some of them, and examine them more precisely than I had been able to previously. They breathed noisily at my doing so, but did not wake. One, I remember very distinctly: he left a strong impression, I think, because some trick of the light and of his attitude was strongly suggestive of a drawn-up human figure. His forelimbs were long, delicate tentacles – he was some kind of refined manipulator – and the pose of his slumber suggested a submissive suffering. No doubt it was a mistake for me to interpret his expression in that way, but I did. And as Phi-oo rolled him over into the darkness among the livid fleshiness again I felt a distinctly unpleasant sensation, although as he rolled the insect in him was confessed.

'It simply illustrates the unthinking way in which one acquires habits of feeling. To drug the worker one does not want and toss him aside is surely far better than to expel him from his factory to wander starving in the streets. In every complicated social community there is necessarily a certain intermittency of employment for all specialised labour, and in this way the trouble of an "unemployed" problem is altogether anticipated. And yet, so unreasonable are even scientifically trained minds, I still do not like the memory of those prostrate forms amidst those quiet, luminous arcades of fleshy growth, and I avoid that short cut in spite of the inconveniences of the longer, more noisy, and more crowded alternative.

* * *

'My alternative route takes me round by a huge, shadowy cavern, very crowded and clamorous, and here it is I see peering out of the hexagonal openings of a sort of honeycomb wall, or parading a large open space behind, or selecting the toys and amulets made to please them by the dainty-tentacled jewellers who work in kennels below, the mothers of the

moon world – the queen bees, as it were, of the hive. They are noble-looking beings, fantastically and sometimes quite beautifully adorned, with a proud carriage, and, save for their mouths, almost microscopic heads.

'Of the condition of the moon sexes, marrying and giving in marriage, and of birth and so forth among the Selenites, I have as yet been able to learn very little. With the steady progress of Phi-oo in English, however, my ignorance will no doubt as steadily disappear. I am of opinion that, as with the ants and bees, there is a large majority of the members in this community of the neuter sex. Of course on earth in our cities there are now many who never live that life of parentage which is the natural life of man. Here, as with the ants, this thing has become a normal condition of the race, and the whole of such replacement as is necessary falls upon this special and by no means numerous class of matrons, the mothers of the moon-world, large and stately beings beautifully fitted to bear the larval Selenite. Unless I misunderstand an explanation of Phi-oo's, they are absolutely incapable of cherishing the young they bring into the moon; periods of foolish indulgence alternate with moods of aggressive violence, and as soon as possible the little creatures, who are quite soft and flabby and pale coloured, are transferred to the charge of celibate females, women "workers" as it were, who in some cases possess brains of almost masculine dimensions.'

* * *

Just at this point, unhappily, this message broke off. Fragmentary and tantalising as the matter constituting this chapter is, it does nevertheless give a vague, broad impression of an altogether strange and wonderful world – a world with which our own may have to reckon we know not how speedily. This intermittent trickle of messages, this whispering of a record needle in the stillness of the mountain slopes, is the first warning of such a change in human conditions as mankind has scarcely imagined heretofore. In that satellite of ours there are new elements, new appliances, traditions, an overwhelming avalanche of new ideas, a strange race with whom we must inevitably struggle for mastery – gold as common as iron or wood . . .

CHAPTER TWENTY-FIVE

The Grand Lunar

The penultimate message describes, with occasionally elaborate detail, the encounter between Cavor and the Grand Lunar, who is the ruler or master of the moon. Cavor seems to have sent most of it without interference, but to have been interrupted in the concluding portion. The second came after an interval of a week.

The first message begins: 'At last I am able to resume this – it then becomes illegible for a space, and after a time resumes in mid-sentence.

The missing words of the following sentence are probably 'the crowd'. There follows quite clearly: 'grew ever denser as we drew near the palace of the Grand Lunar – if I may call a series of excavations a palace. Everywhere faces stared at me – blank, chitinous gapes and masks, eyes peering over tremendous olfactory developments, eyes beneath monstrous forehead plates; an undergrowth of smaller creatures dodged and yelped, and helmet faces poised on sinuous, long-jointed necks appeared craning over shoulders and beneath armpits. Keeping a welcome space about me marched a cordon of stolid, scuttle-headed guards, who had joined us on our leaving the boat in which we had come along the channels of the Central Sea. The quick-eyed artist with the little brain joined us also, and a thick bunch of lean porter-insects swayed and struggled under the multitude of conveniences that were considered essential to my state. I was carried in a litter during the final stage of our journey. This litter was made of some very ductile metal that looked dark to me, meshed and woven, and with bars of paler metal, and about me as I advanced there grouped itself a long and complicated procession.

'In front, after the manner of heralds, marched four trumpet-faced creatures making a devastating bray; and then came squat, resolute-moving ushers before and behind, and on either hand a galaxy of learned heads, a sort of animated encyclopaedia, who were, Phi-oo explained, to stand about the Grand Lunar for purposes of reference. (Not a thing in lunar science, not a point of view or method of thinking, that these wonderful beings did not carry in their heads!) Followed guards and porters, and then Phi-oo's shivering brain borne also on a litter. Then came Tsi-puff in a slightly less important litter; then myself on a litter of greater elegance than any other, and surrounded by my food and drink attendants. More trumpeters came next, splitting the ear with vehement outcries, and then several big brains, special correspondents one might well call them, or historiographers, charged with the task of observing and remembering every detail of this epoch-making interview. A company of attendants, bearing and dragging banners and masses of scented fungus and curious symbols, vanished in the darkness behind. The way was lined by ushers and officers in caparisons that gleamed like steel, and beyond their line, so far as my eyes could pierce the gloom, the heads of that enormous crowd extended.

'I will own that I am still by no means indurated to the peculiar effect of the Selenite appearance, and to find myself, as it were, adrift on this broad sea of excited entomology was by no means agreeable. Just for a space I had something very like what I should imagine people mean when they speak of the "horrors". It had come to me before in these lunar caverns, when on occasion I have found myself weaponless and with an undefended back, amidst a crowd of these Selenites, but never quite so vividly. It is, of course,

as absolutely irrational a feeling as one could well have, and I hope gradually to subdue it. But just for a moment, as I swept forward into the welter of the vast crowd, it was only by gripping my litter tightly and summoning all my will-power that I succeeded in avoiding an outcry or some such manifestation. It lasted perhaps three I minutes; then I had myself in hand again.

'We ascended the spiral of a vertical way for some time, and then passed through a series of huge halls, dome-roofed and elaborately decorated. The approach to the Grand Lunar was certainly contrived to give one a vivid impression of his greatness. Each cavern one entered seemed greater and more boldly arched than its predecessor. This effect of progressive size was enhanced by a thin haze of faintly phosphorescent blue incense that thickened as one advanced, and robbed even the nearer figures of clearness. I seemed to advance continually to something larger, dimmer, and less material.

'I must confess that all this multitude made me feel extremely shabby and unworthy. I was unshaven and unkempt; I had brought no razor; I had a coarse beard over my mouth. On earth I have always been inclined to despise any attention to my person beyond a proper care for cleanliness; but under the exceptional circumstances in which I found myself, representing, as I did, my planet and my kind, and depending very largely upon the attractiveness of my appearance for a proper reception, I could have given much for something a little more artistic and dignified than the husks I wore. I had been so serene in the belief that the moon was uninhabited as to overlook such precautions altogether. As it was I was dressed in a flannel jacket, knickerbockers, and golfing stockings, stained with every sort of dirt the moon offered, slippers (of which the left heel was wanting), and a blanket, through a hole in which I thrust my head. (These clothes, indeed, I still wear.) Sharp bristles are anything but an improvement to my cast of features, and there was an unmended tear at the knee of my knickerbockers that showed conspicuously as I squatted in my litter; my right stocking, too, persisted in getting about my ankle. I am fully alive to the injustice my appearance did humanity, and if by any expedient I could have improvised something a little out of the way and imposing I would have done so. But I could hit upon nothing. I did what I could with my blanket – folding it somewhat after the fashion of a toga, and for the rest I sat as upright as the swaying of my litter permitted.

'Imagine the largest hall you have ever been in, imperfectly lit with blue light and obscured by a grey-blue fog, surging with metallic or livid-grey creatures of such a mad diversity as I have hinted. Imagine this hall to end in an open archway beyond which is a still larger hall, and beyond this yet another and still larger one, and so on. At the end of the vista, dimly seen, a flight of steps, like the steps of Ara Coeli at Rome, ascend out of sight. Higher and higher these steps appear to go as one draws nearer their base.

But at last I came under a huge archway and beheld the summit of these steps, and upon it the Grand Lunar exalted on his throne.

'He was seated in what was relatively a blaze of incandescent blue. This, and the darkness about him, gave him an effect of floating in a blue-black void. He seemed a small, self-luminous cloud at first, brooding on his sombre throne; his brain case must have measured many yards in diameter. For some reason that I cannot fathom a number of blue searchlights radiated from behind the throne on which he sat, and immediately encircling him was a halo. About him, and little and indistinct in this glow, a number of body-servants sustained and supported him, and overshadowed and standing in a huge semicircle beneath him were his intellectual subordinates, his remembrancers and computators and searchers and servants, and all the distinguished insects of the court of the moon. Still lower stood ushers and messengers, and then all down the countless steps of the throne were guards, and at the base, enormous, various, indistinct, vanishing at last into an absolute black, a vast swaying multitude of the minor dignitaries of the moon. Their feet made a perpetual scraping whisper on the rocky floor, as their limbs moved with a rustling murmur.

'As I entered the penultimate hall the music rose and expanded into an imperial magnificence of sound, and the shrieks of the news-bearers died away . . .

'I entered the last and greatest hall . . .

'My procession opened out like a fan. My ushers and guards went right and left, and the three litters bearing myself and Phi-oo and Tsi-puff marched across a shiny darkness of floor to the foot of the giant stairs. Then began a vast throbbing hum, that mingled with the music. The two Selenites dismounted, but I was bidden remain seated – I imagine as a special honour. The music ceased, but not that humming, and by a simultaneous movement of ten thousand respectful heads my attention was directed to the enhaloed supreme intelligence that hovered above me.

'At first as I peered into the radiating glow this quintessential brain looked very much like an opaque, featureless bladder with dim, undulating ghosts of convolutions writhing visibly within. Then beneath its enormity and just above the edge of the throne one saw with a start minute elfin eyes peering out of the glow. No face, but eyes, as if they peered through holes. At first I could see no more than these two staring little eyes, and then below I distinguished the little dwarfed body and its insect-jointed limbs shrivelled and white. The eyes stared down at me with a strange intensity, and the lower part of the swollen globe was wrinkled. Ineffectual-looking little hand-tentacles steadied this shape on the throne . . .

'It was great. It was pitiful. One forgot the hall and the crowd.

'I ascended the staircase by jerks. It seemed to me that this darkly glowing brain case above us spread over me, and took more and more of the whole effect into itself as I drew nearer. The tiers of attendants and helpers

grouped about their master seemed to dwindle and fade into the night. I saw that shadowy attendants were busy spraying that great brain with a cooling spray, and patting and sustaining it. For my own part, I sat gripping my swaying litter and staring at the Grand Lunar, unable to turn my gaze aside. And at last, as I reached a little landing that was separated only by ten steps or so from the supreme seat, the woven splendour of the music reached a climax and ceased, and I was left naked, as it were, in that vastness, beneath the still scrutiny of the Grand Lunar's eyes.

'He was scrutinising the first man he had ever seen . . .

'My eyes dropped at last from his greatness to the ant figures in the blue mist about him, and then down the steps to the massed Selenites, still and expectant in their thousands, packed on the floor below. Once again an unreasonable horror reached out towards me . . . And passed.

'After the pause came the salutation. I was assisted from my litter, and stood awkwardly while a number of curious and no doubt deeply symbolical gestures were vicariously performed for me by two slender officials. The encyclopaedic galaxy of the learned that had accompanied me to the entrance of the last hall appeared two steps above me and left and right of me, in readiness for the Grand Lunar's need, and Phi-oo's pale brain placed itself about halfway up to the throne in such a position as to communicate easily between us without turning his back on either the Grand Lunar or myself. Tsi-puff took up position behind him. Dexterous ushers sidled sideways towards me, keeping a full face to the Presence. I seated myself Turkish fashion, and Phi-oo and Tsi-puff also knelt down above me. There came a pause. The eyes of the nearer court went from me to the Grand Lunar and came back to me, and a hissing and piping of expectation passed across the hidden multitudes below and ceased.

'That humming ceased.

'For the first and last time in my experience the moon was silent.

'I became aware of a faint wheezy noise. The Grand Lunar was addressing me. It was like the rubbing of a finger upon a pane of glass.

'I watched him attentively for a time, and then glanced at the alert Phi-oo. I felt amidst these slender beings ridiculously thick and fleshy and solid; my head all jaw and black hair. My eyes went back to the Grand Lunar. He had ceased; his attendants were busy, and his shining superfices was glistening and running with cooling spray.

'Phi-oo meditated through an interval. He consulted Tsi-puff. Then he began piping his recognisable English – at first a little nervously, so that he was not very clear.

' "M'm – the Grand Lunar – wishes to say – wishes to say – he gathers you are – m'm – men – that you are a man from the planet earth. He wishes to say that he welcomes you – welcomes you – and wishes to learn – learn, if I may use the word – the state of your world, and the reason why you came to this."

'He paused. I was about to reply when he resumed. He proceeded to remarks of which the drift was not very clear, though I am inclined to think they were intended to be complimentary. He told me that the earth was to the moon what the sun is to the earth, and that the Selenites desired very greatly to learn about the earth and men. He then told me, no doubt in compliment also, the relative magnitude and diameter of earth and moon, and the perpetual wonder and speculation with which the Selenites had regarded our planet. I meditated with downcast eyes, and decided to reply that men too had wondered what might lie in the moon, and had judged it dead, little recking of such magnificence as I had seen that day. The Grand Lunar, in token of recognition, caused his long blue rays to rotate in a very confusing manner, and all about the great hall ran the pipings and whisperings and rustlings of the report of what I had said. He then proceeded to put to Phi-oo a number of enquiries which were easier to answer.

'He understood, he explained, that we lived on the surface of the earth, that our air and sea were outside the globe; the latter part, indeed, he already knew from his astronomical specialists. He was very anxious to have more detailed information of what he called this extraordinary state of affairs, for from the solidity of the earth there had always been a disposition to regard it as uninhabitable. He endeavoured first to ascertain the extremes of temperature to which we earth beings were exposed, and he was deeply interested by my descriptive treatment of clouds and rain. His imagination was assisted by the fact that the lunar atmosphere in the outer galleries of the night side is not infrequently very foggy. He seemed inclined to marvel that we did not find the sunlight too intense for our eyes, and was interested in my attempt to explain that the sky was tempered to a bluish colour through the refraction of the air, though I doubt if he clearly understood that. I explained how the iris of the human eyes can contract the pupil and save the delicate internal structure from the excess of sunlight, and was allowed to approach within a few feet of the Presence in order that this structure might be seen. This led to a comparison of the lunar and terrestrial eyes. The former is not only excessively sensitive to such light as men can see, but it can also *see* heat, and every difference in temperature within the moon renders objects visible to it.

'The iris was quite a new organ to the Grand Lunar. For a time he amused himself by flashing his rays into my face and watching my pupils contract. As a consequence, I was dazzled and blinded for some little time . . .

'But in spite of that discomfort I found something reassuring by insensible degrees in the rationality of this business of question and answer. I could shut my eyes, think of my answer, and almost forget that the Grand Lunar has no face . . .

'When I had descended again to my proper place the Grand Lunar asked

how we sheltered ourselves from heat and storms, and I expounded to him the arts of building and furnishing. Here we wandered into misunderstandings and cross-purposes, due largely, I must admit, to the looseness of my expressions. For a long time I had great difficulty in making him understand the nature of a house. To him and his attendant Selenites it seemed, no doubt, the most whimsical thing in the world that men should build houses when they might descend into excavations, and an additional complication was introduced by the attempt I made to explain that men had originally begun their homes in caves, and that they were now taking their railways and many establishments beneath the surface. Here I think a desire for intellectual completeness betrayed me. There was also a considerable tangle due to an equally unwise attempt on my part to explain about mines. Dismissing this topic at last in an incomplete state, the Grand Lunar enquired what we did with the interior of our globe.

'A tide of twittering and piping swept into the remotest corners of that great assembly when it was at last made clear that we men know absolutely nothing of the contents of the world upon which the immemorial generations of our ancestors had been evolved. Three times had I to repeat that of all the 4,000 miles of distance between the earth and its centre men knew only to the depth of a mile, and that very vaguely. I understood the Grand Lunar to ask why had I come to the moon seeing we had scarcely touched our own planet yet, but he did not trouble me at that time to proceed to an explanation, being too anxious to pursue the details of this mad inversion of all his ideas.

'He reverted to the question of weather, and I tried to describe the perpetually changing sky, and snow, and frost and hurricanes. "But when the night comes," he asked, "is it not cold?"

'I told him it was colder than by day.

' "And does not your atmosphere freeze?"

'I told him not; that it was never cold enough for that, because our nights were so short.

' "Not even liquefy?"

'I was about to say "No", but then it occurred to me that one part at least of our atmosphere, the water vapour of it, does sometimes liquefy and form dew, and sometimes freeze and form frost – a process perfectly analogous to the freezing of all the external atmosphere of the moon during its longer night. I made myself clear on this point, and from that the Grand Lunar went on to speak with me of sleep. For the need of sleep that comes so regularly every twenty-four hours to all things is part also of our earthly inheritance. On the moon they rest only at rare intervals, and after exceptional exertions. Then I tried to describe to him the soft splendours of a summer night, and from that I passed to a description of those animals that prowl by night and sleep by day. I told him of lions and tigers, and here it seemed as though we had come to a deadlock. For, save

in their waters, there are no creatures in the moon not absolutely domestic and subject to his will, and so it has been for immemorial years. They have monstrous water creatures, but no evil beasts, and the idea of anything strong and large existing "outside" in the night is very difficult for them . . . '

The record is here too broken to transcribe for the space of perhaps twenty words or more.

'He talked with his attendants, as I suppose, upon the strange super-ficiality and unreasonableness of (man) who lives on the mere surface of a world, a creature of waves and winds, and all the chances of space, who cannot even unite to overcome the beasts that prey upon his kind, and yet who dares to invade another planet. During this aside I sat thinking, and then at his desire I told him of the different sorts of men. He searched me with questions. 'And for all sorts of work you have the same sort of men. But who thinks? Who governs?'

'I gave him an outline of the democratic method.

'When I had done he ordered cooling sprays upon his brow, and then requested me to repeat my explanation conceiving something had mis-carried.

' "Do they not do different things, then?" said Phi-oo.

'Some, I admitted, were thinkers and some officials; some hunted, some were mechanics, some artists, some toilers. "But *all* rule," I said.

' "And have they not different shapes to fit them to their different duties?"

' "None that you can see," I said, "except, perhaps, for clothes. Their minds perhaps differ a little," I reflected.

' "Their minds must differ a great deal," said the Grand Lunar, "or they would all want to do the same things."

'In order to bring myself into a closer harmony with his preconceptions, I said that his surmise was right. "It was all hidden in the brain," I said; "but the difference was there. Perhaps if one could see the minds and souls of men they would be as varied and unequal as the Selenites." There were great men and small men, men who could reach out far and wide, men who could go swiftly; noisy, trumpet-minded men, and men who could remember without thinking . . . ' The record is indistinct for three words.

'He interrupted me to recall me to my previous statements. "But you said all men rule?" he pressed.

' "To a certain extent," I said, and made, I fear, a denser fog with my explanation.

'He reached out to a salient fact. "Do you mean," he asked, "that there is no Grand Earthly?"

'I thought of several people, but assured him finally there was none. I explained that such autocrats and emperors as we had tried upon earth had usually ended in drink, or vice, or violence, and that the large and influential section of the people of the earth to which I belonged, the

Anglo-Saxons, did not mean to try that sort of thing again. At which the Grand Lunar was even more amazed.

' "But how do you keep even such wisdom as you have?" he asked; and I explained to him the way we helped our limited [a word omitted here, probably 'brains'] with libraries of books. I explained to him how our science was growing by the united labours of innumerable little men, and on that he made no comment save that it was evident we had mastered much in spite of our social savagery, or we could not have come to the moon. Yet the contrast was very marked. With knowledge the Selenites grew and changed; mankind stored their knowledge about them and remained brutes – equipped. He said this . . . [Here there is a short piece of the record indistinct.]

'He then caused me to describe how we went about this earth of ours, and I described to him our railways and ships. For a time he could not understand that we had had the use of steam only one hundred years, but when he did he was clearly amazed. (I may mention as a singular thing, that the Selenites use years to count by, just as we do on earth, though I can make nothing of their numeral system. That, however, does not matter, because Phi-oo understands ours.) From that I went on to tell him that mankind had dwelt in cities only for nine or ten thousand years, and that we were still not united in one brotherhood, but under many different forms of government. This astonished the Grand Lunar very much, when it was made clear to him. At first he thought we referred merely to administrative areas.

' "Our States and Empires are still the rawest sketches of what order will some day be," I said, and so I came to tell him . . . [At this point a length of record that probably represents thirty or forty words is totally illegible.]

'The Grand Lunar was greatly impressed by the folly of men in clinging to the inconvenience of diverse tongues. "They want to communicate, and yet not to communicate," he said, and then for a long time he questioned me closely concerning war.

'He was at first perplexed and incredulous. "You mean to say," he asked, seeking confirmation, "that you run about over the surface of your world – this world, whose riches you have scarcely begun to scrape – killing one another for beasts to eat?"

'I told him that was perfectly correct.

'He asked for particulars to assist his imagination.

' "But do not ships and your poor little cities get injured?" he asked, and I found the waste of property and conveniences seemed to impress him almost as much as the killing. "Tell me more," said the Grand Lunar; "make me see pictures. I cannot conceive these things."

'And so, for a space, though something loath, I told him the story of earthly War.

'I told him of the first orders and ceremonies of war, of warnings and ultimatums, and the marshalling and marching of troops. I gave him an idea

of manoeuvres and positions and battle joined. I told him of sieges and assaults, of starvation and hardship in trenches, and of sentinels freezing in the snow. I told him of routs and surprises, and desperate last stands and faint hopes, and the pitiless pursuit of fugitives and the dead upon the field. I told, too, of the past, of invasions and massacres, of the Huns and Tartars, and the wars of Mahomet and the Caliphs, and of the Crusades. And as I went on, and Phi-oo translated, the Selenites cooed and murmured in a steadily intensified emotion.

'I told them an ironclad could fire a shot of a ton twelve miles, and go through 20 ft of iron – and how we could steer torpedoes under water. I went on to describe a Maxim gun in action, and what I could imagine of the Battle of Colenso. The Grand Lunar was so incredulous that he interrupted the translation of what I had said in order to have my verification of my account. They particularly doubted my description of the men cheering and rejoicing as they went into (? battle).

' "But surely they do not like it!" translated Phi-oo.

'I assured them men of my race considered battle the most glorious experience of life, at which the whole assembly was stricken with amazement.

' "But what good is this war?" asked the Grand Lunar, sticking to his theme.

' "Oh! as for *good*!" said I; "it thins the population!"

' "But why should there be a need – ?"

'There came a pause, the cooling sprays impinged upon his brow, and then he spoke again.'

* * *

[At this point a series of undulations that have been apparent as a perplexing complication as far back as Cavor's description of the silence that fell before the first speaking of the Grand Lunar become confusingly predominant in the record. These undulations are evidently the result of radiations proceeding from a lunar source, and their persistent approximation to the alternating signals of Cavor is curiously suggestive of some operator deliberately seeking to mix them in with his message and render it illegible. At first they are small and regular, so that with a little care and the loss of very few words we have been able to disentangle Cavor's message; then they become broad and larger, then suddenly they are irregular, with an irregularity that gives the effect at last of someone scribbling through a line of writing. For a long time nothing can be made of this madly zigzagging trace; then quite abruptly the interruption ceases, leaves a few words clear, and then resumes and continues for the rest of the message, completely obliterating whatever Cavor was attempting to transmit. Why, if this is indeed a deliberate intervention, the Selenites should have preferred to let Cavor go on transmitting his message in happy ignorance of their obliteration of its record, when it was clearly

quite in their power and much more easy and convenient for them to stop his proceedings at any time, is a problem to which I can contribute nothing. The thing seems to have happened so, and that is all I can say. This last rag of his description of the Grand Lunar begins in mid-sentence.]

* * *

' . . . interrogated me very closely upon my secret. I was able in a little while to get to an understanding with them, and at last to elucidate what has been a puzzle to me ever since I realised the vastness of their science, namely, how it is they themselves have never discovered "Cavorite". I find they know of it as a theoretical substance, but they have always regarded it as a practical impossibility, because for some reason there is no helium in the moon, and helium – '

* * *

[Across the last letters of helium slashes the resumption of that obliterating trace. Note that word 'secret', for that, and that alone, I base my inter-pretation of the message that follows, the last message, as both Mr Wendigee and myself now believe it to be, that he is ever likely to send us.]

CHAPTER TWENTY-SIX

The Last Message Cavor Sent to the Earth

In this unsatisfactory manner the penultimate message of Cavor dies out. One seems to see him away there in the blue obscurity amidst his apparatus intently signalling us to the last, all unaware of the curtain of confusion that drops between us; all unaware, too, of the final dangers that even then must have been creeping upon him. His disastrous want of vulgar common sense had utterly betrayed him. He had talked of war, he had talked of all the strength and irrational violence of men, of their insatiable aggressions, their tireless futility of conflict. He had filled the whole moon world with this impression of our race, and then I think it is plain that he made the most fatal admission that upon himself alone hung the possibility – at least for a long time – of any further men reaching the moon. The line the cold, inhuman reason of the moon would take seems plain enough to me, and a suspicion of it, and then perhaps some sudden sharp realisation of it, must have come to him. One imagines him about the moon with the remorse of this fatal indiscretion growing in his mind. During a certain time I am inclined to guess the Grand Lunar was deliberating the new situation, and for all that time Cavor may have gone as free as ever he had gone. But obstacles of some sort prevented his getting to his electromagnetic

apparatus again after that message I have just given. For some days we received nothing. Perhaps he was having fresh audiences, and trying to evade his previous admissions. Who can hope to guess?

And then suddenly, like a cry in the night, like a cry that is followed by a stillness, came the last message. It is the briefest fragment, the broken beginnings of two sentences.

The first was: 'I was mad to let the Grand Lunar know – '

There was an interval of perhaps a minute. One imagines some interruption from without. A departure from the instrument – a dreadful hesitation among the looming masses of apparatus in that dim, blue-lit cavern – a sudden rush back to it, full of a resolve that came too late. Then, as if it were hastily transmitted came: 'Cavorite made as follows: take – '

There followed one word, a quite unmeaning word as it stands: 'uless'.

And that is all.

It may be he made a hasty attempt to spell 'useless' when his fate was close upon him. Whatever it was that was happening about that apparatus we cannot tell. Whatever it was we shall never, I know, receive another message from the moon. For my own part a vivid dream has come to my help, and I see, almost as plainly as though I had seen it in actual fact, a blue-lit shadowy dishevelled Cavor struggling in the grip of these insect Selenites, struggling ever more desperately and hopelessly as they press upon him, shouting, expostulating, perhaps even at last fighting, and being forced backwards step by step out of all speech or sign of his fellows, for evermore into the Unknown – into the dark, into that silence that has no end . . .